Her Mayesty Commissioners

Financial relation between Great Britain and Ireland : first report

Her Mayesty Commissioners

Financial relation between Great Britain and Ireland : first report

ISBN/EAN: 9783742831279

Manufactured in Europe, USA, Canada, Australia, Japa

Cover: Foto ©Andreas Hilbeck / pixelio.de

Manufactured and distributed by brebook publishing software
(www.brebook.com)

Her Mayesty Commissioners

Financial relation between Great Britain and Ireland : first report

Her Mayesty Commissioners

Financial relation between Great Britain and Ireland : first report

FIRST REPORT

BY

HER MAJESTY'S COMMISSIONERS

APPOINTED TO INQUIRE INTO THE

FINANCIAL RELATIONS BETWEEN GREAT BRITAIN AND IRELAND.

Presented to both Houses of Parliament by Command of Her Majesty.

LONDON:
PRINTED FOR HER MAJESTY'S STATIONERY OFFICE,
BY EYRE AND SPOTTISWOODE,
PRINTERS TO THE QUEEN'S MOST EXCELLENT MAJESTY.

And to be purchased, either directly or through any Bookseller, from
EYRE AND SPOTTISWOODE, East Harding Street, Fleet Street, E.C. and
32, Abingdon Street, Westminster, S.W.; or
JOHN MENZIES & Co., 12, Hanover Street, Edinburgh, and
90, West Nile Street, Glasgow; or
HODGES, FIGGIS, & Co., Limited, 104, Grafton Street, Dublin.

1895.

[C.—7720.] *Price ½d.*

FIRST REPORT.

TO THE QUEEN'S MOST EXCELLENT MAJESTY.

MAY IT PLEASE YOUR MAJESTY,

WE, the undersigned Commissioners appointed to inquire into the financial relations between Great Britain and Ireland, and their relative taxable capacity, availing ourselves of Your Majesty's gracious permission to report our proceedings from time to time, desire humbly to present to Your Majesty the following Report of the steps which we have taken in the prosecution of the inquiry entrusted to us.

Having regard to the fact that much of the information required is of a documentary and historical character, we carefully considered and prepared, in the first instance, the requisitions for such information which it would be desirable to address to Your Majesty's Treasury and other public departments.

In accordance with those requisitions we have been furnished with much valuable information, which will be found in the Appendices to this Report, while other information is still in course of preparation.

We have also examined at sittings, held some in London and others in Dublin, 17 witnesses, representatives of public departments and other persons who had a special claim to be heard upon the subject of our inquiry. The evidence of these witnesses is annexed to this Report.

We shall proceed to take further evidence bearing upon the questions referred to us.

All of which we submit to Your Majesty's gracious consideration.

(Signed) HUGH C. E. CHILDERS.
FARRER.
WELBY.
O'CONOR DON.
THOS. SUTHERLAND.
D. BARBOUR.
EDWARD BLAKE.
B. W. CURRIE.
W. A. HUNTER.
CHARLES E. MARTIN.
J. E. REDMOND.
THOMAS SEXTON.
G. W. WOLFF.
H. F. SLATTERY.

29th March 1895.

B. H. HOLLAND,
Secretary.

ROYAL COMMISSION ON THE FINANCIAL RELATIONS BETWEEN GREAT BRITAIN AND IRELAND.

MINUTES OF EVIDENCE,

up to the 28th March 1895,

TAKEN BEFORE

HER MAJESTY'S COMMISSIONERS

APPOINTED TO INQUIRE INTO THE

FINANCIAL RELATIONS BETWEEN GREAT BRITAIN AND IRELAND,

WITH

APPENDICES.

Presented to both Houses of Parliament by Command of Her Majesty.

TABLE OF CONTENTS.

TERMS OF THE REFERENCE TO THE ROYAL COMMISSION.

To inquire into the Financial Relations between Great Britain and Ireland, and their relative taxable capacity, and to report :—

1. Upon what principles of comparison, and by the application of what specific standards, the relative capacity of Great Britain and Ireland to bear taxation may be most equitably determined.

2. What, so far as can be ascertained, is the true proportion, under the principles and specific standards so determined, between the taxable capacity of Great Britain and Ireland.

3. The history of the financial relations between Great Britain and Ireland at and after the Legislative Union, the charge for Irish purposes on the Imperial Exchequer during that period, and the amount of Irish taxation remaining available for contribution to Imperial expenditure; also the Imperial expenditure to which it is considered equitable that Ireland should contribute.

WITNESSES EXAMINED.

ALPHABETICAL LIST OF WITNESSES.

MINUTES OF EVIDENCE

TAKEN BEFORE THE

ROYAL COMMISSION

OF THE

FINANCIAL RELATIONS BETWEEN GREAT BRITAIN AND IRELAND.

Commission Room, Westminster Hall, S.W.

FIRST DAY.

Thursday, 5th July 1894.

PRESENT:

THE RIGHT HON. HUGH C. E. CHILDERS, CHAIRMAN.

LORD FARRER.
LORD WELBY, G.C.B.
SIR R. G. C. HAMILTON, K.C.B.
SIR THOS. SUTHERLAND, K.C.M.G., M.P.
SIR DAVID BARBOUR.
HON. EDWARD BLAKE, M.P.
CHARLES E. MARTIN, Esq.
J. E. REDMOND, Esq., M.P.
THOMAS SEXTON, Esq., M.P.
GUSTAV W. WOLFF, Esq., M.P.
HENRY F. SLATTERY, Esq.

Mr. B. H. HOLLAND, *Secretary.*

Mr. HERBERT HARLEY MURRAY, C.B., and Mr. THOMAS J. PITTAR called and examined.

Mr. H. H. Murray, C.B.

5 July 1894.

Assimilation of Customs duties.

1. (*Chairman.*) You are chairman of the Board of Customs?—(*Mr. Murray.*) Yes.

2. How long have you held that office?—About five years.

3. (*To Mr. Pittar.*) You are Principal of the Statistical Office of the Board of Customs?—(*Mr. Pittar.*) Yes.

4. (*To Mr. Murray.*) We do not wish just now to enter into the history of the Customs as far as it relates to the financial relations between Great Britain and Ireland, but merely to ascertain the mode in which the figures contained in the recent parliamentary returns have been arrived at. I should like, however, to call your attention to one or two general points. The Sixth Article of the Act of Union contains, I believe, provisions as to Customs duties on certain goods imported from Great Britain to Ireland and vice versâ, but declares that with these exceptions all prohibitions and bounties on the export of articles, the growth, produce, or manufacture of either country to the other shall cease and determine, and that the said articles shall henceforth be exported from one country to the other without duty or bounty on such export. That is so, is it not?—(*Mr. Murray.*) I think it is a fair statement of what that Act states. What is called the Second Schedule to that Act, I think, gives a list of a certain number of articles which were to pay ad valorem duties for 20 years.

5. Is it not the case that by the Act of 1823, the 39th and 40th George III., chapter 67, all Customs were assimilated, and the trade between Great Britain and Ireland placed on the footing of a coasting trade?—The 4th George IV., chapter 26, somewhat altered the time during which those ad valorem duties, which were contained in the Second Schedule of the Treaty of Union, were to remain in force. That Act repealed some of those duties, and then limited the time during which the others were to remain in force. But it was chapter 72 of 4 Geo. IV. which to some extent assimilated the tariff of the two countries.

6. That was the final Act, passed many years before all duties were made identical by Mr. Gladstone?—It was the final Act. The Act which finally made the tariff for the two countries alike was an Act which was passed in the sixth year of George IV., chapter 111. That finally assimilated the tariffs of the two countries.

7. Not as to spirits, I think?—Not as to British spirits, but as to foreign spirits. I am referring to the tariff, not the Inland Revenue duties.

8. Previous to 1823 there had been separate Boards of Customs for Great Britain and Ireland, I think?—Yes, there had been.

9. When were those absolutely amalgamated?—There was a Commission appointed in 1817, which finally reported in 1822, I think, recommending the abolition of the separate boards; and that was carried out by an Act of 1823, viz., 4 George IV., cap. 23, which put an end to the separate boards, both in Scotland and Ireland.

Mr. H. H. Murray, C.B.

1 July 1894.

Amalgamation of Customs Boards.

10. After the date of the amalgamation of the boards, and for a long time, the statistics only show, I think, the proportion in which Customs revenue was collected in the three countries?—After the coasting trade was established at the end of 1823 or the beginning of 1824, there were no statistics kept as to the trade between the two countries.

11. There was nothing except the actual cash collection?—The cash collection in each country.

Proceedings to ascertain proportional contribution and consumption of the three kingdoms.

12. No attempt was made till recently to ascertain the proportions in which goods were consumed in each country, and therefore the actual revenue actually contributed by each?—No; it was not till 1890, I think, that the Chancellor of the Exchequer told us that information would be wanted for a committee which it was proposed to appoint.

13. That attempt to ascertain the proportions originated in the Chancellor of the Exchequer's instructions?—It did.

14. Given by him in pursuance of an undertaking to supply the information?—Yes, personal instructions, in some cases verbally, and in some cases by private letters. There were no official instructions sent.

15. Can you produce the instruction or any paper?—The only instruction I can produce happened to be one rather late. We had verbal instructions at an earlier date, but I can produce one which came so late as September 1890. It was a letter which I received from the Chancellor of the Exchequer when he was abroad.

16. Will you read it?—This is addressed to me personally. "I am anxious with reference to the "proposed inquiry into the financial relations between "England, Scotland, and Ireland, that both the "Customs and Excise should give their best atten- "tion to the collection of information bearing upon "the subject. The statistics regarding the con- "sumption of home spirits seem to be reliable, but "we must ascertain all we can about the consump- "tion of the remaining dutiable articles, such as "beer, foreign spirits, tea, coffee, &c., dried fruits, "and tobacco. The Customs should study how they "can best furnish information as to the shipments "from England to Ireland, or vice versâ, of any of "these goods, and the Excise must try inland to "obtain information with regard to consumption. "As regards stamps and other forms of taxation, the "situation is more complicated. I shall take the "matter up immediately on my return to England. "But I am anxious that as much progress should be "made at once as may be possible." That was dated 8th September 1890. A little later on a copy of this was sent to us officially. That is the only official document which we have directing information to be collected.

17. What steps were taken by your Board in pursuance of that instruction?—It was very early known that our figures given as collections were quite unreliable for the purpose in view, and it must have been, I think, in June 1890 that we got instructions to get better information if we could. As regards the movement of British and foreign spirits and unmanufactured tobacco, we could deal with them on account of the system of permits. But the permits at that time were unrecorded, so it was decided to send out instructions that whenever a permit was issued a duplicate was to be taken at the same time, and so far as foreign spirits and unmanufactured tobacco were concerned, these duplicates were to be sent to the Statistical Office for Mr. Pixley to work out, and any duplicates that we got as regards British spirits we sent to the Inland Revenue for them to make up their figures with. That was the first step which we took, and we issued a general order, dated 5th July, giving instructions on that point. (The order was put in, and is as follows):—"Custom House, London, 5th July 1890. Duplicate "permits in certain cases of delivery of spirits and "unmanufactured tobacco. The Board direct that, on "and after the receipt of this order, in every case of "the delivery of foreign spirits and unmanufactured "tobacco, duty paid, from any Customs bonded "warehouse within the United Kingdom, as to which "the permit shows the destination of the spirits or "of the tobacco, as the case may be, to be either of "the other two countries of the United Kingdom "than that in which such spirits or tobacco are "cleared, i.e., England for Scotland or Ireland, "Scotland for England or Ireland, Ireland for "England or Scotland, a duplicate of the form of "permit be made out and forwarded on the day on "which duty is paid, to the Principal of the Statistical "Office, Custom House, London. Code paragraph "160 is to be noted accordingly. By order of the "Board. R. T. PRowse."

18. No goods are the subject of these permits except spirits and unmanufactured tobacco?—No, manufactured tobacco goes free. We have no hold at present over that.

19. I will now refer you to Parliamentary Paper 329 of 1891, pages 6 and 7. At those pages there is a memorandum marked A., prepared by the Board of Customs, dated January 1891. Have you got it before you?—Yes.

20. The four articles of much importance which are the subject of that memorandum are, I think, foreign spirits, tea, tobacco, and wine?—Yes, they are the most important.

21. No mention is made of foreign beer, I suppose?—The importation of foreign beer into the United Kingdom after all is not very much. It only amounts to about 60,000 barrels.

22. It comes in among "all other articles"?—It would be among them. I do not imagine that the importation of it into Ireland is very large.

23. The other articles, besides the four specially named, are cocoa, chicory, coffee, and dried fruits, I think?—Yes.

24. And they are of minor importance?—Yes.

25. Am I right in understanding that in the case of tea, tobacco, and wine, the only period of at all exact statistics upon which the proportion of consumption in each country can be based is that of the four months ending March 31st, 1891?—Of late years. Up to the time the coasting trade was not free there would be the statistics on those points correctly given. But from the time the coasting trade was made free, to 1890, when we got the directions to try and find out as nearly as we could what the actual consumption was in each kingdom, there were no means of arriving even approximately at the facts of the case.

26. Perhaps you would be good enough to read the memorandum on page 31 of that Return?—"The "accompanying adjusted statement of the quantities "of customable articles consumed severally in each "of the three kingdoms in the year ended the 31st "March 1891, has been compiled on the following "basis:—Upon the request of the Board of Customs, "returns were furnished by the railway companies of "the United Kingdom showing the quantities of duty- "paid tea, coffee, manufactured tobacco, and wine "forwarded by their lines for removal to either of "the other divisions of the United Kingdom than "the one in which the goods were booked for con- "veyance in the four months ended 31st March 1891; "and like returns were obtained from the various "shipping companies of the quantities of those goods "removed coastwise between the three kingdoms "after payment of duty. The quantity of each "article on which duty was actually paid in each "kingdom was already known. In order to arrive "at the true consumption it has only been necessary "to add to the quantities cleared for duty in either "kingdom, the amounts brought to that kingdom "after payment of the duty elsewhere, and then by "an inverse process to deduct from the result so "arrived at the quantities duty-paid in that division "for consumption in the other parts of the United "Kingdom. Having in this way arrived at the "consumption in England, Scotland, and Ireland, "of the articles mentioned during the four months "already specified, the proportions so obtained were

"applied to the entire revenue collected under each "head of the tariff during the complete year. As "regards foreign spirits, official information covering "a period of nine months was available, and as it "was considered that the proportions shown by the "longer period would afford a more reliable basis of "estimate, the nine months' proportions instead of "the four months' proportions were used in respect "of that article. Every possible care has been taken "when dealing with the railway and shipping returns "to avoid the inclusion of the same goods twice over. The railway, shipping, and other returns which "have served as the basis of the calculations in the "statement given below were not available when the "figures for the year 1889–90 (page 6 above) were "compiled. (Signed) T. J. Pittar. Statistical "Office, Custom House, June 23, 1891."

27. All subsequent estimates (such, for instance, as this one for 1892–3, on page 5 of the Return of July 1893, 334) are based on this period of four months, are they not?—Yes, with the exception of foreign spirits, because there we had the permits covering the whole time.

28. But, with that exception, that has been the basis of all the former calculations?—Yes.

29. Have you reason to believe that this period of four months fairly represents the average of the year 1890–1 in the case of tea, wine, and tobacco?—I would not say fairly. It only represents it, I think, approximately. It represents foreign spirits accurately.

30. You think it fairly represents a longer period of time?—Approximately it does. It is as near as we can go. It is the only means we have to cover that longer period.

31. Will you explain the important point why the statistics obtained for these four months cannot be obtained continuously, if that is so?—I think we should have got no statistics at all if it had not been for the personal influence of Mr. Jackson, who was at that time Secretary to the Treasury. He had some acquaintance with the directors of one of the leading lines in the kingdom, and it was at his instigation, and, I may say, with his personal assistance, that we got ourselves in communication with Mr. Oakley, the secretary of the Railway Association, and through Mr. Jackson and Mr. Oakley the railway companies were induced to agree to make these returns for a period of three months, beginning December. At a later period also, at Mr. Jackson's instigation, they agreed to do it for one more month, so as to give us a period covering a financial quarter, January, February, and March of 1891.

32. And it would be, in your opinion, too much to ask of the companies to make that more continuous?—It was considered so then, and I doubt very much if we should persuade them to give us any information now such as they then took the trouble to give us. It was done by them, I believe, at considerable expense, and at a great deal of trouble.

33. As to foreign spirits, the proportions of consumption have been ascertained in the Return which I just referred to, 334, 1893, for the year 1892–3. Is that for the whole year?—Yes, that would be for the whole year, 1892–3. The duplicate permit system was in full operation.

34. And from that time will the collection of those statistics as to spirits be permanently maintained?—Yes.

35. Will you explain why that permanent record can be made in the case of spirits and not as to other goods?—The law requires that any quantity of spirits in excess of one gallon shall not be moved without a permit. Therefore any movement of spirits, either foreign or British, in excess of one gallon, must be accompanied by a permit, and we have copies of the duplicate permits now sent to us as regards foreign spirits, and to the Inland Revenue as regards British spirits.

36. And, therefore, without changing the law you cannot insist upon any system of that kind being extended to other articles?—No; we have it as regards unmanufactured tobacco, but that does not cover the movement of manufactured tobacco, and with regard to the movement of manufactured tobacco the Inland Revenue tried to obtain information for us, but they failed. A large number of the manufacturers declined to take any trouble to give them information, and those who did were not in sufficient number to make the return worth anything.

Mr. H. E. Murray, C.B.

4 July 1894.

Returns of spirits, how compiled.

37. Can you tell us (parenthetically) why the law required permits as to unmanufactured tobacco and not as to manufactured tobacco?—I cannot tell you that.

Permit system not applied to manufactured tobacco.

38. There is no tradition in the Customs of the reason for it?—Not that I know of.

39. And you see no particular reason?—The articles have paid duty, and we have had any interest in them.

40. Why should that be the case as to unmanufactured and not as to manufactured?—Because they pay duty upon the raw article and then manufacture it. As soon as they have paid the duty we have lost interest in the article which they have taken out for manufacture.

41. Will you refer to the memorandum on page 7 of 329, 1891. It says there that "the Customs returns show that the manufactured tobacco on which "duty was paid in Ireland, when added to that "received in a duty-paid condition from the other two "kingdoms, amounts to only about 630,000 lbs., "whereas there is an export from Ireland of from "2,000,000 to 3,000,000 pounds of the manufactured "article." Can you tell us how that was ascertained?—I would rather Mr. Pittar should give that information.

42. Let Mr. Pittar give the answer?—(*Mr. Pittar.*) In the case of the exports from Ireland to Great Britain, we applied, in the first instance, to the manufacturers in Belfast and Dublin and the other principal ports of Ireland (but chiefly Belfast and Dublin), and we found that we could not arrive at any very good or reliable estimate of the quantity from what they were able to tell us. We then were induced to look abroad for other information, and we found that as to Belfast, which was the principal port concerned, the Harbour Board there kept accounts of their own for the purpose of their dues, which showed, with very fair completeness, the total quantities of tobacco which were exported from Belfast. We were not able to obtain a similar account in Dublin, and, therefore, we had resort to the shipping companies in Dublin, and from returns which they rendered we were enabled to compile a total for the port of Dublin. In other ports the process varied according as we found were able to get statistics. For instance, at Waterford we obtained them by going through the books of the shipping companies. At Cork we were able to obtain a return from the Harbour Board, and in that way the return of the exports from two to three million pounds was made out.

Mr. T. J. Pittar.

Irish and British tobacco.

43. Is that as to any particular year?—Yes, that was for the year 1889, I think.

44. Before this inquiry was started?—Yes. I may perhaps explain in this way. When the Chancellor of the Exchequer's minute came, directing inquiries to be made, I first of all, by desire of the Board of Customs, communicated with the railway companies in London to see what could be done. They took every possible trouble to satisfy us, but said at once that they could do nothing as to the past. Their records were of such a nature that they did not convey the information in a form that would be of any use for the making of these returns as to the past. But they offered to consider, and ultimately, as you are aware, did effect a method by which statistics were obtained for a short specified period. They offered to consider a method of setting up machinery to do this if the Government urgently desired it, but they said it would be very troublesome. Meanwhile, as that was a matter that involved a good deal of discussion, I went to Ireland at the direction of the Board of Customs to see whether we could get any statistics as to the past that could be laid before the contemplated Committee of the House of

A 2

Commons. Therefore, when I visited Ireland, I selected the year 1889 (the last complete calendar year), and endeavoured to get statistics from the books of those various bodies whom I have named, which would enable us to present figures for a full and complete year, without waiting for the return which the railway companies were considering. That is how the first figures came to be compiled.

44. That accounts for the year being a past year, two years before, and not the year of your inquiry?—Quite so.

45. Coming to the figure of from two to three million pounds, do you think that the quantity can be more exactly ascertained?—(Mr. Murray.) I should doubt it, with the present machinery.

47. You would not go through the process that Mr. Fisher has explained again?—I do not think it would give us anything more accurate than what we have got now, because various deductions have to be made from the figures we did get. We have to reckon the tare of the packages, for instance, which has to be done rather roughly, but it has to be taken off the amount which is said to be exported to England.

48. That is method, I suppose?—It was taken on an average, I believe. But I do not think, unless we get some other legislative powers, we should be able by any process to obtain more reliable information than what we put forward.

49. Passing for the moment from tobacco, you have not found it possible to estimate, according to these papers, even for a short period, the proportions in which cocoa and dried fruits are consumed?—No, cocoa and dried fruits we have no figures about. As regards coffee we get some from the railways, and that enabled us to make coffee rather more accurate than it was before.

50. So that it has been found necessary in a table of contribution to divide the revenue derived from these minor articles in proportion to the population?—To the population.

51. And is that the case as to dried fruits and chicory and cocoa?—Yes.

52. Is it, in your opinion, possible by any reasonable process to obtain the true proportion of contribution as to these articles?—Under an extended system of permit it would be, not otherwise, I think.

53. That is to say, if you extended it from spirits and unmanufactured tobacco to all articles?—Well, to all articles to which it was worth applying it. Some are too small to make it worth the trouble.

54. You would not recommend that?—It depends upon what is required. I should be very sorry to recommend it, because I think it would be a great interference with trade, and most inconvenient to traders. But if it was only for a short time, possibly it might be tolerated.

55. As far as coffee is concerned, we may take it the difficulty has been removed?—I think so, to a considerable extent, but the revenue derived from it is so small. The total revenue is only 190,000*l.* a year for the United Kingdom, and the proportion of that paid by Ireland would be so very small it would be hardly worth while taking any steps about it.

56. Going to the Report of the Select Committee of 1864—there were papers prepared by a Mr. Fisher, who was a journalist, I believe—at 327 of the Appendix to the Report, showing the consumption of tobacco, sugar, tea, wine, spirits, and malt in England, Scotland, and Ireland at various dates. Do you happen to have that?—I saw it the other day, but I did not study it at all. We have it in the office.

57. In your opinion could any return with your present materials and powers, similar to that of Mr. Fisher, be more than very roughly correct?—No, because after 1824 we possess no means of making a return of that nature. As soon as ever the coasting trade became free we had no means of compiling any figures like Mr. Fisher put in. They must have been based upon the collections only.

58. (*Mr. Sexton.*) It might be correct up to 1820, I suppose?—I think it might be correct, I might almost say, to the end of 1823, because the Treasury Minute which established the coasting trade on a free basis was not issued till the end of October 1823. Therefore up to that time there would have been the regular statistics between the two countries.

Mr. R. E. Murray, C.B.

8 July 1894.

Select Committee of 1864. Report of.

59. The average for three years ending 1860 would be speculative?—Quite so. I think I saw that this table was based upon collections. "The Irish returns "are calculated alone on the articles which paid duty "in Ireland, which does not include her entire con"sumption." Therefore these were based only upon the same information as we gave to the Chancellor of the Exchequer before he directed us to try and collect information as to the real amounts contributed.

60. (*Chairman.*) In fact the word in the return put in by Mr. Fisher on that occasion, "consumed," ought more strictly to have been "duty paid"?—Yes, just so, except as I have said up to 1823.

61. I do not know whether you happened to notice the figures given as to tea in 1860, when Great Britain is said to have consumed 64,000,000 lbs. of tea and Ireland only 10,000,000. That would not be a probable figure, would it?—I could not say. It is one-sixth part.

62. (*Mr. Sexton.*) Have you the proportion of population in that year before you?—No. I think that might be fairly accurate. They consume now 22,000,000 lbs. a year, roughly speaking, in Ireland. Then the population was much larger in 1860 than it is now.

Tea consumption.

63. And smaller in Great Britain?—And smaller in Great Britain.

64. I understand you to say that from the time of the coasting trade legislation in 1824, up to the time when this recent adjustment began, you had no statistics except what the Chairman described as the cash collections?—We had no statistics except those of collection.

65. Was this adjustment of Lord Welby's memorandum of 1891 the first methodical effort that was made to ascertain what you call the true contribution of Ireland?—It was the first attempt made to come approximately to it. We knew it could not be a true one, but we made it as near as we could approximately.

Pre-union legislation. No sure means previous to before 1825.

66. Would the figures of the official returns from the time of the legislative Union up to 1824 represent what you now call the true contribution?—They would. We have got figures giving the actual contribution to the revenue, and we have got figures to show accurately the exports and imports of every article up to that time.

67. So that the returns of the Irish revenue from 1800 to 1824 would indicate approximately the consumption in Ireland?—Probably. If the tobacco manufacture was going on in Ireland at that time I should doubt very much if there was the same quantity of tobacco exported to England, so that perhaps the amount of tobacco which was imported into Ireland represented more nearly during that period the true consumption of Ireland.

68. The returns of revenue from 1824 to 1889–90—that is for about 66 years—would represent simply the duty paid in Ireland?—The revenue returns would.

69. And if you endeavoured now to ascertain what was the true contribution of Ireland during that period on the principles recently applied, how would you endeavour to do it?—From 1823 and 1824 upwards?

70. Yes?—We have no means of doing that.

71. So far as revenue relates to articles of consumption, I suppose the only way of adjusting now the revenue for that long period would be to apply some test of comparative population?—That would be a very rough one I am afraid. The conditions of the population would vary so much. It is almost impossible to make out anything reliable upon that basis, I think.

72. The standard of life?—Yes, the standard of life in the two kingdoms.

Mr. G. H. Murray, C.B. — 5 July 1893. — Mode of adjustment.

73. I notice that most of your actual adjustment does really rather depend, when you come to look into it, upon population?—Only as regards cocoa and dried fruits, and "all other articles," and that represents a very small proportion of the total revenue. It is only about 330,000*l*.

74. Yes, but you see, under the head of tea, for instance, that you have made the correction. "This "correction makes the total actual consumption of tea "in that division of the kingdom approximate to the "average consumption of the United Kingdom as a "whole, namely, 4·61 lbs. per head (1889)"?—I beg your pardon. I do not know which return you refer to.

75. I am looking at page 6 of the return 329 of 1891?—Yes, we have got later information than that. On page 6 we had got some of the information from the railways. The later returns were based on the information which we got from the railways during those four months. If you turn to list 334, which gives the contribution for the year 1892–3, you will see that tea, tobacco, and wine were given by proportions ascertained for 1890–91 from railway returns.

76. Does that refer to Mr. Pittar's memorandum on page 31 of the earlier paper?—Yes.

In case of tea.

77. He says there, confining ourselves for the moment to tea, that you obtained from the railway companies a return showing the amount of tea forwarded from one country to another, in the four months ending 31st March 1891, and likewise from the various shipping companies?—Yes.

78. Do I understand you to say that the returns obtained for those four months have formed the basis of all the calculations since?—Yes.

79. There has been no fresh inquiry?—No fresh inquiry. We were directed by the Treasury not to make any further inquiry on that subject about May or June 1891.

80. So that the correctness of the adjustments of revenue in regard to tea for the five years up to March last depends altogether, first upon the correctness of the figures given for the four months, and, secondly, upon the degree to which those figures correctly represent the figures since?—They depend upon the information we obtained from the railway companies during those four months, and upon the amount actually collected.

81. But, of course, the object of the figures is to qualify the conclusions drawn from the amount actually collected?—Yes, but those railway returns enabled us to judge how much was passed back from Ireland to Scotland or to England—how much of the tea which was sent to Ireland passed back again from Ireland, Scotland, and England, and show the true proportion.

82. When you refer to the collection as another element of adjustment, is not that somewhat inaccurate? The collection is the thing we are adjusting?—Yes, I think I should have left out the collection.

83. The collection is what we are adjusting?—Just so.

Adjustment of taxation.

84. Firstly, then, the value of this system of adjustment, so far as tea is concerned, depends upon the absolute correctness of the figures given by the railway companies for those four months?—Yes.

85. And then, secondly, it depends upon the extent to which the figures for those four months may have been truly representative of what happened since?—Yes, we have applied the same proportion which we found in 1891 to some subsequent years.

86. (*Chairman.*) Up to the present time?—Up to 1892–93, the last year for which we have sent in a return.

87. (*Mr. Sexton.*) I should like you to make it more clear to the Commission in what way you applied the figures of the four months to the subsequent years?—I will state it in this way. The adjustments were arrived at in this manner. First, the period taken was the four months to which the railway return was applicable. The total consumption in the United Kingdom of an article, say tea, during those four months was first taken out. I will put in the actual calculation.

Mr. G. H. Murray, C.B. — 5 July 1893. — Adjustment of taxation.

88. How did you ascertain the total consumption?—We got that from our own books at the Custom House.

89. (*Sir David Barbour.*) They show the duty paid which you assume to represent the consumption?—They show the duty paid.

90. (*Mr. Sexton.*) It is by the total duty?—Yes. The quantity which paid duty in England was ascertained. To this was added the quantity which was removed duty paid from Ireland and Scotland to England. From this total a deduction was made of the quantities which were removed duty paid from England to Ireland and Scotland. The total quantity thus consumed in England during those four months was ascertained, and the percentage which they bore to the total consumed during the period in the United Kingdom was ascertained.

91. You have figures which show how the process was carried through?—How the process was carried through.

92. The method you have described appears to be a sound method?—It was the only method we had, I think.

93. You have no doubt of your ability to carry out that principle?—I think as regards tea we were pretty safe, because the tea goes in its own packages, the chest, the half chest, and the quarter chest. There is no mistaking the tea when it is moved. This is the calculation by which the consumption of tea in England, Scotland, and Ireland respectively in the four months ended 31st March 1891 was ascertained. (*See Table on next page.*)

94. It appears there that Ireland consumed one-seventh of the whole?—Yes, something like it.

95. I suggested at the outset that the results appeared to follow very closely the test of population?—I do not object to the population test at the present time; but what I ventured to say just now was I think that the population test, applied at an earlier date, when the condition of Ireland was different to what it is now, would not help us to arrive at any fair conclusion. When you put that question to me some quarter of an hour ago it referred to a much earlier period than the present time.

96. Yes, I began by endeavouring to ascertain from you whether the application of a population test would enable you, for a period from 1824 to 1890, to approximate the adjustments of the more recent years?—I should still, for the reasons I gave, not object to, but place little reliance upon a calculation made on that basis.

97. There appears to be very little movement of tea, scarcely any, from Scotland or Ireland to England?—No, the tea goes to where it is consumed, as a rule.

98. About half of the tea consumed in Ireland is duty-paid there, and the other half is imported from England?—Yes, the great bulk of the duty on the tea which is consumed in the United Kingdom is, in point of fact, paid in London.

Powers of Customs Department to obtain statistics.

99. Do I understand you to say that it would be difficult to obtain for the future by any method statistics to ascertain the figures?—With the powers we have at present got, and which we are willing to enforce.

100. That is to say, you are willing to enforce the powers you have got?—No, I am not. There are powers which we have got, but I should be very sorry to enforce them.

101. It would be desirable, in order that we may know the facts, that we should know what powers you would like?—We have powers over the coasting trade as complete as we could wish to have by statute, but we do not exercise those powers. We leave the coasting trade as free as we can possibly leave it. But every coasting ship is by law bound to keep a cargo book, and in that cargo book it is supposed to enter details of its cargo, but as a rule they never do.

ENGLAND.			
Tea on which duty was paid in England	37,531,997		44,554,578
" imported from Scotland, duty paid	16,423		
" " Ireland "	17,146		
		37,561,566	
Deduct " sent to Scotland, duty paid	3,367,798		
" " " Ireland "	4,445,562		
		[illegible]	
" retained for consumption in England		[illegible]	Per cent. 75·1
SCOTLAND.			
Tea on which duty was paid in Scotland	7,493,993		
" imported from England, duty paid	[illegible]		
" " Ireland "	13,000		
		[illegible]	
Deduct " sent to England, duty paid	[illegible]		
" " " Ireland "	[illegible]		
		[illegible]	
" retained for consumption in Scotland		[illegible]	Per cent. 9·9
IRELAND.			
Tea on which duty was paid in Ireland	[illegible]		
" imported from England, duty paid	[illegible]		
" " Scotland "	[illegible]		
		[illegible]	
Deduct " sent to England, duty paid	17,146		
" " " Scotland "	[illegible]		
		[illegible]	
" retained for consumption in Ireland		[illegible]	Per cent. 14·9

(Signed) T. J. Pittar.

Most of the cargoes, for instance, between England and Ireland are what are called general cargoes, and all they will put in their cargo book is "general cargo." If we were to try to enforce the power which the law gives us against the coasting trade, and compel them to keep these cargo books in the way we might compel them to do, we should hamper trade to a degree that the trade would never stand.

102. There is a duty cast upon the person in charge of the ship. You say there is a cargo book?—The captain of a coasting vessel is bound by law to keep a cargo book in full detail. We do not insist upon that.

103. When you say in full detail, do you mean he is bound to specify the quantity of every article carried?—Yes.

104. Of course, if that law were carried out, it would be a very complete record?—It would be a fair record, but I think if we attempted to carry it out now, after 50 odd years of freedom, we should find ourselves in great difficulty.

105. I am not making any suggestion, you understand, as to the enforcement of the law; I am merely endeavouring to ascertain the facts. The cargo book, if it were filled up accurately as the law intends, would afford precise information as to the quantity of each article on board?—It would.

106. Is it the uniform practice to ignore the law in that respect?—Yes, I may say the practice is uniform. As regards a great number of the steamers which trade between England and Ireland, and many of the other steamers too, they have what they call a general transire, and the condition we insist on their general transire is that we should have access to their books in the office instead of the cargo book being kept.

107. The book being kept in the way the law directs, I think you said the only entry made in the cargo book where ships carry general cargo is simply "general cargo"?—It is very short indeed, and little more than a formal compliance with the law.

108. Giving no particular information?—No.

109. Then instead of availing yourself of the law with regard to cargo, which officially or non-officially has been forgotten by common consent, you apply at the office. Do you mean at the offices of the shipping companies?—Yes. For instance, I may say that when we tried to get the information from the shipping companies we reminded them, in the general order which we issued, of the power which we had got. In the general order which we issued on October 16th, 1890, after directing our officers to obtain the best information they could, we added: "In obtaining the necessary "information it should be explained to the various "carriers that the Board are desirous of interfering "as little as possible with their business, but at the "same time reminding them, where necessary, that "by the ninth section of the Act 42 & 43 Victoria, "chapter 21, they are bound to enter in the cargo "books of every vessel in the coasting trade the "description and quantities of the various goods taken "on board each voyage, and that on the transire "bonded goods must be distinguished from the foreign "goods, and that unless arrangements are made to "otherwise supply the required information, it will "be necessary that these provisions of the law should "be strictly carried out." It was a kind of warning that they should give us the information that we were asking for. Powers of Board of Customs [illegible] from coasting trade.

110. That Act which you are quoting is the Customs Consolidation Act?—The Customs Consolidation Act is 39 & 40 Vict. cap. 36, but it practically contains the powers given in the Act 42 & 43 Vict. cap. 21.

111. I understand, from Mr. Pittar's memorandum of the 29th June 1891, that you applied both to the railway companies and to the shipping companies?—Yes.

112. What is the main railway route for these goods to Ireland?—I should say the greatest proportion go between Liverpool and Belfast, and Dublin and Holyhead, and Greenore. There is also, of course, a considerable line between Bristol and Waterford.

113. Customable goods first imported into the United Kingdom at Liverpool, and then sent to Ireland, would hardly be sent at all by railway, would they?—No, they would go direct from Liverpool to Belfast or Dublin, as a rule.

114. Then I suppose London is the other chief point in England of export to Ireland?—I would not say that. Bristol has got a large export, I believe, to Ireland. I could not answer that off-hand.

115. Would it be the case there as at Liverpool, that the goods would be received at Bristol for shipment and sent by shipment to Ireland? The railways would not intervene?—They might have gone to Bristol from London.

116. That would make London the point of departure?—In many cases it would.

117. Are those customable goods when sent from London to Ireland usually sent by sea?—A large quantity go by sea. I could not say what proportion.

118. The railways concerned would be railways communicating between London and Ireland?—The railways communicating between London and Ireland are in many cases also sea carriers. That is one reason why the information we got from the railways we considered was of so useful a character.

119. Would you say that London is the chief point of export of customable goods to Ireland or Liverpool?—I would not answer that. You see Glasgow exports to Ireland. There is a very large trade between Glasgow and Belfast, for instance, and Glasgow and Dublin. I should have to make inquiries before I could give you any satisfactory answer on that point.

120. I suppose if you name London, Liverpool, Glasgow, and Bristol, then you have named the principal ports?—Yes.

121. Take the London and North-Western Railway Company; they are land and sea carriers?—They are.

122. Would the customable goods sent from London or any other point in England by that railway for export to Ireland be sent by the boats of the companies?—Yes, they probably all go by the company's boats to the North Wall, or to Greenore.

123. So that that company is in an excellent position?—Yes.

124. (*Mr. Wolff.*) A very large quantity goes by Fleetwood, does it not?—I could not say what quantity goes that way without inquiry.

125. (*Mr. Sexton.*) That company has control of the whole route from the point of departure to the point of import?—Yes, it has.

126. They would be in an excellent position to give information?—They would be.

127. In other cases the land and sea carriers are different by the same route?—I think the Great Western has vessels from Milford to Waterford, and I think they also have vessels going to Cork from Milford.

128. But there are cases in which the railway company is a different company from the sea-carrying company?—Yes. I think from Barrow, for instance, there is a distinct shipping company.

(*Mr. Wolff.*) I think not. The Midland Railway Company has vessels at Barrow.

129. (*Mr. Sexton.*) Mr. Pittar says that every possible care has been taken, when dealing with the railway and shipping returns, to avoid the inclusion of the same goods twice over?—Yes, because in the Order which we sent out on the 20th November 1890, when the railway companies had agreed to give us the information, we told the shipping companies "The "shipping companies are to be asked to include "therein only the goods booked locally by themselves "at their shipping offices for transmission to either "of the other two divisions of the United Kingdom, "than the one in which such shipping office is situated," so as to keep clear any goods which were included in the railway returns from also being included in the shipping returns. They were only to include in their returns what they locally booked.

Mr. R. B. [illegible] C.B. July 1894. [illegible] for Irish trade.

130. Do you think that effectual for the purpose?—Well, we hope so.

131. Of course we understand that there have been identical duties on all articles since a long time past in the three countries?—Identical Customs duties. The duties on British spirits, which are Inland Revenue, were different.

Customs duties now equal.

132. Not of recent years?—Not since 1860, I think. I think Mr. Gladstone made them equal.

(*Lord Welby.*) 1858.

133. (*Mr. Sexton.*) They were assimilated finally in 1858?—Yes.

134. Therefore of course it is obvious that the revenue officials have had no possible interest in separating the quantities concerned?—We have had no interest whatever in it.

135. None whatever?—No.

136. As soon as the duty was paid your official interest ceased?—Our official interest ceased.

137. Now a somewhat new state of affairs has arisen, and may develop, and it becomes important to consider how, not for four months but as a permanent matter, the true proportions should be ascertained. Have you any suggestion to make?—I have considered the subject a good deal. My opinion is this, though of course the different trades would oppose it, I think that if information is necessary the system which would give least disturbance to trade would be an extension of the permit system. I would extend it to pretty nearly all the articles mentioned here in this list, except to cocoa and coffee, and "all other articles."

Permit system suggested [illegible].

138. Just a word about that. There are four items in this Memorandum of the Board of Customs, cocoa, chicory, and coffee, and dried fruits, and it appears that the total revenue of the United Kingdom from them in the year is less than a million?—Yes, a great deal less.

139. And then Ireland's share after adjustment is about 100,000*l.*?—About 70,000*l.*

140. So that I do not think we need trouble with any minute inquiry?—I should omit those from any scheme of the kind I suggest.

141. I should propose in any inquiry not to give you any trouble on those heads. Will you kindly give us your opinion as regards the others?—I would be inclined myself to extend it to dried fruits. I do not think there would be any great trouble about that. Foreign spirits we already have accurately under the law. I do not think it would interfere very much with the tea trade, though of course like any other trade they would object.

142. It concerns a very large figure?—Yes, in a large item. Then, as regards tobacco, we have it only as regards the leaf tobacco. What we want is to have it applied to the manufactured tobacco, including cigars.

143. Wine?—I should apply it to wine also, and I think perhaps there would be less objection in applying it to wine, because many of the wine merchants are also spirit merchants, and they are accustomed to the use of the permit in sending out their spirits.

144. A good many of us are non-officials and we have to derive the beginning of our information from you. Could you briefly describe the working of the permit system as it stands?—I have a copy of the permit here. I may say any man who is going to remove unmanufactured tobacco or spirits has to put in what he calls a request, and the request and the permit are, practically speaking, the same document. The upper part of it is the request of the merchant to remove his goods. The latter part is where the Customs or Inland Revenue officer signs, and his signature is the permit. The request and the permit are one document.

Permit system explained.

Mr. F. S. [illegible], C.B.

1 July 1895.

Permit system explained.

145. To move it from where it is at the time?—If it is in London and they want to move it to Newcastle, for instance.

146. Is it under the control of the Customs or Excise?—The Customs or Excise.

147. Before removal?—Before removal. They have to apply for this permit as regards both leaf tobacco and any spirits, foreign or British.

148. Unmanufactured tobacco and all spirits?—All spirits, foreign or home made.

149. Must this be a removal from one of the three countries to another of them?—Yes, it may be a removal anywhere.

150. It cannot be removed at all without a permit?—It cannot be removed anywhere without a permit.

151. Then when you want to adjust the figures as between the three countries, you take the permits that indicate the removal from one country to another?—Yes.

152. You select them?—Yes. I will first take the tobacco permit: "I request a permit to remove from "so-and-so to Mr. So-and-so of so-and-so, in the "county of so-and-so, the quantity of tobacco specified "below; to be sent out by a certain time in the day "and conveyed by a carrier, it may be, or it may be by "ship. Dated so-and-so. Duty paid by so-and-so, "and bond given by so-and-so for the removal." Then below are the marks, the numbers, the net weights, and the packages. Then comes at the bottom, "The "proper duties having been paid, or bond having "been given, the above-named tobacco may be "delivered." This is signed by the Customs officer or the Inland Revenue officer, and the permit goes with the goods.

153. And all goods referred to in such a document are in the absolute control of the Customs until removal?—Under the control of the Customs or the Excise. I do not think they can remove any greater quantity than a gallon of spirits without taking out a permit.

154. Do these permits invariably find their way back to your department?—They did not. They do now, because under the Order which we issued in 1891 we have duplicates to secure complete knowledge.

155. What was the system before that reform?—There was only a single permit which went with the goods, but now we have a duplicate of that permit, which comes to the Statistical Office as regards foreign spirits and unmanufactured tobacco, and as regards British spirits to the Inland Revenue. So that we have got a complete record of the movement of those articles.

156. Are these permits detached documents, or are they in a book?—Detached.

157. Who has the custody of them before they are filled?—They go with the goods which are removed.

158. If a trader wants to remove goods, where does he get the permit?—He would apply to the Inland Revenue or to the Customs officer wherever the goods are.

159. The forms are in your custody?—Yes.

160. (*Lord Farrer.*) If I order six dozen of whisky from Dublin, which has paid duty, is it necessary that the manufacturer should get a permit in order to send it to me in England?—Yes.

161. (*Mr. Wolff.*) Even after it has paid duty and is in his own possession?—Yes, he cannot move it.

162. Not even after he has got it in his own shop?—No, he cannot move it without permission.

163. (*Chairman.*) Suppose that I have in my cellar here in London a cask of whisky, what then?—You are not a dealer. It is the dealer who must do it.

164. (*Lord Farrer.*) If a dealer sends it to a private person he must have a permit?—Yes.

165. (*Chairman.*) Private people do not require permits for moving any amount?—Not that I know of.

166. Either of spirits or unmanufactured tobacco?—I think not, because it is already known to have paid duty.

167. (*Mr. Sexton.*) How does this permit relate to the time of payment of duty. Does it at all?—No. It is a kind of revenue check upon it, that is all.

168. It may have been paid at any time before?—Yes.

169. (*Chairman.*) Is it not the case that the permits practically apply to goods which are duty-paid out of the warehouse?—Yes.

170. And then sent away?—Yes, the goods moved from the warehouse would be moved under bond.

171. Where they are moved from the warehouse to be duty-paid afterwards they would be removed under bond?—Under bond.

172. But the great majority of the cases in which permits are necessary are in respect of goods that are there duty paid?—Yes.

173. On leaving the warehouse and going wherever the consignee wishes to send them?—Yes; and whenever moved they must be accompanied by a permit if they are moved by a dealer.

174. But the cases of permits being required by dealers for spirits or unmanufactured tobacco which has already been removed from the warehouse to their own premises are very few, are they not?—I should not say they are, not so far as my knowledge goes.

175. (*Mr. Wolff.*) Is it not possible that the same whisky has two or three permits issued for it as it is moved from one place to another, and then it appears as if the quantity were greater than it really is?—Each time it is moved by a dealer it would require a permit.

176. Then the quantity named on the permit does not actually show the quantity of whisky?—Yes, it does.

177. But the total quantity shown by the permit does not necessarily correspond with the total quantity which is moved?—You mean the same may be moved twice over. That is so. But the general order as to duplicate permits prevents the same spirit being twice counted in making the "true contribution."

178. (*Sir David Barbour.*) That does not affect the calculation as regards the distinction between England and Ireland?—I do not think it would militate against my proposal, because I think having once gone to Ireland it would stay there.

179. If it were moved out of Ireland there must be another permit?—Yes.

180. (*Mr. Sexton.*) Would there be two permits for moving the same whisky from England to Ireland?—There would not be two at the same time.

181. Would not the one permit accomplish the transfer from one country to another of any particular quantity of whisky?—Without a duplicate, do you mean?

182. If a trader wants to move whisky from one country to another a single permit does it?—Yes.

183. There is no fear that two permits will represent the same quantity of whisky so far as the transmission from one country to another is concerned?—Not at the time that the spirit is moved.

184. I understand the duty may have been paid before the permit was issued?—Yes, it may have been paid and the permit issued when the spirit was removed from the spirit dealer's private premises.

185. I think I understand you to say the spirit referred to in the permit is under your custody or control at the time of the issue of the permit?—If it is in bond it is under our control, but it is not under our control if it is in his private premises. He cannot move it from his private premises without a permit.

186. It may be either in bond or in private control before the issue of the permit?—If he paid duty and took it out of bond, and then wanted to move it after it was taken out of bond, he would have to take a permit for it.

187. Therefore, whether the spirit is in bond or whether the duty has been paid, and the spirit con-

Mr. W. H. [illegible], C.B.

4 July 1894.

Permit system [illegible]. Permit system [illegible].

veyed to private premises, you think the present system is equally efficient to control the moving of it, and for ascertaining the movement of it from one country to another?—Yes, I think so.

188. I understood you to say that if it became necessary to apply precision to this apportionment of revenue, you would extend the permit system?—I would for a limited period.

189. That would be applied to tea, tobacco, and wine?—Yes.

190. And what about foreign spirits?—The law is in full operation as regards foreign spirits.

191. Does it occur to you to make any observations upon the application of the permit system to tea, tobacco, and wine?—I have already said that I think the trade would object to it, but I think there would be least difficulty as regards wine, because most wine dealers are also spirit dealers, and are accustomed to make use of permits.

192. Many wine and spirit dealers are also dealers in tea and tobacco?—Yes.

193. Would that affect the facility of the system?—They would get accustomed to it all the quicker, I think.

194. (*Chairman.*) I think you also added dried fruits?—I should be inclined to try dried fruits. In the United Kingdom they pay about 320,000*l.* a year, and we have at present no statistics at all as to what proportion of that goes to Ireland.

195. (*Mr. Sexton.*) Of course, if the proportionate amount of revenue were to depend upon the efficiency of this system the present system would not suit?—No.

196. It is a mere system of rough estimate?—That is all.

Adjustment of revenue.

197. And the improved adjustments of tea for two years here, involving a sum of a quarter of a million as between one country and the other, could never be allowed to depend upon such calculations as have been made?—I think they are too rough.

198. Would you apply one four-months' period to a number of years?—I believe in approximation, but I do not think it would be sufficient to take any action on.

199. I believe that the net effect of your adjustment is, as regards tea, so far as concerns Ireland and Great Britain (I do not speak as between England and Scotland, there it appears to be very rough indeed); that it approximates to the consumption by population?—Not on tea. We have not taken the tea on the population estimate.

200. Did the results approximate in that way?—I have not worked it out in that way. I can hardly say.

201. When I asked you the question a little time ago you said that that earlier method you stated at page 6 of your paper 329 had been modified by Mr. Pittar's memorandum of 321 of the same return?—Only because in the first return for 1889, 1890, and 1891 I think we had to go upon the approximate figures obtained from the shipping companies.

Mr. T. J. Pittar.

202. Only the first year; I think the second year Mr. Pittar corrected further?—(*Mr. Pittar.*) In the second year we went upon the railway return entirely. In the first year we adopted those methods that I described before as applying to the shipping companies, dock boards, and so on.

203. I am speaking now of tea?—Of tea.

204. Also further increases as detailed at page 31 largely affected the modification of the year before?—Yes, they did.

Adjustment of revenue in case of tea.

205. I see that for the year 1888-1889 the revenue for tea collected in Ireland was 293,000*l.*?—Yes. You are speaking from the first memorandum now, on page 6.

206. Yes—return 329, page 6. The revenue collected for tea in Ireland was 293,000*l.*, and the revenue contributed was found to be 564,000*l.*?—Yes, 564,000*l.*

207. And you arrived at that conclusion by adding the 11,000,000 lbs. of tea on which duty had been paid in England and then, according to the information which came from the shipping companies, exported to Ireland, and 11,000,000 other lbs. on which the duty had been paid in Ireland?—That is so.

Mr. T. J. Pittar.

4 July 1894.

Adjustment of revenue in case of tea.

208. How far did you modify that at page 31?—At page 31 the difference is this; that whereas we had assigned as contributed by Ireland in respect of tea in the first calculation 564,000*l.*, in the second case we assigned only 477,716*l.*

209. A difference of about 90,000*l.*?—Yes, it would be about that.

210. Do you observe that the revenue collected and earned for tea in the second year appears to be 30,000*l.* lower than in the first year?—You observe that you are comparing different years?

211. Certainly. That is what I am saying. The revenue collected in the second of the years was 30,000*l.* lower than in the first of the years?—Quite so.

212. There is a further adjustment for the year 1889-90 in the return of 1891?—That is applying the newer method to it, namely, the Railway Returns.

213. That is applying to the year 1889-90 what you applied in the other return to 1891?—Yes.

214. I observe that the contributed revenue appears to be in each of these just about double the collected revenue by the different methods?—It is not far off.

215. Will you state what was the effect of the application of the newer method, the four months' figures to 31st of March 1891, to the year 1889-90? In the first place the collected revenue, of course, remained the same?—Yes.

216. But instead of holding that Ireland had contributed 564,000*l.*, you have it that they contributed 628,000*l.*?—Yes, that is exactly it.

217. That is to say, the closer investigation you had applied to it led you to the conclusion that Ireland contributed 60,000*l.* more than appeared by the earlier return?—I do not say the closer investigation, but the newer statistical method. We applied another statistical method to it, and the only other that we had, and that resulted in our assigning to Ireland, as contributed by Ireland in respect of tea, 628,000*l.* instead of 564,000*l.*

218. You applied it, I presume, because you thought it a closer method?—No, I think not; we applied it because we had it. As I have already explained, while waiting for these Railway Returns, which took some months to compile, we investigated the accounts of various companies, dock boards, and so on in Ireland for the purpose of getting some figures in the first instance. But those were for the past years. The Railway Returns only applied to the future. They set up certain machinery and applied it to certain four months, and we applied the results which we obtained from those four months to all future years that we had to deal with, because the machinery ceased and was destroyed. We do not express in any of the memoranda, I think, that we think it a better method. Statistically, of course, if one had any better method one would not attempt to defend applying the proportions arrived at upon the figures of one year to the actual figures of another year. But that was the only method that we had at our disposal.

Adjustment of revenue.

219. Seeing that you applied the results of the figures for the four months to the year 1889-90, and substituted those results in regard to the year 1889-90 for the results stated in the earlier return, I suppose your impression was that they gave a better view of the actual facts?—I should not be disposed, as a matter of personal opinion, to say absolutely that I think all the results are more probable. You have perhaps observed that when it is worked out per head of the population it gives a larger amount of duty payments in respect of tobacco per head in Ireland to each individual of the population than it does in England, and at first sight one would not be disposed to say that that is correct. But that is what the railway returns brought out. They were the result

Mr. T. J. Pittar.

5 July 1894.

Adjustment of Revenue.

of machinery set in motion by responsible bodies, railway companies, who had an official system and machinery by which they could carry it out; and I am always disposed to attach more value to results arrived at in that way than to results arrived at by haphazard investigations made by one body here and another body there, which have no kind of machinery adapted for such purposes.

Statistics of imports, how obtained.

220. (*Mr. Martin.*) May I ask if the railway and shipping companies were remunerated in any way for the trouble and expense they went to in making those returns to your department?—No, they were not. I was given to understand at the time that the expense was considerable, and I am prepared to say, from my own knowledge that the trouble was enormous. There were hundreds of thousands of circulars sent out by them, and at their own expense entirely.

221. And you attached considerable importance to the returns made without remuneration, such as you received?—I think so. As I say, railway companies have an organisation of their own, and their discipline is strict with their servants; and from my own experience in a Government office I am more disposed to trust returns which are arrived at by an organisation of that kind than I should be to trust returns based upon miscellaneous information, such as the first returns.

222. (*Mr. Sexton.*) I understand from what you say on page 21 that the figures afforded there by the railway companies and by the shipping companies were given as the result of machinery deliberately established for the purpose?—That is so.

223. They knew what you wanted and the reason why you wanted it?—Yes.

224. And they set themselves upon your initiative to procure the exact facts?—Yes, they did so. They consulted us as to the heads under which we wished information to be given. It was arranged orally, by conference and so on. We gave them the forms, or the shape in which we thought the information would be most useful. They promulgated that information through their Clearing House, which is a central organisation in London having to do with all the railway companies, and then each of the railway companies sent its returns to the Statistical Office.

225. I take it then that the information at page 21 was the best that conference and communication between your department and the carrying companies and their clearing house could secure?—Yes, I think so.

226. May I say they were statistics of the highest efficiency as far as that method could secure efficiency?—Yes, I think so. They did their best for us, and we were of opinion that, being arrived at on that basis, they were statistics that we ought to lay before the Government.

227. (*Mr. Martin.*) Did the railway and shipping companies apply to be reimbursed the expenses they were put to?—(*Mr. Murray.*) They did not.

228. (*Mr. Sexton.*) As you are apparently chiefly concerned on this point, Mr. Pittar, I would ask you this question; whilst this latter method was the result of the deliberate course of action that you have described, I take it that the earlier method described at page 6 was the best information you could pick up on a journey to Ireland which you took yourself?—(*Mr. Pittar.*) Yes, it was. I visited every port in Ireland.

229. In the latter memorandum you speak about the railway and the shipping companies, and in the earlier one, signed by yourself and also by the heads of the department, you speak only of shipping companies?—That was a rough way of speaking of it. There were more returns in the first method made by shipping companies than by dock boards and harbour authorities; but the returns in the first method were not at all confined to returns by shipping companies; they were from any source which we thought most likely to give us the information historically for the year 1889, which was past.

230. Your journey to Ireland was towards the end of 1890, was it not?—Yes, it was about September or October 1890.

231. Your memorandum of it is dated January 1891?—Yes, quite so.

232. You did not content yourself on that occasion with the railway companies; you went to the points of import in Ireland?—Yes, that was so. I had previously communicated with the railway companies, and they were in communication with the Board of Customs during my absence as to the setting up of that special machinery for the future.

233. And the result was the latter method?—Yes, exactly so.

234. In the meantime you went to Ireland and obtained this information?—Yes.

235. Had that minute of yours relation to all the heads of the Customs accounts?—That was so, yes.

236. Tea, tobacco, foreign spirits—which is immaterial as a matter of adjustment of revenue?—Yes, we had only set up the permit method for foreign spirits in July; and as I went to Ireland at the end of September or the beginning of October, we had only three months of the statistics of foreign spirits, and at that time we were therefore obliged to treat foreign spirits very much the same as other articles.

237. You say three months, but I think in your earlier memorandum you say six months?—Because at the time that memorandum was made up you will see that time had gone on to December. But at the time I went to Ireland the registration of accurate statistics for foreign spirits had only been in operation three months; it began on the 1st of July. But by the time this memorandum was made up, which was in January 1891, we had six months of those returns in.

238. You just doubled the results of six months to make the probable results of the year?—That was so.

239. And I understand since then you have actual figures for each year, at least for foreign spirits?—Yes, for foreign spirits. We have no doubt on the subject of foreign spirits.

240. The main purposes of your inquiry in Ireland related to tea, tobacco, and wine; but mainly to tea and tobacco?—Yes, they were the two principal articles.

241. In some cases you obtained information from harbour boards, and in other cases from shipping companies, but I think you only mentioned three places—Belfast, Dublin, and Cork?—speaking from memory—and I think I am correct in this—the only two instances in which we had returns from harbour boards were in the cases of Belfast and Cork, and of course the Belfast return really is the most important of all.

242. Did you examine their books, or did you ask them to give you returns?—We asked them to give us returns.

243. And for what period did they give you returns? for the year 1889–90?—It was for the year 1889 really.

244. The calendar year?—Yes, it was for the calendar year.

245. And you received these returns from the harbour boards of Cork and Belfast?—Cork and Belfast.

246. Did they give you a return in detail, or simply a summary or total?—They gave a return to our collectors at Belfast of the numbers of the packages of each article, and he there made the requisite deductions for taxes, after inquiry on the spot as to each article; and he furnished me with the net return. Very much the same was done at Cork.

247. The tea and tobacco imported?—Not only of tea and tobacco, but of all the other articles except foreign spirits. As to foreign spirits we had another method.

Mr. T. J. Pittar.

5 July 1894.

Statistical returns; inquiry in Ireland.

248. You had a method independently of that inquiry in Ireland?—Independently of that inquiry, yes.

249. I understand you to say the reason why the harbour boards in Cork and Belfast were able to give you what you had to obtain in a looser way elsewhere, was that the machinery for the collection of port dues enabled them to give you that information?—Yes; they were official organisations, and at once recommended themselves to our collectors as organisations from which we should probably get fairly accurate accounts, because their dues were dependent upon accuracy, and where there is a money stake in a matter of that kind it is always more likely to be correct.

250. How did the fact that they collected dues put into their hands the means of giving you the information?—Because, as I understand it, they have different rates of dues on different articles landed and exported, and consequently they keep a register of the quantity of articles landed and exported. That enabled them to give us the returns under heads of articles.

251. In order to collect the port dues on any ship they enter into their books the details of the cargo of the ship?—I believe that to be so. I do not know that their method of collection is by the ship, but at any rate they have a register in which they record the quantity of articles which pass through their books for export and import. Their method I cannot answer for.

252. Are not the dues levied on the ship only?—There are dues levied on ships and dues levied on goods.

253. Of course when the dues are levied on goods my point is still more completely served because when the dues are levied on the goods they have directly to apply those to the goods?—Yes, that is why we thought it was a good method.

254. And when the dues are levied on the ship, would there be any alteration of the amount of the dues because of the nature of the cargo of the ship?—I do not think the dues levied upon the ship would have assisted us in the least. They would probably be upon the tonnage of the ship.

255. In that case the check would be very slight; in fact the means of information would hardly be apparent?—No, there would be no assistance as regards this inquiry from dues levied upon the ship, but only from dues levied upon the goods.

256. Are dues levied upon all goods, or are dues upon goods sometimes taken in the form of dues upon the ship?—I cannot answer that, I have no knowledge.

(*Mr. Wolff.*) If I may be allowed to answer that, I may say that the dues on the ship are totally irrespective of the dues on the goods. The dues on the goods are levied quite independently of any dues on the ship. You can land no goods of any sort at Belfast without having to pay dues and without the harbour officials having a correct list of those goods.

(*Mr. Sexton.*) There are dues upon all goods then, apart from the dues on the ships.

(*Mr. Wolff.*) Quite so.

257. (*Mr. Sexton.*) And therefore the system will be efficient?—(*Mr. Pittar.*) I think so. It recommended itself to me at the time.

(*Lord Farrer.*) They differ in different ports. Different harbour authorities have different modes of charging their dues. It is a very common plan to have certain dues upon the tonnage of the ship, and also dues upon all the goods.

(*Mr. Martin.*) We have no dues at all in Dublin upon goods; we have dues upon ships.

258. (*Mr. Sexton.*) Dublin apparently is very different to Belfast?—Yes.

Adjourned for a short time.

259. As there returns made of the railway and shipping companies quarterly for the four months to March 1891 have determined the adjournment since, it would be important, Mr. Murray, I think, if you would put in any returns obtained from the companies, or records of them that you have, so that we may see in what detail they have given particulars?—(*Mr. Murray.*) Would it answer the purpose which you have in view if an abstract was made of these returns, or would you rather have the returns?

Mr. R. H. Murray, C.B.

2 Feb. 1891.

260. But there is no uncertainty how far they applied themselves to the particulars?—Returns came in from each of the railways, and I think they are made up for the month of November, and then the last returns were made for a period of three months. The returns themselves would be very voluminous. Perhaps it would answer your purpose if you had an abstract of the returns made by each railway for the four months.

261. Yes?—(*Mr. Pittar.*) But in order to agree with the totals we should have to combine with that the returns made by those shipping companies which were not in connexion with railways. It will be understood that they contributed to the general total. If it is wished, in the abstract to be furnished to the Commission, to arrive at the totals which were used in combination, it would not do to leave out of account the shipping companies.

Mr. F. J. Pittar.

262. Would the abstract deal with the different goods?—Yes, it would show the different goods.

263. Now I understand that in Dublin and Waterford you had to depend upon the shipping companies?—Yes, in Dublin and Waterford we depended upon the shipping companies.

264. Did your inquiries relate to every port at which goods would enter?—Yes, to every port. There are not many in Ireland at which there is any considerable coasting trade. My inquiries did relate to every port, and we sent round circulars besides that, with directions from the Board of Customs as to how the companies were to be communicated with, and what inquiries were to be made. Mr. Murray has, I think, already put in the general order of the Board of Customs on that point.

265. You have only named some eastern ports; but there are some western ports like Galway and Sligo?—I do not think I visited Sligo, but I visited Galway. There is some traffic to Sligo. There is a line, I think, from Sligo to Greenock.

266. (*Lord Farrer.*) I suppose that almost all this trade is carried on by certain regular lines of steamship companies?—Yes, for the most part, certainly.

267. There is not much accidental trade?—Very little.

268. So that if you get hold of certain companies you get hold of the whole?—Yes, I think so. And if there be accidental traffic it is not unsafe to assume that it would be the same for that four months as for any other four months.

269. (*Mr. Sexton.*) How was it that you could not get in Dublin any such accounts as you received from Belfast?—I am speaking from memory here, for I have not the papers by me, but in Dublin there was no central authority (so far as I could understand from our collector there) from which a full account could be obtained, such as we had from the Belfast Dock and Harbour Board.

270. (*Lord Farrer.*) Probably in Dublin they take dues upon the ships and not upon the goods?—I think very likely that is so.

271. (*Mr. Sexton.*) And there you had to depend entirely upon the returns given to you by the shipping companies?—Yes, but we inquired also of the manufacturers.

272. Can you say how far shipping companies are able to give you the quantities of different goods?—I furnished the collector of Customs in Dublin with a schedule of the heads under which I wished the information to be obtained, and he moved the companies to make a return. You will easily see that in the case, for instance, of the London and North-Western Railway Company such a return would involve a great deal of work and trouble. That Dublin return took some time to compile and get in.

When it came in we were not perfectly satisfied with the total—(I state this so that the Commission may understand fully the circumstances under which the return was compiled). I have not the figures here, but I know I am not far wrong in saying that the total was about 500,000 lbs. on the chief article, tobacco, given as exported from Dublin to Great Britain. We caused confirmatory inquiries to be made of the manufacturers themselves of how much they sent, and the total given by them was about double that which was furnished by the shipping companies in that case. That made us look with considerable suspicion upon the returns of the shipping companies in Dublin, and to seek about for other means for getting a return, in which, however, we failed. Then it was suggested (though I understand there is some reason to doubt whether that is a good explanation) that though the Dublin manufacturers of tobacco might have sent some 1,000,000 lbs. of tobacco while the shipping companies only carried 500,000 lbs., possibly the difference was owing to some of that million lbs. having gone northward by rail, and having formed part of the Belfast return, for instance.

273. The Belfast export?—The Belfast export. It would be possible, I mean, that 1,000,000 lbs. of tobacco might be sent out of Dublin for Great Britain, and yet that the shipping companies exporting direct from Dublin only carried half a million.

274. Because the other half went out of Belfast?—Yes; we were, however, unable exactly to thresh out that question, and we accepted, for what it was worth, the shipping companies' return.

275. It appears that the contribution of Ireland under the head of tobacco, as tested by the later method of inquiry, is much larger than appeared by the earlier method?—On the same year is it so?

276. I take two successive years?—But then the revenue of the two successive years differed. I do not think it works so much on the same year that we adjusted. I am not quite sure. Yes, there is considerable difference.

277. For the year 1889–1890 the revenue on tobacco was 1,348,000*l*.; for the next year it was 1,404,000*l*., a difference of 56,000*l*. The contribution for the earlier year appears to have been 1,103,000*l*., and for the latter year 1,315,000*l*., a difference in revenue of 56,000*l*. and of contribution 200,000*l*.

(*Lord Welby*.) If you look at Mr. Cheney's return, it is not so much. The figures as given in Mr. Cheney's return are 1,103,000*l*. and 1,230,000*l*. Therefore that figure of 1,230,000*l*. should be compared with that figure which Mr. Sexton has just read out.

278. (*Mr. Sexton*.) It substantiates my point, that the contribution of Ireland under the head of tobacco is larger under the minute or better form of inquiry?—Yes, it would appear so.

279. Now, Mr. Murray, I believe there are some special difficulties in calculating upon tobacco out of Ireland?—(*Mr. Murray*.) There are, because in making any calculation as regards the quantity exported we have to consider the manufactured article, what foreign substances, if I may use the term, have been used in the manufacture of that article besides the leaf which has paid duty. That is one of the points which makes the return so difficult to make. In the manufactured article there is a considerable quantity of water added besides the amount which is in the article at the time it is imported, which is usually supposed to average about 15 per cent.

280. Something like half a million pounds of manufactured tobacco, if I understand rightly, is imported into Ireland?—Yes, so far as I know.

281. Then there is a great quantity of unmanufactured tobacco imported directly into Ireland without passing through Great Britain?—The leaf tobacco has probably gone into Ireland from England, and paid duty in Ireland. There it is so that raw material when turned into the manufactured article that the difficulty arises as to the quantity of foreign matter which has been introduced in the manufacture. I think the deduction made on the quantity exported from Ireland was 20 per cent.

282. There are different rates of duty, are there not?—There are different rates.

283. What are they?—3*s*. 2*d*. on the leaf tobacco, 4*s*. manufactured, 4*s*. 6*d*. Cavendish, and 5*s*. cigars.

284. What do you call unmanufactured tobacco?—The unmanufactured is the leaf—the raw material.

285. Then that raw material is manufactured in Ireland?—It is manufactured in Ireland to a great extent.

286. And results in an export from Ireland of 2 to 3 million lbs. a year?—I think it was ascertained from the railway returns … being in round numbers about 2½ millions.

287. Is there any further fiscal operation on the tobacco after the payment of duty on the manufactured article?—No, none at all.

288. Is it the general result of your inquiries that the amount contributed by Ireland under the head of tobacco approximates to the proportion of the population?—I have not worked it out in that way as regards population. I have got some figures here showing the rate at which tobacco is consumed per head in the shape of money expenditure by each individual of the population. That, as made out in the amended returns for 1889–90, gives the proportion in England at 4*s*. 9½*d*. per head; in Scotland, 5*s*. 1½*d*.; Ireland, 5*s*. 3*d*.; 1890–91, England, 4*s*. 11½*d*.; Scotland, 5*s*. 4*d*.; Ireland, 5*s*. 6½*d*.; 1891–2, England, 5*s*. 1½*d*.; Scotland, 5*s*. 6½*d*.; Ireland, 5*s*. 10½*d*.

289. Is that consumption per head?—Consumption per head, expressed in money expended.

290. As adjusted?—Yes. 1892–3, England, 5*s*. 1½*d*.; Scotland, 5*s*. 6½*d*.; Ireland 6*s*. and a small decimal.

291. It appears that the consumption per head in Ireland is the greatest?—Yes, it is the largest of all.

292. (*Lord Welby*.) That is on the adjusted figures?—Yes, on the adjusted figures.

293. (*Sir Robert Hamilton*.) I think I am right in saying that the figure as first adjusted on page 6 of paper 320, worked out by the population in Ireland, would make the rate per head 4*s*. 8*d*.?—4*s*. 7½*d*.

294. So that there is a rise from 4*s*. 7½*d*. to upwards of 6*s*. in four years?—That is so.

295. (*Mr. Sexton*.) There is another method of adjustment?—Yes.

296. Let me direct your attention to this statement on page 7 of 320 of 1891: "The average amount of "tobacco duty collected per head of the population of "the United Kingdom is 4*s*. 8*d*.; and in England "the amount collected is 4*s*. 8*d*., in Scotland 4*s*. 7½*d*., "and in Ireland 5*s*. 8½*d*. per head. It is known that "duty is paid in Ireland on about 2,000,000 lbs. of "leaf tobacco, which, after manufacture, is sent to "England. If this 2,000,000 lbs. be deducted from "the apparent Irish consumption, the average amount "of duty paid by each individual of the population in "that country becomes about 4*s*. 5*d*. Thus when "allowance is made for the known large export of "duty-paid tobacco from one division of the kingdom "for consumption in the other divisions the result "is to bring the duty paid per head of the population "to something very near the average amount per "head of the whole United Kingdom." That was founded upon the looser inquiry which had relation to the year 1890. It was based on the shipping returns only.

297. And the alteration is due to the method pursued by the department and in connexion with Mr. Fitter's journey to Ireland over the four months of 1891?—Consequent on the railway returns.

298. The closer inquiries seem at least to show a larger consumption in Ireland?—As far as we can gather.

299. As to wine, I notice that the effect of the further adjustment appears to be to lower the apparent contribution of Ireland. Now the question of wine appears to have been dealt with in a very general

Mr. H. B. Murray, C.B.

2 July 1890.

Mr. T. J. Pittar.

Wine consumption and duty.

way?—The shipping companies were only able to give returns of the number of cases, of casks, and of their sizes.

300. And there is a great variety of duties?—Yes.

301. How did you arrange them. (*Mr. Pittar.*) If the question is asked with reference to railway returns, I may say that it was different in the two returns. The plan pursued in the case of the railway returns was this: There are a great many rates of duty on wine. First, we have the wine that pays 1s. a gallon duty and then that which pays 2s. 6d. a gallon duty. Then there comes sparkling wine duty and so on. The railway companies were able to give no information at all of the different rates. They could only tell us that they had got so many packages.

302. They could only tell you it was wine?—They could only tell us it was wine and give us the size of the packages. The size of the packages enabled us to estimate the contents of the package in quantity. The consequence was that we were able to make a quantity calculation as between the three kingdoms without being able to arrive at any knowledge of how much of the stronger and therefore higher duty-paying wine went to one country or the other. We were obliged to assume as a fact that as regards the different kinds and qualities of wine, each country drank equal proportions of the different kinds. We had no choice but to go on an assumption of that kind. That is to say, to put it in a general way, we took it that as large a proportion of claret is drunk in Ireland as is drunk in England, and as large a proportion of the stronger wines, sherry and port, as is drunk in England.

303. How did you estimate the proportion drunk in England?—We assumed that the different descriptions of wine were consumed in the same proportion for the whole kingdom. We took the entire quantity of wine, and then, having ascertained that of the total quantity of wine consumed in the three kingdoms, 85 per cent. was consumed in England, 6 per cent. in Scotland, and 8 per cent. in Ireland (I am discarding decimals), we then simply divided the entire duty, giving 85 per cent. of it as the contribution of England, 6 per cent. to Scotland, and 8 per cent. to Ireland.

304. You take it that 8 per cent. on the whole duty on wine was paid in Ireland?—Yes, because we found that 8 per cent. of the quantity went to Ireland.

305. And you take it that the proportions of the different kinds of wine were the same in the two countries?—We found it impossible to make any distinction as to the different kinds.

306. (*Mr. Wolff.*) Did the railway companies' returns specify the difference between a one-dozen case and a three-dozen case?—Yes, we especially provided that.

307. (*Mr. Sexton.*) There was no other plan open to you but to adopt the one you suggest?—No, no other plan.

308. The generality of the particulars given you by the companies afforded you no better basis?—No.

309. In fact they had no better basis?—They had no better basis. We thought that the basis adopted was substantially fair. At any rate we had no other method.

310. Now, Mr. Murray, apart from the question of the application of the permit system generally, do you suggest any better particulars could be obtained from the companies. We have heard that it was only by the personal influence of Mr. Jackson that they agreed to give this information gratuitously of four months?—(*Mr. Murray.*) Are you speaking of the shipping companies or the railway companies?

Mr. H. B. Murray, C.B.

Powers of Inland Revenue Department over shipping trade.

311. I understood that they both performed the duties gratuitously?—We have no control at all over the railway companies. Over the shipping companies we have.

312. So far as the railway companies are concerned it is a matter entirely of their own pleasure?—Entirely of their own free action.

313. (*Lord Farrer.*) What is your control over the shipping companies?—The regulation, to which I have referred.

314. (*Mr. Wolff.*) Everything must come by ship to Ireland?—Quite so.

315. (*Lord Farrer.*) Where the railway company is the shipping company you have a control?—Yes.

316. And they must carry by ship?—Yes.

317. Therefore you have control over them all?—Yes, but that only applies to Ireland, not to Scotland.

318. (*Chairman.*) There is one test which I do not know whether you applied. Did you look at the relative value per gallon of wine imported into the three kingdoms?—No, that was not taken into consideration at all. We had no means of ascertaining that. We only knew it was wine that went.

319. But as to direct importation you have the value as well as the quantity of the wine?—Yes.

320. Did you look and see whether there was any material difference in the cost?—No, I do not think we made any inquiry. (*Mr. Pittar.*) Perhaps I might answer that question. We did look at that point and we found there was a difference, but not so large a difference but what it was quite possible, if we had been able to ascertain the value of those proportions of wine which were carried between the kingdoms, that that might have redressed the balance, and we could judge nothing by taking the direct imports into Ireland.

Mr. T. J. Pittar.

Wine: value of imports.

321. May I ask you as to the direct import? Which is the strongest or more valuable, the wine that is imported into England, or that which is imported into Scotland, or that which is imported into Ireland?—I cannot at this distance of time state, but a calculation of that kind was made, and I can put it in if required.

322. You might put it in, in answer to my question?—I will make a note of that.

323. (*Lord Farrer.*) May I ask you in regard to tobacco? There is no difference in the duty according to the quality of tobacco is there? It is only as it is manufactured or not manufactured?—(*Mr. Murray.*) It is only according to the raw material.

Mr. H. B. Murray, C.B.

Tobacco, quality of.

324. So that however high the quality, it pays the same duty as if it was of low quality?—Yes, leaf of low quality pays the same as leaf of fine quality.

325. Have you any idea whether the quality of tobacco imported into Ireland has been higher or lower than of that imported into England?—I should assume from what I was told yesterday that the quality of the tobacco imported into Ireland would at least not be inferior.

326. On the whole you assume?—Decidedly not I should say.

327. The quality of the tobacco imported into Ireland is as expensive as the quality imported into England?—I was told yesterday, and it may amuse those who hate the Saxon, that the Irishman is a far better judge of good tobacco than the Saxon is.

328. But that is not the only question; the question is also whether he can afford to pay for it?—My informant told me that he had to supply the South of Ireland and the West of Ireland with a better class of tobacco than he supplied to the stupid Northerner; and in England the ignorant Saxon did not care what he smoked. Therefore I conclude that the quality of the tobacco sent to Ireland would be good.

329. Your figures rather point to the fact that the Irishman pays more per head upon tobacco to the State than either the Scotchman or the Englishman?—The same informant said that for the Irishman in the South especially he had to manufacture a drier tobacco than he had to do for the Northerner—that he really consumed in each pipe he smoked more tobacco than the Northerner would, it being of a drier kind.

330. (*Mr. Sexton.*) Your remark as to the power of the Irishman to apply a particular judgment to the quality of tobacco applies also, I think, to tea?—I

Mr. H. N. Murray, C.B.

3 July 1894.

Tobacco, quality of.

should say it did, because after Mr. Goschen reduced the tea duty he directed us to make inquiry as to whether the benefit of the reduction of duty was obtained in the distant parts of Ireland, and through the constabulary we had a quantity of samples taken in, I daresay, 150 different parts of Ireland. These were analysed in our laboratory, and they were all found to be of good quality—indeed, I may say of high quality—so that the quality of tea drunk in Ireland is certainly good.

331. I understand that the exportation from Ireland to Great Britain of tobacco manufactured from the raw material imported into Ireland, and duty-paid in Ireland, has no fixed effect?—No, not at all.

Permit system explained.

332. I want now to ask you a few questions about this permit system. What rank of officer supplies the permit form to the dealer?—It would be the examining officer with us, probably first or second class, as the case might be; an excise officer, probably of a corresponding rank, it might be as low as assistant of Excise.

333. These permit forms are not bound in a book?—No, they are all numbered.

334. Does the officer who issues the permit form make any permanent record of the issue of it, or the particulars of it?—Not that I know of. I think he has to send us the duplicate, but I do not recollect that he has to make any record of that. I think our surveyor, in checking his account, has to take some note of whether a duplicate permit has been sent or not.

335. (*Chairman.*) Is there no counterfoil?—No.

336. (*Mr. Sexton.*) Is there any reason why an examining officer of the Customs or an equal officer in the Inland Revenue should not record, when he sends the permit, that the dealer has filled up the particulars of the permit in a book?—There is no reason why he should not. It would be adding clerical labour of course.

337. But as a matter of fact it would afford security for accuracy without at all doubting that the officers do forward the duplicates?—He has to record in what is called the register in the warehouse when the permit was issued; but how he would deal with it in the case of goods sent from the private storage of the merchant I do not know.—(*Mr. Pittar.*) There is a central record made. He sends on the duplicate.

Mr. F. J. Pittar.

Mr. H. N. Murray, C.B.

Mr. F. J. Pittar.

338. I quite understand that?—(*Mr. Murray.*) You want a local record.

339. I quite understand that when the permit reaches you or the Inland Revenue they are extremely careful to record it, but I do not yet see how you assure yourselves that every officer has forwarded the duplicate?—We have given instructions about that, and the officers are checked by their superior officers, but I do not think we have any actual record at the stations kept of the permits which are issued. (*Mr. Pittar.*) Perhaps I may answer that question. At the time that the duty is paid upon the goods the document that is put in is called a "home consumption warrant," and there is a column that has been lately inserted since these inquiries commenced, on that form, for the country of destination. If the duty is paid in England, and the article is going to be removed after payment of duty to Ireland, that would appear in that column. That home consumption warrant comes to my office, and the details are there checked. If, for instance, a home consumption warrant came to my office which did not bear the country of destination on it, we should pick it up directly and refer it back to know what the country of destination was; and by that means we have a check which secures that we get a record of every warrant relating to removals between kingdom and kingdom; not in every case,—only the removals between kingdom and kingdom. I am speaking of customable articles now, as duty paid from a Customs warehouse.

340. It relates to Customs simply?—Yes, Customs simply.

341. Does it relate to foreign spirits?—Foreign spirits or British spirits, if they are delivered from a Customs warehouse.

342. The total for a year of these home consumption warrants which you were able to make ought to correspond with the total of the permits issued afterwards for removal?—Yes, if there were another total made; but there is not. We content ourselves with seeing that we get a permit for every case of removal between kingdom and kingdom.

343. I hardly see where the check comes in as regards the total operations of the year?—When the merchant pays duty on his cask of spirits the home consumption warrant comes to my office, and I can see from the column of country of destination whether or not a duplicate permit for that same cask ought to have been issued.

344. And can you identify the cask?—Yes, from the particulars—the marks and numbers would appear. I think you will see they do appear here now on the permit form.

345. Does the office identify the cask?—No, but there are the marks and numbers of the cask, the import particulars of which are stated on the permit, and are also stated upon the home consumption warrant, by which the collector checks it. There is a complete identity established between the two.

346. The permit may be issued a long time after you receive the home consumption warrant?—I am speaking at this moment of permits issued at the time of duty payment from the warehouse. Of course, if the cask of spirits on removal from the warehouse goes direct to a dealer's store, then my observations do not apply. In that case the permit or certificate would be issued at some future date. It may be a year or two hence. It would be issued by the dealer, and checked by the Excise officer.

347. It passes out of your hands?—I cannot answer authoritatively as to the Excise plan of issuing permits, but their method of check I can speak about. Their method of check is this: The permit is torn from a book of counterfoils; that book is in the possession of the trader, and afterwards the Excise officer goes to the trader's store and examines that book. He sees on the counterfoils how many removals there have been between kingdom and kingdom, and he is enabled to furnish to the Central Inland Revenue Office at Somerset House a check by that means. I cannot speak as to details, because it is not my department; but that generally is the system.

348. You do not follow the spirits beyond their exit from the warehouse?—No, not as far as the Customs are concerned.

349. Of course the Excise issue these permits to the dealer?—The Excise issue them. These are numbered books I think I am correct in saying.

350. The dealer can have a book when he pleases?—Yes.

351. Are the leaves of these books consecutively numbered?—Yes, I think so, with a counterfoil.

352. Is there any check upon the dealer at the time of filling the permit?—I cannot answer on that point. I can state my belief, which is this, that he is checked out of his own books. The dealer himself issues the permit and the Excise officer checks him by first looking at the counterfoil book, and he can see from the dealer's own ledgers, which show his stock, what amount of spirit he ought to have in his possession. He has got perfect access to his books and he can check between the counterfoil book, the permit book, and the stock book; and it is because of the necessity for doing that that it is extremely difficult to set up a permit system for other articles.

353. (*Chairman.*) The object of the whole permit system, was it not, originally, a revenue object?—Yes, a revenue object, and not a statistical object.

354. (*Mr. Sexton.*) You think that reference to the amount that the dealer should have in stock enables the officer to determine that the figures put into the counterfoil are the same as those that were upon the permit?—I think so. I do not see where the liability to mistake (I am speaking now of removals from kingdom to kingdom) is likely to come in. The

dealer, if he has removed a cask of spirits to Ireland, can hardly have any motive in putting in, say, Birmingham, instead of Dublin; he will gain nothing by it and there is no object in his putting in a wrong country of destination. The Excise officer will take care that he does put some country of destination in.

355. And he has no object in mis-stating the quantity, has he?—No, I can see no object whatever in his doing so. In fact he has every object in stating the correct quantity, because if he states the wrong quantity the Excise officer will find that the balance in his possession is the wrong balance.

356. The system you have described for the Customs would apply also to the export of spirits from Ireland to Great Britain?—Quite the same.

357. How far does the export of spirits from Ireland to Great Britain come within the jurisdiction of the Customs?—Only in the same way as it does from Great Britain to Ireland. The spirits can be removed in two ways, either under bond or duty can be paid. If removed under bond, they are frequently under the control of the Customs, and must be accounted for at the other end, and the duty paid or an explanation made. If removed after payment of duty, then a permit is issued.

358. You are aware, of course, that an error of great magnitude was discovered in the year 1893?—Yes, I believe that was so, in the figures of the Excise Department.

359. The securities which you have described to the Commission as being efficient existed in Ireland at the time that those errors were made?—No, I think not. Very careful safeguards have been devised since.

360. But at the time the errors were made those safeguards did not exist?—No, at the time the errors were made the safeguards that I am speaking of did not, I think, exist, and certainly the same vigilance was not used. You can understand that after the lapse of some 30 years, when no use whatever had been made of the figures collected, the officers had fallen into perfunctory habits of carelessness, and as regards the record of these Excise permits there was, I believe, no doubt, looseness in one district. I am not speaking from personal knowledge, because it had no relation to the Customs Department. The Inland Revenue can best speak as to this.

361. You can give no evidence of the internal economy of the Excise Department?—Quite so.

362. But you can say whether it was the practice in Ireland before these errors were committed for the dealer to fill up the counterfoil as you have described?—I have little doubt that it was the theory that the dealer should do so, and that it was the theory that the excise officer should carefully check and see that he had done so. I imagine that there were some laches and carelessness in actually carrying out that direction.

363. (*Lord Welby.*) I think it is rather desirable to call the attention of the Commission to one point here. The Inland Revenue officers are the only ones that can explain the causes of that error, and I think you will hear from them that as far as any question of loss of duty was concerned no loss of duty could occur under the system under which the error took place. The fact of the matter was that the error took place in compiling the statistics from those returns. It was a very gross statistical error, but it was an error which did not jeopardise the revenue.

364. (*Lord Farrer.*) I should like upon that to ask you one question. You have had very great experience of collecting statistics quite independently of the revenue?—Yes, I have had some experience.

365. Do you think you can rely implicitly for practical purposes upon statistical returns where there is no question of money or account involved?—When it is in respect of dutiable articles—articles that are subject to duty although it is not a question of the direct collection of duty—I think we can rely upon the returns, but as regards statistics which have no relation whatever to revenue of any kind, I think that we lose a great safeguard which we have in the case of statistics which do relate to revenue.

366. What would be very valuable for statistical purposes where one error counterbalances another, and where on the whole you only want a general result, would be very different indeed in a case where you want to found a practical system of apportioning money upon it, would it not?—Yes, it would.

367. To collect these facts for statistical purposes is one thing, to collect them for the purpose of apportioning a revenue or expenditure between England and Ireland is quite another thing?—Yes.

368. And would require much greater accuracy?—It would.

369. And you think, these articles being dutiable articles, you would have a greater security in that case than you would in the case of ordinary statistics?—I think so decidedly. Being dutiable articles, the revenue officers will be certain to look after them with more or less care.

370. Would have a certain knowledge of them?—Yes, would never, in fact, lose sight of them.

371. (*Mr. Sexton.*) I understand that as soon as it became a question no longer of statistics, but of the possible apportionment of revenue, the error was discovered?—That was so, and checks were applied, not merely in the Excise, but in our own department to make sure that no such slip should again occur.

372. And assuming that the officer correctly extracts from the counterfoil the quantities stated there, you think that his check over the dealer is sufficient to make the whole process reliable?—I think if he carries out his check carefully it must be so. I think under the system which obtains in the Inland Revenue Department that there is practically no doubt whatever that correct statistics would be obtained.

373. (*Lord Welby.*) I think, Mr. Murray, that the Return 329, which we have been discussing, was prepared to assist the Select Committee appointed in 1890 to consider the financial relations between England, Scotland, and Ireland, and that that return simply placed before the Committee such information as the Government possessed or could collect bearing upon the amount and proportion of revenue contributed to the Exchequer by the people of the three countries?—(*Mr. Murray.*) Yes, it was prepared, as I said before, under verbal instructions.

374. The return did not pretend to suggest conclusions on the points referred to the Committee; it was simply intended as a statistical brief which the Committee could analyse, and upon which they could base an inquiry?—It was the best information we could collect to put before any Committee which was appointed.

375. I think the Committee itself only held a preliminary meeting in 1890, and was not re-appointed in 1891, and therefore it did not pursue its investigations?—That was the case.

376. And I think I may put it that this brief that was prepared for the Committee has never, up to the present time, been made the subject of what I should call an independent examination?—That is so.

377. It was intended as a paper to be analysed, and the analysis of which would lead no doubt to various suggestions being made and criticism being addressed to it. Such an examination might probably have led to further suggestions?—It was intended as a kind of starting point more than anything else.

378. So that now, for the first time, this information which was collected by the Government becomes the subject of independent examination?—Yes.

379. I think that from what we know, both you and the Inland Revenue had great difficulties to deal with in collecting this information, and am I not right that you were laying before the Committee such information as you possessed without drawing any conclusions therefrom?—Yes, we drew no conclusions beyond the arithmetical results which followed from the figures we were able to give, such as they were.

Mr. T. J. Pittar. 1 June 1894. Statistics of dutiable articles.

Parliamentary Return 329 of 1890.

Mr. R. E. Murray, C.B. Select Committee of 1890.

B 4

Mr. H. E. Murray, C.B.

4 July 1894.

380. But a more independent tribunal was to judge whether the information was such that conclusions might be based upon it?—Whether the information was sufficiently correct.

381. At the beginning, when you first took up the question, you had no other information except the amount of duty you had collected in Ireland?—None whatever, not authentic.

382. But you had from your own knowledge of business some idea that those amounts did not really represent the consumption in Ireland?—We knew, as a matter of fact, that there were these large manufactories of tobacco in Ireland and that there were large exports of tobacco from Ireland, but we had no statistics with reference to it.

383. At all events that led you to the conclusion it would not do to place before the Committee of 1890 the collection as a safe test of consumption in Ireland?—We told the Chancellor of the Exchequer that, and it was on his learning that, and our telling him that there must be deductions made from that and corrections made, that he told us to commence the inquiries which we made.

384. And it was only from what I may call side information that you were enabled to come to the conclusion that there were interchanges between Ireland and England which would affect very much any conclusion that might be based upon the duties paid in the two countries?—We did not know to what extent the information we got from the railways would check the information we got from the shipping companies. It was by way of a check upon the earlier information we had obtained. This is an extract from a report which Mr. Pitter made to the Board on the first statistics: "These figures are the result of my journey "to Ireland last time, and of the inquiries made at "the same time by the Inland Revenue. They have "no connexion with the statistics now in course of "collection by the railway and shipping companies, "which latter figures when obtained will correct and "stand in the place of these estimates." That was a memorandum which Mr. Pitter put in on the 4th March 1891.

385. That followed as the result of his inquiry?—On the information obtained from the shipping companies. At this time, on the 4th March, we had not got in the final statistics from the railways.

386. Mr. Pitter and the Board of Customs saw some reason to doubt the accuracy of the figures which were obtained on his first visit to Ireland, when he obtained the information from the shipping companies?—It is quite possible the returns of the first month which he got may have shaken Mr. Pitter's mind, because the first returns of the railway companies were rendered for December. For the last three months they were sent collectively. (*Mr. Pitter.*) It was also upon my general knowledge, if I may say so, that the first return was not based upon what I may call a good statistical basis. There was no system properly carried out, and I felt doubtful about it.

Mr. T. J. Pitter.

387. (*Mr. Sexton.*) You refer to the return of 1889?—Yes.

388. (*Lord Welby.*) The return alluded to at page 6 of the Parliamentary Paper 329?—We never at any time intended the first figures as in any way official, but merely as a sort of starting point on which to base other inquiries.

389. And that led you to suggest, as the result of your experience, a further trial should be made through the railway companies?—Not exactly that. I started before I went to Ireland by going to the railway companies. The railway companies, seeing the magnitude of the inquiry, asked for a little time to deliberate. Meanwhile, as Mr. Goschen's demand was pressing, I went to Ireland to get the best figures I could and to lose no time.

390. It was what might be called an intermediate test?—Yes, I think that would very correctly describe it.

391. From the beginning the Board of Customs intended to check the information which they possessed, that information being based solely upon the duties collected in Ireland; they always intended that the *bonâ fide* and final test should be one obtained from the railway companies?—(*Mr. Murray.*) I would not say we went so far as that, but we were not satisfied with the information we had got from the shipping companies, and, as Mr. Pitter has said, he had commenced to negotiate with the railways before he went to Ireland to see what further information we could get from them.

Mr. H. E. Murray, C.B.

4 July 1894.

392. I asked the question because a very considerable modification is shown in the figures based upon the returns given by the railway companies as compared with those which were given as the result of what I call the preliminary examination; and I presume, therefore, that the Commission would be right in supposing that you would sooner rest a conclusion upon the railway companies' returns than upon the shipping companies'?—Yes, for this reason: I think the railway return was built up day by day as the goods were removed; it was compiled at the time the business proceeded, whereas the shipping companies' returns were picked out from their books looking backwards. Now it is always difficult to make a return picked out from books, perhaps not very clearly kept, while, as I have said, the railway companies' return was one which was made day by day as the work was done.

393. I am asking the question first of all in order that we may get into our minds the figures upon which, as far as they go, you chiefly rely, but also because they seem to me to affect very much what is stated in this Memorandum, at page 6 of the Parliamentary paper No. 329. Take, for instance, the article tobacco; the net result of the transfers between Ireland and England is very much less, is it not, under the railway returns than it was under the preliminary returns?—The net returns.

394. If you look at the return at page 6 you will see it gives the result of what I call the preliminary inquiry. The duty collected in Ireland 1,340,000*l*., and it is stated the amount contributed was 1,103,000*l*. When you come to correct that, and it appears corrected in Clancy's return, the contribution by Ireland, which under the preliminary return was stated to be 1,103,000*l*., rises to 1,230,000*l*.?—Yes.

395. Therefore the tendency of your more correct returns was to lead to the conclusion that the consumption of tobacco in Ireland was larger than you thought it was at first?—That is so.

396. In the course of this inquiry allusions have been made to the amount in lbs. weight of tobacco sent from Ireland to England, which have been stated to be 2,500,000 lbs.?—Yes, in round figures.

397. It has not, I think, been clearly brought before us, though it has been mentioned, that on the other side very nearly 1,500,000 lbs. is sent from England to Ireland?—I think it is so stated in one of these papers.

398. But there are figures based upon the preliminary inquiry?—In the memorandum to the preliminary inquiry, page 7, it is stated: "The Customs "Returns show that the manufactured tobacco on "which duty was paid in Ireland, when added to that "received in a duty-paid condition from the other "two kingdoms, amounts to only about 500,000 lbs., "whereas there is an export from Ireland of from two "to three millions lbs. of the manufactured article." But that is not quite the point you are upon.

399. It had been stated that about 2,500,000 lbs. of manufactured tobacco came over from Ireland to England?—Yes.

400. On the other hand, something like 1,500,000 lbs. of manufactured tobacco went from England to Ireland?—I do not now think that is stated in any of these memoranda. (*Mr. Pitter.*) I do not think in any printed memoranda, but those are about the facts.

Mr. T. J. Pitter.

401. May I take it for the moment, subject to this being corrected afterwards, that those figures represent it roughly?—Yes, in round figures, we might say, without being far out, that that is so.

402. Therefore, even upon the rather excessive figures which the preliminary examination showed, the balance is only 1,000,000 lbs.?—Yes.

403. The difference would only be 1,000,000 lbs.?—It is scarcely so much even as 1,000,000 lbs., because when we came in the first inquiry it appeared that 2,500,000 lbs. were removed from Ireland to England, while there was a return the other way of a million and a half, I should say that it is rather to be stated thus. The first inquiry showed that there was exported from Ireland to England 2,500,000; but the first inquiry did not show, I think, sufficiently clearly the amount sent from Great Britain to Ireland. That was one of the reasons which we afterwards had for distrusting the first return. The first statistics gave the return back to Ireland as only about 550,000 lbs., the second, the railway returns, magnified that three times, and made the figure that we have just been speaking of 1,500,000 lbs. That was one of our reasons in the office for preferring the second one, because it is easy to omit something in a calculation of this kind, but if the railway companies gave us an actual return of manufactured tobacco conveyed from England to Ireland in the four months, of nearly the same amount as the first inquiry gave from England to Ireland in the whole year, that was an abundant reason, I think, for preferring the railway return.

404. (*Chairman.*) Could you refer me, if it appears in these papers, to the 1,500,000 lbs., I have not found it?—It is not stated in the papers. I have documents, of which I can put in copies, which will show the million and a half sent direct from England to Ireland, but those which I have here are original.

405. (*Lord Welby.*) The result of this is that on the figures on which the Customs would place the greatest reliance the balance of manufactured tobacco sent from Ireland to England, as compared with that sent from England to Ireland, is represented by only about 1,000,000 lbs.?—(*Mr. Murray.*) Hardly so much.

406. The railway figures rather diminish, do they not, the amount that the shipping returns showed were sent from Ireland to England?—I think the returns of the railway companies did not give quite so much as two and a half millions, it was something like 2,400,000 lbs.

407. I should like to ask you, though I think we have gathered as much already, on the whole you consider the railway companies' figures trustworthy?—As I said before, I prefer an account built up day by day to one which is got by extractions from different books. You may easily miss one when you are extracting from a book; whereas a clerk building up an account day by day is not liable to the same errors.

408. The railway companies would have a knowledge of these great articles of consumption, they would know whether they were sending tea or tobacco?—Yes, certainly. I cannot say whether they know it by the difference in freight or not, but as a rule they would know what they were carrying.

409. And therefore if they told you that their books showed that so much tobacco was sent and so much tea, you, as a critic upon the returns offered by them, would put trust upon that return as approximately right?—Certainly as between those two articles.

410. (*Lord Farrer.*) Have not railway companies accurate knowledge, because from day to day they have to classify the articles and charge them according to their tariff?—They will know, but there is this possibility of error, I believe, although I do not profess to know much about the rates of freight, that there is a different freight charged on different articles so that it might possibly happen sometimes that a consignor sent his goods with the wrong description.

411. The companies have to know under what class to charge, have not they?—Yes.

412. Tea will come under one rate and linen will come under another rate?—Yes.

413. Therefore if the thing is presented to them as tea they would put it in class 2, or whatever the class may be?—I should suppose a sharp practitioner, if he could gain anything by entering his article as one on which he would get a lower freight might in some cases do so.

414. It is discovered and detected, is it not, because it is the railway freight manager's business to detect that?—Yes, it depends, I think, upon who is the consignee.

415. (*Lord Welby.*) Supposing the freight on tobacco and tea were the same, would it not be very possible that traders might substitute one for the other from carelessness?—Not as regards tobacco and tea, certainly not.

416. Why not?—Because the tea goes in in its original packages; it is perfectly well known by sight. It goes in chests, half-chests, and quarter-chests.

417. Do you happen to know whether tobacco is sent in recognisable packages?—I could not answer that. I have not seen tobacco packed for that kind of journey.

418. I asked you the question because, on the whole, it would seem that though, owing to these different rates, there may be some temptation to a trader to misdescribe, yet probably railway companies would, as Lord Farrer has suggested, take very good care that goods are not entrusted to them under false descriptions, if they lose by it?—I should think they might trust their officers to find it out and make it too hot for anybody to do it.

419. (*Lord Farrer.*) It would not be done in large quantities?—No.

420. (*Lord Welby.*) And it would be only large quantities which would affect such considerations as the Commission have before them?—That is so.

421. Therefore I think I may gather from you, on the whole, that you would place very fair reliance upon, say, a year's returns by the railway companies such as you obtained?—I should prefer it for a longer period than the four months to satisfy myself.

422. But from your knowledge you would not be suspicious of any very great error in a return so obtained?—No, I think not. I think it would be fairly accurate.

423. You remember a gentleman who has an immense tobacco trade in Belfast?—Yes.

424. It is said that he pays a very large amount, probably equal to one-half, or at least a very large proportion, of the whole duties collected in Ireland. Now, did you try to obtain from him any information as to the amount of manufactured tobacco which his house alone sent over to England, in order to check the railway returns?—No. Our collector was in communication with him in connexion with the returns which were made by the dock board, or whatever the name of the superintending authority there is, at Belfast; but I do not think the quantities given were in any way checked by this very large manufacturer to whom you refer.

425. Supposing this gentleman were to pay 500,000*l.* or 600,000*l.* of duty (I am not saying that that is the amount), and supposing the duty collected in Belfast were a million, it would be perhaps not an unreasonable supposition to say that at all events his transactions might afford an important check upon the railway returns. If this gentleman told you that he from his own knowledge exported to England half the total amount which the shipping or the dock companies gave you as sent from the port of Belfast, would it not be rather a telling test and check in confirmation of the railway and shipping companies' figures?—No doubt any information he gave in from examination of his books would be a most useful check.

426. May I ask you whether this would be practicable at the present moment?—I should doubt there being any disinclination on that trader's part to give us information on that point. So far as I know, he has not been asked to give that information,

Mr. E. B. Harman, C.B.

4 July 1894.

Tobacco: consumption and duty.

but I do not see why a trader should object to give it. In the case you refer to there would be none, because it is a great house. The parties who might object would be the smaller men, who might not wish to show their hands.

427. You observe I am simply trying to bring before the Commission points by which a test could be established?—You are pointing to another source of information, which might correct or confirm the information we had got; and I may say, with regard to this large trader, who I may say rules the trade in a certain degree, that I doubt whether he would object to give the information, but it is possible it might not be so willingly given by his smaller opponents.

428. As he has such an enormous share in the business of Belfast, if his figures in any way corresponded with, or confirmed those which the railway companies and the shipping companies gave you, would it not be a very strong confirmation of the correctness of that information?—Yes, it would, but in what passed between us he admitted that the sources of information to which we had applied, namely, to what I call the dock board there, possessed absolutely correct information—that we could rely upon the figures we got from them. I think he spoke of being chairman of some steamboat company there, and he seemed to think *quâ* Belfast, we had got accurate figures.

429. Of course you have noticed that the adjustments which you have made in estimating the tobacco consumed in Ireland lead to the conclusion that Ireland consumes per head more tobacco than England?—Yes.

430. Therefore it is extremely important to know whether the facts upon which you arrived at that conclusion can be relied upon or not?—I should like very much to get further information so as to see whether we cannot arrive at something more probable than that the Irish consumption would be as large as these later returns have made it out to be.

431. You have already alluded to that extremely interesting information which this gentleman gave, and I think he also stated that from his knowledge of the trade he was not altogether surprised at the conclusion?—No. He accounted for it, as I have said, by the fact that both the tobacco which he supplies to the South and South-West of Ireland, and the tobacco which he is compelled to supply to the large towns in England (because the Irishman in large towns like Liverpool prefers his tobacco to any other) is good, and in order to satisfy them he is obliged to supply them with dry tobacco which points to a larger proportion of tobacco being consumed in each pipe than in other parts of the United Kingdom.

432. Of course the period over which the railway companies collected their statistics was very short, but have any inquiries you have made, or any information which has reached you, led you to suppose that these four months were possibly an unfair period upon which to base a conclusion for a whole year?—I put that question to this same gentleman, and I asked him whether these *four* months would be a fair representation of his trade during the whole year, and he was accompanied at the time by a gentleman who, I believe, acts for him as manager when he is away in America, and they both said that they thought that the four months would be a very fair criterion.

433. Then, although it would be very much more satisfactory to get a year's returns, you have no reason for supposing that the four months would be an untrustworthy guide for the remainder of the year?—I would rather have 12 months.

434. But still you have no reason for suggesting that the four months are unfair?—No, not *primâ facie*.

435. Do you think the information which you have obtained from the railway companies of those four months is so far trustworthy that, supposing you could extend it over a longer period, the result would be one upon which the Commission might rely?—I confess I am staggered by the quantity of tobacco consumed in Ireland. I do not think the information we got from this gentleman the other day is sufficient to convince me that a dry pipe alone would account for it.

436. Therefore you think the railway statistics are wrong?—I think there must be some source of error in them, though it is difficult to arrive at what it is.

437. (*Sir David Barbour.*) May it not be that that period of four months does not fairly represent the year?—It might be so, perhaps, but I put that question particularly to those gentlemen to whom I have referred, and they both agreed those four months would be fairly representative of their trade.

438. Did they say the four months of that particular year would be fairly representative?—I told him the four months during which we got the returns, in fact he was consulted about it at the time, and both he and his manager agreed that these four months were a fair representation of the trade of the year. I also remember they added this, that they did not think their trade varied 5 per cent. as between one month and another in the year.

439. (*Chairman.*) You noticed of course that they were the four cold months in the year?—They were, it is true, but I am not a smoker, and I cannot say whether smoking men smoke more in hot weather than in cold.

440. (*Lord Welby.*) Would not the doubt which you cannot help entertaining in your own mind about the consumption of tobacco rather tend to lessen in your mind the importance and value of getting a 12 months' return if it would cost much money?—We should see whether there was any variation in the trade of the other two-thirds of the year.

441. May I put it in this way, that it is not so much that you mistrust the figures, but that the figures surprise you so much?—That is another way of putting it.

442. You felt suspicious?—I am suspicious about them.

443. You were speaking favourably, I think, of a power being given you to carry out a system of permits?—Yes. I think that system would give the least trouble and annoyance to the different traders of any system that can be devised if it was only for a limited time.

444. How far would you carry that. Do you suggest that manufactured tobacco, in whatever form it is moved, is to have a permit?—In whatever form it is moved. I think there must be some limit as to quantity just as you have with regard to spirits. You have a limit as to a permit not being required for the movement of a gallon of spirits.

Permit system suggested: tobacco.

445. Supposing I send over to a large house in Dublin for a box of cigars, would that house have to send that box under your system to me with a permit upon it?—It would. That would reduce it to a very low quantity. But I think it was established yesterday that there was no such traffic as that. I think the large trader to whom I have alluded said it would not answer.

446. Our informant did not think as between England and Ireland there was very much such traffic as that, but what I want to come to is, what would you actually propose? Do you propose that the permits should be required in the case of a movement of tobacco within London itself, for instance?—No, it would only be when it was moved from one country to another. Then we should have to fix, as I said just now, a limit below which the permit should not be required.

447. Did not our informant think that Mr. Wills' tobacco was sent over from England to Ireland in small packages?—I think not. I do not think this large trader said that. I think he said Mr. Wills would not supply individuals but would only supply traders.

448. Supposing tobacco is sent over in small quantities, would it not be a very great nuisance to the trader to have to get a permit?—No, I do not think

it would be in a man who once gets accustomed to the permit system.

449. Your proposal is a very far-reaching one?—It is. It is a choice of evils. It is a question what mode of obtaining this information will cause the least trouble and annoyance to the trade and my idea is that it would cause a great deal less annoyance than any system which would place the existing trade under restrictions. It is a question of comparative annoyance.

450. What you contemplate is that the Government should adopt some principle of obtaining statistics?—Yes.

451. And you are comparing your suggestion with your present power, if put into force, of obtaining statistics through the cargo book?—We have the power, but to exercise that power would be such an intolerable nuisance to the trade that I do not think they would put up with it.

452. You mean that if you were to exercise that power it would give such trouble to the trader that he would prefer almost anything else, and you think that as between the two systems the permit would be less troublesome?—I think so.

453. And you would confine it solely as between Great Britain and Ireland to these dutiable goods?—And Scotland and England.

454. (*Lord Farrer.*) Excepting packages of a certain size?—Yes; a certain weight rather.

455. (*Chairman.*) Did you contemplate limiting the permit system to transportation between the different kingdoms?—I should only apply it to goods going from England to Ireland and vice versâ.

456. You have already got it as regards spirits between two parts of the same kingdom?—Yes, but we do not call for this duplicate permit except in cases where the spirits are removed to a different kingdom. The duplicate permits are for the purpose of giving us statistical information, and we do not call for them to be sent in if the goods are removed from one part of England to another part. It is only when they are removed from England to Scotland or England to Ireland or vice versâ.

457. The permit is required?—Yes, but we do not want the duplicate sent up to us.

458. Would you apply the same plan to all the goods sent from one part to another in the same kingdom?—No, I would not apply it there.

459. (*Sir David Barbour.*) What check would you have if you did not apply it to every place? In the case of spirits the check was that the official looked at the dealer's balance, but if you have only a permit in the case of an article sent from Ireland to England, the check is lost, because you do not know how much has been sent to other places?—We could not exercise a check upon the stock of grocers and that kind of people; we could only enforce the practice by a system of heavy fines if it is not. I would not propose to watch the stock of the trader in the way the Inland Revenue do with regard to spirits; but I would impose some heavy penalty.

460. How would you detect breaches of this rule?—Information is often given when people do not expect it to be given, and I think traders would be afraid not to comply with the regulation if there was a heavy penalty. That is the way I would try to work it.

461. (*Lord Welby.*) Supposing a trader in Dublin is sending tobacco over to England, do you think that very likely he would go to the trouble of getting the permit?—It would be so little trouble, and if there was a heavy penalty I think he would rather incur that little trouble than run the risk of detection. That is my impression. I am only speaking from having thought the matter over a little, not from experience.

462. I understand that the permit on raw tobacco is not required as soon as duty is paid upon it?—Directly the tobacco has paid its duty we have no further claim.

463. Am I right in saying that in 1819 or 1820 tea in Ireland was put under the Excise?*—I do not think tea was; tobacco was. The tobacco duties were put under the Excise. Tobacco was certainly for four or five years, but I do not think tea was.

464. From these returns before us it would appear that the consumption of tea in Ireland is that where the Englishman consumes 100 the Irishman consumes 100?—I knew it was somewhere about equal, but I did not know it was exactly equal.

465. Has it ever come to your notice that in 1849 the consumption of tea in Ireland was about 28 as compared with the English 100?—No, I did not know that. But it must be borne in mind that in England (I do not know whether it was ever so in Ireland) the consumption of coffee at one time almost equalled that of tea, though coffee has gone out now. Therefore, if less coffee was consumed in Ireland, it is quite likely that the consumption of tea would be larger than the proportion in England where they consumed coffee also.

466. 1819 or 1820 are apparently the latest years in which you could have an absolute knowledge of the consumption of these goods in Ireland, and one would rather watch the progress of these articles of consumption in Ireland with the light acquired at the time when that information was worth having?—Yes.

467. And of course it is a curious circumstance that the increase should be so large?—Yes; it is a very singular fact.

468. (*Mr. Sexton.*) I suppose it is the case that the consumption of tea in Ireland has very much increased—probably more so than in England?—Yes, I can speak from my own knowledge as to that. One dealer told me that he sold as much as 10 or 12 chests where formerly he only sold one.

469. Has there been a total change in the habits of life there in the last half century?—I think so.

470. (*Sir David Barbour.*) The figures of the collections of revenue on tea, wine, and tobacco have been adjusted with reference to these four months' figures?—Yes.

471. And I think you said in the case of tobacco that you thought four months was a fair average for the year?—I said that the gentleman to whom I spoke thought that any figures which might have been given of his trade during those four months were a fair average of the trade during the rest of the year.

472. Was that as to tea or tobacco?—Tobacco.

473. Does the revenue come in evenly month by month in the case of these three articles, tea, wine, and tobacco?—I could not say. We have not taken it out. We could easily give information as to that.

474. I suppose you did not work out the percentage of adjustment for each month?—No.

475. It was only for the four months?—Quite so.

476. Can that be done?—It could be done, but Mr. Pittar says it would take a very long time, and he cannot take up the work for another week or 10 days, because the office is so busy.

477. I should like to see whether the adjustment keeps about the same, or whether there are serious fluctuations from month to month. If there were, it would raise a presumption that you could not apply the figures of four months to the whole year; but if the percentage of reduction was very small it would be otherwise?—Perhaps Mr. Pittar could speak about that. We could give the information, but it would take a long time to work it out.

478. You have got accurate figures for the adjustment in the case of foreign spirits and home spirits?—Yes. That for foreign spirits is accurate, and, as to home spirits, I have no doubt the Inland Revenue would be able to speak accurately.

479. When you were getting those four months' figures out, did you get figures as to spirits from the

Mr. R. B. Murray, C.B.

5 July 1894.

Permit system, suggested extension of.

Tea: consumption of.

Adjustment of revenue.

* It was subsequently ascertained that tea was put under the Excise not in 1819 but in 1824. It remained under the Excise from 1824 to 1834.

Mr. R. E. Murray, C.B. 5 July 1894. Adjustment of revenue.

railway companies?—I am not sure; I do not see why we should have done so.

480. If you had done so then you might have tested the accuracy of that system by comparing the results with the results you got from the permit system?—I do not think we did that. I do not think the railway companies gave us any information about spirits. We were content with the belief that the permit system was pretty perfect.

481. (*Sir Robert Hamilton.*) The first adjustment which was made and which appears here on pages 6 and 7 of the paper 329 of 1891, was made with the light of all the information that you could collect without having a basis of statistics. You substituted for those figures afterwards the return for the four months; but you did not test it by any outside consideration, you merely took those four months and adjusted the four years by those results?—It is a rough and ready way, I admit.

482. In your first adjustment you made reference to certain tests which would show the probable correctness of your work. For instance, you referred both in the case of tea and tobacco to the average consumption per head, but you adopted without any such test the figures which the four months' returns produced for the four years to which they were applied?—Yes, that is so.

483. Did it not strike you that in certain particulars the difference in the two bases of adjustment made a very great difference in the amount of revenue?—No doubt it did, and I remember Mr. Pittar drawing my attention to it at the time, especially as regards the larger consumption of tobacco.

484. I do not know that I shall go into it; but as regards tea, the revenue, as is stated, for Ireland for 1889–90 was 864,906*l.*, and as subsequently adjusted was 928,671*l.*, making a difference of 63,765*l.*, and raising the contribution per head from a sum less than that of the United Kingdom to a sum considerably more than that of the United Kingdom?—I was not surprised at that as regards tea.

485. As regards tobacco the result was in the same direction. The revenue, as is stated, amounted to 1,403,177*l.*, and, as adjusted, to 1,550,554*l.*, which made a difference in Ireland's revenue of 147,377*l.*; and that adjustment raised the Irish contribution when you calculate it per head from a sum below that of the United Kingdom to a sum very considerably above it. I think it raised it by something like 7*d.* per head?—Yes.

486. If you carry that a little further and adopt your method of adjustment for 1889–90 as correct, and compare that with the figures for 1892–93 we find this result: that while the consumption of tobacco per head has increased in the United Kingdom during those four years by 5·19*d.* that for Ireland has increased by 9·00*d.* Can you give any reason why there should be that great difference in the growth in that period of four years?—No. I should say that during those years Ireland was more prosperous agriculturally than England was. That is the only reason I can give.

487. Do you think that is a sufficient reason?—No, I do not.

488. Then keeping still to those adjusted figures I find that the difference between tobacco revenue collected in Ireland in 1889–90, and what is shown in those returns as contributed by Ireland, amounted to 96,290*l.*, which might be held as representing the amount of duty on Irish manufactured tobacco consumed in England—at least, the net consumption of such?—Do you mean that was the duty upon the quantity exported from Ireland?

489. Yes. The net amount in the year 1889–90. In that year the tobacco revenue collected in Ireland was 1,349,000*l.*; but in 1892–93, when the revenue collected in Ireland was 1,470,000*l.*, the amount that went over to England was only 73,697*l.* So that both actually and relatively there was a reduction in the quantity sent from Ireland to England although the increase of cost per head was going on all over the country, and the collection in Ireland itself was very considerably increased?—I can only again say that it may possibly, as to part of it, have been due to the increased prosperity of Ireland. That would only account for it partly, not to the whole amount, but to a large amount.

490. I understand you to say that you are by no means satisfied that you have got trustworthy results as regards tobacco from the means you took?—I am not. The difference is almost too great.

491. Does any test that you might apply beyond adopting a permit system suggest itself to you?—I think Lord Welby suggested that we might possibly make some personal inquiries of the manufacturers themselves. That would, of course, be one way of checking it; but then if one man refused to give information, and the others did give it, the man who refused to give information would destroy the value of all the information given by the rest.

492. (*Lord Welby.*) You have this advantage, have you not, in Ireland, that the tobacco trade is practically in the hands of five or six men?—I do not quite know how many it is in the hands of, but the great bulk of the duty is paid by five men, two large men in Dublin and two or three large men in Belfast.

493. (*Sir Robert Hamilton.*) You referred just now, in answer to Sir David Barbour, to a return I had asked you to make out showing the amount collected in each month of the four years, so that a comparison might be made between the four months for which we have got statistics and the rest of the period to which the adjustment has been applied?—Yes.

494. Was such a test made by the Commissioners of Customs?—No, it was not.

495. Is it the fact, so far as you know, that the across-channel traffic is pretty equally distributed over the year so as to make any four months a fair test?—I do not know anything to show the reverse.

496. Tea, for instance, comes in largely in certain months of the year?—The arrival of tea is quite different now from what it used to be. In days when China supplied us the tea began coming in in July, and came in very rapidly in the course of a couple of months. But now our main supplies are drawn from Ceylon and India, and the arrivals from those two countries are spread over all the year.

497. You are satisfied that your estimate as regards tea is fairly correct?—Yes, I am quite satisfied about that.

498. What do you say as regards tobacco?—Tobacco I am shaky about.

499. (*Chairman.*) You have spoken of the difficulty of relying on figures where revenue is not concerned. Do you mean that no one is sufficiently interested in checking the accounts, and that the officers become careless owing to want of supervision?—I do not think I said that. It was an observation made by Mr. Pittar, and it had reference, I think you will find, to what took place in the Belfast return made by the Inland Revenue, and they gave as an excuse, if I recollect, in the paper presented to Parliament that not being made for the purpose of revenue the return had been forgotten by one of the officers, and that that had made a large difference.

500. Do you generally agree in the principle that where a return does not touch revenue the officers get more careless?—I think so; where no money is to be got by it there is less care shown in looking after it.

501. Is not that strikingly the case as to the imports of free goods into the country?—Yes, it is there we are entirely dependent upon the information given by merchants' clerks.

502. You will remember that there was a great confusion as to values about 30 years ago?—There was.

503. Is that practically cured now?—I will not say it is practically cured, except in this way, that the mistakes of one year probably correct the mistakes of another.

Mr. E. W. Hamilton, C.B. 4 July 1894. Statistics of tobacco, probability of.

504. Taking them individually, it is very difficult, is it not, to get correct figures?—The values, as given by the merchants of their goods, are more unreliable.

505. (*Lord Farrer.*) The fact is, that the only perfectly accurate statistics are accounts?—You may say that.

506. (*Chairman.*) You said you are better satisfied with the figures as regards tea than the figures with regard to tobacco?—Yes.

507. Why is that?—Because the packages in which teas are sold are so recognisable.

508. The mistakes which occur in the case of tobacco are not so likely to occur in the case of tea?—No.

509. (*Mr. Sexton.*) I have just been comparing the yield of contribution from tobacco from Ireland between 1880, 1886, 1892, and 1893, and I find in each case the increase is 17 per cent. That is the result of the application of the identical test?—No doubt.

510. Then when you speak of an increase, what you mean is that as between the two tests the second test done since the increase, and you consider it more reliable than the first?—Yes, more reliable than the first, though not completely reliable.

511. In fact, so far as you criticise the results of the second test, it is rather that you doubt the accuracy of the results, although obtained on specific information, because you think it unlikely on general grounds that the tobacco may be consumed more largely in one country than in the other?—I will use the word "surprise." I am surprised at the result.

Adjourned to Thursday, July the 19th.

SECOND DAY.

Thursday, 19th July 1894.

Commission Room, Westminster Hall, S.W.

PRESENT:

THE RIGHT HON. HUGH C. E. CHILDERS, *Chairman.*

Lord Welby, G.C.B.	W. A. Hunter, Esq., M.P.
The Right Hon. The O'Conor Don.	Charles E. Martin, Esq.
Sir Thomas Sutherland, K.C.M.G., M.P.	J. E. Redmond, Esq., M.P.
Sir David Barbour, K.C.S.I.	Thomas Sexton, Esq., M.P.
Hon. Edward Blake, M.P.	G. W. Wolff, Esq., M.P.
B. W. Currie, Esq.	Henry F. Slattery, Esq.

Mr. R. H. Holland, *Secretary.*

Mr. A. Milner called and examined.

Mr. A. Milner. 19 July 1894.

512. (*Chairman.*) You are Chairman of the Board of Inland Revenue?—I am.

513. Since when?—Just two years.

514. You have with you two gentlemen, I think, of your department?—Yes; I have Mr. Turner, the Accountant-General of my department, and Mr. Steele, the Chief Inspector of Excise.

Excise duties equalised.

515. We do not propose on the present occasion to do more than ascertain in what way the figures contained in some recent Parliamentary Returns have been arrived at so far as relates to the Inland Revenue, and in the first place I will ask you one or two general questions. When were the duties on spirits made equal as between England and Scotland?—In 1855.

516. And when as between Great Britain and Ireland?—In 1858.

517. Since then the duties both on spirits and beer have been equal in the three kingdoms?—Yes.

Taxes from which Ireland is exempt.

518. Ireland is exempt from land tax, house duty, and from railway duty?—Yes.

519. Ireland also used to be exempt from income tax under Sir Robert Peel's original Act?—Yes.

520. Do you remember when that exemption ceased?—In 1853.

521. Otherwise there is no distinction between the taxation of the three countries?—That is not quite exact; there are a certain number of minor differences.

522. Besides land tax, house duty, and railway duty?—Yes.

523. Could you summarise them in a sentence?—I will mention the more important ones. Ireland does not pay the legacy duty of 10 per cent. on charities comprised in the will of any domiciled Irishman. Then under income tax there was till this year a difference in the charge under Schedule B.; this has just been changed by the House of Commons, which has reduced the charge in England to the same level as in Scotland and in Ireland.

524. (*Mr. Sexton.*) The charge on England was greater than in Scotland and Ireland till this year, was it?—The charge in England was greater than in Scotland and Ireland till this year. Again, the assessment for income tax under Schedule A. has always been on a different basis in Ireland and in Great Britain. In Great Britain the assessment has always been on what the Act of 1842 describes as the "annual value," which is practically the gross value. In Ireland it is expressly laid down in the Valuation Act that it shall be on the net value. I am aware that owing to the fall in the value of Irish land the net there was recently approximated somewhat to the gross in England, but even now there is a difference. The Irish valuation is lower; in almost every case property of the same value would stand at a lower figure in the Irish assessment than in the English assessment.

525. Is that affected by the Finance Bill of this year?—No, it is not, because the same reduction is given in both countries; the allowance has been extended to Ireland. There are some other points which perhaps I had better mention. Ireland is exempt from the patent medicine stamp, which brings in 200,000*l.* in Great Britain. Then the establishment licences are not charged in Ireland. Those are all the things of any real importance; there are besides some trifling differences in stamps, and licences being charged at a slightly different rate, but they

Mr. A. Milner. 11 July 1894.

are very unimportant. I do not think it is a matter of more than a few hundreds a year.

526. (*Lord Welby.*) The establishment licence is not a very small one?—No, I was not saying it was a very small thing. But after mentioning these specific things I say the rest are unimportant.

527. Could you state what the establishment licences are, because it is an important item?—Male servants, 144,000*l.*; carriages, 482,000*l.*; armorial bearings, 76,000*l.*; so that the total of those, excluding dogs, is about 700,000*l.*; the dogs are 414,000*l.* These are the figures for the year ending 31st March 1893.

528. (*Chairman.*) Except as to dogs, which is a peculiar case, all the other charges are paid in Great Britain and are not paid in Ireland, are they not?—Yes.

529. (*Mr. Sexton.*) Can you state at once the amounts realised by taxes levied in Great Britain and not in Ireland, and sum them up so as to give us in one view the difference?—It would take me a little time.

530. (*Chairman.*) You could work that into answer to a question?—It is very easy to supply that, but I could not undertake to do it right off.

531. You have now described, have you, fully, all the distinctions in Inland Revenue taxation between Great Britain and Ireland, or all the main distinctions?—All the main distinctions.

532. All except what we may relatively call trifles?—Yes.

533. Have you with you the Treasury Return 329 of 1891, called generally Mr. Jackson's Return?—Yes, I have it here.

534. That gives on pages 8 and 9 a memorandum dated January 1891, signed by your predecessors, Sir Algernon West and Lord Iddesleigh, on behalf of your Board, showing on page 8 the amount of Inland Revenue actually collected in England, Scotland, and Ireland, and on page 9 an estimate of the amounts actually contributed by each country?—Yes.

535. That is for the financial year 1889–90?—It is.

536. You have also a subsequent return known as Mr. Clancy's?—Yes, Return 93 of 1893.

537. This shows in the same general shape figures for the same year 1889–90, as well as for the two subsequent exchequer years?—Yes.

538. We will return to that presently as we go through the various items; but I presume where there is a difference you consider the figures in the later return, that is, 93 of 1893, to be the more correct?—Yes, the differences are very slight. There were some corrections of detail which, I think, increased the accuracy.

539. But where there are differences the later one is the one to go by, is it?—In my opinion, yes.

540. Was that return published under your own supervision so far as it relates to Inland Revenue?—The Clancy return was.

541. And there had been more time to work out the principles of adjustment?—There had been more time, but I do not know that anything had been done except in respect to the small matters to which you are presently going to refer. In these, on discussion between the Treasury authorities and myself, some slight alterations were made. I may say, generally, this Clancy return was prepared almost immediately after my arrival at the Inland Revenue. I took the basis that I found in the previous return arrived at by the Treasury and my predecessors. I never attempted to criticise that basis, but simply tried to work out the details as correctly as I could.

542. Before the return of 1891 do you know whether there had been any attempt to adjust the incidence of Inland Revenue in the three countries in the case of all the items of revenue?—I recollect, when I was at the Treasury seven or eight years ago, I saw some previous returns in which such an attempt had been made. But I have not been able to lay my hand on them, nor have I been able to find them at the Inland Revenue, nor any trace of correspondence with reference to them, but I cannot help thinking that there are such attempts.

Treasury Returns: adjustments of revenue.

543. (*Lord Welby.*) Are you thinking of the returns moved for by Mr. Maclaren, in which he endeavoured to make a distinction, in which we none of us believed at the time, between England, Scotland, and Ireland?—My recollection of them is that they were very sketchy. I was asked whether attempts had been made, and I think they were made.

544. There were three or four returns moved for by Mr. Maclaren, were there not?—That is no doubt what I am thinking of.

545. But the conclusions shown by these was doubted by everybody concerned in them?—I have no doubt that is so.

546. (*Chairman.*) Can you state on whose instructions your department acted in making the last attempt?—We have no official papers giving general instructions as to the basis on which we were to proceed. There were constant communications both by letter, and still more orally, between the Treasury and ourselves. My predecessor, Sir Algernon West, constantly saw the Treasury on the subject of the lines to be followed in preparing these returns, but there is no single official document which lays down principles for our guidance that I am aware of. Mr. Turner refers to one of a series of letters, but there is no single letter containing full instructions.

547. You were in communication with the Chancellor of the Exchequer, I suppose?—I took the matter up a little less than two years ago. I have a letter addressed to me by Lord Welby, which is the most official thing I have on the subject, which says, "It would be well, I think, to adhere to the principles "of calculation adopted by the Inland Revenue Board "in 1891." (That was before my day. That was in preparing No. 329 of 1891). "Unless you see "reasons for modifying them in any way." I did see reasons for modifying them in the small particulars, to which we shall presently refer, with the approval of the Treasury. Otherwise I took the basis as I found it.

Treasury Returns: Excise.

548. I will go to the first item of these accounts of Excise under this head. The figures seem to be the same for 1889–90, both in 329 of 1891, and in 93 of 1893?—Yes.

549. Except that in the second Return the Excise licences have been removed to a separate head on page 20 of Local Taxation Revenue; that is so, is it not?—Yes.

550. These licences were diverted from the Exchequer under the Local Government Act of 1888, were they not?—1888 in England, 1890 in Scotland.

551. So far as relates to spirits, both 329 of 1891, and 93 of 1893, are subject to the error which is explained in the Report to the Treasury, signed by you and Mr. Robinson and printed as a Parliamentary Return, No. 248 of 1893?—Yes, that is so.

552. I need not perhaps trouble you to read that paper, as all the members of the Commission have copies, but we may take it as read and print it at this point in your evidence?—If you please.

The document was handed in, and is as follows:—

Treasury Returns: Report of Commissioners of Inland Revenue on error in spirit duty.

REPORT of the COMMISSIONERS of INLAND REVENUE to the TREASURY, dated the 6th June 1893, explaining an Error in the Computation of Ireland's Contribution to the SPIRIT DUTY, as shown in the Financial Relations Returns of 1891 and 1893.

Inland Revenue, Somerset House,
6 June, 1893.

MAY IT PLEASE YOUR LORDSHIPS,

AT the time when the Parliamentary Return on the Financial Relations of England, Scotland, and Ireland, presented by Mr. Jackson to the House of Commons in 1891 (No. 329 of 1891), was under preparation, and again when the similar but more recent Return, presented on Mr. Clancy's Motion last

Mr. A. Milner. 17 July 1894. Treasury Return: Report of Commissioners of Inland Revenue as to error in spirit duty.

February (No. 83 of 1893), was being compiled, your Lordships instructed us to furnish you with the details of the amounts, respectively, "collected in" and "contributed by" Ireland under the various heads of Inland Revenue. We regret to state that in the two Reports made by us to your Lordships, in accordance with these instructions, a grave error occurred in the calculation of Ireland's "contribution" to the duty on home-made spirits. The method followed by us in calculating that contribution in both the Reports in question was to deduct from the quantity of home-made spirits charged to duty in Ireland the number of gallons removed, after payment of duty, to Great Britain, and to add to that quantity the number of gallons removed, after payment of duty, from Great Britain to Ireland. The method was just, and the results would have been correct if the removals had been accurately recorded. But the statistics on which the calculation was based were, as has now been discovered, untrustworthy.

The figures of duty-paid spirits conveyed from Ireland to Great Britain and from Great Britain to Ireland were taken by us from a periodical "Return of the quantity of duty-paid home-made spirits removed from one part of the United Kingdom to another part for home consumption." Up to last Easter no doubt had been entertained as to the accuracy of this Return. But when the Return for the financial year 1893-94 was being made up, we were struck by the greatness of the apparent increase in the export of duty-paid spirits from Ireland to Great Britain in 1893-94 as compared with 1892-93. This increase was especially marked in the case of Belfast. No reason being known to us why the exportation of duty-paid whisky from Belfast to Great Britain should have greatly increased during the last financial year, inquiry was immediately made as to the contrast presented by the two Returns; and it then came to light that in one of the four districts into which, for Inland Revenue purposes, Belfast is divided, the quantity of duty-paid spirits exported in 1892-93 had been greatly understated. This error was largely due to the negligence of a single officer. But the fact that so glaring an error had found its way into the "Return of Duty-paid Spirits removed" for 1892-93 aroused our suspicions as to the trustworthiness of these Returns generally; and we were thus led to test their accuracy, first for Belfast, then for Dublin, and ultimately for all parts of the United Kingdom from which there is any substantial export of spirits. A large staff has been engaged for some weeks under the direction of experienced officers in reexamining all the documents on which the Returns for the two years 1891-92 and 1892-93 were based. The result shows that, while no errors of equal magnitude to that first discovered in one district of Belfast have been committed elsewhere, the individual accounts from which the Returns are compiled have, in many instances, been inaccurately made up; and that the figures already published, and accepted without question in our reports to your Lordships at the time of the preparation of the "Financial Relations" Papers of 1891 and 1893 are wide of the truth.

The figures as first reported to us were:—

—	Duty-paid Spirits exported from Ireland to Great Britain.	Duty-paid Spirits imported from Great Britain to Ireland.	Excess of Duty-paid Spirits exported from Ireland to Great Britain over those exported from Great Britain to Ireland.
	Gallons.	Gallons.	Gallons.
1891-2	2,286,171	15,550	[illegible]
1892-3	3,354,103	17,655	[illegible]

The figures as established by the recent re-examination of the original documents are:—

—	Duty-paid Spirits exported from Ireland to Great Britain.	Duty-paid Spirits imported from Great Britain to Ireland.	Excess of Duty-paid Spirits exported from Ireland to Great Britain over those exported from Great Britain to Ireland.
	Gallons.	Gallons.	Gallons.
1891-2	2,214,374	32,393	[illegible]
1892-3	2,605,084	31,532	[illegible]

On the basis of the revised figures, the contribution of Ireland for the year 1892-3 is 2,243,851*l.*, not 2,600,000*l.*, as estimated by Mr. Gladstone (relying upon the amount for the previous year given in the "Financial Relations" Papers of 1891 and 1893) in his speech on the First Reading of the Home Rule Bill.

We can only express our great regret for the occurrence of an error of such magnitude, and it is with no desire to extenuate it that we append a brief account of the manner in which it has arisen.

It is unfortunately impossible to check the figures of the removals of duty-paid spirits from one part of the United Kingdom to other parts for years prior to 1891-2, but there can be little doubt that the faults of system, which have vitiated this Return for the two last years, are not of recent growth, but have affected it more or less throughout the whole course of its existence.

The history of the Return is as follows:—

In April 1858 the duty on spirits in Ireland was raised to the same rate as that prevailing in England and Scotland, and from that time to this the duty has continued at equal rates in the three kingdoms. With the equalisation of the rate it became a matter of indifference to the Exchequer in what part of the kingdom the duty on any particular gallon of spirits was paid. But, on the other hand, it became for the first time necessary, if it was desired to know the true contribution of each of the three kingdoms to the Excise, that the amount of spirits transferred, after payment of duty, from one to the other, should be recorded. Hence in the year 1858-9, the Board of Inland Revenue established an account, intended to show the amount of spirits actually consumed in each of the three kingdoms, as distinct from the amount paying duty in each of them. This account has ever since been compiled quarterly, and a summary of it has been published every three months in the Board of Trade Returns, and once a year in our annual Report.

Unfortunately the details of the account have, as it now appears, been often made up with very inadequate care by the officers responsible for them. The reason, no doubt, is that they were of no importance whatever to the Revenue. The Return in question was a Return of the movement of spirits, which, whatever might become of them, had already paid their full due to the State. Hence the zeal of those engaged in collecting the statistics flagged, and they did not fully examine the documents from which they were compiling.

This was more especially the case with regard to the spirits removed, after payment of duty, from dealers' stores. When duty-paid spirits are removed from a warehouse, they are accompanied by a "permit" drawn up by the officer in charge of the warehouse, and it is easy for him to keep a correct account of such removals. But of the amount of removals from dealers' stores our officers have no other information than that given by the dealers themselves, who are bound by law to send with every consignment of spirits a certificate, stating the quantity and place of destination. The certificates are taken from books supplied to the dealers by the Revenue authorities, and

[illegible]

containing counterfoils, on which the dealers fill in details corresponding to those given in the certificates. These counterfoils are subsequently collected by the officers of Inland Revenue, and it is in extracting the information contained in them, a work which is always laborious and often difficult, that frequent mistakes have occurred. It will easily be understood that, where the quantities under examination are so great, a number of omissions, each individually slight, may collectively produce a heavy percentage of error. For the negligence, which made such a result possible, all parties concerned are undoubtedly to blame.

But the rest of the 'checking' left us a faulty system, and now that the radical imperfections of that system have been fully exposed, we shall adopt means of checking the figures which will ensure accuracy for the future.

We have the honour to be,
Your Lordships' most obedient servants,
A. MILNER.
F. LACY ROBINSON.

543. You refer on page 4 of this paper to an account established by your Board in the year 1888–9 intended to show the amount of spirits actually consumed in each of the three kingdoms as distinct from the amount paying duty in each of them, but I understand from the paper that you think this account cannot be relied upon until the year 1891–2 when a re-examination of documents for that and the following year was made in consequence of the discovery of the error?—It certainly is not absolutely trustworthy. With certain reservations which perhaps I shall have an opportunity of making later, it affords a certain amount of guidance, but no one could pretend for a moment that it was really trustworthy.

[illegible]

544. Why was it impossible to re-examine documents and correct adjustments of revenue for previous years?—The error arose in the certificate books used by traders, when they despatched spirits from one part of the kingdom to the other. These books, when they are taken up by our officers, are subsequently sent to Somerset House, but they are only kept for a couple of years, and we had not got anything like a complete set except for the year in which the error was discovered and the preceding year. All traces of the transactions were destroyed. I might inform the Commission that the number of these certificates is enormous. There were issued for the last financial year from Somerset House, 3,179,770 of them, and the re-examination which we actually undertook was a re-examination of something upwards of 2,000,000 certificates, and even if we had had the books for previous years, which as a matter of fact we had not, I do not know that we had the staff to examine them. It was a very considerable disturbance of the ordinary work to make the examination which we did make and which was complete for two financial years.

545. Going to the last account it seems that in 1891–2, 534,100 gallons of spirits exported from Ireland to Great Britain were not accounted for by permit counterfoils, nor 13,829 gallons exported from Great Britain to Ireland?—I think the last figure is 3,829; the other figure is right.

546. The net result of that was that the contribution of Ireland to revenue in respect of spirits consumed in Ireland was seriously over-stated?—Yes, very greatly over-stated.

547. In the following year, 1892–3, 210,881 gallons exported from Ireland to Great Britain and rather less than a thousand gallons exported from Great Britain to Ireland seem not to have been accounted for?—Yes, those figures are right.

548. Why, in your opinion, was the error so much smaller in the second of those years?—The reason, I believe, was this, that in the second of the two years only what I might call the normal influences making for error existed. In the preceding year those normal influences making for error had been greatly aggravated by the extraordinary blunder which was committed in one of the districts of Belfast; that, I believe, accounts at any rate for the greater part of the difference between the error of the first year and the error of the second. I regard the error shown in the second year as being probably about the average amount of error which ran through these returns for a long period; the error of the preceding year was exceptionally great.

549. And an error in the same direction?—Always in the same direction, necessarily from the circumstances of the case.

550. (*Mr. Sexton.*) Do you say that an error of a quarter of a million of gallons a year would be normal error?—I put it in this way, that something below 10 per cent. is probably the normal error, subject to some observations I shall have to make presently about another influence of very great importance tending to error.

551. (*Chairman.*) Perhaps you will make them now?—They are these, that before the year 1888 this return was confined to removals from excise warehouses and from dealers' stores. The Customs warehouses were altogether omitted. Now that made an enormous difference. In the very first year, in which the Customs warehouses were brought in, it made a difference of nearly 800,000 gallons; that was the year 1888–9. I will amplify that a little. I find that in the year 1886–7 the excess quantities of duty-paid spirits sent from Ireland were 1,894,000 gallons, in the year 1887–8 the quantities were 1,785,000 gallons. The difference there is not more than might very easily occur between one year and another. In 1888–9 there is a jump from 1,755,000 gallons to 2,560,000 gallons, a difference of something like 800,000 gallons, owing to the fact that the spirits taken from Customs warehouses were for the first time brought into account in that year. Therefore, when I say that I think there is a normal error probably of something like 10 per cent., it must not be held to apply to the years immediately preceding 1888–9, in which the error must have been vastly greater.

552. Did that error go through all the accounts?—I think that cause of error existed all along, but I fancy it only became very serious for some years preceding 1888–9, because I do not think—I have no exact statistics on this point, and this is merely hearsay—that the export from Customs warehouses in Ireland was anything like as great, we will say, 20 years ago as it has been during the last six or seven years.

553. Why?—I think I am right in saying there has been increasing tendency in Belfast to clear from Customs warehouses. At any rate, you may take it that there has been a certain shifting of goods between Excise and Customs warehouses in Belfast.

554. Is that part of the general transfer in warehouses, from one department to the other which has been going on for some years?—Yes, in part. But the tendency to clear from Customs warehouses is independent of any such transfer.

555. And that has been more developed within the last few years, has it?—Yes.

556. (*Mr. Sexton.*) Is it a transfer from Customs to Excise control?—No, rather the opposite; there was a transfer of spirits from Excise to Customs control.

557. You convey, I understand, that the error might not have been of such importance in years remote from 1888–9 as in years nearer to it?—Yes; I will tell you why, because I think that in years remote from 1889 there was not so much export from Customs warehouses in Ireland to Great Britain; but this is merely a guess of mine. The certainty is, that in the first year when these Customs figures were brought into the account, they had the effect of increasing the figures of export from Ireland to England by something like 800,000 gallons, the corresponding figures of which in previous years had been omitted.

558. (*Chairman.*) That was before your time?—Yes, that was before my time. I know the effect this had in 1889, because I have looked up the figures, but I cannot tell what might have been the effect of that omission of Customs figures in more remote years.

569. But we understand this inaccuracy was corrected in the subsequent Return for 1893?—Yes, we have got the figures right now for 1891–2 and 1892–3.

570. May we take it that the Return 334 of 1893, known as Sir John Hibbert's Return, gives the accurate figures for 1892–3?—Yes; absolute accuracy is, of course, unattainable, but it is as near accuracy as you can get by any amount of careful supervision and regulation.

571. Careful supervision, having special reference to the discovery of the previous error?—Most certainly.

572. Will you state the exact result of the correction on each of the two years of the mean contribution from each country in respect of spirits, showing in each case the difference and the direction of the error?—For 1891–2, which was the only year for which figures were published, which we subsequently corrected, the figures, as originally published, were, England, 78,[illegible]l.; Scotland, 10,[illegible]l.; Ireland, 8,110,[illegible]l.; the percentages of contribution being, England 79·[illegible], Scotland 10·70, and Ireland 8·[illegible]. The revised figures, after the error had been discovered, were, England, 79,[illegible]l.; Scotland, 10,571,[illegible]l.; Ireland, 7,819,[illegible]l., being an increase of English contribution by [illegible]l., an increase of Scotch contribution by 61,[illegible]l., and a decrease of Irish contribution by [illegible]l.

573. At the end of the Report to the Treasury you say your Board intend to adopt means of checking the returns, which will insure their accuracy for the future. Would you be good enough to explain the means which you have adopted?—Yes; we have both adopted a new system of keeping the accounts, and, of course, what is much more important, we have established a much stricter check upon the men who keep it. As regards the system, in the first place the certificate books, which are filled up by the traders, now contain in the case of each certificate a statement of the part of the United Kingdom to which the spirits are sent, instead of simply the name of the place. That, I believe, was often the cause of error. Our officers guessed, and in some cases guessed wrongly, what part of the kingdom the spirits were going to, but that is a minor matter. What is more important is this, that we now have every officer furnished with a book, especially provided for the purpose, into which he has to enter from the counterfoil of the trader's certificate the particulars of the amount and proof strength of spirit in each case, and the country to which it is consigned, in separate columns, for each country, so that at the end of a certain time, if he has made his calculations accurately, he has nothing to do but to add up his columns, and there is the amount going from that region to each of the other countries. Then, of course, we have a much stricter system of checking, that is to say, every supervisor has to compare a certain number of these counterfoils with the officers' book, and see that he has read them correctly; and also our inspectors, who go out from our head office to look over the work in the different parts of the country, have special instructions to keep a sharp eye on the accuracy of the officer's account and the strictness of the supervisor's check. Of course the greatest change of all is that the service generally is now thoroughly alive to the great importance of this matter, which had been previously much disregarded.

574. I suppose before, the accuracy to be attained was the accuracy of actual cash?—Yes.

575. And now the accuracy of distinction is looked upon as nearly as important?—Yes. I must make this reservation. You can never get that degree of accuracy in an account of this kind which can be got in an account where there is a self-acting check. Still, I do think that a very high degree of accuracy is now attained, and that anything like a serious error would be certain to be discovered.

576. I should now like to take you to your annual report for 1893, and refer you to page 140, where there are tables showing the movement of spirits between the years 1880 and 1893. I suppose only a modified reliance must be placed on those figures?—Yes, a very modified reliance.

577. Might that be also said of the tables on page 13[illegible] of the same report, showing the consumption of spirits per head in each country?—Yes, they are based upon the same figures.

578. Passing from spirits to beer, is there any system of permits as to the movements of beer?—No, none whatever.

579. Will you be good enough to explain the mode by which the adjustment to give the true contribution of each country is arrived at in the case of beer?—Yes, it is arrived at by particulars supplied to us by all the brewers in any of the countries who have an export trade to any other part of the United Kingdom. These particulars were obtained for the whole year ending September 1890, and the figures in the original return, Mr. [illegible]'s return, were adjusted in the proportion derived from those statistics for the year ending September 1890 which we got from the brewers.

580. Then the adjustment for the years 1891–2 and 1892–3 were on the information collected for the year 1889–90?—No, not quite, because we had some further information in the course of the year 1893 which somewhat modified, not to a very appreciable extent, the adjustment of the beer return.

581. But in the main they depended on the old return, did they not?—Yes.

582. Was that the whole of 1889–90, or only for some months?—No, it was for the year; the original figures were for the whole year, but it was for the year ending September 1890. The results of that year were applied to the financial year.

583. Not as in another case only for four months of the year?—No, a whole year.

584. Do you think that this information is complete and trustworthy for that year?—I think it is fairly trustworthy. I do not think it is so trustworthy as, for instance, the corrected spirits return. I think it is much more trustworthy than the old spirits return, because great pains in details were taken by the brewers, but I may say this, that to get anything like real accuracy it ought to be kept from year to year, and not merely the results of one year carried on.

585. I think we might as well take as read, and print at this point in your evidence, the observations with regard to beer and the table of figures given in Memorandum B. on page 10 of the return 334 of 1893?—Yes. I will see that that is put in.

The document is handed in, and is as follows :—

(B.)

EXCISE.

British Spirits (total receipts in 1889–90, 13,[illegible]l.):

Under the Spirits Act, 1880, no quantity of duty-paid spirits exceeding one gallon can be moved from any one part to any other part of the United Kingdom without an "Excise permit." The adjusted figures in the foregoing table are based on the aggregate of such permit returns. The information is regularly printed quarterly in the Trade and Navigation Returns issued by the Board of Trade.

Percentage of incidence: England 80·[illegible], Scotland 2·[illegible], Ireland 17·[illegible].

Beer (total receipt in 1889–90, 9,410,[illegible]l.):

The following figures represent the trade between the three kingdoms, according to information furnished by the collectors of Inland Revenue throughout the United Kingdom, after communication with the different traders in their districts, in response to a

Mr. A. Milner. | In Beer, the ... | Spirits ... | ... | Beer, not ... | Beer; duty and export.

Mr. A. Milne. 19 July 1894. Beer: duty and export.

special circular issued by the Board of Inland Revenue.

—	England.	Scotland.	Ireland.	Total (United Kingdom).
Duty collected in 1889-90	£ [illegible]	£ [illegible]	£ [illegible]	£ [illegible]
Exports:				
England to Scotland	− [illegible]	+ [illegible]	—	—
England to Ireland		—	+ [illegible]	—
Scotland to England	+ [illegible]	− [illegible]	—	—
Scotland to Ireland	—		+ [illegible]	—
Ireland to England	+ [illegible]	—	− [illegible]	—
Ireland to Scotland	—	+ [illegible]		—
Incidence - £	[illegible]	[illegible]	[illegible]	[illegible]
Per cent. -	[illegible]	[illegible]	[illegible]	100·0

As regards exports of beer from Ireland to England and Scotland (which are known to be made almost entirely from Dublin), the information thus received agrees as well as can be expected with the published statistics of the export trade of that port, and the exports from England to Ireland also agree fairly well with the figures given in Parliamentary Paper, No. 163, of 1890. The information regarding export of beer from Scotland is new, but there is no reason to doubt its substantial accuracy. The export trade is principally centred in Edinburgh.

About two-thirds of the beer exported from England to Scotland comes from Burton, and nearly the whole of that going to Ireland.

Licences (receipt in 1889-90, 320,245*l.* imperial, 2,994,413*l.* local):
Shown as collected.

Railway Passenger Duty (receipt in 1889-90, 324,401*l.*):
Shown as collected.
This duty does not extend to Ireland.

Other Excise Duties (receipt in 1889-90, 8,093*l.*):
Shown as collected.

586. Is it not possible to keep a permanent record of the movement of beer between England, Scotland, and Ireland?—Not with our present powers. Such information as we have been able to procure is owing to the obligingness of the big traders, and I do not think we could compel them. Perhaps they might object to give us that information every year. I might add that the information we got was given under pledge of secrecy. We took the total figures, but it was on the understanding that we should not mention the figures of a particular firm.

587. A pledge of secrecy as to particular shipments?—Yes.

588. Would a system of permits be practicable in respect to beer?—I do not say that it would be impracticable, but it would be subject to peculiar difficulties—much greater difficulties than in the case of spirits, for instance.

589. And on the other hand, is the movement of beer between the three countries one of very great importance?—No; about 3 per cent. of the total amount of beer produced is carried one way or the other. I think it is a matter of a couple of hundred thousand pounds, speaking roughly, for the whole trade.

590. I understand that rather more beer comes into England from Ireland and Scotland than goes from it?—Yes, and I fancy that the export from Ireland is increasing; it is mostly due to Guinness, of course.

591. I do not think I need detain you with regard to the other items under the head of Excise, but I pass to the head of Stamps. This subject is dealt with in the memorandum by your department on page 11 of Return 329 of 1891, marked C, which had better be taken as read and printed at this point of the minutes of evidence?—Yes. — Mr. A. Milne. 19 July 1894. Stamps: Death duties.

The document is handed in, and is as follows:—

(C.)

STAMPS.

(1.) Death Duties:—

(I.) *Probate Duty* (total receipt, imperial and local, 1889-90, 4,336,802*l.*):

The authorities of the Legacy and Succession Duty Office are decidedly of opinion that, for practical purposes, it may be assumed that the probate duty collected in each of the three kingdoms corresponds closely with the duty on the property of persons dying domiciled in those kingdoms respectively. It is therefore in accordance with the terms of reference to take the figures of probate duty as collected.

It is right to observe that the per-centages of probate duty collected in the three kingdoms vary sensibly from year to year. For example, the proportion collected in Scotland in 1889-90 was 10·00, and in Ireland 4·66, whereas the averages for the five years to 31st March 1890 were 9·65 and 4·44 respectively.

(II.) *Estate Duty* (total receipt, 1889-90, 790,019*l.*):

The same considerations which apply to probate duty indicate that the estate duty should be allotted as collected.

(III.) *Legacy Duty* (total receipt, 1889-90, 2,723,880*l.*):

This tax is collected in the country where the deceased was domiciled, and, even assuming that it falls on the recipient of the legacy, there is no means of ascertaining in which of the three kingdoms the recipient of any particular legacy is domiciled. This branch of revenue must therefore be taken as collected.

(IV.) *Succession Duty* (total receipt, 1889-90, 1,065,169*l.*):

This may be taken as mainly (*i.e.*, to extent of four-fifths) duty on real property passing by death. The Succession Duty Office reports that the duty, so far as real property is concerned, is almost invariably paid in the country in which the property is situate, and that so far as personalty is concerned, there is no means of ascertaining where the property is situate.

The duty is therefore allotted as collected.

(2.) General stamps (total receipt, 1889-90, 6,126,217*l.*):— Stamps: general.

As only a comparatively small proportion of this item is connected with transactions in real property, the whole of this branch of revenue is treated in this calculation as analogous to taxes on personal property, and has to be apportioned according to what may be considered the true incidence of such taxes on personal property collected in various parts of the United Kingdom. In the metropolitan area (for example) it is known that considerable quantities of property are domiciled for purposes of taxation, although the owners may be scattered throughout the United Kingdom. It will be explained below, under the head of Income Tax, by what means a per-centage correction has been arrived at, with a view to making an allowance for such cases, and the same per-centage allowance there adopted may properly be applied to the figures of General Stamps. Upon this principle, 1·6 per cent. of the total receipt should be deducted from the amount collected in England, 1·4 added to that collected in Scotland, and ·2 added to that collected in Ireland. This correction gives the

Mr. A. M'Gown.

1 July 1896.

Stamps: general.

adjusted figures of General Stamps, England, Scotland, and Ireland, shown in the table subjoined.

—	England.	Scotland.	Ireland.	Total.
	£	£	£	£
Amounts received in 1893–94	[illegible]	[illegible]	[illegible]	[illegible]
Correction to adjust Duty on Transfers of Stock, &c., on London Stock Exchange, &c., affecting Scotland and Ireland:—				
— 1·2 per cent.	[illegible]	–	–	–
+ 1·4 „	–	[illegible]	–	–
+ ·2 „	–	–	[illegible]	–
Total, as corrected £	[illegible]	[illegible]	[illegible]	[illegible]
Per cent.	84·5	7·3	8·2	100·0

Stamps: Probate Duty, &c.; Estate Duty.

592. It is first stated that the authorities of the Legacy and Succession Duty Office are decidedly of opinion that for practical purposes it may be assumed that the Probate Duty collected in each of the three Kingdoms corresponds closely with the duty on the property of persons dying domiciled in those kingdoms respectively, and the same considerations are said to apply to the Estate Duty. Perhaps you will be good enough to state the grounds for that?—The grounds really are nothing more than the universal experience of the officers of the Department, and I think it also stands to reason that that which they declare to be the course adopted by persons taking out administrations, must be the course adopted. An executor would naturally apply for probate in the country in which the testator lived, and not in some other country, unless there were special reasons existing; and as a matter of fact it is found that this is so. Examination was made at one time into probates with the view to this first return, and this was one of the most careful examinations made in connexion with that return. The result is that people as a rule take out probate in that one of the three countries in which the parties die domiciled, and as a rule, and almost an invariable rule, they take out probate for all the property situate in the United Kingdom in that, pay the duty in that country, and then if they have included in their affidavit and included in their duty property situate in one of the other countries, they have the probate re-sealed in that other country as far as the property situated in that other country is concerned. But the duty is paid in the country in which the testator was domiciled.

593. But the amount of re-sealing as between the countries, pretty nearly balances, does it not?—No, it does not. There is a great deal more duty paid in Scotland on English property, and a certain amount more paid in Ireland than is paid in England on Scotch or Irish property.

594. That is important, so far as our inquiry goes, is it not?—Yes, of the very greatest importance; that is all worked out. I place great reliance for what they profess to be worth, on the figures on page 12 of the Financial Relations Paper of 1891, No. 291, Mr. Jackson's paper. I am not speaking of any inference drawn from those figures with reference to income tax or stamps, but with reference to the figures themselves.

Stamps: Probate Duty.

595. The figures at the foot on page 12, giving per-centages, do you mean?—Yes. Of course they are only the figures for one year, but one year in the case of probate duty gives you a very good average.

596. This paper is Sir Algernon West's, but I understand you have looked into it yourself, and endorse it?—Yes. I believe that return was prepared with the greatest possible care, and is of the greatest value.

597. Half of the probate duties now go to the Local Taxation Revenue, I think?—Yes.

Mr. A. M'Gown.

1 July 1896.

Stamps: Probate Duty.

598. Does that explain the difference between the figures on pages 8 and 9 of the return we have been just referring to, in which the transfer to separate Local Taxation Account is not made, and the figures on pages 6 and 7 of Mr. Clancy's Return, No. 93, of 1893, in which it is made for the years, 1889–90?—Yes.

599. The allocation of probate duty seems to be an important point, because the allocation of income tax under Schedules C. and D. is afterwards made dependent upon the proportion so obtained?—Yes, it is a very important point.

600. What is the law about probate duty; must it be collected in the country where the person has been domiciled?—It is rather intricate. Except in the case of Scotland there is no necessity to take out probate in the country in which a man is domiciled; that is to say, supposing a man dies domiciled in England, possessing property in England and in Ireland, his executor may take out probate in either country. It is a matter of experience that he does take it out in the country where the testator was domiciled, as he naturally would. But in Scotland the law is rather peculiar. If a man has property in Scotland, then the executor must take out his probate in the country in which the testator was domiciled, or else the Scotch Courts will not recognise his probate. That is their law; that is to say, if the testator was domiciled in Scotland, his executor must take out the probate in Scotland, but even if the testator was domiciled in England or Ireland, and had Scotch property, the Scotch Courts will insist on probate being first taken out in the country where he was domiciled. It is no good a domiciled Englishman trying to take out probate in Scotland, in the first instance, the Scotch Courts will not recognise it. They say you must first take out probate in the country of domicile, and then we will re-seal it.

601. Is there any reason for that, or is it merely the law?—It is merely the law.

602. (Sir David Barbour.) If a man is domiciled in England and has property in England, Ireland, and Scotland, and probate is taken out in England is the whole probate duty assigned to England and treated as English taxation in these returns?—It is put down as English taxation in these returns.

603. If the person had property abroad, and he was domiciled in England, and probate was taken out in England, would the duty on that foreign property appear as English taxation?—It would not pay probate duty.

604. (The Right Hon. The O'Conor Don.) I understood that in these returns you had corrected that by the re-sealing?—We have not altered the probate duty figures; those figures of re-sealing have been the basis of certain adjustments for income tax and stamps, but we have not altered the probate duty figures, and I am prepared to explain if you like, though it is a tiresome business, why, on the principles on which this return is based, the probate duty figures ought not to be altered.

605. (Mr. Sexton.) I understood that the object of these adjustments due to re-sealing on page 12 was to ascertain by means of the re-sealing how much of the property was really in the country in which the re-sealing occurred, and to separate that property from the rest of the property of the deceased?—I think I mean the same thing as you do, if I may state it in my own language. I think the object was to find out how much property people domiciled in England owned in Ireland and Scotland, how much property people domiciled in Scotland owned in Ireland and England, and so on; to find out the amount of property which a domiciled Englishman, Scotchman, or Irishman, owned in the two countries in which he was not domiciled.

606. (The Right Hon. The O'Conor Don.) But not to alter the amount of the probate duty?—No, not to alter the amount of the probate duty itself, because the rule mobilia sequuntur personam. I do not know whether that is good sense or good

Mr. A. Milner.

19 July 1894.

Stamps: Probate duty.

Latin), was the rule followed in this return. It was the principle of the return that what should be credited to each country was the amount of probate duty paid by the representatives of persons dying domiciled in that country. Therefore, what the domiciled Englishman's executor paid for probate duty was credited to England because it was held to come out of the pocket of an Englishman, even if it was paid in respect of property situated in Scotland and Ireland.

607. (*Mr. Sexton.*) If you had not made this adjustment the whole of the duty upon all the property of the person dying would be attributed to the country in which he died?—It is.

608. Without the adjustment?—We do not make the adjustment, there is no adjustment, and therefore what you say is quite true, the whole of the probate duty is attributed to the country in which the man who owned the property died, although the property might have been in the other countries.

609. Then why do you make the adjustment; do you apply it to income tax?—We think it is the right principle as to probate duty not to make the adjustment; but the examination of the probate duty figures gives us the basis of a very important adjustment for the purposes of income tax.

610. (*Mr. G. W. Wolff.*) With regard to anybody dying in England being possessed of Scotch property, the executor is bound to re-seal, and you can make your deductions from it for other purposes; but if he owns property in Ireland he is not bound to re-seal, and therefore I presume you have no figures for that at all?—Yes we have; we have the figures in this return. You rather surprise me by saying he is not bound to re-seal it. Having taken out probate for all his property in England, he must have it re-sealed in Scotland and Ireland, in Scotland if he has Scotch property, and in Ireland if he has Irish property.

611. I thought you said that the law was rather singular in Scotland?—The point in which Scotland is different to the other countries is this, that if a man has Scotch property his executor must begin the operation by taking out probate in the country in which he is domiciled, but the re-sealing goes on just the same. In the case of Scotland the Scotch authorities insist on your beginning the process in the country in which the man was domiciled; the English and Irish authorities do not. For instance, a man domiciled in England and having Irish property, may begin, if he likes, by taking out probate in Ireland.

612. (*Mr. Sexton.*) I think we now understand it. Although you do make calculations in respect of probate duty, you leave the duty itself unadjusted in the account, but you apply your probate calculations to the adjustment of certain schedules as to income tax?—Yes. Of course if we had to make an adjustment in respect of probate duty, England would have to have rather more credited to her.

613. (*Sir David Barbour.*) Why do you not adjust in the case of probate duty as you do in the case of income tax? If a domiciled Englishman has property in Ireland, probate duty goes to England, but the income tax, I understand, you adjust?—Yes, because the domiciled Englishman pays the income tax, and therefore it ought to go to the account of England. We have adjusted the income tax on the probate figures.

614. But why do you adjust the income tax and not the probate duty?—Because the principle of the return is that England is credited with that which is paid by Englishmen. I do not say it is the right principle; I am merely explaining it. There is a logical principle running through it all—right or wrong—and the idea of this return is that, as far as personal property is concerned, England, Scotland, and Ireland are each credited with the money paid to Imperial taxation out of the pockets of domiciled Englishmen, Scotchmen, or Irishmen. Now income tax, although it may be paid in Ireland, comes out of the pocket of the Englishman who owns that property in Ireland, therefore the adjustment ought to be made for income tax but not for probate duty. But the whole thing is a very small matter, only 80,000*l.* a year.

615. (*Chairman.*) Passing from the law and practice to the actual figures, what do they represent?—The figures themselves are large figures, but their result on taxation is not very great. If an adjustment had been made, the result would have been only to increase the probate duty credited to England by 75,000*l.* by taking 9,000*l.* off Ireland and 66,000*l.* off Scotland.

616. Why is the probate duty taken "as collected" without adjustment. I want you to give the reason in a sentence?—It is taken "as collected" without adjustment because people take out probate in the country of domicile. It follows that the contributions to probate duty of persons domiciled in any one of the countries are accurately represented by the probate duty actually paid in that country.

617. I see that legacy duty and succession duty are taken as collected. Have you anything to say as to that?—Succession duty is taken as contributed by the country in which it is collected, because throughout these returns we have treated taxation paid in respect of real property as belonging to the country in which that real property is situated. We have not adjusted legacy duty, because there are practically no means of doing it that I can imagine. I do not think if there were an adjustment it would make much difference, but I know of no way of adjusting it. All you can do is to attribute the legacy duty paid to the particular country in which the representation is taken out. No doubt there is a small advantage to Scotland and Ireland, as against England, by that system, but it is nothing considerable.

618. (*Mr. Sexton.*) How do you explain the advantage?—Because it follows the probate. What I mean is, if you were to adjust the probate duty, you would have to adjust the legacy duty in the same way. I am not arguing that you ought to adjust the probate duty, but I merely state the fact as it has been from the first.

619. (*Chairman.*) I should like now to pass to the question of General Stamps on page 11. I see that there is a difference between the figures of True Contribution on page 9 of Mr. Jackson's Return for the year 1889–90 and those of Mr. Clancy's Return for the same year. In the first return the figures of True Contribution are as follows: England, 5,391,532*l.*; Scotland, 473,956*l.*; Ireland, 522,729*l.* In Mr. Clancy's Return they are: England, 5,649,810*l.*; Scotland, 406,873*l.*; Ireland, 213,432*l.*; so that the contribution of England is increased in the latter return. Will you be good enough to explain that?—It is very difficult to explain, but I will do my best. The starting point in the whole business is the fact, established by the statistics of re-sealing, that 1·6 of the personal property situate in England belongs to domiciled Scotchmen and Irishmen, namely 1·4, to domiciled Scotchmen and 0·2 to domiciled Irishmen. Then when you come to stamps, in so far as they are taxes on personal property and come out of the pockets of the owners of such property, an adjustment should be made in accordance with this fact. In the Return No. 329 of 1891 it was, I think, erroneously assumed that the bulk of our general stamps were charges on personal property. A closer examination shows that that is not the case. If you will take the analysis of the General Stamp Revenue, given in any annual Inland Revenue Report, you will find that about half of these general stamps do not represent dealings with realised property at all, but commercial transactions, such as bill stamps, receipt stamps, and things of that kind. Of the other half, which do represent dealings with realised property, such as contract notes, stamps on transfers, and so on, about half again belongs to realty. Therefore that is out of the question. The amount of stamp revenue representing dealings with realised personalty is only about one-fourth, of the whole and it is therefore as regards that one-fourth only that the adjustment derived from the probate statistics of re-sealing, which deal only with realised personalty, ought to be applied. Therefore we have so applied it since

the first return; but in that first return we applied the adjustment, as I think erroneously, to the whole body of the stamp revenue.

620. That made a difference so far as England is concerned of 150,000*l*., did it not?—Yes, it was about that.

621. (*Mr. Sexton.*) As to Ireland it was only 9,000*l*. a year, was it not?—Yes, it was very unimportant as between England and Ireland; it is more important as between England and Scotland.

622. (*Chairman.*) Then as to income tax, we had better take as read the Report on page 12 of No. 329 of 1891 and print it at this point in the Minutes of Evidence?—Yes.

The document is handed in, and is as follows:—

(D.)

INCOME TAX.

Under the Income Tax Acts all property and profits are charged at their first source, without regard to the ultimate destination of the profits or income. This method of assessment was introduced with the express object of obtaining secrecy, and of preventing as far as possible the disclosure of the circumstances of the taxpayer. For example, the returns under Schedule D. contain no information as to the proportions in which the profits of any business or concern are divided between the several partners or shareholders.

The difficulties consequent upon this principle of assessment in allotting to the three kingdoms the income tax proper to each are dealt with under the different schedules of the tax.

Schedules A. and B.—(total receipts, 1889-90, 4,221,442*l*.):

The duties under these schedules apply to property with a definite situation in the three kingdoms, and are collected where that property is situate. As to Schedule A., there is no means of ascertaining, by the machinery of the income tax or any other resource at the disposal of Government, where the persons live who are in receipt of the income derived from such property, and there is, therefore, no alternative but to assign these items in accordance with the figures of collection.

As to Schedule B., the assessments are made on the actual occupiers of the land, who almost universally reside where those lands are situated; it is therefore shown as collected.

Schedules C. and D.—(total receipts, 1889-90, 7,733,000*l*.):

It is under Schedule C. that the necessity for some correction of the figures as collected is most obvious, no portion of the amount being assessed in Scotland, and only a small proportion in Ireland.

The schedule includes national securities, home, colonial, and foreign, and some municipal securities. The great mass of these are assessed in London, but they are held by persons domiciled in all parts of the three kingdoms. Owing, however, to the principle explained above, upon which income tax is collected, the machinery of the tax cannot be employed to ascertain where the recipients of interest and dividends reside. It is therefore necessary to resort to other sources of information in order to form any estimate of the true incidence of this branch of taxation, and for this purpose use has been made of information derived from statistics of property assessed to Probate Duty.

It has been stated above that the property assessed to Probate in each country represents with considerable accuracy the property of persons dying domiciled in that country; but the records of the Legacy and Succession Duty Department (which deals with Probate Duty) make it possible to ascertain further with tolerable accuracy how much English property (i.e., property assessed to income-tax in England) is held by individuals domiciled in Scotland and Ireland, how much Scotch property is held by individuals domiciled in England and Ireland, and how much Irish property is held by individuals domiciled in England and Scotland. This information is obtained from the records of "re-sealing," which is, in effect, the official recording in one kingdom of a will already proved, and assessed to Probate, in either of the other two.

The following table, compiled from the records of that Department, gives the required information for the year 1889-90:—

1889-90.	Capital.	England.		Scotland.		Ireland.		Total.	
	£	£	Per Cent.	£	Per Cent.	£	Per Cent.	£	Per Cent.
Gross Probate Duty as collected		3,934,165	85·39	469,934	10·05	187,301	4·56	4,591,430	100
STATEMENT OF RE-SEALING.									
As between Scotland and England.									
In Scotland duty was paid on English property of value	3,390,617	+ 101,109	—	− 101,109					
In England duty was paid on Scotch property of value	1,130,795	− 35,063	—	+ 35,063					
As between Ireland and England.									
In Ireland duty was paid on English property of value	775,143	+ 23,374	—	—	—	− 23,374			
In England duty was paid on Irish property of value	449,055	− 13,450	—	—	—	+ 13,450			
As between Ireland and Scotland.									
In Ireland duty was paid on Scotch property of value	20,454	—	—	+ 818	—	− 818			
In Scotland duty was paid on Irish property of value	44,334	—	—	− 1,340	—	+ 1,340			
		+ 75,911	—	− 33,155	—	− [illegible]			
Adjusted gross receipt		4,009,518	87·14	436,839	8·8	179,336	3·96	4,625,693	
Difference		—	+ 1·6	—	− 1·4	—	− [illegible]		

The results thus obtained show that as between England and Scotland there is paid on English property by individuals who are domiciled in Scotland about 65,000*l.* more than is paid on Scotch property by individuals who are domiciled in England. This 65,000*l.* paid as duty represents property amounting to about 2,180,300*l.*

Between England and Ireland there is paid on English property by individuals who are domiciled in Ireland about 3,894*l.* more than is paid on Irish property by individuals who are domiciled in England. This 3,894*l.* paid as duty represents property amounting to about 129,794*l.*

Between Scotland and Ireland there is paid on Irish property by persons who are domiciled in Scotland about 728*l.* more than is paid on Scotch property by persons who are domiciled in Ireland. This 728*l.* paid as duty represents property amounting to about 24,226*l.*

The general result, therefore, is to show that both Scotchmen and Irishmen hold more property in England than is held by Englishmen in either Scotland or Ireland, and that Scotchmen hold rather more property in Ireland than is held by Irishmen in Scotland. The net result is that 1·4 per cent. of the whole amount assessed to Probate Duty represented property technically situated in England, but owned by domiciled Scotchmen, and ·2 per cent. of the whole represented property similarly situated, but owned by domiciled Irishmen.

If these per-centages may be accepted as fairly accurate where capital is concerned, which is the case with the Probate Duty Assessments, it is not unfair to apply them in the case of income of a corresponding character. It may be added that there is no means of obtaining any per-centages in the case of income of a more reliable character. Incomes derived from such property as is now under view are mainly comprised in Schedules C. and D. (Public Companies, Foreign Dividends, Coupons, &c.), and only a small portion of them are comprised in that part of Schedule D. which is assessed as trades and professions. It may then be argued that for present purposes 1·6 per cent. of the total collected under Schedule C. and the first-named part of D. should be deducted from the sum collected in England; and that, of this amount, 1·4 per cent. should be credited to Scotland, and ·2 per cent. to Ireland.

The per-centage corrections deduced from the probate figures have accordingly, in the annexed tables, been applied to the Income Tax figures under Schedule C., and the part of Schedule D. other than trades and professions, the proportion of English property held by Scotchmen being added to the share of Scotland, and similarly for Ireland.

The remainder of Schedule D. (*i.e.*, trades and professions) is shown as collected, for as the assessments are made at the place where the trade is carried on, or the profession is exercised, it may be taken that the tax is borne by persons resident in the country where it is paid.

Schedule E. (total receipt, 1889–90, 820,448*l.*): Shown as collected.

ALGERNON WEST.
INSPECTION.

Inland Revenue, Somerset House,
January 1891.

623. Do you think it is fair to assume that income tax in respect of property charged under Schedules A. and B. in respect of ownership and occupation of land is paid by the country in which it is collected?—That is the basis of the whole return. The taxation on real property is put down to the country in which it is situated; taxation on personal property is put down to the country in which the owner of that property is domiciled; I do not say whether it is a right or a wrong principle but that is the principle running through the whole return, and therefore this is necessarily so.

624. Without necessarily justifying the principle, you say it runs through the whole account?—Yes.

Mr. A. Milner. 19 July 1894. Income tax assessment.

625. And has it always been so arranged?—Yes.

626. (*Mr. Sexton.*) If an Irish landed proprietor lives habitually or altogether in England, raising his income from land in Ireland, the income tax which he pays is charged as income tax paid by Ireland, is it not?—Yes, it is.

627. And so far as income tax might be regarded as a measure of taxable capacity, the income which he spends in England would be treated as income raised in Ireland and proved for taxable capacity?—If you base taxable capacity on the returns of the amounts actually paid, it would be so.

628. (*Chairman.*) Schedule C. includes Government and other public stocks, home, colonial, and foreign, of all kinds, does it not?—Yes.

629. With regard to Schedule C., the memorandum says that no portion of the amount is assessed in Scotland, and only a small proportion in Ireland. What is the proportion assessed in Ireland?—About 2 per cent. of the whole.

630. Are any foreign dividends and coupons under Schedule D. assessed anywhere except in London?—Yes, there are a few assessed in Edinburgh and Dublin, but the amount is very unimportant.

631. Nothing like 1 per cent. altogether, is it?—No.

632. It is stated in the memorandum at the top of page 12, that under the Income Tax Acts all property and profits are charged at their first source, without regard to the ultimate destination of the profits or income. I suppose that this is the reason why, in the case of the kind of property charged under Schedules C. and D. it is impossible to know directly in what part of the United Kingdom the persons who really pay the tax are domiciled?—Yes, that is so.

633. The adjustment of true contribution in these returns is made from the proportions obtained by the collection of probate duty, is it not?—Yes.

634. Do you assume, speaking broadly, that where people die, there they have lived domiciled?—Yes.

635. That is a reason, I suppose?—Yes.

636. Would you say that this method of estimating the true contribution to income tax under Schedules C. and D. is very satisfactory?—I should say it is very ingenious, but I do not know that I should say it is very satisfactory; satisfactory is too strong an expression. I can think of no better method, but I have not thought much about it yet.

637. (*Mr. Sexton.*) The ingenuity might be very unsatisfactory, might it not?—It might.

638. (*Chairman.*) Do you think it is the best which has been discovered, in the absence of any power of tracing income to its ultimate recipients?—Yes. I do not want to run it down too much. I think, under all the conditions, it was a very clever idea on the part of whoever thought of it, but it is not conclusive of course.

639. On another point I should like to refer you to Mr. Goschen's Report to the Treasury on Local Taxation, which was printed as a parliamentary paper a great many years ago?—Yes, I have seen it.

640. It was reprinted last year, and it contains tables brought up to the year 1868, as to the assessment to income tax under Schedule A. of real property in England, Scotland, and Ireland under four heads of "Lands," "Houses," "Railways," and "Other Property." This gives us a consecutive account in the case of England from 1843, in that of Scotland from 1843, and in Ireland from 1862; and there are also the totals for the United Kingdom in the same form for the same periods. Would there be any great difficulty in bringing these summaries up to the present date for the use of the Commission?—No; I have had it done.

641. It is not printed yet, is it?—No, it has only just been finished.

642. Will you put it in as an appendix to your evidence?—Yes. Do you wish it for land and houses,

or do you want it extended to railways and other property?

643. The old return was as to land, houses, railways and other property, and I think it will be better to continue it in the same form?—We have done so; but all I wish to point out is that lands and houses exhaust Schedule A.; if you go on to railways and other property, then you put into the return a fragment of Schedule D. If it were meant to be an "A" return it ought to be confined to lands and houses.

644. For the sake of symmetrical reasons that would be the case, but for the convenience of the Commission I should think it would be better to carry it on in the old form?—Certainly. The Inland Revenue Report for every year gives full particulars of all the schedules.

645. (*Mr. Sexton.*) Then would that be only a summing up?—Yes, a summing up of certain parts.

646. Does "other property" include everything else?—No, this was a Schedule "A" return. Schedule "A" originally included, and still formally includes, such property as railways, quarries, canals, and so on, but much more property belongs to Schedule D. than we have dealt with in this return.

Adjourned for a short time.

647. (*Lord Welby.*) In the report which you laid before Parliament, explaining the error in the spirit returns, you mentioned that you thought the arrangement you had made was sufficient to insure accuracy; has your subsequent experience confirmed you in the view that you are able to obtain accuracy by the new arrangement?—Yes, I think so. I feel very fairly confident of the accuracy of the returns as now furnished.

648. May we take it that you are satisfied that under the present arrangement the Commission may rely on the substantial accuracy of the figures now presented, and that those figures correctly represent the consumption of spirits in Ireland?—Yes, I feel confident of it.

649. Do you happen to have the figures for spirits in continuation of the last return presented to Parliament for 1893–4?—I have not got them here; they have been sent to the Treasury with a view to the preparation of another Financial Relations paper.

650. Will you have those papers put in as an answer to the question?—Yes.

651. I gather from the report that the system under which duty-paid spirits are transferred from one part of the kingdom to another may be divided under two heads, namely, the duty-paid spirits removed from warehouse, and secondly, the duty-paid spirits removed from dealers' stores?—Yes.

652. In order that the Commission may fully understand the means you have for ascertaining the movements of spirits, could you tell us how, under those two methods, spirits are transferred?—Do you mean how the account is kept?

653. How the account is kept?—I speak generally of removal from warehouse as distinct from removal from traders' stores; under warehouse I include such a thing as distiller's stores. The difference is this, that in removing from a warehouse the warehouse books—books kept by our officers, so-called warrant books—show the amount of spirits entered in the permit. Before a man can remove spirits from a warehouse he must have a permit, that is to say, he makes out a request-note addressed to an officer to take out a certain quantity of spirits at such-and-such a strength, and when that note is signed by the officer it becomes a permit, and goes away with the spirits.

654. May I take it that so far the record is more perfect than it is in the case of spirits removed from dealers' stores?—Yes, it has been practically absolutely perfect with regard to warehouses.

655. Then with regard to the error that arose, am I right in supposing it arose more from the transfers of spirits from dealers' stores than the transfers from warehouses?—Almost entirely in the transfer of duty-paid spirits from dealers' stores. Any error that occurs in the account of removal from warehouse must be a clerical error of the smallest possible consequence. It was in the account made up by our officers from the books kept by the traders that error arose. The traders kept these books, and the officers were expected to take out particulars from the books kept by the traders. There were an enormous mass of them, and it was difficult to extract the particular figures in question; the officers were not aware of the importance of the work and they did it rather carelessly, and that is where the error arose.

656. As far as the process itself is concerned, the process itself is perfect, so far as anything of the kind can be perfect, namely, that each consignment of spirits, whether sent from warehouse or from dealers' stores, is accompanied by an official document signed by a public officer, and the particular spirits will not be delivered without the production of this document?—It is not signed by a public officer in the case of the spirits removed from a dealer's store; it is made out by the dealer himself. In the case of spirits removed from a warehouse it is made out by the person owning the spirits, but it bears the officer's signature showing that it is correct in its details, and we have in our books a copy of the particulars.

657. Taking a cask of spirits sent from Dublin to Liverpool, how does your officer in Liverpool satisfy himself, before he allows that spirit to be removed for consumption, that it has been duty-paid. He sees this permit, I suppose?—The permit, or the certificate, as the case may be, ultimately reaches the hands of our officer.

658. Does that permit contain any counter signature of a public officer?—The spirits are accompanied either by a permit when they have gone out of warehouse, or by a certificate when they have gone out of dealers' stores, but the certificate drawn up by the dealer bears no signature of a public officer, and the trader is responsible for its accuracy. He is compelled by law to state certain particulars, and he is under severe penalties if he makes a mistake; but we do not interfere, and we have not seen, I think, for 40 years interfered, with the free movement of spirits from dealers' stores accompanied by a certificate drawn up by the dealers.

659. Supposing a man had a cask of illicit spirits, and he sends it out, would it be possible for him, since the dealer draws up the document, to forge the certificate. I ask the question because I do not understand from you that this certificate has undergone the scrutiny of any person at the point from which the spirits are sent?—No, I do not think it has. Of course it is an official document; we supply these books of certificates to the trader.

660. I only want to see how far it is possible there might be mistake or otherwise?—As Mr. Steele says, the certificates are on special paper and specially printed, so that it would be probably easy to detect one of these documents if it were forged, but it has not undergone any check on our part before the spirits are despatched.

661. (*Mr. Wolff.*) If he has one barrel of illicit spirits and one barrel duty-paid, cannot he put them both on the same certificate?—No doubt he could.

662. (*Lord Welby.*) I want to get the difference between two methods, one of which, I understand, is perfectly satisfactory, and the other, which is open possibly to doubt. At the same time you have no reason to think, have you, that it is abused?—No, I do not think so.

663. (*Chairman.*) What is the trader's interest in being accurate?—Of course his first interest in being accurate, is that he is under severe statutory penalties if he is inaccurate.

664. Who watches him?—We watch him, because it is always possible to get hold of a certificate at the other end, after it has accompanied the spirit; the man to whom it is sent has to enter the spirit in

Mr. A. Wilson.

10 July 1895.

Spirits, movements of.

his stock book, and he would not, except by a regular system of comparison with the person who sends, accept the thing if the details were wrong, because his stock book would be wrong, and his stock is checked by his stock book.

665. (*Lord Welby.*) May I ask if there are any complaints on the part of the trade against the present permit system?—No, I do not think there are. Mr. Steele would know that better than I do. I have never heard of any.

666. These consignments are usually made in considerable quantities, are they not?—Sometimes they are quite small consignments.

667. I am asking this question with a view to a question that I will put shortly, but I will tell you the reason why I ask it. It is this which has been suggested to the Commission. That in order to ascertain the true consumption of Ireland, the permit system should be very widely extended. Now you will see why I ask the question whether you have any complaints in that particular branch of trade in which the permit system is most stringently established, and I gather you do not think so?—Complaints are not made to my knowledge. It may be that they are so used to it now that any inconvenience which it causes is accepted.

668. Of course the revenue purpose is the original and chief purpose?—That is the original and chief purpose.

669. Except for that necessity do you consider the permit system one that interferes, I will say, unduly with the movement of spirits?—I think in the case of spirits it does not interfere much.

Beer: want of statistics.

670. Passing to the case of beer, I understand that you have not any very satisfactory statistics of your own? —No, we are entirely in the hands of the traders, and they are not obliged to furnish any official statistics. The statistics we have got from the traders were merely statistics that they gave us to oblige us. I believe they were carefully prepared, but they are not official.

671. Has it ever occurred to you whether you might get a check upon these statements by getting a return from railway companies and shipping companies?—I do not think we have ever done it.

672. We know there would be great difficulty in doing it, because we know the information which was obtained from the Customs was only obtained through the intervention of Mr. Jackson?—Some figures were got with regard to the export of Irish beer in the year 1890, which in a general way confirmed the figures given us by the Irish brewers.

673. Is not that a very important check and a very important element in our calculations, if you can get, we will say from the traders themselves, a return of what they send out, and if from other sources, either from dock companies or from shipping companies, or from other persons independent of those traders, you get a statement which practically confirms the traders?—Certainly I should think such a check would be of great importance.

674. At the present moment you are relying for your statements as to beer upon the return of the traders, very much as the Customs have relied upon the statements of the railway companies for their figures as to tobacco and tea?—Yes, I think so, except that we took a whole year and they took four months.

675. May I ask, if you wanted to be sure that the figures were thoroughly to be relied upon with regard to beer, would you wish to extend the inquiry to another year. Supposing you base your calculations of 1893 upon figures obtained in 1890, there must be an element of uncertainty there, and I ask, would you, in order to be able to say you were satisfied as to the general correctness of your figures, like to have those figures tested by a fresh return from the traders, say every third year?—Yes, I should like it very much. I do not know if they would like it.

676. Are you aware that no such complete means as you have in regard to spirits exist for checking the movement of other duty-paid goods so as to ascertain the actual consumption in Ireland?—Quite so.

677. And from what I have said just now, and you are aware yourself, the only figures we have are those based on the four months of the railway companies' returns?—Yes.

678. I think we have heard from the Customs that in itself they would place considerable reliance upon those statistics, but when they come to see the result as applied to tobacco they were very much surprised? —Yes.

Permit system: suggested extension of.

679. And though they had no ground upon which they could suspect the railway companies, at the same time the result was one that startled them, and therefore they were disposed to recommend an extension of the system of permit. Perhaps I might drop any extension of the system of permit, except so as tea and manufactured tobacco. Would it be your opinion that the system of permits could be adopted with regard to those goods, without raising a very great outcry?—I can say nothing at all about tea; I am afraid I do not know anything about it. As regards tobacco, I should think you would have to restrict it to a certain number of large dealers. I do not think you could apply a hard-and-fast rule that no tobacco could be sent without a permit to all the large number—20,000—I think of licensed dealers in tobacco.

680. I suppose in many cases tobacco is sent in very small parcels?—Yes, in very small packets.

681. May I take it that in your view, with very small packages a permit system would be almost impossible?—I think so; I think if you would ask Mr. Steele, who has great experience in this matter, he might be able to throw more light on it than I can.

Mr. J. Steele.

Tobacco trade.

(*Mr. Steele.*) We have between 500 and 600 tobacco manufacturers, and you would have very little difficulty in applying such a regulation to them. Of course they send very often small quantities too, and you would have that difficulty there, but if you go outside those and deal with two or three hundred thousand tobacco dealers in the country, I think the thing would be utterly impracticable; it would be very vexatious to anyone, and it would be very costly.

682. (*Lord Welby.*) If that be the case, am I not right that the chief part of the trade—might I say two-thirds of the trade—in manufactured tobacco in Ireland is in the hands of five or six houses.

(*Mr. Steele.*) That is so. Perhaps one town at any rate, say Belfast, may take the half of the trade in round numbers.

683. (*Lord Welby.*) Then do I gather you say that five or six houses have half the trade?

(*Mr. Steele.*) Yes, practically, half the Irish trade.

684. (*Lord Welby.*) Supposing those five or six houses were to give the amount of manufactured tobacco that was sent over in the year, would you feel satisfied that you might take that as a fair and accurate indication of the whole?

(*Mr. Steele.*) I may say that we have got this. We have these figures for the whole country as to imports into Ireland, and as to exports from Ireland of manufactured tobacco.

Mr. A. Wilson.

Tobacco: exports and imports of.

685. (*Lord Welby to the Witness.*) Have you got these figures lately?—We have them quite lately, within the last fortnight.

686. Does it include the great Belfast house?—Yes; in fact, Belfast is by far the greatest exporter, and next Dublin.

687. Can you give us the particulars?—I will give you the totals, because there have been corrections up to the last moment in the details. The totals as we have them are—sent from Ireland, 4,619,000 lbs.; sent to Ireland, 1,430,000 lbs. Now we have reduced this manufactured tobacco, if I may use the expression, to leaf; that is to say, the amount of leaf which it will represent unmanufactured, at the ratio of 125 to 100, and we find that the leaf equivalent would be—

Mr. J. Wilson.

18 July 1894.

Tobacco: consumption and movement of.

sent from Ireland, 3,521,000 lbs., and sent to Ireland, 1,137,000 lbs., showing a balance sent from Ireland to Great Britain of 2,384,000 lbs.

688. That would be in the raw leaf?—Yes, that which has paid duty.

689. Do you happen to have the amount of manufactured tobacco which has paid duty in Ireland?—The amount is 9,417,000 lbs., and deducting the 2,384,000 lbs., it leaves 7,033,000 lbs. as the quantity consumed in Ireland.

690. At that rate that would diminish very much the amount per head would it not, which would be deduced from the figures obtained by the Customs?—I fancy it would, but I have not had time yet to compare them very carefully. Taking the population at 4,607,000 in Ireland, it works out at 1·52 lbs. per head.

691. (Mr. Sexton.) What year is that for?—1893–4.

692. Is there any corresponding information for 1892–3?—I think not.

693. I think we had better have this put in, and also a calculation of the effect it would have on the true contribution of Ireland in 1892–3?—Very well, I will put it in.

694. (Lord Welby.) I think that these figures throw some doubt upon the four months' figures obtained from the railway company, do they not?—Although, as I say, I have not been able carefully to compare them, as I have not had time, I may say, after having seen the other figures, that these figures rather astonish me.

695. Do you happen to have at hand what the consumption of Great Britain is?—I do not think I have.

696. (Mr. Sexton.) Were these particulars obtained since Mr. Murray and Mr. Pittar were examined here?—Yes, they have been quite recently obtained.

697. (Lord Welby.) When your calculations are completed will you see if you can put in a return which would apply this correction to the figures we already have before us?—Yes, I will see if that can be done. I should like to say that these figures have been collected during the last fortnight or three weeks. I have the greatest confidence in the persons who have collected them, but I have not had time to look over them myself or to ask any questions which I might think necessary with regard to them; therefore I should like to have the whole matter gone over carefully; and the figures I have put in to-day would be subject to subsequent correction if I find that they require amendment in any way. I feel bound to make that reservation, and I think the application to 1892–3 had better be reserved until I can guarantee these figures as far as I am able to do so.

698. (Mr. Sexton.) Of course the position is that the Customs officials to whom the matter appertains and who were examined here, have great confidence in their system?—Yes.

699. Now we are confronted with figures over certain months which are not exhaustive?—Yes, they are practically exhaustive. Of course they will be in evidence for what they are worth, without its being stated how they were obtained. I think that will be the best course to take.

700. (Chairman.) Has Mr. Murray seen those figures?—No, I should like him to do so.

701. Perhaps you will undertake that he shall see them?—Yes.

702. (Lord Welby.) With these figures before you as to which I understand you have not made up your mind, or tested them, assuming that they prove as trustworthy as you think they are, would that amount of information satisfy you, and so that would you be prepared to tell the Commission that you thought we might accept these figures as indicating the consumption of Ireland without further extension of the permit system?—That is a question I could not answer until I have been over them a little more carefully than I have had time to do yet. I may say the final figures only reached me this morning, but I knew pretty well what the result was going to be.

Mr. J. Wilson.

18 July 1894.

Tobacco: consumption and movement of.

703. Do you exercise a superintendence over the tobacco trade now?—Yes, the superintendence exercised is very considerable.

704. What form does it take?—Constant inspection of the manufacturers' premises by our officers, and also visits from our analysts, which take place about once in two or three months.

705. But the visiting for the purpose of taking samples for analysis or general visits of that kind would not keep you informed of the movement of manufactured tobacco out, would it?—There are daily visits made by our officers for the purpose of general inspection. The visits which take place once in two or three months are for the purpose of analysis by our chemical staff.

706. Could your officers who visit daily take an account of the amount exported from each house they go to?—I should think they could, but I do not think we have any power at present.

707. You would have to have a power for it, would you?—We would have to have a power for it.

708. I am only suggesting for consideration what may be an alternative?—I perfectly understand that.

709. Would you think it would be practicable, as your officers are in constant relation with these, that they might take an account, which might be a valuable check?—Speaking at first sight, the question is new to me, I do not see why that should not be possible.

710. (The Right Hon. The O'Conor Don.) What is the difference between a warehouse and a dealer's store?—A warehouse is a place where spirits are kept under the superintendence of revenue authorities in bond, and a dealer's store is simply a place where a dealer who has cleared his spirits from bond keeps them for the purposes of his trade.

711. This permit system applying to the dealer's store you say is kept for the purpose of revenue. In what way is the revenue concerned when once the duty is paid?—It is to the interest of the revenue to be able to come down upon spirits wherever they are in the kingdom and to find out where they came from; to know the whole history of them. It is a most valuable and important check on illicit distillation. You can always come down on a dealer's stock and ask him to account for every bottle of spirits he has got, and the history of the spirits has to be on record. That is the importance of a permit and certificate system. If goods are taken out with a permit from a bonded warehouse they have equally paid duty; they pay duty when they leave the warehouse, but still it is very important for us to have a record of their movements.

712. Do you think the dealers keep very accurate books of their stores?—I think very accurate.

713. Then the error which arose in the returns presented was not in any way due to erroneous books being kept?—No, it was due to the counterfoils of the books being inaccurately examined.

Income tax assessments.

714. In the beginning of your evidence to-day you mentioned certain sources of revenue which were derived from taxes that were raised solely in England and not in Ireland, and amongst others you mentioned that Ireland had an advantage in consequence of the mode of assessment of the income tax?—Yes.

715. Would you kindly tell us how the income tax under Schedules A. and B. is assessed for England?—In Great Britain it is re-assessed every five years. In Ireland, except in exceptional cases, the valuation made about 40 years ago is still the basis of the income tax assessment.

716. Before we leave England, I want to know exactly upon what it is assessed. You say it is assessed every five years; what is the basis of the assessment?—Upon the annual value, as defined in the Income Tax Act, 1842.

717. How is that value ascertained?—Wherever you have a gross rent, it is on the gross rent.

Mr. A. Milner.

18 July 1894.

Income tax assessment and valuation.

718. Without any deduction for local taxes or local rates?—Yes, there is a deduction for tithe and land tax, and a deduction for rates when they are paid by the landlord, but no deduction for landlord's outgoings, such as repairs and insurance.

719. But there are deductions for the rates where they are paid by the landlord?—Yes, there are deductions for the rates where they are paid by the landlord.

720. In Ireland, as you mentioned, the income tax under Schedules A. and B. is assessed upon the tenement valuation?—Yes.

721. Do you know when that tenement valuation was made?—A general valuation was made in 1852 or 1853. I think it is Griffith's valuation.

722. Forty years ago?—Yes.

723. (*Mr. Sexton.*) It was not completed for a long time?—No, it began in the year 1852.

724. (*The Right Hon. The O'Conor Don.*) The Act was passed in 1852, and it took about 10 or 12 years to complete?—Possibly.

725. At all events in the last county valued in Ireland the income tax is now levied on a valuation made 30 years ago?—Yes, except in cases where there is re-assessment; there is power of re-assessment in the Act, but it is only in the case of new constructions that a new assessment is actually made.

726. Is there any power whatever to re-assess valuations in Ireland, except upon buildings, railways, and property of that description?—Yes, I think there is power.

727. Is there power, for instance, to re-assess the value of land itself?—I think there is, but it has never been used.

728. I think you are mistaken?—I may be, but I think not.

729. The income tax therefore at present is levied upon this valuation made over 30 years ago?—And where the rent has fallen below that valuation, upon the rent.

730. How long has that been in existence?—It is in the Act of 1853.

731. The proprietors have now the option of paying upon the rent instead of on the valuation, have they?—They have always had the right, and they do pay on the rent, and not on the valuation, when the rent is below the valuation.

732. In every case?—It is the general rule.

733. In what proportion have you found them to pay on the rent instead of on the valuation?—I could not say the exact numbers, but I should think in most cases they still pay on the valuation, because the rent is not below it.

734. Is it not the practice for the collectors of income tax to send in the assessment based upon valuation?—Not universally.

735. How are they guided in sending it in, on the rent, instead of on the valuation. What are the directions they get with regard to making up the account which they send in to the proprietors of land for the payment of income tax?—I fancy that the landowner has himself to satisfy the surveyors in cases where the rent is below the valuation, and that otherwise the valuation would be assumed to be the proper figure of income tax assessment. It is open to the owner to show that, as a matter of fact, his rent is below.

736. Then it comes to what I said a moment ago. Do not they apply for the tax on the valuation, and if the owner considers he has a claim to have it reduced, he makes that claim?—I should not think it would be necessary for him to make it every year; in the first instance, he must make a claim, and show that his rent is lower than the valuation.

737. How long has that been in operation?—For about 10 years we have made the concession of charging income tax on the rent as the landlord received it. I am not quite sure when the system began, but it was 1881 or 1882.

738. And now it appears that in many cases the rent is below the valuation?—It does; not in the majority, but in a certain number of cases.

Mr. A. Milner.

18 July 1894.

Income tax assessment and valuation.

739. Supposing we take the case of land in the owners' hands, has not he to pay the income tax on the valuation?—Yes.

740. And if the land in the hands of tenants has fallen in value, does it not appear likely that the owner in such cases has been paying on too high an assessment?—I should think it possible that there were some cases.

741. I think you stated that even at the present day notwithstanding the fall in the value of land in Ireland, and all over the United Kingdom, still Ireland has still an advantage in this mode of assessment of the income tax?—That is the opinion of all the tax officers who know Ireland best. They think that even in the case of land the number of instances in which the valuation is below the rent, are still the great majority, and enormously so in the case of houses. But it is not denied that, especially as regards land, there are cases in which the rent is below the valuation.

742. But if the valuations were at all correct in the beginning, is it not the fact that land has fallen very much in value within the last 30 years?—Yes. But one contention is that it was a very low valuation in the beginning, as compared with the English. It was a net and not a gross valuation.

743. When you say net valuation, was there anything deducted except the local rates from the Irish valuation?—The matter is a little complicated. As regards houses, the Act says "the rent, after deducting "the cost of repairs and insurance and other necessary "expenses." As regards land, the valuation was based upon the price of certain staple articles of agriculture produced at the time.

744. But the values were fixed on the assumption that it was the full rent after deducting the local rates?—That is not at all clear. The words of the Act are not at all clear as to agricultural land, but the fact is certain, according to all the information I can derive from those of my officers who know Ireland best, that for many years the valuation was very much below the rent, and that it still is below the rent in most cases. A large number of figures as to judicial rents have been taken out, and those judicial rents, more frequently than otherwise, are above the valuation, but there are cases in which they are below it.

745. Can you tell us what was the rate of income tax for those years which you have given, from 1889 to 1893; was it a uniform rate all the time?—No, it was 6*d.* in 1889–90, 6*d.* in 1890–91, 6*d.* in 1891–92, 6*d.* in 1892–93, but it was 7*d.* in 1893–4.

746. Then during the whole four years it was a uniform rate of 6*d.*?—Yes, we have not got the 1893–94 figures yet.

747. Have you remarked that according to these returns the income tax under Schedules A. and B. in Ireland has fallen considerably between 1889–90 and 1892–93, whilst the receipts in England have considerably increased?—Yes, but those are net receipts; we have not for some years been getting anything like the assessment in Ireland. There are great arrears in the income tax collection in Ireland.

748. How are those arrears allotted? In these returns you put down the actual amount collected in each year?—Yes.

749. And if you collect arrears in any given year they will appear as returns for that year?—Yes, it would be a complicated matter in the case of Irish Schedule A. income tax to assign it to the year to which it strictly belonged, because many of the owners are very much in arrears in the payment of the tax.

Taxes from which Ireland is exempt.

750. With regard to these other taxes, land tax, house tax, and railway duties, have you ever made a calculation as to the probable amount which would be collected under those taxes if they were applied to Ireland?—No.

Mr. A. Milner.

751. I suppose it would be a very inconsiderable amount?—I cannot imagine any basis on which we could apply the land tax to Ireland.

752. Put aside the land tax, and take the other taxes, such as establishment licences, armorial bearings, and so on?—It would be very easy to calculate how much the house tax would bring in; it would not be anything very large certainly.

753. With regard to the local taxation revenue which I see in these returns, is that collected separately. It is contained in the last table in each of these returns. Is it collected separately from the other duties on beer, spirits, and so on?—No, they are collected together; for instance, the duty on spirits is 10s. 6d., of which 6d. a gallon is credited to the local taxation and 10s. to the Imperial Exchequer; they are credited together by us.

754. Is the amount collected in each country applied to the services of that country?—Of local taxation revenue?

755. Yes?—I think you must ask the Treasury about the distribution of the revenue. We are mainly concerned with the collection.

756. (*Mr. Sexton.*) 80, 11, and 9, are the proportions for England, Scotland, and Ireland?—That is as to probate.

757. I shall take some considerable time in putting my questions, and, if convenient, I will postpone my examination until a date suitable for everybody. Perhaps you will be able to attend again?—Yes.

757a. (*The Right. Hon. The O'Conor Don.*) With regard to those allowances. Under Schedule B. in England, under the present Budget, an allowance is to be made, is it not?—Yes.

758. Will you explain what those allowances are?—It is an allowance under Schedule A. An allowance has been made from the assessment on lands under Schedule A. of one eighth of the amount of the tax, and from the assessment on houses, of one sixth of the amount of the tax. This is supposed to represent, roughly, the cost of repairs, insurance, and landlords' outgoings, speaking generally.

759. Why should not it be extended to Ireland?—It has been extended to Ireland.

760. When?—It is extended to Ireland in the Bill.

761. I thought from these returns it was exclusively confined to England?—No, it is extended to Ireland.

762. Why is there a blank then in the return as regards Ireland?—I cannot conceive that the return can be affected by it in any way.

763. There is no estimate here in this return?—What return are you referring to?

764. (*Mr. Sexton.*) The explanation is that the return was issued at a date earlier than the date of the Bill?—Yes; there was an alteration of the Bill in committee, which brought Ireland in. I did not know which return the Right Hon. gentleman was referring to.

765. I understand that when in Ireland the valuation is already one eighth lower in the case of land, and one sixth in the case of houses, of the rent, no allowance would be made?—Neither in England, Ireland, or Scotland, is any allowance made in such a case.

766. But when it approaches to one eighth or one sixth of the rent the whole allowance is made?—Yes.

767. (*Sir David Barbour.*) In the case of certain stamp revenue there is no adjustment based on statistics as to probate duty, I understand?—Yes.

768. I suppose there is a good deal of stamp revenue collected on documents relating to property abroad?—Yes, there is.

769. That would be chiefly collected in London, I fancy?—Yes.

770. And the probate statistics do not deal with property which is held abroad; I understood you to say there is no probate duty paid on such property?—Not on property that is technically foreign, but there is a great deal of property situated abroad which, because it is registered in England, or transferable by delivery of bearer bonds in England, is subject to probate duty even if it is foreign. But if in order to transfer the property you have to go before some foreign court or to perform any act abroad, that excludes it from probate.

771. In the case of that foreign property which is transferable here, there would be no necessity for re-sealing, would there, in Scotland or Ireland, if it was registered in London?—No.

772. So that practically the probate statistics would not refer to that property?—Yes, they would; all that property would go into the probate statistics.

773. But not into the re-sealing which is what you base the adjustment on?—Quite so.

774. So that you have to assume that that property would be divided between the three countries very much as the property is divided with respect to which re-sealing is necessary?—I do not think I quite follow that.

775. You say that in case of probate a certain amount of re-sealing is necessary on account of property held in other portions of the United Kingdom?—Yes, but if any foreign property was held by a domiciled Irishman or Scotchman his executor would take out the probate in Ireland or Scotland, even though that foreign property was registered or transferable in England. The executor would pay the duty on that foreign property in Ireland or Scotland, and get the probate re-sealed in England if necessary, so that it all comes into re-sealing in one way or the other.

776. As regards the income tax, you apply the same sort of adjustment. Do you think it is fair to apply that to certain sections of the income tax?—Yes, we apply it to what you might call realised personalty, because it is only to realised personalty that those probate statistics apply.

777. But you do not think it is perfectly accurate, do you?—After all it is only approximate.

778. What you say is, having made the adjustment the figures are more accurate than they were before?—Yes, a great deal more accurate.

779. And I suppose you would admit that owing to the fact that the three kingdoms are united and that London is the metropolis, there is a certain tendency for revenue which might fairly be attributed to the other countries to be collected in London?—Yes, but that is the kind of tendency which these corrections are intended to counteract; but there is that tendency.

780. And I suppose you would admit it is impossible to make perfectly accurate corrections?—Yes.

781. For example, take pensions paid from the revenues of India, such pensions would be all paid in London, wherever the pensioner might be domiciled, and the income tax collected here. That is an example of the correction which it would be impossible to work out and carry out to the full extent?—Yes, it would be.

Adjourned to Thursday, 8th November 1894.

THIRD DAY.

Thursday, 8th November 1894.

Commission Room, Westminster Hall, S.W.

PRESENT:

THE RIGHT HON. HUGH C. E. CHILDERS, *Chairman.*

Lord FARRER.	BERTRAM W. CURRIE, Esq.
Lord WELBY.	W. A. HUNTER, Esq., M.P.
The Right Hon. THE O'CONOR DON.	CHARLES E. MARTIN, Esq.
Sir ROBERT HAMILTON, K.C.B.	J. E. REDMOND, Esq., M.P.
Sir THOMAS SUTHERLAND, K.C.M.G., M.P.	THOMAS SEXTON, Esq., M.P.
Sir DAVID BARBOUR, K.C.S.I.	G. W. WOLFF, Esq., M.P.
The Hon. EDWARD BLAKE, M.P.	HENRY F. SLATTERY, Esq.

Mr. B. H. HOLLAND, *Secretary.*

Mr. A. MILNER re-called and further examined.

Mr. A. Milner.

8 Nov. 1894.

Revenue: adjustment of.

782. (*Mr. Sexton.*) The department of the Inland Revenue of which you are the head collects about three-fourths of the entire revenue raised from taxes, does it not?—Yes, about three-fourths.

783. In fact, you collect the whole tax revenue except the duties on Customs?—Yes.

784. Until inquiry was instituted in 1890 at the instance of Mr. Goschen, in all questions of attributing revenue to any of the three countries concerned, the revenue was always taken as collected, was it not?—Yes, I think so.

785. Up to 1824 when the separate systems were abolished, the revenue collected in each country did show, I suppose, what you would call the true revenue of the country?—Up to 1817, was it not? I am not very strong on the early history.

786. I think the separate Boards were abolished about 1822, were they not?—Yes, I think so.

787. From that time up to 1890 in attributing revenue to England, Ireland, or Scotland, you simply took the revenue as it was collected in each country, did you not?—We simply regarded collection. We did not attempt to attribute the true revenue to each country. Of course we were aware that the collection did not correspond with the actual amount paid by the inhabitants of each country, but we took no notice of that.

788. But in discussions on revenue, the revenue collected was usually what was referred to as the basis of discussion?—I should think so, generally.

789. When Mr. Goschen undertook to appoint the Committee, which never proceeded, and never inquired, he entered into communications with the Treasury, and the Treasury with the Departments, and I gather from some of your answers that the methods of adjustment pursued in the financial relations papers were founded upon the terms of the reference by the House of Commons to the Committee which never inquired?—I am not quite certain. I was not either at the Treasury or at the Inland Revenue, or even in England at the time, and I am not quite sure whether the preparation of the financial papers in the first instance was founded on the terms of that reference. I could not speak positively about it. The records in our department of official communications between the Treasury and us on the subject can hardly be said to exist, they are so scanty, but of course I am aware that there were constant communications in private letters, and verbally between the Treasury and the Inland Revenue in establishing the basis on which that return was made. It was a matter of very constant discussion.

790. But the House of Commons itself gave no instruction, did they?—Not that I am aware of.

791. Nor did the Government as such?—No.

792. Any rules of adjustment which you have applied to these financial relations papers were either determined between the Treasury and the Departments or evolved by the Departments for their own guidance?—All of them had the approval of the Treasury, certainly; all were the subject of discussion with the Treasury. I remember that even the small alterations which I made in the basis of the Returns were only made after consultation with the Treasury.

793. Those small alterations referred, I think, to two points, did they not, as to the proportion of general stamp duty which really relates to personalty?—Yes, that is one point, and the other is as to the application of the adjustment derived from the examination of the probate figures to the income tax assessments under Schedule D. We extended the application a little, but these are very small matters.

794. The part of the income from trades and professions which you believe to be interest on capital?—Yes, that is so.

795. You have somewhat dwelt in a part of your evidence upon what are, in fact, certain small exemptions of Ireland from taxation, and certain advantages which you conceive Ireland has in the matter of taxation?—Yes.

796. Did you intend those statements to refer simply to the fact that these differences existed, or did you intend them to convey any view that upon the whole system of taxation, considered as a whole, Ireland enjoys an advantage?—Oh, no; they were particular answers, I think, to particular questions. The particular question I was asked, if I remember rightly, was whether there were any taxes imposed in Great Britain which were not imposed in Ireland.

797. And you were giving to the particular question a particular answer, were you?—Yes.

798. The general system of taxation in these countries has long ago become, generally speaking, what the Act of Legislative Union contemplated should be established in certain contingencies; that is, it is an indiscriminate system. It is a system of equal taxes in both countries upon the same subjects of taxation, is it not?—Yes, subject to the limitation of certain taxes to particular parts of the United Kingdom.

799. Subject to what I may call relatively small exemptions, but the great scheme of taxation is one which the Act of Union calls indiscriminate; that is to say, it levies equal taxes upon the same subjects of

taxation in both countries whether as to articles of consumption, property, realty, or personalty, or transactions?—Yes. I must once more make a reservation. With regard to the tax on land, although it has been nominally the same, you know I hold that, owing to a different system of valuation, there has been really a discrimination in favour of Ireland.

800. I am speaking now generally; I shall come to that presently. Such a system of taxation rests, does it not, on the assumption of equal taxable capacity?—I do not know on what assumption it rests, or rested.

801. At any rate, being indiscriminate it ignores any difference in capacity, if any exists, between the people of one country and the other, does it not. It assumes, does it not, that the people of one country are as well able to pay as the people of the other; in fact it taxes the two countries as if they were one?—Yes, it taxes the two countries as if they were one.

802. As you have spoken of particular small exemptions as conferring advantage, which might be taken to mean advantage on the whole, it becomes necessary to inquire whether a system of equal taxes upon the same subjects of taxation in two countries differently circumstanced may not operate very unequally. Take the return for the Financial Paper, 1892–93. I do not think we have yet got the Paper for 1893–94, though many months have elapsed since the financial year ended. I am referring to No. 334, Sir John Hibbert's Return. May I put to you upon the subject of the operation of a system of equal taxes upon the same articles a suppositious case which I think has been often put before: Suppose France and England were joined in a fiscal union subject to an indiscriminate system of taxes, France, I think, drinks much more coffee and England more tea than coffee; suppose there were a system of equal taxes on the same articles, a heavy tax upon coffee, but the same in both countries, and a lighter tax upon tea, but the same in both countries, the effect, of course, would be that France, because it used more coffee than tea, would bear the heavier burden, although the system is nominally equal?—Yes, certainly.

803. That makes it clear that a system of taxes nominally equal can be actually oppressive where no care is taken to adjust the different taxes according to the degree in which the articles are consumed in either country, does it not?—It may be.

804. Will you kindly direct your attention to page 7 of the Return to which I have referred and to the column headed "Revenue net receipt" and so on. The population of England is, I believe, between six and seven times the population of Ireland?—I think about six times, but I have not the figures before me.

805. The figures last Census were: Ireland, 4,700,000; England, 27,000,000. If you look at the columns headed "England" and "Ireland" respectively, under the head of "Spirits," there you will see, I think, that whilst the population of England is between six and seven times that of Ireland, the consumption of spirits in England is between four and five times that of Ireland?—It is.

806. The consumption per head is, therefore, considerably less in England than in Ireland?—Yes.

807. Then take the next article, "Beer." You see there that the population of England being between six and seven times that of Ireland, the consumption of beer in England is about 14 times that of the consumption in Ireland?—It is.

808. That is to say, proportionately more than double?—Yes.

809. Now the taxation upon a gallon of whiskey at present is 11s., is it not?—Yes, 10s. 6d. for the Imperial Exchequer and 6d. for the local bodies.

810. Shall we take the Imperial taxation?—Yes, 10s. 6d.

811. That is the taxation upon about 60 gallons of beer, is it not?—Yes, upon about 60 gallons.

812. Now the tax on spirits, let us say, represents from two-thirds to three-fourths of the selling price of the article, does it not?—Yes, quite that. I do not mean the selling retail price, but the selling wholesale price.

813. What is the usual price of a barrel of beer of 36 gallons?—I should say about 40s.

814. The tax on that is 6s. 3d., is it not?—6s. 3d.

815. That is to say, that whilst the tax upon spirits, which is the article more generally consumed in Ireland, is equal to from two-thirds to three-fourths of the price, the tax upon beer, which is overwhelmingly the article of consumption in England, is only about a sixth of the price?—Yes, about a sixth.

816. The article, therefore, more commonly consumed in Ireland is heavily taxed upon by the fiscal system, and the article very commonly consumed in England by comparison is very lightly touched?—I should not say beer was lightly touched; I do not think the brewers would agree with that. It may be comparatively lightly touched.

817. In comparison with the tax and the price?—Yes.

818. I have also seen a comparison of the amount of alcohol which gave out the same results, which shows that beer is taxed five times as lightly as spirits, having relation to the amount of alcohol?—I should think that was an over-statement, but I am not prepared to say without examining it.

819. If the taxation upon spirits was as light by any test of comparison you choose to institute as the taxation upon beer, or if, on the other hand, the taxation upon beer was as heavy as the taxation upon spirits, would not there be such an alteration in the figures of these two columns against England as would greatly alter the incidence of taxation as between Great Britain and Ireland?—Certainly.

820. So we see that under a system of equal taxation of the same articles there may be an arrangement pointed to heaviness of consumption of one article in one country and to lightness in another which produces unequal effects?—Certainly. I may be permitted to say, though perhaps it is not strictly relevant to your question, in order that it may not lead to misunderstanding, that you might reduce the tax on spirits, and you might increase the tax on beer, but to increase the tax on beer to anything like the amount of the tax on spirits would undoubtedly kill the beer revenue right away.

821. Of course it is a question of degree?—Yes. That is, of course, apart from the particular subject of your inquiries. But I cannot help making that reflection.

822. (*Sir David Barbour.*) It would also affect the spirit duty, would it not?—Yes, it would affect both.

823. (*Mr. Wolff.*) If you increased the beer duty you would probably increase your revenue from the spirits?—I think you would.

824. (*Sir David Barbour.*) And perhaps you would not increase the revenue from the beer?—It is a question of degree, of course.

825. (*Mr. Sexton.*) Mr. Wolff suggests that anything you might lose on the taxation of beer you would gain on the spirits?—You would gain something.

826. On the other hand, if you lightened the tax on spirits to make up for a proportion of the tax on beer, that would not destroy the consumption of spirits, would it?—Certainly not.

827. Which seems to make heavy increases?—The last increase does not seem to have agreed with it.

828. It stood a good deal, did it not? That was the object with which my question was pointed, to make it clear that under a system of equal taxes upon the same subjects of taxation in two countries, it would be quite possible to throw the whole burden of taxation upon one of the countries, and, as we see, it does in fact work out some considerable inequality. That, I think, puts into the foreground the three questions as between Great Britain and Ireland at present, and I think it puts in true perspective in the background these infinitely smaller questions of exemption and advantage to which reference has been made. I should be thankful if you would, and

Sir R. Giffen. [illegible] Nov. 1894.

Tax on spirits and beer in the two countries. [illegible]

Taxes from which Ireland is exempt. [illegible]

perhaps you now can give precisely the particulars of the exemptions and advantages to which you referred in your former evidence?—I was asked when I was here before to give a list of the amounts of the taxes which are paid in England and Scotland and which are not paid in Ireland. I think a copy of that was sent to the Secretary of the Commission some time ago. Perhaps that will make it unnecessary for me to go into the details; the total amounts to about 4,000,000*l.* a year.

829. I see a small item here, "Patent medicine duty," which realised 213,000*l.* in the year. Is there no duty paid on patent medicines in Ireland?—No.

830. Who pays the duty in England?—The vendors. They have to put a stamp on the bottle.

831. Not the manufacturer?—I do not quite know. The manufacturer might affix the stamp, or the vendor might affix it; all we do is to insist that it shall not be sold without the stamp.

832. But if a man in Ireland buys a bottle of patent medicine, does he not pay for the stamp just as if he were in England?—No, because patent medicine sent out from England to be sold in Ireland is not charged; it is allowed to go out free without the labels, just as if it went to a foreign country.

833. The total of the taxes levied in Great Britain and not levied in Ireland amounts, as you say, to about 4,000,000*l.* a year. These are the railway duty, the establishment licences, certain stamps, the land tax, and the inhabited house duty. Have you made any calculation as to what would be the yield of those taxes, or of corresponding taxes, if they were applied to Ireland?—I am sorry to say that the materials do not exist for making a calculation which would be worth anything at all. I can make a round guess, but I am not in a position to do more, and it would take a good deal of time and investigation to get at the facts. For instance, it is very difficult for us to know how many male servants and carriages there are in Ireland; it would be a very difficult matter indeed to adjust the land tax. We have no figures enabling us to adjust the inhabited house duty.

834. You may guess, may you not, that the Inhabited House Duty beginning at houses of 20*l.* value, would be in Ireland trivial?—Between 30,000*l.* and 50,000*l.*, I think; that is a very large margin; but I have not the materials to speak definitely.

835. That is about one-fortieth of the British yield?—Yes, it would be very small.

836. Will you give your guess on the corresponding duties in Ireland, if they were levied?—I should say 150,000*l.*

837. (*Sir David Barbour.*) I see Scotland gives 360,000*l.* and you think Ireland would give considerably less?—Yes, I think Ireland would give considerably less.

838. (*Mr. Sexton.*) These are all direct taxes, are they not, except perhaps the railway duty?—Yes, I suppose you would call them all direct taxes.

839. Now the direct taxes which you do levy in Ireland, that is to say the stamps and the income tax, do yield about four per cent. of the whole revenue of the United Kingdom under those heads, do they not? I see here, for instance, in the same account, 1892–3, that stamps yield 609,000*l.* against a total of 13,788,000, which is 4·4 per cent.?—Right.

840. And the income tax yields 662,000*l.* out of 15,139,000, which is 4·2 per cent?—Yes.

841. The mean between the two would be 4·3?—Yes.

842. If you apply that to the direct taxes here, which are not levied in Ireland, and take 4 per cent. on 4,100,000*l.*, that would give 160,000, would it not?—Yes.

843. Showing that your guess comes extremely near?—I have not guessed it that way, but still I am glad to be so far confirmed.

844. The experience of direct taxes shows that you are extremely close to the mark?—Yes, I think it is a fair guess, but it is only a guess.

845. Then your surmise, backed by the actual results of direct taxation, seems to go far to establish, does it not, that the difference in favour of Ireland, by reason of the non-levy of those taxes in Ireland, amounts to perhaps 150,000*l.* a year?—Yes.

846. At page 10 of this Return it is shown that in the year 1892–3, there was levied in Great Britain and surrendered for the purposes of local taxation under the head of licences, 3,600,000*l.*?—Yes.

847. And in the same year there was collected in Ireland, under the head of licences (page 6), 193,000*l.*?—Yes, 193,000*l.*

848. Which was not surrendered for the local uses of Ireland, as the money was in England and Scotland, but was appropriated to Imperial expenses?—Yes.

849. It appears, therefore, that under the present arrangement, Ireland, under the head of licences, is a loser to the extent of 193,000*l.* a year?—I think you ought to take the whole arrangements for local taxation together.

850. I know the view of the Government was, when by the Acts of 1888 and 1889 the Imperial licence revenue was in England and Scotland surrendered to local uses, that Ireland was entitled to an equivalent?—Well, you know more about that than I do.

851. At any rate, the arrangements for local taxation stand by themselves, do they not?—Yes, and must be judged as a whole.

852. But the licence revenue in Great Britain is surrendered to local uses, and the licence revenue in Ireland is not?—Yes, there is a very trifling amount in Great Britain which still goes into the Imperial Exchequer.

853. And as against the sum of 193,000*l.* a year which, if an equal rule were established, would be available for the local uses of Ireland, the contribution made to it from the Exchequer is only 40,000*l.* a year under that head, leaving a net loss of 150,000*l.*, which is about equal to the gain which arises from the non-levy of those taxes. I think I may pass from what you call the exemptions. Now there are certain advantages which you said Ireland enjoyed—not exemptions, but advantages—and one of these has relation to Schedule B of the income tax; that advantage, however, has disappeared this year, has it not?—The advantage which Ireland used to derive along with Scotland from a different rate of taxation under Schedule B has disappeared, but I am not sure that it would be correct to say that Ireland has no advantage now under Schedule B, for this reason: that the exemptions under Schedule B apply to a far greater number of cases in Ireland. Practically, no farmer is taxed at all under Schedule B unless his rent is something like 400*l.* a year.

854. Where are you speaking of?—Of the whole country; this is common.

855. I fear it interests Irish farmers very little then?—They do not pay under Schedule B, and therefore I think Ireland does get off lightly under Schedule B. I admit it is a small item.

856. The whole yield in Scotland is 25,000, and in Ireland 19,000*l.*, so I think it may be left?—Yes.

857. You hold that the Irish landowner has an important advantage under Schedule A, I understand?—Yes, an important advantage.

858. Do you say so important advantage?—Yes, an important advantage under Schedule A. I do not say it is of immense importance as applying to the whole set of figures; but so far as Schedule A is concerned the advantage is an important advantage, and has been a very important advantage.

859. There is no doubt that there has been a very continuous fall in land values in these countries since 1877, is there?—I should say since 1879.

860. 1877 was the highest year in England, was it not?—Yes, it was the highest, but the steep down grade only commenced about 1880.

861. If the assessments under Schedule A in Ireland ever conferred an advantage upon the Irish landowner, it would have been, I suppose, before that fall in values began. When do you suppose that the

Sir A. Milner.

9 Nov. 1894.

Taxes from which Ireland is exempt.

Advantages enjoyed by Ireland.

advantage would have been at the greatest?—I think the advantage was at the greatest between about 1860 and 1877.

862. In 1864 a Select Committee of the House of Commons reported on subjects cognate to those which now engage our attention, and they reported unanimously: "With regard to the Income Tax "under Schedule A in Ireland it has not been proved "to the Committee that the Irish taxpayer enjoys any "important advantage in consequence of the tax being "assessed upon the net Government valuation of land "and houses instead of upon the gross rent as in Great "Britain"?—That was in 1865.

863. It was?—That is just before the period during which I think the great advantage was enjoyed.

864. How do you explain that?—I think there has been some advantage all along, but it has been greatest in the period to which I refer.

865. Perhaps you will state your view of the difference which exists under the principle of assessment under Schedule A between England and Ireland?—I think I stated it before. There are two great differences. In the first place, the English Act defines "annual value" in a manner which makes it practically equivalent to gross value.

866. The English assessment, as I understand, is upon the rent actually received, less the local rates?—No, not less the local rates. The rates are paid by the tenant, you see. It is gross rent.

867. And if the landlord pays any rates, he may take them off, may he not?—Yes.

868. Then it is the rent less the rates when the rates are paid by the landlord. Now in Ireland what is the position?—The net annual value is taken irrespective of rent, the effect of that being that the valuation was much below the rent.

869. No doubt, but the rent might have been too high, might it not?—But that has nothing to do with the present question. I say in England we followed the rent, in Ireland we did not, we went much below. That is quite independent of whether the rent was too high; it may have been too high in England for all I know.

870. What was the net value in Ireland; was it the rent which the landlord might expect to receive less the amount of the outgoings for management?—I would not speak positively, because my Department has never had to make the valuation in Ireland.

871. Just so; the subject is very obscure, and conclusions upon it ought to be cautiously approached?—Yes, but I am quite prepared to give you my evidence for what I have stated. But let us clear up first this point about the basis of the valuation. The Irish Valuation Act, which the income-tax authorities do not administer, but which the Irish Valuation Commissioners administer, says repeatedly "net annual value." In dealing with houses, it distinctly says the basis is to be the tenant doing all the repairs.

872. Which he does as a matter of fact?—Yes, I daresay. But in England, whether the tenant does the repairs or not, the house is valued as if the landlord did them. Therefore, it is valued higher than it would be in Ireland. I am informed that the valuation of houses in Ireland is almost universally a low one. As regards land, the valuation has remained practically unchanged.

873. Land has remained absolutely unchanged, has it not?—I think it would be too much to say absolutely unchanged; a little land may have been brought into cultivation, but in the main the valuation has not been altered on land since 1866.

874. (*The O'Conor Don.*) Before you go further, you spoke of land being brought into cultivation. If land had been brought into cultivation that had not been valued before, can it be valued now in Ireland; can there be any change whatsoever made in the value of land?—I would not speak positively. Looking at the position in England in the year 1865, the value of lands was 46,000,000*l*. In the year 1877 it was 52,000,000. That is the effect of a system under which there is a regular re-valuation. As compared with that, The O'Conor Don tells us that there was no change at all in the valuation of land in Ireland. Yet the increase in value between 1865 and 1878 was a general increase.

875. (*Mr. Sexton.*) You have recalled the zenith year in England, 1877?—Yes.

876. Since 1877 the value of land in England, which in that year was 52,000,000*l*., has fallen in 1893 to 41,000,000*l*., has it not?—Yes, it has.

877. And that reduction is founded, as I understand, upon permanent reductions of rent and not at all on temporary abatements?—Yes.

878. So that probably that 11,000,000*l*. does not at all measure the full value, because all the temporary abatements are outside the 11,000,000*l*.?—They are.

879. Is not that an extraordinarily striking proof of the recent fall in land values; looking to Ireland in the year 1877, which was your zenith year in England, the value of land was 10,000,000*l*. almost exactly?—Yes.

880. And last year it was 9,973,000*l*.?—Yes.

881. There it is stereotyped?—Yes.

882. Now if there were in Ireland, as there is in England, a system of periodical revision every five years instead of a stereotyped, antique valuation, is it not evident that the same fruitful causes arising since 1877, which brought down the assessment from 52,000,000*l*. to 41,000,000*l*. in England, would also strike at least one-fourth off the total valuation in Ireland?—I think that is very likely, but I am equally convinced that the valuation in Ireland, if we had had the English system, would in 1877 not have been 10,000,000*l*. but something very much higher. Sir Richard Griffith, in 1871, estimated that a re-valuation then would have added 30 per cent. all round; and Mr. Ball Greene, in 1876, estimated that a re-valuation would have added 33 per cent. all round. I agree with Mr. Sexton that there would have been a great fall since 1880 in the Irish valuation, but it would have been a fall, in my opinion, from a figure vastly higher than this stereotyped valuation to a figure about equal to that valuation.

883. Are you aware that in 1886 Mr. Giffen, who was a somewhat competent inquirer, wrote an article in the "Nineteenth Century," in which he said that Ireland, as compared with England, is strictly valued, and is over valued?—I do not recollect Mr. Giffen saying that, but it would not alter my opinion, I am afraid.

884. Nor would the opinion of the Select Committee, you say?—The opinion of the Select Committee does not affect me, because that deals with the earlier period.

885. (*The O'Conor Don.*) Do you agree with the Select Committee as regards that earlier period?—I am inclined to think (of course I say this with great reserve) that the valuation was always low for land in Ireland; but where I think Ireland got the great advantage under Schedule A was about those 15 years from 1865 to 1880, and since then it has had an advantage, but a constantly declining advantage, and to-day under "Land" I should think the advantage was very slight, if any; under "Houses" I believe it still to be very considerable.

886. If the Irish valuation was deliberately designed to fix the level of value much lower than in England, that must have been as apparent in 1864, when the Select Committee inquired, as at any other time, must it not; the valuation had then been just completed, you know?—There are two points to be kept quite distinct; one is the point whether the basis has not always been lower in Ireland than in England; and the other is the point whether Ireland has not gained greatly by not having re-assessments. The first is a matter on which I have my opinion. I think Ireland always has had an advantage, but I do not insist on it. But what is clear to me is that Ireland did gain greatly by not having these re-assessments.

887. That is during the period of crescendo, of ascending value?—Yes. The fact is that to-day, after all this fall, taking the judicial rents all round, they

Mr. A. Milner.

8 Nov. 1894.

[illegible]

Mr. A. Milner.

4 Nov. 1895.

Income tax assessments and valuation.

are rather above the valuation as it has always existed; then how much must the rent have been above the valuation before any of those reductions took place?

888. No doubt the rents were, as a rule, considerably above the valuation, but I should be rather disposed to warn you against taking the level of the rents in Ireland, that is, until the courts began to have any control of them, as any test of the equity of the valuation?—I am not saying that at all. I am only saying that if in England the rent of a piece of land had gone up between 1853 and 1880, 50*l*., the landlord would have been assessed on those 50*l*. extra, whether he had a right to them or not; that is the basis of the English valuation. It is admitted that when rent went up to an equivalent degree in Ireland it did not affect the valuation at all. Here we have judicial rents fixed on a large number of properties, now amounting to rather more than the valuation which has existed all along.

889. When you say "rather more," do I understand you to say that in all the cases in which there are judicial rents, that is to say in the case of six millions of rental in Ireland, the judicial rents and the valuations do not approach each other?—The judicial rent is near the valuation, but on the average it is above, though only a little above it.

890. I suppose you are aware that the valuation was very unequal?—Very unequal.

891. And whilst the counties valued in the earlier years, when the country was depressed and local rates were high, were valued rather low, the counties valued in the later years were valued relatively high; so that it is hard to put a general application with regard to it?—The average is very close. For instance, may I just give you these figures. They are the figures of all the lands on which judicial rents have been fixed up to date: "Former rent, 5,975,000*l*.; judicial rent, "4,732,000*l*.; valuation, 4,341,000*l*."

892. That shows, at any rate, that with regard to about one-half, I should think, or approximating to one-half, of the value of Irish lands, there is now no particular advantage, at any rate in being valued upon the valuation. You might as well, as in the case of the English landlord, be valued on the rent, might you not?—Even now the Irishman has an advantage. If the rent is below the valuation he is charged on the rent, and if the valuation is below the rent he pays on the valuation.

893. But I am pointing out to you, with regard to what was a sum of 6,000,000*l*. of rent, that it matters nothing to the Irish landlord now, at any rate since these courts came into operation, whether or not he is valued on the rent or the valuation, because they are pretty much the same?—It does matter. He has an advantage still in being assessed on the valuation, because where the valuation is below the rent he gets the advantage of it, and where the rent is below the valuation he gets back the difference.

894. But does it not approach the vanishing point nearly where the rent and the valuation are so close to each other?—No, it does not, because in this total the inequalities balance one another; but in the practical working of the Act, as I point out, they do not, because where the rent is above the valuation it is of no benefit to the Revenue, and where the rent is below the valuation the landlord has the privilege of paying only on the rent. Therefore these figures do not represent the advantage which even now the Irish landlord gets under this system.

895. The whole question hinges upon a matter difficult to decide, and that is, how far the original valuation differed from what would be the rent of such land in England?—That is a question open to dispute. What it seems to me is not open to dispute in the face of the figures is, that in the interval between the original valuation and to-day there was a considerable period during which, as compared with England, Ireland benefited at least 20 or 30 per cent. on the Schedule A valuation, owing to the fact that there was no re-assessment. May I point out to you that the former rent of 6,000,000*l*., which we were speaking of, must infallibly, if it had been English land, have got into our income tax assessment. We do assess on the rent in England, but in the case of Irish land the Revenue never got into the assessment, which remained at 4,000,000*l*. odd.

896. (*Mr. Martin.*) I apprehend, when you say that Ireland benefited during this period by the lower valuation of the land, that you refer to your Department alone, not to the equity of the case; that is, if the land in Ireland were too highly rented, your argument, looking at it from an equity point of view, would not hold good, would it?—I do not think I quite follow that.

897. In other words, if the land were rented 33 per cent. too high, then your Department would have had no right to levy the extra taxes on that extra valuation?—Of course, all we look at is this: certain people in Ireland put 6,000,000*l*. into their pockets and pay income tax on 4,000,000*l*. I call that an advantage to them as compared with people in England who put 6,000,000*l*. into their pockets and pay income tax on all of it.

898. (*Sir David Barbour.*) When you say Ireland benefits by this, you mean a certain class of the Irish people, of course?—A certain class, of course.

899. And some of these Irish landlords might be Englishmen, I suppose?—Quite so.

900. If they were absentee landlords Ireland, as a whole, would not benefit in any way, would it?—No.

901. (*Mr. Sexton.*) We are discussing the question of the landowner—the Irish landowner and English landowner?—I am discussing the question of the assessment of land. It does not concern me whom the land belongs to, or whether it is held in small or large holdings. I am talking now simply of the question whether Irish land has not been undervalued for income tax.

902. We are discussing the question of whether or not the particular class of persons who paid income tax in Ireland under Schedule A. were better treated than the corresponding class in England?—No, I am discussing the question whether the State got the same share from the yield of Irish land that it did from the yield of English land, and I say that it did not.

903. If we were discussing the question of the general benefit, of course it might be pointed out that the valuation in Ireland included houses and other improvements made by the tenant, not by the landlord, which would not be made by any tenant in Great Britain, and that the assessment in Ireland, so far from being a proof of taxable capacity, might be taken as a proof of poverty. But these questions are apart; we are now on the relations between the State and the particular class of persons who pay a particular kind of tax in Ireland and in England?—No, I am looking at the relations between the State and a particular kind of property. In this question of assessment it does not interest me at all, from my point of view, who the owners are. There is so much value from which I want to get my tax, so much annual income, and I say there is an annual income in Ireland of 6,000,000*l*. from which I only get the same tax as I should in England from a much lower amount.

904. Whatever conclusion one may come to about the valuation, I think your case from your point of view is sufficiently made out when you are able to show that the rent is higher. You say that if that land had been in England a man would have paid on the rent, but being in Ireland he did not pay on the rent but on a lower thing, the valuation; is not that so?—Yes.

905. And you really do not claim to come to a conclusion, do you, whether the valuation was too low or too high, but when you say it, it is lower than the rent, and if he had been an English landlord the tax would have been paid on the rent?—Yes.

906. That really involves no conclusion as to the justice of the valuation. No doubt, if in those

Mr. A. Milner. 8 Nov. 1894.

successive years when valuations were going up, from 1865 to 1877, there had been fresh valuations in Ireland conducted by the same persons and on the same principles as the original valuation, there might have been some increase. It is equally evident, I think, is it not, that the fall from 1877 to 1893 has been far greater than the ascent in those previous years to which we have referred, and if there had been a periodical revision between 1877 and the present time in Ireland, the 10,000,000, or whatever the valuation was, would have gone down unquestionably by much more than one-fourth if, not only the permanent reductions, but the temporary abatements, which were so chronic as to be permanent in their nature, were taken into account?—I beg your pardon. The temporary abatements would not affect the gross assessment either in Ireland or in England. Any relief afforded for temporary abatements is given by a repayment without altering the gross assessment.

907. At any rate, upon the fall in value simply, the Irish valuation would have been immensely reduced, would it not?—It would have been immensely reduced from the highest point; but my contention is that it is proved that it would not have been reduced below the present figure.

908. You suggest that, but the whole question is this, whether the increase in the valuation in years of increasing values was so much less than the decrease in the sixteen years of falling values, that the net valuation at the end of it all might not be considerably less than now?—I do not see how the valuation could be less than now in the face of the facts about the judicial rents. No valuer who had got the principles of English valuation in his mind could possibly put the valuation below the judicial rent, and it still is below it.

909. The valuation is still below it, is it?—Yes, it is still below. I quite agree that if you had had the English system in Ireland there would have been an enormous fall in the valuation of land in the past fifteen years, only it would have been from a much higher figure than that which you actually see for the years 1879 and 1880.

910. The summing-up of it is, is it not, that the rent in Ireland is higher than then the valuation, that if the Irish landlord were an English landlord he would have to pay upon that rent, but as he has the option of paying on the valuation, he is better off than the English landlord; but whether the rent is higher or lower, you are not in a position to say, are you?—It is a question of rent, is it not? For instance, the English landlord may be content with a lower rent than the Irish landlord, and many people contend that the proportion of profit which the English landlord receives is lower than that received by the Irish landlord?—May I ask you a question?

911. Certainly.—You think that the value of land has fallen in Ireland since 1880?

912. Unquestionably, in all these countries it has. —There has been a very great fall in all these countries?

913. Yes, a very continuous and heavy fall.—Then in that case a rent fixed on the principles on which the judicial rent is now fixed would have been higher than the present judicial rent, and therefore it would have been much higher than the present valuation.

914. (*Lord Farrer.*) In the case of temporary abatements of rent in England, of which there have been so many, do you still get income-tax upon the full rent without taking into consideration the abatement?—No. We should repay the landlord the tax on the rent abated, but it would not affect the figures which you see in this table, which are figures of gross assessment.

915. (*Mr. Wolff.*) But still the landlord gets back the proportion of tax, does he not?—Yes, he gets it back in England.

916. Not in Ireland?—Yes; in fact he never pays now in Ireland except on what he actually gets.

917. He pays on the valuation, does he not?—No, he pays on the rent, where it is below the valuation; and if he does not get the rent he does not pay at all.

918. I presume that is the same in England, is it not?—That would be so if he got no rent at all. But he has not the same option as in Ireland of paying either on the valuation or on the rent.

919. (*Mr. Blake.*) Let me ask you whether you have any figures which will show from year to year the additional amount of fall in value of land occasioned by those temporary abatements?—They might be worked out, I think.

920. That would add very seriously probably to the total fall in the value of land in each country, would it not?—It would.

921. (*Mr. Sexton.*) If you can show for the year 1877 how much of the 52,000,000*l.* assessment was represented by further remissions granted and temporary abatements, and then were to apply the same principle to the year 1893, we should really see what the actual fall in the value of land as tested by rent has been in England at that time, should we not?—Yes, we could do that.

922. It is manifestly much heavier than appears?—What we could give you would be the actual net receipt from Schedule A. in the two years in England after the repayments had been made.

923. Which, multiplied by the tax, would give the assessment?—Yes.

924. And that no doubt would show a considerably heavier fall in value than appears by this assessment. I mean that the remissions under the head of temporary abatement were much heavier in the year 1893 than they were in 1877, a prosperous year?—Yes. If we were to look at the net receipts from Schedule A. both in England and Ireland, they would show something very much less than the tax on the gross assessments—in Ireland even more so than in England. I have got some figures here on that point, but they are only for one or two years.

925. (*Chairman.*) For how many years can you put in such a return?—I have the last three or four years worked out now.

926. Could you make a return from the common point of 1877 or 1879?—I do not know if we could. I am not quite sure how far we can go back, but would it do if we could get some specimen years further back instead of trying to carry it through the whole period?

927. (*Mr. Sexton.*) If you want to judge the complete swing of a pendulum you must take the beginning and the end—1877 and 1893 or 1894?—I will try and do it, but I cannot promise. There is one point which the Accountant-General of the Inland Revenue calls my attention to, and that is, that unfortunately we must take land and houses together, because our accounts would not show the repayments on different parts of Schedule A., but only on Schedule A. as a whole.

928. That would make it, I think, practically useless, because the valuation of houses, which in Ireland is stereotyped, is in England extremely buoyant and bounding?—Quite so.

929. For instance, the valuation of houses which in 1877 in England was 90,000,000, is now over 127,000,000?—Yes.

930. (*The O'Conor Don.*) Is there much repayment under the head of "Houses"?—A good deal is given up by Schedule of Discharge.

931. (*Mr. Sexton.*) Can you endeavour to confine it to "land" and "houses" connected with the working of land?—I will see what I can do, but I am afraid I can give no promise.

932. How would the same thing work out in Ireland?—My impression is that it would reduce the Irish assessment more than the English. I mean to say that the loss through non-payment of rent and arrears, and one thing and another, is heavier in Ireland than it is in England.

933. (*The O'Conor Don.*) Could you make such a return under Schedule B.; would that give you the

amount of the reduction?—Yes, but it would be hopelessly misleading under Schedule B., because of the enormous number of total exemptions. You see Schedule B. only affects a farmer of a certain class; it only affects an infinitesimal part of the farmers in Ireland.

934. (*Chairman.*) It is the wish, I think, of the Commission that you should give us the abatements on land distinct from houses?—I will see what I can do.

935. And approximately at the same period?—Yes.

936. (*The O'Conor Don.*) As far as Schedule B. is concerned, that under Schedule B. is a certain proportion of the tax under Schedule A., is it not?—Yes, of the gross assessment.

937. If you lower the gross assessment under Schedule A., do you not lower the assessment under Schedule B.?—Certainly.

938. Do you lower it in the case of a temporary abatement as well as in that of a permanent one?—No, you lower neither A. nor B. in a temporary abatement.

939. You repay to the landlord the excess?—Or, in the case of Ireland, we never get it. This is the difference in the systems; in England the tenant pays the income tax, and he deducts it from his rent; in Ireland the landlord pays the income tax. Under the system at present in force the Irish landlord does not pay the income tax when he does not get the rent; whereas in England when he does not get the rent as somebody else has paid the income tax, the landlord must seek repayment.

940. But that has been in force in Ireland only during the last few years, has it not?—Since 1881.

941. Supposing, recurring again to Schedule B., that the temporary abatement is made to a tenant, does he pay the income tax on the gross rent all the same? Is any abatement given under Schedule B. Income Tax, in consequence of the temporary abatement he received from the landlord?—No.

942. But if the abatement is a permanent one receives an abatement on the tax?—Yes.

943. (*Mr. Sexton.*) Passing to the return of income tax, I wish to ask one or two questions with the view of showing the stationary condition of Ireland in contrast with the progressive state of England, and in view of the fact that an equal system is considered to be suitable. In the year 1862 if you look at the Irish return papers you will see that the total assessment of Ireland under these heads was something over 13,000,000l.?—Yes.

944. And of that it appears that 12,500,000l. were from land and houses?—Yes.

945. Leaving only 1,000,000l. for the others?—Yes.

946. In 1893, after 30 years, the assessment had advanced only from 13,000,000l. to 15,000,000l., of which 13,500,000l. were land and houses?—Yes.

947. Leaving only between 1,000,000l. and 2,000,000l. for the rest?—Yes; but the other heads have nearly doubled, have they not. They have increased 80 per cent., I should think.

948. Now, in the same year, 1862, the English assessment, by comparison with the Irish of 13,000,000l., was 120,000,000l.; that is about nine times the Irish, is it not?—Yes.

949. Of which 97,000,000l. was land and houses, leaving 23,000,000l. over?—Yes.

950. In the year 1893 the gross assessment under these heads in England had become 221,000,000l., that is, having been nine times the Irish in 1862, it had advanced to more than 14 times the Irish in 1893, 15,500,000l. as compared with 221,000,000l.?—Yes.

951. And whilst the Irish assessment still continued to be almost wholly an assessment of land and houses, the assessment of land and houses in England was 168,000,000l., out of 221,000,000l., leaving no less than 53,000,000l. of assessment under other heads?—Yes, but the great advance in England was in houses.

952. No doubt a very considerable advance was in houses, but railways, as you see, advanced enormously from 12,000,000l. to 30,000,000l., and other property from 9,000,000l. to 22,000,000l., an extraordinary progress?—Yes, but not so very different from the Irish progress, is it? I mean railways have advanced from 790,000l. to 1,571,000l. in Ireland. Of course we are dealing with much smaller figures, but that is nearly double.

953. Upon the gross, you see, England having been nine times more than Ireland in 1862, had become 14 times more in the later year, had it not?—Yes. But again I point out that the enormous increase in houses has a great deal to do with it. I wish an Irish valuer could be called as to the Schedule A. assessment of house property in Ireland.

954. The enormous increase of houses in England means the increase of a thriving industrial population, does it not?—Yes, and a constant re-assessment bringing them up.

955. Do you suppose that any re-assessment of the houses in Ireland would very materially have altered the proportions?—Yes, I think it would have altered them.

956. Do you happen to know the City of Dublin, for instance?—No, I am not speaking from personal knowledge.

957. I know it very well, and I should say that over a great part of Dublin a fresh valuation would greatly lower the figure?—Would you say the same of Belfast?

958. I do not think a fresh valuation would alter them much in Belfast.—I have no knowledge of Ireland, but my information is that the valuation of houses in Ireland is extremely low compared with England. I give that for what it is worth. The income tax officials are unanimous on this point. They are not valuers, it is not their business, but they have great experience all the same.

959. (*The O'Conor Don.*) Are not houses re-valued in Ireland when they are rebuilt and improved?—New constructions, yes.

960. All new constructions are valued up to the latest stage?—Yes, but the Act distinctly says on the net value; in England it is on the gross.

961. (*Mr. Sexton.*) The questions I have put to you on this Return are intended to show, and I think your answers have shown, that Ireland is comparatively stagnant, that the valuation advances slightly at long periods, whilst the valuation of England is buoyant and progressive in the extreme, and an equal system of taxation on the same commodities which treats these communities as of equal capacity to pay is one that requires serious investigation. I asked you at the beginning whether it was not the fact that the rules of adjustment were due to the language of the reference to the abortive committee of 1890. That committee was instructed under the first head to report the amount and proportion of revenue contributed to the Exchequer by the people of England, Scotland, and Ireland respectively. Is that the first time in your knowledge when these words "Contributed and contributed by the people" were used?—Yes, that is the first time I know anything about it.

962. Revenue was previously regarded as something raised in each country, not further adjusted?—No, I think not.

963. You did say something about efforts being made at the Treasury, when you were there seven or eight years ago, did you not?—I think Lord Welby identified them.

964. Lord Welby identified them in very remarkable language, because Lord Welby said there were some terms drawn up in which nobody believed, I think. It appears they pointed to conclusions, or were intended to point to conclusions, which conclusions no experts of the Treasury were disposed to accept. It was this language "contributed to the Exchequer by "the people of England, Scotland, and Ireland respec-"tively" which led you to make the adjustments which have been made, I presume?—Yes, no doubt.

965. For the purpose of these adjustments the revenue which you collect, and which is really all the

Mr. A. Milner.

5 Nov. 1894.

Adjustments of revenue.

duce and customs, the revenue of the country, divides itself into realty and personalty, and taxes on consumption; these are the heads, are they not?—Our main heads are Excise, Stamps and Taxes.

966. I am speaking now of the description of the property which governs the adjustment of it; realty is one; original realised personalty is another; taxes on consumption another?—Yes.

967. We may settle out of view the land tax, house duty, railway duty, and also, I think, the licences, which are credited where they are collected, being local in their nature, and there remain for purpose of adjustment the excise, the stamps and the income tax, is not that so?—Yes.

968. What would you call the heads of realty under excise, stamps and income tax?—Do you mean which of these taxes fall on realty?

969. Which of these are realty?—Schedule A. is a tax on realty.

970. And Schedule B. may be classified in the same way as relating to realty, may it not?—I should not call Schedule B. a tax on realty. It is like Schedule D., a tax on profits.

971. For the purpose of our present discussion in relation to adjustment, it is practically a tax on realty, because the tax is tied to the place, is it not?—Yes.

972. Is there anything else? What are the death duties?—The succession duty is on realty.

973. And the rest is personalty?—A small part of the estate duty is on realty, but for practical purposes you may ignore it.

974. And in the case of general stamps I think you by your own calculation came to the conclusion that one-fourth of the general stamps are related to realty?—Yes, about one-fourth.

975. The rule of adjustment which you have applied to realty is this: that a tax levied upon real property is to be credited to the country in which the property exists, is not that so?—Yes, regarded as a contribution of the country in which the property exists.

976. Or "a contribution from the people of that country," as the return says?—Yes.

Income tax: assessment and yield. Taxable capacity.

977. From this point of view Schedule A becomes of vast importance, and whatever may be thought about the treatment of the individual landowner in England and Ireland under Schedule A., there are very important questions connected with it, because, as you know, in the Act of Legislative Union and in Mr. Gladstone's speech on the Home Rule Bill in 1886, and in the whole interval between and since, the produce of an income tax, or the assessment to an income tax, has been often referred to as a proper measure or test of the relative taxable capacity of two countries subject to the same income tax. All income tax upon Irish land, no matter where the man may be who receives the rent or appropriates the rent, is credited in these accounts as tax contributed by Ireland; is that so?—Yes, certainly; it comes out of Irish property.

978. There are many Englishmen and English landlords who own land in Ireland, are there not, and live in England?—Yes.

979. And spend their incomes in England, the tax they pay being credited to Ireland?—Yes.

980. And the assessment upon which that tax is levied being part of the Irish assessment, if that tax or assessment were taken as a measure of the relative capacity of Irishmen to pay taxes, it would include income spent not in Ireland but in England, would it not? That is to say, it would treat as part of the taxable capacity of Ireland income which really in the fact is part of the taxable capacity of England?—That is a very difficult question to answer, I feel, and perhaps it is not important that I should answer it.

981. I put it to you that if the relative yield of income tax in Ireland and England is used as a measure of taxable capacity——?—Of the taxable capacity of Ireland?

982. And of England relatively?—Then it is a right measure.

983. You think it a right measure, do you?—I should think so. It is the annual value of Irish land; to whom that land belongs is quite another inquiry.

Mr. A. Milner.

5 Nov. 1894.

Income tax assessment of each class. Taxable capacity.

984. But do you think it a safe measure of the taxable capacity of the two communities at large, or are you speaking of it only as a measure of the taxable capacity of the income tax paying class of either country?—I am not thinking of a class; I am thinking of the country as a whole.

985. It appears from this account that of the 80,000,000 raised from taxes in England, over 11,000,000 come from income tax?—Yes.

986. That is nearly one-fifth of the whole taxation, is it not?—Yes.

987. And of the six millions and a half raised in Ireland half a million comes from income tax—that is about one-twelfth?—Yes; that does not at all surprise me.

988. Does it not follow that the diffusion of wealth is very different in England to what it is in Ireland?—Certainly.

989. That the income tax paying class is relatively a much smaller class in Ireland than in England?—Certainly it is.

990. And, therefore, that the yield of income tax in Ireland, where the class is relatively only half as great as the corresponding class in England, cannot be taken as a safe relative test of the ability of the community at large, that is of the multitude outside the income tax paying class?—Of course, income tax assessments cannot possibly be a test of the capacity of the multitude who are outside such assessments to pay anything.

991. But if you found that the proportion of income tax levied in England bore the same relation to the total tax revenue in Ireland, and in England, then you could say that the income tax paying class were equally strong factors in both communities, that there was a tolerably even diffusion of wealth, and there might be a presumption that the two communities might be in an analogous condition; but when the income tax paying class is double as large in one country as the other, is not there a contrary presumption?—I think it is perfectly evident that the two communities are not in analogous positions as regards wealth or the distribution of wealth.

992. Still pursuing this question of the value of income tax yield or assessment as a measure of capacity, I pass from the Englishmen who are Irish landlords to the Irishmen who are landlords in Ireland but who live out of it. You know that since the time of Sir William Petty, and before it, there have been many estimates made of the proportion which they bear to the total of landlord class in Ireland, and since the time of Edward III. legislation in this country has been directed to stop it. At the present time there are estimates which hold that about one-third of the rental of Ireland is taken out of that country and spent in this by men who prefer to live here. Now the tax they pay is credited to the Irish tax, is it not?—Yes.

993. And forms part of the Irish measure of capacity whenever anyone chooses to take the yield of income tax as a measure?—Yes.

994. The income upon which that tax is paid is included in the Irish assessment, is it not?—Yes.

995. Does it not follow, when such a test is applied, that the result is altogether illusory, and that some millions of income is added to the Irish assessment which is really English income and spent in England?—The income may be spent in England, but it is derived from Ireland. It is Ireland that produces that wealth, and if you are going to measure the taxable capacity of Ireland and England, you must credit Ireland with the whole produce of her soil as much as you do England with the whole produce of hers.

996. I think that is rather technical?—No, I think this is substantial. Surely in arriving at what is the taxable capacity of Ireland, must you not look at that which Ireland produces; is not that what you

Mr. A. Milner. 8 Nov. 1895. Taxable capacity.

ultimately come back to?—All that the State can tax is a share of the produce of industry and agriculture.

997. I should submit, with all deference, that it depends not so much on what is produced in any country as upon what becomes of what is produced in any country; in other words, upon how much of what is produced in any country remains in it for the benefit of the people and the population, and how much of it is spent there?—This is really not a question for me. I differ from you, but I think it is a question for the Commission, and not for me. May I put it in this way: Supposing you were to lay down the proper distribution of taxation as between England and Ireland with regard to the part of the world where the Irish income at the particular moment happened to be spent, you might make an arrangement which a year or two years would render absolutely inapplicable. We will say Ireland produces 10,000,000*l.* (taking any figure) yearly income from land; that comes out of the land of Ireland; it is part of the produce of the soil. To-day, we will say, one-third of that is spent in England; if you were in any permanent arrangement as between the two countries to add that one-third which is to-day spent in England to England's share of wealth and taxable capacity, the whole thing might be rendered null and void in a year by that one-third being retransferred to Ireland. The only permanent measure, surely, of the taxable capacity of the two countries is the average production of the two.

998. I should think that the only two reasons why the produce of an income tax can be regarded as a measure of capacity at all are these: either that in the two countries the income tax paying class are in about the same relation to the taxpayers as a whole, which might argue relative capacity, or else that the income upon which the tax is paid is part of that general fund of the community from which the taxes are derived. If that general fund, or any part of it, is transferred from one country into another, it ceases to be a fund for that purpose?—Quite so.

999. (*Lord Farrer.*) You, of course, are very well acquainted with the case of Egypt; Egypt has a considerable debt, has it not?—Yes.

1000. The owners of that debt are people who reside out of Egypt, are they not?—Yes.

1001. If you were considering the taxable capacity of Egypt as a whole country, should you deduct what is paid as interest to the holders of that debt?—Certainly not.

1002. (*Mr. Sexton.*) But if you were considering the relative taxable capacity of Egypt and of England, I suppose the money is paid into England, is it not?—It is mostly paid into France.

1003. Then if you were considering the taxable capacity of Egypt and France, if certain millions of money were paid out of Egypt into France, anybody appearing in the interests of Egypt would be apt to complain, would he not, if those millions transferred to France every year were treated as moneys of Egypt, available to yield taxation and not as money of France?—Probably.

1004. (*Lord Farrer.*) You would probably hold, would you not, that in considering what was the taxable capacity of a country to which Egypt owed a debt, you would have to consider the property they had invested in Egypt?—Certainly.

1005. And, therefore, it would come into their taxable capacity, would it not, as well as into the taxable capacity of Egypt?—It all depends on whether you are looking at the taxable capacity of a country at a given moment or at what you might call its permanent taxable capacity. If you ask what taxation Egypt is able to bear to-day, of course you would have to take into account the fact that so many millions are paid over to the French. But if you were going to consider, from a broader point of view, and for a longer period, the taxable capacity of Egypt, the accidental temporary diversion of part of Egypt's revenues into the pockets of Frenchmen would not affect the case. Egypt is capable of producing so much a year from land; that is what you must look to in determining the comparative wealth of Egypt and other countries. Of course, if Egypt were for ever and a day going to hand over half its land revenue to pay the debt, that would alter the case. I agree with Mr. Sexton that if it could be proved that half the revenue derived from Irish land had always been, was now, and would in the future always be consumed in England, that would alter the case; but the mere fact that some of it may be to-day and may not be to-morrow does not.

1006. (*Sir David Barbour.*) Would that alter the case? Supposing half the rent of Ireland were paid to English landlords and spent in England, that would not prevent an Irish Parliament from taxing that to any extent they liked, would it?—No, it would not.

1007. So that they could draw upon it, could they not?—They could.

1008. (*Mr. Sexton.*) Supposing that the war indemnity from France to Germany were a permanent indemnity to be paid every year for ever, would you as an economist consider the annual produce of that war indemnity as part of the taxable capacity of France or part of the taxable capacity of Germany, it being paid over from one country to the other?—It would be part of the taxable capacity of France.

1009. Although payable for ever?—No, I mean the other way; it would be part of the taxable capacity of Germany.

1010. I would point out to you also that there are a number of persons in Ireland who have purchased their farms by loans from the Treasury and they now pay to the Imperial Treasury every year about half a million sterling; that would represent a part of the rent of the country, would it not?—Yes.

1011. And the income nevertheless is not an income devoted to Irish uses, but becomes Imperial?—Yes.

1012. Then there is another matter of immense importance which I think the Commission would do well very seriously to consider. It is thought that a proportion of the value of Irish land, not less than one-third, and some people think approaching one-half, is represented by money lent by insurance companies and other corporations and private lenders in England. Now the interest on these loans is part of the income tax assessment, is it not?—Yes.

1013. But the tax is credited to Ireland, is it not?—Yes.

1014. And the income upon which the tax is paid is sent over here and, according to my view, it forms part of the taxable capacity of England; so that, under these several heads, Englishmen who are landlords in Ireland, Irish landlords who prefer to live out of Ireland, tenant purchasers who pay the value of the land annually to the Imperial Treasury, and British mortgagees who have lent one-half or one-third the value of Irish land, I think it follows that neither the yield nor the assessment of income tax can be seriously regarded in the circumstances as they stand as any measure of relative capacity, though these circumstances are all proper to be considered no doubt in that connexion?—I do not think the income tax would be a measure of the capacity of the people living in Ireland at this moment.

1015. (*Sir David Barbour.*) Do you think the income tax is ever a proper measure of the capacity of a whole people to pay taxes when there is a very high limit of exemption?—Not the smallest.

1016. May I ask what the limit of exemption is now?—160*l.* a year.

1017. In some poor countries I imagine that if the income tax were taken as the test and the minimum taxable income were fixed at a high figure, there would appear to be almost no taxable capacity?—It might be so. In many parts of Egypt certainly there would be no taxable capacity.

1018. (*Mr. Sexton.*) It is quite conceivable, I think, that in a country, say, wholly independent on agricultural industry, a class of persons may be able from one circumstance and another to take to themselves so much of the profit of the soil or the industry that there would be little or no taxable capacity left,

Mr. A. Milner. 4 Nov. 1895. Taxable capacity.

and that the position of the income-tax-paying class might, in fact, instead of being a test of capacity be in itself a very proof of incapacity?—Just so.

1019. All this springs out of the rule of adjustment that taxable capacity is to be credited to the country in which the property is situated; and the reason why I have pressed you so much about it is that Mr. Pitt and Lord Castlereagh at the time of the union, and many persons since, have referred sometimes to the yield of the tax and sometimes to the assessment of the tax in the two countries as the best measure of relative capacity. I think Mr. Pitt at the time of the union lamented that there was not an income tax in Ireland?—It is a very good test of the relative capacity of the countries, but not necessarily of the inhabitants of them.

1020. I hardly follow that distinction. A good test of the powers of the land of the two countries?—Yes.

1021. But of the distribution of income, not?—No.

1022. (*Lord Farrer.*) I suppose if you were to make deductions from the taxable capacity of the country on the ground that the persons who receive the income live out of the country, then you must also, when you are treating the other side of the account, and seeing what Ireland does pay, treat that as something which she does not pay?—Certainly, as something she does not pay.

1023. (*Mr. Sexton.*) In fact, according to the best study I can give to the subject, if you were to make the income tax any measure of relative capacity you would have to take out of the Irish tax and out of the Irish assessment all that is taken away by English landlords who have land in Ireland; by Irish landlords who live out of it the value of tenant purchasers' holdings, and also that part of the value of the land represented by British mortgages. You would have to deduct all those things from the Irish assessment, and add them to the English assessment, in order to give the relative taxable capacity at the time, although I agree with you that the circumstances might change?—Yes.

Adjustment of income.

1024. (*Mr. Sexton.*) Now I pass from realty to realised personalty. What are the heads in your account which you describe as realised personalty?—Schedule C of the income tax is on realised personalty; Schedule D is largely on realised personalty. A certain amount of the general stamps are on realised personalty; probate is on realised personalty; and legacy duty is on realised personalty.

1025. Now as to the rule of adjustment for realised personalty. Realised personalty is, I think, a more important part of the income of England than realty, is it not?—Yes, much more important.

1026. The assessment of land under Schedules A. and B. is 160,000,000*l.* The assessments under C. and D. are 312,000,000*l.*?—Are you taking that from our report?

1027. Yes?—Then that is no doubt correct.

1028. The rule of adjustment for realised personalty appears to be the converse of that for realty, does it not?—Yes.

1029. Realty follows the country, whereas realised personalty follows the person?—Yes, that is the basis of these returns. For the purposes of this return realised personalty is treated as belonging to the country in which the owner of that personalty habitually resides.

1030. I think you said in answer to a question put by the chairman at the last meeting that you assumed the fact of domicile from the fact of death?—Yes.

1031. That you assume the country in which a man dies is the country in which he has been domiciled?—No, we assume that the country in which the executor takes out probate is the country in which the dead man was domiciled. If an Englishman went over to Dublin and happened to die there, his executor would take out probate in London and not in Dublin. All we assume is that the country in which the executor takes out probate is the country in which the dead man habitually resided.

Mr. A. Milner. 4 Nov. 1895. Adjustment of income.

1032. In other words, you assume that the country in which he dies is the country in which he had lived, do you not?—Not that the country in which he dies is the country in which he had lived, but that the country in which his probate is taken out is the country in which he lived.

1033. I think you also hold that the fact of death in a country is evidence that a man was one of that community?—No, that is not an assumption of our return.

1034. All that is necessary for your purpose is that the duty is paid in the country of the death, is it?—That the probate is taken out in the country in which the dead man was domiciled, and that, I believe is the general rule.

1035. And the domicile is inferred from the fact of death?—No, from the fact of probate being taken out in that country.

1036. As the probate duty is paid it collects the duty on the whole realised personalty en bloc, it is in the country in which the probate is taken out, then is it not?—Yes.

1037. Without regard to the re-sealing?—The re-sealing does not affect the duty.

1038. But it identifies the property?—Yes, it identifies the property.

1039. It happens, therefore, that the mode in which the probate duty is collected accords with the principle which in your opinion ought to prevail; that is to say, that it brings all the duty into the country in which the probate was taken out?—Yes, it brings all the duty into the country in which the man was domiciled; it causes the duty to be attributed to the country in which the man was domiciled.

1040. So that if we were concerned with probate duty alone you would not think it necessary to make any adjustment because the duty as paid effectuates the principle?—Yes.

1041. But then there is other realised personalty; there is realised personalty in other circumstances not connected with death, that is to say Schedules C. and D. of the income and part of the general stamps, and the duty upon these is so collected in the case of income tax where a profit arises, and in the case of general stamps where a transaction occurs, that the tax does not attribute itself in the same way as probate to the country where the tax-payer is domiciled?—No, it does not attribute itself.

1042. Is that the true explanation?—Yes.

1043. And have you got to make that uniform in the case of general stamps and income tax? The principle settles itself, of course?—Yes, that is so.

1044. Then in order to determine how to adjust the proceeds of general stamps under Schedules C. and D., not being able to disentangle under the head of general stamps or of income tax, you were obliged to resort to the information at your hands in connexion with probate, were you?—Yes, that was it.

1045. You took, I understand, a certain year, and you took the wills proved in that year so far as they related to personalty?—Yes.

1046. And you found that the personal property held in England by persons domiciled in Scotland or Ireland exceeded the personal property held in Scotland and Ireland by persons domiciled in England in a certain proportion?—Yes.

1047. And that became the proportion of adjustment?—Yes, that has been the basis of adjustment ever since.

1048. The financial results are trivial, are they not?—Very.

1049. But the questions of calculation and even of principle involved may be considered of great importance. You said that one year gives a good average for probate, did you not?—It would have been better to have had several, but it was a very laborious business examining the statistics.

1050. I notice in the Report attached to Paper 329 of 1891, before you went to the Inland Revenue, that

Mr. A. Milner.

8 Nov. 1894.

Adjustment of revenue.

it was shown that the yield of probate varies very much from year to year?—Yes, the total yield, no doubt, varies very much, but I should think the total yield would vary very much more than the distribution between the countries.

1051. I see here that the yield in Ireland for the actual year taken as the basis of adjustment was very nearly ½ per cent. less than the average yield for the five years up to that time, whilst on the other hand the yield for Scotland in that year was ⅔ per cent. more than the average for the five years; so that you see the basis of one year is very uniform, is it not?—Yes.

1052. It would never do as a permanent test, would it? You found in regard to realised personality—that is, the whole of Schedule C. of the income tax, and all Schedule D. except four-fifths of the trades and professions—that the amount to be added to the Irish contribution was ·2, that is one five hundredth part of the whole?—Yes, that is it, ·2.

1053. Schedule C. and Schedule D. included the whole of the stocks of the country, consols, and all the other public stocks, did they?—Yes.

1054. And also, I think, the Indian stocks, Colonial stocks, stocks of corporations, and everything?—Yes, everything of that sort.

1055. It includes almost all industrial enterprises, does it not?—Yes.

1056. And all public companies and railways?—Yes.

Income tax assessment and adjustment.

1057. The assessment to Ireland itself under Schedule C. without the adjustment was only a trifle of 700,000*l.* as against 39,000,000*l.* in England, was it not?—Yes.

1058. That is about one fifty-fifth, is it not?—What page are you looking at?

1059. It is page 32 of your last report. The assessment in Ireland without this adjustment under Schedule C. is short of 750,000*l.* as against 39,000,000*l.* in England?—Yes.

1060. That is, I think, about one fifty-fifth, or so, is it not?—Yes, it is about one fifty-fifth.

1061. That fact suggests some reflection as to relative taxable capacity when you pass away from land and inquire into other sources of income and means of taxation. Can you tell me how it is that this Schedule C. includes corporation stocks; do you see it?—Yes.

1062. Where are they assessed, in what part of the kingdom?—A good many of them are assessed in London.

1063. I suppose the whole of the National stocks, the colonial stocks, and the foreign stocks are assessed in London?—Yes, at the Bank of England; not the whole of the foreign stocks, but the whole of the English stocks, and a number of colonial stocks.

1064. Where are Guinness, Son, & Co. assessed?—In Dublin.

1065. Are there many Irish companies assessed in London?—Companies carrying on business in Ireland?

1066. Yes, for instance, you often see meetings of railway shareholders held in London?—No, I do not think such Irish companies are assessed in London. You will find them in Irish "Schedule D., Public Companies."

1067. Would it be possible to furnish the Commission with a list of the places in which companies are registered and assessed?—Certainly. Of course you would limit it to companies of considerable dimensions?

1068. Yes.—It would be perfectly easy.

1069. If we had it for Irish corporations, too, I should be glad. The Dublin Corporation has 1,250,000*l.* of stock; Belfast has, I think, nearly 1,000,000*l.*; Cork and Waterford have stocks also have they not?—Yes.

1070. How is it that Ireland is only assessed to a total of 700,000*l.* under Schedule C., seeing that Schedule C. ought to include all these corporation stocks, which in Ireland alone would be more than a [illegible] in spite of this?—That 5*l.* per cent. represents the interest, not the capital. But I am not quite sure under what head Irish municipal stocks are assessed. I will find that out.

Mr. A. Milner.

8 Nov. 1894.

Income tax assessment.

1071. Will you kindly inquire?—Yes. I do not quite know why they do not appear here.

Adjourned for a short time.

1072. (*Mr. Sexton.*) In connexion with corporation stocks in Ireland, I was drawing your attention to the fact that on page 32 of your last Report the total assessment of Ireland under Schedule C., which deals with all public investments, was only 700,000*l.*, as against 39,000,000*l.* in England?—Yes.

1073. I notice now, that under the sub-head of "Municipal Corporation Stocks" there is no assessment in Ireland?—No, I see there is not in this Return.

1074. But there are unquestionably, are there not, in Dublin, Belfast, Cork, and Waterford stocks amounting to 2,000,000*l.*?—Yes.

1075. Dublin 1,250,000*l.*; Belfast, Waterford, and other places, better than a million?—May we take it as 60,000*l.* a year which would be the sum to be assessed?

1076. The income would be 60,000*l.* a year, you mean?—Yes.

1077. There is no assessment, is there, of these corporation stocks?—No. I will find out what head it has got under. They are not inscribed at the Bank of England, I suppose? If they were of course they would go into the London assessment, but I will clear up that point. I cannot tell you without reference to our books.

1078. What presses upon me is that the adjustment which you have founded upon the circumstance that Irishmen who died in a certain year were proved to have been possessed of personality in England to a certain extent (taking it as a rule as to all personality held by Irishmen out of Ireland) comes only to ·2, which amounts to only one five-hundredth part of 38,000,000*l.*?—Yes.

1079. One five-hundredth of 38,000,000*l.* would be another 700,000*l.*, would it not?—No, it would be about 70,000*l.*

1080. Therefore by your adjustment it would only add to Ireland's [illegible] 70,000*l.* some 70,000*l.* more, would it not? But if it turns out on inquiry that there are Irish Corporation Stocks of the value of 2,000,000*l.* a year, at 3½ per cent., that would give to them 70,000*l.*, what becomes of all the other personality undoubtedly held by Irishmen in Great Britain?—We adjust on about 38,000,000*l.* of property under Schedule C. I do not see that the fact that there are 70,000*l.* of income on Irish municipal stocks in the 38,000,000*l.*, even if such should prove to be the case, at all invalidates the correctness of the adjustment. It may or may not, but it does not follow.

1081. There may be 70,000*l.* worth of Irish stock in this, but if you adjust only by giving one five-hundredth part of the total to Ireland that would give Ireland only 70,000*l.* of adjustment upon the whole body of Schedule C., is not that so?—Yes.

1082. (*Sir David Barbour.*) It is a net adjustment, is it not, after deducting what is supposed to be on the other side of the account?—Yes, it is a net adjustment.

1083. (*Mr. Sexton.*) That is to say, you deduct the 15,000*l.* of Irish property from 25,000*l.* of English property, leaving 10,000*l.*; but still, however you arrive at it the effect is the same, that you only add to the assessment made in Ireland one five-hundredth part of the personality that is in England?—On balance, yes. That is to say, we do not assume that only 500,000*l.* worth of English personality is held by Irishmen, but that on balance, after you have set off Irish personality held by Englishmen, the proper figure is ·2 per cent.

1084. It appearing that the Irish property held by Englishmen in that particular year paid 15,000*l.* for

Mr. A. Milner.

8 Nov. 1894.

Income Tax: assessment and adjustment.

duty, and the English property held by Irishmen came to about 24,000*l.* of duty, it would seem that the property held by Irishmen in England was between two and three times the amount of the sum which formed the basis of the adjustment. The total property held by Irishmen in England was 24,000*l.*, and the balance on which you adjusted was 9,000*l.*, so that it would appear that the total property was two or three times the amount adjusted upon?—Yes.

1084. I confess in face of the fact that there is unquestionably 70,000*l.* a year of Irish property under one head alone under Schedule C. unaccounted for in the Irish adjustment, I still regard with something more than doubt—in fact, I reject the idea—that any adjustment which gives Ireland only 70,000*l.* out of the whole of Schedule C. can even approximate to what is just. It is perfectly obvious, I think, that there must be something more required. Will you look into that?—Yes.

1085. I submit to you that when we pass from the schedules relating to land, which is the sole industry of Ireland, and come to those schedules which represent the accumulated wealth invested or employed in enterprises, the barrenness of Ireland and her slender resources become more apparent. You see that in Schedule C. the assessment is only one fifty-fifth part of the English assessment, and even if you take the '2 and add the five-hundredth part, which is 70,000*l.* more, the total assessment would be 800,000*l.*, which would still not be very different, one-fiftieth or so of the English assessment?—But do not I understand you to contend that the adjustment ought to be greater?

1086. That is not yet admitted. If it were admitted that the adjustment ought to be greater we will go upon that basis, but now I am going upon your figures?—I think the adjustment is pretty right myself, but I thought you were taking two conflicting points at the same moment.

1087. My view is that the Irish assessment ought to be greater; your view is, however, that it ought not to be greater, and I am taking you upon your own view, which is that the assessment is about one-fiftieth under Schedule C.?—Schedule C. being a small part of the total tax.

1088. No doubt it is a comparatively small part. Now we come to Schedule D., and there the assessment for trade purposes is 127,000,000*l.* for England and 1,000,000*l.* for Ireland, and the total assessment under Schedule D. is 277,000,000*l.* for England and 9,000,000*l.* for Ireland?—It is 312,000,000*l.* for England and 11,000,000*l.* for Ireland.

1089. I am looking at the net?—It is doubtful whether you ought not to look at the gross, but looking at the net it is 274,208,000*l.* and 9,475,000*l.*, as you say.

1090. And you would adjust that according to the best of your knowledge by taking one five-hundredth part, not of 277,000,000*l.*, but of 177,000,000*l.*, because you leave out four-fifths of the trades and professions which has nothing to do with realised personalty, and that would add about a third of a million to the 9,000,000*l.*, making about 9,300,000*l.* as against 277,000,000*l.*; it does not greatly alter the proportion, does it?—It makes more than 9,000,000*l.*, does it not?

1091. One five-hundredth part of 177,000,000*l.* is about a third of a million?—Yes, it comes to nine and three quarter millions.

1092. Still it would not be any more than one-fortieth on the whole of the income of England on that schedule, would it?—Yes, more than a fortieth, it would be more than a thirtieth.

1093. About a thirtieth?—Yes.

1094. And that schedule, of course, is infinitely more important than Schedule C., because the total assessable net income of England being 512,000,000*l.* there is 277,000,000*l.* comprised in Schedule D.?—That is the most important schedule.

Adjustment of Income.

1095. And the proportion of Ireland is not more than one-thirtieth of the whole?—I do not know. One twenty-seventh, or one twenty-eighth, I think it is; it is worked out in some of our tables.

Mr. A. Milner.

8 Nov. 1894.

Adjustment of Income.

1096. It approximates to one-thirtieth; it might be one twenty-eighth perhaps, but you will not make it one twenty-eighth out of the figures here?—May I look at the Financial Relations Return, No. 334? Whether we take the assessment or the yield is, I suppose, a matter of indifference. Income Tax Schedule D., contributed by England, 4,587,000; contributed by Ireland, 145,000*l.* It is a good deal more than a thirtieth.

1097. Contributed by Ireland, 145,000*l.*, contributed by the United Kingdom, 4,728,000*l.*, is it not?—I thought you said how much was the contribution of England.

1098. Perhaps it would be better to take Great Britain, England and Scotland together?—Then it is about a thirtieth; in fact, it is a little less than a thirtieth.

1099. I think not. If you take the contribution of Ireland off the total, you come to 4,583,000*l.*, which would be between a thirty-first and a thirty-second, would it not?—Yes, that is so.

1100. Can you suggest, as a permanent arrangement, anything better than this, which I think you have spoken of with questionable admiration as an ingenious arrangement, though not one which you would like to commit yourself to?—I cannot think of anything better; I certainly think it would be desirable to examine another year or two on the same principle, but though I do not think the system a very perfect one, I think the results are not far out, judging from the general idea one has of the comparative industrial wealth of the countries.

1101. Do you mean that the distribution of personalty, as disclosed by the wills proved in a single year, between the three countries is as good an average or estimate as you could make of the whole of the personalty existing?—I do not like to say for a single year; I think the single year is the weak part of it, and we really ought to have two or three years more, but of course it is a very difficult return to make out, and the adjustment in any case will be slight. You see that the result of it all is only a matter of 10,000*l.* or 20,000*l.*

1102. The importance that I attach to it is rather pointed to the relative taxable capacity as disclosed by the adjustment than to the yield of the income tax?—Yes, I think it might be desirable to extend the consideration of the statistics of re-sealing.

1103. And so far as concerns the immediate object of the adjustment it does enable you, in your opinion, does it, to square the adjustment for income tax, and for a certain part of general revenue, in that which probate already does by being paid wholly in the country of domicile?—Yes.

1104. I have dealt with the realty and realised personalty; I suppose realised personalty may be called interest on capital, may it not?—Yes.

1105. Then the other personalty in Schedule E. and the remainder of Schedule D. we need not deal with, because it is from year to year in the place where the person lives, is it not?—Yes.

1106. Then there only remains the question of the taxes on consumption. Now the adjustment of taxes on consumption has a far more material effect, of course, upon the revenue of Ireland than any other?—Yes, much more important.

Beer: adjustment of Revenue.

1107. I will take first the least important of the two, the adjustment on beer. On page 8 of the Return No. 334, for 1892–93, it appears that there was collected in Ireland as duty on beer 778,000*l.*?—Yes.

1108. But that the true contribution, as you have adjusted it, is 590,000*l.*?—Yes.

1109. In other words, the revenue as collected has been reduced by 188,000*l.*, or about one-fifth of the whole?—Yes.

1110. The process that you have applied to this has been, I believe, that you have taken the beer upon which excise was paid in Ireland; you have added to

F 4

Mr. J. Wilson.

8 Nov. 1894.

Beer: adjustment of figures.

that amount beer sent from Great Britain on which excise has been paid in Great Britain, and you have deducted from it any excise beer sent out of Ireland to Great Britain?—Yes.

1112. As I understand the adjustment is founded upon inquiries made of certain brewers as to their operations in the year ending September 1890?—Yes, in the year ending September 1890.

1113. And I gather from some observations made in the report of your predecessors to the Treasury that those inquiries were made at Dublin, at Aberdeen, and at Edinburgh?—Yes.

1114. The beer trade is centred in those three towns, is it?—Yes; there are some other very important brewers besides, but not brewers that export very much. I may say, however, in connexion with this matter that since the last meeting of the Commission we have once more obtained a whole year's figures, not from selected brewers, but from all the brewers.

1115. For what year?—For last year.

1116. Up to March 1894?—Yes, and the percentage, if you disregard what comes after the decimal point, is exactly the same as the per-centage of the figures which we collected from a limited number of brewers for the year 1890, showing I think, that a very near approach to accuracy was made on that occasion.

1117. Have the brewers again requested you to regard their communications as secret?—Yes, that is part of the bargain.

1118. You see that involves a question of nearly 200,000*l.* of Irish revenue per annum?—Yes.

1119. And under those circumstances I think it would be important to consider whether the permit system could be applied without inconvenience, would it not?—I do not think it can. I think not only that it cannot be applied without inconvenience, but I am afraid I do not yet see how the permit system is to give us the facts which we require; because, you see, there is this difference between beer and spirits: when spirits are exported from one country to the other, if you know the strength of the spirit which is being exported, you know also the duty it has paid. All you have to look at is the proof strength. But when beer is being exported there is no indication about the beer to tell you what was the original gravity of the wort out of which that beer was made; consequently the consignment does not tell you anything about duty. A consignment of spirits bears its duty on the face of it; you know the amount, you know the proof strength, and you can say, "That spirit paid so much duty"; but in the case of a consignment of beer you cannot tell at all how much duty the wort, out of which that beer was made, has paid. You might get the original gravity of the beer by analysis, as Mr. Steele points out to me, but that reduces the thing to an absurdity. The idea of analysing a sample of every barrel of beer before it goes away!

1120. How could the brewers tell you so precisely?—Because they know from their books the amount of wort at a particular gravity which had gone to make up their beer.

1121. Then they tell you not only how many barrels they send from one country to another, but also what was the specific gravity of the wort, do they?—Yes, barrels reduced to standard gravity of 55.

1122. You have to take it entirely on trust, have you not?—Entirely.

1123. (*Sir David Barbour.*) Have you any reason to suppose that the returns are at all inaccurate?—No reason whatever; they are perfectly disinterested in the matter and they have a great interest in helping us from the constant relations which we have with them; they are always willing to oblige us in any way that does not hurt themselves.

1124. (*Mr. Sexton.*) So that really it was not by the number of barrels they exported that you were at all enabled to decide what ought to be taken off the revenue of Ireland; but it was altogether by an arbitrary communication made to you as to the amount of the specific gravity of the wort concerned in the exportation?—Barrels of a certain strength, you might say.

Mr. J. Wilson.

8 Nov. 1894.

Beer.

1125. You have tried close and continued inspection on the introduction of spirits, have you not?—Yes.

1126. Would it be possible by inspection to determine the specific gravity of the exports?—By analysis it would. Are you speaking of spirits or beer?

1127. Of beer?—You could only determine by analysis in the case of beer. In the case of spirits you can determine the proof strength at any moment.

1128. But in the case of an establishment like Guinness's, which has the export of Ireland mainly in its hands, does the specific gravity of the wort vary?—Yes, I think it does.

1129. Is not the product a uniform product?—No, I think they work at a number of gravities, and sell in different ways.

1130. So that a permit system, even if established whilst it might give you the quantity exported, would leave one to determine the factor necessary to calculation, I understand?—That is it; that is precisely the difficulty which we feel.

1131. And that could only be afforded by analysis either of the particular beer exported or of other beer in the brewery which could be judged to be of the same specific gravity?—Yes.

1132. Now I pass to the question of spirits which is of course the main question; and it appears on page 7 that whilst the collection on the excise of spirits in that year was 3,918,000*l.*, the contribution is held to be only 2,101,000*l.*, giving round figures; in other words you deduct 1,800,000*l.*, or pretty nearly half the revenue, or approximating to half the revenue, in respect of Irish spirits exported to Great Britain over British spirits exported to Ireland in that year?—Yes. Spirits.

1133. Since the year 1860 when the spirit duties for the three countries were first assimilated, your Department has produced an annual Return which purports to give, or has been relied upon as giving, the actual consumption of spirit in each of the three countries, has it not?—Yes.

1134. What is the Return; it is a return of duty on home made spirits exported from one country to the other, is it not?—Yes.

1135. That return was always looked upon as enabling anyone interested to adjust the collection upon spirits in any of the three countries, and to give the true contribution, was it not?—I do not know in what light it was regarded; I never heard of it myself until two years ago.

1136. Your attention, and the attention of all of us, was very specially drawn to it two years ago, was it not?—Very specially.

1137. By the discovery which you made that the export of spirits from Ireland to Great Britain for 1891 and 1892 had been very materially understated?—Yes.

1138. In the Report signed by yourself and Mr. Robinson, addressed to the Treasury, you give this account of the way in which the discovery was made: "Up to last Easter no doubt had been entertained as "to the accuracy of this return, but as the only return "the title of which is 'A return of the quantity of "'duty paid on home made spirits removed from one "'part of the United Kingdom to another, part for "'home consumption,'" (an absolutely comprehensive title) "but when the return for the financial year "1892–3, was being made up"—at Somerset House, I suppose?—Yes.

1139. "We were struck by the greatness of the "apparent increase in the export of duty-paid spirits "from Ireland to Great Britain in 1892–3, as compared with 1891–2." I understand that to mean that Mr. Robinson and yourself, or both of you, in supervising the return for 1892–3, were struck by the apparent great increase in the export from Ireland for that year?—It was our Accountant-General, Mr. Turner.

1140. The Accountant-General really was the discoverer, was he?—Several of us noticed it; I do not know really who first discovered it, but there were

Mr. A. [illegible].

8 Nov. 1894.

Spirits.

several of us who made the same observation about the same time.

1141. It was a discovery made in the office without any suggestion, was it?—Yes, without suggestion from outside—I noticed no mention of it appearing in the Press or anywhere until at least three weeks after we had begun to take steps to put the thing right.

1142. It stood in this way: you had before you the statement that in 1891-2 the export was 3,080,000 gallons, and you saw that for 1892-3 there was an export of 3,354,000 gallons, and you said to yourselves, "Why is there a larger export this year by 270,000 "gallons than last year from Ireland of spirits?" Will you look at page 5 of your evidence?—Yes, that was it. That was exactly the question we asked, "Why is there this large change?" because at this time the importance of this return had been forced upon us in connection with the preparation of the financial relations papers.

1143. You said, "Why does Ireland send 270,000 "more gallons of spirits to England than she sent last "year," did you?—Yes.

1144. And upon that question you directed a full investigation, did you not, of all the facts to take place?—Yes; it all came out gradually. It was not quite immediately we found out the extent of the inaccuracy. First we asked certain questions, and the answers were not satisfactory, and then we asked further questions, and so things went on until we became convinced that the whole return was on an unsound basis.

1145. Out of every six gallons which had been exported in 1891 and 1892 one gallon was missed out, was it not?—Yes.

1146. Amounting to 630,000 gallons altogether?—Yes.

1147. And in the second year the actual export was a quarter of a million more than appeared?—Yes.

1148. What adds decidedly to the importance of this is your observation that this error, or some such error, may have affected the returns since the beginning, because that being your opinion we can no longer look at the return with any confidence, can we?—I am afraid not with any confidence.

Spirits: permit system.

1149. Now it becomes necessary for this reason to investigate very closely the circumstances under which this error arose in order to determine whether or not it was such an error as was likely to have pervaded a series of years. Are the permit forms used in warehouses, and the certificate forms used by dealers, issued in the first instance from Somerset House?—Yes.

1150. All of them?—All of them.

1151. Are the permit forms bound together in books or detached?—At distillery warehouses they are in books.

1152. Numbered consecutively?—Yes, numbered consecutively, I think.

1153. Are there counterfoils?—Yes, at distillery warehouses. At other warehouses the permits have no counterfoils, but the particulars on the permits are copied from the warehouse books. Thus there is a complete record in our books; that is the point. As regards the clearance from general duty-free warehouses, there are records in our books of the places, the amount, and the destination, which correspond with the particulars on the permit.

1154. What officer issues the permit upon the request of the dealer?—The dealer makes out his own permit, or rather he makes out a request note, which, when countersigned by our officer, becomes the permit.

1155. At the request of anyone?—It is checked by the officer in charge of the warehouse.

1156. Each such officer has a warrant book in which he enters the particulars of the permit at the time of issuing the permit, I suppose?—The particulars on the permit are copied from the warrant book.

1157. He then periodically summarises the contents of the warrant book, does he?—Yes.

1158. And forwards the return to Somerset House, I suppose?—Yes. It reaches us through the collector.

1159. And in that way you make up quarterly and yearly the amount exported under permit?—Yes.

Mr. A. [illegible].

8 Nov. 1894.

Spirits: permit system.

1160. And I understand you to say that there has been no substantial error in the permit branch?—No, none, nor was there any likelihood that there would be, you see, because of necessity there is a very careful record. Our officer had at the moment when the spirit went out, a perfect knowledge of all about it, and in fact was bound for the accuracy of the stock to keep a complete record himself.

1161. How often was he bound to forward to Somerset House the summarised particulars of the warrant book?—I am not quite sure. The return is made up quarterly for the Board of Trade. We used to receive the returns at Somerset House from the collectors, who are our principal officers in each district, quarterly, but whether they made them up quarterly or monthly I do not know.

1162. Can you say whether the amount of spirits exported from Ireland under permit was a substantial part of the whole export?—Yes, a substantial part of it.

1163. What part of it?—I can give you some indication of it in a minute from some papers that I have here.

1164. It would be important if you would. Taking the total export at about 3,300,000 gallons, how much was passed from Ireland to Great Britain under the permit system as distinguished from the certificate issued by the dealer?—These papers will show you, more or less. I have here the figures of the Belfast Collection, which, as you know, is by far the most important.

1165. I think if, at your convenience, you could put in anything showing how much of these spirits came under permit every year it would be desirable?—You may take it from me it is a very considerable amount.

1166. Can you mention any figure now?—I should think about half.

1167. (*Chairman.*) You can put the figures into your answer, can you?—Yes.*

1168. (*Mr. Sexton.*) Therefore I may infer that as the permit branch covers one half of the export, and as there have been no errors in the permit branch, but there was a regular record made, the returns since 1825 would be correct so far as concerns the liquor exported under permit?—Under permit from Excise warehouses.

1169. One half of the whole; that would be correctly given, would it?—Yes.

1170. And the errors, therefore, would have arisen under the other half of the exports under the certificate of dealers?—Yes. I am not sure if I was not wrong in saying half went under permit. I think it is not so much; however, the figures shall be given.*

1171. Now, with regard to the certificate trade, you also issue the certificates from Somerset House in books bound, numbered with counterfoils, do you not?—Yes.

1172. And they are issued by these first-class officers, I suppose, on the request of the dealers?—No, the dealer makes out his own certificate, and fills up a counterfoil, and our officers afterwards take up the counterfoils; our only guide is the counterfoil.

1173. Who gives the book to the dealer in the first instance?—Mr. Steele tells me the officers give them to the dealer on a request from the dealer.

1174. I suppose you have a strict system of accounting at Somerset House for the number of books given out, have you not?—Certainly.

1175. The dealer gets the book on request then?—Yes.

1176. May I ask you whether all permit forms and all certificates eventually find their way back to Somerset House again?—No, they would not; they go away with the spirit; the counterfoils all find their way back.

* *Note by Witness.*—The figures were for 1891-2:—Removals under Excise permits from one part of the United Kingdom to another, 2,480,719 gallons. Removals of like nature under certificates from dealers' stocks, 1,625,783 gallons.

1177. What becomes of the permit form eventually?—The permit form goes with the spirit.

1178. But what becomes of it?—The permit form may disappear in this way: the spirit may be sent to a private individual; he has no interest in keeping the permit form or certificate, and throws it into the fire, or does anything he likes with it; it is only of importance to the man who is himself a spirit dealer, and has to account for his stock. He has to keep that permit or certificate in order to show where he got his spirit from.

1179. I understood when spirits are moved under a permit, even before delivery, some officer has to see the permit?—I do not think so; Mr. Steele will explain this better.

1180. Perhaps Mr. Steele will kindly explain it to us?—(Mr. Steele.) In the case of spirits sent to a licensed person he is bound by law to enter the quantity in his stock book; the officer comes periodically, and he takes up those permits, but a permit going to a private person is lost, we have nothing to do with it at all.

1181. And those that are taken back go to Somerset House again, do they?—Yes.

1182. The dealer in filling up a form is subject to no scrutiny or check, is he?—No, not in filling up a certificate.

1183. Nor is the filling up of the counterfoil?—No.

1184. When does the officer deal with the counterfoil; is it from the book when it is used up, or by casual visits to the store?—It used to be when the book was filled up; but now the counterfoils are taken up regularly every month.

1185. What was done at the time of the error?—At the time of the error they were taken more or less haphazard.

1186. Did the officer go to the store and extract the particulars there, or did he take the counterfoils to his office and do it in his office?—He goes to the store as a general rule. If it is a very large place, he has the option of taking them to his office, but as a general rule the quantities are extracted on the premises.

Mr. A. Milner.

1187. Did he simply add up the counterfoils on a scrap of paper?—He takes them down in his book. (Mr. Milner.) He was left to his own devices, more or less, at the date of the error.

1188. He simply added up the counterfoils, sent them to the collector, and the collector sent them on to you, I suppose?—Yes.

1189. I am still at a loss, I confess, to know whether this extraordinary omission of 600,000 gallons out of 3,300,000 gallons was due to wrong transcription from the counterfoils or to omission of particular counterfoils or omissions of whole books, or omission of officers to make returns at all?—No, they all made returns; it was due to omissions of various kinds, mainly omissions to take out from any book all the counterfoils which related to spirits going out of the country. The officer's orders were to take particulars of all the counterfoils of spirits sent out of the country whether it was from Ireland to Scotland or England, or from Scotland to England and Ireland, as the case might be; but what happened was this: under the old loose system, when the officers were allowed to do this as they pleased, and before they had books into which they entered all the particulars from the relevant counterfoils, they would go through them somewhat carelessly, and in many cases the counterfoil itself did not indicate quite clearly in what part of the country the place of destination was; it did not say such-and-such a place, England; such-and-such a place, Scotland; but simply described it by some common name, say, Kingstown, which might be in England or Ireland.

1190. I saw an observation which rather surprised me, namely, that the officer might have mistaken the country?—Yes, they sometimes mistook the country. Some of the officers whom we called upon for explanations complained that they had insuperable difficulties in finding out sometimes which the country was; but the main cause of error no doubt was this: that the officer went through the book hastily, and only took down the particulars of those counterfoils as to which he was quite certain that they related to removals to one of the other countries, and, no doubt to save himself trouble, he often gave himself the benefit of the doubt, when he was not quite sure, by leaving out a particular.

1191. That was one class of error; then there would be counterfoils perhaps omitted?—There would be counterfoils omitted.

1192. And books?—Not whole books, I think; but this I think very likely happened: if an officer took up an Irish book and found that the first 12 or 15 counterfoils all related to Ireland, and he was in a hurry or disposed to be lazy, very likely he said: "Oh, this man deals only in Ireland," and did not go on examining the book, although there might have been counterfoils relating to England or Scotland further on.

1193. Then the officer made no record in any book, did he?—He did make a record, but he did not make a record in a book prepared for the purpose; he made his own notes in his own way.

1194. On a scrap of paper, one might say?—They might have been on scraps of paper; I think they very often were.

1195. There was no permanent record?—No permanent record in the hands of the officer.

1196. And the counterfoils you did not think it was necessary to preserve?—No, we did not preserve them after a certain time.

1197. As the permit system has been correct all through apparently, can you say now if the certificate system, conforming to the permit system, may be relied upon to give accurate results?—There can be only a small margin of error under present conditions.

1198. Probably in the future you will not destroy the counterfoils so soon, will you?—No.

1199. Will you tell the Commission what was the amount of the exceptional error committed at Belfast in the year 1891–92 by one officer. The total error was 530,000 gallons for the year, was it not?—Yes.

1200. How much of that was attributable to what you call the exceptional or special error at Belfast?—Might I put the answer to that question into the evidence?*

1201. Have you any idea how much it was?—Yes, I believe it was between 300,000 and 350,000 gallons.

1202. Half the error?—I am not sure. Certainly a large proportion of it.

1203. You used an expression on the last day which I am unable to follow. You spoke of a probable normal error existing throughout the period of the return?—Yes.

1204. And I think you said that it would be perhaps about 10 per cent. of the whole export. Now, in the first place, we have to separate the permit system, in which there was no error, from the certificate system, do you mean 10 per cent. of the certificate total?—No, I mean 10 per cent. of the excise total, both permits and certificates. Excise only, remember. I am not dealing with the Customs for the moment.

1205. You had before you, I think, only two years, 1891–2 and 1892–3. You had no counterfoils nor details for any previous year, I understand?—No.

1206. And the fact that you had before you when the investigations were concluded was, that one year was wrong by 630,000 gallons and the other year was wrong by 300,000 gallons; how, out of such data, did you construct your theory of a normal error extending over 40 years?—I do not think I said a normal error extending over 40 years. I certainly intended to indicate that I thought no conclusion could be drawn with regard to the earlier period.

1207. "I regard the error shown in the second "year" (that is an error of 300,000 gallons a year) "as being probably about the average amount of error

* Note by Witness.—The exceptional or special error in one station at Belfast for the year 1891–2 amounted to 345,000 gallons, out of a total of 515,000 for the whole of Belfast.

Mr. A. Wilson.

5 Nov. 1894.

Treasury statement: error in spirit duty.

"which ran through these returns for a long period." That was your evidence?—Yes, but I think I qualified it.

1208. "The error of the preceding year was "exceptionally great"?—Yes, that, of course, is evident.

1209. Was there any particular Belfast error in 1892-3?—There were any number of Belfast errors, but nothing exceptional; nothing more than the ordinary accidents which happened to these returns everywhere, owing to the laxness of the system; whereas there was an exceptional Belfast error in 1891-2, because a particular officer fudged his whole return boldly.

1210. What did he do?—He took a pencil and wrote down as much as pleased him; he estimated it.

1211. I am very curious to know exactly what he did?—He estimated. I believe he admitted himself that he estimated; he could have done nothing else.

1212. In what form was he obliged to send in a return to the collector; was it a total?—Yes, he simply sent in a total.

1213. Of gallons for the period?—Yes.

1214. Every quarter?—Yes every quarter.

1215. Did he in each quarter put down what he thought proper, without investigating the consignments?—I cannot remember whether he did it each quarter, but he certainly did it in several quarters, so that that sole error amounted to a very large figure, and, no doubt, greatly increased, and, as I said, abnormally increased, the total error for the year.

1216. It was a large part of the 200,000 gallons, was it?—It was more than the 200,000 gallons, I think.

1217. His share of it?—I must go back, if you please. When I spoke of between 200,000 and 300,000 gallons I referred to this particular district, not to all Belfast. The total error in Belfast in that year was much larger, but the balance is what I call the normal error.

1218. How much of the 630,000 gallons was due to Belfast?—A very, very large proportion.

1219. Two-thirds of it?—More.

1220. Three-fourths of it?—I believe it was almost wholly in Belfast.

1221. Do you mean that the 630,000 gallons almost wholly arose from Belfast?—Yes. These figures will have to be put in. I do not want to get them wrong on the notes, but you may take it the error which vitiated our calculation was almost wholly due to Belfast.

1222. No attention was called to these errors of 1891-2 till the year 1892-3 had also expired, and until you were actually engaged at Somerset House in making up the returns for that later year?—That is how it happened.

1223. How did it happen, then, that these officers at Belfast who had made such errors appeared to have made no such errors in the second year?—That is the whole point, and that is how the thing came out. The particular man who made these colossal errors, which I distinguish from the normal error, had come to grief over some other returns in which his inaccuracy had been found out.

1224. During 1892-3?—At the end of 1891-2 He was reduced, which is the severest punishment in the service next to dismissal, and transferred to another station. Consequently when the year 1892-3 came on he was no longer in his old Belfast station, and the returns for that station were more accurate. His error had taken the form of huge omissions; he had enormously under-estimated the amount of spirit going out from his station, and the consequence of his removal was that the amount of spirit going out from that station, and with it the total figure of removals from Belfast appeared greatly increased in the following year, 1892-3. That was the year we found it out, because we said to ourselves, "What has happened at Belfast that the export is so "much larger?" There was really no great increase of export; in fact, there was a diminution, as it turned out.

Mr. A. Wilson.

5 Nov. 1894.

Treasury statement: error in spirit duty.

1225. In fact, both years were understated, as it turned out?—Both years were understated.

1226. How long had this officer been there?—I think he was only there one year or two years. I am not sure though.

1227. Where had he come from?—I could not tell you.

1228. Does it not come out quite clearly that the great bulk of this error was a personal error, due to inefficiency or neglect of a solitary officer, and that no theory of any normal error was to be founded upon it?—No, not at all, because, putting altogether aside the bulk of this man, when we came to examine the figures we found them wrong all round, and almost always wrong in the direction of under-statement—necessarily so.

1229. Almost necessarily so?—Almost necessarily so, because no officer in stamping his work would put in certificates of spirit removed to another country when no such spirit had been removed. What he did was to miss out a certain number, either from laziness or because he had not the means to see exactly.

1230. But when a return has been 30 years in existence, and when the exports have, as they have, greatly increased and multiplied in that time, and when the natural tendency to become careless as to the use of this return is so apparent as years went on, does it not occur to you that probably the errors which grew so much in those years may have been trivial in the more early years?—Not only do I think that likely, but I think it is almost certain, and that is why I object to its being supposed that I suggested I thought this normal error extended over 30 years. I think it probably went back a considerable number of years, but I do not think at the beginning there was much error.

1231. And you would probably say, looking at the increase in the bulk of export, and also to the tendency to carelessness if it is not checked, it is an error which would diminish as you go back?—As far as routine figures are concerned, I think the error would diminish as you go back.

1232. Now I come to the question of the new and rather startling evidence you gave as to the exclusion from the return of spirits exported from Customs warehouses from Ireland?—Yes. Spirits exported [illegible]

1233. Have you a table of the exports of spirit from Ireland since 1888?—Yes, I have it here somewhere, but the fact is I had to bring such an enormous mass of papers, not knowing exactly on what points the examination would turn, that it is rather difficult to find a particular table in a moment.

1234. I understand that the exports under the supervision of the Customs were wholly under the permit system?—Yes, I think so, wholly on the permit system.

1235. And would, therefore, be a matter of permanent record; I mean there were warrant books corresponding to yours, in which the officer entered particulars?—That I could not tell you. The Customs would know that.

1236. At any rate the Customs did not supervise the export from Ireland otherwise than from warehouses; they had nothing at all to do with dealers' stores or certificates, had they?—No, nothing at all to do with dealers' stores; it was all from warehouses. Here is the return for which you were asking. (*The return was handed to Mr. Sexton.*)

1237. Where is the column which shows the figure affecting the adjustment? In, the course of your evidence you said that up to the year 1888-9 the spirits exported from Ireland under the supervision of the Customs had not been included in the return?—Spirits exported from Customs warehouses.

1238. And that was the only way they did export?—Yes.

1239. I understand you to say they had nothing whatever to do with the certificates of dealers, and

Mr. A. Milner.

8 Nov. 1894.

Spirits: consumption and movement of.

that they are only exported there under the permits from the warehouses?—Yes.

1240. And I therefore assume by analogy that they must have made a permanent record, as you have made a permanent record?—Of course I do not know for how many years they kept their books. I think you have hardly an idea of the enormous mass of this material.

1241. I have; but considering the importance attached to the statistics of consumption even before the revenue came into question, I should think the Customs would not be likely to omit to keep a total for the year. The Customs Department were aware that the Board of Trade publish quarterly, and that you publish every year, a return which purports to give the total export of duty paid spirits from Ireland to Great Britain, were they not?—I cannot tell whether they were or not.

1242. You have no doubt, have you, that the heads of the Customs Department look at the Inland Revenue Report?—I cannot answer that question in any way.

1243. They were aware, no doubt, that this return was relied on as the means of ascertaining the statistics of consumption. Did they ever suggest to you that there were figures of export under their supervision which were essential to complete that return?—No, not that I am aware of. I am speaking of a time long anterior to my connexion with the Inland Revenue, and cannot speak very positively, but I cannot see anything in the correspondence about it.

1244. Is there any record that the Inland Revenue who made up the return ever said to the Customs: "We have to present to Parliament a return of the "spirits exported from Ireland. Will you tell us how "much has been exported through you in order to "complete our return"?—That is what we did say in 1893.

1245. But the returns have been going on from 1858?—This is no doubt how it happened, that the Customs were not included in the return; it was a return of duty-paid British spirits transferred from one country to the other. At the time when the return was instituted in 1858 no British spirits were cleared from Customs warehouses. The practice of clearing them from Customs warehouses only commenced in 1864.

1246. I see the return had been going on six years before there was any export from Ireland?—Yes, and therefore, no doubt, when first of all there was this clearance from Customs warehouses of British spirit it probably was a very small affair, and it had not occurred to anybody that the introduction of this new element was making the return valueless. By that time whatever small interest had attached to the return when it was first called into existence in 1858 had probably died out. As I have often explained, it was a purely statistical return on which no revenue depended, and that was the cause of its neglect by the Inland Revenue Department, which had no statistical branch at all or anybody specially concerned with statistics. When it was started it was started on the right basis; for six years it continued on the right basis; by the time that a new element came into the situation, which made the basis of the return wrong, it had already probably fallen into neglect. That is the only explanation I can offer on what I do not know by my own experience.

1247. There has been scarcely a year for the last 15 years since I came into the House of Commons that that return has not been used by someone or other as a basis of conclusions as to relative indulgence in spirits in Great Britain and Ireland, which is now proved to be rather erroneous?—Yes, quite erroneous.

1248. I wonder the officers of the various Departments did not think it their duty to look more closely into the matter. Is there any record which will show from 1864 to what extent the Customs supervised the export of spirits from Ireland? Surely it would be possible to deduce it in some way, would it not, from their revenue returns?—I cannot see myself how it would, but it is a question which should be addressed to them.

Mr. A. Milner.

8 Nov. 1894.

Spirits.

1249. Of course you will admit the importance of endeavouring to put that return on some firmer basis?—Yes, certainly.

1250. I think you said that what sustained your view as to the importance of the omission was the jump in the number of gallons between 1887-8 and 1888-9; are you quite certain that that was due wholly or mainly to the introduction of the customs?—Mainly; I could get the figures as to that and will add them to my answer.*

1251. It was a large jump, but not the only jump, and it would be important to see how far it was due to revenue and how far to the omission of these Customs figures. For example, between 1888-9 and now, for instance, it has increased from 2,800,000 gallons to 3,500,000 gallons?—That includes the jump from the wrong figure to the right one.

1252. Yes, but it is a jump all the time of a million in a few years; it is a jump from 2,800,000 gallons to 3,500,000 gallons, and it leaves me to doubt whether a jump of 700,000 gallons in one year is to be accounted for wholly by the omission of the Customs figures?—I think we can make that quite certain by reference to the fact.

1253. Your notion is that during the greater part of this period the exports under the Customs was comparatively slight, is it?—My notion is that it steadily increased, that at first it was slight and that in the years immediately preceding the discovery of the omission of the Customs figures it had become very large; but I cannot say what the rate of increase was.

1254. What led to this? Why was not the export of spirit, the duty on which is collected by the Excise Department, conducted by them; was it a matter of convenience?—It was a matter of convenience to the trade, no doubt. I think the amalgamation was regarded as convenient to the trade and, as in many cases, what is convenient for the public and the revenue, is fatal to statistical accuracy.

1255. Convenience and symmetry are not very agreeable to each other?—No.

1256. There was a transfer of business then from the Excise to the Customs. I think I remember that a good deal of the business was handed over on some points?—I think there has been a considerable transfer both ways. What happened was that the Customs were allowed to take our spirits and we to take theirs.

1257. Can you arrange with the Customs to give us some account of the time at which and to the extent of which this business of supervising the export of spirits from Ireland passed into their hands so as to enable us to conclude how far the returns have been affected by these facts?—We will do our best.

Tobacco: consumption and movement of.

1258. I have only one matter left to ask you about, but it is a matter of some importance. Your evidence, otherwise confined I think to the Department of Inland Revenue, branched off at one point to a subject which is more immediately for the consideration of the Customs; it is the question of the duty on tobacco. Now, taking again this return for 1892-3, the duty collected in Ireland on tobacco was 1,470,000*l.*, and the contribution of Ireland as tested by consumption was 1,397,000*l.*?—Yes.

1259. Now we have had three different methods of computation applied to this subject of tobacco?—Yes.

1260. In the first place, Mr. Pittar, in the very clear and able evidence he gave, described the efforts he

* *Note by Witness.*—As a matter of fact the inclusion of the Customs figures accounts for almost the whole of the apparent increase in the exportation of spirits from Ireland between 1887-8 and 1888-9. This export was, for 1887-8, when the Customs figures were excluded, 1,810,780 gallons. For 1888-9, when these figures were included, it amounted to 2,604,496 gallons, an increase of 793,716 gallons, of which the amount going out of Customs warehouses was 743,485 gallons. In the subsequent year, the export from Customs warehouses had risen to 916,326 gallons.

Mr. A. Milner. 9 Nov. 1894. Tobacco—consumption and movements of.

made when he visited Ireland in the winter of 1890 to get a basis of calculation, and he did get the figures for 1890 as well as he could get them, but being retrospective they were of less value than if they were current. That was at first applied, and then the railway and shipping companies concerned in the cross channel trade gave actual facts from day to day as to the actual carriage for four months. Upon those four months the calculations have been founded, and, as I understand, the Customs Department, although they noted the increase involved in the second mode of computation, did not very seriously question it; in fact, Mr. Murray, the head of the Customs, accounted for it by the partiality of the Irishman for dry tobacco, that he likes dry tobacco and smokes more of it. Now you produced on the last occasion in answer to Lord Welby some new figures not from public authorities in Ireland but from some manufacturers, which were said to apply to the year up to March 1894, and therefore did not admit any preceding figures which had been under consideration?—Quite so.

1261. Can you either apply Mr. Pittar's first method and the second method adopted by the Board of Customs to the year 1894, or apply your new figures to the preceding years, and tell us exactly what is the effect upon Irish consumption and Irish revenue of your new figures?—Yes, our new figures could be applied to preceding years, but the calculation would have to be worked out.

1262. The effect of it is, I think, to estimate a larger export from Ireland to Great Britain, is it not?—Very much larger.

1263. And I think a somewhat larger export from Great Britain to Ireland?—Yes, I think so; but at any rate the balance of export from Ireland to Great Britain is very much larger than was got at from the Customs figures.

1264. Then what you may call the apparent revenue of Ireland is proportionately diminished?—Yes, by about 200,000*l.* a year. The revenue as contributed is reduced by about 200,000*l.*

1265. Is that by comparison with Mr. Pittar's first method or by comparison with the second method?—By comparison with the second method; by comparison with the first method it is nothing like so large. The second method put up the contribution of Ireland on tobacco very considerably; it increased it very largely.

1266. I do not think it increased it so largely as you have now diminished it?—No, not quite so largely.

1267. This third method puts the contribution at its lowest, does it not?—Yes.

1268. By far?—I will not say by far, but it does put it at its lowest.

1269. Have the Customs been consulted upon these new figures?—Yes.

1270. Have they expressed any view upon them?—Would you ask Mr. Pittar what he thinks?

Mr. Thomas J. Pittar re-called and further examined.

Mr. T. J. Pittar. Tobacco; consumption; new figures.

1271. (*Mr. Sexton.*) Bearing in mind your former evidence as to your first method, and as to the reasons you have for preferring the results of the second method, what do you now say upon the third set of figures?—I think the figures that the Inland Revenue have prepared, and which they have shown to us, are decidedly better figures. I think there are grounds for supposing that they are more accurate.

1272. Will you state the grounds?—It is generally in this way: that the results in the first place are more reasonable and probable; that, statistically, is a ground to begin with. They bring out a consumption per head of the population which is more in accordance with what one would expect to find.

1273. As how?—For instance, by what I will call the Railway Returns—by what you have called the second method—the consumption of leaf-tobacco per head of the population was 2·11 lbs. in Ireland.

1274. For what year was that?—For the year 1893–4. It now brings it down to 1·62 lbs. That is very close to what it brings out the English and Scotch consumption. The English consumption comes out at 1·62 lbs. and the Scotch at 1·61 lbs.; but I wish to say that there are some little differences not yet threshed out between the two Departments (we have not had yet time to work them out), which may slightly alter these figures, but not in a material degree, I think.

1275. That would altogether take away the force of the observation as to the practice of smoking drier tobacco in Ireland, would it not?—I heard that observation made myself by one of the largest Irish manufacturers, and I think it must rest on his responsibility.

1276. It was the largest manufacturer who said it, was it not?—Yes.

1277. I know the man very well, and there is no one better competent to give an opinion?—Quite so.

1278. It is evident that when three modes of inquiry officially carried on for two or three years produce such very different results, that we must press the matter to some better issue, and with a view to that I think it would be well that you should give us a return, showing, for each of the years since 1889–90 up to last March, by the two methods (I suppose we may cast off the first method now) what was the total consumption of Ireland—what was the total of exports and imports, and the balance, the resulting true contribution, and the rate per head of consumption in England, Scotland, and Ireland?—Very well.

1279. That will enable us to see how far the revenue has been affected by the new method of computation?—It will take a little time first of all for us, with the authorities of the Inland Revenue, to thresh out our differences. We had better do that first, and I apprehend it will take perhaps two days to do that.

1280. (*Chairman.*) How soon may we have the return?—Very soon after that—in a fortnight I should think we should be able to do it. I understand that the return you want is a comparative return between the two methods, showing by how much the Irish consumption, or the consumption for each country, differs under the one method and the other method.

1281. (*Mr. Sexton.*) Showing the effect of the two methods upon export, import, balance, revenue, and consumption per head in England, Ireland, and Scotland?—Quite so; but I do not know whether you understand that the new inquiry of the Inland Revenue has been directed solely to the one article of tobacco.

1282. I am speaking solely of tobacco?—I mean it is not all the articles named in those two tables.

The witness withdrew.

Mr. A. Milner re-called and further examined.

Mr. A. Milner. Tobacco trade.

1283. (*Mr. Sexton.*) Who conducted these recent inquiries?—Mr. Steele really had it all in his hands; it was done by the excise officers. The information is entirely derived from the manufacturers. We have asked the Irish manufacturers how much they have exported to England and Scotland, and vice versa. That is the basis upon which we have proceeded, just as we did with the beer.

1284. Have you asked the English manufacturers how much they export to Ireland?—Yes, we have asked them all round.

1285. For the financial year?—Yes, for the financial year; they have taken enormous pains about it.

1286. Did they give you details or totals?—Totals.

1287. Only totals?—I think only totals. Each gives his own totals.

Mr. A. Milner.

4 Nov. 1894.

Tobacco trade.

1288. Each gave you just one figure?—(Mr. Steele.) They were taken from their books.

1289. But what did they give you—one figure for the year, showing the total of their export?—Yes. (Mr. Milner.) To each country.

1290. When were these figures given—within the last few weeks?—Months; the last time I was here we had received a lot of them, but not all, and we gave you then an approximate account of the results; but, as I said then, we were not ready. Now, as far as the returns from the manufacturers are concerned, I believe we have them all complete.

1291. Is the information given subject to the same pledge as the information with regard to beer?—That would be implied in any case, I think.

1292. I suppose there is no objection to tell us who the manufacturers were, though you may not state the figures?—We have all the manufacturers—we have taken them all.

1293. How many of them are there in Ireland?—I think the whole number is 527 altogether in the United Kingdom.

1294. And you have applied to them all, have you?—We have applied to them all.

(Mr. Steele.) There are only about 22 in Ireland.

1295. (Mr. Sexton.) There is so much conflict on this point that I should like to ask you in conclusion, whether you think the permit system could be applied to the tobacco trade without much inconvenience or to the main bulk of it in relation to the manufacture?—(Mr. Milner.) Yes, I should think it might. Of course, I do not like putting anything on traders that is not necessary for revenue purposes if I can help it, considering how much we have to harry them.

1296. But if there were no other satisfactory way of determining the partition of the revenue I suppose it would become no greater inconvenience than it does in the spirit trade, would it?—Yes, I think it would. I think I should be inclined to take the word of the traders; perhaps they might agree to let us examine their books; that is conceivable.

1297. There might be an examination of the books by those concerned on either side, you think?—Yes.

1298. But you would be disposed to take their certificate back by an examination of their books as sufficient evidence of the amount of the export, would you?—I think so.

Income tax assessments.

1299. (The O'Conor Don.) Referring to the return which Mr. Sexton referred to at the beginning of your examination, this return of the income tax giving the amount of the assessment on lands, houses, railways, and other property from the year 1814, do you know the return?—Yes, I have it here.

1300. Does the first column of that return include the metropolis?—Yes, the item is very unimportant, of course; but the metropolis is included in the first column.

1301. I see in the year 1852 there is an asterisk. Between 1851 and 1852 there was a drop, and there is a note: "The decrease in the valuation did not "arise from the actual diminution in value, but from a "difference in the mode of stating the accounts by "reason of which properties which have been pre- "viously included under the head of lands were "classified under other heads." What are those properties, and under what other heads were they included?—I am sorry to say I did not look that up. I do not remember.

Income tax assessment and valuations.

1302. Is the column the gross valuation of the lands?—This is the valuation, the gross assessment.

1303. Have you got your last report before you?—Yes.

1304. Will you look at page 36, "Assessment on lands." I see there that the assessment for England and Wales for the year 1893 was 40,894,818*l.*?—Yes.

1305. That does not agree with the return which you have given which is 41,000,000*l.*?—It does not.

1306. What is the reason of the difference?—The reason of the difference is that in this table we have included with lands certain payments in the nature of tithe, not being tithe rentcharge, which are excluded in the figures that you quoted from our annual return. Our instruction was to follow the basis of the older [illegible] in preparing this memorandum. In order to do that we had to include with lands certain payments, the nature of tithe amounting to between 200,000*l.* and 300,000*l.* a year which were included in the older assessments, but which strictly ought not to have been included under lands; and to that extent our annual report and the statistical abstract is more correct than this memorandum. But as I say, it is all between 200,000*l.* and 300,000*l.* a year. If you look at the appendix to our Inland Revenue Report, page 23, you will see that in a footnote.

Mr. A. Milner.

4 Nov. 1894.

Income tax assessments and valuations.

1307. Is the first column in the gross assessment to income tax?—Yes.

1308. That is practically the rent, is it not?—Yes, in England and Scotland it is rent.

1309. Then may we take it that the first line shows the increase or diminution of rent in England or Scotland in those successive years?—Yes.

1310. Will you look at page 32 of your annual report. You allude there to the decrease in the value of land in the different countries, and amongst others you have a decrease in Ireland, and you say, "The "decrease in Ireland is stated to be due to the new "poor rate valuation"?—Yes.

1311. What is that; has there been any new poor-rate valuation in Ireland?—There cannot be a new poor-rate valuation. It is an error. There must be some change in the valuation, of course, but there is no general new valuation.

1312. I did not understand what was meant by "new valuation"; you say there is none?—No.

Spirit and beer duties.

1313. (Lord Welby.) In some of the evidence given stress has been laid on the very large amount of spirit duty which is paid in Ireland as compared with the duty on beer which the Englishman generally pays. Is there not another way of looking at it? Would you agree to this form of stating it: the population of England and the population of Ireland, I think, is, as Mr. Sexton put it, something like 6·4 to 1. If you take the whole of the revenue paid on drink by England and Ireland respectively, namely, spirits and beer together, I make it that the English contribution is 14,480,000*l.* and the Irish contribution is 2,152,000*l.* The proportion between these two gives a slightly greater excess to the English consumer, namely, 6·7 to 1 as against 6·4 to the other in proportion to population. I will not ask you to examine the figures, but, subject to correction on that point, do you admit that that is a fair statement?—Yes, I think so, from that point of view.

1314. That is to say, when you take the whole contribution of the Englishman and the Irishman to the drink duties, the proportion which appears so very heavy against Ireland when it is confined to the spirit duties is practically equalised?—You mean that the two countries contribute in about the same proportion to the drink duties as a whole.

1315. Yes?—That seems to be so.

1316. (Sir David Barbour.) The same proportion per head of the population, I understand?—Yes, the same proportion per head.

1317. (Lord Welby.) A good deal of stress was laid upon the fact that at different times income tax might be taken as a good test. Do you happen to recollect that the last time when these matters were brought forward in Parliament Mr. Gladstone, in making his statement, alluded to the income-tax, but he specially spoke of it as a test of a very imperfect and unsatisfactory character, and therefore he grouped along with that the subjects of valuation and of death duties?—I do not remember that he said that.

1318. It is within my recollection, and I am only calling your attention to it, because I think perhaps a little too much stress has been laid upon the importance which has been placed upon the income-tax there as a test. I want to put one question on the subject of the error in the spirit duties. Before 1853 there was a trade in the export of spirits from Ireland to England, was there not?—Yes.

1319. When the duties were different?—Yes.

1320. And then I suppose spirits were exported under bond or upon re-payment of duty?—Not necessarily under bond.

1321. But on re-payment of duty?—On re-payment or an extra payment. If they were taken from the country which had a lower rate of duty they paid the difference on leaving, and in the opposite case there would be a re-payment of the difference between the rates.

1322. Therefore while the duties were different in 1857–58 I suppose you would have an accurate statement of the amount of duty paid on spirits exported from Ireland, would you not?—You can have an accurate statement of the amount of spirits consumed in each country, because the different rate of duty shows it.

1323. But would you not be able to see how much was actually exported from Ireland?—Yes, you could tell it.

1324. If you took that as the basis under that return which you have handed round in manuscript, I see that in the first year of the new system the balance exported is 730,000 gallons?—Yes, between 700,000 and 800,000 gallons.

1325. Would not a comparison between the last year of the old system and the first year of the new be some clue as to whether at the commencement of the new system the returns were fairly accurate?—Yes, I think it would.

1326. (*Sir David Barbour.*) I think you said that the taxation on spirit was comparatively high and on beer comparatively low, did you not?—It is much higher on spirit in proportion to the value of the article, or in proportion to the quantity of alcohol.

1327. So that the Irishman who drinks spirit pays more taxation than the Englishman who drinks beer, other things being equal?—Yes.

1328. But the Englishman who drinks spirit and not beer is subject to the same disadvantages as the Irishman?—Yes.

1329. If then you wanted to adjust the incidence of taxation fairly the adjustment would have to be between the spirit-drinking man and the beer-drinking man, and not necessarily between the Irishman and the Englishman?—No.

1330. And that could only be done, I suppose, by lowering the duty on spirits and raising the duty on beer?—I do not know of any other way.

1331. Even after that had been done there would be a certain inequality, because the teetotaller, whether he was an Irishman or an Englishman, would not pay anything?—No, he gets off now.

1332. Unless you put a special tax on him?—Just so.

1333. Does not that rather point to the conclusion that if you raise revenue by putting a duty on articles of consumption, the taxation necessarily falls with a certain amount of inequality on the different members of the community, according as they do or do not consume the article, or as they consume a larger or smaller quantity?—Yes, unless you were to tax a universal article of consumption.

1334. And that might not be consumed by everybody in the same proportion, so that there still would be inequality?—No.

1335. (*Sir Thomas Sutherland.*) Has not the object, both in the taxation of beer and spirits, been to extract the utmost amount of revenue out of the consumption?—Yes.

1336. So that it would be impossible to apply an equality of taxation on the two?—From a purely revenue point of view, of course, it would be madness.

1337. (*Mr. Wolff.*) I suppose you are aware that although we do not pay the same tax on dogs in Ireland as in England, we do pay a dog tax?—I am not officially aware of it. There is a local tax, I believe, of 2s. 6d. a dog, but it is not paid to the Exchequer, nor have we anything to do with it.

1338. (*Chairman.*) I should like to ask you a question upon a matter of some large figures. Will you look at the return which you have in your hands, which has been prepared under the authority of the Board? The increase of assessment of lands and houses, taken together, as between 1862 and 1893, first of all in Ireland, is about what per cent.?—Land and houses taken together between 1862 and 1893?

1339. Yes, I have the figures here. They are about twelve millions and a quarter in 1862 and about thirteen millions and a half in 1893?—Yes.

1340. That gives a total, I think, of about 11 per cent., does it not?—Yes.

1341. The increase in the assessment of lands and houses in Great Britain during the same time is between 110 millions and 189 millions, as I have it, if you will be kind enough to verify it?—Yes.

1342. So that the increase in the assessment of Irish land and houses in these years is about 11 per cent., and in Great Britain it is 71 per cent.?—Yes.

1343. Or between five and a half or six times as much in Great Britain as in Ireland increase?—Yes.

1344. Can you give me the same figures for Schedule D.? Can you give me the assessment under Schedule D. in 1862 in Ireland and also in Great Britain, and the assessment under Schedule D. in 1893 in both countries?—I will put them in in answer to the question; I cannot give them to you at this moment.

1345. Can you roughly give us at this moment the percentage?—I could not give that even roughly without referring to my tables.

1346. But the increase is vastly more in Great Britain, is it not, than in Ireland?—Yes, but I think it is not in the same proportion as the increase I have already given, but I could not say.

1347. And you could give us, perhaps, also the assessment for all taxable purposes in Great Britain and Ireland?—Yes, certainly.

1348. I should like to have those figures on the notes?—Quite so; I understand you mean all the schedules of the income tax?

1349. Lands and houses first, Schedule D. second, and then of all the schedules?—Between 1862 and now?

1350. Between 1862 and 1893?—Yes.

1351. (*Mr. Martin.*) Does the tithe rent-charge payable in Ireland find its way into the Imperial exchequer?—Do you mean whether it would be charged to income tax?

1352. No; does it find its way to the exchequer in any way?—I do not think it does.

1353. It is something very equivalent to the land tax in England?—The vital difference to me is that I get the land tax in England, and I do not get the tithe rent-charge in Ireland.

Mr. J. E. Keys, 6 Nov. 1895.

Spirit duty.

Income tax assessments.

The witness withdrew.

Adjourned to to-morrow at 11 o'clock.

Commission Room, Westminster Hall, S.W.

PRESENT:

THE RIGHT HON. HUGH C. E. CHILDERS, *Chairman*.

LORD WELBY, G.C.B.	CHARLES E. MARTIN, Esq.
The Right Hon. THE O'CONOR DON.	J. E. REDMOND, Esq., M.P.
Hon. EDWARD BLAKE, M.P.	THOMAS SEXTON, Esq., M.P.

Mr. B. H. HOLLAND, *Secretary*.

Sir EDWARD W. HAMILTON, K.C.B., called and examined.

Sir E. W. Hamilton, K.C.B. [illegible]

1354. (*Chairman.*) What office do you hold in the Treasury?—I am Assistant Secretary to the Treasury.

1355. I believe you have prepared a memorandum which you hand in for the use of this Commission, in which you review the financial relations of Great Britain and Ireland from the time before the Union; and you have also made some record of the fiscal changes that have been effected since. You have divided your memorandum, I think, into three parts?—Yes; I took the period during which Ireland enjoyed legislative independence; then the period between 1801 and 1817, as representing the period during which there were two separate Exchequers under one Legislature; and then the period subsequently to 1817 down to the present time.

1356. We will take the first period first. Will you describe, if you please, the power of the Crown to deal with the surplus revenue before 1782?—I think it may have been said to have been a constitutional right in the Crown to dispose of the surplus revenue of Ireland in the last century.

1357. Was that modified in any way?—It was modified, I think it may be said, by legislation.

1358. In 1782, how was it modified?—The military aid of Ireland had been placed on a more distinct basis by an Act of the Irish Parliament passed in 1769.

1359. When that change took place, had the Government of England any special proposal to make as to the surplus?—I think it is clear that when legislative independence was granted to Ireland in 1782, they had proposals under consideration for securing from Ireland some more direct contribution to Imperial expenditure; but they thought it an inopportune moment to bring them forward.

1360. Lord Rockingham and the Duke of Portland, I think, were then the authorities?—Yes.

1361. And they contemplated some change, but did not carry it out?—I think they contemplated placing the contribution of Ireland on a more direct and distinct basis.

1362. That was prevented by the excited state of feeling at that date, and nothing, I think, was done?—That is the case, I believe.

1363. What was it that Mr. Grattan proposed then?—Mr. Grattan proposed a distinct grant in aid of the Royal Navy of 100,000*l*. in 1782.

1364. Was that carried?—Yes, it was carried.

1365. A little later, in 1783, what was the proposal involved which led to a good deal of debate as to military expenditure?—There was a proposal relating to the number of troops borne on the Irish establishment, which were 12,000, I think, at that time, and the number that might be withdrawn for temporary service out of the country.

1366. Mr. Grattan opposed the change, did he not?—No, Mr. Grattan did not oppose that change.

1367. He opposed the change to reduce the charge?—Yes; that was a year later, I think.

1368. And Mr. Grattan commanded a majority, did he not?—Yes, that is so.

1369. (*Mr. Sexton.*) I believe the Irish Parliament agreed to the proposal that a certain number should be available for service out of Ireland?—Yes.

1370. (*Chairman.*) Then shortly afterwards a financial proposal came before the authorities both in England and Ireland, I think, with reference to the commercial relations between the two countries?—Yes, there was a proposal by the English Government in connection with the commercial proposals.

1371. That proposal was not carried through, was it?—It was not carried through (though it was originally accepted by the Irish Parliament) in consequence of the alterations which were made in the resolutions by the British Parliament. Owing to the alterations, the Irish Parliament rejected the entire proposal.

1372. Those alterations were made, were they not, by the British Parliament in compliance with strong pressure from the commercial interests in England?—Yes, that was so.

1373. Then the proposal of a contribution which was made later, attracted great attention on the part of both the English and Irish Government, I think?—That was the only proposal for placing the contribution of Ireland on a more distinct and definite basis.

1374. That was not after the commercial proposals, was it?—No, in connexion with the commercial proposals.

1375. It was not after the defeat of the commercial proposals?—No; those commercial resolutions underwent so great a change in the British Parliament that they then became very unacceptable to Ireland, and the consequence was that the whole of them dropped, along with this proposal of Mr. Pitt's, that there should be a distinct contribution from Ireland towards the expenses.

1376. So that both the proposals came to nothing, both the commercial and the financial proposals?—Yes.

1377. Now after that arose the question of the military establishment in Ireland?—I think it may be said that no change took place in the military establishment between 1785, when the resolutions were dropped, until the French War broke out in 1793, and then there was a move made in the direction of getting a larger contribution, directly and indirectly, out of Ireland.

1378. Did that affect the naval expenditure, or the military expenditure only?—I think it must be said to be military expenditure.

1379. What was the result of that movement?—The result of that movement was, of course, that an enor-

mous military expenditure was imposed on Ireland during the last seven years of last century.

1380. You say "enormous"; it really was very large in Ireland, was it not?—Yes, it was very large. Of course the difficulty I have had is to try and ascertain how much of that large increased expenditure was due to the French War, and how much was due to the internal disturbances of Ireland.

1381. You have given in your paper, at page 8, a table, I think, showing the Irish Revenue and expenditure from 1782 down to the Union?—Yes.

1382. That Table, while showing a revenue of from 1,000,000l. up to 2,000,000l., and finally in 1800 to 3,000,000l., has to be balanced against an expenditure for many years of about the same as the revenue, but in the last years giving a deficit of 2,000,000l. or 3,000,000l.?—That is so.

1383. What does the careful examination of this Table show; what two facts do you elicit from it?—I elicit from it that the expenditure was largely in excess of the revenue raised, and that that large expenditure was due to two main causes, one, the war with France, and the other, the disturbances in Ireland.

1384. In the first 10 or 11 years the finance of Ireland was good in that respect; there was a slight surplus, was there not?—I think it may be said that the account was just about balanced.

1385. But in the last six or seven years there was a very heavy deficit?—Yes, a heavy deficit.

1386. Is there any one particular year that you would wish to call attention to, or two years together, that illustrate that very much?—No; I think that the two principal features to be borne in mind are that 1793-94, that is the year of the outbreak of the French War, was the first year in which this extraordinary military expenditure was incurred, and then from the year 1797-98 must also be taken into account the expenditure in respect of the Rebellion in Ireland.

1387. The military expenditure during those seven or eight years would have been only about 4,500,000l. had it been according to the former normal condition, would it not?—Yes, that is, I think, a fair estimate.

1388. Whereas as a matter of fact it is nearly 21,000,000l.?—Yes, that is so.

1389. Passing from the expenditure to the accumulation of debt, can you give us any salient figures comparing the first years, the years of peace, with the last years?—It will be seen from the tables given in the paper that while during the first twelve years it may be said that there was comparatively little increase of debt, yet during the last few years the increase was enormous. The aggregate increase amounted to nearly 27,000,000l.

1390. The aggregate increase having been nothing to speak of down to 1793 became 25,000,000l., I think?—I make out that the total increase during those 18 years—or during the time of the Grattan Parliament—the Irish debt was increased by 26,623,000l.

1391. (Mr Sexton.) And during all the period from the establishment of the Irish Parliament up to the outbreak of the French War it was only about 1,000,000l.?—That is so.

1392. (Chairman.) Then as to the unfunded debt, was there any very large increase at the same time in that?—I was speaking of the funded and unfunded together. It was 25,500,000l. on the funded, and 1,000,000l. or 1,250,000l., roughly speaking, on the unfunded debt; that makes a total of 26,500,000l. and 26,750,000l.

1393. Passing from those figures, could you tell us what the proportion of the population of Great Britain and Ireland was at the time of the Union?—The Commission will kindly understand that I have got at present no authentic figure from the Registrar-General. I am not sure whether it is not already before the Commission, because the Registrar-General promised to make some calculations. I think the Commission are aware that in those days there was no census taken, but according to the best authorities which I have consulted I put the respective populations of the two Kingdoms at 10,500,000 for Great Britain and 5,000,000 for Ireland.

Sir R. W. Hamilton, K.C.B.

6 Nov. 1894.

Relative populations.

1394. Practically very nearly two to one?—Yes, two to one.

1395. The revenue at the same time of Great Britain was how much?—It may be put down at the time of the Union at about 31,500,000l. and Ireland at about 3,000,000l.

1396. That is in the proportion of about 10½ to 1?—Yes, of about 10½ to 1.

1397. So that the revenue per head of the population at that time was how much in Great Britain?—According to that the revenue per head of the population of Great Britain was just about 3l., and in Ireland about 12s. per head.

1398. (Lord Welby.) May I say that you make that calculation always with a reserve that the population of Ireland is so uncertain?—Yes, I only take those rough figures of 10,500,000 and 5,000,000.

1399. (Mr. Sexton.) The British population is ascertained by census, is it not?—Yes.

1400. (Chairman.) Taking the figures of expenditure which you have given us, the proportion of British to Irish expenditure was about 8 to 1, was it not?—Yes.

Relative expenditure and debt.

1401. Now taking you to the debt—the funded and unfunded debt (it is not worth distinguishing them) at the Union of Great Britain and Ireland was how much?—A little over 15 to 1.

1402. But how much was it in figures?—It was 446,500,000 in Great Britain and 28,500,000 in Ireland.

1403. The proportion being about what?—A little over 15 to 1.

1404. There is also besides the regular debt the annuity debt, but does that affect the question very much?—Not very materially, but the capital value of annuities which depend on actuarial calculations ought not to be lost sight of.

1405. The figures are 13,000,000l., add to a [redacted] and a third about?—Yes, 1,250,000l.

1406. Taking the annual charge connected with the debt at that time for Great Britain, it was how much?—It was 21,300,000l. odd, and in Ireland about 1,250,000l.

1407. The proportions being what?—About 17 to 1.

1408. May we say that that was the position financially of Ireland at the time of the Union?—Yes, relatively to Great Britain.

1409. Then the Union was proposed, I believe, in 1799 and 1800?—Yes.

Debates in Irish Parliament, 1800, on financial provisions in Act of Union.

1410. What were in outline the financial proposals?—That Great Britain and Ireland were to contribute towards the joint expenditure or what may be called imperial expenditure, in the respective proportions of 15 to 2; and that each country should defray the charges in respect of its own debt previously incurred.

1411. The first proposal for the Union failed, did it not?—The first proposal failed in Ireland.

1412. The second proposal was carried, was it not?—Yes.

1413. The second proposal, so far as finance was concerned, was practically the same as the first proposal, was it?—It was the same in principle.

1414. Can you tell us what Lord Castlereagh said during the debate in Ireland as to the financial proposal in 1800? Will you be so good as to give the Commission the principle of the financial arrangement as he described it?—I think the most important part of his statement was the basis upon which he made the calculation of the respective contributions towards the imperial expenses of the two countries. He took the average annual value of imports and exports in the two countries, and he took the average annual value of dutiable articles consumed in the two countries. Then he took the average of the two proportions, which he made out to be as nearly as possible 7½ to 1, and those were the proportions which he proposed, and which were eventually carried in the Act of Union.

Sir E. W. Hamilton, K.C.B.

8 Mar. 1895.

Debates in Irish Parliament, 1800, on financial proposals in Act of Union.

1415. That double calculation of the imports and exports on the one side and of the consumption of dutiable articles on the other, was the basis of the financial arrangement of the Union, was it?—That is so.

1416. (*Mr. Sexton.*) Have you been able to find his figures verified by any public records of the period, as are they simply in his speech?—The calculations are to be found in his memoirs, but how they were made I cannot say definitely. The conclusion which I was led to form on reading the notes of them in his memoirs was, that some special calculation was made *ad hoc*.

1417. But there is no record of that in the accounts of the period, is there?—No.

1418. (*Chairman.*) Taking the 7½ to 1 as the basis, there were some very important details, I believe, one as to the debt. Will you explain that to the Commission?—The main principle was that while Great Britain and Ireland should each bear the charges of their respective debts incurred prior to the Union, thereafter they should contribute in their own proportions towards the debt incurred jointly for both countries.

1419. Then as to the $\frac{15}{17}$ths and the $\frac{2}{17}$ths division, was that to be capable of revision?—Yes, that was to be capable of revision at the end of 20 years.

1420. Then with respect to any possible surplus, what provision was made?—An Irish surplus might be applied in one of several ways—in remission of taxation, to local purposes, in making good a deficiency of Irish revenue in time of peace, or building up a reserve fund to relieve Ireland's contribution in time of war.

1421. He contemplated also further loans, I think. How were they to be dealt with?—According to the strict interpretation or most natural interpretation to place upon the Articles of Union, it would appear that what was contemplated by the framers of the Union was, that the debt should be jointly incurred, and that the charge thereafter should be in the respective proportions of 15 to 2; but, as I point out later on in my memorandum, it was impossible to work that system and at the same time carry out the terms of the Act of Union.

1422. There was a very sanguine possibility hinted at, I think, by Lord Castlereagh, that the debt might be extinguished, was there not?—Yes, it was the British debt, I think, that he thought might be materially diminished.

1423. And not the Irish debt?—I do not think that comes out very strongly, but I think it was generally thought that the British debt might come down very materially.

1424. In the event of the debt being extinguished, was any change to be made in the financial arrangements?—I think what was contemplated was that the debt of Great Britain would come down to the proportion of 15 to 2, and in that case there seemed to be no reason why any separate financial arrangements should be kept up, and why the taxes should not be indiscriminately levied and, in fact, the two Exchequers consolidated.

1425. Going into the financial calculations, Lord Castlereagh gave it as his opinion, I believe, that the arrangement was beneficial to Ireland, did he not?—Yes, that was apparently his view at the time.

1426. Will you give the Commission the large figures upon which he based that view?—He made a calculation, taking a year of war like 1799, that the expenditure in Great Britain had been 32,750,000 to 6,500,000*l.* in Ireland, and he showed that, had this expenditure been met by the two countries in the Union proportion of 15 to 2, Great Britain's share would have been somewhat greater, and Ireland's share somewhat less; in fact, he made out according to those calculations, of course on the assumption that the war expenditure would continue at the same rate as it was in 1799, that Ireland would have saved about 950,000*l.*

1427. (*Mr. Sexton.*) Ireland's expenditure in that year having included the whole cost of the Rebellion?—Yes, that is so.

1428. (*Chairman.*) Then as to the peace establishment, what did he do?—Then he took the peace establishment and he made a simple calculation according to which he thought that the peace establishment of Great Britain might be put at 7,500,000*l.* and that of Ireland at 1,500,000*l.*, and if that 9,000,000*l.* were borne in the respective proportions of 15 to 2, it would likewise have given Ireland a relief of something approaching 500,000*l.*, (441,000*l.* his calculation was); but of course these are purely hypothetical figures on the part of Lord Castlereagh.

1429. After a long debate Lord Castlereagh's resolutions were carried by a large majority, were they not?—That is so.

1430. And that, I think, was followed by a debate in Committee, in which Mr. Speaker Foster made a very famous speech?—Yes, it was a speech of very great note.

1431. What was the main financial objection which he took to Lord Castlereagh's calculations?—He thought that Lord Castlereagh's calculations were based upon great fallacies, and that instead of Ireland being likely to gain under the Union arrangements financially she would become much more heavily burdened.

1432. He referred to the debt arrangements also, I think?—Yes, he did so. He made out that in the six years ending 1799 the British debt had been increased by 180,000,000*l.*, while at the same time the Irish debt had been increased by 14,000,000*l.* The liabilities, therefore, he pointed out, of the two kingdoms had been augmented by 200,000,000*l.* Ireland's share of these joint liabilities under the Union proposals (viz. $\frac{2}{17}$ths) would have been 23,530,000*l.* instead of 14,000,000*l.* which was the actual amount incurred in Ireland.

1433. After the debate in Committee the next important debate was on the third reading, I believe, when Mr. Grattan made a great speech?—Yes.

1434. Can you give the Commission any leading figures contained in Mr. Grattan's speech?—He likewise took exception to Lord Castlereagh's statements. He pointed out that Lord Castlereagh had stated the Irish revenues for the year at the time of the Union to be about 2,800,000*l.*, and with that figure there had been a margin of revenue over normal peace expenditure; but he further pointed out that this margin had disappeared, because Lord Castlereagh had arbitrarily estimated the establishments at 1,500,000*l.* and not 1,000,000*l.* I have not been able to verify Lord Castlereagh's figures. They appear to have been very hypothetical, and so I do not think I should attach any great importance to them myself.

1435. (*Mr. Sexton.*) The figures, I think, were never examined by a Committee of either Parliament?—I believe not; there is no trace of how Lord Castlereagh got his figures—at least, I cannot find any.

1436. (*Chairman.*) The measure passed through the House of Commons, I believe, and then was discussed in the House of Lords, but not at such great length?—No. In the Irish House of Lords, you mean?

1437. Yes, I am speaking of the Irish Parliament. But there was a famous protest, was there not?—Yes, that is so.

1438. Which is very remarkable, is it not?—Well, it states the case very fully from the Irish point of view. It may be a little exaggerated in places; but I have given it at length in my paper.

1439. Have you compared at all the anticipations in that protest with the outcome?—I think I did at one time, but I do not think I could give the Commission the results at this moment, because I have forgotten how I worked up the calculations.

1440. Was it your impression that there was great force in that protest?—I think they were more nearly right than Lord Castlereagh was in his forecast.

1441. Do you happen to know who drew up that portion?—No, I am afraid I do not.

1442. (Mr. Sexton.) It was agreed, I think, by two-thirds of the whole number who voted in the division, was it not?—Yes, by 20 votes.

1443. (Chairman.) The Act of Union passed in what month? Do you remember?—The address embodying the terms of the Union was voted by both Irish Houses in March 1800.

1444. And it came before the British Parliament in April, I think?—Yes, after the address had been received from the Irish Parliament.

1445. Mr. Pitt made a long financial speech, I think?—Yes, he explained the financial provisions in a long speech with the other provisions of the treaty of Union.

1446. Is there any part of his speech which, from a financial point of view, you wish particularly to refer to?—I think, perhaps, the most remarkable part was that he evidently himself felt that, but for the difference in the two debt charges, an amalgamation at that time of both the Exchequers would have been rightly proposed. I think that clearly comes out.

1447. Which amalgamation?—The amalgamation of the two Exchequers which was eventually contemplated under certain circumstances in the Act of Union. I think that would have been proposed at the time, had it not been for the very great difference between the respective debt charges of the two countries.

1448. The Departmental amalgamation. But would that have included uniformity of taxation?—I take it so.

1449. You think that was Mr. Pitt's meaning, do you?—Yes; my general impression is that he would have proposed financial uniformity for the two countries, had it not been for the great difference relatively of the respective debt charges.

1450. (Mr. Sexton.) What it would have included would have been power to the Imperial Parliament to decree uniformity of taxation, I suppose?—Yes.

1451. (Chairman.) I need not go through the history with you and stages of the Act of Union Bill in the British Parliament, but it was adopted practically without change, was it not?—That is so.

1452. And came into force?—Yes.

1453. Will you give us in summary the terms of the financial arrangements as set out in the 7th section of the Act of Union?—Yes.

1454. (Mr. Sexton.) And in connection with that I think it would be convenient if you dealt now with a matter to which you have already referred, namely, what in your opinion is the reason why it became impracticable, as the Union arrangements worked out, to treat the debts as joint debts?—Yes, I will do so, if you would like that now. Perhaps I might briefly refer to the various provisions in the seventh article in the Treaty of Union. The first subsection of the seventh article provided that the interest and sinking fund of the debts which had been incurred by Great Britain and Ireland previously to the Union were to continue to be separately defrayed by each kingdom. It then provided that for the next 20 years the two countries should contribute to the Imperial expenditure in the proportions of 15 to 2, or 7½ to 1; or perhaps a better way of stating it is in the proportions per cent. of 88·24 for Great Britain, and 11·76 for Ireland. At the end of that time, unless it had been provided that the joint expenditure of the United Kingdom was to be indiscriminately defrayed, then there might be a revision of the two contributions, and it was pointed out that the basis which Lord Castlereagh took might form the basis of any future revision. There were alternative bases pointed out: one was the respective values of British and Irish exports; another was the amount of dutiable articles consumed in both countries; a third was the combination of those considerations; and a fourth alternative was this——

1455. The third one was the one which Lord Castlereagh adopted or purported to adopt, was it not?—Yes, and the fourth was the respective incomes of each country as measured by the income tax, which at that time of course did not exist, because the income tax only applied to Great Britain. Then a revision was to be subsequently made on this basis at intervals of not more than 20 years, or less than seven years. I may mention that during the time of the separate Exchequers between 1800 and 1817 there was no revision made, and I do not think there was any revision suggested. The Commissioners will see that there were endless inquiries made into the working of the system, yet apparently there was no specific proposal made to reduce the actual contributions between 1800 and 1817, though of course it would have been open under the terms of the Act of Union, because the term prescribed was a maximum period of 20 years and a minimum period of seven years.

1456. (Mr. Sexton.) That does not apply to the first period, does it; it was only at the expiration of 20 years, in the first instance?—I must be mistaken, I beg pardon.

1457. The flexible provision came in after the first twenty years?—Yes you are quite right. Perhaps I might now go through the other heads of the financial article. The Irish revenues were to be constituted a consolidated fund on which the pre-Union debt charge was to be made the first charge, the remainder, of course, being applicable to defray Ireland's contribution to the Imperial expenditure.

1458. (Mr. Sexton.) There is nothing there about other separate charges than the charges for the pre-Union debt, is there?—No, but other charges were put into the article itself. I think it is in that paragraph. I was only looking, for the moment, at the summary.

1459. I am pointing out to you that in the article governing the disposition of the consolidated fund there is no provision for any separate charge except a charge on the pre-Union debt?—That is quite true. Then there was a provision for the disposal of any surplus after Ireland had met these respective charges out of her revenue; but curiously enough there was no provision for meeting any deficit. I think it is in connection with the absence of that provision that the great contest has been with respect to the raising of debt during the period between 1800 and 1817, because it is obvious that it would have been impossible for the terms of the Union to have been carried out had Ireland had no separate power of borrowing; for, if she had a deficit, the only way in which she could possibly contribute her quota was by borrowing. There could have been no other means of carrying out the terms of the Union. I think that is quite clear; but I think it was a most remarkable omission in the terms of the Union that that was not clearly provided for.

1460. (Chairman.) There is nothing, is there, to show how that omission came about?—No, there is nothing to show it certainly, and as I say, I think it is due to the absence of that provision that there has been so much controversy about the way the debt at that time was raised. That, I think, was the point that Mr. Sexton wished brought out.

1461. (Mr. Sexton.) Might not the absence of a provision of that kind be accounted for by what appears to have been the general expectation in the British mind, at any rate, of a surplus rather than a deficiency?—There is no doubt that nobody anticipated or could have anticipated this enormous deficit, which was, of course, due to the tremendous expense incurred in consequence of the French War, which lasted nearly 15 years afterwards; but at the same time I think it a most remarkable omission to make in a financial arrangement of this kind, that where it was laid down distinctly how a surplus was to be disposed of, no provision was made as to how a deficit was to be met.

1462. Your point is that the charges which fell on Ireland exceeded so much any revenue which could be raised that there was no other way except to borrow?

Sir E. W. Hamilton, K.C.B.

9 Nov. 1894.

Act of Union, its finance.

Sir E. W. Hamilton, K.C.B.

6 Nov. 1894.

Act of Union, 7th Article.

—I do not say that that was contemplated when the terms of the Union were drawn, because the framers of it never for a moment contemplated that Ireland would be saddled with this enormous expenditure. But my point is that it is a remarkable omission that, while Ireland was to be saddled with a quota of the Imperial expenditure, nothing was said as to how she was to meet it, if her revenue proved insufficient. I admit there was a provision by which it was shown that if the debt were raised in different proportions in the two kingdoms, then it was not to be a joint but a separate debt; but it was very curious, I think, that there was no distinct provision about enabling Ireland to borrow separately in order to meet a deficit.

1462a. If there had been a specific provision for meeting a deficit the promoters of the Bill would have found very difficult inquiries, because there would have been a suggestion from the people of Ireland of what possibly might happen?—That might have been the case, and it was hinted at by several Irishmen at the time. I think Mr. Grattan was one of them, if I recollect rightly.

1463. (*Chairman.*) The omission of that provision has been one of the greatest difficulties in discussions ever since, has it not?—I think that is so.

1464. What is your next point?—I think I need not refer again to this extremely difficult and obscurely worded provision about the debt incurred subsequent to the time of the Union; I pointed out, I think, how the difficulty as to interpreting it arose. Then there was a distinct contingency provided for in the next subsection, which was the amalgamation of the two Exchequers if the respective debts of the two countries became proportionate to the respective contributions to Imperial expenditure; that is to say, if the British and Irish debts became as 15 to 2, either by a reduction of the British debt or by an increase of the Irish debt, in that case the two Exchequers might be consolidated, and taxes indiscriminately levied.

1465. When did the consolidation actually take place?—It actually took place in the year 1816, or rather as from the 5th of January, 1817.

1466. Before that there were four or five Committees, I think, were there not?—Yes, there were Committees sitting perpetually. The first Committee sat in 1805; the next in 1808; there was another Committee in 1811, and that sat continuously until 1815.

1467. (*The O'Conor Don.*) May I ask you a question upon the point that you referred to in answer to Mr. Sexton about there being no provision to raise a separate debt to meet a deficiency of contribution. Will you look at article 8, page 16; is there not to a certain extent there a provision for it, "Provided that "if at any time in raising their respective contributions hereby fixed for each country the Parliament "of the United Kingdom shall judge it fit to raise a "greater proportion of such respective contributions in "one country within the year than in the other, or to "set apart a greater proportion of sinking fund for the "liquidation of the whole or any part of the loan "raised on account of the one country than of that "raised on account of the other country, then such "part of the said loan for the liquidation of which "different provisions shall have been made for the "respective countries shall be kept distinct, and shall "be borne by each separately." Is not that to a certain extent a provision?—It may be said to be so to a certain extent, but I do not think it covers my point. The ordinary interpretation to place on it is that if a loan of 34,000,000*l*. were going to be raised and Great Britain was not to be saddled with 30,000,000*l*. of it and Ireland 4,000,000*l*. of it, then there might be some difference in the proportions of the debt charge; but it makes no special provision for Ireland going into the market and raising on her own account a debt by which she could discharge her liabilities to Great Britain.

Act of Union.

1468. But does it not come to the same thing if they raise a joint debt?—I hardly think so. My contention is that that provision to which you are referring at the present moment really has reference to a joint debt raised in different proportions. I am referring to a debt raised separately by Ireland on her own responsibility, and on her own account, and I do not think it can be said that that was provided for in the Treaty of Union.

Sir E. W. Hamilton, K.C.B.

6 Nov. 1894.

Act of Union.

1469. But would not this be an alternative for that; it would be one way of meeting a deficiency in Ireland or in either country. You said there was no way of providing for a deficiency?—You might get over it in this way. The article you are referring to is this: "Provided that if at any time in raising their "respective contributions hereby fixed for each "country the Parliament of the United Kingdom "shall judge it fit to raise a greater proportion of "such respective contributions in one country within "the year than in the other," and so on. A greater proportion for Ireland might be *nil* for Great Britain, the whole charge falling upon Ireland. But is not that rather straining the words of that section?

1470. (*Mr. Sexton.*) The point of it appears to be that if a sum of money were raised for the joint service, and, if for any reason the burden of the contribution referred to in the Union was not put upon either country in regard to its share of the debt, that country should be held accountable for its part of the debt in future so as to protect the other country with regard to its part?—Yes, I think so.

1471. It refers to a joint debt?—Yes, it refers to a joint debt, but I was speaking of a separate debt.

1472. (*Chairman.*) Will you kindly recur to the work of those Committees. What was their object?—Their primary object was to find out what was the true proportion that was due from Ireland, I think.

1473. And that took from 1805 to 1816, did it?—Yes.

1474. (*Mr. Sexton.*) Before you go to the question of the Committees I should like to ask, looking, for instance, to the disestablishment of the Irish Church by the Imperial Parliament, which was to be maintained for ever by one of the articles of the Act of Union, have you any doubt as to the constitution or power of the Imperial Parliament at any time during the 20 years which followed the Union, or at any time after the Union, to revise the terms of the financial contributions?—Certainly not. Of course Parliament could always amend its own Act, but I do not think any proposal was definitely made, or a Bill introduced to amend the Act of Union in that respect between 1800 and 1817. I cannot find any trace of a proposal made in Parliament to that effect.

1475. It has been seldom mentioned in the discussion of this question, but it appears to me to be obviously the way to deal with the difficulty as soon as it became clear, that the terms imposed upon Ireland were such that no revenue she could raise would satisfy her wants?—It may, of course, be held that Ireland was not sufficiently taxed—that she did not raise enough by taxes.

1476. Does not your own record of the history of the period show that additional taxation imposed within the period reduced the income instead of increasing it?—I have come to the conclusion, speaking entirely for myself, that Ireland was taxed as heavily as probably she could reasonably be expected to be taxed, without leading to the result which may ensue from over-taxation, that is to say, a diminished revenue.

1477. There is no doubt, is there, that the Imperial Parliament at any time after the Union could have revised those terms, and dealt in that way with that question?—No doubt.

1478. (*The O'Conor Don.*) And it was the Imperial Parliament, was it not, which decided what taxation should be levied in Ireland?—Yes.

Committees of 1805, 1808 and 1811-1815.

1479. (*Chairman.*) Now to go back to the question of the Committees. After incubating for 11 years, practically, what was the outcome of them?—They came to the conclusion that as the debts had then not

only because in the proportion of 15 to 2 but of about 15 to 2, the contingency contemplated by the Act of Union for the amalgamation of the Exchequers had arisen, and, therefore, the two Exchequers might properly be consolidated, and the taxes indiscriminately imposed in the two countries; in fact, that they should be one country financially; that Ireland should from that time be under the same financial system as Great Britain.

1480. You have described the debate on the Bill which was brought in upon that resolution; have you anything to add to what you have said in your paper? —No, I do not think so, unless any honourable member of the Commission wishes to ask me a question upon it.

1481. The Irish Chancellor of the Exchequer agreed with the English authorities, I think, and there was practically no discussion?—No, there was apparently very little discussion in the House at that time.

1482. (*Mr. Sexton.*) What was the position at that time of the Irish Chancellor of the Exchequer; was he a member of the British Government?—Yes, he was a member of the British Government, I suppose.

1483. He went in and out with them?—Yes, I imagine so. I daresay you are aware that the Chancellor of the Exchequer to this date has a separate seal for Ireland; the Chairman will know that. There are still two separate seals.

1484. (*Chairman*). You have given us the tables of the Revenue and expenditure of Great Britain and of Ireland in those years, and you have given us a summary of them in your paper. Does any point occur to you specially to mention to the Commission?—I may mention that I have got out some more details that work up to the same figures, which I thought it might be interesting to the Commission to see. They show the expenditure and likewise the revenue in greater detail, and I hope to be able to place them in the hands of the Commission before long; but they have been very complicated to work out.

1485. (*Mr. Sexton.*) I suppose the returns which you were so good as to undertake to present will be soon forthcoming?—Yes, I think so; at any rate for these early years; I should say we have some difficulty about the years prior to the Union, but for those years in question I think we have practically finished the returns.

1486. (*Chairman*). You have also given tables of the separate debt charges, and you have given a very useful table here of the difference in duties at that time?—Yes.

1487. There were two duties in Scotland, I think, which is not generally known?—Yes, that is curious.

1488. One for the North of Scotland and the other for the Lothians?—Yes.

1489. And there were differences of duty for different kinds of spirits?—Yes.

1490. (*Mr. Sexton.*) Before you pass from this section it would be well if you would state the effect of Table 5, that is, the effect of the 15 to 2 proportion working during the 16 years upon the debt of Ireland and upon the debt of Great Britain?—The effect was that, whereas when the Union was proposed the respective debts of Great Britain and Ireland were in the proportion of about 15 to 1, they were in 1817, when the Exchequers were united, in the proportion of 6½ to 1.

1491. The figures being what?—The figures being these; in 1801 the total debt of Great Britain was about 446,300,000*l*., and Ireland about 28,500,000*l*., whereas in 1817 the debt of Great Britain had risen to 737,000,000*l*., and that of Ireland at a still greater rate to 112,300,000*l*.

1492. The debt of Great Britain increased by two-thirds of itself and the debt of Ireland quadrupled?—Yes, just about quadrupled.

1493. (*Chairman.*) What do you say about the debt charges in the next summary table?—The debt charge in Ireland likewise increased proportionately much more rapidly than that of Great Britain. At the time of the Union the debt charge of Great Britain was nearly 21,500,000*l*., while that of Ireland was about 1,250,000*l*. When the Exchequers came to be united in 1817 the debt charge of Great Britain was a little over 40,000,000*l*., while that of Ireland had risen to as much as nearly 5,500,000*l*.

1494. One had doubled nearly, and the other was quadrupled about?—Yes.

1495. (*Mr. Sexton.*) The revenue of Ireland having been at the time of the Union about 3,000,000*l*. a year, the debt charge alone of Ireland at the end of 16 years had become 6,000,000*l*. a year?—Yes. For the last year 1816–17 it was over 6,000,000*l*.

1496. The debt charge alone at the end of 16 years was double what the whole revenue of the country had been at the time of the Union?—Yes.

1497. (*Chairman.*) I do not want to go from the sequence of your paper, but I should like to ask you how could that in fairness have come about?—Do you mean the enormous debt charge?

1498. No, the enormous difference?—Because Ireland, on the one hand, had had to borrow so enormously in order to defray her contribution to the Imperial expenditure.

1499. (*Mr. Sexton.*) It is really a question of whether the proportion of 15 to 2 should ever have been imposed at all, is it not?—Yes, that is of course one of the points of discussion. It must be remembered that Great Britain raised proportionately much more out of taxation than Ireland did.

1500. Upon that point it is true that Great Britain did raise very large sums, but was it not ascertained by one of the Committees that the taxation of Ireland, leaving out debt altogether, had increased within the 16 years more than the taxation of Great Britain?—Relatively, yes, I think that is so.

1501. In Great Britain it had about doubled, and the taxation of Ireland, if I remember, was between four and five times what it had been, was it not?—I should have thought it was rather putting it too high in saying four or five times. For instance, if I take the revenue of Great Britain for the first year after the Union there were about 35,000,000*l*. raised. Of course part of that was not taxes, but was other revenue besides taxes, but the greater part of it may be said to have been raised by taxes. In 16 years' time it had reached 63,000,000*l*., that is not of course quite double. But in Ireland the revenue was in 1801–2 about 3,000,000*l*., and in the last year it was about 5,300,000*l*.

1502. The 3,000,000*l*. included all the Rebellion charge. I was referring to the normal taxation of Ireland?—But then you have to go back to the time before the Union. According to the figures I have just given, the increased amounts raised by revenue in Great Britain and Ireland respectively were very much about the same relatively.

1503. So therefore you think no argument can be founded upon it?—I think not, if you take the period between 1800 and 1817.

1504. (*Chairman.*) I was going through the tables which you have given of the differences between the rates of taxation in Great Britain and Ireland. First of all, on page 28, you give the difference in spirits, I think?—Yes. A more interesting, and really the more important one is the table with reference to home-made spirits which is on the previous page, page 27. Of course the home-made spirits represent a far larger amount than the foreign spirits.

1505. On the home-made spirits the excise duty had risen from between 2*s*. and 3*s*. in Ireland, to 5*s*. and 6*s*., and in England from between 5*s*. and 6*s*. to 10*s*., or between 10*s*. and 11*s*., I think?—That is so.

1506. And in Scotland the duty was at two separate rates, but they were not very far from the Irish duty?—They were much higher than the Irish duty at the end of that period.

1507. (*Mr. Sexton.*) Do you say that the taxation of home-made spirits in England less than doubled within the time?—Yes, and certainly more than doubled in Ireland.

Sir E. W. Hamilton, K.C.B.

[illegible]

1508. The figures a good deal more than doubled in Ireland, did they not?—From 2s. 5d. to 5s. 7d.

1509. It became 5s. 7d., so that Ireland then was taxed more heavily relatively than Great Britain, was it not?—The increase was greater.

1510. (*Chairman.*) Then in reference to foreign spirit the table is curious. In some respects Ireland was taxed even higher than England in some years. I think in 1808, for instance?—I do not think very much can be made of that table. I have not the figures as to what the amount yielded was, but I think it must be very small.

1511. Have you any remark to make upon variations of the tea duty?—No, I do not think so. The duty, it will be observed, was not materially different in the two countries.

1512. (*Mr. Sexton.*) I think there was a substantial difference during the Union in the high period time; it was 50 per cent. in Great Britain and only 20 per cent. in Ireland; and in 1814 that advantage entirely disappeared, is not that so?—Yes, I admit that.

1513. (*Chairman.*) Have you any remark to make on the table as to malt?—No, I think the Commissioners will observe during that period that there was no material difference in the two duties. Of course England was higher than Ireland, but by the time of 1815 and 1816 England and Ireland were practically on the same basis.

1514. Then with regard to tobacco?—With regard to tobacco Ireland got no doubt a slight advantage at the commencement of that period, but towards the end it was on all fours with Great Britain.

1515. (*Mr. Sexton.*) At the commencement it was 1s. and 1s. 8d., and at the end it was 3s. in each country?—Yes.

1516. (*Chairman.*) Then with respect to the income tax, what have you to say?—That was not levied in Ireland at all.

Exports and imports.

1517. You give, I think, also a table of the exports and imports, which is interesting considering that it was one of the bases of the revision of the Act of Union. Have you any remark to make upon what it came to in 1816?—It would seem that the value of imports and exports had grown in Great Britain from 67,000,000*l.* to 81,000,000*l.* in the course of the 15 years, while in Ireland they had practically stood still, there being only an increase of 500,000*l.*; that is to say, from 10,300,000*l.* to 10,800,000*l.* These are what is called the official value of imports and exports. I have purposely left out Lord Castlereagh's figures, because I am unable to find out upon what basis he made his calculations at the time of the Union.

Expenditure.

1518. That finishes so much of your paper as refers to the revenue. You then take the expenditure, and you refer to the paragraph in the 7th article, in which specially it is "provided that the remainder of "the revenues of Ireland, after the charge in respect "of the interest and sinking fund of the pre-Union "debt, shall be applied towards defraying a proportion "of the expenditure of the United Kingdom." Have those words led to much difference or controversy?—No, I do not think it can be said that they led to any great difference or controversy, but it is a point that might very well be taken. I point out that really it made comparatively a very small difference. I have not been able to see why these particular services were selected as separate charges for Great Britain and Ireland respectively, but it will be observed by the table I give at the bottom of page 33 that the total was 35,000,000*l.* in the two countries, the aggregate amount; and if that 35,000,000*l.* had been taken exactly in the proportion of 15 to 2 the difference would not have been very great. Ireland would have had a little turn from it, so to speak; she would have gained about a quarter of a million.

1519. (*Mr. Sexton.*) If they had been joint charges?—Yes, if they had been treated as joint charges; but, as I say, I really do not know why, as they appear to be imperial services, they were taken to be separate services. I have no means of ascertaining.

Sir E. W. Hamilton, K.C.B.

3 Nov. 1894.

Expenditure.

1520. (*Chairman.*) Nothing of importance arises upon it, I think, does it?—No, I do not think any great point has been made of it.

1521. Then, with respect to the debt in the period we are discussing, what have you to say?—That is the point, of course, to which I have already referred.

1522. Have you anything to add to what you have said?—No, I do not think so. I think I have said all I wish to bring out [illegible] that point, unless there is anything else you [illegible] like to ask upon this particular provision.

Effect of consolidation of Exchequers.

1523. Passing from the period of [illegible] Union to 1817, and coming to the last period, how would you express tersely the effect of the absolute union of the exchequers in 1817? What was the operation of the absolute union of the exchequers?—The immediate effect was that Ireland, so to speak, was forgiven a very considerable sum which, under the terms of the Union, she would have had to make good to Great Britain; and really what it came to was that Parliament said, "We shall be content to get from Ire- "land what we can; we will pay the whole of the "Irish expenses, and we will take whatever surplus "revenue there is in Ireland towards meeting the "imperial expenditure"; therefore, from that time there was no fixed quota from either country towards meeting imperial expenditure.

1524. (*Mr. Sexton.*) I do not understand that Ireland owed anything to Great Britain at the end of the time, though she had a separate debt of a very large amount and was in danger of bankruptcy?—Yes, but at that time she could not possibly raise revenue sufficient to pay what was due to Great Britain under the terms of the Union.

1525. That would be a matter for the future, but at the moment the state of affairs was that owing to the inability of Ireland to raise by revenue the amount of her liability which she had incurred from year to year, there had been incurred on her account debts amounting to 112,000,000*l.*, and she was responsible for that amount?—She was also arrears with her contribution, and there was actually 2,000,000*l.* remained.

1526. But the question was a question of [illegible] the contingency to be faced at that time [illegible] was that debt [illegible] be dealt with, was it [illegible]?—No doubt.

1527. And of course, a state of affairs might soon have been reached when it would not have been possible to have raised any money on account of Ireland?—It is quite conceivable that things might have gone from bad to worse.

1528. (*Mr. Martin.*) [illegible] I understand, the Irish debt raised after the Union was raised by the English Chancellor of the Exchequer?—No, it was raised by the Irish Chancellor of the Exchequer partly in Ireland and partly in Great Britain, but I think the responsibility of raising it must be said to rest on the Irish Chancellor of the Exchequer; I mean so much of the debt as was separate, and purely Irish debt.

1529. What proportion did it bear to the rate of interest paid by the Chancellor of the Exchequer for England?—I am afraid I have not got those figures by me at this moment, but we can easily furnish them, if required. Of course the credit of Ireland was not equal to that of Great Britain at that time.

1530. (*Mr. Sexton.*) Of course as Ireland could neither perform any legislative or executive act after the Act of Union was passed, every act done was done under the imperial authority?—No doubt; but what I meant was that the debt raised separately for Ireland primarily rested on the credit of the Irish revenue. I presume the imperial credit was behind it, but at the same time the fact that Ireland had been in a perpetual deficit in those years must have made her borrow on much more exorbitant terms than she would, had she been able to make ends meet.

1531. I suppose the borrowing after two or three years passed was almost wholly in the British market? —No doubt.

1532. (Chairman.) At any rate from 1817 everything was amalgamated, though the duties were not equalised: the whole of the finance of Great Britain and Ireland was amalgamated into one, was it not?—All the revenue raised in England, Scotland, and Ireland was then paid into one common fund, which was called the consolidated fund of the United Kingdom, and out of that the interest on the debt as well as the expenditure was paid. The interest on the debt, whether raised in Ireland or Great Britain, constituted the first charge on the fund.

1533. One of the objects of the amalgamation, or at any rate what had necessarily to follow amalgamation, was the uniformity or the approach to uniformity of taxation, was it not?—Yes. I think uniformity may be said to have been certainly contemplated by the Treaty of Union.

1534. I think that was expressly stated, was it not? —Yes, "indiscriminately defrayed," I think is the expression, which may be said to cover that point.

1535. I should like to take you through what was done in that respect dealing with page 39, and what follows in your paper. You have given us details of the different equalisations or approximations of equality. The tobacco duty was equalised almost directly, was it not?—Yes.

1536. How were the stamp duties dealt with?—There were so many rates of duty that it would be almost impossible to give them in detail, but the whole amount was somewhat insignificant and they were finally assimilated and levied at the same rates in the two countries in 1842; but it is not a material point. The really two material points are the spirit duties and the income tax.

1537. The spirit duty is the most important of all, is it not?—Yes.

1538. Could you give us a short account of the time which it took to equalise the spirit duty, and the steps which were taken. We had the rates of duty just now down to 1817; will you start from there and tell us the main steps that were taken?—The striking difference, of course, to commence with, is that shortly after the consolidation of the two exchequers, that is to say about 1823, the duty was levied in England at the rate of 11s. 8d. per gallon; in Ireland it was only 2s. 4½d.

1539. (Mr. Sexton.) About one-fifth?—Yes, only about one-fifth. Then there were several attempts made to slightly raise the spirit duty in Ireland so as to bring it a little nearer to that of Great Britain, but it may be said that these attempts failed until the year 1853 when Mr. Gladstone made a proposal, which was accepted by Parliament, to raise the duty from 2s. 8d. to 3s. 4d.

1540. The English duties having been first reduced by about one-third were then raised a little and brought up to 7s. 10d. and the two stood at 7s. 10d. and 3s. 4d. in 1853?—Yes. I think the material date to bear in mind is 1853, when the commencement of the assimilation of the duties in the two countries took place. It was quickly effected; because, whereas in 1853, when Mr. Gladstone made the first serious step in that direction, the duty in Great Britain was 7s. 10d., and that in Ireland 3s. 4d., by the year 1858, only five years later, it was uniform in the two countries, viz. 8s. a gallon.

1541. Twopence was added in England and 4s. 8d. in Ireland?—Yes, that is so in that short period.

1542. (Chairman.) Whatever the reasons may have been, this process was completed, I think, in 1860, was it not?—No, in 1858. From that time the duties have been levied in the two countries at exactly identical rates.

1543. The next great difference was with respect to the income tax, I think?—That is so.

1544. Neither England nor Ireland had income tax after the war, had they?—No.

1545. When was the British income tax imposed? —The income tax was re-imposed in Great Britain in 1842, but it was only imposed for the first time in Ireland in 1853. | Sir E. W. Hamilton, K.C.B.

6 Nov. 1894.

Equalisation of taxation.

1546. Between 1842 and 1853 there was no Irish income tax, was there at all?—No.

1547. (Mr. Sexton.) Was there an income tax between Waterloo and 1842?—No, it was almost the first tax that was taken off after the peace was concluded.

1548. (Chairman.) There was a famous division in the House of Commons, I believe, and the Government were defeated?—Yes, that was the case; that was in 1816, I think.

1549. You have given us the figures, which I need not go through now. Were there any other taxes which have been equalised?—No, I think we have referred to all the taxes which are worth referring to. Of course the Commissioners are aware that there are several taxes levied in Great Britain during that period, in fact ever since the consolidation of the two exchequers, which are not levied in Ireland.

1550. Very soon after the final equalisation of the spirit duty, I believe the question of Irish finance came very prominently before Parliament in two or three important debates, did it not?—Yes, that is the case. | Debates on Irish finance in 1834, 1853, 1863 and 1864.

1551. Do you remember when the first was?—The first was earlier than that period, long before the question of raising spirit duties or levying the income tax in Ireland arose; it was in 1822.

1552. I am speaking of later than the Reform Act? —Then I think the most important is the motion that was made by Colonel Dunne in 1853.

1553. (Mr. Sexton.) Mr. O'Connell's motion came after the Reform Act?—Yes. I thought you meant after the assimilation of the duties. Mr. O'Connell's motion was in 1834, two years after the Reform Act.

1554. (Chairman.) What was the outline of the grievance which Mr. O'Connell expressed?—Of course his main point was that Ireland had been saddled with too heavy a quota during the time of the separate exchequers between 1800 and 1817; and he also maintained that, even since that, Ireland had not got her share of remissions of taxation.

1555. What was the answer; who answered him? —Mr. Spring Rice, Secretary to the Treasury, answered Mr. O'Connell at the time. It is a very elaborate speech, one of the longest speeches to be found in Hansard.

1556. What was the result of the debate?—The result of the debate was that it came to nothing; there was no action taken upon the motion.

1557. Is there anything remarkable in that debate which you wish to mention to us?—No, I think not, I think the case was better argued, that is, in a more practical form, later on in some subsequent discussions.

1558. (Mr. Sexton.) I notice that Mr. O'Connell said that the quota of Ireland under the Act of Union instead of being 2 to 15 should have been 1 to 16 in the opinion of the Irish Lords who were opposed to the Act of Union?—Yes, that is the case.

1559. (Chairman.) If there is nothing specially arising out of that debate, will you kindly mention the next?—The next was when Mr. Gladstone proposed to extend the income tax to Ireland. Colonel Dunne brought forward again the question of Irish finance, pointing out that of course this would have the effect of making the Irish case a still harder one than it had been before.

1560. Is there anything in Colonel Dunne's speech, or in Mr. Gladstone's reply, which is of special interest?—I think not, because Mr. Gladstone mainly went back upon the time of the Union, and I do not think there was anything specially new which he brought out in his speech. He evidently thought at the time that Ireland was not paying more than her fair share at any rate.

Sir E. W. Hamilton, K.C.B.

9 Nov. 1894.

1561. (*Mr. Sexton.*) I think he assumed all through that there was what we may call an equal taxable capacity between the two countries. He said that Ireland did not pay anything that England and Scotland did not pay, but England and Scotland paid a considerable number of things Ireland did not pay. That would look as if Mr. Gladstone founded himself on the maxim that the taxable capacity was equal in both countries. He did not go into the question, did he?—I think it may be said that he founded his assumption on the fact that there was no material difference in the taxable capacity of the two countries.

1562. (*Chairman.*) The next debate on this subject, I think, was upon Colonel Dunne's renewed motion in 1863?—That is so.

1563. To which Mr. Gladstone replied also?—Yes, he then again argued the case.

1564. Is there anything special that you wish to call our attention to in that debate?—I may say that in this speech Mr. Gladstone demurred to (what he called) having public money expended on geographical principles. He regarded Great Britain and Ireland as that time as separate counties in England; therefore he declined to argue that Great Britain and Ireland could be treated as financially separate, and he strongly maintained that in Ireland's own interest fiscal equality was the goal set to keep in view. In fact, he referred to the previous separate exchequers as an unsatisfactory state of things, and intimated, in concluding his speech, that all that he could see by which he could redress the proposed inequality was by increased liberality towards Ireland in the shape of making loans of public money.

1565. You call special attention in your paper to a speech of Mr. Longfield, and to two particular figures he gives. Do you not think that they have great weight?—Yes. These are taken from Hansard. I have not checked them to see whether they are accurate.

1566. Have you taken them from his speech?—Yes, I have taken them from his speech. If they are correct they are striking figures, no doubt.

1567. As between 1842 and 1862 he makes out the taxation of Ireland per head to have doubled, does he not?—He does make that out, no doubt. Of course that was to a certain extent due to a very large fall in the population during that time.

1568. Was there any answer in debate to that, do you remember?—No, I do not think there was.

1569. (*Mr. Sexton.*) What would be the figure per head now, 12s. 6d. in 1842, and 25s. in 1862, was it not?—I am not quite certain what those figures of revenue are, 4,000,000*l.* and 7,000,000*l.*; they are very round figures, and what they represent I have never analysed, but, roughly speaking, the present taxation per head of population is about 1*l.* 10s.

1570. It is a couple of shillings a head more than it was in 1862, is it not?—Yes.

1571. I think it must be before that?—In a Parliamentary paper which will be before the Commission almost at once now, it would appear that in the year 1860, which was two years before one of the periods to which Mr. Longfield refers, we make it out to be about 1*l.* 6s. 6d.

1572. (*Chairman.*) You make it about 30s. now, do you not?—It depends on whether you take the whole revenue or merely the taxes. I make out that in 1892–93, if you take only the revenue raised by taxes, it comes to about 1*l.* 2s. per head of the population.

1573. (*Mr. Sexton.*) And for the whole true revenue how much would it be?—For 1892–93 it would be 1*l.* 18s.

1574. (*Chairman.*) The next debate in Parliament I think was in the following year, also on the motion of Colonel Dunne?—Yes, the question was again brought forward by Colonel Dunne.

Select Committee of 1864–65.

1575. And he succeeded, did he not, in getting a Committee appointed?—A Committee was nominated.

1576. What should you give as the outcome of that Committee?—I do not think there was any very definite conclusion formed, if I may say so. I hope I may not be thought disrespectful towards any member of this Commission who was upon that Committee.

1577. (*Mr. Sexton.*) I suppose The O'Conor Don was in the minority, and your language is not too strong to imply that the upshot of it was somewhat negative?—Yes. I think they disposed of the question of whether Ireland had been very unfairly treated during the time of the separate exchequers between 1800 and 1817. They saw the immense difficulties of treating Ireland as a separate entity in the way of taxation, and the only way in which they thought that material relief could be afforded to Ireland was by making larger loans to Ireland.

1578. (*Chairman.*) Was that practically what it came to?—Yes, I think so.

1579. There were really no suggestions made at all?—No, there was no practical recommendation made which could be made the subject of legislation.

1580. They were sort of palliatives, but nothing very definite, were they?—No.

1581. (*Mr. Sexton.*) Events were not always quite relevant to the subject. The chairman, when his report was rejected, retired and never came back; Colonel Dunne left the Committee and never returned, so that the report was considered and decided upon in the absence of the chairman, was it not?—I think the report was Sir Stafford Northcote's, if I remember rightly.

Subsequent proceedings in Parliament.

1582. (*Chairman.*) What followed in Parliament on the subject; was the motion renewed for an inquiry?—Nothing came of it, I should say.

1583. There was no motion for an inquiry, was there, until within the last few years?—I think it may be said that no action was taken at all upon the report of the Select Committee of 1864–65 unless it may be said that an impulse was indirectly given to the loan system in Ireland by that report. The Land Improvement Acts were amended, I believe, very shortly after that, and there were larger loans made in Ireland for that service.

1584. Sir Joseph McKenna moved in Parliament, did he not, once or twice?—Yes, subsequently he did.

1585. But nothing was done immediately afterwards?—No.

1586. In 1864 and 1867 Sir Joseph McKenna, I think, moved, and later in 1878 again?—Yes.

1587. Then practically that is the history of the Parliamentary action on this subject, is it?—Yes. It has never engaged the serious consideration of any Government since the report of the Committee of 1864–65, until we come down to 1890, when the Government of the day proposed to appoint, as the Commission are aware, a Committee to inquire into the financial relations not only of Great Britain and Ireland, but of England, Scotland, and Ireland.

Adjourned for a short time.

Table of revenue collected, per head and per capita.

1588. (*Chairman.*) You have prepared in the latter part of your memorandum some extremely important tables of the utmost value, and I should like to ask you a few questions on these now. The first table shows "the Revenue collected in Great Britain and Ireland "respectively, in each year from 1817–18 to 1893–94 "(i.e., the net receipts, after repayments, drawbacks, "and allowances have been deducted, but without any "deduction on account of collection expenses and of "certain other charges, which were formerly met out "of revenue in its progress to the exchequer, instead "of being voted, as now, and charged on the general "revenues of the United Kingdom)." That return is, I understand, to be supplemented by another, and, later, one with some other deductions, is it not?—We are going to give you more in detail these figures, and, likewise, we are going as far as we can to adjust them in order to bring out what we consider the best basis of arriving at the true revenue of each kingdom.

1589. But these are the true net receipts?—Yes, as collected.

1590. Quite so, that of course is the safest?—But it is very misleading.

1591. I have examined these very carefully, and I would ask you not as to every line, but as to every fourth or fifth line, which will enable one to judge of the general result. I take first 1821; in that year the percentage of British revenue was 92·14, and the percentage of Irish revenue was 7·86?—Yes.

1592. That produced by the population basis per head, 3l. 17s. 10d. for Great Britain, and 13s. 8½d. for Ireland?—Yes.

1593. I then take five years further, 1826. The percentage of Great Britain's revenue is 92·11, and of Irish Revenue 7·89?—Yes.

1594. That gives 3l. 8s. 8½d. per head for Great Britain, and 12s. 4½d. per head for Ireland?—Yes.

1595. The next year I take is 1831, with 92·20 per cent. for Great Britain, and 7·80 for Ireland. That gives 3l. 1s. 8½d. per head in Great Britain, and 10s. 11½d. per head in Ireland. Then I go five years further and take 1836; the percentage for Great Britain is 90·80, and the percentage for Ireland 9·10?—Yes.

1596. That gives per head a revenue payment in Great Britain of 2l. 12s. 2d., and in Ireland of 11s. 6¼d. I go next to 1841; the percentage for Great Britain is 92·06, and for Ireland 7·94. That gives 2l. 11s. 6½d. per head in Great Britain, and 9s. 11½d. in Ireland?—Yes.

1597. In 1846, the percentage for Great Britain is 91·85, and for Ireland 8·15, which gives 2l. 13s. 1½d. for Great Britain, and 11s. 3d. for Ireland. In 1851 the percentages are 92·84 for Great Britain, and 7·36 for Ireland, or 2l. 10s. 11½d. per head in Great Britain, and 12s. 10½d. in Ireland?—Yes.

1598. Then going to 1856 (there is a broken year between which it is not necessary to refer to), the percentage is 90·41 in Great Britain, and 9·49 in Ireland, which is 3l. 17s. 10d. per head in Great Britain, and 1l. 2s. 4½d. in Ireland?—Yes.

1599. In 1861 the percentages are 90·64 in Great Britain, and 9·36 in Ireland, the per head result being 2l. 15s. 2½d. in Great Britain, and 1l. 2s. 8½d. in Ireland. In 1866 the percentages are 90·44 in Great Britain, and 9·56 in Ireland, being 2l. 9s. 11d. per head in Great Britain, and 1l. 3s. 8d. per head in Ireland. In 1871 the percentages are 89·63 in Great Britain, and 10·37 in Ireland, being per head 2l. 9s. 8½d. in Great Britain, and 1l. 6s. 11½d. in Ireland. In 1876 the percentages are 89·25 in Great Britain and 10·75 in Ireland, the per capita expenditure being 2l. 9s. 2½d. in Great Britain, and 1l. 11s. 4½d. in Ireland. In 1881 the percentages are 90·51 in Great Britain, and 9·49 in Ireland, or 2l. 11s. 2½d. per head in Great Britain, and 1l. 15s. 10½d. in Ireland. In 1886 the percentages are 90·46 in Great Britain, and 9·54 in Ireland, or 2l. 11s. 7d. per head in Great Britain, and 1l. 14s. 10d. in Ireland; and in 1891 the percentages are 90·43 in Great Britain, and 9·57 in Ireland, or 2l. 12s. 8½d. in Great Britain, and 1l. 19s. 1½d. in Ireland. As to the figures of computation per head we do not, of course, ask you to say at once that they are correct, because they ought to be checked, but they are taken mathematically from the figures you have given?—Yes.

1600. The only question I would ask you upon that is, to what would you attribute the enormous proportional increase in the per head revenue of Ireland as compared with Great Britain?—To two general causes, one being the closer assimilation of duties in the two kingdoms, and the other, the great increase in population of Great Britain and the decrease in population of Ireland since the time of the famine.

1601. (*Mr. Sexton.*) Assuming the capitation figures to be correct, the general effect of your return may be stated thus: that the taxation per head in England, which in 1821 had been 3l. 17s. 10d. per head, had in 70 years, that is to say, in the year 1891, become 2l. 12s. 8d. per head; it had decreased by nearly one-third?—Yes, according to those figures.

1602. And, on the other hand, the inhabitant of Ireland who in 1821 paid 13s. 8d. for taxes, paid in 1891 1l. 19s. 1d.; that is, his rate had trebled?—Yes, according to these figures, but they do not, of course, show the incidence of taxation correctly, because we have every reason to believe that in the early years you ought to deduct a sum of something like a million from the British revenue and credit it to Ireland, whereas in the later years you ought to deduct something approaching one million and three quarters from the Irish revenue and add it to Great Britain's revenue. I am afraid I have overstated the figure for 1890-91; it is about 1,330,000l., and I think that is understating the case rather than overstating it. I should take 1,330,000l. off 9,212,000l., and add that sum on to 87,887,000l.

1603. (*Mr. Sexton.*) Which alters the British proportion very little?—But it would, of course, make a difference in Ireland.

1604. It would turn the Irish figure from 1l. 19s. 1d. to about 1l. 13s. 6d., would it not?—I do not know what the population figures are; I have not the census figures with me.

1605. The census is 4,700,000 for 1891. Even subject to that amendment, it does appear that the capitation rate in Great Britain, between 1821 and 1891 decreased about one-third, and, on the other hand, the capitation rate in Ireland increased more than double, does it not?—Yes, I think that may be safely said.

1606. (*Chairman.*) You give us in Table II. "the "true revenue of Great Britain and Ireland respec- "tively in 1819-20 and 1892-93," that is corrected, I suppose, by the last correction?—By what has been already laid before Parliament.

1607. Does that include the correction as to tobacco?—No, not about tobacco. We cannot correct the figures back.

1608. Then in Table III. you have given a summary of Table II., and that also does not provide for that correction, does it?—No; it provides for the correction as regards spirits, but it does not provide for the correction as regards tobacco; in fact, I have no figures before me as to that at present; the Customs have made no report to me.

1609. (*Mr. Sexton.*) Nor is the subject in a position for correction; there are several figures in conflict, are there not?—Yes, I believe so.

1610. (*Chairman.*) Then you give us another table, "Table IV., showing the estimated amounts by which "the revenue collected in Ireland has been more or "less than the true revenue of the country"; that is correct up to the present information, is it?—The figures in that particular column, I must explain, are merely taken from a Parliamentary paper, which will be in the hands of members of the Commission almost immediately. Some slight corrections may have to be made to them, but the results will not be materially affected.

1611. (*Mr. Sexton.*) I see in Table III. you do give figures for capitation, with all the adjustments you can make?—Yes.

1612. In the year 1819 the inhabitant of Great Britain paid 3l. 13s., which had fallen in 1893 to 2l. 4s. 6d., a fall of considerably more than one-third. In the year 1819 the inhabitant of Ireland paid 14s. 6d. for imperial taxation, which in 1893 had increased to 1l. 9s., or nearly exactly double?—Yes, you may say exactly double.

1613. (*Chairman.*) Table V. is an adjustment as between collection and credit to the proper country, is it not—true revenue and collected revenue?—Yes.

1614. No remark, I think, arises upon that, does it?—No.

1615. (*Mr. Sexton.*) I should like to know how, between the period from 1853 and the period when you began your recent increase in 1890-91, you adjust in the interval?—That I could hardly explain, because it is very complicated. It is explained in a

Sir E. W. Hamilton, K.C.B.

8 Nov. 1894.

Tests of revenue collected, proportions, and per capita.

True revenue of Great Britain and Ireland.

memorandum which we are going to lay before Parliament in pursuance of an order given by the House of Commons last Session. The memorandum is completed.

1616. Can you include that memorandum amongst our papers?—If you wish, it can be handed in.

1617. (*Chairman.*) Has it been laid before Parliament?—We shall lay it out in the course of a week or 10 days, I hope.

1618. And it will come into the papers, will it?—Yes, and of course we can hand it in as a paper for the Commission as well.

1619. Table V. there is some confusion about, is there not?—Yes, I am afraid so. I have two tables numbered V; I shall have to correct and re-number them.

1620. I will refer to it as Table V. (*b*); that is "Expenditure incurred on local services in Great "Britain and Ireland respectively, in 1819–20 and in "1892–93," showing that the expenditure in Ireland is a good deal beyond its proportion. That is the object of the summary of the table, I suppose?—The object was to show the relative expenditure of the two countries.

1621. The summary of the Table seems to show that there is a higher expenditure on local purposes per head in Ireland than in Great Britain?—Yes. Table VI. shows the calculation per head.

1622. And that is calculated and shows the great increase which has taken place in the expenditure on local purposes in Ireland?—That is so. Table VI. shows the contributions to Imperial expenditure from the two countries.

1623. (*Mr. Sexton.*) It shows that the inhabitant of Great Britain in 1819 paid 3*l.* 8*s.* 4*d.* for Imperial as distinguished from local purposes, and that figure had fallen to 1*l.* 14*s.* 11*d.*, or less than half, in 1893. The inhabitant of Ireland in 1819 paid 16*s.* 10*d.*, which 16*s.* 10*d.* had only fallen to 9*s.*, or only one-fifth, whereas the English contribution had fallen by one-half?—That is so.

1624. (*Chairman.*) Now Table VII. is a return "showing true revenue of Great Britain and Ireland "respectively, in 1892–93, under its principal heads—" "net revenue" in each, its "percentage" in Great Britain and Ireland respectively, and the amount per head of the population. You give the aggregate (I need not take you through each of the items) of revenue as 2*l.* 12*s.* 10*d.* per head of population in Great Britain and 1*l.* 12*s.* 11*d.* per head of population in Ireland, or, excluding what is not taxed revenue, the net taxed revenue is 2*l.* 4*s.* 8*d.* in Great Britain and 1*l.* 8*s.* in Ireland?—Yes.

1625. Those we may take as your final figures, I suppose, carefully corrected?—Yes.

1626. (*Mr. Sexton.*) How is this affected by what Mr. Milner said about the remission before 1888–89; this is for the year 1892–93, is it not?—Yes.

1627. And I suppose the customs exports from Ireland of spirits is included?—The figures which you have before you here in Table VII. include the correction that it was necessary to make with respect to spirit duty.

1628. (*Chairman.*) Then on page 62 you say that "a comparison of the true revenue collected by the "State in one country with that of another appears "to be by itself an incomplete test of the incidence "of fiscal burdens on their respective inhabitants; because a rate levied by a local authority is much a burden on the person liable to pay it as a tax imposed by the Government"; and you think it is "proper that account should be taken of "the relative amounts raised by means of local rates "in Great Britain and Ireland; more especially as "the State bears" the whole charge of the police in Ireland, "while the cost of the British police "mainly constitutes a charge on rates. It is not "possible to separate completely the proceeds of "rates from the proceeds of charges for gas and "water undertakings; but the sums derived from "these charges may be held to be analogous to part "of the revenue collected by Imperial officers." Then you give the figures of the "amount raised "from (1) rates, and (2) gas and water undertakings" in Great Britain as 53,000,000*l.*, or a little more, in Ireland at 3,300,000*l.*, so that the proportion per cent. is 93·29 in Great Britain and 6·71 in Ireland, or 1*l.* 8*s.* 1*d.* per head of population in Great Britain and 13*s.* 1*d.* per head in Ireland?—Yes.

Sir E. W. Hamilton, K.C.B.

4 June 1895.

Incidence of taxation.

1629. (*Mr. Sexton.*) Do you include those payments by persons to private gas and water companies even where the gas and water is not in the hands of the local authorities?—No, it is only when they are in the hands of the local authorities.

1630. It is not correct to say, is it, that the entire cost of the Metropolitan Police is borne by the State; about one-third of it is borne by local taxation, is it not; the vote is for the net cost, is it not?—Yes.

1631. There is a deduction of about 150,000*l.* paid out of the local rates?—Yes.

1632. (*Chairman.*) Then you sum up the exchequer and local revenue together to a grand total in Great Britain of 127,[illegible],000*l.*; in Ireland of 10,454,000*l.*, altogether 137,[illegible],000*l.*, or, taking it per head of population, 3*l.* 11*s.* 2*d.* in Great Britain and 2*l.* 3*s.* in Ireland?—Yes.

1633. Then you give the details of the expenditure out of exchequer revenue in Great Britain and Ireland, and you arrive at the grand total of 23,1[illegible],000*l.* in Great Britain, and 5,1[illegible],000*l.* in Ireland. That is the ordinary civil expenditure of the country, I suppose?—Yes.

1634. (*Mr. Sexton.*) I suppose it follows the system suggested in the Financial Relations Papers?—Quite so; it does.

1635. (*Chairman.*) And you then give a "Table "showing the present cost of administering Great "Britain and Ireland respectively," the final line of which shows 1*l.* 11*s.* 9*d.* per head for Great Britain, and 1*l.* 11*s.* 9*d.* for Ireland. Then you give in Table X. the contributions derived from Great Britain and Ireland respectively to Imperial expenditure, and you state that the total expenditure on Imperial services is 62,087,000*l.*, and you divide the contributions of Great Britain and Ireland in this way: the total adjusted revenue expenditure 95,000,000*l.* odd in Great Britain, 7,000,000*l.* odd in Ireland; the total local expenditure 29,000,000*l.* odd in Great Britain, and 5,000,000*l.* odd in Ireland; balance, available for Imperial expenditure, 58,000,000*l.* in Great Britain, and 2,000,000*l.* in Ireland; and you say that that shows a proportion of 96·53 per cent. of contributions for Great Britain, and of 3·47 for Ireland, the contribution per head of the population being 1*l.* 11*s.* 11*d.* in Great Britain, and 9*s.* in Ireland?—Yes.

Contributions to Imperial expenditure.

1636. And you observe that there is a difference to be accounted for between the two accounts of the Imperial services but I do not think I need read those to the Commission; they are not important?—They are not.

1637. You then give certain other tables of comparison: "Property assessed to probate and succession "duties in Great Britain," 163,573,000*l.*, and in Ireland close upon 8,200,000*l.*, giving 95·42 to Great Britain and 4·58 to Ireland?—Yes.

Tests of relative wealth.

1638. You give the net value of property assessed to succession duty as 90·62 per cent. for Great Britain, and 9·38 per cent. for Ireland; and the net value of property, taking the average of two years from March 1891, assessed to probate and succession duties, as 211,000,000*l.* odd for Great Britain, and 12,000,000*l.* odd for Ireland, the actual percentages being 94·33 per cent. for Great Britain, and 5·67 per cent. for Ireland. That is as to property passing at death. Then as to property subject to property and income tax under Schedule A., you give 166,000,000*l.* as the letting value of lands, tenements, and hereditaments in Great Britain, and 12,000,000*l.* in Ireland. I am taking these sums in round figures. Profits

Assessments to death duties and income tax.

[illegible] made by occupiers out of husbandry, under Schedule B., 21,000,000l. for Great Britain, and 2,000,000l. for Ireland. Income derived from Government Stocks, &c., under Schedule C., 30,700,000l. for Great Britain, and 740,000l. in Ireland. Profits derived from trades and professions, under Schedule D., 302,000,000l. from Great Britain, and 9,000,000l. in Ireland, the decimals being 97·04 for Great Britain, and 2·93 in Ireland. Official and other salaries, or pensions, under Schedule E., 35,900,000l. for Great Britain, and 1,780,000l. for Ireland; and then the summary [illegible] this is a figure which of course you have taken great pains to check, have you not?—Yes.

1639. 667,000,000l. for Great Britain, and 30,800,000l. for Ireland, or percentages of 95·47 and 4·53. Do those figures represent, strictly speaking, the property of Great Britain and Ireland?—Yes, that may be said to be so. I may say that those figures are given on the authority of the Inland Revenue Department.

[illegible] 1640. Then going to the head of capital (I will not read it in detail) "the estimated amount of capital in "Great Britain and Ireland respectively in 1885," was 9,490,000,000l., and 447,000,000l. in Ireland, the proportions being 95·55, and 4·45 per cent.?—Yes.

1641. (*Mr. Sexton.*) I notice that in the side head to that table you refer on the estimated amount of capital in Great Britain and Ireland to a work of Mr. Giffen's?—Yes.

1642. What is the date of that book?—It was about 1887 or 1888.

1643. Because I remember distinctly that in his article in the "Nineteenth Century" in March 1886, he put the Irish capital not at 447,000,000l., but at 400,000,000l., and he said that he thought he rather overstated it at 400,000,000l.?—I notice that.

1644. Perhaps you can let us have an extract from the book to support that estimate?—Perhaps the Royal Commission may wish to examine Mr. Giffen himself, but I am not responsible for his figures in any way.

1645. Here it is in the "Nineteenth Century." He puts the capital of the United Kingdom at 9,500,000,000l.; that is about the same figure as you give; and then he says: "I have to refer to Irish "capital later on, and I estimate it at 400,000,000l." So you see my memory was correct?—Yes, but I took these figures because they were more up to date.

1646. He makes a further reference to Irish capital. Later in the article he says: "The whole capital of "Ireland must be inconsiderable, probably not over "400,000,000l., the principal items being value of "land 160,000,000l., houses 60,000,000l., tenants' "capital, 80,000,000l., railways, 36,000,000l., furni-"ture of houses and other movable property, "20,000,000l., and other capital, 44,000,000l., making "a total of 400,000,000l.," and he says that 400,000,000l. is probably over the mark?—Yes. I took this later book of his, because it was much more elaborately worked out, and I thought it was probably the result of longer investigation than he gave in writing the article. I think he explains in his book how he arrives at his figures.

Railway receipts. 1647. (*Chairman.*) Then the next table shows "the "average gross receipts derived from railways in Great "Britain and Ireland respectively, in the years 1891, "1892 and 1893," Great Britain 78,000,000l. and a little more, Ireland 3,000,000l. and a little more, or 96·06 per cent. for Great Britain, and 3·94 per cent. for Ireland?—Yes.

Savings Banks and Post Office. 1648. Then Table XV. gives the amounts with which depositors in savings banks were credited in Great Britain and Ireland: Great Britain 116,000,000l., Ireland 6,000,000l., or roughly 95 per cent. and 5 per cent. relatively. Then comes money orders issued in Great Britain and Ireland in 1893; the amounts are 23,207,000l. for Great Britain, and 1,361,000l. in Ireland, or 94·46 per cent. and 5·54 per cent. respectively?—Yes.

1649. Then postal orders 95·27 per cent. in Great Britain, and 4·73 per cent. in Ireland; and the number of letters, newspapers, book packets, circulars, samples, and post cards delivered by the Post Office in Great Britain and Ireland respectively in 1893–94, 2,633,500,000 in Great Britain and 140,350,000 in Ireland, being a proportion of 94·95 for Great Britain, and 5·05 for Ireland. Then Table XIX. shows the number of telegraph messages, the percentage being 94·38 for Great Britain, and 5·62 for Ireland. The number of paupers is an inverse proportion: 89·71 per cent. in Great Britain, and 10·29 per cent. in Ireland. Then you adopt, I suppose, without being responsible for it, Mr. Leone Levi's estimate of the total income?—I would rather not say "adopt"; I cite the figures; I do not pretend to form an opinion upon them.

1650. That gives the total income per head of the population as 36l. 11s. 10d. in Great Britain and 16l. 15s. 2d. in Ireland, and Mr. Giffen's estimate, which you also print without either adopting or giving any authority to, gives 33l. 7s. 5d. in Great Britain and 14l. 6s. 8d. in Ireland?—Yes.

1651. (*Mr. Sexton.*) I see that both these great authorities agree, so far as income is a standard of taxation, that the capacity of Great Britain is more than double the capacity of Ireland?—That would be the case if you take them as standards. Taxable capacity.

1652. That is, of course, the capacity of an individual Englishman is more than double the capacity of an individual Irishman?—Yes, taking it in that way.

1653. (*Chairman.*) Then you make a few remarks on the general question. You say, "It is quite con-"ceivable that an Irishman with a weekly wage of "only 10s. or 12s. may have a larger margin to spend "as he pleases than an Englishman or Scotchman "with a weekly wage of 18s. The Irishman may be "able to house himself more cheaply. He may have "less to spend on his fuel. His food may be cheaper. "His clothing may cost him less. Therefore the "amount of a man's income is not necessarily a test "of his capacity to bear taxation. Perhaps a better "test of the amount which the taxpayer can afford to "pay for being governed, protected, and educated, is "the residue of income remaining after bare neces-"sities of life have been met." Would you enlarge upon that a little?—Of course all these tests are fallacious to a certain extent, but I thought income by itself was a distinctly misleading test, because, as I say, it does not necessarily represent what a man can afford to pay. Then I made some further calculations for what they are worth, to show what a man does spend, or what he is estimated to spend, both in Great Britain and Ireland, upon what may be considered to be not absolute necessaries of life. I thought, on the whole, that perhaps might be a fairer test of the taxable capacity of the two countries than taking the income of the population. Both calculations must be founded on hypothetical figures.

1654. (*Mr. Sexton.*) Mr. Giffen and all the authorities practically agree that the best basis is the income after you have subtracted from the income what they call a minimum allowance for the cost of the necessaries of life; is not that practically what you do?—I do; but though the figures so far as they are derived from the income tax are trustworthy, I think when you come to make out the earnings of the working classes they are very hypothetical, and I should not like to express any opinion upon them.

1655. (*Chairman.*) You give some illustration of some particular taxes, do you not?—Yes. Further on I give a calculation as to what the individual Irishman and the individual inhabitant of Great Britain is estimated to spend on certain dutiable articles, such as tea, tobacco, spirits, and beer. Perhaps it may shake one's confidence a little in the accuracy of figures, but I find the Irishman spends rather more in tea per head of population than does the inhabitant of Great Britain. Consumption of dutiable articles.

I 2

Sir E. W. Hamilton, K.C.B.

6 Nov. 1894.

Consumption of dutiable articles.

1656. 11s. 10d. for the Irishman you give, and 10s. 1d. for the Englishman?—Yes.

1657. (*Mr. Sexton.*) I think the Customs witnesses here do not cast doubt on that conclusion, do they?—No, I do not think they do; and I have heard it confirmed by outside authority. They think on the whole that the Irishman consumes more tea per head of the population than does the inhabitant of Great Britain.

1658. (*Chairman.*) And not nearly so much tobacco?—According to these tables I make it more, but I expect after the adjustments it would probably come out about the same.

1659. And you give a similar calculation as to spirits and beer with a different result. However, I will not question you about those figures?—The calculation is given with great diffidence.

1660. (*Mr. Sexton.*) Can you state shortly the results as to spirits and beer?—As regards spirits, I make out—the Commission will understand I am speaking now of the estimated amount spent per head of the population in Great Britain and Ireland upon spirits and beer—that in Great Britain the inhabitant would spend 1*l.* 9*s.* on spirits, whereas in Ireland he would spend 1*l.* 6*s.* 6*d.* In beer, of course, the difference is very material. I make out that the inhabitant of Great Britain would spend 2*l.* 12*s.* in beer, whereas in Ireland he would only spend 1*l.* 7*s.* 2*d.* If I bring these figures together, that is to say, all the alcoholic drinks, I make out that the inhabitant of Great Britain would spend 4*l.* 2*s.* in his drink, and the inhabitant of Ireland 2*l.* 12*s.* 8*d.*

1661. (*Chairman.*) That is drink only, is it?—It is drink only I am speaking of. Then I add up all these dutiable articles, and I make out that the inhabitant of Great Britain would spend on those articles, including tea, tobacco and alcoholic drinks, 5*l.* 4*s.* 8*d.*, and the inhabitant of Ireland 4*l.* 0*s.* 1*d.*

1662. (*Mr. Sexton.*) According to Mr. Giffen the 4*l.* which the inhabitant of Ireland spends comes out of a total income of 14*l.*, and the 5*l.* which the inhabitant of Great Britain spends comes out of a total income of 35*l.*; is not that so?—Yes.

1663. In the case of Ireland, this particular expenditure would be about one-third of the income, and in the case of Great Britain it would only be one-eighth?—That is so.

Public Loans.

1664. (*Chairman.*) Then you have a table here of public loans in Great Britain and Ireland in which you give the balance outstanding on the 31st March 1893?—I think that might be misleading; the simplest way of stating it is this: Amount advanced in Great Britain from the commencement of the loan system 67,000,000*l.*, and 42,000,000*l.* in Ireland. In Great Britain there has been repaid nearly 41,000,000*l.*, in Ireland a little over 20,000,000. There has been remitted a little over 1,000,000*l.* in Great Britain and 10,700,000*l.* in Ireland.

1665. (*Mr. Sexton.*) Chiefly in connexion with the famine?—A large portion, no doubt, is in connexion with the famine.

1666. (*Mr. Martin.*) Does that include the 4,000,000 which were remitted by Mr. Gladstone?—Yes; 4,000,000 were remitted by Mr. Gladstone in the year 1853. That was incurred in connexion with the famine.

Sir E. W. Hamilton, K.C.B.

6 Nov. 1894.

Summary.

1667. (*Chairman.*) Then finally in Table XXVIII. you give a summary which is so valuable that perhaps you would not mind reading it in detail?—Of course I give these simply as tests for what they are worth, and I have summarised them like this: Of property assessed to death duties in Great Britain, the percentage is 94·33, and Ireland, 5·67; of property assessed to income tax on the average of three years 95·45 Great Britain, 4·55 in Ireland; estimated amount of capital (this figure refers to 1885, which is the latest figure I have) 95·55 in Great Britain and 4·45 in Ireland; gross railway receipts on the average for the last three years, 96·06 in Great Britain, 3·94 in Ireland; savings banks deposits (31st December 1893) 94·93 in Great Britain, 5·07 in Ireland; amount of money orders issued (1893), 96·46 in Great Britain, 3·54 in Ireland; amount of postal orders issued (1893), 95·27 in Great Britain, 4·73 in Ireland; number of letters, &c., delivered by Post Office (1893–4), 94·07 in Great Britain, 5·93 in Ireland; number of telegrams forwarded (1893–94), 94·38 in Great Britain, 5·62 in Ireland; number of paupers relieved, 89·71 in Great Britain, 10·29 in Ireland. Then the estimated total income, according to Mr. Leone Levi in 1882–3, was 92·85 in Great Britain, 7·15 in Ireland; and, according to Mr. Giffen's estimate relating to the same period, it was 94·33 in Great Britain, and 5·67 in Ireland. Then I estimate the expenditure on dutiable articles. Tea in Great Britain, 86, in Ireland, 14; tobacco in Great Britain, 86·20, in Ireland, 13·80; spirits, 88·77 in Great Britain, 11·23 in Ireland; beer, 93·97 in Great Britain, 6·03 in Ireland. The total of such expenditure so estimated is 90·42 in Great Britain, and 9·58 in Ireland.

1668. (*Mr. Sexton.*) These estimates refer to the price of the article, not the duty, do they not?—This is what I calculate to be the amounts expended on dutiable articles of consumption. I give the basis of my calculations in the memorandum.

1669. (*Chairman.*) Now give us the population?—The population, taking the middle of 1894, is 87·83 in Great Britain, 12·17 in Ireland, and as regards the true taxation, that is the taxation after the adjustments have been made, the figures are: indirect taxes 88·18 in Great Britain, 11·82 in Ireland; direct taxes 95·90 in Great Britain and 4·10 in Ireland; total taxes 91·74 in Great Britain, 8·26 in Ireland; and the contribution to imperial expenditure for 1892–93 was upon these figures estimated to be 90·43 in Great Britain and 2·47 in Ireland.

1670. (*Chairman.*) Until we have the complete returns which are promised us by the Treasury we will not further examine you?—I should hope to be able to let you have them in a tolerably complete form by certainly the time of the meeting of Parliament. I daresay I could give you part of them before.

1671. (*Mr. Sexton.*) Perhaps each separate return might be circulated without waiting for the others?—Certainly.

The witness withdrew.

Adjourned.

FIFTH DAY.

Wednesday, 5th December, 1894.

At the Benchers' Chambers, Four Courts, Dublin.

PRESENT:

THE RIGHT HON. HUGH C. E. CHILDERS, *Chairman*.

LORD WELBY.	CHARLES E. MARTIN, Esq.
THE RIGHT HON. THE O'CONOR DON.	THOMAS SEXTON, Esq., M.P.
SIR DAVID BARBOUR, K.C.S.I.	GUSTAV W. WOLFF, Esq., M.P.

Mr. R. H. HOLLAND, *Secretary*.

Mr. HENRY A. ROBINSON called in, and examined.

1672. (*Chairman.*) Would you be good enough to give us the nature of your office?—I am a Commissioner of the Local Government Board for Ireland.

1673. I propose to ask you some general questions as to local taxation in Ireland first, and then to go to the points which you will deal with bearing upon our present Inquiry. In the first place would you explain to us the objects to which local taxation is applied in Ireland?—The chief branches of local taxation are the Grand Jury Cess, the Poor Rates, and the taxes levied by Municipal Authorities. The Grand Jury Cess is applied to roads and bridges, to the erection and repairs of Court and Sessions houses, Salaries of County Officers, Annuities of Superannuated Prison Officers, Contributions to Infirmaries, Hospitals, &c.; Maintenance of Lunatic Asylums, Extra Police, Valuation, and various other heads of expenditure. This tax is not likely to increase very much, and has not increased very much during the last ten years. The Poor Rate is applied to the maintenance of the poor in workhouses, out-door relief, the maintenance of poor persons in institutions for the Blind and Deaf and Dumb, and in extern hospitals, emigration expenses, expenses under the Medical Charities Act and the Vaccination Acts, the Registration of Births, Deaths, and Marriages, for Sanitary purposes, and for Burial Ground Expenses, Expenses under the Superannuation Acts, Labourers Acts, Contagious Diseases (Animals) Act, the National School Teachers Act, and the Parliamentary Franchise, the Jurors, Explosives and other Acts. I think we must look for an increase in the poor-rate because the tendency of recent years in connection with remedial legislation is to place its administration on the poor rates. During the last four or five years a great many Acts of Parliament have been passed, and the cost of the administration of these to a great extent has been placed on the poor rates. A very important one of these was the Labourers Act. Municipal taxation is applied to the general improvement of towns, paving of streets, cleansing, watering, lighting, supplying water, sewerage, and other similar matters. Then there are also tolls, fees, and dues levied by harbour commissioners, which are applied to harbour purposes, such as maintenance of the harbours, the improvement and repairs of lighthouses, providing floating lights, buoys, beacons, &c., the payment of rents, taxes, &c. There is also a tax for the Dublin Metropolitan Police which is eightpence in the pound in the Metropolitan District. The other taxes are Petty Sessions Stamps and Crown Fines, the Dogs Licence Duty, Fees of Clerks of the Peace and Clerks of the Crown, certain tolls in respect of inland navigations, and light dues and fees under the Merchant Shipping Act.

1674. You are able to put in a table showing the expenditure during a series of years, are you not?—Yes, the gross amount of expenditure from Grand Jury Cess presented for in 1893, was 1,488,815*l*., and it has not varied very much during several years. In 1881 the amount was 1,348,584*l*.

1675. And you give us in the table the details of the application of these monies?—Yes, for one particular year. Maintenance of roads and bridges for last year came to 751,858*l*., and that is the principal charge on the county cess. The cost for erection and repairs of courthouses was not so high, being only 7,344*l*. Salaries of county officers is a large item, 103,573*l*. Prison expenses (which consists of assessing to Bridewell keepers and other persons, and various other small matters) amounts to 13,117*l*. The contributions to infirmaries and hospitals increased during the last ten years, amounting to 80,778*l*. in 1893. Maintenance of lunatic asylums has increased from 114,586*l*. in 1884 to 157,164*l*. in 1893. Lunacy, I believe, is on the increase, and better accommodation is required for lunatics at the present day. The Imperial Exchequer contributes a good deal towards the maintenance of lunatics at the present time, viz., four shillings per head per week where the cost exceeds eight shillings, under certain conditions. Then the cost of extra police amounted to 37,348*l*.

1676. The cost for extra police is a falling charge, is it not?—Yes, it has fallen from 52,814*l*. in 1884 to 37,348*l*. in 1893. Then valuation is a fixed sum of 5,000*l*. a year paid by the counties. The payment of debts incurred under the Relief of Distress and other Acts, came to 81,786*l*. in 1893, and there is a charge of 3,343*l*. to the police for weights and measures. The Grand Juries are the local authorities to consider under the Weights and Measures Act, 1878, and the police are inspectors. Then unclassified expenditure has increased very much, from 148,114*l*. in 1884 to 234,043*l*. in 1893. I think the cause of the increase under this head is principally owing to the new Parliamentary franchise which has entailed heavy duties on Clerks of the Peace and other officers, but the jurors' expenses, the cost of collection of the cess, compensation for malicious injuries, and various other items are included in this amount. These are all the heads of outlay in connection with county cess.

1677. Altogether coming to about a million and a half, and slightly increasing?—Yes.

Mr. Henry A. Robinson.

8 Dec. 1894.

Poor Law Relief.

1678. Not very much?—Not very much.

1679. Then you can also put in a table, I think, showing to what extent local revenue is derived from rates, and to what extent from other sources, over that period of ten years?—Yes, the expenditure by Boards of Guardians in the year 1893 amounted to 1,397,032l., but after excluding the portion thereof defrayed from loans, and deducting the probate duty grant and other Parliamentary grants, the net expenditure falling on the poor rate amounted to 1,028,122l. The cost of in-maintenance in the workhouses in 1893 amounted to 302,036l., and the table which I have handed in shows that the outlay under this head is not increasing, and has not increased during the past ten years. One reason for that, I think, is that the cost of provisions has gone down very much, and that contracts for workhouses can probably be obtained on more favourable terms than ten years ago.

1680. (*The O'Conor Don.*) The numbers have not diminished, have they?—The numbers have rather diminished. On out-door relief the expenses have rather increased during the past ten years; they have gone up by nearly eight thousand pounds. The expense now for out-door relief is 158,566l. The cost of maintenance of poor people in institutions has also rather increased, I do not think because more are sent there but because the charges made by those institutions have slightly increased. The cost at present to the Poor Rates for that is 15,387l. Emigration expenses have gone down very much.

[illegible]

1681. (*Chairman.*) Why is that?—In 1884 the return was 14,921l., and last year it was 178l. only. In 1884 a great deal was done in the way of State aided emigration.

1682. (*The O'Conor Don.*) Are these figures families who emigrated or individuals?—Those figures are pounds which emigration has cost.

1683. (*Mr. Wolff.*) Have you the numbers of individuals?—I can get them. During 1884 a large sum was provided by the State for emigration, so it is not quite fair to take that as a criterion of the ordinary expense of emigration at that period. But taking the amount in the following year, viz., 1,377l., I think that gives what the average was in the way of assistance in an ordinary year from the Poor Rates. Of recent years the American authorities have been far more strict in regard to the admission of immigrants, and they have passed an Act, one of the clauses of which provides that no person who is likely to become a public charge or a pauper should be allowed to land. In those days it was the habit of the Boards of Guardians, if they had people in the workhouses who desired to emigrate to relatives in America, to assist them to do so, and the Local Government Board consented to the proposed expenditure; but now we are prohibited from issuing our consent if the proposed emigrants are paupers. If a person be in a workhouse and it is proposed to send that person out to a relative, perhaps husband, wife, or child, we cannot authorise the expenditure of money for the purpose, it would be a violation of the United States Emigration Act; and for that reason the amount has fallen very low. The next item is salaries and rations of officers, which has increased very much. I think the number of officers has increased in the workhouses. All other poor relief expenses remain very much the same. The expenditure under the Medical Charities Act has increased slightly, but a large portion of that is paid by Government. In fact only one-half the salaries of all medical officers and one-half the cost of medicines in workhouses and dispensaries in Ireland falls on the Poor Rate, the other half is provided for by vote of Parliament. The Registration of Births, Deaths, and Marriages is about 10,000l. a year, and that remains practically stationary. Under the Sanitary Acts the expenditure has increased very much, and in recent years especially. In 1893 it amounted to 80,280l. and in 1884 it was 58,844l. The condition of the people has improved; the sanitation of the country is very much improved, but one reason of the very great increase from 57,000l. in 1892 to 80,280l. in 1893, is no doubt the fact that the cholera scare made local authorities very attentive to sanitary matters. The Burial Grounds Acts cost about 7,000l. a year; and the Superannuation Acts, 14,114l. The cost of the Labourers Acts has increased from 3,992l. in 1884 to 106,015l. in 1893, but the expenditure incurred in the erection of labourers' cottages is defrayed by means of loans obtainable from the Commissioners of Public Works. I think a great deal more remains to be done under those Acts.

1684. (*Mr. Sexton.*) I suppose 1886 was the first year in which the Acts came into operation?—In 1884.

1685. I mean into active operation?—Yes, I should say that there was not very much done before 1886. Then the cost of the Contagious Diseases (Animals) Act was very high in 1884, 34,995l.; that has gone down considerably to 9,210l. The assessment under that Act is the only rate which is not levied on a particular Union in accordance with the requirements of the Union, as it is uniform over the whole of Ireland. The cost of the National School Teachers Act has increased from 12,590l. in ten years to 19,865l. The cost of the Parliamentary Voters and other Acts has increased very much, from 14,327l. in 1884 to 34,298l. in 1893. That is due to the fact that under the new registration of voters the officers of local authorities have very much heavier work, and incur more expense than formerly. The repayment of loans has increased from 26,359l. in 1884 to 87,558l. in 1893. I think, as I said before, that the Poor Rate is likely to be an increasing quantity in consequence of the cost of the administration of nearly all Acts of remedial legislation being placed on the rates; but while the average Poor Rate in a Union might be low owing to the fact that rates are made on Electoral Divisions, the rate on a particular Division might be extremely high and very oppressive.

1686. (*Chairman.*)—Taking the whole of the table the increase is not large, is it?—No, about 100,000l.

1687. Then I will go to the next table, which is "Expenditure of Town Authorities" during the same period.—That is an increasing expenditure. The Town Authorities have done a great deal in the way of improvement of recent years, and they can now get money by the issue of stock, on much better terms than formerly. The total expenditure of the towns was in 1893, 1,362,339l., and in 1884, ten years ago, it was 1,044,582l. The principal increase was under the head of paving and repairs of streets, cleansing, and in the providing of water supply. Making sewers and drains, also shows a considerable increase to 145,149l. in 1893 from 60,328l. in 1884, but a great part of this expenditure is defrayed from loans obtained under the Public Health Act.

1688. The last item but one, payments in respect of borrowed money, includes both interest and repayment of principal, I suppose?—Repayment of interest and principal.

1689. (*Mr. Sexton.*) I suppose the same remark applies to a similar item in the previous return?—Yes, just the same.

1690. (*Chairman.*) Then passing from that to "Expenditure of Harbour and Pier Authorities during the last ten years," what have you to say as to that?—That is not provided for by a tax felt by everybody like the Poor Rate and Grand Jury Cess. It remains very much the same; in fact it is rather less now than it was ten years ago. The amount of expenditure in 1893 by Harbour Authorities was 461,491l.; in 1884 it was 486,301l.

1691. The yearly expenditure on works has fallen off considerably, I think?—Yes, it has.

1692. On the other hand the expenditure in respect of past works, interest, and repayments, has increased?—Yes, it has increased.

1693. Then you put in a return as to the Dublin Metropolitan Police?—Yes, the total cost is about 51,000l.; and, as I have already stated, there is a rate

Mr. Henry A. Robinson, C.B.

4 Dec. 1894.

Dublin Police.

of eight pence in the pound in aid of this expenditure. This is the maximum rate authorised by the Act (1 Vic., cap. 25).

1694. (*Mr. Wolff.*) That is a tax falling only on Dublin, is it not?—On the Dublin Metropolitan Police district which extends considerably beyond the boundaries of the city.

1695. (*Mr. Sexton.*) I suppose it comprises the area served by the force?—Yes, exactly so.

1696. (*Chairman.*) Then there is a small amount, not varying very much, the amount of the Petty Sessions stamps?—Yes, that is a tax which the people contribute to in all parts of Ireland. The amount of Petty Sessions Stamps and Crown Fines in 1893 was 51,571*l.*, and that was applied to the payment of Officers of local courts, the Reward fund for the Police, Cattle Disease account, and to Treasurers of Boroughs, and private parties.

1697. Then there is Dogs Licence Duty?—Dogs Licence Duty has increased somewhat, from 34,065*l.* in 1884, to 40,334*l.* in 1893. A portion of this Duty goes in aid of town rates and a portion in aid of Grand Jury Cess.

1698. (*Chairman.*) Unlike what is the case in Great Britain, it is a local matter entirely, is it not?—I do not quite know how it is arranged in Great Britain.

1699. (*Mr. Wolff.*) It is inland revenue in England.—In Ireland it goes partly in aid of county and town taxation.

1700. (*Mr. Sexton.*) What is done with the Fines and Fees Fund, three-fourths of which is derived from the Dog Licences?—The salaries and retiring allowances of the Clerks of Petty Sessions are charged on the Fund, and to secure them from variation consequent on fluctuation in the amount of fines levied at Petty Sessions and in the sale of stamps, the Registrar of Petty Sessions Clerks is authorised by 44 and 45 Vic., cap. 16, to deduct from the Dog Licence Duty such sum as the Lord Lieutenant may order in any one year, and to add it to the Fund.

1701. (*The O'Conor Don.*) That is the remuneration, is it not, for the Petty Sessions Clerks?—Yes, for their salaries, emoluments, and retiring allowances.

1702. What is the rate of the Dog Tax?—Half-a-crown.

1703. Is not the rate 2*s.*, and sixpence on each separate registration which goes to the Petty Sessions Clerk?—The duty is two shillings for each dog, and there is a sixpenny Petty Sessions stamp affixed to the certificate of registration issued to the owner. Any number of dogs may, however, be included in the certificate.

1704. In each registration sixpence goes to that fund?—The amount transferred to the Petty Sessions Clerks Fund was 16,164*l.* in 1893.

1705. (*Chairman.*) About the same as it was ten years ago?—Yes, practically about the same.

1706. Then you deal with the question of fees and other emoluments received by Clerks of the Peace?—The fees of the Clerks of the Peace and Clerks of the Crown (exclusive of receipts from Grand Jury Cess and from the Imperial taxes), amounted in 1893 to 3,724*l.*

Navigation.

1707. Then the expenditure in connection with inland navigation is very much the same?—About the same, 5,534*l.*; very much the same. Then there are certain Light dues, and fees received under the Merchant Shipping Act, 1854, applied to the purposes of the Mercantile Marine Fund amounting to 19,874*l.* in 1893 against 18,680*l.* in 1884, but these scarcely affect the general tax payer very much.

1708. These tables with which you have now dealt in short, I believe cover the whole ground?—They cover the whole ground.

Sources of income.

1709. Would you be good enough to tell us whether you could put in tables showing to what extent the local revenue is derived from rates, and to what extent from other sources?—Rates on real property amounted in 1893 to 2,952,104*l.*, and I think that comes to about 4*s.* 5*d.* in the pound on the valuation for Ireland; then "Tolls, Fees, Stamps, and Dues" came to 474,035*l.*, and rents and "other receipts" to 271,810*l.*, the total amount being 3,697,949*l.*

Sources of income.

1710. That during the last ten years has been nearly a constant sum, has it not?—Yes, and it represents 5*s.* 3*d.*, I think, on the valuation of Ireland.

1711. (*Mr. Sexton.*) Is the payment from the Imperial taxes shown below part of the total addition?—No, it is deducted.

1712. Then it is part of the total addition?—In the figures I gave, payments from Imperial taxes were not included.

1713. Is it part of the 3,697,000*l.* or is it to be added to it?—It is to be added to it.

1714. Then the total expenditure is 4,000,000*l.*?—Yes, the total receipts applied to expenditure.

Contributions from Imperial taxes.

1715. (*Chairman.*) Can you give us the movement in the amount of contributions from Imperial taxes?—The amount in 1893 received from Imperial taxes was 369,314*l.*, and in 1884, ten years ago, it was 115,035*l.* The principal reason of the increase is the grants under the Probate Duties Act, 1888, which began in 1889.

1716. But that would account apparently for about 100,000*l.*, would it not?—101,000*l.* in the case of Counties alone.

1717. Then there is a considerable increase besides that?—Yes, there is an increase of considerably more than that amount in Towns and Poor Law Unions. In regard to Union Authorities also, I may observe that the whole cost of Workhouse Teachers' Salaries is paid by the Government to Boards of Guardians.

1718. (*The O'Conor Don.*) The whole cost?—All the schoolmasters and schoolmistresses are paid out of the Parliamentary grant; and I also think that the expenditure of Union Authorities on salaries of sanitary officers has rather increased.

1719. (*Chairman.*) For these different reasons the grant from the Imperial Exchequer has increased about a quarter of a million, has it not?—Yes, a quarter of a million roughly speaking.

Local loans.

1720. Can you put in a statement showing the total amount of loans for local purposes raised, paid off or outstanding, and the purposes for which such loans were authorised?—Yes. The amount of loans which were brought into the accounts during the year 1893 was 588,401*l.*, and it has been greatly increasing. In the year 1884, taking Counties, Poor Law Unions, Towns and Harbours, the amount of loans received in that year was 302,602*l.*, and it has been always increasing. The highest was in the year 1890 when the loans amounted to 1,692,078*l.*, but I rather think that that must be due to some very large loan to some Town Authority, probably Dublin.

1721. That was exceptional, was it?—Yes.

1722. (*Mr. Sexton.*) That would be explained, I think, by the payment off that year of the debt due to the Government and the substitution of stock, would it not?—Yes, that is so.

1723. (*Chairman.*) Then it is a mere matter of account?—It is a mere matter of account, but it was brought into the account. Still it is increasing, undoubtedly.

1724. From year to year?—From year to year.

1725. (*The O'Conor Don.*) Do these figures include all loans granted to any authority?—Yes, to Counties, Poor Law Unions, Towns, and Harbours; but they only give the new loans brought into account, they do not take in the total amounts outstanding.

1726. The loans are made by the Board of Works, are they not?—Either by the Board of Works, or they may be borrowed from private sources, or by the issue of stock.

1727. (*Mr. Wolff.*) But supposing that a Harbour Trust borrows from a private bank or corporation in London, would that be included?—Yes, any loan which appears on the face of the accounts furnished to the Local Government Board would appear in this statement.

Mr. Henry A. Robinson, 4 Dec. 1894. Local loans.

1728. (*The O'Conor Don*). Does it include the advances for the guaranteed railways?—Advances to what bodies?

1729. To the promoters?—No, I do not think so, we do not audit the accounts of those at all.

1730. (*Chairman*). Then you put in a table as to the outstanding loans?—Yes, at the close of the financial year, against Boards of Guardians and Town and Harbour Authorities. We have not been able to get the amount against counties outstanding. As to Boards of Guardians there was 1,369,409*l.* outstanding, and of this 1,126,502*l.* was money advanced under the Labourers Acts, and under the Public Health Act there was 235,744*l.* advanced.

1731. Which are the outstanding loans which you say are not included in that amount?—The counties and towns are not included in this particular item.

1732. Have you got any reference as to them?—Yes, as to towns.

1733. How much do they amount to?—I have not got the information for the counties, we were unable to get it, but the total amount due at the close of the financial year in 1893 in respect of loans obtained by town authorities was 4,564,044*l.* The total amount exclusive of counties altogether, but taking in Poor Law Unions, towns, and harbours now outstanding is 8,621,831*l.*

1734. That does not include the counties, you say?—No.

1735. Can you give a rough estimate as to that?—No, I am afraid not; we were unable to get that information in the short time at our disposal, but I will endeavour to obtain it.

1736. (*Mr. Sexton*). Do you mean that you have asked for it and did not get it, or that you have no records?—It is not brought into our audited accounts.

1737. You have not asked the counties for it?—No, we have not asked the counties for it; there was such difficulty in getting the information for this inquiry ready in time that we did not press for it.

1738. (*Chairman*). Do you mean that the counties do not render any statistical account?—The Local Government Board audits the accounts of the counties, but the counties do not bring into each half year's account the amount outstanding of the loans; they only bring in the amount of the interest and principal paid during the half year.

1739. And they do not even give you in the statistics how much the total outstanding loans are?—The information which we are dealing with we endeavoured to get out of our own statistical department, and just as the work was approaching completion we found that we had not got this particular information.

1740. Possibly before we have done our work here you will get it?—I will ask the Treasurers of the Counties to obtain it.

1741. (*The O'Conor Don.*)—Do not the county presentments in each case state the instalment of the loan for which the annual payment is made?—They do, but they do not state what still remains outstanding of the original loan.

1742. But they state that there is so much paid, being, say, the twenty-first instalment for the repayment of a loan of so much, do they not?—They put down the principal and interest of the loan, but they do not give us any more information than that.

1743. It would be very easy, would it not, to calculate how much is remaining if you know how many instalments have been paid, and if you know the sum of the original loan and the amount of each instalment?—If it was done on the annuity system perhaps it would.

1744. Does not each county presentment set out the amount of the annual instalments, the amount of the original loan, and the number of that instalment?—I am not quite sure whether it does or not.

1745. (*Sir David Barbour.*)—How can you completely audit the interest payment unless you know the amount of the loan and the amount of the interest payment?—By the receipt.

Mr. Henry A. Robinson, 4 Dec. 1894. Loans by counties.

1746. The receipt satisfies you, and you do not go into the further question?—I am not sure if the auditors do this or not.

1747. They accept the receipt as sufficient, and take it for granted the local authorities have not paid too much?—I am not very clear about their procedure.

1748. To make a more complete audit it would be necessary to know the amount of loan and the rate of interest, would it not?—Yes; I am not quite familiar with the process.

1749. (*Mr. Sexton.*)—In case you found any improper payment in those accounts have you not power to surcharge?—I think so, except in the case of counties. I am not quite sure with regard to the county—they do not come under our control to the same extent as the Boards of Guardians do. I think if a judge once *fiats* a presentment we cannot surcharge it. If the money had been wrongly applied—if money has been, in the opinion of the auditor, wrongly applied but if it had come before the judge and the presentment had been *fiated*, I do not think the auditor can surcharge.

1750. Does the audit precede the order of the judge or follow it?—I think it follows it.

1751. (*The O'Conor Don*).—Are you sure of that?—I am not at all familiar with it.

1752. I think you will find that it follows it?—I think so.

1753. (*Chairman*)—Evidently you yourself would like to see that gap completed?—Yes.

1754. (*Mr. Sexton*).—The judge deals with the county expenditure, and the account deals with the closed Poor Rate, so that the audit must follow the judicial action?—Yes.

1755. (*Chairman*).—You have also put in a table showing the total advances for certain purposes, such as waterworks and purposes of that kind, coming to rather above two millions. Have you any remark to make upon that?—No, the amount, as you say, for waterworks, sewerage, streets, public baths, and scavenging amounts to 2,158,653*l.*

1756. (*The O'Conor Don*).—Advances to whom?—This was advanced to sanitary authorities.

1757. (*Chairman*).—You can also, I believe, put in a table of the loans sanctioned by the Treasury for the labourers' cottages?—Yes, 1,419,663*l.* Loans for labourers' cottages.

1758. And you divide that between the provinces, do you not?—The amount advanced to Munster was 825,230*l.*; to Leinster, 573,629*l.*; to Connaught, 9,039*l.*; and to Ulster, 11,745*l.*

1759. How is it that two out of the four provinces have had so much larger a sum?—In Connaught the labourers are nearly all small holders of land. That is one reason; they are not *bona fide* labourers, and do not depend on their labour so much as they do in the other places. In Ulster the Boards of Guardians have not adopted the Act to any considerable extent, and an Act has been brought in now to take the power out of their hands and place it in the hands of officials of the Local Government Board.

1760. For Ulster particularly?—For any place where the Labourers Act is not brought into operation.

1761. (*Mr. Sexton*).—You have had that Act some time, have you not?—We have. It was passed in 1891.

1762. Have you acted under it?—Yes.

1763. (*Chairman.*) Then passing from the county authorities to the town authorities, what is the total amount of loans obtained by them outstanding?—The total amount of loans due from the town authorities was 4,564,044*l.* Loans by town authorities.

1764. And of that how much applies to Dublin?—At the close of 1893 the debts of the City of Dublin, including a balance due to the Treasurer, amounted to 1,326,323*l.*, of which 1,055,365*l.* was stock issued under the Act of 1890.

1765. (*Mr. Sexton.*) Dublin and Belfast would be more than half of it, I suppose?—The debts of Belfast amounted to 1,035,059*l.*

1766. (*Chairman.*) Then what is outstanding on the harbour authorities' loans?—2,478,178*l.* The total as I have said before is 8,624,631*l.*

1767. Exclusive of the counties?—Exclusive of the counties.

County Cess.

1768. Then I pass from these more statistical figures to ask you to explain to the Commission the process. What is the mode of assessment to local rates in Ireland?—The Grand Jury Cess is a poundage rate on the valuation, assessed on the occupier according to the barony in which the property occupied is situated. But under the Landlord and Tenant Act of 1870, section 66, it is provided that in the case of tenancies created after the passing of that Act, where the valuation of the property occupied does not exceed 4*l.*, the County Cess shall be payable by the Immediate Lessor. In the same Act provision was made enabling occupiers under any tenancy created after the passing of the Act to make in respect of County Cess, a deduction from rent similar to that allowed in the case of the Poor Rate—viz., one half.

Poor Rate.

1769. Then as to the Poor Rate?—As to the Poor Rate that is a poundage rate on the valuation of the holding assessed, and the occupier and owner share this rate equally when the valuation of the holding is above 4*l.* In cases where the valuation is at or under 4*l.*, the owner pays the whole of it. There are certain exceptions. In the case of houses let in separate tenements, section 10 of the Act of 12 and 13 Victoria, chapter 104, provides that persons receiving rent in respect of hereditaments exempt from rating are liable to be rated in respect of such rent to the extent of one half the poundage rate on the Electoral Division in which the hereditaments are situated. Section 63 of the Act 12 and 13 Victoria, chapter 91, provides that in the City of Dublin the owner of property of which the valuation does not exceed 8*l.*, or which is let to weekly or monthly tenants, or in separate apartments, shall be rated instead of the occupier.

Then all Boards of Guardians are Rural Sanitary Authorities. The Poor Rate is levied on the Electoral Divisions, and there is a separate rate for each Electoral Division, and a certain number of the charges are Union at large charges, and a certain number are Electoral Division charges. Maintenance in a workhouse and out-door relief may be charged to an Electoral Division or to the Union at large according to the chargeability of the person who received the relief.

1770. One question as to the Electoral Divisions; would these remain the same?—Yes, the Electoral Divisions will remain the same. They were originally I believe, made to be as far as possible coterminous with the properties, so that each property should contribute as far as possible towards the maintenance of its own poor.

1771. But whatever other changes have been made the Electoral Divisions are constant, are they?—Yes, there have been a few small changes made with a view to bringing Electoral Divisions wholly in the same county, but as a rule Electoral Divisions have remained the same since the original Poor Law.

1772. (*The O'Conor Don.*) The Unions are not coterminous with counties, are they?—No, but an electoral division cannot extend into two counties.

Other Rates.

1773. (*Chairman.*) Then as to the Municipal rate?—Before leaving the Unions I should state that there are other rates which fall upon electoral divisions which would tend to bring up the charge on electoral divisions considerably higher than the average rate over the entire Union. The charge under the Labourers Acts may be an electoral division charge or it may be a charge in any area which the Board of Guardians can fix. Then there is the Medical Charities and Dispensary Houses Acts—the expenditure under these is charged to a certain number of electoral divisions which together are formed into a Dispensary district, and the sanitary expenses may be levied on a special area, or over the Union at large, as the local authority may fix. Other charges, with a few exceptions, are placed on the Union at large; but, nevertheless, these particular charges may be sufficiently high to render the poor rate in a particular division oppressive.

Mr. Henry A. Robinson, 3 Dec. 1894. Other Rates.

1774. Is the tendency of legislation to move to the Union generally or not?—Yes, I think it is. The last Act on the subject, the Poor Law Rating Act of 1876, was in that direction.

1775. And there is nothing more recent than the Act of 1876?—No, nothing more.

Municipal Rate.

1776. Then would you go to the Municipal rate?—The Municipal rate is levied generally upon the occupier; it is a poundage rate on the valuation. The towns are constituted under four enactments: there is the 3 and 4 Victoria, chapter 108, the Municipal Corporations Act, 9 George IV., chapter 82, 17 and 18 Victoria, chapter 103, and there are besides special Acts for certain towns. Under the Municipal Corporations Act the rate is levied on the owners, occupiers, or tenants of hereditaments situated therein, subject to the provisos contained in the Section with regard to hereditaments under the value of 5*l.* Section 10 of the Act 3 and 4 Victoria, chapter 108, directs that the maximum Borough rate in any Borough shall be one shilling in the pound, and, except in certain cases specified in the Section, it limits the Borough rate in Boroughs in which the Act 9 George IV., chapter 82, is in force to three pence, subject to the provisos contained in the Section. In the case of towns under the Act 9 George IV., chapter 82, the rate is levied off the owners, occupiers, or tenants of property within the town, and for the purposes of the rate, the property is classified as follows:—(*a*) Tenements valued at 5*l.* and under 10*l.*; (*b*) Tenements valued at 10*l.* and under 20*l.*; (*c*) Tenements valued at 20*l.* and upwards. In the case of (*a*) the rate cannot exceed 6*d.* in the pound. In the case of (*b*) the rate cannot exceed 9*d.* in the pound. In the case of (*c*) the rate cannot exceed 1*s.* in the pound, and premises under 5*l.* are exempt from rating under the Act. In towns under the Towns Improvement Act (17 and 18 Victoria, chapter 103) the rate under that Act is made on the occupier where the valuation of the property occupied exceeds 4*l.*, and, except in certain cases, on the Immediate Lessor when it does not exceed that amount. The rate is limited to 1*s.* 6*d.* in some cases, and 1*s.* in others. Where the clauses with respect to water have been adopted the 1*s.* 6*d.* rate is levied, and where they have not been adopted the 1*s.* rate. A large number of the governing bodies of towns are also urban sanitary authorities, and there is no limit to the rate which may be imposed under the Public Health Act. Then there are expenses incurred under the Housing of the Working Classes Act, and various others.

1777. How are they defrayed?—Under the Housing of the Working Classes Act they come out of the rates of the local authority; but Section 24 of the Act removes for the purpose of Part I. of the Act which deals with unhealthy areas, any limit in respect of the local rates; and Section 43 also removes the limit for Part II. of the Act which deals with unhealthy dwelling-houses; these remove the limits on the local rates; so that practically under these Acts the administering authorities may levy any rate.

1778. Then as between leaseholders, owners, and occupiers, is there anything remarkable?—No; there is no distinction made between landlords and occupiers, and it is generally a matter of arrangement between them.

Difficulties in levying rates in poor districts.

1779. Is there any general difficulty found in regard to these rates?—No; not any general difficulty, but in the poorer Unions all round the western seaboard there is found considerable difficulty in levying rates there, and of course the County Cess is sometimes very oppressive. Now, in the County of Kerry the County Cess is extremely high. The average in the County of Kerry for the five years ended in 1893

Mr. Henry A. Robinson.

5 Dec. 1894.

Differences in levying rates in some districts.

was in the Barony of Clanmaurice 6s. 1½d. in the pound, which is very heavy. Now in Corkaguiny it was 6s. 4d. in the pound.

1780. (*The O'Conor Don.*) Have they any guaranteed railway there?—Yes; but the guarantee rate is not in any case levied over the entire area of a barony. Dunkerron, North, was 4s. 6d. in the pound, and Dunkerron, South, 4s. 1d.; Glanarought, 4s. 9d.; Iraghticonnor, 4s. 3d.; Iveragh, 5s. 5d.; Magunihy, 3s. 10d.; and Trughanacmy, 4s. 9d.; those were the average.

1781. (*Mr. Sexton.*) They have two guaranteed railways there, have they not?—I think three.

1782. Which have imposed a heavy charge?—The heaviest rate was 1s. 6d., which was assessed in 1893 on a portion of Glanarought and South Dunkerron Baronies, and the lowest 2d., which was levied in a portion of Magunihy in 1892.

1783. And there was also the compensation in the fatal accident case on the Tralee line which fell on the cess-payers?—I do not think that that occurred during the years for which these figures are averages.

1784. (*The O'Conor Don.*) Would not that necessarily raise the average?—Yes, it might of course, but I think it has been rather a stationary quantity.

1785. (*Lord Welby.*) Could you tell us what amount of that rate was due to the light railways?—The averages I have given do not include the rate for these railways as it is not assessed on the whole of a barony in any case.

1786. (*Mr. Sexton.*) In some Baronies it was certainly the greater part of the whole rate?—It did not exceed 1s. 6d. in any of the five years ended in 1893. In the Barony of Corkaguiny the County Cess was 5s. 11d. in 1889; 6s. 5d. in 1890; 6s. 3d. in 1891; 6s. 9d. in 1892; 5s. 1d. in 1893, and the average is 6s. 4d. I am not quite sure of the year when the accident took place.

1787. About three years ago, I think?—The County Cess was very high even before that.

1788. What would be the Poor Rate in those places?—Of course the Board of Guardians might not strike what was necessary, but if you take what the poundage of the total charge on the Poor Rate was on the valuation that will tell you what it ought to come to. In Dingle Union it was in 1890, 3s. 5d.; in 1891, 3s. 4d.; in 1892, 3s. 4½d.; in 1893, 3s. 5½d.

1789. Will you give us one year for each of the baronies?—It is not levied by baronies. It was up very high in Dingle, to 3s. 10d. in 1890; 3s. 10d., 1891; 3s. 10d. in 1892, and in 1893 it was a very high rate, and of course, in some particular divisions, it was higher. Take the case of an occupier of a holding valued at about 7l. a year paying 7l. in rent. If his tenancy was created prior to the passing of the Landlord and Tenant Act in 1870 he would have to pay in addition to his rent 42s. for the county cess and half of the poor rate, which came to say about 14s., so that for rates he might be paying about 2l. 16s.

1790. Then it would appear that in Kerry the small occupier first pays his rent, then he pays perhaps a sum approximating to 10s. in the pound on his land for these local rates before he begins to pay any Imperial taxation?—Not quite 10s. in the pound, because you must take off half the poor rate, you see, but you might very safely say he would have to pay 8s. in the pound before contributing to any other taxation.

1791. Can you say in what division and what year the poor rate ran highest?—The poor rate ran highest in those distressed districts in 1886, because there was a very large amount of out-door relief given there, and the rate which would have been necessary ran up to 11s. or 12s. In that year the rates in the Electoral Divisions of Clifden Union were 5s. 3d., 4s. 11d., 6s. 11d., 6s. 10d., 7s. 5d., 5s. 11d., 4s. 3d., 6s. 3d., 5s. 4d., 7s. 6d. 8s., 6s., &c.

1792. You see in cases like those arising concurrently with such a charge as that you have described would give a charge of 10s. on the occupier, would they not?—Certainly, they would in a particularly bad year like that.

1793. (*Mr. Wolff.*) When you say a particularly bad year like that, and the rates go up like that, what percentage of them gets collected?—In taking these unions where the rates are very high, taking for example a union like the Belmullet Union (where they strike very high rates), out of 3,519 occupiers, 3,068 are under 4l., so that the landlords there pay nearly all the rates, and in a bad year when the rents are not coming in very well it is extremely difficult to levy the rates, you have to proceed against them in the superior court. Very often cattle are not saleable and if you go to the land it is very doubtful whether you recover.

1794. (*Chairman.*) Do you mean cases arise in which the works have to be foregone in consequence of the difficulty in raising the rates?—I think in all these poor unions round the west coast the Local Government Inspectors have always felt that they were bound as far as possible to discourage these Boards of Guardians from acquiring loans for sanitary and other purposes: they felt they could hardly recommend them to the Treasury when they knew that the Guardians would not be able to discharge them.

1795. Do you think to any considerable extent necessary works have been foregone or abandoned for that reason?—In these few unions on the west coast I think undoubtedly sanitary improvements have been more or less at a standstill owing to the oppressively high rates they have.

1796. (*Sir David Barbour.*) Because the people cannot pay for them?—Because the Guardians cannot pay for them without unduly burdening the taxpayer.

1797. (*Mr. Sexton.*) Would you forbid a necessary sanitary work upon an apprehension of that kind?—No, I do not think we would. Certainly we would not refuse to sanction a loan if we thought the public health and the safety of the people demanded it. The Board of Works, of course, only look into the financial ability of the people to pay, and they might not grant it although we might recommend it.

1798. (*Lord Welby.*) I think several loans of that kind have been granted in consequence of the Local Government Board pointing out the necessity of the work?—Yes; if we ever pointed that out I am sure they would give way, but we ourselves have been obliged to refuse to sanction loans.

1799. (*Sir David Barbour.*) But if these unions do not pay their way, in the long run what happens—do they always pay in the long run?—No, they do not.

1800. Then what happens?—They get deeper and deeper into debt. The history of these unions in the last ten years is a very curious one. Since 1879 they have had periodical relief under the Distress Acts, and have been assisted by grants from the Imperial Government.

1801. (*Mr. Sexton.*) They get no grants, do they?—They have got grants to pay off their debts in some few cases.

1802. (*Chairman.*) What is the extreme remedy when the district gets into an impossible state of raising their liabilities?—I wish I could see it.

1803. Is there any remedy by law—any extreme remedy?—Do you mean if a union gets so hopelessly embarrassed that it cannot go on? That has occurred, and the Board of Guardians have been superseded and paid officers appointed.

1804. There is such a remedy, is there?—Yes; if affairs come to a dead-lock and the financial state of those unions is such that no one will advance money for the relief of the people, and no money is forthcoming for out-door relief in a bad season, under such circumstances the Local Government Board may dissolve the Board and appoint paid officers.

1805. Has that been done?—Very frequently.

1806. (*Sir David Barbour.*) But how do you get money even in that case if the people are not able to pay?—The paid officers who are appointed collect the

Mr. Henry A. Robinson.

4 Dec. 1894.

Difficulties in levying rates in certain districts.

rates much better. They insist upon the collection of the rates, and they are probably more economical in that way than the Guardians are as a rule, and in a few cases they have got grants to assist the unions.

1807. (*Lord Welby.*) Can you tell us in the case of Belmullet the amount of arrears of rates in any recent year. You spoke of Belmullet as a very high rated union in which the larger number of holdings were under £4, and in that case you said the burdens fell upon the landlord, but in bad times when rents were badly paid that led to a great difficulty, and I want to know if you can give us any idea of the amount of arrear that had accrued in such a union as that?—The amount of the debt outstanding at the present time?

1808. Yes. I want to find out to what extent arrears in such a case as that accumulate?—I have not got at present a return of the indebtedness of these unions at the end of the financial year, but I can get it with very little difficulty. I can show you what the financial position of these unions was on the 29th of September, but I have not got the information with me now.

1809. (*The O'Conor Don.*) Could you give us a return of the amount of grants made to these unions?—Yes. I have here a return showing the poundage on total expenditure in most of these distressed unions from 1880 to 1893, which I can hand in.

1810. (*Chairman.*) Will you put that in as one of your returns?—Yes. I shall be able to give a return showing the indebtedness of all these distressed unions at the conclusion of the financial year.

1811. (*Mr. Sexton.*) When you supersede a Board and send down Vice-Guardians they are paid out of the local rates are they not?—Yes, and notwithstanding that they have generally managed to make a better collection of the rate, and to leave the union in a good financial position when they go away.

1812. (*Mr. Martin.*) Are Vice-Guardians permitted to incur debts to their bankers, say?—They may do everything but give money for emigration purposes.

1813. The ordinary Guardians are not allowed to incur debts to their bankers are they?—Oh, yes; the greater part of these unions, or the principal part, were indebted to their bankers, but they are not allowed to pay interest on over-drafts for current expenditure; they may pay interest to the treasurers for loans for any sanitary purposes, or for any purposes for which they are authorised to contract loans, but not for meeting the ordinary every-day expenditure of the unions.

1814. (*Sir David Barbour.*) I suppose they cannot contract a loan without sanction?—No.

1815. (*Mr Martin.*) But they may over-draw their account?—Yes.

1816. (*Sir David Barbour.*) Would they be allowed to over-draw their account without sanction?—Oh, yes, they do.

1817. (*Mr. Wolff.*) What guarantee would a banker have in giving them an overdraft?—Well, he has got the rates.

1818. (*Chairman.*) He does not like to lose the account, I suppose?—I suppose that is so. There is a good deal of competition in all these towns and they like to have the Union account.

1819. (*Sir David Barbour.*) And I suppose it is quite certain that in the long run the money will be paid from some source?—Yes, in some cases that have come under my notice the workhouse has been seized by the creditors in recent years, and the Local Government Board have sent down an inspector who has bought the furniture up on their account.

1820. (*Chairman.*) Has that been a reason for superseding the Board of Guardians and substituting paid Guardians?—Not in itself; it might be a reason, but I do not know whether it happened to be a reason in those particular cases. But certainly at Belmullet and Swinford, and at Westport, Clifden, and Oughterard workhouses, the furniture and fixtures were seized.

1821. (*Sir David Barbour.*) No doubt the Board of Guardians would not be superseded unless there was some fault on their part?—They should not be.

Mr. Henry A. Robinson.

4 Dec. 1894.

Difficulties in levying rates in certain districts.

1822. (*Mr. Sexton.*) In a union like Swinford or any of those unions where the occupiers are under £4 and the bulk of the rates are paid by the landlords, this state of things which you have described might arise from default of the landlords in paying the rates, might it not?—Yes, and there is much more difficulty in getting the rates from the landlords than from the tenants on the land sometimes, because the landlords are very hard up. Some of the properties are in Chancery and the rents behindhand, and it is altogether extremely difficult; but of course these cases round the west coast are exceptional and do not apply to the whole of Ireland.

1823. (*The O'Conor Don.*) Are the rates in these cases under 4*l.* a charge on the land?—They are a charge on the land if you fail to get them from the immediate lessor. You can proceed against the occupier, and he is then enabled to deduct the whole of the rates from the rent when he pays it, but the Board of Guardians do not like taking that step.

1824. Do not the Boards of Guardians shrink from taking that step, as a rule?—Yes, they do.

1825. And is not there very great trouble in carrying that course out under the present law?—It is, because the tenants have not been in the habit of paying it, and they do not understand being suddenly called upon to pay taxes which it has not been their practice to pay.

Claims of very high rates.

1826. (*Chairman.*) Do you receive at the Local Government Board many complaints from particular districts as to the excessive rates?—Yes, the Boards of Guardians complain very much. Often when they consider estimates for rates they say they are too high, and cut them down as far as they possibly can; but that generally leads to a higher rate having to be levied the following year, and we always endeavour in a good year to induce the Guardians to levy a rate sufficient for the expenditure of the Union.

1827. Are the complaints from the Boards of Guardians or from individuals?—From both.

1828. Do you get many complaints from individuals?—I think the Boards of Guardians generally represent the views of their constituents, and the complaints we hear are generally made through the Guardians themselves at the Board rooms.

1829. If there is a very strong complaint do you send an inspector down?—No, it is not necessary; because, when the clerk to the Guardians prepares an estimate of the rate which will be necessary to carry on the union for the financial year, the estimate is sent to the Local Government Board, it is checked by the Local Government Board, and, if they see that it is too high or too low, they write and inform the Guardians; but if, on the other hand, it appeared to be correctly and carefully prepared, they would be able to answer any complaints which were made to them by the people.

1830. At the time then the complaints are made, generally the rate has just been struck or is being struck?—Yes, about that time. We have received memorials from time to time complaining about the rates, and the collectors have often informed us that in these poor districts they have experienced great difficulty in levying the rates from the occupiers. Of course there are occasions when there may be in some of these districts a variety of other taxes. For instance, I remember in my time, when I was an Inspector of the Local Government Board, the rates in the Belmullet electoral division being 13s. 5d. in the pound.

1831. (*Lord Welby.*) About what year was that?—That was about 1885. For instance, there was a poor rate coming to 3s. 6d.; there was a sewerage rate of 6d.; there was a waterworks rate of 9d.; there was a county cess of 4s. 2d.; and there was the injury to Mr. Carter, which was 3s. in the pound; and a road rate 2s. 6d. Of course a road rate is more a payment for value received; and in addition there were some small sums for malicious injuries; but altogether the

Mr. Henry A. Robinson, C.B.

6 Dec. 1894.

Cases of very high rates.

amount which was collected from the ratepayers at that time was 13s. 5d., that was in 1883.

1832. (*Chairman.*) Was that about the worst case you know of?—That is the highest rate I have known to be collected.

1833. The highest rate since the Famine, I suppose?—Yes.

1834. (*Lord Welby.*) Did that seed rate apply to many of the Unions which you have been mentioning?—That was the seed rate of 1880, and nearly all the Unions participated in that. I may say that the poor rate which was levied in that year was not sufficient to meet the requirements, but having regard to the very high taxation from other sources the Guardians reduced it, but it ought to have been 2s. higher; so what they ought to have levied in that year was 15s. 5d. in the pound.

1835. (*Mr. Wolff.*) Was that paid?—Yes, the 13s. 5d. was paid.

1836. (*Lord Welby.*) What would be the rates at the present time in Belmullet as compared with that figure?—Belmullet has improved; of late years they have become more economical.

1837. (*Mr. Sexton.*) A good deal of that 13s. 5d., the county cess and the compensation in Carter's case would fall upon the occupier, would it not?—All but 3s. 5d.

1838. No matter how small the occupation was?—No.

1839. Ten shillings in the pound fell upon the occupier, even the 4l. man?—Yes, nearly 10s. in the pound.

1840. Did they manage to pay it?—They did—they did indeed. I was asked what the estimate of rates was for Belmullet, they vary from 3s. 2d. in the pound to 2s. 11d. in the pound, 4s. 6d. on some divisions; 1s. 8d. was the lowest I found.

1841. (*Lord Welby.*) You do not mean to put the 1s. 8d. in recent years as against the 10s. 8d. in that very bad year, do you?—I am only giving the poor rate, 1s. 8d. as against 3s. 5d.

1842. Can you give us what the total would be as compared with the 13s. 5d.?—No, I am afraid I have not got the barony cess at the present time, but I believe it to be about 3s. 6s. in the pound, it is very high there.

1843. Looking at the seed rate which has practically ceased, and the compensation to Carter, and the fall in poor rate, it would probably bring the poor rate down about half, would it not?—No; a 3s. 5d. poor rate is a low rate.

1844. I thought you said just now it had fallen to 1s. 8d.?—Only in one particular division, that was the average rates: now the rates in Belmullet are as follows:—In one division it is 3s., the next division 2s. 11d. (this is the last estimate for 1892), 4s. 6d., 3s. 5d., 2s. 10d., 2s. 5d., 3s. 4d., 2s. 1d., 2s. 2d., 4s. 4d., 5s., 4s., 4s. 9d., 3s. 8d., and 1s. 8d., those are the poor rates on the different divisions in a prosperous year.

1845. (*Mr. Sexton.*) Then you say that the county cess is high in that barony now, do you not?—Yes.

1846. How much is it, it was 4s. 2d., you said, in 1883, I think?—Yes, quite right; the average for the past five years was 3s. 4½d.

1847. Then there is a new seed rate Act?—Yes.

1848. Is there a rate under that in the Belmullet Union?—They have collected a good deal of that; there is a 1,000l. outstanding now, I think.

1849. What is the rate in the pound there for it usually?—It was not so much a rate in the pound, those who received seed were rated for it in accordance with what they got.

1850. But they all got something I suppose?—They all got different amounts.

1851. Assume it kept 3s. 5d., then you would have still as against 13s. in that year about 10s. or 11s. without any special compensation rate, would you not?—Yes, but not on the occupier, there would not be 10s. on the occupier or anything like it.

1852. But all except that poor rate would be on the occupier?—But the occupier pays little or no poor rate there.

1853. (*Lord Welby.*) There would not be more than 6s. or 7s. on the occupier, would there?—That is what there would be, taking the seed rate.

1854. (*Mr. Sexton.*) It would be more than that if there is a seed rate, and they pay all the county cess besides, 4d. county cess, and seed rate, you say, half-a-crown, but you cannot count the Belmullet people as paying any poor rate, a few only of them pay that.

1855. 300 of them, you say, pay the poor rate?—Yes.

1856. (*The O'Conor Don.*) Is the seed rate a rate?—No, it is payment for value received.

1857. They receive the potatoes and they pay the price?—Yes.

1858. (*Chairman.*) Will you put in your evidence the total of that Union?—Yes, I have given Clifden, for instance where the rates, so far as the poor rates are concerned, are probably higher.

1859. (*Lord Welby.*) Is there any seed rate being paid now in Belmullet?—Yes, they are collecting it still.

1860. It is very nearly paid off, is it not?—The Unions that received loans under the recent Seed Act have paid back nearly all the amount they received of the 240,408l. advanced. I think at the present moment there is, roughly speaking, only about 3,000l. unpaid.

1861. (*Chairman.*) It did not bear interest, I think, did it?—No.

1862. (*The O'Conor Don.*) When was it made?—In the spring of 1891. It has been very well paid.

1863. The condition was that it was not to be repayable I think for a year or two, was it not?—Two years, one instalment in August after the striking of the rate, and the next the year afterwards.

1864. The previous loan was repayment by four instalments. That was the 1880 seed loan, so that this loan has been practically paid off within the time limited by the Act, has it not?—Well, it ought to have been paid off in 1892, and we are getting near 1895 now.

1865. (*Mr. Wolff.*) Has the 1880 loan been paid off?—I think there is 12,000l. of that still outstanding.

1866. (*Chairman.*) Now we will pass to a little history, and I shall be glad if you will give us the history of the introduction of the Poor Law system, particularly with respect to its financial aspect, when it was introduced, and what the result has been?—There was no poor rate at all in Ireland until the Act of 1838 was introduced. In the 2nd of Anne (Cap. 19) there was an Act for erecting a workhouse in the city of Dublin for employing and maintaining the poor thereof, and there was a rate of 3d. in the pound in the city of Dublin and the Liberties for that purpose. That was the very first one for the relief of the poor. Then there was an Act of George II. in 1735 for establishing a workhouse at Cork similar to the one in Dublin, and the rate charged on that was a rate charged on all coal and culm imported into Cork. Then houses of industry were subsequently established.

1867. Do you happen to know who had the control of the affairs of those workhouses?—Yes, it was in the hands of the Corporation, both in Dublin and in Cork.

1868. (*Mr. Martin.*) Were not these houses of industry established more with the view of sequestrating vagabonds rather than for relief of destitute people?—Yes, they were rather for tramps and mendicants. Ireland was overrun with them at that time as there was no poor law.

1869. And they seized them and compulsorily forced them into these institutions?—Yes, they had the power to detain these people, and the whole legislation at that time was with a view of suppressing mendicancy and vagrancy. Then there was an Act by which people were entitled to beg.

Mr. Henry A. Robinson. 3 Dec. 1894. History of Poor Law system in Ireland.

1870. (*Chairman.*) Got licence to beg, you mean?—Got licence to beg. They went about with badges, and those badges gave them the right to beg. It was the Act of 11 and 12 George III., cap. 30. This Act enabled the corporations to grant badges to the helpless poor, and they had a licence to beg within certain limits, and that was the only relief there was for that kind of people.

1871. (*Sir David Barbour.*) I suppose the object of that would be to repress criminal vagrancy?—Yes. Only to allow the deserving poor to beg, and to prevent anybody else from begging.

1872. (*Lord Welby.*) Was that an Act general in Ireland or only applying to certain corporations?—I think it was of general application throughout Ireland, but it was only put into operation, I think, in about fourteen or fifteen cases. The corporations were to be enabled to build hospitals to be called houses for the relief of the poor, and Grand Juries were to be enabled to raise a certain sum of money in each county and county of a city or town. Each of these enactments was more or less in the nature of a poor law, but no regular provision was made until 1838.

1873. (*Mr. Sexton.*) Was the Act of George III. an Irish Act?—It was.

1874. 11 and 12 George III. would have been 1772. He came to the throne in 1760. Was it an Irish Act?—Yes. The next Act was the 45th of George III., which enabled the Grand Jury of each county to raise from the county at large a sum to be applied, in addition to subscriptions received, in providing medicine and medical and surgical aid and advice to poor people. Then the 46th of George III., chapter 95, enabled Grand Juries of counties to levy certain limited sums to be applied towards building houses of industry, and an Act of the following year authorised a further limited sum to be presented for fever hospitals wherever such had been established. Then the 54th of George III. chapter 112, and 58th George III., chapter 47, enabled Grand Juries to contribute out of their rates towards these fever hospitals and the cost of dispensaries. Then the Act of 6th George IV., chapter 102, authorised rating for maintaining deserted children until their admission to the Dublin *Foundling Hospital*. That I think was the last Act before the Act of 1838 was passed.

1875. (*Chairman*). Will you give us some figures showing the total indoor and outdoor, and the total number of poor in receipt of relief for some periods which you are prepared to give?—In 1852 and 1853 the country was first recovering from the famine, and at that time the numbers relieved in workhouses were very high—259,436. That number went down very considerably, until about the year 1862–63, when it was raised to 253,718.

1876. It fell very much between 1852 and 1857, I think, did it not?—Yes.

1877. What was the cause of that?—I think the people were better off at that period—I think that was the reason. The people recovered, and I think were in a better position at that time.

1878. (*Mr. Sexton.*) Then they are in now?—That is just a question.

1879. Because the figure for this year is much higher than any figure between 1853 and 1883—for thirty years?—Yes.

1880. It is higher this year than for thirty years after 1853?—That is the total number relieved, but that does not altogether give a very fair indication of the pauperism. You must take the average daily number. The total number relieved in the workhouse represents the total number admitted, as the same person might be admitted several times in the course of a year.

1881. That might happen at both periods?—Yes; but at the same time the only fair way is to find out what the average daily number in the workhouse is, and the daily average number from 1852 to 1893 in the workhouses has remained very much the same.

1882. (*Chairman.*) Will you give us the total for periods of five years?—I think it is better to take the average daily number for the reason I have stated, that it is more reliable. In 1852–53 the average daily number in workhouses was 129,390.

Decrease of indoor relief.

1883. That was indoor relief?—Yes, and Institutions for the Blind. The next period of five years it dropped to 43,781. The next period of five years up to 1863 it rose to 58,201, but there was a scarcity in 1862—it was a very bad year. Then it fell again the next five years to 54,195; then up to 1873 it was 47,325; up to 1878 it was 47,749; up to 1883 it was 51,097. 1882 was a bad year; there had been a bad failure in the potato crop. In 1888 it was 45,103; and in 1893 it was 41,546. But the outdoor relief has increased considerably during that period. The average daily number in receipt of outdoor relief has increased from 1,245 in 1852–3 to 59,127 in 1892–3. In 1853 the average daily number was 3,012; in 1858 it was 1,365; in 1863, 6,245; in 1868, 14,949; in 1873 it was 27,509; in 1878 it was 33,547; in 1883 it was 53,635; in 1888 it was 8,508; and in 1893 it was 59,127. Of course there is not the test of destitution where a person receives out-door relief that there is in the case where the person goes into the workhouse.

Increase of outdoor relief.

1884. How would you account in a few sentences for the average number and the percentage of population in receipt of indoor relief being, if anything, on the decrease, whereas the average number and the percentage in receipt of outdoor relief has increased so enormously as it has during those years? Will you put your answer into two or three sentences?—I think that the Boards of Guardians have got into the way more of giving outdoor instead of indoor relief, there is not the same test of destitution as to outdoor relief, and, therefore, there is more laxity with regard to the administration of outdoor relief than there is with indoor relief. And I think when any union starts a system of outdoor in preference to indoor relief the tendency of the relief is to increase very much; that the people get to be dependent upon it; and if one per cent. of a certain union receives this outdoor relief the other persons who think that they are equally entitled to it come forward and claim relief who never would, perhaps, claim relief in the workhouse.

1885. I put to you the very important question—do you think that that is evidence of increased distress in Ireland during those terms of years?—As to the outdoor relief?

1886. Yes; the enormous increase of outdoor relief?—I think that when the standard of living has increased very much it is much harder for the older class of people—persons who are qualified to receive outdoor relief—to get along than it was many years or about 20 years ago, when the style of living was very cheap and the people lived altogether on potatoes.

1887. I ask the question more with respect to the steady increase, not only in the few years, but over the whole series of years in the number on the average in receipt of outdoor relief which has risen from ·04 to 1·27, showing a steady increase from year to year. What in your mind does that indicate, only the greater general luxury and therefore the inability of the old people to keep pace with it, or greater general comfort?—Yes, I think it indicates that to a great extent,—the inability of the old persons to keep pace with the improved comfort of the population. But of course outdoor relief cannot be given to landholders in Ireland and to able-bodied persons, so that therefore it would not indicate in the same way that there is a very great increase in the poverty of the landholders.

1888. (*Lord Welby.*) It would represent, therefore, a large amount of comforts given to the old people?—Yes, I think so.

1889. (*Sir David Barbour.*) Is it not due to greater liberality in granting outdoor relief, or, say, greater

Mr. Henry A. Robinson.

6 Dec. 1894.

Increase of outdoor relief.

charity: that is the main cause, is it not?—Yes, I think the Board of Guardians prefer very much of recent years to give outdoor relief.

1890. Do the same authorities manage the business now who did so in former years?—Yes.

1891. But they have in the course of time become more lax, liberal, or charitable?—Yes.

1892. (*Lord Welby.*) The class of people who are Guardians now has altered to some extent, has it not? Has not the control passed into the hands of smaller farmers, and have not the gentry rather retired from the duty of recent years?—Yes, *ex-officio* members do not attend as much as they might.

1893. (*Chairman.*) Did they attend in former days?—I believe they did.

1894. Were there particular Guardians who specially concerned themselves with the questions of outdoor relief?—I think you will find that to be so now. I think there are a few leading members on Boards of Guardians who, as a rule, take greater interest in it; but ever since I have had any connection with the Poor Laws, in 1876, the *ex officios* have not been very regular in their attendance at Boards of Guardians.

1895. (*Mr Sexton.*) Except when an office had to filled?—Very likely.

1896. (*Chairman.*) You know in England the *ex-officio* Guardians do attend particularly to this special point?—Yes.

1897. (*The O'Conor Don.*) Is it not the custom in Ireland for the Guardian of the poor law electoral division to look after the outdoor relief in his own division?—He ought to, but very often a Guardian may be elected for a division which he does not live in at all, and which he may know very little about; so that generally speaking they take the sense of the Board on the question, whether relief shall be afforded to a particular case.

1898. (*Mr. Sexton.*) I would suggest to you that there are two causes for the growth of outdoor relief which have not been mentioned—one is the extraordinary emigration of the young from Ireland leaving an undue proportion of old people in the community; the other is the extraordinary number of evictions within the last ten years, and the outdoor relief in consequence of them, and that the people did not go into the workhouse?—You see they can only be afforded exceptional outdoor relief for a month in cases of eviction.

1899. But when large numbers of people are evicted constantly that month will amount to a great deal, will it not?—You may be right. I have not the figures of the evictions.

1900. (*The O'Conor Don.*) Do you admit that there has been an extraordinary number of evictions?—No; I do not know anything about the number of evictions.

1901. (*Mr. Wolff.*) Emigration certainly has gone down within the last few years, has it not?—Yes.

1902. (*Sir David Barbour.*) I imagine that the greater liberality on the part of the Guardians represents not a change of opinion on the part of the Guardians alone, but a general change of local opinion. I presume the Guardians represent the local opinion?—Yes, I think there is that opinion.

1903. (*Lord Welby.*) Does this greater liberality in the way of outdoor relief form a policy of the Local Government Board or a policy of the Guardians?—The Local Government Board are prohibited by law from interfering in cases of individual relief.

1904. In the case of a large extension of relief would not the Local Government Board interfere and ask the reason of it?—No; the auditor might call attention to the fact that the Guardians had been increasing the relief very much, and the Local Government Board would then write to the Guardians, and suggest the propriety, perhaps, of taking those people off the relief lists at certain periods of the year, and revising their relief lists, and doing all they can so that abuses might not creep in; but it is only in a general way that we can give them advice.

Mr. Henry A. Robinson.

6 Dec. 1894.

Increase of outdoor relief.

1905. (*Chairman.*) Does the Local Government Board put pressure on the Boards of Guardians to keep the amount of their outdoor relief down?—Yes, as much as they possibly can.

1906. Do they do that by circular?—By circular; by representations made by the Inspectors to the Boards of Guardians, and also by the auditor who calls attention to the fact in any case where he thinks that the amount given has been growing or has been excessive or extravagant.

1907. Has that been the constant policy of the Local Government Board?—Yes, since outdoor relief has been increasing.

1908. (*Mr. Sexton.*) When would you say it really came into operation—not in those years which are represented by very small figures—would you?—No, it extends principally, I think, from about 1872, say after 1870.

1909. It would be well, would it not, to bear in mind that outdoor relief has been practically upon one level ever since 1882, with the exception of the bad year of 1886?—Yes.

1910. (*Lord Welby.*) 1872 is a very favourable year, is it not?—Yes.

1911. (*Mr. Sexton.*) It was only developing then?—Yes.

1912. (*Sir David Barbour.*) The Local Government Board cannot go beyond the tender of advice in such a matter?—That is so; they have no legal power to do more.

1913. (*Lord Welby.*) Supposing that the auditor reported very extravagant expenditure, has the Local Government Board any power then?—He would probably surcharge it himself.

1914. But that must be expenditure which is practically illegal, must it not?—Extravagant. If they gave a person a very much larger amount of relief than was necessary to maintain that person for a week—say, if they gave him 2*l.* where 2*s.* would have been sufficient—then I think the auditor might surcharge the difference between that amount and what was given in an ordinary case.

1915. (*Mr. Martin.*) As a matter of fact, do they surcharge in those cases?—Yes; I have seen frequent cases where outdoor relief has been surcharged.

1916. (*The O'Conor Don.*) What are the classes who are entitled to outdoor relief?—A person must be temporarily disabled by accident or illness, or permanently disabled by infirmity, or a widow with two children. Then, in the event of the workhouse being full, outdoor relief may be given to able-bodied people.

1917. And with regard to those holding land?—They are ineligible.

1918. To what extent?—A quarter of an acre.

1919. Has there been any alteration of the law in regard to that?—No, except under the Relief of Distress Act of 1880, and under that Act that limit was relaxed, and also under Distressed Union's Act of 1886.

1920. Those were only temporarily?—Yes.

1921. (*Mr. Sexton.*) You have said that you often appoint Vice-Guardians to administer the affairs of unions; I should like to ask you whether you have found that the appointment of Vice-Guardians has exercised much effect on the incidence of outdoor relief?—Yes.

1922. Considerable?—Considerable.

1923. The central officials, as I may call them, in Dublin take a more rigid view of the necessity of outdoor relief than the local men, do they not?—Yes, I think they have. I think in every case they have been much more careful and have felt that they have been bound to keep down the expense as much as they possibly could, and they have reduced the outdoor relief.

1924. Can you say whether that has not resulted in the increase of indoor expenditure, and that there has been no increase of inmates?—There has been no in-

crease. I may mention a case in one union, showing that the cutting off of outdoor relief has not so resulted, where about 400 people were cut off relief suddenly because the treasurer refused an overdraft. They were cut off for one month, and there was no large increase of the number admitted to the workhouse. I think the class of persons, widows with two legitimate children, who get outdoor relief, are not people who would go into the house. It is given by the Guardians with a view to a little comfort.

1925. I suppose there is such a strong aversion to going into the house?—Yes.

1926. And that the necessity of the person is not an indication of distress?—There is no doubt that in the case I mention when the Guardians struck off the relief they did not go in.

1927. (*Chairman.*) What is the effect of relief being given?—It disfranchises the recipient.

1928. (*Lord Welby.*) I suppose the Vice-Guardians are not put in until the union is in a bad financial condition?—That is so.

1929. And that economy is absolutely necessary apart from sentiment in the matter?—Yes.

1930. (*The O'Conor Don.*) Are not the individual amounts given to the recipients of outdoor relief very small as a rule?—Yes.

1931. And inadequate to support them of themselves?—Yes, they vary from 1s. 6d. to 2s. 6d. a week.

1932. Is it not even a shilling a week sometimes?—Yes; I have seen that.

1933. (*Sir David Barbour.*) I suppose people who have been in the habit of supporting themselves, however poorly, will not go into the unions if they can possibly help it?—No.

1934. (*Chairman.*) Viewing the whole matter, can you tell us whether the Local Government Board have any distinct views as to the recent tendency of affairs in Ireland in the matter of pauperism, and whether it is in the opinion of the Board an increasing amount or a stationary or a decreasing amount, taking Ireland generally, or taking any of the provinces?—We have always considered that during the last ten years the ordinary pauperism of the country has not decreased; it remains stationary. The population has decreased but the ratio of pauperism to population remains stationary.

1935. Is that general, or can you make exceptions for particular parts of Ireland?—No, I think that is the general rule.

1936. In Ulster, for instance?—I think it has remained much the same in every case.

1937. Taking the whole of Ireland and taking the provinces separately, pauperism has been about constant—has it?—Yes; the ratio of paupers to the population has remained about the same. It was 2·19 in 1882 and it is 2·17 now.

1938. (*Sir David Barbour.*) And that includes persons in receipt of outdoor relief?—Everything.

1939. (*Mr. Wolff.*) That is the proportion, is it?—Yes, the ratio of paupers to the population.

1940. (*Chairman.*) And that opinion do you give confidently?—Yes.

1941. And is it the opinion of your colleagues?—Yes, it is the opinion of the Board.

Economic conditions, comparison with former times.

1942. Can the Board produce any information from their inspectors' reports which has a direct bearing upon the economic conditions in Ireland, and changes in the standards of life of the population during recent years?—I have been looking through some of the reports of the inspectors and I think the period during which the march of improvement among the poorer classes in Ireland was the greatest was from the famine years to about 1872 or 1873. I think, judging from the reports of the Commissioners who introduced the poor laws into Ireland and comparing them with the reports made by Arthur Young of his visit to Ireland, there was very little improvement between 1780 and 1830. The population had increased enormously from 2,800,000 in Arthur Young's time to about 6,000,000 or 8,000,000, and the houses that they were living in at the time of the famine, reported upon by these Commissioners were exactly of the same class as those described by Arthur Young—mud cabins with neither window nor chimney and no furniture. The difference was that in his time the people always had a sufficiency of potatoes and milk, but at the time of the Commissioners' Report there was a vast growing and unemployed population who were really in a state of fearful misery. There were more agricultural labourers in Ireland on the introduction of the poor law than there were in Great Britain according to the reports, although I believe there were only about 14 million acres under cultivation in Ireland and 34 million acres in England. The cost of living Arthur Young describes as having been about half in Ireland what it was in England. Then the population was decimated by cholera and fever, and starvation at the time of the famine, but after that was over, and from that period on to about 1872, as I have said before, the greatest improvement has been known. To begin with, prices of agricultural produce were very high about double what they were in the famine years. The country had been opened up, education had made its way, and the people lived altogether upon the produce of the land—upon potatoes and oatmeal—and they were a little better dressed perhaps. Cattle commanded a good high price, labour cheap, and altogether the houses were of a better class; the mud hovels were swept away and stone houses were built there.

1943. Are you speaking of up to 1872?—Yes, that is the time when I think the greatest improvement was made. The people lived well within their means, paid their debts to the shopkeepers—they had very few debts, comparatively—and fortunes were made up to 1874 by the price of cattle. Then the price of cattle began to go down after 1873. There was American competition; the failure of the potato crop followed and the people got into debt, and then occurred a period of great depression. After that period I think it is very doubtful whether the march of improvement continued to the same extent. The security of tenure and reduced rents, under the Land Act of 1881, of course, has been an immense advantage to them in every way, but I doubt whether on the whole they are better able now to make both ends meet than they were in 1873. Of course it is a matter of opinion, some people will tell you that they are and some will tell you that they are not; but I think if you take the case of the people who are under 15*l.* valuation, my own opinion is that there is not very much improvement in their financial condition. I think their standard of living is higher, but the question of whether they are able to make both ends meet and keep clear of debt I doubt. Of course they have the reduced rents, and the cost of living is very much lower than it was before. There are more wage-earners in America, and more money coming from that source, and a greater number of cattle; but, on the other hand, the standard of living has increased enormously.

1944. (*Chairman.*) That is in their favour, is it not?—Yes, they are living better. But I am talking now about their ability to live on the land compared to what it was.

1945. (*Sir David Barbour.*) But the change in the standard of living is in itself an improvement, is it not?—Yes, certainly. The prices of agricultural produce have gone down very much; wool has gone down very much; the price of corn has gone down very much.

1946. (*Mr. Sexton.*) And of stock and the produce of stock?—Yes; it has gone down compared with 1873, which was the highest year. Compared with 20 years ago all that has gone down.

1947. (*Sir David Barbour.*) You are speaking of farmers now, I suppose?—Altogether, because they are all practically farmers to whom I allude. For instance, they don't live on potatoes now as they used to. Their potatoes form, perhaps, one meal a day and part of a second for part of the year; but 20

Mr. Ernest A. Robinson, [illegible]. 9 Dec. 1895. Economic condition, comparison with former times.

years ago they lived on them almost altogether. They now use tea, bread, and they spend a great deal more on dress and tobacco than they did; so that I think if a farmer came to balance up at the end of his year (which I do not suppose he does) he would find he is no better off, but has as great difficulty to live in his present style as he had then.

1948. Then your view is that he is decidedly better off?—His condition is much more bettered—more civilised.

1949. (*Chairman.*) But his balance is smaller?—His balance is smaller.

1950. (*Sir David Barbour.*) Is it not the habit of all people to live up to their incomes?—I am inclined to think that this man has rather gone beyond it. In a way they are better—they are better up in all the controversies of the day and better educated, but somehow I do not think the condition of their houses and surroundings has improved; you see the same miserable out-at-elbow style of agriculture—the men going to England, the women and children doing a very little drudging and farming in the winter months, the cattle in the houses, the manure heaps before the door in just the same way; I think, in proportion to their incomes, the class I refer to pay more in the way of indirect taxation than almost any other class of the community.

1951. (*Chairman.*) But what we wanted specially was your view of the condition of the people as to comfort; that is considerably higher than it was, is it not?—Undoubtedly the people, so far as their style of living goes, are in every way more civilised and more comfortable.

1952. Their dress is decidedly better, is it not?—I do not know whether you would call it better, but it is more expensive. For the old picturesque cloak which was handed down from mother to daughter they have substituted shoddy garments which do not last quite so long.

1953. But where they specially have not made any laying by for a rainy day, you think they are worse off?—Yes, I think they are less able to resist a bad year than they were in those days; I think that is shown by this, that between the famine years and 1879 the poor law was always able to meet the exigencies of distress, but since 1879 there have been five or six Relief of Distress Acts. I think the people who have made the most are the people who are above that class, say from 12*l.* to 15*l.* valuation upwards. I think in every way those people have improved; they have done more in the way of building, and their whole surroundings have improved in every way. I think the younger generation are not sticking to the land there, they are placed in various professions, going into trades, shops, and so on.

1954. Then would you say at the top of the scale people are not as well off as they used to be?—At the top of the scale I think they are improving more than the others, that is speaking of farmers. Again these violent oscillations in the prices of cattle are very hurtful to the small people. Cattle farming seems to be more a gambling transaction now than a safe investment. The larger men are able to turn over their cattle more often and are better able in the buying and selling of them to make a profit than the small people are. The people whose condition is most improved during the recent years, and who benefit most by the low prices of provisions, are the labourers. The wages of labourers are considerably higher than they were twenty years ago; they can buy provisions at a far less price than before, and under the operation of the Labourers Acts their condition has been materially improved, although of course a good deal remains to be done.

1955. (*Chairman.*) Then the higher class of farmers and those corresponding with them in other matters are better off than they were; the small farmer lives better, but saves no more, is that so?—Yes.

1956. And the labourer as a rule is better off?—Yes, he gets higher wages and pays less.

1957. (*Mr. Wolff.*) When you talk about the higher class of farmers, what is the average at which you would begin?—It is very hard to take an exact line, but I take them from 15*l.* down and 12*l.* up.

1958. Of course 15*l.* is not a very large amount, is it?—No, but there are comfortable men paying that.

1959. (*Mr. Sexton.*) Would that be the rental for about 20 acres?—It varies.

1960. As an average?—Yes, I think it would be from that upwards.

Adjourned for a short time.

1961. (*Chairman.*) There is one further question I was going to ask you, and that is this—It is, I think, important that we should have some information as to what the budget, if I may use the expression, of a poor family living in a pauper or low-quarter house is—what they may be expected to receive, and what they may be expected to spend in the year. Can you give us good information on that point?—Yes; I think I can get that for you through the relieving officers.

1962. In different parts of Ireland?—Just so.

1963. (*Mr. Sexton.*) I think the family budget of an ordinary agricultural labourer in Ireland, and of an ordinary small farmer, without any special relation to the congested district question, would be better?—Quite so.

1964. (*Chairman.*) We have a congested district budget, I think?—Then you don't want that.

1965. No; we want it for the average country districts in different parts of Ireland?—Just so; the labourer and the small farmer of under 4*l.* and over.

1966. It is especially the 4*l.* and under that we care about, but you may make it as broad as you please?—Just so. From each of the four provinces?

1967. (*Mr. Sexton.*) In whatever form the evidence would be of most general application to the population at large?—Quite so.

1968. (*Lord Welby.*)—You have given us some figures on the subject of the poor relief since 1852; can you tell us anything before that date as to the extent to which indoor relief was given, and whether it was very largely given between 1838, say, and the famine?—It was very largely given. There was a failure of the potato crop in 1844–45, and, I think, 1846 was the great failure. In 1847 there was distress in some parts of Ireland, and also in 1848 and 1849. In all those years you may say that the workhouses were full to overflowing. Poor Relief before 18[illegible].

1969. I want to obtain, if possible, some information as to a period before the famine; we know that the famine was a most exceptional period, but take 1842 or 1843?—The workhouses were not completed at that time; the Irish Poor Law were hardly in full swing, I think, before distress was upon the people.

1970. Then during that time you had a very large population struggling for means of subsistence, and how were their wants met?—Their wants were not met. According to the reports of the Commissioners they were undergoing an amount of suffering which it is almost impossible to describe. The practice of subdivision had gone on to such an extent that the holdings were reduced to the smallest modicum on which it was possible for a human being to gain subsistence. There was no form of relief open or accessible to all parts of the country, and if they had not their potato patch the people found their way into the towns and there was a great deal of misery; it was really a case then of having some land or employment or starving.

1971. There are no means of instituting what I may call a fair comparison of the action of the poor relief for a time before the famine and subsequent years?—No, there are not.

1972. I did not quite catch you, but you said, I think, that the holder of a quarter-of-an-acre is not entitled to outdoor relief?—He cannot be afforded outdoor relief by the Board of Guardians, but in the

case of sudden or urgent necessity before his case has been reported to the Board by a relieving officer, the relieving officer may afford him relief for a week.

1973. (*Mr. Martin.*) For any less a quantity than a quarter-of-an-acre is he entitled?—The relieving officer might afford relief to anybody in case of sudden emergency, until his case is brought before the Board of Guardians.

1974. (*The O'Conor Don.*) Might he afford him relief in money?—In kind.

1975. (*Mr. Sexton.*) The quarter-of-an-acre clause would exclude a good many from relief would it not?—Yes, it would exclude labourers.

1976. (*Lord Welby.*) You have given us instances of very high rates drawn, I think, almost completely from the west and congested districts. Can you give us what I may call some average and typical instances of the incidence of rates in parts outside of congested districts?—I think if you take good and bad together throughout the other parts of the country, you might say that the average rate was from about 1s. 3d. to 1s. 9d.

1977. Poor rate?—Yes.

1978. What would it come to including all rates, do you suppose?—The average of county cess for the whole of Ireland you may put down at 1s. 9d.

1979. Then, if that is the case, the average rating outside the congested districts probably would not amount to above 4s. in the pound?—No, it would not.

1980. Of which some part or parts of the poor rate, at any rate, would fall on the landowner?—Yes.

1981. Therefore if we go outside congested districts, may I take it as your opinion that the rating is not very heavy on the occupier?—There are no difficulties experienced outside the congested districts in levying rates—at least we have never found any difficulty.

1982. I would go one step further and ask you whether in your experience you consider the average to be a high rating, putting the congested districts aside?—Outside of towns I do not think it is oppressive at all.

1983. When you give that average of 1s. 3d. to 1s. 9d. and so on for poor rate, and 1s. 9d. for county cess, does that include towns?—No, only poor rate and county cess. I am not quite sure whether the poor rate is very accurate, but I am quite sure that the average of 1s. 9d. is fair for the county cess.

1984. Those figures apply to rural districts and not to towns?—Quite so; the towns of course are rated very much higher.

1985. I observe that in giving some of those very highly rated districts, Belmullet, for instance, you gave us ninepence as the rate for water, but that is a rate for value received, and therefore stands on rather a different footing from the other rates, does it not?—They all have to contribute towards it; whether they receive any value from it or not they all have to pay the rate. A contributory district might take in, say the area of an electoral division, and the rate might be paid by some persons who really very seldom used the water. But the area over which the cost of this is assessed is as far as possible the area in which the people who benefit by it live.

1986. In the average districts of Ireland outside the congested districts, I suppose there are not very many exceptional rates, are there? For instance, in those districts do the light railways' contributions fall heavy?—No. I think you may say east, of a line drawn from Lough Swilly to Cape Clear, that the light railways do not bring up the cess there very much. But of course in every poor law union if the average rate is a shilling, or whatever it may be, there are some particular electoral divisions comprising a large number of people in which the rate must necessarily be considerably higher than the average union rate.

1987. But in judging from the local taxation, or what I may call the taxable capacity of Ireland, you would really have to divide Ireland into two parts. You could not judge the country east of the line which marks the congested districts and the country west of it by the same standard, could you?—No, I think not. I think the east and the west are two different countries.

1988. I was rather struck by your statement as between 1871 and the present time. If I understood you rightly, you did not think there had been a very great improvement in the housing of the poorer classes in Ireland. Let me state what I understood you to say: that between 1849 and 1871 there had been a great improvement, but you thought that it had been rather stationary since then?—Yes, I say they have not continued to improve at the same rate as they did between those years. I went further and said, I think, that in the poorer districts there is very little improvement in the houses and surroundings in the last twenty years.

1989. That is the point I want to learn from you, because in this most valuable collection of statistics of Dr. Grimshaw's there is a comparison which is a more or less rough one, of the different classes of houses, namely, first, second, third, and fourth?—Yes.

1990. Of course we have to bear in mind that emigration has been going on, and probably that most of the emigrants have been from the lowest classes, but these figures appear very striking. In the fourth class, which I suppose is the class everybody would wish to see disappear, from 1871 to 1891 the number has fallen from 156,000 to 20,000?—I think you must take into consideration the class which I am not referring to, the labouring class. I think the labourers' temporary dwellings have been levelled and in place of these there are houses of much higher class than the class you refer to now. I think in regard to the agricultural tenants, although they have built outhouses and offices and done a good deal in that way as far as the cleanliness and surroundings of their own particular houses are concerned, I cannot see very much improvement.

1991. That is what I want to come to, but I will finish with this fourth class. You see if the improvement of the face of the land of this fourth class were to go on at the rate at which it went between 1881 and 1891 they would practically disappear by the time the next census was taken?—Is that so?

1992. They diminished from 1871 to 1881, from 156,000 to 40,000; and from 1881 to 1891, from 40,000 to 20,000; and going on at that rate they would of course disappear in 1901. I am only speaking that as applying to the class you have not got in your mind, namely, the labouring class. At all events it indicates a considerable improvement with regard to that class. Then with regard to the third class, always bearing in mind that there has been a diminution of population, I see that the third class houses in 1871 were 363,000, and in 1891 they were 312,000. Therefore you see that the third-class, which is a rather inferior class of house, has diminished, though probably not more than compared with the decrease of population. But when you come to the higher classes, in 1871, the second-class house, which I suppose to be a fair house, has risen from 291,000 to 395,000, that is between 1871 and 1891?—That is my experience.

1993. Is not that a proof of considerable amendment in the housing of the farmer class?—I think I said that I considered the better class of farmers had improved in every way with regard to houses and everything; I am quite of that opinion.

1994. Then your criticism, as I take it, would rather fall on the third class, which is represented by 363,000 in 1871, and by 312,000 in 1891?—I am not quite sure what the meaning of the different classes is, but no doubt it would be that. No doubt it would be a third-class house if you take a labourer's cabin to be a fourth-class house.

Mr. Henry A. Robinson. 4 Dec. 1894. Housing of poorer classes.

1995. (*Mr. Sexton.*) I understand that anything excepting the old mud cabins without a window or a chimney is a third-class house?—That may be so, I am not clear about it.

1996. (*Lord Welby.*) I will read Dr. Grimshaw's words upon it:—"This system of classification was devised by Sir Thomas Larcom, who divided all houses into four classes; the fourth class includes all single-room houses, constituted of mud or perishable material." That would rather meet the case of the labouring class of which you spoke?—Yes.

1997. And that I think we may take as really disappearing from these figures, may we not?—They are much better now.

1998. "The third a better class with from two to four rooms and windows. The second" (which is the one to which I call your attention as showing such a large improvement) "a good farmhouse in the country or a small townhouse having five to seven rooms and windows?—I think the Registrar-General's statistics bear out what my evidence was; that the third-class had not improved very much, and that the mud cabins have disappeared. The better-class farmer, what is called the second class, are certainly improving very much.

1999. Therefore, we get to an agreement on the point, and taking this table of the division of houses, we know the point to which your criticism goes?—I think so.

Effect of evictions on Poor Law Relief.

2000. Some allusion was made I think to the fact of evictions as accounting possibly for the large increase of poor rates since 1871; has the number of evictions been very large of late years?—I have not the statistics of them.

2001. I mean if the evictions of late years have not been very numerous it would scarcely account in a great degree for the large mounting up of the outdoor relief; would it?—Just so.

2002. I did not gather that you laid very much stress on that argument, because I inferred that you thought the increase really was a consequence of the increased comfort of living, and the general sentiment of the people who administered the poor law that the elderly people were entitled to greater comfort?—That was one of my reasons or ideas for that increase.

2003. (*The O'Conor Don.*) With regard to that last question asked, is it not the custom of the Board of Guardians to give special relief in the case of evictions, for a certain time after the eviction?—One month from the date of the eviction.

2004. Is not the question then of the number of evictions brought under the notice of your Board, in consequence of these special grants for that purpose?—No; it is not given under our Board at all, except in the bulk. Remember, there is no distinction made in the numbers on outdoor relief or the particular Act under which the relief is afforded. Each case would come under the notice of the auditor, and if there was anything to which our attention should be called he would do it.

2005. Would it not be in the power of your auditors to find out whether these sums had been very largely granted of late years?—Every single case of relief comes under the notice of the auditor.

2006. Special grants in evicted cases have not been brought before your Board as particularly arising in late years?—No.

Houses of the poor.

2007. With regard to the houses, I understood you to answer Lord Welby that the mud cabins were chiefly inhabited by labourers?—I am very sorry to say there are a great number of them inhabited by labourers still.

2008. But are they not also very often to be found on the holdings of small occupiers of land?—In what part of the country?

2009. In the poorer districts?—They are nearly all stone there.

2010. In the poorer districts?—You may see a few here and there, but they are exceptions. A mud cabin without a window or chimney is entirely an exception in these days.

Mr. Henry A. Robinson. 4 Dec. 1894. Houses of the poor.

2011. Do you think that the houses of the smaller occupiers of land have really not improved of late years?—I think that as a rule they live in exactly the same class of houses as they did in 1874.

2012. But you admit they have built out-offices, I understand?—In that way I see an improvement. I say they are doing something in the way of building barns, and so on.

2013. Before the out-offices were built the cattle and pigs had to be in the house with the family?—But they are still.

2014. Where the out-offices are built, do they not keep them in the out-offices?—They do, but the out-offices are very often a shed for a cart. I include everything in "out-offices." Of course if they have accommodation for cattle the better class men will keep them in these out-offices; but I say the practice still prevails of keeping the cattle in the houses.

2015. Do you think that that practice has diminished at all?—I think it has to a certain extent.

2016. (*Lord Welby.*) The advance of education itself would tend to diminish the practice, would it not?—Yes.

2017. (*The O'Conor Don.*) In the first part of your evidence you alluded to the probability of the poor rates increasing, or a tendency in the poor rates to increase?—Yes.

Purposes other than Poor Law Relief.

2018. And I think you mentioned that the poor rates were now burdened with taxes for a great number of purposes quite distinct from the relief of the poor?—Yes.

2019. Will you give us an idea of the proportion of the poor rate which is payable for what I will call real and essential poor relief, and for these extraneous subjects?—When the poor law unions were laid out for the first time, I notice that the Commissioners on the Boundary Commission referring to what the probable cost of administration of relief would be, said that they thought about sixpence in the pound ought to be the cost.

2020. That was only an estimate, I suppose?—Yes; as a matter of fact so many extra things have been put upon it that there are very few unions where sixpence is the average. Do you want the amount of the total poor relief expenditure?

2021. I want the proportion of the total poor law expenditure that might be properly called expenditure for relief of the poor?—Out of a total expenditure of [illegible] the amount which was for poor relief expenditure simply was [illegible].

2022. Then about a third would be for purposes not peculiarly for the relief of the poor?—Yes.

2023. And it is upon that class of expenditure that you are looking forward to increase, is it?—Yes, by other Acts of Parliament placing other charges on the poor law; I mean to say the tendency is when there is any remedial legislation, if any local authority has to bear the costs, that it should go on the poor rates. That has been the practice, and, I think, we must look more or less to a continuance of that, because Boards of Guardians are more easily dealt with than Grand Juries.

Increase cost of workhouses.

2024. I think you also said that one of the causes of expense was that the number of officers in workhouses have increased?—Yes, they have increased.

2025. What is the reason for that increase?—I do not know about the number of officers having increased, but the amount paid to them has increased. Prices of living have rather gone up, and they have received increased salaries. Then, on the other hand, there is a much better class of nursing and supervision for the sick than there was thirty or forty years ago, and Boards of Guardians are more ready to appoint ward-masters, and to have a better system of supervision over the workhouses than in those days, and I attribute it to that.

2026. Have not the number of workhouses diminished?—Yes, by a few.

2027. How many have been abolished?—Four unions have been amalgamated.

Mr. Henry A. Robinson, C.B. 4 Dec. 1894. Superannuation of Union Officers.

2028. (*Lord Welby.*) Have not you rather an expensive system of superannuation for your poor law officers?—I do not think so. It is not very much more expensive than the scale laid down by you for the Civil Service.

2029. I have a recollection that we at the Treasury thought it a somewhat extravagant scale; that we thought it in excess of the Civil Service scale, which we think a very liberal scale?—You intimated that to us, and in making orders for superannuation for Union Officers we have endeavoured, as far as possible, since that date to confine it to the scale which was laid down by the Treasury.

Mode of assessment.

2030. (*The O'Conor Don.*) You have informed the Commission about the mode in which the taxation of the unions is divided between electoral division and the union charges; is it not the case that if the charge upon the electoral division amounts to a certain sum the excess becomes a union charge?—Only for indoor relief.

2031. That is not extended to the outdoor relief?—No.

2032. When was that Act passed?—In 1876.

2033. Have there been many cases in which it has been put into operation?—Yes.

2034. What is the amount to which the rate must rise in an electoral division in order to get the excess transferred to the union at large?—If the rate of any particular electoral division for in-maintenance exceeds the average rate over the whole union for in-maintenance plus half the average rate, the balance goes over the union at large.

Contagious Diseases (Animals) Act.

2035. Will you explain to the Commission how the expense for the Contagious Diseases (Animals) Act is arranged?—It is a general rate all over Ireland.

2036. At a given rate per pound?—Yes, usually a farthing in the pound on the valuation.

2037. How is that apportioned between the unions afterwards?—That is done by the Veterinary Department of the Privy Council, who administer the Act, but I do not know what their procedure is.

2038. You do not know how they administer it?—No, we have nothing to say to the veterinary work.

2039. It is given in aid of a union where any contagious disease breaks out, is it not?—Yes.

2040. Is there an unlimited amount given in any union; is there no limit to the amount given to any particular union out of this national rate?—I am not quite sure, but I think if the necessities of the case involve a larger amount being paid to a union than was contributed by that union, they would do it if necessary. I am not quite sure about it, but that is my impression.

2041. Your impression is that there is a connection between the amount subscribed by the union to this national rate and the amount it gets?—No, that there is not. My impression is that it deals altogether with the necessities of a particular case without reference to the union in which the expense occurs.

2042. Is this rate an annual one?—Practically so.

2043. What is the amount?—It varies. It was 14,000*l.* on the last occasion.

2044. I do not mean the total amount but the poundage?—It must not exceed one-halfpenny in the pound in any one year.

Local loans.

2045. Turning to another subject, with regard to the loans that have been advanced to these different public bodies, can you put in a return showing the amount that has been lost to the Treasury by these loans, if any?—I think that the Treasury have lost very little through loans advanced on the recommendation of the Local Government Board, but I am afraid that we could not put in that; it would have to be the Board of Works who would afford that information. I have told you that the amount which up to the present has not been recovered out of 800,000*l.* advanced for seed is 12,000*l.*, but some of this will be recovered, and it is still in course of collection.

2046. Do all the loans advanced to public bodies to which you have referred come under your board for audit?—Yes, except those to harbour authorities.

Mr. Henry A. Robinson, C.B. 4 Dec. 1894. Local loans.

2047. And it was to those loans alone to which you referred in your evidence, I suppose?—Yes.

2048. You did not refer to loans given for drainage purposes?—Arterial drainage?

2049. Yes?—No.

2050. And to advances made to landlords or tenants?—No, we have nothing whatever to do with it; it is all done through the Board of Works.

2051. So that the loans of which you have spoken to-day are simply loans which your Board audits?—Exactly.

Levying rates in distressed unions.

2052. You have spoken of the cases in the distressed unions where it has been almost impossible to levy the rates, and you have also stated that the payers of those rates were the landowners and not the tenants?—Yes.

2053. Was it not the fact usually in those cases that the landlords had not received their rents? You stated that the landlords refused to pay the rates of those tenants under 4*l.* for whom they were liable to pay?—I cannot answer that definitely to say whether it was always or was not always the case, but in those cases where there was a great difficulty in levying the rates there was also a difficulty in recovering the rents; more than that I cannot say.

2054. Do you not think it would be an improvement to have the rates leviable upon the land for poor rate, as it is for the county cess, directly?—Do you mean for the occupier to pay poor rate?

2055. Yes, for the occupier to pay the poor rate and then deduct the whole of it in the case of those holdings under 4*l.* from his rent as he does now in the case of holdings over 4*l.* where he deducts half?—No, I should be sorry to see that; it would cause much more difficulty in the collection of the rate. At present they get it from one lessor in one take, and it is a much more convenient arrangement.

2056. (*Sir David Barbour.*) You gave instances of places in which the local rates were very high and there were great difficulties in collecting those rates. I suppose such places form only a small percentage of the whole country?—Yes; you may take it that those are the unions bordering on the West Coast of Ireland—on the sea coast.

2057. And in those parts I believe the land is not very productive?—No.

2058. There is a great deal of mountain land and rock, is there not, there?—Yes.

2059. And the climate is wet, I believe?—It is a very nice climate.

2060. Is it good for agriculture?—I think so.

2061. The population is large in proportion to the amount of cultivated land, is it not?—Yes, it is. The valuation per head of the population in some of those districts is extremely low.

2062. But the population is not very large in proportion to the total extent of the land?—Oh, yes; there is an enormous amount of waste land there.

2063. There are no manufactories, are there?—No, except in the North; in the North some flax is grown.

2064. I do not think they manufacture it in the North-west districts, do they?—I think flax is grown there, and there are small Scotch mills.

2065. I think the factories are more to the East even in the North, or to a great extent, at any rate. Consequently then the people are very poor, are they not?—Yes, extremely poor.

2066. And there is a good deal of pauperism?—Yes.

2067. I suppose the expenditure on roads is heavy in a district of that sort in proportion to the wealth of the country?—Yes.

2068. In a thickly-populated country a road might serve a thousand houses while a road of equal extent in a thinly-populated tract would serve fewer houses?—I think it is a good deal harder to keep up the bog roads; more has to be done on them than on a road with a solid foundation.

Mr. Henry A. Robinson.

4 Dec. 1894.

Incidence of Imperial taxation.

2069. Then the rates are high and difficult to collect, because the people are very poor?—Yes.

2070. And for the same reason the Imperial taxation falls harder upon them than it does upon rich people in the wealthy districts?—Yes.

2071. I suppose they are not affected at all by the income tax?—No.

2072. And the duties on property do not affect them much—that is, death duties and stamp duties.—No.

2073. The duties that fall upon them are the tea duties, the tobacco duties, and the spirit duties?—Those are the principal duties.

2074. If you wish to relieve those districts in any way, an exemption of Ireland generally from the income tax would not do so?—No, you would not relieve those particular districts.

2075. But, I suppose, if they could be relieved of the tea duty, the tobacco duty and the spirit duty, or if these could be reduced, there would be pro tanto an improvement in their condition?—Yes, they would have to pay less.

2076. But it would not put them in a prosperous condition, would it?—They would have more money to spend.

2077. But, looking at their position now, do you think that if they paid no tea duty, spirit duty, or tobacco duty they would be well off?—I think they would be in a much better position.

2078. But do you think that they would be in a satisfactory condition; they would be better off, no doubt?—I do not think it would be a complete remedy for the state of things which exists there at present.

2079. And if you took off those duties you would lose a great deal of revenue, would you not?—Yes.

2080. And you would relieve a great many people from taxation who really do not require relief, or do not require it in the same degree?—It would relieve a great many to whom it is not so oppressive.

2081. And some to whom it is not necessary at all?—I daresay.

2082. So that if anything were to be done for those people it would require to be done as a special case which specially affected them, rather than that something should be done which affected all Ireland?—I daresay that would be so.

2083. There is no doubt that there are a great many paupers in England?—Just so.

2084. And there are a great number of people on the verge of pauperism in England, are there not; I suppose the tea and tobacco and spirit duties fall as heavily and as hardly on those people in England who are on the verge of pauperism, as they do on the people in a congested district in Ireland?—I do not fancy they consume so much spirits.

2085. But in so far as they do, am I not right?—Of course.

2086. And in so far as they consume all those things the burden falls just as hardly upon them as upon the people of Ireland?—Yes.

2087. (*Mr. Sexton.*) You are aware that the reference to the Commission does not deal with classes of individuals in either country but with each country as a community, are you not?—Yes.

2088. The Commission is instructed to report upon the capacity of Ireland as a whole, compared with Great Britain as a whole, and not as to the relative condition of classes of individuals in either country?—Yes.

Effect of evictions on outdoor relief.

2089. Upon the question of evictions, is it not a fact that the landlord is bound to give notice of the eviction to the relieving officer of the district?—Not less than 48 hours.

2090. And the relieving officer would become aware of the fact of an eviction?—Yes.

2091. And in that way the Board of Guardians?—Yes.

2092. And so within the ambit of your department there is knowledge and record of an eviction?—No.

2093. You could procure it from the Guardians?—Yes, I suppose we could if we wrote to the Guardians. The relieving officer may, or may not, lay the notice on the table of his Board.

2094. But the Guardians may call for it?—They may.

2095. Have you been long a Commissioner?—I have been a long time connected with the Board; I have been four years a Commissioner.

2096. And before that you were an official?—Yes, for ten years.

2097. For the last fourteen years you have had direct experience of the condition of the people?—More than that; since 1875. Before that I was in another post.

2098. Have you any doubt that the evictions in Ireland, or the dispossessions, whatever may have afterwards become of the evicted persons, say in the last fifteen years, have been very far more numerous than within our generation previously, say since 1870?—Really I have not gone into the statistics at all; it does not come under our notice. There have been a great many of them, but I would be very sorry to bind myself down to any positive statement on that subject.

2099. Assuming the prevalence of evictions for those years, would not the effect of the evictions, looking to the probable condition of the evicted persons, afterwards lead to an increase of out-door relief?—Yes, certainly; if a large number of people were evicted, and they all got relief, the returns would show it.

2100. Do you know enough of the social condition of Ireland to know that if a family are evicted they must come on charitable benevolence?—Quite so.

2101. So that that social condition would account undoubtedly, for a considerable increase in the incidence of out-door relief during the time which has been known as the land struggle, would it not?—It would be great or little in accordance with the relief afforded under those circumstances.

2102. (*The O'Conor Don.*) Before we pass from that, do you think it would be possible for your Board to furnish to the Commission any return which would show the number of persons in receipt of out-door relief consequent on evictions?—For how many years past do you mean?

2103. (*Mr. Sexton.*) For about fifteen years?—I do not know whether they could.

2104. (*The O'Conor Don.*) Or, if you cannot do it for such a length of time, say for five years?—I will see if it can be got, but I do not think it can, as the outdoor relief is not put under separate headings in that way; it is all on the application and report books, but if it can be got it shall be got.

2105. (*Mr. Sexton.*) I understand from you that the administration of the poor law is expressly conducted by the elected Guardians?—Yes.

2106. And they are usually tenant farmers, are they not?—Yes.

2107. Of course above the £4?—Yes.

2108. And therefore liable themselves for half the poor rate?—Yes.

2109. And if they unduly expend money the burden falls to that extent upon themselves and their neighbours in the same position?—Well, so far as outdoor relief is concerned it does not; it falls on the particular electoral division. But then, of course, the whole board have the administration of the outdoor relief in their hands; it is not a general charge over the whole union.

2110. A particular Guardian if he assented to unnecessary outdoor relief would be open to attack from his neighbours, would he not?—He would if they were ratepayers.

2111. I refer to those who are ratepayers. Great stress has been thrown on the question of house accommodation. It is the fact, is it not, that the total number of houses in Ireland has decreased by more than one-third since the first census in the year

Mr. Henry A. Robinson. 9 Dec. 1894. Houses of the poor.

1841?—Yes, I believe that is so from the Registrar-General's return.

2112. That is to say that the reduction in the number of houses has been proportionate to the reduction in the number of people?—Yes.

2113. Then, we notice that the reduction of the fourth class houses is almost the same as that of the total number of houses. The total number of houses decreased by 456,000, and the mud cabins by 470,000?—Yes.

2114. Then it would appear that the great diminution of the mud cabins has not resulted from any organised or deliberate effort of any kind at social improvement, but it simply means that when the family were turned out and drifted away, or went to America or the workhouse, the mud cabin was levelled and disappeared?—I do not know.

2115. Is it not open to that inference? If you find that the reduction in the number of mud cabins is about the same as the number of houses that have disappeared, and that a third of the population corresponding to that number of houses have emigrated, does it not rather look as though when the poor family left the place the mud cabin disappeared?—That is quite open to argument.

2116. (*Lord Welby.*) But is that quite consonant with what one has read on the subject? Is it the case that emigration has been entirely confined (no doubt it has to a large extent) to the class who were occupying mud cabins. For instance, taking the north, one has heard—I think my recollection is right—that a large number emigrated from the north?—I would not say that it has been entirely confined to the people who had mud cabins of recent years, but there is no doubt that before the famine the majority of the cabins were made of mud, and there is no doubt that they were all cleared away at the time of the famine.

2117. (*Mr. Sexton.*) We have heard from Dr. Grimshaw that emigration from Ireland is on the decline; it follows the failure of the potato crop, but he says when the potato crop is good it is not so great. That being so, have you any doubt that emigration was mostly by those who had mud cabins?—I should imagine that the emigration during the famine years was among the people who occupied the mud cabins.

2118. The old class of small Irish tenant?—Yes.

2119. Who emigrated because of hunger at the time of the potato famine and was the occupier of a mud cabin?—Certainly.

2120. And the population of that class to a great extent has disappeared, and there has been a corresponding diminution in the number of mud cabins?—Yes.

2121. Nothing is to be inferred in the way of social improvement from that fact, but simply that the poor dwellings of the expelled people have disappeared?—I think also there is a greater improvement than that. I think when there was a sub-division of land and a man settled down, instead of building himself a mud cabin he put up a stone cottage with a chimney and a window to it.

2122. I am coming to that. There are still 50,000 of these mud cabins, are there not?—Yes.

2123. There are still 312,000 of what you call third class houses?—Yes.

2124. And I have still to note that there are 55,000 families having only fourth class accommodation, and 359,000 having third class accommodation?—Yes.

2125. There you have 400,000 families out of a total of 900,000 who are living either in the mud cabins or something only just better?—Yes.

2126. Because I understand that Dr. Grimshaw's third class is anything that has more than one room; no matter how miserable the hovel may be, if it has more than one room it is a third class house?—Yes.

2127. Therefore we have a number of the population still living in houses of the fourth class?—Yes; but you may have a very good third class house. I have seen a good many of these third class houses which are by no means uncomfortable houses.

2128. But still it would include anything that is better than the old windowless, chimneyless mud cabin, would it not?—Yes.

2129. The evidence then is very uncertain as to the condition of the people so far as the houses are concerned?—Yes.

2130. "The fourth class includes all single room houses constructed of mud or perishable material; the third and better class with from two to four rooms and windows." So that anything with two rooms and a window is a third class house. With regard to those who did not emigrate but who remained, what happened was that as time went on they substituted as occasions served a better dwelling of some kind for the mud cabin?—Yes.

2131. The farmers of Ireland provided themselves with these houses; the landlords did not build them, did they?—The farmers built them themselves.

2132. Very often with their own hands?—Yes, themselves and their families.

2133. Can you draw any inference as to the condition of a farmer, with regard to income, expenditure, and surplus, from the fact that he built that class of house for himself sometime or other within the last thirty years?—In what way?

2134. As to his present condition, does the possession of that house enable you to draw any inference that he is now in a better social or financial condition than he was in before he built the house?—No.

2135. It is quite a delusive idea, is it not, to suppose that the industry of the man at some indefinite time in the past in providing himself with a house argues anything whatever as to the superiority of his general condition now compared to what it was in the past?—I think it shows that he is more alive to the decencies of life, and is anxious to provide better accommodation than his fathers had before him.

2136. Of course the fact that until very recently a farmer was liable to be rented upon the house he built for himself would operate as a bar to such improvements, would it not?—Yes; I think so.

Economic condition compared with earlier times.

2137. I understand you to say generally as to the condition of the farmers that they did improve from the Famine up to 1871?—I should go further and say up to 1876, or so.

2138. But have been falling rather backwards since?—No; I would not say they have been falling backwards, but I do not think they have gone on in the same proportion improving.

2139. There is a good deal of debt you say to the shopkeeper?—Yes, there has been ever since 1876.

2140. And is still?—And is still. I do not think they are getting credit to the same extent. I think credit has shrunk of recent years.

2141. And the shrinkage of credit argues the existence of debt?—Yes.

2142. And they borrow from the banks?—Yes, and from the gombeen man.

2143. We hear so often the same old figures about bank stock and railway shares and Government Stocks in Ireland that I should like to ask you whether you have any reason to think that the farmers in Ireland hold any of this class of property?—If you mean the average man occupying a third class house I do not think he has much railway stock or bank stock; and I do not think the larger men invest their money in that way. I think what they have they invest in cattle rather than that.

2144. What comes more directly under your observation I should think is that they are in debt and constantly endeavouring to borrow from the bank?—Exactly.

2145. You have spoken of the change in the habits of the people, and the mode of living?—Yes.

2146. Is the change in the mode of living anything more than what you would call the ordinary movement of civilisation?—It is the progress of civilisation.

M

Mr. Henry A. Robinson.

4 Dec. 1895.

Economic conditions, comparison with earlier times.

2147. The ordinary progress of civilisation?—Yes.

2148. Which it would be safer to call a change than an improvement?—It is a decided improvement, I think.

2149. Is it a decided improvement to eat poor baker's bread and drink inferior tea rather than eat oatmeal porridge and milk?—They do not drink inferior tea, but the very best tea they can get.

2150. Is even the best tea an improvement on porridge and milk?—Bread and butter and tea.

2151. Do you say they eat butter?—A few of them do. I think that is an improvement compared with potatoes and nothing but potatoes, especially having regard to the fact that they cannot put any confidence in the potato crop.

2152. I put it to you in this way, that before the famine the habits of the people were different, they dressed in homespun and fed on the produce of their farms to a great extent, oatmeal, milk, and butter, and in more recent years they buy their clothing and resort to baker's bread and tea?—Yes.

2153. Would not that be more correctly described as a change than as an improvement?—It is a change, but at the same time I think when you come to consider how very uncertain the potato crop is that it is improvement also, and, I think when you read about the way in which they were all seated round a bowl on the floor, and the pig forcing his way in, and all eating the potatoes together in 1830, and go into a house now and see them sitting at a table with bread and milk and tea, you would admit that it is a decided improvement.

2154. (*Sir David Barbour.*) I suppose the people think tea an improvement and choose this mode of living of their own free will though it is more expensive?—Yes, I think they would not think it respectable otherwise.

2155. (*Mr. Sexton.*) It is a change of habit due to a change of feeling or opinion, they do what they prefer?—Just so.

2156. All that about the pig forcing his way in is rather a satirical observation, is it not?—No, I believe the report of the Committee in those years was that they had no furniture or beds or anything in the houses but themselves and their live stock.

2157. The change of the mode of living renders the small farmer less independent in this sense, that before the Famine he was able to provide himself with food and clothes by his own labour, whereas now he requires money to buy them?—I should say immediately after the Famine because before the Famine the evidence is that he was unable to feed himself with food of any sort.

2158. You are speaking of immediately before the Famine?—I am speaking of after the time that the war prices declined, from 1820 down to the Famine.

2159. Have you any reason to doubt the opinion of the Commissioners of Lunacy that the substitution of tea for oatmeal has produced an increase of lunacy?—That is in the North, is it not? I can quite understand it in the North, because they drink their tea in a different way to what they do in other parts of the country. They put it on to stew early in the morning and drink it strong and black and bitter. In the other parts, the West and South, I think they know how to make tea. I do not know whether lunacy has increased owing to tea drinking in the North.

2160. The change in the mode of life has imposed a heavier cash expenditure on the farmer, has it not?—Yes, undoubtedly.

2161. And in that sense might render him less able to bear fiscal burdens?—Yes, while he lives as at present.

2162. You spoke of the reduction of rents. You are aware, I make no doubt, that the judgments of the Land Courts apply to something like one-third only of the whole valuation of Ireland?—I was not aware of that.

2163. It is a little more than one-third; the rents of the remainder have not been reduced?—Is that so? I ought to be better up in those figures but I have enough to do of my own work.

2164. The rents where they have been reduced have only been reduced on the average 20 per cent. Would that reduction, do you think, enable the farmer to meet the state of agricultural facts which has arisen since 1878?—I think you must remember that there are other advantages he has, that the class of food which is now substituted for the potato is extraordinarily cheap; but, as I said before, I do not think he is any better able to bear taxation now than he was twenty years ago.

2165. One farmer out of every three has got twenty per cent. off his rent, the other two have got nothing off, and they have had to face since 1873 an extraordinary fall in yield—about one-third or one-half of the principal crops, and together with that an unprecedented and still continuing fall in price?—The prices of nearly everything have fallen since 1878.

2166. Fallen heavily?—Yes, but that was an extremely good year. Prices I am glad to say are a little up this year.

2167. Then the farmer has to pay higher wages, has he not?—Well, the poorer class of tenants do not employ much labour. The large farmer makes use of more machinery, but any labour he does employ he undoubtedly has to pay higher for it.

2168. Taking it altogether, the debts due to the shopkeepers, the restriction of credit at the banks, the heavy fall in prices in the last twenty years, the heavier fall in yield and the higher wages he has to pay—taking it all round, is there anything in such a matter as a better house or a change in an article of food that would entitle anyone to say that the Irish farmer is in as all as good a condition as he was about twenty years ago?—He is in an improved condition, I say in the way of living, but, as I have said before, he is no better off.

2169. The mode of living has changed?—The mode of living is better and his clothes are better.

2170. But the position of the man with regard to income and expenditure is certainly more precarious, is it not?—Yes, I think it is of those small men.

2171. As to the condition of the labourers, they lived mostly on the produce of the land about them, potatoes, did they not?—I think they lived on the wages they earned and got a small patch of potatoes from the farmers to till.

2172. They lived so much on the produce about them that the wages were hardly essential—the necessaries of life were supplied from the produce, were they not?—I do not agree with you. I think they lived principally on the wages they earned.

2173. In those old times the wages were only sixpence a day, were they not?—I thought you were referring to 1878.

2174. I meant the old times?—I do not know how they made a living at all. Their wages were from sixpence to tenpence a day, and there was no employment for a very large proportion of them.

2175. The labourers have higher wages now, have they not?—Yes.

2176. And I suppose they pay higher rents now?—They pay the Guardians for their cottages about a shilling a week.

2177. I am speaking of the labourer in general?—I do not know that they do; I do not think they pay very much more; they do not pay more than they did before the Act was first brought in. In fact I think the tendency of the farmer is rather to improve the condition of the labourer for fear that the cottages might be put upon him.

2178. What you have said about the change in the mode of life of the farmers I think applies also to the labourers in a certain degree, does it not?—Yes, it does.

2179. They purchase clothes and food?—Yes.

2180. They do not depend so much on home industry for their clothes, do they?—I do not think the labourers have ever made their clothes much; I think they mostly always bought clothes; they had no

Mr. Henry A. Robinson. [illegible] Dec. [illegible]

[illegible]

sheep or stock. They would buy their clothes and so forth and things.

2181. (*The O'Conor Don.*) Do the farmers object to the labourers getting better cottages?—They do not object to them getting better cottages so long as the cottages are not put upon their land.

2182. (*Mr. Martin.*) The farmer has to contribute to the cost of these cottages, has he not?—Yes, very considerably.

Labourers' Acts.

2183. (*Mr. Sexton.*) As to the Labourers Acts, can you explain why it is that the administration of the Acts having gone up in cost from 125,000*l.* in 1886 to a quarter of a million in 1888 has fallen again to 100,000*l.*?—What are you referring to now?

2184. Your return of expenditure?—I think the great weight of the work done under the Labourers Acts fell on those three years, and it has been rather diminishing of late years. Of course when a vast number of the labourers were housed as they had been up to that date, naturally there was not so much to be done.

2185. To what extent has the condition of the labourers in Ireland been affected by the Labourers Acts?—This shows you the expenditure. I did not bring the number of houses which have been built, but a very considerable number have been built.

2186. Can you tell me the number?—10,352 actually built, 640 in progress of erection, and 1,945 additional authorised.

2187. What is the average cost of a cottage and plot of land?—About 125*l.* I should think.

2188. That would give us between 11,000 and 12,000 houses out of this sum of money, would it not?—It would. I think I can give you the exact number.

2189. It would not be more than 12,000. Have you found it?—I have a map here showing the cottages which have been built in each union.

2190. At 125*l.* a house you would get 8,000 houses for a million pounds, and the money here was a million and a half, so that would give 12,000 houses?—I think you are rather over it—that is my impression—because some of them might not be able to get contracts on such favourable terms. How many did you say?

2191. I said it might be 10,000 or 12,000.—The number of cottages authorised is 12,937.

2192. (*Mr. Wolff.*) That is the total number which have been built, is it?—It includes the number either built or in course of erection. The average weekly rent is about 1*s.* 3*d.*, so I put it rather too high.

2193. (*Mr. Sexton.*) That is relatively a very small number after some ten years' working of the Acts, is it not?—It has been going on at high pressure, I can tell you that much.

2194. But there would be a very considerable number still in need, would there not?—I admit that there are, and schemes are coming in every day for inquiry and are being inquired into.

2195. (*Sir David Barbour.*) There are two provinces, you say, in which the Act has not been applied?—That is so. In Ulster the Act has not been taken up.

2196. (*Mr. Sexton.*) I should say that only a small proportion of the labourers of Ireland are not properly housed?—A small percentage.

2197. Yes, a tolerably small percentage?—I do not know what the number of labourers is.

2198. It would be a very large number?—I cannot say.

2199. Some hundreds of thousands?—I am sorry I cannot say. Dr. Grimshaw might be able to speak certainly. I do not know the exact number, but certainly the Act is being administered at the present moment very actively.

2200. What is the average rent paid, 1*s.* 3*d.*?—Yes, 1*s.* 3*d.* is about the average.

2201. What is the average annuity payable per 100*l.*?—The usual number of years selected for repayment is 50, and the annuity in that case is 4*l.* 9*s.* 2*d.*

2202. It is more than 3*l.* 5*s.*, is it not?—I think that each cottage costs the Guardians about 5*l.* a year —probably more—about or thereabouts. I cannot be very sure without looking it up.

2203. That is to say, after the rent has been received and credited to the extent of 1*s.* 3*d.* a week or 3*l.* 5*s.* a year, there is about 35*s.* a year to be made good from the rates?—Yes, or more, I should think. I have not the figures at my finger's end, but I am sure in any case the principal and interest would lead to a loss to the ratepayers of about 3*l.* a year, I should say roughly.

2204. Of course that constitutes a great impediment to the development of the system. The mere fact that the rent recoverable is substantially less than the liability incurred by the Board is in itself an impediment to the development of the system, is it not?—Yes, certainly.

2205. Are you aware whether there is dissatisfaction felt with the expenses of the system under the Acts, including the expense of your inquiry, and so forth?—There is a great dissatisfaction at the expense of the Acts, but I do not know that the expense of the inquiry is great; it only consists of the shorthand writer's notes; nothing is charged for anything else. The Inspector's going round and the cost of making his report is not charged to the rates.

2206. Would it not be a matter of cardinal importance with respect to the comfort and health of the people and to their taxable capacity if the class of houses to be provided under the Act could be more generally provided for the labouring population?—Yes.

2207. Either by cheapening the procedure or in any other way?—Yes, it would be a great matter if the procedure could be cheapened in any way.

2208. I have no doubt your Board would be very willing to co-operate in any suggestion or device to bring about such a purpose?—You may be sure of that.

2209. As to Connaught you say, I think, with accuracy that the labourers are mostly small occupiers, and therefore the Acts do not apply; but what is the explanation about Ulster?—The explanation about Ulster is that the Guardians do not approve of the Act, so far as I see, and object to put it into operation; but I do not know what their objection is beyond that. As a matter of fact, they have not put it into operation to any considerable extent.

2210. Ulster is the most populous of the four provinces, is it not?—You must take into consideration that there is a vast manufacturing population there.

2211. It has a vast agricultural population, and I see you have spent only 11,000*l.* there, which would give about a hundred houses in Ulster?—Very few at the present moment. The Inspector of the Local Government Board is now the Sanitary Authority for one or two unions under the Labourers Act. It is under the new Act—the Act of 1891, I think.

2212. You say it arises from the indisposition of the Guardians to act?—I think so.

2213. Have the labourers put forward representations?—Yes.

2214. Many?—Yes, they are all making representations, trying to urge on the Guardians to take up their case, and of course until the year 1891 there was no remedy.

2215. Have you acted in many cases in Ulster?—Yes, we have a great many cases in now. The procedure, first of all, is this: the inquiry is held to ascertain what reasons the Guardians have for not building; then the Inspector makes a report and calls upon the Guardians to build a certain number of cottages, giving them a reasonable time to build them in—some six months, say. In the event of the Guardians declining to do that, the Guardians are superseded as the Sanitary Authority, and the Local Government Inspector himself becomes the Sanitary Authority, and has to prepare a scheme. There are some schemes now in course of preparation in regard to some of the unions.

M 2

2716. I see you have only adopted four schemes in all Ulster at present, is that so? There are a great many more coming in, I believe.

2717. May we entertain a hope that you really mean to examine your powers?—Yes, we are bound to do so.

2718. I think it is apt to be forgotten, is it not, in comparing the condition of the labourer in Ireland with the condition of the labourer in other parts of the United Kingdom, that the labour market is very precarious?—My impression is that a great many of the labourers in the summer months cannot be got; and two or three months in the winter they are half starving.

2719. Is not it an aspect which ought to be kept in mind, that his occupation is intermittent and precarious, and his daily or weekly wage is no criterion of his income?—Yes. Of course in harvest time the wages are very high; the labourers in the towns are the people who are the worst off.

2720. Their condition is extremely uncertain everywhere, is it not?—Of course the men who are in constant employment all the year round, who are bound men to farmers, are well off, comparatively speaking.

2721. But they are a small percentage of the whole, are they not?—I think on every big farm there are a few of the kind.

2722. I see that the total of these local rates is about three millions of money upon a valuation of eleven millions and a half?—Fourteen millions, is it not, including the towns?

2723. Yes; that would be 4s. 2d.?—Yes.

2724. And you have given cases in which the local burden has reached 13s. 3d. in the pound?—That was an extreme case. I was asked what was the highest I was aware of.

2725. I suppose cases are by no means uncommon, especially in a bad or in a congested district where extremely heavy local rates, especially poor rates, fall upon a rather small number of rateable occupiers and become very oppressive?—The poor rates in bad years, undoubtedly in some of those districts I have referred to, on the occupier who pays poor rates, press heavily, because he has the cess to pay besides, and the man who feels it the most is the man who is nearest to the 4l. limit—the 5l. man. Of course he has county cess and heavy poor rates to pay, and there may be pressing divisions in those unions where the rate is very much above the average.

2726. The ordinary case is that the local burden is much less than the Imperial burden. As a whole the local burden is very much less than the Imperial burden, and I suppose in England and Scotland that represents the usual state of affairs: the local pressure is less than the Imperial, but in these districts in Ireland the local burden is very often a multiple of what the Imperial taxes would reach, is it not?—I would rather like to work that out before giving a definite answer. They contribute a good deal you know in the way of indirect taxation.

2727. But it would not reach any such figure as you gave with regard to Belmullet, would it?—If you consider how much a man contributes in the way of tobacco and whiskey, and so on in the year, I think he would pay more in the way of Imperial taxation than in local taxes. Assume that he pays a shilling a week for tobacco.

2728. I understand you to say that the loans recommended by the Local Government Board have not resulted in much arrear?—I think they have been wonderfully well paid.

2729. I should like to have that testimony clear. These debts have been incurred under circumstances of extreme difficulty by the unions in the west, have they not?—Yes.

2730. Is it not the fact that the repayment has been wonderfully good and the arrear is very small?—I think it has been very well recovered, especially under the last Act—the 1890 Act.

2731. And all these stories about defaulting Boards and debts not paid, and so forth, are pure romance; they are paid?—The reason of defaulting Boards is simply because the Boards have failed to strike rates which would meet the current expenditure. I think there is a great deal owing to the Treasury in some of the poor unions, and we receive a good many applications from the Board of Works to call the attention of the Guardians to the fact that they are behindhand in instalments on loans. That comes in constantly and you have to press them to levy a rate which will cover the instalments due, and very often they make a rate which will not provide for the instalments due.

2732. I have not gathered from your evidence that there is any heavier arrear on the loans advanced to Boards of Guardians than to other local authorities?—I do not quite know what is outstanding.

2733. Is there any impression on your mind that Boards of Guardians owe heavier arrears to the Treasury than other authorities do?—No, I think not—I think on the whole the loans advanced to the Boards of Guardians have been paid very well.

2734. I put it to you that the payment of the seed loan of 1880, and still more the seed loan of 1890, which has been more recently paid, has been most remarkable?—I think so.

2735. There are 160 unions in Ireland, are there not?—159.

2736. It might be as well as we hear so much about suspensions of Boards, which is another favorite topic in certain quarters, to know how many there are which have been suspended in a year, say?—I suppose there have been about ten during the last ten years; that is all.

2737. About ten in ten years—one a year?—Oh, no; there might have been four or five all at once.

2738. But ten in ten years?—There may have been one or two more. I cannot answer off hand. That is all I can think of at present.

2739. (*The O'Conor Don.*) For what length of time have they been suspended?—For the making of two rates, generally.

2740. (*Mr Sexton.*) The suspension would be due to financial difficulty and bad times, I suppose?—It might—any default. They are never suspended unless it is absolutely unavoidable.

2741. I wish to put a question or two about the constitution of these local bodies, and especially as to your jurisdiction. The county funds are administered not as in Great Britain, by elected bodies, but by Grand Juries?—Yes.

2742. And the Grand Juries are nominated by the High Sheriff?—Yes.

2743. They are not continuing bodies, are they?—No.

2744. They are created and dissolved twice a year, are they not?—Exactly.

2745. Their responsibility is very slender then?—Yes, the greater part of the work is in the hands of the officers who carry on the county work.

2746. A permanent committee of the officials?—Yes.

2747. What control have you over those?—None.

2748. None at all?—No, none over Grand Juries; they are not under us.

2749. You have simply a power of audit?—Simply a power of audit and certifying their accounts, that is all.

2750. In case you do not approve of any expenditure can you surcharge?—The mere fact of our approving is nothing, the Judge approving of it makes it perfectly legitimate.

2751. It seems a somewhat barren function then?—I think it is necessary.

2752. But what would they care if you have no power to make your disapproval felt?—I think if anything was wrongly applied and brought under the notice of the Judge of Assize, notice would be taken of it.

[illegible]

2253. (*Lord Welby.*) Do you publish the Auditors' Report?—Yes.

2254. And there is therefore the fear of publication?—Yes.

2255. (*Mr. Sexton.*) So that with regard to this sum of a million and a half a year spent by Grand Juries, which is a good deal more than one-third of the whole local taxation of Ireland, there is no supervision in regard to economy to the taxpayer, excepting such as may be afforded by the Judge of Assize?—Yes, there is no central authority over them at all, and the check of course is the audit of the accounts and the publication. Of course any cess-payer may object to the fiating of any presentment.

2256. The fiating of any presentment before the Judge?—Yes.

2257. But when the period has closed and the Grand Jury dissolved and the audit held, even supposing the auditor then said, "This is improper or illegal," what redress has anybody?—I am not quite sure; I do not think that anything which has been passed by the Judge can absolutely be surcharged by the auditor.

2258. Do you know of any reason why the county rate should not be subject to a revision, supervision, audit and surcharge, if necessary, just the same as the union rate?—By whom?

2259. By some one?—I see no reason why it should not be so.

2260. (*The O'Conor Don.*) Before you pass from this, you stated in answer to Mr. Sexton that all the county expenditure is passed solely by the Grand Jury nominated by the High Sheriff?—Yes.

2261. Can the Grand Jury pass any presentment except for some exceptional work that has not been previously sanctioned by the Presentment Sessions?—They cannot originate anything.

2262. They cannot alter any presentment passed?—No, they may refuse it.

2263. They either pass it or throw it out?—Exactly.

2264. Therefore with regard to the great bulk of the sum to which Mr. Sexton has referred, the powers of the Grand Jury are as you have stated, either powers of rejection or approval?—Exactly.

2265. All works approved of by the Presentment Sessions?—Yes.

2266. If there were any such system of audit which would result in surcharging somebody for a presentment which ought not to have been passed, on whom would that surcharge be made?—It would have to be made, I presume, upon the magistrates and the cesspayers. I was referring rather to the whole organisation than to the particular Grand Jury, the Presentment Sessions, of course, being a part of that organisation.

2267. (*Mr. Sexton.*) Probably the cure would be to have a continuing body who might be surcharged?—Yes.

2268. (*Lord Welby.*) Could not the surcharge be made on the people who ordered the payment?—I have never known the magistrates to be surcharged—I do not quite see how it could be done.

2269. It may not be law laid down, but so far as it goes you could surcharge, could you not, upon the actual people who have ordered the payment?—I suppose it could be done.

2270. (*The O'Conor Don.*) Is not the Judge really the person who orders the payment?—The Judge orders the payment.

2271. (*Mr. Sexton.*) But you see no probability of payment?—No. It is open to any cesspayer to oppose any presentment—they are called out by baronies, and he can make opposition before the Judge fiats.

2272. (*The O'Conor Don.*) They are called out publicly in court, are they not, before the Judge fiats them?—Yes.

2273. And if anyone chooses to object the Judge will hear the objection?—Yes.

2274. (*Sir David Barbour.*) Then I understand there are three authorities dealing with this matter—what is called the Presentment Sessions, then the Grand Jury, then the Judge?—First of all there is the Presentment Sessions held for each Barony separately, and for the county at large before each assizes, then the Grand Jury, and the Judge.

2275. (*Mr. Sexton.*) The Presentment Sessions is practically controlled by the magistrates, is it not?—The magistrates and the cesspayers.

2276. But the magistrates have a right to act, of course, and the cesspayers are chosen by ballot on the spot?—Yes.

2277. The same class which constitutes the Grand Jury controls the Sessions?—It is part of the system.

2278. I understand now how it is you are unable to inform us as to the amount of debt now outstanding in counties; they are not even under obligation to inform you, I suppose?—No.

2279. Have they any power to borrow?—They were given power to borrow under the Relief of Distress Act, and the Relief of Distress Amendment Act for Baronial Works, but that Act has expired.

2280. Have they to refer to any authority in case of borrowing?—They ought to refer to the Board of Works.

2281. Not to you?—No.

2282. Have the county authorities any power in times of distress to provide employment?—None under existing law, beyond that they can afford employment in the way of making ordinary roads which may be required by the people, but not in the way of any special distress works, like they did under the old Distress Act. They cannot carry out any work of that kind purely for the purpose of relief; they can only carry out works which are required by the particular counties, and carry them out in the way prescribed.

2283. They may adopt the ordinary services, but cannot take any special action?—That is so.

2284. As to the unions, you have a much more drastic supervision, have you not?—Yes.

2285. The unions are constituted, I believe, one-half of magistrates ex officio?—Yes.

2286. And the other half of elected ratepayers?—Yes.

2287. Elected upon a property franchise?—Yes.

2288. Which may give one vote to the occupier and thirty or thirty-six to the owner, or up to thirty at any rate?—Yes, up to thirty, but only in the case when the owner is also occupier and immediate lessor. The occupier, of course, may have more than one vote—it depends upon the valuation.

2289. You audit their accounts, and have power to surcharge?—Yes.

2290. Would the sums surcharged over the unions of Ireland in a year reach any considerable amount?—They are very careful—the mere fact of that power existing is quite sufficient to make both the Guardians and their officers extremely careful.

2291. Then I may infer, as you have power to surcharge not only for illegal but for extravagant expenditure, that the administration of the funds by the Guardians is economical?—Yes, I think they try to keep it within the bounds as far as possible.

2292. What special powers have Guardians to cope with distress arising?—They have first of all the power of affording outdoor relief to the classes I have mentioned in the earlier part of my evidence. Then for the ordinary classes they have the workhouse, in which any person may receive relief, and then the relieving officer has power in case of sudden and urgent necessity pending the order of the Board of Guardians to afford relief.

2293. And the outdoor relief is for a limited time. May it continue for an unlimited time?—The outdoor relief which the Guardians give may continue for an unlimited time.

2294. Is it usual to give outdoor relief to families?—Not if they are in occupation of land.

2295. So that therefore the provisions for outdoor relief would not apply to farmers in any degree, would

Mr. Henry A. Robinson.

4 Dec. 1894.

Boards of Guardians.

it?—No, except in sudden cases of urgent necessity when a man might be starving.

2296. The poorest occupier with only a quarter of an acre of land would be debarred from outdoor relief then?—Yes.

2297. (*The O'Conor Don*). With regard to the exceptional cases where men are starving, the relief must be given in kind and not in money?—In kind and not in money.

2298. (*Mr. Sexton*). They have no power to levy a rate or to borrow for the purpose, say, of providing a supply of seed?—No, they have no Act at present for that purpose.

2299. And in order to enable either the counties or the Guardians to provide works to give employment to labourers or to provide seed, is there no other way than by legislation?—No.

[illegible]

2300. I see that the cost of administration as to towns has increased much more than any of the other local bodies?—Yes.

2301. I suppose that is due to greater energy in necessary works of sanitation?—Yes, and the fact that there is room for more improvement in the towns.

2302. The towns in past times have been somewhat neglected?—Yes.

2303. Many primary essential things were required to be done?—Yes, the improvement is always a very gradual and slow process, but I think they have been made more alive to the necessities in recent years, especially since the cholera was threatened than previously.

2304. The municipalities have power to issue stock, have they not?—Yes.

2305. Some of them under special Acts?—Yes.

2306. And any of them, I should think, with the sanction of your Board under a recent public Act?—Yes.

2307. Have you been asked to grant the sanction?—Yes.

2308. In many cases?—I cannot remember the exact number at present. We have been asked.

2309. Have you granted it?—Yes; I cannot remember the number at present.

2310. I believe it is the case that in the principal cities, Dublin, Belfast, Cork, and Waterford, the issue of stock which is a resort from Imperial to local credit has resulted in a considerable saving to the rates?—Yes, it has been very successful, no doubt.

2311. And Imperial credit was dispensed with to the credit of the community?—Yes.

Cost of workhouse inmates.

2312. There is one other question as to which I should like to get some information from you. What is the average cost of the maintenance of an inmate in an Irish workhouse?—It varies.

2313. What is the average?—It varies from 3s. to 4s. a week, including clothing.

2314. Nothing but what the inmate wears and eats?—The highest in Ulster is 3s. 9d.

2315. Have you struck any average for the country?—The average for Ulster is 3s.; the average for Munster is 3s. 2½d.; for Leinster, 3s. 7½d.; and for Connaught, 3s. 6d. For the whole of Ireland it is 3s. 4d.

2316. 3s. 4d. a week for the whole of Ireland?—Yes.

2317. That would be 8l. 13s. 4d. a year for the whole of Ireland?—Yes.

2318. I notice that the average daily number in the workhouses for 1892–3 was 41,000?—Yes.

2319. If you divide that number into the cost of maintenance, 333,000l., you get 8l., which corresponds with what you have said?—Exactly.

2320. Then if you want to ascertain the full cost of an inmate, really, I should think, you have to add to that the cost of the officers, which, I suppose, you might put instead of rent if the person were living outside?—Nearly the whole cost of the establishment. You mean the establishment charge?

2321. (*Chairman.*) It is about 15 per cent.?—Yes.

2322. (*Mr. Sexton.*) Salaries and rations of officers and every expenditure—would that be it?—Yes.

2323. That makes 651,000, and dividing 41,000 into that figure, we come to the result that the average cost of an inmate in an Irish workhouse is 16l. a year?—Yes, about that figure if establishment expenses are included.

Mr. Henry A. Robinson.

4 Dec. 1894.

Rates in different parts of Ireland.

2324. (*Mr. Wolff.*) You have told us that Ireland as regards the poor law and relief and so on you may almost divide by a line from Lough Swilly to Cape Clear?—Yes.

2325. That on the east of it the average was a 1s. 5d. rate?—I do not think I said that. I said that the average of the county cess in Ireland was about 1s. 9d.

2326. I misunderstood you—you cannot give the average of the poor rate then?—No, I have not got it now. Do you want it on those two districts?

2327. I would like it on those two, and I would like it over the whole. If we are to compare the expenditure and ability to pay of one country with another we ought to have such information, I think?—I will get it for you.

Labourers Acts.

2328. I was going to ask also about the Labourers Act, which you have told us has not been taken up in Ulster; can you give us any reason why it has not been taken up in Ulster?—I really cannot say why the Guardians have not taken it up, beyond that they seem to think the labourers are already properly provided for.

2329. Is it your experience that they are properly provided for?—No, it is not my experience; but I think the Guardians contend that they do not require additional accommodation or do not require improved accommodation. There is very great resistance on the part of the Guardians to the Act.

2330. There must be some portions in the west of Ulster which are no better off as regards the labourer than these other parts?—The labourer, as a class, does not exist in those very poor parts as in Donegal. There they are small occupiers, but in Ulster the labourer lives on rich lands, where large farms are held by one man. I think the poor people you refer to in Donegal are not labourers—they are small holders.

2331. (*Lord Welby.*) I do not think you have given us the figures. Can you give us what has been the expenditure out of loans made by the State on farmers' dwellings and labourers'?—I can give you labourers' dwellings, but I cannot give you farmers' dwellings—that does not come under us at all.

2332. Does that come under land improvement?—Yes. Under labourers' dwellings the amount remaining outstanding is 1,125,500l.

2333. Can you give us the total that has been advanced?—1,236,222l.

Fall of prices.

2334. I want to call your attention to one point. You mentioned, and I have no doubt with very good reason, that the price of stock having fallen was a reason why the farmer, on the whole, had not got such a paying capacity, for whatever purpose it might be, as formerly. Looking at Dr. Grimshaw's figures, I arrive at this conclusion—that, taking the time when they had the highest price—namely, between 1884 and 1888—and dividing it by the population, what it comes to is that the valuation of stock at that time was about 11l. per head of the population, and in 1889 to 1893, 12l.?—Yes.

2335. Of course that is due to there being a much increased stock?—Yes.

2336. My test is a very rough one, but you see on that basis the farmer has as great a paying capacity as in the higher time, has he not?—I was not comparing it in that way. The comparison I instituted was more between the years during which I said there had been a great improvement—that is, between 1851 and 1874—than between the years 1882, 1883, and onwards.

2337. I am not asking you to accept these figures; they are figures given by Dr. Grimshaw, and he gave in 1851–55 the value of all descriptions of live stock as 30,000,000l.; in 1866–70, 39,000,000l., which is the date on which I base my 11l.; in 1884–88, 55,000,000l.; and in 1889–93, 54,000,000l. You see the prices

[illegible] 5 Dec. 1894.

these given carry out your view that there has been a considerable fall per head between 1866-70 and 1886-91?—Yes.

2338. But that to the farmer is made up by an increase in the number of the live stock?—I see what you mean.

2339. When you were talking of tax-paying capacity I understood you to say in answer to a question, or you rather expressed an opinion, that the consumption of tea at present drew very largely on farmers' resources now as compared with the time, say, before the famine, or 1851-53. Your answer left it upon my mind that the consumption of tea rather burdened and diminished his tax paying capacity; was that so?—Yes.

2340. We must be careful how we use that. Let us go back and consider what was the farmer's position; at the time you were speaking of the tax upon tea was probably 3s., 2s. 6d., or 2s. 2d.—it was certainly 2s. 2d. late in the fifties?—Yes.

2341. I suppose the price of tea itself was considerably higher than than it is now—for the sake of argument let us say 2s. higher—and that the farmer was paying 4s., out of which 2s. went to the revenue. At the present moment I do not suppose I am very far wrong if I say the value of tea is 2s. of which 6d. goes to the Government?—Yes.

2342. Now I think we can hardly say, can we, that if the price of an article is diminished half and the duty is diminished 75 per cent., that the position of the consumer is not better and that so far he is in a better tax-paying position than he was?—But he did not pay at all in those years.

2343. Perhaps so. I will next put to you the case of sugar at that time. Wherever you go you will find that the removal of the duty on sugar has been one of the greatest boons during the present century. That tax has entirely gone, and surely therefore the tax-paying capacity of the consumer has increased through that relief. I only use the argument for the purpose of putting the matter right, because it seems to me a very dangerous ground to say that, because you find a man under much more favourable circumstances so far as price goes, with a larger command over articles of comfort, therefore his tax paying capacity has diminished?—I do not think I said that; what I said was this, I think that class of small occupier at the present time contribute more in the way of indirect taxation in proportion to their income than any other class of the community.

2344. In answer to Mr. Sexton I thought you rather admitted it?—If I did I did not quite see the point.

2345. (Mr. Sexton.) I thought what you said was this, that the change in the mode of life, the change in the mode of diet, involved a rather higher cash expenditure than the domestic habits of the last generation involved, which might render them less able to bear a fiscal burden?—Yes.

2346. (Mr. Wolff.) As a matter of fact do they not contribute more to the imperial revenue now under a 6d. duty on tea than they did formerly when the duty was 2s., in that they now consume a considerable quantity and they formerly consumed none?—Just so.

The witness withdrew.

SIXTH DAY.

Thursday, 6th December, 1894.

At the Benchers' Chambers, Four Courts, Dublin.

PRESENT:

THE RIGHT HON. HUGH C. E. CHILDERS, *Chairman*.

LORD WELBY.	CHARLES E. MARTIN, Esq.
THE RIGHT HON. THE O'CONOR DON.	THOMAS SEXTON, Esq., M.P.
SIR DAVID BARBOUR, K.C.S.I.	GUSTAV W. WOLFF, Esq., M.P.

MR. B. H. HOLLAND, *Secretary*.

SIR JOSEPH M'KENNA called, and examined by Mr. Sexton at the request of the Chairman.

Sir Joseph M'Kenna. 6 Dec. 1894.

2347. (*Mr. Sexton.*) You have sat for many years as an Irish representative in the Imperial Parliament, have you not?—About twenty-two years.

2348. And you have given particular care and study to financial questions, have you not?—Yes.

2349. You now propose to offer evidence to this Commission upon some of the questions referred to it?—Yes.

2350. Especially upon the main question which is the relative taxable capacity not of any classes or interests in Great Britain and Ireland as compared with each other, but as compared between Great Britain on the one hand and Ireland as a whole on the other?—Yes. In the course of that investigation I have discriminated between England and Scotland, but that was owing to the accidental form in which the returns from which I had to work were made out, but the case remains that if you add the product of Scottish revenue to the product of English revenue you get that of Great Britain, and I have made my comparisons on that basis in the end, but incidentally as I went along I have brought out the fact of Scotland suffering somewhat as we have suffered.

2351. In the course of your evidence to-day you will be good enough to bear in mind that the units are not England, Scotland, and Ireland, but Great Britain and Ireland. You propose to found your case upon certain matters of financial record contained in Parliamentary Papers, Nos. 407 of the Session 1874, No. 108 of 1886, and No. 38 of Session 2 of 1886?—Yes, and others as I go along;—I do not found the case on those solely.

2352. But those in the first instance?—Those in the first instance.

2353. Will you give us the titles of these papers and describe their contents?—I will as I go along; it will involve extreme labour to go into them now; they will be found on the face of my evidence. I will submit myself at once to cross-examination on the matter, and I will give evidence in favour of the whole memorandum.

2354. I had better myself read to you the titles of these papers, and you will say whether I describe them correctly. The first is a return of "Revenue and "Population" of Great Britain and Ireland for the years 1841, 1851, 1861, and 1871, being No. 407 of

Sir Joseph M'Kenna. 3 Dec. 1894.

the Session 1874, and a similar return brought down to 1881–82 and 1884–85, being No. 166 of 1886; a Parliamentary Paper, No. 35, Session 2, 1886, containing (1) "A return of the gross amount of revenue "raised by taxation in Ireland for the years 1800 to "1840, both inclusive"; (2) a like "return for the "years 1841 to 1880, both inclusive"; and (3) a return of the amount of loans from the Imperial Exchequer for Irish purposes from A.D. 1800 to the 31st March, 1886, distinguishing amounts paid off, remitted, and outstanding at the last mentioned date? —Yes.

Points with respect to Act of Union.

2355. Before you enter into details I understand that you wish to lay down some points with respect to the Act of Union which you consider in dispute?—I do not. I make an assertion upon that part and give evidence upon the general fact instead of laying it down as a matter of pleading, which it would be too lengthy for this Commission to entertain.

2356. You wish to state them, do you not?—I wish to state the facts as concisely as Mr. Gladstone stated them to the Duke of Argyll. I wish to state that the proposition which was made, and the purpose to be carried out, and which, I believe, was carried out by the passing of the Act of Union, was that subsequent to the consolidation of the two Exchequers we should be treated relatively to our taxable means the same as Great Britain.

2357. Will you look at paragraph 5 of your memorandum on the first page. Be so good as to state the effect of that paragraph. There are four articles there. I desire you to give the Commission as we proceed the substance of the memorandum?—What particular point do you ask me upon?

2358. The whole of it.—Ask me a question upon it.

2359. I desire you to state to the Commission the substance of the paragraphs. You will understand that the memorandum you have handed in is the basis of your evidence?—Just so. Then I will read 1, 2, 3, and 4 as my answer to that. "1st.—No living statesman is accountable for the enactment of the Act of "Union. 2nd.—The Act of Union was carried "through the Irish Parliament by corrupt means. "3rd.—Even were it still in question whether the Act "of Union had not been so carried, the financial conditions enjoined, imposing on Ireland an obligation to "contribute until the amalgamation of the two "Exchequers (an event which did not occur until 1817) "two-seventeenths to the Imperial Revenue was "inequitable to Ireland, being manifestly disproportionate to the relative resources of the two islands. "4th.—That whatever may have been the injustice of "that obligatory condition, no such compact exists or "has existed under the Act of Union or otherwise, since "1817, but all distribution of burden thenceforth "rested, and now rests, with the Parliament of the "United Kingdom." That is the most condensed form in which I can give the status quo at present complained of.

[illegible]

2360. The practical effect of that is that under the Act of Union an excessive contribution was imposed upon Ireland, and that in 1817 that arrangement ceased?—Yes.

2361. And that since then the obligation of Ireland was to contribute according to her means?—Yes; under the Union.

2362. Passing on, how do you say that the excessive character of the contribution imposed upon Ireland by the Act of Union was made manifest?—There is a subsequent paragraph which I will refer you to for that.

2363. I am taking you through your paragraphs as they stand?—As I understand, your question is how do I make out that Parliament had a free hand after the consolidation. Those were the terms of the Act of Union.

2364. No, I am at present asking you how you make out that the contribution imposed upon Ireland by the Act of Union was excessive?—Because the effect of it was that she was run into debt four times; her debt was quadrupled, and the debt of England was not even doubled.

2365. Moreover, the revenue exacted from Ireland in the seventeen years during the separate exchequer was far in excess of the revenue she paid before the Union?—Yes, far in excess. She paid, according to the best authorities open to me, the average for the ten years immediately antecedent, 1,500,000*l.* a year or a fraction short of that.

2366. I put it to you from a paper issued to this Commission by the Treasury last July, which shows that the total revenue of Ireland including from one to three hundred thousand pounds of miscellaneous, which was not taxed, ranged from 850,000*l.* in the year 1791 to 3,100,000*l.* in the year before the Union?—I do not know upon what that is founded, but I daresay it is quite correct.

2367. The tax revenue of Ireland in the first seventeen years of the Union ranged from 2,500,000*l.* in the years 1801–2 to 5,000,000*l.* in the year 1816–17? —Yes.

2368. Do you contrast, therefore, a revenue before the Union varying from 800,000*l.* a year to 3,000,000*l.* with a revenue afterwards which I have given?—I do not go into that, but no doubt it is so. I have stated that it is an open case, but I did not go into it. I took the starting point at the Union, and I contrasted the first fifty years of the Union with the taxation ever since.

2369. But you have referred in passing to the fact? —Yes, I do not want to block that question with respect to those who wish to go into it.

2370. That the revenue of Ireland, which never exceeded 3,000,000*l.* before the Union, became 5,000,000*l.* in those seventeen years after the Union. —It became practically much more than 5,000,000*l.*, because there was an enormous annual deficit which was charged in the nature of debt.

2371. I am speaking simply at this moment of revenue raised by taxes. There was in addition to that a deficit upon each year of the seventeen varying from four and a half millions in the first year to ten millions in 1813–14?—That deficit had a right to be spread as a matter of account over antecedent years. It was not in that particular year, but they were making up accounts and everything was brought in. There was a legitimate reason for the Accountants of the Treasury to bring that in, and therefore that particular year was swollen.

2372. It ranged from 3,000,000*l.* a year, 4,000,000*l.*, 6,000,000*l.*, 8,000,000*l.*, up to 10,000,000*l.*, did it not? —Yes; it made the Irish debt which was 26 or 27 millions up to 1801 108,000,000*l.* at the seventeen years.

2373. In addition to the excess of revenue?—In excess of taxation.

2374. The excess of revenue raised by taxes?—Yes. But let me keep myself perfectly clear on that and not be subject to misrepresentation. That 108,000,000*l.* was not paid by Ireland. It was paid by a debit in the Consolidated Account, and therefore all we suffered by so much of the Irish revenue as was raised by loan was in proportion to our own share in the partnership of the general Estate of the United Kingdom which took on the debts of both realms.

2375. You distinguish between the case of the revenue raised by taxes and the debt recorded against the country?—Yes.

2376. You remark, that the deficiency created as against Ireland between 1801 and 1817 was never forgiven by the financial authorities of the United Kingdom?—It was never forgiven.

2377. What did they do in regard to it?—They debited the whole amount to the exchequer of the United Kingdom.

2378. During the seventeen years?—No, at the end of them.

2379. I am speaking now of the progress of the seventeen years?—During the seventeen years they kept up a separate account for the the debt of Ireland.

2380. They kept alive the exchequer of Ireland for the purpose of recording debts against it?—Evidently, the Chancellor of the Irish exchequer as an executor to the dead exchequer of Ireland, was there to agree to the taxation which was put on, and to the loans that were borrowed.

2381. And so much of the contribution of two to fifteen as was not raised by taxes during that period was recorded against Ireland as debt?—Yes.

2382. Do you consider that the ultimate consolidation of the two exchequers was contemplated and intended by the promoters of the Act of Union?—I do.

2383. Do you believe from your study of the records if it had been possible for them to have consolidated the exchequers at the time of the Union, they would have done it?—Yes, and it would have been much more beneficial to Ireland if they had.

2384. But they desired and intended to do it?—No; they were ashamed, or they were afraid of the public opinion which would be aroused by coupling a debt of 25,000,000*l.* with a debt of 400,000,000*l.* odd, and the theory upon which they proceeded was this: that Ireland was twice as rich, had twice as much money as she really had, and if they were not to treat her in that fashion they would have had no claim for the two-seventeenths. They made an assumption that Ireland was able to pay two-seventeenths, and upon that basis they proceeded as if the debt of England might come down before the debt of Ireland went up, and when the proportion of the two-seventeenths came about in the Irish debt they would be consolidated. I do think (as a matter of conjecture) that the officials who framed that scheme were quite distinct from the statesmen, who, for the most part, knew nothing about it at all, but the permanent officials of the Treasury tell them what to do, they do it; they tell them what they are to say, they say it; they tell them what they are to sign, and they sign it. That is my experience of public life, and it is my experience of what takes place in private companies. The majority of the people who are only a short time in office have to be coached by others. For instance, I believe that the whole of the 1853 coaching was done by the permanent officials of the Treasury at that time.

2385. Will you for the moment confine yourself to the point that the promoters of the Act of Union wished to consolidate at once, but they did not think it safe to propose to put a contribution upon Ireland of one to seven and a half, her debt being only one to sixteen?—Yes.

2386. Whatever strong opinion you hold about what occurred in the first seventeen years after the Union or up to 1853, you propose, I understand, to address yourself chiefly to what has happened since 1853?—I address myself to the comparison which bears upon the two periods.

2387. And to the hardship inflicted upon Ireland, particularly in the second period?—I do; that is what I have made up my statement upon.

2388. Will you take up the return of September, 1856, and give the substance of it as stated in your memorandum?—What paragraph do you refer me to?

2389. Paragraph 8 of your memorandum.—I show that for the first fifty years the average was 4,363,816*l.* including all the riots and injustices of the Union, and I treat the periods from 1851 to March 31st, 1856, five and a quarter years, as a period of transition, whilst the taxes of Ireland were being judiciously raised, slowly raised, to compare with the figures for England. I strike that period of five and a quarter years out and I compare the twenty-five last years of the return from the 31st of March, 1856, to the 31st of March, 1881, and I show that for that period it had risen from 5,400,000*l.* to 7,300,000*l.* The average had risen from 4,360,000*l.* in the first fifty to 6,700,000*l.* on the twenty-five years.

2390. There is a misprint in the memorandum; it should read "5 years to the 31st March, 1881," not "from 31st March, 1881"?—I suppose so—I am not quite sure. It is only a mistake in the print, I think.

2391. "From" should be read "up"?—Yes, "from" should be "to."

2392. The salient fact which you have desire to present is this, that not only did the quinquennial average rise during the first seventeen years after the Union, but also that, the annual average for the first fifty years being 4,360,000*l.*, the annual average for the almost succeeding twenty-five years was 6,700,000*l.*?—I do not follow you.

2393. They are your own figures on the face of the memorandum before you. What does your paragraph show to have been the annual average of Irish taxation for the first fifty years after the Union?—4,360,000*l.*

2394. What does your paragraph show to have been the annual average for the last years up to 1881?—6,700,000*l.* for the twenty-five years.

2395. The point therefore is, for the latter period the annual average increased by more than one-half of the former?—Yes, and was still on an ascending scale, because the last two are 7,274,000*l.* and 7,344,000*l.* The two last quinquennial periods show an ascending scale.

2396. The quinquennial averages in the later period show even a more rapid advance than is indicated by the whole average?—Yes.

2397. This is the revenue of Ireland as collected, is it not?—No, as returned. I do not know about what they collect. I do not go behind the Parliamentary papers, and I do not go behind the accounts of the Treasury.

2398. Quite so, but it is returned by the Treasury as the revenue collected in Ireland?—No, it is not returned by the Treasury as collected; it is returned by the Treasury as received from Ireland, and there is no evidence whatever of any distinction being drawn at that period between that which was collected in Ireland and that which was collected in England.

2399. Have you read the evidence of Sir Edward Hamilton, the Treasury witness?—I have. I have not read it critically through, but the most part of the evidence I read of Sir Edward Hamilton was very clear, very efficient and evidently given with the object to state everything as fairly as he possibly could and as truly as he could. I am not in collision with Sir Edward Hamilton so far as I know.

2400. I wish to draw your attention to the fact that the case made by the Treasury before the Commission, the case at least alleged by the Treasury, which they will try to prove and intend to rely upon is this—that from 1830 to 1870, owing to the fact which they represent, that the duties paid in England upon goods consumed in Ireland were much higher annually than the duties paid in Ireland on the goods consumed in England, that the revenue as stated in those and other returns was less than the true revenue of Ireland by considerable sums per annum. I do not ask you to discuss that question now; I merely ask you to note it?—Oh, yes, but do not put it as my evidence because I disagree with it.

2401. Quite so; but it is alleged by the Treasury, and we shall have to face it in the course of the Inquiry.—If you wish to cross-examine me upon what the Treasury allege, let me have the particulars of what they allege. I do not question anything they allege now because it is not before me to do so.

2402. Quite so; you adhere to these figures?—I give this memorandum as evidence from first to last, and everything in it is from first to last a statement of fact and true, and everything in it as a statement of account is true to the best of my knowledge, belief, and skill.

2403. (*Lord Welby.*) Where do you take your figures from?—From Parliamentary returns, and I mention them as I go along in the memorandum.

2404. (*Mr. Sexton.*) You take them from a Parliamentary Paper, No. 88, Session 4, 1856, "A Return of the Gross Amount of Revenue raised by Taxation in Ireland" for certain years?—Yes.

Sir Joseph M'Kenna.

4 Dec. 1894.

Imposition of income tax on Ireland.

2405. (*Lord Welby.*) A paper for which you moved, Sir Joseph, did you not?—Yes.

2406. (*Mr. Sexton.*) I have looked myself into Sir Edward Hamilton's figures, and I think that even applying his adjustments so far as we are able to apply them at present (because the details are not before us) the calculation you make as to the excessive taxation in the next fifty years is not materially disturbed. You wish to call attention to the financial situation at the time when Sir Robert Peel considered and put aside the idea of imposing an income tax upon Ireland?—Yes. Mr. Roebuck brought forward a motion to extend the income tax to Ireland, and made a very strong and very able speech, as most of his speeches are strong and able, and exhausted the subject in what he said. Sir Robert Peel put it aside in a statesman-like fashion, but not perhaps as frankly as he would have done if he were an Irish statesman and not an English statesman; but he acted upon a sense of justice quite as complete as if he were an Irish statesman and a fair one. He declined to extend the taxation there, although he was at that time minus in the Treasury 2,150,000*l.*

2407. You say that although he had to meet a deficit exceeding two millions in the year 1842 he yet refused to extend the income tax to Ireland?—Yes.

2408. Then you say that in 1853, eleven years afterwards, Mr Gladstone did impose the income tax at a time when he had a surplus of over two millions?—Yes. I have stated all the circumstances of that year in a general way. I have stated them further on in the memorandum.

2409. But you understand that all the material facts in your memorandum have also to be got into your evidence?—Quite so; and that in the advantage of your examination of me, and the more it is in the nature of a searching cross-examination the more I welcome it.

2410. I only propose to elicit the state of your mind upon the matters disclosed in your memorandum. I leave cross-examination to others. What was the justification stated by Mr. Gladstone for imposing the income tax upon Ireland?—He pooh-poohed the idea of Ireland not getting more by the remission of the Consolidated Annuities than the whole volume of taxation which he was putting upon them, which has lasted ever since.

2411. What was the nature of these Consolidated Annuities?—The Consolidated Annuities were a creation by statute; numbers of the unions and the counties I believe also as counties and some unions as unions borrowed from the Treasury or Board of Works, monies which were due undoubtedly to the United Kingdom on the terms of their first contracts in some way. They were complaining very much from time to time, when these were put upon the basis of an annual payment that was to cease after a given number of years; these were called Consolidated Annuities. There were 250,000*l.* a year, not for all time, but for a given period, which I do not recall to my mind for the present. It was a very fair calculation that the amount which stood to the debit of the unions in 1853 at about 4,500,000*l.*, and was repayable by 250,000*l.* a year; assuming that there was a debt at all, that was a fair commutation. It would have ceased long since if it had been going on.

2412. There was a debt of 4,500,000*l.* due by certain districts?—Yes.

2413. And these districts—not all Ireland—had to pay 250,000*l.* a year for the terminable period?—Yes.

2414. Mr. Gladstone cancelled that debt and imposed instead of it, as he said, the income tax?—Yes.

2415. And proceeded to increase the spirit duties?—Yes.

2416. What do you say was the financial effect as against that remission of the imposition of the income tax?—Up to the period that I have taken, the exactions up to 1881, the amount that was paid was more than ten millions greater than the amount which was claimed to be due on the Consolidated Annuities capitalised.

Sir Joseph M'Kenna.

4 Dec. 1894.

Imposition of income tax on Ireland.

2417. You make out that up to 1881 from 1853 Ireland paid under the income tax about 15,000,000*l.*?—She paid 14,900,000*l.* odd in that time, and that constituted more than the whole of the advances to Ireland that were put down in the Return No. 3 of September 17th, 1886, including the 4,500,000*l.* for which it was a *quid pro quo* apparently.

2418. The amount stated in No. 3 of the Return as having been remitted is about 10,000,000*l.*; over 10,000,000*l.*, is it not?—Yes.

2419. And that 10,000,000*l.* of which we still so often hear as a matter remitted to Ireland included the four millions and a half, the remission of which was held to be an equivalent for the imposition of the income tax?—Yes.

2420. You proceed to refer to the usual argument that is offered in defence of the imposition of the income tax in Ireland. What do you say in reply to it?—What I say in reply to it is this, that when the volume of taxation on any country is excessive at the time. The effect of adding to it an income tax, although that *per se* it is one of the fairest taxes, is just as much an injustice as if it were a tax on boots.

2421. Then you say that before the income tax was imposed upon Ireland, Ireland certainly was paying—to put it at the lowest point—at least her full share of the tax?—I put it that she was paying her share. If you were really cross-examining me I should say she was paying about double her proper share.

Taxable capacity of Ireland.

2422. Will you state the figures given in paragraph 14 of your memorandum. I may first read to you, in view of the answer you have given, your own words in paragraph 15: "I have, therefore, only to "show that, prior to the imposition of the income tax "on Ireland, the levy on her of other Imperial taxes was "at least proportionately equal to the levy of Imperial "taxes on Great Britain, including the income tax." That was the question I put to you just now?—Yes. Then we were, before that imposition was put upon us, paying the one-thirteenth of the gross revenue of the United Kingdom raised by taxation, and I think it is beyond the powers of sophistication to make out that the one-thirteenth of the wealth and taxable income of the United Kingdom belonged to us at that time.

2423. You state that the revenue raised from Great Britain in 1851 was over 42,000,000*l.*?—Yes.

2424. And from Ireland in the same year just about four millions?—Yes, we paid one-thirteenth of the whole.

2425. Then you proceed to urge that it is proved by the returns of the United Kingdom, and the yield that the taxable property and income of Ireland in 1851 was not equal to one-thirteenth?—No.

2426. Do you happen to have by you the exact proportion it was?—I do not.

2427. But it was less than one-thirteenth?—Yes.

2428. And you add that the taxable property and income of the people of Ireland is not now one-eighteenth?—Yes.

2429. I believe the yield of the income tax is only one-twenty-fourth at present?—I am not speaking of the income tax yield there, I am talking of the estimate of the property irrespective of what tax it yielded.

2430. The assessment?—What the schedules return as being the incomes of the various scheduled classes.

2431. That is the assessment?—Yes.

2432. At present that is about, I think, one-twenty-second, is it not?—I have not gone into that.

2433. You proceed further to analyse the return of September 17th, 1886?—Yes.

2434. And you point out that the average annual contribution to the Imperial revenue by Ireland from the Union till 1817 was over four millions and a half?—Yes; up to 1817 it was over four millions and a half.

Sir Joseph N. McKenna. 3 Dec. 1894.

Effect of consolidation of the Exchequers.

2435. Then you point out the two things that affected Ireland—first, that her revenue in that period was in excess of what it had been before the Union, and, secondly, that she was debited with a debt, the difference between 28,000,000*l.* and 107,000,000*l.* in that time?—Yes.

2436. What remark do you make in paragraph 16 upon the effect of the consolidation of the Exchequers and the opening of the new partnership account?—The consolidation of the Exchequers put a close to a vicious system of over-taxation for the purpose of trying to make up an impossible revenue just as we may endeavour to debit a tenant with an impossible rent, and it put a period to that by debiting the whole debt to the consolidated Exchequer of the United Kingdom as an admission in fact that that increase arose from a system of over-taxation which produced a debt not chargeable against the individual partner, but chargeable against the firm, so to say.

2437. (*Lord Welby.*) Over-taxation would not produce a debt, would it; it would be rather under-taxation that would lead to a debt. Taxation cannot produce a deficit?—Yes, taxation produces deficit because the revenue raised by taxation was not equal to the amount.

2438. Do you not want to put it in rather a different form. A high tax cannot produce a deficit. I only want to put it a little clearer although I see what you mean?—I understand, but I think that the distinction is too subtle for people, generally speaking, to take into account. The Irish were debited with a deficit to make up the taxes that were assessed against them; two-seventeenths was the taxation. It was not on the individual ratings or assessments that they were taxed; they were taxed two-seventeenths as between Great Britain and Ireland.

2439. That is the point, they were not taxed two-seventeenths, because they did not pay two-seventeenths, therefore, that was not the rate of taxation?—As between Great Britain and Ireland there were no taxes, but there were two-seventeenths that Ireland was bound to make up of the gross expenditure, whatever it was, of Great Britain or the United Kingdom rather; and the debt that Ireland was run into was a matter of taxation, because it was an assessment of two-seventeenths under the Act of Union; and why I welcomed the consolidation in this *ex post facto* fashion was because it put a period to that vicious system of running up a debt which had no good in it except one which I did not put forward; and that good was, it made Ireland a drawing post when the Chancellor of the Exchequer wanted money, and required to issue a loan.

2440. (*Mr. Sexton.*) You present the case, do you not, in this way. The Act of Union made Ireland liable to an excessive contribution of two out of seventeen to the Imperial revenue?—Yes.

2441. And the effect of that was first, that her revenue was more than doubled by bringing up taxes to straining and breaking point, and, secondly, that after that oppressive revenue had been collected, there was also a debt raised up against her of 84,000,000*l.* in the seventeen years?—80,000,000*l.* And that was in a certain sense according to accountancy paid, because it was placed to the credit of the taxation of the two-seventeenths imposed or contributed, or whatever you choose to call it, and which was debited finally to the consolidated debt of the United Kingdom.

2442. It continued to be a debt of Ireland until the consolidation?—Yes, exclusively.

2443. Now you state here a double effect of the consolidation first, that the fixed ratio came to an end, do you not?—Yes.

2444. Secondly, that when the fixed ratio came to an end under the Act of Union it was altered, as you judged the future ratio ought to be, to "the actual taxable means of each island"?—That, the Union articles provided for, as plainly as could be provided for beforehand.

2445. You say "I submit these conditions were "embraced in the Act and Articles of Union"?—Yes.

2446. Would you allow me now to put to you for the convenience of the Commission as a matter of record the language of the article of the Act of Union dealing with the subject. May I state it to you now?—Yes.

Article 7 of the Act of Union.

2447. Article 7 of the Act of Union after first providing that when the debts came into the same proportion as the contributions certain things might be done, then proceeds in this way "If it shall appear "to the Parliament of the United Kingdom that the "respective circumstances of the two countries will "thenceforth admit of their contributing indiscrimi- "nately, by equal taxes imposed on the same articles "in each, to the future expenditure of the United "Kingdom"?—Yes, that is the 7th article of the Act of Union on which I rely, as establishing the affirmative of what I suggest.

2448. You interpret that as enacting that indiscriminate taxation should not be imposed until equal taxable capacity was proved, do you not?—Yes, I do.

2449. That condition being satisfied, as you believe it never was satisfied, the Act then proceeds to enact that in that event "it shall be competent to the Par- "liament of the United Kingdom to declare that all "future expense thenceforth to be incurred, together "with the interest and charges of all joint debts con- "tracted previous to such declaration, shall be so "defrayed indiscriminately by equal taxes imposed on "the same articles in each country." Now did the Imperial Parliament ever, at that time or since, make that inquiry?—They never did.

First proposals of 1853.

2450. Did they even make that declaration?—No, not that I am aware of.

2451. Without the satisfaction of the condition, without the inquiry and without the declaration prescribed in the Act of Union, they proceeded to do the thing which should only follow upon all these things?—Mr. Gladstone on that occasion in 1853 refused the Committee which was moved for by Colonel Dunne. Now he grants this Commission, and I am grateful to him for it, and return him the full acknowledgment of what no man can deny he has, the courage not merely of his opinions but of his recantations.

2452. On the point before us you submit that the Imperial Parliament never did inquire, as directed by the Act of Union, whether the respective circumstances of the two countries admitted of indiscriminate taxation?—No, they from time to time touched the fringe of the case in one way or the other, but it never was inquired into.

2453. And they never made the declaration required by the Act of Union that the circumstances had come to such a point?—I do not know about that quite.

2454. Now the enacting words of the Act of Union are these—"And thenceforth from time to time, as "circumstances may require, to impose and apply such "taxes accordingly, subject only to such particular "exemptions or abatements in Ireland, and in that part "of Great Britain called Scotland, as circumstances "may appear from time to time to demand." Would you represent that these words of the Act of Union direct that from time to time and for all time the circumstances of Ireland should be taken into account in imposing taxation?—I do not think it would be rational to say they were not to be taken into account.

2455. I put these last words to you with the view to elicit from you whether you think that these words of the Act of Union impose upon Parliament for all time the duty of having regard to the capacity of Ireland in imposing taxation upon her?—I will not say that. "All time" is a very long period.

2456. "As circumstances may appear from time to time to demand"?—Yes, they have no right to stereotype a tax for Ireland without previously proving that it was just, and that it was required in order to establish a parity of treatment.

Sir Joseph M'Kenna.

4 Dec. 1894.

2457. That is precisely the point I am putting, that under the terms of the Act of Union, so far as they may be held to amount to an obligation or a treaty, the Imperial Parliament was bound from time to time, and without limit of time, only to impose upon Ireland such taxation as her circumstances fairly allowed?—Yes, when the Exchequers were consolidated.

Effect of consolidation of Exchequers on taxation.

2458. You say that the consolidation in 1817 did not bring an increase of taxation?—No, it brought no increase.

2459. Will you refer to the figures on that head?—Yes. The figures on that head are these:—The taxation was 4,800,000l. a year on an average for the seventeen years, and the taxation for the fifty years, including that seventeen years, was only 4,300,000l. a year, so that there must in the thirty-three years have been a very considerable reduction in the taxation of that thirty-three years to bring down the average of the first seventeen included in the fifty to 4,300,000l., 500,000l. a year less.

2460. Now, having shown that, as the case appears to you, the taxation of Ireland in the seventeen years after the Union was higher than in the remaining thirty-three years of the first half century, will you now proceed to compare the taxation of the first fifty years with the twenty-five that followed?—Yes.

Taxation in 25 years preceding 1881.

2461. Give us the figures. I am proceeding with your memorandum in order as the paragraphs stand.—If the circumstances had remained the same with respect to population and taxable ability for the last twenty-five years as in the first fifty years, the twenty-five years taxation, up to March, 1881, would have been 108,089,285l., but instead of that sum the Imperial taxation of Ireland for the twenty-five years amounted to 168,741,237l., all which extraordinary increase of burden, as shown between 1856 and 1881, due to the legislation and new system laid down in 1853, and has to be considered in connection with the fact that the additional burden had to be borne by a dwindling population, which had commenced to fall away before any additional burden had been cast upon it, and the following will show with what results:—The population of Ireland in 1841 was 8,222,664; in 1851 it had fallen to 6,552,385; in 1861 to 5,798,967; in 1871 to 5,412,377; in 1881 to 5,144,983; and in 1884–5 to 4,962,693; and the pressure of taxes measured per head of the population, which was 9s. 7d. in 1841, had risen to 12s. 3d. in 1851, although the total revenue raised in the latter year by taxation in Ireland had been only fractionally (and, I may add, accidentally) greater than in 1841. The taxation was seriously increased between 1851 and 1861, so in the last mentioned year it rose to 1l. 2s. 6d. per head. In 1871 it rose to 1l. 6s. 3d.; in 1881 to 1l. 6s. 9d., and in 1884–85 to 1l. 11s. 3d. per head. What occurred during those years in respect to taxation in England I treat of very shortly hereafter in paragraphs 29 and 30.

2462. You point out incidentally that a Committee of the House of Lords recommended the remission of those consolidated annuities, the existence of which was treated as the reason for the income tax?—Yes.

2463. Your view is, is it not, that the taxation of Ireland, as it existed before the income tax was imposed, was a heavy taxation for Ireland?—It was an excessive taxation.

2464. And you consider that you would be entitled to say that the taxation as it existed before the income tax was imposed, should either have been sensibly reduced at that time or else that a considerable part of it ought to have been devoted to purely Irish uses?—Yes.

2465. You consider that the effect of the increased taxation in 1853 and subsequent years was most prejudicial—most unfortunate for Ireland?—Almost destructive.

2466. You have said already that a tax abstractedly fair may be very unjust by reason of the mode and time of its application?—Yes.

Sir Joseph M'Kenna.

4 Dec. 1894.

Taxation in 33 years preceding 1881.

2467. You make no objection to the income tax itself, do you?—On the contrary. Even at the cost that it was to them I welcome it because the income tax enables the whole unfairness to be exposed at once.

2468. It supplies in your judgment a good standard of measurement?—Yes.

2469. You cite the opinion of Sir Francis Baring, who was a Chancellor of the Exchequer, upon the fiscal ability of 1853?—Yes.

2470. He was of opinion that it was not fair to relieve Great Britain to the extent of a million and a half, only imposing 400,000l. of new taxes, and at the same time to place an additional taxation of 413,000l. upon Ireland?—Yes; because at that time there was only 10d. a gallon additional whiskey tax put on, and Sir Francis Baring did not get the opportunity of viewing the policy in its entirety.

2471. It was only 8d.; the tax had been 2s. 8d., and it was made 3s. 4d.?—Yes.

2472. What was the immediate financial effect of the increase? I will put it to you in this way. The spirits consumed in Ireland in the previous year were 7,500,000 gallons?—Yes.

2473. And an eightpenny tax was added with the immediate effect of the increase of a quarter of a million?—That would be so assuming the consumption remained the same.

2474. I am taking the preceding year and assuming it remained the same. Of course the spirit duties, which had been 2s. 8d. in 1853, and were then increased 8d., became 10s. in the course of five years?—Yes.

2475. What did Mr. Gladstone say in regard to the greater advantage to be derived by Ireland of the remission of the annuities over the disadvantage of the new tax?—Mr. Gladstone said "The taxation we propose for Ireland would in the first two years be considerably higher than the taxation we propose to remove, but if we look to the time when, as I have said, Parliament will be in a position to part with the income tax, Ireland will enjoy, and enjoy for a long term of years, a much larger remission of consolidated annuities than it will have to bear of additional burdens in the shape of spirit duty." Mr. Gladstone of course believed all that; I give him credit for believing it; but I show what the twenty-five years of the income tax have done—not only paid off the 4,500,000l., but have paid 10,000,000l. back of all that Great Britain plumes itself on having extended in the way of reliefs and loans to Ireland.

2476. He indicated there that the income tax would be temporary, but it has proved to be permanent?—Yes.

2477. He did not indicate there any intention to increase the spirit duty further?—No.

2478. And there was no indication given in 1853 of an intention to force up the duties upon the liquor chiefly consumed in Ireland, and to keep them at a very low point on the liquor chiefly consumed in Great Britain?—No.

2479. You press the point, do you not, that in the thirty-three years from 1851 to 1884 and 1885 the taxation per head in England, a progressive and wealthy country, was reduced by 6s. 2d. a head?—Yes.

2480. And that in the same time the taxation per head upon the people of Ireland, an unprogressive country and one of the poorest in the world, was increased by 19s. per head?—Yes.

Relative taxable capacity.

2481. In proposing to take the assessment or the yield of income tax as the standard of measurement, you do not at all leave out of mind that the disparity between the capacity of Ireland and Great Britain is probably greater in the classes below the income tax than amongst the income tax classes?—No doubt. I do not leave that out of mind at all, understand.

2482. But you state it here?—Yes.

2483. Of course you bear in mind, I suppose, Mr. Giffen's measurement—that the yield between Ireland and Great Britain is as 1 to 24?—Yes.

2484. Mr. Giffen's estimate of the relative taxable capacity of Ireland and Great Britain as a whole including the income tax is 1 to 33?—Yes.

2485. But you say that pending any proofs that may be obtained of the gross body of income, you will proceed at present on the basis of the income tax?—Yes. That is all I base my comparisons on.

2486. Upon the subject of the duty on liquors you do not suggest the imposition of differential duties, do you?—No, I do not—I think that is a matter that can be very easily managed between the officials on the one side of the water and those on the other. They can have the same duty and afterwards make an allowance to the country from which the excessive taxation is extracted.

2487. It is often suggested in these discussions upon taxation that any complaint of the excessive taxation of Ireland, if attended to, would involve differential duties, but you say it would not?—Not in the slightest; there is no reason for it whatever.

2488. You say that even if it be admitted that the taxation of Ireland is excessive, the excess could be met by applying it either in the relief of Irish local taxation or in the hands of an Irish local authority for Irish public uses?—Quite so.

2489. And you are of opinion, are you not, that provided the excess was applied in that way it might tend to make taxation popular?—Quite so.

2490. Will you kindly explain the precise effect of the fiscal policy of 1853—firstly, as between the beverage usually consumed in Ireland and that consumed in England, and secondly as between the drinks of the rich and the drinks of the poor?—The beverage of Ireland was spirit, and in 1853 the duty was 2s. 8d. a gallon; and at that time the main duty on beer was the malt duty and the hop duty. These have been abolished and have been commuted into a tax of 6s. 3d.—now raised to 6s. 9d.—a hogshead on the beer. On an analysis it is found that the 6s. 3d. was equivalent to about 1s. 10d. a gallon on the alcoholic equivalent in proof spirits.

2491. I believe it is 6s. 9d. now; there is no great difference, is there?—It will not amount to 2s., and I have treated the taxation upon beer as one-fifth of the duty upon alcohol in whisky.

2492. I believe it will be found that the relation to the prices of the alcohol is also pretty much the same—that the disparity is as great if you consider the price as if you consider the alcohol?—Quite; the unfair disparity is enormous.

2493. I should like to get that in the simplest way. Beer is the usual drink in England; whisky or spirits is the usual drink in Ireland?—Yes.

2494. Now, if a man buys a shilling's worth of beer, what he buys is tenpence worth of beer and twopence worth of tax, is it not?—Yes.

2495. If he buys a shilling's worth of whisky, what he buys is only twopence worth of whisky and tenpence worth of tax, is it not?—About that—that is roughly stating it.

2496. That is certainly a very great disparity, is it not?—Yes.

2497. The case of spirits is somewhat greater even than I stated, because the duty has been raised from 2s. 8d. in 1853 to 11s. now?—I have stated everything as far within the facts as would leave the results sufficient to satisfy anyone with a sense of justice that the case I made was a just one.

2498. You have brought the increase up to 1858, but there has been some further increase since. It is now 11s., is it not?—Yes.

2499. You have stated the case as between spirits and beer; now will you state the case as to wine?—Before 1853 (and it remained unaltered at that time) the duty on all wines was on the liquid measure, irrespective of alcoholic strength, but, as science became more advanced in the bureaus, it was thought it would be well to apply a standard of alcoholic duties, and, accordingly, port and sherry, which were the heaviest taxed wines, after 1853, were let in at 2s. 6d. the gallon—that is to say, a strength of 42 was let in at a duty of 2s. 6d. a gallon. The French and German wines were let in at a strength of 30 or 32, at 1s. a gallon, and that made the disparity which I have set forth in one of these paragraphs.

Sir Joseph M'Kenna. 8 Nov. 1895. Effect on fiscal policy of 1853.

2500. On the wine?—Yes. In paragraph 35 I say "I must now say something in respect to the duties "on wines. Before 1853 the duties levied on wines "were fixed at rates per liquid gallon, irrespective of "alcoholic strength. The duties were, however, in fact "much heavier (as to the alcohol which the wine con- "tained) than the duties levied on spirits either in "Great Britain or Ireland were then or are now. Wines "were then, as they are now, the alcoholic beverage of "the rich; they were and are proportionately con- "sumed most in England, less in Scotland, least in Ire- "land. Since 1853 the duties on wines, measured "now by an alcoholic standard, have been lowered, "some to half the previous duty, others to a third, "others to a fifth. Spanish and Portuguese wines, in "proportion to the alcohol they usually contain, were "placed on a scale equivalent to a spirit duty of 6s. "per gallon; French and German wines, in proportion "to their usual alcoholic strength, at the equivalent "of 4s. a gallon spirit duty. Slight alterations "recently made bring some of the wines down to a "duty of 3s. 4d. per gallon in relation to the equiva- "lent of each gallon of proof spirits which they con- "tain; thus it happens that the Irishman, too poor to "pay for wine, but requiring, or thinking he requires, "some stimulant, has to pay in respect to the whisky, "which he usually mixes with water, 200 per cent. "higher duty than his richer neighbour, who can "afford to drink sherry, has to pay on the spirits con- "tained in the latter."

2501. So that not only was the popular drink in England favoured at the cost of the popular drink in Ireland, but the liquors drunk by the more wealthy classes and drunk by them more in England and Scotland than Ireland were also particularly favoured?—Yes.

2502. You have given here the financial effect as between the year 1851 and the year 1890 of the dealing with the spirit duty, have you not?—Yes.

2503. In the year 1851 the consumption of spirit in Ireland was seven million gallons and a half?—Yes, 7,500,000 gallons.

2504. The population being then about six millions and a half. The tax upon that seven-and-a-half millions of gallons at 2s. 8d. per gallon was something in excess of one million sterling for the year?—Yes.

2505. In the year 1890, the population having fallen to slightly over 5,000,000, the consumption was 5,075,000 gallons, that is one third less than the consumption of 1851; but the duty having increased in the interim from 2s. 8d. to 10s. a gallon, the duty on the lesser quantity of whisky was two millions and a half sterling for that year, having been only a million in the earlier year?—Yes.

2506. Ireland paid a million and a half more duty on 5,000,000 gallons than in the previous year she paid on seven millions and a half?—Yes.

Excessive taxation of Ireland.

2507. You say that Ireland, therefore, under these heads of taxation—not raising any question now as to what happened before 1853, but limiting yourself to what happened since—has been drained of over 3,000,000l. a year?—Yes.

2508. And you say that she has been taxed to this extent entirely for the good of the Imperial Exchequer?—Yes.

2509. And you say she has not been taxed for any current necessities of the State?—Yes.

2510. Then you point out that within the period during which this sum of 80,000,000l. in excess has been imposed on Ireland the National Debt has been reduced 74,000,000l.?—Yes.

2511. And whilst, as you say, you cannot ear-mark the application of any particular sum of money, yet

Sir Joseph M'Kenna. 4 Dec. 1894. Excessive taxation of Ireland.

you notice the coincidence that an excess of taxation of Ireland by 60,000,000*l.* stands side by side with this reduction of the National Debt?—Yes. I have no hesitation in saying that I can depose that of the 76,000,000*l.* paid in that period of 25 years, 60,000,000*l.* of it came out of extra-taxation of Ireland, and only 16,000,000*l.* out of the rest of the United Kingdom.

2512. You say that at any rate, no matter whether you ear-mark a particular sum or not, that of that 76,000,000*l.*, 60,000,000*l.* was provided by Ireland, and only 16,000,000*l.* by the rest of the United Kingdom?—That is so; and that is assuming that before they started in 1853 and for the first 50 years of the Union it was a fair taxation.

2513. I put it to you that you do not at present for the purpose of this argument debate any question as to the period before 1853?—No.

2514. At this point I observe that you cite a speech of Mr. Gladstone in 1853 in which he dealt with the state of affairs at the consolidation of the exchequers?—Yes.

2515. And pointed out that the charge for Ireland's debt at that time exceeded her total revenue?—Yes.

2516. And that this was a state of affairs which was put an end to by the Act of Union?—Yes.

2517. But he omitted to state, did he not, that it was the Act of Union which caused it to arise?—He did not know it or he would have stated it; he knew nothing at all about it. The Irish members at the time lost themselves very much through positive ignorance in ascribing the fraud of the Union to the consolidation of the Exchequers as if it was a fraud, which I do not say it was. Having taken that view they attacked the consolidation without any sufficient grounds as it appears to me, and Mr Gladstone then took up consolidation and Union and all, and defended them as if they were all one, and the things that were done in 1817 he attributed to the Union, and he attributed it with relation to the Union. That is, as I say, evidence of the utter misunderstanding there was when this additional taxation was levied on Ireland. There was nobody, it appeared to me, to understand what the consolidation meant at the time in the House.

2518. The understanding of difficult questions is not universal in the House at any time, is it?—I am not aware of that, but the people outside, curiously enough, made some strange mistakes. John Francis Maguire was a member for Ireland who took up the strongest opposition at that period to the increase of the spirit duties, and when he got back to Cork, expecting to have the congratulations of his friends on his maintaining his own spirit at any rate, he found that he was tabooed by the people who were in the whisky trade. One man said—"My good friend, "Maguire, do you think I am going to be offended with "the Government for having put 8*d.* additional value "on every gallon of 15,000 gallons of whisky that I "have got out of bond." Mr. Maguire asked me what reasoning there could be with a country that took that view of things. He multiplied, I said, 8*d.* by 15,000, and he knew he had that in his pocket which was an advantage. I said "Why did you not answer him "properly?" He said, "I could not, I am not Maguire "and M'Kenna together or I would have done so."

2519. A closer study of the Act of Union and its effects in recent years has fundamentally altered the opinions of Mr. Gladstone in regard to its financial provisions, and its provisions as a whole, has it not?—Quite, I believe.

2520. He is entitled to that statement?—Quite.

2521. In paragraph 41 you deal with the question which I suggested to you some time ago, and which of course the Treasury will press upon us, as to the effect upon the revenue of the payments made in England for duty on goods consumed in Ireland, and the payments made in Ireland for duty on goods eventually consumed in England?—Yes.

2522. Will you kindly state the substance of that?—Let me explain what I am about to say upon that. Under any view of the case, the Treasury view or any other, assuming that we do actually pay all the duties we get credit for in Ireland, we are nevertheless shown to be the smallest consumers of any equal population of the United Kingdom.

Sir Joseph M'Kenna. 4 Dec. 1894. Consumption in Ireland and Great Britain.

2523. Consumers of what?—Of all things subject to duty except tobacco—we are slightly excessive in our consumption of tobacco.

2524. What about tea; what do you say as to tea?—I believe we get all the tea duty-paid from England, and there it figures on the opposite side.

2525. Some I think is paid in England, and some in Ireland; but as to the point of consumption, do you say we consume more or less pro rata?—All that is shown in our favour as consumers, and supposing you are proving that the Irish were a prosperous people, and you said, Look at all they consume there, and you gave them credit for all the duty they pay and for the consumption of these dutiable goods, then I say they are not prosperous; because giving them credit for all this, they are the lowest consumers of dutiable goods of any people of the United Kingdom.

2526. (*Mr. Wolff.*) Per head, you mean?—Per head.

2527. (*Mr. Sexton.*) Per head or individually—either way?—Yes, per head or collectively.

2528. They certainly consume vastly less beer in proportion than is consumed in Great Britain, do they not?—Yes.

2529. And they undoubtedly consume less alcohol than is consumed either in Scotland or England per head?—In Scotland they have a million less population and they consume I think much more by a million and a quarter gallons than Ireland does of whisky. But as between England and Scotland or as between Ireland and Scotland what we have to say is this—that, as the returns show, we are the smallest consumers of all these dutiable articles. The case presses strongly in our favour; but if we do not consume all which the returns show we consume, on the other hand, much which is duty-paid upon in England, is consumed in Ireland, and does not go to our credit in the Custom House Returns; and I believe that there is a good deal more consumed in Ireland of dutiable goods which have paid the duty in England, than there are of dutiable goods consumed in England of which the duties have been paid in Ireland. I treat that in this way. I say "But perhaps it will be urged "that the case is not in reality so bad as it looks. It "will be admitted that the case comes out badly on the "Parliamentary returns, but it has been urged that "some of the duties collected in Ireland are really paid "by persons resident in England, as, for instance, in the "case of spirits, which may happen to be 'duty paid' "in Ireland and consumed in England. To that "suggestion I reply: I believe the balance of such "transactions would be on the other side, that is to "say, I have no doubt that there is more duty paid "in England, in the first instance, on goods consumed "in Ireland, such as tea, coffee, brandy, and wine, than "there is of duty paid in Ireland in the first instance, "on articles consumed in Great Britain. I am "strengthened in this view because, with the single "exception of tobacco, if we set down the whole con-"sumption which the duties indicate as being paid by "the Irish people, the latter are, nevertheless, shown to "be, of all the divisions of the United Kingdom, by "far the most frugal consumers not only of alcohol but "of all other articles paying customs or excise duties, so "that if they consumed less than is apparently shown it "would be strong indication of their poverty being the "greater." Then I show that even if there were 500,000*l.* (half a million) more duty paid in England or less duty paid in Ireland than the returns show, or than we could attribute to the consumption by Ireland, and therefore to the actual payment, it would not raise the proportion of income tax in England to the one-fifth of the gross taxation, and it would not bring the Irish taxation down to be less than thirteen times her income tax.

Sir Joseph M'Kenna. 4 Dec. 1895. Consumption in Ireland and Great Britain.

2530. The Treasury represents to us by their returns and in their statements that the amount of duty paid now in Ireland upon goods consumed in England is far larger than the amount paid in England on the goods consumed in Ireland. Do you not think it would be very desirable that in a matter of this importance steps should be taken to devise such means of record as would put the matter as far as possible beyond doubt?—That is a question which the officials must settle for themselves as a recommendation and not on my recommendation. I do not think there is any difficulty about it at all.

2531. It would be unsatisfactory of course that conflicting statements should be made without some precise evidence?—I go upon what is on the records; I go by the returns, and I say if there was a difference, and there never has been a difference of £300,000 shown, it would not substantially alter the case which I make on this paper.

Taxable capacity of Ireland.

2532. Now, I come to the method which you propose for ascertaining the taxable capacity of Ireland, and I will describe it to you by way of question. Tell me whether I state it correctly or not. You take the total income tax imposed in the United Kingdom?—Yes.

2533. You then take the total revenue raised in the year?—Yes.

2534. You deduct the income tax from the total revenue, and you find the balance of taxes other than income tax?—Yes.

2535. You then find the proportion between the total of the income tax and the total of the taxes other than the income tax?—Yes.

2536. And you say that the true proportion of each country is the proportion of the income tax raised in that particular country multiplied by the proportion which the income tax raised in the whole kingdom bears to the income tax required in that kingdom?—I do not take that as the simple way in which I put it. I say that if you take 1*l.* of income tax, wherever paid, as a unit, the 1*l.* of income tax would require 5*l.* 4*s.* of a complementary or supplementary system of taxation to make up the revenue that was required in the year I have analysed—that is 1884–85.

2537. You say for every 1*l.* of income tax raised in the United Kingdom there must be 5*l.* 4*s.* of other taxes raised?—Yes.

2538. That is on the revenue of 1884–5?—Precisely. I only take that as an illustration. Then if each of the realms raised 5*l.* 4*s.* in proportion to this every 1*l.* of income tax it raised it would make a precise par between all the countries. The 5*l.* 4*s.*, in addition to each 1*l.* of income tax, would precisely make up the revenue of 73,000,000*l.* odd, which was raised by taxation in that year. Then I went on to see how far they had raised it and in what countries. England and Wales only raised 4*l.* 12*s.* 3*d.* as a complementary addition for every 1*l.* of income tax. Scotland raised 6*l.* 15*s.* for every 1*l.* of income tax. Ireland raised 12*l.* 11*s.* for every 1*l.* of income tax, and there is no possible mode of doing anything except nibbling at that. They can only nibble that this did not come in or that did not come in, and against all those nibblings I say that the unscheduled classes represent fifty times more taxable capacity, or, as Mr. Giffen thinks, fifty-three times more taxable capacity in Great Britain than a similar class in Ireland. I put them all out of account, and, nevertheless, I find that we are paying, under the circumstances I have pointed out, 12*l.* 11*s.* for every pound Income Tax, in contrast to 4*l.* 12*s.* 3*d.* which is all that England and Wales pay, and 6*l.* 15*s.* that Scotland pays, in comparison to their similar units of Income Tax.

2539. The actual amount paid by Ireland in that year was 7,163,000*l.*, was it not?—Yes.

2540. Her income tax for that year as actually raised was 571,000*l.*?—Yes.

2541. And you say that the other taxes in Ireland and Great Britain should have borne the same proportion to the income tax raised in each country as the other taxes for the United Kingdom bear for the kingdom, namely, 5*l.* 4*s.* for each 1*l.*?—Yes.

Sir Joseph M'Kenna. 4 Dec. 1895. Taxable capacity of Ireland.

2542. And you say, therefore, that the revenue to be raised for Ireland in that year in addition to her income tax should have been not 7,163,000*l.* but 2,972,000*l.*—Yes, in addition to the income tax.

2543. (*Sir David Barbour.*) I understand you to hold that the people of Ireland are, man for man, much poorer than the people of England?—Yes.

2544. And, however we may question the accuracy of certain figures, there can, I believe, be no doubt that that is the case. It is beyond argument, is it not?—Yes.

Expenditure in Ireland.

2545. You have called attention to the great increase of taxation in Ireland. Do you know if it is the case that the expenditure of money in Ireland for the purposes of government has also largely increased?—No doubt, and in England too, but I do not know that it has increased more than in England.

2546. I wish to give you certain figures which I find in page 33 of Sir Edward Hamilton's memorandum. He puts down the Irish expenditure for 1819-20 as 1,512,000*l.*, and for 1892-93 he puts down the Irish expenditure as 5,540,000*l.*, an increase of about 4,000,000*l.*?—Yes; those are Sir Edward Hamilton's figures. I am not prepared to accept that computation at all as being a *bonâ fide* increase.

2547. Are you prepared to contest it?—I am.

2548. Have you got any figures you would like to put in?—Not here.

2549. Will you put them in afterwards?—I will show that that is not so. In that he assumes the Constabulary to be an Irish establishment.

2550. No doubt he does?—That was an Imperial establishment in 1814 before the consolidation of the Exchequers. I am not prepared to be examined on this point as to what Sir Edward Hamilton says, but I am prepared to give an indication to this Commission in every way I can on the ground of all that sort of figuring and computation. In 1814 the Constabulary were established in Ireland, and the Constabulary was, after considerable discussion on the subject, formally and regularly for good reasons put on the joint exchequer of the United Kingdom; and the whole of the argument derived from that will vanish into utter insignificance, on consideration of the one fact that when we compare all the things that are cast upon England, she only pays 4*l.* 12*s.* 3*d.*, whilst Ireland pays 12*l.* 11*s.* in complementary taxation to the income tax unit of one pound.

2551. I observe that Sir Edward Hamilton puts down the Irish contribution to Imperial expenditure proper as 3,658,000*l.* in the year 1819–20, and as only 2,104,000*l.* in 1892–93, being 10*s.* 10*d.* per head in the former year, and only 9*s.* in the latter. Do you know if those figures are correct?—I am sure they are not, in the sense they should be taken by this Commission not analysed.

2552. Those figures you will find on pages 33 and 34 of his memorandum, if you care to put in other figures in opposition to them?—I have not seen those figures; and although in a general way I have looked over Sir Edward Hamilton's evidence, I am not in a great many things disposed to agree with him.

2553. Those figures are taken from the tables at pages 33 and 34 if you wish to examine them. You have made a calculation for 1884–85, and you come to the conclusion that Ireland was over-charged about 4,000,000*l.* sterling?—4,210,000*l.*

2554. Do you think she is still over charged to that amount?—I am quite sure she is, and even more than that amount.

2555. At the present day?—Yes, at the present day.

2556. I refer to this matter because Sir Edward Hamilton makes out that Ireland's contribution in 1892–93 to Imperial expenditure proper was only 2,104,000*l.*?—I do not understand what he means by "to Imperial expenditure proper." Does he mean that there is no Imperial expenditure in Ireland?

Sir Joseph M'Kenna. Expenditure in Ireland.

2557. No, he does not mean that, but he draws a distinction between Imperial expenditure proper as distinguished from certain expenditure incurred in Ireland itself and for Irish purposes, such as constables and pensions, courts of justice, law and justice?—Courts of justice is as much Imperial expenditure in Ireland as Imperial expenditure in Great Britain; and why should he differentiate there?

2558. But he draws a distinction between expenditure such as that incurred on the Army and Navy, and expenditure incurred on we will say courts of justice in Ireland?—Just so; but he makes fish of one and flesh of the other. I object to that altogether, except that it is presented to me in a fashion in which I can deal with it as an issue. Whatever I call Imperial expenditure is what the statute law passes, and the United Kingdom calls Imperial expenditure. Whatever that is I go by, and the amount has been increased in Ireland by Imperial legislation, and it does not follow that the thing would be agreed to at all if it were put in any other way than as Imperial expenditure.

2559. Then I understand you do not accept these figures of Sir Edward Hamilton's?—No, I do not.

2560. Because if it were the case that Ireland only contributes 2,000,000*l.* to Imperial expenditure proper, and that she is over taxed 4,000,000*l.*, it would follow that if the excess taxation of 4,000,000*l.* were remitted or returned to her in some form Ireland would not only fail to meet her own expenditure but would receive a subsidy of 2,000,000*l.* yearly from Great Britain to enable her to do so?—The official calculations upon these matters are the calculations of experts who wish to show the thing in favour of the Government under which they live, and it is fair enough to view all their evidence with that consideration, that they are faithful and good subjects, trying to do their best according to their lights; but it would be a most monstrous thing to found any system of differentiation between the Imperial expenditure now from what has been found since 1800.

2561. Then you do not accept these figures?—No, I do not.

2562. You will find them at pages 33 and 34 of Sir Edward Hamilton's memorandum if you wish to controvert them?—I do not accept it.

2563. (*Mr. Martin.*) Are you familiar with the history of the period between 1800 and 1816 as to the loans that were created on account of Ireland?—As compared to the generality of people, perhaps I may say that I am familiar with them.

2564. Can you tell us what rate of interest these loans were raised at, as compared with the rate of interest that English loans were raised at, at the same time?—They were raised at somewhat less favourable rates than the English loans.

2565. At a lower rate of interest?—I mean to say that they offered better terms to the lenders than the English securities.

2565A. (*Mr. Wolff.*) At a higher rate?—At a higher rate; yes, but not to any extent that was unreasonable.

2566. (*Mr. Martin.*) Because I find nearly a hundred millions raised at that time, and it would be important to know?—Yes; there were about eighty out of 108,000,000*l.* raised in the period between the passing of the Act of Union and the consolidation in 1817, and the manner in which that 108,000,000*l.* was dealt with, was on the whole (as a rough and ready mode of dealing with it, and as bearing the statute in mind also), the nearest approach to fairness that the Chancellor of the Exchequer had at the time of dealing with it.

Adjourned for a short time.

2567. (*The O'Conor Don.*) You stated to the Commission that the Income Tax in 1853 was extended to Ireland upon the distinct understanding that it was imposed in lieu of the consolidated annuities, is not that so?—Yes.

Sir Joseph M'Kenna. Income-tax.

2568. And it was stated by Mr. Gladstone, was it not, that the income tax then imposed was of a temporary character?—Yes.

2569. Was it not laid down in the Act by which the Income Tax was extended to Ireland that it should expire within a similar limit?—I apprehend that there was a period of expiry in the Income Tax, at whatever time it was passed, and I think it has been renewed from time to time since.

2570. Was it not the fact that the Act passed in 1853, the 16 and 17 Victoria, chapter 34, enacted that the Income Tax should be enacted only for seven years?—That is so.

2571. And for the first two years it was to be at 7*d.* in the pound, the next two years at 6*d.*, and the last three years at 5*d.*?—Yes.

2572. And then it was to expire?—Yes.

2573. Those were the conditions upon which it was imposed?—That is so.

2574. But, as a matter of fact, did it not turn out that not only the Income Tax continued but the rates of Income Tax were very largely increased?—Yes.

2575. Was it not the fact that in the year 1854 the duty was increased by one half?—I cannot say that.

2576. This is a return I might put into your hand and I would like to get it on the notes. If you will look you will see the different increases of Income Tax up to the year 1860, the date at which it was supposed to expire?—Yes, that is so.

2577. In 1854 the duties were increased by half?—Yes.

2578. In the following year there was an addition of 2*d.* in the pound placed on the Income Tax?—Yes.

2579. And the rate was increased to 1*s.* 4*d.*?—Yes.

2580. In 1857 there was a reduction to 7*d.*?—Yes.

2581. Then in 1859 there was an increase of 4*d.*, making a total of 9*d.* in certain cases?—Yes.

2582. So that the understanding upon which the Income Tax was passed in lieu of these annuities was not carried out?—It was quite illusory.

2583. If this debt of 4,500,000*l.* on account of loans granted to Ireland had not existed, I presume we would be justified in assuming that the Income Tax certainly would not have been imposed in 1853?—It was not even sought for upon any other grounds, because Mr. Gladstone's own words I thought sufficiently important to record, and they are on the face of my memorandum.

2584. He had a surplus that year?—Yes.

2585. And therefore he would not have thought of imposing additional taxation on Ireland if he had not some ostensible idea of giving a remission of grant?—I fully believe that.

2586. Therefore it would not be fair to say that this sum of 4,500,000*l.* has been forgiven to Ireland?—Oh, no; it is preposterous to say that.

2587. (*Lord Welby.*) I think you told us in answer to Mr. Sexton that the average revenue of Ireland for the ten years before the Union was about 1,300,000*l.*, did you not?—Yes.

Irish revenue before the Union.

2588. Would it not be rather more correct if you were to state that figure on the basis of the income before the French war really began, because if you take the ten years before the Union, including several years of war, you will find that the revenue was considerably higher, I think?—I do not think I should mix up, under any circumstances, the two questions together—war or peace. I agree that Ireland should be taxed as much in connection with the Union as she could bear relatively to Great Britain; and I do not make the complaint once the Union was carried, and imposed, so to speak, on the English Parliament as well as on the Irish Parliament—when one was vested with the power and the other was merged—I do not believe they made a very bad use of it between 1800 and 1817; and to state it shortly, I take Lord Rosebery's view of Mr. Pitt and his policy, and not Mr. Gladstone's—I do not believe there was

any intention in carrying out that Union to defraud Ireland.

2589. Observe, I was not asking any question of opinion.—It is desirable that, as far as possible, the Commission and the witnesses shall proceed on more or less agreed figures, and my question was simply one of fact—namely, that the figures before us show that the average revenue of Ireland during the ten years before the Union was not 1,500,000*l.*, but in round figures 3,000,000*l.* I was venturing to suggest to you that if you restricted your statement to the income before the heavy expenditure of the French war began, probably your figure would be in agreement with the papers before the Commission. In Sir Edward Hamilton's paper, page 2, there is a statement of the revenue of Ireland for each year from 1782–83 to 1800, and if I take the ten years before the Union, beginning with the year ending 25th of March, 1791, the revenue is stated as follows:—

	£
1791.	[illegible]
1792.	[illegible]
1793.	[illegible]
1794.	[illegible]
1795.	[illegible]
1796.	[illegible]

I stop there to show that so far the figures before the Commission and your statement would be very close together?—Yes.

2590. Now I go on to 1797. Then the revenue was 1,703,000*l.*; in 1798 the revenue was 2,034,000*l.*; in 1799 the revenue was 2,115,000*l.*; in 1800 the revenue was 3,017,000*l.*, and I think if you take these ten years and put in those very large sums of the last three years representing war expenditure, not only would the sum be larger than you give, but also it would hardly state your case so strongly as it might be stated, if confined to the revenue of Ireland before the expenditure on the French war began?—Well, I put it strictly chronologically as I find it. I found 15,000,000*l.* (and the inquiry I made was outside altogether Parliamentary returns) was more than the total revenue of Ireland for the ten years up to the Union, but the last two or three years, although running up to 3,000,000*l.*, did not disturb the average, because it was much less than 1,500,000*l.* for the early parts of the ten years. But I do not think I was called upon to differentiate between the amount of that revenue or taxation of Ireland before or subsequent to the French war. I think that is a very fair item for others to comment upon, and I do not object to any reasoning that is founded upon it for the increase between 1800 and 1817, but after 1817 there were no analogous reasons.

2591. (*Mr. Sexton.*) It may be taken that the return shows, at any rate, that if you do not include the miscellaneous revenue, the tax revenue was considerably under an average of 1,500,000*l.* for those years; but if you do include the miscellaneous revenue, the lotteries, and everything, the average for those ten years was about 1,500,000*l.*?—Yes.

2592. (*Lord Welby.*) I would ask you whether we ought not also to pay some attention to the expenditure for the time before the Union, because the expenditure of those ten years which was met by the Irish Parliament was considerably in excess of that sum?—Yes, it was, but not raised by taxation.

2593. It was on an average 3,000,000*l.* a year?—Yes, including money raised by loans.

2594. Therefore I would put to you that that point ought also to be borne in mind in considering the financial condition of Ireland before and after the Union, speaking simply of a matter of fact?—Well, I do not quite understand what paragraph of mine you desire to modify by my answer or the extent to which you wish to modify it.

2595. My point is this: I understood you to say in answer to Mr. Sexton that you took as a basis of comparison between the finance of the two periods the income of Ireland before the Union which you put at 1,500,000*l.*?—Yes, the revenue.

2596. Then, I say, would it not be fair also to take into consideration the expenditure of Ireland during that time?—Yes, it would be. I don't object.

2597. Merely as a basis of consideration—I am not now drawing any conclusion from it?—Quite so.

2598. And that I find amounted on an average for that ten years to 3,000,000*l.*, though of course if you were to adopt what I venture to suggest to you to take ten years before the French war broke out, it would be considerably less?—Yes.

2599. Do you object to my suggestion that the expenditure should also be taken into consideration?—I do not think it enters in there. It is a very proper subject for the Commission to take into consideration as explanation of the *prima facie* force of anything that I have put forward. Of course I could not object to that, and on the whole my case is made, I admit, in a certain sense *ex parte*—it could not be otherwise than *ex parte*—but in making that *ex parte* statement I have not excluded any fact that has naturally, or as the subject of inquiry has come within my knowledge, I fail to be able to reach a better comparison than that which I have made in favour of Great Britain. I am very strongly in favour of putting this case as moderately as I can. It is not well to throw the hatchet too far, and I rather throw it to the bounds at which I can throw it again and overpass it.

2600. At all events will you not agree with me that in judging the financial condition of a country, it is fair to take into consideration not only revenue but the expenditure?—I think so—in England as well as in Ireland. The deficiency was made up in Great Britain as well as in Ireland by loans, and the result of it was that England had about twenty times the indebtedness that Ireland had, and that, about at that time, represented the relative means of the countries.

2601. I think in speaking of the Act of Union, with reference to clause 7 of the Act, you gave an interpretation, or at least I understand you gave an interpretation, of the words used there—"according to "the means." If you will remember in clause 7 it says—"If it shall appear to the Parliament of the "United Kingdom that the respective circumstances of "the two countries will thenceforth admit of their "contributing indiscriminately by equal taxes imposed "on the same articles in each, to the future expenditure "of the United Kingdom, it shall be competent to the "Parliament of the United Kingdom to declare that all "future expenses thenceforth to be incurred, together "with the interest and charges of all joint debts "contracted previous to such declaration, shall be so "defrayed indiscriminately by equal taxes imposed on "the same articles in each country, and thenceforth from "time to time, as circumstances may require, to impose "and apply such taxes accordingly, subject only to such "particular exemptions or abatements in Ireland, and "in that part of Great Britain called Scotland, as "circumstances may appear from time to time to "demand," and the enacting words are "in the existing "circumstances"?—Yes.

2602. I am not in the least objecting to it; but it is an interpretation of yours, is it not, that that meant actual taxable means?—That is what I understand by it.

2603. The words "actual taxable means" are not used in the clause of the Act, are they?—I do not think the science of international finance was understood in those days at all, and they made use of general terms where they ought to have been more specific, but we cannot deal with that now. I believe that the Union was carried by promises in both Parliaments that Ireland should be treated as a portion of the United Kingdom in the sense that she was not to pay more according to her means than Great Britain had to pay.

2604. All I am putting to you in my question is this, that though there may be different interpretations,

Sir Joseph N. M'Kenna.

6 Dec. 1894.

Interpretation of Act of Union.

and fair interpretations as to what the respective circumstances of the two countries should mean, we have no knowledge now that those respective circumstances were not considered by the Government of the day very carefully. It is very true, and I think stress has been laid on the point, that no inquiry preceded the amalgamation of the Exchequers. That, according to our present view, would have been a very proper proceeding, but there is no direction to that effect?—There was no occasion to have done so, inasmuch as there was no attempt in 1817 to move the taxes forward to the English or British scale. If that attempt had been made, of course some of the representatives of Ireland would have said—"there must be an inquiry before we do "that," but in fact whatever were the rights as to making inquiry and founding legislation upon it, no inquiry was made, and therefore I imagine we had from 1817, and have at this day, a right to go back upon what has been done in connection with the terms of the Union, and I am prepared to contend against all men that the seventh Article of the Articles of Union has been systematically violated, but in respect to the period between 1817 and 1853; for those 36 years there was no attempt made to put such taxes on Ireland as would call her attention, or would call the attention of her representatives to the fact that the Articles of Union were being misapplied or were being transgressed.

2605. Quite so; and I think many of us would agree that an inquiry at that time would have been very desirable. All I say is, that the words as they stand did not direct such an inquiry. It was not a breach of the treaty of Union that such an inquiry did not take place, was it?—I say no actual breach of the treaty was made by legislation until 1853, but a breach of the treaty in this sense was incurred; conditions were allowed to continue which ought not to have been allowed to continue, from 1817 forward until 1853.

2606. Then I think so far we are fairly agreed that whatever was desirable, whatever actually took place at that time, was not a breach of Article 7?—In 1817?

2607. Yes?—No; I accuse the framers of the consolidation of the Exchequers in 1817 of nothing.

Irish debt.

2608. I think you then spoke of that immense debt that was accumulated between 1800 and 1817 as not forgiven but recorded?—How it was recorded was this:—In accordance with another Article of the Articles of Union it was incorporated in the debt, so to speak, of the firm of the United Kingdom, and taken from the debit of the partner.

2609. Therefore Ireland was not called upon to pay it?—She was not called upon to pay it. She was not called upon to make any separate contribution on account of it.

2610. Therefore there is no injury done to a person who is not asked to pay a charge that might be raised against him?—No, there is not.

Contribution under Act of Union.

2611. Now, a great deal of discussion has taken place upon the fact that the treaty of Union contemplated a contribution from Ireland of two-seventeenths?—Yes.

2612. Which is held, I may say generally, to have been excessive. I do not think you will find that many people will dispute that now. But as a matter of fact, during the period of the French war I find that the actual charge on Ireland was only about two-thirds of that proportion—that is to say, instead of her paying even during all the weight of the French war, two-seventeenths, she only paid one and a third seventeenths. That is my calculation. I do not ask you to accept it, but I want to place upon record that during all that time, the taxpayer of Ireland never at any time contributed anything like two-seventeenths?—Quite so, but her constitutional government, either before the Union or since the Union, in the person of the Chancellor of the Exchequer, Mr. Corry, who officiated at that time, contracted debts for Ireland which stood in place of taxation. But I deny they stood in place of taxation in the sense of Ireland being entitled to complain of the treatment apportioned to her because it was a corollary of the Union for which those who consolidated the Exchequers were not accountable. I was the first, I think, who specifically undertook to defend, and to defend when it was not very popular to do so, the consolidation, and whereas Colonel Dunne, our old friend, had an idea that we were very much cheated in that consolidation, I, for his sake—I was not in Parliament myself at the time—went into the whole facts of it. At the time his committee sat I went into the whole facts, and I think I convinced him that there was no injustice done, but a great deal of injustice put an end to by the consolidation, and I do not take the extremely strong views that some people take about the intentions of Pitt and Castlereagh with respect to it. Their intentions were not carried out and it would have been better if they had been—if we are to understand their intentions by their language in the House of Commons, in the House of Lords and out of it. Ireland was to receive a beneficial consideration on every point which tended to increase her taxation, and we did not get that, but it was denied to us I admit through ignorance. I do not introduce the charge of intentional injustice at all.

Sir Joseph N. M'Kenna.

6 Dec. 1894.

Contribution under Act of Union.

2613. You went on to make rather a striking comparison between the weight of taxation in Ireland and Great Britain, and I think you took the years 1841 to 1881. In answer to Mr. Sexton, taking it head by head, the incidence of taxation was comparatively very light I may say in 1841 and very heavy comparatively in 1881?—Yes.

2614. I would ask you does not that want some qualification. If you take alone without qualification the incidence of taxation upon people, leaving out of view entirely the fact whether the people have become in the interval poorer or richer, will you not get to a wrong conclusion. Let me give you an instance of what I mean. I will take such a place as the colony of Victoria. Before the gold discoveries you had there a small, sparse, squatting population, probably very little administered, and paying very few taxes. Probably in such a case you would find out that the incidence of taxation at that time was extremely small?—Yes.

2615. But take it thirty or forty years later when there was a great population, and what I am now dwelling upon, an improvement in wealth, you would find out that the incidence of taxation was very much heavier per head, for instance perhaps 5s. per head at first, and perhaps £2 in the second, but it would be wrong to draw the conclusion from that fact that the individuals were relatively more heavily taxed at the later period than the first, would it not?—If there was no contrast to show how they were taxed there might be a good deal to reflect over in the suggestions you make, but as we know how they were taxed, that the specific article of whisky, which was taxed 20 per cent. more fifty years ago than beer was taxed, was made use of as a medium for further taxing the Irish people, and that they were taxed to the extent that on an economy and a moderation of consumption of two million and a half gallons, by the peculiar system that was introduced, a million and a half more pounds sterling were exacted in a single year from the Irish people than they had been paying in 1851 on the larger quantity, and the nation which was a consumer of alcohol in another form, in the form of brewed drinks, in respect of the alcohol were allowed to remain as they were, paying 2s. or less than 2s. on the equivalent of a gallon of proof spirits. There is one item that explains the grievance to the extent of perhaps nearly two-thirds of the whole case.

2616. I quite admit the reasonableness of your dwelling upon the large increase in the spirit duty; but I want to put in a caveat against the assumption that comparison of the incidence of taxation per head in the two periods taken by itself is a just measure of the taxable capacity?—If you can show

Sir Joseph N. McKenna.
4 Dec. 1894.
Comparative incidence of taxation before Act of Union.

that the condition of the people had improved between those years—and there are no statistics more than twenty-five or thirty years ago—there are no absolute statistics to show that the people are as well off now as they were in 1853.

2617. I think the year you took was before that, was it not? Was not the comparison between 1841 and 1881?—No, 1851. I think it is due to the Commission to explain that I was only anxious to put the first 80 years of actual taxation, and Mr. Fowler, who was very kind to me, said that he would do everything he could to facilitate me in getting the true statement, splitting it up from 1841 to 1881. I presume it was for the purpose of giving it to separate heads of offices to make it out for him. I had to restore it and have restored it in my reduction to quinquennial periods, so the periods I want, that is to say, I carve the 80 years into three periods, the first 20 years of the Union, the next 32 which constituted what I call the period of transition, and the last 33 years of the return which Mr. Fowler gave and that enabled me to make a short cut upon the question by showing that if we had continued as we were we would only have paid 108,000,000*l.* as against 216,000,000*l.* for twice the period of the first 20 years of the Union, in place of which we paid 169,000,000*l.* on the last 33.

2618. Of course you are aware that there is a contention that the condition of the people of Ireland has considerably improved in the interval?—There are statistics that go to the extent of showing that some people have improved and there are fewer poor, and I do not contend there has been no improvement, because there has been some. Ireland has had some of the advantages of science, and knowledge and education, and is reaping them by much slower degrees, but it is nothing comparable to the advance in the taxable means of Great Britain.

2619. That is a fairly arguable question, but I want to put this as a qualification upon a comparison of the incidence of taxation per head. If the condition of the people remaining in Ireland has improved, their taxable capacity in 1891, might—I will not say it is—be larger and better than it was in 1851, might it not?—I do not want to say anything to discourage the people of Ireland in the most hopeful view of their state but I think they have largely gone to the bad, and I think although there may be more money—and undoubtedly there is more money in the banks, and there is about the same in Government stocks held in Ireland—the amount of the poverty relative to the numbers of the people has increased, notwithstanding the diminution of the numbers of the people. A contrast of the 6s. 9d. contributions per head in Great Britain with the 13s. increase per head of taxation on the people of Ireland, I think, almost dispenses with all syllogistic reasoning on the subject.

2620. Without pressing that point very far I will give one single figure as an illustration of what I mean. With the comparatively large population that there was in 1851 they had according to the summary of statistics which has been given us very nearly 3,000,000 head of cattle while the comparatively small population of 1890 had 4,780,000. To the outside person that looks like an increase of means and not only an increase of means absolutely but a very large increase of means relatively, does it not?—If you could not point to new imposts put upon them or old imposts increased in their incidence you are quite right, but inasmuch as new imposts have been put upon them, and as the old imposts have increased in their incidence you are wrong.

2621. That is a subsequent question. At the present moment I am only giving some instances in support of my opinion that the mere comparison of the incidence of taxation between 1851 and 1891 is an unsafe one to rely entirely upon?—If it was pressed as proof to demonstration of everything, I would reject it, but that is not so. It is one of a series of circumstantial evidences which go to assert what I have proved otherwise and that is, to begin with, an increase of taxation relative to its former imposts and without the sanction or authority as I conceive of the Articles of Union on which we were consolidated into one United Kingdom.

Sir Joseph N. McKenna.
4 Dec. 1894.
Comparative incidence of taxation before Act of Union.

2622. You give it as fact as an illustration, but if you would permit me to offer other illustrations, it might tend in the opposite direction?—I do not exclude from my own consideration anything of the kind you suggest, but I think I have given them all full value in the conclusions I have arrived at. My arithmetical figures have a right to be displaced by arithmetical figures and not by reasoning, because I show that such and such money was got by the Exchequer, and such and such money was beyond the proportion which was collected from Great Britain.

[Luncheon.]

2623. I think, Sir Joseph, in speaking of the time when Sir Robert Peel imposed the income tax you attributed as a reason, unwillingness on his part to place (for reasons which were sufficient for him) the income tax on Ireland?—Contemporaneously with the initiation of this discussion, which began I believe very nearly thirty years ago, I read all the debates and I did my best to possess myself of what Sir Robert Peel's reasoning was on the matter from what he said and also from what he did not say, and whilst he kept some things back which I think a statesman in his position who was endeavouring to accommodate all sides as much as he could was justified in doing, I calculate that he would have yielded to the arguments that were very trenchantly put forward by Mr. Roebuck in 1842, if it were not that the Articles of Union bound him not to do so—honestly and fairly bound him not to do so, and that Ireland had been taxed up to her full measure at the time. But I admit he did not specifically say that, and I would not expect any Chancellor of the Exchequer to say so or to introduce a new element of dispute; and therefore he did not say so. But there stands out the fact that before the famine in putting on an income tax for England he declined to do so for Ireland, in the face of a deficient Exchequer and in the face of a very rallying Radical cry, to have Ireland included in the taxation. That was four years before the famine 1846–47. In 1853, six years after the famine, and with these famine loans staring the Government in the face, they extend the income tax as a quid pro quo for giving up a beggarly £4,500,000, which the loans, if you please, had recommended to be forgiven altogether as being a visitation on the United Kingdom or a visitation on the Empire of which Ireland was a part.

2624. That may have been a reason in Sir Robert Peel's secret mind for it, but may I refer you to the reason which he alleged, which can be verified from Hansard, namely, that he exempted Ireland from the tax on the ground that the machinery for its collection was not ready to hand in that country as it was in Great Britain. Ireland had not been subject to the former income tax, and she had no assessed taxes at all. The collection of the proposed income tax would therefore have required the devising of new machinery. You will know what an important consideration that was. We in England had the whole machinery of commissioners and collectors of these taxes ready to hand, and could entrust the collection of income tax to them, which was an important point. Then he went on—"Such a step was a serious one to take in the "peculiar state of society in that country, and was one "which he did not feel called upon to adopt, more "especially as the tax was only to be temporarily levied. "As, however, Ireland was, in his belief, to benefit as "much as any part of the Empire by the reductions of "taxation which he proposed, he held that she should "bear her fair proportion of the increased revenue "which had to be raised. This end he proposed to "secure by adding one shilling a gallon to the duty on "Irish spirits (this was the increase to those duties "which had to be abandoned within twelve months), "and by equalising the stamp duties in Ireland to those

Sir Joseph M'Kenna.

4 Dec. 1894.

Income tax.

"in England." The history of that bit of taxation was that in the following two years he had to repeal that extra shilling, therefore so far there was the counter-tax which he proposed abolished?—Quite so.

2625. And further before 1850 so far from there being an increase of stamp duties the whole of the stamp duties, especially those upon land, had been lowered in Great Britain and Ireland, and were lower than they were in Ireland before the imposition of the income tax?—I admit the lowering of the stamp duty which affected those who passed small bills in Ireland, and I admit that it was a very liberal measure, but it cost the Government nothing, because since then the stamp duty payable on bills of exchange in Ireland has rather increased than lessened.

2626. But these stamp duties refer to all the deeds upon land; they were the stamp duties, if I remember aright, that came under the heading of deeds, and I think it was upon those that the tax was raised. I think also it was in 1848 or 1849 that a large reduction took place in that branch of taxation ending by the rates of duty being less than they had been before the imposition?—I quite admit that, and I admit all these popular details, so to speak (popular with some people, but not popular with me), of what England pays and Ireland does not pay. As for the assessed taxes I dismiss the subject altogether, for my complaint is not of any particular tax. The assessed taxes are just as honest as any other taxes we pay, it is the volume of the entire I object to. Where is the use of saying England pays such and such a thing and Ireland does not pay it when, as complementary to the income tax and to supplement the moneys that are necessary for the United Kingdom Ireland pays 12l. 11s. as against 4l. 12s. 3d. paid by England in complement to each pound Income Tax. Everything is contained in that, it is like a man's account with a banker for a hundred years, the whole thing is summed up in the balance, and the whole taxation of Ireland is summed up in the balance. What I say is this, as to any taxes that are equally unobjectionable and equally objectionable (if there be objection to any tax), that the sum of those taxes which are cast upon Ireland are transcendentally unfair, and in 1874, when the subject of French taxation for the purposes of the German war indemnity arose, I stated and I proved that the amount of additional taxes at that time cast upon Ireland was relatively greater than the ransom of France.

2627. My question did not refer to the general question at this moment of whether Ireland is too much taxed or not, I was only wishing to place on record and bring before you, reasons for thinking that Sir Robert Peel was not actuated only by the feeling that the income tax ought not to be imposed upon Ireland, because I show you that he gives quite a different reason for not doing it in his speech, but further than that, I want also to get upon record that the increase of taxation which he did put on as a substitute, in seven or eight years disappeared. Now, with your leave, I will just pass on to Mr. Gladstone. I understand you to say that Mr. Gladstone put the imposition of the income tax as a set off against the consolidated annuities?—Yes; I decline to put it down upon my own statement, and I put it down on what he says himself in the house.

2628. I was going to suggest a small amendment to bring us together. He put it rudely as a set off; it was not a set off absolutely, was it?—Of course it is not a set off unless it is a legal set off, but it is rhetorically a set off, and it was one of the grounds on which he carried it, and carried the Irish members with him, because the Irish members were as willing to assist the Government of the day as any one else.

True measure of taxation.

2629. But it was a very considerable set off at the moment to Ireland, against the imposition of the income tax. I am not arguing that as it stands now, it can even be treated as in the main, a set off. I am not quite clear whether I arrived at your view with regard to the statements that have been made, that the revenue collected in Ireland does not represent the revenue paid by Ireland?—I think the revenue paid by Irishmen was greater, not less (it is contended that it is less) than what appears from the returns, not from the returns being in any degree tampered with or modified, but because, as a matter of fact, a very large portion of the dutiable articles are purchased by dealers in Ireland from wholesale merchants in Liverpool and in London, and those, for the convenience of trade, when the sums are not very large, such as three or four or ten chests of tea, they think it better to take out of bond and send as best they can, rather than wait for the facility of transferring them in bond and letting the purchaser or consignee take them out of bond and pay the duty. I think they find it far more convenient to send small parcels, duty paid, than otherwise; and I think that is availed of to a much larger extent than on the other side, for instance, on whisky being sent to England or malt duty being taken here on porter, ale or beer consumed in England. I think we probably pay not half a million less than we appear to pay, but half a million more than we appear to pay, but that is a calculation which I dismiss, because it is without proof. But, *prima facie*, I intend to rely upon the returns as to what they show, until they are absolutely disproved by the counter case which may be set off.

Sir Joseph M'Kenna.

4 Dec. 1894.

True measure of Ireland.

2630. I quite understand that opinion, and up to a certain point there is probably no difference of opinion between you and the Revenue officers. It is admitted on all sides that a large amount of the tea consumed in Ireland comes over duty-paid, but we must draw a distinct line upon that point between what is mere opinion and what is actual knowledge. Have you any facts upon which you rely from which you are able to say that you think the two sides balance, or is that only opinion?—That is only an opinion formed after taking the best evidence I could, and I am conscientious in the matter, not leaning to what would be the popular view of my side of the question. I believe, although I have not insisted on it for a moment, that there is half a million more paid in duty by Irish consumers than is shown in these returns without any reflection upon the officers of the Government in the matter, because they have no watch over duty-paid goods.

2631. On what do you base your opinion that it is 500,000l. more than 400,000l. or 300,000l. or 700,000l.?—I arrive at it by taking the item in round numbers, which I have never heard exceeded on the other side.

2632. What item is that?—I believe that 500,000l. is as much as has ever been stated to have been paid in duty in Ireland for English consumers. In all large transactions there is so obvious an interest in not paying. On whisky for instance there is obviously an interest not to pay duty, but to leave it in bond as long as the purchaser or consignee can do without it, and has it for sale. It is getting improved value and he has not the 10s. a gallon to expend upon it, so that I think that, except for small parcels like a couple dozen of whisky sent to friends in England at Christmas or something of that kind, it is not a very large thing at all.

2633. But still that is only an opinion?—That is only an opinion.

2634. You know this subject has been very closely investigated by the officers of the Revenue, and that first of all their investigations led them to discover a very great error in their statistical returns which of course we admit at once. You are aware of that, are you not?—Yes.

2635. But that led to a very careful investigation by the Revenue officers, and as the result they have arrived at the conclusion that a very large sum—over a million—is so paid, that is to say on whisky made and paid duty in Ireland, but transferred to England and consumed by English consumers. But from what you say to me now you challenge that and

Sir Joseph M'Kenna.

8 Nov. 1895.

True burden of Ireland.

you throw the whole of these investigations to the wind, do you?—Yes.

2636. You do?—Yes, I do, and I will tell you why. What accounts for the small quantity consumed in Ireland? I find the collateral evidence tending to my view of the case all through. Admitting that we get credit for everything that is shown to be paid, we are nevertheless left the smallest consumers and smaller consumers than ever we were.

2637. Of whisky?—Yes, that is so.

2638. I am delighted to hear you are getting so temperate here, but I want to come back to this point for it is rather a serious matter. You are aware, are you not, that there is a very minute record kept of the movement of the spirits by the officers?—Yes.

2639. And it is by means of this record and (what I want to lay stress upon) this amended record, as applied to the year 1892–93, that the revenue officers have come to the conclusion, not upon any question of opinion, but upon absolute documents, that such and such duty paid spirits went over. Now that is a fact. Of course it is open to you to say that they falsified the facts, or that they made a mistake about them; but here you have an actual record kept of the movements of the spirits. I think it wants, does it not, something more than a mere opinion as against that to say that that fact is all wrong?—But, I am not driven to a matter of opinion, I am going to the returns that come, and they have a right to be displaced by returns that show the facts. If an attempt is made to diminish or discharge some of the duties that are returned as so much duty collected in Ireland, it must be, I submit, on the scale of submitting a pro and con account—a debtor and creditor account—how much tea, how much brandy, how much wine, how much of any other dutiable article is duty paid in England and consumed (and consequently, of course, paid for) in Ireland. That should be shown, and if that is shown I would walk a long way to get the exact facts, wholly irrespective of whether they told for or against me. But in the meantime I go upon this fact. We are not shown to consume any more than, or as much as, during the period when we had a corresponding advantage in the spirit duties, when, as a matter of course, they were all paid for in Ireland that were consumed in Ireland. The consumption per head, and the consumption generally is lessened from that; and as between the people themselves the consumption by Ireland of all dutiable articles, with the exception of tobacco, is less than it is in any other of the three realms.

2640. But still I would call your attention to the fact, confining ourselves to spirits, that every drop of spirit is followed by record; it is followed from Ireland to England, and followed from England back to Ireland. Therefore you have got, unless there is falsification, an absolute record; and the result of that record is, I should venture to submit, unless you are able to show that there is fraud in the matter, a fact of which we should take note, and as against this there is only an opinion that inasmuch as Ireland consumed a certain amount of whisky thirty or forty years ago, they must consume the same now?—I do not assume that; I assume they consume less, and I believe they do consume less; but I assume they do consume as much as is shown short of the amount of dutiable articles, and the duty that is paid upon dutiable articles in England, that are consumed in Ireland and undoubtedly paid for by Ireland.

2641. Still I have to come back to the fact that you have every movement of the spirits followed and recorded, and it is on that record that the conclusion is arrived at that this very large amount of whisky is consumed in England, and therefore for which of course the English consumer pays; I would put it to you, unless you have some special facts, is it not rather a strong circumstance to reject?—I reject the whisky supplementary duty to be attributed to England, unless I get an estimate of all the dutiable articles that are duty paid in England and consumed in Ireland. I want the two together, and I would submit it to the closest test of examination open to me.

2642. Very much the same kind of investigation has been taking place with regard to tobacco. There have been two investigations, first on the basis of the information given with regard to it by the shipping companies and by the railway companies, and that produced a result (though we believe it to have been perfectly fairly drawn out) which seemed doubtful. That has been followed by a closer investigation with the aid of the great tobacco manufacturers, and the result of that shows, as recorded in some of these papers, what is sent to England and what is got back. There, to a certain extent, we come to fact again?—The contention to favour my views is this, that we are not much more, though we are some what more, temperate in the use of intoxicating liquors than we always have been, and I ground that argument, because it is only an argument, upon this, that we are nevertheless admitting that all is paid by us, which *primâ facie* the returns show the smallest consumers of these articles, and if we consume so much less than we formerly did, or the people of England, Scotland and Wales do now, we have a right to be treated upon the view that we do so, because the duties have impoverished us to the extent that we are not able to afford as much as our English or Scotch neighbours. You have to contend against this fact, that we are shown to be the most moderate consumers and the most inordinate payers of duty relatively to our means.

2643. I want you to follow the care which has been taken to investigate these figures?—I am sure all reasonable and fair care has been taken by the officers, and I impute not the slightest tendency in the world to practise any deception.

2644. But out of this inquiry the Government have arrived at certain conclusions which are not based merely upon opinion but are based upon a careful record of such information, which I venture to put to you in the case of spirits is almost complete, in the case of tobacco is very strong indeed, and in the case of other articles is not so strong, though still evidence which I think most people would be fairly ready to accept, and so that the result is that there is a considerable balance of duty paid in Ireland on articles consumed in England, and so far that conclusion is at variance with your statement, which I think is only based on opinion. I venture to put to you that these inquiries are worth more than the best opinions which are not based on facts?—But my calculations are not based on mere opinion, because if you add to our normal consumption in former years in the proportion of tax increase, and if we continued to consume the same quantity—you would find it would amount to a good deal more than is actually paid according to the returns now questioned; and, in fact, in order to make out that we do not pay this duty upon whisky you must make us inordinately temperate compared with what we were formerly, and compared to what the English and Scotch are to-day.

2645. If the record shows that it is not a question of opinion but a question of fact, that the Irish do not consume so much whisky as they used to do, it is fair to conclude that they do not?—We have a right to rely on the statistics furnished us, and so long as those statistics are consistent there is no reason why we should not found our arguments upon them and not upon the argument that the duty has become so high, and we are not able to pay it and do not consume so much.

2646. I am not disputing your right to form the other opinion, I only want to bring forward that your argument is based on an opinion or an analogy of what happened before?—No, it is not. I go by the returns; I sustain it by the analogies.

2647. Then you refuse to accept these returns?—If a different case is to be presented, just as Mr. Sexton

Sir Joseph M'Kenna.

4 Dec. 1894.

True revenue of Ireland.

presented the case with respect to the 400,000 gallons or pounds sterling—I do not know which it was he made his calculation upon,—that has to be presented in a proper statistical paper, giving the history of everything of that kind, and another paper presented with it that will give the history of all the duty-paid articles in England that are subsequently consumed in Ireland, because they have been exported to this country, or imported by this country duty-free or duty-paid.

2648. You mentioned just now the small consumption in Ireland. Are you aware that at the present moment the figures, as far as they go, leave it to be concluded that where the Englishman consumes in tea 100, the Irishman consumes 114. I do not call that a small consumption as I understand you to contend. That is to say, the Irishman consumes per head considerably more tea than the Englishman?—Just so.

2649. You were saying just now that the Irishman was comparatively a small consumer of dutiable articles?—Yes.

2650. I take one article, and mention to you that according to the best information we have, where an Englishman consumes tea in the ratio of 100, the Irishman consumes it in the ratio of 114?—That should be taken in comparison with all articles in the nature of teas, such as coffee and cocoa; the average of all these should be taken, and I venture then to say it would not be found that they consume more. But the consumption of an article that is strictly a temperance article does not enter into my mind at all. I am speaking now of the intoxicating liquors—that is what is present to my mind, and I will be only too much gratified to believe that the proportion of tea is as you say. What is it?

2651. It is the percentage, the English being 100, and the Irish 114 per head?—I will be quite prepared to believe that that is so.

2652. Therefore you see it was not quite fair to say that the Irishmen are very small consumers of dutiable articles, was it?—Not on that particular article; I said of all articles except tobacco, and I should not mind in the least degree if it was founded on proof, and I am not prepared to reject any proof offered under fair conditions—to say with the exception of tobacco and tea, because these are the beverages and indulgences of poor people.

2653. You have pointed with good reason to the fact of the great increase of taxation which has taken place in Ireland since 1853?—Yes.

2654. Is there any figure which you would put that at?—Yes.

2655. Will you give it?—The Parliamentary Return will give it. I confine myself to the Quinquennial summary of the Parliamentary Return of 1880. You will find it in paragraph 8 of my memorandum.

2656. That gives a rather large sum, and I want to get at what would be the annual increase. If you will look at Sir Edward Hamilton's memorandum, page 29, you will see that he there states the taxation of 1851 at 4,214,000*l.*, which is very nearly your average, and if you look over-leaf, in 1894 the taxation has risen to 9,554,000*l.*, from which a considerable deduction has to be made, from our point of view, on account of spirits?—Just so.

Expenditure in Ireland.

2657. That deduction would carry it down to something over 8,000,000*l.*, and therefore I agree that the sum received from taxation in Ireland is nearly double in that period. But on the other hand, have you considered the extent to which that has been applied to Ireland, that is to say, by how much the expenditure in Ireland has been increased?—Is not the expenditure that you are claiming to have increased in Ireland the statutable expenditure of the United Kingdom and passed as such through the Imperial Parliament.

2658. Whatever it is it is spent in Ireland and on Irish objects?—Have you made any estimate of how much of the gross revenue and how much of the gross loans raised on the credit of the Imperial Parliament and of the United Kingdom is spent in Great Britain, as compared with Ireland? The expenditure of people who are paid salaries and purchase the necessaries of life, and a few of the luxuries of life is a very small consideration to a people, unless they amount to a large and a numerous class, they do not amount to much, it is like the quartering of soldiers in a town; the soldier consumes as much as he pays for, and what he pays for is mostly a marketable article which could be sold in the next big town if the soldier was not there at all, so that the amount which is paid or expended out of the revenues of the country in that way does not account for very much.

Sir Joseph M'Kenna.

4 Dec. 1894.

Expenditure in Ireland.

2659. I will put my question in a rather different way. Out of the largely increased sums collected, I would put it to you have you considered how much has gone towards what we shall all admit as common expenses—that is to say, the Debt and the Army and Navy? I find that in spite of this very large increase of taxation, the sum so available, we will say, for those services, was, in the year ending 5th January, 1850, 2,613,000*l.*, in the year ending 31st March, 1890, it was 2,634,000*l.*?—Those are at present Imperial charges which you desire me in my mind to digest as if they were local expenditure, and which England or the Great Britain exchequer is entitled to credit for.

2660. No, not at all. What I put to you is this: Removing all those questions of charges as to whether they are Imperial or not, I ask you to consider whether those figures which make up the sum available for Army and Navy and National Debt, was in the year 1850, 2,613,000*l.*, and in the year 1890, 2,630,000*l.*?—That is the most illusory combination of figures that was ever got up.

2661. Were you acquainted with them before?—Remember this: I have subjected the whole to an exhaustive analysis, and I have found that, in addition to the income tax for the Empire at large, every person paying 1*l.* income tax should get somehow or other out of his own pocket or out of the pockets of the classes that are not scheduled for income tax, 5*l.* 4*s.*; and I have shown that if they got 5*l.* 4*s.*, neither more nor less, it would produce exactly the sum which would be required in 1884-85. That is brought to an arithmetical figure of great accuracy, and is there, before all the great experts in the matter to analyse. Then I follow that up by saying how much do they produce? Scotland has got exactly the same kind of treatment, but she happens to be richer and can better afford it; she has more means; so if she made up 5*l.* 4*s.* and England made up 5*l.* 4*s.* and Ireland made up 5*l.* 4*s.*, the whole money would be found which the Chancellor of the Exchequer required and collected in 1884-85. I select that year and submit it to analysis which will stand the test of the twenty provosts of twenty colleges.

2662. That hardly answers my question?—Pardon me, I have a right to be heard in this, because it is an explanation. As against that did they each pay the 5*l.* 4*s.*? No; England paid 4*l.* 13*s.* 3*d.* in addition to the 1*l.* of income tax; Scotland being also hit on the spirit duty in comparison to the hitting of England and the beer duty, paid 6*l.* 15*s.* as her complement, Ireland paid 12*l.* 11*s.* There is no getting out of it at all; in fact it is only peddling with the whole question to argue it on any other base but that. Then I have not only that circumstantial evidence, which is also based on authentic documents, and then the increase of the duty upon the articles that are absolutely consumed in Ireland, but you say they are less now than they were, so it is the worse for your argument.

2663. I will put my question in this way: A certain amount of revenue is levied, and out of that revenue, there is disbursed upon what I call, at the moment, local services, namely, the civil expenditure in Great Britain and Ireland respectively, so much. No arithmetic can get over that. The remainder is the only sum which is available for the payment of the interest on the National Debt and the charge of the Army and Navy, both of which, are common charges. In regard to that, I put before you that,

after those civil charges have been defrayed in Ireland, perhaps wastefully—that I have nothing to do with at the present moment—out of the sum collected in Ireland, the amount remaining as a contribution towards the debt of the Army and Navy in 1849-50 was 2,913,000*l*., and in 1889-90 was 2,874,000*l*. Therefore, out of this very large amount of taxation, England has not taken for what I may say common purposes of the United Kingdom, namely, more in 1889-90 than she did in 1849-50, or only a few thousand pounds more?—You must please consider this, that that is not a question to be put to me until you have shown what England and Scotland defray.

2664. I am only asking the actual facts. It is quite open to say that the local expenditure in Ireland is wasteful?—I should like to see that produced in print and in a State paper—then I will meet it. I do not accept it now in any shape or way. I challenge it as wholly illusory. We are to compare things as they were at the time of the Union; and I go with you to this extent, that I will challenge nothing before 1853, and I will assume, if you choose, that you have done the best you could for Ireland up to 1853, and I say that, at any rate, you are accountable for any excess of taxes put upon Ireland since 1853, because you have put it upon Ireland knowing the necessity of the Union terms, which I do not wish to dwell upon at all. There might be worse terms, but I do not want to dwell upon them. Having done that, you come and take a paper that I found no argument upon, and say that additional taxes have been laid on Ireland which produce 3,000,000*l*. to 4,000,000*l*. more than they did in 1853; you tell me that they have been collected, and you tell me that, if they have been collected, they have been largely expended in Ireland. I want a United Kingdom return to show, then, how much is expended in the same way and after the same fashion in Great Britain, out of Imperial taxes.

2665. There has been a good deal of discussion with regard to the drink duties, and I want once more to get it upon record that, whether the Irish drink whisky and the English drink beer, practically the Englishman pays to the revenue more per head on strong drinks, beer and spirits, than the Irishman; and I will repeat these figures to you in order to have them upon record. The Briton, if I may call him so, pays in drink revenue altogether, the population being this year 33,000,000, 25,150,000*l*., made up thus: home spirits, 11,151,000*l*.; foreign spirits, 3,757,000*l*.; and malt, 9,846,000*l*. The Irishman pays 3,028,000*l*.; namely, home spirits, 2,134,000*l*.; foreign spirits, 385,000*l*.; and beer, 509,000*l*.; making 3,028,000*l*. That was the bill paid by a population of 4,706,000. The relative incidence comes in the two countries very close, but I think you will find the Englishman paid per head rather more than the Irishman?—I suppose that is made out and given in as evidence to this Commission, but, at the same time, I protest against it as evidence at all.

2666. (*Mr. Sexton.*) The expenditure upon the local charges of Ireland has been ordered and framed by the Imperial Parliament as a matter of Imperial policy, has it not?—Yes.

2667. Would you admit that the amount of that expenditure could be pleaded to justify taxation in Ireland above the amount which ought be proved to correspond to her fair relative capacity?—Under no circumstances whatever. For instance, take the constabulary, which is a great point upon which reliance was placed. That was carried in 1814, before the consolidation of the exchequers. In 1836, I think it was, or while William IV. was on the throne, there was another readjustment made, and in 1853 there was a complete revision of everything that Ireland ought to pay and ought not to pay, as far as Parliament could give it in debates, but not further than that. Then is it not a preposterous thing to think that a legislature, which is now called upon to make a new arrangement for the future and that submits to a condition like this, to analyse what ought to be done, should rely upon their own misapprehension of moneys from an Irish point of view, set up the taxation of this country, and set it off as against something that we are bound to pay, not upon the terms upon which it was first enforced, that is, as partners in the United Kingdom, but on our own account. What reason would there be? But I will take the case again, and I say that they surcharge beyond what we ought to pay on the twenty-five years more than 60,000,000*l*.; and all that has been applied, not for the necessities of the State, but towards 15,000,000*l*. reduction of the National Debt in the purchase of consols to the extent of 60,000,000*l*., and the income represented from that 60,000,000*l*. Irish extra taxation, so applied is equal to the fee simple, or is equal to the purchase of an annuity to cover all the items that are made up in that additional charge since 1853.

2668. I want to put your reply in one word. Would you put it in this way, that the amount which the Imperial Parliament spends in Ireland as a part of the United Kingdom cannot reasonably or justly be pleaded for calling upon Ireland, as a partner in the United Kingdom, to raise more than her fair share of the taxation?—Yes; I should like to add something.

2669. In other words, expenditure merely cannot justify excessive taxes?—The amount levied in Ireland by the Imperial Parliament, but now applied as part of the Imperial expenditure of the United Kingdom, cannot be relied upon now as if it were a local assessment of Ireland herself. And I contend if it were set up originally as Imperial, it must so stand at this inquiry.

2670. But the point raised by Lord Welby was not revenue, but expenditure?—I say the amount levied off Ireland by the Imperial Parliament.

2671. That is revenue?—No, but now part of the Imperial expenditure of the United Kingdom cannot be relied upon as though it were a local assessment of Ireland herself; and if it was so set up as Imperial, it must so stand at this inquiry.

2672. And the amount expended in Ireland cannot be held to justify taxation in itself excessive?—The amount levied off Ireland by the Imperial Parliament, but now applied by statute law as part of the Imperial expenditure of the United Kingdom, cannot be set up now as if it were a local assessment of Ireland herself, and I contend that if it were set up as Imperial, it must so stand at this inquiry; and the amount expended in Ireland cannot be classed as Irish expenditure merely because so spent there, nor, in my opinion, can it be considered except in connection with the separate account of analogous expenditure for Great Britain not Imperial, save in the sense as all expenditure by Act of Parliament is Imperial.

2673. (*Chairman.*) After your extremely interesting evidence and very fatiguing examination, I will ask you only two questions, and they will be general questions, and will not, I think, give you any difficulty to answer. The first is this—Having regard to the principle and provision that $\frac{2}{17}$ths of the Imperial revenue should be contributed by Ireland, the old principle of the Act of Union, may I ask you what in your opinion should be the fraction now so contributed?—The fraction that would satisfy me would be far short, considerably short, of what I should bring out honestly as a mathematician or arithmetician in figures. I think a twentieth of the expenditure would be an extremely loyal vote, if it depended upon a vote, for Ireland.

2674. That is a very clear answer, and I am much obliged to you for it. The other question that I want to ask you is this—At page 8, sections 32 and 33 of your Report, you say that you are not an advocate for making indulgence in intoxicating liquor any cheaper than it appears to be at present. This is the material part:—"Nor am I by any means an advocate for return to the old system, whereby diverse rates of duty were charged on liquors consumed in the several divisions of the United Kingdom." Then in the following paragraph you say—"On this branch of

Sir Joseph N. M'Kenna.

6 Dec. 1894.

[illegible]

"the subject of taxation I desire to explain that the "unequal incidence of particular duties admits of being "corrected without alteration of the duties as levied." Then you give reasons for it. In answer to Mr. Sexton you explained very plainly that you were against (using the common well understood word) differentiation in such matters?—Yes.

2675. Will you allow me to ask you, in reference to the answer you just gave me as to the proper fraction to be debited to Ireland, without asking you to construct a Budget, which, of course, neither you nor we have any authority to do, what in general terms in your view would be proper subjects of duty, and as to, not the exact rates, but as to a comparison with the present rates of the incidence of taxation upon you?—If I understand the question rightly it means this—What would I think the fair proportion if we continue as Imperial what is now Imperial, and continue as local what is now local, and that we do not go upon the question of having to pay our own way, which in my opinion would be a disastrous thing for England. I think we should continue everything to be disbursed by the Imperial Government analogous to what is now disbursed. I do not say identical, but analogous to what is now disbursed. And, sir, remember this, that all the local taxes of England and all the local expenditure in England, not the local taxation, but local expenditure in England for Imperial purposes, are immensely greater in proportion to the revenue than ours is. I would say that preserving the integrity of the United Kingdom, whether there was to be subordinate (71 Rule) legislatures or not, but preserving in any case as Imperial establishments, all those institutions which are now so treated and maintained out of the revenue of the United Kingdom, I should say that a contribution to the last mentioned revenue of an annual sum equal to a twentieth of the sum which had to be raised by the Chancellor of the Exchequer of the United Kingdom would be a reasonable proposition, whether made on the part of Ireland, or on that of the Chancellor of the Exchequer of the United Kingdom, as a settlement by some arithmetical proportion, subject to revision at certain periods. The gross revenue raised in Ireland on the tariffs of Customs and Excise, and on income tax, should, subject to the deduction of that one-twentieth of the gross revenue which had to be raised for the United Kingdom, be applicable to the separate uses of Ireland subject to the control of Parliament.

2676. That is to say, that on the large question of levying of duties in England, Scotland, and Ireland you are conservative in keeping them at their present rate, and you would apply a financial adjustment outside that?—Yes.

The witness withdrew.

Adjourned to to-morrow at eleven o'clock.

SEVENTH DAY.

Friday, 7th December, 1894.

At the Benchers' Chambers, Four Courts, Dublin.

PRESENT:

THE RIGHT HON. HUGH C. E. CHILDERS, *Chairman*.

LORD WELBY.	CHARLES E. MARTIN, Esq.
THE RIGHT HON. THE O'CONOR DON.	THOMAS SEXTON, Esq., M.P.
SIR DAVID BARBOUR, K.C.S.I.	GUSTAV W. WOLFF, Esq., M.P.

Mr. B. H. HOLLAND, *Secretary*.

DR. T. W. GRIMSHAW called in, and examined.

Dr. T. W. Grimshaw.

7 Dec. 1894.

2677. (*Chairman.*) I believe you are Registrar-General of Ireland?—I am. Before you go further, sir, I should like to point out one or two things which ought to be corrected in the papers which are before the Commission. For instance, in this programme of papers there are the words "hearth may," instead of "hearth money." The next correction is in the statement with regard to the rough estimate I have made of agricultural values. You will see the values per head of the mean population on pages 4 and 5 of the printed extracts from my statement, Tables IV. and VI. After the first (or second as the case may be) figure in the pounds in these Tables, there is a comma, which should have been a decimal point. It has had the effect of multiplying these two tables by a thousand. These are pounds and decimals of pounds. Another point affecting the figures, and a very important one, I should like to mention, on page 46 of Part I. of my pamphlet on "Facts and Figures about Ireland." I discovered a day or two after publication that there was an error, and an erratum slip was issued. I find that in some copies which were purchased for the purposes of this Commission, and sent to my office, the erratum slip has been inserted in Part II. In Part II. it has no meaning. It is a very important item. If you look about two-thirds of the way down the page you will see "Government Stock" and "Railway Capital." The total for 1880 is put down as 72,000,000*l.* odd; it should be 62,000,000*l.* odd. The erratum slip was issued a year and a-half or more ago, and it was only the other day I found it had been put into the wrong book.

2678. (*Mr. Sexton.*) You are 10,000,000*l.* poorer than you thought, are you?—From that point of view, yes. It is a very important error, because although it does not alter the conclusion between 1880 and 1851 except in amount, it reverses the result between 1880 and 1881.

2679. (*Chairman.*) Now I will go back to the questions I was putting to you. How long have you held your office?—For fifteen years last September.

2680. You belong to several statistical societies I think?—Yes; I am ex-President of the Statistical Society of Ireland, a Fellow of the Royal Statistical Society and of the International Statistical Institute.

2681. And you have given great attention to statistics generally, and, among other works, you have prepared the "Facts and Figures about Ireland" which we have before us?—Yes.

Dr. T. W. Grimshaw.

1 Dec. 1899.

2682. What are your duties as Registrar-General?—My duties are of a mixed character. Mine is partly an administrative department and partly a recording department. In the administrative department I have merely to administer the laws with regard to births, marriages, and deaths; and as head of the recording department I collect and issue reports upon births, marriages, and deaths, emigration, agriculture, railway traffic, banking and shipping matters; and, as a special thing, I edit (and compile to a certain extent) the criminal and judicial statistics of Ireland. That is done for the Chief Secretary's Office, and is not one of my duties as Registrar-General.

Census of Ireland.

2683. When was the first Census of Ireland taken?—The first complete Census of Ireland was taken in 1821. There was an attempt to take a Census in 1813, but it was a failure. Of course I am chief of the Census Department, the taking of the Census being part of my duties as Registrar-General.

2684. The estimated figures of the population in the years preceding the Union and up to 1821 is a matter bearing upon the historical portion of the inquiry we are making; will you state shortly what are the sources of information upon the subject, and give any estimates of the population at different dates between 1782 and 1821, and put in any figures or tables which you can?—I have here a table which I hand in, written up to 1891 (*handing in Table* (3)). There was great difficulty in estimating the population of Ireland prior to the taking of the Census of 1821; there were various guesses made at it from time to time by Sir William Petty, Arthur Young and others; but the first substantial effort that was made was by Mr. Gervais Parker Bushe in a paper which he sent to the Royal Irish Academy. I have a copy of his paper here, which I hand in (*handing in the same*).

2685. (*Mr. Sexton.*) He was a Commissioner of Inland Revenue, was he not?—He was a Commissioner of Inland Revenue. With that paper he wrote a letter which was addressed to the then President of the Royal Irish Academy, Lord Charlemont, which I also put in (*handing in the same.*)

2686. (*Lord Welby.*) As Commissioner of Inland Revenue he also looked after the hearth duty, did he not?—Yes, that was part of his duty.

2687. (*Mr. Wolff.*) What is the date of that paper?—It was written in the year 1789 and was published in the year 1790, I think, in the proceedings of the Royal Irish Academy. Mr. Bushe tells the state of affairs, the defects which he found, and states very frankly that his collectors had not done their duty and that things were very much wrong. He then proceeded to his conclusions—and the conclusion he arrived at was that in the year 1788, which was the year he was working his paper on, the population of Ireland was 4,040,000. In the Report of the Census Commissioners for 1821 there is an account of the various attempts that were made to estimate the population of Ireland. I have an extract from that, but I suppose it is not necessary to read it. It is to be found on pages vi. and vii. of the Census Report. It is a very interesting paper and the conclusions are all contained at the end of it, where there is a short table giving a list of the population of Ireland as estimated by these various persons from time to time.

2688. (*Chairman.*) Beginning with Petty?—Beginning with Petty, and ending with the incomplete Census of 1813.

2689. Will you read those main figures?—It begins with the year 1672, when Sir William Petty gives the number as 1,320,000. Then there is South's estimate of 1695, 1,034,102. Then there are four estimates by Mr. Dobbs, 1712, 1718, 1725 and 1726; those are 2,099,000, 2,169,000, 2,317,000, and 2,309,000. I leave out the hundreds. Then there was an attempt made in 1731, through the clergy of the Established Church, to get a Census—that was 2,010,000. Then come the hearth money collectors' calculations in 1754, 1767, 1777, and 1785. Those were 2,372,000 in 1754, in 1767, 2,544,000, in 1777 2,690,000, and in 1785, 2,845,000.

Dr. T. W. Grimshaw.

1 Dec. 1899.

Census of Ireland.

2690. (*Lord Welby.*) I see that there is a very large difference between the figures which you have given upon the basis of Bushe's amended statement for 1785 and those figures you have just read. In your figures 1785 is 3,850,000, and the figures you have just read as given by the Hearth Commissioners are 2,845,000, a difference of very nearly a million?—Yes. The next one is Mr. Bushe's calculation in 1788, of 4,040,000; that is the number I mentioned before. Then in 1791 the hearth money collectors' calculation, which I believe to be the more correct, is 4,206,612.

2691. (*Mr. Sexton.*) Mr. Bushe's calculation was also founded on the hearth money, was it not?—Yes, but Mr. Bushe knew he was only making estimates. He gives in his paper which I have handed in, statements showing that he could not rely on a large number of returns and he proceeded to correct them, and that is an estimate founded on his corrections. In 1792 the Rev. Dr. Beaufort made an estimate.

2692. (*Chairman.*) Who was he?—I really do not know. His estimate was 4,088,000. Then there was Mr. Newenham, who wrote a very good account of the state of things in Ireland, and his estimate for the year 1805 was 5,395,000. Then there was the incomplete Census of 1813, with estimates added for incomplete parts, amounting to 5,938,000. Mr. Bushe having called attention to the defects in the earlier estimates and having made a general disturbance about them, and being the head of the department which had the control and collection of the hearth money, naturally called upon people to do the thing right in the future; and the consequence was that there was a new estimate made on what was believed to be a more reliable basis. That was in the year 1791, after Mr. Bushe had made this work over the incorrect returns. That return gives 4,206,612 I believe that to be the nearest approach to accuracy that we have. Of course it would be impossible to say now that it is absolutely accurate, but it is the most reliable figure to be had for the last century.

2693. (*Lord Welby.*) Might we judge from that that in all probability the estimates from 1712 all were under the mark?—I should think so, but it would be very hard to say.

2694. (*Mr. Sexton.*) I suppose they became rather more precise as time went on?—I think nearly all those estimates of Newenham and others were founded on the same figures—the hearth money figures. It is the same set of figures turned over and over again.

2695. They estimated the population from the number of houses?—Yes.

2696. (*Mr. Martin.*) What possible facilities had Newenham for making an estimate of population; he was merely a writer?—He was merely a writer; and if you read his book you will find his estimate was made on the hearth money collection, and so with Mr. Bushe.

2697. (*Lord Welby.*) But he had the advantage of Mr. Bushe's correction then, had he not?—He had; he quotes Mr. Bushe in his book. So that that 4,206,612 appears to be the only return of population that was taken under anything like strict rule. Therefore I take it that that is the best thing we can get, although it may not be true. Now we know that the Census of 1821 was reasonably correct and probably as good as any Census of that date was likely to be. If we take the population by that Census and the population according to the hearth money, after Mr. Bushe had introduced, as he believed, a more correct system, we find that the average increase per annum of the population would have been 1·615 per cent. per annum.

2698. (*Mr. Sexton.*) From what date to what date?—From the hearth-money return of 4,206,612 in 1791 to the Census population of 1821. The Census population of 1821 was 6,801,827. If those figures are gone into in a general way you will find the average increase was 1·615 per cent. per annum.

P

Dr. T. W. Grimshaw.

7 Dec. 1894.

Census of Ireland.

2699. (*Lord Welby.*) The figures all lead up to that; but is not that a very large increase; do not we reckon in England it would be about 1 per cent. per annum?—Yes, it is a large increase, no doubt.*

2700. (*Chairman.*) But is not that allowing for a very large emigration from England?—Yes. My own impression would be that it was rather a large figure, but, as I have said, these are the two best figures we could get.

2701. (*Mr. Wolff.*) Is not the increase partly accounted for by the better collection of statistics? The early enumeration of population, you say, was incorrect?—That is prior to 1791. I am starting with what is generally believed to be the best thing to be had prior to Census time. The estimate on that basis is in the Table which I hand in [*handing in Table* (1)], and is as follows:—First of all, estimating that as a fair view of the question, and adding on the 1·8 per cent. from year to year, starting with the 1791 population, you would get an estimate for the Census year of 1821 of 6,802,000—the enumerated Census was 6,801,000—so that it looks as if the thing was fairly correct. You arrive at one figure by estimating and at the other by actual enumeration, and the result is the difference is so very slight between them that it looks as if the calculations at all events had been very correctly made. That would give the population for those periods. But you will observe that in the table I have handed in, it goes backwards as well as forwards. We reversed the process and went back to the year 1780, and proceeding on the same basis, the population for 1780 would have been 3,526,661; for 1781 it would have been 3,583,641; for 1791, 4,206,612; for 1801, 4,937,553; for 1811, 5,795,446; and for 1821, 6,802,409. That is the series of figures which the Secretary asked me to supply to the Commission.

2702. (*Mr. Sexton.*) The average increase between 1780 and 1821 is not 1·815, it is 1·6151?—I did not work it out myself, but it was done by the most accurate statistician I know of. [See Note at foot.]

2703. It is important that that should be corrected. Lord Welby called attention to the presumption that the figure was rather high, and now I point your attention to the fact that it is 1·6151?—I see in this paper that I have in my notes the "5" is put in as a correction.

2704. Will you look at this Table?—That apparently is a mistake, because this checked figure is 1·615, and whatever has been there previously has been scratched out and 5 put in, which I tell you is the correct number.* Of course I need scarcely tell you I do not make these calculations myself, but they were made by one of the most accurate men I know of, Mr. O'Neill of my department. The only other point I would call attention to in connection with that is that the population was about the same in the middle of 1895 as it was at the time of the Union. In 1801 it was 4,937,553; in the year 1895, to the middle of the year, the estimated population was 4,626,568. Perhaps it would be useful for the Commission to have that point before them. That appears to be as near as we can go to the corresponding population after the Union as at the time of the Union. I have here a copy of a remark of Arthur Young's about the estimates. He said he did not believe any of them; that they were worthless; but that was before Mr. Bushe's time. He, writing in 1779, says:—"As "to the number of people in Ireland I do not pretend "to compute them because there are no satisfactory "data whereon to found any computation. I have "seen several formed on the hearth tax, but all compu-"tations by taxes must be erroneous; they may be "below but they cannot be above the truth. This is "the case of calculating the number in England for "the house and window tax. In Ireland it is still "more so from the greater carelessness and abuses in "collecting taxes." That is Arthur Young's remark on the subject.

2705. (*Chairman.*) Arthur Young was sceptical about statistics, was he not?—Yes, but there were no reliable returns in his time.

2706. (*Lord Welby.*) I think before the close investigation which you applied to it, Mr. Lecky came to the conclusion that between 1780 and 1800 the population of Ireland varied from 4,000,000 to 5,000,000?—I think so.

2707. (*Mr. Sexton.*) That would confirm the computation both of Mr. Bushe and the subsequent one of the House of Commons?—Yes; I think you may take it these figures I have given now are likely to be correct—in fact the nearest thing we can get. I do not think there was anything reliable until 1791, when Mr. Bushe tried to enforce exactness on his collectors.

2708. (*Chairman.*) Will you now proceed in the order in which you have prepared your papers?—Owing to the fact that the population of Ireland was decreasing, of course there is a difficulty in making estimates on the same basis that you use in making them for an increase of population. Latterly I have pursued the system of taking the population as estimated from the births, the deaths, and the emigration. These are all very accurately known, and my estimates now, instead of being made by the increase or decrease between Census periods, are made on the actual figures for each year. I have a table here, which has hitherto been published in my quarterly reports and in the annual reports as a standard; but in this revision which has been made for this Commission I have come to the conclusion that those figures prior to 1821 should be dropped. They are not of much value because we have nothing to compare with them, but the Census population for the modern periods is founded on very good ground indeed. The Census Commissioners for 1841 had some doubts as to their estimates.

2709. (*Chairman.*) You have not given us the figures yet from 1821 to 1847?—Would you like the figures for each successive Census period.

2710. Yes; we have got up to 1821 but we have not got them any later?—I have not the Census for 1831 here; the Census for 1841 was 8,175,124; for 1851 6,552,385. [The population in 1831 was 7,767,401.]

2711. Then you were on the down grade?—Yes.

2712. I want you to give us a general account of the years when the population was still rising and the percentage?—I will give these figures first: in 1861 the population was 5,798,967; in 1871 it was 5,412,377; in 1881 it was 5,174,836; in 1891 it was 4,704,750. [*Table* (3) *handed in.*]

2713. Now give in one figure from 1821, up to which year you have given us very full figures, the maximum year. I think the Commission would be glad to have the percentage of increase in the same way as you have given it up to 1821?—I do not know that I have calculated that exactly, I shall have to refer to the Census report. I have the rate of decrease here between 1841 and 1851, in the table which I have just put in.

2714. But you have not the rate of increase before we got to the decrease?—I can find it afterwards.

2715. Will you put that in your answers?—Yes, I will take a note of it. The maximum year is 1845.*

2716. (*Mr. Sexton.*) What was the figure for that year?—The estimated population in 1845 is 8,295,061.

2717. (*The O'Conor Don.*) How was that estimate arrived at?—That was arrived at as explained at foot of table already handed in (Q. 2684).

2718. (*Chairman.*) That was the maximum population of Ireland, was it?—That was the maximum population of Ireland as far as can be ascertained.

* Note to Qs. 2702 et seq. The number 1·615 was a copyist's error in the heading, the rate is 1·615, and the Table handed in calculated at 1·615, is perfectly correct.

* The respective rates of increase for the four years 1842–5, as estimated, were 0·4, 0·9, 0·4, and 0·2 per cent. of the population in the preceding year.

Dr. T. W. Grimshaw. 7 Dec. 1894. Census of Ireland.

2719. (*Lord Welby.*) Upon the system which you have now given up, that is to say, upon the increase in each year?—Yes, as formerly estimated.

2720. (*The O'Conor Don.*) It is not upon the improved system which you have lately adopted?—No, it is not.

2721. (*Mr. Sexton.*) Did it apply the average annual increase from 1831 to 1841 to the years between 1841 and 1845?—It was applied on up to 1841, and then the system referred to in Table (2) was followed.

2722. (*Chairman.*) The system pursued in order to get this estimate for 1845 I understand was this, that you applied the average annual increase between 1831 and 1841, as ascertained by the Census, to the years between 1841 and 1845?—No; on the system detailed in Table (2).

2723. Are those all the figures you wish to put in as to the movement of the numbers until 1841?—I have a quotation from my pamphlet here on the point put to me about 1845, which I will read. It also bears on the present estimate. The estimated population to the middle of the present year is 4,600,000. Now this is what I have written in my pamphlet: "The "estimates show that the population of Ireland "diminished from 8,200,000" (leaving out the odd hundreds) "in the middle of the year 1841 to "4,718,000 in the middle of the year 1890, exhibiting "a loss of 3,482,000. The Census figures show that "the population stood at 8,175,124 in 1841, and "5,174,836 in 1881, being a diminution of 3,000,288 "in forty years, or at the rate of 36·7 per cent up to "and including 1881. The rate of diminution from "Census period to Census period in these forty years "was a decreasing ratio. Between 1841 and 1851 "the rate of diminution was 19·8 per cent; between "1851 and 1861 it was 11·5 per cent; between 1861 "and 1871, 6·2 per cent; and between 1871 and 1881, "4·4 per cent only; while between 1881 and 1891 "there was a greater tendency to decrease than in the "previous decade, the population having fallen from "5,174,836 in the former to 4,704,750 in the latter "year, being a decrease of 470,086 or 9·08 per cent." The point there is that the decrease between 1881 and 1891 was a greater percentage than between 1871 and 1881.

2724. (*Mr. Sexton.*) About double?—Just about double; I may say exactly double.

2725. (*Chairman.*) Does that complete the figures?—This extract goes on: "There can be little doubt "that immediately before the famine, namely in the "year 1845, the population of Ireland amounted to "about 8,295,000 or about 85,000 more than in 1841. "From 1845 to the year 1877 a steady decrease in the "population took place. In the latter year it rose "slightly" (this is a very important point) "the "increase for the year being about 8,000 as compared "with the year 1876. The decrease recommenced in "the year 1878, and has been going on in varying "proportions ever since. I wish specially to direct "attention to this increase."

2726. (*Lord Welby.*) Are those figures arrived at on your system of comparing births, deaths, and emigration?—They are arrived at on the new system.

2727. (*Chairman.*) Are those the main figures which you wish to put before us as to the general rise and fall in the population during the last century?—Yes; I may mention I have left out the 1831 figure as I have not got it at the present moment; but the estimate in this Table (2) is practically correct.

Systems of estimating population.

2728. (*Lord Welby.*) May I ask you whether you have compared your more accurate principle of estimating the progress of population between two Censuses with the old method of estimating it by the mean, and whether there is a great difference?—There was a very great difference. At the time of the taking of the Census in 1881 I got Mr. O'Neill, my principal statistical man, to make an estimate on the old system. I made an estimate on the new system, and we got clerks to check the two figures. I was only 82,000 out in the estimated population of Ireland; he, I think, was 134,000 out.

Dr. T. W. Grimshaw. 7 Dec. 1894. Systems of estimating population.

2729. (*Mr. Sexton.*) And yours was the new system?—Mine was the new system. I do not mean to say that was his view; it was not; but it was just a test as to how the two systems worked. We had got all the materials then for testing them, and we found the test was very close indeed following the new system.

2730. But the maximum error of the superseded system was only 134,000 in 5,000,000?—It was not very great.

Changes in urban and rural population.

2731. (*Chairman.*) As I said just now, those are the figures that you wish to put before us as to the movement of the population of Ireland in the aggregate?—Yes.

2732. Will you be so good as to state to us whether the decrease since the maximum is greater in the rural districts than in the towns or cities?—It is greater in rural districts.

2733. Will you give us some figures in support of that answer?—First of all, I should like to explain that in the Irish Census it has been the custom to divide the population into what is called civic and rural. A civic population means the population of any town of 2,000 and upwards—that is a good sized village; the rest are looked upon as rural populations. I have a series of tables here, and in table (4), which I hand in, I have headings for the population of towns of 2,000 and not exceeding 10,000 from the year 1821 by each census on to the last, with the increase and decrease. I have then given the population of towns of 10,000 and upwards, which we look upon as the large towns of Ireland, with the increase and decrease. I have also given in Table (5) the rural population of Ireland, and from these tables I can state now in reply to your question where the increases and decreases are, comparing country, small towns and large towns with one another. I think that is what you wish.

2734. Yes; will you give us the figures?—I have already given you the total population of Ireland. The rural population in 1821—that is all the population outside towns of 2,000 and upwards, was 5,858,000, leaving out the hundreds; in 1831, 6,657,000; in 1841, 7,039,000; in 1851, 5,352,000; in 1861, 4,687,000; in 1871, 4,311,000; in 1881, 3,929,000; and in 1891, 3,460,000.

2735. (*Mr. Sexton.*) That includes all the towns of less than 2,000 people?—Yes, it does. The maximum was in 1841, 7,039,000, you may say 7,000,000 in round numbers.

2736. (*Mr. Sexton.*) Can you get no nearer to the absolutely rural population; must you include the places of less than 2000?—It is with difficulty it is done, owing to the want of distinct boundaries. You see in taking boundaries of this sort you have to make a guess at it, and this period was even before the Towns Improvement Act, which made definite boundaries for many places of 1,500 inhabitants and upwards; but there are no definite boundaries at all for many of these places, and they had to be taken according to the common report of the people, who considered the place to be a town. It is in that way a little defective, I admit.

2737. (*Sir David Barbour.*) You draw a distinction, do you not, between the rural population and the agricultural population; the population depending on agriculture for their livelihood?—I think you may take it that the whole of the rural communities are agricultural.

2738. But there would be a number of shop-keepers, shoemakers, blacksmiths and so forth included, would there not?—Of course, but I cannot distinguish them; I can give you the proportions of persons employed in the various industries; I have that for the whole country, but this is the rural population, not all necessarily agricultural labourers or farmers. With regard to the increases and decreases during that

Dr. T. W. Grimshaw.

7 Dec. 1894.

Changes in urban and rural population.

period (of course we do not know them before 1821), the increase of rural population between 1821 and 1831 was 707,000; in 1841 it was 383,000; in 1851 there was a decrease of 1,708,000; 1861 a diminution of 678,110; in 1871, a diminution of 418,340; in 1881, a diminution of 291,700; in 1891, a diminution of 462,676. The point to be observed there is that the first two periods are increases; the other five are diminutions. Now the civic population of towns of 2,000 and upwards in 1821 was 913,000; in 1831, 1,100,000; in 1841, 1,133,000; in 1851, 1,216,000; in 1861, 1,140,000; in 1871, 1,201,000; in 1881, 1,248,000; in 1891, 1,244,000. I will now take the increases and decreases in that column. In 1831 there is an increase of 187,000; in 1841 an increase of 34,000; in 1851 an increase of 83,000; in 1861 a diminution of 76,000; in 1871 an increase of 60,000; in 1881 an increase of 44,000; and in 1891 it remained practically the same, a diminution of 1,000 only.

2739. (*Lord Welby.*) Is it not rather a surprising fact that the town population should have increased between 1841 and 1851, at a time when the whole population had decreased so very much?—Yes, it is so. There is a peculiar feature with regard to that. The people in the famine times in 1848, rushed into the towns; so that the large towns show an increase of population in the year 1851, which immediately decreases again, as you will observe. There is a diminution in the following Census, and it was the rush into the towns of the starving people which is the explanation of it.

2740. (*Mr. Sexton.*) There is an increase in the towns between 1841 and 1851; there is a diminution?—No; there is an increase of 83,000. It is in 1861 the decrease comes.

2741. (*Lord Welby.*) May I ask you with reference to that, has increase of town population any bearing on the diminution of fourth-class houses?—I think it has; those probably would be inhabitants of fourth-class houses.

2742. (*Mr. Sexton.*) Of course Belfast was increasing very rapidly between 1841 and 1851?—It was; I shall be able to give you those figures.

2743. (*Chairman.*) Can you analyse any further these increases and decreases?—I was going to distinguish the large towns from the small. In the large town populations there is a slight discrepancy, which I can explain. In the earlier years the population was given for Parliamentary boroughs instead of municipal boroughs, and it makes Cork look, for instance, as if it had gone down tremendously, whereas it did not in reality. I have taken towns with a population of 10,000 as the standard of a large town in Ireland, because Dr. Ogle, who was superintendent of statistics, at the office in London, considered that a fair line to draw between strictly rural and strictly town populations; and I came to the conclusion, if that is the opinion in England, it should be still more so in Ireland. As to the towns above 2,000, and not exceeding 10,000; the population in 1821 was 399,000; in 1831, 473,000; in 1841, 514,000; in 1851, 543,000; in 1861, 478,000; in 1871, 438,000; in 1881, 432,000; and in 1891, 399,000. That is dealing with towns of between 2,000 and 10,000 population. Now the way these deal with regard to increase and decrease is this: between 1821 and 1831, there was an increase of 74,000; between 1831 and 1841 of 41,000; between 1841 and 1851 of 29,000; the increase was diminished. Then it becomes a decrease: between 1851 and 1861, 73,000 was the diminution; between 1861 and 1871, 34,000 was the diminution; between 1871 and 1881, 6,000 was the diminution; between 1881 and 1891, 33,000 was the diminution. Of course these towns of between 2,000 and 10,000, although not so closely dependent upon the state of the rural inhabitants as the smaller ones, are nevertheless, closely allied to them.

2744. (*Sir David Barbour.*) Was the decrease in these towns greater or less than the average decrease of the whole population, or about the same during the same period?—I could not tell you that without making a calculation; it has not been calculated.

2745. It can be done, I suppose?—Yes; I will put it in.

2746. (*Mr. Wolff.*) I suppose, with the exception of a few purely manufacturing towns, the rest of the towns depend as much on agriculture as the rural districts?—I take it that that is so. All these small towns depend on the rural population.

2747. (*Mr. Sexton.*) Generally, unless a town has an independent manufacturing industry, it depends on the rural population, does it not?—Certainly. The next point is the populations of towns of 10,000 and upwards—what we may call really the large towns of Ireland. In 1821, in these towns there were 514,000; in 1831, 636,000; in 1841, 621,000; in 1851, 675,000; in 1861, 670,000; in 1871, 765,000; in 1881, 815,000; in 1891, 845,000. The way they go with regard to increase and decrease is—from 1821 to 1831 there was an increase of 122,000; between 1831 and 1841, a diminution of 15,000, between 1841 and 1851, an increase of 54,000; and—this is the point Lord Welby was asking about—in 1861 there was a diminution of 4,470 only; in 1871, an increase of 95,000; in 1881, an increase of 49,000; and in 1891, an increase of 30,000 nearly.

2748. (*Mr. Sexton.*) Those towns must be very few; can you name them?—Yes.

2749. (*Chairman.*) How many towns are there exceeding the 10,000?—Sixteen.

2750. Will you enumerate them?—When I say 16 I mean in 1891. Dublin (including Rathmines and Rathgar and Pembroke Townships), Kingstown, Belfast, Cork, Limerick, Londonderry, Waterford, Galway, Newry, Dundalk, Lisburn, Drogheda, Wexford, Lurgan, Kilkenny, Sligo.

2751. (*Mr. Wolff.*) I see that five of those you have enumerated have gone below 10,000, which had been in 1841 above 10,000.—But I have only read those which have stuck to 10,000 or have risen to 10,000 since 1841. Of course, you will observe in those there are included a group of towns which practically is Dublin—that is the city—Rathmines and Rathgar, Pembroke and, you may say, Kingstown.

2752. (*Mr. Sexton.*) They are suburban towns?—Yes. Of course there are other Dublin townships all round not up to 10,000 which would not come into that list at all.

2753. (*Chairman.*) Does that exhaust that branch of the inquiry?—Unless you wish me to go into particulars of those that have gone up and down. This table gives it. There are several other towns in this list which have gone down, and some did not exist at all in 1841.

2754. (*Sir David Barbour.*) Then the movement of population in these 16 towns has not been uniformly in the direction of increase or decrease?—No, that is the aggregate.

2755. (*Chairman.*) Will you give us the aggregate population of those 16 towns?—In 1891 it was 844,349.

2756. I think that completes the figures as to what you call the civic population, does it not?—I have here another table (Table III.) which goes back to 1821, which corresponds with the one I have been referring to; but, as I have mentioned the populations of Dublin, Cork, Limerick, and one or two other towns, are not comparable because they are parliamentary boroughs and not municipal boroughs, and we cannot distinguish between them at that time.

2757. Can you give us shortly the relation between the increase and decrease of what you call the civic districts in the aggregate and the rural districts; have you put it together?—Do you mean the percentage?

2758. The decrease in the rural population between 1841 and 1891 was at the rate of how much per cent. per annum?—50·4 per cent.

Dr. T. W. Grimshaw.

7 Dec. 1891.

Proportion in urban and rural population.

2759. (*Mr. Sexton.*) The rural population between 1841 and 1891 decreased by just one-half, you may say?—Yes.

2760. (*Chairman.*) What are the corresponding figures for the small and unimportant, and the large urban populations?—I do not think I can give you that.

2761. Will you calculate it and give it afterwards?—I can give you the increase of the total civic populations—that is of towns of 2,000 and upwards—but I cannot give you those of above 10,000. The former shows 9·7 per cent. increase.*

2762. The decrease of the rural populations you have stated to be 50 per cent.—Yes. The corresponding figure for the urban populations, without distinguishing the classes, is 9·7 per cent. increase.

Diminution by provinces.

2763. (*The O'Conor Don.*) Can you give us the diminution of the population by provinces?—I can.

2764. Distinguishing the different parts of Ireland?—I have it here, county by county.

2765. But have you made it up by provinces?—Yes; it is done by counties, provinces, and totalled.

2766. Will you give, in a short way, how much the percentage of diminution is in each province between 1841 and 1891?—In the province of Leinster the decrease was 39·8; Munster, 51·1; Ulster, 33·1; Connaught, 45·9.

2767. (*Mr. Sexton.*) And all Ireland 42·3?—Yes, all Ireland 42·3.

Causes of diminution of population.

2768. (*Chairman.*) Can you give us what, in your opinion, is the cause of the diminution of the population of Ireland during the period to which you have been referring—50 years, practically?—I look upon it altogether as a question of the decay of the potato, and the consequent emigration movement.

2769. Will you enlarge that a little? The famine, of course, was the beginning, but can you enlarge a little as to the time since then?—In this paper which I have prepared, I have taken that as a sort of basis, and taken it for granted.

2770. We want tersely your opinion upon the matter.—On page 9 of Part I. of my pamphlet, the whole thing is given. Would you like me to read that?

2771. No. Will you give tersely the summary of your opinion? As to the original cause, you have stated it; but what do you think the continuous diminution of the population is due to since?—It has not been exactly continuous. For instance, in the year 1879 we had another failure of the potato, and there have been less serious failures since. Of course, there was immediately an increase of emigration. We had very good times about the year 1876, and the population is believed to have been increased, that is so far as an estimate can show it; by the vital statistics of the country an increase is shown in the population. The emigration was very low; for instance, in the years 1876, 1877, and 1878 it was only 7·1, 7·2, and 7·7 per 1,000 of the population, which is a very low number; and if you will look at the year 1876, you will find there was a very good harvest, and there was no inducement to run away and seek for labour elsewhere. The potato crop gave an extremely high yield.

2772. (*Mr. Sexton.*) The best for 20 years, I believe?—The best for 20 years. I think the decline in emigration was due to the large potato crop, which was then the staple food of the country; and there were also the waste potatoes, which went for feeding pigs, which is a very important thing amongst the small people. I found in comparing these statistics that whenever you have a plentiful potato crop, you almost always have an increase in the number of pigs in the following year, which is a great matter for these small agriculturists. That will be found to be the case following the good year of 1876; you had a good harvest, an increase of population, and evidently an overplus of food, because the pigs increased in number and consumed the balance of the waste potatoes and so on. That will be found to be pretty nearly true always when those circumstances arise.

2773. Those are very clear and excellent reasons for the exceptional either increase or stationary character of the population; but during the great majority of the years of that half century the population diminished almost continuously. Will you give your opinion of the causes of that continuous diminution, which is the principal question we have to consider on this part of our inquiry?—My opinion is that it is the great reliance which was placed on the potato. It was very seldom that you had such a year as 1876 to keep up the population. Then there is another point, which is a valuable point, which does not depend upon this country at all. Most of our emigrants go to the United States of America, and when wages rise and things are prosperous there, there is an attraction, so you have the two elements; you have the attraction of good times in America, and you have the bad times in Ireland. If these are combined you have the reason of emigration to the United States. Things have altered now, as you know, with regard to emigration into the United States, which must have its effects, because people cannot go there now, simply because they are poor. They must go with prospects, either with money in their pockets or having established friends to go to.

2774. (*Lord Welby.*) Has that diverted any of the emigration to some of our colonies?—I could not say that, but I think it is possible it may have done so.

2775. (*Chairman.*) Will you sum up the two causes which you consider chiefly contribute to the steady decline of the population?—The uncertainty and frequent failure of the potato crop is one, and the attraction by good times in America is another.

2776. There may be other minor causes, but these are the two principal causes of the diminution of the population, you think?—Yes; and another attraction to America is that there is a great number of Irishmen settled there, and families prefer to go where they meet their friends, of course.

2777. (*Mr. Sexton.*) I think there is a third major cause, is there not: the absence of manufacturing industry in Ireland; so that when the rural population become destitute there is no refuge for them?—That is admitted; it is want of employment.

2778. (*Chairman.*) Then you say there are three principal causes for the diminution of population: the continuous difficulty as to the potato crop, the attractions of emigration generally, and thirdly the want of manufacture?—I mean the United States particularly.

2779. (*Sir David Barbour.*) Has it not been affected also by the fact that there are now greater facilities for emigration—that is to say, that there is a quicker passage, and that the cost is less?—There are increased facilities, of course; and, for instance, one of the ways in which I account for the greater decrease of rural population between 1881 and 1891 is that there was a great deal of assisted emigration—for instance, there was Mr. Tuke's fund—and people could get off more easily during that period.

2780. There is better information now generally as to the rates of wages obtained in foreign countries, and there are also greater facilities for moving from one country to another, are there not?—Certainly.

2781. (*Chairman.*) Do these all count as branches of the three main heads you have given?—Yes, but of course they apply to the whole world, not only to Ireland.

2782. (*Mr. Martin.*) Would not you consider that the great depression in America during the last few years has also had the effect of deterring emigrants from going to the United States?—Yes, there is a fall in emigration.

2783. Owing to the want of prosperity in the United States?—Yes; I have a table here showing the emigration year by year from the year 1870 up to

* The population in towns having 2,000 and under 10,000 inhabitants declined 7·3 per cent., and the population in towns of 10,000 and upwards increased 16 per cent.

Dr. T. W. Grimshaw.

7 Dec. 1894.

Causes of diminution of population.

the year 1894 (Table I.) The estimated emigration for this year (we have eleven months of it in) is 36,046. That figure is about 12,000 under that for last year, and is the lowest for any year since, at all events, 1841.

2784. (*Chairman.*) Those are all parts of one question. Emigration in some years has been greater and in other years less; the attractions have been greater, the facilities have been greater, or the impediments may have been greater. The three causes you have mentioned are in your opinion the main causes for the diminution of the population, are they not?—Yes.

2785. (*Mr. Sexton.*) I should like to get on record your statement that you consider the potato crop to be the regulating factor of emigration from Ireland?—Yes, and more strongly in former days than now.

2786. (*Lord Welby.*) That is absolutely true as to the time between 1845 and 1851; but of late years has not the entire dependence of the population on the potato diminished very much, and therefore so far it would be an important factor, but not so important a factor, would it?—I think the importance of it is diminishing every year.

2787. It is still an important factor, but not so important as it used to be—that is to say, the population is not so entirely dependent on the potato as it used to be, is it?—Certainly not. My notion is now that the deterrent effect, as contrasted with the effect on the other side, is less important relatively than the attractions. In former days the repellent effect was most important; now the thing has balanced, and they have to consider whether they will be better off if they go.

Increase of population in Great Britain.

2788. Although the population of Ireland, from the main causes you have enumerated, has fallen off almost continuously during the last half century, you are of course aware that the population of Great Britain has increased, also almost continuously, during that period?—Yes.

2789. What reason would you give for the difference in the movement of the population in the two countries?—First of all you have extensive manufactories in England. The great point about England at the present time, as compared with Ireland, is that in England two-thirds of the population are town population.

2790. (*Chairman.*) Are you counting on the basis of towns with 2,000 inhabitants and upwards?—I am referring to the big towns, and that means, in fact, that the people who are employed in manufacturing industries in Ireland, about one-fourth of the population, are inhabitants of considerable towns—not one-fourth in the 10,000 inhabitants towns, but about one-fourth in the urban sanitary districts.

2791. On the same principle of comparison it is two-thirds in one case and one-fourth in the other?—Yes. If there had been the same state of things in England, and three-fourths of the population had been agricultural population, I have no doubt you would have had diminution. As a matter of fact, the country population of England has diminished. Some of the counties in England which are dependent altogether on rural industry have largely diminished in population.

2792. (*Mr. Sexton.*) The difference is that they go into the towns of England, not out of England, is it not?—Exactly; they migrate to the towns. There are not sufficient towns or centres of industry to migrate to in Ireland, and therefore people have to go to other countries.

Emigration from British Isles.

2793. (*Sir David Barbour.*) Is not there also a considerable emigration from England?—Yes, there is.

2794. A large emigration?—Yes.

2795. (*Lord Welby.*) Then may I take it that you think the fact of the Irish population diminishing to the extent it has is natural?—I do.

2796. (*Sir David Barbour.*) I see it is stated here, in a pamphlet before me, that in 1890 the number of English and Welsh in the United States, as shown by the Census, was 745,000; in Canada, in 1881, 160,000; and in the same way in the Australian colonies, 499,000; so that there must have been a considerable emigration?—I do not deny that, but not in proportion. I can give you the numbers of Irish in some of those colonies, according to the latest returns.

Dr. T. W. Grimshaw.

7 Dec. 1894.

Emigration from British Isles.

2797. Has there been also an emigration from Ireland to England?—Yes, there is to a certain extent. There are a large number of Irish persons settled in England and persons of Irish parentage.

2798. (*Chairman.*) Is that emigration to England continuing now. It was very large?—I do not think it is so great as it was. I forget when looking at the books the number, but I think the number of Irish-born residents in England, according to the last English Census, is about the same as it was before.

2799. (*Sir David Barbour.*) Do you recollect the figure?—I do not.

2800. Perhaps you will put it in afterwards?—I will.* That is, of course, Irish-born people; we do not know how many persons there are of Irish descent. Do you wish it for England only?

2801. For Great Britain.—Very well.

2802. (*Chairman.*) In your opinion, therefore, the great cause of the remarkable difference between the movement of the population in Great Britain and Ireland—increasing fairly rapidly in Great Britain, diminishing now slightly in Ireland—is the absence of manufacture in Ireland?—Not the absence, but the want of sufficient employment—of course we have some manufactures.

2803. Is manufacture in Ireland increasing at the present time?—Yes, I think so. I think I can show you that presently when you come to those points.

2804. You have some facts upon that, have you?—I have. I do not know whether with regard to the potato point you wish me to say anything. On page 11 of my pamphlet, Part I., I mention the state of things in 1879, when there was the greatest breakdown there has been since the famine.

Potato crops.

2805. (*Mr. Sexton.*) You gave the effect of a good year, and you wish now to give the effect of a bad one?—Yes. This, of course, was the worst year we have had since the great famine. I say: "This year "almost immediately succeeded the prosperous period "of 1876–77. If we look at the statistics of the years "1879 and '80, and compare them with those of the "years 1876–77, we shall find a complete contrast. "As in the former case we look at the conditions of "the year 1879 to account for the circumstances "which arose in 1880. In 1880 we find a decrease "of about 63,000 in the population, caused chiefly by "a large emigration in that year and towards the end "of the year 1879. The emigration rate for 1880 was "17·6 per 1,000 of the population, being higher than "for any of the thirteen preceding years, and only "exceeded since in 1883 when it was 21·7, although "it was nearly equalled in 1882 when it was 17·4, "and in 1887 when it was 17·1. Now, let us look "at the year 1879. First, let us examine the yield "of the crops. Wheat was only 11·4 cwt. per acre—a "yield far below the average. The yield of oats, also, "was very low; but when we come to the staple food "of the country, we find that the yield of potatoes in "1879 was the lowest on record, namely, 1·3 tons per "acre. If we apply the test of the surplus or waste "portion for feeding pigs, we find that in 1880 the "pigs were the lowest number on record, except the "years 1847 and 1849 (the year 1848 not being "known). In 1890 the yield of potatoes fell to 2·3 "tons per acre, the lowest on record since 1879; and "in 1891 the pigs fell to 1,358,000 from 1,570,000 "in 1890, and the fall continued the following year "to 1,118,000, thus showing a result similar to that "which followed the greater failure in 1879. The "emigration rate did not rise, showing less severity "in the crisis than in that of 1879."

* In 1881 the number of Irish born persons in Great Britain was [illegible], in 1891 it was [illegible].

Dr. T. W. Grimshaw.

7 Dec. 1894.

Estimate of total wealth of Ireland since the famine.

2806. (*Lord Welby.*) May I ask what you call an average potato crop. You say that 1·3 tons per acre is very low, and 1·3 is low?—About 3½ tons to the acre is the average.

2807. (*Chairman.*) Passing from the purely population statistics to those of wealth, I shall be glad if you will tell us whether, according to the figures which your statistics are a summary of, the wealth of Ireland in your opinion has increased or diminished since the famine. Do you think that the individual Irishman has more or less to spend than he had at that time?—I consider that the total wealth of the country has increased.

2808. The population at that time was rather over 8,000,000?—Yes.

2809. And it is now between 4,000,000 and 5,000,000, is it not?—It is 4,600,000 odd.

2810. Do you think from the statistics you have collected that the 4,000,000 are as well or better off than the 8,000,000 in the year 1847, and if in the aggregate they have more individually. Do you think the proportion of wealth is greater or less?—Of course one follows from the other. The aggregate, I say, is greater so far as we can ascertain, and therefore averaging the thing over the whole community the amount per head would be greater.

2811. You answer my first question by saying that the aggregate is greater?—Yes.

2812. That there is a larger amount of wealth now enjoyed by the 4,500,000 than there was in 1847, by the 8,000,000?—Yes, of course; do not understand me to say that I think every man in Ireland is better off than he was.

2813. We are taking averages, of course. Will you give us shortly your grounds for that opinion?—The statistics that I have collected for the past fifty years I find in nearly every case point to increased wealth, manufactures and commerce; and that while agriculture has not been so remunerative as a whole in consequence of foreign competition, and consequent fall of prices, the population has so diminished in rural districts and so many improvements in agriculture have taken place that the existing agriculturists are better off than those who preceded them.

2814. Have you any other remark to make on that point?—I do not know that I have, except to answer any questions with regard to the various things. That is the result of investigating all the figures I could get put together. We have an increase of manufactures; our banks, railways and all the tests you can apply show increased wealth.

Increase of wealth per head.

2815. If the aggregate wealth has increased and the population is only half, or little more than half, we may estimate that in your opinion the Irishman is twice as well off on the average as he was then. How would you modify that?—I think it would be scarcely fair to make such a wide statement as that.

2816. In what way would you modify that?—I should not like to fix a ratio all round in that way. I have taken various heads and gone into the amount of savings, of railway capital and manufactures per head, but I should not like to say how much the average individual would be better off than before.

2817. (*Sir David Barbour.*) What do you mean by twice as well off?—I take it that it means a man gets twice as much income.

2818. But supposing prices have risen, he might not be now as well off?—He might not.

2819. And if prices have fallen?—As a matter of fact, prices are down—that is, the prices of the necessities of life are lower—therefore that would not come in in this case; but I take it as a general rule that a man who gets a larger income and has a larger income to spend, unless there is some drawback, is better off.

2820. Certainly; I am merely asking you if you could define what you mean by twice as well off?—It was the Chairman's phrase, not mine.

2821. (*Mr. Martin.*) Have you made any estimate as to the percentage of increase in the wealth of the country in the last 50 years?—No, I have not. I have not attempted that. That is like an estimate of increase of income. In these pamphlets I have put down exactly what appears to be the result of the calculations.

Dr. T. W. Grimshaw.

7 Dec. 1894.

Increase of average wealth per head.

2822. I have a note here that the average wealth of the country has increased, and it would be very interesting if we had some estimate of what percentage it had increased by?—That is a thing I would not attempt myself.

2823. (*Chairman.*) I therefore get, as the starting point, your general opinion that the aggregate wealth of Ireland has increased, that the population has greatly diminished, and that therefore, per head, there is more wealth enjoyed by Irishmen than was the case 50 years ago; but that you do not think a sum in mathematics can be made of that, showing that every man of the population was double, or in any other proportion, as well, as he was then?—That is my answer. I could not undertake to estimate the wealth of the country in that way. Of course it comes very much to the same thing as making an attempt, which has been made elsewhere with a certain amount of success, to get at the total income of the community. I think those are very fallacious estimates, and not things I much rely upon. For instance, Mr. Giffen, who I suppose is one of the best statisticians in the world, has done it, but he has had to make such a number of allowances, averages and so on, that I think it cuts away a great deal of the foundation of his estimate.

2824. But we attach great importance to your opinion, and we shall be glad to know, as far as you can give it, what in your opinion is the additional prosperity of Ireland in respect of personal wealth compared with what it was half a century ago. You cannot give us, I understand, any idea at the present moment?—No, I could not. It is a very interesting thing to speculate upon, no doubt.

Classification of houses.

2825. In your tables you have given an emigration table; then Tables IV. and V. deal with inhabited houses. I should like to know what in your opinion is the bearing of the statistics of inhabited houses upon the comparative well-being of Ireland between the dates we have discussed. They are divided into four classes, I think?—Yes, they are divided into four classes; that was a classification made by Sir Thomas Larcom. I think Mr. Robinson gave you that evidence.

2826. We want your view, which is of course an independent view.—The Census Reports from 1841 to 1891 give the houses classified; the system of classification was devised by Sir Thomas Larcom, who classified them in this way—The fourth class includes all single room houses constituted of mud or perishable material; the third, a better class with from one to four rooms and windows; the second, a good farm house in the country or a small town house, having five to seven rooms and windows; and the first class, all houses of a better description than the preceding.

2827. (*The O'Conor Don.*)—When was that classification made—in what year?—In 1841—that was for the Census of 1841.

2828. Was not there a tremendous gap between the lowest class and the next above it—mud cabins of only one room, and the third class that includes houses with from two to four rooms?—There is a considerable difference, but you must remember that there are mud houses with two rooms, and they would come into the third class.

2829. That is what I say; the division does not seem to be a very correct one?—But for comparative purposes it is the same all through at each Census.

2830. (*Mr. Sexton.*) Any mud cabin with a partition if it had one pane of glass in it would be a third class house, would it not?—It would.

2831. (*The O'Conor Don.*)—And on the other hand a very comfortable farm house with four rooms might be a third class house too?—It might be. The classification which is most perfect is the accommodation classification, which is founded upon this—it is a

Dr. T. W. Grimshaw.

7 Dec. 1894.

Classification of houses.

much nearer correct estimate of the conditions under which the people live than the classification of the houses themselves. You see you have four classes of accommodation given in table 4 of Part I. of the pamphlet.

2832. (*Chairman.*)—Will you state the character of the movement which is in the direction of improvement in the 50 years to which your table on page 18 refers?—The way in which it points generally to improvement is in the class of accommodation more than in the class of house itself; because you may have a very large house with so many families in it that the families are no better housed than in a house with one room. There is one correction I wish to make. You will observe in the pamphlet on page 17 there is this remark:—"It is right here to point out that in "1871 a somewhat different plan of tabulation was "adopted which accounts for the apparent increase of "the fourth class houses and of the number of families "with fourth class accommodation in that year." The meaning of that is that in the tables for 1871 the classification adopted on previous occasions is departed from to a certain extent, many houses which in former Censuses would have been tabulated as the third class being then included in the fourth, which latter was sub-divided into two groups, one consisting of fourth class houses built of brick or stone, the other of mud cabins. It would probably have been a better classification if it had been continued. It meets the very thing the O'Conor Don referred to; it would have made five classes in fact. (*Table VI. handed in.*)

2833. (*The O'Conor Don.*)—Was that system adopted only with regard to that one period?—Only with regard to that one period; and it was partly done by mistake and partly by the good intentions of some of the people in the office, I think. It led to an error of comparison in the figures.

2834. Was it for a period of ten years or only one year?—For the year of the Census only. Of course it is only the Census figures we are dealing with.

2835. (*Lord Welby.*) And the Census of 1881 goes back to the old classification?—The Census of 1881 goes back to the old classification. That was a quotation from the Census Commissioners Report, and I think I might add this further from it:—"We have "considered it advisable to return to the classification "followed in 1841, 1851, and 1861, and the houses "now included in the fourth class are exclusively "those built of mud or perishable materials."

2836. (*Mr. Sexton.*) The effect of what you say is that the records and percentages for 1871 are comparatively worthless for the purposes of comparison as far as concerns the present fourth class of houses?—They are.

2837. (*Chairman.*) Making due allowance for that, what does your table point to as to the improvement in the condition of the people?—It points to this. The accommodation is what I apply as the test. I do not care so much for the houses themselves as for the accommodation.

2838. What do you mean exactly by the difference between the accommodation and the houses in which the accommodation is provided?—Perhaps the best plan would be to read an extract, but before doing so I would point out this, for instance—that about the worst accommodation a man can get, which is worse than a mud cabin—is a small room in a tenement house in a big city with a family in it. That man is worse off, in my opinion, than a man in a mud cabin in Connemara; so that accommodation is the real test. I say "in order to apply a test so as to ascertain the conditions under which the people actually "live, a further classification into four classes of "accommodation is made. All families living in fourth "class houses are said to occupy 'fourth class accommodation,' as also are all those in third class houses containing more than one family, all in second "class houses containing more than three families, and all in first-class houses containing "more than five families. 'Third class accommodation' consists of third class houses occupied by one family each, second class houses with "two or three families, and first class houses with four "or five families. 'Second class accommodation' consists of second class houses occupied by one family, "and first class houses with two or three families. "'First class accommodation' consists of first class "houses occupied by only one family."

Dr. T. W. Grimshaw.

7 Dec. 1894.

Classification of houses.

2839. (*Lord Welby.*) Therefore the question is really the number of families occupying a house?—Yes; for instance, we have cases of ten-roomed houses in Dublin where there are ten families in the house. Those people, of course, are just in the same condition as people living in mud cabins. Now, comparing 1841 and 1891 (we could not fairly introduce the intermediate stages on account of the disturbances) of first class accommodation, there were 31,000 in 1841 and 62,000 families in 1891.

2840. (*Chairman.*) Give the other extreme?—In the second class you have 241,000 families in 1841 against 434,000 families occupying this kind of accommodation in 1891. The third class in 1841 was 574,000 families, and in 1891 there were 359,000. The fourth class accommodation in 1841 was 625,000, and in 1891 55,000 families. That is to say, the first class accommodation is double, the second class accommodation has nearly doubled, the third class accommodation has been reduced nearly one half, and the fourth class accommodation has been reduced to about one-twelfth.

2841. The proportions are not quite the same as in the other classification?—No, they are considerably different.

2842. But they both point to very much the same result, do they not?—Yes.

2843. How do you define that result?—There are two conditions. First of all, the people who emigrated were the people—or most of them were the people—who occupied the third and fourth class accommodation.

2844. (*The O'Conor Don.*) That is to say, whole families emigrated?—Yes; a family, you know, in the census may mean only one person.

2845. (*Mr. Sexton.*) Whilst the decrease in the number of houses and the decrease in the number of inhabited houses since 1841 is about the same—440,000 and 450,000—the decrease in the number of families in Ireland is nearly 100,000 more?—Well, you know a family is a standard family—it does not mean necessarily that there is a father and mother and a number of children.

2846. But there are 100,000 more domestic groups broken up than live in houses, are there not?—A bachelor or a widow living by himself or herself would be a family. The point I was upon was this. A large number of the people who inhabited the third and fourth class accommodation were emigrants. They went away altogether and their houses fell into ruin. But the figures show a considerable improvement as to the people inhabiting first-class accommodation; they doubled, and the people with second-class accommodation have nearly doubled. There are, as we know, a large number of people living in houses of the third class accommodation, and it may be assumed from the fact that the fourth class has almost altogether disappeared, that a large number of them have gone into better houses; but of course the bulk of the diminution of the fourth class is owing to emigration.

2847. (*Lord Welby.*) On the question of amelioration, may I ask are you satisfied that a family decently housed lives necessarily in a second-class house?—There are some very good third-class houses.

2848. If they live in a second-class house they do not want very much more?—Not if they have it all to themselves.

2849. I am taking your 434,000 families with second-class accommodation, and I am putting to you whether a family with second-class accommodation is not well housed?—Yes.

2850. Then if that is the case may I put it in this

Dr. T. W. Grimshaw. 7 Dec. 1894. Classification of houses.

way that in 1841 only one family in six and a-half was well housed, and in 1891 more than one in two was well housed?—Yes, I think that is a fair statement.

2851. Is not that considerable evidence of an improvement in the state of the people?—Certainly. I have no doubt that the people are improved in house accommodation, and the improvement in towns is very considerable, as well as in the country.

2852. (*Sir David Barbour.*) You might say enormously improved?—Yes.

2853. (*Mr. Sexton.*) With regard to towns, does it not occur to you that the improvement in the first class of houses would be due to the growth of the townships about Dublin, the development of Belfast, and the general practice of building suburban residences for professional men and so on, about the various towns in Ireland?—Yes.

2854. That would account for the first class?—Yes.

2855. Would not the development of the second class be generally accounted for by the development about Dublin and Belfast?—It may be so.

2856. On the point Lord Welby has put, the difference would be greatly accounted for by the urban development of certain cities and townships, would it not?—Yes. I have some papers here containing tables from the second part of my pamphlet, showing each county by itself, and in those house accommodation comes after population, and you can find for each county how it has proceeded at each Census.

2857. (*Mr. Wolff.*) With regard to the class of houses, do you know the ordinary class of house that an ordinary operative workman lives in, in a large town?—Yes.

2858. Are those second or third class houses?—They would come in between the two.

2859. They must be one or the other?—Most of them would be third class.

2860. They are fair enough houses, are they not?—Yes.

2861. (*Chairman.*) Most of them, you say, would be third class as to accommodation?—Yes.

2862. (*Mr. Sexton.*) The second class includes small town houses, having from five to seven rooms and windows, does it not?—Yes.

2863. (*Mr. Wolff.*) Then the bulk of them would be second class, would they not?—No, a great many of them would be third class. For instance, take the artisans' cottages in Dublin, built by the Corporation or Artisans' Dwellings Company, those would be third class, most of them.

2864. Then the increase of the second class house cannot be accounted for by the increase of the towns as regards their working population?—Not with regard to their working population. I think that might be fairly said as to most of them.

2865. (*Mr. Martin.*) You do not count sculleries as a room in these artisans' houses, do you?—No.

2866. Then, though these artisans' dwellings that Mr. Wolff knows of, and that I know of, all have very good accommodation in the shape of sculleries and out-offices, still they may come under the third class category?—Yes.

2867. (*Mr. Sexton.*) It would affect the fact of any investigation into the condition of the rural population?—It might; but if it were desirable we could take out those counties where there were few large towns, and you could see how the thing stands.

2868. It would be very desirable if you would endeavour to distinguish the improvement in house accommodation which is urban and suburban belonging to the professional classes, and that which appertains to the farmer and to the labourer?—I should not like to pledge myself to do it, but I will make an attempt.*

2869. (*Chairman.*) But you can approximate to it, distinguishing the towns from the villages, can you not?—No.

2870. (*Mr. Sexton.*) Will you endeavour to distinguish between the improved accommodation of farmers and labourers, and of others which if you like means a distinction between urban and rural. What I want to ascertain is what is the proportion of this improvement which may be properly ascribed to an improvement in the agricultural class, whether you are speaking of farmers or labourers?—Of the agricultural labouring class?

2871. Yes; how much of the improvement may be attributed to the improved housing of farmers and labourers, and how much to the urban and suburban element?—Quite so. Do you think it will do if I endeavour to distinguish between the improvement in the houses of the agricultural class, and the urban and suburban class?

2872. If you mean by agricultural labouring class both farmers and labourers, it will do?—The agricultural classes. You must understand I do not pledge myself to do it, because when it comes to boundaries and districts it becomes impossible.

2873. (*Sir David Barbour.*) If you cannot do it for all Ireland you can do it for a district, perhaps?—Yes; for instance you could take Leitrim, which has not a town in it of any size.

2874. (*Lord Welby.*) Taking a simple method of doing it, I suppose you can give the number of first, second and third class houses, first of towns over 2,000, second of towns over 10,000, and, third of the rest of Ireland?—I could give it for the very large towns; I could do it for Dublin, for instance.

2875. (*Chairman.*) We understand you will do what you can, and you will put it into some one's hands quickly?—Yes.*

2876. I think I have not asked you this general question. Taking the two tables, Table V and Table VI, the results of which in some respects are not very different, what conclusion do you draw from a comparison between 1841 and 1891?—A great improvement in the house accommodation of the existing population.

2877. Can you describe that improvement by simple figures in any way?—Not otherwise than by the figures I have given you.

2878. Can you say the accommodation is twice as good, or three times as good, or once and a half as good on the average, or in any other similar way?—Only by classes. Notwithstanding the great decrease in the population, there are twice as many people well housed in the first and second class as there were in 1841.

2879. But I want a general and popular answer if you can give it. What should you say was the increase in improved accommodation, classifying it as to present accommodation, and classifying it under the old system?—I should not like to put it in a mathematical form.

2880. I will not ask you for the answer now, but can you, thinking over these tables, give anything like a figure of that kind. It is so much easier to remember than a detail of small figures?—You see it is very hard to put a thing into a mathematical expression, as it were, which is not capable of being put into figures. Taking Dublin for instance, I know there is a vast improvement in the housing of people, but I could not say the people are twice as well housed as they were fifty years ago.

2881. And there is no figure by which you can express that improvement, is there?—I think not, except by giving these details of accommodation, which are the best information we have on the subject.

2882. Statistical tables are of no use to common

* In the civic districts in 1841, the distribution of the families according to house accommodation was 7 per cent. first class; 22·4 per cent. second class; 33·3 per cent. third class; and 36·7 per cent. fourth class; the corresponding percentages for 1891 were 10·[illegible] first class, 51·[illegible] second; 33·7 third; and [illegible] fourth. In the rural districts in 1841, 1·[illegible] per cent. had first class accommodation; 10·3 second; 42·[illegible] third; and 43·[illegible] fourth; the respective percentages for 1891 were [illegible], 47·[illegible], 43·[illegible], and [illegible]. In the civic and rural districts combined the percentages were, in 1841, first class [illegible]; second 16·[illegible]; third [illegible]; fourth 43·[illegible]; and in 1891, first class [illegible]; second [illegible]; third 18·[illegible]; and fourth [illegible].

Dr. T. W. Grimshaw. 7 Dec. 1894. Classification of houses.

minds unless they can be summed up in some very short expression?—I would not like to put it in that way. Mr. Sexton, who knows about the state of things in Dublin probably better than I do, knows perfectly well that the accommodation has vastly improved,—more within the last twenty years than the last fifty years, but I do not think he would be prepared to say the people are once and a-half or twice as well off as they were.

2883. Supposing one fifth of the population of Dublin are as badly housed as in any city, what was the case in 1841?—I might make a guess at it by looking into the figures.

2884. And nobody but you can do that?—I wrote a paper on the subject, showing how they had improved, but I also showed they were very badly off still.

2885. (*Mr. Sexton.*) A number of houses in Dublin that in 1841 were first class houses, giving first class accommodation, have since become third or fourth class houses, have they not?—Yes, in a sense; of course the classification of the house has not been altered, but the accommodation enjoyed by its occupiers has, as there are several families where there was only one.

2886. And the people who lived in them have gone to the suburbs in first class houses there, is not that so?—That is so. For instance, there is a line of street now undergoing that process—Gardiner-street; it is a long stretch of wide good street which had very good houses—those were all first class houses, but a very large proportion of them—I would not say how many—are now inhabited by people with fourth class accommodation.

2887. (*Sir David Barbour.*) Can you give for the two periods the total percentage of the population of those periods having first class; the percentage having second; the percentage having third; and the percentage having fourth class accommodation—that is to say, at the earlier period it might be one per cent., and at the later two. I mean the percentage of the population of the period?—I have got that done for each county in these tables.

2888. Will you put that in later on?—Yes. (*See Table VIa.*)

2889. (*Mr. Sexton.*) There is one very curious result to be deduced, is there not, from your table VI. Your table VI. shows that the number of families having first class accommodation is fewer than the number of first class houses by 8,000; the number of families having second class accommodation is fewer than the number of second class houses by 12,000; but conversely, in the third and fourth class the number of families having accommodation of those classes is greater than the number of houses. Would it be right to say that 8,000 of the first and 12,000 of the second class—that is, 20,000 in all—have been lowered out of that class by reason of 47,000 families and 35,000 families occupying those 20,000 houses, and putting them into the third and fourth class of accommodation?—I should think that is a natural inference as you put it. I would like to go into it more closely than that, but I think you are correct.

Adjourned for a short time.

Agricultural classification of cultivation.

2890. (*Chairman.*) You have put in a number of tables in connection with land and agricultural statistics, chiefly in connection with the latter. Will you take 1841 as your starting point, and state whether the area under cultivation has increased or diminished?—Here is a table (*handing in Table VII.*) I may mention that it extends to the year 1891. It was compiled for each census period, and I have put in, so far as is known, the land figures that came in to the middle of 1894. I have not put them in there, but I can add them afterwards, if desired.

2891. Will you give us the salient points?—This table is headed "Division of land," it contains land under crops, woods and plantations, barren mountain land; bog and marsh, waste land, &c.—that is including towns and other places not used for agricultural purposes. I have here an abstract of what it contains, "the amount of land in use for agricultural purposes in Ireland has increased in the fifty years covered thereby. In the year 1841, according to the Census report for that year, the waste lands of Ireland amounted to 6,295,971 statute acres. In the year 1891 the amount was only 4,901,756 acres; or, in other words, 1,585,216 acres, or 7·6 per cent. of the whole surface of Ireland had been reclaimed in fifty years. It will be observed from the table that the decrease of waste land between 1841 and 1851 was 1,073,039 acres; between 1851 and 1861 it was 692,224 acres; and between 1861 and 1871 it was 217,050 acres, or 6·0 per cent. of waste land, and 1·4 per cent. of the area of Ireland. Between 1871 and 1881 an apparent increase of 412,910 acres took place; and between 1881 and 1891, there would appear from the table to have been an increase of 172,304 acres" (that is 0·66 per cent. of the total area of Ireland). The conclusion naturally to be derived from that was that there was a decrease of the land in use. A more detailed examination however shows that up to the year 1876 there was a general decrease of waste lands, and from 1876 up to the present the returns apparently point to a steady increase of waste lands. I have it all printed here, but the fact is, to be short about the matter, there was not sufficient care observed in picking out waste in cases of holdings where there were parts of waste mixed up with good arable land, and there were more strict instructions given to the enumerators to carefully pick out all the waste pieces from the other parts. The result of that increased accuracy was to give an apparent increase of waste. The increase, however, is a very small thing, only 0·66 per cent. in the 10 years 1881–91. The first figures are taken from the census, and the rest from the agricultural statistics. Another point is that if cattle increase in a given area to a considerable extent, the cattle are put on land which may not have been used for some years, and that land would then be included as pasture and used land; whereas, if the cattle were off it, it is of such inferior quality that the enumerator would put it down as waste. That accounts for a good deal of variation, and testing it by a number of cases, we found that in a good many cases where there was a decrease of waste land it was accounted for by the fact that cattle were turned upon it. The amount of the variation is slight, and is not of much consequence; but it looks as if there was a decrease in the use of the land, whereas it is not really so.

Dr. T. W. Grimshaw. 7 Dec. 1894. Classification of cultivation.

2892. Dividing the aggregate figures between tillage and pasture, what has been the movement during the last fifty years?—The tendency is to the increase of pasture and diminution of tillage.

2893. (*Mr. Sexton.*) How is it you have not got the crops and grass divided in 1841, as you have in the subsequent periods?—It was not done. The returns were not made up in that way. Of course that was not done as an annual business then; it was taken at the census, and the crops were not taken at all on that occasion.

2894. (*Chairman.*) Can you state since 1841, in periods of ten years, how the acreage of cultivation, pasture, and tillage together compares with the population per head?—Yes. I have a table here in which I have got the census from 1841 to 1891, and the populations of towns of 10,000 inhabitants and upwards. Taking those from the total population of the country I get a balance, and I have then here the acreage per head of the total population. Then I have acreage of arable and pasture land per population, and I have the average acreage of arable and pasture land per person of the rural population.

2895. What is the outcome of that?—The average acreage per person of the whole population in 1841 was 2·5; in 1851, 3·2; in 1861, 3·6; in 1871, 3·8; in 1881, 4; in 1891, 4·5.

2896. That shows a progressive improvement, does it not?—It shows an increase of acreage per head of

Mr. T. W. Grimshaw, 7 Dec. 1894. Classification of acreage.

the population, but then I come to compare it with the acreage to rural population—that is, without the towns of 10,000 inhabitants.

2897. (*Mr. Sexton.*) What table is that?—Table VIII. of the "Facts and Figures." It is all in the same table, but I think that is the answer to the Chairman's question.

2898. Before you leave Table VII. of "Facts and Figures," I notice that between 1861 and 1891 the land under crops fell by just a million acres, and in the same period—thirty years—the land used in grass increased by 700,000 acres, leaving 300,000 acres to be accounted for, which seems to have gone to waste?—That is the point which I was explaining. It did not go to waste, all of it; about half of it was dealt with in the way I was mentioning. There were towns, roads, railways, and various things made in that time which took a great deal out of it. There are a great many things to be taken into consideration besides waste, but, according to the figures appearing on the face of the table, the waste has increased, and I pointed out that the apparent increase was only 0·6 per cent.

2899. (*The O'Conor Don.*) The apparent increase of waste?—Yes; but I also explained how that came about—that some years ago a more careful instruction was issued to the enumerators.

2900. (*Chairman.*) Then you will put in those figures and tables?—Yes.

2901. Have we got before us tables, not per head, but actual tables of the comparative tillage?—I think, Table VII. is the one which you mean.

2902. (*The O'Conor Don.*) That is exactly the same as in your pamphlet?—It is; but I would like to add to that, if the Commission wish, some figures. I have the figures for 1894. For 1894 the crops are 4,937,179 acres; grass, 10,305,107; woods and plantations, 311,224; barren mountain land, bog and waste land, roads, &c., and towns, 4,870,834; total, 20,333,344.

2903. (*Mr. Sexton.*) Showing a little less waste, a good deal less grass, and something more of crops?—Yes. There is an increase of crops that I was not able to give you before, because they are the agricultural statistics of the present year and were not checked.

2904. (*Chairman.*) That compares this year with last year, does it?—That compares this year with 1891. Of course, if you wish for it year by year, it can be given.

2905. (*Sir David Barbour.*) Might I ask if the increase in the waste land which took place between certain periods took place in one year or was spread over several years?—It was spread over several years.

2906. But if the enumerators were more strict did that strictness take some years to develop?—It did. I may tell you whenever you start anything new of this kind it takes several years to develop it.

2907. (*Chairman.*) You can put the figures in for the years between 1891 and 1894, can you?—Yes, I will do so.

2908. (*Mr. Sexton.*) For the first time since the beginning there is now a falling off in the grass, I notice?—I wish to point out that these figures have not been fully checked as yet.

2909. As you give them what I say is the result, is it not?—Yes, as regards the years given in Table VII.

2910. For the first time since you began to enumerate there is a falling off in the grass, is there not?—That is comparing those particular periods, but there are other intermediate years where variations have taken place.

Values of crops and live stock.

2911. (*Chairman.*) Then going to values can you give us any particulars as to the values of crops and the values of live stock. I think you have got the statistics in groups of five years, have you not?—That contained in the printed statement which has been circulated.

2912. I should like you to give the figures for the four periods—1851-1855, 1866-1870, 1881-1885, 1889-1893?—The four periods are 1851-1855, 1866-1870, 1884-1888, and 1889-1893. The value of the crops for the first period were 58,837,000*l.*, for the second period 43,365,000*l.*; for the third period 35,751,000*l.*; and for the fourth period 34,643,000*l.* That is a decrease on the estimated value.

Mr. T. W. Grimshaw. 7 Dec. 1894. Values of crops and live stock.

2913. Are those market values?—They are market values, as nearly as can possibly be ascertained.

2914. (*Mr. Sexton.*) Are those the values of the total crops without any deduction whatever?—Without any deduction whatever. The stock is 39,148,000*l.* for the first period; 53,630,000*l.* for the second; 55,821,000*l.* for the third; and 54,312,000*l.* for the fourth. The totals are—97,985,000*l.* for the first period; 106,995,000*l.* for the second; 91,570,000*l.* for the third; and 88,955,000*l.* for the fourth.

2915. (*Chairman.*) Of course these periods are not consecutive. Can you say whether they are fair samples?—I believe them to be fair samples.

2916. How did you take them?—The way I took them was this: In writing the pamphlet I have handed in—which was an address to the Statistical Society—I say, in the first place, it is a speculative inquiry and not like the things which we have been dealing with up to the present, which are absolute facts. This to a certain extent consists of estimates and values which I believe to be as near as I can give, but may not be absolutely accurate. Then the reason why the first three periods are taken is this:—At the time I read this paper I had thirty-eight years to go upon, and I divided that as nearly as I could into five year periods. I took the first, the last, and the middle period without any reference to any special circumstances connected with them. Before I took the periods I had all the five year periods that I could make out put together and averages struck for each of them, and I selected by that rule, taking the first, the last, and the middle of those periods in that way, so that there is no choice made in any of the periods.

2917. Do you think that that affords a fair idea of the movement during those years?—I think so. Of course in 1851-55 there was the Crimean war, and some of the prices might have been high. The sixties were good years—some of the years between 1860 and 1870 were rather favourable years for agriculture—that is a tolerably good period. Of course the last period we come to was when depression was extending, and the fourth period I have given, because it was the last I could make up before the sitting of this Commission.

2918. The result of the table would be that whilst the total value of the crops of Ireland has decreased by about 24,000,000*l.* per annum during the last forty years, the total value of live stock has increased by about 15,000,000*l.* per annum?—Yes, that is so.

2919. So that the total value of the agricultural wealth of Ireland, crops and stock together, has been, roundly speaking, in the quinquennial period 1889-1893 (the last which we have discussed), 9,000,000*l.* less than it was in the period 1851-1855, 18,000,000*l.* less than in 1866-1870, and over 2,000,000*l.* less than in the period 1884-1888?—Yes, I think those are the figures.

2920. I asked you before whether these were the market values. Can you give us any information as to precisely how they were arrived at?—The way in which I proceeded was this:—I ascertained the average annual amount of agricultural produce and live stock in Ireland during each of these five years periods.

2921. (*Mr. Sexton.*) How did you ascertain that?—From the agricultural statistics.

2922. I want to know how much is actual and how much is speculative—you took the actual crop of each year, added it up and divided it into five, did you?—Yes. I took the prices published in Purdon's Almanack. I have here Purdon's prices for a number of years. I have not got them up to the last year, but that is the main standard I have taken in making these calculations. Purdon's Almanack is a well-

Mr. T. W. Grimshaw.

7 Dec. 1894.

Values of crops and live stock.

known publication, and is believed to be very carefully compiled.

2923. When the price of a crop or head of live stock varied in the same year from time to time, how did you arrive at the average of the year?—I took Purdon's averages.

2924. Does he give a yearly average?—He gives a yearly average of the highest and lowest prices. He publishes them from week to week in the *Farmer's Gazette*, and they are generally believed to be the best prices that can be got—we cannot go very much behind them.

2925. (*Lord Welby.*) Do you take a mean price?—I take a mean price between highest and lowest.

2926. (*Chairman.*) An arithmetical mean price without reference to the quantities?—Yes.

2927. (*Lord Welby.*) For instance supposing for nine months there had been a low price and the remaining three a high price, the mean would hardly represent a real mean, would it?—You are correct in a certain sense, but I take Purdon's average highest and lowest prices and find a mean between those myself. You see Purdon does not give the mean.

2928. (*Mr. Sexton.*) If the price at the time of year when crops and stock are commonly sold, happened to be considerably lower than the price at a time of year when they are not much sold, the effect would be to some extent misleading, would it not?—No doubt, it would; but that I leave to the experts. I do not deal with the market prices myself; I take them as I get them.

2929. (*Chairman.*) You do not think that the figures require material correction, and that they are not among the many fallacies that one is liable to?—This is a mean of prices without reference to variations, but the way in which you, as it were, counteract any fallacy in making a comparison is, that that variation or that error if you may so call it, would be just the same in one year as another. It is not likely that the error would be greater at one time than another, so that for the comparative purposes it is practically correct.

2930. It is sound for the purposes of comparison though not absolutely correct for the purposes of quantity?—Quite so. I have told the Commission, you know, that I look upon this as rather a speculative inquiry.

2931. (*Mr. Sexton.*) The quantities may be said to be actual though the prices are average?—Yes, the quantities of the yield of the crops are absolute.

2932. (*The O'Conor Don.*) How do you average the price of stock amongst the different classes of one year old, two years old, milch cows, and so on?—I consulted salesmasters and others as to the ratio which should be given between them. I got opinions from various people.

2933. You do not know the principle upon which that ratio is based, do you?—No, I have carefully left that be done by persons who understand it. I do not profess to understand that.

2934. (*Chairman.*) Do you know that in England and elsewhere there have been great controversies as to the value of this class of statistics?—I know that.

2935. And that Ireland has had the reputation of having better statistics, particularly of this class, than we have in Great Britain. Do you adopt that suggestion?—Which class do you mean? I do not know that in the question of prices and that sort of thing we are better off.

2936. I mean as to agricultural statistics generally?—I think so, but that is because we have been working at them longer.

2937. Then you would on the whole give faith to these figures, would you?—Oh yes, the agricultural statistics figures certainly.

2938. It is notorious that the English agricultural statistics are open to a good deal of controversy?—They are collected on a totally different principle. In the case of the statistics in Ireland the enumerator goes to the people themselves, and if there is an error it is made by the individual. In England a man writes out a return, posts it to the Inland Revenue officer, and a great many do not make returns at all, you have to estimate those.

Mr. T. W. Grimshaw.

7 Dec. 1894.

Values of crops and live stock.

2939. Do you not collect them in Ireland through the Constabulary?—Yes, the constable goes to the individual and asks him "How much of this, that and "the other have you got?"—and as a rule the constable knows pretty well the person he is dealing with. They are all known personally to him, and he would enter into conversation with a man and ask him "Are you "quite sure of this, and quite sure of that?" and there is no reason to believe that there is any attempt made on a large scale to deceive in this matter. This is matter in which the public do not look on the policeman as a policeman at all; under those circumstances they look upon him in a very friendly light.

2940. (*Chairman.*) They look upon him as a statistician, do they?—From the inquiries I have made I find that the number of people who object to give information to policemen on questions of that sort are very few indeed. There are a few turn up every year and those people generally speaking send in their figures direct to the office. The constable reports that those gentlemen do not wish to give any information to him, gives their addresses; a private letter is sent to them, and they almost invariably send the information to me. There is no general objection to it.

2941. As between values and quantities do you consider the decline after the 1870 period is due to the decline in prices or the decline in quantities or to both causes combined?—I do not understand the question.

2942. The fall in quantity is from 104,000,000*l.* in the period 1866–1870 to 93,000,000*l.* in the period 1889–1893. Is that chiefly quantities or prices or both?—That is value—that is prices. Of course, in the question of tillage products you have both elements. Tillage products are decreasing, and their price is decreasing too.

2943. But taking the aggregate figures of crops and stock where you have a fall of 10,000,000*l.* between the 1870 period and the 1893 period, do you consider that is mainly due to fall in price or to fall in quantity?—To fall in price.

2944. (*Mr. Sexton.*) It appears in the case of the crops to be due to both causes?—In the case of crops it is due to both causes certainly.

2945. But in the case of stock there is rather an increase neutralised by fall in price?—There is an increase in stock.

2946. Rather neutralised by fall in price?—Yes.

2947. There is one question I should like to ask you about Table C. The crops in the quinquennial period being the crops of that period and nothing else it is evident that the value in each column is a distinct matter from the value in another column, but in the case of the stock you value in each year the total stock then existing. Is it not obvious that a part, and probably a substantial part, of the value of the stock therefore overlaps from one period into the other and is repeated?—Of course, there would be a balance carried from the last two years of one period into the other, but that is not exactly carrying over the balance. The question of the amount sold is dealt with further on in this paper.

2948. But in this line of four figures of stock each of the three figures that come after the first would include some portion of the value of the preceding figure, would it not?—Certainly; but then it would have something at the end that would belong to it, you see. There is a balance carried from one to the other—you are quite correct.

Values per head of population.

2949. (*Chairman.*) You have compared also these values with the population at various periods, and I think you have worked out a table, have you not?—That is a table in the printed memorandum I have put in. The value of crops per head of the population for 1851–1855, the first period, would be 9·44*l.*; for 1866–70, 8·29*l.*; for 1884–1888, 7·21*l.*; for 1889–1893, 7·40*l.*

Dr. T. W. Grimshaw. 7 Dec. 1886. Average per head of agriculturists.

2950. And the stock?—The stock would be 9·347*l.* for the first period; 10·902*l.* for the second; 11·115*l.* for the third; and 11·6*l.* for the fourth. Combined that would be 13·790*l.* for the first; 19·208*l.* for the second; 18·732*l.* for the third; and 19*l.* for the fourth—the last two are very much the same.

2951. What conclusion do you draw from the figures for those four periods?—The conclusion to be derived from them is, of course, that during the last of the four periods the average per head of the agricultural community must be so much higher per annum than it was before, in the ratio of 19 to 13.

2952. That is a very remarkable result, is it not?—Yes, but of course it depends on the diminution of population.

2953. (*The O'Conor Don.*) Is there any real increase in the wealth of the people per head. I see here you state that although the aggregate value of live stock and so on has diminished, the agriculturists themselves as a class were individually better off in the second than in the first period—is it true that any one was individually better off. The way to test it is this: supposing, instead of this decrease in the population there had been an increase—say, for instance, due to increase of manufactures—in that case the tables would turn the other way?—They would.

2954. And would show that the agricultural population was worse off, would they not?—An increase of manufacturing industries and an increase of population employed in industry would not work in that way.

2954A. But this comparison I understand is made with the whole population of the country, is it not?—Yes, this one is.

2955. If instead of the whole population of the country having diminished, the whole population of the country had increased, through, as I suggest, the establishment of manufactories, do you mean to say that the agricultural class would be worse off on account of that?—No.

2956. You state here that they are better off in consequence of the diminution of the population?—Of course we know that the produce of the agricultural class is not the produce of towns.

2957. (*Sir David Barbour.*) Might I ask if you could distribute the agricultural wealth over the agricultural population per head?—I have done it in one of the tables I have handed in.

Occupation of the people.

2958. (*Mr. Sexton.*) I do not think you have yet said whether your functions in regard to the Census include any computation of the total number of people in Ireland who are engaged in or dependent on agricultural or pastoral pursuits, have you?—Oh, yes.

2959. What is the number?—199 per 1,000 of all the population are engaged in agriculture.

2960. (*Chairman.*) Practically a fifth?—A fifth of the population—yes.

2961. (*Sir David Barbour.*) For **what year may I** ask?—That is from the 1881 Census.

2962. (*The O'Conor Don.*) A fifth of the population, is that all?—Yes, that is employed.

2963. (*Mr. Sexton.*) Men?—And women, if returned as agricultural labourers. For instance that includes farmers, agricultural labourers, herds, and all persons employed in agriculture.

2964. (*Chairman.*) And their children?—No.

2965. (*Mr. Sexton.*) I asked if you had made a computation of how many of the 4,900,000 individuals in the country are dependent on agricultural pursuits. Mr. Giffen took it at 3,000,000 in 1886, but I suppose his information would not be precise?—I will answer the question to-morrow. I think it is 3,100,000, but I do not like to make a guess.

Definition of agricultural class.

2966. (*Chairman.*) When you speak of people engaged in agriculture, do you include both landlords and occupiers?—I include in the agricultural community all persons who are dependent on the land for their subsistence—landlords, tenants, labourers, and all.

2967. In dealing with the produce you take it in the aggregate only. Do you give any consideration as to how much goes to the farmer himself and how much goes to the large proprietor, the landlord?—No, I have not gone into that.

Dr. T. W. Grimshaw. 7 Dec. 1886. Distribution of agricultural wealth.

2968. You have never computed that at all?—No.

2969. Of course it is of very great importance in making the calculation of what the Irish produce is?—Perhaps I am not correct in saying that I never went into that. I did go into it.

2970. Have you made an estimate?—I have here a paper upon that question which was prepared at the request of Sir Robert Hamilton when he was Under Secretary for Ireland.

2971. Will you give the salient points in it?—This is not for the individual agriculturist. He asked me whether I could give an estimate of the income of Irish agriculturists as well as landlords—I remember that was the way the question was put. I set to at that time to collect, from all sources I possibly could, information, and a gentleman who was at that time in my office, but who is now, unfortunately, dead, collected information from all kinds of traders supplying agricultural machinery, supplying seeds and various things, and the result was that, treating Ireland as a whole, the value of the whole Irish agricultural produce in 1885 was 23,873,818*l.*

2972. (*Mr. Sexton.*) Stocks and all?—No; crops only.

2973. (*Sir David Barbour.*) Is that the gross value or the net value?—That is the gross value, without the various deductions made.

2974. (*Mr. Sexton.*) Will you say what the deductions were specifically—under what heads?—Seed is put down as 3,000,000*l.*; oil-cake, maize, &c., for feeding purposes, 1,108,000*l.*; artificial manures 400,000*l.*; agricultural implements, 250,000*l.*; vehicles and harness, 500,000*l.*; hay for use of horses and cattle, 5,000,000*l.*; turnips, 1,700,000*l.*; mangolds, 375,000*l.*, oats for horses, &c., 3,000,000*l.*—that makes 15,333,000*l.*; labour, 8,200,000*l.*; rent, 11,000,000*l.*—that was putting it down on the valuation of the rural districts of Ireland. That totalled to 34,533,000*l.*

2975. Deducted from a gross of what?—The 23,000,000*l.* in crops, and it assumes the crops were sold off in the year.

2976. Gross crops?—Yes. Then the estimated value of the live stock sold of all kinds for that year was 14,797,000*l.*

2977. (*The O'Conor Don.*) That includes sheep, pigs, and everything else?—Yes.

2978. (*Mr. Sexton.*) That makes a total produce of what?—Perhaps it will be best for me to read it as it stands. "The estimated gross value of the crops grown in Ireland in the year 1885 is 23,873,898*l.*; the value of milk and its products is taken as 14,174,810*l.*; that of the wool clip as 330,745*l.*; and of the eggs as 656,180*l.* The sum obtained for the live stock sold is estimated at 14,797,758*l.* The total value of the crops and of the live stock disposed of during the year would, upon this calculation, amount to 61,833,491*l.* The cost of production may be classed under three heads—(*a*) seed, artificial manure, food for live stock, and wear and tear of vehicles and implements; (*b*) labour; (*c*) rent and taxes. The estimated expenses under these heads are—(*a*) 15,333,000*l.*; (*b*) 8,200,000*l.*; (*c*) 11,000,000*l.*; total, 34,533,000*l.* Deducting this sum from the value of the crops and live stock as given above, the net income of the agriculturists of Ireland for the year would appear to have been 27,300,491*l.*"

2979. (*Chairman.*) As against how much going to the landlord?—I have put down the rent as 11,000,000*l.*; and putting down the rent at 11,000,000*l.* would mean, if a man owned his own land, he would have to allow so much for his rent.

2980. Can you make any calculation nearer than that?—I do not know that I can. Of course this was before the Land Acts; but this is really an illustration of how a thing of that sort might be done, but, like the other paper, it is speculative.

2981. (*Sir David Barbour.*) You say the income of the agriculturist is so much, and that does not include rental, I understand, because the rent has been taken off?—It does not.

2982. It does not include labourers?—No.
treated Ireland as a farm under one farmer.

2983. That is the profit of the farmers?—Yes.

2984. Their income?—Yes; that is treating Ireland as one farm under one farmer.

2985. That is 27,000,000*l.* for the farmers, and you allow 11,000,000*l.*, I think, for the landlords?—There is 11,000,000*l.* put down as rent.

2986. That is allotting it to the landlords?—Not necessarily. For instance, say you were to call the rent 11,000,000*l.* Now there are a certain number of people who have bought their farms; their rent would be put down, it would be so much interest on the money sunk in the purchase.

2987. The total of that is the 38,000,000*l.*, the farmers' profits and the landlords' profits, or rent as it not?—Of course, if there is 11,000,000*l.* paid in as rent, you have to add it to the 27,000,000*l.*

2988. And the labour is how much?—8,000,000*l.*

2989. Then that makes 46,000,000*l.* altogether, roughly?—Yes.

2990. And that agrees pretty well with Mr. Giffen's estimate. He says from 40,000,000*l.* to 45,000,000*l.*?—Quite so.

2991. (*Mr. Sexton.*) Of course the people who have bought their farms under the Purchase Acts since 1870 are paying their amounts to the State, and that would stand in the form of rent?—Yes, and it would come to the same thing; but it is another of these experimental things.

2992. (*Chairman.*) We receive that as a very conjectural estimate?—Yes, it is, very. The substance of this paper was published in some of the newspapers at the time.

2993. I should like to ask some questions about the potato crop. Is the potato much less staple in Ireland than it used to be?—I think so; I think they are eating other things.

2994. Have you any reason to think that the small farmer in Ireland consumes more or less of his own produce than formerly?—The small farmer?

2995. The producer generally?—The producer, generally, I should say, consumes less, because there are very few people, I should think, comparatively speaking, who eat their own meat, for instance. The consumption of things in that way has probably diminished, but I am not sure.

2996. Should you say there was a smaller amount eaten by the farmer nowadays than there was forty years ago?—I think it is very likely there is. For instance, it was the practice of a farmer in former days to send his grain to a mill and have it ground, and then eat it. Now he buys it at a shop. Milling as a trade has gone down.

2997. I suppose there is a decided increase in the quantity of meat eaten from a farm?—I do not think in those days they ate much meat at all.

2998. (*Mr. Sexton.*) They never did in Ireland, I think?—Practically they did not.

2999. (*Chairman.*) They do now, do they not?—There is more meat consumed in Ireland than there used to be, no doubt.

3000. (*Mr. Sexton.*) Does the farmer in Ireland, except those of a very limited class, consume meat or butter to any extent—small farmers?—I think they consume very little; I cannot say.

3001. They even sell the milk, do they not?—No, I do not think they do. I found on going through the country myself that a great quantity of milk was consumed. In Donegal the other day I was enquiring about it. There their habits have considerably altered, and I found many of the people I spoke to there, who were well-to-do small people, who were weavers as well as farmers, stating that they lived altogether almost on milk, bread, and potatoes; that they consumed a great deal of bread and porridge.

3002. (*Chairman.*) You know the opposite is the tendency in Great Britain, namely, to send away a great deal more of the milk and to use much less at home, do you not?—I know.

Food of the people.

3003. And that tendency is not found in Ireland?—I do not think so.

3004. (*Mr. Sexton.*) Do you not think what you say about Donegal would be explained by the circumstance that the houses there are so bad that people cannot make butter for want of accommodation?—It is not a dairy country, except in East Donegal.

3005. But where the small farmer has facility for making butter, does he consume the milk?—I do not think he does in the South, and where there is a fine dairy country I should say he does not; he makes the butter and sells it.

3006. (*Lord Welby.*) You were saying that the farmers were not so dependent as they used to be on potatoes. In some of your statistics in Part 2 you give the extent under crops in statute acres in each year. Looking down the column of figures, I see that in 1849 there are 719,000 acres under potatoes, and in 1850, 875,000 acres. Then coming down to later years, in 1888 I see 804,000; in 1889, 787,000, and in 1890, 751,000; so that there is no very great difference in the acreage under potatoes in the extremes of the two periods?—Yes, but there is a great drop from the time prior to the famine.

Potato crops.

3007. The figures are not given for that period. There is a curious figure here in 1847 of 284,000 acres with the enormous produce of seven tons per acre?—I do not believe in that produce.

3008. I drop that out, and I want to ask you in regard to these figures which more or less run together. If the farmer cultivates very nearly as many acres as formerly and consumes less, I suppose he sells more in the market towns?—Probably he does, but I am not quite sure.

3009. The number of acres under potatoes runs very much the same in the years from 1849 to 1853 as they have done of late?—But then potatoes at that time were a complete failure.

3010. Down to 1853 or 1854?—They had not recovered from the famine at that time. If you look at the potato acreage in the intermediate periods you will see it runs very much.

3011. But the point I want to put to you is this: From your Summary of Statistics, Part 2 of the table in Book I., it appears that the farmer now keeps very nearly—I do not say exactly—the same number of acres under potatoes as he did, but he does not use so many potatoes for his own consumption and that of his family. How do you account, then, for the fact of his having so much under potatoes? I suppose the only way you have of accounting for it is that he has a larger sale in towns?—I suppose so.

3012. (*Mr. Sexton.*) But taking together the fall in yield and the acreage, you see 284,000 acres in 1847, which yielded seven tons an acre?—I do not believe that it yielded seven tons an acre.

3013. Now we have 751,000 acres at two tons an acre?—Quite so.

3014. (*Lord Welby.*) But the average per acre is about three and a-half tons?—I believe that six or seven tons to be apocryphal altogether.

3015. (*The O'Conor Don.*) As an average?—Yes.

3016. Of course a particular portion may have yielded that?—Yes, but that was not the yield of potatoes in Ireland at any time, I should think.

3017. (*Chairman.*) What classes in Ireland do you consider that the loss caused by depreciation of prices chiefly falls upon?—On the agricultural class: of course the consumer is better off.

Incidence of agricultural depression.

3018. (*Mr. Sexton.*) On the farmer?—On the farmer.

3019. (*Chairman.*) On the occupier especially?—With a very small man who consumes altogether his own produce, or nearly altogether his own produce, market prices are of no consequence.

3020. It depends on whether the rent is produced, does it not? It may fall mainly on the owner?—I

Dr. T. W. Grimshaw. 7 Dec. 1894.

am afraid I do not understand your point. I understood you to ask upon whom the loss fell; it falls of course on the farmer, on the agricultural community at large.

3021. But would you include in the agricultural community, the landlord, where there is a landlord?—Yes, and of course the landlord has lost his rent if it is reduced.

3022. Looking at the table which you have given us of the fall of produce mainly in prices, how much of that do you think has fallen upon the occupier, and how much on the landlord?—I could not tell you.

3023. You cannot make an estimate at all?—Of course the rents have been reduced.

3024. (*Mr. Sexton.*) Your table 1 in the printed statement laid before us shows that between 1881 and 1893 the fall in the value of crops was 14,000,000*l.* a year, and that that was only neutralised to the extent of 15,000,000*l.* by the increase of stock, leaving a net annual loss of 9,000,000*l.* Now we know as a matter of record that the rents have only been reduced by 1,190,000*l.*?—Yes, if you include all the stock, not the portion disposed during the year.

Export of live stock.

3025. (*Chairman.*) That is the figure I wanted. Can you give us any figures as to the amount and value of the classes of live stock exported from Ireland to Great Britain?—Yes, I have taken three important items—Cattle, sheep, and pigs. In 1893 the number of cattle exported was 643,373; the pigs, 436,371, and the sheep, 705,399. The values put upon these by an experienced salesmaster in Dublin were:—Cattle, 6,111,903*l.*; pigs, 1,369,713*l.*; sheep, 1,234,273*l.* Total, 8,715,925*l.*

3026. For what year was this?—Last year, 1893. The values are 9*l.* 10*s.*; 3*l.*, and 35*s.* I may mention that the gentleman who made this estimate says there is a certain number—not a very large number—of those pigs which he thinks might have reduced the average somewhat below the 3*l.* He told me of a circumstance I never knew before, that there are a certain number of the smaller make of pigs that go to London, and not to any other part of England, which weigh less than the average pig, and he thinks he might have put that figure a little too high.

3027. The total is how many millions?—The total, according to that, is 8,715,925*l.*

3028. Do you think that is a fair estimate?—I think it is a fair estimate, subject to that slight qualification.

3029. (*Mr. Sexton.*) What proportion does that bear to the total of these animals sold or consumed within the year? What is the total of cattle, pigs, and sheep sold or consumed within the year?—I cannot give you that for last year.

3030. Can you give it for any year?—No, I could not, except as to the year referred to; it is not put in that way at all, so that the things are not comparable with one another.

3031. Can you give us any figures which would show us what proportion the export from Ireland bore in any year to the total consumed and sold?—No, I could not do that; I should have to get it taken out specially.

3032. Because the amount of export seems to me to go far to negative any presumption that the meat is consumed by the producer to any extent?—I do not think it is consumed to any very great extent. I wish to explain that the reason I took those three items was that they might be compared with the item which I know of occurring 90 years ago—that is the number of cattle exported for the year ending the 5th January, 1804, was 28,532, and the value 276,663*l.*; the pigs 19,276 and the value 55,684*l.*; the sheep 7,489, and the value 13,093*l.* The total value of that was only 335,440*l.* In tables of export, which are very interesting tables, in Newenham's Ireland, which might be very interesting to the Commission, the exports of Ireland are divided into what he terms the products of land and the products of labour. He does not admit the word "labour" as applied to land at all. These are collected from returns of that date.

Dr. T. W. Grimshaw. 7 Dec. 1894. Export of live stock.

3033. (*Mr. Sexton.*) I suppose by "labour" he meant manufacture?—Yes. He gave the total value of the products of land exported from Ireland, at 4,332,794*l.* 7*s.* 8*d.*; and the products of labour at 3,549,088*l.* 4*s.* 4*d.*; the total value being 8,901,000*l.* The total value of all the exports of Ireland for that time was 8,341,497*l.*

3034. (*Chairman.*) What conclusion do you draw from that?—That it is something less than the value of all the cattle last year. The cattle exports last year are more value than the whole exports of Ireland ninety years ago.

3035. The whole of the export trade of Ireland—not to Great Britain only?—Practically all those cattle go to Great Britain.

3036. (*Lord Welby.*) It was less than the value of cattle exported last year?—Yes, less than the value of cattle exported last year by 414,000*l.*

Decline of population.

3037. (*Chairman.*) You connect the decline of population to a certain extent with the change from tillage to pasture, but from which cause you have not told us. Has it produced a decline in the population or is it the result of a decline in the population?—Of course they are dependent upon one another. If tillage falls in value, agriculture declines and the people must go.

3038. But it acts both ways?—Unless they consume their own produce as they did in the potato eating days.

East and West of Ireland compared.

3039. You have also in your heads of evidence spoken of the social economic conditions of the east and west of Ireland. You divide the east and west by that famous line, I think, which you have described more than once?—That is an important point I think, but whether it comes into the question of taxation I do not know. The way in which this division of the country came into my mind in the first instance was during the great potato failure of 1879, and I was at that time one of the secretaries of the Duchess of Marlborough's Fund. It became necessary then to see what part we should primarily devote our attention to. Under the Distress Act there were certain unions scheduled, but that did not take place until a little after we had begun operations, and from what I knew of the country I came to the conclusion that we might draw a line from Londonderry, or just to the west of Londonderry, down to Skibbereen, and so we might be prepared at all events to deal in the first instance with all west of that line as a distinct province which was clearly likely to be affected by the distress.

3040. (*Mr. Sexton.*) How many counties were there to the west of that line?—There are practically eight; there are all the counties of Connaught, Donegal——

3041. (*The O'Conor Don.*) Do you mean the whole of the counties or only portions?—If you take the counties that are practically on the west side of it, that would mean the five Connaught counties—Donegal, Clare, and Kerry.

3042. Following the area of those counties pretty closely?—Yes; it is a rough thing, but it is done in that way. This matter attracted my attention to such an extent that I thought I would go systematically into an investigation of the country from that point of view, and I divided Ireland into two provinces, an eastern and a western province, and compared them in a pamphlet which I wrote. It was a Statistical Society's paper; they are contained in the first edition of that table which is in Part 2 of the Facts and Figures. The paper on which that is founded was made a comparison between 1841 and 1881 originally, now it is a comparison between 1841 and 1891. When the question of the Purchase of Land and Congested Districts Bill came before Parliament, I was asked by the Government to assist them in making out what would be likely to be a congested district, and it was determined that this should be done by taking the Government valuation, dividing it by the population, seeing what was the average valuation, and then ascertaining the number and condition of the

Dr. T. W. Grimshaw.

7 Dec. 1894.

East and West of Ireland compared.

people above and below that average. It was assumed that those who were above it did not require any congested district legislation, and that those below it might, and accordingly the congested district clauses of the Bill were drawn up. In designing that I undertook to plan a map for the Government, and this was the map (*producing same*) upon which all the reds are at and above average, and all the blues are below average. Anyone looking at the map will see that the dark blue is all along the west coast of Ireland; and when you come to draw the line which I originally drew for another purpose, you will find all the dark blue is on the western side of it, confirming wholly the view taken by me years before as to the state of things.

3043. (*Mr. Sexton.*) The darker hue on the west coast indicates a heavier congestion?—Yes.

3044. And what follows the coast line all round?—It follows the coast line all round, and goes away inland too.

3045. (*Chairman.*) The bright red is the most prosperous part?—The bright red is the most prosperous part.

3046. And the dark blue is the worst?—And the dark blue is the worst. I have here a map of the same kind made up to 1891. This map which is in the Census Report of 1891 is made on the Census of 1891. This was the only guide the Government had at that time, but when we got the Census revised, the rate in the Bill was struck from the new figures.

3047. (*The O'Conor Don.*) Do either of these maps show the boundaries of the congested district?—No, they do not. The congested districts consist of certain places where a certain percentage of electoral divisions are present which have a valuation below 1*l.* 10*s.* 0*d.* per head of the population. However, that I think you will get from another gentleman who I believe is to come before you.

3048. (*Lord Welby.*) I see the blue comes very much round to the east coast in the north?—It does; there are some very poor parts of the country there. This is the main table I had prepared upon that point, but besides that I have a series of tables here where every county is given separately, and if there is any test or comparison between the two parts which you wish to apply, it can be done from those tables.

3049. (*Chairman.*) Is there any way in which you would practically apply that division of Ireland into these two parts for legislation?—I was going to point out the leading facts with regard to east and west. "The population east and west were respectively in "1841, 5,372,000 and 2,793,000. In 1891 they were "3,091,000 and 1,614,000; the general decrease of "population in Ireland having been 45·5 per cent. for "the period, it was 40·6 per cent. for the eastern and "47·1 per cent. for the western group. In the case of "rural populations the decrease in the east was 52·1 "per cent., in the west 47·9 per cent. In the town "population (of towns of 2,000 inhabitants and up-"wards) there was an increase of 15·2 per cent. in the "east, and a diminution of 33·9 per cent. in the west."

3050. (*Mr. Sexton.*) It was all diminution and no increase in the west?—Yes, the towns increased in the east and the towns diminished in the west.

3051. (*The O'Conor Don.*) And are there any towns in the west of any importance?—Not many, but those I speak of are towns with a population of 2,000 and upwards. In 1841 the town population of the east was 17·1 per cent. of the total population; in 1891 it was 33 per cent., or nearly double the proportion. In the west the town population in 1841 was 5·7 of the whole; in 1891 it was only 7·1.

Taxable capacity.

3052. (*Chairman.*) Do you draw any conclusion as to policy from that division of the country into east and west?—Looking at it from the point of view of the Commission it is quite clear that people who live under those circumstances are not so well able to bear taxation as those who live in the eastern part.

3053. You think that the west cannot bear taxation?—I should think not as well as the east.

3054. Will you carry your conclusion a little farther. What do you wish to impress upon us by that?—I do not wish in any way to tell the Commission what they ought to do, but I think as those are altogether agricultural populations, if the taxation is to be regulated so as to fall lightly on the people who are worst off, it ought to fall much more lightly on the agricultural community than on the urban community or manufacturing community.

Dr. T. W. Grimshaw.

7 Dec. 1894.

Taxable capacity.

3055. You have no actual specific practical proposal to make to us, have you?—No, I have not.

3056. (*Sir David Barbour.*) Do you know how you would carry that out?—I do not know, I am not a Chancellor of the Exchequer.

3057. But you think it desirable that it should be done?—I think it would be very desirable.

3058. And you have no doubt it could be done, but you are not prepared to say how?—No.

3059. (*Mr. Wolff.*) Does not that apply equally to a great many parts of the counties lying east of the line as to those which you said were poor?—It does, but I merely take that as an example of the contrast. Of course there are lots of places in the east which are badly off, and also in England. If you take the east of England at present I daresay it is worse than it is here.

3060. (*Mr. Sexton.*) You come here to give facts, and not to suggest remedies?—I do not like to venture any opinion.

3061. (*Lord Welby.*) Do you mean to carry your view to this point, that the people to the west of the line are to be taxed lighter than those to the east, you do not mean that a man with 2,000*l.* a year living to the west of the line is to be taxed lighter than a man with 2,000*l.* a year on the east?—I do not know; if he derived it from work I think he ought to be.

3062. But a man only pays tax on what he gets?—You mean income tax?

3063. Yes; and I am supposing a man gets 2,000*l.* a year. When you talk of the difference of taxation a great difficulty arises in assessing it. Taking the case of a man with 2,000*l.* a year west of the line and a man with 2,000*l.* a year on the east, you do not mean to make any distinction between one and the other, do you?—Not to that extent. For instance, I do not suggest you should alter the income tax, but there are many taxes which hit land and agriculturists which are not directly levied on them. Take for example the taxes on spirits and beer. They are indirectly a tax on agriculture. They tax commodities the raw materials for which are drawn from the land, and when you tax beer you tax malt, when you tax malt you tax grain, and when you tax grain you practically tax the agriculturist.

3064. (*Chairman.*) But you do not suggest there should be a difference of taxation on articles of that kind in the east and west, do you?—No, I do not. I do not suggest, for instance, that a man should pay a lower duty on his whiskey in Dublin that he does in Galway.

3065. (*Sir David Barbour.*) If you reduce the taxation on spirits and beer with the object of relieving agriculture, might I ask on whom you would throw the taxation required to make up the consequent loss of revenue?—I do not know, I was only giving an example.

Occupations of the people.

3066. (*Lord Welby.*) I think you will admit it is a difficult question to suggest differentiated taxation?—Most difficult. I would be very sorry to have to be on the Commission to decide the question. May I say that I have just found the figure that Mr. Sexton asked about as to those who were dependent on agriculture. It is 2,320,000.

3067. (*The O'Conor Don.*) 2,320,000 of the population?—Yes.

3068. Is that men, women, and children?—That is men, women, and children.

3069. (*Mr. Sexton.*) Does that include farmers, labourers, herds, and all those?—Here is the way in which it is made up: "The total number of persons

Dr. T. W. Grimshaw.

1 Dec. 1894.

Occupations of the people.

"with stated occupations, exclusive of the domestic "class, is 1,590,556; the number of persons returned "as engaged in agriculture amounts to 915,795, to "which is added the estimated number (70,000) of "those agricultural labourers who were returned in-"definitely as 'labourers.' We then find by calculation "the proportional number of the indefinite and non-"productive class (2,359,071, including 'wives and "children') in the agricultural community; the result, "1,334,337, is added to the estimated number "(985,795) of persons engaged in agriculture, which "gives a total of 2,320,132 as depending on agriculture "in Ireland in 1891."

3070. That is less than half of the population?—Those are directly dependent.

3071. Do you say that more than half the population of Ireland are not living by agriculture?—Not directly, because I consider that about three-fourths of the population are dependent on agriculture, but you may add the inhabitants of the small towns to those as indirectly dependent.

3072. You told us that the number of people living in towns of 2,000 and upwards was a million and a quarter, and on the other hand, a figure, which I may call 3,500,000, are rural. If 3,500,000 are rural, how comes it that there are only two million and a quarter agricultural?—Directly dependent.

3073. (*The O'Conor Don.*) What do you mean by "directly dependent"?—The farmers and their families, and all specifically returned in the Census as such.

3074. What happens to the balance?—They are engaged in various other occupations, such as keepers of shops, or, as one of the members suggested, tailors, blacksmiths, and those sort of people.

3075. (*Mr. Sexton.*) In the towns of 2,000 and upwards you have only a million and a quarter altogether, and that leaves 3,500,000 in rural life; of that 3,500,000 would you deduct a million and a quarter?—I would take something over a million as engaged in other occupations. You must recollect, for instance, that a cart-maker in a country village is dependent on agriculture, the village smith and the village shopkeeper are dependent on agriculture.

3076. (*Chairman.*) You do not count them in?—No; I said "directly."

3077. (*Lord Welby.*) He is not actually engaged in agricultural pursuits, though he may live by what is really agricultural labour?—Yes.

3078. (*Mr. Sexton.*) The distinction which is made is between industries other than agriculture, and by agricultural industry. You can hardly say that a man making linen in Belfast, or spirits in Dublin, was making a living by agriculture; whilst, on the other hand, a small craftsman in a village, dependent entirely on the farmers for his work, might be said more directly to depend on agriculture?—He is one of the persons whom I say is indirectly dependent. Of course everything, in a way, is got out of the ground.

3079. (*Chairman.*) He would be in your million and a quarter persons indirectly dependent, would he?—Yes, he would.

3080. (*The O'Conor Don.*) Are those figures taken from the Census?—Yes, from the Census of 1891.

3081. (*Mr. Sexton.*) Will you give us the direct, the indirect, and the total?—Directly, the number is 2,320,000.

3082. (*Mr. Wolff.*) You have put down the rural population in the first table, in No. 3 of your book, at 3,431,000?—Then the difference between that and those directly dependent ought to represent those who are indirectly dependent.

Development, linen trade.

3083. (*Chairman*). I now pass to certain articles of manufacture. Will you give us some figures as to the progress of the linen trade?—The progress of the linen trade is measured generally by looms and spindles, and I have here the number of spindles and looms which were known to be going at certain periods.

Dr. T. W. Grimshaw.

1 Dec. 1894.

Manufactures, linen trade.

These figures have been supplied to me by the Flax Association of Belfast. In 1841 the number of spindles was 250,000; in 1850 it was 326,000; in 1851, 390,000; in 1859 it was 632,000; in 1861 it was 593,000; in 1871 it was 866,000; in 1881 it was 878,000; and in 1890 it was 827,000.

3084. (*Mr. Wolff.*) Have you nothing beyond that?—I think I have. The number of spindles in 1891 was 827,000, the same as in 1890. In 1892, 838,000, and in 1893, 847,000.

3085. (*Mr. Sexton.*) That is less than it was in 1881?—Yes.

3086. (*Chairman.*) There was a great development up to 1871 or thereabouts, was there not, and since then the increase has been very slight?—Yes. Then as to the number of power looms we have only broken records; but in 1850 there were 58; in 1854 there were 1,871; in 1859, 3,633; in 1864, 8,187; in 1868, 12,969; in 1871, 14,834; in 1872, 18,169; in 1873, 19,155; in 1874, 19,331; in 1875, 20,152; in 1877, 20,598; in 1879, 21,153; in 1880, 21,177; in 1881, 21,779; in 1882, 22,274; in 1883, 23,677; in 1885, 24,303; in 1886, 24,520; in 1887, 24,786; in 1888, 24,973; in 1889, 25,360; in 1890, 25,350; in 1891, 26,190; in 1892, 26,232; and in 1893, 26,733. Those are what are used generally as the measure of the progress of the linen trade.

3087. Can you state how many people are employed in the cultivation of flax and in its manufacture?—No, I could not. There can be figures made up from the Census of the different trades—that is, the different designations of employment in the flax mills. We could divide them into weavers and hacklers, and so on, and make up the population for those engaged in the flax trade, but it would be rather a difficult thing to do.

3088. You have no statistics at hand of the total number of people who depend upon the linen trade, have you?—No, I think not. Of course the Board of Trade could give the numbers employed under the Factories Acts.

Beer and spirits.

3089. Is there any other principal article of manufacture which shows a remarkable progress. How about beer and spirits—can you give us any information about the progress of breweries?—Beer and spirits I have set out in those tables also, and I have here averages I took by five-year periods, which I thought would be more instructive to the Commission.

3090. What we want chiefly to know is the movement of the trade—how many people are employed, and whether they are increasing or not?—I cannot tell you the number of people employed.

3091. (*Mr. Sexton.*) It ought to be very easy to find out both as to the beer and spirit trade, they are so confined. It is a question of people employed in Belfast and a few towns about, and people employed in Dublin, is it not?—Very much so. Of course the classification of occupations in Census returns is very misleading to use for purposes of that sort; because an owner or manager will be put down as a brewer, and under the brewing trade everybody connected with it almost would be put down as brewers.

3092. You have not got available statistics for us showing the number of persons employed in the great manufactures, have you?—No.

3093. (*The O'Conor Don.*) How is it that you got that information with regard to the woollen trade?—It is taken from the Board of Trade return. With regard to the flax trade, of course it can be done; because you can get it from the factory inspectors of the Board of Trade.

3094. (*Chairman.*) But, as a matter of fact, you have not got it?—I have not got it; but it may be assumed, if the output of any industry has increased or decreased, that the employés have increased or decreased proportionately. I have some figures here with regard to whiskey and beer in five-year averages and in ten-year averages, and in another table I give

Dr. T. W. Grimshaw. 5 Dec. 1894.

Beer and spirits.

it from year to year. The ten-year average from 1841 to 1850 would be 7,147,000 gallons.

3095. (*Mr. Sexton.*) Spirits distilled?—Yes. From 1851 to 1860, 8,011,000 gallons; 1861 to 1870, 5,710,000 gallons; 1871 to 1880, 10,733,000 gallons; 1881 to 1890, 10,614,000 gallons. [*Table XVIII. handed in.*]

3096. Has your attention been drawn to the evidence we have lately had on this question of spirits as touching the consumption? There were two statements made in London—one that there had been serious errors in the computation of exports from Ireland, and the other that the spirits exported by the Customs department from Ireland had not been properly recorded before 1888. If that is so, that would greatly affect the point, would it not?—But these are figures as to the material produced. I have a table which was given me by the Inland Revenue, as to the amount consumed, but I am told it is all wrong. With regard to beer, the average number of barrels of beer brewed from 1841 to 1850 was 741,000; 1851 to 1860, 928,000; 1861 to 1868 (eight years), 1,378,000; 1871 to 1880, 1,930,000; 1881 to 1890, 2,214,000.

3097. In what part of Ireland are the principal breweries?—In Dublin.

3098. And in which part are the principal distilleries?—In Dublin. There are distilleries, of course, in other places. There is a distillery in Belfast, and some small breweries and distilleries in Cork and other places.

Fishing industry.

3099. Now will you go to the question of fishing. Is the fishing industry a rising industry?—No; fishing is a very decaying industry. You will find in columns 66 and 67 of the large tables the fishing given from year to year.

3100. Will you give us the salient figures, please?—If it is taken by five-year periods, in the same way as I have done before, the average number of vessels and boats between 1861 and 1865 was 10,715; in 1866 to 1870, 9,260; in 1871 to 1875, 7,472; in 1876 to 1880, 5,880; and 1881 to 1885, 5,968. Of the men and boys employed, the numbers were, in 1861 to 1865, 45,839. [*Table XX. handed in.*]

3101. What are they now?—From 1885 to 1890 there were 22,183, about one-half.

3102. The fishing industry is a decaying industry, is it?—Apparently it is; there is a good deal being now done to improve it.

3103. Do you know what is attributed generally as the reason for it?—I think it is very likely owing to the decrease in population, and therefore the somewhat increased demand for labour, the result of which is that fishing being rather a hazardous occupation, many of these fishermen, who were partly farmers, I am inclined to think, prefer the more easy life of working on land than working at sea. That is the only explanation I can see of it.

3104. (*Mr. Sexton.*) Is it not a fact that owing to the want of harbours and piers on the western coast, and the frail character of the boats, the people are unable to pursue the fishing industry to any extent?—Yes; but that applied before. No doubt those are things that contribute to make it an occupation not so agreeable as working on land.

3105. (*Chairman.*) Do you think it is decaying now—is the diminution going on?—I forget how the matter stands just at present. I see there is an increase now. The number of vessels and boats in 1890 was 5,655, in 1891 it was 5,103; it rose to 6,142 in 1892, and the last return shows 6,516, so that there has been an improvement. In the same way as to persons employed in 1890, it was 22,987, and it is now 24,813, so that there is a tendency to improve. At the time I wrote that pamphlet it was going down steadily.

3106. (*Mr. Sexton.*) The whole policy of the development of harbours has occurred since, has it not?—Yes, since the earlier years I have been dealing with.

Railways.

3107. (*Chairman*). Will you give the Commission, as to railways and railway traffic some information—is the railway mileage increasing?—Yes. The statistics of the railways, of course, has a reference to various points—to capital, mileage, and receipts.

3108. First of all as to mileage—is the mileage increasing?—The mileage has steadily increased. Of course railways were not developed at all in 1841–45, but the mileage was then thirty-five miles altogether, taking the average of those five years.

3109. How is it now compared with ten and twenty years ago?—If you compare the average of the five years 1886–1890, the mileage is 2,626 miles, and for the period 1861–1865 it was 1,079 miles.

3110. What addition to the mileage will the light railways give?—I could not tell you that exactly.

3111. Are any of them open yet?—Oh, yes, there are some of them open.

3112. To any considerable extent in mileage?—I could not distinguish the mileage of the light railways from the full-gauge lines.

3113. Can you tell me the mileage for this year, 1894?—No, I cannot give you the mileage for 1894; I think I can do it for 1893. The mileage for 1893 was 2,741.

3114. Compare that with the previous date which you gave?—The last figure was 1890, 2,643 miles. [*Table XXI. handed in.*]

Foreign trade and shipping.

3115. Is the foreign trade of Ireland diminishing or increasing?—The only measure we have of that is the entrance and clearance of ships by tonnage, and if you measure ships by tonnage, the average tonnage of the shipping entering in the foreign trade was, for the period 1841–1845, 220,000 tons, and for the last period I have here, the average was 848,000 tons.

3116. Can you give it at present?—The foreign trade entered for the last year I have, that is 1893, was 989,000 tons, and for the year before 1,040,000, and for the year before that 990,000.

3117. It is about stationary then, roughly?—It has increased as compared with five years ago.

3118. (*Mr. Sexton*). It has declined during the last few years, has it not?—The year 1890 is the highest on record.

3119. (*Chairman*). Going back a few years further, what was it in 1880?—In the year 1880 it was 1,000,000.

3120. Will you repeat again what you gave for last year?—989,000.

3121. Then practically for the last ten or twelve years it is stationary?—Practically it is.

3122. (*Mr. Martin*). I think in 1870 you will find it is 680,000 only.—In 1870 it was 700,000 only. Of course that is only foreign trade, and does not represent the trade of the ports at all.

3123. (*Chairman*). Have you any statistics as to the coasting trade?—Yes.

3124. What is the movement, is it increasing?—It is increasing very considerably.

3125. (*Mr. Wolff*). With regard to the coasting trade, you say "coasting trade with cargoes only," does that include all the channel steamers which carry passengers and cargo?—Certainly.

Woollen trade.

3126. (*Chairman*). Will you give one or two salient figures with regard to the coasting trade, or you may perhaps take the woollen trade first?—The woollen factories are measured by spindles in the same way. The number of factories, the spindles, looms, and persons employed in the year 1874, the first year I have here, is as follows:—In 1874, 80 factories; in 1878, 74; 1884, 141; and in 1889, 82. [*Table XIX. handed in*].

3127. (*Mr. Sexton.*) What became of the 60 factories which fell off between 1884 and 1889?—I have never been able to find that out. I believe that number 141 is wrong; because if you look there is no corresponding falling off in spindles. Those figures I am not responsible for. The spinning spindles, 51,948 in 1874; 46,705 in 1878; 70,323 in 1884, and 64,009 in 1889. For the same periods the figures as to doubling spindles were 2,626, 4,912, 5,551, and

11,428: power looms, 307, 413, 763, and 920; persons employed, 1,506, 1,975, 3,136, and 3,413.

3128. Are those the figures up to this year?—No; the last year is 1882.

3129. Lower down on page 33 of Part I. of your pamphlet you give the later figures. Will you incorporate them in your evidence. Tell us what is the difference between the table and the statement below it?—The number of persons enumerated in the census periods 1871, 1881, and 1891 as occupied in the woollen trade were respectively 5,198, 7,210, and 6,650.

3130. (*Chairman.*) That is woollen and worsted trade, is it?—That is woollen and worsted trade. That is a very indefinite term, because it includes people working at home and various things.

3131. (*Lord Welby.*) You are not able to tell the difference between those two classes, are you?—No.

3132. I see the power looms increased, particularly by very large numbers in the linen trade?—Yes.

3133. I suppose in reality a power loom possesses a much greater power of working up and represents therefore a much larger amount of work done, than a spindle, does it not? A power loom I take to be a machine worked by steam, and probably, therefore, turning out a great deal of work as compared with a spindle?—But the spindle is worked by steam too?—It is spinning.

3134. A power loom would be a more powerful machine, would it not?—It is a different thing—the spindle represents the spinning.

3135. What happened before there were power looms in the earlier days?—It was all done by hand. Of course a spindle in a spinning frame does far more work than anybody with hands would do, and so a power loom would do more work than a man with a shuttle.

3136. (*Chairman.*) I omitted to ask you, with respect to spirits, the amount consumed in Ireland so far as it is estimated now?—I have a table on that subject somewhere here, but I am informed by the Inland Revenue people it is not correct; so I do not offer it as evidence.

3137. We have had evidence as to that (incorrectness), but I only want to get on the note from your statistics what you state it at?—It is stated here from 1881 up to 1891.

3138. What is the relative amount in the two years?—I have not an average.

3139. Give us three years?—In 1881 there were 5,154,053 gallons consumed; in 1886, 4,154,670; and in 1891, 4,321,146; but I am told that those figures are all wrong.

3140. (*The O'Conor Don.*) Did you not get them from the Inland Revenue?—I got them from the Inland Revenue privately. I wrote for them, and they were sent to me while I was writing this pamphlet.

3141. (*Chairman.*) Will you now go back to the figures as to the coasting trade?—Do you wish the figures of vessels entering?

3142. Either—practically they are the same?—The coasting entered in 1841–1845 is 1,940,000 tons; in 1851–1855, 2,720,000; in 1861–1865, 3,700,000; in 1871–1875, 4,560,000; and the last period, 5,187,000.

3143. (*Mr. Sexton.*) Again there has been a fall in the last three quinquennial periods?—There was a fall in the average. The latest return in the coasting trade entered shows 5,396,000 tons.

3144. (*Mr. Martin.*) Is that for 1893?—That is for 1893.

3145. (*Chairman.*) I did not ask you about the shipbuilding trade—that has been developed a great deal, has it not?—I have here a table of the tonnage of shipping of the principal ports in Ireland, entries and clearances.

3146. Give us the salient figures, please?—The most important points are, that nearly all the ports, taking them all over, show an increase, and in some cases the increase is very great. For instance at Belfast in 1847 the tonnage entered was 466,000, and in 1892 it was 2,134,146.

3147. Is that the total tonnage of the port?—No, entered. The total tonnage entered in Belfast in 1847 was 463,000, and in 1892 it was 2,134,000. In Cork in 1847 it was 260,263; it is now 898,430. Dublin was 616,313 and is now 1,700,457.

3148. Have you any statistics with regard to shipbuilding?—Yes. I have figures supplied to me for my pamphlet by Sir Edward Harland; there was difficulty in getting regular official returns. The result of that statement was that in the year 1841 the number of tons of shipping built in Ireland was 1,042; in 1851, 1,840; in 1861, 7,543; in 1871, 16,974; in 1881, 24,945; and in 1891, 103,454.

3149. Where is the principal shipbuilding carried on?—In Belfast.

3150. (*Mr. Sexton.*) Only there; is there not any other shipbuilding?—Not much, I should think. I may mention that in the year 1814, I see from some old returns I came across, the tonnage of shipbuilding was 1,973; in 1821, 2,133; and in 1830, 2,341.

3151. Can you give us any details as to savings banks deposits and the deposits in other banks—banking capital?—I have banking capital and deposits, and cash balances in joint stock banks, and deposits in savings banks, both by trustees and the Post Office savings banks. Perhaps the quickest way will be to read the extract:—"We find that the capital of the joint stock banks of Ireland has increased from an average of 6,334,000*l.* in 1846–50 to an average of 7,024,000*l.* for the years 1888–92." Then the business of these banks, measured by the deposits and cash balance, in 1851 amounted to 8,263,000*l.*, which is equal to 1·3*l.* per head of the population. In 1861 it was 15,005,000*l.*, equal to 2·6*l.* per head of the population, being an increase of 6,742,000*l.*, or 81·6 per cent.; in 1871 it was 27,348,000*l.*, or 5·1*l.* per head, being an increase of 12,343,000*l.*, or 82·3 per cent.; in 1881 the amount rose to 30,161,000*l.*, or 5·8*l.* per head, being an increase of 2,813,000*l.*, or 10·3 per cent. as compared with 1871; and in 1890 the amount was 31,385,000*l.*, and it is still rising. It was 35,852,000 in 1893. That is with regard to deposits and cash balances in the joint stock banks.

3152. Will you give the figures with regard to the savings banks?—The savings banks have been steadily rising; the average for the years 1841 to 1844 in the savings banks (that was before the Post Office savings banks existed) was 2,343,000*l.*, and for the decennium 1841–50, 2,181,000*l.*; while for 1886–90 it was 5,241,000*l.*, and for 1891–93, 6,477,000*l.* Taking the period over which the combined statistics extend, we find that the total amount in the savings banks in 1863 was 2,167,000*l.*; in 1890 it was 5,996,000*l.*, or nearly treble, with a smaller population. The average amount per head of the population was for 1863, 0·4*l.*; for 1890, 1·2*l.*; and in 1893, 1·4*l.*

3153. Then as to the investments of Irish capital, what are the salient figures?—The main capital may be taken to be invested in Government stock, banking, and railways. The main feature on that point is that these investments in Government stock have decreased in bulk, whereas the investments in other kinds of stock, railways, and banks have increased.

3154. Can you give the figure as to each?—It is difficult unless I read you the extract just as it is.

3155. It will be sufficient if you give the salient figure: by how many millions have the investments in Government stocks diminished, and by how many millions have the investments in other stocks increased?—The investments in Government stocks have diminished by 11,483,000*l.* between the years 1881 and 1893. In railway stock the increase was 13,677,000*l.*, so that, allowing for the portion of increased railway capital which was subscribed by English investors, it may fairly be assumed that the money withdrawn from the Government funds in

Dr. T. W. Grimshaw.

3 Dec. 1895.

Shipping and trade.

Banking.

Investments of capital.

Ireland generally went into Irish railways, probably largely in the form of debenture and preference stocks as representing trust funds. If to the above we add another of the ordinary securities for the investment of money, namely, bank shares, we have an addition of 4,987,000*l.* of banking capital in 1861, of 6,947,000*l.* in 1871, of 6,604,000*l.* in 1881.

3156. What does that come to in the aggregate?—In the aggregate, under those various heads, it comes to 65,874,000*l.* in 1861, 70,063,000*l.* in 1871, 72,837,000*l.* in 1881, and 70,108,000*l.* in 1890, showing a total increase between 1881 and 1893 of 4,330,000*l.*

3157. The percentage, of course, on investments in the aggregate is not by any means so great as the percentage of increase in savings banks deposits?—No, it is not; but I wish to point out that these figures, of course, are all taken at par—there is no allowance whatever made for the increased value of stocks. Of course a lot of the money that is sold out of Government stocks at or very close to par was invested at a premium in money on these debenture stocks. The only one I touched was the banking stock, and I find that the market value of stocks and shares of all the Irish banks was on the 30th of November last (that is according to the last monthly list) 18,818,000*l.*, whereas the paid-up capital was only 7,009,000*l.*, more than double; so that that does not represent the real selling value of these shares at the present time.

3158. (*Mr. Sexton.*) Are the ordinary shares of the railways included here at their nominal value?—Everything in that list is included at its nominal value.

3159. Then it is clear some millions should come off the railway stock, because we all know that the original shares of the Irish railways mostly stand at below their nominal value?—But the total of the whole thing stands at par.

3160. But of the whole stock, how does it stand?—It is considerably above par; it is sold at a premium.

3161. (*Sir David Barbour.*) Your figures do not include, as I understand, investments in ordinary joint stock enterprises?—No.

3162. And they do not include investments in similar joint stock enterprises in England by Irishmen?—No.

3163. Nor in English railways or foreign railways?—No.

3164. Or in foreign government stocks?—No; this is simply taking a look at these particular points, merely to illustrate the point as to what had become of the Government stock.

3165. It may have gone to foreign investments?—It may; it was to account for what I could lay my hand on.

3166. There can be no doubt that there are large investments in foreign railways and so on?—No doubt whatever; and it is generally believed that Irishmen hold a great deal more money outside the country than Englishmen do in Ireland.

3167. (*Chairman.*) I think I have gone through with you now the principal statistics. Would you say, from your own study and experience, that the wealth of Ireland is increasing?—I think decidedly so.

3168. Is the wealth of what is vulgarly called the upper classes increasing?—I should think, as to those who are engaged in trade and commerce, yes.

3169. Taking them all round?—I should think it would be taken for granted that the Irish landlords, who would be classed among the upper classes, are worse off decidedly; but if you take the merchant class and the traders, they are better off.

3170. Is the wealth of what is popularly called the middle classes increasing or decreasing?—I should say increasing—that is a matter of opinion.

3171. And in respect to the poor, do you think they are better off?—They are better off—their wages are higher.

3172. I think the opinion has been expressed to us that the farmer is not doing much better than he was, but that the labourer is—is that your opinion?—The farmer is not any better off, except in this respect, that the farmers have become bigger men, and are engaged in a larger business—that is, the number of small holdings has steadily diminished, and the farms have been consolidated. The average Irish farmer now is doing more business. He has more land and sells more than an average Irish farmer did forty years ago.

3173. Does the phrase that the rich are not doing as well, and that the poor are doing better, the converse of what one hears elsewhere, apply to Ireland?—I do not think that the poor are getting poorer.

3174. Do you think the rich are getting poorer?—I think the landowners are, but nobody else.

3175. Taking the aggregate, as I have said before, of the class which is vulgarly called the upper class, you think they are not getting richer?—If you include among them all the traders and merchants I should say that that part of the upper classes are better off, but when you come to the landed proprietors I say they are worse off, and it is a notorious fact.

3176. But you would put on the other side of the scale, whether farmers or labourers, that you think that class are doing better?—I will not say that a farmer is doing better, because I have shown already to-day that I think the value of his produce has decreased, but the farmers at present are a more prosperous set of men a great deal than the farmers forty years ago—they are more substantial men, is, perhaps, the best way to put it.

3177. And the labourer you think is decidedly better off?—Yes, decidedly. I have some returns which I collected privately of labourers' wages in past times, and the present labourers' wages, which are published in my agricultural reports for each Constabulary district in Ireland, and they show an enormous increase. I could give that return. It was published in the Cowper Commission. The return was collected by writing letters to private persons.

3178. (*The O'Conor Don.*) Could you say in a general way what the percentage of increase is?—No, I could not; but you see the wages are wonderfully low in many of those cases.

Adjourned to to-morrow at 11 o'clock.

Dr. Grimshaw's evidence is continued at question 3962 (Ninth Day).

EIGHTH DAY.

Saturday, 8th December, 1894.

At the Benchers' Chambers, Four Courts, Dublin.

PRESENT:

THE RIGHT HON. HUGH C. E. CHILDERS, *Chairman*.

LORD WELBY.	CHARLES E. MARTIN, Esq.
THE RIGHT HON. THE O'CONOR DON.	THOMAS SEXTON, Esq., M.P.
SIR DAVID BARBOUR, K.C.S.I.	GUSTAV W. WOLFF, Esq., M.P.

MR. B. H. HOLLAND, *Secretary*.

MR. WILLIAM L. MICKS called in and examined.

Mr. W. L. Micks. 8 Dec. 1894. Population.

3179. (*Chairman.*) You are secretary to the Congested Districts Board in Ireland?—Yes.

3180. Do you lay upon our table sundry returns, and the first report of the Board?—Yes.

3181. I will take the returns in order; the first is a table showing the acreage, Poor Law valuation, and population of congested districts in Ireland?—Yes.

3182. Before we pass to the next, have you any remark to make which you consider of importance in connection with that table?—These congested districts are not territorial divisions which are known already; they are divisions of natural areas comprising several electoral divisions which are shown on page 3 of the same return. These districts were formed having regard to geographical circumstances chiefly, mountains intervening, also rivers, and in some cases people were of different occupations in adjoining parishes with which in many cases districts coincide. In one parish some of the men are migratory labourers, and in the next parish no people go at all to work in England and Scotland; so having regard to various different circumstances and to natural boundaries, these districts were formed by the Congested Districts Board.

3183. The congested districts consist of an entire electoral division, do they?—In some cases they are divided. You will see on page 8, for instance, parts of electoral divisions.

3184. Are these parishes practically?—They are very nearly parishes in many cases.

3185. Have you any other remark to make upon this first paper?—The totals at pages 6 and 7 show some matters of interest.

3186. Will you point out what they are?—The area of all congested districts in statute acres is three and a half millions.

3187. What is that compared with the whole area of Ireland?—The whole area of Ireland is 20,138,000 statute acres.

3188. It is about a sixth then?—Yes. Then the Poor Law valuation is 547,000*l.*, as compared with, you may say, 14,000,000*l.* in round numbers.

3189. And the population?—The population is 542,000, as compared with 4,704,000. The number of families is 98,129 in the congested districts, and the number of inhabited houses in all Ireland is 870,578. The next four columns in the return have reference to valuation and poverty. The first column shows the number of holdings above 4*l.* valuation in the congested districts, and also those who have no land at all. 12,924 is the number of families having holdings above 4*l.*, and of those who have no land. The number of families on holdings exceeding 2*l.* and under 4*l.* is 26,645; and the number of families on holdings under 2*l.* valuation is 28,270. Then in addition to that, in the next column there are a number of families put down who are in very poor circumstances, who approach the border line of pauperism; there are 17,312 families in that condition.

3190. And the average Poor Law valuation is what?—The average Poor Law valuation is 1*l.* 0*s.* 2*d.*, as compared with 3*l.* 15*s.* 8*d.* for the entire of Ireland.

3191. Taking the different columns together, this deals with about an eighth only as between land and population all round, does it not?—I did not work it out in that way exactly, but as regards population, it is about a ninth. There is another matter which I might point out. The Poor Law valuation per head of population varies very much in these districts. On pages 2 and 3 you will see Nos. 10, 11, and 12, Tory Island, Gweedore, and the Rosses; their valuation per head is 7*s.* 4*d.*, 6*s.* 0*d.* and 6*s.* 8*d.* That is not exactly a test of poverty, because you will see in the case of the Rosses, No. 12, you have only ninety-four families who are reported to be in very poor circumstances, out of 2,330.

Congested districts; supplementary industries of inhabitants.

3192. (*Mr. Sexton*). Have they any supplementary industry?—Yes, they have migratory labour, and the women knit a great deal; and along the coast they have kelp making and some fishing.

3193. (*Chairman*). Passing to the next paper which is marked No. III., you give there the principal occupations of the inhabitants of the congested districts. Have you anything to remark upon that?—I think nothing in addition to what is stated in the column for occupations; that states really in a general way as much as I can say.

Recommendations by Congested Districts Board.

3194. Then paper No. IV. gives generally the recommendations which have been made to the Board for the improvement of the circumstances of congested districts?—Yes, by means of engineering works. A number of other recommendations have been made for the development of industries—fishing, weaving, and things of that sort.

3195. But recommendations are made, are they not, for works in respect of all the districts practically?—Yes, practically all.

3196. Is there anything special which you would call our attention to?—From what point of view?

3197. As a matter of fact in these recommendations is there anything abnormal in any particular recommendation?—Railway extensions are recommended.

Mr. W. L. Micks.

7 Dec. 1894.

Recommendations by Congested Districts Board.

in a great many cases, and in the opinion of the Board nearly all these railway extensions that are mentioned are highly desirable.

3198. Apparently the great majority of the recommendations are of the same character?—They are, and they are very largely as to road-making and the opening up of backward districts.

3199. And a good deal of pier-making too?—Yes, pier-repairing, drainage, and reclamation.

3200. That is simply drainage, I suppose?—That is arterial and main drainage.

3201. Then there is a certain amount of reclamation recommended, is there not?—Yes; that is very largely recommended, but it has not been taken in hand by the Board yet.

3202. There is nothing else to call attention to then in connection with No. IV., is there?—No, I think not.

Budgets of typical families.

3203. Then as to the report of the Board, are there any points which you think would be especially of interest to this Commission?—On page 32 there are given twelve family budgets.

3204. I was going to put a question to you upon that subject, but before coming to that, is there anything in the report which you think we ought to notice particularly?—I think not. Perhaps Dr. O'Donnell will give evidence upon anything of that kind.

3205. We shall be glad of your evidence upon it.—I do not know quite the scope of the inquiry. These budgets, I think, will apply to a very large proportion of the people living in those districts.

3206. I will take you to these budgets. How many are there?—There are twelve.

3207. From how many pounds' receipt to how many pounds in the year do they range?—In the twelfth the people are so poor as to make only a little over 8*l.* a year in cash. Then from their own produce they make hardly as much more.

3208. Have you formed any estimate, not only as to the congested districts, but as to the other agricultural districts, what the budget of an ordinary farmer may be taken to be?—It varies in nearly every district, I think.

3209. There is no approach to a normal average budget?—I think not.

3210. It depends on the nature and the character of the holdings and the habits of the people, I suppose?—Yes.

3211. Given the receipts, can you estimate pretty fairly how the expenditure should be divided?—Yes.

3212. But you cannot give any general estimate for the income of a small farm?—In different parts?

3213. Yes.—It varies a good deal. You have to take the quality of the land, and whether it is altogether pasture or altogether tillage, or partly of each.

3214. Who may be said to be specially responsible for these budgets?—I am responsible for some of them myself.

3215. Will you take one or two of them?—I think I can answer questions about most of them.

3216. Some of them are very nearly the same, but take one or two which are normal.—The average is 29*l.* odd.

3217. The average of the twelve?—Yes. I do not think much turns on the average.

3218. (*Mr. Sexton.*) That is the cash receipt average?—Both cash receipt and expenditure—the balance.

3219. But not including the home produce?—No, not including the home produce. The home produce averages 16*l.*

3220. (*Chairman.*) And you assume, do you, that nothing is set aside for saving, and that the whole of the produce is consumed in some way?—There are a few people who save, but they are very few—there are not many.

3221. Is it the experience of the savings' banks in the West of Ireland that there is not much coming in from that class of farmers?—I cannot answer about the savings' banks' returns. There are a few people who save money, but the number who save is not very large in my opinion.

Mr. W. L. Micks.

7 Dec. 1894.

Budgets of typical families.

3222. At any rate, in forming an estimate of the condition of these districts, you are bound to assume that very little is set aside?—Yes; people find it very hard to make both ends meet; in fact, a great number of families fail to make both ends meet.

3223. Will you take one of these budgets which you think is the most typical?—No. 3, page 33, is a poor district. They have small farms there; they make a little by fishing, and the women make a little by sewing and knitting.

3224. The aggregate receipt is how much?—About 27*l.*

3225. That would represent how many acres, probably?—That would represent tilling about 2½ or 3 acres; then they have a small run for a couple of cattle—the holdings are very small in that locality.

3226. Which they generally enjoy in common with others?—Yes, the mountain in common; and then they have fields of tillage and meadow for their own use.

3227. You take that one as typical?—It is typical of that kind of small holders who also fish.

3228. You assume that the expenditure is little more than the receipt, I suppose?—These budgets were made out quite independently of any attempt to balance; each side of the account was made out separately, without any attempt to reconcile them or make a balance.

3229. In some cases do the families save a little?—In that district hardly any people save—that is, the district of South Donegal.

3230. And in this case particularly there is a deficit, I think?—Yes, and that is rather the character of the neighbourhood; they are a little behind always.

3231. Is that a district from which the people go in the autumn to England?—No; they never go to the harvest or summer work in England from that district.

3232. What is the exact district?—It is Teelin; fishing has been developed there a good deal; the Board have established two or three curing stations there, and the earnings from fishing have largely increased.

3233. From some parts of Donegal a considerable number go to England, do they not?—From No. 4 they go over to the harvest. As soon as they have their own crops in they go over and do not come back, in many instances, till Christmas Day.

3234. I see you estimate the earnings away from home at as much as 10*l.*?—Yes.

3235. Is that a fair estimate for any considerable part of Ireland?—I think that is fair for the districts of the Rosses, Gweedore, and Cloghaneely. Very often two or three from the family go. That is a family average, not a man's average.

3236. I should like to take No. 3, and go through some of the items. On the receipt side I do not notice anything remarkable. There is a large item for "Fish"?—It is much larger now.

3237. As an average?—Yes, it is very much larger as an average; men very often are able to make two or three pounds a boat for a night's fishing where there was no sale for the fish before.

3238. Then 8*l.* is a low average?—At present it is. At the time this was made in 1891 or 1892 it was about a fair average.

3239. I am surprised to see so much given, not only in that one but in some of the other little budgets for the proceeds of eggs?—Yes; it is not a cash transaction; in Donegal they very rarely get cash over the counter for the eggs they sell, but get tea, sugar, and tobacco in exchange.

3240. It comes to the same thing, that in the long run they sell their eggs at a little less than the market price, and buy on the other side at a little loss?—But the balance of advantage is on the side of the trader.

3241. In No. 1, I see, for instance, the figure is 7l. 10s.?—Yes; that is a place where the better-off families have a good deal of poultry—Belmullet, county Mayo.

3242. Is that a fair average?—I should think it is rather high, but that is the evidence we have from a competent judge.

3243. Going back to No. 3, I see nothing very salient on the receipt side?—Knitting was rather low at that time; the M'Kinley tariff had come into force and it affected the embroidering industry.

3244. Has that revived again?—It has a little, but has not gone back to the old state.

3245. Is that one of the districts where the women are always knitting?—Yes, they are always knitting and embroidering when they can get work; but the supply of work very often fails.

3246. Then on the other side I presume the rent is about normal?—That is the average rent.

3247. Then tea and sugar?—Tea is a relatively expensive article; the people always pay the highest price for tea.

3248. And the consumption of tea is increasing in Ireland, is it not?—It is very large; they always have the teapot on the hearth stewing there.

3249. (Mr. Sexton.) What is the usual price of the tea?—It varies from 2s. 4d. to 3s. They buy a very high-priced tea there.

3250. (Chairman.) They like high-priced tea?—The wholesale price no doubt is much lower.

3251. (Sir David Barbour.) Is the tea of a good quality?—I have often drunk it, but it seems to me the way they prepare it is not wholesome, as the tea is so bitter.

3252. (Mr. Sexton.) How do they buy it—in pounds, half-pounds, or ounces?—According to their means; if they have fair credit they get it in the larger quantities; and very often they get it in exchange for knitting and eggs.

3253. (Chairman.) Are these the shop prices which you state on both sides here?—Yes, they are the shop prices.

3254. Clothing is very small?—Clothing does not involve a large expenditure; a great deal of it is home made; there are weavers in that district. You see flannel and tweed on the receipt side of No. 3. Every family has a web, and as a rule, from 60 to 100 yards a year are woven by or for each family.

3255. Then tobacco is 2l. 7s. 8d.?—Yes, that is a very large item.

3256. Is it the consumption of tobacco that is very high, or are the prices high?—No, it is the consumption that is great. That is a family average.

3257. Is that normal, do you think, for a family?—It is rather higher in some parts of Donegal and in some parts of the west too. That is about normal; a shilling a week is a fair sum to take—in fact it is low.

3258. A shilling a week for a family?—Yes.

3259. What is a family supposed to consist of?—They have about one and a half smokers in a family, averaging it.

3260. In this part of Donegal do the women smoke much?—Very little; they snuff sometimes.

3261. They do in some parts smoke a good deal, I think?—Only the very old women smoke as a rule.

3262. Then you may say that that for a family in ordinary circumstances, deriving its money from farming, and to a certain extent from fishing, is a fair budget?—I think it is. They get a little also from weaving flannel.

3263. Will you point out to me any other?—There is a budget of a very poor family—and there are others of the same class—in No. 2. The cash receipts are 9l. 14s. from all sources. The expenditure is estimated at 10l. 19s., and the home produce varies from about 12l. to 17l. a year. Those are people in the Barony of Erris, County Mayo; they are perhaps the poorest people in the country.

3264. The amount of rent and county cess is 1l. 12s.; that is a very low average, I suppose?—The holdings are wretched.

3265. May I ask what are clerical charges?—The dues they pay to their clergy.

3266. (Sir David Barbour.) Is this a budget of an actual family, or is it a sort of average?—It is more a budget of an actual family. First the budgets of a number of actual families were put together, and a great many of them coincided so largely that you might almost take it as an actual budget.

3267. What number do you take for a family?—The census average of the place.

3268. What would that be?—About five and a fraction.

3269. (Chairman.) I see in No. 2 tobacco is a great deal less than in No. 3?—Yes, they have very little money to buy tobacco to smoke in district No. 2.

3270. And clothing is a good deal more; but they do not make so much as in No. 3, I suppose?—No, they have very little means. That is a place in which fishing has been started too, and they are making more from fish now than formerly.

3271. Which parish do you specially point to in No. 2?—I know Donegal pretty well.—No. 2 is in Mayo; it is a division called Knockadaff.

3272. Will you take another which you think is typical?—No. 5 is typical of inland—Mayo and Galway, in the Swinford district, say.

3273. Where there is nothing earned from fishing?—Nothing from fishing.

3274. But the young people go to the English harvest?—Exactly.

3275. What items in that do you give?—Migratory labour is put down there as 8l. I am inclined to think that is rather low, but at all events it is not an excessive average.

3276. I think the English farmers' estimate is that they pay about 10l. a man?—I never went so high as that; I have gone as high, taking one year with another, as 10l. a family, and that means a fraction over a working man.

3277. Then you are prudent in this case in taking the 8l.?—I think so.

3278. (Sir David Barbour.) Is that the profit after paying the expenses of a family?—The profit after paying the expenses of a family and getting a suit of clothes. They very often come back with a suit of English or Scotch clothes.

3279. (Chairman.) Is the 8l. or 10l. net?—It is cash brought or sent home.

3280. Do you know from Donegal and the west generally what is the railway and steamer fare to and from England and Scotland?—It varies very much; a great many men can get over for half-a-crown by steamer from the west coast of Donegal, but from some parts of Mayo it comes to about a pound, I suppose.

3281. Do you know what an Irish labourer pays for his passage to and from the east coast of England?—No, I do not know, but it is very low.

3282. Not a pound?—I should say a pound would cover most. I think a good many of them borrow a pound for their trip, just to see them over until they get to their destination. The shopkeepers very often lend them a pound to go over.

3283. Is there any item you suggest we should specially look at in No. 5? There is one that attracts my attention. Besides flour, you have shop bread?—Yes.

3284. I do not think that occurs in many of the other budgets; what is the distinction?—The flour they make their own cakes out of, and shop bread is bread brought round in bakers' carts, which they buy from the baker on the road.

3285. Is that first-class bread, as a rule?—No, it is not first-class, but it is wholesome bread as a rule.

3286. Is it not the Irish custom, as it is in parts of England, to eat nothing but the best bread?—No, they cannot get it really well made in the country; it is

Mr. W. L. Micks. 4 Dec. 1894. Budgets of typical families.

not anything like, for instance, the bread we get in Dublin.

3287. Some of the poorest of the labouring classes in England will eat nothing but first-class bread?—I believe the Irish country bread is a good, wholesome bread, though it is not good in colour. There is one omission from No. 5, I think. There is put down for rent and county cess 6l. 5s. I believe that refers only to the land on which the house is. Now, the plots are very small, and the rent is relatively high, and every man there has to buy grass for his cow, and hay for the support of his cow in the winter, which is really a second rent, in addition to the agricultural rent that he pays.

3288. I see, apparently, there is no weaving done there?—No, nothing to speak of.

3289. Everything is bought entirely?—Yes.

3290. (*Mr. Sexton*). Is the second rent mentioned in the account?—No; as I say, it is not.

3291. Then there would be a deficiency in that account instead of a surplus if the second rent had been put in?—Yes.

3292. (*Chairman*). How much do you say they would have to pay?—I fancy they would have to pay fully 3l. for their grass and hay.

3293. (*The O'Conor Don*). How is it, if that be so, that in the receipts, which I presume represent sales, they appear to sell hay?—Well, they do not sell much. You see, they buy a piece of meadow, cut it, and save the hay for themselves, but they may get rid of their surplus. You see, the amount put down for it is very small—only 10s. for surplus hay and straw; that may be chiefly straw.

3294. Would it be surplus hay and straw outside their own holding?—That 10s. is a receipt for hay and straw sold.

3295. But not grown upon their holding, according to your statement?—The straw would be grown on their holding.

3296. But whatever proportion of that is hay would not be grown on their own holding?—That is my opinion.

3297. (*Mr. Sexton*). I understand you to say that the hay they sell would be surplus?—That is my conjecture, but I fancy it would be mostly straw.

3298. (*The O'Conor Don*). Is this an individual case or an average one?—That budget was not prepared by me, but it is a typical case. The circumstances of the people in that district are very much alike; they are nearly all settled on reclaimed bog, and go over to work in England. The good land in the district is nearly all held by grazing farmers, and these people have to rent grass at a high rate, and buy hay at a high rate from the farmers round them, being on reclaimed bog themselves.

3299. (*Chairman*). Is there anything in Nos. 6 or 7 to which you would like to call attention?—No. 6 is a budget for people living in the island of Achill.

3300. That is, I suppose, as poor as any district?—There they are exceedingly poor, but I do not think they are as poor as the people in the north of the county Mayo.

3301. As to No. 7, have you anything to say—I see a large item for knitting?—Yes, that is Glenties, in the county of Donegal.

3302. (*Mr. Sexton*). It is an organised industry, is it not?—Yes; the M'Devitts and a number of other merchants have gloves, stockings, and other woollen garments knitted there.

3303. (*Chairman*). Is that industry being extended at the present time?—I fancy it is extended as far as it can go.

3304. Is it remunerative?—Yes. The M'Devitts are wealthy people, having a branch house in Leicester, I think, and they work from Leicester to Glenties, backwards and forwards. There are other merchants as well.

3305. I see there is a large item on the expenditure side for tea?—Yes, and I think that is got by the people selling their knitting; they do not get cash from some of the knitting merchants; some of the merchants who carry on the knitting business never pay in cash; they have grocery shops and pay in a kind of truck way.

3306. But you incorporate that as if it were a cash transaction, do you not?—Yes. Some of the merchants pay cash always; the M'Devitts, for instance, pay cash.

3307. Then in No. 8, there is a very large item of the same character?—That is in connection with the shirt industry in Derry. That is a district where materials for shirts can be sent out to the country people.

3308. There is a large charge in that budget for luxuries?—Yes.

3309. It is almost the only one in which you have given that item?—The amount spent by the country people on that item is just a monthly expenditure, once a month at the local monthly fair. As a rule they do not drink in their own houses or during the day.

3310. That is 4s. spent once a month, is it?—I think that would be about it.

3311. (*Mr. Sexton.*) It is the only budget in which you have an entry for spirits?—Yes.

3312. Does that indicate that there is much total abstinence?—There is a great deal of total abstinence in the county of Donegal.

3313. (*Mr. Wolff.*) I see 1l. 19s. for snuff in two of the budgets?—Yes; in some places snuffing is carried on far more than in others.

3314. (*Chairman.*) Among the younger people?—I never see the younger people snuff, but old men and women do.

3315. Is that a declining expenditure practically?—They take to it in their old age.

3316. Those who have not been snuff-takers when young, take it as they advance in age?—I cannot say. One sees old people snuffing. I do not know whether the people take to it at a certain age or not.

3317. Then in No. 9, is there anything remarkable?—Not very much—no. Embroidery you see is rather a profitable industry there.

3318. The item for tea I see is very normal in these budgets?—Yes.

3319. A great many of them are about 5l.?—They are—they are about the same.

3320. (*Mr. Sexton.*) It is about a pound of tea a week?—Yes.

3321. (*Chairman.*) No. 12 is a very remarkable budget; the expenditure of a family in the poorest possible circumstances?—Yes, but before you pass to that, may I say as to No. 10 budget, that that applies to a district where they have little or nothing except a little flannel weaving; it is in Glencolumbkille, county Donegal. A great many of the people have emigrated from there, and they send back money to that district.

3322. (*Mr. Sexton.*) It is the only budget in which you have noted remittances from America?—There are many other places where you can put it in, but it is a difficult thing to put it in as a typical receipt.

3323. (*The O'Conor Don.*) What part of the country does budget No. 9 deal with?—No. 9 is Killybegs; No. 11 is County Kerry, Castlegregory.

3324. (*Mr. Sexton.*) Inland?—No, the sea coast.

3325. There is no fishing, is there?—Not much.

3326. There is none in the budget?—No, it is most inland; there is very little fringe.

3327. (*Chairman.*) Then I come to No. 12, that is the budget of a family in the poorest possible circumstances?—Yes, it is really only two or three cases in the mountain glens of Donegal. I put it in not as a typical budget, but to show that the people were struggling on in such a state as that.

3328. (*Chairman*). They are 2l. on the wrong side, I see?—Yes; it means that they drift to the workhouse or leave the locality in some way before long.

3329. These budgets are all in congested districts, are they not?—They are all in congested districts,

The Board to which I am Secretary have no connection with any district outside the congested districts.

3330. You have not referred to any district outside your special administration?—No. I was a Local Government Inspector in a good many districts in Ireland, and of course I have no idea of comparison.

3331. (The O'Conor Don.) I think you have told us about all these budgets, excepting No. 4. What district is that in?—That is the Rosses, county Donegal.

3332. (Lord Welby.) What is No. 3?—Tonlin.

3333. (The O'Conor Don.) Taking No. 3 upon which you gave your detailed evidence, what is the employment of the people generally?—They till between two and three acres, and in the months of January, February, and March they have very good cod and ling fishing. Then in the summer again they have salmon fishing in the open sea by drift net, and later on they have a little haddock, and herring, and mackerel fishing, but not very much. Their principal fishing is in the first three months of the year, and the Congested Districts Board buy these fish from them and cure it cured.

3334. (Mr. Martin.) Would 15l. be too much as an estimate for their present income from fishing?—I think it would not be enough.

3335. (The O'Conor Don.) 8l. is what you have put down?—I think it is far more than that now, it has improved.

3336. How many acres of land have they altogether in this typical case?—A very few acres. They have very small holdings; they would not have more than four or five acres; the land is very much exhausted, and whenever a failure of the potato crop happens, it shows in that district. In some cases the same land has been growing potatoes, without a year's rest, since the famine time.

3337. When you speak of acres, do you speak of statute acres or Irish acres?—They are the Scotch acres, Cunninghams acres.

3338. And is it the Cunningham acres you refer to when you refer to the number of acres?—It is, in a rough way.

3339. Is the half of their holdings in tillage?—Yes, about half—more than half.

3340. Would the remaining half support a bullock or heifer?—But then they have a mountain run as well.

3341. Have they a mountain run in addition to these four or five acres?—Yes, a mountain run for sheep and stock.

3342. What would be about the proportion that each occupier would have of this mountain run?—They would never reach the full limit; they never have stock enough to put on.

3343. I suppose these mountain runs are held in common?—They are held in common.

3344. And the proportion is regulated by a certain number of beasts and sheep, is it not?—In a great many cases it is, but there are a number of places where there is no interference. A man may put on as many as he likes, because they never reach the point of over-crowding the mountain.

3345. Then the mountain would really carry more than it has on it?—In a great many cases that is so; in this case it is so.

3346. But you do not know in this case what would be the proportion that this individual would have a right to place upon the mountain if he had the cattle?—No, I do not.

3347. How do you estimate the produce? I see you have "Corn, 15s."; how is that estimated?—It was estimated on the price at the time, oats so much a stone—I suppose then it would have been about 10d. a stone.

3348. In ascertaining how much is produced by the tillage, how do you proceed?—That would be the sale of the surplus.

3349. Do the people use the oats themselves?—They use some of the oats—they use them for a pony if they have one, and for food, and so on.

3350. Do they grind it into meal and so on?—Very little; there is a mill about five miles off, and they send a little there, but chiefly Indian meal is used.

Mr. W. L. Micks.

6 Dec. 1893.

Budgets of typical families.

3351. Are these statements as to the receipts and the expenditure taken from the statements of the people themselves?—Partly so. I have taken a number of these budgets myself, and they are partly taken from the people themselves and partly from information got from the shopkeepers and from every available source, rent receipts and so on.

3352. I find that in many of these cases the expenditure exceeds the receipts. How can that go on for a number of years?—It shows that the budget, I think, is not quite right. It is an attempt at making the best budget, but there has been no attempt to reconcile the two sides. The instructions were to find out what was received in money and what was spent in money as far as possible, without any attempt to cook or balance.

3353. But does it not show that there must be some error?—Yes, to some extent there must be some error.

3354. Because they could not go on year after year in that way, could they?—I think it does; the excess is very little.

3355. Little or great it is a fact, is it not?—The budget is not put forward of course to show an exact cash account, it is an estimated budget. The estimate is evidently a little wrong in some minor detail.

3356. (Mr. Martin.) You do not take into account in any of these returns the aid and assistance which is given to these people in money or kind from subscriptions?—No, I do not. I do not think it does come in.

3357. (The O'Conor Don.) Taking this typical case of the Swineford district, I see there is nothing at all in that budget put down for spirits?—No.

3358. Do you know the number of public houses in Swineford?—I am sure it is large, but this is dealing only with country people whose expenditure would be made on the fair day.

3359. But is not the expenditure in the licensed houses in the towns mainly made up of country expenditure?—I should say very largely.

3360. It is not made up of the expenditure of the population of the towns, is it?—A great many of the town people are regular drinkers, but country people as a rule are not.

3361. The country people, as you state, no doubt only take these refreshments upon market and fair days, but is not the great bulk of the spirit sold upon those days?—I should think the larger part of it is.

3362. Do you think you would put down as a typical budget of the Swineford district, one in which there is no expenditure upon spirit?—I think it would be fairer to include a sum of say 2l. a year in most of these budgets for luxuries of different sorts.

3363. How long do these migratory labourers stay in England, as a rule?—They go over as soon as they have got their own crops in. They go over in May perhaps, and a great many of them are coming back about now, and up to Christmas. Some come back earlier, in October, November, and December.

Migratory labourers.

3364. They stay about five months then?—Yes, and some, more especially the Donegal people, stay a longer time, in Scotland, for instance, they get work on the railways and elsewhere.

3365. And during those five months they support themselves in England as well as lay by this amount of money which you have put down here?—Yes.

3366. Do they send over anything during that time to their families?—That I include in the cash receipts. A man may come back very often, and does come back, with only 1l. or even less in his pocket; he has sent it all on before him.

3367. In the case of No. 3, how many acres of land would the holding contain?—I should say about 4 or 5 acres of land.

3368. Statute or Irish acres?—I am not speaking from personal knowledge. I did not make that

Mr. W. L. Micks.
9 Dec. 1894.
Migratory labour.

budget myself, but it was made by a very competent Inspector, Mr. Doran. I think the rent is high there.

3369. You do not mean that the land about Swineford is let at 1*l.* an acre?—I do not say that, but I say the rent is relatively high though.

3370. But if the area is only four acres, and the rent and county cess come to 4*l.* 5*s.*, the rent must be about 1*l.* an acre, must it not?—Yes, it would be so—that looks high.

3371. You cannot verify it?—No, I cannot verify the acreage. I have been on a number of those holdings, and they seemed to me to be very small holdings, and what makes me say four acres is that they have not got grass on the holdings as a rule.

3372. There is no mountain land there, is there?—Oh, no.

3373. Why is the congested district divided into these particular very small districts. What is the purpose of the division?—They are chiefly natural areas; one would notice that more plainly in Donegal. If you turn to the map which you will see on page 12, there are inlets of the sea and mountain chains which divide these areas into natural districts.

3374. Are these districts separated from non-congested districts, or do they join together?—A great many of them are touched by nothing else except congested districts.

3375. What I ask you is if they form part of a whole together, why have you divided them into such minute portions?—Because the livelihood is got and earned in a different way. Take the parish of Dunloe and Lettermacaward where there are migratory labourers, and on the other side of the river hardly any man at all go to England and Scotland, which is because they have rather better land on the south side of the river, and are able to make farming pay.

3376. Have they larger holdings?—They have larger holdings, and better land.

3377. And where these labourers go to England, I presume, the holdings are extremely small—that is to say, the portion that can be tilled?—Yes.

3378. And there would not be occupation for them at home?—Oh, no; they could not live in the place if they did not make money from migratory labour. Their farms would not support them at all.

3379. What do these migratory labourers generally do during the winter?—The months of November, December, and January are perfectly idle for them; they have nothing to do, except a few people along the shore who catch herrings just now. It is one of the problems the Board has to face, to try and find some employment for these people during the winter months of November, December, January, and February.

3380. Can you say how many months of the year they are employed working on their own holdings?—They are employed during March, April, and May, we will say; then the women and younger people, and old people keep the holdings going for the rest of the time.

3381. So out of the twelve months the able-bodied man is only employed three months on his own holding?—That is about right.

Mode of ascertaining the budgets.

3382. (*Lord Welby.*) Were these budgets made for any particular year; what year would they apply to?—They were made in the years 1891 and 1892.

3383. Will you tell us how you arrived at the information, for instance, as to groceries. One lb. a week, which seems to be the average for tea—is a very large consumption, is it not?—Yes, it is very large, but the shopkeepers have shown me their books over and over again, and therefore I can say that the information is positively correct.

3384. Then getting it in that way through the shopkeepers, you had a check on the information—you did not get it from the people themselves?—Oh, no; I got it from a great many different sources, and checked it.

3385. Also if you got the information from the shops, you got the real prices?—Yes.

3386. I ask the question with the view of knowing whether you got it from the persons who paid or the shopkeepers?—I got the prices from the shops, but in a great many districts it is a case of barter.

3387. In that case how would you arrive at the price?—They barter on a money basis; they say, "The market price of eggs is 7*d.* a dozen, and we will "allow you at the rate of 6*d.* a dozen, and you pay us "for tea at the rate of 2*s.* 6*d.* per lb."

3388. I observe a difference in the budgets; for instance, there are one or two with no clerical charges?—I think that is simply an omission on the part of the official who made the budget.

3389. Therefore we come to this conclusion, that there has been no cooking of the accounts. You have taken the statements as they are made, and that is a complete budget of expenditure, according to what they told you?—Yes. Budget No. 6 is one which I made myself in very careful detail.

3390. And do you refer to that as one of the more complete ones?—Yes; it is one that I took a good deal of trouble over myself.

3391. I see in several cases there is an item for manures, which does not occur in others, and seeds?—Yes.

3392. Now I see a considerable amount of fish sold, and you told us that was a growing industry; may I ask whether that is due to the opening up of communication?—No; it is due to the fact that the Congested Districts Board have started curing stations. They buy all the cod and ling that are brought in, and as many herrings as they can, having regard to their plant, barrels, and salt at the different stations.

3393. With regard to light railways, I see from the map that you divide these congested districts into three—one in the north, one in the west, and one in the south?—Donegal forms one really, then I should say sea-coast Mayo and Galway form another, inland Mayo and Galway form a third, and Cork and Kerry a fourth.

3394. How do these light railways affect the congested districts—are there railways either completed or being pushed forward now into each of these districts?—There is a railway to Killybegs, which has been open for some time.

3395. Is that the only one in that district?—There is another to a place called Glenties which is not yet open; it will be very soon open, though.

3396. That will be two railroads in the northern district?—Two in Donegal only.

3397. And one has been open for some time?—Yes.

3398. Have you found any benefit from it?—Buyers go to the fairs, and therefore better prices are given for the cattle, and poultry can be sent off.

3399. Is there much fish trade?—Not much fresh fish traffic.

3400. The fishermen depend on the Board as the buyers?—Yes, for some classes of fish; salmon, plaice, whiting, lobsters, and so on goes, undoubtedly, by railway in a great many cases, but some places are too far from the railway. When a place is ten miles from a railway fish does not go as a rule.

3401. Therefore the value derived from the opening up of these communications, great as it is, one must take with the limit that unless the seller is near the railway it is not of much use to him?—Yes; a little further extension of the railway is what is necessary.

3402. Are there any railways in this western district?—Yes, there is a railway from Westport to Achill; that is opened to Mallaranny, and the receipts are very encouraging there indeed. Then you have a big railway from Galway to Clifden, which is not open yet. Then there is an inland railway, too, in process of construction in the co. Mayo.

3403. And in the south?—In the south there is one to Dingle, another to Cahirciveen.

Mr. W. L. Micks. 3 Dec. 1894.

Light Railways.

3404. Are these opened?—Yes.

3405. May I judge that your opinion is that they are answering the object for which they were constructed?—They are doing a great deal of good.

3406. And your view would be that they want further extension?—Certainly.

3407. But even if they were extended, I still gather that it would only be a limited area to which that would be of use?—The extension of railway from Killybegs to Glencolumbkille, which is only ten miles, would mean a fishing trade for the line, and we would not have to cure fish there. A great deal would go fresh to market, and at a better price.

Poor Law Relief.

3408. Do you think in the case of these budgets which are not in equilibrium there is any out-door relief given?—No, the out-door relief is given chiefly to old people, very often old maids.

3409. And these people having holdings would not be eligible, would they?—No, except in cases of sickness, but very little out-door relief is given; in Donegal hardly any.

Rents.

3410. Some of these rents are high. You were describing one just now of very nearly £1 an acre?—I should not like to give positive evidence about that.

3411. We have heard your opinion about it; I want to ask you if have they been into court yet?—Yes, I am sure they have.

Migratory labour.

3412. With regard to migratory labour, is it pretty stationary—year by year do an equal number of men go, or has it declined?—It is an equal number. Great numbers of the men go to the same farms in England or Scotland from year to year—they wait until they get a letter asking them to go.

Congested and non-congested districts.

3413. I know you have large experience in Ireland as to the congested districts; these budgets you take as simply typical of the very bad districts, but you would not generalise from them as to the condition of non-congested districts, would you?—There are very much poorer budgets I am sure for the labouring population in Limerick, Tipperary, and North Cork.

3414. In districts which are not congested?—Yes, the richest districts in Ireland, and the budget there would be very much worse for the labourers.

3415. But not for the farmers?—No.

3416. Would your view be—supposing anything was done to the west of the congested districts line that it ought to be done through your Board, or how; that is to say, would you recommend a considerable extension of your powers?—I do not know what would be the view of the Board upon that.

Condition of labourers.

3417. (*Mr. Sexton.*) I think you have said that the ordinary budget of a labourer in Ireland would be still worse than these budgets?—I am excluding that very last budget, budget No. 12; but I say that the ordinary labourer in a very large part of Cork, Limerick, North Kerry, Clare, and Tipperary is in shocking poverty, owing to want of permanent employment. I have seen the most abject poverty among these people.

3418. Then there are a great number of labourers worse off than a good many people described in these budgets, are there?—I think the agricultural labourers of that part of Ireland are a great deal worse off than the congested districts people.

3419. As to a congested district, there are two conditions which must happen in order to form a district, I understand; the first being that the valuation per head in the electoral division must be less than 30s.?—Yes.

3420. And, moreover, although that may be the case, it would not be a congested district unless the population made up twenty per cent. of the county?—Yes.

3421. Therefore for two reasons the area of your congested districts may be far from indicating the local area of congestion?—It does not indicate the congestion at all in some parts, because in Mayo and Galway, for instance, the greatest poverty possible among small occupiers of land exists in non-congested districts, and the reason these districts are not congested under the Act is that there is very good land held by large farmers and graziers in the districts; and taking the valuation as a test the district is not scheduled as congested.

Mr. W. L. Micks. 3 Dec. 1894.

3422. But it is probable, is it not, that there are many electoral divisions in Ireland, the valuation of which is less than 30s. a head of the inhabitants, but because they do not contain 20 per cent. of such, they are shut out?—Just so. Clare is not a congested country, but there is a great deal of poverty in it.

3423. On the other hand, a county may contain a great number of persons valued below 30s., but because they are not grouped together there is no congestion?—Because there is rich land adjoining them; in a great number of cases poor villages are not scheduled as congested. If townland, instead of electoral division, were the area, a good deal of good could be done I think.

3424. The point which I wish to elicit, and which I think I have elicited from you, is that there is a large body of people in Ireland, who are pretty much in the same condition as these people, who by reason of not satisfying the two particulars of the conditions, are not regarded as being in a congested district?—Quite so.

3425. I see the average number of a family is rather nearer six than five?—Yes.

Income of the Board.

3426. There are 98,000 families, and 17,000 of them next to pauperism. What is the annual income of your Board?—41,250*l*.

3427. That is only at the rate of about 8s. for each of those families?—Yes, if you put it in that way.

3428. Very inadequate, I should think, to make much impression on the question?—Quite inadequate; it is worse than inadequate, because it is disappointing; people do not realise how small the income is, and the Board are expected to do a number of things they have not the means to do.

3429. You have power under your Act, with the concurrence of the Treasury, to use a portion of your capital, have you not?—There is that power.

3430. Have you used it?—We have not.

3431. Have you asked the concurrence of the Treasury?—No.

3432. The Board has not come to any conclusion upon that point?—They have not.

3433. Have they considered the point?—I have heard it mentioned.

3434. Because it seems worth consideration. You have a million and a half of capital, and if you could more rapidly produce a permanent effect, it would be desirable?—We might find ourselves without any capital if we did that.

Food and mode of life.

3435. It would depend on the amount you spent, would it not? You have not said yet what is the ordinary dietary of the inhabitants of these districts?—I can give the dietary for each district.

3436. I simply want the best idea you can give in a few words, without aiming at extreme precision in each case?—It varies at different times of the year. When potatoes are in season; potatoes are largely used, we will say from the middle of August to the middle of March is the potato season.

3437. At other times is the food meal?—Yes.

3438. What meal?—Indian meal.

3439. Never oatmeal?—Yes, a little, but nothing like as much.

3440. A little fish?—A little fish as a relish, but not as an article of food.

3441. They cannot afford to use it as food?—Very rarely. Then they use a little bacon fat; they call it "kitchen," as a rule.

3442. The fish would be herring, I suppose?—Or dried ling.

3443. Speaking of drink, I have heard that most of the people are total abstainers in Donegal?—Yes, great numbers.

3444. So that they would not drink either on market or fair days?—They would not.

3445. In any case, the drinking is very much con-

Mr. W. L. Micks. 3 Dec. 1894.

found, you say, to the market and fair days?—I never saw any sign of drinking or saw drink in the houses.

Food and mode of life.

3446. As a matter of fact I believe they do not keep drink in the houses at all, do they?—They do not so far as my observation goes.

3447. The drinking may be disproportionate on the market or fair days, but it does not exist at other times?—No; the reason it shows on market days, I think, is that some people rarely eat anything—they only drink to refresh themselves.

Work of the Board.

3448. I notice in Return No. 3 a great variety of industries in Donegal, and in a county like Leitrim nothing whatever. Donegal has five or six industries, some inland, some on coast, and others inland, and Leitrim nothing?—Yes.

3449. That seems to indicate the vast importance of organising small industries, does it not?—Yes.

3450. The Donegal people are naturally the people for this increase of industries, looking at the size of the items for knitting, embroidery, sewing, and so forth, which in many cases make the budget right?—Yes. The people of Donegal are a very distinctive people. Take the hand of a Donegal woman; it is quite different to the hand of others, it is quite refined from the constant use of the needle. If you put the needle into the hands of an ordinary woman in the southern districts of Ireland, I believe she would not be able to use it in the way most of the Donegal women do.

3451. Does not the extent to which they are made solvent by these home industries indicate to you the vast importance of endeavouring to organise these domestic industries elsewhere than in Donegal?—Yes, and efforts are being made in that direction; but the progress must be very slow.

3452. It would be important to proceed with it, would it not?—Yes.

3453. Women anywhere in Ireland can be taught to knit and sew and weave, I suppose?—The young girls could.

3454. I notice that amongst the various proposals made to you for expenditure, there is none for the provision of boats and gear?—We keep that going; we can meet all the fair demands we have out of the Sea and Coast Fishery Fund and out of the Irish Reproductive Loan Fund, and no reasonable application is refused.

3455. Do I understand all the propositions on this list received the assent of the Board?—No, these are proposals which have been made to the Board by their inspectors and others.

3456. Have the inspectors approved of most of them?—Some roads, of course, are not approved of.

3457. Have you made an estimate of the cost of carrying out all these proposals?—I have tried, but it is apparent it would soon consume our income.

Mode of preparing budgets.

3458. As to the amount of the deficiency existing; of course a deficiency for a small sum may go on from year to year on credit?—Yes; but there are some places where the people sink down and get a load of debt round them—there is no doubt about that.

3459. The existence of a deficiency is in itself no ground for impugning the accuracy of a budget, is it?—No. I think in this case it rather goes in favour of the budget.

3460. It seems to me to show that the facts were ascertained without any particular attempt to square them?—Quite so.

3461. As to the rent—I believe it is very well known that when land, even bog land, has been laboriously reclaimed, a rent of 1l. an acre is not uncommon?—I would rather not speak on that question.

3462. However, these budgets were made up by people of competence and reliable people who did their best to ascertain the facts, I understand?—They were very carefully made up.

3463. The people who made them up saw the rent receipts?—They saw the rent receipts.

3464. And inquired at the shops?—Yes, they inquired among the people, and they were persons who were acquainted with the mode of living of the people; they were not strangers sent down to examine, but persons who had years of experience of the country.

Mr. W. L. Micks. 3 Dec. 1894.

Incidence of taxation on poor.

3465. May I ascertain from you in a few minutes the effect of the fiscal system of these budgets. Taking No. 1, I see there is a surplus of 11l. 1s. 4d., and the duty paid is—on tea, 15s.; on tobacco, 1l. 19s.; total, 2l. 15s.; is that correct?—Yes.

3466. That is 2l. 15s. duty out of a surplus of 11l. Then No. 2 budget shows a deficit of 1l. 3s. Taking groceries at 10s. and tea, 7s. 6d., say duty 1s. 3d.?—That is tea and sugar.

3467. Then tobacco, 1l. 6s.; duty, 18s. 6d.; total duty levied on that family, 1l. 0s. 9d.; the deficit on the account being 1l. 3s.?—Yes.

3468. Then No. 3 budget shows a deficit of 3l. 4s. 9d.; duty on tea, 16s. 6d.; tobacco sold, 2l. 7s. 6d., the duty being 1l. 15s., showing a total duty levied of 2l. 11s. 6d. on a deficit of 3l. 4s. 9d. Then No. 4 shows a deficit of 1l. 15s.; tea, 6l. 1s. 4d., duty on that, 1l.; tobacco, 3l., duty on that, 2l. 5s.; duty levied on that family, 3l. 5s.; showing a deficit on their account of 1l. 15s.?—Yes.

3469. Then No. 5 budget shows a surplus of 1l. 7s.; tea and sugar, 3l. (say tea 2l. 10s.), duty 8s.; tobacco, 1l. 10s.; duty, 1l. 2s. 6d.; duty levied on that family, 1l. 10s. 6d.?—Yes.

3470. Then No. 6 shows a deficit of 8s. 6d.; groceries, 3l. 12s. 7d.; say tea, 3l.; duty levied on same, 10s.; tobacco, 2l. 12s.; duty thereon, 1l. 19s.; total duty levied on that family, 2l. 9s.?—Yes.

3471. No. 7, deficit, 7l. 0s. 11d.; tea, 5l. 4s.; duty on tea, 17s.; tobacco and snuff, 4l. 11s.; duty, 3l. 6s. 3d.; total duty levied on that family, 4l. 6s. 3d. Then No. 8, deficit, 1l. 4s.; tea, 5l. 4s.; duty, 17s.; tobacco, snuff, and whiskey, 6l. 11s.; duty thereon, 5l. 4s. 3d.; total duty levied on that family, 6l. 1s. 3d.?—Yes.

3472. No. 9, deficit, 1l. 0s. 7d.; tea, 5l. 4s.; duty on tea, 17s.; tobacco and snuff, 2l. 16s. 1d., duty, 2l.; total duty levied on that family, 2l. 17s. No. 10, deficit on the account, 5l. 7s.; tea, 5l. 17s.; duty, 19s. 6d.; tobacco and snuff, 9l. 6s.; duty, 2l. 12s.; total duty, 3l. 11s. 6d.?—Yes.

3473. No. 11, surplus, 2l. 18s.; groceries, 4l., of which tea would represent 3l., taking a most favourable view, would it not?—3l. 10s.

3474. Duty on tea, 10s.; miscellaneous expenditure, 3l. 7s. (of which tobacco would be, say, 1l. 6s.); duty, 15s.; total duty, 1l. 5s. Then No. 12 shows a deficit of 3l. 6s.; groceries 4l., of which tea would probably be 3l.?—Tea and tobacco say 3l., or say 1l. for tobacco and 2l. 10s. for tea.

3475. Duty on the tea, 8s. 4d.; duty on the tobacco, 15s.; total duty on that family, 1l. 3s. 4d. The total cash receipts of that family appear to be 8l. 3s.; and the expenditure, 11l. 9s., showing a deficit of 3l. 6s.?—Yes.

3476. Now I would ask you if you would be so good as to summarise from the fiscal point of view these twelve budgets in order to inform the Commission whether the results which I have myself obtained by summarising them are correct. I find there is a surplus on three of the budgets, that the surplus was 15l. 1s. 10d., and the duty paid by these three families was 5l. 0s. 6d. There was a deficiency on nine of the budgets of 2l. 19s. 6d., but they had to pay duty amounting to 25l. 14s. 3d., so that there would have been a surplus of 7l. 4s. 9d. but for the duty. But the most important fact I deduce is this, that the income per head of all the twelve families for the year, including the home produce as well as the cash they had to live upon, was 6l. 17s., and upon these people there was a duty of 31l. 14s. 9d. You have been an Inspector of the Local Government Board, and I believe you are aware that the cost of maintaining a pauper in an Irish workhouse is 8l. 13s. 4d. a year?—That is about the cost, I believe.

Mr. W. L. Micks, M.A.

6 Dec. 1895.

[illegible]

3477. About 2*l.* more than the average receipt of those people upon whom 32*l.* duty has been levied in the year?—Yes.

3478. (*Lord Welby.*) You would make a certain qualification to the answer to Mr. Sexton's question, would you not?—Mr. Sexton brings the deficit in that budget to an exact arithmetical comparison with the duty paid. I think we gathered from you that you would not tie yourself down to those deficits as being reliable?—As regards the deficits, yes; but as regards the amount of duty and the consumption of the articles it would be dangerous to say that the figure is a certain figure.

3479. And to say, bringing the whole figures together, that such and such was the money result relying on that deficit as if it were an ascertained fact, would be unreliable?—Quite so.

3480. (*Mr. Sexton.*) But that would not disturb the relation between the total receipts and the duty levied, would it?—That is what I mean.

3481. (*Sir David Barbour.*) There is very little put down as expenditure on spirits in these budgets?—Very little. There is a great deal of total abstinence in these districts. In some parishes, for instance, the whole parish are total abstainers.

3482. I suppose on the whole the expenditure is rather understated?—I think it would be fairer, as I have said, to add a trifle more for luxuries.

3483. Is there any illicit distillation in those districts?—There is none in Donegal; it has been completely put a stop to there. There is a little in Mayo, and there is a little in Galway.

3484. There was a good deal some years ago, was there not?—There was in the north part of Donegal; in the diocese of *Derry* there is a little still.

3485. I was thinking more of Mayo and Galway?—There is some still, but not what there was. It is carried on chiefly on the islands off the coast where the islanders can see the revenue boats coming, and set things right before they are visited.

3486. I recollect travelling there some years ago on a public conveyance, which pulled up at a house in order that the foreigners might see an illicit still; do you think there is less of that now?—Very much less.

3487. As regards tea and tobacco, I think the duty on tobacco is taken at three-fourths of the price?—Mr. Sexton took it at that; I have no means of knowing if that is correct.

3488. Do you know what the price of the tobacco is on the average?—About 3½*d.* an ounce.

3489. And the tea?—Half-a-crown a pound I think you can average it at.

3490. And the duty can be calculated from that, I suppose?—Yes.

3491. These people receive certain remittances from their friends abroad, do they not?—In some places they receive a steady amount, but in other places the people do not emigrate at all.

3492. I suppose it would be impossible to get the exact figures of those remittances?—Some of the men from Donegal go across to America for part of the year, and come back.

3493. But you could not get the exact figures of any remittances of that kind?—They can be got, of course, at the Post Office.

Light Railways.

3494. How were these railways promoted—not by your Board, were they?—No, before the Congested Districts Board was started, in 1890 or 1891.

3495. Do you know what assistance Government gives?—Yes. I was one of the Commissioners or Inspectors appointed to inquire into what should be done.

3496. Will you tell the Commission what assistance the Government gave?—They practically made the lines.

3497. Did they find the money?—Yes.

3498. Does Government bear the loss?—As a rule the Railway Company, of which these light railways are extensions, work them, and in some cases there is a local guarantee for working expenses which falls on the county.

Mr. W. L. Micks, M.A.

6 Dec. 1895.

Light Railways.

3499. Does the Government bear the interest on the expenditure?—As far as I know Government do not bear anything except the initial cost of the construction.

3500. They find the money, but do they charge interest on it?—No; it is a free grant. There are some railways in the South that were made under the old Act of 1883, but a large number of railways that were made in 1891 were made with free grants for which the Government charge nothing.

3501. I think you said that these railways did a great deal of good?—They do a great deal of good.

Condition of labourers.

3502. You also said that the condition of the labourers in some parts of Ireland was even worse than is shown by the budgets to which you have referred?—It is most wretched; I never saw greater poverty; there are plenty of men who cannot get employment at all; they simply hang round, while a child will be employed as a herd, and a girl to milk cows.

3503. What are the wages of a labourer there if a man gets employment?—There is practically little employment; they are called labourers, but now the farmer is driven rather tight and he and his family are out in the fields making hay and doing everything, where before he had labourers doing it.

3504. But these labourers cannot live permanently on a want of employment?—I have not been there for four years, but at that time they were very badly off.

3505. Had they been long out of employment?—Yes.

3506. How do they live?—A great many of them live on the quarter acre which they get from the Guardians. A great many of them have a house from the Guardians for which they pay from eightpence to a shilling per week, and the quarter acre is attached to them, but a man gets very little employment.

3507. But some men must get employment?—Yes.

3508. What would be the rate of wages when you left?—It depends; a great many men all the year round would not get more than, say six shillings or seven shillings per week in some parts, and their diet.

3509. Which would be equivalent to three or four shillings more, I suppose?—Yes; three or four shillings; that is very low.

3510. That brings it to nine or ten shillings a week?—But those would be men who had employment all the year round.

3511. Can you suggest any means of improving the condition of these men?—I should like to see them getting larger allotments, larger grants of land.

3512. In fact they would then cease to be labourers and have a small holding, would they not?—Yes.

3513. Can you not think of any other way?—No.

Work of the Board.

3514. As regards the amount of income which the Congested Board has at its disposal, you say that that only comes to 5*s.* a family per year, which of course is small?—It is very small.

3515. But you do not make grants of money to families?—No, and there are a large number of districts where a shilling has not been spent by the Board—whole districts.

3516. You use the money, as I understand, for the most pressing districts?—Yes.

3517. And in giving the people the means of improving rather their own condition than in making direct payments to them?—We do not make direct payments to them at all.

3518. You give them the means of improving their condition by their own exertions?—We buy stallions, bulls, rams, and so on for improving the breed of live stock.

3519. And you leave it to them to improve their condition by their own exertions?—Yes.

3520. Which is a much better plan than giving money, is it not?—Yes.

Mr. W. L. Micks. 8 Dec. 1894. Incomes of families on the poorest.

3521. Mr. Sexton calculated the duty these people pay, and which no doubt is high in proportion to their income; assuming that duty to be entirely remitted, do you think their condition would be satisfactory?—I think they would consider it a great improvement.

3522. But still their condition would not be from our point of view satisfactory, would it?—It would be so much better.

3523. But only so much better. If a family had, we will say, an income of 9*l.* 16*s.*, like family No. 2, and you improved their condition by 2*l.*, you think that would be a substantial improvement?—It would be a tremendous thing for those people, it would be equivalent to having their land rent free nearly.

3524. If a family got 9*l.* 16*s.* you think it would be immensely improved in condition by an addition of 2*l.* A family that has an income of 42*l.*, that is No. 1, must, therefore, be in extremely good circumstances already?—They are much better off; they are comfortably off people comparatively.

3525. And even people who have 27*l.* at present must be very well off?—Oh, no, they are poor.

3526. Then the people who obtained 11*l.* 16*s.* instead of 9*l.* 16*s.* would still be poor, would they not?—Yes.

3527. (*Mr. Martin.*) With reference to the answer to Sir David Barbour as to the light railways, I apprehend you refer only to the railways that were inaugurated by Mr. Balfour last year?—Yes.

3528. And you do not refer to the baronial guaranteed railways?—I do not refer to the railways made under the Act of 1883, I think it was, but even some of the railways made under Mr. Balfour's grant have baronial guarantees.

3529. But the bulk of the light railways I apprehend are baronial guaranteed railways, and are you right in assuming that the Government supplies all the money for those railways, or any portion of it even?—I am only speaking of the light railways which were made under the grant when Mr. Balfour was Chief Secretary here.

3530. But the great majority of the light railways that have recently been constructed in Ireland, I apprehend are made in the ordinary way, with the exception that the Government guarantee 2 per cent. after the baronies have paid their 2 per cent., and that the capital is found in the usual way?—The Glenties line and the Killybegs line were made free by the Government, also the Achill line. All these lines were made free; the Clifden line too.

3531. (*Mr. Wolff.*) I was going to ask a question about the recommendations for the congested districts; I see they are confined almost entirely to road making?—Yes.

3532. That employment can only be very temporary, I suppose?—Yes, I do not think much good comes from road-making.

3533. It is a sort of out-door relief?—I think it is.

3534. But at the end of a year or two there must be an end of it?—There must be an end of it.

3535. There is another thing put down here I see; you propose to build a factory?—Yes; but a great many of the roads are necessary; there are a great number of places where the people have to go two or three miles across mountain sides with their pigs and cattle in order to get to market.

3536. Do you consider when these roads are made you will permanently improve the district?—Distinctly; the people will get carts, will improve their land and bring lime to it, and so on.

Mr. W. L. Micks. 8 Dec. 1894. Work of the Board.

3537. And will be actually able to earn a larger income?—Certainly. For those particular districts where the road accommodation is fairly good, I quite agree with what you say as regards making roads for short cuts, and for such reasons, but when opening up a district it is of importance to make some roads.

3538. Is the Congested Board doing anything for the fisheries?—A great deal.

3539. Are you supplying nets?—We are supplying nets and lines and boats on loan. We do not give the cash; we pay the boat builder, the manufacturer of nets and lines, send the goods to the country, and hand them over to the fishermen in the presence of the coastguard officer, or other local official, so that we are thoroughly satisfied that the gear and boats reach the proper persons for whom they are intended.

3540. And you find no trouble about getting those things taken care of or returned, do you?—They become the property of the men and they pay us back the price of them.

3541. And they do pay?—Yes. There are cases where we have to proceed against people, but on the whole the repayments are very good.

3542. And on the whole do you think your Board could do a great deal more good if it had more means?—As far as the fishing is concerned we have enough, I think.

Condition of labourers.

3543. (*The O'Conor Don.*) In answer to Sir David Barbour, you stated that in certain parts of the south of Ireland the labourers were extremely badly off?—Yes.

3544. And that there was no permanent employment for them?—Very, very little.

3545. Do you mean to say that the Boards of Guardians build cottages for labourers where no permanent employment is obtainable?—I say that the people are living there for generations and have a certain amount of employment. As Local Government Inspector I have reported on a great number of cases myself, and the objection was often raised, but I always felt, as to the people who were there, that it would improve them to give them a house and land, and put them in a better condition.

3546. I thought it was always one of the conditions of building labourers' cottages that it should be shown that there was employment for the labourer there?—If you want to bring a fresh labourer into the district you would have to show a necessity for him, but if you found a labourer in the district, a man who was keeping himself alive with great difficulty by the labour of himself and of his family, I never thought it a valid objection that he was not making a comfortable subsistence.

3547. I only wanted to know the fact whether cottages were built for labourers in districts where no permanent labour was required?—Where there was not sufficient employment to give him a comfortable livelihood, certainly.

3548. But where there was not sufficient employment to support him, even in as good a state as these people in the distressed districts?—The labourers, in my opinion, there were much worse off.

The witness withdrew.

Mr. John Chaloner Smith called and examined.

Mr. J. Chaloner Smith.

1 Dec. 1894.

Relative taxable capacity of Ireland.

3549. (Chairman.) You are President of the Institution of Civil Engineers of Ireland, are you not?—Yes, until the close of this year.

3550. Have you given great attention to some fiscal and taxation questions connected with the relative taxation of Ireland and Great Britain, and do you base upon those calculations certain proposals in connection with railways?—Yes.

3551. I should like to ask you to put into a few words, for our information, the facts contained in your very interesting paper, and will lead the way to enable you to do so. First of all, you consider, did you not, that of the taxation of the United Kingdom, Ireland contributes, as collected, 11·7 hundredths, or, as presented, 9 hundredths?—Yes.

3552. You say that, according to the Report of the Select Committee of 1865, the contribution of Ireland to taxation was in 1822 as 8·7 to 91·3, and in 1864 as 9½ to 90½?—Yes.

3553. You say that taking the revenue from taxation as imposed in Great Britain and not upon Ireland for the five years ending 1817 at one hundred and one millions, makes an average for each of those years of twenty millions, and that for the year ending 31st March, 1864, it was very close upon four millions, taking the round figures only?—Yes.

3554. Therefore you say that during the period between 1817 and 1864 the amount of abatements from equal taxation made to Ireland was reduced by four-fifths?—Yes.

3555. And that this was brought about partly by a remission of the special taxation of Great Britain, and partly by additions to the special taxation of Ireland?—Yes.

3556. The income tax imposed upon Ireland in 1853 gave in 1864 a proportion of Irish to British income of about 8 to 92?—Yes. That had to be done in consequence of the difference of the valuation of land in Great Britain and Ireland, and the Committee decided that that was as nearly as possible the proportion.

3557. And your conclusion is that comparing this proportion with that of the actual taxation, which was nearly as 9½ to 90½, it would appear that in 1863-64, as judged by the criterion of the income tax, 1½ per cent. of the entire taxation of the United Kingdom was raised in Ireland, which should have been raised in Great Britain?—Yes.

3558. You repeat the figures that the proportion of Irish to British income, as given in the Treasury return of this year, would be as 4·7 to 95·3 per cent.?—Yes.

3559. And comparing that proportion with that of the actual taxation, as estimated to be contributed, which is as 9 to 91, you would conclude that Ireland is now paying 4·3 per cent. of the entire taxation of the United Kingdom, which, as judged by the criterion of the income tax, ought to be paid by Great Britain?—Yes, as judged by the criterion of the income tax.

3560. Do you say that this proportion of income tax in Ireland and Great Britain of 8 to 92, and of 4·7 to 95·3, as given in the 1863 account and in the 1894 account, shows that there has been a serious diminution between those dates in the relative taxable capacity of Ireland?—Yes.

3561. And that the diminution from 9½ out of 100, to 9 out of a 100 does not correspond with it?—Yes.

3562. Therefore, you say, that the circumstances contemplated in the Treaty of Union as to adjustment of taxation have arisen?—Yes.

3563. You say that there are numerous reasons against an increase of the present exemptions or abatements allowed to Ireland in taxation, and that the intention of the Treaty of Union can be carried out without reference to that, and you argue that the relative taxable capacity of Ireland should be augmented, and the more the plan for accomplishing that is of a reproductive character, the less would be the cost to the United Kingdom?—Yes.

3564. That summarises your argument, does it?—Yes.

Reports of Royal Commissions on Irish railways.

3565. Now I come to your proposals. You refer to the reports of three Royal Commissions during Her Majesty's reign in favour of the State providing cheap railway transport in Ireland?—Yes.

3566. Parliament has given some aid in the making of Irish railways, but the great bulk of their cost was defrayed by the investments of private persons; and railways in Ireland, as well as in Great Britain, having been constructed under the powers and conditions of their Acts of Parliament, are now carried by companies who work them on the ordinary commercial principles?—Yes.

3567. You say that in 1836 the first of those three Royal Commissions, with Mr. Under Secretary Drummond at its head, urged that every precaution should be taken, and every measure adopted, which would contribute, on the one hand, to the encouragement of the capitalist; and, on the other, to secure to the country the full and entire benefit which the railway system is capable of affording?—Yes.

3568. At that time large exemptions or abatements from equal taxes were being made to Ireland, and the Royal Commissioners based their advice on the grounds that the State would derive an enormous profit on the greatest contemplated outlay, through equalisation of taxation in the article of excise, which is not the case now. In 1868 you say that the second of these Royal Commissions recommended the purchase of the Irish railways by the State, and the reduction of the rates thereon to the Belgian standard; and anticipated that the increase of traffic caused by this reduction would, at the expiration of 11 years, pay all losses and interest on borrowed money, and leave a balance in favour of the Exchequer?—Yes.

3569. You say that the bearing on the case of the reports of the Royal Commission of 1836, and of the Select Committee of 1865, does not appear to have been considered?—I do not know whether it was as regarded the reference to the Commission, or whether it was that they were not considered.

3570. You refer to the proposals in Parliament as to the purchase of Irish railways in 1873 and also in 1874?—That is given in the report on Irish Public Works of 1888.

3571. You say that in 1884 you read a paper; will you tell us where?—I have the paper here—there are copies in the room—and there shall be a number placed on the table for the use of the Commission.

3572. It was read before your Institution of Civil Engineers, was it not?—Yes.

3573. You read that paper for the purpose of showing that the railway rates might be reduced to the public by the State taking upon itself the loss caused by the reduction, and that it was not necessary to incur the outlay required for the purchase of the railways, or for the State to take upon itself the obligations attaching to the companies?—Yes.

3574. That view, I believe, you hold very strongly?—Yes. I saw that the purchase of the railways was the great objection, and I wanted to see how it could be done without that.

3575. You notice that in 1888 the report of the third of the three Royal Commissions, to which you refer, did not advise the purchase of Irish railways by the State, but proposed a reduction of the rates to the public through a State guarantee, and that it does not seem to have been observed that a guarantee of gross receipts makes no allowance to the companies for working the increased traffic?—Yes, therefore I did not think that a gross guarantee would be fair.

3576. You refer to a Royal Commission presided over by the late Duke of Devonshire in 1867, which

Mr. J. Chaloner Smith. 4 Dec. 1894.

Reports of Royal Commissions on Irish Railways.

decided by a large majority that it was not expedient for the State to purchase the railways either in Great Britain or in Ireland, but that, as the railway companies had the best opportunities of judging whether rates could be reduced, they should be left to carry out such experiments at their own risk?—Yes.

3577. That was the recommendation of the last Commission's or Parliamentary Committee on that subject, was it not?—Yes, I think that is the last to which I allude, though there have been various Commissions since.

3578. I am taking the three Commissions together?—Yes. That of 1867 was not one of the class which recommended cheap railway transport in Ireland.

Railway Returns.

3579. Then you say that the Railway Returns of the Board of Trade for 1867 and 1893 show that the public in Great Britain have availed themselves of these facilities to a much greater proportionate extent than the public in Ireland; that between those dates the number of passengers carried increased in Great Britain by 230 per cent, and in Ireland by only 69 per cent. Then you compare the average fares for each passenger and say that they have been reduced in Great Britain from 12·6d. to 7·7d., and in Ireland from 15·7d. to 13·4d.?—Yes.

3580. Then you also say that the gross receipts from this great reduction have increased in Great Britain by 106 per cent., and in Ireland by 78 per cent.; and the net receipts have increased in Great Britain by 75 per cent., and in Ireland by 63 per cent.?—Yes.

Proposal as to reduction of railway rates in Ireland by State aid.

3581. Then you say that these statistics tend to confirm the income tax returns in affording proof of the decline in the relative taxable capacity of Ireland. But you think that they give grounds for a reasonable anticipation that a measure for reducing railway rates to a scale in conformity with the wants of the people of Ireland, would call forth her capabilities, arouse her latent industries, and check the decrease in her population, arising from an excess of emigration, which you think is chiefly caused by the want of profitable employment in Ireland, as compared with Great Britain?—Yes.

3582. And you say that if those experiments were made in Ireland and succeeded it might lead to results favourable to its consideration elsewhere?—Yes.

3583. Then you say that the amount of public money required would be very large, but not nearly so large as that already expended by private enterprise in the construction of railways in the three Kingdoms?—Yes.

3584. I have summarised, I think, your points, have I not?—Yes.

3585. Will you be good enough to give us also in a summary form as far as you can the exact recommendation which you would make to this Commission?—With regard to the railways?

3586. On the whole question. I have summarised the reasons—you need not go back upon them—now I should like you to summarise the recommendations you would make?—The object was, and is, that a cheap railway transport should be provided. In order to do that, the first project which was brought forward was, that the State should purchase the railways, lower the rates, and become the owners of the railways. That has for a precedent many cases on the continent and elsewhere. If that were done the State would not only have to pay the outlay on the railways but they would also have to bear the loss consequent on that reduction, and the project which I have embodied in my recommendation is that the State should bear the loss caused by the reduction, but that it should bear no other loss whatsoever. I think it most probable, from these railway returns and from the general progress of the country, that the loss caused by the reduction would be greatest at first, and would then by degrees diminish until it finally disappeared; that the railway companies then would have been helped over the stile, and that they could go on at the lower rates as they are doing now at the higher, without any assistance from the State.

Mr. J. Chaloner Smith. 4 Dec. 1894.

Proposal as to reduction of railway rates in Ireland by State aid.

3587. (*The O'Conor Don.*) You propose the State should aid the railway companies to lower the rates, do you?—That the State should bear the loss of the reduction.

3588. (*Chairman.*) Perhaps you will give seriatim the purport of the several recommendations you make?—The first recommendation I make is that the State should settle a schedule of rates, and I say that these should be entitled "the standard." The second would be that the return of all traffic for a certain defined past period, it may be three years or one year, or any term that is desired, should be calculated and summed out at the standard rates, and that the result of that calculation should be deducted from the gross receipts of the companies during that defined past period. That is a fixed sum. It has passed the companies and cannot be interfered with, and when the result of the calculation is deducted from that, the balance would be entitled "the maximum deficit." That deals with existing traffic. I then go on to future traffic receipts, and for each period of the same length as the defined past period, I propose to deduct the result of calculation, which can be done in divisions of proportionate parts of period and receipt. Then I propose that the balance left after that should be divided between the companies and the State. A portion should go to the companies in order to pay them for the cost of working the increase of traffic, and a portion should go to the State to be applied in reduction of the maximum deficit. The next recommendation is that the companies should not be permitted to vary their charges from the "standard" rates, or to reduce the number or the speed of their trains without the consent of the State, but that with the consent of the State they may do so. Then that the companies should give every information as to traffic in their possession or procurement, and that the accounts should be all duly audited, and when so audited, the State should pay to the companies the balance between the maximum deficit and their proportion of the increased traffic.

3589. Those are your several proposals, are they?—Those are my several proposals.

3590. Then you also are prepared to state what in your opinion would be the financial result of those, are you not?—That is an estimate as affecting Ireland which I make.

3591. Of course this is all as affecting Ireland?—Yes. Supposing the average reduction of rates made in Ireland were for passenger traffic, including its various branches, fifty per cent., and that the reductions made upon all classes of goods traffic, minerals, cattle, and so forth, was one-third, then the deficit arising from that, taking for the defined past period the year 1892, would be about £1,273,000, and supposing the thing carried out, the State would then have a right to deduct from that deficit whatever their proportion of increase of traffic might be.

3592. What, roughly, do you estimate that would be?—The conditions under which they would be are these: what it would cost to a railway in carrying traffic is not affected at all by the rates received; consequently if a railway receives a proportion of the gross traffic, the greater the reduction in the rates, the higher the proportion the company are entitled to receive; but on the other hand, railway companies have found that it is often very profitable to them to make large reductions in rates in order to secure additional traffic; in fact, that the proportion of working cost to gross receipts for additional traffic is less than that for existing traffic, and it occurred to me, supposing the reductions which I mention were something like those adopted, it would be near enough to the mark, as a trial for a short period, to allow to the companies 55 per cent. of the gross receipts of additional traffic for working, and to allow 45 per cent. of the gross receipts of that additional traffic to the State.

3593. Then according to the calculation that the

[illegible]

Proposal as to reduction of railway rates in Ireland by State aid.

total railway returns are approaching three millions and a quarter, and that that reduction of 30 per cent. was made, how much do you think the State would have to find—what would be, first of all, the increased traffic?—That is simply a matter of estimate. I really could not give that because it depends on so many circumstances.

3594. You have not formed any estimate, have you?—No; but I think in her present state, Ireland getting such an impetus as that would have the power of increasing wealth generally, and that the increase would be very considerable, very important, and very marked.

3595. The immediate loss to the State on such a plan would be about a million and a quarter, would it?—A million and a quarter on the first year is the maximum.

3596. Supposing the traffic doubled owing to from one-half of the rates and fares being taken off, what do you estimate the loss would be then?—Supposing it doubled at the standard rates, the receipts would be about two millions.

3597. Taking it that on the present traffic the loss would be a million and a quarter, what would it be if the traffic was doubled?—Taking, for round numbers, the present gross traffic at "standard" rates at two millions, if doubled the increase would be two millions also. Dividing this, for round numbers, equally between the companies and the State; that would then allow a million to the State for their proportion, which would reduce the maximum deficit to a quarter of a million in the case which you take.

3598. The maximum increased deficit, do you mean, or the maximum deficit?—The actual deficit; the State would only have to pay, in the case you put, one-quarter of a million.

3599. The State would have to pay, as things are, a million and a quarter, would it?—I do not think they would have to pay that, because I think the very first year it was tried there would be a large increase of traffic.

3600. But say a million and a quarter as a maximum?—Yes.

3601. Whereas when the rates were reduced and the thing was in working you anticipate a reduced deficit from a million and a quarter to something like a quarter of a million, is that so?—Certainly. In the case you gave me that the traffic would be doubled, I make out that what would have to be paid by the State would be only a quarter of a million.

3602. I put it if the traffic were doubled?—Precisely. None of us know what it may be; it is impossible to tell.

Irish taxation to be reduced.

3603. I understand then in a few words what you suggest is this: you say that Ireland at present is overtaxed to a certain amount?—Yes.

3604. And that instead of remitting any of the existing taxes you would propose that a remission should be given to the people of Ireland in the form of reduced fares for carrying themselves and their goods whenever they want?—Precisely so.

3605. And that that remission should be given out of the taxation which is now excessive?—Precisely so.

3606. Then you go on to show that although at the start this alteration in affairs might result in requiring the whole amount to be paid by the State, after a time it would be recouped by the increased traffic?—Yes, and I may fortify that by the opinion, if you will be good enough to read it, of the Royal Commission of 1868. They said they anticipated that the increase of traffic caused by the reduction, which in that case was to be to the Belgian standard—mine is a little more than the Belgian standard was at that time, but I do not know that it is more than the Belgian standard is now—at the expiration of eleven years would pay all the loans and interest on the borrowed money for the purchase of the railways.

3607. And this reduction of rates would be tantamount to a remission of taxation which would meet all the classes of the community?—Yes.

[illegible]

Income tax a test of national wealth.

3608. (*Sir David Barbour.*) Do you say that Lord Castlereagh expressed the opinion that the return from an income tax would be the best criterion from which to judge the proportion in which Great Britain and Ireland should contribute revenue?—Yes.

3609. Do you think that Lord Castlereagh was such an authority on matters of finance that we should accept his dictum without examination?—I do not presume to say any such thing, but it was he who carried the Treaty of Union, and it is valuable to have his ideas because it shows the grounds on which the Treaty of Union was carried.

3610. You would admit, would you not, that the real question at the present day is not what Lord Castlereagh said on the subject nearly a hundred years ago, but whether or not what he said was sound?—Precisely so, and applicable to the present time.

3611. The income tax evidently affords a perfect criterion of the income of the persons who pay it?—Yes.

3612. Do you think it affords any information as regards the incomes of the people who do not pay it?—Inferentially it might, but nothing to go upon.

3613. Nothing directly?—Oh, no, that should be ascertained.

3614. And even in the wealthiest country the number of people who pay income tax when the minimum limit is 160*l.* a year must be very small as compared with the number of people who do not pay it?—Quite so, as far as numbers go.

Proposed action of State.

3615. I understand you to recommend that State interference should be employed according to your scheme in order to secure a reduction of railway rates in Ireland—that is what you recommend, is it not?—I do not know that "interference" would be exactly the word.

3616. I will say State "action"?—Precisely, State action.

3617. And you have no doubt that such reduction in railway rates would be a great gain to this country?—Not the slightest doubt.

Construction of light railways.

3618. Do you also think it would be a great gain if the Government were to construct, or to promote the construction of, light railways in the more distressed portions of the country on such terms as would leave the question of rates in the hands of the State?—The light railways are all branches in the extreme parts of Ireland, and there is no doubt that facilities given by the State for constructing those are exceedingly valuable; but I think there is nothing that can be conceived that would more promote the traffic on those light railways than a reduction in the charges on the main lines of which these light railways are extensions.

3619. You would like in short to have both these schemes, would you?—Certainly.

3620. And if you could not get both you would like one, or as much as you could get?—I do not really see why there should not be both.

3621. You recommend both these schemes—think highly of them—but would be glad to get as much as you could?—I think they are both parts of Mr. Drummond's great plan.

3622. Which you approve of?—Indeed I do.

Irish expenditure.

3623. There have been various suggestions made for improving the conditions of Ireland either by remitting taxation or by expending public money; have you heard of any proposals for meeting the cost or the loss of revenue by effecting economies in existing State expenditure in Ireland?—That would be a subject quite beyond me.

3624. But you have not heard of any such proposal?—The effect of such a proposal would be this. At present the civil expenditure in Ireland is enormous as compared with expenditure either in England or Scotland, and it certainly does seem to me that economies might be made in it, but the result of

Mr. J. Chalmers Smith.

4 Dec. 1895.

Irish expenditure.

these economies would be that so much less money would be spent in Ireland.

3625. But still if the economies are in themselves expedient, the mere fact that less money would be spent in Ireland would not lead you to oppose them if they were just and proper economies?—That is a question entirely for Parliament.

3626. I will give you the official figures of the cost of the internal administration, excluding the cost of collection of taxes and post-office services, in Great Britain and Ireland, respectively, for the year 1892-93. I take these figures from a Memorandum by Sir Edward Hamilton. The cost for Great Britain is put at 12,240,000*l.*; that is the internal administration; and for Ireland at 4,192,000*l.*, which you will see is rather more than one-third?—Yes.

3627. I do not say that these figures prove that the Irish expenditure is unduly high, but considering the relative population and wealth of the two Islands, do you not think that those figures suggest the expediency of an inquiry into the matter?—I do.

3628. And I imagine you would be of opinion that the Parliament of the United Kingdom might be more willing to assist the people of Ireland in the matter of railways if we began by cutting off any expenditure in Ireland which could be shown to be excessive or unnecessary?—Yes; but perhaps you would allow me to remark this—The expenditure of Ireland is a portion of the expenditure of the United Kingdom; and the Treaty of Union and the Act of 1816 taken together prove that that expenditure is to be indiscriminate; that is to say, supposing so much was spent in Ireland, it is not to be charged to Ireland, it is to be charged to the United Kingdom; therefore the whole question is a matter for Parliament. They have absolute power to spend the revenue of the United Kingdom wherever they wish, and it is entirely in their discretion how much they will expend in Ireland.

3629. But I suppose Parliament might be more ready to agree to a scheme involving increased expenditure in Ireland if at the same time it could be shown that other expenditure which was not so necessary could be reduced in Ireland?—I should not like to take the liberty of giving any opinion upon that. I think it is entirely a question for the Parliament of the United Kingdom—the whole thing.

Income-tax as test of relative wealth.

3630. (*Mr. Sexton.*) Whatever may have been the ability of Lord Castlereagh as a financier, I believe there is very little doubt that Mr. Pitt was a financier of some note in that branch of science?—Yes.

3631. Mr. Pitt as Prime Minister had, no doubt, something to do with drawing the Act of Union?—Yes. My idea about it is, that the cause of the Treaty of Union was the permanent obligation laid upon England to present an unbroken front to her enemies.

3632. Mr Pitt, as Prime Minister would, no doubt, have dictated the draft of the Act?—Yes.

3633. You refer, I think, in your Memorandum to the Act of Union. I will read for you the language of Article 7. After providing that for twenty years there should be a fixed contribution, the Act goes on to say what should be done afterwards, and one of the alternatives to fix the revenue afterwards was this:—A comparison of the amount of income in each country, estimated from the produce for the same period of a general tax?—Yes.

3634. "If such shall have been imposed on the "same descriptions of income in both countries; and "that the Parliament of the United Kingdom shall "afterwards proceed in like manner to revise and fix "the said proportions according to the same rules or "any of them, at periods not more distant than twenty "years, nor less than seven years from each other; "unless, previous to any such period, the Parliament "of the United Kingdom shall have declared that the "expenditure of the United Kingdom shall be de"frayed indiscriminately, by equal taxes imposed on "the like articles in both countries." That was one of the modes of discovering the capacities of the two countries?—Yes.

Mr. J. C. Smith.

4 Dec 1895.

Income-tax the test of relative wealth.

3635. Then Pitt himself in a speech delivered in the Imperial Parliament, in moving the clause, said:— "And even after that limited period the whole con"tribution from time to time might be made to de"pend on the comparative produce in each kingdom "of such general taxes as might be thought to afford "the best criterion . . . . . of their respective "wealth." And in the Act itself he denoted the income-tax?—Yes.

3636. So that that no doubt is the evidence upon which you, in your Memorandum, felt at liberty to say that the income-tax was the tax selected by the framers of the Act of Union as the best criterion of relative capacity?—Yes.

3637. Lord Castlereagh as a financier, no doubt, must take a modest place as compared with Pitt, but in the Irish Parliament he acted for the Government and for the experts who advised the Government, and he said in explaining the Message from the Lord Lieutenant on the 5th of February, 1800, that "he "conceived the best possible criterion would be the "produce of an income-tax levied on the same descrip"tion of incomes in each country, and equally well "levied in both. In the absence, however, of that tax "in Ireland, resort had to be made . . . . to some "other test." So that it was only in the absence of an income-tax that the Government of that day failed to lay it down as the mode of fixing the incomes?—Quite so.

3638. I think you lay it down as a principle that the taxable capacity of Ireland, as ascertained from time to time, ought to be the measure of her contribution of taxation?—Certainly.

Act of Union, its provisions of Article 7.

3639. Do you rely upon those words in the Act of Union—that the contributions as fixed by the Union were to be altered when it should appear to the Parliament of the United Kingdom "that the respective "circumstances of the two countries will thenceforth "admit of their contributing indiscriminately, by "equal taxes imposed on the same articles in each to "the future expenditure of the United Kingdom, it "shall be competent to the Parliament of the United "Kingdom to declare that all future expenses thence"forth to be incurred, together with the interest and "charges of all joint debts contracted previous to such "Declaration, shall be so defrayed indiscriminately by "equal taxes imposed on the same articles in each "country"?—I think I may observe that I could not well understand the Treaty of Union there until I had read the Act of 1816, and the Act of 1816 made the thing very clear to me indeed. It puts the entire financial question as to the Treaty of Union into the smallest possible compass. The Treaty of Union, and it together decide that the taxation of the United Kingdom shall be discriminate, because it allows exemptions or abatements to Ireland. It also enacts that the expenditure of the United Kingdom should be indiscriminate, and under those circumstances the whole financial question seems to have resolved itself into this—whether or not the taxation paid by Ireland was such as circumstances appeared to demand, and that appears to me to be precisely tantamount to what you have observed, that the taxation should be in proportion to the taxable capacity.

3640. There were further words in Article 7 of the Act of Union which I think form the foundation of your argument, that after the fixed contribution had been given up, and after the indiscriminate taxation had been decreed, it still remained the duty of the Imperial Parliament?—I think the taxation was discriminate. I draw the distinction between taxation and expenditure.

3641. I am speaking now of the provision of the Act of Union. The Act provided that after the fixed contributions had been given up, and after what was called indiscriminate taxation had been introduced?—Of course the taxation would be indiscriminate if there were no exemptions or abatements.

3642. I understand, but allow me to come to the point of these words. After this taxation, whether you call it discriminate or not, had been introduced, the Act of Union instructed the Imperial Parliament "thenceforth from time to time, as circumstances may "require, to impose and apply such taxes accordingly, "subject only to such particular exemptions or abate-"ments in Ireland, and in that part of Great Britain "called Scotland, as circumstances may appear from "time to time to demand." Now you say under that it is the duty of the Imperial Parliament from time to time, and without limit of time, to consider whether the circumstances of the time do demand a revision of these exemptions and abatements?—Precisely.

3643. And an allowance to Ireland?—Precisely.

3644. Without going into percentages at all, your general argument is that the yield of the income tax of Ireland as compared with the income tax of Great Britain, the test devised by Mr. Pitt, by Lord Castlereagh, and the Act of Union, is between four and five per cent. to 100 of the whole?—Yes, at the present moment.

3645. I may venture to suggest to you that the test of an income tax is certainly not favourable to Ireland as against England, because, as you know, a great proportion of the rent of the country and the interest on mortgages on Irish land held in England is taken out of Ireland every year?—Yes, but I am not so familiar with those matters as you are.

3646. Still I think it is obvious, is it not, when you ask the test of an income tax, you do not ask anything unduly favourable to Ireland?—I think not.

3647. The yield of an income tax being four or five per cent., you say the contribution of Ireland to revenue approximates to double that?—Yes.

3648. And instead of lowering the taxes, which might produce fiscal embarrassment, you would prefer that the overplus exacted by way of revenue should be turned to useful purposes in Ireland?—Yes, so as to increase the taxable capacity of Ireland, and in that way I think the intention of the Treaty of Union would be carried out. I do not know whether you have observed the intention of the Treaty of Union—it was conveyed in a message from the Sovereign, and is cited in the Act of the Irish Parliament which passed the Union. The intention is stated to be to promote and secure the essential interests of Great Britain and Ireland.

3649. Do you think, if the amount now taken in excess from Ireland, or a part of it, were returned in some such mode as this, that the effect would be to increase the taxable capacity of Ireland, so as eventually to render the taxation more just?—Yes.

3650. And amongst the uses which you consider desirable, the one which has the leading place in your mind would be that the State should, within certain limits, indemnify Irish railway companies against loss in respect of a reduction of rates and fares?—Precisely.

3651. And you think that the present rates, especially on goods, do act as an impediment to trade and prosperity in Ireland?—Certainly.

3652. (*Sir David Barbour.*) The Parliament of 1800 settled that Ireland was to contribute in the proportion of 2 to 15, did it not?—For twenty years.

3653. That was the proposal made by the Government at that date?—It was the proposal carried in Parliament.

Mr. J. Joseph Smith.

4 Dec. 1894.

Relative taxation.

3654. Which was seriously attacked at the time?—It was.

3655. I do not know whether you hold that the proportion was in point of fact excessive?—It is a curious thing, but I saw during the present week, in a pamphlet, a statement that a proportion of 1 to 7½ might have been perfectly just in the year 1800, but immediately afterwards it ceased to be so in consequence of Ireland not improving.

Proposed reduction of railway rates.

3656. (*Mr. Wolff.*) I do not wish to enter into those matters with regard to the Union; but as to putting the railways into the hands of the Government, and making, in fact, as it were one large company of it, I understand you have calculated certain deficits that would have to be paid by the Government if the fares were reduced as you have suggested?—Yes; that is, a deficit on all the railways together.

3657. It would be a million and a quarter, and might come only to a quarter of a million. Have you made any allowance for the enormous saving there would be by having one management over all these railways instead of separate managements for the whole of them?—That, to my mind, is a question absolutely for the railway proprietors themselves. Unless the State purchase the railways, the State cannot amalgamate them. There is no compulsory mode of doing it without taking very extreme measures; but it may safely be left to the proprietors of the railways themselves to amalgamate amongst each other.

3658. But I understand that your proposal is that the State should take the railways?—No.

3659. That is it merely to compel the reduction?—No; that it should simply bear the loss of the reduction. My proposal is not what you suggest exactly.

3660. Then, at all events, you would be giving up a great source of saving, would you not? If the State were to take the whole of the railways and manage them, you would not be able to carry out the scheme you suggest?—It is open to the State to take them if they thought proper to do so.

3661. Would not that be a much more economic plan?—No; I do not think it would. It was computed during the Commission of 1868 that there would be a saving of working expenses and that there would be a saving of debenture interest, which together came to 122,000*l.* a year; but since that time the entire of the mortgage debt has been turned into permanent debenture stock, and cannot be interfered with. That knocks 68,000*l.* a year off the 120,000*l.* Then there have been a great number of railway amalgamations made. The Great Northern Railway here has absorbed some five or six different companies; and if that is allowed to go on, it would reduce the number of companies to a very small proportion; in fact, the English managers, when they came over here, generally recommend that the number of companies should be reduced by amalgamation amongst themselves to three leading companies.

The witness withdrew.

Adjourned to Monday next, at 11 o'clock.

NINTH DAY.

Monday, 10th December, 1894.

At the Benchers' Chambers, Four Courts, Dublin.

PRESENT:

THE RIGHT HON. HUGH C. E. CHILDERS, *Chairman*.

LORD WELBY.	CHARLES E. MARTIN, Esq.
THE RIGHT HON. THE O'CONOR DON.	THOMAS SEXTON, Esq., M.P.
SIR DAVID BARBOUR, K.C.S.I.	GUSTAV W. WOLFF, Esq., M.P.

Mr. B. H. HOLLAND, *Secretary*.

DR. T. W. GRIMSHAW, recalled.

Dr. T. W. Grimshaw. 10 Dec. 1894.

3662. (*The O'Conor Don.*) Taking first the question of population, you told us on the last occasion you were examined, that the returns show that the population of Ireland has steadily decreased since 1851?—Yes, with the exception of one year, when there was an estimated increase. I think I mentioned it before—it was in the year ending with the middle of 1877; it is to the middle of each year that we estimate the population.

3663. That was a very trifling increase, was it not?—It was a very small increase.

Emigration.

3664. But, still there was a large amount of emigration in that year, although it had diminished from the previous year?—There was a diminution of emigration in that year.

3665. But that quite coincides with the question I asked you, that there has been a decrease in the population every year, owing to emigration, does it not?—In that particular year the estimate is that there was not a decrease.

3666. I thought that the proportionate amount of emigration in that year was less than in other years?—Yes; it was so much less as to fall below the natural increase of the population. Would you like the particulars?

3667. No, I do not think it affects the question very much?—It was in 1877.

3668. Was the emigration in that year less than the natural increase of the population?—It was.

3669. You stated also the causes of this emigration, and I think you set it down to three causes?—I think we came to the conclusion that there were three causes.

3670. Will you just repeat them again?—The failure of the potato crop, the want of means of living at home, in fact the want of sufficient manufactures within the country to enable the people to get employment, and the attraction of higher wages and better times, mainly in the United States.

3671. Do you not think that the latter reason will operate to bring about emigration no matter what may be the condition of Ireland, namely: the attraction to America, and the fact that almost every family now has relatives in the States?—Certainly. The attractions of America are acting on every country in Europe; it is not peculiar to Ireland.

3672. Has not almost every family now in the country parts of Ireland, relatives and friends in the United States?—I could not say almost every family, but I think it is very probable.

3673. Then might not we count upon it as almost a certainty, that there will continue to be a large amount of emigration every year as a regular settled incident of the year?—I think the chances are that it will go on, but, in diminishing quantity, because as the population here is thinned, wages rise, and there is not the same attraction to go elsewhere. It is quite impossible, I think, to make a forecast of that sort.

Loss caused by emigration.

3674. Assuming that the emigration continued at anything like the present rate, I would like to ask you a few questions as to its consequences. First of all, I suppose every emigrant who leaves this country takes out of it a certain amount of value. The emigration of every emigrant costs the country a certain amount per head, does it not?—I do not understand the point. Do you mean that the person who emigrates is worth so much capital or value to the country?

3675. No, I am taking the actual cost of removing to the United States?—Yes, it costs somebody some money. Formerly the money was very commonly sent over by friends in America, but I believe there is not quite so much of that as there was, but that I have no certain knowledge of. It is commonly reported that the people do not get quite so much assistance to go across as they formerly did.

3676. Irrespective of any assistance they may get from America, may we not take it as almost certain that they themselves spend a considerable sum consequent upon their going to the States, which sum would not be spent if they remained at home?—Certainly, it costs them something, but I doubt whether it can be called a considerable sum.

3677. Would it be too much to estimate it at £5 a head?—I should say not.

3678. I find by your tables that the average emigration of late years has been about 80,000. The emigration for the ten years ending 1889 was 80,000?—Yes; but I have here an average for the last five years, and it is only 51,169; there has been a considerable decrease.

3679. If we calculate the number of emigrants at the figure of 80,000 there would be an annual loss to Ireland of half a million sterling, and at the figure you give of 50,000 something over a quarter of a million, would there not?—Of course there would be that money spent, but the question of loss is another thing.

3680. If it be spent in paying the passage of these people to America, is it not a general loss to the country?—It is so much money spent out of the country, of course.

Dr. T. W. Grimshaw.

22 Dec. 1884.

Returns of emigration.

3681. And if it continues it is an annual drain on the resources of the country?—It does not follow that it is a loss, because a man whose labour is not turned to the best advantage in the country is a loss while he is in it. Any man who cannot earn his living is a loss or a cost to the community. I should not like to be taken as saying that because a person spends so much money in emigrating, the money he has spent on that emigration is a loss, because if he is a man who cannot get adequate means of supporting himself in this country he is a loss to the community as long as he stays here.

3682. That is to say if those people remained at home there would be a greater loss to the country?—There might be. I do not mean to say there is. If the people remained in the country and were employed there would be a gain, because they would be earning money, that is if they were employed at adequate remuneration, but if they are not able to maintain themselves, and if they have to obtain assistance from others or are unable to pay their debts, and so on, they are a loss to the community.

3683. You must not understand me as endeavouring to make you state that it would be a gain to the country that emigration should cease. I only want to point out to you the fact that this money spent in removing the people from this country to America proves that a certain amount of the income of the country is taken out of it in removing them?—That is a fact of course, but I do not want to be taken as stating that that is necessarily a loss of money. Of course it is an expenditure of money; there is no doubt about that, I quite admit that.

3684. Have you any record to show whether any large number of those who have gone to America return to Ireland?—We have no record of it, but there is no doubt that some of them do.

3685. Is not that very much increasing?—I do not know; I have no knowledge of that; that might be ascertained by future Census returns. For instance, if we find a number of American citizens in Ireland who had been born in Ireland; but there is nothing in the returns at present to confirm that view, though it may be perfectly true.

3686. I am not talking now of persons returning to live permanently in Ireland, but has not the communication between Ireland and the United States become so very easy that considerable numbers who have gone to America come over again and spend some months in visiting their friends?—Oh! yes, that goes on all over the world.

3687. How are those persons registered when they return to America; are they put down as emigrants?—That depends upon circumstances.

3688. Do you know how the emigration statistics are taken on this side?—They are taken at every port by an enumerator appointed for the purpose.

3689. (*Chairman*). When people have emigrated and come back and re-emigrated, do they appear as emigrants; do they appear as persons re-emigrating?—If they are persons merely departing from the shores of the country they do not appear as emigrants at all.

3690. Are they counted when they go back as emigrants?—Certainly not, unless they state they are; if they state that they are leaving Ireland permanently they would be put down as emigrants.

3691. (*The O'Conor Don*). Supposing they say they are leaving permanently?—Then, they may not have been emigrants before. The number of such cases would be insignificant, because any one of us may say we are going to America permanently, but when we got there we might find it desirable to come back. Of course persons may emigrate three or four times in their lives, and some do.

3692. Then these cases might be repeated as units?—It is quite possible, but that must be an insignificant thing. It is one of the errors that statistics are liable to. The same may apply to the Board of Trade returns for England and Scotland; it is a thing which cannot be avoided.

3693. The question whether they are emigrants or not is taken from their own statements, is it?—They are asked whether they are leaving the country permanently, and a person who is leaving the country permanently is put down as an emigrant. That is the definition of an emigrant.

Agricultural statistics, mode of collection.

3694. Leaving the question of population, and coming to your agricultural statistics, I think you said that you thought they could be relied upon as far as quantities are concerned?—Certainly.

3695. As far as quantities are concerned are they not collected from the people themselves?—They are derived through questions addressed to the people themselves. The enumerator brings a form which he has in his hand, he asks the person so and so, and so and so, according to the information which is required.

3696. Have you every reason to believe that they are correctly collected?—I have.

3697. Do you take any steps to check the accounts given to the constabulary in any way?—They are compared with the previous years' accounts, and if there are discrepancies found, and it looks as if the variation is unnatural or unlikely, the matter is gone into further; queries are sent down, and the enumerator is required to account for the whole area of his district. He has got the area of his district on a map, and if he finds that he has not had sufficient area, or an area that is too large returned, he goes back over it all again and finds out who has put in too much acreage, or who has put in too little. Sometimes a man will say, "I have so many acres,"—it may be too much or too little, he may either consciously or unintentionally make a mistake, but that would not deceive the enumerator; he must account for every bit of his holding, and unless he planned to deceive the enumerator, which there can be no conceivable reason for doing, he could not do so, because the area of each farm is accounted for.

3698. Do the same enumerators go to the same districts every year?—I think they generally do. I do not choose the enumerators, the enumerators are chosen by the constabulary officers, who are superintendents of enumeration, according to what they believe to be their fitness.

3699. Are they paid anything?—No, they are paid any expenses that they incur, and if they have to perform duties which under the constabulary regulations would entitle them to extra pay, they are paid extra; for instance, if a man has to stay out all night, which is not an uncommon thing, he gets an allowance. If he has to walk more than a certain number of miles he gets an allowance. If he is away from his barracks more than a certain number of hours at one time he gets an allowance. It is, in fact, a subsistence allowance.

3700. Do these allowances, do you know, come to much?—I think it is something like 900*l.* a year.

3701. All over Ireland?—All over Ireland, but I could not tell you without looking into the estimates.

3702. Is that paid by your office or by the constabulary?—Formerly it was paid directly by my office, and all the accounts were checked in my department, but that was found to be inconvenient, and now an estimate is made by the constabulary authorities of how much the service is to cost, and that estimate is put down in my vote as a bulk sum. Then I pay over to the constabulary from the monies voted by Parliament for my department that amount or the amount it comes to; of course it might not exactly correspond with the estimate, but it would be dealt with in the usual way; if it is under, of course I surrender the money.

3703. What is the amount of the vote for your department?—About 16,000*l.* a year.

3704. Is this the only remuneration which the enumerators receive?—They get no remuneration beyond their ordinary pay strictly speaking; what we

are speaking of is merely a subsistence and expense allowance; that is what it comes to—it is an allowance, not a payment.

3705. (*Sir David Barbour.*) Is it the same allowance as they get when employed on other duty?—It is exactly the same. There are certain constabulary regulations laid down for certain services, such as having to be out all night, lodging, and so on, and these are allowed to them on the same principle exactly as if they are on agricultural statistics duty or Census duty. The Census work is done on exactly the same principle.

3706. (*Chairman.*) This branch of the service is not an unpopular one, is it?—No.

3707. There is no suggestion that it is underpaid, is there?—I do not suppose the Constabulary men think they get enough.

3708. For these particular services, I mean; I do not mean the pay of the constable as a whole, but is this service an unpopular one for the men to perform?—I think not; I should say not; in fact I have been given to understand that it is rather popular, because it takes them off their regular routine police duties, and they cease for the time being to be regular policemen.

3709. There is no suggestion that the enumeration is bad because the service is not sufficient to pay for it?—Certainly not.

3710. (*The O'Conor Don.*) How do you ascertain the yield of produce?—The yield of produce is ascertained by estimators in much the same way that it is done in England; that is, certain persons are selected for each district—the district selected is an electoral division—that is with the view of having these statistics in as convenient a form as possible for compilation. If an electoral division extends into two or more Constabulary districts an arrangement is made by the Inspectors as to the district in which it shall be taken, and in each electoral division the officer returns from inquiries among practical farmers what the average yield of the crops should be in that division. That return is applied to the acreage returned at the previous enumeration, and the result is the estimated yield of the crop.

3711. Is not this information also obtained through the Constabulary?—It is obtained through the Constabulary officers.

3712. It is not then the enumerators who ascertain this?—Yes; it is some of the enumerators who make the inquiries.

3713. And the information as to the yield, I suppose, is mainly obtained from agriculturalists—farmers in the district?—Yes, altogether from persons engaged in agriculture.

3714. Then, I suppose, they have no interest in exaggerating the amount of produce?—None whatever; there is no reason why anyone should falsify the returns, so far as I can see.

3715. If there is any reason for falsifying the returns, I suppose, it would be in the direction to make out that the produce was not up to the real amount that it was?—It might possibly be so.

3716. Do you think on the whole it gives you a fair, true, correct idea?—I do, as nearly as can be; of course nothing short of actually weighing and measuring everything on every farm could give an absolutely accurate return, but that is an impossibility. I can, if you like, put in the Regulations for guiding these men in collecting information. Here are the General Instructions for the men and the officers, and here is the Circular which is issued in the autumn in order to get the yield of the crops. Then I have the form which is sent out with it. In addition to that we send out a form for any notes that the officer may wish to make—as, for instance, why the crops are good or bad, and what has happened in their districts. We are sometimes told that the weather has been the cause; sometimes we are told that there have been ravages of insects, and so on.

3717. Turning to the tables which you gave in your evidence on the last occasion, I shall have occasion later on to call your attention to what I consider some errors in the mode of their compilation; but before doing so I wish to take them as they are, and to ask you some questions regarding them. The Table C in your paper as to the values of agricultural output shows that, comparing the period of 1851 to 1855 with the last period, 1889 to 1893, there was a loss in the value of crops of 23,900,000*l.*; and, again, in the value of cattle an increase of 15,000,000*l.*, leaving a net loss of 9,000,000*l.*?—Yes.

3718. Mr. Sexton asked you on Friday whether, with this loss of 9,000,000*l.* in the value of produce there had been only a reduction of a million and a half on rents. You, I presume, have nothing to say as to the question of the reduction of rents?—I think Mr. Sexton said a million and a quarter. That I take it is the reduction under the Land Acts; but I do not know that that represents the entire reduction of rents; there are heaps of reductions besides those under the Land Acts, and we do not know what they are of course. Reduction of rents.

3719. Do not your tables refer to the whole of the land of Ireland, both of small owners, large farmers who do not come under the Land Act, and peasant proprietors?—Everybody.

3720. And this reduction of rent which has been referred to, applies only to a small proportion of the whole area?—It is about eleven per cent. of the valuation; we do not know what the rent is. Of course, we can find out from the Land Commission returns what the rents of the holdings which were reduced amounted to, but there is no such thing as a return of the rental of Ireland.

3721. I do not want to ask you any question bearing upon the accuracy of the statement with regard to the reduction of rent. I will ask you to assume that it is true, and I merely want to draw your attention to its connection with these tables. Although there has been, according to the tables, at first sight an apparent reduction of 9,000,000*l.*, is it not true that the percentage of reduction between these periods was only 9 per cent., combining the crops and the live stock; you will see it stated on the top of page 4 of your printed statement?—I have no doubt that is quite correct.

3722. Leaving a net loss of practically 9,000,000*l.*, or 9·1 per cent.?—Yes.

3723. The reduction of the rents made by the Sub-Commissioners in that period was about twenty per cent., was it not, on an average all round?—Do you mean on the showing of the Land Commissioners' tables?

3724. Yes?—Yes, I think it was a little over twenty per cent.; I forget the amount, but I have a table which will show it.

3725. So that, taking these tables and assuming them to be correct, although there has been only a reduction of nine per cent. in the value of produce, we have reason to believe that the reduction made in rents was twenty per cent.?—Yes, of the rents as they were at the time of hearing, but I cannot say, except from general knowledge, what the exact reduction of rent has been, even by the Land Commissioners. I have in the judicial statistics for one year what it would be, but unless I made it up for the purpose I could not tell exactly what has happened. I know the generally received opinion is that it is slightly over twenty per cent.

3726. I wish you now to look at Table A. If you compare the first period in Table A, 1851-55, with the last period, 1889-93, and look at the item "Potatoes," you will see the enormous difference in price calculated upon the value of potatoes in the first period from the second. One is about 5*l.* a ton and the other not 3*l.*; is not that so?—Yes. Values of crops and live stock.

3727. Is not that price of 5*l.* a ton an abnormally high price for potatoes?—Yes, but that was believed to be a very good time. I believe it is a high price,

Dr. T. W. Grimshaw. 18 Dec. 1894. Values of crops and stock.

but those are the prices which I found in published authorities. You know I do not collect prices.

3728. I know that, but I only want to point out to you that the figure in the first period of 5l. a ton is, according to all the other periods, a very abnormally high price for that particular description of produce?—I presume it is, in fact, I know it is.

3729. Is not what I put quite clear as a matter of fact?—Yes, it is quite clear.

3730. Is it not usually considered a sign of a good year in Ireland when potatoes are cheap? Are not they usually consumed by the people?—They are largely consumed by the people.

3731. A great proportion of the potatoes are consumed by the people, are they not?—Yes.

3732. Would it, therefore, be of any very great advantage to them that they should be at a very high price?—Certainly not.

3733. And if we take the price of potatoes in the first period, and diminish it to the ordinary price of 3l. instead of 5l., would not that do away with the entire difference of 9,090,000l. of loss?—I have no doubt it would. I could not say exactly unless I calculated it out.

3734. I have calculated it out?—I have no doubt you are correct—I think it is highly probable. I would say, generally, that that is the conclusion to be arrived at.

3735. So that the entire amount of this 9,090,000l. representing apparent prosperity in the first period as compared with the last, is due to the very high prices at which you have taken potatoes in the first period as compared with the last one?—No doubt that is so.

3736. I also see that in your paper, if you look at page 1, you state that the prices during the first period were greatly influenced by the Crimean War. You say "In the first period there is a distinct "disturbing cause, which influenced prices during the "years 1854-55, namely, the high prices caused by the "Crimean War"?—That is believed to be the case.

3737. At all events, during that period the Crimean War took place?—Yes.

3738. And the prices rose?—Yes. It would not raise them over the whole period; there was no war between 1851 and 1853.

3739. But it raised them?—Probably during a short portion of the period.

3740. Would you say that that is scarcely a fair period to take, and that the second period of 1866-70 would be a fairer period to take for comparison?—I do not think so. I mentioned that as a disturbing cause, but I do not say it disturbed the thing so as to make it unfair. I do not think it is unfair, because the Crimean War only prevailed during a portion of that time, and in 1851 the times were bad. All farmers will tell you that the sixties were a particularly good time.

3741. The period from 1860 to 1870 was a very good time?—Yes, portions of it; they speak of the sixties being the very best time they ever had for farming for some time during fifty years or so.

3742. Then let us take the period of 1860 to 1870. I said at the beginning that I had to call attention to what I considered an error in the mode of compiling these tables, and I think I had better allude to it now. In these tables where you combine the annual value of the crops and the live stock, that is to say Tables A and B, you take the value of the live stock, do you not, as if it were an annual product instead of being to a certain extent composed of capital?—Are you alluding to Table B?

3743. Table A gives you the annual value of the crops?—The value.

3744. The value of the crops raised in that year?—Yes.

3745. Table B gives you the value of the live stock that existed in the country in that year?—Certainly.

3746. But is it quite fair to compare the value of the live stock with the value of the crops, inasmuch as the live stock to a certain extent is capital, and the crops we may regard as income, as the produce of the year?—Certainly not. I say so on the next page. In the paragraph near the middle of the next page I say: "It is not, however, quite fair to deal with crops "and stock collectively in this manner, as in the ordinary "course of business of the farmer, the crops (except "those portions reserved for seed), are for sale or con"sumption within the year, whereas the live stock are "only for partial sale or consumption each year, although "some of their products such as milk, butter, eggs, and "wool are for sale or consumption every year." This is only given for what it is worth. I should mention I think, that this is really a reprint of the paper I read before the Statistical Society, and it was a subject for discussion and was discussed by several very good agriculturalists who were there.

3747. I want to ascertain what it was worth and to make it as far as possible a table that can be compared. To make these tables accurate for the purpose of comparison, ought not we to reduce the value of stock to what we might estimate to be the proportion of its increase each year?—That is like the statement I put in the other day of the income derived. Of course, you would have to take each class of animal and as far as possible estimate how much of that class was sold each year. I think you said "increase," did you not?

3748. It may be an incorrect mode of expression to call it "increase"?—Of course, the increase would be in one sense the same thing, because that is what you have to sell afterwards. The increase of the stock in one year, would, of course, form a marketable produce for the next year or the year after, according to circumstances.

3749. Now, I want to take these tables of years for these particular periods and to turn them into what I would call more accurate tables for comparison by reducing the value of the stock to the proportions which you gave us the other day. I think the proportions were two-sevenths of the cattle, two-sevenths of the sheep, the entire pigs, about one-tenth of the horses and two-thirds of the poultry?—Yes.

3750. And you omitted altogether the asses and goats—they are not a very large item?—Practically they are not disposed of to any very great extent.

3751. But taking the goats, for instance, they are used like the potatoes, by the people, are they not?—They are.

3752. However, they do not amount to much and I do not want to complicate the account by arguing upon them. Now let us take the third table. In the period from 1851-55 taking the crops at the amount put down 53,337,000l., and stock 39,348,000l., two-sevenths of the cattle would come to 6,834,000l.?—Yes.

3753. Taking the crops at 53,337,000l., two-sevenths of the cattle would be 6,834,000l.; two-sevenths of the sheep 1,295,000l.; the whole of the pigs 1,449,000l.; one-tenth of the horses 338,000l., and two-thirds of the poultry 375,000l., making a total of 63,637,000l. for that period. These figures of mine may not be correct, but you can check them to see if they are incorrect. Have you followed me?—Yes; I think I know what you are upon, but I am not quite sure.

3754. I am reducing your Table B by the amounts that you yourself told us the other day you had adopted when you were making out the estimate of the income of the farmers of Ireland?—I suppose you understand I did not make that out at all; that was made out by various experts. I undertook to try and get the information for the Government of the day in the best form I could, but it is not a thing I would consider myself competent to deal with, nor have I any experts attached to my department except figure experts.

3755. But assuming that those proportions are right, what I wished to do was to reduce these Tables A and B in the same proportion so that they might fairly be compared together?—Yes.

3756. Perhaps if you will do that and put it in it might give us a fair idea?—You do not ask me to do it now?

Dr. T. W. Grimshaw.

29 Dec. 1893.

Values of crops and stock.

3757. No, I have it done here, perhaps incorrectly, and I make out that if those two Tables were reduced in the manner I mention, the result would be that there would be a decrease in the income and value between the first and second periods, that is to say, 1851–55 as compared with 1866–70, of 10·2 per cent.; between the same period and 1884–88 of 24·1 per cent., and between that period and 1889–93 of 32·6 per cent. Then comparing the second period, 1866–70, with the other two periods there would be a diminution in the first of 17·7 per cent., and in the second of 19·6 per cent. Then comparing the third period, 1884–88, with 1889–93 there would be a decrease of only 2·3 per cent. Those are the figures that my calculation works out to, and I should be glad if you would check them?—I have made an estimate somewhat of that sort on page 5.

3758. You have there made an estimate of the proportion of the product of crops and stocks sold or disposed of?—Yes, that is on the same lines, I think.

3759. (*Mr. Sexton.*) It is exactly, when you add the products of the stock?—Yes. Is not that so, O'Conor Don?

3760. (*The O'Conor Don.*) It is somewhat on the same lines, but I do not think it produces exactly the same figures as the deductions you gave us of two-sevenths, and so on?—I have not made a comparison exactly, but this statement here was based on a revision by a calculator of the chromograph paper which I have handed in headed "Income of Irish Agriculturists in the year 1885." I doubt if there is very much difference between what the O'Conor Don has said and that statement.

3761. (*Mr. Sexton.*) If you compare the figures in Table B and Table E, the stock sold varies from period to period. There appears to be no inflexible rule from period to period?—There would not be—it would depend on whether the proportion of cattle to sheep and sheep to pigs varies, and that would produce a variation. The ratio to the total would not be the same in each period because the relative number of live stock of different kinds must vary.

3762. (*Chairman.*) Are you familiar with the English agricultural statistics?—Yes.

3763. They bring out a very careful calculation, do they not, a combination of value and quantity?—Yes, they have that in an appendix.

3764. (*Sir David Barbour.*) Does your phrase "disposed of" include consumption by the producer?—Yes, it does. It does not necessarily mean "sold." It is sold or otherwise disposed of.

3765. (*Mr. Sexton.*) It means everything, does it; the whole value of the crops left after the cattle have been fed?—It does, practically.

3766. (*The O'Conor Don.*) Then Tables A and B as they stand, show, do they not, a reduction between the last two periods, 1884–88 and 1889–93, of a little over 2 per cent., if you combine the two together?—It is more than 2 per cent.; it is 2,624,000*l.* out of 91,879,000*l.*; it is nearer 3 than 2 per cent.

3767. It is between 2 and 3 per cent.?—It is between 2 and 3 per cent., but it is nearer 3 than 2.

3768. Then, if you will look at Table A alone, there the diminution in the value of crops between those two periods is a little over 3 per cent.; it is 3·1, is it not?—It shows a reduction from 35,600,000*l.* to 34,500,000*l.*

3769. That is slightly over 3 per cent.?—Yes, that is slightly over 3 per cent.

3770. If you will look at the different items in the period 1889–93, you will see that in wheat there is an increase in the value, is there not, as compared with the period of 1884–88?—There is an increase in the total, but a decrease in price.

3771. I am putting the total value?—Yes, because there was more wheat produced.

3772. In oats there is a very large increase, is there not?—Yes, there is an increase.

3773. Then in barley there is an increase?—Yes.

3774. The next two items are very unimportant; they are about the same?—Yes.

3775. Then, passing over potatoes, there is an increase in turnips, is there not?—Yes.

3776. Then there is an increase in mangel?—Yes.

3777. And a slight decrease in flax?—A decrease of about 10 per cent.

3778. The only two items that remain in the table are hay and potatoes?—Yes.

3779. And in those items there is a large decrease, is there not?—Yes.

3780. The total decrease between the period 1884–88 and the period 1889–93 is due to a decrease in the value of hay and potatoes, all other crops practically showing an increase—is not that so?—Yes, that is about it.

3781. Those two crops of hay and potatoes are crops that are usually consumed, are they not?—Yes, a great portion of them.

3782. They were not sold?—A good many potatoes were sold; the hay was practically nearly all consumed in the country, but nevertheless much of it was sold.

3783. An increase in the price of hay, therefore, is of no great consequence one way or the other to the farmer, is it, if the yield is good, if they consume it all themselves?—But they do not. The individual farmer who grows the cattle does not necessarily grow the hay his cattle eats. There is a great deal of hay bought and sold; in Dublin alone there is an immense market in hay, and a great quantity changes hands in Dublin.

3784. But, generally speaking, throughout the country do not the farmers consume their own hay, putting aside the large cities?—There is no doubt a great many of them do so, but nevertheless there is an immense quantity changes hands, and there is some exported.

3785. (*Chairman.*) Farmers may consume it, but not necessarily the same farmers, you say?—Not necessarily the same farmers.

3786. (*Sir David Barbour.*) If it passes from one farmer to the other, that does not affect the aggregate income of the farming class, does it?—No, it does not. But of course if hay is cheap and stock dear, the cattle farmer would get the best of it; whereas if the reverse was the case the man who owns the hay would get the best of it.

3787. (*The O'Conor Don.*) The produce of the hay in the last period, as compared with the last period but one, is considerably larger, is it not?—It is somewhat larger.

3788. So that the difference in value is due to the reduction in price and not to the reduction in yield?—Yes.

3789. With regard to potatoes, we have the rather curious anomaly, I might almost call it, of a reduction in yield and also a reduction in price; is not that so?—Yes, that is so.

3790. Does it not usually follow that when there is a large amount of produce there is a reduction in price?—Yes: but I fancy that there are more potatoes grown for sale than there used to be, in proportion to the quantity consumed.

3791. Would that result in a fall in price?—If you flood the market with any article it would reduce the price.

3792. (*Sir David Barbour.*) Do you mean that other food, such as grain, has taken the place of the potato amongst the farmers?—I should think so; there is more bread eaten now.

3793. So that there is not the same demand for potatoes?—I should think so; there are more potatoes put on the market, I think, than there used to be, but that is a mere opinion of mine.

3794. (*The O'Conor Don.*) But the amount of potatoes grown or produced appears to be rather less for the one period than the other, and yet the price is lower?—I would account for it in the way I have stated, and that is the only way I can account for it. Of course there was a decrease in the population.

Dr. T. W. Grimshaw.

29 Dec. 1893.

Values of crops and stock.

Dr. T. W. Grimshaw. 14 Dec. 1894. Values of crops and stock.

3795. Might not it be accounted for in this way, that this is an average of years, and that in one year there was a failure and in another year a high price?—Yes, there may have been bad and good years. I could find that out. I have tables here which would show the yield of potatoes in particular years if you would like me to refer to them.

3796. I do not want to trouble you about it. On the whole, if we take these tables to be correct, would not they show that the fall in agricultural values between 1854-58 and 1859-63, which was only 2·8 per cent., was almost entirely due to a fall in the prices of hay and potatoes, and a smaller yield in potatoes, and that all other crops increased in value?—Yes, that appears to be the result of your analysis of them.

3797. Do you think that these fluctuations in the values of crops have really much to do with the comparative capacity of Ireland with Great Britain with regard to taxation?—No, because the fluctuations are very much of the same nature in both countries. You may have a good year in Great Britain and a bad one in Ireland, and vice versa; but I should think, taking them altogether things come to pretty much the same all round.

3798. I think you stated that the period between 1860 and 1870, which you called the sixties, was a very good period?—Yes, it is generally spoken of by farmers as one of the best times; if you ask a big farmer he will say that the sixties were the best years in his time.

3799. The commencement of that period, I believe, was not very good, from 1860 to 1865, was it?—I was not appointed until the year 1879, and I cannot say of my own knowledge.

3800. Who was your predecessor?—My immediate predecessor was Dr. Burke, but he only held office for three years before he died.

3801. Who preceded him?—Mr. Donnelly.

3802.—Mr. Donnelly you are probably aware gave evidence before the Taxation Committee in 1864?—I believe he did.

3803. Of which, unfortunately, I am old enough to have been a member, and before that Committee he told us that the values of all crops and stock and everything in Ireland were diminishing. He stated that the decrease in the value of stock of all sorts between 1855 and 1864 nearly equalled three millions?—That was a bad time I suppose.

3804. We may take it that Mr. Donnelly was correct in the statistics he had before him, may we not?—I should think he ought to have been.

3805. He had the same figures that you have?—These figures which I have here are his figures so far as numbers go.

3806. I will read to you the summary of his opinion upon the state of things immediately preceding 1864. He said he considered that there was a general decrease in the agricultural produce of the country, and with the exception of barley there was a decrease in the market value of every item of agricultural produce; and he further stated that in his opinion the wealth of Ireland had diminished since 1859. This was the opinion of the Registrar General at that time arising out of the examination of these figures of produce and of prices, and yet that was about the middle of a period, which you say has since been regarded as the highest period of prosperity in Ireland?—No, I said the Sixties; I did not say that particular period, and I find that 1862 (and Mr. Donnelly's figures are before me) is an extremely bad year. The yield of potatoes in 1859 is put down at 4·4 tons per acre; and in 1862 it was only 2·1.

3807. As a matter of fact, those years immediately preceding the Committee of 1864 were bad years, were they not?—In 1861, if we take potatoes, it was a very bad year, the yield being only 1·6, the next year the yield was 2·1; 3·4, the rate for 1863, is about the average. The next is a good potato year, 4·1, which is above the average.

3808. But that is the statement of Mr. Donnelly, is it not?—Yes.

3809. And yet those years from 1860-64 form part of that decade, which afterwards became one of the best decades of modern times?—Yes, that is generally stated to be so.

3810. Would not you draw from that the inference that we cannot from a particular number of years come to the conclusion that the agricultural prospects of the country are altogether going to the bad?—I do not think that agriculture is altogether gone to the bad, but farming is depressed. But did I understand you to say that Mr. Donnelly was comparing the particular year of 1862 with the particular year of 1855?

3811. Mr. Donnelly compared first the actual increases and decreases between 1855 and 1863, and there he made a general statement that the wealth of the country in his opinion had diminished since 1851?—Of course, if it were measured by those two years it would be so, but I would not go by any single year in a matter of that sort. Of course in the tables attached to my paper you have everything done by five and ten year periods, and when the Commission is considering the question, they will have it all before them.

Comparative circumstances of poorer classes in Great Britain and Ireland.

3812. Irrespective of these questions of the fluctuations in the values of agricultural produce and live stock, do you not think that it is beyond dispute that the average wealth of the classes below the income tax limit is much lower in Ireland than in Great Britain?—Are you speaking of the agricultural class or of the whole class of the community?

3813. The whole class of the community.—Certainly the English people are better off because there are a large number of artisans earning high wages, and the average there would give a much higher figure, of course.

3814. First, comparing the agricultural classes of the two countries whose incomes are under the income tax limit, take labourers and small farmers in England and compare them with those in Ireland?—I do not think they are any better off in England than they are here. I doubt if they are; from what little I have seen of them they are very much depressed.

3815. Is not the agricultural rate of wages much higher in England than in Ireland?—It is higher, but in some parts of England it is very low. I could not tell you without looking into the reports of the Royal Commission on Agriculture, but it struck me in reading those reports that Irish labourers and small people are better off than I expected to find them in comparison. That was the impression I derived, and I read nearly all the reports.

3816. (*Sir David Barbour.*) The O'Conor Don asked you about the average income of the agriculturists under 160*l.* a year; that would include the small farmers and the labourers; would not the proportion of small farmers to labourers be different in England to what it is in Ireland?—Very different.

3817. The proportion of small farmers to labourers would be greater in Ireland than in England, would it not?—Yes.

3818. And that would rather tend to raise the Irish average as compared with the English average of small farmers and labourers, would it not?—It would. Of course Ireland is largely a country of small holdings, and on the small holdings there are practically no labourers; the work is done by the people themselves.

3819. (*The O'Conor Don.*) And consequently taking the whole of the population all round there would be a much larger proportion of what may be called a poorer class in Ireland than in England, would there not?—Do you mean of agricultural occupiers?

3820. I say taking the whole population all round, artisans and every one else having incomes under 160*l.* a year?—Sir David Barbour asked me only about agriculturists and agricultural labourers.

3821. But if there be a larger proportion of agricultural labourers and small farmers, as Ireland is

Dr. T. W. Grimshaw. 16 Nov. 1894.

mainly an agricultural country, do not you think it follows that there is a larger proportion of the whole population with incomes under 150*l*. in Ireland than in England?—I think I said so, because owing to the number of artisans in England who approach very closely, and sometimes go up to the income tax limit, you will have a much higher average of that class than you have here.

3522. And there is a much greater proportion of that class in Great Britain than in Ireland?—Certainly.

3523. (*Mr. Sexton.*) I suppose you know the income tax in Great Britain is one-sixth of the revenue and in Ireland only one-twelfth?—I do not know that as a fact. I have never looked at it in that way, but I should think it is so.

Income of Irish agriculturists.

3524. (*The O'Conor Don.*) I come now to another point, namely, the income of the Irish agriculturist?—I wish to repeat the caution that I am not personally responsible for these figures.

3525. The return was made in your office, was it not?—It was made by one of my clerks.

3526. Have you confidence in him?—Yes, he was a very clever statistician and a very careful man.

3527. Did he consult any external authorities with regard to it?—Some hundreds I believe, a very great number.

3528. Did he not endeavour to make it as accurate as he could?—He endeavoured to make the statement as accurate as he could. Of course the difficulty about consulting authorities on a matter of that sort is this, that when you are dealing with a matter of that kind in the Dublin office you are practically confined to Dublin people. You must take the Dublin market prices from the Dublin suppliers of agricultural implements, and so on. It is of course a very low standard.

3529. Although you did not make up this return yourself, are you in a position to be able to explain to the Commission the principles upon which it is compiled?—It is all stated in the paper. Shall I read the paper? I put it in on the last occasion. Is it to be taken as read?

3530. We may take it as read. The reason I asked the question was this: I thought if I were to ask you a question why these particular percentages were adopted you might answer that you did not know anything about it?—I had got good reasons for everything at the time. I think I mentioned that that was prepared in reply to a request of Sir Robert Hamilton who asked me if I could do that sort of thing; I told him I would see what could be done, and that is the result; but I have very little belief in speculative statistics. When you come to put opinions into figures they are very fallacious.

3531. (*Sir David Barbour.*) I suppose you would say that speculative statistics are not really statistics at all?—Practically so.

Values of produce taken from [illegible].

3532. (*The O'Conor Don.*) The prices of agricultural produce in this and in your returns I believe are taken from "Purdon's Almanack," are they not?—Yes, as far as possible.

3533. It is stated here that they are taken from "Thom's Directory," and I suppose "Thom's Directory" is taken from Purdon, so that it is precisely the same thing?—Those maintained standards over a great number of years of certain prices, whereas the prices varied, but that I think was all allowed for in those returns.

3534. Will you tell us how the average of these prices is ascertained in "Purdon's Almanack"?—I should like to read that from Purdon, if you please, because when I take a thing on some one else's authority I do not like to put it forward as my own. He says:—"The following tables show the range "of prices of agricultural produce in the Irish mar-"kets from 1851 to 1893, both years included. These "prices have been taken chiefly from the market "reports published in the 'Farmer's Gazette.' The "prices of grain are those of the Dublin market. The "prices of flax are taken from the reports of the "Belfast market. The prices of butter are taken from "the quotations of firsts, seconds, and thirds in Cork "butter market. The prices of beef, mutton, pork, "potatoes, wool, hay, and straw are Dublin prices. "The prices given of eggs are the wholesale prices "current during the summer months in the Dublin "market. The two prices given after each item of the "above are not the extreme quotations of the whole "year, but the mean of the highest and lowest "quotations for twelve months, or the season, as the "case may be. The prices of milch cows, two-year "old and one-year old cattle have been taken from "the reports of country fairs held during the months "of May and June in each year and published in the "'Farmer's Gazette.' The prices of lambs are those "current during May and June in the Dublin "market."

Dr. T. W. Grimshaw. 16 Nov. 1894.

Values of cattle and live stock.

Values and deductions of live stock.

3535. Then would it not appear that these prices are taken in the places where prices are likely to be the highest?—Yes, most of them; and in anything I have written on the subject I have always said that probably these prices as they are taken in the best markets are higher.

3536. Although for the purposes of comparison between one year and another, the same system having been adopted with regard to both, this may not have much effect, yet when you come to make up a table of the supposed income of the Irish farmer, is it not a matter of consequence to remember that the prices of produce are taken in the highest markets?—Certainly. I did not say in the highest market, because a number of the cattle prices are throughout the country—the highest market would naturally be Dublin. "In the best markets" are the words I used.

3537. Passing from the prices of the crops and going to the table of deductions of live stock, can you explain to the Commission the principle upon which these deductions of two-thirds, and so on, were made?—That is the amount sold off.

3538. Yet, the cattle for instance are taken at two-year-olds?—That was got through salesmasters and agriculturists.

3539. Do you base it on the authority of those people?—I base it on the authority of people who are believed to be experts.

3540. Not on any knowledge you yourself possess?—Quite so; we have never collected any information on the subject.

3541. The same with regard to the sheep?—Yes, with regard to the whole table.

3542. Would it not appear singular that the same deduction should be made with regard to sheep as cattle. Taking sheep as a whole, are not they disposed of and reproduced very much quicker than cattle?—I believe they are, but I understand that the persons who made these estimates had to make allowances for calves and lambs which vary in proportion as to their sale, and so on. I believe that is the explanation. I remember the question being asked at the time. The different proportions between the calves and lambs that were sold and the number that were allowed to grow up varies very materially. I do not know exactly what it is, but the explanation offered was something of that sort. I believe there was something of the same sort offered with regard to pigs.

3543. Then I suppose it would require an expert in your opinion to explain the reason of these particular things?—I do. I do not consider myself competent to explain the minutiae of that table; I am not any more competent to do it than I am to state why a particular article ought or ought not to be of such a value in the market. We do not collect statistics of that sort in my Department. Of course if we did, it would be a different matter.

3544. In the memorandum headed "Income of Irish Agriculturists" in the year 1893 you take the income at about one-tenth of the capital?—It is about one-tenth; it is ·107.

Dr. T. W. Grimshaw.

18 Dec. 1894.

Values and quantities of live stock.

3845. What proportion of these horses do you calculate as agricultural horses?—I could not tell you without looking at the returns, but I could get that information. I may mention that the horses in the Agricultural Returns are classified as "agricultural," "unbroken," and so on, under separate heads.

3846. In what proportion, I want to know?—I could not tell you; I should not like to trust my memory on the subject.

3847. Do you think that the sum of 832,000*l*. would be a fair sum to put down for the value of horses actually sold in Ireland in a year?—I should think at that time it was, but I think it is a great deal more now. I think horse breeding has increased in the country since that time.

3848. Have you any statistics which would show the proportion of live stock, cattle, sheep, and pigs, disposed of in Ireland in a year which are disposed of by being exported to Great Britain or other countries?—I have a table of the exports; they are regularly kept. I have no tables showing the proportion.

3849. I see at the end of your paper, page 6, you give the exports of cattle, sheep, and so on, for the year 1893?—Yes, it is there, but I have a table here giving the exports for a series of years which I think I have handed in.

3850. I am sorry you are not able to give me the proportion, because I wanted to ask a question arising out of the proportion of cattle and sheep and pigs. What proportion of those disposed of in the year are disposed of by being exported to Great Britain and other countries. Can you say in a rough way whether it was one-half, or a third, or two-thirds?—In 1893 the number of cattle exported was 643,000, of calves 45,000, of sheep and lambs 1,106,000, and of pigs 454,000. You see we do not know the total number disposed of in any year.

3851. Take the proportion of cattle and sheep in the country then?—The total number of cattle in the country in 1893, which is the year I have given the exports for, was 4,464,000; that would give one-seventh of the cattle exported. It is more if you add the 45,000 calves to it, which ought to be added to it as a total. You may call it 700,000 out of 4,500,000; that is nearer a sixth than a seventh.

3852. According to this calculation of the income, two-sevenths is what are used or disposed of in the year?—That is not for this year; it is for the year 1852.

3853. But I should have imagined the proportions would be the same for other years, would they not?—The exports of cattle in 1852 were about 56,000 less than last year.

3854. What was the total number in the country—was it less, because that is the point?—Somewhat less.

3855. Then would not the proportions be very much about the same?—It was less by about 335,000, so that probably it would come to the same thing.

3856. The question is the proportion rather than the value. I will take it for argument's sake at one-seventh, because it will correspond so easily to the two-sevenths. If one-seventh is exported and two-sevenths represent the total amount disposed of in the year, would it not follow that half of the cattle were not used in the country?—Yes.

3857. Would you think that that is probably a correct estimate?—I think it is very likely it is; I have not checked one thing against the other, but I should think very likely that is about true. Of course taking figures and looking at them in that way is rather a dangerous thing to do.

3858. I think the figures as to sheep show rather a curious anomaly. Take the sheep exported at about the same proportion?—The sheep exported in 1893 amounted to you may say 1,108,000 in round numbers.

3859. That does not agree with the figures you have given in this paper, if you look at page 6, you say at the bottom "sheep, 700,000"?—That is sheep without lambs; the lambs are not included in that figure.

3860. Are the lambs included in the sheep in the calculation of the income of the farmer which you have given?—They are; you see the note at the bottom of Table G of the statement was made for a different purpose altogether; it was made for the purpose of comparison, and the reason it was put in that form was that there was a corresponding figure ninety years ago, which I compared it with. We do not know whether there were any lambs or calves included in that, so I exclude them from the estimate. There may have been, but we do not know as a fact.

3861. Let us take then the figures as you make them out now?—This table I have here is compiled from the Privy Council Returns.

3862. What is the number of sheep?—The number of sheep and lambs exported last year, 1893, was 1,107,960.

3863. Out of how many?—4,411,000—about a fourth.

3864. So there would be a larger proportion of sheep exported than of cattle?—Apparently.

3865. And if we take these figures of two-sevenths as the amount disposed of within the year a much greater proportion of the sheep are used out of Ireland than of cattle?—Yes, apparently so.

3866. Surely that cannot be true. It cannot be true that there is a greater proportion of the cattle used in Ireland than of the sheep, can it?—But that includes cows.

3867. You say that these $\frac{2}{7}$ths of the amount used every year show the proportions of all classes of stock, cows, heifers, bullocks, and everything else used or disposed of by being either exported or killed, and used in the country, and in the same way you show the total amount of sheep and lambs disposed of either by being exported or used in the country, and yet these tables of exports would show that a very considerably larger proportion of the sheep are exported and used out of the country than of the cattle?—But it is a fact that they are. One fourth of the sheep last year were exported as a matter of fact. That is not a question of theory at all; it is not an estimate at all. It is a fact that out of 4,431,000* sheep and lambs in Ireland, there were 1,107,000 exported.

3868. That is a fact, but it is not yet proved that $\frac{2}{7}$ths is the proper proportion of the whole which are disposed of within the year?—It is not on my authority; I never said it was so.

3869. I know it is not on your authority. I only want to question the accuracy of it. Is it not evident from the number that are exported in proportion to the number existing in the country that the $\frac{2}{7}$ths is entirely too low a proportion of the number of sheep used in the year in the country?—I do not follow you. The $\frac{2}{7}$ths there mentioned does not mean that they are used in the country; it says, disposed of altogether.

3870. That is what I say. According to these tables, $\frac{2}{7}$ths of the whole of the sheep are disposed of in the year either by export or being used in the country.—That is the statement which is made to me.

3871. I am perfectly aware of that; I am not disputing that it was made to you; I only want to show that it appears to me it must be wrong, because if only $\frac{2}{7}$ths of the sheep are disposed of within the year, and it appears by the statistics that one-fourth of the entire sheep in the country were exported, it follows that a very small proportion of the sheep were used in the country. Mr. Sexton has, with his quick head, made out the figure at $\frac{1}{28}$th.—It may be so; but that is not for the same year, to begin with. There were 31 per cent. less sheep in Ireland when that return was made out. It shows that it does not do to compare one year with another in that way.

3872. I am not comparing the total number of that year with the total number this year; I am merely

* A considerable number of lambs, those used or exported before the collection of the Returns, escape enumeration in the Agricultural Statistics which show only the number in the country about the middle of June, but all those exported are in the Export Tables.

Mr. T. W. Grimshaw.

16 Dec. 1895.

Values and quantities of live stock.

comparing the proportions used within the year. I presume that, if 2/7ths was the proper proportion in the year 1886, it has not varied very much since then—has it?—I really do not know. These figures are very materially different. There were 21 per cent. less sheep in Ireland at that time than there were last year, so that the matter is a very different one indeed.

3873. Does that in the slightest degree alter the proportion? Supposing it was correct to state that in the year 1885 3/7ths of the sheep, and only 2/7ths, were disposed of within the year, is there any reason for supposing that the proportion of sheep used within the year has increased or diminished or altered?—I should think, when the number of sheep was so totally different to what it is now, those figures are very likely to vary.

3874. Do you think the proportions are likely to alter every year with the increase or decrease?—Certainly. That, I believe, is owing to disease, which had partly injured the stock and partly made it unprofitable, and the consequent restrictions on their movement. I think that is the cause of it, and if that were so, it would materially alter the proportion of buying and selling.

3875. Does it not follow, if that be true, that this table of income is absolutely unreliable for any year except 1885?—I never said it was reliable for any year in particular, and 1885 is the only year it can be applied to, I would not apply it to any other year.

3876. Not in the same proportion?—Certainly not; I would not attempt to do so. It was made for that year especially, and it was looked upon as a sort of experimental and rough estimate which gave a general idea, but nothing more.

3877. (*Mr. Sexton.*) The language used here is very general, namely, that these proportions are turned out and disposed of each year.—That is, applied to that particular year only.

3878. (*The O'Conor Don.*) I cannot understand upon what grounds the proportions should change. I can understand the numbers changing, but why should the proportions change to any appreciable extent?—I see now before me one of the changes. The number of sheep exported in 1885 was 622,000; the number now is 1,107,000, nearly double, whereas the stock has only increased by one fourth.

3879. (*Chairman.*) May I help you to this extent? The quantity exported depends very largely upon the price at the place to which they are exported, and a heavy fall in price would greatly reduce the export; would it not?—Certainly.

3880. And again on the other hand, a great rise in the price of stock of any kind at the places to which that stock is customarily exported would raise the export very much; would it not?—Certainly, but there is the matter of fact, showing how these ratios vary. The export between 1885 and 1893, has nearly doubled but the stock has only increased one fourth.

3881. (*Sir David Barbour.*) If two-sevenths were taken as the normal number sold and disposed of every year, it might be inferred that the average age of the sheep and lambs disposed of was about three and a-half years, might it not. Do you not think that is rather a high age?—I should think it is too high.

3882. Therefore, the normal fraction disposed of would probably be more than two-sevenths?—I should think it very likely is so.

3883. (*The O'Conor Don.*) I was going to ask that question in another form. Have not these proportions really been based upon the period of time at which these different classes of stock re-produce themselves?—I presume they have been to some extent.

3884. That is not altered in the slightest degree by the number in the country, is it, if sheep re-produce themselves in two years and cattle in three and a half years?—In this case where there is a much smaller proportion exported than there is in another year, it must be quite clear that there is an accumulation. The people in Ireland will not eat those animals simply because they are there, they would be kept.

3885. I think I have troubled you enough upon these tables, and I shall have only a few more questions to ask you.—May I mention before you go farther, that if that document which has been so much used with regard to the income from Irish agriculture, had been considered a reliable and efficient document, it would have been published; but it was never meant to be put forward as an authoritative and official document. If it had been so, I would have included it in my next report as a very valuable article, but I did not think it is reliable enough to publish.

3886. Do you not think it would be of great importance if we could ascertain what is the average income, meaning by "average," from year to year, of producers in Ireland?—I do, I think it would be very important indeed.

3887. Can you suggest any means by which this can be, I will not say perfectly accurately, but approximately ascertained?—I do not know, unless we tried to collect returns all over the country from reliable persons. It might be done in the same way as we get the estimates of the crops, but that is done under a very well-organised system.

3888. But leaving all these estimates of the crops and the value of the crops, do you not think that a fairly reliable table could be made out upon the principle of this one?—I do not think with the information I have before me, it could. You see there are a great number of things which have to be taken off; the cost of manures, the value of horses and vehicles, and all that kind of thing. I should have to go into the rate of wages regularly and systematically. I get statistics of wages now for the agricultural statistics, but there were none returned in former days.

Classification of agricultural population. Labourers and farmers, etc.

3889. With regard to the question of labour, which you have stated at 6,200,000*l.*, does that amount include the entire labour, including the labour of the farmers themselves, or is it merely hired labour?—Their own labour is allowed for in that, I think—I am pretty sure it is allowed for, but I would not be positive about that.

3890. You state, in the paper on the income of Irish agriculturists, that the number of labourers is taken at 300,000?—Then it cannot be included in it.

3891. If it is not included in it, on the other hand is it not entirely too large a sum? Are there 300,000 hired labourers in the country?—Yes, I should think so.

3892. Do you mean to say that there are 300,000 agricultural labourers in Ireland?—I think there are, but I cannot answer that question right off.

3893. You think there are?—I think there are; but I can supply the information as far as can be estimated, but it is a difficult thing to distinguish one labourer from another. It is a question which has been raised before, and it is practically impossible to do it. The labourers in towns are sometimes agricultural labourers—they sometimes go out of town to work, and they are altogether a very fluctuating body. For instance, it is a remarkable fact that the great proportion of labourers in Dublin were at one time agricultural labourers—they all come in from the country.

3894. You told us on Friday that the total agricultural population, men, women and children, connected directly with the land was 2,500,000?—Yes, that is an estimate.

3895. That included all the small farmers as well as the labourers, did it?—Yes, people directly dependent upon the land.

3896. That being the total number of men, women and children, one-fifth of that number would give you the number of men, would it not?—No, males and females are pretty nearly equal in that number. The females exceed the men by a small number.

3897. Would it not give you the number of grown-up men connected with agriculture?—It would give you the number of heads of families, but that would not mean the number of grown-up men.

Dr. T. W. Grimshaw. 10 Dec. 1884. Classification of agricultural population, farmers and labourers.

3898. It would give you the number of heads of families?—Yes.

3899. Then there would be only 400,000 heads of families connected with agriculture either as small farmers or labourers?—Yes.

3900. Do you mean to say out of that number 300,000 would be hired labourers?—I am afraid I do not understand the question.

3901. You told us a moment ago that in your opinion there were 300,000 hired agricultural labourers?—I would rather you did not go into that question, because I gave you a number which I said I was not sure of; I am not prepared to answer that question.

3902. (*Mr. Sexton.*) There are 480,000 agricultural holdings and that would account for two and a half millions without any labourers, counting five to each holding, would it not?—It would give you two millions and a half of people, but that does not touch the question at all.

Classification of agricultural population.

3903. I should have thought it did touch it very closely?—I should have thought it was really at the very heart of the question. Perhaps it is not; but that is my impression?—There are a great number of people who are occupiers of land who are agricultural labourers.

3904. A very small proportion?—A very large number.

3905. (*The O'Conor Don.*) They are not hired labourers, are they?—They are. They work on adjoining farms. There are great numbers of people who have agricultural holdings who do so. For instance, there are 33,000 agricultural holdings in Ireland under one acre; those are all inhabited by agricultural labourers in all probability.

3906. Are these all included in the 486,000?—The total number of agricultural holdings according to this return here [Agricultural Statistics] is 527,000. In round numbers there are about 500,000, or slightly under, occupiers of land in Ireland according to the Census return. A man may have two or three holdings and be counted over again.

3907. (*Sir David Barbour.*) Does a small piece of land occupied by a labourer count as a holding?—Yes, if there is any agricultural produce on it it is counted. This is done with the view of accounting for the agricultural produce.

3908. (*Mr. Sexton.*) I want to put this point to you. You only give us 2,300,000 as the population directly connected with the land?—Yes, estimated.

3909. That allows for only about 400,000 men, taking one in five as the head of the family?—Yes.

3910. How can you make out of that 460,000, however you combine them, nearly 500,000 agricultural holders and 300,000 labourers, even though you assume that a large number of the holders are labourers as well?—I do not say these people are farmers. A man who has an acre of land is not a farmer.

3911. But if the total agricultural population is only 2,300,000, that only allows for half a million of men altogether, does it?—Oh no, there are a great many adult persons besides the head of the family. I think you are assuming that the head of the family is the only grown-up male person in the family, but that does not follow at all.

3912. (*Chairman.*) When you spoke of 300,000 did you mean heads of families or men employed as labourers?—I was asked the question whether there were 300,000 agricultural labourers in Ireland and I said I thought there probably were; that means all men who are engaged in agricultural labour.*

3913. (*Mr. Sexton.*) But a farmer is not usually a labourer?—Very often he is.

3914. Usually not?—I think the small farmer usually is.

3915. He may be in Connaught or some limited part, but not throughout Ireland?—They are returned as farmers' sons very often in the Census.

Dr. T. W. Grimshaw. 10 Dec. 1884. Classification of agricultural population.

3916. (*The O'Conor Don.*) Are the farmers' sons included in this 300,000 males mentioned in this paper?—What paper are you speaking of?

3917. This paper in blue ink, headed "On the Income of Irish Agriculturists." You see it states the number of labourers as 300,000; are the farmers' sons included in that number?—I daresay a proportion of them are.

3918. And their labour is put down at 10s. a week as if they were paid as hired labourers?—You cannot tell whether a man is a farmer's son or whether he is a labourer; but if a man is returned as an agricultural labourer he is put down as such, totally regardless of what his father may be.

3919. What I wanted to ascertain, and what has brought about these last questions that you have been asked is this: you have set down a sum of 6,000,000*l.* for labour, and the paper you have handed in says that that is made up by a calculation of 300,000 males and 30,000 females at a certain rate of wages?—Yes.

3920. Then I asked you whether that included the labour of the farmer and his family?—No; not in that sense. I did not understand your question exactly previously. If it is stated in that paper to be the number of agricultural labourers, that is, the number in 1881, it is an absolute fact; it is not a question of opinion at all.

3921. (*Sir David Barbour.*) You mean the number of hired labourers?—No, the number of people who returned themselves as agricultural labourers. We do not know the conditions of hire or employment. If a farmers' son says "I am an agricultural labourer," he is written down as such in the Census, whether he is paid, or whether he is not. It is a question of whether the person is so returned in the Census.

3922. (*The O'Conor Don.*) But do not you see if we are to use a paper of this description, as of any value at all, it is most essential that we should know whether on the expenditure side of the account the amounts set down for labour include the labour of the farmer and his family, or only hired labour?—I believe it only includes hired labour.

3923. But the answer to my question is, is it not, that it is most essential that we should see which it does include?—I think it is most desirable.

3924. Does not the value of the paper very much depend upon whether it be hired labour or the labour of the farmer and his family?—But it is labour paid for by the farmer.

3925. Therefore it would not be the labour of the farmers' own sons upon his own farm?—Do you mean estimated?

3926. Yes.—Certainly not.

3927. This 6,000,000*l.* is the complete outlay, is it?—Certainly; it is certainly meant to be that; it is not a mere estimate of number in that case. The wages are taken as we have got the return for them, and we have then the number of persons whom we believe to be employed as agricultural labourers; one is multiplied by the other, and that is the result.

3928. Then, returning to the point, it seems to me extraordinary that there should be such a very large number as 300,000 males and 30,000 females, 330,000 altogether of persons paid as hired labourers in agricultural pursuits in Ireland; when the total number, including all the holders of land, is only 460,000 heads of families?—But 460,000 heads of families you must remember is not a number comparable with the other figure at all. There are a large number of the 330,000 who are not heads of families.

3929. I will not press you any more upon it. Suppose you have a family it does not follow that it is the father and mother only of the family who work as agricultural labourers, everybody above 15 or 16 is an agricultural labourer.

* The number of males entered under the heading "Agricultural Labourer, Cottager," in the Census of 1881 is 187,379, and the number under "Farm Servant (indoor)" 104,436. Of the males in the rural districts, who were vaguely returned as "Labourers," it is estimated that about 70,000 were agricultural labourers.

Dr. T. W. Grimshaw.

28 Dec. 1894.

3930. You have put in a return of the rate of wages; the return shows the alteration in wages in three periods, 1800, 1840, and 1886?—Yes, and it is on that return I may mention that the value of labour is based.

Wages of Ireland.

3931. You have shown that between these periods there have been considerable increases in the wages of labour?—Yes.

3932. But between 1840 and 1886 you have no intermediate period?—No, I have not.

3933. We all know that 1840 was before the great famine?—Yes.

3934. It is a matter of notoriety of course that between 1840 and the period after the famine there was a considerable increase of wages, but it would be more interesting, and I think more valuable, to know whether there has been any increase in wages say within the last ten or the last twenty years than comparing the present period with the period before the famine?—There were no wages statistics collected until recently. I now collect wages statistics which are published in the Agricultural Return, but it will take many years before that return is fit for making comparisons; that is the first systematic attempt to collect wages statistics that has been made in Ireland.

3935. When was the return first begun?—I think it has been going on now for four or five years. [In each year since 1890.]

3936. Are you in a position to give us any information as to whether, say since 1860, there has been any substantial increase?—No, I could not say.

3937. What do you think?—I am pretty sure there has been an increase, but I could not say.

3938. Do you think the increase has been steady and gradual or has there been a sudden rise, and then a stagnation?—I think it has been a steady rise.

3939. Continuously going on?—Since the famine I should think there has been a steady rise. That is a mere opinion. I have no evidence on the subject, but I dare say some evidence can be got, although I do not know of any just at present.

3940. Your predecessor, Mr. Donnelly, in his evidence before the Committee to which I have before referred, stated that there had not been much appreciable increase in wages up to his time?—Well, I suppose he had evidence to that effect; but I do not know of any such evidence. I may mention that this chronograph paper was a personal affair altogether. I wrote to individuals private letters at very great labour, and I got that result. I may mention also that a number of people throughout the country sent me old accounts, pages out of their account books, lent me books, and so on, showing these and some other matters which I have been asked about.

3941. But they did not give you any information as to an intermediate period?—I did not ask for it.

3942. Do you not think that such a return would be a more interesting return now than one going back to such an ancient date?—It would, but at the time I collected this information the question under discussion was the old prices, and as I divided these things by the famine I took 1840, as being altogether clear of the famine, for the purpose.

3943. You have informed us that your department is now making a collection?—Yes, I have the last year's return.

Adjourned for a short time.

Growth in taxation.

3944. (*Mr. Sexton.*) I think we had better obtain at the outset a clear idea of the growth of Irish taxation. You are aware, no doubt, that the local taxation of Ireland in 1866, the first period given in your return, is 2,300,000*l.* I will ask you to assume my figures. The local taxation was 2,500,000*l.* with a population of five and a half millions, or 8*s.* 4*d.* per head, and it has grown in 1895 to 3,000,000*l.*, which is 15*s.* a head. Imperial taxation in 1841 was about 10*s.* a head, and it is now 30*s.* Assuming those figures to be correct, the gross taxation per head at the former date would have been 18*s.*, and at present it is 42*s.* per head. Your evidence has not gone much upon the question of relative taxable capacity, has it?—No; of course what I have done as requested by the Commission is to take these two pamphlets of mine and put them into evidence.

Dr. T. W. Grimshaw.

28 Dec. 1894.

Taxable capacity.

3945. You have only aimed, I think, at giving data which might be held to bear more or less upon the question of the Irish side of the comparison between Ireland and Great Britain?—Yes.

3946. Of course if you had come here to give evidence of relative capacity your attention would have been called to the estimate that Great Britain receives 400,000,000*l.* sterling a year from invested capital alone, and also that whilst land is all important, everything in Ireland, the land assessment is only $\frac{1}{15}$th of the income tax assessment in Great Britain. These are very vital facts in the way of comparison, are they not?—Yes.

3947. You have been asked some questions about the English artisans and labourers. Have you any doubt (you are not officially aware) that the wages of artisans and labourers are materially higher in England, and that the employment is more regular?—I really do not know whether they are higher for similar occupations or not. I believe they are, but I do not know it as a fact; and as to the constancy of employment I do not know that it is more constant. Really I do not know it to be a fact, and I doubt it. I believe the wages are higher, but I doubt whether the employment in any particular occupation followed in England is more constant than employment in the same occupation followed in Ireland.

3948. Of course the population in England is an advancing and progressive population, full of energy and activity, and the fact that the assessment of income tax is fifteen times the assessment on the land alone indicates great energy and variety of employment, does it not?—Yes; but of course those are subjects which I have not arranged for giving evidence upon. I could ascertain those facts, but there are other witnesses much more competent than I to deal with them. I repeat what I said before that two-thirds of the people in England reside in towns. Only about one-fourth of the people in Ireland reside in towns, and that practically means that they reside more in the centres of industry in England than they do here, and it means employment in industrial occupations.

3949. Taxation being an annual burden, and the fiscal system of these countries resting, as it does, in England mainly, and in Ireland almost wholly, upon articles of consumption, it appears to follow, does it not, that the income of the taxpayer, out of which he has to buy those articles, must be a practical test of his capacity to bear taxation—in the first instance it must be the test to which we refer for his capacity to bear taxation, must it not?—I do not exactly follow you.

3950. I am distinguishing between capital and income?—You are now taking an individual.

3951. Yes, or I will take the country?—If an individual is a richer man than another individual, the richer individual is better able to pay taxes than his less rich neighbour. Is that your proposition?

3952. I will take two men of the ordinary population; the man who has better wages or a larger income is better able to pay taxation upon certain articles of daily consumption than the man whose income is narrower, is he not?—Upon articles of necessity.

3953. Upon articles of consumption?—"Consumption" is a very wide phrase. I do not want to give an opinion without knowing exactly what the point I am upon is. If you take a man who has a large income, there are certain things that he must have in order to live; and a man with a small income must have certain things in order to live; either of them can live on articles that the richer man does not care to live on, but the poorer man cannot help it, he must.

Investment of capital.

3954. Whatever the richer man chooses he is better able to afford?—Yes, that is what he chooses.

3955. At any rate taxation being an annual burden it is not to the capital of a country that you must look, but to the income of the people, in order to ascertain their capacity to bear the annual burden?—Yes, but of course that is a question which economists discuss as to whether the taxation should all come out of income, or should be shared equally between income and capital; that is a big question.

3956. I am taking it as it stands. The income does come in Ireland to the extent of 16s. out of every 1l. from consumption?—I do not know whether that is the proportion.

3957. Will you be good enough to assume that the fiscal system in Ireland rests upon articles of consumption; then it follows, does it not, that it is the test of the people's capacity at large?—Certainly. I admit that on your statement of facts.

3958. It is well known that the income as adjusted by the Treasury, is 6¾ millions. You have 1¼ millions from stamps and income tax, and 5½ millions from food and drink, have you not?—Yes.

3959.—Do you accept the principle that income tax begins when a minimum allowance has been made for the cost of subsistence; that is to say, that the tax payer should not be taxed upon that which is absolutely required for bare necessities of life, but that the taxable capacity begins when that allowance has been made?—Oh yes, I think that is a fair statement; it is a generally received opinion, and I think it is a fair statement.

3960. Although the question of capital is rather far removed from the question of capacity to bear taxation, you have been asked some questions about capital in Ireland, and you have stated that the amount of Government stock, bank stock, and railway stock has declined between 1861 and 1890?—No, not declined.

3961. It was 73,000,000l. in 1861, and 70,000,000l. in 1890?—That is the original value.

3962. Yes, the holding?—No, no. I beg your pardon, I think you are mistaken in what I said upon that subject.

3963. Look at page 46 of your pamphlet. At the bottom of the page you say nearly 73,000,000l. in 1861, and 70,000,000l. in 1890, and that the amount has only increased by 3,000,000l. during the last thirty years?—That is not what I stated, with all due respect. The object of this statement in the pamphlet is to account for what has become of the Government stock, which has decreased in Ireland, and I ask the question here what has become of this capital. "If "we compare the capital at different dates it will be "found to be" so and so.

3964. I have asked you a particular question, and it is dealt with at the bottom of page 46.—I beg your pardon, the point is this: You say the value has declined, but the value has not declined, with all respect to you.

3965. The amount?—No; the amount of original par stock which is held is less, but the saleable value of that stock is far more.

3966. The saleable value may have altered. I should say some shares have fallen back and some have advanced?—The great majority has advanced.

3967. I was putting a question as to the nominal amount.—But it is not the nominal amount really; that is the original par price at which these things were issued.

3968. That is the nominal amount, is it not?—Yes, you may call it the nominal amount if you like.

3969. That is what it is called, and it has fallen off 3,000,000l. since 1861?—Yes, somewhat over 3½ millions.

3970. And increased by only 3,000,000l. in thirty years?—That was not the question you put in the first instance, if you will excuse me.

3971. It was the question I intended to put.—The railway stock and the bank stock are increased very considerably in value; far beyond that amount in value.

3972. The fact that the nominal amount of stock has not greatly altered and has declined in a certain period does not indicate a very buoyant condition or great extension of enterprise, does it?—If you will observe, that diminution is altogether in Government stock. These figures do not indicate the amount of capital held in the public companies in Ireland.

3973. I am dealing now with Government stock, banks, and railways?—Government stock has gone down, taking it at its nominal value, and railways and banks have gone up.

3974. But the whole amount of the nominal capital has not materially increased, has it?—I beg your pardon, that is the nominal capital of the three items.

3975. I am speaking of these three. The whole amount of the actual nominal capital under these three main heads has not substantially increased?—Yes, under one of these main heads.

3976. But taking the three heads together; take the total—it has not, has it?—But I do not want this paper to be taken as meaning something that it is not intended to mean at all. It was written to explain what may have become of the Government stock that was sold.

3977. I am not enquiring into what you have written on another part; I am addressing a simple question on the result which you have yourself totalled at the foot of the page, and that result I have put in my question to you.—Well, the answer to the question directly is this, that the total nominal value of Government stock, bank stock, and railway stock, all added together, is less than it was; but that has nothing to do with the capital of the country.

3978. (*Sir David Barbour.*) Can you refer me to the page where you have given that information?—It is on page 46, but that is one of the points which I corrected at the opening of my evidence. I stated that, that 72,000,000l. near the middle of the page should be 73,000,000l., and as that is carried out into the next amount the 80,000,000l. ought to be 75,000,000l., and the percentages at the top of the page should be correspondingly altered.

3979. (*Mr. Sexton.*) This property represents the accumulation of generations—the savings of past times of prosperity, does it not?—I do not know what it represents at all. I do not say anything of the sort; it only represents the money that the people had to invest at the time it was invested. I know nothing of the time at which that money was saved.

3980. But would it not be a fair presumption to say that it forms a large part of the property of those who invested it, that it has come down for a considerable time, and that there was no sudden saving or gain?—I should say the contrary.

3981. Why?—Excepting wealthy people in Ireland, or the people who hold land, it is the merchants and business people who have increased in wealth, and it is probably they who have invested their money in these stocks.

3982. But had the people saved nothing in the last generation or the generation before?—I do not say they did not, but I should think nothing like what they save at present.

3983. But do you not think that the savings in the last generation and before then have assumed the form of this investment?—What has passed as the Government stock probably has, but the Government stock is the only item that could be of that nature, because joint stock banks and railways did not exist then to any considerable extent.

3984. But the savings of earlier times may have been transferred from other investments into this, this being considered the most acceptable at the present time?—It may be, but I know nothing about it; I have no knowledge of it.

3985. You have no evidence against it?—I think

the evidence against it is that these things did not exist in old times, therefore the money could not have been put into them then. It is probable, in fact it is pretty certain, that some of the money which was invested in Government stock has been put into railways, banks, and other securities.

3986. But surely these three main heads of investment represent, no doubt, the bulk of the savings of those who made these investments, do they not?—Not generations ago, necessarily.

3987. The bulk of all their savings and property?—But that would imply that the savings in former days were much greater than they are at present.

3988. No, not at all.—I do not understand you then.

3989. I am only implying that these sums probably represent the greater part of the accumulation of the classes who invested in them, and that you cannot put a limit of time upon it; you cannot say that these sums were made or saved within a limited time?—Of course I cannot fix the time at which these investments were made.

3990. You cannot put a limit upon it?—I cannot, of course, fix a time when these investments were made—of course not.

3991. Now these investments in Ireland are held by a very limited class, are they not?—I do not know who holds them. I have not gone into the question of the names on the registers.

3992. But one sees occasionally accounts of the number of shareholders in these concerns. Would you think the total number of these investors would reach one per cent. of the population of Ireland?—I do not know; I have no idea. I never went into it: but the smaller people do not use these means of investment; they put their money into the savings banks, and keep it there from year to year. They do not invest in this form.

3993. I am speaking of this form?—I should think these are not the sort of things which small people would deal in. A small man when he saves a little money in the country probably increases the stock on his farm or something of that sort; he would not go into the money market probably to speculate or invest.

3994. The course of these investments from year to year, whether you regard nominal amount or market price, does not appear to be greatly affected by their general prosperity or depression, does it; they seem to hold their own independently of what is going on say in the agriculture of the country?—I take the increase in the value of stocks to be a proof of increased general wealth and prosperity.

3995. But I am putting it the other way. Would you say that a good year like 1874 or a bad year like 1879 would impress its character upon the prices of these particular stocks?—I do not know that it would; I have never looked into that point. I could not tell whether it would or not.

3996. So that the state of these stocks appears not to be particularly symptomatic of the general condition of the country?—Certainly it is. If you have all your railway investments at a higher price and paying as good or better dividends than before, it certainly indicates an improved state of the country, because these concerns live by the use the people make of them.

3997. On the other hand the agricultural population might be suffering as they did in 1879, without any very great change in the position of these securities?—Railway stocks and those things were not good at that time.

3998. As to the deposits in the Joint Stock Banks do you think that they are made to any great extent by the three classes into whose condition we have been inquiring, the landlords, farmers, and labourers?—The labourers do not use Joint Stock Banks at all I should think.

3999. And landlords just as little in Ireland I should think?—I do not know that, except that they have very little money to lodge; they use the banks, but probably not to accumulate money in.

4000. The depositors also probably are a very limited class?—I do not know that it is a large class as between landlords and labourers.

4001. Do you think the farmers are large depositors?—Certainly.

4002. Do you not think their relations are more that of borrowers?—They lodge a good deal of money, and borrow money too.

4003. What do you think is the usual relation of an Irish farmer to an Irish bank; is he borrower or lender?—I do not know, but I know as a matter of fact they can pay money with cheques.

4004. Of course you are not able to take any account of his debts to the bank?—I know nothing about them.

4005. But you would not pledge yourself to any very emphatic statement as to which side the balance lies upon between his borrowing and lending, would you?—I would not venture any statement on a subject like that.

4006. The deposits in these banks are 31,000,000*l.*?—Yes.

4007. That is just about the loss in the annual value of crops as given in your Table E, between the first and the third of these periods, so that your Table E leads to the inference that in the period from 1884 to 1889 the loss in the annual value of crops was equal to the whole amount deposited in the Joint Stock Banks?—Do you put that as a question?

4008. Yes?—Well, I should say as a matter of fact it has no relation whatever to it.

4009. The two things exist in the same country?—They do, but it is a mere coincidence that the numbers are the same.

4010. If anyone leans upon the fact of the existence of 31,000,000*l.* of capital in the Joint Stock Banks in proof of the capacity to bear taxation, there is some relevancy, is there not, in pointing at the same time to the fact that the class who have to consume the taxable articles have lost 27,000,000*l.* a year?—It is legitimate to say one class had 27,000,000*l.* and the other 31,000,000*l.*, but do you imply it is their 31,000,000*l.* that has got into the banks?

4011. Not at all; it would be impossible for me to lead you into any such absurdity; but when the existence of capital is more or less relied upon as proof of taxable capacity in a country, I am entitled to point out that those upon whom the burden mainly falls lost 27,000,000*l.* a year by reason of the fall from 43,000,000*l.* to 16,000,000*l.* in the value of crops—that is all I put?—The only thing is that I do not see that the two things are related.

4012. Why is capital in the Joint Stock Banks mentioned at all in this Inquiry?—I do not know; that is for the Commissioners to say.

4013. Exactly; you put it into your brief and you seemed to think there was some relevancy in it?—No, I was asked to put everything into my brief, which was suitable for giving evidence upon. The request made to me was that I should take my two pamphlets and make them a brief of evidence, and I have put a lot of information into this brief in consequence, which, I believe, nobody has asked me any questions about, and which I am not likely to be asked any questions about, and which have been got from other sources. I have been briefing my pamphlet to the Commission.

4014. If you say the deposits in the Joint Stock Banks have nothing to do with the subject, I will not press it further?—I do not say so.

4015. Then they are relevant?—Of course.

4016. Then you say they have something to do with it after all?—That is not what I said, I think you mistook the words I used. I said I did not wish it to be understood that I am consenting to an opinion that there is a co-relation between the loss in agriculture and the increase of deposits in banks.

4017. But I think you will agree that the fact of the existence of 31,000,000*l.* in the banks is a fact of slight importance as proof of taxable capacity, in comparison with the fact that the occupiers of the

country have lost 27,000,000*l.* a year on their crops?—Of course, one has produced distress of a certain character and the other has not. I do not know as to the relative importance of the two things, because they point to different classes.

4018. They do, but the revenue depends on articles of consumption, and if you leave the farmers with only one-third of the income, does it not bear more closely on the subject than the question of the money in the banks?—It does bear closely on the subject, no doubt, but I do not consider they are correlated in the way that you appear to make them correlated.

4019. There is no further correlation than that the two facts exist in the country, and the fact in relation to the banks is of infinitesimal importance as compared with the matter of power to bear taxation?—That is a matter of opinion.

4020. Do you contend that the existence of the 31,000,000*l.* in the banks is only a matter of opinion—I must ask you to give me your view as to whether the existence of the 31,000,000*l.* of deposits is at all of comparable importance in regard to the capacity to bear taxation, upon articles of consumption, with the fact that the crops of the farmers in this country between 1855 and 1888 fell, upon the average, 27,000,000*l.*?—I think that is quite too involved a question to answer. It is a very involved question.

4021. Is the capital sum of 31,000,000*l.* as important in regard to taxation upon articles of consumption as a revenue loss of 27,000,000*l.*?—But that 31,000,000*l.* is not capital in the ordinary sense.

4022. It is deposited?—That is the floating capital that is used for transacting every day business; it is not invested capital you see; it is floating capital, which makes all the difference in the world.

4023. I am sorry to press you, but do you consider the existence of such a sum of floating capital as having at all as important a bearing on the question of taxable capacity as a loss of 27,000,000*l.* a year in the agricultural revenue?—I am not at all sure which is the most important. One is, to a large extent, the money of traders and the other is the money apparently of agriculturists; both traders and agriculturists consume articles and it is a very difficult question to deal with. You have made up your mind on the subject but I would be very sorry to make up my mind without considering it closely.

4024. One is floating capital not varying much from year to year; the other is 27,000,000*l.* of loss per year. The deposits in the Savings Banks are about 5,000,000*l.* that is about half a year's taxation, is it not?—I do not know.

4025. You do not know that the taxation of the country is 10,000,000*l.* a year, 7,000,000*l.* Imperial and 3,000,000*l.* local?—I think it is about that.

4026. If you will kindly take it from me that the taxation of Ireland is 10,000,000*l.* a year, then the deposits in the Savings Banks amount to about six months' taxation of the country?—That may be.

4027. Do you know that only one person in twenty in Ireland has a Savings Bank account?—I forget what the number is. Very likely it is so.

4028. As against one in six in England?—I know there are not nearly so many but I do not know the ratio.

4029. Have you any particular idea as to the class of people who invest in Savings Banks; would you say they are domestic servants and small officials and others who have salaries, or would you say that they are to any great extent farmers and labourers?—I should think they consist of the working classes of every kind.

4030. But the gross amount is only little more than 1*l.* per head of the population, is it not?—I think so.

4031. Mention has been made in your evidence of other industries connected with the land, would it be correct to describe the other industries of Ireland as merely local?—Of course every industry is local to a certain extent.

4032. The land industry is national you might say?—Yes, but that is not generally called an industry; it is spoken of as "Agriculture." We speak of agricultural pursuits and industrial pursuits.

4033. It is hard work at any rate?—It is, but by "local" you mean that it is fixed in particular places.

4034. Precisely—in localities?—Yes.

4035. The spirit industry may be said to be limited to Dublin, Belfast, and Cork, may it not?—It is mainly limited to Dublin.

4036. The beer industry is chiefly confined to Dublin, is it not?—Chiefly to Dublin.

4037. The linen industry is confined to Belfast and a few towns in that region?—Belfast and a good many towns round about there.

4038. The shipbuilding industry may be said to be confined to Belfast, may it not?—Yes.

4039. And the woollen industry employs only about 7,000 hands altogether?—There are more than that employed now, but I could not get a recent return. That of course is not fixed in any one place; you have some in Dublin, some in Belfast, some in Cork, and some in Limerick; there is no great woollen town so to speak as there is a linen town and brewing town.

4040. Then the economic scope of these industries is that they provide profits for a certain limited number of firms, and wages for a small fraction of the population of Dublin, a much greater proportion of the population of Belfast, and two or three small towns, is it not?—Yes, but you know there are a great many towns in the north of Ireland besides Belfast engaged in the linen trade—towns of 10,000 inhabitants and upwards which I have classified as large towns in my evidence.

4041. You have made some very difficult and laborious inquisitions into this complicated question, and have done them with very great care, though I cannot agree with your conclusions; could you furnish the Commission with any estimate of the probable profits and wages yield of these minor and local industries?—I could not; I have not attempted to work that out. The wages, for instance, of the linen industry are all published in the Board of Trade returns of wages, which were recently issued. They were published for different periods, and some of them go back a good way. At one time I was studying that question, and I thought of going into it, but I had not time to do it, the number of heads under which persons are engaged is so great. For instance, in the flax industry there are hacklers, roughers, spinners, and weavers, and so on. There may be twenty different things, and you have to deal with them all separately; so that it becomes a very difficult question to come to any positive conclusion about it. Of course a conclusion could be arrived at, but it would be laborious. I may tell you, that a lot of these things are not things undertaken by any department. Nearly everything in this pamphlet has been compiled either by myself or at my expense; it has not been done for Government.

4042. The total output of the spirit industry, the beer industry, the linen industry, and the shipbuilding industry is known, and all you would have to do would be to estimate the value of it and estimate the cost of production?—Yes, it could be done.

4043. Personally, I should be glad if you would do it.—The wages question is the one which is the great difficulty—how much is distributed in wages.

4044. That also is the subject of specific tables.—It is a very difficult question.

4045. I should be glad if you could do it; we shall have to get it done by someone, and I have no doubt you are the most competent person to do it.—You know you have to collect returns first before you start at anything of that sort, and check them.

4046. (*Mr. Martin.*) Have not the Government, within the last couple of years, got such a return from the employers?—Yes; and it is from those alone that the information can be compiled.

4047. (*Mr. Sexton.*) I wish to turn now to the question of the population of Ireland at the time of Population

X

the Union. You have handed in a paper, on which you start from a conjectural estimate made by Mr. Bushe in the year 1791?—Yes.

4048. And assuming that the population advanced in the then ratio from 1791 to 1821, that would have given an increase from 4,200,000 to 6,800,000, which is equal to 63 per cent.?—I think that is it.

4049. That would be a very large increase in thirty-one years, would it not?—It would. I admit that that figure, 1½, is higher than is usually allowed for increase of population.

4050. You have yourself made the observation that these estimates of the last century were under the mark?—Probably. The fact is, that in Mr. Bushe's paper, which I handed in, he shows where he knows defects to have existed, and he assumes a great many others to exist, but the 4,200,000 is not taken from Mr. Bushe's paper.

4051. What I submit to you is that it might be safer to argue back from the ascertained figure of the Census of 1821 than forward from any conjectural figure preceding the Union. The ascertained figure for the Census of 1821 is 6,800,000?—Yes.

4052. And for the Census of 1831 it was 7,760,000?—Yes.

4053. That is an increase of fourteen per cent. in the ten years?—Yes.

4054. Have you any reason to suppose that the rate of increase in Ireland was very different between 1801 and 1821 to what it was between 1821 and 1831?—There is no ground for it except the supposition that those were correct populations just in the same way as I would say, if I take 1881 and 1891, I estimate the population between those two periods on the supposition that those two numbers are accurate, and the estimate that I have handed in, which you referred to in the first instance, is on the supposition that the hearth-money returns after Mr. Bushe's statement had been made are correct.

4055. Quite so; it rests on a conjectural estimate—And we believe the 1821 population to be as correct as anything that could be got at that period.

4056. Taking the 1821 and 1831 populations as correct, we have fourteen per cent. increase between these two years, have we not?—Yes.

4057. Applying that fourteen per cent. backwards I find if the population had increased at the rate of fourteen per cent. in each ten years from 1801 to 1821, it would have been 5,960,000 in 1811 and 5,230,000 in 1801?—Yes.

4058. Which comes pretty near to what you call a very good account of Ireland given by Mr. Newenham, who says that in 1791 it was 5,000,000 odd?—Yes.

4059. Would you say that probably is a reasonable estimate?—That probably is a reasonable estimate, but that has been done; I have the figures here.

4060. I would ask you this—Do you think working backward from the ascertained figure of the Census of 1821 and applying the rate from 1821 to 1831 is likely to be more correct than the one founded upon the conjectural estimate of Mr. Bushe of 1791?—There is a doubt expressed by the Commissioners of 1841 as to its accuracy. The Census Commissioners of 1841 considered the Census of 1821 was somewhat under, and the Census of 1831 was somewhat over the proper number. That threw some doubt upon it, and another thing that threw some doubt upon it was that in order to check it we tried to take the figures out by sexes, and the result of estimating by sexes would have been to bring out a false ratio altogether, so that there appeared to be something wrong in the estimate.

4061. However, you see no cause, do you, to impeach this mode of proceeding?—It is a perfectly legitimate mode of proceeding—it is what most people would do, in fact.

4062. I turn to ask you your opinion of the causes of the present economic state of Ireland, and I would ask you whether those causes are the repeal of the corn laws and the famine. I would suggest to you that the repeal of the corn laws was very beneficial to England, and put Ireland in a difficulty by contracting the market?—Of course the repeal of the corn laws may be considered as an injury to home agriculturists, and, as must be admitted, Ireland is an agricultural country, therefore, of course, if one is admitted and the other is admitted, it must have been injurious to Irish agriculturists.

4063. I was not speaking in any sense as implying opinion; I was asking your opinion as to the cause of the economic condition?—I say, of course, it must be admitted, viewing the fact that you have free trade in corn, it is injurious to the pocket of the man who grows corn here. That is quite clear, but the question of how it benefited the whole community is another question altogether. It does not follow that it would have been an advantage to the Irish consumer any more than to the English to have dear corn.

4064. But Ireland was a mainly agricultural community, was it not?—Yes.

4065. And the effect was, of course, to stimulate the substitution of pasture for tillage?—Yes.

4066. Then came the potato failure on the top of the repeal of the corn laws?—Yes, but besides the repeal of the corn laws you must take into consideration the greater facilities for transit which have cheapened corn far beyond anything that might be attributed to the repeal of the corn laws.

4067. At any rate the repeal of the corn laws taken by itself at that time did stimulate the change from tillage to pasture?—Yes, of course, and there were bounties on Irish corn brought to Dublin in old times.

4068. Just so. Then came the potato failure. Was the potato failure an unforeseen calamity, or were there warnings of it?—I have not gone into this very carefully, but I believe it is quite admitted that signs of the disease in the potato existed for several years before the absolute famine took place—in fact all the accounts one reads of it say so.

4069. Before 1844?—I think before 1844, from what one can read.

4070. But no effectual steps were taken to avert the catastrophe?—I believe not; but those were different times from the present.

4071. To me the most painful and memorable passage in your book is where you say that the deaths caused by the famine and by its effects and the diseases consequent thereon amounted to 729,000.—That is believed to be the case. Of course there was no registration of deaths at that time, so that that figure cannot be taken as a fact, but it is not likely to be over-estimated.

4072. Then the immediate effect of the famine and of the repeal of the corn laws taken together was that great clearances of the people were effected from Irish land. Some of them, I daresay, went of their own will, and others were put out in great numbers?—Of course that was the result of the decrease of tillage and of the production of corn, and so on.

4073. Then pasture began to be substituted for tillage and farms consolidated?—Yes.

4074. One of the effects of that, no doubt, was a contraction of the labour market?—Certainly.

4075. Which lasts to the present day?—Certainly.

4076. Because one herd can manage as much land as twenty labourers used to do?—Yes; I have gone into that in the pamphlet, I think.

4077. Would I be right in saying that another effect was that Irish farmers were divided into three classes—the mixed tillage and pasture farmer, the farmer who depends almost entirely on tillage, and the stock farmer who has very little to do with tillage—the grazier, as we call him?—Yes, that would be a classification; but the man who depends wholly on tillage is a very rare individual.

4078. There is a very large class of men who depend

[illegible]

mainly on tillage, is there not?—They are more the small people who consume their own produce to a large extent.

4079. But the class exists, does it not?—Yes, but they are generally small holders who, of course, do not occupy a great area of the country.

4080. I ask you that question, because it appears to me that such tables as your Tables D and F in your printed statement as to values of output are mere arithmetical exercises where you apply the whole population as reduced to the amount of crops and stock?—Yes.

Economic condition of Ireland.

4081. It suggests an equal diffusion of wealth or income which, of course, is merely an abstract idea when we remember the division of these farmers into these classes?—Yes, of course it does, if you take the country as a whole—this [the pamphlet] is meant taking the country as a whole. One of the points in my paper was to deal with Ireland as much as possible as a whole. These were the original lines of the paper.

4082. In fact all that these Tables D and F mean is that the population of the country has grown less during the interval than these figures would indicate?—No, I mean a great deal more than that.

4083. What more do they mean?—They mean precisely what they say—that the average per head of these items is so much more.

4084. But what is the practical value of that, considering that there is no such division in existence of the income as that suggested by the paper?—But that would apply to everything you apportion to the population.

4085. Very well, it is an impeachment of the doctrine of averages?—It is.

Reduction of population.

4086. The effect of that economic system on the population of Ireland has been to reduce the rural population since 1841 by one half, has it not?—Yes.

4087. I have the figures here—the rural population has been reduced by quite one half, and the whole population by not far from one half?—Yes.

4088. And you are aware, of course, that it is still diminishing?—Yes, it is believed to be at present.

4089. And has diminished in the last decennial period twice as much as in the previous one?—Yes.

4090. And Great Britain is increasing at the rate of three to four millions a decade?—But the diminution in the current decade is probably less, because emigration is less.

4091. The population of Ireland now and since 1878 is less than it was at the time of the Legislative Union in 1801, is it not?—I think I stated it for 1885. In 1885 it was about the same as the estimated population at the time of the Union, and it has been diminishing since, therefore, of course, it is less now.

4092. Do you know of any other old settled country in which the population at the end of the century is less than it was at the beginning?—I do not think I do—I do not. I could not give you any country as an example.

4093. You have spoken of the emigration movement as a movement without parallel in modern history?—Yes.

4094. I suppose if you went to ancient history, such as the dispersal of the Jews, you might find something like it?—Very likely.

4095. Population is usually considered a factor in national prosperity, is it not?—Yes, because it is always assumed that a population will not stay unless there is employment for it.

4096. And the absence of population argues want of employment?—It does.

Pasture and tillage.

4097. As to the extent to which pasture has been substituted for tillage you cannot say, between 1841 and 1851, because you have no figures, what it was?—No.

4098. But even since 1851?—There is a steady increase of pasture and a diminution of tillage—there is no doubt about that.

4099. In 1851 I find from your returns that tillage was two-thirds of the pasture and in 1894 it is less than half?—Yes; that is about right.

Dr. T. W. Grimshaw. 18 Dec. 1894. Pasture and tillage.

4100. That is taking the extent in acres. Does it occur to you from the tables you have put in and from your knowledge of the subject that the substitution of pasturage for tillage in Ireland appears to have reached its limit?—I do not know that it has.

4101. It appears by the table upon page 19 of your pamphlet, that the area under crops has been falling heavily ever since 1861 up to 1891, but that it has increased by over 100,000 acres in the last three years?—Yes; there are fluctuations, of course.

4102. But there was a double movement. On the other hand the amount in pasture had increased heavily from 1861 to 1891, and has decreased by nearly 100,000 acres in the last three years, so that there is a movement now from pasture towards tillage, as disclosed by your returns?—There is at present. But I was answering the general question rather which you put first of all. I think, that that is a thing as to which one cannot make up one's mind whether it is going to continue or not—you see there are variations from year to year and it would not be safe to make a forecast from these figures.

4103. The fall in crops in previous periods is so substantial, and the increase in grass so heavy that it seems to argue a very settled course of diminution on the one hand and increase on the other hand up to 1891?—Yes.

4104. And now a turning point appears to have been at last reached?—Yes.

Values and quantities of crops and stock.

4105. I think there is some reason for it in your Table B of your printed statement. I do not compare the value of stock in the last decennial period with the first, because the first was a period when the stock system was undeveloped in Ireland. I think it is fairer to compare it with the second period, 1866 to 1870. There you see that the capital value of stock in Ireland in each year from 1889 to 1893 was 3,000,000*l.* less than in each year from 1866 to 1870, although the numbers of the stock were much greater, and the land devoted to them a million acres more?—Yes, as regards the stock, but the area devoted to them is not a million acres more.

4106. That argues a reaction, does it not?—Of course, it means that stock growing is not so valuable in proportion as it used to be.

4107. It appears to suggest to me, and I submit it to you under your correction, that the original movement from tillage to pasture promoted by the repeal of the corn laws is now being neutralised by that greater facility of transit of which you spoke as applied to the supply of live stock and dead meat to Great Britain?—It may be so, it is not improbable; but I would not be prepared to make a forecast on that at present.

4108. Now the case is more serious with regard to tillage as disclosed in your Table A. There we may compare the first period and the last. It shows that whilst the average annual value of the crops of Ireland in every year from 1851 to 1855 was 58,500,000*l.*, that value had fallen in every year up to 1889–93 to 34,000,000*l.*?—Yes, there was a great fall.

4109. An enormous fall?—Yes.

4110. Some attempt was made by the O'Conor Don to affect the comparison by suggesting that the price of potatoes was put too high in the first period?—Well, it is possible, of course.

4111. The price is put at about 7*d.* a stone at the time of the Crimean war?—Yes.

4112. Did the war affect the price of potatoes in Ireland?—I cannot tell; it may have done.

4113. It may have promoted an export of grain?—I could not tell you. There is a general belief that prices were high at that time.

4114. You say, yourself, that in the first period prices were influenced by the higher prices caused by the Crimean war?—I say it was a disturbing influence

Dr. T. W. Grimshaw, M.D. 28 Dec. 1894. Values and quantities of crops and stock.

Of course when there is a great war of that sort, in which the country is engaged, it must have a disturbing effect.

4115. Agriculture is a life of vicissitudes?—Yes.

4116. Ups and downs is the very essence of it?—I think the weather has more to do with it than war, as a general rule.

4117. But you cannot object to any particular quinquennium, because there was a high price for an article in that period?—The question of war is generally introduced when you deal with the cost of provisions, because it has an effect, and there is no doubt that a great deal of the prosperity of the grain-growing farmers in Ireland in the early part of the century was owing to war—not only in Ireland, but all over the United Kingdom.

4118. Taking it altogether—not only the Crimean War, but the fact that you stated that potatoes were probably not thrown so much on the market at that time as at the later periods—there is no more reason to impeach any of the prices at that period than at any of the others, is there?—I do not want to impeach the prices, except that the farther you go back (and there is always that point to be taken into consideration) in the compilation of the almanacks from which these prices are taken, the less accurate they are likely to be; they are improving every year. The accuracy of all publications of that nature has become much greater. For instance, the publication of prices in newspapers, and so on, is much more accurate than it used to be.

4119. Taking the table altogether, I am disposed to think that the taking of the prices in good markets put the value of the crops at probably higher than their real level?—Probably; I admit that, but that would not invalidate a comparison.

4120. Certainly not. It would touch the value of each year, would it not?—It would, but not the comparison.

4121. I think I may suggest also that your method of proceeding (which I daresay was the only one you had available), namely, to take the highest price and the lowest price of the year and striking the half-way between the two as a mean price, also gives a higher value to the crop than the real value, for this reason, that the lower prices are apt to prevail when the crop or stock is put on the market, and the higher prices at the time of year when sales are not much made; so that, if you take half-way between the two, it is evident that you put a higher price upon the produce than was obtainable at the time it was sold; do you not?—That might be so.

4122. (The O'Conor Don.) Is that actually what is done? Is the highest price and the lowest price taken and a mean between them come to?—As I read it from the heading of Purdon's Table it is not done by means; it is done by averaging the highest price and the lowest price from month to month; and then, my prices were taken as a mean between his estimated highest and lowest.

4123. But that is not the actual highest and lowest in the year?—Oh, no. He gives a highest and lowest average price, and I have taken a mean between them.

4124. (Mr Sexton.) We are getting a little complicated. I think that a mean even between the average highest and the average lowest would probably indicate a higher value, would it not?—It is a figure of very doubtful value, I admit.

4125. And that would apply to the annual total for each year, and for each quinquennium, would it not?—Yes; the point is that in making the comparisons it would not make any difference.

4126. Not the slightest, if you pursued the same system throughout, but it would in estimating the positive yield for the year or for the quinquennium?—Of course it would.

4127. (Sir David Barbour.) Do I rightly understand that you did not take the mean prices of twelve months and add them together and divide by twelve, but that you took the mean between the highest and lowest average prices in each year?—No. The monthly figure Purdon gives is the average for the year.

4128. (Lord Welby.) He first of all finds the average for the month, and then carries it on for the year?—No; he makes yearly averages of the highest and of the lowest monthly prices.

4129. (Mr. Sexton.) How were the prices taken from Thom's Almanack?—They were taken as they actually appeared.

4130. How did you get the average?—They averaged them I think.

4131. (Mr. Martin.) Could it be that Mr. Purdon in compiling his list of prices states that say 13s. to 14s. 6d. means the best quality of oats, and that the second quality of oats is a different figure?—No, because he takes a mean of the prices as they stood on different times.

4132. But it might mean the mean of those prices at those times?—I cannot tell you what he means. What Purdon says himself is this—"The two prices "given after each item of the above are not the extreme "quotations of the whole year but the mean of the "highest and lowest quotations for twelve months or "the season or as the case may be."

4133. (Chairman.) I should understand that to mean that he takes each month, or each period where there is a season and averages the means of those periods?—I should think so.

4134. (Mr. Sexton.) He does not take note of the value of sales in each month, does he?—No

4135. What I would suggest to you simply is this, that the time of year at which the great bulk of crops or stock is thrown on the market is apt to be the time of year when the lowest price prevails, and therefore by taking any average between that time and the times when there were smaller sales and higher prices you give to the whole produce of the year a higher value than the real value?—Yes; but that depends upon the extent Mr. Purdon gives to the phrase "season." He may leave off those prices when there is not a large supply, and he may consider the season to be the time of a plentiful supply, that we cannot tell.

4136. I suggest to you simply that the average would rather act to increase the value of the crop in view of the fact that the throwing of the bulk of the crop on the market at one time tends to lower the prices?—Yes, just so.

4137. I think you do not dissent from what I have said, do you?—I think it is quite possible.

4138. Does your department supply the figures of yields of crops in Ireland for the Statistical Abstract?—Yes, they are derived from our returns.

4139. Because I notice in recent years, and I suppose it goes further back, that the yield of important crops is given as far higher for Ireland than for Great Britain. Is the cultivation under far more favourable conditions?—Sometimes; it depends on what year you have got. For instance, if you took 1847, it was much better in Great Britain than it was in Ireland.

4140. The first I notice is 1890: barley in Great Britain was 31·75, and in Ireland, 39·07 per acre; oats in Great Britain, 39·27; in Ireland, 40·87; beans, 28·61 to 34·05. Then in the next year barley was 35 to 37; beans 32 to 43. In the next year barley was 34 to 41; oats, 38 to 44; beans, 29 to 43. In 1892, wheat was 26 to 29; oats 38 to 42; beans, 32 to 37; and in 1893, last year, wheat was 25 to 30; barley, 28 to 36, and oats, 35 to 44. These differences in yield which, no doubt, govern the computations of value, appear to be greater than can be easily accounted for, considering the great skill and care and expense in regard to English agriculture?—That may be.

4141. (Mr. Wolff.) Are those statistics given for the statute acre?—They are for the same acre. They are all statistics given for the statute acre.

4142. (Mr. Sexton.) Having touched upon the yield and the price I again throw emphasis on the fact that the loss of the farmers per annum in the last five years, compared with the first five years, was

Decrease of Irish agriculture.

Dr. T. W. Grimshaw.

11 Dec. 1894.

Progress of Irish agriculture.

34,000,000l., that is a loss equal to what you estimate to be the rent and the whole wages for labour, and 5,000,000l. added?—Very likely, I suppose it is. I did not go into it in that way, but I suppose it is as you say, but that only refers to crops; you exclude stock.

4143. The wages of labour have also greatly increased between 1855 and 1893, have they not?—Yes, I have no doubt they have.

4144. And the increase of wages of labour not being included in this computation has to be added to the 34,000,000l. loss?—Yes; but there is one thing about that which I mention in this pamphlet, namely: that the increase of agricultural machinery has done a great deal to counterbalance the loss that the farmer is at by the increased price of labour.

4145. I lately had the opportunity of examining in London, before a Committee of the House of Commons, several very competent men, personally and directly acquainted with agriculture, and the opinion of some of them was, that the use of machinery applies only to what you might call the largest and most important class of holdings, and that it does not apply to the bulk of the holdings?—Of course it does not so much apply to the small holdings.

4146. And, therefore, it would not in the greater number affect the question of expense, would it?—But then you see the very small holders do not pay much in wages, and you come to another difficulty.

4147. Of course, but what they do pay in wages would amount to a very large sum?—Yes; but these things cut both ways.

4148. The only relief in regard to rents, which has been afforded, at any rate by the operation of the law, has been a reduction of 1,250,000l.; about 6,000,000l. of the rents have gone into the Courts, and have been reduced 1,250,000l.?—But then there have been a great many reductions besides the Land Court reductions, and those under private agreement, registered in the Land Courts. We do not know what that amounts to.

4149. My figure includes the agreements registered in the Land Courts?—Yes, but we do not know how many rents have been reduced by arrangement between landlord and tenant irrespective of the Land Acts.

4150. I should think it very unlikely that a tenant desiring security in his tenure would be content with an agreement outside the Court which gives him no security, when by going into Court he would get his 15 years' term?—There have been a great many of such reductions, I believe. There are three charities which I happen to be on the Board of Trustees for, and reductions have taken place on all of them without going into the Land Court or registering them.

4151. So far as the remedial measures carried by the Legislature affect the situation this loss of 34,000,000l. a year from 1889 to 1893, together with any increase of cost of labour, has only been relieved by the operation of the law to the extent of 1,250,000l. a year, has it not?—Yes; that is of course as to the ascertained fact.

4152. I should like to ask you at this point a question having some relation to the notion that the decrease in the number of the people or of the farmers, in some way which I can hardly quite understand, produces prosperity in seasons of loss. These farmers having lost 34,000,000l. in those five years from 1889 to 1893, how does the fact that there are fewer farmers now than there were in the earlier period make their loss any smaller?—That is not a loss necessarily—it is a diminution of profits which makes all the difference in the world. If a man gets two farms and makes only half as much out of each of them as he did out of one in former times he has got as big an income. His total transactions bring him in as large an income, and he personally is just as well off as he was on the one farm at high prices. He may have more trouble to make it, but financially it is the same to him.

4153. But was the smaller number of farmers better off in 1894 on the 34,000,000l. of receipts from crops than the larger number of farmers were in 1855 upon 38,000,000l.?—I do not know; I cannot tell you that.

4154. I think it is a very nice question?—I do not know; you must take the point into account that if a man gets say 100l. a year from a farm at certain given prices, and he takes two farms and gets 100l. a year profit out of the two farms at lower prices, he is just as well off, except that he has more trouble to do it.

4155. Yes, in the case of the particular man undoubtedly, if he gets a smaller income from each of the two farms than he had from one he is as well off, but taking the country at large, and taking a larger number of farms with an income of 38,000,000l., and a smaller number with an income of 34,000,000l. from crops one does not quite see how the conclusion is readily drawn that the people are better off in the latter period?—I do not think I said they were better off, did I?

4156. No. I think you guarded yourself very carefully in regard to the individual. You said that there was more wealth in the country, though I fail to see how these returns prove it, and you guarded yourself very carefully as to the position of the individual. May I observe that the collocation of these two Tables A and B is, I think, somewhat misleading, the O'Conor Don called attention to the point?—I mentioned it myself, I think.

4157. But the mere mention of it perhaps hardly enables us to realise exactly what it means. The crops in the first line of Table C are distinct annual values separate from each other, are they not?—Yes.

4158. The stock in the second line is really capital which is turned into revenue at the rate of about one-third a year?—Yes.

4159. And the remainder goes over?—I have got that stated here in the middle of the next page.

4160. I know that you have perfectly realised the point, but I want that we should realise it as well as you do?—I think every one on the Commission understands that.

4161. I am not quite sure that I understand it myself yet. I should like to know whether I do or not. The meaning of it is that these amounts of stock are not to be taken as independent of each other, but that each succeeding period includes from two-thirds to three-fourths of the figure of the value of the stock in the previous period?—Yes, there is a certain carrying over. You cannot cut a thing short and say that that is cleared off. But that applies to everything, because grain that is grown in one year is probably not sold until the next. In every business you have a turn-over from one year to another both of debts and credits.

4162. But in accounts you do not usually add together, in order to ascertain a man's position, his revenue and his capital?—No, you do not; you do not deal with the capital at all; that is in the tillage business; I am not saying you do not deal with it at all, but practically you do not deal with it.

4163. I think in order to get any clear idea upon it it is necessary to pass on to your Table E and there the case becomes, I think, worse for the agriculturist. The principle of that table is gross annual income without considering expenses, that is to say, you put into that table all the crops that remain after the stock have been fed?—Yes.

4164. You do not put into it the crops that pass into the form of stock in the year, but you put into it the crops that remain after a portion of them has been given to the stock?—Yes.

4165. Then you put in the portion of the stock sold or disposed of in the year?—Yes.

4166. Then you add the products of the stock?—Yes.

4167. That gives you the position of the farmer from period to period, taking note only of the amount of crops consumed by the stock as an item of expense?—Yes, that would be it.

Sir T. W. Grimshaw.

24 Nov. 1894.

Incomes of Irish Agriculturists and Values.

4168. Then in this case it appears that comparing the two last periods, the income from stock (we are not now upon capital, but upon income) of the Irish farmer in each year of the latter period was lower than his income from stock in each year in the former period by nearly 7,000,000l.?—That is the last period mentioned here as compared with the middle period.

4169. Yes?—Yes, that is so.

4170. And I apprehend that the period for 1889-93, when you put it into form will show a further decline, because the factors of which it is composed, namely, the values of stock and crops in the first and second tables are, in the case of crops, 1,000,000l. lower, and in the case of stock, 1,500,000l. lower?—Of course it will be less if the cost of the production of the stock be the same.

4171. Then in the case of crops, the loss of the farmer appears to be more considerable than when we are considering gross produce, namely because here we see that the annual value of crops has fallen from the 1855 period to the 1888 period by no less than 27,000,000l.* a year, or about two-fifths of the whole? —Yes, there is a very great fall.

4172. That is surely an extraordinary thing?—I believe it is true for all that.

4173. I have no doubt in the world it is. That means that double the annual rent of the country, as measured by you, has been thrown into this immense gulf of loss in the five years from 1884 to 1888, and the total shows that one-fourth of the gross income of the country, from crops and stock together, has decreased between the earlier and the later period, and that the farmer now taking the 1893 period as being worse than the 1883 period is worse by 80,000,000l., or 20,000,000l. a year—that is one-fourth of the whole, taking crops and stock together, than he was at the period up to 1855. That, so far from indicating anything like prosperity, indicates something which would appear more certainly to spell ruin, would it not?—I do not exactly see your point; of course the decrease is enormous; but are you dealing with Table E altogether?

4174. Yes, I am dealing with Table E?—There is of course a difference between 54,000,000l. and 72,000,000l. Really that is the decrease in the total.

4175. It is one-fourth—it is a decrease of 18,000,000l.?—Yes.

4176. Which is just the amount which you allow for the rent of the country, and the expenditure on wages for labour in each year?—Yes, about that.

4177. That is a tremendous loss?—It is—it is a great fall.

4178. I think I must ask you a few questions upon the account which has been handed in, showing the net profit of the producer—the account prepared by an officer under your supervision. The gross value of crops which you take at 30,000,000l. for the year 1865 is calculated, I understand, from prices taken from Thom's Directory?—Yes, I think so.

4179. Were they not at hand in Porter's Almanack? —I cannot tell you why Thom's Directory was chosen.

4180. Did the two differ?—I do not know.

4181. May I ask you again what material does Thom afford for the average price?—He gives a table of prices. I think he has altered the form of table since then, and I doubt if this present Directory will give it.

4182. The stock sold and the produce of stock sold in the year you take as amounting to more than half the capital value of the stock?—I believe there is an alteration made in the method of calculation, and I will look it up.

4183. (*Chairman.*) Will you add the information to your answer?—But there was no distinct question put to me. I was simply looking at the book to see where it was got.

* This is the difference between crops disposed of after feeding live stock, and it cannot be taken separately from the stock, as Ireland is treated as one farm, and the number of the stock was far greater in the later than in the earlier period.

4184. (*Mr. Sexton.*) My point is whether it is such an average that it was an average taken between two prices of the year, or whether it was a mean average of a series of prices within the year?—I will look it up. Sir T. W. Grimshaw. 24 Nov. 1894. Incomes from Agriculture and Values.

4185. At any rate I suppose the remark would apply equally that these averages, seeing that the lowest price usually prevails from the greatest quantity sold, would be to increase the apparent value of the produce?—I do not know how it is done exactly; I could not tell you unless I looked at Thom; I should have to get a Thom of that year.

4186. You put the live stock sold and the produce of the stock sold within the year at what appears to be a very high figure of more than half the total value of all the stock existing in the country, and that is caused in a great degree by the very round figure applied to the milch cows. You put down each milch cow in the country, the number being 1,400,000, at 10l. a year, and you put down 14,000,000l. of the farmers' income as due to that calculation. Are you aware whether there is any careful examination and well founded basis for the assumption that every milch cow in Ireland is worth 10l. a year to the farmer?—That was the estimate which was given. I happen to know where that was got, but it was given confidentially.

4187. I will not ask you to disclose anything confidential, but the matter is a public matter?—It was stated on very good authority.

4188. I think it will be the subject of considerable scrutiny and debate in the country. I understand you to say that the proportion of total stock under each head sold from year to year is not considered to be invariable, but varies from year to year according to the total number of stock, and to other circumstances? —I daresay it does.

4189. What is the meaning of saying that all the pigs are disposed of every year. If all the pigs are disposed of every year there would be no pigs for a second year, would there?—As to that, that is, of course, a question of increase from year to year. That is the statement that was given, and I believe that it was founded on very good authority, but I cannot vouch it myself. Pigs.

4190. (*Sir David Barbour.*) I suppose there are a number of young pigs born in the course of the year?—There are a number of course, and I presume it was considered a sufficient number by the estimator to balance the thing.

4191. (*The O'Conor Don.*) But will not a pig produce young in about eight months from the time of its birth?—I believe so, but I should not like to say for certain. I ought to know as a physiologist, but I really do not know.

4192. (*Lord Welby.*) The pigs existing at the commencement of the year are added to by the number born within the year, and taking away at the end of the year the pigs existing there would remain the new generation born for the year?—Yes.

4193. (*The O'Conor Don.*) A whole generation of new pigs can easily be brought into the world in the year, can they not?—Yes, it can.

4194. And therefore it is quite possible that the whole existing might be sold at the end of the year, and yet you might have the same number as at the beginning?—I think so, I think that is the explanation.

4195. (*Mr. Sexton.*) Why are they put down at 1l.?—That is the price put upon them.

4196. That is not the price of a pig, is it?—The price of the pigs passing over to England last year was supposed to be 3l., but a young pig in those days probably was not worth anything like 1l.

4197. (*The O'Conor Don.*) What is 1l.?—I mean a new-born pig.

4198. (*Mr. Sexton.*) All the pigs, young, old, and middle-aged appear to be included in this number, and are put down at 1l.?—They are.

4199. That admits of some explanation, does it not?—There are such a large number that are worth very little—that is the explanation. I noticed at the time that it was a very low price indeed.

Dr. T. W. Grimshaw.

13 Dec. 1894.

Estimate of Irish agricultural values.

4200. The only other remark worth making is that one-fourth of the fowls are put down as laying hens. I thought always that the head of a family amongst hens did not bear so large a proportion to the population as one to four. You say that every one of those hens laid one hundred eggs, and you put down a figure of two-thirds of a million. I think that is a sanguine estimate, is it not?—It is not my estimate; it may be sanguine.

4201. It was the best estimate that could be made at the time I suppose?—Yes.

4202. No doubt as time goes on, if further efforts are made in the same direction, the facts might be more closely approached?—If the thing were done officially and returns called for from all markets, and things of that sort, and the hens were distinguished from chickens in the Agricultural Statistics, which they are not, you might get a different result, but there has been no official collection of information as to anything of the sort.

4203. The estimator made the best attempt he could, I suppose?—He did.

Milk and eggs.

4204. (*The O'Conor Don.*) Upon this point I find in the income paper you have included the value of milk as 14,000,000*l.* Is the value of milk and eggs, to which Mr. Sexton has just referred, included in these tables of the value of live stock to which we were alluding at the beginning—namely, Table B in your statement giving the number and value of live stock? Do you include in that the value of milk and eggs?—No, not in that particular table.

4205. Then that very important item, amounting to 14,000,000*l.* for milk and a very large sum for the eggs, is not included in the values stated there?—It is not included there.

4206. (*Lord Welby.*) But if that is not included, must not that be carefully noted when such conclusions as Mr. Sexton has drawn about the loss to the farmer are taken into consideration?—Most decidedly, but I think Mr. Sexton has taken that into consideration.

4207. (*Mr. Sexton.*) In Table B there is no reference to the produce of the stock; it is only the capital value of the stock?—Yes.

4208. In Table E you first have the net amount of crops after the stock has been fed out of them?—Yes.

4209. Then you have the amount of the stocks sold or disposed of within the year added to the whole product of the stock within the year?—Yes.

4210. Under the head of "stock" you add together the amount of stock sold within the year, and add the produce of the stock to that?—Yes.

4211. (*The O'Conor Don.*) Does that include the item of milk?—Yes, certainly.

4212. (*Mr. Sexton.*) Milk, butter, cream, cheese, everything?—Oh, no; I do not separate them like that.

4213. But they would all be included, would they not?—They would all be included in the 10*l.*

4214. In fact, it is the gross average income from all sources of the Irish farmer, taking note only of one item of expenditure—that is to say, the crops consumed by the stock, and all other items of expenditure are excluded?—I am not quite clear as to that.

4215. It is described in this sentence below Table E—"We see here that, after allowing for the portion "of the crops consumed by the stock, the estimated "average value of the crops and stock, and products of "stock sold or otherwise disposed of, was" so and so; so that it evidently includes it?—In giving that 10*l.* a year which is mentioned in the other paper it includes everything that can be got out of the cow. There was no attempt to find out how much butter and cheese and milk was sold—that was not attempted.

4216. I thought it a very heavy figure, including everything?—That was the figure which was given to me, as I have said, by a very experienced man.

4217. I will put to you now a few questions on the credit side of the estimate for 1850. The estimate for seed is only 2,000,000*l.* Do you consider that a full estimate for seed for Ireland during the year?—It is as given to me. I do not know anything about it; I have not an opinion upon the subject.

4218. Then, artificial manures, 600,000*l.*—less than 1*l.* a farmer?—A great number use none whatever.

4219. But a great many use many pounds' worth, do they not?—They may do.

4220. Now, I see that the crops consumed by the stock on the expense side of this account amount in value to 11,000,000*l.*, out of a total gross value of crops of 29,000,000*l.* You will observe that the portion of the crops reserved in your estimate in the year 1885 to feed the stock was 11,000,000*l.* out of 29,000,000*l.*, or more than one-third of the whole?—Yes.

4221. The total average annual value of the crops raised in Ireland from 1851 to 1855 was 45,000,000*l.*?—No; for 1866–70.

4222. Now, will you turn to Table E. For the period 1866–70 the total value of the crops there, after the stock had been fed out of them, is, say, 28,000,000*l.*?—Yes.

4223. Which shows, taking the difference between 28,000,000*l.* and 45,000,000*l.*, that 17,000,000*l.*, or considerably over one-third, went to feed the stock?—That is very likely.

4224. In the next period—1884 to 1888—the crops were of the total value, according to Table A., of nearly 36,000,000*l.*?—Yes.

4225. If you turn again to Table E. you will see the amount of crops left after the stock had been fed out of them was only 16,000,000*l.*—that is to say, 20,000,000*l.* went to feed the stock—very much more than half?—Yes.

4226. How is it that in the year 1885, which was a year comprised in that same quinquennial period, when, out of an average crop of 36,000,000*l.*, 20,000,000*l.* went to feed the stock, here, with a crop of 30,000,000*l.*, only 11,000,000*l.* goes to feed the stock?—That is an average. You are applying the whole average to an individual year—you must average everything. The calculation is not applicable—you are applying an average to an individual year.

4227. But I have shown you that in the preceding quinquennial period, out of a total of 45,000,000*l.*, 27,000,000*l.* only was left, so that 18,000,000*l.* out of 45,000,000*l.* went to feed the stock, even at a time when the stock had not developed to the figures which they reached in 1884–88, and what I press upon you is, the average annual value of the crops in those five years being 36,000,000*l.*, that 20,000,000*l.* went each year for the feeding of the stock, which is 2,000,000*l.* over half the total?

4228. And in this particular year, 1885, which is one of the five years dealt with, out of the 30,000,000*l.* of crops produced, only 11,000,000*l.* is set down on the other side as having been expended by the farmers to feed the stock—a difference so extraordinary that I cannot realise how it can be accounted for, because it is only two-thirds of what the average for the quinquennial period would be including that year with the others?

4229. (*Lord Welby.*) Is not that accounted for by the fact that the value of the stuff consumed by the cattle is taken at a very much lower price in one year than the others?—Of course it is, to some extent.

4230. (*Mr. Sexton.*) I think if this account is revised it will show that 15,000,000*l.* to 16,000,000*l.*, instead of 11,000,000*l.*, must have been used for feeding the stock, and I would submit that for your consideration in case of further inquiry?—Quite so.

4231. (*Chairman.*) You have quite caught the point, have you?—Yes.

4232. Perhaps you would like to add something to your evidence on that afterwards. It is the most material difficulty on the table?—If that is considered a material difficulty it is based on a document which I do not vouch for, which, as I say, was prepared as a basis

for discussing and considering the question. This is not an official document of my department—it is a private thing arranged for, as it were, as a basis for Sir Robert Hamilton and myself to talk about, and as a document of that sort (all the materials for the making of which have disappeared) it is not exactly the thing to ask me to revise it. It would be impossible—at present it could not be revised.

4233. (*Mr. Sexton*). I hope you understand that I do not hold you in the least degree responsible for the paper?—I am responsible for handing it in here, but I hand it in as a paper that might be useful to the Commission not as a document issued by my department.

4234. (*Chairman*.) We quite understand that; and, if you will allow me to say so, I rather think with a little more time you would be able to modify the difficulty with regard to it; but it is a great difficulty?—Of course.

4235. (*Mr. Sexton*.) The paper, although in its particulars it may be erroneous, is most useful in enabling us to take the first step in ascertaining what is the net income of the producers of crops in Ireland. The only other point I want to ask you about is, the charge for rent, you put that down at 11,000,000*l*.?—That is Griffiths' valuation of Ireland without taking towns of 10,000 inhabitants and upwards.

4236. I rather thought in your pamphlet you put it down at 11,400,000*l*.?—Perhaps I did; there may have been some addition for houses and so on.

4237. Taking rent first, you are no doubt aware that the official records show that 4,600,000*l*. of the valuation was dealt with in the Land Courts?—Yes.

4238. And the rent corresponding to that amount of valuation was 5,900,000*l*., that is one-fourth over the valuation?—Yes.

4239. If we may assume that the remainder of the valuation corresponding to 6,700,000*l*. exceeds the valuation to the same extent that would add 1,700,000*l*. to the remainder, making 8,400,000*l*.?—Yes.

4240. Which added to the revised rents would [illegible] 13,000,000*l*.?—It might be.

4241. I mean upon the assumption that the rents which have not been revised were at the same level as those which have been?—Yes.

4242. Then as to the taxes, the county cess [illegible] 1,500,000*l*. was payable entirely by the occupiers?—I had no means of dealing with those separately—the rent and taxes are put down together.

4243. You say that the rent and taxes are so and so, and you arrive at the total by making a deduction, and adding roughly a certain amount for taxes?—Yes.

4244. But I say the proper amount was not added because the occupier pays 1,500,000*l*. of county cess, and he pays all the poor rate over the 4*l*. valuation—that would be 2,000,000*l*.—then added to 13,500,000*l*., which upon the basis of the proceedings of the Land Court seems to be a reasonable figure for rent would make the charge for rent 15,000,000*l*. instead of 11,000,000*l*., would it not?—That may be so, but it is not my opinion: it must be remembered that the 11,000,000*l*. valuation includes all towns with less than 10,000 inhabitants.

4245. Upon that assumption it would increase the charges here by 5,000,000*l*. for the cost of feeding cattle out of the crops, and by 4,000,000*l*. for rent and taxes which would reduce the net income of the producers from 27,000,000*l*. to 18,000,000*l*. But even taking the net income of the producers as you have put it at 27,000,000*l*. you say the rural population of Ireland is 3,415,000 as distinguished from the civic population?—I think so.*

4246. And what you have said to us to-day about the labourers seems to confirm very strongly what you suggested on Friday, namely, that the population of the small towns under 2,000 must be really practically as much dependent on the land as the farmers are?—Very much so.

* Note by witness—3,440,000.

4247. Because, you see, we have 486,000 farmers, some of whom, no doubt, are labourers?—Yes.

4248. But you have also 300,000 labourers, these labourers not being to any considerable extent, I think, farmers' sons?—These are not; the farmers' sons are another class—I have them here.

4249. It is obvious then that to get at the population dependent upon the exertions of the farmers and the labourers for support, you must get at a much larger figure than the 2,300,000?—I said "directly dependent." "Directly dependent" was the phrase.

4250. But in point of fact the practical question is, is there any other fund from which the rural population of Ireland of 3,400,000 can live, except the fund derived from agriculture and pastoral industry?—No, I presume not.

4251. Then I reach the final stage of my examination (and I wish to thank you for the attention you have given to the questions I have put to you) by asking you whether even if my estimate of 18,000,000*l*. for income be wrong, and the estimate of 27,000,000*l*. be right, this sum divided between the rural population of 3,400,000 gives an average income of 8*l*. per annum?—Very likely it does; I have not done the sum.

4252. Will you kindly say what the 3,400,000 divided into 27,000,000*l*. comes to?—What is the 3,400,000?

4253. It is the rural population?—But that includes all the village shopkeepers all over the country.

4254. It does, but they all subsist on the same fund, do they not?—Oh, no; that is assuming that the income does not pass on to the other people, who make use of it as it passes through their hands.

4255. But in measuring the total of national wealth, we think of the creation of wealth, not of the passage of it, and in this inquiry we are considering the creation of wealth?—But that is getting into another question altogether, with all respect to you. If the farmer earns so much money, and pays the blacksmith and shopkeeper, the blacksmith and shopkeeper earn the money which the farmer had previously earned, and the shopkeeper probably pays the wholesale dealer—that is his income, and so it goes on.

4256. But there is no fund out of which any of these people can derive any income except the 27,000,000*l*.?—But it is income paid over and over again to different people.

4257. No doubt, but the fund out of which they derive their income is the 27,000,000*l*., which divided between the rural population gives an average of 8*l*. per head, does it not?—But that is not an admissible division.

4258. Is it not quite as admissible as your divisions in Tables D and F of the value of crops and stock over the whole of Ireland?—Quite so; but I do not say that that is what the people live by, or what they are worth. That is the ratio to the people.

4259. Divided in the same spirit as an average, is it not the same?—But you asked me, as it were, do I think that that is what all these people have to live out of.

4260. You said a moment ago that there is no other fund out of which they can live?—In that sense there is not.

4261. Very good, in that sense I put it to you?—But when you come to divide that——

4262. I am not coming to divide it. I am asking you to give me the average which that fund affords, spread over the rural population. I do not ask you to draw any further inference. What is the average of the fund derived from agricultural and pastoral profits divided over the rural population?—That is, of course, a matter of arithmetic. I forget what figure you gave me.

4263. It is 34 into 270—it is very near 8*l*. Then, if you add the wages for labour to that, it would be, say 35,000,000*l*., which would be about 10*l*. per head, taking the wages for labour and the profits on agriculture together?—Yes.

is the value you are
d ?—37,000,000l.
e from ?—That is on
have handed in.
the average of gross

nans are not ?—The
e Irish agriculturist.
of his personal expenses
true ; but our income
fore.
able capacity begins,
income an allowance
dence ?—But I do not
is the income of any

the average in your
me of any individual
is a different matter

come provided by the
and pastoral industry
it is not—at least I
saying it is what is

the rural population
?—That is the money
ulation, but that does

nly earning, is it not ?
is the only earning of

of earning, is there ?
a country it does not
es into that country
a sum circulates over
an income repeatedly

es in Ireland ?—And

we have to take the
ct sources of national
e with the other, and
ons and repetitions ?—
that is the income of
case if you do I say

nt. The question I
n average of the total
tural industry of the
al population ?—Of
f arithmetic. If you
rings out that figure,

to individuals, but it

ou give your answer
wo pages of the paper
taxation which you
as if Mr. Sexton will
ion again to you after
, I think you will be
so on ?—My answer is

upon that ?—I say if
000,000l. the answer
t that is not the total
ion of Ireland—the
is circulating among

your explanation ?—

Perhaps you will define
al population" ?—All
in the towns of 2,000
tion as distinguished

any attempt to calcu-
?—I did, but I gave it

4284. You think it is not possible to make such a calculation with accuracy ?—I do not. I think it is impossible.

4285. Would you go so far as to say that the total capital is or is not less than 400,000,000l., or would you rather not express any opinion upon the subject ?—I would rather not give you any opinion upon it.

4286. I want to ask you whether or not the total taxation of Ireland is not made up of the aggregate of the taxation falling on the individual members of the Irish community ?—I think so.

4287. It could not be anything else, could it ?—It must be so, of course.

4288. And if the taxation of Ireland as a whole is unfair as compared with that of Great Britain, does it not follow necessarily that taxation must fall unfairly on at least some members of the Irish community ?—Certainly.

4289. If every member of the Irish community were fairly taxed, the country as a whole would be fairly taxed ?—Certainly.

4290. Has it come to your notice that the taxation on an Irishman having an income of, we will say, 1,000l. a year is unfair, as compared with the taxation falling on an Englishman having the same income ?—No, I should think not.

4291. Do you think there is any unfairness in the case of persons in the two countries having a smaller income, say of 500l. a year ?—No, but you are coming down now to the agricultural community.

4292. I would ask whether you think there is any unfairness with regard to the agricultural community ?—But that does not apply to Ireland solely—it applies all over the United Kingdom.

4293. Then do you think that the agriculturists are unfairly taxed ?—I think it is a question.

4294. Can you say in what respect you think they are unfairly taxed ?—The articles which would bear upon them most would be beer and spirits—not the tax paid on beer and spirits which they consume—but indirectly taxing agricultural products which are in a very depressed state. I think that is one of the cases where an agricultural community might be hit by a tax of that sort. I do not mean to say that as to the spirit which a man who is worth 500l. a year buys he is over-taxed in that.

4295. Do you think, taking two men with 100l. a year each in the two countries, they are differently treated, or that one is unfairly taxed as compared with the other ?—They appear to me to be treated exactly in the same way individually.

4296. And the same rule I suppose would apply to two men in the two countries with 50l. a year ?—I think so.

4297. If there is any unfairness in taxation it is not between the individual Irishman and the individual Englishman, but between the poor man and the rich man ?—Yes, I think that fairly expresses it.

4298. I will go back to what you said about the whisky duty falling rather hardly upon the agriculturists—that was a point we discussed the other day. You think, I understand, that the spirit duty falls hardly upon the agriculturist, because he gets a smaller price for his oats or barley, or whatever is used to produce the whisky ?—Yes.

4299. If you reduce the demand for his produce he gets a lower price ?—Yes.

4300. In order to increase the demand for the raw material there must be more whisky drunk ?—Yes.

4301. Do you think it is desirable to take off the tax in order to increase the consumption of spirit in the hope of ultimately conferring a benefit on the agriculturist ?—Certainly not. I think if you could diminish the amount of the spirit consumed you would benefit the community.

Emigration.

4302. I wish to ask you a few questions about emigration ; you have given figures with regard to emigration from Ireland ?—Yes.

4303. You are no doubt aware that emigration is not peculiar to Ireland although there is probably no

Dr. T. W. Grimshaw. 10 Dec. 1894. Emigration.

country in which it has been carried to the same extent?—Yes.

4304. There has been emigration from England, from Scotland, from Sweden and Norway, from Germany, and from Italy?—Yes.

4305. I have got figures here which show that, from 1841 to 1889, 3,000,000 persons of Irish descent arrived in the United States of America as emigrants, and that during the same period 3,002,000 people of German birth arrived in the same country?—Yes.

4306. Showing that there was nearly as large an emigration during that period to the United States from Germany as from Ireland?—Yes.

4307. But of course that emigration was relatively to population much larger from Ireland?—Yes, of course Germany is much larger in population.

4308. Are you aware that a number of Irishmen move to Great Britain every year in search of labour, and return after some months?—Yes.

4309. Are you aware that there is a similar migration of labourers in other countries, and notably in Italy?—I know there is.

4310. And that the Italians move at certain seasons in the year into France, Switzerland, and Austria, and return later on?—I am quite aware of that.

4311. You are no doubt aware also that there is practically no emigration from France?—Yes, there is scarcely any.

4312. And you know that France is a country of great natural resources, and that the people are frugal as a rule?—Yes.

4313. That the population is either stationary or declining, but practically stationary?—The rural population is declining.

4314. And I suppose you would think that this state of things accounts for the absence of emigration there?—Certainly.

4315. Are you aware that taxation is very high in France?—I believe it is.

4316. So that high taxation, if the population is not increasing and the country is fairly prosperous, does not necessarily lead to emigration?—No; it is not driving the people out of the country in that case.

4317. Do you think (as a matter of opinion, of course), that the Irish people who have emigrated, and their descendants, are, as a body, better off than they would have been if there had been no emigration, and they had remained in this country?—I do think so—very much better off.

4318. Do you think that the people of Ireland who did not emigrate, and their descendants who are still here, are better off owing to the fact that the pressure on subsistence was reduced by the emigration of a large number of other inhabitants?—I do.

4319. You gave certain figures in regard to the amount of manufactures of certain articles in Ireland—linen, and so forth; there is no doubt, is there, that the total amount of manufacture in Ireland is relatively small compared with other countries?—Yes, that is so.

4320. I should like to know how you account for the comparatively small amount of manufactures that exist in Ireland?—I think the principal reason is that we have not got the supply of the raw material—we have not got coals in Ireland, and so on, or minerals to any great extent.

4321. Do you think then that the tendency is for manufactories to be set up at those places where there are natural advantages for carrying on manufactures?—Yes, certainly.

4322. You know, of course, that there is a vast extent of manufacturing industry in England and Scotland?—Yes.

4323. I daresay you are also aware that there are large tracts in England and Scotland where there are no manufactures?—Yes; I know that.

4324. Do you think that those facts corroborate the opinion you have already expressed that manufactories are set up at those points where there are natural advantages which make it profitable for them to be set up there?—I do.

4325. I believe a great many Irishmen, and a great many people of Irish descent, are employed in the manufacturing districts of England and Scotland; are they not?—Yes, there are a great number. I could not say how many, but there are a great many.

4326. The number is large?—Yes.

4327. I think we may fairly assume, may we not, that these persons emigrate to England and Scotland, and still remain there, because they found that by so doing they could better their condition?—I presume that is the reason—there is no other reason.

4328. I suppose you would say it would be quite useless to establish manufactories in places where they could not be conducted at a profit?—Certainly; I would never propose to establish a manufactory where it would be carried on at a loss.

4329. Manufactories must be, and only can be, established at places where they can be carried on at a profit—that is an axiom?—Yes.

4330. And, under such circumstances, does it not appear to you that there is no other reasonable course except to establish manufactories at places where the business can be carried on at a profit, and to allow the population to migrate to those places?—Certainly; they must either go to the employment or the employment must come to them.

4331. And if the employment will not come to them?—They must go to it.

Adjourned to to-morrow at 11 o'clock.

Dr. Grimshaw's evidence is continued at Question 4399 (Eleventh Day).

TENTH DAY.

Tuesday, 11th December, 1894.

At the Benchers' Chambers, Four Courts, Dublin.

PRESENT.

THE RIGHT HON. HUGH C. E. CHILDERS, *Chairman.*

LORD WELBY.	CHARLES E. MARTIN, ESQ.
THE RIGHT HON. THE O'CONOR DON.	THOMAS SEXTON, ESQ., M.P.
SIR DAVID BARBOUR, K.C.S.I.	GUSTAV W. WOLFF, ESQ., M.P.

MR. R. H. HOLLAND, *Secretary.*

DR. O'DONNELL called and examined.

4332. (*Chairman.*) Your lordship is Bishop of Raphoe, I think?—Yes.

4333. And you have been a member of the Congested Districts Board for how long?—For two years.

4334. But you wish to give your evidence on your own responsibility, and not as representing the Board, as I understand?—Yes.

4335. How would you define Ireland in respect of its occupations; what would you define Ireland to be, a country of what kind?—An agricultural country.

4336. An agricultural and pastoral country?—Yes.

4337. What would you lay down as the first rule with respect to Ireland's capacity to pay taxes?—As Ireland is in the main an agricultural country and the bulk of the population depends upon agriculture, the prosperity of the country turns on the question of whether agriculture flourishes or not; accordingly when agriculture flourishes the population as a whole thrives and the country is able to maintain a condition of prosperity, but, if agriculture ceases to be remunerative, Ireland has neither commerce nor manufactures on which to sustain its population.

4338. What has been the condition of Ireland as to its agricultural condition within the last few years?—In my opinion the agriculturists of Ireland have been losing money.

4339. For some years past?—Yes.

4340. In what respect is the Irish agricultural system specially deficient?—There is a radical blot on the Irish agricultural system arising from the fact that there has been a strong tendency towards removing the tillage population from the good land and planting the inhabitants down in large numbers on very inferior soil. Until that process is reversed I do not think agriculture can thrive in Ireland, nor the country as a whole be prosperous.

4341. Is there any other main cause for the want of prosperity in Ireland?—It goes with the preceding cause that very many of the agricultural holdings in Ireland are of low valuation. Those of lowest valuation are commonly found in districts where the potato is to the largest extent the staple article of food, and where at the same time that crop is most liable to be destroyed by blight. The result is that a season in which blight affects the potato crop is one in which a large number of Irish agriculturists are brought face to face with a very serious state of things.

4342. What proportion of the Irish agricultural holdings, do you remember, are below the line of £4?—A fourth of the agricultural holdings are below the line of £4.

4343. In the West and North-West particularly is not the proportion still greater than that?—Yes. In the county Donegal and the county Mayo one-half of the agricultural holdings are rated under £4.

Dr. O'Donnell. 11 Dec. 1894. Defects of Irish agricultural system.

4344. Do you remember the number, roughly?—Out of 29,534 agricultural holdings in Donegal, 14,948 are rated at £4 and under; in Mayo out of 33,128 agricultural holdings, 16,668 are rated at £4 and under; in Galway out of 32,018 agricultural holdings, 14,186 are rated at £4 and under.

4345. With respect, then, to those three counties it may be stated in general terms that half, or nearly half, the holdings are of 4*l.* or under, may it not?—Yes.

4346. Then, with respect to the seasons, is there a considerable proportion of bad seasons in Ireland?—The seasons in which the crops fail occur often in Ireland. For instance, in recent times, 1879 was an extremely bad year, 1882, over a great deal of the country, was a bad year; in 1888 the potato crop failed very seriously in Donegal and in other parts of Ireland; in 1890 it was worse; in 1892 it was also bad in Donegal. The extent of the failure of the potato crop in 1891 all over the country was not less than half a million tons; while in 1890 the deficit in this crop fully reached one and a half million tons.

Failures of crops.

4347. Would it be extravagant to say that one-third of the seasons, particularly with reference to the potato crop, are thoroughly bad in that part of Ireland?—I can answer that question best, I think, by giving you my own experience. I have been in Donegal since 1888; 1888 was a bad year; 1890 was a bad year; 1893 was a bad year; and the potato crop is not this year, in the poorer parts of Donegal, more than a third of a fair crop.

4348. Could you give a value below which the occupier cannot even be expected to pull through in an average bad year?—Taking the agriculturists generally, I think those rated under 10*l.* have, as a class, a good deal of difficulty, but the class that go down in a bad year like 1890, and cannot at all get on, even by means of credit, without public help, is the class of those rated at 6*l.* and under.

4349. And you would put 6*l.* as the line below which a farmer cannot pull through in a bad year, would you?—Yes, speaking of them as a class, but not of individual farmers.

4350. As a class, you say, the farming tenants cannot pull through?—Yes; and although that class is a more numerous one in the congested districts than elsewhere, undoubtedly in what is spoken of as

Most Rev. P. O'Donnell, D.D.

13 Dec. 1894.

Failures of crops.

the eastern half of Ireland the farmers so rated have a great deal of difficulty in a bad year. No doubt their land is somewhat better and it is not so subject to blight as that along the western coast, where the rainfall is excessive and the storms of the Atlantic do a great deal of harm; but anyone who looks at the report of the Mansion House Relief Committee on its work during 1880 will see that agriculturists in the east of Ireland, owing to the failure of the potato crop, made applications and received substantial relief from the collections of the gentlemen composing that committee. For instance, agriculturists in Down and Antrim and Meath, Wexford, Tipperary, and Waterford were aided in that way. Perhaps it would give the Commission a fuller idea of what is really needed to pull the people through such a disaster as overtook them in 1879 if I read a short extract from the proceedings of the Mansion House Committee:— "It must be recollected that the Mansion House Fund "was only one of many agencies employed to mitigate "the crisis. Beside the 180,000*l.* subscribed to this "fund, sums amounting to about 500,000*l.* more were "distributed between the Duchess of Marlborough's "Committee, the 'New York Herald' Fund Committee, the National Land League, the Canadian "Fund Committee, and the Philadelphia Food Committee. The largest share of the American subscriptions—according to one calculation, 200,000*l.*— "was forwarded to the Irish Bishops for separate distribution; 26,330*l.* was thus remitted to the Archbishop of Tuam alone. The individual remittances "from America and Australia to friends in Ireland "will be, perhaps, moderately estimated at 150,000*l.* "more. If to this magnificent tribute of 830,000*l.* of "private charity we add the 189,720*l.* claimed to have "been issued to landowners for relief employment, the "55,937*l.* returned as the expenditure upon baronial "relief works, and the extra charges for outdoor "relief, which are probably under-estimated at "200,000*l.*, we shall have in round numbers 1,250,000*l.* "applied to the alleviation of seven months' distress "without being able to do much more than satisfy the "immediate cravings of want; and this, without "taking into account that some 4,000,000*l.* of rents "and debts were, if not wiped out, at least suspended "during that time; that 500,000*l.* more were loaned "for seeds; that therefore four months' food was "available at the commencement of the crisis, and "that an unusually early harvest shortened its continuance for fully three weeks longer, at a juncture "when every form of charity was exhausted. Nor "can we truly say that with all that timely warning, "glorious generosity, zeal, organisation, and immense "expenditure like those we have enumerated could "do, there has not remained much suffering, and that "it is to be feared some contributory elements of the "increased mortality of the year."

4351. That great distress and that marvellous amount of charitable relief arose out of the failure of 1879, I think?—Yes.

4352. Could your Lordship say what you think the amount of the failure of the crop that year could be taken at in figures?—The official estimate, I think, puts it at 10,000,000*l.*

4353. And for the three years?—For 1877, 1878 and 1879 at 20,000,000*l.*

4354. How much of that is represented by the loss on potatoes?—Upwards of 11,000,000*l.* of that sum.

4355. The average value of the potato crop is what?—About that time the average was about 9,000,000*l.* a year.

4356. And the actual valuation of 1879 was what?—Three and a half millions.

4357. So that in that year alone five millions and a half was lost?—Yes.

4358. So that you would say as to the failure of the potato crop in various extents of the country that it is the cause of poverty and of serious obstacles to the improvement of agriculture?—Certainly.

4359. In 1882 do you remember what the yield of potatoes was?—The yield of potatoes in 1882 was one and a half million tons short of what the yield had been in 1881, or of what it was afterwards in 1883.

4360. 1882 was a particularly bad year, was it not?—Yes.

4361. Do you remember how much the yield of the potato crop reached altogether in that year?—I have not got the figures, but it did not reach 2,000,000 tons.

4362. May we say then altogether as the result of the answers to the last questions, that the people were only kept from starving by the munificence of the relief they received?—Quite so.

4363. When you come to 1885, was the potato crop short again in that year?—I have no distinct recollection for 1885 or 1886 as I was not much mixing with the people then, but in 1886 there was a bad crop of potatoes.

4364. In coming down to 1890 was the potato crop short then?—Yes, in 1890 the potato crop was short by one and a half million tons of its usual yield.

4365. And in 1892 was it still short?—Yes, it was still short.

4366. Was it specially short in particular districts, or was the failure general throughout every part of the country?—The failure was worst on the western sea board where the rainfall is heaviest and the storms severest.

4367. I think your lordship assisted in distributing a large sum of money in 1892 and 1893, did you not?—Between 1888, 1890, and 1893 I was the medium of distributing 6,000*l.* or 7,000*l.* either for food or for seed. The money was given not so much in those years as in the spring seasons that followed them.

4368. But it was given in reference to the failures of those years, was it not?—Yes; and in the year 1891 following 1890, the Lord Lieutenant and the Chief Secretary organised a relief fund which amounted I understand to about 50,000*l.*

4369. The Congested Districts Board was appointed by the late Government I think as the outcome of that state of things?—Yes. It was appointed under the second part of the Land Act of 1891.

4370. Will you give briefly its purpose and its income?—The purpose of the Board was to improve permanently agriculture, fishing, and other industries in the congested districts.

4371. Its income was how much?—41,250*l.* a year, being the interest at $2\frac{3}{4}$ per cent. on 1,500,000*l.*

4372. What was the unit of area?—The unit of area is the Poor Law electoral division, and poor law electoral divisions to be scheduled under the Congested Districts Board should be rated in this way:—the total number of inhabitants in the electoral division divided into the valuation of the division should give a sum of less than 30*s.* per head, and next, the electoral division should be situated in a county in which at least 20 per cent. of the inhabitants was found in such divisions.

4373. Can you remember the number of divisions?—423.

4374. What proportion of the total land of the country was in the congested districts?—About a sixth.

4375. And what proportion of the population?—About a ninth.

4376. And what proportion of the valuation?—About a twenty-fifth or twenty-sixth.

4377. Then the proportion of the valuation was a very small one, showing how very poor the districts were?—Yes.

4378. How would you describe roughly the holdings; of what proportionate sizes were they, or what sizes were they?—They vary a good deal in size; sometimes mountain grazing is attached to the holding, and sometimes it is not. Generally the holdings have an average of two acres of tillage, in some

Most Rev. Dr. O'Donnell.

21 Nov. 1895.

Operations of Congested Districts Board.

places four or five acres, and in extent vary from an acre to twenty acres, five or six being the average.

4379. With reference to the fourfold classification of houses with which we are familiar now, what was the character of the houses generally in the congested districts?—The houses are generally third-class houses.

4380. Very few fourth class?—Not so many fourth-class houses.

4381. What other sources of income besides agricultural income would the people living in the congested districts have?—There are some secondary sources of income, and it is unfortunate that they are not more widely diffused. In most parts of the congested districts, as things are and until the people are brought back to better soil, they cannot well make a living out of their holdings. Some fish, some migrate for labour, some make money by kelp-burning; and then, for the women, in one district there is knitting, in another shirt-making, and so on; but these industries are very circumscribed as to the area in which they are found.

4382. In the congested districts is the fishing a languishing industry, or is it improving?—The fishing industry at present is improving, through the operations of the Congested Districts Board. Until the establishment of the Board the industry languished.

4383. Does the Board make direct grants for the purpose of improving fishing?—The Board gives boats and gear to fishermen of good character, with the obligation of repayment by fixed instalments.

4384. There is no absolute grant given?—There is no absolute grant given.

4385. Does the Board do anything in the way of providing small piers and accommodation affecting fishing, or is that work confined to another department?—At present the Board is expending a good deal of its income on piers and roads, especially on fishing piers. I should rather say that it is spending a sum of 50,000*l.* out of a little fund which, in addition to its annual income, has been placed at the disposal of the Board. That fund is made up of the Irish Reproductive Loan Fund and the Sea and Coast Fisheries Fund. The surplus of these two funds is placed at the discretion of the Board for expenditure.

4386. Have the funds themselves been wound up, or do they still exist in their separate conditions?—They have been transferred to the control of the Congested Districts Board.

4387. With respect to the women's work, knitting, shirtmaking, and things of that sort, is the Board giving money to assist that?—No. Here and there the Board has given money to assist the starting of a factory in the congested districts, but not anything directly to the workers. In a few places the factories are looked upon as so many training schools, and on that principle, for the number taught in those factories, a capitation grant for a fixed number of years is allowed by the Board; but there is no such thing as direct payment from the Board to any worker.

4388. Is the amount of work of that kind by women, especially knitting (which everybody who has visited that country cannot help observing is very general), increasing in amount?—The knitting industry is one that is very widespread in Donegal, and for that the Congested Districts Board has been able to do very little. It was a pretty well-established industry there, and it goes on perhaps not so flourishingly as it did a few years ago; but yet it gives employment to a considerable number of people. The wages are extremely small; rarely would a woman receive more than twopence halfpenny for knitting a pair of plain socks.

4389. That means practically how much a week? How much is a woman who is not overburdened with a family able to earn?—A hardworking woman, besides doing her household work, would knit a pair a day; and if she had nothing else to do, she would knit three pairs in two days.

4390. That would mean about eighteenpence a week?—Yes.

Most Rev. Dr. O'Donnell.

21 Nov. 1895.

Operations of Congested Districts Board.

4391. That does not include the value of the stuff, does it?—No. The yarn is given out to the great bulk of the people who are engaged in the knitting industry. Occasionally the people in that part of the country spin their own wool and make stockings or dispose of the wool and sell it in the local market. That of course is a much more profitable business than working at the yarn which is given out by the hosiery merchants, but it is not by any means so profitable as it was years ago.

Food and mode of life of the people in Congested Districts.

4392. Passing from that point to the question of the food of the people in the congested districts, has your lordship any special remark to make for the advantage of the Commission?—The food of the people in the congested districts and, indeed, generally, of the agriculturists throughout the part that I am familiar with, has greatly changed, just as the fashion of the people's clothes has changed or the material out of which the clothes are made; it has changed and become more expensive, and in my opinion is not better.

4393. More white bread is eaten, I suppose?—More white bread is eaten and more tea consumed, but not more meat—less meat. I should say that the Irish farmer with a valuation of under 10*l.* a year practically is a vegetarian.

4394. Does your lordship go so far as to say that he consumes little of the cheaper forms of meat, bacon, and so on?—On Sunday he may have bacon, but those who are valued under 4*l.* rarely have any kind of meat except two or three times in the year. In the congested districts the food is farinaceous or vegetable food.

4395. We have evidence that there is a large increase in the consumption of tea; is that so in the congested districts?—It is; the change that has come about in the food of the poorer people of the congested districts is pretty much of this kind. The substantial part of their food is composed of potatoes as long as they have a supply. When the potatoes fail the main article of food is Indian meal.

4396. Has the prejudice against Indian meal quite disappeared?—To a large extent it has. Sometimes the poor people have milk, but often they have not, even with their stirabout, and the nature of this food and the want of milk have had a great deal to do with the large use of tea in the poorer parts of the country. When a man has pretty hard work to do and has for his dinner only potatoes or stirabout, a little tea with some bread after is really a necessary of life in order to enable him to go to his task with anything like spirit, and consequently in the congested districts at two of the three daily meals it is not unusual to have tea and bread, either in supplement of the food which I have described or as a substitute for it. Occasionally, in fact frequently, during the spring and autumn when the work is hard, there is an evening refection also of tea.

4397. A good deal of the tea consumed in all parts of Ireland I presume is not very judiciously made, is it?—I do not quite agree with everything that is said in regard to that. People generally say that the tea is kept until the tannic acid is well abstracted. I do not think that is largely the case at all. I think the people make their tea much more judiciously than that.

4398. At one time there is no doubt the astringent character of the ordinary tea in an Irish cottage was very marked indeed, was it not?—Yes.

4399. And that has improved, you think?—Yes, I have myself not observed tea made in the unsatisfactory way many persons say it is.

4400. Passing from tea to tobacco, has the consumption of tobacco increased or decreased in the congested districts?—I suppose for a number of years past it has been pretty stationary.

4401. Is the price felt to be very high?—It is. It is a large draw upon the small incomes of the people, but their food is so poor and so little strengthening that a strong man who has got this meagre fare for his meals and his work to do naturally Tobacco.

Dr. O'Donnell. 13 Dec. 1895.

Tobacco.

turns to a little tobacco to raise his spirits, or get himself into working order for his task.

4402. At the small shops in those districts what is the price of an ounce of tobacco?—Threepence.

4403. I suppose your lordship is aware that that would be considered very high in our part of the Kingdom—the price there is between twopence and twopence farthing?—I do not profess to give the price accurately.

Prices of meal.

4404. Has the Congested Districts Board's attention been called to the question of the high prices of the necessaries of life in that part of Ireland?—No doubt; these things frequently come up for discussion, and little by little I am sure prices will be a good deal reduced. In fact, in regard to meal and flour (which also latterly I am glad to say is more largely consumed in the congested districts owing to the reduction in price than it used to be), the competition now in sale is so considerable that if the people have ready cash to pay they can get them for a very reasonable price.

4405. There is real competition in the villages and small towns, is there?—Yes, certainly. Along the coast for cash prices the people can get such food as meal and flour very reasonably; but they have not yet been able to command the market in the same way with regard to groceries, or to the same extent, and generally the price paid for provisions by those people is high, very high, if the business be not a cash but a credit transaction.

4406. The Congested Districts Board have attached to their report some very interesting calculations, family budgets, I think, they are called, have they not?—Yes.

Income and expenditure of the poor.

4407. With respect to the income and expenditure of the twelve classes who have been chosen, did your lordship take much interest in the formation of those estimates?—Indeed, with the formation of them I had nothing to do; but I have looked into them carefully and I know that they very accurately describe the condition of the people in those districts. I would make just this remark about those budgets, that there are a few things of great interest, from a financial point of view, to the people, to which they do not make reference and could not. There is a district in Donegal, comprising four or five parishes, out of which an enormous number of people migrate to Scotland and to East Donegal for labour, and the wages which, with great toil, they secure are on the whole good wages. Counting those who go twice a year, 4,000 labourers migrate annually to Scotland, and I am sure also at least 5,000 labourers come to East Donegal and the county Derry and Tyrone for employment out of a district which I may widely describe as West Donegal, and chiefly out of four parishes in West Donegal. Owing to the income from migratory labour these industrious people have a little money which otherwise they could not possibly have, and without which they could not live. Now in Gweedore and in the Rosses, the centre of that district, the valuation per head does not exceed 5s. 6d., yet these families have with the shopkeepers an accumulated debt of 10l. each against them, besides what they may owe in arrears for county cess or for rent; and I am sure the debt elsewhere is not less, because in that district, owing to the migratory labour, they have a considerable means of earning money. In addition to that you will note that these tables, which are very accurate, do not cover any expenditure for death, or sickness, or marriage; so that you see even where there is not a loss shown at the end of the year, various expenses may occur to account for this large debt. In the whole of that country it is no exaggeration to say that the small holders have an accumulated debt in the shops of 10l. each family.

4408. (Mr. Wolff.) Does not that get paid off from year to year. It is not allowed to increase continually, is it?—It is much more before the labourers go to Scotland or elsewhere, and it is reduced when they come back. I should say this accumulation has grown within comparatively recent times.

Dr. O'Donnell. 13 Dec. 1895.

Increasing indebtedness of the poor.

4409. (Chairman.) That is to say the credit that given them is better than it used to be in past days?—Yes. You see although their valuation is so small, yet they have this way of earning money, and they are extremely regular in paying their debts as far as they possibly can. They are most honest, truthful, and industrious, and of course they have now got security in their little holdings, and consequently the shopkeepers, as far as they can, will give them credit.

4410. Do you think that they are running too much into debt to the shopkeepers? Do you think that that is the tendency?—Too much, but not more than they can help.

4411. But too much as an economical arrangement?—Yes. And I may say this, that in the town of Letterkenny, where I am situated, I have talked this matter over with farmers in the better part of Donegal—in Eastern Donegal, where the land is held in large farms and is as well tilled as in any part of Ireland, to say the least of it. Speaking to these large farmers in East Donegal about the backward movement of the people in the poorer parts, I have been assured by them that they are going down hill much more rapidly than the people in the poorer districts. They assure me that they are losing money from year to year, and although they are not people who will individually tell one how their account stands, they say of themselves as a class, and it is well known there, that they are largely in debt to the banks, to building societies, and to the merchants in Derry and other considerable towns.

4412. What would your lordship say was the average of the receipts of a farmer according to the twelve budgets which have been produced?—The average receipts are 29l. 11s. 7½d.

4413. Besides the value of the produce consumed by the family?—Yes.

4414. And the two together would come to about how much?—The average value of the produce is 11l. 14s. 7d., and the two together would amount to 41l. 6s. 3d.

4415. The expenditure (which of course must only be compared with the cash receipts) would be about how much?—The expenditure is 29l. 15s. 11½d.

4416. And does that include all the items; you mentioned, I think, that that did not include burial expenses?—It does not. Of course the 29l. 11s. 7½d. represents cash receipts; the 29l. 15s. 11½d. represents cash outlay. The 11l. 14s. 7d. may be looked upon either as a receipt or as outlay; it is both; the occupier takes this value out of the soil and expends it.

4417. I would ask you one question about what are called clerical expenses: what is the average amount received by the Church from a holding?—You will notice that in those returns clerical expenses are put down in three or four cases only, and not in the others. If you take the amounts charged in all the returns, and add them together, and divide by the total 12, you will, I think, have a fair idea of the clerical charges, family by family. I suppose they come to six shillings or seven shillings.

4418. I think those that were given average about six or seven shillings?—There are many who are charged nothing at all, others are charged more, and others some considerable amount. These charges, of course, cover everything, not only the maintenance of the priests, but also the contributions for the erection and maintenance of churches. You see in Ireland the Catholic population, which is three-fourths of the whole population, support their clergy without any aid whatever from any public fund; even in the poorest districts the number of clergymen must be considerable, and in one way or other some means, usually very slender means indeed, must be found for the support of the clergy, and no other means can be found except these contributions.

4419. Then the estimate of 6s. or 7s. which is given

Dr. O'Donnell, D.D. — 14 Dec. 1906. in some of the budgets is a fair one all round, is it?—I think it would be a fair one for small occupiers.

Taxation and the poor. 4420. Having then this income and this estimate of expenditure, what would you say was the financial condition of these poor people, and is it possible to expect from them any additional contribution to the public revenue?—It has been already calculated that they pay a large sum into the public revenue, but considering that they have not the means of subsistence all round, it seems indefensible to put a tax upon them.

4421. What they pay to the public revenue is almost exclusively the duties on spirits, tea, and tobacco, and some other small things, is it not?—Yes, in Donegal, with which I am most acquainted, it is chiefly a duty on tea and tobacco. Except in the towns the people do not drink at all. These migratory labourers that I spoke about are almost to a man total abstainers. I think, when calculated, the amount of duty charged on tea, tobacco, and spirits in the congested districts would be 2*l.* 16*s.* or near 2*l.* 16*s.* per family, and as there are one hundred thousand families, that would come to upwards of 300,000*l.*, raised from these people.

4422. I suppose your lordship would not wish to see any considerable diminution in the price of spirits?—I have never considered how far an increase in the duty on spirits is any means of preventing the consumption of spirits. I do not know how far an increase of duty prevents consumption, but taking in the other dutiable articles, whether spirits are good for these people or not, it is not right to put a tax on a community where the people of the community have not already secured to them the ordinary means of subsistence.

4423. With respect to tobacco and tea, which are by all accounts harmless articles of consumption, you would hold with any reasonable reduction in their price, would you not?—Certainly.

4424. Do you consider that the large consumption of tea is due to any unknown cause?—Within the last thirty years quite a change has come over the dietary of the people generally, and I believe it is not a change for the better. The dietary is not more substantial than it used to be with the farming class, but it is more expensive, and it is impossible, by any mere logical process, to get the people to change the habit which they have now formed.

Advances and grants of public money. 4425. Can you put into a few sentences the correlation in your mind, or the want of correlation, if I may use the expression, between the taxation of the country in these respects which you look upon as heavy, and the boons which it has received in the shape of advances and grants of money?—I consider that the advances and grants of money to these districts hitherto have not been very much. No doubt the operations of a Board such as the Congested Districts Board, will result in a material improvement of those districts, especially if the Board were provided with money sufficient to attain its object. But it is my opinion that the poorer districts of the country, apart altogether from their being too heavily taxed, have a claim to be pulled on with the rest of a large progressive community of which they form part. If a certain portion of a country be unfavourably circumstanced it seems right that the resources of the State at large should be available to pull on that section within reasonable limits, provided the people in the poorer parts show themselves to be industrious. Now in the congested districts the people are undoubtedly very industrious; and, moreover, it is to be noted that for years past they have been paying duty on tea and tobacco, although their incomes certainly were not such as even to supply them with the necessary means of a proper livelihood. The accumulation of that tax paid by them if expended upon those districts would undoubtedly completely transform them. It is my own opinion, and I believe it is the opinion of many others, that the proper remedy for most of the evil that is to be deplored in the congested districts would be to transfer from the bad land where the people are crowded the most industrious of the population and give them holdings on grass land, which is now very largely in many parts of the country being thrown back upon the hands of the proprietors, inasmuch as it is not paying as grazing tracts. It would require, of course, to accomplish that on a large scale, that some tribunal in the country should be endowed with compulsory powers to take land, such at least as the Parish Councils have in England; but one can see on a small scale how the process may work out from the operations of the Congested Districts Board on the Pinnock Estate, where lately there has taken place an enlargement of holdings that promises the very best results. The Board bought a property for 7,000*l.* on which there was a very large grazing farm; that grazing farm the Board carved up into small holdings; on some of those holdings it built houses and gave them to tenants who migrated from other parts of the estate. The lands vacated by those tenants were given to the occupiers of adjoining farms. Then again the Board sometimes enlarged a holding by making an accommodation road between a portion of this grazing tract and the holding which an occupier previously held, and assigning it to him. These operations have been carried out by the Board, and after fencing and draining and building houses, improving generally the condition of the tenants, and making them tenant purchasers, the Board instead of losing by the transaction has a sum of over 300*l.* to expend for the benefit of the people.

Policy of migration. 4426. Then may we understand that in addition to these different classes of local improvements your lordship would advocate what used to be called migration as a wise policy?—Certainly. I think I do not take the view of many in regard to the process by which the Irish population has gone down. It is my opinion that the dominating factor in bringing about such a result was the clearance of the good lands, because it was thought that cattle and sheep would pay better on the land than tillage farming. You can see that since 1841 the population of Meath and Tipperary has gone down much more than the population of Donegal or Mayo. Now Meath and Tipperary are both purely rural counties. The land there is better for tillage than the land in Donegal or Mayo. The potato crop there is less subject to blight, yet in the period between 1841 and 1891 the population of Meath came down by more than half; the population of Tipperary by more than half; while the population of Donegal has decreased only by a third, and the population of Mayo has decreased only by a third; and if we come to Mayo and to Donegal you will find that whereas the population of both has been swept away from the comparatively good land, it is not impossible to find in either tracts of bog on which the population has actually increased. I take it then that the dominant factor in the decrease of population has been the clearance off the best land of tillage farmers to make way for cattle and sheep. I think now the tide has begun to turn; foreign competition, the cheap freights across the Atlantic, the quick passage, the coming of butter from New Zealand, all these have had such an effect on the price of Irish stock, that the tendency is not likely to continue of getting the land out of tillage, and putting flocks upon it.

4427. And the automatic or semi-automatic system which has been going on for some time, which has diminished the population in an insignificant or inadequate degree, you think should be supplemented by some system of direct encouragement to migration so as to clear those inferior lands, which cannot be cleared in other ways?—That will absolutely be needed. By far the best system for most of the land in the congested districts with which I am acquainted would be the following:—If the grazing land were so cut up as to give the occupier at least three or four acres of good land, and a mountain range besides for his cattle, he

Most Rev. P. O'Donnell, D.D.

13 Dec. 1894.

Policy of emigration.

could combine agriculture with the raising of rough stock, and he could also reclaim with advantage the moorland. A man who has only moorland could scarcely ever reclaim it with advantage—never if he has to pay for the labour. But if he has a small tract of pretty good land, he can change his seed from that to the reclaimed bog, and when the potato crop fails on the bog it is not so likely to fail on the clayey soil. Then a year that is bad for crops may not be so bad for stock, and if he has a valuation, or a holding that is fairly rented, over 6*l.*, there is every reason to hope that with economy he would be able to pull through. At all events the class so circumstanced could meet the disastrous effects of a bad year, and would not be thrown on the world's charity.

4428. Passing to another subject, is there much absenteeism in your lordship's diocese?—Yes, and I consider absenteeism is largely responsible for the non-progressive condition of this country, and especially of the congested districts. In a poor country like this it is an enormous loss when the great bulk of 11,000,000*l.* of rent is spent out of Ireland, and that loss is especially felt because the country is an agricultural one. This income is derived from the land, and some portion of it should be expended in making the business of agriculture, out of which the money really comes, pay. If the owners were resident and gave prizes for good cultivation, for improved houses, for making drains—even small prizes—the improvement would be enormously great. I notice that on the Palmerston property in Sligo, which was once owned by Lord Palmerston, the houses are fairly good—the reason being that Lord Palmerston, who was a very good landlord, gave prizes to those who kept their houses neat and built them in a stable way.

4429. Does your lordship look to any specific method of bringing about any reformation in respect of absenteeism?—It would be more for the Commission to decide than for me to suggest whether gentlemen who derive their incomes from agriculture and reside abroad, should not bear more of the country's taxation than if they remained at home and discharged those duties which would enable the tenantry on their estates to prosper.

Incidence of taxation.

4430. (*Lord Welby*). Did I understand your lordship rightly in dealing with the question of taxation, that practically in these very poor districts, and with this very poor population, there should be no taxation? Your words rather seemed to me to imply that, and I want to ascertain whether your view is that they should be exempted from taxation, or whether it is a question of degree?—I do not see the ground on which people whose incomes are such as we have been considering can be taxed, but I have not suggested that there are not in the congested districts many people here and there who are capable of paying taxes.

4431. Your lordship will see the extreme difficulty there would be, especially when taxation is on articles of consumption, in legislating, so that certain people should be exempt on account of poverty?—Evidently it is a practical difficulty.

4432. It is almost an insuperable difficulty, is it not, in detail?—That is, of course, a matter on which I could not form an opinion. It is for those who work out taxation to say how the remedy can be practically applied; but the strong fact in the case seems to be that these people really have not the means of supporting themselves and their families, and, consequently, the ground for taxing them does not seem to exist.

4433. Of course the most important point in all these questions is to arrive at a practical recommendation, and I wish to bring before your lordship the extreme difficulty that would occur in attempting to give effect to such a suggestion as that which would mean the exemption from taxation of a certain class. Of course that is possible in the case of direct taxation, but where it is indirect taxation it is almost impossible, I think, to draw a distinction between the different classes of consumers?—I have no doubt an Irish authority would be the proper department to work out such a question as that.

Most Rev. P. O'Donnell, D.D.

13 Dec. 1894.

Incidence of taxation.

4434. But your lordship sees the difficulty, do you not?—Yes; and it is especially difficult I think when such things are managed at a distance, as they are now.

4435. The point has possibly not had your attention, but it has been very often brought forward that Ireland (I think I may put it as broadly as that) got no benefit from the legislation which followed the imposition of the income tax—speaking of the income tax in England,—and that that tax was put on in order to benefit branches of trade which were almost purely English. Have you ever considered among other things what has been the effect of putting on the income tax in England, with its corollary, of extension to Ireland; that though undoubtedly it was in the first instance used largely to take off the burdens on raw material, and manufacture in England, at the same time by means of it very large reductions have been made in the taxation of those articles of consumption which are the comfort of the poorest?—Yes, I consider that income tax also in Ireland properly imposed would be the fairest of all taxes, provided that the other taxes which in Ireland appear to be in excess, came down proportionately.

4436. I would draw your attention to one or two points merely to show that the poor Irish consumer has been considerably aided in obtaining those articles which I think we should all agree are in the main great comforts?—It seems to me that if the taxation on the articles that are consumed in Ireland remains excessive, the income tax has not effected that change; it should perhaps have done it, but I do not think it has accomplished it. I myself consider that the amount of income tax which is raised in any country is about the fairest indication that you could have of the taxable capacity of the country. Certainly, taking the two countries together, Ireland and England, the proportion of taxable capacity seems not unfairly to be determined in that way, but so far as I know when the income tax was extended to Ireland, the duty on the articles consumed in Ireland, instead of going down, actually increased.

4437. We will not take the produce of the income tax in the United Kingdom at the present moment, but I will take it at some little time back, at the time when the produce was 1,500,000*l.* at a penny, which is taking a moderate sum, because now it is over 2,000,000*l.* When you take into consideration the exemptions which are granted to the lower classes of income tax payers you will see even with a tax of sixpence that means 9,000,000*l.* or 10,000,000*l.* a year, and that tax both in England and Ireland has been the means, or has given the Chancellor of the Exchequer such a surplus that he could reduce the taxation on articles of consumption. Now let me take this case and put it before your lordship. Take tea in those years which have been frequently referred to, the years 1859 and 1860, the calculation was that the Irish taxpayer paid about 700,000*l.* on tea, and the calculation is now that he pays something over 600,000*l.* In the meantime, and very much through the operation of the English income tax, the surpluses thus afforded have enabled the Chancellor of the Exchequer to reduce the tax upon this most legitimate article of consumption, tea, from 1*s.* 5*d.* to 6*d.* If the tax had remained at the rate at which it stood in 1858–60, either the Irish consumer must have gone without the tea which he now consumes, or his contribution to the revenue instead of being 600,000*l.* would be about 2,000,000*l.* I would venture to put before your lordship that that is a very considerable result to have been obtained, and that so far the argument is fair that the imposition of the income tax in England, because the income tax in Ireland would not have enabled it to be done, has been the means of putting a very considerable benefit on the Irish consumer?—It seems to me that all that is regrettable is that the income tax did not effect a very much larger diminution of the duty on those

Dr. O'Conor [illegible] — [illegible] — Incidence of taxation.

articles of daily subsistence. The income tax is a very fair tax quite apart from other taxes; its being imposed I am sure should commend itself to every one; but in Ireland we have to take into consideration not only the operation of the income tax but the operation also of all other taxes which are levied with it; and I believe it is a fact that the proportion between the income tax levied in England and the other taxes is not at all so great as the proportion between Irish income tax and the other taxes levied in Ireland.

4438. I think that is rather going to a different subject. The point I want to bring before your lordship is with regard to these figures. Without asking you to take any responsibility for them, but to accept them as my statement for the time being, would you admit my argument, that by means of the large sum given to the revenue by the income tax, the Chancellor of the Exchequer, or the Government of the United Kingdom has had it in its power to reduce, and has reduced very considerably, the duty on articles that ought to be largely consumed, and thereby has conferred benefit upon that class of the United Kingdom, in which the Irish consumer has shared?—Yes, it seems to me to be a very good argument in favour of the imposition of the income tax.

4439. I am not asking whether you think it has gone far enough, I want to bring before you what has been the tendency of legislation, that by means of the income tax a considerable benefit, perhaps not a sufficient one, has really been secured to the Irish consumer?—I should only say that it is a poor way to relieve an unfair imposition of taxes by imposing another which, considered by itself, is a fair one.

4440. But, still the Irish taxpayer has been relieved upon my figures, has he not. I will repeat them once more. If the tax had remained as it was in 1859–60, he would have had to pay 2,100,000*l.* a year to the revenue, whereas, he now pays a little over 600,000*l.* That is a very considerable relief, is it not, in that time?—Did the population go down during that time?

4441. Yes, and that only shows that the consumption of tea has been larger in order to bring it up to such a sum as a tax of 600,000*l.* I now pass to another point. I have no doubt your lordship will admit that one of the greatest comforts of people with small wages, is sugar?—Yes.

4442. It is calculated that the Irish taxpayer in 1859–60, had to pay to the revenue as much as 530,000*l.* on sugar, on its then consumption; that duty has been entirely swept away, and swept away in great measure by the same agency as the tea duty has been lowered, namely, the imposition of the income tax in England, and the securing of an extra income of 10,000,000*l.* or 12,000,000*l.* a year, which has thereby enabled the Government to take off and reduce greatly the duties on articles of great comfort in life to the benefit of all the lower class of consumers; therefore, the tendency of the last forty years has been distinctly in the interest of the consumer, and that benefit I put to you has been obtained in great measure by the imposition of the income tax in England, securing as it did that large revenue?—I do not think it can be questioned that the operation of the income tax, considered in itself, is one which tends to work out fair results.

4443. (*Mr. Sexton.*) I think you have said you consider it the fairest of all and the best test?—Yes.

Relative [illegible] of England and Ireland.

4444. (*Lord Welby.*) There is one other point I should like to bring before your lordship. We know that Ireland is a poor country, and the argument has been used that England is a rich country, and that, therefore, Ireland should be very much exempted from taxation; but does not that argument assume a good deal too much? England is not a rich country in that sense. I have no doubt your lordship has seen such a book as that of Mr. Booth's, with its fearful pictures of poverty in London, such poverty as one hardly dreams of in Ireland. Do you not think that ought to be taken into consideration, and that you should be slow in accusing of [illegible] that everybody in England is rich, and that, therefore, the English poor should bear a large amount of taxation which Ireland cannot bear?—It seems to me no one should assume that everybody in England is rich, or that there is not a very large poor population in the most progressive countries, as things are in this world. In every large city there is almost necessarily a very large poor population, but, I do not think that should affect the point in taxation, which is due to a far distant and non-progressive country which does not share at all in the progress, and the advantages that are attendant on proximity to a large capital. If you wish to see how the thing works out, although there are unemployed in London, Manchester, and other cities, people go in thousands from the county Mayo across the channel to England to get work; and you will find young girls from Achill [illegible] to [illegible] thronging the boats from Achill, and going drowned in their endeavour to reach Scotland to earn a little money to help their parents to subsist. So that, all told, England seems to be the country where progress is going on, where there is circulation of money, and where there is employment.

4445. You see, in dealing with this question, the argument is not put on the ground of economy, but the general assumption is that the large increase in the demands of modern communities requires an enormous public revenue, and that public revenue must be levied somehow. You cannot carry on these great works of education and all the works which are now being demanded, without money, and it must be levied somewhere. If Ireland were exempt, extra taxation would be laid upon England, and you could not raise that revenue by direct taxation, because you would exhaust the source from which it is drawn. The consequence would be that you must increase the duty on the consumer in England; and I venture to say to anybody who has read Mr. Booth's book, it would be a very awful thing to say you should increase the duties on the articles which are consumed by these masses of very poor people in London in order to obtain that money?—It does not appear at all necessary that an indirect tax should be levied in that way. The income tax might be increased, and it would not be a tax upon the necessaries of life at all.

4446. I do not think any person who has anything whatever to do with the finance of the country would follow you there. However, the point of the thing is this; you must look at the enormous sums which are raised by indirect taxation, must you not?—In any case the industries of Ireland and the commerce of Ireland are so few and so small compared with the resources of England throughout, that it could not make so very much difference to impose in England such taxes as are necessary in order to strike a just balance with Ireland, and that would be, I think, seen to be especially needful if the amount which is credited against Ireland as being allocated for local taxation were properly considered. It is put down against Ireland, for instance, that 15,000*l.* from the Imperial Exchequer is allotted to hospitals in Ireland, but the largest and most useful hospital in Dublin cannot have a penny of it, as the Archbishop of Dublin pointed out the other day; and so on with other moneys which are allotted to Ireland and put down against Ireland. There is an immense sum of money expended on the Royal Irish Constabulary to keep them, not so much for Irish purposes, but as a semi-military Imperial force, dependent on the executive (which is the arm of the Cabinet) in Ireland, and not subject, as a police force in England is, to the local authority; it seems to me that the money is not used for Irish purposes at all, but for what is conceived to be a wise Imperial policy, whether it be so or not.

4447. I think the point your lordship takes deserves most careful consideration, but it does not quite touch the point I was bringing before you and which I wished to suggest to you—namely, the [illegible] amount of poverty, quite as great and I venture to say

greater than that in Ireland, which exists in England and which the practical statesman would have to deal with if the burden of moderate taxation be transferred from Ireland to England?—The only answer I can make would be that it seems to me to be the duty of practical statesmen to so transfer the extra revenue raised in Ireland to England as not to press on the poorer class in England.

Absenteeism.

4448. (*The O'Conor Don.*) I think your lordship stated with regard to absenteeism, that 11,000,000*l.* of the rent of the country was spent out of Ireland?—No, I stated that the rental was 11,000,000*l.*, and that a very large proportion was spent out of Ireland.

4449. I thought you said it was a great loss to Ireland that 11,000,000*l.* of the rent was spent out of the country; I wanted to be certain about it; it is a large proportion of it and not the entire, you say?—Yes.

4450. Then you quoted, as an example of an estate that was especially well managed, the estate of Lord Palmerston?—In the particular respect, that the houses have improved. I do not know the details of the management at all, but I have heard that he gave prizes, and I noticed that the houses were improved.

4451. But you quoted that as an example, showing what good a landlord might do if he devoted his attention to his estate?—Yes.

4452. But was not Lord Palmerston an absentee?—If he were an absentee he must have been very well locally represented. I have spoken to a man who received from Lord Palmerston, when he was Prime Minister of England, and had most pressing cares on his shoulders, an autograph letter about some little complaint as to the details of his farm. Whether he was there or not he took a great part in the management of his estate.

4453. Does not that show absentees may take as much part in the management of their estates as many who are resident?—If they are all Lord Palmerstons.

4454. But it shows that there is no impossibility of an absentee being as good a landlord as a resident, does it not?—Of course it is not impossible, but one swallow will not make a summer.

4455. But you happened to quote, as the example of the Irish landlord, an absentee?—No, not in connection with absenteeism, but prizes for houses.

4456. I understand that in illustrating the benefit of a landlord attending to his property, you gave the instance of Lord Palmerston. An absentee landlord might be able to do as much good to his tenants if he really attended to them, if such a man as Lord Palmerston, overwhelmed with public business, was able to have his estate so well looked after, might he not?—Yes, but I assume no one will venture to hold that absentee proprietors are capable, as a class, of discharging their duties to their tenantry.

4457. (*Mr. Sexton.*) If they would allow their incomes to be spent in Ireland, your lordship would object much less to their absence?—Very much less.

4458. (*The O'Conor Don.*) With regard to the enlargement of the holdings, I believe you are very much in favour of enlarging these small holdings?—Yes.

4459. And you quoted an example of the French estate, which has been lately purchased by your Board and divided amongst the tenants?—Yes.

4460. What provision is made against the future subdivision of these holdings?—The last paragraph of our last Report states that our Board has at present under its careful consideration the making of such regulations as we consider best to prevent subdivision.

4461. But you have not yet drawn out these regulations?—No, but we have frequently talked them over on the Board.

4462. Do you not think it is a very difficult thing to secure?—I do, unless with precaution. It is my own personal opinion that there should be some official in the country responsible for inquiring into and looking after this evil of sub-dividing holdings that are purchased under the Land Commission.

4463. What is the condition of one of these holdings purchased under the Land Commission in which the occupier, or the owner, as he now is, dies without a will. What is the legal condition of that holding—is it not personal property?—I can only say that we have been able to sell to the representatives of a deceased man as conveniently as to the man himself.

4464. I am not talking of where you are selling to the representatives of a deceased man, because he may be for that particular purpose made the sole owner of what he purchases; but I am taking the case of a man who has purchased his holding and who dies without having made a will, leaving, we will say, seven or eight, or perhaps ten children—some of them in America, some of them in Australia, some in England, and perhaps one or two at home—some daughters married, and so on. What is the legal condition of that man's holding? Is it not personal property, which should be divided amongst his ten children?—I am sure I do not know enough law to answer very accurately; but I do believe that if peasant proprietary were established in this country on a sound basis, there would not be at all the tendency to subdivision which existed some time ago. Many of the people would emigrate and be better educated than they were. They should be better taught in industrial arts, of which kind of education there has been very little in the country.

4465. If you will take it from me that it is the law that it is personal property, and that its value should be divided amongst all the children, I ask you how is the sub-division to be prevented?—That again is law. I do not see the great inconvenience, when a case of that kind occurs, in having the little holding sold out, every member of the family receiving his share, and the purchaser occupying the place of his predecessor in title.

4466. Then the purchaser will come into that holding having paid what we would call the full competition value for it?—Yes.

4467. And that competition value is the full competitive value in the country?—Yes.

4468. And will not that new owner then be in a worse position—or at least in as bad a position—as a tenant, paying the highest competitive rent?—He need not be. All the people in the country are not absolutely without money. We have returned Americans now and then; they build pretty good houses along the coast, and occasionally they have money to buy a farm, and such men may be able to buy the land and work it.

4469. He may be able to buy it, but will he not have paid for it a price, the interest on which would be equal to the highest competitive rent?—Yes, but the same difficulty arises about every man who buys land.

4470. Is the remedy which you would propose to prevent subdivision, that at the death of every holder the holding should be sold?—I have never considered the question of how subdivision should be best prevented beyond what I have stated.

4471. With submission to your lordship, I think it is a very important question for your Board to consider?—It has been under consideration.

Food of the people.

4472. With regard to the food of the people in the congested districts, you gave an enumeration of the different articles of food that entered into their daily consumption; but I think you omitted one which is probably of considerable importance; do not they use eggs?—Not largely at all; by no means; the eggs go for the groceries.

4473. What would be the amount of tobacco used per day or per week by a family of this class to which you have referred?—Possibly a shilling's worth of tobacco a week. I think that would be high, but in many families it would come to a shilling and in some sixpence and in some ninepence. I consider a shilling too high and would put it at ninepence.

4474. You say it is 3*d.* an ounce?—Yes.

Dr. Grimshaw, C.B. 24 Dec. 1894. Food of the people.

4475. That would be four ounces a week?—Three ounces a week would represent 9*d*.

4476. That would be about what they would use in the family?—Yes, taking one family with another.

4477. And how much tea?—In the part of Donegal that I know best there is about 5*l*. worth of tea consumed per year in the family.

4478. But how many pounds in weight; what is the price of tea in that district?—2*s*. 6*d*. per pound.

4479. Is not that a very large price for tea? Is it of very good quality?—It is fairly good quality; it is sold in small quantities; and I suppose the dealers in that way require to sell it at rather a large price.

4480. (*Mr. Sexton.*) Is it parted with for eggs mostly, is it not?—Frequently.

4481. And that makes a higher price, I should think?—Yes.

4482. (*The O'Conor Don.*) Because it is to a certain extent bought on the credit system?—Yes.

Failures of crops.

4483. With regard to the yield of the potato crops, you have mentioned the very great falling off in the produce and value of these crops in different years, which you have estimated at 10,000,000*l*. I think, have you not?—Yes, in one year, for all crops.

4484. With what did you make that comparison?—I took the comparison from Dr. Hancock's papers.

4485. You say that is a falling off from the usual yield; but would it not appear from your evidence that the usual yield is as often bad as good?—It was a falling off from the preceding year, I understand.

4486. Because out of the twelve years you have mentioned you have given five or six that were bad; therefore the return which you call the usual yield must have been not a usual yield but a yield of an exceptionally good year?—I said the crop in 1879 was 10,000,000*l*. short of its value in the preceding year. These other years that I mentioned as bad were specially bad for the potato crop, not necessarily so bad for the other crops.

4487. The words I thought your lordship used at the time were that it was short of the usual yield; and what I wanted to ascertain was what you understood to be the usual yield. What was the usual yield of the potato crop when you made that comparison between some years and others; do you make the comparison between a particularly good year or a comparison between all the years, good and bad, on an average?—As I went on making my statements, I stated the ground of the comparison, I think.

4488. It would not be fair, of course, to compare the yield of a bad year with that of a particularly good year, and to say that the loss was 10,000,000*l*. or anything else?—No, quite unfair.

Indebtedness of people.

4489. Is credit given more freely now by the shopkeepers than it formerly was? I understood you to say that it was, and it is quite new to me if it is so?—I think if you take the debts as the test, undoubtedly credit is more freely given now.

4490. Do you think the people are more in debt now than they were in 1880, say, or 1881?—Yes, they are, there is more of an accumulated debt.

4491. Accumulated since then, a new debt since 1880?—I was not actually in contact with the people in 1880 and 1881, but I know that the debts have accumulated, and are now such as I have described.

4492. And yet shopkeepers are more willing now to give credit than they were?—I do not think I have made any statement to the effect that they are more willing to give credit; but undoubtedly the fact that the tenants have got fixity of tenure and are surer of their holdings has been a reason for the giving of credit when otherwise it would not have been given.

Work of Congested Districts Board.

4493. The operation of your Board is practically confined, is it not, to a small portion of the congested districts?—Yes.

4494. There are a great number of districts for which you have been able to do nothing?—A large number; and a great many clustered areas that are in a very poor condition are not scheduled under the Act.

Dr. Grimshaw, C.B. 24 Dec. 1894. Work of Congested Districts Board.

4495. But even of those that are scheduled there are numbers that you have absolutely done nothing at all for, are there not?—That is so.

4496. And I presume that is from want of funds?—Chiefly from want of funds. We were anxious to do something for the very poorest districts while at the same time keeping in view the importance of promoting those industries and schemes that promise best for the permanent improvement of the districts as a whole.

4497. Then I may take it that you do not consider that your Board has got a sufficient amount of income?—It has not for its work.

4498. What additional income do you think it ought to have to be able to properly carry out throughout the whole district what you are endeavouring to do now in the restricted area?—Really I should not like to answer a very important question of that sort without giving it more time than I have ever bestowed upon it.

4499. Your Board have never considered the subject?—No.

Incidence of taxation.

4500. (*Sir David Barbour.*) Your lordship referred to certain estimates of the receipts and expenditure of typical families in the congested districts upon which I wish to ask you a few questions. I understand that you would like, if it were possible to do so, to exempt these poor people in the congested districts from the taxation on tea and tobacco and, perhaps, also from the taxation on whiskey?—Yes.

4501. Lord Welby asked you certain questions about the difficulties that would be experienced in exempting them from taxation. In the first place the poverty of Ireland, as we are all sorry to know, is not confined to these districts. There are people just as poor outside them, are there not?—Yes.

4502. And they would have an equal claim to exemption, would they not?—Yes.

4503. And although the proportion of poor people in England and Scotland is not so great as in Ireland, still there are people who would have as good a claim to exemption from these duties in England and Scotland, are there not? For instance, we know that there is a great number of paupers in England and Scotland; and as there are paupers there must be people on the verge of pauperism. Those people would have as good a claim in proportion to their income as people in Ireland to exemption from duties on tea and tobacco, would they not?—I take it that paupers do not pay duties of any kind.

4504. I am speaking of the people on the verge of pauperism in England and in Scotland; they would have a claim to exemption, too, would they not?—It is for those who have immediately to deal with the poor in England and Scotland to consider the question for them. I should greatly rejoice at any benefit bestowed on them; but the case immediately before me, and with which I am daily in contact, is that of the poor in the congested districts in Ireland, who form the great bulk of the population in those districts, and where incomes are so small that it does not seem that they have resources capable, by any fair standard, of bearing taxation.

4505. I quite understand your argument, but you suggest, do you not, that it would be a good thing to exempt them from taxation if it were possible to do so?—Yes.

4506. And I wish merely to bring out the difficulties in the way of adopting that remedy. I do not wish to argue that it is not desirable to adopt some remedy; but you would admit it is very desirable the remedy adopted should be a feasible remedy and a good remedy, would you not?—Quite so.

4507. And you will admit, I think, that if you exempt certain people in Ireland from paying tea duty and tobacco duty, there are a certain number of people in England—perhaps not a very great number—who would have an equally good claim, and do possess an equally good claim at the present moment, to exemption?—You assume that those people in

Dr. O'Donnell. 31 Dec. 1894. Incidence of taxation.

England have only the same means of earning a livelihood.

4508. I assume that they are in the same position as regards income and as regards comfort?—It seems to me there is a very great and very important element to be weighed in such a case, and that is the possibility for the family, supposing it to be industrious, to earn income.

4509. Therefore you think if it is possible for the family to earn an income they ought not to be exempt, do you?—I think when you are dealing with large populations it is an important element to take into consideration that these people not merely do not earn incomes, but that they absolutely cannot.

4510. So long as they remain in their present position?—So long as their position is not improved.

4511. So long as they remain in the country where they now live?—They need not be moved much in order to have their position improved.

4512. But until there is some improvement, less or more, it is impossible, you think?—Yes, it is.

4513. Assuming that the poorer people in Ireland were exempted by the Legislature from the tobacco duty and from the tea duty, it would be necessary to exempt all the people in Ireland, would it not, from that duty?—Really I can offer no opinion of the least use in regard to the practical working out of finance schemes.

4514. I wish to point out to you that if a certain number of people were entitled to get their tea and tobacco free of duty, there would be unlimited facilities for smuggling. There would be no reason why a man who was entitled to get it free of duty should not purchase it and sell it to a man who was not entitled, would there?—It seems to me there is not much in that, because notwithstanding such a possibility as that the making of illicit whiskey was quite common in Donegal, but there is no such thing now.

4515. I think that is a different question. If certain people were entitled to get whiskey free of duty, and certain others had to pay duty, I think you would find there would be great facilities for smuggling?—It is difficult to say how these things can be worked out practically, but I believe it can be done. While the position remains as it is it has been found quite possible to get the population to give up illicit distillation.

4516. Then it comes to this, that while you would like to see these people exempt from taxation you are not prepared to state any plan by which that exemption could be carried out in practice?—It comes to that; but I must add that I do not consider it would be for me to work out such a scheme.

4517. I should like to call your attention to the case of the two poorest of the typical families. The two poorest, I think, are No. 2 and No. 12. In No. 2 the cash income is 9l. 16s. only?—Yes.

4518. And the value of the produce consumed by the family is between 12l. and 17l.—we may take it at 14l. 10s. on an average?—Quite so.

4519. That gives that family an income of 24l. 6s.?—Yes.

4520. Which of course is very small?—Yes.

4521. That family does not appear to consume much tobacco or tea, but I make out that they pay about 1l. in duty on tea and tobacco?—Yes.

4522. If that duty of 1l. was remitted, of course it would be a gain to these people; but it would be only equivalent to raising their income to 25l. 6s., would it not. The present income is 24l. 6s., and if they were 1l. better off they would practically have an income of 25l. 6s.?—For those poor people 1l. is a big sum.

4523. I admit that when a person has that small income 1l. is a good deal?—Yes, and if you have 500 such people in a parish the retention of 500l. in the parish rather than the removal of it from the district is a great advantage.

4524. Of course I admit all that. The exemption would practically bring their income up, for the purposes of argument, to 25l. 6s., but they would be still very poor?—Yes.

4525. And you would not be content to see them remain with that income. You would desire to see the income made still more, would you not?—Yes.

4526. Up to what limit do you think you would like to raise their income; what would satisfy you, and at what income would you say that it was unnecessary that more should be done at the public expense?—I do not think an estimate of that in the rough can be made. If the resources which might possibly be developed in the congested districts were uniform throughout it might be done; but in one place there is fishing to be developed, in another place there might be established a weaving industry, and in another place the opening of a fine stratum of granite is practicable, and so on. You have to take in connection the income and the class of expenditure of the families. The class of expenditure is entirely different for these different families. Some for instance have to get fishing gear; others have to provide 1l. to enable them to go from a remote part of Donegal or Mayo to the English or the Scotch harvests, and so on.

4527. But taking that family which is stated to be a typical family and not an actual family, if their income is raised, at what figure would you say they were fairly well off? Something very considerably more than the present figure, no doubt?—Yes, quite.

4528. How much?—It would depend on the number of people in the family.

4529. We are taking typical families with five or six people in them?—If they had an income which would give pretty much the same to each person as is expended, perhaps, on the poor in the workhouse, it would greatly improve their condition.

4530. Say 50l.?—That would be a very material improvement.

4531. Then you think, if they had 50l., in all probability expenditure at the public cost would not be necessary any longer?—Yes.

4532. You see that means an increase over their present income of 26l.?—Yes.

4533. So that the remission of taxation to the extent of 1l. would only improve their position by $\frac{1}{26}$th of the improvement which you desire to see?—No doubt; but remember that when people are in a critical condition, it is often the last straw that breaks the drudge's back.

4534. Quite so; but I am trying to bring out the fact that though the remission of this taxation might involve the loss of a great deal of the public revenue, it would not by any means raise the people to a satisfactory position?—No, if you look upon it as merely involving the effect upon an individual family; but if you assume that the duty levied upon these districts is 200,000l. a year, and the accumulation of that 200,000l. is expended in the district, or even that it is expended year by year, I can only say that, in my opinion, these congested districts would soon cease to be a charge to any public department.

4535. Do you mean if this taxation were remitted?—I have said if the 200,000l. which the taxation represents were expended in the locality.

4536. In providing means for enabling the people to help themselves?—Yes.

4537. But not if it was merely remitted to them?—I have not considered how that would work out, but I can see that the 200,000l. left in these districts would mean an enormous improvement.

4538. But it would not bring their incomes up to what you would like to see them?—No, not necessarily.

4539. In fact, do you not think it would be fair to say that it is not the taxation that makes these people poor, but that these people being very poor, the slightest increase to their burdens falls heavily on them?—That is true. I should, however, like to add the qualification that we are dealing with taxation now, and the fact that they are bearing taxation which seems to be beyond their power, in this connection at all events, seems a very remarkable grievance.

4540. I think you said, in the abstract of your evidence, that the people were really unable to bear the local taxation, much less the Imperial taxation?—That is so; in fact, the work our Board is doing is an evidence of it. You see, we are forced to make roads that the Grand Jurors have not made, for the development of trade, and to enable people to manure their lands and to come to markets, because we deem such roads absolutely necessary.

4541. Will you look at No. 3, "Estimate of Receipts and Expenditure." The cesses and taxes there are 11s.; do you observe that?—Yes.

4542. The expenditure on tea is 5l. 4s.?—Yes.

4543. The expenditure on tobacco is 2l. 12s.?—Yes.

4544. The expenditure on snuff is 1l. 12s.?—Yes.

4545. And the expenditure on whisky, &c., is 2l. 8s.?—Yes.

4546. Making a total, I believe, of 12l. 3s. Of course these people are poor, and these are their little luxuries, but do you not think it is putting the case somewhat too strongly to say that such a family cannot bear the local taxation when their local taxation is only 11s.; and the expenditure on tea, tobacco, snuff, and whisky is 12l. 3s.?—I notice that the whisky bill is exceptionally high; and possibly, too, the tobacco bill is a little high; but it may be, for instance, that there was a marriage in that family, and on the occasion of it the supply of drink was unusual.

4547. But I understood that these estimates of receipts and expenditure are typical; that is to say, they are the average receipts and expenditure of a number of families for a number of years?—No doubt; but when any one goes to make inquiry in any district in this country, or any other, the information he receives is largely coloured by the facts immediately preceding the collection of the information.

4548. You did not make the estimate, did you?—No.

4549. Now I wish to ask you a few questions upon the very excellent work of the Congested Districts Board. You have no doubt, and I have not met anybody who has any doubt, that that Board is doing very good work so far as it goes?—It is doing very excellent work.

4550. Can you foresee a time when, owing to the improvement of the condition of the people in the congested districts, it would be possible to dissolve the Board and leave the people to their own resources?—We have not at all arrived at the stage when one could make such a calculation. The fact is, we have been only able to touch very lightly beyond the fringe of congestion; we have tried to do a good deal for the fisheries; we have tried to promote industries and agriculture, and a little migration; and in all our projects we have aimed at attaining something like a commercial status in the end. But when our operations will so tell upon the districts as to leave them independent and self-supporting, it would be really difficult at this stage to say.

4551. You are not within measurable distance of it at the present time?—No.

4552. I think I understood you to say that you thought it would be impossible to raise these people to a satisfactory condition so long as they remained where they are now; and that you would like to see, at any rate, some of them transferred to the better districts in every fair way, and allotments given them there?—Quite so; the development of the industries, fisheries and quarries, and so on, in the congested districts, would provide for a certain part of the population; but the great bulk of them cannot be permanently benefited, except by migration schemes.

4553. And I imagine you hold the opinion that any form of assistance which would be merely relief, enabling them to tide over temporary distress, would not in the long run be satisfactory?—There is no one in Ireland interested in improving the people who would go in for any relief whatever of an eleemosynary kind, except when it is actually wanted to ward off starvation.

4554. Such relief brings no permanent improvement, of course, and in other respects does not do good?—No.

4555. And what you would like to see would be a permanent improvement in the condition of the people, brought about by means which would give them opportunities of improving their position by their own exertions?—Quite so.

Adjourned for a short time.

4556. (*Mr. Sexton.*) Your lordship has done the Commission the favour to attend to-day, I understand, chiefly in order to give testimony of facts and grievances within your knowledge?—Yes.

4557. And in addition to offer such suggestions as your experience, which is large, enables you to make towards improving the condition of the people?—Yes.

4558. You have said emphatically that eleemosynary aid is not your aim, but rather such provision as law or administration can make for enabling the people to be solvent and self-supporting?—Quite so.

4559. Your lordship's own action in associating yourself with the Congested Districts Board, and in labouring in their work of practical improvement, shows what you desire is not that the condition of the people should be improved by relief, but that they should be enabled to help themselves by assistance to which I understand you consider that the results of losses and their condition gives them a special claim?—Yes.

4560. In offering the Commission the assistance of your evidence, your lordship does not undertake the function which belongs to those who have the experience and the expert assistance of legislators to suggest the particular form of the remedy to be applied?—I could not undertake such a task.

4561. There are those whose duty it is to undertake it?—Yes; those who are responsible for the government of Ireland, for the time being, seem to me to be under an obligation to look to such things.

4562. I wish to remind your lordship of the inquiry which this Commission is directed to make. We are to inquire into the financial relations between Great Britain and Ireland and their relative taxable capacity, and to report upon what principles of comparison and by the application of what specific standards the relative capacity of Great Britain and Ireland to bear taxation may be most equitably determined, and what so far as can be ascertained is the true proportion under the principles and specific standards so determined between the taxable capacity of Great Britain and Ireland. Your lordship perceives that under this reference each country is treated as a unit separate from the other?—Quite so.

4563. And that so far as this Commission is concerned, under this reference, Ireland may be treated as if she had a legislature now?—Yes.

4564. And that the legislatures of the two countries were arranging under one fiscal system the best method of determining the equitable taxation of each?—According to the capacity of each nation.

4565. As a unit?—Yes.

4566. Some of the questions put to you to-day must, I think, in view of this reference have perplexed your lordship?—Yes; to some extent the questions seemed to turn on the condition of some individuals or occasionally of small sections of the people rather than upon the condition of the people at large; but at the same time I could scarcely in any way complain of such questions because I am especially identified with one particular part of the agricultural population which is in a very poor condition. I am a good deal in contact with agriculturists generally, but my special knowledge is of the congested districts.

4567. It is true that your lordship has given evidence specially as to the congested districts, because your personal experience has lain there, but I observe in the course of your evidence that you applied the weight of your testimony not simply to

Dr. O'Donnell.

11 Dec. 1895.

Work of the Congested Districts Board.

Object of the inquiry and capacity of the witness to the Commission.

Dr. O'Donnell.

11 Dec. 1895.

[illegible]

the congested districts but to the occupiers throughout Ireland whose valuations are not over £4?—Yes; and I have been resident in Donegal, in a town which is really on the margin between two very different countries—the congested districts in the mountains of Donegal, where the land which is tilled is perhaps some of the poorest which is under cultivation, and East Donegal which is highly tilled and is also occupied by a most industrious population.

4568. But in this inquiry when we refer to the condition of particular classes of the people in particular localities we do it not so much to establish a particular case as to offer the best illustrations that can be found of the contention that the country as a whole is over taxed?—I quite understand that your object is to get a full conspectus of the state of Ireland in all the departments of Irish industrial life, in order to ascertain what the real taxable capacity of the nation at large is.

4569. Precisely, and when you are asked whether some people in England and Scotland may not be so poor as to have a claim for reduction or remission of taxation, if poverty be a claim, does not such a question appear to your lordship to involve a misconception of the true nature of this Inquiry?—It does seem to imply that when we talk of the poorness of certain districts in Ireland we are talking of a limited poverty that is found in conjunction with very large and considerable wealth, whereas speaking of the poor districts of Ireland the facts are put forward and the circumstances explained to show that the condition of these people is a very large and a very constant ingredient in the state of things in Ireland.

4570. And part of the general question of the over taxation of Ireland?—Yes.

4571. And suppose as the result of this Inquiry it were found that Ireland is over-taxed, whether or not a remedy was applied, would not the question of the relation of taxation between the rich and poor of Great Britain remain another and a different question?—It is an entirely independent question and I daresay it is a question too which might be very profitably considered for Ireland by a local legislature acting for the Irish people themselves.

4572. Your lordship I think was put the point. The question of the incidence of taxation as between the rich and the poor in either country, either country in this Inquiry being treated as a unit, is an absolutely distinct and different question from the capacity of either country as a whole compared with the other?—It is.

4573. And the introduction of [illegible] only tend I should submit to you to [illegible]?—No doubt it has that tendency.

4574. It has been suggested to you as a difficulty that if some were exempt in Ireland all would have to be exempt. Does it occur to you as reasonable in an Inquiry to determine whether Ireland relatively to England is over-taxed to introduce a question of that kind as a difficulty?—Of course I would not conceive that it is for a witness to point out the practical means by which an acknowledged wrong could be righted. For one like me giving evidence the province seems to be to state and prove the wrong if it exists and leave to others the redressing of it.

4575. The evidence you have given in evidence of grievance and it does not necessarily involve, as I understand, either the imposition of differential duties of necessity between England and Ireland or the total exemption of any one in Ireland?—Quite so.

4576. It does not of necessity involve it?—By no means; on luxuries.

4577. The wisdom and the ingenuity of legislation may find other remedies?—Yes.

4578. Let the grievance, if it exists, be first established and let the remedy be found?—Quite so.

4579. That in your judgment would be the sequence?—That would be my opinion, and I have stated already that I conceive for the Irish people, in such a matter an Irish authority would be the best to make such an arrangement.

4580. You were asked with regard to these poor people in your part of the country, whether taxation makes them poorer whether it is not that they are poor already. Does that appear to you to touch the question before us as to whether or not they are over taxed. Is it a question for us as to whether the taxation makes them poor or whether being as they are, the taxation upon them as individuals of the Irish community is unduly heavy as compared with the average taxation upon individuals in Great Britain?—The latter is undoubtedly the correct aspect of the case. These people are poor and they are made poorer by taxes, and the point at issue seems to be how far it is wrong or right to impose taxes upon them.

4581. Again Sir David Barbour directing your attention to Budget in the appendix, noted the fact that people with a cash income of [illegible] and home produce of from [illegible] to [illegible], paid a taxation of [illegible], and he asked you if the [illegible] were remitted would the family be much better off. You replied that you thought they would be somewhat better off, but if taxation be excessive is it an argument of any force to suggest that if the excessive taxation were remitted the people would not be much better off; is that a reason for continuing taxation?—No, I conceive if [illegible] be due to me it should be given to me, even though it is known I am going to throw it away.

4582. Quite so; it is a question of equity, and not of the subsequent condition of the person wronged when equity is done?—Yes.

4583. Your attention was also directed to Budget 8, and to the entry of whiskey on the expenditure side?—Yes.

4584. Am I right in saying that this is the only Budget in which such an entry appears?—It seems to be the only one.

4585. And I understand your lordship to say that in the part of the country with which you are specially acquainted the people, especially the rural community, are total abstainers?—They are total abstainers as a body.

4586. And that the oppressiveness of taxation in that part of the country is not due in any material degree to indulgence in spirituous liquor?—It falls on tea and tobacco.

4587. The items of excisable and customable articles on the credit side of No. 8 were added up, but when we analysed them they do not appear immoderate. The entry for tea is [illegible] (3s. a week), being less than a pound of tea a week for what may be a large family?—Yes.

4588. The entry for tobacco is [illegible] a week—there may be two or three [illegible] in the house, may there not?—There may be.

4589. The entry for snuff is [illegible] a week—there may be, as there often are, several old people in the family?—Yes, old women use snuff, and sometimes it happens that in the family there are two or three generations of people living in the same house, and for such a family of course the consumption of such articles would be unusually large, especially of tea, tobacco, and snuff.

4590. Under these circumstances do these items appear to you to call for any particular comment?—No, I think these budgets, taken one with another, give a very good conspectus of the condition of the people in the congested districts.

4591. In official language the excisable and customable articles are often spoken of and dealt with as luxuries, are they not?—Yes.

4592. I would turn for a moment to your lordship's account of the dietary of the families of whose conditions you have knowledge. I understand it to be this—from the potato harvest up to the spring they live almost wholly upon potatoes, do they not?—Yes.

4593. Except a comparable article the home produce is potatoes?—The home produce is potatoes.

4594. They live upon potatoes sometimes with buttermilk?—Yes.

4595. And sometimes without it?—And sometimes without it.

4596. When the potatoes are exhausted they resort not to oatmeal but to Indian meal, do they not?—Indian meal comes in gradually superseding the potatoes at one meal in spring, and then taking their place possibly at the three meals. I have stated, however, that tea and a little bread were common at two of the meals.

4597. Is the oatmeal too dear to be used?—Oatmeal is very seldom bought by small Irish farmers. When it is used it is generally a product of the soil, and in these poorer districts it is much more common to sell off the oats or use them in another way. In fact a mill to grind oats is not at all a common thing to find in the congested districts. There are such mills here and there, but I know myself parishes in which not a single farmer grinds his oats.

4598. They are driven to resort, when the potato crop is out, to Indian meal, which, I believe, is considered to be about the lowest form of human food, is it not?—Yes, they resort to Indian meal.

4599. And in eating the Indian meal, as in eating the potatoes, they often consume it without milk, do they not?—Yes. On these little patches the fodder for cattle is very deficient, especially in the winter, and in some years the fodder is so late that the cattle are scarcely able to stand in spring.

4600. Has the scarcity of milk in that region had anything to do with the introduction of tea?—Undoubtedly. You see it is very difficult even for the poor to consume potatoes and water, or Indian meal and water, and consequently tea and bread accompany these meals as far as the people can provide them. Latterly it often happens that when potatoes disappear from the morning meal, tea and bread are the dietary if the people are comparatively well off. Now and then they may have a little butter, but it is not common among such families as you have made use of in these budgets.

4601. A dietary of potatoes or of Indian meal, with or without milk, from year's end to year's end, must have a very depressing and stagnating effect upon the people, must it not?—Yes, alone it certainly would.

4602. Then your experience is that they are driven by the nature of this diet almost below the level of savage life—to have a drink of tea and to take a smoke?—Undoubtedly; if a person had a little meat for dinner he would not have at all the same craving for a drink of strong tea as he has if he has to take his potatoes without any relish at all.

4603. Your lordship stated that these poor occupiers do not have meat at any time except two or three times a year?—That is quite the case, and when they have fish it is salt fish, and it is not so much used as food as for a relish.

4604. On the other hand, in Great Britain, I believe, there is no doubt that the mass of the population do habitually eat butcher's meat?—I am not familiar with the condition of the people, but I have heard frequently from persons who have travelled in America that the hard-working classes there have meat for every meal to which they sit down, and I suppose the same thing obtains to a large extent in England. I know, indeed, in Scotland, when our men go over there, their food is vastly improved beyond what it is in Ireland; they have meat once or oftener during the day.

4605. And I understand your view to be that in the case of a man who diets liberally or sufficiently upon beef, or bacon, or cheese, or other such products, while to him tobacco or tea may be really a luxury, to the creature who is eking out life on potatoes without milk or Indian meal without milk they may almost become necessities?—It seems to me that they have become for that class of people necessities—they need something like a smoke or a drink of tea to make them forget the bad meal and to put them in the humour to work again.

4606. I turn to some questions put to you by the O'Conor Don. Your evidence as to absentees was this, I think: you said you thought the bulk of the rental of Ireland was taken out of it?—That is my opinion, at all events.

4607. The O'Conor Don invited you to suggest a cure?—Yes. And might I say in connection with that matter that if I wished to give an instance of what a resident landlord could do for the people I should not have taken the instance which was a little discussed. In the instance I put forward I meant to show what could be done in the way of improving houses by means of prizes. The best instance I know of what a resident proprietor could do is afforded by the late Earl of Leitrim in Donegal. His predecessor was really a tyrant, but the late Lord Leitrim, who died a few years ago, lived largely among his people and worked hard for them. He established steam communication between his estate and Glasgow, brought his tenants into contact with the Glasgow market, encouraged them in every effort and every public project they took the least interest in, and gave a living lesson of what a man with a heart, residing among the people, could do.

4608. Some Irish landlords, like the O'Conor Don, do reside in Ireland. Taking your own county, what is the practice of the landlords in Donegal? The Commission is now aware of the condition of the people there—what is the practice of the landlords in Donegal in the spending of their rental?—None of the large landowners live in Donegal, and I am not aware that there is any considerable expenditure tending to the improvement of agriculture in the localities going on from their resources.

4609. Do they come even for the shooting season, or do they rent the shooting?—Occasionally they come for the shooting; the shooting is good in Donegal, and it is sometimes let, but sometimes the proprietor comes and lives in a shooting-box during the season.

4610. Is any material part of the rent from Donegal spent upon the improvement of the soil?—No.

4611. Then I take your lordship's view to be that if the landlords of Ireland, as a body, had practically accepted the obligations which are carried into effect by the landlords of England and of Scotland, and had lived for the most part of their lives in Ireland and spent the main part of their rents there, many of these people would have been in a less acute condition of poverty?—The condition of the population would have been different and the relation of Irish tenants to Irish landlords, I think, would be practically one of devotion.

4612. Of course, if the bulk of a rental of say 15,000,000*l.* a year—I think it can be scarcely less—had been spent in the country as it is in wealthy England and comparatively wealthy Scotland, the effect would have been that the people would be better housed, the soil would be improved, and made more productive, and the labour market would have been fuller?—Quite so.

4613. And all these influences would have acted to prevent this growth of extreme distress with which we are now concerned?—That is certainly the case.

4614. Now, as to the cure your lordship is no doubt aware that the Legislature of England though in some respects it has not shown any careful spirit with regard to the affairs of Ireland has, even in old times, engaged itself with the question of Irish absenteeism, and has passed many Acts actually levying penalties and taxes on Irish landlords to compel them to live in this country?—I do not know much of the progress of such law.

4615. But your lordship knows that if an Irish Legislature had existed, it would have been found no difficult matter to enforce ordinary obligations as to property upon absentees?—The ordinary

11 Dec. 1894.

[illegible]

Absenteeism.

obligations should be enforced. Of course for the existing generation of men some allowance is to be made on the score that their incomes are very largely consumed by the payments on mortgages. That is one of the unfortunate results of absenteeism to a large extent in the past, but in any case it seems an obvious conclusion that those who derive large incomes from agricultural land should try and make the source of their contributions a little bit reproductive.

4616. The fact that a man's ancestors have sunk, or he himself has sunk, his property under a mortgage would be no reason in your judgment why the balance of the rental, small or large, should be withdrawn from the country which produces it?—Certainly not, and although it makes, as I have said, some difference as regards the responsibility of individuals it makes absolutely no difference with regard to the result on Irish agriculture; however the money goes out of the country, the country suffers.

Enlargement of holdings and prevention of sub-division.

4617. The O'Conor Don, I think, with special reference to some of your endeavours on the Congested Districts Board to enlarge small holdings, asked you how you were going to prevent sub-division?—Yes.

4618. Your lordship is, no doubt, aware that with regard to judicial tenants and the tenants who have purchased under the various Purchase Acts effectual measures have been devised for that purpose?—I am aware of that.

4619. And that tenant who has purchased under any of the Purchase Acts cannot sub-divide without the leave of the Land Commission?—And during the term of the annuity.

4620. That carries us on half a century?—It does.

4621. I think the statesmen of the twentieth century may be left to settle their own difficulties?—We have an abundant crop of them for the fag end of this century.

4622. (*The O'Conor Don.*) But when you say "cannot"—they are forbidden to do it; but practically cannot they do it?—Of course, they have to pay their annual instalments to the Land Commission, and very properly the Land Commission is the authority to prohibit any subdivision. How far there are violations of the law I really do not know, but I am quite in accord with the opinions of those who hold that there should be a strict supervision in such things, and really if there is subdivision, without the exercise of such supervision, it will not be the people who are to blame but the public authority that has neglected its duty.

4623. Is there any supervision at present?—I am in no way in contact with the department which should supervise—I know there ought to be.

4624. (*Mr. Sexton.*) Eviction being the legal penalty of a breach of condition if a tenant-purchaser violates that condition, as your lordship has clearly pointed out, the blame lies on the public authority which fails to execute the law?—The temptation to divide is sometimes pretty strong for a man; anybody may fancy his circumstances are special, and unless the law is strongly enforced there will be sub-division.

4625. With regard to the statutory tenants, who are now 300,000 in number out of 480,000, it is a condition of the statute that no tenant who has acquired a statutory term shall sublet or subdivide?—Quite so.

4626. He incurs the penalty of eviction if he does?—Yes.

4627. And that is an effectual remedy, is it?—Yes. The law provides for both cases, and it is apparently the duty of a public department to look after the observance of the law.

4628. Has your lordship any doubt that the wisdom of the legislature if it has dealt sufficiently with the case will deal with other cases?—It seems to me a matter which only requires looking after; it is not so very difficult, I may say from my own personal experience that the tendency to subdivide has very much gone out; but at the same time there is enough of it left to demand constant care from the public authority.

[illegible]

Enlargement of holdings and prevention of sub-division.

4629. (*The O'Conor Don.*) Do you think that public opinion would support an eviction in the case of subdivision?—It depends very largely on the locality.

4630. (*Mr Sexton.*) And on the circumstances of the case?—Yes; on the circumstances of the locality and on the circumstances under which the eviction comes about.

4631. (*The O'Conor Don.*) But there are cases, I presume, in which public opinion would not support the eviction of a family on account of subdivision?—I take it that if the public authority is one in which public opinion reposes confidence, then anyone violating a statutory condition will not be pitied if he suffers the penalty.

4632. (*Lord Welby.*) Supposing a purchasing tenant makes a private agreement, it would be to his interest that it should not be known—do you think it is a very easy thing for a public authority sitting here to ascertain whether the rule against subdivision is carried out?—Cure would be difficult, but prevention certainly is not. In fact, with the present police force and the various officials there are, it should be rather easy.

4633. I would rather put it to you from your lordship's knowledge of the country—would the subdivision be a matter of notoriety, do you think? To me it would seem to be not altogether a difficult thing to make it a private arrangement, which would not be matter of notoriety?—It seems to me supervision would be quite in accordance with the general feeling of the community. When once the people knew there was care being taken about it, and that the defaulters would be prosecuted or suffer, I do not think there would be much danger of subdivision.

4634. (*Mr. Sexton.*) It is not an abstract question, or one that depends entirely on forecast. We have absolutely a good many years' experience of the working of the Purchase Acts, and there are several conditions, the violation of which entails eviction. Your lordship is, no doubt, aware that the Land Commission from year to year have had to proceed to eviction and sale of farms?—Yes.

4635. And have done it?—And have done it.

4636. And there has been no difficulty whatever?—I believe they cannot complain of loss in that way.

4637. (*The O'Conor Don.*) Do you know if they have ever evicted for sub-division?—I do not know much of the history of the matter. Perhaps if they have not evicted for subdivision it would show that there has been very little of it.

4638. (*Mr. Sexton.*) Is there any reason to suppose that an eviction for sub-division in clear breach of an engagement would be much more difficult than an eviction for non-payment?—I think the people would expect, in fact, the public authority to insist on the observance of the statutory conditions in those cases.

Failure of crops.

4639. The O'Conor Don asked you some questions which appeared to be pointed in a critical spirit to your lordship's estimate of the pressure on account of the failure of the potato crop in certain years. We have the advantage here of referring to official figures. We have had the estimate of the Registrar General of Ireland, that the average yield in a fair year is three and a half tons per acre?—Yes.

4640. Your lordship first mentioned the year 1879?—I did.

4641. I find that the yield of the crop in that year was 1·3 tons per acre?—Yes.

4642. That would be about a third of the average?—Yes, a third of the usual yield.

4643. And I think, if I remember rightly, a third was the proportion your lordship named in your evidence of the value of the crop in that year?—I recollect giving the diminished value of the potato crop in that year, and off the usual value almost two-thirds had gone.

Sir T. O'Donnell, Bart.

11 Dec. 1894.

Incidence of taxation.

4644. I think you said it amounted to 3,000,000*l.*, as against an average of 9,000,000*l.*?—3,500,000*l.* as against an average of 9,000,000*l.*

4645. The second year to which you referred was 1883. In the two years between the periods the yield was 3·4 tons per acre, in 1884 four tons per acre, and in 1885 the yield was 3·4 tons per acre?—Yes.

4646. The next year to which you drew special attention was the year 1890. I shall have to read the yield between 1882 and 1890:—In 1883 it was 4·3; in 1884, 3·8; in 1885, 4·5; in 1886, 3·3; in 1887, 4·3; in 1888, 3·4; in 1889, 3·0; and in the year to which your Lordship called attention 2·3, so that your Lordship has the satisfaction of knowing that the official returns entirely confirm your evidence?—That is so.

4647. From some questions put to you by Lord Welby, it might have been inferred that your Lordship suggested that the income tax was too high?—I, of course, do not make such a suggestion.

4648. Lord Welby put it to you that the imposition of income tax was justifiable on the ground of benefits conferred upon the consumers. Your lordship so far from objecting to the imposition of the income tax, in fact in the course of your evidence cited the income tax as the fairest tax, and as affording the best test of relative capacity, did you not?—I only regret that the income tax had not been made the vehicle of removing other taxes which fell so heavily on consumers.

4649. Your lordship would not be sorry to see a heavier income tax upon the landlords who draw the rent out of the lands of Donegal, and only come there for the grouse?—It would be more equitable that they should pay a pretty heavy part of the taxation.

4650. We must look a little more closely at this question of income tax. Your lordship is perhaps aware that whilst only three-fifths of the taxation of Great Britain, that is 12*s.* in the pound, is drawn from the people, and 8*s.* in the pound from property (at least it was so until this year) in Ireland, 16*s.* out of every 20*s.* comes out of the consumer's pocket, and only 4*s.* out of those who hold the property of the country?—I have read that.

4651. That establishes at once a very great difference between the treatment of the inhabitants of Ireland and the inhabitants of Great Britain, does it not?—It does.

4652. Your lordship knows that before the imposition of the income tax the rate per head of taxation in Great Britain was considerably higher than it is now?—Yes.

4653. So that one of the effects of the imposition of the income tax, or at any rate one of the facts that has followed, has been a reduction of taxation per head on the inhabitants of Great Britain?—Yes; whereas the per head taxation of Ireland has been increased.

4654. Take Great Britain first and let us look at the period since the Union. At the period of the Union the inhabitants of Great Britain paid 3*l.* 3*s.* per head, and now they are paying about 2*l.* 4*s.* Great Britain having been in the interim the most progressive country in the world, and the one that accumulated the most wealth. Ireland having been in the interim undoubtedly the least progressive and the poorest country, the taxation of 10*s.* a head at the time of the Union has now become 2*l.* 2*s.* per head?—Yes.

4655. So that the Englishman has got rid of a third of his taxation since we became united, and we have had ours quadrupled?—Yes.

4656. The beauties or benefits resulting from an income tax are not so clearly perceived by us, and we may be pardoned for not seeing them so clearly when we see that the inhabitant of a wealthy country has got rid of a quarter part of his taxation, and that in spite of the income tax our taxation has gone up?—Yes.

4657. Of course the effect of the income tax has been to remove the pressure of a certain part of the taxation from the [redacted] to the owner of property?—That is so.

4658. But what is the relevancy of urging it when we find that the consumer has still to pay an increased modicum of taxation?—It has no relevancy in that connection.

4659. Then look at the relation of income tax to the beverages which are consumed respectively in Great Britain and Ireland. Your lordship is no doubt aware that at the time of the imposition of the income tax the duties on beer and on spirits were much more nearly upon a level than they are at the present time?—Yes, I am aware that since then the tax on whiskey has gone up very considerably.

4660. But now the income tax having been imposed for the good of the consumer, as we are told, and beer being the ordinary beverage of an Englishman, an Englishman can now go and give a shilling for beer and drink ten pennyworth of it, paying two pence tax. If an Irishman has a shilling to spend and desires to spend it on his beverage (and no legislature has a right to dictate to him whether he shall or not), he gets two pennyworth of spirit only and pays ten pence tax?—That is so.

4661. Does it appear to your lordship just or tolerable that the ordinary beverage of one of the two countries should be taxed to five-sixths of its price, and the other only one-sixth?—To my mind the question of temperance does not enter into the matter at all. I should greatly like to see the temperance and total abstinence movement spread all through Ireland, but that is not a matter for legislation. People have a perfect right to consume in any country a drink that is not evil in itself within reasonable bounds, and the Irish people who do consume whiskey rather than beer, should not have their consumption of whiskey taxed more heavily than is the consumption of beer in a neighbouring country where beer is the favourite drink.

4662. The Legislature having to deal with two countries, the one a poor country and the other a rich one, has no right to take advantage of the difference of taste and consumption in the two countries, in order to penalise the beverage of the poorer people, and to leave the beverage of the rich one partly free of duty?—If one might discriminate, one would think it should be in the opposite direction.

4663. Lord Welby put it to your lordship whether your meaning was that some people in Ireland should be exempt from taxation. I understand your lordship to say that your evidence does not necessarily lead to any such conclusion. I would call your attention to the statement made by the Treasury witness, Sir Edward Hamilton. In his memorandum laid before the Commission he said:—"The estimates" (these are the estimates according to Mr. Leone Levi and Mr. Giffen)—"unquestionably bring out in a very "striking manner the relatively small income which "the average Irishman enjoys, as compared with the "income enjoyed by the average inhabitant of Great "Britain; but the taxable income is the income "remaining after allowance for the minimum necessary "to maintain a population upon a given standard of "living." Then he goes on to say:—"A better test of "the amount which the taxpayer can afford to pay "for having Government protection and education is "the residue of income remaining after the bare "necessaries of life have been met." Now the question to which your lordship has directed yourself to-day is not whether some people in Ireland ought to be exempt, but whether the people in Ireland generally, and especially those of whom you have special knowledge, have, after meeting the bare necessities of life, to quote the language of Sir Edward Hamilton, any residue, or any substantial residue, which may be made the subject of taxation?—They have no such residue—they are going into debt.

4664. The fact that the cash expenditure exceeded the cash receipt in several of those budgets was

Dr. O'Donnell.

18 Dec. 1895.

Incidence of taxation.

ingeniously made an argument for doubting the accuracy of the budget—is it any argument for doubting the accuracy of the budget?—None whatever.

4665. Your lordship has testified that each family budget owes 10*l.* on the average?—In that poor district where the valuation is so small.

4666. Therefore in cases where the cash receipt of the year is less than the cash expenditure, the explanation is that the family is in debt?—Yes. There are three parishes in Donegal—the two Rosses parishes and Gweedore—where I am sure the debts to shopkeepers alone amount to 30,000*l.*

4667. I should like to ask your lordship when you say that the yield of the income tax is a good test of relative capacity, whether in the case of Ireland the yield of the income tax, if taken as a measure of relative capacity, should not be adjusted so as to take out of it—first, the rents withdrawn from Ireland by absentees or English landlords who have land in Ireland (the tax upon which rents is included as Irish tax); and secondly, the interest upon mortgages held in England, which interest is withdrawn from Ireland?—That seems obvious to my mind.

4668. But if the yield of income tax was so adjusted as to leave a balance representing the part of the assessment to income tax which is actually spent in Ireland, and if the yield transferred to Great Britain were added to the taxable capacity there, then the yield of income tax in the two countries might be a fair test of the relative capacity to bear taxation?—So it would, because it should be a fair tax on income above the necessaries of life in each country.

Pressure of population on inferior soils.

4669. I understood your lordship to convey that you think the condition of most of the people in this country, not alone in Donegal, but very much throughout the country, upon tracts of mountain and bogland, is largely responsible for the repeated failure of the potato?—For the failure to such an extent as to throw a large portion of the population into a condition of general want.

4670. I should be very glad to ascertain clearly from your lordship how, in your judgment, this strange spectacle of the emptiness of plains of good land and the congestion of population on mountain sides and bogs came about—was it simply the result of a belief on the part of the landlords at a former time that they could use the lands more profitably for pasture?—That is decidedly my opinion. If one looks up the records of clearances, one will find that the clearances were generally on good land, and the people, if they remained in the country, had to congregate on the bad land. In a book published not long ago by the late A. M. Sullivan, called "New Ireland," there is a description of an event that occurred in the year 1843 in the diocese of Meath. An eye-witness describes how he was present when 700 people were evicted and left on the roadside in one day, and out of the 700 people no head of a family, except one, owed a shilling of rent. In four years a fourth of those people were dead, and there was nothing for the rest but to emigrate penniless or to go into the workhouses; and I must say, for myself, I consider that way of thinning the population of Ireland unnatural in itself and in its consequences. It was unnatural, in the way in which it was done, to substitute bullocks for men of thrift; and it was unnatural in its consequences because nothing can be more unnatural, I conceive, than to fling families penniless on the quays of Liverpool and New York. I am sure events of that kind tended largely to swell what is called agricultural crime in Ireland. Many a young fellow, pretty well reared, was simply maddened by the thought of his father and mother being thrown on the roadside, or perhaps his sisters driven into the purlieus of one of the big cities, and under the influence of that feeling did deeds that no one can justify.

4671. Is it not the natural and reasonable use of a country to sustain its own people?—It seems to me to be a miserable record for a great nation in contact with a poorer one, after nearly one hundred years, to have its best land depopulated—its population not increased, and, besides, to have the record of so many famines, one of them involving the destruction of nearly a million human lives.

Dr. O'Donnell.

18 Dec. 1895.

Pressure of population on inferior soils.

4672. In the view of the statesman, does your lordship think that the extirpation of the people under such conditions is compensated for by what is called output—that is, by summing up the number of bullocks, sheep, and pigs, and dividing them over the dwindling population left, and calling it an average income?—If that were the true aspect of the case, and the destroying angel slew two-thirds of the population of Ireland, the remainder would be very well off indeed; but there is another view of the case. It seems to me no doubt that, counting crops and herds, we have a larger sum to put opposite each individual now—that is to say, the agricultural business in Ireland is a bigger business than it was years ago; but it does not at all follow that it is a more profitable business. Now the rent is very little less than what it was before, the taxes are not less, but in many cases are going up, and the price of labour in East Donegal has greatly increased, notwithstanding the employment of machinery. Even on the big farms the tenants employ very little power except a reaping machine and a threshing machine. Then it seems to me, also, that the price of produce has gone down so much, and ways of living, without being improved ways, have become so much more expensive, that we have not the agriculturist of Ireland in a better monetary condition, but in a much worse monetary condition than before, and I am perfectly sure, taking the agriculturists generally, the farmers are steeped in debt throughout the whole country.

4673. We know from official figures that the profits from stock have gone down enormously less than the profits from agriculture. Even if it were not so, 5,000 graziers and 50,000 herds could work Ireland comfortably for pasture; but would that be a satisfactory condition for the country, even for the living?—No matter how much land a grazier has, he can manage it with a man and a couple of dogs; but that employment of land gives nothing to the tailor or shoemaker or other artisans, and there is very little consumption of tea, not much of tobacco, and soon; so that, from any public standpoint, it would seem that to devastate a country of its human inhabitants in favour of cattle is an unnatural and improper use to put it to.

Special remedy in congestion of population.

4674. If such a set of circumstances had attacked the British people your lordship has no doubt they would have found their way out of it other than by expatriation of themselves?—Yes, I do not think that such events as have occurred in Ireland would have been allowed to go on had they occurred in Yorkshire or had they occurred in any part of France without an adequate redress being provided by the Government.

4675. However, in the fifty years since the famine it appears that the economic conditions which then tempted the landlords to substitute cattle for people have been changed and modified by foreign competition, improvements in transit by opening to the whole world the markets of Great Britain, and that tracts of pasture land in many parts of Ireland are being thrown back on the hands of the landlord?—That is quite the case. I know there is a very large tract of grazing land in the county Donegal, and by all accounts it is not at all paying at present. I know as a matter of fact in the West that these tracts of land are being thrown back; but that state of things will be a very long time in bringing about the transfer of the population from the congested areas to the grass land under proper conditions, unless there is some public authority in the country vested with the power to take these lands at a fair value and to divide them amongst a population that will be in a true sense an agricultural and a pastoral population.

Dr. O'Donnell. 12 Dec. 1906. Suggested remedy for congestion of population.

4676. It would appear that even the conditions of political economy do not any longer dream the lands in pasture?—In this country it would be very difficult I think, even for the discredited science of political economy, to set up a justification for the existing arrangement as to Irish land.

4677. The present congestion of the people on these tracts of bog and mountain sides reclaimed from a state of nature by their hands, lays them open year after year to the failure of the crop upon which they chiefly depend, because of the poor nature of the land, I understand, and the boisterous climate in the west of Ireland. The very operation of law and selfishness which placed them on those lands renders them particularly liable to the potato failure, I understand?—That is so.

4678. Therefore if only for the purpose of relieving the community and the benevolent from repeated calls on charity, it would be desirable that these people should be transferred to land upon which they could live, would it not?—I think from the point of view of the public good it is the beginning and to a large extent the end of any process of improving this country.

4679. And I understand your lordship to be of opinion that pastoral lands are now forthcoming and available provided that powers of purchase exist?—That is my opinion; but I must not be taken as saying that those pasture lands could be obtained and transferred at a reasonable price, and with reasonable facilities in any large quantities unless a compulsory power of purchase is vested in some tribunal.

4680. I understand it is very difficult to procure any land in Ireland at a fair price unless you have powers of compulsory purchase?—And, considering the past use of this land, it is not an easy matter to restore it to the descendants of those who formerly occupied it.

4681. If the compulsory powers to purchase lands for this great purpose were given there would be no practical difficulty in placing land under the Land Purchase Acts, or any similar Act to be passed, at the disposal of an authority for the purpose of distribution?—No. Credit would be a necessary requirement, and I do not see that there should be any difficulty about it.

4682. Your view I take to be that these purchases of land should be made under such conditions as would not involve loss; that the purchasing tenants should recoup the authority at least the amount spent upon the purchase?—That is my view, else it could never be carried out on a large, broad scale. The land could be bought, could be re-distributed, drained, fenced, given back to the occupiers as tenants, and afterwards those tenants could be converted into tenant purchasers without, apparently, any loss to the department that effects the transfer, as is shown by the instance of the Ffrench estate.

Instance of the Ffrench estate.

4683. I think it would be of value that I should in a few words ask your lordship to put before the Commission the financial aspect of the transaction relating to the Ffrench estate. I have the figures. I understand that you bought the estate for 7,600l.?—That is so.

4684. And sold it for 9,400l.?—That is so.

4685. That being sixteen years' purchase of the rent?—Yes, sixteen years' purchase of the rent. We bought under fourteen years' purchase and sold at sixteen, but we sold a very different article from what we bought.

4686. You spent 474l. on building and repairing houses, 378l. on roads and fences, and 318l. on drains?—Will you allow me to say that those houses, of which you have plans attached to this report, were built at an expenditure of 85l. each, and they are houses in which practically anyone might live. The tenants there worked like men, did all the unskilled labour gratis and very willingly, as far as these houses go.

Dr. O'Donnell. 12 Dec. 1906. Inspection of the Ffrench estate.

4687. That estate was a very striking example of this congestion, and also of the existence of land which might be used to relieve the congestion? As I understand, it was an estate of seventy-five tenants, with an average rental of 3l. apiece, and one grazing tenant, who had 350 acres to himself?—That is so.

4688. You took the grazing land?—We took the grazing land.

4689. And distributed it among the others?—The grazing tenant had no particular rights on the land. We made some equitable arrangement with him to satisfy him, and the grazing land we used in the ways that I have already described. Out of some of it we carved new holdings altogether, other parts we added to the neighbouring farms, and the remainder we joined to holdings at a distance by means of an accommodation road.

4690. And whilst fifty of these tenants before this transaction were under 3l. valuation, and therefore under the level of solvency, as you take it, all of them, except eight, are now over 5l. valuation, and of the eight, six are old people who cannot work a larger holding?—That is so. In all cases of the kind there will be families exceptionally situated, and it is not necessary for these that an ordinary provision in land should be made. I may say that we found the people there most reasonable and ready to co-operate in every way with the operations of the board. There were only two tenants who did not buy—one of them was absent in England or Scotland, and practically not approachable; the other is a tenant who cannot arrive at an arrangement with a son-in-law of his. It is a case for which practically there is no remedy, because there seems to be some slight mental defect.

4691. So that here, by the use of the public credit, you bought an estate in the Encumbered Estates Court; you sold it at a price to the occupying tenants which, even if you had made an expenditure of 1,600l. in improving it, still left a considerable surplus?—Yes, it left us a surplus.

4692. The Chairman desires that you should give the Commission the total expenditure and the total receipts in these transactions?—It appears on page 10. The amount paid for the estate was 7,600l.; building and repair of houses, 474l.; roads, fences, &c., 329l. 11s. 7d.; drains, &c., 318l. 8s. 3d.; redemption of charges, &c., 350l. 3s. 10d.; legal expenses, 400l. 3s. 4d.; incidentals, 163l. 6s. 1d.—total, 9,639l. 6s. 1d. Then receipts—sale of seventy-five holdings, 9,390l.; value of two holdings unsold, 118l.; payments for occupancy of three tenant purchasers, 150l.; arrears of rent, 423l. 3s. 4d.; grazing and sale of hay, pending sale to tenants, 220l. 3s. 7d.; incidentals, 3l. 17s. 6d.—total, 10,316l. 3s. 5d.

4693. (*Chairman.*) What does that sum up on both sides?—Expenditure 9,639l. 6s. 1d., receipts 10,316l. 3s. 5d.

4694. (*Mr. Sexton.*) You have transformed these tenants from being a body of cottiers liable to become paupers in a bad year into a body of substantial and self-supporting tenants?—Tenant purchasers, whose instalments after 49 years are at an end.

4695. And whose instalments after the five years' insurance have been paid will be less for the large holdings they are to have in the future than the small holdings they had in the past?—That is so.

4696. Is there any reason why by use of the public credit, especially with compulsory powers of purchase, such a beneficent transaction might not be multiplied in many parts of Ireland?—I do not see any reason in the world. This was our first experiment—we were very anxious to make it a success, and I need not say that every member of the board went into it with great heart. We had the services of an extremely competent representative in the district, Mr. Doran.

4697. For some other parts of your work the provision of harbours, the provision of boats, the stimulation of domestic industry, the establishment of factories, and soforth, you would no doubt need con-

Dr. O'Donnell.

18 Oct. 1894.

Increase of thrift in poor districts.

siderable funds; but for this particular work it would appear that if the adequate legal powers were granted the credit of the State might be safely and sufficiently employed for the purpose?—Yes; I have no doubt that these people are very good for their instalments, in fact there are marks of incipient prosperity already about their holdings.

4698. Do you think the settlement of these Irish difficulties would be accelerated if the advice and opinions of men who know the country were more often taken by those who have the responsibility of the administration of legislation?—This Irish board seems to be getting on pretty well with its work now.

4699. I am rather disposed to think from your lordship's evidence that you cherish the opinion that in these difficulties in the administration of Ireland the old maxim applies, and if there be an earnest will it is not impossible to find the way?—I think so. I think these Irish difficulties are best solved by the practical skill of the Irish people. The natural custodians of any nation's prosperity are her own sons.

4700. It is a fact perhaps worth emphasising, that at a time when Ireland was undoubtedly more prosperous than she is at present, under domestic legislation the taxation was from 4s. to 5s. per head, whilst now, under conditions deplorably different, the taxation is two guineas for each inhabitant of the country?—Yes.

Enlargement of holdings.

4701. (*Mr. Wolff.*) You have said that the tendency was to force the small farmers on to the bad land away from the good land, and that the remedy was to put them back upon the good land. Is there any good land in the neighbourhood of where they live or would you have to transport them altogether to distances?—It would add enormously to the difficulty if there were not good land in the neighbourhood. As a rule there are suitable tracts at no great distance from the congested populations.

4702. Could you get these tracts without special law or without special legislation empowering you to oust the people who hold them at present?—We can get them steadily—but I think not for our operations in any large quantity. We got the Ffrench estate, I think we have got another estate, and so on. Of course, really in the beginning we were not anxious to begin operations on a large scale—we wanted to go surely and steadily at this work, because the making of it a success is of the most enormous importance in doing anything for the congested districts. I do not think we could get land in large quantities. That is my private opinion, but of course, I do not speak for the Board in these cases at all.

4703. The Ffrench estate has been, as you have described it, a very great success?—It seems to be so.

4704. Is not that success greatly owing to the energy and ability which your board has brought to bear upon that individual case, and which you could hardly expect to be equally exercised when these operations are carried on on a very large scale?—For any work of such importance as this, constant work, constant exertion, and great pains are necessary, and should not be dispensed with.

4705. But could such lands be found to any large extent?—I think so.

4706. At all events to carry such a work out as a general policy, not only for relieving Donegal but all Ireland, you think it could not be done without special legislation?—That is my present opinion.

4707. The number of tenants on that estate I think you said originally was 78?—Yes.

4708. Are there more or fewer now?—I think there are 77 now.

4709. So that in reality you have as many as ever there were?—Yes; we were able to have three or four new holdings cut out of this grass land.

4710. Would it assist the operation of the improvement at all if the English Agricultural Holdings Act was extended to Ireland, do you think?—I do not know enough about the English Act to give you an answer to that.

4711. It would be much better, would it not, than instituting a new local board?—I have understood that the parish councils in England have the power of compulsory purchase of land, and something like parallel powers would be of great assistance I am sure in these districts.

4712. (*Sir David Barbour.*) Your lordship said that the people in Donegal and the very poor people generally use tea and tobacco because their other food is very inferior?—Yes.

4713. And especially because they could not get milk?—Yes.

4714. Have they a less supply of milk now than they had in former times?—I would not undertake to say that at all.

4715. Do you think the supply of milk was probably always deficient?—Undoubtedly it was; and I will explain what I said before when I said that the use of tea in Ireland thirty or forty years ago was comparatively small, but now has become pretty general. The practice grew up of compensating for the want of milk by the use of tea. Of course I do not know that it does add very much to the well-being of the people, but it is a change in dietary—a costly change—that has come with the times, as other such changes have come, and we have to take account of it.

4716. (*Chairman.*) Does much milk go from the congested districts into the large towns?—Not from farmers of this class. In the towns the inhabitants are supplied by pretty large farmers. Of course throughout the congested districts there are such farmers.

4717. (*Mr. Martin.*) In your replies to Sir David Barbour I took you to express an opinion that you considered in certain very poor districts of Ireland the people should be exempt from the payment of any excise taxes. In view of the difficulty that he pointed out in collecting or in making such differential taxation, would it commend itself to you as equitable if a similar amount were expended in these districts in reproductive works—were returned to the people as it were?—It seems to me that it would be very equitable to estimate how much these people paid in taxes beyond their taxable capacity, and to expend that sum. I cannot see a sufficient ground on which to continue taxing these people, as they have not the taxable capacity.

4718. But if it were returned to that particular district in reproductive works, would not that commend itself to your lordship?—Of course there is the difficulty that the individuals who are taxed may not benefit by such a return.

4719. (*Chairman.*) Do the purchasing tenants on the Ffrench estate, for instance, become freeholders, or are they still under obligations to the board?—In the first place they are tenants to the board as landlord. The board sells as landlord—they are the board's tenants, and then they become tenant purchasers with the obligation to pay instalments until the purchase money is paid up.

4720. How long does it take on an average under the scheme before the purchaser becomes really a freeholder?—Forty-nine years is the term.

4721. And during that term are you satisfied with the relation of the tenant to his great landlord?—During that period he is really out of our hands, except for the purpose of friendly intervention; he has to deal with the Land Commission for the payment of his instalments; we do not receive back the instalments.

4722. The operation is conducted by the Land Commission like any other purchase?—Yes, in regard to sale we occupy the position of an ordinary landlord.

The witness withdrew.

4723. (*Chairman.*) You were in the public service; are you still?—No, I have retired under the age rule altogether from the public service.

4724. You were a Poor-law Inspector, were you not?—I was.

4725. And you were Assistant Commissioner under the Labour Commission?—Yes, I was Poor-law Inspector and Local Government Inspector for more than thirty years, and I was afterwards Vice-Chairman of the General Prisons Board. Since my retirement I acted in 1892 and 1893 as an Assistant Royal Commissioner on Labour.

4726. You are in a position, I understand, to give us information as to the condition of the poor in Ireland for a great many years?—Yes, I have been personally familiar with it for a very large number of years.

Condition of the poor in 1845.

4727. How would you define the condition of the poor to have been, say, as far back as 1845?—That is immediately before the famine?

4728. Yes?—Nothing could have been very much worse than it was then. The population was then over 8,000,000—about 8,300,000 was, I think, the estimate made of it. There were 591,505 holdings in Ireland at that time, and of these nearly half, 310,000, were holdings of between one and five acres in extent. There was besides these a very large number under one acre; but in the census of 1841 the particulars of those were not given, so I do not know what it was.

4729. What was the food at that time?—At that time the food, I may say, consisted almost entirely of potatoes. There were three classes of the community that at that time may have been said to depend almost exclusively upon potatoes for their diet. There were a very small class of farmers of from one to five acres, which comprised a very large number of very poor people, who may be said to have been dependent upon potatoes. Then came the cottier class, holding houses on the farms of their employers with small patches of land attached to them, ranging from a rood to an acre of land. Sometimes they had a rood, sometimes half an acre, and in certain cases it came to an acre. For that they paid, generally speaking, not by money but by so many days' labour, and those as a rule were exacted at periods of the year when labour was of the most value to them, consequently their opportunities for supplementing their income in other ways was very limited. Then below that there was a third class who did not come under the head of cottiers, but who were simply labourers, living where they could and how they could, and who were dependent almost entirely upon what was well known in Ireland as the con-acre system; they got patches of ground from some neighbouring farmer which was either manured by the farmer, or in some cases was taken unmanured; and, in both cases, they either paid for it in money or by labour, which was a very common form of doing it. Their resources were exceedingly limited—their employment was very uncertain—and in certain parts of Ireland they were almost entirely dependent for the means of paying both for their houses and the land on the sums they made by migrating during certain seasons of the year to Scotland and England, and also to parts of Leinster.

4730. Was that migration much larger at that time than it is now?—Very much larger, because at the present time the migration may be said to be confined to some of the western counties—Mayo, Galway, Sligo, Roscommon, and Donegal are almost now the only counties which contribute to migration, whereas in former times they came from further south.

4731. Was the migration at that time, would you say, in the aggregate double what it is now?—I should certainly say it was a great deal more than double. The numbers that migrated at that time were very considerable, but I have no means of giving any absolute estimate of what they were.

Houses.

4732. What was the nature of the accommodation in their huts or houses?—Most wretched; they were mud cabins, consisting sometimes of one, two, or three rooms, but mud cabins of one room were very common, and the condition as to repair and in other respects was exceedingly miserable.

4733. And was the rent high?—Yes.

Wages.

4734. What were their wages?—The wages would range when they were paid in money (and they took probably the same basis in calculating when it was to be paid by labour) in the south and west of Ireland, from probably 6d. or 8d. to 10d. per day; but it has been stated, and I believe truly, that in the slack season of the year people in the west of Ireland were sometimes not at all unwilling to accept a lower scale, and there have been cases in the winter season where as low a rate as 4d. was paid.

4735. And they eked out those very poor wages with what?—They, generally speaking, having an exclusively potato dietary, were able to feed a pig and fowls, and in that way they made some reasonable addition to their income, and in many parts they made a substantial sum, as I have said, by migration.

4736. Then, as to clothing and bedding, what would you say?—The clothing and bedding were of the most miserable description. I can give you no higher authority than this. You are, no doubt, aware that at the end of 1843, before the famine, a celebrated Commission was appointed, known as the Devon Commission. They made a report, I think, a few months before the famine (in February, 1845), and if you will permit me I will read to you one or two passages in which they describe the condition of the labourers. They say—"In adverting to the different classes of occupiers in "Ireland, we notice with deep regret the state of the "cottiers and labourers in most parts of the country, from "the want of certain employment. It would be im-"possible to describe adequately the privations which "they and their families habitually and patiently endure. "It will be seen in the evidence that in many districts "their only food is the potato, their only beverage water, "that their cabins are seldom a protection against the "weather, that a bed or a blanket is a rare luxury, and "that their pig and manure heap constitute their only "property. When we consider this state of things, "and the large proportion of the population which "comes under the designation of agricultural labourers, "we have to repeat that the patient endurance they ex-"hibit is worthy of the highest commendation, and "entitles them to the best consideration of Parliament." This report is dated February, 1845. The first appearance of the blight in Ireland took place late in the autumn of 1845, so that this was some months previous to it.

Failure of potatoes.

4737. What was the result of the commencement of the potato blight?—I may explain that the failure of 1845 was a comparatively partial one; but it was nevertheless of very considerable extent, and of great severity. The early crop of that year had escaped entirely. That part of the crop was estimated to be about a sixth of the entire. Of the remainder the destruction was very considerable, but nevertheless there was a very fair reserve left, so that the pressure in the early part of 1846 from that failure was by no means what it came to some months afterwards. That was met at once by the establishment of relief committees, where food was either sold at a reduced rate or was given gratuitously where the circumstances justified it. In addition to that, public works were, to a certain extent, established in parts of the south

Mr. W. P. O'Brien, C.B.

18 Dec. 1894.

Failure of potatoes.

and west for the employment of the labouring poor. I am now speaking of the early months of 1846.

4738. Later in 1846, and in the following years 1847, 1848, and 1849, what was the movement, if I may use the expression, in respect to Irish distress?—In 1846 the potato crop might be described as a total failure; from one end of the country to the other the cry was the same. At the end of July it was described as being in blooming luxuriance, but only a little later it was blasted, and turned black from one end of the country to the other. Then the calamity became of vastly greater magnitude, and the relief measures that were adopted to meet it were also on a commensurately increased scale of magnitude.

4739. How was it in the following year, 1847?—The potato crop escaped remarkably well in 1847, and the other crops were particularly good; but in 1846 I may explain that the idea was that the failure of 1845 was merely a passing cloud, and they all cherished the hope that it would pass away, and they would be rewarded by an extra bountiful crop in the ensuing year; consequently enormous exertions were made in 1846, and the amount of land sown was exceptionally large. In 1847, in consequence of the experience of the failures of the 1845 and 1846 crops, the extent of land sown with potatoes did not amount to more than a sixth of that of the previous year, so that though the disaster of 1847 was a very much modified one in every way, the relief it brought was very partial for the reason that people had not planted so largely.

4740. In 1848 and 1849 was a larger acreage sown in potatoes; was the produce larger?—In 1848 there was a considerable increase, and immediately after 1848 the tendency was to a further increase, but I do not know what the exact figures were.

4741. Then we come to 1851; what was the state of things then?—In 1851 it may be said that there was throughout the country generally a greatly improved state of things, but to that there were very marked exceptions. I was Poor Law Inspector in the county Clare in the years 1849 and 1850, and most unquestionably the famine came in those years there with more severe effect, in the way of mortality and disease, than in any of the preceding years; but, throughout the country generally, the year 1851 showed a decided tendency towards improvement.

[illegible]

4742. What in 1851 was the state of things as to population?—I think in the middle of 1851 the population showed a total diminution of about 2,000,000, speaking from recollection. Probably the best indication of when the tide began to turn and things improved may be taken from a report I made several years ago for the Committee on the Local Government and Taxation of Cities and Towns, in which there is a table going back as far as 1848 showing the total out-door relief expenditure, the daily number of persons in workhouses, and the number of persons in receipt of out-door relief. I see from that return that in 1852 the expenditure, which in 1848 on out-door relief had been 738,443*l.*, fell to 491,700*l.*, and the number of persons in the workhouses in the same time had diminished from 128,295 to 104,000.

4743. Then in 1852 there was a modified recovery, was there not?—There was then a distinct tendency towards recovery, but, as I stated just now, it prevailed in most parts of the country, but was not universal.

4744. What was the policy of the Government as regards poor law during that term?—In what respect do you mean?

4745. Generally, what were the changes which were made in the poor law administration?—In 1846 and 1847 the relief of the poor was administered entirely through temporary agencies; there were relief commissioners appointed for the purpose, and the Board of Works played an important part in it; and up to August, 1847, the relief administered was chiefly done through these temporary agencies. In 1847 the original poor law only admitted of relief being afforded in the workhouses, and it was only in the session of 1847 that that was changed, and power given to afford out-door relief.

4746. Was that a matter of great discussion and difficulty?—I do not think so. My recollection is that considering what had occurred in the country it met with general acceptance, and it was regarded on all sides as inevitable, that some such change in the law should be made; and, as far as my recollection will bear me back, I do not think in either House of Parliament, though there may have been some discussion about the able-bodied people, it was objected to. There was one change made in the Bill in passing through the House of Commons which prohibited anybody holding more than a quarter of an acre of ground getting relief, but excepting as to such details as that, I do not think there was any modification made in it.

4747. (*The O'Conor Don*). Getting out-door relief you mean?—At first the provision was as to getting any relief; but they were afterwards—in 1862—allowed to be relieved in the workhouses.

4748. (*Chairman*). Will you tell us what main changes of policy took place between 1851 and 1871?—After the famine time the whole expenditure became a local one. Up to that time it had been largely defrayed by the executive government, but from that time it became a charge on the local rates, and was administered by the local bodies.

4749. Was there any change made as to the area upon which the expense fell?—Yes, at the time of the famine the universal cry was that the size of the divisions operated to prevent the landlords and others interested in property from giving work to the people depending upon them. They said "it is no use our "employing our people, because we are in partnership "with others who will not do it, and we shall have to "pay all the same." In consequence of that a very strong agitation was got up, and the demand at that time was, for individualising responsibility. Accordingly the Government of the day appointed three boundary commissioners. It was also stated that the poor law unions were too large which operated to prevent guardians attending from a distance, and that the details of business were so great that the boards could not discharge their duties sufficiently, and it was asked both that the divisions should be made smaller and the unions increased in number. A commission was appointed, consisting of Sir Thomas Larcom, who was afterwards Under Secretary for Ireland, a Royal Engineer Officer, and Mr. C. S. Crawford, Poor Law Inspector. They commenced their inquiries in 1848, but it was only in 1850 that their report was acted upon, and in 1850 the number of poor law unions was raised from 131 to 163, and the number of electoral divisions was changed from 2,049 to 3,438.

4750. Going back to 1848 may I ask you to state the changes in the administration. I thought you said there were no great changes. Making that the starting point, will you give us what great changes in the administration took place between 1848 and the time of the appointment of the commission of 1871?—Of course there was the out-door relief administration, which was thrown entirely upon the poor law at the end of 1847. In 1847 it continued very heavy, but the numbers afterwards in the usual course declined both in the out-door relief and subsequently in the workhouses.

4751. It was those changes in administration of the poor law that I was asking you about. What changes took place after that and up to 1871?—I do not know that there were any particular changes; there were various changes made from time to time

in points of detail in the law, and giving additional powers for doing various things. I do not think the main principles of the law as they were adopted in 1847 underwent any great change; but under this new rating of electoral divisions, after the famine the number of cottier tenements diminished enormously—by nearly one-half, I think—and the result was that a very large number of those who had been previously resident in rural districts became residents in the towns. The effect of that was that the town rates became very heavy—oppressively so, and a very prolonged agitation followed that. The town people naturally complained, and said it was entirely owing to the clearing out of the people of the country, who, after they had been a certain time in the towns, became chargeable upon them. They complained very loudly, and in consequence of their agitation a Union Rating Committee, as it was called, was appointed. I think the evidence was taken in one session, and the report made the following session. They took a very large body of evidence. The committee consisted of seven Irish members on each side—those who were advocates of and those who were opposed to union rating, with one English member on each side, and the chairman was the Chief Secretary of the day, Lord Hartington. They went very elaborately into the whole thing; but, as well as I recollect, Lord Hartington had the deciding voice in the matter, and the others were equally divided. Union rating had been adopted in England in 1865, and they recommended that it should be adopted in Ireland.

4752. Was it adopted?—In the year 1876 there was a modification of it adopted; they also made a provision about blind and deaf and dumb, and classes like that; but the principle of electoral division rating has been maintained intact up to the present day.

4753. In 1871 your attention was specially called, was it not, to the condition of the labourers?—Yes; the session of 1871 was the session when Mr. Gladstone brought in his first Land Bill, and it was in connection with that that the several poor law inspectors were instructed to report on the condition of the agricultural labourers, which we accordingly did.

4754. What became of those inquiries?—I do not exactly know; there was some provision in the Land Act with reference to labourers' houses, but my recollection is that it proved inoperative; the machinery provided did not work, and it led to no result.

4755. Then coming down to quite recent times, what was done about the condition of the labourers?—The great complaint on the part of the labourers for years was the wretched condition of their house accommodation and the want of any land on which they could grow crops. They complained that for a great part of the year they could get no employment, and having no potato crop and no other resources, they were left in a state of the direst misery, and their houses were of the most wretched description. That topic was dealt with very fully, as may be found on reference to the reports of the poor law inspectors at the time. My own report on the condition of the houses was, at that time, as strong as I could make it. There was nothing done at that time at all, except, as I say, that there was some provision, as to which I am not very clear, in the Land Act about labourers' houses, but nothing notable was done for the labourers until 1883; between 1883 and 1891 there were a series of Acts passed which enabled the Boards of Guardians to provide houses for the labourers, with half a statute acre attached to them, and in some parts of Ireland, in Leinster and Munster, those provisions have been very largely availed of, but not in either of the other provinces to any great extent—in Connaught very little, and in Ulster very little.

4756. What would you say now is the condition of the labouring class compared with what it used to be thirty years ago?—I have no doubt whatever that the condition of the labourers is substantially and in many directions improved, as compared with ten or fifteen years ago; as compared with the time when I wrote my report on the labourers in 1871, the condition of the labourers has undergone a very marked and substantial improvement.

Mr. W. P. O'Brien, C.B.

11 Dec., 1894.

Present condition of labouring classes.

4757. Are wages higher?—Wages are higher, and, what is probably of more importance, employment is more constant, owing to the great emigration which has taken place amongst the class of able-bodied men.

4758. Is their food and clothing cheaper?—Their food is cheaper than it was fifteen years ago, and their house accommodation, in the two provinces I mentioned, at all events, has undergone considerable improvement; and carrying with them, as they do, those plots of ground, they are enabled to keep pigs and fowls to provide them with food during the months they can get no employment.

4759. Then you say the condition of the labourer class is much better now than it was a few years ago?—I have no hesitation whatever in saying so, so far as my own experience is concerned, and so I have stated in my report to the Labour Commissioners.

4760. Now, taking the other classes concerned in agriculture, especially in small villages, has their condition improved as much as the labourers' condition?—Labourers in the towns are not all in as good a condition as the labourers in the country. A great many of the town labourers, I may explain, are of the class of what are called loafers, who do not care to get systematic employment, and prefer living from hand to mouth by getting casual jobs at high rates; but there are in all towns a considerable number of men who are industrious, steady, and anxious to get employment, and they feel, where their work is not constant, greatly the want of having allotments or gardens.

Other classes.

4761. Then as to the class above them, who are not called labourers, the small farmers, and those even above them, the lower class of employers—has their condition improved?—As regards the farmers generally, it may be said that after the effects of the famine passed away they had a long series of years of decided prosperity; they had high prices for butter and agricultural produce of every kind, and the farmers did extremely well. During that time a change took place generally, I think, in the style of living of the farmers, and when recently the times got bad, I do not think that scale of living correspondingly altered. When I was on the Labour Commission, I took especial pains at every union I visited to ascertain facts from those I knew to be good, reliable authorities, and the result of my inquiries was this, simply:—That the very large farmers were fairly well able to bear the reverses that had come upon them; that as regards the others, about twenty-five per cent. might be said to be fairly safe and solvent, but that as regards three-fourths of them, they were more or less in debt to the shopkeepers and others. It was further explained to me that even though many of those had deposits at the bank, that was not a proof that they were not in debt and difficulties, because they appeared to have, as far as I could gather, an almost superstitious dislike to part with their deposit receipts, and also possibly the showing of the receipt enabled them to get credit in various ways; but the result of my inquiries as regards the majority both of the small and middle class farmers now, in consequence of the great fall that has taken place in prices, the advance in wages and increase in local taxation, is that their condition is worse than it was ten or fifteen years ago.

4762. Is there any connection, in your mind, between the improvement in the condition of the labourers and the non-improvement in the condition of those to whom you have just referred?—The addition of wages to the labourers, which has so much improved their condition, has detracted from the resources of those who employ them; and again, the labourers who have been assisted by getting those valuable houses and plots of ground, have got them at a very substantial cost to the ratepayers of the districts in which they reside.

Mr. W. P. O'Brien, C.B.
18 Dec. 1894.
Local taxation.

4763. How has the local taxation in Ireland stood, say, taking thirty years ago and ten years ago?—The local taxation in 1864 was 2,538,280*l.*

4764. (*Mr. Sexton.*) Does that include everything—rates and everything?—All the local taxation. Grants are deducted from that; that is the amount which had to be paid.

4765. (*Chairman.*) Now take twenty years later—1884?—In 1884 it had come to 3,788,546*l.*

4766. That is an increase of nearly 50 per cent.—Yes.

4767. Then will you take from 1884 to the present time?—It has fluctuated, but last year it got up to 3,617,564*l.*, that is about 170,000*l.* under the amount for 1884; but I found that that was caused by the circumstance that in 1893 a grant of 248,000*l.* was received under the provisions of the Probate Duty Act of 1888.

4768. Do I take it from you that the increase in local taxation indicates any falling off in the well-being of those who pay it, or otherwise?—I consider that any increase of taxation means a diminution of their resources, and so far it goes to explain the fact generally represented to me that their condition now is not at all so satisfactory as it was fifteen years ago; but that is only one element in the consideration.

4769. It is, in your opinion, one element?—Decidedly.

4770. Has there been any change in the valuation?—The Irish valuation has never been revised; there was the original tenement valuation under the Act of 1852 that extended its operations from 1853 to 1868, the northern parts being those that were last valued, and the southern and western earlier. In that Act there was a provision that there might be a revision at the end of fourteen years, but there never has been any revision, and the only change from that time to this has been the adding of new property and removing other property.

[illegible]

4771. Is there anything which indicates to you the cause of the diminishing resources of the farming class?—Yes; in my inquiries under the Labour Act everywhere they told me the land was starved, that it wanted lime, draining, and fencing, and a great many other things; but they said: "As we stand at "present, even if it could be shown to us as clear as "daylight that it would be to our advantage, we have "not the means, and labour is so high at the present "time that it is out of our power to do it;" and as another indication of that, I found a general tendency to diminish the extent of tillage, the explanation being this—"We cannot afford to pay for labour, and we are "obliged to diminish our tillage"; and tillage has consequently in many of the districts been considerably on the decline.

4772. That then indicates to you a worse condition of the farming classes, does it?—Yes.

4773. Does that re-act on the labouring class, do you think?—Certainly, in this way: the first complaint of the labourers was about their houses. In those unions where that has been remedied, the complaint now is that they have not constant employment. Sometimes they tell you (no doubt they very often exaggerate) that they are seven and eight months a year without employment; but from the very best sources of information, as land agents, who had no interest in misrepresenting the state of things to me, I learnt that for four months of the year the condition of the labourers was a very hard one, that there was little or no employment going on, and unless they had plots of ground or something of the sort their situation was a bad one. In some unions the tillage has been enormously reduced, in fact it is all grazing, and they told me the labourers were certainly, as to the majority of them, for four months of the year without much employment, but where houses have been granted to them on an exceptionally liberal scale, they have that resource to fall back upon.

Mr. W. P. O'Brien, C.B.
18 Dec. 1894.
Effect on labourers.

4774. May I sum up your evidence up to this point in these words that, in your opinion, for the last thirty years, the condition of the labouring class has been steadily improving, but that that improvement is checked now, and that they are not improving, and that on the other hand the condition of the farming class has not improved, but is now going backwards?—Decidedly.

4775. I take it that that is the sum and substance of what you have said?—Exactly; I think the labourers' condition is stationary at present, except in one direction, namely, that there is a tendency going on to improve their house accommodation. I think that has become a matter of great interest I hope from the labours of the Labour Commission to some extent, but at all events the fact is that there has been increased activity observed of late in providing better houses for them, and so far there is a material improvement in their condition. As regards the effect of providing house accommodation for the labourers by the rate-paying classes, I am not quite sure whether the Commission are aware that though rents are paid by the labourers, they fall very greatly indeed below the amount that those cottages cost the ratepayers, and therefore in every union where a cottage is provided it substantially amounts to a loss to the ratepayers of about 3*l.* a year.

4776. I suppose you are aware that that is the case in England and Scotland as well, and that is universal?—No doubt; but that is an additional charge on the ratepayers. The labourers have been improved by it, but so far as it goes it operates against the farmers as ratepayers.

4777. (*The O'Conor Don.*) You have stated that the rate of wages has very much increased?—Within the last ten or fifteen years. Wages.

4778. Do you think that that increase has been a progressive one?—I think that for some years past there has been no change; but as compared with some ten or fifteen years ago, there has been a decided increase.

4779. Was there any decided increase ten or fifteen years ago as compared with the price of labour before the famine?—Certainly. In point of fact, before the famine you know as well as I do that in the west and south of Ireland there really was very little money changing hands, for they generally paid their rent by so many days' labour; and where they were paid in money in the west of Ireland, 8*d.* and 9*d.* were the common rates, ranging in some better places to 10*d.*; but I have heard of cases in the West of Ireland where in winter the rate went as low as 4*d.*

4780. What do you consider to be the average rate of wages for the agricultural labourer now?—Labourers must be divided, in considering their position, under two heads, the large class of farmers and the gentry pay their labourers exclusively in money; the middle class of farmers almost as a rule, or in the great majority of cases, give the labourer his diet, and give him money wages in addition to that. In some of the districts the diet now exacted is an exceedingly good and expensive one, costing, I should think, to the farmer who employs the man, a great deal more than the difference between the wages he gives and the current rate where they give no diet. Still the farmer, for various reasons, prefers having the labourer to diet. Where the labourer gets no diet the scale of wages may be said to range from 8*s.* to 12*s.*; 12*s.* would probably be the amount in the neighbourhood of large towns, but 9*s.* and 10*s.* I think may be taken as the usual rates that prevail. I think, speaking generally, from 9*s.* to 10*s.* may be the amount. With the diet, they may be said to range from 4*s.* to 7*s.*, but 5*s.* and 6*s.* are the most usual rates. In the county of Wexford, which is an exceptionally prosperous district, they almost entirely diet the labourers, and their money payment is

Mr. W. P. O'Brien, C.B.

11 Dec. 1894.

Wages.

exceedingly low—5s. and 5s. 6d. a week, but the diet given is exceedingly liberal.

4781. How long should you say it is since the wages ranged from 9s. to 10s. a week?—I do not think there has been any change probably for ten years.

4782. No practical change for the last ten years?—I think not.

4783. You say you found the farmers have abstained from draining and improving their lands to a great extent on account of the great expense of labour?—So they told me themselves.

4784. And yet that the labourers were idle for four months and sometimes six months of the year?—They allege that, but on the best authorities I could consult I have no doubt in my mind that for four months of the year a very large proportion of them have hard times. Of course where there was a really good worker or good man he could calculate on pretty uniform employment throughout the year; but as to those who did not come under that category, their employment for four months in the year was very precarious. There are some districts in Ireland it was represented to me in which a good labourer need not be idle for the whole year; but they suffer again in this way—in wet weather and on church holidays, when they will not work, the wages for those days are stopped, and in that way there is a considerable loss.

4785. But are not these two statements contradictory—on the one hand that the farmers cannot drain their land because wages are too high, and on the other that the labourers cannot get employment?—That is exactly what the farmers say; they say "if "these men were willing to take moderate wages, such "as we can afford to pay, we would employ them"; but the labourers refuse to give way on that point; they will not accept a low scale.

4786. They prefer remaining idle for four months?—Certainly; that was represented to me at several places. If they were willing to take low wages they could often get them, but they will not take them.

4787. (Mr. Sexton.) What wages would they get?—You may take it as general where they are not dieted it would be 9s. to 10s., and from 6s. to 7s. where they are dieted; but 9s. probably in the poorest parts of the country would be about what they would get, and they will not take less.

4788. In the case of conflict between labourer and farmer what wages does the farmer offer, and what does the labourer want?—In the winter time probably the farmer would expect them to take 9d. or 10d. a day.

4789. (Mr. Wolff.) And they would rather be idle than take it, would they?—Yes, and that is very intelligible, because they feel probably that if the precedent was once established, and 9d. or 10d. became recognised as a reasonable scale of wages to pay, they would stick at it, and would not get more at other times. At all events the fact is so, and it has been represented to me, in various districts, that they prefer refusing employment to taking it at a reduced rate.

4790. (The O'Conor Don.) Is not there at present considerable difference in agricultural wages in winter and summer?—Of course, as regards harvest time they command very exceptional wages, also at hay and seed time, but I do not think that in any parts of the year the scale goes below what I have mentioned.

4791. But is it not the fact that for the short days in winter the farmers do not pay the same rate as they do for the longer days in summer?—I do not know that they go much below the 9s. or 8s. rate at any season.

4792. Is it your experience that there is no change between the winter and summer wages?—There may be several cases where they give less. In the cases I speak of I am not giving you the precise sums, but I have no doubt about the representation that was made to me—they would not take the wages the farmers could afford to pay; what the amount was I cannot say. In spring and harvest the wages greatly exceed the rates I have named.

Guardians' cottages.

4793. You have told us that the rents the labourers pay for the cottages built by the Guardians do not at all repay to the Guardians the interest on the money they borrowed for building those houses. Can you give us the amount of extra rates payable by any union in consequence of the building of these cottages?—They cannot exceed a shilling in the pound for labourers' cottages.

4794. (Lord Welby.) The charge can only be a shilling in the pound?—Yes, on the valuation.

4795. (The O'Conor Don.) A shilling in the pound on the valuation of the electoral division?—Exactly; the local authority are invested with the power under the Act to fix the area, but you are right in supposing that that is what is practically the area. Now I find in my report upon the Kilmallock Union this—"The total "number of cottages for the erection of which the "necessary official authority was obtained is 544, this "being the largest number yet approved of in any union "in Ireland; of these, 460 have been already completed "and occupied; the remainder having been, for various "causes, with the particulars of which I am not "acquainted, unavoidably abandoned; but a fresh "scheme providing for 330 more has been recently "submitted and enquired into, and only awaits the "decision of the proper authorities for its final ratifi-"cation. The full cost of the cottages erected has not "been precisely ascertained, but it is estimated to be "about 130l. for each cottage; or about 59,800l. in all. "The rents, which are it is satisfactory to learn as a rule "paid with reasonable punctuality, only amount in each "case to 2l. 8s. per annum; and as the charge on the "rates for interest, cost of collection, repairs, &c., is "estimated to amount to 7l. 9s. 6d., this, it will be seen, "represents an annual loss to the union of 5l. 1s. 6d. "for each cottage."

4796. On a total amount of what?—7l. 9s. 6d.

4797. How many cottages were there?—They were in course of building; there had been already completed 460, and the actual expenditure was 59,800l.

4798. (Lord Welby.) In that one district?—No, in the whole union, but the charge was assessed on the electoral divisions separately.

4799. (The O'Conor Don.) You told us that the loss to the union was 5l. a cottage?—Yes.

4800. I want to know what was the total loss to the union?—I do not know how many cottages they have built since. The number then was 460.

4801. That gives 2,300l. as the loss to that union?—At that time, yes.

4802. What was the average expenditure of that union altogether?—I have been out of touch with the poor laws now for fifteen years, and I do not know. It is a union in which the land is very rich and valuable; it is an exceedingly rich grazing territory and the rates do not come very high there compared with other places.

4803. Do you know what proportion of the total expenditure this payment of 2,300l. for the cottages amounts to?—That could only be got from the Local Government Board. I have no figures as to that.

Local taxation.

4804. You have stated that the local taxation has risen enormously since 1865?—Yes, I have given you the figures.

4805. Can you give us what you believe to be the causes of that great increase?—I can, I think there have been several causes. In the first place there has been a very large increase in county taxation, owing to expenditure on lunatic asylums. When I made my report on local taxation I found the expenditure for lunatic asylums in 1865 was 97,654l. and here I find that the expenditure for 1891 was 272,816l. 15s. 3d., so that in that one item there has been a large increase. Then there are other items, such as cattle plague and out-door relief, which has increased very largely; it has undergone an enormous change in Ireland—new items have also been added. There have

2 B

Mr. W. J. O'Brien, C.B. 16 Dec. 1894. Local taxation.

been sanitary questions under the Public Health Act, a system of drainage, and a variety of other things, which have contributed, one by one, to increase the taxation. The sanitary expenditure has been very considerable. Then the salaries of officers underwent a change, and there was a great deal of change made in the dietary in the workhouses. There have been altogether a great many different things contributing to bring about the change which has taken place.

4806. (*Sir David Barbour.*) I think you said that the condition of the labourers was very bad before the famine?—Certainly, nothing could be worse; I quoted to you the best authority I know of. I must explain to you that the Devon Commission not only took a large body of evidence, but they also made personal visits, and saw things for themselves.

4807. The condition of the very small farmers was wretched, too, was it not?—It was, they were only a grade above the labourers.

4808. And their food was chiefly potatoes?—Yes, and as the Devon Commission says, their drink water, and, as they say further, a blanket or a bed was then a rare luxury.

Food, &c.

4809. I believe it is the case now, is it not, that there is a great deal of tea consumed?—Yes, and I am sorry to say consumed in a very objectionable way, because it is kept stewing the whole day.

4810. But it is in point of fact consumed?—It is, there is no doubt about it.

4811. That is an entirely new addition to the diet, is it not?—Quite a novelty.

4812. I do not know whether they drink more whisky and smoke more tobacco?—In almost every union I visited I always had the labourers to meet me in the different districts, and I examined them themselves as well as examining the farmers, and I generally tried to ascertain from them what their expenditure was under different heads; I cannot say I got much information about the whisky, it was rather a delicate point, and I cannot say I touched upon it much; but as to tobacco my estimate was very much what the Bishop of Raphoe said—6d. to a 1s.—probably 9d., would represent the average. They all smoke, and probably an average of 9d. a week would represent the expenditure on tobacco.

4813. I think you said that owing to various causes land was not being drained now to any extent?—The farmers themselves told me they were doing as little as they could to the land. Numbers of respectable farmers have said to me—"I admit I am not farming "properly, but I cannot afford to do it."

4814. The cultivation is not so high as it was in the years 1870 or 1875, is it?—I think not.

4815. I suppose the main cause of that is not the high price of labour, but the low price of produce?—The two combined; the price of produce having diminished, the high wages demanded operate in the same way.

4816. There has been some evidence given to the effect that grass land is going back to tillage, because pasture is not profitable; do you agree with that?—I found no indication of that at all.

4817. Of course it might be the case in particular districts, might it not?—Some cases may have occurred, but I can only say that I visited thirteen counties under the Labour Commission; I made very careful inquiries, visited every part of the districts, and I found no case of that sort. I cannot say there may not be such cases in other places.

4818. It is quite certain it has not gone on to any large extent?—It has not as regards Leinster or Munster.

Comparison of present time with time before the famine.

4819. (*Lord Welby*). In what form would you sum up your experience, comparing first of all the time before the famine with the present time. As I understand you, before the famine the classes of agriculturists consisted of farmers, cottiers, and labourers?—Yes.

4820. I want to see if I follow you rightly. Practically the effect of the famine and subsequent action almost abolished the class of cottier?—The cottier was almost swept away altogether.

Mr. W. J. O'Brien, C.B. 16 Dec. 1894. Comparison of present time with time before the famine.

4821. I want to get from you, if I can, what your view is of the agricultural classes of Ireland before the famine of which you had experience and the present time?—Since the famine they had a series of years of undoubted prosperity, and their general condition improved considerably, but in recent years it is not so.

4822. I want your idea as to the present time and the time before the famine?—I should think they are better off now. There were an enormous number of exceedingly small holdings at that time, but they lived much more cheaply at that time, and in that way they were better off; but they live much better now than they did then. At that time the very small class of farmer scarcely lived better than the labourers, and even the farmers a grade above that had very much the same diet; fresh meat was not much indulged in amongst them before the famine. Their consumption of meat was very moderate, but now that class of farmer would have meat at certain times, and has to give his labourers meat also. That is one of the things they complain of so much, that they have to give the same diet as they themselves have to the labourers. A very respectable farmer that I examined in the Cashel Union in County Tipperary, which is a very good union, told me this which I will read from my report:—"An extensive practical farmer in the "Cashel Union thus described to me his experience "in this matter. He says 12 or 14 years ago a "labourer would have potatoes and milk for break"fast, potatoes and butter for dinner, and oatmeal "stirabout for supper. Now we farmers must give "them bread and butter, and often eggs for breakfast, "meat for dinner, four or five days in the week, and "the others butter and very often tea for supper." That I take it represents the state of things. The labourers get the diet the farmers themselves have, and that diet I take to be considerably in excess of what the farmers of the same class had before the famine in Ireland.

4823. What size farm would that be?—This man was a substantial man, I think. I do not know what his acreage was.

4824. I do not know whether you noticed it, but if I heard the Bishop of Raphoe aright, he gave it as his experience that meat was almost unknown in his part of the country?—Yes, I am quite sure that is the case there. It so happens that Donegal is the one county in Ireland of which I have no knowledge at all. I have never set foot in it, and I know nothing about it; my evidence is intended to apply to the South and East of Ireland, as to this.

4825. At all events so far as the districts you know are concerned, you would not express yourself in the same terms as the Bishop of Raphoe did about the non-consumption of meat?—I think the farmers live better now. I am not able to speak positively of course, but I should say one of the reasons why they are depressed now is that they began to live better, and they have not changed their mode of living with the fall in times and prices.

4826. But still from your experience on the Labour Commission, do you think it would be right for this Commission to assume that what the Bishop of Raphoe said about Donegal, and about meat never being used there, would be a fair representation of the state of things all over Ireland?—I will take Wexford. The Secretary of the now extinct Labour League, who had specially intimate acquaintance with the special affairs of his class, says in relation to men being paid partly in labour and partly in money: "The food of the labourer's family is wretched, and "consists of Indian-meal stirabout and buttermilk; "less than one-fourth of the labourers are paid en"tirely by money wages, 8s. and 9s. a week. I

Mr. W. P. O'Brien, C.B.
21 Dec. 1894.
Comparison of present with state before the famine.

"consider the labourers should have 2s. a day "without diet; they cannot do on less."

4827. (*Lord Welby.*) Who says that?—That was the evidence of a very intelligent man in good employment himself; he was the caretaker of some Corporation land there. He had been a labourer, and was a man of exceptional intelligence, and his evidence was that in that county where I was taking his evidence, the practice is to diet the labourer and pay small money wages.

4828. That conflicts with the statement of the farmer whose statement you read before?—No. This applies only to the families of the labourers. He says the families suffer, not the men, where the labourer is paid partly in money and partly in diet. The following is the evidence given by one of the Secretaries of another Labour League in the same county—Wexford—as regards the labourers themselves. He says: "The breakfast given by farmers is generally "stirabout and milk or bread and milk; no tea except "in rare cases. Dinner, meat two or three times a "week, American meat with potatoes. Supper, tea "and bread, potatoes and milk. At 4 o'clock they "also get tea and bread; that is four meals." That I take it fairly represents the diet of the labourers themselves.

4829. That is your view of it?—Yes.

4830. Am I to understand that you draw a distinction there between the food given to the labourer himself and that of his family who are living outside the farmer's house, who are fed very poorly?—Precisely. I call attention specially to the case of Wexford, which is an exceptionally prosperous agricultural district, two of the baronies of it being amongst the most prosperous agricultural districts in Ireland. In my report what I call attention to most strongly is this: that while the labourers there get an exceedingly good diet, such as I have just described, the families have to subsist on exceptionally low money wages. The scale paid in Wexford, in addition to diet, is less than I found almost anywhere else I visited, rarely exceeding 4s. or 4s. 6d.; and, in point of fact, if it were not that the women happen to be exceptionally industrious and thrifty, I do not know how they would exist at all. But the wives rear poultry and manage to help on the earnings of the head of the family, otherwise I do not know how they would exist.

4831. I have heard it said that two hens will pay the rent; what do you say as to that?—Well, the class of fowls they rear in Wexford fetch very high prices indeed.

4832. May I take it that that is your opinion of the districts generally which you know?—Certainly.

4833. Which would amount to this, that as a rule the labourers' families live on rather poor diet?—That is where the arrangement is that the labourer is not paid all in money, the condition of his family is much worse than in other cases; but the strange part of it is that both the farmers and the labourers themselves appear to prefer the arrangement. The labourer's preference is a selfish one, namely, that he gets fed better than he would at home; but as regards the practice, to his family it is injurious. If a man has four or five children, and only gets 4s. 6d. a week, and he has to pay for rent and clothing, the difficulty is to understand how they can live at all, under those circumstances.

4834. Going back to the question of your experience as to the condition of the people before the famine and now, I suppose one may take it that before the famine there were comparatively few of what I may call decent sized holdings?—Considerably more than half were under five acres, because of the 690,000, the total number of holdings, 310,000, were from one to five acres; and the number under one acre must have been very considerable, as it comprehended the whole of the cottier class, which at that time was an overwhelming one.

Mr. W. P. O'Brien, C.B.
21 Dec. 1894.
Comparison of present with state before the famine.

4835. The whole history of the famine and the diminution of the population of the country is a most melancholy story—about that we shall be all perfectly agreed; but do you think that there would have been an improvement in the physical and material condition of the Irish if there had been no famine—I am so afraid of putting a question in a form which might lead one to think that I thought the famine a blessing—supposing there had been no famine, would not you have anticipated that the population, as it then stood, in the absence of some very great changes, would have gone from bad to worse?—If there had been no famine I take it the population would have gone on increasing, and I do not know how they could have existed at all; they had already come to such a point of misery that I do not see that there was anything lower to go to; I do not see how any human being could exist under conditions more distressing than those which existed at the time of the famine.

4836. You hardly agree with Mr. O'Connell, who said he wanted to see 16,000,000 people in Ireland?—If the whole population were to be dependent, as they were then on the produce of the land, I do not know how the thing could have been done. I think nothing could have been worse than the condition of certainly a great deal more than a third of the then population of Ireland. I take it that the number at that time was over 3,000,000 who were living in that abjectly wretched condition, and there can be no more authoritative opinion than the one I gave you from the Devon Commission, which took enormous pains to get at the facts.

4837. You were mentioning that a change had taken place in the migration; that the migration which used to take place in the West and South is now almost confined to the West. Can you give me any reason for the change?—The class that used to migrate have emigrated very largely, and left the country altogether. Migration.

4838. But that part of the South from which migration no longer takes place belongs to rather a poor district of Ireland, and one from which the emigration has not been so great as in other parts, does it not?—The emigration has been very considerable, generally, in Kerry and that part of the country. I have not got the exact figures, but the reduction of the population in Kerry has been considerable.

4839. And you think it arises from that, do you?—They do not migrate to England and Scotland. The only exception I found to the cessation of migration in the south of Ireland is rather a peculiar one. The Kilmallock district is a dairy district, and about St. Patrick's day in each year the lads and lasses come from West Cork and Kerry to Kilmallock; they are hired to the farmers for nine months, and at the end of that nine months they go back to Kerry, and remain for three months, then go back again. That is the only thing in the shape of migration that I found while I was engaged on the Labour Commission.

4840. I did not quite follow you on a very interesting subject—that of the Labourers Dwellings Acts—we have had a great deal of information placed before us on the subject of the dwellings in Ireland generally, and most of us are very much struck by the fact of the disappearance which you will no doubt have watched, of the old class of houses, the fourth class, the great improvements in class 1 and class 2, and what I may call the more or less stationary character of class 3. I am now dealing with what Dr. Grimshaw has called our attention to, namely, the accommodation rather than the actual number of houses. Taking his figures there are 932,000 families in Ireland, of those over half, or fully half, are housed in the first and second class houses, and I think we may consider that there is no immediate necessity for improvement in those. The fourth class is dying out very rapidly, and therefore we are left with the third class as the class which need re-housing. I have been rather struck by seeing that though the Labourers Labourers' dwellings.

Mr. W. P. O'Brien, C.B.

11 Dec. 1894.

Labourers' dwellings.

Dwellings Acts have not been in operation a very long time, they have only, as you inform us, been adopted in some places?—There are cases in Connaught and Ulster, but they are not extensive.

4641. I see from the returns that no less than 1,100,000l. has been laid out in labourers' cottages?—Yes, it is a very large sum.

4642. I do not know if you know—I will not trouble you if you do not—what is about the average cost of a labourer's cottage?—From 120l. to 130l., all expenses included.

4643. There you see a very great movement forward, do you not?—Of course it is.

4644. By that means the class of houses to which all well-wishers of the Irish population would not object are rapidly being removed, and that has been the result of this Act, which has been in operation for ten years?—Yes, that has been the chief means; there has been very little improvement made in that class of houses through any other agency.

4645. Then you put as a make-weight against that that though this is a very great advance and improvement in regard to that class, at the same time the result of it has been a loss to the ratepayers?—Certainly.

4646. And you think that that falls upon the farmers?—Most certainly; 5l. a cottage per annum where they carry out the Act actively comes to something very substantial.

4647. Did I gather that the charge of a cottage re-built in this way comes to about 5l. a year?—It comes to 7l. 9s. 6d., and the rent receivable is 2l. 8s., leaving a loss of 5l. 1s. 6d. I must tell you the rents are not absolutely uniform. I came across unions where they were only 8d., 10d., and 1s. Some guardians are more liberal than others, but they range from 8d. to 1s. a week.

Local taxation.

4648. You gave us some very instructive figures about the increase of local taxation—do you happen to know whether the local taxation increases more in the towns proportionately than in the country?—It has increased very considerably in the towns, because they have been applying the Public Health Act very actively in the towns.

4649. It is for that purpose I ask the question?—No doubt the town expenditure must have been very considerably increased from what I know generally of the number of cases where they have brought water from a distance and had an improved system of drainage, and so on.

4650. That is rather an important point when you point out and dwell on the fact that the increase of local taxation has fallen heavily on the farmers, and when you support that by these striking figures, it is rather necessary to examine them and see how far that increase really affects the farmer?—The town areas in Ireland are very unequal. I served upon a Boundary Commission for re-arranging the Municipal Boundaries of Ireland in 1878-9, and there was found to be an enormous disparity. In some places the towns are strictly the town limits, but in others they extend and have a very wide rural district attached to them; so that in some cases the farmers would have to pay a share of the cost, though, of course, they do not enjoy the advantages in the same way as others.

4651. To a certain extent that has to be borne in mind, has it not?—No doubt.

4652. For instance, the local taxation of Belfast, Dublin, and Cork might comprise a very considerable amount which does not fall on the farmer, might it not?—Of course the farmer would not pay unless it happened that his district is included in the municipal area.

4653. You have given a fair description of what you considered to be the general movement of the agricultural classes, and you have called our attention to the fact that many things have told against the farmer, but there is one point you did not mention which I think is rather an important one, namely, that the farmer is a consumer as well as a producer, and that the cost of his living has fallen?—No doubt that is so, as far as he is a purchaser of what he consumes.

Mr. W. P. O'Brien, C.B.

11 Dec. 1894.

Local taxation.

4654. And that there is not only a fall in the price of his own articles of production, but all the way round in all commodities?—No doubt.

4655. That is a point which should be taken into consideration on the other side, is it not?—Yes, of course he shares in that.

Poor law relief.

4656. We have heard a good deal about the increase of outdoor relief, and we have been told with regard to that that in reality the increase is due chiefly to a desire on the part of the guardians, to which in the main the Local Government Board have not been opposed, to increase the comforts of the people to whom outdoor relief is given; would you agree with that?—The increase in the outdoor relief has been more a change of practice than one resulting from anything in the condition of the country during the time it has taken place. After the famine I may say outdoor relief ceased nearly altogether. The lowest was in the year 1856 when it came down to 2,344l. in the whole of Ireland—it had practically disappeared. The first year when any substantial increase took place was in 1862 when it came to 14,000l. After the famine, the people had got so frightened and the fear of outdoor relief was so great at that time, that the practice was generally to take what were called auxiliary workhouses, instead of giving outdoor relief. It was felt that it was demoralising the whole population, and embarrassing the ratepayers, and the effort everywhere was to get rid of it. They, therefore, took an extra number of workhouses in the southern and western unions, and the effect was that gradually the outdoor relief was reduced until it was brought down almost to nothing, as I say, 2,344l. in 1856. Some years after that, about the year 1865, I remember, letters began to be written in the papers; and one board here and another board there began to give relief, and from that time onwards you will observe the amount has kept on increasing year by year, while the workhouse numbers fluctuated in accordance with circumstances. They responded to the conditions of the seasons, they were elastic, and became larger or smaller as the seasons were more or less favourable; but the progress of the outdoor relief every year increased, until at last, from being 2,000l. a year it came up to 200,000l. As I have said I have been out of touch with the poor law since 1879, but what I formerly found to be objectionable in the mode of giving outdoor relief is this: that they did not give nearly enough in cases of sickness. Where the head of a family was struck down I always thought it was to the interest of the ratepayers as well as the family that their household should not be broken up, and to meet that liberal relief should be given. Liberal relief was not given usually, but instead of that a system began of giving wretched doles to people of 6d. and 1s. a week which simply assisted them to live by begging. I remember once at a union in the west of Ireland a man had been struck off the outdoor relief list, and I happened to be in attendance when he asked to be replaced. He had had 1s. 6d. a week for a long time, and I asked him how he managed to live on that. His answer was he paid a 1s. a week for lodging, 6d. a week for tobacco, and he begged the remainder. I said that I thought a system of relief, such as that, was alike injurious to the ratepayers and to the recipients. My view was that if outdoor relief was given it should be given liberally, but that that system, as an aid to begging, was thoroughly objectionable. I should apprehend from the progressive increase I have mentioned here that probably the same system more or less prevails to the present day, but that I cannot speak to. Most certainly when I

Mr. W. P. O'Brien, C.B.

11 Dec. 1894.

Poor law relief.

was in the habit of attending boards of guardians the system of outdoor relief I thought was not a beneficial one; it was not enough to support the recipients, and simply gave an impetus to mendicancy, which ought to have been discouraged.

4857. May I take it that you are not quite satisfied with the result?—I am referring to an experience fifteen years old, and I cannot tell what has occurred lately; but in former times the mode of giving outdoor relief was such as I thought not at all satisfactory.

4858. (*Mr. Sexton.*) If Mr. O'Connell ever spoke of 16,000,000 as a possible population of Ireland, I presume he would have had in his mind the development of Ireland?—I do not see how it could by any possibility be accomplished otherwise.

4859. Ireland at one time had many successful manufactories, had she not?—No doubt; that was before my time.

4860. And at one time, I believe, they were suppressed by imperial Acts of Parliament?—No doubt; that is a matter of record. Acts of Parliament were passed which had a destructive effect upon the manufacturing industry of the country.

4861. And if the manufacturing industries of the country had progressed since 1800 as they did before, another 8,000,000 might not have been an excessive population?—That would admit of indefinite expansion, no doubt.

Local and imperial taxation before and after the famine.

4862. Comparing fifty years ago and now, what was the local taxation of Ireland before the famine?—I have been quoting from those returns that Dr. Neilson Hancock first compiled. They do not go back further than 1865.

4863. Do you suppose it was more than 1,000,000*l.* about the time of the famine?—I should suppose it was not very much more. For instance, the poor rate expenditure was very small at that time, the county cess was low, and the town expenditure, I should think, was the lowest of all; so that the local taxation of Ireland before the famine must have been comparatively very moderate.

4864. Now it is reaching 4,000,000*l.*?—It is very close to it.

4865. And you know that the two rural heads of poor rate and county cess cover nearly 3,000,000*l.* of it?—Yes.

4866. And tolls and harbours only a small fraction?—Yes, very small. The taxes on real property, I think, amount to about 80 per cent. of the whole expenditure.

4867. The imperial taxation, which was about 4,000,000*l.* before the famine, is now 7,000,000*l.*?—Yes.

4868. That is to say, that the whole taxation per head has a good deal more than doubled?—Certainly.

4869. The sketch you have given of the condition of the labourers before the Union rather presents a picture of a primitive state, does it not?—I did not say before the Union; I said before the famine.

4870. Quite so; it rather presents a picture of a primitive state?—Yes. The labourer lived in a state of absolute serfdom; he contracted to give so many days' labour, and the farmer was a hard taskmaster, I am afraid, and the universal statement is that he took pains to exact that number of days at the only seasons of the year when labour was of value.

4871. The labourer bartered the main part of his labour for food, for a house, and sometimes a bit of land?—Yes.

4872. And the balance he received in cash of 8*d.* or 9*d.* a day?—I do not know that the cottiers got any cash; they migrated and all that, but I think the farmer got such work done as he required. There were a certain class who got money who did not get land from the farmers.

Dieting system.

4873. Then we have a class of labourers now who are employed by the large farmers, dieted by them, and the balance of their hire—9*d.* a day about—paid in cash?—It varies. Where they give diet the limit is from 4*s.* to 7*s.*, but I think 5*s.* to 6*s.* you may take to be the commonest rate.

4874. I may say 10*d.* to 1*s.*?—Yes.

Mr. W. P. O'Brien, C.B.

11 Dec. 1894.

Dieting system.

4875. In that case a labourer occasionally gets some meat, you say?—Yes; I gave you two cases where they undoubtedly got it.

4876. Do you think that would happen in the houses of small occupiers?—Certainly not the small class, but the small classes of farmers do not employ labourers, they do the work by themselves and their families, and in the busy season a practice prevails in a great part of Ireland of assisting each other—they go and help each other.

4877. At any rate the practice of dieting only prevails amongst the large farmers?—Not the very large farmers, we may say the middle class of farmers.

4878. When the labourer is dieted, does it not occur to you that his family are really worse off than if he received his wages in cash?—Certainly. I have adverted in the strongest terms in my report to that very circumstance. I say I think the system is very bad. I read to you the evidence of a most intelligent man, who had been a secretary to the Labour League, who said the condition of the families is wretched, but the diet the man himself gets is excellent.

4879. It would be better for the family if the man got 10*s.* than a few shillings with diet?—I should think so. One labourer I asked who did not get diet "How do you get on?" He said, "My wages are "10*s.*; I have eight in family; I spend 1*s.* for rent, 1*s.* "for milk, 9*d.* for fuel, 4*d.* for light, 1*s.* for tobacco, and "that leaves me 6*s.* 6*d.* for the diet of the family of "eight."

4880. The condition of the labourer before the famine almost excluded the use of money, did it not?—Almost entirely.

4881. It had nothing to do with fiscal systems or money?—Quite so.

4882. And even now when he has any diet he has to purchase some things?—Yes.

Margin of taxable income.

4883. Now, if we take the formula laid down by Mr. Giffen and other experts, that the taxable income of a man is the income remaining, after allowance for the minimum necessaries to maintain him upon a given standard of living is made, do you conceive that these wages, with diet in one case, or without diet in the other, will allow any appreciable balance after any civilised standard of living has been applied to the case?—Certainly not; the mystery to me is this. I see the Commission have been trying to get budgets. Now I tried by every means I could to get some of the most intelligent workhouse masters and relieving officers to make up a labourers' budget for me. They undertook the duty with alacrity, but when they took down the figures they found the outlay was so greatly in excess of the known income, that the thing could not balance at all. So far from leaving any margin, it is a mystery to me how they are able, with their large families, to live. I asked several most intelligent men who came before me in Wexford, "Can you explain to me this—the "labourers' wages are 6*s.* and 6*s.* 6*d.* a week; they have "a great number of children—can you explain to me in "what way they manage to live?" but they one and all admitted to me they could not tell.

4884. It would rather appear, would it not, that any duty paid by a man of this class upon tobacco or upon tea must in some way be subtracted from the necessities of living?—That is obvious, and the consumption of tea has become very considerable—it has become an article in general use.

Labourers' dwellings.

4885. I understand that there are only 12,000 of the houses which you referred to?—I am not sure if they have built 12,000 yet, but it was certainly over 10,000.

4886. Dr. Grimshaw tells us there are 300,000 agricultural labourers taking them altogether. It would appear, therefore, would it not, that scarcely the fringe of the question has been touched?—In some of the unions they have done a good deal; but

Mr. W. P. O'Brien.

11 Dec. 1894.

Labourers' dwellings.

in the Queen's County for instance, which is a rich county, the number of houses built is very insignificant indeed, and some of the other counties have done very little. Kilmallock, which I have given you, is the largest district, but there are a great many others, even in Leinster and Munster, where there has been very little done as yet. Some of the houses I personally visited on the Labour Commission, when they alleged to me that they lived in wretched houses, and I found that they let in the rain. I always, after I had completed the inquiry, got a policeman to show me the house itself, and I satisfied myself that the house accommodation in a large measure was extremely wretched, as alleged.

4887. Taking those 11,000 houses and the total number of labourers, there would appear to be a large number who want houses?—Quite so.

4888. And apart from the better social condition of the man there is the question of the acre of land too? —The holdings, with all the houses that were built up to the time of my going out, were limited to half an acre; in 1892 an acre was allowed, but the Act was not retrospective. It enabled the guardians in any future schemes to extend the land to an acre, but it had no retrospective bearing, which created an intense feeling of dissatisfaction, because some of the labourers said, "Why should not I have as much as my neigh-"bour?"

4889. Do you think the acre should be given all round?—I think if you give it at all it must be done all round. I think it is practically unworkable, to have the two running concurrently. If one of the labourers gets an acre, the others will never be satisfied with half an acre.

4890. But of course such losses as those in the case of Kilmallock create an obstacle to the system? Yes, that is one of the things. I do not think any of the houses have been built at a cost of much under 120*l*.

4891. Do you think by giving greater powers to the local bodies, less intervention to the body in Dublin, and so on, and cheapening the cost of houses, you might get the thing done for a price which would bring it very nearly to the amount of the burden upon the rates?—The impediments complained of at present have more reference to the time, than to the cost of building. The complaint generally when I was going round was that the time lost from the incipient stage to the closing of the scheme was about two years. There were so many notices to be given at particular times, and so many forms to comply with, which almost all the Clerks of Unions whom I consulted told me were really useless. I got three of the most intelligent Clerks to send me statements in writing of what their experience was of the impediments, and I incorporated those in my report.

4892. Suppose it were admitted that the taxation of Ireland was excessive, and the question were dealt with, not by way of reduction of taxation, but by way of the application of a portion of Irish revenue to Irish uses, do you think a useful way would be to apply it to an extension of this system?—I think so; it is a matter of the greatest importance I think to the contentment and comfort of the labouring classes in this country that they should be properly housed. If you are going to give relief at all I do not know any better form that you can give it in than to lighten this expense. I do not think any of the labourers can pay more than a shilling a week, but if it could be so arranged that this would pay back to the Guardians the expense that they had to bear, it would be a most decided boon.

Mr. W. P. O'Brien.

11 Dec. 1894.

Labourers' dwellings.

4893. An acre of land carefully tilled would give the man enough to live upon with his wages, would it not?—As regards the acre and half acre there is a great diversity of opinion; many people think that if they got an acre they would become farmers, and would be quite independent, and that they would be no use as labourers at all. The labourers on the other hand say "half an acre is no use, because we "must have a rotation of crops, which half an acre "does not admit of our growing." Some people think the acre would be a decided disadvantage, and that the labourers would get independent of the farmers, snap their fingers at them, and refuse to work for them, but would grow potatoes, and live upon them; the labourers say otherwise.

4894. There are always people ready to venture that kind of prophecy, are there not?—Those are the different views.

4895. (*Chairman.*) How much land would you say would be a proper quantity?—Labourers are in very different positions. Take a man who has a couple of sons who are able to help him in the culture of the land, he could get on very well, but if a man only had young children he would not have the same facility. I think, however, you must have a uniform system, and now that Parliament has sanctioned an acre I do not believe you will have satisfaction and contentment until you give them the acre, and as the object was to make them a contented and comfortable class, that object will not be attained unless they get it.

4896. You think the general application of the acre would go far to make them contented, do you? —I think so.

4897. Then the general picture you present as between the farmer and the labourer is that the farmer out of lower prices for his produce has to pay higher wages?—Yes.

4898. And that the reason of his paying higher wages is because he has contracted the labourer, and that he in turn has contracted the labour market; so that on the one hand the labourer has higher wages, and on the other hand less employment?—Certainly.

The witness withdrew.

Adjourned to to-morrow at 11 o'clock.

ELEVENTH DAY.

Wednesday, 19th December, 1894.

At the Benchers' Chambers, Four Courts, Dublin.

PRESENT:

THE RIGHT HON. HUGH C. E. CHILDERS, *Chairman*.

LORD WELBY,	CHARLES E. MARTIN, ESQ.
THE RIGHT HON. THE O'CONOR DON,	THOMAS SEXTON, ESQ., M.P.
SIR DAVID BARBOUR, K.C.S.I.	GUSTAV W. WOLFF, ESQ., M.P.

MR. B. H. HOLLAND, *Secretary*.

DR. T. W. GRIMSHAW recalled and further examined.

Dr. T. W. Grimshaw.

19 Dec. 1894.

Mode of estimation of agricultural values.

4899. (*Lord Welby.*) May I take it that the paper you laid before the Commission the day before yesterday is intended as a convenient summary of the agricultural statistics which your department possesses. I refer to the paper which works out the 19,000,000*l.*—the blue paper?—That paper of course does not depend solely upon Departmental statistics. That paper consists of two things: the agricultural statistics collected by my department, which I treat as facts, and the opinions of other people applied to those facts. The agricultural statistics are, of course, collected for my office by the constabulary, who are lent to me for the purpose. They are all dealt with by my staff, and they are as accurate as such means can possibly make them. But the rest of the statistics, the prices, and so on, that are applied, and the proportion sold, and so on, are all mere opinions of other people, not mine. They are opinions of persons who profess to be experts, and their opinions are as good as can be got. I have not collected prices. Some years before I was Registrar General, for some three years, prices were collected for that particular purpose from market clerks throughout the country: but those were not continued by the Government, and any prices that are collected now officially are collected by the Land Commission. As you are aware, after the Cowper Commission land rents were to a certain extent dealt with on the ground of the existing prices of agricultural produce; and with the view of having a record to guide them, the Land Commission have collected statistics of prices, which of course, to a certain extent, are in their infancy, because they have only been going on for a short time. No doubt, those in future years will be very valuable and useful; but at present we cannot use them at all for comparison with past years.

4900. In fact might I put it that your department can only collect information under a few heads, and that in drawing up this paper of which you are speaking, you have had to rely for many particulars on estimates which it is impossible to base upon actual information in your possession?—Certainly, that is so.

4901. For instance, you get particulars on which you can rely, because they are collected by and on behalf of your department, as to the nature and extent of crops, the number of live stock, and so on?—Yes, and produced.

4902. But the values attached to them are the subject of an estimate which at best can only be a presumption?—Certainly.

4903. And which must be subject, therefore, to qualification in different districts and under different circumstances?—Certainly.

4904. I mean by that that though put together they may be a fair summary, yet at the same time it would be dangerous to draw too minute conclusions from them?—Yes. I understand you mean that they should not be applied locally, that is it would not do to say that those ought to be the prices in some particular locality.

4905. To illustrate my meaning, you put down the produce of the hay crop at 4,156,096 tons, worth 9,351,216*l.* That represents, subject to some margin of error, the crops as you may say officially obtained?—The amount of produce officially obtained, but the value is not official.

4906. I was only putting the value to give the figures; but the amount of the crop is as reliable as any information of that kind can be?—Certainly.

4907. And for that your department would take a certain amount of responsibility?—We take all the responsibility that can be attached to anything of the sort.

4908. On the other hand, you put down hay [illegible] valued at the round sum of 8,000,000*l.*?—Yes.

4909. This is, no doubt, carefully drawn up, but that is a conjecture?—It is a conjecture; it is not my conjecture; it is the conjecture of two or three persons who were asked what they thought it ought to be.

4910. And so far that does not rest on any facts such as those on which the actual crops are based?—Certainly not; it may not be a fact at all, but it is as near as we could get.

4911. And without more information than the Commission possesses, it would not be safe to rely upon that figure as absolutely accurate?—Certainly not. Why I brought it here was because I thought it might be of assistance to the Commission; and when I was asked to give evidence my view was that anything I knew of that I thought would be of use to the Commission and which was in my possession, I should bring forward. I have done so, but I bring it forward with that very great caution which I wish to be observed in compiling a statement of that sort.

4912. I will take again the estimate of the expenditure on manures and various charges of that kind which make up the expenditure side of the account. Much of the accuracy of that depends upon the accuracy of Mr. Harris, does it not?—Yes.

4913. No doubt Mr. Harris is a statistician who takes a good deal of trouble, but different people might not unreasonably put different values upon the absolute accuracy of his calculation as applied to those particular heads?—Certainly, I look upon Mr. Harris in the light of an expert.

4914. If you rely upon the opinion which an expert forms, you must bear in mind, must you not, that it is merely an opinion, which may or may not be accurate, and before one accepts it implicitly one would like to

Dr. T. W. Grimshaw. 12 Dec. 1894. Mode of collection of agricultural statistics.

know a good deal more about the basis on which he arrived at it?—Certainly.

4915. You would not take any statistician's word implicitly?—Certainly not; but his was the most recent figure, and you may perhaps remember it was discussed a good deal at the time. It was published in the "Economist."

4916. You and I should be agreed, should we not, as students of statistics, that such calculations can only be considered as giving an idea of a statistical problem?—Certainly.

4917. And then in mere self-defence it is necessary to insist on the necessarily imperfect nature of the statistics, and also that it is dangerous to generalise too closely upon such figures?—Certainly.

4918. In illustration of what I mean I will put this to you. In taking their statistics the Customs officers see the actual packages containing the goods and the invoices of their contents, but we know that on non-dutiable goods there is room for error, although the Customs officers actually handle the goods themselves when brought in, but with a certain allowance for error of that kind they get a fair account of any particular item, such as eggs?—Yes, I think that is quite correct.

4919. But still those statistics are liable to a considerable margin of error. Can we speak with the same confidence when we estimate the value and number of eggs produced in the great country of Ireland, and must not we regard such a value as that of 556,000*l*. as probably the best estimate which can be formed, but still an estimate based on little more than conjecture?—That is all, it is only based on conjecture.

4920. Again you estimate for labour in the rough. Is it not dangerous and would you not shrink from making yourself responsible for a calculation which based conclusions on necessarily uncertain figures of that kind?—Certainly, I would not be responsible for that at all. At present I get with the agricultural statistics the rate of wages in the various districts; but that is quite a new thing and it would require a great mass of material of that sort, and a great deal of consideration before you could arrive at any accurate statement with regard to it.

4921. The point I am leading up to is this. We must not particularise, as I venture to put it, too rashly upon these things. It would not be right to come to the conclusion and to give it the weight of your opinion that these figures really mean that every man, woman, and child gets 6*l*. a year to spend, and that is all they have. It is too broad a conclusion to rest upon so narrow a basis, is it not. I ask you whether you would feel safe in arriving at so important a conclusion upon what I venture to put before you as uncertain data?—I think that is pretty much the same question that Mr. Sexton put to me the other day, is it not, that is if you divide the money over the agricultural community. I do not think you can take it so positively as that.

4922. I wish to know if you are content to put such a conclusion as that forward on your responsibility?—Certainly not, and I think (the Chairman will correct me if I am wrong) I disclaimed altogether the idea that that was the income of the agricultural community, and that that was merely the money circulating as it were.

4923. If you were told that such a conclusion was to be based on the paper which you have laid before us, and that on that conclusion possibly a system of financial policy was to be modelled, may I put it before you that it would be desirable before that conclusion was accepted, that it should be much more closely discussed?—It would have to be very carefully sifted, I do not see myself that we have the material for coming to an exact conclusion. I do not think we have.

Investments of Irish capital.

4924. We had some interesting information from you and an interesting discussion on investments beginning with the noticeable fact that the amount of consols held in Ireland had diminished, and you gave us some reason for it, and some explanation of that fact?—An explanation of what may have become of the money.

Dr. T. W. Grimshaw. 12 Dec. 1894. Investments of capital.

4925. You alluded to banks also; but in the main your argument was addressed to Government stocks and railways, I understood?—There were three items, I said the Government stock had diminished by so much, I then said there are several well known investments which can easily be ascertained on public stocks, that is railways and banks. I only took the two as possible examples which are perfectly well known, and I said that a large portion of the money which was withdrawn from the Consols might be accounted for in that way.

4926. Of course now-a-days as we all know, there is an enormous amount of investment outside those heads, general investments?—Yes, in my pamphlet I say "besides" so and so, I only take those two principal items that we know. It would be impossible to find out all the investments in small companies and so on.

4927. Do you remember that after the conversion of Consols that took place it was a well accepted fact that in England a large amount of sales took place of Consols, that people, being disappointed with the return the Consols then gave, transferred their money to various other securities such as those you allude to, and as to which you would have no positive information?—Yes.

4928. You remember the criticism that many benefits and one evil attended the conversion, namely, that many people were tempted owing to the small amount of consol interest to go into investments which were not safe?—Yes, I read a great deal of literature on the subject at the time, and heard a good deal about it.

4929. Do you not think something of the same kind may have acted on Irish investors?—Certainly.

4930. Therefore unless we had a considerable amount of information on the subject of those investments it would not do to base too positive conclusions as to the reason for the diminution in the holding of Consols would it?—Certainly, it was more by way of accounting for a certain amount of the money that had gone out that I gave those figures.

4931. Several of us have heard of cases, no doubt, in which there have been considerable transfers from one or two English companies to Irish?—Certainly, it has occurred.

4932. It is difficult to get information upon the point, but I do not know whether you have noticed some of the papers that have been laid before the Commission, showing the amount of income tax that is probably levied in England on the investment of Irishmen. To put it shortly to you. Probably in the gross 50,000*l*. a year in income tax is paid in England on the investments of Irishmen. That represents a very considerable sum, does it not?—Yes, of course it does. I have not gone into it myself.

4933. I am putting these points to you in support of my conviction that there are very large investments of Irishmen in other securities except Consols and railways, and therefore that a conclusion based on the diminution of sales as showing the diminution of the wealth of Ireland is not trustworthy?—That would not prove any diminution of wealth, I think. It would be only conjectural.

4934. There is another point upon which a good deal of stress has been laid, namely, the fact of the diminution in the value of the Irish agricultural produce?—Yes. Value of agricultural produce.

4935. I should like to qualify the deduction so drawn, and to put it in this way:—If there were fifty people where formerly there were 100 you would naturally expect the produce of those fifty people to be somewhat less than the produce got by the labour of the 100. With a diminishing population you would in the first instance look for a diminution apart from the price or amount of produce from their labour, would you not?—Of course fifty

Dr. T. W. Grimshaw.

people could not produce as much as 100, supposing them all to be working at the same rate, and with the same energy. Taking it generally, no doubt your statement would be a correct one.

4936. I think you gave us some interesting information on the subject of the famine itself. Do you know the pamphlet on "The Irish Crisis" which is attributed to Sir Charles Trevelyan ?—Yes.

4937. I think you come pretty much to the same conclusion as he did as to the result of the famine ?—Yes, I consider that his statements appear to agree with mine.

4938. That pamphlet is constantly spoken of as a standard of information, I believe, on the subject, is it not ?—Yes, and it is a good standard on the subject.

4939. Before your interesting "Facts and Figures" one has to go back some time before we find statisticians who employed themselves upon these comparisons of different dates, but I think there was a time about thirty years ago when Dr. Hancock gave himself very much to that study, did he not ?—Yes, in fact a good many of these things I am doing officially were done by Dr. Hancock; the early returns with regard to banks were all compiled by Dr. Hancock, and they were taken from his calculations. He used to prepare for the Government half-yearly a statement of bank statistics with regard to Joint Stock Banks and Savings Banks, and his figures which were contained in those were checked over and were transferred to those different columns of Facts and Figures. Then Dr. Hancock, in the year 1863, was asked by the Government of that day to report upon the supposed decline of Irish prosperity, and he wrote a report for the Government, which I have here, which is done very much upon the same lines as the paper I have written.

4940. That was a very well-known paper and attracted a good deal of attention, I think ?—Yes.

4941. My object is to call attention to it and to ascertain from you whether in some respects your papers are not a continuation and improvement upon it ?—They are a good deal in continuation.

4942. (*Chairman.*) Has this report of Dr. Hancock's been printed and presented to Parliament ?—It was printed, but I do not know that it was laid before Parliament. This copy which I have here is not a Parliamentary copy, but like other papers it may have become so afterwards. It is printed by the Government printers in Dublin, and is addressed to the Under-Secretary.

4943. (*Lord Welby.*) Would it be right to say that Dr. Hancock arrived at the conclusion that there had not been a progressive decline in the prosperity of Ireland from the time the immediate effect of the famine passed off ?—Certainly, that was Dr. Hancock's conclusion. He began very much in the same way that I did by taking the figures from the time following the famine, and going into them all much in the same way as I have done, but of course he had not anything like the material available that I have had to do it with.

4944. He had not the material; of course your information goes over a much longer period ?—Yes, the material was not easily accessible at that time, and has been picked up from other sources since. Of course I had thirty years more than he had to go on.

4945. I do not know whether there are any remarks you would like to make further on your evidence, or give any further exemplification of it. For instance, I think it has been admitted there has been a slight increase in the labourers' wages. I am not sure whether your view is that there has not been a considerable one ?—I mention the return of wages taken in 1860, and in the agricultural statistics, which I think I handed in, we are now publishing wages tables. I have not attempted to analyse them and compare them one with the other.

4946. I gave that as a sample; I wanted to know whether you would wish to supplement your answer ?—I do not know that I have anything further to say about it.

4947. (*Mr. Wolff.*) I think you stated that one of the causes of distress or want of progress in Ireland is the absence of manufactures ?—Not the absence, but the comparatively small amount of manufacture speaking in comparison with Great Britain.

Want of coal in Ireland.

4948. And which you attribute to the want of iron and coal in Ireland ?—Mainly.

4949. But of course there is a very considerable amount of manufacture in Ulster, is there not ?—Yes, there is.

4950. Would you attribute in a great measure the fact of the manufactures being there and not in the rest of Ireland to the fact that Ulster is close to the coal producing districts of England and Scotland ?—I have no doubt it has a good deal to do with it, and the same applies to a certain extent to Dublin. In fact it applies as it were to the east of Ireland as compared with the west, they are so close to the coal producing districts that where coal is necessary for the manufacture, as it always is, it is more easily obtainable than it is in the west.

4951. There were at one time one or two mills in Dublin and Wexford, and so on, but they have all been abandoned, have they not ?—Yes, most of them.

4952. Do you think that was owing, in some degree, to the extra cost of coal there to what it would have been for Ulster ?—I should think it probable, but there may have been other causes. Of course the carriage of coal by steam colliers of considerable size makes the coal available at once in the ports to which those vessels come; therefore the facilities would be greater for carrying on a manufacture where your coal was landed on the quays as the actual terminus than elsewhere.

4953. At the same time, in Ulster the manufacturing district extends 30 or 40 miles away; does it not ?—Yes, and some of the most rising towns in Ulster have increased very much.

4954. If I press this point a little it is because one so very often hears in England that it is impossible to establish manufactories in Ireland outside of Ulster, on account of the cost of coal. I find on looking at the freights from the shipping ports in England going down from Glasgow to Garston, which is a large shipping port, that from two of those ports you can ship coal cheaper to Dundalk and Dublin than you can to Belfast ?—I think that may be so.

4955. From three of them it would be dearer, but the total difference would be only about 3d. a ton either way, and I find that the shipping of the coal to Cork or Waterford would be only about 1s. 6d. a ton more, and if Welsh coal were used it would be only 1s. more; therefore you can hardly say that the difference in the cost of coal prevents manufactories being established in the south and east of Ireland if they are established in Ulster, can you ?—It should not prevent it, but if it is 1s. 6d. a ton more for Cork and Waterford that is so much against them.

4956. I suppose you are aware that the cost of coal is one of the smallest items in the cost of production of flax ?—I am.

4957. That in the manufacture of a bundle of yarn, costing from 3s. to 5s., the cost of coal is only 1½d., so that the cost of coal does not enter into the question to any great extent. Therefore if it is not the cost of coal which prevents this manufacture being established in those parts of Ireland, do you know of any other reason ?—I do not; I cannot account for it.

4958. Is there anything, do you think, in the difference of race between the inhabitants of Ulster and other parts of Ireland which causes it ?—Of course the people of Ulster are a different race from the people in the South.

4959. And you can see no reason why we cannot hope in future to establish these industries ?—That would be expressing an opinion of the capacity of Ulster-men in comparison with Southerns—I have no facts whatever to go upon.

4960. At all events it is not the difficulty of the cost of coal which prevents it to any great extent ?—Not according to your statement.

Dr. T. W. Grimshaw. 11 Dec. 1894. Values and quantities of crops and stock.

4961. (*The O'Conor Don.*) In connection with a return which I asked you to put in, I forgot to hand you a statement which I wished put in. I was making a comparison between Table A. and Table B in your printed statement, and as Table B contained what I consider the capital value of all the live stock, I prepared a table reducing Table B by the proportions which you gave us, namely, two-sevenths for cattle and so on. I have given you that table since, and I would ask you to verify it and see whether the figures are correct?—I have your table here, and will do so.

4962. If these figures are correct would not the percentages appear to decrease between the different periods which you have given as to the value of produce in Ireland. Looking at the bottom of the paper, and comparing 1884–88 with the last period, 1889–1893, you see the decrease in value is 2·3 per cent.; and comparing the 1866–1870 period with 1884–88, it is 17·7, and comparing it with 1889–1893, it is 19·6 per cent.?—Yes.

4963. Then, as compared with 1851–55, the reduction in the period 1866–1870 would be 10 per cent.; the reduction in the third period, 1884–1888, would be 26 per cent.; and the reduction in the fourth period, 27·6 per cent.?—I have no doubt those figures are right.

4964. (*Mr. Sexton.*) How does this new paper differ from Table C?—It does differ a little.

4965. Is it not the same thing?—It has the same object in view.

4966. There is no great difference in it?—There is some difference.

4967. I want to know what function this new return discharges which is not already discharged by your Table C?—I understand that the O'Conor Don wishes to apply his own test to it, and he asks me to do it in a particular way from that table.

4968. Do you mean he applies the proportion in 1885 to all the quinquennial periods?—Yes.

4969. But your evidence was that the proportions varied from year to year?—I believe they do, but I do not wish to discuss with the Commissioners whether it is right or wrong that this paper should be handed in. The O'Conor Don asks for it.

4970. But it ought to be clearly understood that the test he applies to the value of stock sold within the year is the test upon which you have already thrown doubt in reply to Lord Welby in regard to the year 1885, and your evidence is that that test cannot be safely applied to years in general, because the proportion varies from year to year?—Just so.

4971. (*The O'Conor Don.*) It is not the stock sold but the stock disposed of during the year?—Yes.

4972. Either by home consumption or sale?—Either by home consumption or sale.

4973. When Mr. Sexton says it is made up by my own calculation is it not made up on the calculation of the proportions given in that paper that you handed in?—Certainly.

4974. The proportions are not my own in any way?—No, they are the speculative proportions which I have mentioned.

4975. (*Mr. Sexton.*) They are proportions admitted by you to be inapplicable to any year but 1885 and of doubtful applicability even to that—is that so?—That is so.

4976. (*The O'Conor Don.*) But would not the proportions of stock, for instance, of cattle and sheep, having a certain average length of life before they were turned to the use of man, be the same for any year?—I should think they must be approximate to the average.

4977. It is not a question of the amount sold but it is a question of the amount disposed of, and as sheep are generally used before they come to the age of three, or mostly used at or under two years old, and as cattle hardly ever have a life of more than three and a half years, there must be some definite proportion in which stock of all descriptions are disposed of in a given period?—Yes, I think your statement is quite fair. In putting in this paper, of course, it must be referred to in the answer to the O'Conor Don.

4978. (*The O'Conor Don.*) This is simply and solely what it is?—It is applying a test to the paper you handed in which was prepared by a competent gentleman, to the figures you gave in one of your tables, that is all; is not that so?—That is so. It is the gross annual value, calculated on the estimates for 1885, which have been referred to, without, on the one hand, taking account of milk, wool, or eggs, or, on the other, making any allowance whatever for cost of production.

The following table was handed in:

Description.	Periods. (000 omitted.)			
	1851–1855.	1866–1870.	1884–1888.	1889–1893.
	£	£	£	£
Crops,	58,537	45,868	36,755	34,918
Cattle (2/7ths),	6,836	11,222	10,858	9,867
Sheep (2/5ths),	1,396	2,668	1,875	1,924
Pigs,	1,480	1,592	1,236	1,877
Horses (1/10th),	853	673	668	936
Poultry (2/3rds),	273	637	694	770
Totals,	69,370	62,597	51,263	50,107

As compared with the period		In the period
1851–1855,	There was a decrease in income value of 10·3 per cent.,	1866–1870
" "	" " " 26·1 "	1884–1888
" "	" " " 27·6 "	1889–1893
1866–1870,	" " " 17·7 "	1884–1888
" "	" " " 19·6 "	1889–1893
1884–1888,	" " " 2·3 "	1889–1893

The witness withdrew.

Sir Richard Sankey called, and examined.

Sir R. H. Sankey, K.C.B.

11 Dec. 1894.

Amount of loans made.

4979. (*Chairman.*) You are the head of the Board of Works in Ireland, I believe?—Yes.

4980. You come here, do you not, in the first place, to put in certain tables with respect to loans affecting and in connection with public works?—Yes.

4981. The first of your tables deals, I think, with the open loan service, does it not?—The open and closed loan services.

4982. Will you explain that table to the Commission?—It is a table which deals with all the loan services of the Board under loans secured on undertakings, loans secured on rates, loans secured on lands, miscellaneous, and also loans made from the Irish Church Fund, secured on rates and lands.

4983. Commencing from the 1st and 2nd of William IV., I think?—That requires a little explanation. The Board of Works since its formation in 1831 took over certain closed services on which there had been advanced 12,[illegible]l. forming part of the sum of 16,983,912l. shown on Table II., to have been advanced in closed services; the advances on open and closed services giving a gross total of 32,[illegible]l.

4984. Those loans have been provided for out of what funds?—The loans that the Public Works have made since the year 1831 have been provided for out of the Consolidated Fund to the extent of 33,645,403l., and 1,869,933l. from the Irish Church Fund.

4985. (*Lord Welby.*) Up to what date is that?—Up to the 31st of March, 1894.

4986. (*Chairman.*) That is from the starting point and represents the loans you took over since 1831?—Yes.

4987. And embraces the whole of your loans since?—Yes. Putting it in round numbers about 37,000,000l. have been advanced by the Board in the way of loan since its formation in 1831.

Loans secured on undertakings.

4988. Omitting the Church Fund for the moment and going to the loans made from Imperial Funds, will you give some particulars to the Commission?—The first class consists of loans secured on undertakings. The total amount of loans under that head is 2,686,236l., made under the 1st and 2nd William IV., chapter 33, and dealing with loans to local boards, for inland navigation, for railways, quarries and mines, harbours, docks, reclamation of waste lands, labourers' dwellings in towns, and housing of the working classes.

4989. These are all secured on enterprise are they?—On the undertakings.

4990. Some have I think an additional security, have they not?—Yes, under labourers' dwellings in towns, on which 189,111l. and housing the working classes, 502,121l. were advanced, the loans are secured on the undertaking, and whatever collateral security could be got in addition.

4991. And in certain cases, for instance, loans for harbour purposes, are not they secured on the rates as well as on the harbour receipts?—Under certain circumstances they are. I have a list of the harbour loans.

Loans secured on rates.

4992. Passing from those to the loans which you denominate as Class 2, how much are those, and what is their general character?—These are secured on rates. The total amount of loans on those amounts to 6,340,024l. They are made to grand juries for roads and bridges, court-houses, etc.

4993. Are they exclusively secured on rates?—Yes. There are loans for public buildings and public libraries also secured on rates, loans for fishery piers and harbours under the Fishery Piers and Harbours Acts, Public Works loans, under the Act 57 George III., cap. 34; repairs to post roads and bridges, repairs to fishery piers and harbours, maintenance of navigation works, lunatic asylums buildings, artisans dwellings; public health, under the Public Health Acts; emigration; under the Labourers Acts; and Dispensary Houses.

Sir R. H. Sankey, K.C.B.

11 Dec. 1894.

Loans secured on rates.

4994. Are these all exclusively secured on rates?—Exclusively on rates.

4995. And they amount in the total to how much?—A little over 6,300,000l.

4996. (*Lord Welby.*) You said labourers' dwellings; do you mean labourers' dwellings in the country?—The loans that come under those Acts are like the public health loans, emigration and others, recommended to us by the Local Government Board; we only act as a loans department. We do not investigate the nature of the security, which is the rates, or go into any detail as regards the character of the building, or other circumstances. The Local Government Board has the whole initiation, carry it through, and merely make use of us as a loans board with the sanction of the Treasury; we have to make the loan and recover it afterwards.

4997. (*Chairman.*) Some of these loans are in aid of grants, are they not?—Yes.

4998. Taking the loans for lunatic asylums there is a large amount advanced, is there not?—Yes, over one and a half a million of money has been advanced up to the close of this account.

4999. Is that an increasing amount?—Yes, a seriously increasing amount; within the last three years there has been a very great increase in the amount of provision for the lunatic poor, and the Board of Control have been exceedingly active in dealing with the subject, with, so far as we can see at the present, the probability of very nearly half a million of money having to be advanced in addition to what is shown here.

5000. Raising the total amount to more than 2,000,000l.?—Yes, the amount here is 1,591,522l.; the liabilities from my own knowledge of the Board, as I happen to be *ex officio* on the Board of Control, would certainly warrant me in saying that the amount to be expended on lunatic asylums will not be far short of 500,000l. in excess of what is here shown.

5001. The next item I think is for artisans' buildings, that is limited in its application, is it not?—Yes.

5002. To how many towns, do you remember?—That was limited, speaking from memory, to Cork and Dublin. It is a closed Act and we now lend under other Acts, the Acts of 1890 and 1885.

5003. Advances for artisans' buildings are now made under the general Acts, and not under the local Acts?—Yes.

5004. Then taking the very large item which follows, No. 13: Loans for Public Health purposes, will you give us some information about that?—The total of loans under the Public Health Acts at the present moment amounts to 2,078,046l. All the loans made under this Act of 37 and 38 Victoria, chapter 93, and the 41 and 42 Victoria, chapter 52, are made on the recommendation of the Local Government Board, the only test that we apply being that of the borrowing power of Union and Towns which is limited to twice the annual valuation.

5005. Is that a growing head of loan?—I can give the figures from 1890 down to 1894. In 1890 we advanced 110,000l.; in 1891, 70,500l.; in 1892, 99,000l.; in 1893, 138,200l. and in 1894, 138,000l.

5006. I notice that in one year the amount was very much larger than all the others?—Yes.

5007. What was the reason of that?—We have not reasons before us; it is merely recommended to us to make the loans. We act as a loans department, and do not go behind the reasons of the Local Government Board.

5008. Do you not know as a matter of fact what the reasons were?—No, we have no knowledge of them. We know of the class of work, but not the circumstances. We are not consulted; we have nothing to say to the works, or their execution, only to make the loans.

5009. Do you mean that you, as a department

Sir R. R. Jackson, K.C.B. 27 Dec. 1894.

Loans expended on ...

charged with the actual work, are not consulted as to its utility or probability of its being remunerative?—No, they have their own special establishment headed by a very able Engineer, Mr. Cotton, for examining into all the matters connected with the Public Health Act; they take all the responsibility of making the inquiries, seeing the work properly carried out, and so forth; we have no responsibility.

5010. No reference is made to you before so large an expenditure is made?—None whatever. In making our recommendation to the Treasury we have to show that the law is observed in regard to the valuation, and as to the amount of loan being within the conditions of the Act. Beyond that we have nothing further to do than this, that where land has to be acquired we have to appoint the arbitrator.

5011. Then what do you say as to your 21st item, expenditure under the Labourers Acts?—That falls under the same remarks; we have no responsibility further than making the loan. Our whole duties are confined to the Labourers Dwellings Act and the Housing of the working classes under the Act 29 and 30 Victoria, chapter 44; 48 and 49 Victoria, chapter 72; 53 and 54 Victoria, chapter 70; and 56 and 57 Victoria, chapter 33, that is loans secured on undertakings.

5012. I have gone through the leading heads of Class 2, I think, have I not?—Yes.

Loans for drainage.

5013. What are your loans under Class 3?—The loans here are principally those that have been made under the old Act of 1842, with reference to arterial drainage, navigation, and so forth, and again under the Act of 1863 for river drainage and 1866 for maintenance.

5014. The main item is for arterial drainage, is it not?—Yes. But there was a distinct change of policy with regard to the Act of 1842, under which the Board planned and carried out the works. There was a very large sum expended, to the amount of 2,092,083*l*., chiefly owing to the famine of 1847. These works were carried out during the famine, and owing to a great number of causes, which it is unnecessary to state, a special Commission was instituted; constituted of two of my predecessors. They closed their proceedings in 1856, and it was decided with Treasury sanction that 1,307,383*l*. should be written off or remitted from the amount that was expended. Then a change of policy came as embodied in the Act of 1863 (the Act of 26 and 27 Victoria, Chapter 88), under which local boards of drainage undertake to promote works, after due inquiry by an Inspector appointed by the Board of Works. These Bodies have as a fact carried out a number of these large works to the value of 816,944*l*., none of which was remitted. The whole charged upon the owners.

5015. Is that the only outstanding balance upon that account?—The arrears altogether on that account at present due amount to 14,416*l*.

5016. The account practically in that respect then is unclosed?—There remains not called up 371,044*l*.

5017. And that has not yet been claimed?—Quite so; but the arrears amount in reality to 14,416*l*.

Loans for land improvement.

5018. Now we will go to the next item—advances to landowners?—That is the most important service under which the Board have made advances. They are chiefly made under the Act the 10th of Victoria, cap. 32, the Land Improvement Act, which deals with drainage, farm-houses, farm-labourers' dwellings, and so on. It is an Act enabling owners and others who are qualified as such with certain terms of lease to borrow. The total amount advanced under that Act has been 4,105,137*l*. In addition to that sum of four million odd, out of the Church Fund, we have advanced 973,819*l*. for improvement to lands, and thereby have advanced in all to owners over five millions sterling.

5019. Of that there has been repaid how much in round numbers?—Out of the 4,000,000*l*. odd 1,213,490*l*. has not come under repayment yet.

5020. But how much has been repaid, I ask?—A little over 3,000,000*l*. has been repaid out of the 5,000,000*l*.

Sir R. R. Jackson, K.C.B. 27 Dec. 1894. Loans for land improvement.

5021. What was the rate of interest on those loans and what is it at present?—As regards the Land Improvement loans originally it was fixed at 3½ per cent. for 22 years. Subsequently the period was enlarged and the interest continued at 3½ per cent. for 35 years with a sinking fund of 1½ per cent. so that during the currency of the loan the whole charge, including sinking fund, was 5 per cent.

5022. Instead of 6½ per cent., which it was originally?—Yes; the charge under the Act of William was limited to a term, to 35 years. As improvements, however, this character were exhausted or would be likely to be exhausted within 25 years, it was deemed more prudent that the limitation of the loan should be 22 years.

5023. Is your item 23 advanced out of the Church Fund or is it separate?—It is out of the Local Loans Fund. That is quite another class of loan. Under the Land Law Act of 1881, sections 19 and 31, we have advanced 534,337*l*. since the introduction of the Act.

Loans to tenants under Act of 1870.

5024. Then you have also made advances to the tenants, I believe?—Those are the advances to the tenants. Under the Act of 1870 we were authorised to advance to certain tenants for the purchase of farms a certain proportion of the purchase value leaving the tenant to find the remainder, and under that Act we advanced to 818 tenants the sum of 518,932*l*. The operations under that Act have ceased altogether.

5025. Was there any limit to the amount which might be advanced to one tenant?—Yes; speaking from memory, the limitation was, I think, that the Board advanced two-thirds of the purchase money, or three-fourths, I am not quite certain, leaving the tenant to find the residue.

5026. That concludes your third class I think, does it not?—Yes.

Miscellaneous loans.

5027. What is the fourth class?—The fourth class are the miscellaneous loans—glebe loans, loans for building schools, for seed supply, and so forth. The Glebe Loans Act is a renewable Act at the present moment, and will, I presume, be perpetually renewed. We have made advances upon 1,199 glebes, to clergymen of all persuasions, to the amount of 804,363*l*.

5028. Was that under the Church Act?—It is a special Act.

5029. What is the outstanding amount at present?—Out of 804,363*l*. advanced there has not yet come under repayment 349,364*l*.

5030. Is that being regularly repaid?—Yes; there are no remissions, you will observe, under that.

5031. There is no practical difficulty in getting it repaid, is there?—No.

5032. Then there are advances I see under an old Act for schools, which represent a small amount: then I come to the seed advances under your class four?—The seed advances are made under the 43rd Victoria, cap. 1. We have advanced under that Act 617,562*l*., of which there remains uncollected at the present moment 12,087*l*. Under the later Act of 1890 we have advanced 274,370*l*., of which, at present of this year, there only remain 3,125*l*. outstanding. I should explain that in this return we show 12,437*l*. as uncollected, and was at that moment not brought into account, but since then we have recovered an amount of 9,000*l*., leaving only 3,125*l*. remaining to be collected.

5033. What will be the ultimate, if any, failure to obtain repayment?—That is a matter chiefly dependent on the Local Government Board, who have given us a great deal of assistance and advice in regard to these repayments. We are now concerned with regard to this balance of 3,125*l*. only.

5034. May I say parenthetically that the seed loans have been very well repaid?—They have been very fairly repaid. Of course we anticipate a certain possible amount of failure.

5035. But the percentage will not be 1 per cent., will it?—No, I think not.

5036. They were loans without interest, were they not?—Yes, they were loans without interest.

5037. Then there is a large item for National school teachers' residences—do you know under what Act that was advanced?—That was under 33 and 34 Victoria, chapter 82; we made 670 loans for 147,279l.

5038. Are they, as to repayment, upon the same terms as the others?—Yes, but we have different classes of these residences, viz.:—200l., 225l., and 250l., and we make advances under this Act for them.

5039. Can you summarise in a few figures the transactions under these four classes, either including or not, whichever is most convenient, the Church Fund advances?—I can give it separately. The total amount advanced from the Consolidated Fund up to the present moment has been 38,452,409l.

5040. Of that has been repaid how much?—Of that has been repaid principal 23,790,470l.

5041. And remitted how much?—The amount remitted is 7,965,938l.

5042. And the amount outstanding is how much?—The amount outstanding is 7,856,007l.

5043. Now we will go to the Church Fund?—Under the Church Fund we have made advances for public health, burial works, relief of distress, improvements to lands, arterial drainage, and schools (altogether 2,041 loans), for 1,269,932l. The amount repaid is 502,583l.; the amount remitted is 23,336l.

5044. Is that absolutely remitted?—Yes. The amounts have been written off.

5045. (*Lord Welby.*) Sanctioned by Parliament, I suppose?—Yes. The amount that has not come under collection is 739,932l.

5046. (*Chairman.*) Before we pass from these public transactions may I ask you whether, in your opinion, the repayment is as good as could have been expected, or whether there is in your department much disappointment at the result?—That would have to be judged a good deal by the class of loans. The general state of arrears for the four years are given in our last return. Perhaps I might summarise them first by saying that the total arrears in 1891 were 503,790l. of all classes of loans; in 1892 they were 551,276l.; in 1893, 548,274l., and in 1894, 561,887l. In answering the particular question which you have put to me it may be as well to say that the railway loans are chiefly answerable for the state of arrears. The arrears there were, respectively, for 1891, 348,253l.; for 1892, 388,766l.; for 1893, 424,124, and for 1894, 439,345l. The railway loans, perhaps, had better be dealt with as a separate class, but I may generally explain that, owing to the periods at which they were made, they have not proved up to the present satisfactory—at least a very large number of them—and it has been impossible to collect all the interest. There is a very large amount of accrued interest, as to which I should have to go into very considerable detail to explain. It is the fact that a large number of these railway loans are at present in an unsatisfactory condition. We are receivers now at the present moment and working with agreements, you may say, two lines that we had to take over. In both those cases the year's interest on the loan is to a very great extent realised.

5047. Were those old loans?—Yes—that is, prior to the Act of 1883. We had been making loans under general Acts up to 1883, when the new legislation came in, followed by that of 1889. Since the Act of 1883 two loans have been made under the old Acts, but a large number of loans were made prior to that, some of which have practically been lost.

5048. To how many companies were those loans made?—To twenty-three companies, irrespective of loans made under a subsequent Act to enable certain lines under the Act of 1883 to carry on and complete their works.

5049. The Act of 1883 was the first Light Railways (Ireland) Act, was it not?—I will not say it was the first Light Railway Act, but it was the first Act in which the principle of local guarantee was recognised as an essential part of the scheme. It was then followed by the Act of 1889, when the advances were made in another way altogether.

5050. Summing up your table, the total amount advanced, including the church loans, was close upon 40,000,000l.?—Yes.

5051. Of that there has been repaid, let there out, 24,300,000l.—avoiding the smaller figures?—Yes.

5052. And the total amount remitted is just 8,000,000l.?—Yes, close upon 8,000,000l.

5053. The total amount in arrear is altogether 500,000l.?—Yes. At the present moment the total amount in arrear is 561,887l., exclusive of £197,128l. principal written off.

5054. That is close enough, taking it in round figures. The amount not yet due is a little over 8,000,000l.?—Yes.

5055. That is the current loan account of the Government of Ireland, is it?—Yes, both advanced from the Consolidated Fund and from the Irish Church Fund.

5056. You put in also a table as to the rates of interest. Have you any particular remark to make upon it?—The rates of interest vary for every class of loan, and we have given, I think, a paper showing the corresponding numbers to the general statement. Opposite every number there is the rate of interest. Under certain numbers the rates of interest vary.

5057. Have you any special remark to make upon it?—No, I have no remark to make. We are entirely under the instructions of the Treasury as regards the rate of interest—we have nothing to say to it.

5058. Then you have also given a return showing the issues during the last five years on the principal loan service?—Yes.

5059. Does anything occur to you upon that as useful to bring before the Commission? It is a detailed account?—No. 3 Statement as put in deals with the Labourers' Dwellings and Housing of the Working Classes as one main head, Public Health Acts as a second, Lunatic Asylums as a third, Land Improvement under the Act of 1881 as a fourth, and then the Labourers Act. We thought those were the most interesting headings to give the facts under. We have given the progress of advances since the year 1890 up to the present time to show as far as possible the movement under each head.

5060. You have not given it here, but I suppose there will be no difficulty in giving the sum total. You have given it separately for each year?—Yes, we can do so.

5061. Will you give the sum total of the entire amount of the loans under these heads?—Yes.

5062. Then Table VII. is a table of the amounts of the different rates of interest. I think I might ask if there is anything particular to say upon that. The first two items are trifling. The first large amount as to which the rate of interest is given is 4 per cent., the amount being 1,500,000l. Does anything occur to you to mention upon that? Why is so large an amount as 1,500,000l. issued at 4 per cent.?—These are loans chiefly made on undertakings under the Act of William IV. and also the railway advances.

5063. Is the railway advance, as a rule, an advance at 4 per cent.?—The railway advances originally were made at 5 per cent., and in the year 1883 that was reduced by Treasury Order to 4 per cent., at which rate it still remains. A very large proportion, also, of the harbour loans has been made at 4 per cent. Where they were at 5 per cent. they have been generally, but not altogether, reduced to 4 per cent.

5064. Is $3\frac{1}{2}$ per cent. the normal rate?—That has been the normal rate. It generally applies to that very large item, land improvement.

5065. Then I see there is $3\frac{1}{4}$?—That is in advances principally for the housing of the working classes. The rates at which we are permitted to make advances for this service are $3\frac{1}{4}$ per cent. with a term of twenty

12 Dec. 1894.

years; 3½ per cent. with a term of thirty years; 3¾ per cent. with a term of forty years; and 3½ per cent. with a term of fifty years.

5066. Then in Table VIII. you have given the amounts provided by Parliament in each year since 1884–1885, and I notice that the largest amount was the amount voted in 1885–1886 of 1,500,000*l.*?—Yes.

5067. And the smallest amounts are 800,000*l.* in each of the last two years?—Yes.

5068. The amounts actually issued do not appear to be much more than half the amounts authorised?—That is so.

5069. I suppose you make an estimate of how much would be required for your department?—We make the best estimate we can, and there is no doubt about it that it has not borne a very much better proportion than one-half in reality.

5070. Do you think it is a prudent arrangement to ask for double what it turns out you ought to ask?—We did not exactly go upon that principle. You see, the number and the character of the loans vary from year to year very much. I may mention, as regards the land law loans, that they varied in a peculiar way. In the year 1882–1883 we only made advances to 746 tenants; in 1883–1884 they suddenly rose to 3,276. In 1884–1885 they stood at 2,160, since which they have gone down to a minimum of, in 1889–1890, 395 loans only. Latterly, in 1893–1894, showing a little more life, they have risen to 496.

5071. (*Mr. Sexton.*) Are these loans to landowners or tenants?—These are loans to tenants. I was merely showing the great fluctuation which has occurred. In various other ways we have to keep a considerable margin for our loans fund, so as not to have to call on the Treasury to supply us with more funds.

5072. (*Chairman.*) Looking cursorily at the return which you have given us, I should say that the amount advanced is not quite equal in any of these years to the amount of principal repaid, but that the principal and interest, as a rule, exceed the amount advanced in the year?—Yes. Last year, the amount actually repaid in principal and interest was 767,000*l.*

5073. So that it is a gradually growing amount. The total amount advanced gradually increased from year to year, but, including the interest repaid, you do not quite require on the average as much as you receive if the two sides were treated as one account?—Yes, that is the case.

5074. I have taken you through the statistics which you have placed in my hands. Are there any others which you wish to mention to us before we pass to the question of administration?—No, there is nothing further.

Rate of interest.

5075. (*Lord Welby.*) Is it not the case that the rate of interest which you charge is 4 per cent., except where there is a special Act authorising a different rate?—Yes. Of course the Treasury have authority to vary that even as regards the Act of William, and they have, under certain conditions, varied it; but as a rule 4 per cent. is the normal rate, except, as you say, under special Acts.

5076. I was under the impression that the Act of William limited the powers of your board to 4 per cent.?—4 per cent. for a term of twenty-five years, but that was subsequently dealt with by the 6th and 7th William IV., chapter 108, and under section 16 of that Act the Treasury is authorised to vary the rate of interest, so that the interest shall be at least 10*s.* per cent. above the value of exchequer bills. The wording of the Act is rather peculiar. It is not quite clear whether it would be applicable at present, but they had that power, and it has been so exercised.

5077. Do you know at all how that worked out. I am under the impression, but I speak only from memory, that at that time exchequer bills were never below 1½*d.* a day—they bore interest at a daily rate?—I am not able to give you the circumstances. I know there is a moot-point as to the extent to which that power is limited now, because the Act merely expresses that it shall not be less than 10*s.* per hundred, in addition to the price of the exchequer bills.

5078. And is that Act still in force?—That Act is still in force.

5079. Have you ever turned your attention to the fact as to what the average rate of interest which you really get back upon your loans is. I may perhaps remind you that some years ago the Treasury paid some attention to that point, and the conclusion to which they came was that the interest received, I think, did not very much exceed, if it exceeded at all, 3 per cent.?—That would be a difficult subject to go into, because every class of loan would have to be considered. I should be afraid to give an opinion about that.

5080. You have never seen those papers, have you?—I think I have seen some calculations.

5081. Perhaps I may say that we took every class of loan, we took the sums actually received and worked them out, and I think, speaking from memory, that practically the rate of interest obtained turned out to be somewhere about 3 per cent.?—Yes.

5082. It may have been below that; but it was an endeavour to ascertain what, from 1840 or 1850, had been the real financial effect of the loans made through your board?—Of course looking through the table we see that the vast proportion of loans have been made at over 3½ per cent.

5083. But then looking at it as a financial proceeding you have to take what is received and not what is charged?—Yes. There is so much that is problematic about the railway account that I do not know exactly how it would come out.

Glebe loans.

5084. If you take the sums actually received you get to facts, but as you have not the facts before you, I will not press you upon the point. Taking the classes of loans, I think you said that the Glebe Loan Act was a perpetual Act?—No, it is renewed from year to year.

5085. You spoke of it practically in the nature of a perpetual Act?—Yes.

5086. Is it not the fact that it will eventually lapse?—One would assume so, we have already advanced for 1,199 glebes, more than half a million sterling.

5087. Do you know at all what number of glebes it might refer to, because it extends to all denominations, does it not?—Yes, pretty nearly. The Church of Ireland for instance has had 279 glebe loans; the Catholic Church has had 645 loans; the Presbyterians 207 and the Wesleyans and others 68 loans.

5088. You do not know at all what the number of glebes to which it might apply are?—No, I have no knowledge.

Seed loans.

5089. The Chairman asked a question about seed loans, and I think he put it to you that the loss on seed loans, which are advanced without interest, would come within one per cent. Is it not the case that the amount now outstanding on the first seed loan is considerably under one per cent.?—The amount hitherto uncollected is 13,097*l.* out of 647,562*l.* advanced.

5090. If that amount was not collected the loss would be a larger amount than one per cent.; would it not?—It is less than two per cent., but it is not at all clear that this will be absolutely lost. Its collection is deferred under advice received from the Local Government Board; and is a matter more for their consideration than for ours.

5091. But looking at the length of time, I suppose the proportion of that amount which is likely to be recovered is not a big one, is it?—I am not at all certain. I do not see why any portion of it should be remitted. The Local Government Board have not treated it in that light. They have looked upon the collection as deferred, and they hope to be able to recover it eventually.

Sir R. K. [illegible], K.C.B. — 12 Dec. 1906. — Public Health Loans.

5092. On that loan, if you did not recover any of that amount the loss would be about two per cent.?—Not quite.

5093. In dealing with the Public Health Loans I think that in some cases the Local Government Board have pointed out when the already existing liability of the area upon which the loans were to be secured was very heavy, and that you have called the attention of the Treasury, have you not, to the risk that would attend the loan?—Yes, under certain circumstances we have.

5094. You have felt it your duty to point out the financial risk, though at the same time I think I am also correct in my memory, am I not, you have been willing not to make it a subject of opposition?—Quite so. I may say that in respect of those loans we have invariably consulted and act as far as we possibly can, under the advice of the Local Government Board.

Railway loans.

5095. (*Chairman.*) I omitted to ask you three questions about railways. You put in, do you not, a statement having reference to the light or narrow gauge railways?—Yes.

5096. You also put in a statement as to the railways constructed under the Act of 1889 and the grants by the State, by the county, or by the baronies?—Yes.

5097. You also put in an abstract of the guarantees by counties and individuals?—Yes, the latter extends over a much wider period.

5098. (*Lord Welby.*) I have not the figures before me in the returns put in. Will you give us the figures of these advances and grants. May I ask first of all whether in your return under the head of loans to railways you class together the old advances before the Light Railways Act passed with the advances under the Light Railways Act, or do you separate them in the accounts you publish?—We separate them.

5099. Can you give us the amount of the advances and the amount outstanding under the old Acts, as apart from the amounts advanced under the Light Railways Act?—The total amounts advanced for railways were 1,193,636*l.*, of which there is principal outstanding 733,477*l.*, and interest in arrear 134,797*l.*

5100. Has there been any part of those loans remitted?—Yes, there has, and that is a point I shall dwell upon immediately; but before passing on I may mention that in that are included certain railways, first of all, the West Clare, the Clogher Valley Tramway, and the Cavan, Leitrim, and Roscommon Light Railway, and the Cork and Muskerry Railway, and the West Donegal Light Railway, which had to take advantage in 1886 of a special Act of Parliament under which the Board were authorised to advance 196,000*l.* in order to allow these undertakings to be completed. The Companies having failed in financing these railways an Act was passed in 1886 which enabled the Board to take shares in each of these railways, which shares the Board have held and have been engaged in selling ever since; and now I am glad to say that the selling value has improved so much that there is very little left in reality to recover—I do not think there is more than 30,000*l.* which is not recovered.

5101. (*The O'Conor Don.*) Were these particular lines mentioned in this special Act of Parliament to which you refer?—Yes, I think so.

5102. It was a special Act for these particular lines—it was not a general Act enabling you to take shares in these light railways?—I have the actual Act here. It was "an Act to amend the Act of 6 and 7 William "IV. for the purpose of enabling any such company "as aforesaid to give such security as in this Act "mentioned, and such company may, notwithstanding "any provision of any Order of Council confirmed by "Parliament before the passing of this Act, issue and "allot as paid-up shares or stock of the company, "which shares or stock shall by virtue of and for the "purposes of this Act be deemed to be taken as fully "paid and shall be entitled to the full benefit of any "baronial guarantee attached to any other portion of "the paid-up capital of the company, provided that "nothing in this Act shall be construed as extending "any baronial guarantee to any amount," and so on. It did not as I find specify the exact railways, but the companies came to us, placed the shares in our hands. We advanced against those shares, and have held them ever since and have been engaged in selling them.

Sir R. K. [illegible], K.C.B. — 12 Dec. 1906. — Railway loans.

5103. (*Lord Welby.*) Are these the only companies that availed themselves of the provisions of that Act?—Yes.

5104. Now that you have sold the larger part of those shares what position do these companies occupy?—The whole of their share capital is hypothecated. These companies form an exception to the general statement I made, but I class them as advances, because as a matter of fact we did advance the amount as represented by shares.

5105. At the same time if these shares have been in greater part sold we must exclude those lines?—They will be paid off very soon, I think, entirely.

5106. What amount is there outstanding?—About 30,000*l.*

5107. (*Mr. Martin.*) Are the shares of these lines at a premium?—Yes. The fact is they could not finance themselves at all at one time in 1886, and the Treasury came to their support. They might possibly have got rid of their shares at par, but having had previous offers, I believe, from some financiers of placing the capital at a substantial premium, they declined to go on; when, owing to the circumstances of the time, they saw loss staring them in the face, and asked the Government to assist them, which Parliament did, by passing that Act; and now, I think, the shares are standing at 130.

5108. (*Sir David Barbour.*) Did you take up the shares at par?—Yes, we received them at par.

5109. (*Mr. Welsh.*) Have they paid a dividend?—The Treasury have allowed them to write off a certain number of shares for the difference between the sale value and the par value.

5110. (*Lord Welby.*) You are satisfied with getting back what you gave for the shares?—Yes, that is it.

5111. Will you tell us under what head you charged the purchase money. Did you charge it under the same head as advances, and did you advance the money from the same fund?—It was advanced from the consolidated or rather the local loans fund.

5112. But it was advanced as part of loan money?—Yes.

5113. And therefore as the matter now stands we need not take much more account of that?—I think not. It is a disappearing sum.

5114. The figures you have given of the whole railway loans are 1,193,000*l.* advanced, of which 733,000*l.* is outstanding?—Yes.

5115. I think you were going to tell us about a certain amount remitted after we had dealt with these exceptional lines, were you not?—I should have to go through them all. There are fourteen railways to which we have made advances, and in each the circumstances vary considerably. If the Commission desire to have an explanation upon the matter I can go shortly through it.

5116. Are you not able to tell the Commission even in a round figure whether there has been any actual remission of a portion of the loans?—I may mention the only one. A railway we sold the other day to the Pembroke Company—called the Rosslare line—the proper designation is the Waterford and Wexford line, on which the Board had advanced originally 53,000*l.* That amount has been remitted in the Public Works Loans Act, the line has been sold for 10,000*l.* nominally, that is to say that should the earnings equal a certain amount the company may have the power of purchase within three years for the value of 10,000*l.* It may be assumed that here we may get back 10,000*l.* out of the 53,000*l.*

Sir [illegible], K.C.B. 12 Dec. 1895. Railway loans.

5117. And that would be equivalent to a remission of 43,000*l.*, would it not?—Yes. As a fact, I think the last Loans Bill has written off only 38,000*l.*, but I presume the whole will be written off with the exception of the 10,000*l.*

5118. Have there been any remissions on any other lines?—There are one or two lines as regards which negotiations for sale are going on, and possibly it may not be very desirable that the whole of the facts should be disclosed.

5119. I was rather alluding to anything that has been done. Nothing more than that has been written off, I understand?—I may say that one or two have been paid off altogether. The loans on the Ballymena and Larne Railway and that of the Bessbrook Extension have been paid off, and also very nearly that for the Dun Valley Railway, the loan on another line. I may say we are in treaty for disposing of several lines—four lines altogether—but I think, perhaps, it may not be desirable to say anything about it. I find I am a little mistaken. Two Railways are under Receivers, and are being worked by the Board, who have taken possession as mortgagees. As to another there is an Act about to be passed in Parliament for the sale—that is the Clara and Banagher line. The advances by the Board of Works in that case were 57,917*l.* I may say that the sum realised will be very much under that.

5120. Will you please confine yourself to what has actually been written off?—There is no other.

5121. Therefore we may say at the present moment as far as statutory powers go that out of the 1,153,000*l.* only 43,000*l.* has been written off?—Yes, 38,000*l.* I should say exactly, because that is the amount specified in the Loans Act of 1892.

5122. One more question upon that point. Am I not right in thinking that the larger part of this outstanding amount is, as far as the dates for which the loan is granted go, considerably in arrear?—Yes, very considerably.

5123. Now passing on to the light railways, what amount has been advanced for them. There was nothing before the Act of 1883, was there?—As regards light railways I may say the question is one that covers three periods. Before 1883 there were five narrow gauge lines constructed in the north of Ireland to the extent of 109 miles, and the advances in regard to these I am afraid I cannot state accurately. That was the first period, and I do not think perhaps it concerns us much, but I merely mention the fact that there were these 109 miles of narrow gauge lines made in Ireland under advances made by the Board of Works, covering a period prior to the Act of 1883. They were practically the leading narrow gauge lines of Ireland, and it was that no doubt which led up to the idea of the instruction conveyed when promoters came forward under the Act of 1883 that they were to confine themselves to a three-foot gauge.

5124. Does the money which was advanced to them form part of the 1,195,000*l.*?—No, because the aid given does not come in as a capital sum. The arrangements under section 9 of the Act of 1883 were that the Board of Works or rather the State came in support of the baronial or county guarantee to the extent of 2 per cent. Where for instance the guarantee was 5 per cent. the Board of Works were authorised on that being paid by the counties to contribute to the extent of 2 per cent., and where the guarantee was 4 per cent. the Board of Works came in support to the extent of 2 per cent.

5125. Did that apply to the pre-1883 railways?—No.

5126. I want to understand with regard to those pre-1883 railways; did the State make any advance?—The 109 miles were made I think in all cases by Board of Works Loans.

5127. Where do you find that charge in your account. Do we clearly understand that those narrow gauge lines previous to 1883 were included under railways on which the advances were 1,195,000*l.*?—Yes.

5128. The 1,195,000*l.* was advanced entirely on undertakings, was it not; there was no charge on the rates?—In some cases there were charges on the rates. I put in a paper showing that in a great number of cases the local guarantees were given before 1883.

5129. Passing to the railways made under the Act of 1883 do I understand that no advances were made to them but only guarantees?—That is so, perpetual guarantees.

5130. Is that paid out of the vote?—Yes. There is now a special head for railways under which we pay the amount of guarantee to the extent of 2 per cent., and we also pay in some cases of guarantee under the Act of 1889, as I shall presently explain.

5131. Under the Act of 1883, therefore, you are paying 2 per cent.?—Yes.

5132. Is that so in every case or are there any railways in which the receipts have been sufficient to reduce that charge?—There are several cases in which the 2 per cent. has not and will not be entirely called up. The first is the Loughrea line that is worked by the Midland and Great Western Company on a special agreement of 55 per cent. of the receipts. In that case we save a certain amount on the guarantee. I do not know whether it is desired to go through all these cases, but I might summarise the results by saying that there are four railways in which we estimate there will be a considerable saving on the 2 per cent.

5133. I will put it to you in this way: can you give us what the amount chargeable is and what the amount paid is?—I may mention that the guaranteed capital of the whole of the railways constructed under the Act of 1883 amounted to 1,384,112*l.*—the total Treasury liability of 2 per cent. would amount to 29,682*l.* As I have mentioned there are several of the railways being worked under working agreements on which we have undoubtedly a saving. There are also such lines as the West Clare, West Donegal, Cork and Muskerry, Dublin and Blessington, which are being worked by the owning companies which show a saving upon the 2 per cent. You may say practically therefore ten companies now that will in reality show a saving on the 2 per cent.

5134. How many companies are there altogether?—There are sixteen.

5135. And of these ten in some shape or other show a reduction?—Yes.

5136. Are they all in full working order?—All.

5137. Can you tell us what you paid last year?—I am afraid I am not able to give the amount at this moment; I should say about 15,000*l.*

5138. (*Chairman.*) You can put in the exact amount in correcting your evidence, can you not?—Yes.

5139. (*Mr. Martin.*) In any case is it not the fact that you do not pay until twelve months after the deficit has been ascertained?—It depends upon the time at which the Assizes take place and Presentment Sessions occur. Whenever that occurs soon after the half year the payment is rapidly made, but I do not think on the whole the delay would be more than three or four months at the outside.

5140. I understood the baronies had to present in the first instance, and to pay up their 4 per cent., and that they recovered from you whatever was the deficiency?—Yes, up to but not exceeding 2 per cent.

5141. So that I apprehend you would not be called upon for payments in respect of 1892 until, say 1893?—I do not think as a rule the delay is more than, at the outside, three or four months, and there are arrangements made, I may say, in regard to the West Clare and other railways, by which the dividends are paid regularly half yearly.

5142. Quite so, but I think they are always in arrear, are they not?—No, I do not think that is so as regards the latter lines though it is the case as regards the majority; which are in arrears, but not to a great extent.

Sir [illegible], K.C.B. 12 Dec. 1895. Railway loans.

Sir R. H. Sankey, K.C.B.

12 Dec. 1895.

Railway loans.

5143. (*Lord Welby.*) I think I can gather what Mr. Martin means, namely, that if there is a State liability of 36,000*l.*, and you only paid 18,000*l.*, that 18,000*l.* would not represent the sum payable on account of that year, because payments are made in arrear?—He is quite right in regard to that.

5144. As against that I began by asking if all these railways were in full working order?—Yes.

5145. Supposing whatever figure you put in that you have estimated 18,000*l.* as the sum you have actually paid, would you consider the difference between that and 36,000*l.* a fair indication of the amount to which the railways earn a diminution of the Government liability?—No, certainly not, but that owing to certain of the lines not being completed and working and to the delays which have been alluded to and which I have mentioned as being three or four months, the 2 per cents. in certain cases have not come fully up as against the last year.

5146. I think probably that would represent the difference in the simplest form. Can you tell us now, taking any year you like, the last year you have the accounts complete for, what is the liability for the year, and what is the actual charge, so that we may see what is really the saving by the earnings of the line?—If you will allow me I will take a note of that, and will put the answer in.

5147. The next point is the financial result of the Act of 1889. Do I understand that the Act of 1883 is no longer in operation?—The Act of 1883 placed at our disposal a sum equivalent to 40,000*l.* a year; the Act of 1889 places a further sum at our disposal of 20,000*l.* a year, or it might be taken as a capital sum of 600,000*l.* plus 3,000*l.* a year. A subsequent Act placed 5,000*l.* a year at our disposal. The total sums under the three Acts amount now to 65,000*l.* a year. As regards the Act of 1883, there have been no means for capitalising that yearly charge, but under the Act of 1889 the capitalisation is effected in this way, that the National Debt Commissioners advanced to us sums which eventually will reach 600,000*l.*, probably by the end of this year, and they have arranged for extinguishing this by terminable annuities in ten years. They recoup themselves in that way, and it will come in as a charge and be got rid of off the public accounts.

5148. I want to ascertain what actually has been the financial result of the Act of 1889. I suppose railways now commencing do not come to you under the Act of 1883 pure and simple, but they prefer to come under the more recent Acts, under which the terms are somewhat more favourable, are they not?—All the money under the Act of 1883 has had to be absorbed by the residue of the works that were required under the Act of 1883. That is, putting it in round terms in this way, I mentioned that 25,000*l.* was properly proportionable to the works under the Act of 1883; there remained then a certain sum which has been appropriated to the Act of 1889.

5149. Then the Act of 1889 is now the operative Act?—Yes, with its 600,000*l.* capital plus 2 per cent. unappropriated under the Act of 1883.

5150. Therefore, what I may call the surplus available under the Act of 1883, is now included under what is really the operative Act of 1889?—The Act of 1883 is entirely exhausted, and we have invariably to inform Grand Juries before whom any schemes come that the Act is exhausted.

Adjourned for a short time.

5151. Now, let us pass to the Act of 1889. What are the conditions under which a railway company gets your assistance under that Act?—Under the Act of 1889 there were three conditions under which assistance could be given by the State. The first, where the promoters of the light railway are an Irish railway company having a railway open for traffic; second, where the promoters have made an agreement, approved by the Treasury, for the maintenance, management, and working of a light railway by such railway company; or, third, where the promoters, in making application to the Grand Jury of any county under the Act, proposed that a barony or baronies in the county shall guarantee the payment of dividend on a portion of the paid-up capital of the light railway, pursuant to the provisions of the Tramways and Public Companies Act of 1883. The first condition as to Irish railway companies promoting these lines was not complied with excepting in the case of three short lines, the Downpatrick and Ardglass line, eight miles in length; the Bantry Bay Extension, one and three-quarter miles in length; and the Baltimore Extension of seven and three-quarter miles in length. With those three exceptions no railway in Ireland was so promoted.

5152. Then condition No. 1 only applied to three short railroads?—Yes. Promoters came forward for all the others; that is to say, for twelve lines; but the conditions that they should give sufficient guarantees, approved by the Treasury, for the maintenance and management and working of these lines having failed, Mr. Jackson, the Financial Secretary of the Treasury, came over and arranged with the parent companies to construct and work certain lines under given conditions. Agreements were made with the Midland Great Western Company for the Galway and Clifden line, for the Ballina and Killala line, and for the Westport and Mallaranny line; also with the Great Southern and Western Railway Company for the Killorglin and Valentia line and the Headford and Kenmare line; and again with the Belfast and County Down line for the Downpatrick and Ardglass line.

5153. You mentioned in the first instance, under condition No. 1, the eight-mile Ardglass line; is that the one you are referring to now?—Yes, that was the one. I made a mistake with regard to that. That left it in reality two lines. The Stranorlar and Glenties line of twenty-four and a half miles, and the Donegal and Killybegs line of eighteen and three-quarter miles. These have since then been constructed with narrow gauge by the Board of Works, and an agreement has been subsequently made with the Donegal Company for working both lines.

5154. Does that make up your twelve?—Not altogether, because since then two lines have been added in relation to the relief of distress. The first of these is the Collooney and Claremorris line of forty-seven and a half miles in length, and the Achill Extension of eight and a quarter miles. As to the first of these lines, the Collooney and Claremorris, an agreement has been made with the Waterford and Limerick line for constructing and working. The Achill Extension line has been constructed by the Board of Works, and an agreement has now been made with the Midland Great Western Company to take it over and work it in perpetuity. I may mention one fact more, and that is, that of the 237 miles made under that Act only forty-three and a quarter miles are narrow gauge, the rest being of the standard gauge.

5155. The twelve lines are represented by a mileage of 237 miles?—Yes.

5156. Can you give us what the cost of that 237 miles is, and to what extent and to what degree assistance was rendered by the State towards their construction?—The Agreement with the Treasury in most of these cases took the form of a certain amount of grant, leaving the companies free to exercise their own judgment as to raising the standard of the line, that is to say, putting in rails of greater weight, reducing the curves and gradients, and so forth, so as to enable them to work these lines as part of their system. Without application to the companies, it would be impossible to say what is the difference chargeable to the actual construction of the line. But I have given in a table the amount of all, the Government grants, in the whole amounting to 1,159,300*l.* That is a grant supplemented by local guarantees in six cases previously under the Act of

1883, which was read with the Act of 1889. These local guarantees are as follows:—The Killorglin and Valentia line and the Headford and Kenmare line had respectively local guarantees to the amount of 70,000*l.* and 40,000*l.* capital.

5157. (*Sir David Barbour.*) At what rate of interest may I ask?—That came in under the Act of 1883—4 per cent.—with the Government coming subsequently in support with 2 per cent. so that in addition to the amount actually given as capital grant the Government came in with 2 per cent. as against those two sums. The guarantee for the county was 4 per cent., of which they met 2 per cent. from rates, and the Government the other 2 per cent. I may mention with regard to the Killorglin and Valentia line that the amount of the capital grant was 55,000*l.*, the amount of the local guarantee was 70,000*l.* on which the baronies bear 1,400*l.* and the Government 1,400*l.*

5158. There was a grant of 55,000*l.* by the Government, was there?—Yes, of capital grant.

5159. Does the Government charge any interest for that?—That is a free grant.

5160. And besides that on the company's capital there is a guarantee of 4 per cent.?—Yes, part of which is borne in the same manner as in the Act of 1883 by the Government to the extent of 2 per cent., so the grant is 55,000*l.* plus a capitalised amount equal to 1,400*l.* a year.

5161. (*Lord Welby.*) Have you any idea what the cost of that line was?—No, except that we have had serious complaints from the company that they have been subject to very heavy expenditure, and it has cost them a great more than they expected. That is all we know.

5162. Do you know what the estimate originally was of the line upon which the 55,000*l.* was granted?—The estimated amounts in these cases were respectively the share capital as declared under the Act of 1883, in the case of the Killorglin and Valentia line at 125,000*l.* and in the case of the Headford and Kenmare 110,000*l.*

5163. What was the grant in the case of the Headford and Kenmare line?—50,000*l.* Then proceeding with the others, the Downpatrick and Ardglass line got a free grant of 30,000*l.*, and there was a local guarantee of 17,000*l.*, but without a Treasury contribution; there was a special arrangement there.

5164. Therefore there is no further State liability than the grant?—There is no further State liability. The Stranorlar and Glenties line of 24¼ miles in length got 116,000*l.* in capital grant, and there was a county guarantee of 1,000*l.* That was to ensure their meeting the deficit and working expenses should any arise; but as it has now been arranged under Treasury agreement the locality is not called upon for anything, or will not be so called on for anything in future. The Donegal and Killybegs stands on exactly the same footing.

5165. (*Sir David Barbour.*) In those cases does the Government take any profit from the line, or is it a perfectly free grant?—It is a perfectly free grant.

5166. If there was a profit would they take it?—No, it is a free grant.

5167. To whom?—Practically to the working company.

5168. Does the company raise any capital?—The company raised no capital in either of these cases; The Board of Works are constructing the lines, and they have to hand them over to the satisfaction of the parent company.

5169. Does the company get the line and construct it?—The company gets the line which we construct; and not only so, but there is a guarantee in the case of the Stranorlar and Glenties for six years that there shall be no deficit to meet on the working.

5170. (*Lord Welby.*) Who gives that guarantee?—The Treasury give that in their agreement.

5171. Therefore there may be for those six years a demand on the Vote?—Yes. The Donegal and Killybegs line of 18¾ miles is on somewhat different conditions. The capital sum there granted was 115,000*l.*, and similarly a local guarantee of 1,000*l.*; but in that case the localities will not be called upon for anything, nor will the Government to meet any deficit in working expenses. On the Collooney and Claremorris line the Government have given a grant of 150,000*l.* and the localities have given guarantees amounting to 130,000*l.*; that is divided between the counties of Mayo, which gives a guarantee of 40,000*l.*, and of Sligo, which gives a guarantee of 90,000*l.*

5172. (*Mr. Martin.*) And the Government counter guarantee there half that; is not that so?—There are very special arrangements connected with this line. Under the Mayo presentment the county to a very great extent countered themselves out of all loss in reality, by requiring that there should be a payment to this company of 800*l.* a year which practically will lead to their having to meet nothing; and the Government meeting one per cent. But in regard to Sligo there is not the same understanding, and under certain arrangements they might have to pay something, though not much. I may summarise it by saying that whereas the Government grant in capital was 1,159,000*l.*, in respect of all the lines the local guarantees were given upon 325,000*l.* in the aggregate.

5173. (*Lord Welby.*) The idea was that those two sums should really construct the lines, was it not?—Yes, the companies being allowed to supplement them in any way they thought best.

5174. But that would be at their own risk, would it not?—Quite so.

5175. (*The O'Conor Don.*) They were bound to do so?—They were.

5176. They entered into a binding agreement to do so, did they not?—They entered into a binding agreement to do so with the Treasury, copies of which I have, in which they bound themselves to give certain services, to complete the line to the satisfaction of the Board of Works and to work the line in perpetuity, giving a certain service, generally two trains a day each way.

5177. (*Lord Welby.*) I think I should not be correct in saying that the Treasury were liable for two per cent. on that 325,000*l.*, because in one or two cases that you mentioned, the Treasury was not brought in, was it?—No, they have contracted themselves out so far as those are concerned. They may be answerable to the extent of one per cent. with regard to portion of Collooney line, and also as regards the Stranorlar and Glenties they have undertaken a liability for six years.

5178. Probably you may say for the time being there is something like 4,000*l.* a year in question, 2,000*l.* on the Killorglin and Valentia line, and the other two would carry the Treasury liability up to, say, 4,000*l.* a year, would they not?—Yes. The general idea the Board have is that the Treasury, as a fact, will not be called upon to meet much. Both the Killorglin and Valentia and the Headford and Kenmare are good lines.

5179. Are these lines open yet?—All but the Stranorlar and Glenties, which ought to be ready for opening in about a month, also the Achill Extension about the same time.

5180. So far as you have any knowledge of them, are those railways answering the expectation formed of them?—They have been opened for such a short time that the companies have not reported the results.

5181. I am not at this moment asking financially, but I am asking as far as traffic goes, whether it is viewed with satisfaction?—We have not sufficient information yet. That will probably come out in the report of the different companies at the shareholders' meetings. We have practically nothing to do except to supply the amounts under agreements.

Sir R. H. [illegible], K.C.B.

12 Dec. 189[illegible].

Railways.

5182. The upshot is that in these extensions of lines, which you can hardly represent as commercial lines, practically the Government have found by far the larger amount of capital?—Yes, that is the case.

5183. Turning to another subject, am I right in understanding that as far as the labourers' cottages are concerned in the rural districts you are simply the bankers of the Local Government Board?—That is so. Under the Labourers Act we simply make the loans. As regards both the Public Health Act and the Emigration and Labourers Acts, we act under the advice of the Local Government Board; and on being sanctioned by the Treasury we make the loan, and know nothing more about it. We know nothing about the details of the work, and have no responsibility whatever.

5184. Therefore you have no opinion on the operation of the Act or the necessity for extending it, or on the reasons which have led some parts of Ireland to adopt it, and other parts not to do so?—No, we have no information of that. I can give the Commission the relative expenditure according to locality generally, if they desire. In reference to the matter of the labourers' dwellings, the total sum sanctioned to be advanced under the Labourers Act was 1,419,863*l.*

5185. That is in the rural district?—Yes.

5186. That is up to 1894, is it?—That is up to 1894. Only forty-five unions took advantage of the Act in Munster, the authorised advances in that case being 925,330*l.* In Leinster thirty-eight unions took advantage of it to the extent of 873,029*l.* In Connaught seven unions took advantage of it to the extent of 9,056*l.* In Ulster four unions took advantage of it to the extent of 11,743*l.* In all, ninety-four out of 159 unions alone took advantage of the Act.

5187. As the matter stands you have no opinion as to the reason for that great difference between the provinces, simply because your advice in the matter is not asked?—Yes; we have no opinion on it.

5188. Do you consider it a good arrangement that with regard to these loans you should be in no respect an adviser, but a simple banker?—Unless we had a very considerably extended architectural and engineering staff, it would be very difficult for us to take upon ourselves the responsibility. The Local Government Board, on the other hand, have a special staff for this particular duty, and take all the responsibility.

5189. (*Sir David Barbour.*) You referred to certain old railway loans made before 1883; part of those loans has been repaid, part has not been repaid, and there are certain arrears of interest outstanding. Were those loans made generally on the security of the railway, or on the security of the railway and the rates?—You will understand that these loans were made in reality on the undertakings—that is to say, when a railway company has failed to make up the whole of its share capital, and requires additional assistance, it comes to the Board of Works, which institutes very searching inquiries; and when satisfied that the net receipts of the line are quite sufficient, in their opinion, to justify the loan, they are empowered under their general Act with sanction of the Treasury to advance to the extent of one-third of the capital, on the condition that one-half the company's capital has already been called up and paid.

5190. That is the point I wish to bring out. The Government only advances a third of the capital?—Yes. That was the general rule, but in regard to some lines there have been also local guarantees.

5191. But do I understand that the condition of one-third of the capital applied to all the railways?—Yes, that was the general condition.

5192. So that the estimates of income must have been very much out if the Government did not get back its money?—The estimates, no doubt, were out in many instances.

5193. (*The O'Conor Don.*) Was the capital paid up?—As regards capital paid up, we had an assurance of that, because we took care to get a reply to our queries; each case was very carefully investigated, and there was no doubt about the proper proportion of the capital being paid up.

5194. (*Sir David Barbour.*) Then there were five old light railways before 1883; the Government lent money to those railways; there was also a certain amount of guarantee, and they have done very well, I understand?—One of them has already paid off the whole of its loan. There is another now from which we hope, I might say in a few days, to get the whole of the loan paid off by their being able to place their debentures. The other three are not in a good condition.

5195. Are there any arrears with regard to those? —Yes.

5196. Then there were certain railways made with a guarantee of 4 per cent.—a guarantee falling partly on the barony and partly on the Government; does not 4 per cent. seem to you a very high guarantee in the present day?—Considering the nature of the guarantee, it being a purely local one, hampered as Mr. Martin has explained by delays with regard to the payments, the grand juries decided themselves that they would in some instances present for plans a 5 per cent. guarantee, and in others only 4; it was concluded, I presume, that they could not raise money with a less guarantee.

5197. Two per cent. of that guarantee is a Government guarantee, which is the best guarantee you could get; and 2 per cent. is a guarantee on the rates, which is almost as good as that of Government; and I rather think 4 per cent. debenture stock of a good Irish railway would be at between 30 and 40 per cent. premium, would it not?—As a matter of fact I think they have arrived at par. I think the West Clare line, for instance, which has a 4 per cent. guarantee, stands now at par. I have not seen the last quotation, but there is no doubt that the 5 per cent. guarantees are standing at 120 or over.

5198. The Government could borrow the money now at what rate?—Perhaps I had better not answer that question.

5199. If the Government borrowed the money and lent it at 2½ per cent., taking the risk of 2 per cent. upon itself, that would leave a risk of only ½ per cent. to be borne by the rates?—The Treasury will be able to say better whether raising money at 2½ per cent. would warrant loans being made at that amount.

5200. As regards the light railways that have been made, I understand that the Government gave certain grants, that in some cases there were certain guarantees or local responsibility, that the parent company then made the railways and are entitled to any profits that may come from those railways?—Yes.

5201. And in some cases there is a guarantee against loss on the working for a very limited period, is there not?—Yes.

5202. Of course the construction of one of those light railways is indirectly a gain to the parent railway as it tends to bring traffic to it?—No doubt.

5203. So that at any rate for the parent railways it seems to be a very good bargain?—That remains to be seen.

5204. (*The O'Conor Don.*) I should like to follow up this question of the railways first; but before I do so I must remark that some members of the Commission are under difficulties in not having your figures before them until we met to-day. With regard to these railways, to put it shortly, under the Act of 1883 was not a sum which was supposed to realise an income of 40,000*l.* devoted to the purpose of assisting in making light railways?—The whole amount 40,000*l.*, placed annually at disposal by the Act of 1883, was not taken up under that Act.

5205. I know that it was not, but did not the Act provide a capital sum which would produce an annual income of 40,000*l.*?—The Act provides that 2,000,000*l.* shall not be exceeded, but the question did not come up at all in the matter, as the guarantee was always in the form of a per centage.

Railway loans.

Sir R. E. Sankey, K.C.B.

21 Dec. 1894.

Railway lands.

5206. But the amount which the Treasury could guarantee could not exceed a certain annual sum, could it?—Quite so.

5207. Was not that sum 40,000*l.* a year?—That sum was 40,000*l.*

5208. The mode of procedure with regard to these guarantees was this, was it not? The proposed line was promoted in the first instance before the Grand Jury?—Yes.

5209. And an estimate was made of the amount of capital that would be required to construct the line?—That estimate was put by the promoters before the Grand Jury, with copy of the Report of.

5210. I am talking of the promoters. The promoting company laid an estimate before the Grand Jury of the probable cost of making the line?—Yes.

5211. Are you aware that the amount of that estimate almost invariably depended upon the amount of interest that they asked for from the Grand Jury, whether it was 5 or 4 per cent?—There is no doubt that it was treated in a great measure as a financial operation.

5212. And was not the result this, that where lines are said to have been constructed at a 4 per cent. guarantee, in reality they were constructed at a 5 per cent. guarantee; because if the Grand Jury gave a guarantee at 5 per cent. the capital for constructing the railway would have been diminished?—I am not sufficiently aware as to the facts, but I think it may be fairly concluded that the amount was inflated.

5213. On account of the rate of interest being placed at 4 instead of 5 per cent.?—I cannot say exactly what was the cause of it, but they were more or less exposed to the difficulty that the actual amount at such prices was probably never ascertained accurately.

5214. Does it not come to this, that practically all these guaranteed lines have been promoted and made on the assumption that 5 per cent. interest would be payable on the capital?—No doubt that was part of the assumption.

5215. As Sir David Barbour has pointed out to you, is not that interest of 5 per cent. a very high rate of interest, considering that there is a Government guarantee to a certain extent at the back of it?—I am not able to express an opinion, as of course that in some measure depends upon the validity of the baronial guarantee.

5216. At present the shareholders who invest their money in these guaranteed railways have no direct communication with the Treasury at all, have they?—None.

5217. Or with you?—None.

5218. They receive their dividends from the county?—Yes, entirely.

5219. And the county has, in the first instance, to raise the total amount of the interest, to pay it to the shareholders, and then to come to you to be repaid half of that amount if it does not exceed 2 per cent?—That is so. Under section 3 of the Act.

5220. You stated, and I think it might be as well to have it quite clear, at the beginning of your evidence, that the Treasury contribution was 2 per cent.?—Yes.

5221. Is that necessarily so, practically I know it is?—I know it is up to 2 per cent.

5222. It cannot exceed 2 per cent?—No.

5223. And it cannot exceed more than half?—It cannot exceed more than half, and it cannot exceed 2 per cent.

5224. So that if they were able to borrow money at $3\frac{1}{2}$ per cent., the Treasury then would not contribute 2 per cent.?—I assume it was taken at the time that it could not be raised at less than 4 per cent., and the circumstances showed that that was correct.

5225. But as a matter of correct statement, what the Treasury undertook to do was to pay half the interest, provided it did not exceed 2 per cent.?—Quite so.

5226. If this Treasury contribution had been given in a more direct form, do you not think that the railways might have been constructed at a much cheaper rate to the ratepayers?—That was the opinion of the Royal Commission which sat and reported in 1888. They made certain distinct recommendations, that, among the rest—that there should be a direct guarantee of 3 per cent., with certain other conditions attached to it.

5227. And if that had been done, would there not have been a very great saving of money to the country in general?—Not unless there could have been some machinery by which you could ascertain the exact and proper amount to be paid for all the works; there was no machinery for doing that, or for ascertaining the exact cash value of the different works.

5228. Have you not experienced railway engineers connected with your Board?—We had no connection with that part of the subject—none whatever—and no such duties were imposed upon us. The County Surveyor was the sole person who was the judge as to the work being carried out properly; the Board of Works had no responsibility and no duties with reference to it.

5229. I am not asking you whether you had this responsibility or duty thrown upon you, but do you not think it would have been of advantage to the country that some public department like yours should have had that duty thrown upon them, and that it should not be left to the chance estimates of the promoters?—That is the opinion of the Royal Commission.

5230. Therefore the result of the mode that was adopted with regard to these contributions to any loss that might arise from the receipts of the railway has been, probably, that the lines have been constructed at a much greater cost than they otherwise would have been?—No doubt, so far as can be judged, they have been constructed at a larger price than they ought to have been; but from the average cost of these lines (very little exceeding 4,000*l.* a mile, properly equipped) it is not so clear that a very large loss has been sustained. Some loss probably has occurred, but not a very large amount.

5231. Do you think that these lines have all been properly carried out and properly equipped?—We have no means of ascertaining.

5232. You have heard of the Dingle railway, have you not?—I have heard a great deal about it.

5233. Were you in any way responsible for that; did it come under your department in any way?—To this extent, that the lines and the estimates were examined, and a report made to the Lord Lieutenant for the use of the Privy Council.

5234. Before the Privy Council passed the line?—Under this Act we give a report to the promoters, which they present to the Grand Jury, as regards the merits of the line from an engineering point of view. We also under the Act have got to submit an estimate of the proper cost of that line, or rather the share capital, for the information of the Privy Council; but that is not given either to the promoters or to the Grand Jury.

5235. I think you stated that many of these guaranteed shares are now selling at over par?—Yes, the 4 per cent. shares.

5236. At about 120; and that the 4 per cents. are at about par?—I think they are above par.

5237. And, therefore, the advantage that has arisen from the discovery that has been made that the security is a good one, which would have been apparent if the Treasury responsibility had been a direct one, has passed into the hands of the shareholders in these guaranteed lines instead of going to the benefit of the ratepayers?—That is so.

5238. With regard to the results upon the lines that have been guaranteed, I think you said that the annual responsibility of the Treasury with regard to the guaranteed lines was 2 per cent. upon a capital of 1,234,000*l.* That was the liability if none of them paid?—It was a liability of 23,482*l.* per annum.

5239. That is the liability if none paid?—Yes.

5240. And you stated that the charge last year had been only 15,000*l.*, did you not?—That figure I was unable to give accurately, and I shall have to supply that.

5241. It was about 18,000*l.*, in round numbers, was it not?—I would not charge my memory with it. I have the correct figure now, which I find to be 19,500*l.*

5242. That would show that about 6,000*l.* had been paid by the lines, would not it?—Yes, as affects last year.

5243. Mr. Martin asked you whether those figures could be depended upon, inasmuch as the payment by the Grand Juries was always six months, and sometimes a year in arrear. If that was so, would not the account be still correct, because you would have in one year the balance outstanding from the previous year?—That would be the case had all the railways been for some years in working condition; but as regards others that were not quite complete, or had only just commenced working, it would be fallacious.

5244. Have not all the railways that were made under the Act of 1883 been in working order for at least two years?—The Ballinrobe and Claremorris and South Clare Lines have only had one years' working; the Fermoy and Mitchelstown only three years' working, and so on.

5245. But with the exception of those, the amount that would come in in any one year would be the real deficit which you had to make up?—It might or might not be the case. Our accounts close on the 31st of March each year, which is the end of the financial year, whereas the Grand Jury only make their payments after the Assizes, which may fall immediately after that time, and the consequence is that a payment may fall upon one year or the other; and unless that was analysed properly you would not be able to see exactly the working of it.

5246. But although these lines have been for such a short time in working order, it would appear from your statement that they are already paying about 20 per cent. of the liability incurred to the guaranteed shareholders—they are paying 6,000*l.* a year out of 25,000*l.*, are they not?—I do not think that that 6,000*l.* could be calculated upon, owing to the difference of dates at which the accounts are made up; and my own impression is that it would be considerably less than that.

5247. Can you give us any idea of what you think they are paying?—Of course that is somewhat problematical at present. I may say this, that possibly on the five lines made under the Act of 1883 which are worked by parent companies there may be calculated a saving of 1,500*l.* on the Government guarantee. Then under certain conditions as regards the others, I think I may safely say that there would be another 1,500*l.*; so that I think it would not be unsafe to say that there will be a saving of 3,000*l.*, if not 3,500*l.*, upon the Treasury guarantee.

5248. But is it not generally found in practice that when a new line of railway is opened, for the first few years it does not pay very well—it takes time in fact, to create traffic. Is not that the experience in nearly all railways?—That is necessarily so. I have before me now the facts as regards a great number of these lines over six and seven years in working, but still there is no very great improvement. For instance, taking in each case the first half of the year for the Clogher Valley, in 1889 the receipts were 2,940*l.*; in 1893 they were only 2,905*l.*, showing hardly any improvement. For the Cavan, Leitrim, and Roscommon in 1889 the gross receipts were 3,104*l.*, and in 1893 they were 4,072*l.*—that is one of the lines I am calculating a certain saving from, for there you see there is an upward movement. From the West Clare in 1889 the gross receipts were 2,547*l.*, and in 1893 they were 4,070*l.* There again we calculate on a certain amount of saving. For the Skull and Skibbereen Line in 1889 the gross receipts were 1,1[illegible]*l.*, and in 1893 they were 979*l.* There is also one that we make a certain allowance in favour of. For the Cork and Muskerry (a very favourable example) in 1889 the receipts were 5,237*l.*, and in 1893 4,3[illegible]*l.*

[illegible]

5249. Is it not your experience that those lines which are worked in connexion with the main lines are those that are doing best, such as the Claremorris and Ballinrobe(?), [illegible] and [illegible], and so on?—They seem, I think, to have a better train service; but in other respects, of course, I am not able to express an opinion.

5250. Are the lines that pay least of the ordinary gauge?—I would not say so; for instance, the Clogher Valley has a narrow gauge, and the Cavan and Leitrim and West Clare are the same.

5251. Are these narrow gauge railways worked by any of the main lines?—No; they are independent lines, with independent stock, establishments, and so forth.

5252. I think you spoke in the beginning of your evidence about these guarantees being perpetual. Is that the case with regard to all of them?—Yes.

5253. The guarantee for the county contribution is perpetual in all these cases, is it not?—Yes.

5254. Supposing these independent companies that have made no arrangement with any existing large company found that they could not work the line, and that in fact, the working expenses were greater than the receipts, what would happen?—Where the working expenses are deficit for two years, under section 10 of the Act, the Grand Jury become owners of the line, and then, under an Order in Council, a committee of the Grand Jury can be appointed to manage the lines, they taking possession of the line. I had better read the Act, perhaps: "If at any time the receipts "from the undertaking are insufficient to defray the "expenses of management" (this is the 1853(?) Act, 16 and 17 Victoria, chapter 43(?))——

5255. (*Chairman.*) Is that still in force as to the later lines?—It is the leading Act as regards the Act of 18[illegible]—"and will efficiently maintain" (that is to say, where the receipts were not equal to the working expenses) "and work the undertaking, then such sums "as may be necessary for those purposes shall be con-"tributed from time to time." Then it goes on to say: "and if they have been called upon to pay, and "have during a period of not less than two years, to "be fixed by Order, continued to pay, money for "maintaining or working the undertaking, then the "undertaking and all the property of the company "connected with it shall become the property of the "Grand Jury, subject to any liabilities affecting such "undertaking or property, and the undertaking shall "be maintained and worked by the Grand Jury at "the cost of the guaranteeing baronies, and the Order "shall also provide for the manner in which the "undertaking is to be so maintained and worked."

5256. (*The O'Conor Don.*) So that if the line, for instance, has been badly made, and the company fails and the traffic on it is not sufficient, the Grand Jury are bound, at the expense of the ratepayers, to take over these lines, with all their liabilities, and to maintain them and work them in perpetuity?—Yes. They can allow them to become derelict if they like; there is nothing in the Act to prevent that.

5257. Is there not?—I assume not.

5258. I thought they were bound to maintain?—Yes; I am making a mistake—that is so.

5259. (*Chairman.*) The Grand Jury cannot close them, can they?—No; they are obliged to keep them open.

5260. (*The O'Conor Don.*) Supposing they did not fulfil that legal obligation, what would happen?—I do not know exactly.

5261. At all events, so far as the guaranteed shareholders are concerned, whether the line is worked or not, or whether it pays or not, the Grand Jury are bound to pay them the guaranteed interest?—The rates are obliged to meet the guaranteed interest.

5262. And if the rates did not meet the guaranteed interest, the Treasury would contribute nothing, would they?—That is so.

5263. (*Lord Welby.*) Do you happen to recollect whether, at the time the arrangement was made under which the baronial guarantee was given, subject to a repayment by the Treasury of 2 per cent., it was not the object of the Government to secure that the locality had such a lively interest in carrying out the line that it was willing to undertake some risk with regard to it?—Exactly; that was the object.

5264. And though it might be cheaper in some respects had the Government undertaken the whole risk that advantage would have been lost?—No doubt that was the policy of the Act of 1883.

5265. (*The O'Conor Don.*) Would not that object have been equally attained if the Treasury contribution was a direct guarantee to the shareholders and the county guarantee a direct one for its share?—The opinion of the Royal Commission was in that direction.

5266. And if that were done, even if the Treasury half contribution were a direct one, could not the money have been raised at a much lower rate?—That I cannot say.

5267. You do not think that a direct obligation from the Treasury to pay the shareholders would enable money to be raised in the London Market where most of it was raised at a lower rate than when the primary obligation came from a Grand Jury in Ireland?—I do not see how that is to work at all, if you ask me the question, because the Treasury in making a direct payment of that kind would also undertake to keep the whole of the undertaking open and the line in working order. They would not undertake to guarantee absolutely and in perpetuity that it should be kept in working order; they could not undertake any responsibility of that kind. By the Act they cast the whole responsibility of keeping the line open and working in perpetuity on the Grand Jury.

5268. (*Mr. Sexton.*) But would not that responsibility of keeping the line open and working it in perpetuity be thrown on the Grand Jury equally well if the Grand Jury contribution to the shareholders was a direct one and the Treasury contribution to the shareholders also direct?—I do not quite understand the question. Is the Treasury guarantee in your sense a guarantee in perpetuity whether the line is to be kept open or not?

5269. So far as the Treasury is concerned, yes?—Then that would be a guarantee in perpetuity for a line that might be shut up at any moment.

5270. The obligation resting upon the county to keep it open in the same way as it does now?—I do not see how, myself, the obligation would act; but that is entering into a problematical point.

5271. (*Chairman.*) The O'Conor Don asks what should happen in the case of a railway which did not pay its working expenses. Supposing its receipts were 5,000*l.* and its expenses were 7,000*l.*, what would happen in such a case?—If the Treasury guarantee of 1½ per cent., as the O'Conor Don has put it, were given in perpetuity, the Treasury would in that case, I presume, be bound to go on in perpetuity for all time, whether the line were kept in working order or not.

5272. And the security to the public (the Treasury is the public, you know), would be the power of somebody to force the Grand Jury to keep the line in working order. Is not that the purport of your answer?—Yes.

5273. (*The O'Conor Don.*) And is it not exactly the same now. What guarantee is there that the counties will fulfil these obligations thrown upon them of keeping the line in working order?—The Grand Jury are liable for the 5 per cent., and I presume would be open to an action by any shareholder of the company on account of that 5 per cent. If they did not keep the line open the Government would not come in support with the 2 per cent., and in such a case the Grand Jury would have to put upon the rates the full 5 per cent. without the support of the Treasury at all.

5274. The difference is in the one case as compared to the other that the county now would have to pay the whole of the guarantee to the shareholders in case it did not keep the line open?—Precisely.

5275. And in the other case they would only be liable for the half?—That is it, according to the baronial guarantee.

5276. (*Chairman.*) And a little more. And the county would have to be protected against in some way—I do not know what way—to compel them to keep the line open?—The shareholders of the company have no interest in the line at all; they are merely practically as a financial concern of a particular kind; they are not in the least interested as to whether the line is open or closed. All they know is that they are guaranteed by the county a certain rate of interest; if they do not receive that, I presume the courts are open to them.

5277. But there is this qualification, is there not, they are interested to this extent, that if the line produces more than the amount of the guarantee, then their interest would begin, but up to that point they have no interest?—That is so; they share with the county. If the earning was six per cent. they would get half per cent.

5278. (*The O'Conor Don.*) Turning to the first part of your evidence, you told us that the total amount of advances made by your Board was in round numbers 38,500,000*l.* and that about 8,000,000*l.* of that had been remitted. I see, in turning to these details, you divide them first into the accounts that are closed and the accounts that are open?—Yes.

5279. Of the accounts that are closed, I think 6,470,144*l.* was remitted; is not that so?—Yes.

5280. Will you kindly look through the items of that amount and you will see that amongst those items the large sum of 4,284,000*l.* had been advanced for the employment of the labouring poor; is not that so?—Yes, 4,797,444*l.*

5281. And if you will look down further in the column, almost at the end, you will see that 787,778*l.* is under the heading of consolidated annuities?—Yes.

5282. May I take it that those two items both constituted what are called the "consolidated annuities"?—I presume that not only these, but some other items come in to the same category, probably a larger amount than you name.

5283. We have been informed by previous witnesses that the consolidated annuities amounted to about 4,500,000*l.*, and that these consolidated annuities were remitted by Mr. Gladstone in 1853, in consideration of the imposition of the income tax, and the increase in the spirit duty. If the amount received from these two taxes there has very largely exceeded the amounts of remission, would not we have a right to deduct from the total amount of loans remitted; that amount of 4,500,000*l.* from the 6,470,000*l.*?—I am afraid I cannot throw any light upon that.

5284. I only want to ascertain from you the fact that in the 6,470,000*l.* remitted, the sums known as the consolidated annuities are included?—Yes.

5285. I now turn to the sums remitted out of accounts that are open. Taking Class 1, the loans secured upon rates, they amount to 6,580,000*l.*, do they not?—Yes.

5286. Out of that there is remitted 179,000*l.*; is not that so?—Yes, those figures are correct.

5287. Then you will see the greater portion of that sum is made up of the sum of 177,000*l.*, and in 176,000*l.*, in respect of public works loans, under the 57th George III. Can you tell us what those loans were for?—I am afraid I cannot throw any light upon it, but I will see what information I can get. I see, on reference to a statement I have here, there were "Repairs to Parish Churches," "Roads, Dublin to Navan," "Grand Canal Company," "Limerick

"Bridge," "Cork Street Improvement," "Fancy "Canal," "County Mayo Courthouse," "County Kil-"kenny Roads," "Youghal Bridge," and certain other items.

5288. Must not there have been loans of very old date?—Yes, these are all of very old date.

5289. And you still keep those accounts open, do you?—We still bring them forward in all our statements, year by year, bring forward past transactions.

5290. (*Mr. Sexton.*) So long as there is a balance payable at the foot of them?—We bring forward the whole, whether or not; we show the total amount advanced and the total amount remitted.

5291. You bring them along as an open service, do you?—The amounts we bring forward include the closed services, and they, of course, would necessarily form part of the total amount advanced.

5292. The closed services are added at the end of the return, but you regard as an open account, I understood, an account in regard to which, though advances may have ceased, you have a balance open as repayable?—There is nothing repayable as far as closed services are concerned.

5293. I mean although you do not continue to make loans under the head, it remains an open service as long as there is a balance repayable?—Quite so.

5294. (*The O'Conor Don.*) I only wanted to point out that nearly the whole of this 179,000*l.* of loans which have resulted in a loss to the State are of a very old date?—Yes, very old.

Rates of interest.

5295. May I take it that the loans secured upon the rates have, on the whole, very good security?—Yes.

5296. If that be so, let us turn to the table of interest which the Board of Works charged for these loans. Look at No. 9 for instance, advances made to the Grand Jury. You make advances to the Grand Juries for roads, bridges, court-houses, and bridges between counties, and I see the rate of interest which you charge for these advances, with the exception of that on court-houses, is 5 per cent.?—Yes.

5297. Five per cent. on what you admit yourself is very good security, is a very large charge to be made by the State, and does not the State in fact make a profit upon it?—That is a matter as to which we are entirely under the directions of the Treasury.

5298. I am not for a moment accusing you of having framed this rate of interest, but as a matter of fact does not the Treasury or the public Exchequer make a profit, and a very considerable profit upon these loans advanced upon what you admit is very good security?—I can only judge by the price of consols, and there would be apparently a gain, but on the other hand the losses must be taken into consideration.

5299. But do you think it is fair to one public body which can give good security to charge a very high rate of interest because the Government may think it expedient to lend money to another body or company where the security is very bad?—Those are questions I would rather leave to the Lords of the Treasury.

5300. I want to ask you in connexion with these especial advances made for the building of lunatic asylums which you have told us about, whether they are not only at present a very large amount but an increasing amount?—Yes, it is a growing amount.

5301. I see that you charge for those advances $3\frac{1}{4}$ and $3\frac{1}{2}$ per cent.?—On lunatic asylums they charge $3\frac{1}{4}$ per cent. for a term of 30 years and $3\frac{1}{2}$ per cent. for a term of 50 years.

5302. The interest charged is at those rates?—Yes.

5303. Were the advances to lunatic asylums at any time made without interest?—I am not aware that that was the case—not in my time.

5304. Was there any change in the law in the year 1877 with regard to them?—That I am unable to answer.

5305. You may take it that advances were made up to 1877 for building lunatic asylums without any interest?—I am not acquainted with the fact.

5306. And you cannot give us any reason for the change, can you?—No.

5307. Has it not been recognised by the State by paying so much a head for the maintenance of lunatics in the asylums that this charge for lunacy generally is one of an Imperial rather than of a local character?—I am not aware of the reason.

5308. You are aware that they do pay a certain amount towards the maintenance of lunatics in asylums, are you not?—The fact has not come under my cognisance on the Board.

5309. If that were so, would you not think it very extraordinary that the State should charge for the advances made for the building of these asylums a rate of interest on which they are making a profit?—I am not able to give an opinion upon that.

5310. With regard to the advances now made to private persons for the improvement of land, either to tenants or the owners—have you had much loss?—Under the Act of 1842, as I have already mentioned, out of advances for river drainage works amounting to over 2,000,000*l.* there was remission of 1,200,000*l.*

5311. Was not that remission mainly in connexion with public works on the Shannon and large drainage works of that sort?—Some upon the Shannon, but upon a large number (I think there were 131) of those drainage works carried out under the Act of 1842, chiefly in the fifties. Owing to various circumstances difficulties arose, to investigate which the Government appointed a Special Commission, consisting of Sir Richard Griffith and Sir John G. M'Kerlie, and in 1859 they made their Report recommending this remission.

5312. Were not those works carried out under the Board of Works?—Those works were carried out under the Board of Works as relief of distress; that was the raison d'être.

5313. So that we have that much more addition to make to remissions of a charitable character, such as moneys advanced for exceptional distress?—Yes.

5314. My previous question had rather more reference to the advances made for the land improvements to owners or occupiers. Have you had much loss on advances made to owners or occupiers?—Out of a sum of over 4,000,000*l.* advanced for land improvement to owners, under the 10 Victoria, chapter 32, there has been no remission.

5315. Are they much in arrear?—The total of the arrears up to the present moment is 41,214*l.*

5316. Out of how much?—Out of an original advance of over 4,000,000*l.*, and a not yet called-up sum of 1,213,000*l.*

5317. Have you any reason to believe that you will lose any considerable portion of those arrears?—Judging from past experience, no.

5318. Have you found any difficulty in collecting the instalments from the tenant occupiers?—Yes, to some extent.

5319. How do you collect—have you agents to collect the money or how is it collected?—It is collected by the accountant and solicitor acting together. These loans, as you are aware, are not well secured, the tenants' loans being made upon a very different security to that of any other. They are made merely upon the tenants' interest and he may be evicted at any time. It has shown itself not to be altogether a good security—and Parliament passed the P. W. Loans Act, 1882, the purport of section 5 of which was that we are to levy a poundage of one shilling in the pound, on all arrears in respect of Loans made since the passing of that Act. That has been and is acted upon now in reference to all arrears of one month after becoming due.

5320. Have you found that to have a beneficial effect?—A most beneficial effect, and we hope that it will have a very great effect in preventing any further arrears.

5321. Are the advances made to the tenant at the same rate as the advances had previously been made to the proprietors?—Yes. That is to say the loan has a currency of twenty-two years; the rate of interest is 3½ per cent., and 3 per cent. to provide a sinking fund, so that during the twenty-two years there is a total charge for interest and sinking fund of 6l. 10s. for every 100l.

5322. The interest being 3½ per cent.?—Yes.

5323. Have not we here again a profit made by the State on these advances, because they can borrow money at a much lower rate than 3½ per cent.?—I cannot venture upon an opinion, as to the rate of interest but will give the losses. The total number of loans up to the current year was 11,330 for a total sum of 884,337l., and on that total sum up to the present date there has been a loss of close on 13,000l., that is to say, there are 10,000l. arrears which it will be probably very difficult to collect, and 2,340l. which has been written off in the Public Works Loans Acts.

5324. I must ask you one question more with regard to lunatic asylums which I forgot to ask when dealing with the subject. You are a member of the Board of Control, I believe?—Yes, by the Act.

5325. And has not the Board of Control the absolute decision as to what amount shall be spent upon buildings?—They have complete control over all new works and additions.

5326. And the local authorities who become responsible for the payment of the money advanced have really nothing to say to the amount that must be spent, have they?—They have no statutory obligation cast upon them, though as a fact the Board of Control invariably consult them upon every single portion of the charges.

5327. They do not invariably act upon the opinion expressed by them, do they?—No, because the Board of Control are responsible under Statute.

5328. With regard to the loans under the Public Health Act, I think you said there was a limit to the amount which could be borrowed to twice the valuation?—Yes.

5329. The limit to which they can borrow is twice the amount of the valuation, is it not?—Yes, that is statutory under the Public Health Acts—at least I believe it is so.

5330. The Chairman asked you a question with regard to your preparing the estimates for the year, and he called attention to the fact that you generally asked for a much larger sum than it turned out afterwards you required. Might I ask you how those estimates or votes are made out—are they made out in detail, or is it a bulk sum that you ask for?—We ask for a bulk sum, and a bulk credit.

5331. Which of course is made up by you in detail beforehand, is it not?—Yes, necessarily, on the best information we can get.

5332. Can you apply that bulk sum to any one item of the service without the Treasury's permission?—The Treasury give us sanction for every item. Not one escapes the Treasury, and their definite sanction is given for all advances; and we have to prove that it comes within the Statutory provisions.

5333. With reference to a particular case, which I daresay you know of, last year in connection with a certain drainage work in Ireland, it was stated to the Drainage Board that you had not applied for a sufficient sum of money to carry on the works?—Yes.

5334. And yet it appears from these returns, to which the Chairman has referred, that last year you had applied for about twice the amount that it turned out you required to expend. Can you explain how it was that you were unable to supply this particular undertaking with the required money, upon the ground that you had not put a sufficient sum in the votes?—We judged according to what we thought was the ability of the Drainage Board to carry out the works, and we provided what we thought would be equal to their competence for expenditure.

5335. Yes; but you provided, you see, on the whole for a much larger amount than you required; and how was it that then you were not able, until the financial year was out, and new estimates could be presented, to advance the money?—The savings which arise upon various items of the vote are applicable, under Treasury approval, for appropriation to one or other of the sub-heads of the vote.

5336. You had, according to these papers, a surplus of, I think, 440,000l. How was it that you were unable to get the Treasury sanction to the application of that surplus savings, as you call it, on the other vote to this one, where you had made too low an estimate?—The fact of the matter is, under the River Bann Acts there was a State free grant of 30,000l. for those works. That grant had to be provided for in two or three years' votes, and the item that you question appeared upon the votes, and does not form any part of the loan services at all. It was part of a grant that had to be provided for in our Public Works vote for the year, and it has no reference whatever to the particular provision for loans at all. It was part of the grant—part of that 30,000l.—that is how that matter arose.

5337. The result of the provision not having been made was, was it not, that the Drainage Board had to borrow the money from the bank at a considerable loss?—Yes, that was the case.

5338. And they have been consequently at that loss through the estimate made at your office of the amount that would be spent within the year being too low?—The Treasury, I think, have guaranteed you the amount of that loss of interest, so that you do not sustain any loss on the 30,000l.

5339. I am not aware of that?—I think that is the case.

5340. (*Mr. Sexton.*) How is remission effected?—By Treasury order.

5341. Do you initiate the proceedings, or do you simply advise upon the initiative of the Treasury?—The Treasury see all the details of our arrears, and, on full inquiry, they provide for the remission. Formerly it was done by a Treasury order; now the remission is written off in the various Public Works Loans Bills.

5342. The Treasury acting, I suppose, upon your advice and recommendation?—It is a matter settled by the Treasury on the statements that we lay before them.

5343. Comparing the repayments made by landlords and by tenants, to which the O'Conor Don has just referred, I draw your attention, first, to item 39 in class 3, of Paper 1. It appears there that over 800,000l. has been lent to tenants for the purchase of their farms?—That is under the Act of 1870. There we only act as a loan department.

5344. What were the terms under that Act?—The terms were, if I recollect correctly, that we advanced two-thirds of the amount of the purchase money that had been agreed on between the landlord and tenant, the tenant to provide the remaining third, one-third or possibly it may have been one-fourth; I am not quite certain about the proportions.

5345. How was the advance repaid?—The advance was repaid on the usual terms.

5346. Would that be twenty-two years?—No, at 5 per cent. for thirty-five years, that is to say, 3½ per cent. with 1½ per cent. sinking fund.

5347. Out of the owing sum of 800,000l. there has been no remission whatever, and only an arrear of 8,000l.?—That is so—principal arrears.

5348. That is a good collection, is it not?—Yes.

5349. Then, under the Act of 1881, the Land Law Act, the terms are forty-nine years at four per cent., are they not?—Under the 1881 Act the loans made to tenants are at 6l. 10s., with a term of twenty-two years.

5350. For improvements?—Yes.

5351. Those are rather exacting terms, are they not?—It is three and a half per cent., with three per cent. sinking fund, making 6l. 10s. with a term of twenty-two years.

Sir R. G. C. Hamilton, K.C.B.

11 Dec. 1886.

Loans for land improvement Act of 1870.

5352. For every 100*l.* advanced, the tenant has to pay back 6*l.* 10*s.* for twenty-two years?—That includes sinking fund.

5353. But he has to pay it. We know from the administrators of the Land Acts that they generally only allow five per cent. for sums spent upon improvement. They find the improvement usually estimated by a payment of five per cent., or a remission of the rent, and here the tenant would be under a payment which would exceed the usual allowance. Under these circumstances it does appear that out of a total sum of 814,000*l.*, a writing off of 2,000*l.* and an arrear of 6,000*l.* ?—No, an arrear of 10,000*l.*

5354. Is not that an unsatisfactory result, considering the bulk of the debt and the depressed times in Ireland?—It was not the exact amount of the arrears we judged by, but by the way in which those arrears grew. It was considered that there was a tendency for those to increase, and that as the loans advanced the difficulties of collection would become more and more.

5355. Let us compare them with the loans to the landowners, who are presumably in a better position to pay than the small tenants. You have advanced to the landowners over 6,000,000*l.*, and you have written off from the Local Loans Fund 12,000*l.*, that is more than four times as much as you have written off for the tenants, and there is an arrear also of 17,000*l.* Is that subject to any further increase?—I do not quite follow you—the total amount written off the 6,000,000*l.* is nothing.

5356. There is 12,000*l.* written off the assets of the Local Loans Fund. I am now upon item 25?—Yes. The amount written off is 12,360*l.*—you are right—the principal 17,763*l.*, and interest arrears 11,092*l.*; but that is on a very large amount—on 6,000,000*l.*

5357. The two sums due on the amount borrowed by the tenants amount to considerably over 1,000,000*l.*?—They are under quite different circumstances and Acts. Under the Act of 1870 the security is the land, and under the Land Law Act the security is the tenant's interest merely, so that it would be impossible to mix the two things up together.

5358. I am thinking more of the condition of the people who have to pay, and not so much of the nature of the security. I am comparing the punctuality and extent of the payments, having regard to the condition relatively of the people who have to pay, and it does not appear to me that the payments by the tenants as compared with those of the landlords are open to any animadversion, especially as I see under the Irish Church Fund Loans, on page 8, there was a further loan made to landowners for improvement of land, amounting to nearly 1,000,000*l.*, and that 1,000,000*l.* was lent, I believe, at 1 per cent., was it not?—That was lent at 1 per cent. for relief of distress, and the conditions, of course, under which those loans were made were totally distinct from those on which the ordinary land improvement loans were made under the Act of 10th Victoria. The circumstances of the time were different altogether, so that I think it would be inadvisable to mix these two sums together. Everybody of course is aware that under the relief of distress the conditions never can be satisfactory.

5359. I suppose they improve the lands with the money which they get at 1 per cent.?—Yes; but what I mean is this—that in the year 1880-1881 sums up to perhaps 2,000,000*l.* sterling were advanced by the Board of Works with necessarily an insufficient establishment, and it would have been impossible to have exercised under the pressure of distress the same amount of supervision as under ordinary circumstances. Time does not admit of it. Loans which are made in the ordinary course of business are totally distinct.

Railway loans.

5360. Under the two heads, the remissions and arrears of loans to landowners amount to 56,000*l.*, and under the two heads the tenants' arrears are about 16,000*l.* Did I understand you to say that the State liability incurred in connection with the railways is equivalent to a sum of 65,000*l.* a year?—The total sum under the three Acts amounts to 65,000*l.* a year.

Sir R. G. C. Hamilton, K.C.B.

11 Dec. 1886.

Railway loans.

5361. Of course the greater part of that is now incurred?—Yes; you may say that the whole of the funds under those Acts are exhausted.

5362. In regard to the liability as to the railways from year to year, did I understand you to say there is a tendency rather to diminish the sum payable by the State?—No, I do not say that. I think on the whole there is generally or may be a slight improvement, though it is very difficult to say that is is anything very absolute. As I mentioned before the loans made before 1883 are not satisfactory. Many of those loans were made for the purpose of relief of distress.

5363. I understood you to say that in a recent year you incurred actually about three-fourths of the gross liability that might have been imposed upon you—18,000*l.* out of 25,000*l.*?—That was with reference to the Act of 1883.

5364. I was taking all the Acts together?—No, that was merely under the Act of 1883. The 2 per cent. provided under the Act of 1883 amounted to a little over 19,000*l.*, and that did not come up to the amount that the 2 per cent. would have given 25,000*l.*; it was 6,000*l.* less in reality, that is to say, the Treasury in that particular year were called upon to pay less by 6,000*l.* than the 2 per cent. guarantee.

5365. Have you made any calculation or have you any amount of the possible maximum that might be thrown upon the ratepayers in any year under all the Railway Acts?—No. That is very difficult, because over and above having to meet the guarantee of 2 and 3 per cent. respectively, they have also to find a sum for any deficit of working expenses beyond that, and that of course varies with each locality and each railway.

5366. Does the local guarantee ordinarily carry with it a liability not only to find the dividend in the first instance but also any deficiency of receipts to defray working expenses?—Under the Act the Grand Juries are to find not only the interest but any deficit of working expenses.

5367. I understand that when and so far as the guarantee falls upon the rates it is payable altogether out of the county cess?—It is levied in the same way I believe—I am not familiar with the machinery.

5368. That is a rate wholly paid by the occupier, is it not?—The occupier I think down to the 4*l.* valuation or something of that kind—I am not quite certain. The landlord I believe pays all below 4*l.* and half of that above.

5369. I think the occupier pays in every case, except where a new tenancy has been created?—These are points that I am not sufficiently acquainted with.

5370. Have the ratepayers ever had any control over the incurring of the liability?—I do not know the amount of control they have exercised, excepting as to the influence they can bring to bear on the Grand Jury.

5371. But legally the power rests altogether with the Grand Jury, so far as locality is concerned, does it not?—Quite so.

5372. And all the ratepayer has to do is to pay the liability when it arises?—I do not know what amount of influence they can bring to bear.

5373. I am speaking of the law now?—The law is that the Grand Jury provides the amount.

5374. Did I correctly understand you to say that in the event of a line becoming derelict and ceasing to be worked if the guarantee is perpetual, as I believe it usually is, the county is liable for ever to pay the dividend?—Yes.

5375. And if they allow that to happen your liability ceases, does it not?—Yes.

5376. And the county pays the whole dividend?—Yes.

5377. Without limit of time?—Yes.

[illegible] K.C.B. 12 Feb. 1894. Railway loans.

5378. Has your attention been drawn to the liability incurred in the case of the Dingle line?—I know something about it, but it is not a matter that comes before our Board.

5379. You would not be concerned further than as regards your moiety of the dividend, would you?—Nothing further.

5380. I believe as a matter of fact they had to pay not only their share of the dividend, but also a heavy deficiency on working expenses, and also compensation for injury and loss of life?—They had to pay those sums, and I believe they were compensated to a great extent by a free grant from the Treasury.

5381. There was a special arrangement made, was there?—Yes.

5382. I know that in two of the baronies at least in county Kerry the cesspayers have been placed in an extremely difficult position, by reason of the liabilities arising on some lines?—In one barony I am aware they have; in the Corkaguiny barony they have been subject to a heavy charge; but I cannot say that any others have gone beyond 5d. or 6d. in the pound.

5383. In one barony, I think, it was something like 5s., was it not?—I have the incidents here.

5384. I should be glad to know what was the burden?—In regard to the Dingle Railway, which is an extreme case, the barony of Corkaguiny in the year 1892 had to meet a poundage of 2s. 3·45d. The Clanmorris barony, for the same line, had to meet a poundage of 4s. 0·28d., and the Trughanacmy barony, 2s. 4d.

5385. Was that for only one line?—That was for one line. They vary—2d., 4d., 6d., and 7d., and so on. There is one rather heavy one, 9½d. Corkaguiny is quite an exceptional case.

5386. Apart from the question of deficiencies arising on working expenses, what would be the gross liability of the cesspayers in Ireland in any year, assuming a total failure to pay dividends?—Take an average of about 4½ per cent., on the total amount of guarantee.

5387. 4½ per cent. on 269,000l.?—No, it would be on 1,000,000l. The two Acts have got to be taken together. There is the 1883 Act and the guarantees under the 1889 Act. I think I had better give you that information afterwards. It will have to be worked out.

[illegible] 5388. On the subject of loans for labourers' cottages, you lend the money at 3½ and 3¾ per cent., according to the term of years in which it is to be repaid?—Yes.

5389. Has the Local Government Board the administration of the loans?—The Local Government Board have got the administration entirely of all the Labourers Loans Acts under item 21—that is to say, under the Act of 46 and 47 Victoria, chapter 60. The Board of Works have solely to deal with items 7 and 8, labourers' dwellings in towns, and the housing of the working classes, under Acts of 1866 and 1885.

5390. In the case where the Local Government Board is the administering body, what is your function; do you simply pass on any application to the Treasury?—Simply, as the Loans Department, we have to see to the security, to see that the law is observed as regards the proportion that the loan bears to the total indebtedness of each union, and to make a recommendation to the Lords of the Treasury, who give us their sanction, on receipt of which we make the loan.

5391. Do you intervene by recommendation, or otherwise, in every case?—Under certain circumstances we correspond with the Local Government Board, and take their views in cases of difficulty; but, ordinarily, we act for ourselves and make recommendations to the Treasury.

5392. You reserve to yourselves the right to say whether the loan ought or ought not to be granted, do you?—Yes, being a Loan Board we have to see to the security and all other safeguards.

5393. (Chairman.) You have plenary responsibility?—Yes.

5394. (Mr. Sexton.) Do the plans which are used of the houses and so forth proceed from your Board?—Under the Local Government Board we see none of the plans for labourers' cottages in rural districts, or anything of that kind—they have their own machinery and their own staff of officers. With regard to the others, the promoters bring up the designs; each design is examined by the technical staff in our office in detail. [illegible] 12 Feb. 1894. Labourers' dwellings.

5395. Has your attention been drawn to the extent to which the allotment of loans exceeds the amount derived by the Guardians from the labourers?—No, we have no information whatever on that subject.

5396. I understand that the function of your Board in regard to loans is in itself not administrative. You cannot determine whether or not a loan shall be granted, or alter the terms or conditions upon which a loan may be granted?—We have to be guided entirely by Acts of Parliament, and within the terms of those Acts we go into each case; see to the security, make all inquiries necessary, and when we have decided that the loan shall be made we make a recommendation to the Treasury, who give their sanction. [illegible]

5397. But you have no discretion whatever of your own, have you?—No, we merely have to report to the Treasury.

5398. The Treasury, I believe, under various statutes possess a tolerably wide discretion in regard to relaxation of terms, do they not?—Yes, I should say that they had every discretion.

5399. (Lord Welby.) I think if you look at the Loan Act of 1877 or 1878, I forget which year it is, which now regulates it, you will see that the discretion of the Treasury is limited as to terms of loan and as to power of remission also, there is a discretion but it is very much limited under the Act?—I was merely alluding to the fact that as between our office and the Treasury we are entirely under their guidance. I did not for a moment wish to question the fact of the limitations placed by Act of Parliament upon the discretion of the Treasury. I was merely speaking with regard to our own position.

5400. (Mr. Sexton.) Would you not put it that you are under their control, and that they are a good deal under your guidance?—I hope our recommendations carry given weight.

5401. I heard you say to-day, for instance, in regard to one or two classes of loans, that both the rate of interest had been reduced and the term of years extended by a Treasury order?—Yes.

5402. That would indicate a very important discretion to the Treasury, would it not?—That is no doubt conferred by the Statute.

5403. Would it be possible do you think to give the Commission in a paper, or otherwise, the extent to which the Treasury may modify at any time the terms upon which loans have been or may be made?—I only know of certain Acts under which the Treasury can exercise power. I mentioned one, the 6th and 7th William IV. under which they can, but I am not aware of many others in which they can exercise their powers. We take our instructions in all such matters entirely from the Treasury.

5404. As to remissions, we often hear of these remissions in connection with Irish taxation, in fact we have never done hearing of them. Can you explain how it is that in Table 2, remissions on closed services no rate of interest is given and no indication is given of what rates of interest the borrowers had to pay, whilst the loans were current?—I am afraid I cannot give any information on that subject. Remissions.

5405. I suppose the records of your Department are complete with regard to these loans?—Yes. I have had a note placed in my hands just now which shows that in most cases there was no interest on these closed loans.

5406. It is almost impossible for any one at this time

looking at Table 2, to appreciate the circumstances under which the loans were made, is it not?—Yes.

5407. Can you give us any particulars which will enable us generally to see when the loans were made, to what bodies of persons, and under what circumstances they were remitted?—As far as I understand these loans commenced in 1817, and were made prior to the formation of the Board of Works in 1831. I daresay the records might throw some light upon it.

5408. It would be very convenient taking the main heads under which large sums were remitted if you could let us know when the money was lent, the bodies and persons to whom the money was lent, and the circumstances of the remissions?—Yes.

5409. I think perhaps if you could also apply that to the remissions upon the unclosed accounts, which, though they are more recent, are not more familiar to many of us than the remissions on the closed accounts, it would be desirable?—In all the open accounts you have information as to the rates of interest, dates, amounts, and so on, you have that information.

5410. Certainly, the information is popular, but for instance I see a remission of 10,000*l.* for inland navigation, and 74,000*l.* for harbours and docks; one is not able to appreciate the circumstances under which the remission was made simply by reading the title?—You wish the details of those.

5411. Yes, some particulars?—Very well, you shall have them as far as possible.

5412. The circumstances, the time, the rate of interest, the persons, who received the money, and the reason why the balances were remitted?—Perhaps Mr. Sexton, you are not aware that we have 25,000 open accounts at the present moment.

5413. I know you have, and I do not wish to ask anything unreasonable, but I thought you might be able to indicate the general character of the remissions in a narrow space?—I will see what we can do.

5414. The arrears upon the open accounts with regard to four-fifths of the amount are due to these railway loans, are they not. The total arrears are how much?—561,887*l.*, of which the amount due to railway loans is 429,934*l.*

5415. How many of these railway companies are there?—Sixteen.

5416. I notice they have paid 460,000*l.* under the head of principal, and comparatively a very large sum, 313,000*l.* for interest, so that it would rather appear that the rate which you charge these railways, 5 per cent. up to 1883, and 4 per cent. since, must have a good deal to do with their inability to meet their engagements?—That is a point as to which the Board is entirely under the guidance of the Treasury.

5417. If you have any power of initiative I suggest you might employ it very well, in considering with regard to these loans in Table 7, due by public bodies or quasi public bodies whether 4 per cent. is not a high rate considering the value of money?—I am afraid I have not the data for considering that question.

5418. You do not feel that you can take it upon yourself to take any action upon that subject, do you?—No.

5419. The rates of interest as well as the terms of repayment vary very greatly in regard to services of tolerably equal public utility, do they not?—Yes, that is the case.

5420. And I notice in Class 2 that the rates payable by the companies for loans to Grand Juries are nearly all higher than the rates payable by Boards of Guardians—they range from 4 to 5 per cent. merely in the case of Grand Juries, and in the case of Boards of Guardians from 3 to 4 per cent. Do you know of any reason why that disparity should continue to exist?—The difference is not quite so much as that; the generality of the loans to Grand Juries are at 4 per cent.; the generality of the loans to Guardians are at 3½ per cent., so that there is not such a very great disparity; but at the same time there are disparities, and, as mentioned before, the Board of Works has no authority or power to deal with any question of interest.

Mr. R. W. Horsley, C.B.

14 Dec. 1893.

Rates of interest.

5421. I observe that in the table of the average rates of interest payable on the advances before the Local Loans Fund was established the money was provided out of the Consolidated Fund?—Yes.

5422. Since the year 1877, was it?—No, since the year 1887 when the Local Loans Fund was created; all that has been by advances from the Commissioners of National Debt who made the advance to us.

5423. The Local Loans Fund is floated at three per cent., is it not?—I believe so.

5424. At par?—I believe so.

5425. And I see that the average rate chargeable is 3*l.* 11*s.* 2*d.*?—That covers cost of administration and losses of all kinds.

5426. It would be something like half per cent. or a little more than half per cent. on 8,000,000*l.* a year. I mean, taking only the percentage which you pay for the money and the percentage which you receive, leaving out of account losses?—That would have to be a matter of detail and calculation; I am not able to give exactly what it would come to.

5427. I understand the Local Loans Fund is one Imperial Fund for the three countries?—Yes.

5428. Are Irish losses earmarked as against Irish receipts, or is the whole fund applicable to any loss no matter where arising?—That I do not know.

Railway loans.

5429. (*Chairman.*) I wish to ask you one question upon a point which I do not think is quite clear with respect to the light railway account. I have been analysing it during the last few minutes, and if you turn to pages 74 to 77 of your report you will see you give the cases both of railways which pay their working expenses and the railways which do not pay their working expenses?—Those are all the railways under the Act of 1883.

5430. I am speaking of the Act of 1883. Will you be good enough to tell me whether I am right in the calculations that I have made that in point of money, though not quite in point of numbers, as many of those railways do not pay their working expenses as do pay them?—Rather more pay than those that do not pay.

5431. And taking the last completed year of which you have an account here, that is 1892, half of the total number of 16 railways do not pay their working expenses?—Yes.

5432. What will become of them. Is it likely that the Baronies will be obliged to put into operation the extreme penal consequences of the Act?—The Act as I understand acts automatically, that is to say, that where the working expenses are not paid for two consecutive years, an Order in Council is obtained under which the railway passes into the hands of and is administered by a Committee of the Grand Jury.

5433. But it is a highly penal process, is it not, to take a railway away from its natural managers, and putting it under a public body. Will that necessarily occur, or is there any power to postpone so severe an operation as that?—As at present constituted, the several companies have no direct interest in managing these lines. The Grand Jury on the other hand having to find the money have a very direct interest, and the only question is whether in regard to their body they are able to appoint a sufficient number of experts as directors to manage the line.

5434. I hope the number of directors is not so much an element in the case as the efficiency of the management?—Yes, of course, efficiency of management is the essential matter.

5435. (*Mr. Martin.*) There is a case at the present moment, is there not, of a line being managed by the Grand Jury?—Yes, there is.

The witness withdrew.

Adjourned to to-morrow at eleven o'clock.

TWELFTH DAY.

Thursday, 13th December, 1894.

At the Benchers' Chambers, Four Courts, Dublin.

PRESENT:

THE RIGHT HON. HUGH C. E. CHILDERS, *Chairman*.

LORD WELBY.
THE RIGHT HON. THE O'CONOR DON.
SIR DAVID BARBOUR, K.C.S.I.

CHARLES E. MARTIN, ESQ.
THOMAS SEXTON, ESQ., M.P.

MR. B. H. HOLLAND, *Secretary*.

Mr. MURROUGH O'BRIEN called, and examined.

Mr. Murrough O'Brien. 13 Dec. 1894.

5436. (*Chairman.*) You are, I believe, a member of the Land Commission?—Yes.

5437. But you do not come here to give evidence in a representative character?—No, I am here to give evidence in my personal character.

5438. To give your own opinions on facts which you have collected yourself. I think the paper which you have laid before the Commission is an enlargement of a pamphlet which you published some time ago, is it not?—It is an enlargement of writings published in the press.

5439. And then republished as a pamphlet, I think?—Yes.

Financial arrangements at the Union.

5440. Going directly to your paper, you describe the financial arrangements at the time of the Union as objectionable to Irishmen on several grounds?—That appears to be a matter of history.

5441. The main arrangement was that Ireland's contribution to the Imperial revenue should be $\frac{2}{17}$ths of the whole, I think?—Yes.

5442. The recorded protest against that you refer to, but you do not give it in detail?—I do not give it in detail because a great deal of it has been gone over already, and I did not think it necessary to cite the history of the Union arrangements.

5443. In your opinion, was that protest well founded and justified by results?—It appears to have been justified by the results.

5444. In 1800 what was Great Britain's debt per head?—The amounts stated per head for Great Britain is 42l., and for Ireland it is 5l. 12s.

5445. But that proportion was very much varied at the time of the Union of the Exchequers. I think Ireland's proportion was much larger, was it not?—At the time of the amalgamation of the Exchequers the Irish debt had quadrupled; the British debt appears to have only doubled. Having read the proceedings of the Committee of 1864 it seems impossible to make out from them whether the accounts were kept strictly in accordance with the terms of the Union or not, and I should have thought it was impossible to disentangle those accounts at present.

Effect of identical taxation.

5446. Since the amalgamation of the Exchequers the taxation of the countries has greatly been assimilated, I think?—The taxation is almost identical in both countries now.

5447. You do not think therefore that indiscriminate taxation and identical taxes necessarily mean equality of taxation?—The circumstances and social conditions of Ireland are so very different from those of England that I do not think identical taxes would necessarily apply to the same incidents in both countries.

5448. How would you in a few words express the nature of the grievance on that point?—I think the position of Ireland is as if a person with 200l. a year had to keep up an establishment in forced partnership on the same scale, and in the same style, with another person with 10,000l. a year, contributing a proportion of every outlay which the richer partner chose to make. The modest competence that would amply suffice for all the necessities of the first, if living independently, would be ruinously insufficient for the poorer person in such a partnership.

5449. What was the provision of the 7th Article of the Treaty of Union as to the revision of the financial arrangements?—That after twenty years the contribution to the revenue by each country was to be ascertained by a comparison of the income of each country from the produce of a general tax, if such had been imposed. No such tax existed until 1853, when the income tax was extended to Ireland.

5450. So, in your opinion, that provision of the Treaty of Union, though not an absolute provision, expressed an arrangement which has not been carried out?—That has not been carried out.

Treasury Financial Relations returns.

5451. You refer to the Parliamentary paper which presents the Treasury view of the financial relations, and you have given us a summary table showing us the amounts of the percentages of the contribution of each country. Would you give us the salient points of that—not so much the figures as the percentages?—It appears from the Treasury tables in Paper 329, of Session 1891, that Ireland's contribution to the Imperial revenue was 8·27 per cent. in 1889–1890, 8·46 per cent. in 1890–91, and 8·22 per cent. in the year 1891–1892. The amount returned by the Treasury as expended on Irish services was 17·24 per cent. in the first year, 17·90 in the second year, and 17·64 in the third year, leaving as the contribution to be made by Ireland to the Imperial services 4·03 per cent. in the first year, 3·64 in the second year, and 3·04 in the third year.

5452. That may be said to be the Treasury view of the financial arrangement?—That appears to be so.

5453. Will you now take the Treasury estimate of the taxation per head?—The Treasury estimate made in that paper of the taxation per head for Ireland was in the year 1889–1890, 1l. 12s. 5d., of which 10s. 11d. is estimated to have been contributed to Imperial services; in 1890–1891 the taxation of Ireland was 1l. 14s. per head, of which 9s. 5d. is estimated to have been contributed to Imperial services, and in 1891–1892 the taxation per head in Ireland was 1l. 13s. 6d., of which 8s. is estimated to have been contributed to Imperial services.

5454. How would you sum up the Treasury view

as given in these calculations?—That paper indicates that Ireland, from the Treasury point of view, is becoming of less value from year to year in the way of contribution to Imperial services. The cost of administration appears to be growing greater, and the contribution, therefore, remaining for Imperial services is gradually growing less.

5455. But, in your opinion, you say that is a fallacious conclusion. Will you point out in what respect?—I think the classification in the paper is difficult to criticise, because the head of account does not always indicate what the services actually are; but a great many items are classed as Imperial services to which Ireland contributes, and it appears to me that they should have been classed as English or British services.

5456. Do you think that Ireland does not derive adequate benefit from a good many points of expenditure?—I think Ireland, a purely agricultural and pastoral country, has no need of a great many of the services which are supplied for the benefit of the Empire as a whole.

5457. As a part of the Empire, you do not suggest that Ireland should not pay at all for those services, but you think that the charge is too great?—I think the charge is too great. We have no commerce practically, no industries practically, no foreign relations as a separate country, and I do not think that the army, navy, and expenses in connection with foreign relations should be charged in full to Ireland.

Civil expenditure in Ireland.

5458. Then do you also think that a good deal of the civil expenditure is excessive, having regard to Ireland's requirements?—I think there is an excessive cost of administration in Ireland, because in many departments there are two establishments; there is an establishment in Dublin and an establishment in London.

5459. With respect to what are more strictly Irish services, do you think the charge for some, such as the police, is excessive?—The cost of the police in Ireland appears to be enormous in comparison with crime. Crime is on the whole slightly less in Ireland than in the rest of the United Kingdom, but the cost of the police is about three times what it is in Great Britain. The police admittedly are kept up for Imperial purposes and not local purposes; such a large force would not be required for the suppression of crime.

5460. Does that criticism of yours extend to other civil establishments in Ireland which you think are kept up on too large a scale?—I think the whole Imperial expenditure administered in London chiefly benefits Great Britain, not Ireland.

Taxation per head.

5461. And you do not think that the comparison between the Irishman's taxation of 34s. against the Englishman's of 53s. really is a strong support of the present arrangement, because Ireland, though paying less per head, is a much poorer country?—The average income in Ireland would be very much less than the average income in Great Britain, and therefore the taxation per head is naturally a great deal less, and I think should be still smaller as the margin for taxation in Ireland on the average income is very much less than the margin for taxation in England.

Relative wealth of Great Britain and Ireland.

5462. You have constructed a table from the Inland Revenue Report of 1890–1891. Will you give us the proportions which, according to that report, the income tax assessment indicates as the comparative wealth of Great Britain and Ireland?—In round numbers Ireland's proportional estimate on the basis of the income tax assessment, would be 1 to 21·3, and the income indicated per head for England would be 17*l*., against 8*l*. 10*s*. in Ireland. The same table gives the assessment of houses and messuages. Houses have often been taken by economists as one of the best evidences of capability of people for taxation. The assessment of houses in Ireland to the rest of the United Kingdom is as 1 to 34, and the value of house property, according to the assessment, would be 4·4*l*. in England and 0·87*l*. in Ireland.

5463. The most favourable item to Great Britain on the three main contributions is the property assessed to probate and succession duty and I think the Irish proportion stands higher in regard to that than as to income or personal property?—A good deal of succession duty is paid on estates that are owned by people who are not resident in Ireland, and presumably resident in England, and therefore it would not indicate that the proportion taken on that basis would be a just one.

5464. (*Mr. Sexton*). I notice that the columns containing the assessment are headed "United Kingdom" and "Ireland" respectively; then the columns containing the calculations are headed "England" and "Ireland"?—Yes, I thought it more useful to compare England and Ireland per head.

5465. The comparison we are engaged on here is one between Ireland and Great Britain?—I did not take out the figures for Great Britain, because at first the Treasury tables gave a separate estimate for Scotland, and I imagined that possibly Scotland was coming into the inquiry, and in the notes I made I thought it more useful to compare England and Ireland.

5466. But if in these final columns you had compared not Ireland and England, but Ireland and the United Kingdom, the proportion of Ireland would be smaller. Obviously if the first of the two columns had included Scotland or had included the whole of the United Kingdom, the proportion of Ireland to that would have been smaller than it is to England merely, would it not?—I am not sure whether on the assessment per head it would be so.

5467. (*Chairman*). Of course the comparison could be made by deducting the total Irish assessment from the United Kingdom assessment. That would give the Great Britain assessment, and that might be compared with the Irish assessment?—Yes.

Assessments in Great Britain and Ireland compared.

5468. You complain of the over-assessment in Ireland as compared with the notoriously under-assessment of certain classes of property in England. Will you enlarge upon that a little?—The assessment in Ireland is made upon a different principle from the assessment in England. In England the assessment is on the estimated rent of the premises, with certain deductions that are made for repairs, outlay, tithes, and land tax. I think they are all taken off from the assessment when made in England. The valuation in Ireland was made under an Act passed in 1852, and was completed about 1864. It was supposed to be made on an estimate of what the land would produce, and a certain scale of prices was given, but the material for applying that scale of prices was not given—that is to say, the cost of production was not brought into account, as laid down in the Act. Everyone acquainted with the history of the Valuation in Ireland knows that it followed the rents to a large extent. The valuers who were employed in making the assessment—which has never been changed as regards land since it was made under the Act of 1852—were directed to collect and note the rates of rent payable. Practically that is the only way in which an assessment could be made, and I think the assessment made in 1852 indicates generally what the rents payable then were, and really the assessment was not made on an estimate of what the land would produce.

5469. Then Griffith's Valuation, though it may be called sound for its purposes, would not be sound as a factor in a calculation comparing the assessment of Ireland with the assessment of Great Britain?—I think in comparing the assessments you must take into account the difference of principle upon which the two assessments were made; but I do not think that Griffith's system, which is not in use in any other civilised country, was a sound one.

5470. In England you have collected some facts as to under-assessment, have you not?—The under-assessment of mansions is a thing that has been repeatedly drawn attention to. Very large mansions that have cost 200,000*l*. or 300,000*l*. are often assessed at less than villas in adjoining towns. That is not the case to the same extent in Ireland. The under-

Mr. R. Barry O'Brien.

27 Dec. 1895.

Assessment specially in Great Britain and Ireland compared.

assessment of land has been especially noticed in the proceedings of the London County Council, and I may mention as an illustration of the immense under-assessment on the large residences that escape from any assessment, the evidence given to the Valuation Committee of the London County Council in 1892. Mr. Harper, a well-known valuer, giving evidence to them, says: "The annual value of all vacant land (in "London) which is not assessed I have put down very "moderately at 1,500,000*l.* annually." The Committee's Report stated that in the parish of Kensington there was vacant land worth for sale 1,750,000*l.* practically not rated at all. In Paddington, he said, there was 300,000*l.* worth not rated at all, and in West Hampstead 1,000,000*l.* worth at least. This is taken from the Report of the Valuation Committee of the London County Council in 1892.

5471. (*Sir David Barbour.*) Was that land producing any income at the time?—It was not, and for that reason it was not rated; but that was estimated to be the saleable value of the land.

5472. (*Chairman.*) How would that compare as to Irish assessment?—I am not aware of any similar cases. For instance, we have not land of that immense value in towns; most Irish towns are decaying.

5473. Summing up the figures to which you have had access, and which you have considered, what do you say as to the amount which should be taken off Schedule A in Ireland, in order to make it compare with the reduction made in Great Britain?—I do not think I am prepared to give any exact figures on the subject, because that could not be got without making a valuation which would represent in each country the actual value of the property. I took these cases for the purpose of comparison, to show that the Irish assessment is higher than the English assessment, which excludes such very large values as these.

5474. I think in your paper you say that 2,000,000*l.* at least should be taken off Schedule A in Ireland?—I say that 2,000,000*l.* at least should be taken off for the fall in the value of agricultural land, to compare with the 13,000,000*l.* that has come off agricultural land in the last thirteen years in England. May I also draw attention to the under assessment of railways? Of course I am not able to compare the railways myself, but I took some public papers and representations made by Mr. Hedley, one of the largest valuers in the North of England, in 1878. Among some of his reports I find he says—"Comparing the valuation and amount of rates payable by "the Dublin, Wicklow, and Wexford Railway, with "the amounts paid by the two largest English Rail-"way Companies, the London and North Western "and the Great Western, it will be seen that the rates "paid or payable by the former are enormously in "excess of the latter, and that the difference is solely "to be attributed to the 'parochial principle' of "rating in England." Comparing different parts of the London and North Western Railway system with Irish Railways, he says, the assessable value of the Dublin, Wicklow, and Wexford Railway, in proportion to the receipts, is eleven times greater than that of the Shrewsbury and Hereford.

5475. (*Mr. Sexton.*) Does that mean that they pay eleven times as much as they would if they were in England?—I give you what he says; I do not know at this moment that I am prepared to interpret it further.

5476. (*Lord Welby.*) You see it turns on a rather curious word "assessable." I think we ought not to jump to the conclusion that it means they paid eleven times more?—I think the meaning of the whole of his whole report is that the Irish railways are assessed higher than the English railways; how much higher I do not think is clear. He gives a few instances, of which this is one.

5477. (*Chairman.*) Of course that instance is a comparison between one of the main lines from the Metropolis in Ireland and an essentially branch line in the country between Shrewsbury and Hereford?—

Mr. R. Barry O'Brien.

27 Dec. 1895.

Assessment specially in Great Britain and Ireland compared.

It is a comparison of one of the least prosperous of Irish lines whose stock has been down under thirty within the last twelve months, with a prosperous branch of the London and North Western Railway.

5478. (*Sir David Barbour.*) This inequality of assessment, I understand, refers only to local rating, and not to assessment to the income tax?—I think the assessment to the income tax for England is largely based on the local ratings.

5479. Would it not be on the profit of the company?—No; there is the rating to the poor rate, and rating to the county rate and the rating to the income tax in England, and practically they are very nearly the same.

5480. (*Mr. Sexton.*) I understand you to be discussing altogether the income tax assessment and nothing else?—The income tax assessment chiefly.

5481. (*The O'Conor Don.*) But is not the income tax upon railways paid upon the dividend, and not upon the valuation?—The real property of the railways is assessed under Schedule A, and they are rated separately for the part of the line in each parish and the stations in each parish. Then they would be rated for income tax on the profits of the railway as well—that would be under a different Schedule. I may also point out that in a later pamphlet showing the under assessment in England, which I think has to be taken into account in comparing the two systems, Mr. Hedley says—"Whilst the strictest "supervision is exercised over expenditure, the "assessment of properties to the rates is seriously "neglected. Whilst the Guardians may not expend "a few shillings contrary to the consolidated orders, "or to the prejudice of the ratepayers, they may, by "neglecting the proper assessment of properties, "prejudice the ratepayers to the extent of many "thousands of pounds." He then points out that in six Unions of Durham, collieries were underrated to the extent of 120,000*l.*; and to show that these irregularities extend to other properties he gives the rents paid and the rateable values in 113 cases in a Union being valued by his firm. In some instances the valuation is one-eleventh of the rent; the rents of the whole lot are 190 per cent. higher than the rateable values—3,943*l.* rental, against 1,359*l.* rateable value.

5482. (*Chairman.*) That is an extract from Mr. Hedley's pamphlet, is it?—It is an extract from the pamphlet published in 1882.

5483. (*The O'Conor Don.*) In connection with what was that pamphlet published?—In connection with rating.

5484. (*Lord Welby.*) To whom was that report made by Mr. Hedley?—It is a publication of Thomas F. Hedley, Surveyor and Valuer, and a Fellow of the Statistical Society.

5485. (*Sir David Barbour.*) It refers only to local taxation, I think?—It refers only to local taxation.

5486. (*The O'Conor Don.*) But the assessment is practically the same for Schedule A under the Income tax, is it not?—Practically the same; there are different deductions made in each case.

5487. (*Mr. Sexton.*) But the assessment which he describes in that book is substantially the income tax assessment, or approximately so, is it not?—Yes, nearly so.

5488. (*Chairman.*) Then I come to the effect of the large amount of absenteeism. How much do you say should be deducted from the Irish assessment, in comparing the wealth of the two countries, in respect of absenteeism?—I think it is impossible to give an estimate exactly of the amount of the absentee drain from Ireland. It has been an economic evil of great magnitude at various times; and various estimates have been made as to the amount. I do not know whether I may quote some of the earlier estimates made in 1729 in a pamphlet published by Prior. The absentee rental was estimated at 627,799*l.* out of a rental of 2,000,000*l.* In Swift's time he estimated

Absenteeism.

Mr. Murrough O'Brien.

12 Dec. 1894.

Absentee rentals.

that one-third of the rents of Ireland were spent in England. Mr. Butler Bryan, who was a member of the House of Commons, I think, estimated before a Committee of the House of Commons in 1830 that 3,000,000*l.* was the amount of the absentee rental. A return was obtained in 1872 on the motion of Mr. Patrick Smith for the purpose of showing the number of absentee landowners in Ireland and the rental. That referred only to rural properties, and that gives substantially as the absentee rental 2,500,000*l.* That does not include the London companies, apparently, in the north of Ireland; it does not include absentee landlords who own property in towns; and the return was known to have been very defective by people who examined it at the time, because there was great difficulty in classing people as absentees. There are many people who have residences in Ireland, but who rarely, if ever, come there, and practically spend their incomes entirely out of this country.

5489. Whether the total amount should be taken at 3,000,000*l.* or 5,000,000*l.*, which appears to be the largest estimated figure, a deduction ought to be made?—Yes. I should take it at 4,000,000*l.*, but I do not think that would exhaust the absentee drain. We know that there are large numbers of people resident in England who hold mortgages on Irish property. Mr. Giffen estimated the amount held by the insurance companies alone at 14,000,000*l.* in 1886; I do not know what means he had of getting at it, but probably, he had some means.

5490. (*The O'Conor Don.*) Do you know by whom that return was made out?—This return was taken, I fancy, from the Valuation Office.

5491. (*Mr. Sexton.*) Would there be any practical difficulty in ascertaining what landlords in Ireland are habitual absentees?—There would be no difficulty whatever in obtaining it if a return was ordered by name. It could be given, of course, by the Valuation Office. They have got what practically amounts to a domesday book, giving the owners of property all through Ireland. That would give some indication, but would not give all, because there are many persons who are returned in their books as owners of property who are paying large head rents to people in England, that is to say, some of these large estates were granted out in perpetuity to residents but part of the proceeds go to pay absentees.

5492. The police could find out, I suppose, as easily as they can find out how much wheat is grown per acre?—I think it could be done approximately. I see that the return is signed by Mr. Greene, a Commissioner of Valuation.

5493. I wish to ask whether you know of any way in which the amount of mortgages upon Irish land or other realty, held by persons living out of Ireland, can be ascertained; is there any register or record from which it could be ascertained?—I do not think there is any public register of mortgages in Ireland that could be used for that purpose.

5494. (*Chairman.*) The residences of the mortgagees are not given in any public document, are they?—I do not think they are; it would be, as far as I know, perfectly impossible to do it.

5495. And it would involve considerations which might lead to great fallacies?—Yes.

Assessments under Schedule D.

5496. Passing to Schedule D, you remark in your paper that a good deal of taxable personal property escapes notice in a great country like England—and a great city like London particularly—which would not escape notice in Irish towns?—I think that is the case in all very large and wealthy communities. There is a greater tendency for assessments which are practically self-made by returns of the owners of the incomes to be concealed, whereas in smaller and less wealthy communities what everybody has is more or less known, and it is more difficult to avoid concealment.

5497. Taking, however, the amount of the income tax assessment, you have calculated the rate of assessment in Ireland in 1890–91 as how much in the pound?—The rate of Imperial taxation in Ireland in 1890–91 was 6*s.* in the pound, while for England and Wales it was only 3*s.* 1*d.*

Alleged over-payment by Ireland.

5498. And you deduce the conclusion from that that Ireland has been paying more than double what she should?—I think she appears to have been paying, certainly of late years, more than double what she would have paid under the Articles of Union.

5499. You make that excess payment about 4,000,000*l.* a year, and you capitalise it at about 300,000,000*l.* sterling?—It comes to a very large sum. If you take 2,000,000*l.* a year, payable for 90 years since the Union, at 3 per cent. compound interest, it would amount to over 1,000,000,000*l.*; and if you take it at 4,000,000*l.* for 30 years at the same rate, it would amount to 190,000,000*l.*

Criterion of the incomes.

5500. There was no tax analogous to the income tax, which Lord Castlereagh said was the best criterion of the relative means of the two countries, till the middle of the century. That now exists and you consider that that criterion is at least, if not a perfect one, one which can be referred to, do you not?—I think they are the only figures we have as to the comparative wealth which are in any way correct figures. As regards the whole of the United Kingdom income tax assessment, except Schedules A and B, the tax is practically assessed in the same manner, and the assessment is probably uniform, except so far as it is more easy in England for incomes to escape taxation.

5501. But for the reason which you give, you say that the aggregate income shown by the produce of such a tax is only a criterion of the taxable property of the wealthy?—That is all. I think it can only be taken to apply to people who have taxable incomes; and if you could ascertain the income of each person in England and each person in Ireland, the two countries could be compared. You cannot do that; but we can with a certain amount of accuracy ascertain the incomes payable by the classes who are above the limit of taxation.

Benefit of Imperial expenditure.

5502. And you lay stress upon the fact that the Irishman receives less benefit from the great items of expenditure per head than an Englishman receives?—I think it is very clear that most of the Imperial expenditure is made for the benefit of Great Britain. Its enormous commerce and industry require an expenditure which Ireland should not be bound to contribute to the same extent as Great Britain.

5503. (*Sir David Barbour.*) Are not there a great many Irishmen engaged in the commerce and industry of Great Britain?—I take it that, as far as Irishmen have gone and settled in England, they become practically Englishmen.

5504. Are not there a great many Irishmen in British dependencies engaged in commerce, trade, and so on?—Nothing like the same proportion that there is of Englishmen. The great mass of the Irish emigrants have gone, as is well known, to the United States, and an Irishman gets no particular advantage if he goes to Australia; a Swede or a German may go there just as well, and become an Australian citizen, and benefit by every advantage that the colony can give him.

5505. Then, taking an English landowner, say, with a thousand a year, in a non-manufacturing district, what advantage has he over an Irish landlord with a thousand a year?—I think that an English landowner must be looked on as one of the English community, and the English community, as a whole, benefit by the Imperial expenditure to a greater extent than Irishmen do.

5506. (*Mr. Sexton.*) You are aware, are you not, that the reference to this Commission is a comparison of the two countries and not of single individuals?—Certainly; but I do not think an Irish landlord does get the same advantages from the Imperial expenditure or from the expenses of legislation in England as an Englishman does.

5507. (*Chairman.*) Going now to the incomes below the income tax line, you say that the average of

Mr. [illegible] O'Brien. 12 Dec. 1895. Migratory labourers. [illegible]

these incomes is much smaller, and that small properties are more rare than in Great Britain; is that the result of a careful calculation?—That appears now to be the case from all the statistics that are available. I have given later on some tables in which I took nearly all the figures in which there was any comparison given in the Statistical Abstract, and I find that in everything the amount per head is less for Ireland than it is in England or Great Britain.

5508. You quote Mr. Little's Report to the Labour Commission as to the wages of agricultural labourers?—I refer to that Report and give the reference, because his report is summarised in the Journal of Agriculture; but that does not take into account a vast number of people who are not earning wages at all. The dearth of employment is so great that a large number of Irish labourers go every year to England. There are returns showing the number of agricultural labourers who are described as migratory, who go every year; but that gives a very insufficient idea of the numbers who actually go, because there are a vast number of people who go who are not agricultural labourers. They go for a month up to six months, and some stay a year or two working at public works, factories, and railway works in England. I notice in the return of migratory labourers that from County Down there are only thirty-four labourers set down as going from that county. I should think there are many parishes that send a great many more migratory labourers—though not necessarily agricultural migratory labourers—to England every year.

Cost of emigration.

5509. You give one figure which a little surprises me. You give 1,000,000*l.* as the amount spent annually on the outfit and passage of the 60,000 or 70,000 emigrants who leave Ireland, that is 15*l.* a head; is not that excessive?—I do not think that is excessive, because, besides the passage and outfit of an emigrant, he generally takes a little money with him. A great number of the emigrants who go out cannot land in New York without a penny in their pocket or they would become paupers.

5510. (*Mr. Sexton.*) They would be sent back now, would they not?—They would be sent back, and in past years, when they were not sent back, it was known it was not safe for a man to go without a penny in his pocket.

Mr. Giffen's statement.

5511. (*Chairman.*) You refer to Mr. Giffen's figure as to the taxable income of Ireland as compared with the taxable income of Great Britain, and to an important conclusion which he draws; do you adopt that conclusion?—Mr. Giffen is much more competent to form an opinion than I am, but the conclusion he comes to seems to be fully borne out by all the figures I have been able to collect.

5512. And that conclusion in a sentence, is what?—What he says is, that the conclusion he came to, writing absolutely from a British point of view, was that Ireland as a poor country was disproportionately taxed, and that although the taxes of the United Kingdom are nominally indiscriminate, nearly the whole taxable income of the Irish people was absorbed by the State, and that under such conditions there could be little accumulation in Ireland.

5513. And the ruling figure of his calculation is that if equality of taxation existed the average Irishman would pay a seventh of the amount paid by the average inhabitant of Great Britain?—Mr. Giffen does not say that, but I draw that conclusion from his figures. He says that the average Irishman's income, which he thinks probably overestimated, is 14*l.* 6*s.* 8*d.*, and the British average income is 33*l.* 7*s.* 8*d.* If you take 10*l.* for the subsistence off each of those incomes, it would leave the Irish taxable income at 4*l.* 6*s.* 8*d.* and the British at 23*l.* 7*s.* 8*d.*; and I think roughly that indicates that if an Irishman paid a seventh of what an inhabitant of Great Britain did, equality of taxation would prevail.

5514. He estimates the average capital at 80*l.* per head in Ireland as against 302*l.* in Great Britain. It must be remembered that since his figures were given Great Britain has rapidly increased in wealth, and Ireland, I think, has become poorer.

Mr. [illegible] O'Brien. 12 Dec. 1895. Taxes on drink.

5515. Passing to taxes on drink, as to which you say there is so great an inequality of taxation, can you put into two sentences your calculation?—The standard of taxation for drink is its alcoholic strength, but that does not apply to beer which is largely drunk in England, and is less so in Ireland. The figures I have taken were taken for the year 1891, and from them it would appear that the duty paid in respect of the spirits drunk per head by Englishmen was 8*s.* 6*d.*, for beer 6*s.* 6*d.*, and 10*d.* for wine. In Scotland it would be 17*s.* 5*d.* for spirits, 1*s.* 8*d.* for beer, and 4½*d.* for wine. In Ireland it would be 11*s.* 3*d.* for spirits, 2*s.* 7*d.* for beer, and 5½*d.* for wine. If taxation was levied on the alcohol in beer at the same rate as on spirits an Englishman would pay 19*s.* 6*d.* instead of 15*s.*; a Scotchman 20*s.* 5*d.* instead of 19*s.* 1*d.*, and an Irishman 27*s.* 11*d.* instead of 14*s.*

5516. You refer to Sir Edward Hamilton's account of the financial relations between Great Britain and Ireland which has been published, and you think Sir Edward Hamilton's objections to the arrangements in 1800 were proved to be well founded?—I think Sir Edward Hamilton's paper shows that clearly, and it does not require any further evidence. It led to the bankruptcy of Ireland.

Causes of poverty in Ireland.

5517. Excessive taxation in your view is one of the causes of the poverty of Ireland. Will you name one or two others?—I think that excessive taxation, by which I mean that 4,000,000*l.* or 5,000,000*l.* a year is taken away from Ireland without any beneficial return, is one cause, and in itself alone would be a cause of poverty, for the resources of Ireland are not very great. But there have been a number of causes co-operating. Another has been the absentee drain which I have already referred to.

5518. You quote Arthur Young with reference to the penal laws, do you not?—Yes, I think the penal laws also had a great effect in the earlier part of the century and that the effects of those laws still remain.

5519. Arthur Young said that the laws discouraging thrift and industry contributed more to prevent progress in Ireland than all the other causes together. "Where," he says "is there a people in the world to "be found industrious in such a circumstance? If a "Catholic should accidentally gain wealth, the whole "Kingdom could not afford him an opportunity of in-"vesting it. These laws were directed," he said, "not against the Catholic religion, but against the "industry and prosperity of whoever professes that "religion. How is agriculture to flourish, manu-"factures to be established, or commerce to extend, "under a system which drove out of the Kingdom all "the personal wealth of the Catholics, and prohibited "their industry within it?" He was a Protestant himself, I think?—I do not know—I believe he was.

Local taxation.

5520. Therefore, what I have just read is stronger evidence as to the past state of things. Then will you go to what you wish to bring before us as criticising Sir Edward Hamilton's statement with regard to local and Imperial expenditure in Ireland which you say is interesting?—Sir Edward Hamilton's figures I think show that, but I do not think his comparison of the local taxation in each country is a fair one, for we do not obtain the same services in quality or quantity as Great Britain does—we have not a reformed Local Government; we have not so extensive a system of municipal government. In roads, streets, bridges, drainage, water supplies, parks, markets, public lighting and libraries, artisans dwellings and municipal enterprise, Ireland is far behind the rest of the Empire.

5521. (*Mr. Sexton.*) Do you think the addition of local taxation to Imperial taxation in relation to this Inquiry has any tendency to be misleading?—I do not know that I have considered that point. I have

Mr. Murrough O'Brien. 15 Dec. 1893.

Cost of Irish administration.

been saying this, that I think the taxation in England is better applied—they get more value for their local taxation than we do, therefore if you compare the amounts you must also compare the services obtained for the taxes paid.

5522. (*Chairman.*) According to the Treasury classification, Irish administration costs more than British, but what are the reasons for that to which you would point?—I think it is clear that Ireland is more distant from the centre of government, and is practically charged with a double set of establishments, in Dublin and in London. But the principal reason is that Ireland is, and always has been, governed in opposition to the wishes of the Irish people, and much of the expenditure charged against Ireland is really for Imperial purposes.

Criticism of tests suggested by Sir E. Hamilton.

5523. Then you repeat your criticism on the tests as given by Sir Edward Hamilton as to the death duties and income tax, and Mr. Giffen's estimates of income and capital, and you state two considerations; will you mention those?—Sir Edward Hamilton's tests of the capacity for taxation are taken from the official statistics for death duties and income tax. In these, I think he should have adjusted the death duties and income tax by allowing for absenteeism, and making an allowance for the difference in the systems of assessment. He also quotes Mr. Giffen's estimate of national capital and income.

Relative cost of living.

5524. As to the relative cost of living in England and Ireland you reply to Sir Edward Hamilton's suggestion that as a matter of fact the Irish working classes have to pay less for necessaries than the English working classes, and that they may therefore have a larger balance for luxuries. How do you deal with that?—Sir Edward Hamilton suggests that if the Irish working classes have smaller incomes, their houses, fuel, clothes, and food cost less than an Englishman's, and that an Irishman, out of 10*s.* or 12*s.* a week, may have more to spend on "luxuries" than an Englishman earning 18*s.* a week. The idea of a labouring man having "a margin to spend as he pleases" out of 10*s.* a week, which is more than an average agricultural wage in Ireland, is ludicrous. As to fuel, English coals are burned over a large part of Ireland, and so far the Irishman's fire costs nearly fifty per cent more than the Englishman's. Arthur Young said turf was the most expensive kind of fuel, and it costs more now to win turf equivalent to a ton of English coal than the coal would cost, except in particularly favourable conditions. An Irishman's house, clothes, and food cost less than an Englishman's, not always less, merely because they are infinitely worse. Nearly every article of common use is imported from England.

5525. And you quote Mr. Senior's remark that Ireland is "a country in which the mass of the people "are worse fed, worse lodged, worse clothed, and worse "paid than in any other country he had visited"?—I think that would apply to Ireland in comparison to almost any of the civilised countries in Europe that I have seen.

5526. And you quote also Arthur Young's sarcastic remark as to cheapness?—I may draw attention with respect to the cost of living to the Report of the Commissioners appointed to inquire into the condition of the Civil Service in Ireland in 1873. They reported that the cost of living was not less in Dublin than in London—"living" including house rent as well as articles of consumption.

5527. (*Mr. Sexton.*) Would you not say that the cost of living is rather more in Dublin than it is in London?—My own experience, gathered from people who have lived in the same way in Dublin or in the suburbs of Dublin, and in London, that is to say, not living in expensive houses in London, is that the cost of living is higher in Dublin than it is in London.

5528. (*Lord Welby.*) Have you any facts upon which you can base that statement, because the information I have does not carry me to the same conclusion, and I should like to know whether you have studied that question, and have based it upon any facts beyond what, no doubt, is your opinion from what you see about you?—No; I refer first to the Report of the Civil Service Commission in 1873, and I also say that people whom I have known living in London and in Dublin have told me that it was dearer living in Dublin or the suburbs of Dublin than it was living in London in a house of the same kind.

Mr. Murrough O'Brien. 15 Dec. 1893.

Relative cost of living.

Consumption of dutiable articles.

5529. (*Chairman.*) You dispute Sir Edward Hamilton's test derived from the per head expenditure on tea, tobacco, spirits, and beer, and you say in the first instance that he omits wine. Does that make very much difference?—It is not large; but if the articles of consumption are to be taken as a test I think that all articles should be taken, and it affects his test to some extent, but I think the test is entirely unfair.

5530. (*Sir David Barbour.*) Do you think that in fixing the rate of taxation for spirits, beer, and wine, regard should be had to the quantity of alcohol, and to nothing else?—I do not think so, but I say that alcohol is apparently taken as the test. Spirituous liquors and wines are practically taxed according to the amount of alcohol in them, but a notable exception is made in the case of beer and porter.

5531. Do you think there ought to be no exception in the case of beer and porter?—I think I would take into account in estimating the financial capacity of Ireland and England, that the Englishman's drink is practically exempt as compared with the Irishman's drink. Nearly half the revenue of the country comes from drink.

5532. (*Mr. Sexton.*) Are you aware that the disparity is as great in relation to price as to alcoholic strength?—No, I have not taken that into account.

Public loans.

5533. (*Chairman.*) Then as to the argument as to liberality to Ireland in the matter of loans, how do you meet that?—I think that the loans which have been made are to a large extent a concession to the complaint of Ireland that she was over taxed, and they were also made to Irish local governing bodies, because they had not the same power as English bodies have for raising funds on their own security. An instance of that is the Dublin Corporation. For many years, until they got an Act passed in Parliament, they were unable to consolidate their loans. Of late years many of the towns and townships have had the power of raising money on their own account, and have been able to do so; but I think the principle of making loans, very often at a rate of interest higher than what the Imperial Treasury might lend at, is an exceedingly bad one, and leads to an enormous drain. I may take as an instance, perhaps, the loans made on the security of the Church Fund. The Church Fund loans vary in amount, because they have been paid off; but at present the church property is paying on about 4,000,000*l.* to the National Debt Commissioners three and a-half and three and a-quarter per cent. In fact the interest on the loans outstanding on the 31st of March, 1891, at three and a-half and three and a-quarter per cent. is 148,343*l.* If that money was lent as it might be—the security being ample, because a large part of the debt has been paid off—at two and a-half per cent., the amount would only be 107,536*l.*, that is to say, there is 40,000*l.* a year being taken to pay interest at a rate that is over the market rate for public money. These loans were made for public purposes, or to some extent for charity.

5534. (*Mr. Sexton.*) We had it stated yesterday that all the Treasury loans to Ireland carry an average rate of 3*l.* 11*s.* for interest, amounting in all to 8,000,000*l.*?—I think this is a particularly bad case, because the National Debt Commissioners are paid three and a-half per cent., and have been paid it from the very beginning. The loans amounted to 9,000,000*l.* at one time, and the rate of interest was higher. But when it comes to making a grant out of the same fund to the Congested Districts Board, all they get on the 1,500,000*l.* allotted to them is two and three-quarters per cent.

5535. Do the National Debt Commissioners take the difference?—The National Debt Commissioners got three and a-half and three and a-quarter per cent. on the loans they have made on the security of the Church Fund, but the Congested Districts Board, to which 1,500,000*l.* was allotted, get two and three-quarters per cent. on that, which reduces their income by the figure you have had already.

5536. (*Mr. Sexton.*) It reduces their income by one-half per cent. on 1,500,000*l.*?—I do not suppose the money is worth two and three-quarters per cent., and my argument is that we should only pay the National Debt Commissioners two and a half or two and three-quarters per cent., which would make a difference of 40,000*l.* a year to the Church Fund.

5537. (*Chairman.*) Do you think the interest in that sense should be regulated by the state of the market?—I think the rate of interest on loans made by the Imperial Treasury for what are practically public purposes, and for purposes that affect the peace and security of the Empire, as many of these loans have, should be made at the lowest possible rate. I think that the rate of 3½ per cent. probably was a fair rate when this loan was contracted, but it has long since ceased to be so; and if the rate had been reduced the Irish Church Fund would have had 40,000*l.* or 50,000*l.* a year more for the past few years.

5538. On the other hand, if the value of money in that sense had been very much increased you would not have been favourable to raising the rate, would you?—That case has not occurred, but I think very often these loans are so much money misspent, and leave Ireland in debt to England. For instance, the money lent on the security of the Church Fund to buy potato seed, when there has been a potato famine, has practically been thrown away, as far as any remuneration goes, because the potato seed cost so much in a year of distress that the crop in the following year was worth little, or no more than the amount of the seed put into the ground in the year of distress and scarcity.

5539. You sum up this part of your case by saying that Great Britain is increasing in population and wealth, whilst Ireland is decreasing in population and probably in wealth, and that if allowance were to be made for the present over-assessment under Schedule A, it would be found that Ireland's assessment has increased hardly or not at all, but at the same time Great Britain's assessment has increased by nearly double?—It has doubled.

5540. As regards Ireland's assessments under Schedules A and B, you refer to the fact that 1844 was a year of low prices. What conclusion do you draw from that?—I refer to the year 1844 because that was the year in which a Committee sat on the same subject I believe. Ireland's assessment was then brought into the inquiry. The assessment of land has not changed since then, but the prices of produce have fallen enormously. I give you the fall of prices, taken from the past record of prices. I quote Barrington's farm prices. Store cattle have fallen 32 per cent.; fat cattle, 23·5 per cent.; sheep, 31·7 per cent.; mutton, 22·5 per cent.; beef, 31 per cent.; butter, 18 per cent.; pork, 20·5 per cent.; flax, 39 per cent.; wheat, 20 per cent.; and barley, 22 per cent. Oats have increased slightly. These are the falls up to the year 1893, and since then prices are, I think, on the whole lower. Mr. F. A. [illegible] 13 Dec. 1894. Fall of prices.

5541. You give your opinion that the amount per head of income, property, and business transacted are much better tests of the capacity of a nation for taxation than the amounts per head consumed of such common articles of use as tea, tobacco, spirits, and beer. Do you adhere to that view?—I think, referring to Sir Edward Hamilton's tests, that property is a better test of wealth than a man's consumption of articles of common use, which he must have. Property a better test of wealth than consumption.

5542. That is to say, you adopt what appears to have been Mr. Pitt's view at the time of the Union?—I am sorry to say I am not acquainted with that view.

5543. You then put in four tables, which are long and interesting. What are the salient points upon those tables to which you wish to call our attention?—I may explain that I thought the only way of comparing the property and wealth of the two countries was to take the figures given in the Statistical Abstracts so as to get comparative figures. Table I. shows the proportion of Irish income and property per head to be 0·38*l.* to 1·1*l.* of the United Kingdom, and that the average Irish income is about one-third per head of the average English income. Table II. gives a comparison of the business and wealth of England and Ireland. Table III. the amount of revenue contributed by England and Ireland; and Table IV. the population of England, Scotland, Ireland, and the United Kingdom in 1892. Tables of comparison.

5544. That is a summary of the results of the four tables. Is there any particular item in them in addition to those summary results to which you would like to call our attention?—I do not know that I am at this moment prepared to make any other remarks; I simply give you the figures.

The tables were handed in, and are as follows:—

I.—COMPARISON of NET INCOME TAX ASSESSMENTS and RECEIPTS in the UNITED KINGDOM, ENGLAND, and IRELAND; the Amount per head of Population in England and Ireland (Inland Revenue Report to 31st March, 1893); Increase or Decrease since 1879 of Gross Assessments (Statistical Abstract, 41st No.); Income Tax and Death Duty Receipts for five years (Parl. Paper, 1893).

	United Kingdom.	England.	Ireland.	Proportion Ireland to U.K.	Per Head.		Increase or Decrease in Gross Assessments since 1879.	
					England.	Ireland.	England.	Ireland.
	£	£	£		£	£	Per cent.	Per cent.
Schedule A.	173,603,714	[illegible]	12,714,727	1 to 14	[illegible]	[illegible]	+ 129	+ [illegible]
" B.	[illegible]	[illegible]	2,436,[illegible]	1 " [illegible]	[illegible]	[illegible]	− 15	Nil.
" C.	[illegible]	[illegible]	[illegible]	1 " [illegible]	179	[illegible]	Not given separately	
" D.	[illegible]	[illegible]	[illegible]	1 " [illegible]	[illegible]	[illegible]	+ [illegible]	+ [illegible]
" E.	[illegible]	[illegible]	1,740,[illegible]	1 " [illegible]	[illegible]	[illegible]	Not given separately	
Total	[illegible]	[illegible]	[illegible]	1 to [illegible]	[illegible]	[illegible]	+ [illegible]	+ [illegible]
	£	£	£		£	£		
Assessments of Houses and Mortgages.	[illegible]	[illegible]	5,715,[illegible]	1 to [illegible]	[illegible]	[illegible]	+ [illegible]	+ [illegible]
Net Receipts, Income, and Property Tax, 1892–3.	[illegible]	[illegible]	[illegible]	1 " [illegible]	[illegible]	[illegible]		
Do. for five years, 1889 to 1893. Parl. Paper, [illegible]	[illegible]	Great Britain, [illegible]	[illegible]	1 " [illegible]				
Death Duties for five years, 1889–93. Parl. Paper, [illegible]	[illegible]	[illegible]	[illegible]	1 " [illegible]	[illegible]	[illegible]		

EXCHEQUER REVENUE contributed by ENGLAND and IRELAND respectively, as given by Parl. Paper 334/93, for year to 31st March, 1893, and the Estimated Revenue for year to 31st March, 1893 (Parl. Paper 115/94), and the poundage which the Revenue for 1892–3 amounts to on the Income Tax Assessment of each Country.

	England.	Ireland.	United Kingdom.
	£	£	£
Revenue contributed, 1892–3. Parl. Paper 334, 1893.	71,[illegible]	7,384,184	80,153,[illegible]
Poundage Rate on Income Tax Assessments.	2s. 9d.	1s. 6d.	3s.
	£	£	£
Estimated Revenue, 1893–4,	74,[illegible] 000	7,729,000	84,175,000

II.—COMPARISON of the WEALTH and PROGRESS of ENGLAND and IRELAND from the principal tables in which separate accounts are given for these countries in the Statistical Abstract (41st Number, 1894). The figures are taken from the last year given in the Abstract.

Table in Stat. Abstract.	Property Assessed, &c.	United Kingdom.	England.	Ireland.	Ireland's Proportion to U.K.	Per Head. England.	Per Head. Ireland.
	Value of Property Assessed under D Income, &c.	£ 000 omitted.	£ 000 omitted.	£ 000 omitted.		£	£
[illegible]	1. Professions Only.	[illegible]	[illegible]	[illegible]	1 to [illegible]	[illegible]	[illegible]
	2. [illegible] Only.	[illegible]	[illegible]	[illegible]	1 to [illegible]	[illegible]	[illegible]
[illegible]	Post Office Savings Bank Capital,	£ [illegible]	£ [illegible]	£ [illegible]	1 to [illegible]	[illegible]	[illegible]
[illegible]	Trustee Savings Bank Capital,	[illegible]	[illegible]	[illegible]	1 to [illegible]	[illegible]	[illegible]
[illegible]	Government Stock held for Depositors in Trustee Banks,	[illegible]	[illegible]	[illegible]	1 to [illegible]	[illegible]	[illegible]
[illegible]	No. of Accounts P. O. Banks.	No. [illegible]	No. [illegible]	No. [illegible]	1 to [illegible]	[illegible] persons.	[illegible] persons.
[illegible]	Do. Trustee Banks.	No. [illegible]	No. [illegible]	No. [illegible]	1 to [illegible]	[illegible] persons.	[illegible] persons.
[illegible]	Railway Capital,	£ [illegible]	£ [illegible]	£ [illegible]	1 to [illegible]	£ [illegible]	£ [illegible]
[illegible]	Net Receipts,	[illegible]	[illegible]	[illegible]	1 to [illegible]	[illegible]	[illegible]
[illegible]	Registered Companies — Paid-up Capital,	[illegible]	[illegible]	[illegible]	1 to [illegible]	[illegible]	[illegible]
[illegible]	Building Societies' Liabilities,	[illegible]	[illegible]	[illegible]	1 to [illegible]	[illegible]	[illegible]
[illegible]	Industrial and Provident Societies' Capital,	[illegible]	[illegible]	[illegible]	1 to [illegible]	[illegible]	[illegible]
[illegible]	Licenses Collected,	[illegible]	[illegible]	[illegible]	1 to [illegible]	[illegible]	[illegible]
[illegible]	Tonnage of Shipping of Ports entered at Principal Ports,	Tons. [illegible]	Tons. [illegible]	Tons. [illegible]	1 to [illegible]	Tons. [illegible]	Tons. [illegible]

Mr. [illegible] O'Brien. 12 Dec. 1895. Tables of statistics.

III.—Amount of Revenue contributed by England and Ireland in 1892-3 in respect of Stamps and the several Income Tax Schedules: the Proportion of Ireland's Contribution to the total U.K. Revenue under these heads, and the amount per head of population contributed by England and Ireland in thousandths of £1. Parl. Paper 334 93.

No. of Table in P.P. 334.	Head.	Amount Contributed by: United Kingdom.	England.	Ireland.	Ireland's Proportion to U.K.	Amount per Head in £'ths: England.	Ireland.
	Stamps.	£	£	£			
5	Probate Duty,	[illegible]	[illegible]	[illegible]	1 in [illegible]	[illegible]	[illegible]
6	Legacy Duty,	[illegible]	[illegible]	[illegible]	1 in [illegible]	[illegible]	[illegible]
7	Succession Duty,	[illegible]	[illegible]	[illegible]	1 in [illegible]	[illegible]	[illegible]
8	General Stamps,	[illegible]	[illegible]	[illegible]	1 in [illegible]	[illegible]	[illegible]
9	Total Stamps,	[illegible]	[illegible]	[illegible]	1 in [illegible]	[illegible]	[illegible]
	Income Tax.	£	£	£			
11	Schedules A and B,	[illegible]	[illegible]	[illegible]	1 in [illegible]	[illegible]	[illegible]
12	Schedules C, D, and Government Stocks, Public Companies, Dividends, &c.	[illegible]	[illegible]	[illegible]	1 in [illegible]	[illegible]	[illegible]
13	Schedule D—Trades and Professions,	[illegible]	[illegible]	[illegible]	1 in [illegible]	[illegible]	[illegible]
14	Schedule E—Public Offices and Salaries,	[illegible]	[illegible]	[illegible]	1 in [illegible]	[illegible]	[illegible]
15	Total Income Tax,	[illegible]	[illegible]	[illegible]	1 in [illegible]	[illegible]	[illegible]

IV.—Population of England, Scotland, Ireland, and the United Kingdom in 1893, with percentage of total Population, and Increase or Decrease since 1879 (Statistical Abstract, 1894, 41st No.).

—	England.	Scotland.	Ireland.	United Kingdom.
Population,	30,060,763	4,124,691	4,593,677	38,778,031
Proportion of Population of United Kingdom,	77·5%	10·6%	11·9%	100
Variation since 1879,	+18·6%	+11·0%	−11·6%	+11·8

Proportion to Population in England, Scotland, and Ireland of Births, Deaths, Marriages, Emigrants, Police, Committals, and Convictions (Statistical Abstract, 1894, 41st No.) in 1893.

—	England.	Scotland.	Ireland.
Births,	1 in 33·5	1 in 33·3	1 in 43·5
Deaths,	1 in 53·9	1 in 51·6	1 in 55·4
Marriages,	1 in 137	1 in 153	1 in 211
Emigrants,	1 in 231	1 in 183	1 in 98
Police,	1 to 730	1 to 923	1 to 343
Committals for Trial,	1 in 2444	1 in 1781	1 in 2081
Convictions,	1 in 3065	1 in 2166	1 in 3335

5545. (*Mr. Sexton.*) Will you look at your Table No. IV. It appears from that table that the number of police in England is 1 to 730 of the population; in Scotland, 1 to 923; and in Ireland, 1 to 343?—Yes.

5546. With regard to births, deaths, and marriages, it appears that in Ireland now the marriage rate is more than one-third less than it is in either England or Scotland; that the birth rate is about one-third lower than in England or in Scotland, and that the death rate is pretty nearly the same?—The death rate is a little lower for that year, but for the previous year it was higher.

5547. Ireland was once regarded, and was in fact,

I believe, in the last generation, a country where the people married early?—For the last three or four Censuses the Commissioners have drawn attention to the fact that early marriages are exceedingly rare in Ireland. I do not know whether that was gone into in the earlier years of the Census, but if you refer to the last two or three reports you will find that statement.

5548. In England it is given in your table as 1 in 137; in Scotland, 1 in 152; and in Ireland, 1 in 211?—It is something like that. I have given at the end of the paper another estimate taken from the Return of the Registrar-General of England of the number of persons married in the three countries. That appears on the last page of my paper.

5549. You give there the average number of persons married, of births and of deaths to each thousand persons living in the twenty years from 1871 to 1891, and it shows that out of every thousand persons in England 15·6 were married in that time; in Scotland, 13·9; and in Ireland only 9 per cent.?—Yes; I think that puts it clearer.

5550. Taking a period of twenty years the average per year was in Ireland more than one-third less than it was in Scotland, and more than two-fifths less than in England?—Yes, it is something like that.

5551. (*Sir David Barbour.*) May I ask if the marriage-rate would not be affected by the large emigration from Ireland?—Certainly, that is one of the causes.

5552. The birth-rate also appears from the last page of your paper to be as much lower than the birth-rate of England and Scotland as the marriage-rate. The births were 34·0 in England; 33·6 in Scotland; and only 24·0 in Ireland?—That is so.

5553. The birth-rate approximates more nearly to the birth-rate in England and Scotland than the marriage-rate does; is not that so?—I think so.

5554. (*Chairman.*) Coming again to the question of comparing the Irish income tax assessment with that of England, would you sum up, as you do on page 16 of your paper, the result from your point of view?—I have given an estimate of the way in which, I think, the income-tax assessment should be adjusted in order to arrive at a proper comparison of the wealth so far as is indicated by that of England and Ireland. I think a fourth should come off Schedules A and B, partly for the over-assessment of Ireland in comparison with Great Britain, and partly to correspond with the reduction of 13,000,000*l.* that has come off the assessment of land in Great Britain in the last twelve years. These would bring Schedules A and B to 11,278,820*l.* From this I should take off 4,000,000*l.* (that is, as far as I can judge, an under-estimate) for the absentee rental and drain, leaving the net amount for A and B, 7,278,821*l.*, and making the adjusted total 16,000,000*l.* odd.

5555. (*Mr. Sexton.*) What about the interest on mortgages?—I am unable to form any opinion of what the amount would be. The only figure I am aware of is Mr. Giffen's estimate of 14,000,000*l.*, as representing the mortgages held by English Insurance Companies in Ireland.

5556. What I want to make clear is that you are not allowing for it here?—I do not think that the 4,000,000*l.* would allow for the mortgages, because we have no means of ascertaining them except that. Besides mortgages, there are, of course, a number of annuitants on Irish estates, living in England, which would not appear as mortgages, but so far as that remittance of absentee rent goes to England, we get nothing for it except a bundle of rent receipts.

5557. (*Lord Welby.*) Are you aware that of late years the number of such mortgages to which you refer has steadily diminished. I am speaking of course of Irish mortgages held by the Insurance Companies?—I am sure they are diminishing as rapidly as they possibly can, because the companies press on the sales of estates on which they have mortgages if they think there is any possibility of calling their mortgages in.

5558. I only note in passing, that the information I have received is that that number of mortgages to which Mr. Sexton has referred has very much diminished?—I apprehend they would call them all in if they could.

5559. (*Mr. Sexton.*) Lord Welby may not be aware that there are a couple of thousand estates in the Incumbered Estates Court, which cannot be sold, and it would be hard, I should think, for any English company to realise its mortgage?—Very hard, because even if they hold the first mortgage the estate will not be sold unless the ———— Judge and the later mortgagees consent.

5560. (*Chairman.*) Then on page 20 of your paper you say that the extent of over taxation, though the thing itself is obvious, is very difficult to estimate?—I do not think any exact estimate can be made, though it is quite clear to my mind that Ireland has been over taxed for many years.

5561. You give the causes of that over taxation and speak of the excessive cost of British administration, but you do not feel able to give us what in your opinion would be the fair proportion of taxation if the whole facts were arrived at?—I did not think it was my province to give an actual figure. I cannot say I have no opinion on the subject, but, I think, before arriving at any figure, it would be desirable to have as much further information as can be got as to the absentee drain.

5562. Possibly such further information may to a certain extent result from this Inquiry?—Certainly.

5563. You say that no adjustment is possible unless the past overpayments are taken into consideration?—I think the overpayments through taxation have been a very potent cause of the existing Irish poverty; and one cause of the perpetual difficulty with Ireland is her poverty. Mr. Giffen, in the article which I have referred to, holds that that is the entire cause of the discontent in Ireland, and evidently the abstraction of 4,000,000*l.* or 5,000,000*l.* a year from a poor country like this would be quite sufficient to keep it poor.

5564. Then on the question of expenditure I gather from your paper that you do not concur in the opinion that Ireland is as much interested in a strong navy as Great Britain?—Ireland having practically no commerce, I do not think does require a navy, and before the Union I believe she had no navy, and did not contribute to the English Navy.

5565. But with reference to the present state and condition of things under which Great Britain and Ireland depend for the supply of food from abroad, and the necessity for a strong navy, you do not think that applies to Ireland because Ireland would gain by exporting to England a large amount of food at a high price?—Anything that closed the ports of the world to England would be an advantage to Ireland, as, owing to her proximity to England, we could probably send food there.

5566. Do you think that under any conceivable state of politics such a principle could be adopted in settling the strength of the military and naval forces?—Certainly; I think the reasonable way to settle Ireland's contribution would be to estimate either what proportion of the Imperial revenue she should pay, and let her pay that, or adjust it from time to time according to circumstances.

5567. You compare with Great Britain and Ireland the arrangements in force as to Sweden and Norway, do you not?—Sweden appears to me of all European countries, to be that most similar in its population and circumstances to Ireland. The population is 4,784,981. Sweden has a good deal of commerce and mineral wealth, and a considerable trade. Her revenue is under 5,400,000*l.*; her army costs 1,148,000*l.* and her navy 342,000*l.*, both together about as much as the Irish police cost. Norway, with a population somewhat less than half Ireland's, namely 2,001,000, has a revenue of 2,800,000*l.* Her army costs 436,000*l.*; her navy 144,000*l.* These two countries have a larger amount of merchant shipping than any European country

Mr. Murrough O'Brien. 13 Dec. 1895.

Comparison with Sweden and Norway.

except Great Britain. Comparing Ireland's condition with these countries, it must be remembered that Ireland has neither shipping commerce, or neighbours against whom it would be necessary to keep up armies and navies.

5568. (*Sir David Barbour.*) Have you compared the scale of taxation in those in Sweden and Norway with the scale of taxation in force in Ireland?—I do not quite understand what you mean by the scale of taxation, but I should take Sweden to be pretty much of the same value as Ireland—that is to say, the capital value of real property in Sweden is estimated at about 220,000,000*l.* That would be somewhat more than any estimate made of the capital value of Ireland.

5569. By the scale of taxation I mean the rate of duty on property and the rate of duty on articles of common consumption?—That is to say, the proportions in which these different subjects contribute to the revenue?

5570. No, the rate of duty, say on spirits in the two countries respectively, and on tobacco and tea?—I have not done so, but there is a very recent report on the finances of Sweden from the Foreign Office, which probably gives that information.

Summary of conclusions.

5571. (*Chairman.*) Let me give shortly your summing up. First of all as to the causes of Ireland's poverty, you think it is "over taxation," "drain of "absentee rental," "bad laws, chiefly those which "have prevented agricultural improvement and enter-"prise, and now maintain a system of land tenure "under which no prudent person, whether landlord "or tenant, ought to lay out money in the permanent "improvement of land"; and "the fall in agricultural "prices and farm profits." That is your summary on page 311?—Yes.

5572. Then you mention as the symptoms of poverty: "A continually diminishing population," "decaying towns and villages," "emigration," "mi-"gration of labourers for temporary employment to "Great Britain and the United States," "annually "recurring distress, and periodical famines"; "per-"sistent and unabated social and political discontent," "the appearance of the mass of people—their houses, "clothes and food"?—Yes; that is my summary of what I conceive to be the causes and symptoms of Ireland's poverty.

5573. You say you doubt whether Ireland has increased in wealth during the last thirty years, and that the symptom of increased prosperity per head and the diminishing population is no evidence of real increase of prosperity?—That is so.

5574. (*Mr. Sexton.*) And you do not at all accept the system of adding up animals and dividing them over per head of the people as a proof of the prosperity of the country, do you?—I do not think that indicates prosperity at all, because it may indicate that a country is reverting to the state of an American ranche as part of Meath has.

5575. (*Chairman.*) Then you say that "No poor "agricultural country such as Ireland could stand "the continued drain of excessive taxation she has "been subjected to, and of remittances to absentees "without the economic effects of such remunerative "payments becoming evident," and you give reasons for that which I will not go into now. Then you say, as to Ireland's chief industry, farming, she suffers far more than England from the agricultural depression which is now prevalent everywhere?—I think she suffers quite as much as England does, for the distress of the agriculturist is admitted and evident; there is no reason why she should not.

Mr. Murrough O'Brien. 13 Dec. 1895.

Advantages of English farmers.

5576. And you then set out in great detail the natural advantages which the English farmer has over the Irish farmer, which enables him to treat a time of agricultural depression more effectively than an Irishman?—Yes; owing to the large urban population, the English farmer has better markets within easy reach, and his produce is worth more than the Irish farmer's at the points of final consumption, the large English towns; for the Irish farmer has to bear the cost and risk of carriage. The English farmer has a more abundant supply of manure from the large towns and villages, and can, therefore, farm more highly and grow heavier crops. He can get his feeding stuffs, artificial manures, agricultural implements and appliances, more cheaply than the Irish farmer, for most of these things are imported to Ireland from England. Above all the English farmer rents his land fairly equipped with buildings, roads, gates, fences, and thoroughly drained. The farm equipments are renewed and maintained by the landowners, often out of other resources than the rental of the agricultural estate.

5577. You point out that in England to a great extent improvements fall on the landlord, whereas in Ireland almost exclusively they fall on the tenant, and this in the time of depression is very much to the disadvantage of the tenant, irrespective of other considerations. I have put it very shortly, but that, I think, is the purport of the paragraph at the end of page 224?—Yes.

5578. You point out that the farm buildings are usually frail and thatched, costly to maintain, uncomfortable and unhealthy for man and beast; that the farms are imperfectly fenced, insufficiently drained, without gates or proper farm roads. The cost of production is, therefore, much more to the Irish farmer, and is much more onerous, particularly in bad times, than it is to the English farmer; and you wind up with a sentence which perhaps you would like to read?—Yes. I say: "It is no wonder then "that Irish farms and homesteads have deteriorated "in condition and repair, for the farmer has had less "to spend in maintaining them. It is an arithmetical "impossibility that the volume of business in country "towns should not have decreased, for both landowners "and farmers have had very much smaller incomes to "spend of late years, and the fall in price of articles of "common consumption has not been so great as to "counterbalance the fall in profits of the landed interest."

Physical ability compared.

5579. You say that the physical ability of the population, as well as their occupation, counts for much in measuring their means of wealth and capacity for taxation—that the population of Ireland is mainly rural, and should be more robust than the urban population of England, but that the reverse is really the case, and that the annual elimination by emigration of the most able and enterprising part of the population is one of the causes of this; and you say that this is shown by the larger proportion in Ireland of blind, deaf mutes, and insane or idiotic persons, and by the proportion of persons living who are over sixty-five years of age; for, though the absolute proportions of the latter are almost the same in England and Ireland, a more proper comparison would be between Ireland and the rural districts of England?—Yes. "The following figures, from the general report of the "Census for England gives a comparison of the civil "condition, occupations, infirmities, and pauperism in "the three divisions of the United Kingdom, and the "figures from the Registrar General's report show "the average births, deaths, and marriages for twenty "years, to 1882."

The following table is handed in :—

Mr. Murrough O'Brien.

21 Dec. 1894.

Physical and other comparisons.

Condition or Occupation.		England.		Scotland.		Ireland.	
		Males.	Females.	Males.	Females.	Males.	Females.
Single,	Proportions per 1,000 living.	620	596	663	631	696	641
Married,		345	329	304	290	265	262
Widowed,		35	75	33	79	39	97
Professional,		33		38		44	
Domestic,		66		30		31	
Commercial,		48		45		29	
Agricultural and Fishing,		46		63		200	
Industrial,		353		356		140	
Unoccupied,		355		359		545	
Persons sixty-five years old and upwards at Census, 1891, per 1,000 living.	Urban districts.	40·1		Not ascertained.		47·2	
	Rural districts.	65·6					
Blind,	Proportion per 1,000,000 living.	809		695		1,186	
Deaf and Dumb,		493		538		718	
Mentally deranged,		3,356		3,341		4,904	
In receipt of indoor relief,		6,200		2,834		9,029	
In Prison,		587		656		481	

5580. (*The O'Conor Don.*) May I ask you whether you have seen the return given to us by Mr. Milner of the assessments under different schedules of the income tax?—I have seen it, but I have not examined it, because it came to me after I prepared that paper, which I had to do in rather a hurry.

5581. If you have that return it would be desirable probably to consider it before the Commission examine you again?—Certainly.

5582. You will see in the first column that the assessment on "lands" in England and Wales was at its highest point in 1880, and that since then to the present day, the reduction is, I think, 20 per cent.?—Yes; I have taken the figures as to the reduction from the Inland Revenue Reports from year to year.

5583. I wish to ask you one question, which has nothing to do with the statistics you have given (but it struck me rather as a strange statement) with regard to the advances that were made for the purchase of seed potatoes in 1879. I understood you to say that you considered that that was a waste of money?—I think it was, from an economic point of view, an unremunerative expenditure of money. I do not say that particularly of 1879, because there have been many seed loans, but in some years the cost of the potato seed, for which the individual or the union goes in debt, has amounted to as much as the whole crop would have been worth in the following year, but the repayment of the loans continues a debt on the union or the individual for years; therefore I say that it increases the poverty. In the time of distress and famine the proper thing to do is either to tax the locality, if it will bear taxation, which some localities will not bear, or give to support life, but not to lend when a man is in distress, and say to him—"No, I will "not give you anything, but I will lend you 10*l.* at 4 "per cent. and you shall pay it off in so many years." I do not think that is wise.

Seed loans.

5584. (*Lord Welby.*) Those seed loans were made without interest, and a loan without interest is a boon, is it not?—Just so.

5585. (*The O'Conor Don.*) Was not the advance made partly with the object of getting a new class of seed into the country?—In 1889 the champion potatoes were introduced; they cost 10*l.* to 15*l.* a ton, and according to the Registrar-General's figures, the return from an acre of potatoes would not be more than four tons per acre. The four tons per acre in the following year would not be worth as much as the seed cost the year before, when the seed was at its highest price.

Adjourned *sine die.*

Mr. Murrough O'Brien's evidence is continued at Question 9489 (Fifteenth Day).

THIRTEENTH DAY.

Thursday, 21st February, 1895.

At B Committee Room, House of Lords.

PRESENT.

THE RIGHT HON. HUGH C. E. CHILDERS, *Chairman*.

LORD FARRER.	BERTRAM W. CURRIE, Esq.
The Right Hon. THE O'CONOR DON.	THOMAS SEXTON, Esq., M.P.
Sir THOMAS SUTHERLAND, K.C.M.G., M.P.	HENRY F. SLATTERY, Esq.
Sir DAVID BARBOUR, K.C.S.I.	

Mr. B. H. HOLLAND, *Secretary*.

Mr. J. G. BARTON, M.I.C.E., F.S.I., called and examined.

Mr. J. G. Barton. 21 Feb. 1895.

5586. (*Chairman.*) Will you tell the Commission the title of your office?—The office I administer is the Valuation Office and Boundary Survey Office of Ireland.

5587. How long have you been in that position?—Between two and three years—two years and eight months.

5588. And before that I think you were in the public service?—I was connected with the Board of Works for some time previously.

System of rating before 1830.

5589. Before the year 1830 can you tell us what the general system of the applotment of the grand jury cess was to the local rates?—It varied in different counties, but the general system was somewhat as follows:—After each assize the sum to be levied on the whole county was divided amongst the several baronies according to the computed area of each. This was further divided amongst the town lands, or plough lands, according to their calculated area, which was in many cases incorrect.

Valuation of 1830.

5590. When was the first Government Valuation of Ireland for the purposes of rating made?—It commenced in the year 1830 and was completed, with the exception of six counties, in the year 1846.

5591. In this valuation what was the unit valued?—There was a scale of agricultural prices on which the valuation was based.

5592. (*Mr. Sexton.*) The town land was the unit?—Yes, the town land was the unit.

5593. (*Chairman.*) And the valuation was based upon certain prices, was it not?—Yes.

5594. Will you mention those prices?—Wheat at 10s. per cwt., oats at 6s., barley 7s., potatoes 1s. 7d., butter 65s., beef 33s., mutton 34s. 6d., pork 32s. 6d.

5595. Were those the average agricultural prices at that time?—They were the average agricultural prices in certain maritime markets of Ireland.

5596. What was Sir Richard Griffiths' main object in settling that principle at that time?—His object was to make the valuation as far as possible relative, so that valuations made in different parts of the country at different times should be relative one to the other.

5597. What was the character of the instructions given to the valuers at that time?—Generally that they should value the land on a liberal scale, that is to say, as if to be let to solvent tenants on leases for 21 years. The soil and subsoil were to be examined in each case. Land of the same quality in the same locality, though badly farmed, was to be valued at the same rate as similar land well farmed, clean, and in good order, but all the permanent improvements, such as drains, fencing, roads, &c., were to be taken into consideration, so that the industrious farmer who tilled and manured his land well should not be taxed more than his indolent neighbour, similarly circumstanced, who did not take advantage of his situation. The valuation being a permanent one, due regard was to be paid to temporary deterioration. Grass lands were to be valued as such and at a price per acre proportional to the number of cattle, sheep, &c., they were capable of grazing; the usual prices per head paid in the neighbourhood being taken into consideration. Allowances were to be made for local circumstances, such as altitude, access to quarries, seaweed, &c., and vicinity to towns.

Mr. J. G. Barton. 21 Feb. 1895. Valuation of 1830.

5598. As to buildings, what was the valuation of those?—It was to be determined by measurements, and where the rent was ascertainable that was to be ascertained. The Act provided that all houses were to be valued at the rent for which each could be let by the year, deducting therefrom one-third of such rent, and further, no house of an annual value less than 5*l.* was to be included in the valuation lists. This deduction of one-third of the rent was doubtless intended to cover the cost of maintenance and repairs, and the taxes. Mills and factories were to be included in the valuation lists, but water power was not to be valued, except in so far as actually used, nor was machinery to be rated.

5599. Public property was exempt, was it not?—Public property was exempt, and property used for charitable purposes was exempt.

5600. Were the results of the valuation published?—They were published and issued to each of the counties as completed.

5601. Was there any machinery for appeals from valuations?—There was; the machinery was as follows:—Any vestry or barony dissatisfied with the valuation could appeal to a committee nominated by the grand jury in accordance with the terms of the Acts, and this committee might confirm, amend, or order a re-valuation of the lands regarding which the objection was raised.

5602. When was the valuation commenced, and where?—In 1830 it was commenced, in the north. Londonderry and Tyrone were the first counties valued, and then it gradually worked down south.

5603. When did it stop?—In 1846.

5604. How many counties had been valued then?—All of Ireland, with the exception of six counties; 26 in all.

5605. (*The O'Conor Don.*) Which were the six?—The six were Limerick, Cork, Tipperary, Waterford, Kerry, and County Dublin.

5606. (*Chairman.*) Who paid for the valuation?—The cost was in the first instance borne by the Consolidated Fund, and afterwards it was repaid by the counties.

5607. When did you say the work was stopped?—In 1846.

Tenement valuation of 1846.

5608. What was the next step after the stoppage?—Consequent on the passing of the Poor Law Act of 1838 (1 & 2 Vict. cap. 56) it was necessary for the levying of poor rates to have a tenement valuation.

5609. That tenement valuation commenced when?—In 1846.

5610. Was it completed?—Only so far as the six counties not valued under the first Acts are concerned.

5611. Then either under the Act of 1836, or the Act of 1846, the whole of Ireland has been valued so to speak?—Yes, the whole of Ireland has been valued under those two Acts.

5612. What was the unit of valuation under the second Act?—There were two units of valuation, there

was a townland unit and there was a tenement unit. Valuation was to be carried out in townlands on the scale of prices as laid down in the first Act of 1826, which we have been dealing with, and it also was to be valued on a rent value for tenements. This valuation was never published. The Act of 1852 was passed before it was completed, and it was then brought in line with other valuations made under this latter Act.

5613. What did the Act of 1852 provide?—The Act of 1852 provided for the valuation of the whole of Ireland in tenements on a scale of prices.

5614. And that consolidated the whole of the previous valuations did it?—I do not know that I can say it exactly consolidated them, but it brought the valuations made under the Act of 1846 into line with it.

5615. Will you describe the basis of this second valuation Act?—In the second valuation the tenement was the unit. The Act provided for one uniform valuation of land and tenements in Ireland which may be used for all public and local assessments, and other rating, which was to supersede the townland, and tenement valuations made under former Acts, and was to be used for the collection of the grand jury cess as well as for the poor rates.

5616. Will you give us the exact words of the Act which define the rateable properties?—The rateable properties were defined thus: "All lands, buildings and open mines; all commons and rights of common, and all other profits to be had or received or taken out of any land; and in the case of land or buildings used exclusively for public, scientific, or charitable purposes, as hereinafter specified, half the annual rent derived by the owner or other person interested in the same, so far as the same can or may be ascertained by the said Commissioners of Valuation; and all rights of fishery; all canals, navigations, and rights of navigation; all railroads and tramroads; all rights of way and other rights or easements over land, and the tolls levied in respect of such rights and easements, and all other tolls."

5617. There were some provisos to that, were there not?—Yes, there were "Provided always that no turf bog or turf bank used for the exclusive purpose of cutting or saving turf, or for making turf-mould therefrom, or fuel or manure, shall be deemed rateable under this Act, unless a rent or other valuable consideration shall be payable for the same; And provided also, that no mines which have not been opened seven years before the passing of this Act shall be deemed rateable until the term of seven years from the time of opening thereof shall have expired; and no mines hereafter to be opened shall be deemed rateable until seven years after the same shall have been opened; and mines *bonâ fide* reopened after the same shall have been *bonâ fide* abandoned shall be deemed as opening of mines within the meaning of this Act."

5618. What is the special exception to increase of rating in respect of reclamation?—Section 14 provides that no land or hereditament is to be rated in respect to any increase in value arising from drainage, reclamation, or embankment from the sea or any lake or river made or executed within seven years before the making of such valuation or revision.

5619. The lists of the valuations were to be published in the most ample way, were they not?—Yes, and issued to the various rating bodies.

5620. What was the appeal?—The appeal was in the first instance to the Commissioner of Valuation himself, and he had then power to send down a valuer, one of his staff who had not been employed in the case before to report to him, or he could examine it himself, and he could then alter the valuation or amend it. If the parties were not satisfied, then they could appeal to quarter sessions.

5621. This is the valuation which is popularly known as Sir Richard Griffiths' valuation, is it not?—Yes.

5622. Was it in your opinion a very perfect and complete one?—I think it was a very fair valuation.

5623. It was very costly, was it not?—Yes, for the purpose it was intended, I should say it was.

5624. What did it cost?—[illegible]

5625. A very large staff were employed under Sir R. Griffith?—That is so.

5626. (*The O'Conor Don.*) I do not think you mentioned what the first valuation cost, did you?—The first valuation cost 150,000*l*.

5627. (*Chairman.*) Can you give in a few words an account of the way in which the work of the valuation was carried through?—In the first instance instructions were issued to the valuers, which instructions were very carefully drawn up by Sir Richard Griffiths, and approved of by the Lord Lieutenant. In these instructions directions are given as to what the valuer is to do in every case he may have to deal with. I think the instructions are very ample and very complete. The valuer having received his instructions, proceeded to the country. He first took into consideration the value of the land separately from that of the buildings. He bore in mind that the total valuation of the land and buildings, exclusive of taxes, was not to exceed the fair letting value to a solvent tenant. The nature of the soil and subsoil and the underlying rock was to be considered, and from this was calculated the annual outlay to which a tenant might be liable and the average value of the produce according to the scale of the Act, the valuer from these data arriving at the nett annual value of the tenement. Local circumstances were to be taken into account. These were: Climate as affected by altitude; the proximity to, and facilities for, acquiring sea weed for manure, turf bogs for fuel, and limestone quarries for lime, proximity to market towns, their size and commercial importance; land under plantation and wood was to be assessed according to its agricultural value, and turf bogs where used for pasture were to be rated as such, but where the turf was sold the gross produce was to be estimated, and the expense of cutting, saving, and sale to be deducted, the balance, after allowance for tenants' profits, being the nett annual value. In the case of mines, quarries, and potteries, the expenses of working and proceeds of sales on the average of four years, were to be taken as the basis. As regards fisheries, the nett proceeds were taken as the value, and for railways, canals, &c. the rateable value was to be determined from the nett profits, making due allowances for interest on tenants' capital, tenants' profits, depreciation of stock, and working capital. The valuation of the stations and other buildings was to be ascertained separately and deducted. Superfluous roads were to be considered and valued as waste. The valuation was checked by the chief valuers, who drew a line across the district which had been valued by the local men, and re-valued for half a mile or so on each side of the line. In this way the checking under the Act of 1852 was carried out, the checking in the former valuation having been done by three valuers working together.

5628. The work of this valuation was commenced, I think, in 1846?—Yes.

5629. And completed when?—In 1865. The last county, Armagh, was issued in 1865.

5630. I need not take you through the valuation duties of a surveyor, but will you give them in regard to buildings in general terms?—In making a valuation of buildings the full measurements were to be taken and the value of the buildings was to be calculated from tables which are given in appendices to the "Instructions to Valuers." The rent was always to be ascertained, and the cost of the building calculated, this was a check to the rent, it is also the only way in which a valuation can be made where there is no rent paid the occupier being the owner of the house, a nominal value was to be put upon buildings which had become useless from their being unsuitable for the purpose for which they were built. Deductions were to be made in the case of large country mansions,

Mr. J. G. Barton.

Valuation under Act of 1852.

Instructions to valuers.

as the cost of these was usually out of proportion to the rent at which they could be let.

5631. The primary and main object of the valuation was with respect to local taxation, was it not?—Entirely. At the time the Act was passed there was no income tax raised in Ireland. It was not until 1853 the Income Tax Act was passed.

5632. And the Imperial Treasury had nothing to do with the valuation?—No, except paying the bill and the appointment of the Commissioners.

5633. (*The O'Conor Don.*) Did the Treasury pay the bill; was it not paid by the counties?—The amount was afterwards refunded by the counties.

5634. It was in reality paid by the counties?—Yes.

5635. (*Chairman.*) But there is a marked difference, is there not, between the state of things when the valuation was commenced, and the state of things when it was completed?—I presume you refer to the fact of the valuation being higher in one part of Ireland than another?

5636. Yes. Will you explain that?—The prices on which this valuation was based, which I did not read before, but which I had perhaps now give, as explaining this, are set out in the 11th section, of the 1852 Act; they are wheat, 7s. 6d. per 112 lbs.; oats, 4s. 10d.; barley, 5s. 6d.; flax, 49s.; butter, 65s. 4d.; beef, 35s. 6d.; mutton, 41s.; pork, 32s. These prices were taken from the general averages of prices ruling in 40 market towns in Ireland during the years 1849, 1850, and 1851, just as Ireland was recovering from the famine. The last valuations were completed in 1865, when the country was very much more prosperous, and when prices had risen very largely. The basis of the valuation is confessedly that scale of prices, and it would naturally be supposed as the valuation went on, and the value of crops increased, that the valuation would remain the same. Such is not the case. The valuation in the south of Ireland is confessedly higher than in the north. I think it is to be accounted for, to a certain extent at any rate, by the following reasons:—The principle on which this valuation was made was really the rent value which the lands or houses would bring. It is supposed to be a fair rent value. The Act prescribes that the valuation of houses shall be taken as the fair rent that they bring one year with another. I think it was the intention at the time that land should be valued on the same basis, so as to have an equal rating; but rents in Ireland, at that time, were not very equal, and it was felt, I think, that if the rent basis only was adopted an unequal valuation would be made. Therefore, the way in which the rent was to be arrived at was settled by the Act thus: That it should be worth the produce of the farm, less the cost of production, and less the rates and taxes, and a due allowance for the tenant's capital. I think, generally, that was the principle adopted. When the valuation commenced in the south rents were very low. When it had reached the north they were considerably higher, and I have no doubt that that must have influenced the valuers when they were making the valuation. When they commenced in the south the country was just recovering from the famine, and the farming was bad; the farmers had little or no capital and they did not get from their land as large an amount of produce as the Ulster farmers were getting when the valuers were at work in the north. The result was that the amount of produce per acre, the land value being equal, was not quite the same; it was greater in the north. I think that must have influenced the valuers. Further, the prices in the schedule, which I have read you, favour butter, beef, and the produce of grass lands more than they favour the agricultural land, and therefore the greater proportion of land in the south, compared with the north, being grass, that would make the valuation lower there than it is in the north.

5637. Does this inequality, which you have described, seriously affect the equal and fair assessment to taxation?—Not for local purposes.

5638. But it does for income tax purposes, which were not at the time thought of?—That is so.

5639. Then with respect to the revision of the valuation, will you tell us how that was provided for in the original Act?—There was an Act passed in 1854, which provided that an annual revision of the valuation was to be made. The mode of procedure was as follows:—On the 15th of November each year, every collector of poor rates in each union makes out and delivers to the clerk of the union, to be by him laid before the board of guardians, a list of all tenements or hereditaments in the said union, and within his district where the valuation shall require revision for any of the following reasons:—First, where the limits of the tenements have been altered; and second, where any property, the annual value of which is liable to frequent change, such as buildings, fisheries, railways, canals, &c. requires to be increased or diminished. Further, any ratepayer in the union may, before the same date, deliver to the clerk of the said union a list of any tenements, the valuation of which shall, in his opinion, require revision. These lists, after being open for public inspection for 10 days are transmitted to the Commissioner of Valuation to be dealt with. A revision of all cases thus brought under my notice is then made by officers of the department, who go down to each union, meet the rate collectors, and go through the lists with them, after which they visit each farm or house where revision is called for, and raise, lower, or otherwise alter or confirm the valuation as the case may require, but under no circumstances, except where a clerical error is discovered, may the total valuation of the lands, independently of the buildings, within each respective town land or other denomination be increased or diminished.

5640. When is this revision taken in hand?—Every autumn it commences.

5641. And it lasts how long?—We complete in August. The lists must be issued before the summer sessions to the grand juries.

5642. What is the average annual cost of the revision?—The average annual cost is 23,000*l*. Of this [illegible] is repaid by the Irish counties; and 1,000*l*. is from fees. We issue certificates of valuation and maps showing holdings to the public, and to the courts, and the amount we receive annually for these is about 1,000*l*., leaving a balance of about 11,000*l*. to be paid by the Treasury each year.

5643. At what figure would you estimate the number of changes annually made in the lists?—Taking the average of the last two years, the cases dealt with were as follows:—Alterations of farm boundaries, divisions of tenements, &c. 8,800; new houses valued, 6,300; houses re-valued on account of structural alterations, 2,700; valuations reduced or struck out owing to fall in rent value or dilapidation, [illegible]

5644. (*Mr. Sexton.*) Does that refer to houses?—That refers altogether to houses, or other rateable property liable to change.

5645. But unconnected with land?—Unconnected with land. Then railways, canals, fisheries, &c. 500.

5646. (*Chairman.*) Have you any remark to make about the effect of the annual revision work?—I wish to say that, except where structural alterations have been made, the valuations of existing houses are not brought, as a rule, under the notice of the department, except where they have decreased in value. Then they are brought under our notice by the ratepayers; but, as a rule, the rate collectors do not bring them under our notice unless some structural alteration has been made.

5647. It is only therefore a partial valuation, is it not?—It is only where structural changes have been made, or the value has depreciated.

5648. Not where it has risen?—Not where it has risen, as a rule.

5649. If a fresh valuation were taken in hand *ab initio*, would there be, in your opinion, a great change?—Yes, a considerable change.

5650. Can you give an estimate of that?—I estimate that there would be an increase in the valuation of from 15 to 20 per cent.; but of course, this

Mr. G. A. Barton.

13 Feb. 95.

Revision of valuation.

Probable effect of new valuation.

Mr. J. G. Barton. 2 Feb. 1895.

Assumed increase in value of houses.

is only an estimate. Sir Richard Griffith estimated it at 20 per cent.

5051. Is that for the whole?—Yes.

5052. 20 per cent. rise?—Yes.

5053. (*The O'Conor Don.*) Over what? Over the present valuation, estimating it for land and houses?—I estimate it here for houses.

5054. (*Chairman.*) For houses, do you say, the rise would be as much as 15 to 20 per cent.?—Yes.

5055. There has been no change in the valuation of land, has there?—No.

5056. (*Mr. Sexton.*) When did Sir Richard Griffith estimate that the value of land, if made anew, would be increased?—I think it was in 1869.

5057. When giving evidence before the Committee of the House of Commons?—I think so.

5058. (*Chairman.*) All the improvements on land, of late years, are not allowed for in the re-valuation at all, are they?—No, there has been no change in land since the valuation was made in 1852.

Comparison of valuation with judicial rents.

5059. Comparing the valuations with the judicial rents, so far as they have been fixed, what is the result?—I have prepared a table, Appendix No. VIII., in which I have shown up to the 31st of March 1893 the total number of cases in which judicial rents have been fixed, their acreage, tenement valuation, former rent, the percentage above or below the valuation of that former rent, the judicial rent, the percentage above or below the valuation of that judicial rent, and the percentage of reduction in rents. Taking the total it would appear that some 288,054 cases were dealt with up to that date; containing some 8,076,151 acres (that would be about half of Ireland, roughly speaking). The tenement valuation of these was 1,861,793*l.*, the former rent was 2,873,692*l.*, which was some 26·13 above the valuation. The reduction is taken as a unit in this way: The judicial rent was 4,733,263*l.*, which was 1·33 above the valuation.

5060. (*Mr. Sexton.*) That is treating both as units?—Yes, the valuation is the unit all through. The reduction in the rent is 20·7 per cent.

5061. Will you refer to your Appendix IX., at page 23 of your *précis*, and describe it?—That appendix is more or less founded on Appendix VIII. You will see a portion of it is headed "Portion which has been "dealt with by Land Commission." On that as a basis I have deduced the fact that certain savings to the payments of income tax have been made in Ireland.

5062. (*The O'Conor Don.*) What do you mean by savings in income tax?—I mean the advantage to the landowner in being able to pay on the valuation, or the rent, instead of, as in England, on the rent only. The heading of the table is this: "Table showing "approximately the saving in the assessment on "which income tax is paid on landed property in "Ireland under Schedule A., owing to same being "based on the valuation where it is below the rental, "the basis of assessment in Great Britain."

5063. (*Mr. Sexton.*) You assume that the standard of rental in Ireland and in Great Britain is the same, do you?—Yes, I assume that the standard of rent in Great Britain and Ireland is the same.

5064. (*Chairman.*) Will you give us a summary of this table?—The summary is as follows:—The approximate amount of assessment on which tax was saved prior to the Act of 1881 was 2,559,900*l.*, and at present it is 276,380*l.*, of course, less whatever deductions are usually made.

5065. (*Mr. Sexton.*) This rather important calculation rests entirely upon assumptions of an arbitrary character, does it not?—I have explained that in my paper later on.

5066. You assume, in every case prior to 1881, the valuation was lower than the rent, and that the landlord paid the income tax on the valuation?—No, I do not assume that.

5067. But you assume that prior to 1881 the valuation was lower than the rent?—Yes, on the whole.

Mr. J. G. Barton. 2 Feb. 1895.

Comparison of savings under judicial rents.

5068. And that the landlord preferred to be assessed upon the valuation?—Yes, he preferred, in the generality of cases, to be assessed upon the valuation, because it was the lower; where it was not lower he was assessed on the rent.

5069. Then you say that, at present, the saving is very slight indeed, about 110,000*l.* a year, being the difference between the rents fixed in the Land Courts, and the valuation of the lands?—Yes, in the portion dealt with by the Land Courts.

5070. A couple of thousand a year in income?—That is all for the portion.

5071. But when you come to the larger calculation, that rests upon the assumption that the rents of Ireland, which have not been dealt with in the Land Courts, bear precisely the same relation to the valuations of those lands that rent and valuation do to those which have been dealt with?—Exactly. I have explained that, I think, in the last paragraph of my *précis* of evidence.

Incidence of taxation as between landlord and tenant.

5072. (*Chairman.*) We will now pass from these calculations to the facts as to the incidence of taxation. Will you tell us what the rates are which the landlord now pays?—The landlord pays at present half the poor rate, where the valuation is over 4*l.*, and the whole where it is under that amount; half the county cess in the case of new tenancies under the Act of 1870, or where an agreement to that effect is made; and tithes and income tax.

5073. And as to house property?—As to house property, it depends entirely upon the locality; but in making the valuation we, in all cases, deduct both the rates and the maintenance, when paid and done by the landlord.

5074. Do you say that as regards land in a valuation for local taxation, an addition to the occupiers' interest would have to be made?—I think so.

5075. What sort of percentage do you think?—I would not like to say any particular amount, but I think if a tenant pays a sum of money to go into his holding, that should be taken into account in making a valuation for local purposes, in the same way as a fine may be paid by a man who takes a house.

5076. (*Mr. Sexton.*) But when that valuation is also used for imperial purposes, for the purpose of assessing income tax, do you say that a landlord should pay income tax upon property created by another man who is not liable?—No, I am talking now about local taxation.

5077. The heading points to income tax years, does it not?—I qualify that sentence by saying "In valuation for local taxation." I think that is the beginning of the sentence.

5078. But you would not apply it to income tax, would you?—No.

Local taxation of Ireland.

5079. (*Chairman.*) What does the local taxation of Ireland consist of?—Grand jury cess, poor rates, and other rates paid to boards of guardians, town rates, the Dublin police tax, and the Belfast Water Commissioners' rates.

5080. How much do they amount to altogether?—The real property tax amounts to 2,971,104*l.*; that was in 1893; tolls, fees, stamps, and dues 474,932*l.*; other receipts 271,910*l.*; bringing the total up to 3,717,946*l.*

Government contributions.

5080a. Does the Government in Ireland contribute, as it does in England, to any extent, in aid of local rates?—Yes, it does.

5081. Will you describe what they do?—All Government property, which is legally exempt from rating such as barracks, Government offices, &c. is valued in the same manner as other rateable property, and on this the Treasury grant a bounty equal to the amount of the local rates, less the proportion paid by the landlord, where a rent is received in respect of the lands or premises. Under section 2 of the Act 17 Vict. cap. 8, and section 2 of 19 & 20 Vict. cap. 63, the landlord is liable for county cess and poor rate on half the annual rent he derives out of any exempted property. The Government property in Ireland,

Mr. J. G. Barton. 21 Feb. 1895.

which in 1852 was valued at 97,000*l.*, now stands at 145,000*l.*, being an increase of nearly 50 per cent.

Comparison of rental to valuation.

5082. And the contribution in aid of local rates is how much?—30,000*l.*

Licensed premises.

5083. Have you any remarks to make about licensed premises?—They are generally valued at a very low rate. In Ireland we do not take into account the licences.

5084. Can you compare them with the valuations in Great Britain?—No, I do not think I can.

Assessment of lands and houses.

5085. Will you describe, with a little more minuteness, the arrangement as to the assessment of income tax in Ireland on lands and houses?—As the tenement valuation in Ireland forms the ground work for the assessment of income tax payable under Schedules A. and B. I have thought it well to show how this basis compares with that on which these duties are assessed in Great Britain. Under the Income Tax Act of 1853 the owners of lands and houses in Ireland are assessed under Schedule A., and the occupiers of lands under Schedule B. Under Schedule A. the person assessed may, in the case of any holding where the valuation is higher than the rental, elect to pay on the latter, and if he so elect he may deduct such poor rate as he is liable for, but should he pay on the valuation only such proportion of this as will, with the valuation, make up the rent. A deduction for sea walls is also sanctioned by section 37 of the Act. Further, if the owner pays on the rent, the difference between this and the valuation is reckoned towards the liability of the occupier.

5086. (*Mr. Sexton.*) That is if the occupier happens to be liable to income tax, is it not?—Exactly. Owners of rentcharges may deduct these from their taxable property. Under a Treasury Order issued in 1881 owners of property in Ireland are not liable for income tax on the portions of their estates on which rent has not been paid. The very largely increased amount which has been written off through the schedule of discharge since that date would seem to show that prior to it a considerable sum had been paid as tax for lands on account of which no rent had been received. The total valuation of the lands and houses in Ireland (excluding railways and other rateable property not assessed for income tax under Schedule A.) amounted in 1871 to about 12,800,000*l.* On this the income tax under Schedule A. at 1*d.* in the pound would be 53,333*l.*, which was practically the amount actually charged that year to duty. In 1893–4 the valuation of similar property was about 13,630,000*l.* on which the tax at 1*d.* in the pound would amount to 56,791*l.*, but the amount charged to duty was only about 53,000*l.* This reduction, instead of an increase, is no doubt partly due to sales to the occupiers under the Land Purchase Acts, the properties so sold ceasing in nearly every case to be assessable, and partly to the fact that in consequence of the general reduction of rents, many landlords are now assessed on the rental rather than on the valuation. The falling off in the net produce of the tax is even more marked, for whilst this in 1871, at 1*d.* in the pound, amounted to 39,500*l.*, it had fallen in 1893 to 41,849*l.* This further reduction is, in my opinion, chiefly due to the rebate allowed since 1881 in the cases where the rents are not paid.

Appendix IX.

5087. (*Chairman.*) Then you put in Appendix VIII.?—Yes, Appendix VIII. is the appendix which we have just been through, showing the judicial rents. I should like to read what I say about Appendix IX. In Appendix IX., I have endeavoured to show to what extent the landowners of Ireland benefited prior to the judicial reduction of rent, and at the present time, by being allowed to select either the valuation or the rental for assessment, instead of being limited to the rental, as in Great Britain. The value of this table largely depends on the accuracy of the following premises: First, that the rental of those lands which have not been brought within the purview of the land courts both before 1881 and now bears the same proportion to the tenement valuation as it does in those that have. From my own experience and knowledge of the country, I am inclined to believe that this is the case. I have consulted some of the leading land agents in Ireland who would be conversant with this question, and they generally agree with me.

Mr. J. G. Barton. 21 Feb. 1895.

Judicial rents.

5088. (*Mr. Sexton.*) The cases that have got to the land courts are about 300,000 in number, and they deal with about one half the land, do they not?—Yes.

5089. Can you give us any more details as to the nature of the evidence upon which you came to this important conclusion?—I have put the question to one or two gentlemen, and they have agreed with me generally. One reason which made me come to this conclusion is that I know in Ireland, rents have been reduced voluntarily by the landlords to a very large extent on the same lines as they have been judicially reduced. Those are cases which have not gone into court at all. I believe that is the case in a good many counties, and I think that there has been an average reduction of about the same amount as the judicial rents.

5090. Do you represent that the tenant in Ireland, has, in numerous cases, accepted a reduction from year to year upon something like the scale which has been given in court, and has not gone into court to secure the permanent reduction for 15 years?—I know of a good many such cases.

5091. (*The O'Conor Don.*) In those cases does not the tenant secure a reduction for 15 years by having it registered?—Yes, if it is registered, but not, if it is not.

5092. (*Mr. Sexton.*) I understood you to speak of cases where the agreements have not become judicial?—Certainly. Of course if it is registered it comes into the first part of the table. This is merely my opinion from the information I have gathered on the subject.

5093. (*Lord Farrer.*) The result of the whole is that if the Irish landowner has had any advantage over the English landowner, in consequence of being taxed upon the valuation, that advantage has now been reduced to something very small indeed; that is so, is it not?—That is so. Then second, that the valuation of each county as set out in column 1, was the sum on which the owners were assessed in 1881, and that this or the net rental, as set out in column 2, whichever is lower, is that on which they are now assessed. Those are the two assumptions.

Assessment under Schedule B.

5094. (*Chairman.*) Then with respect to schedule B., what remarks have you to make?—Under schedule B. the occupier is assessed on the valuation of his holding at one-third of the tax, this being assumed to be the amount of his net profit. Prior to 1876, if the entire assessable income of the occupier were derived from his holding, he would not (assuming that there was no other liability) have been assessable for income tax, unless his valuation amounted to 300*l.* or over. Of holdings of this valuation in Ireland there are only about 1,800 outside those in the cities and towns. In 1876 the incomes exempt from tax were raised to 150*l.*, so that since that date unless the occupier derived an income from outside sources, or had two or more holdings, he would not be subject to the tax except his valuation was at least 450*l.* There are under 900 valuations of this amount, or exceeding it, in the whole of Ireland after those in the cities have been deducted, there being no assessment on those under this schedule. It is however, apparent from the amount of the tax that there are a considerable number of persons occupying holdings of less value than 450*l.*, who, having other sources of income, are rendered liable and pay income tax under Schedule B. There are a very large number of landowners in Ireland who are assessed under Schedule B., in fact I think the tax is principally paid by the landowners. Under the Finance Act of 1894, sec. 34, the limit of exemption was raised to incomes of 160*l.* per annum.

5095. There is a further provision in the Finance Act, is there not?—Yes; under the Finance Act of

Mr. J. G. Barton. 24 Feb. 1894.

1894, as I say, it is provided (section 35) that owners of land in Ireland paying income tax under Schedule A. may deduct one-eighth of the annual value, and those paying on house property one-sixth, except in cases where the amount of the assessment is more than one-eighth or one-sixth respectively below the rent, after deducting from such rent any outgoings that may be by law deducted in making the assessments. From Table 10 it appears that Ireland should contribute $\frac{1}{21}$ of the total revenues if income tax be taken as a basis for determining the relative taxable capacity of the two countries.

5696. That is, if that was the general principle?—Yes.

5697. In this Table X. do you make all the necessary allowances?—Yes, in this table. Items (a) "Amount actually charged to Duty under Schedule A." and "Amount charged to Duty ... Schedule B. in Great Britain" are taken from the Income Tax Returns. The item (b) is based on the amount paid by the Land Commission under the Purchase Acts, equal to the fall in the amount charged to Duty between 1880 and 1892.

5698. (Mr. Sexton.) Why do you put that in, that property has ceased to be assessed, has it not?—It has; but in order to make a comparison I thought it advisable to take it because such a transfer of property has not taken place in England.

5699. In England although he remains the tenant he has the capital. I am puzzled to understand why property which has passed into the hands of non-income tax paying persons should be deemed to be a part of the just measure of relative capacity due to the payment of income tax in the two countries?—I considered it that the fairest way to arrive at a equitable basis would be to take it before these sales had taken place. This was exceptional legislation. In another 10 or 15 years the income tax under Schedule A. might disappear altogether, the whole country having been sold to tenant purchasers.

5700. But for 49 years the annuity which represents what the land formerly was passed out of the country and goes into the Imperial Treasury and is no part of the wealth of Ireland?—It is not assessable for income tax. I am merely making a comparison on the basis of income tax.

5701. But when property is in the hands of persons who are not liable to income tax, and the only fund derivable from property passes out of Ireland, I find it difficult to understand on what ground you regard a tax which would have been paid upon that same if the land had remained in the hands of the landlord as a part of the test afforded of the income tax paying capacity of Ireland?—I do not think that land that has passed into the hands of the tenants under the Purchase Acts has become any less valuable. It certainly does not pay tax, but it has not become any less valuable.

5702. (Chairman.) What is practically the difference if Mr. Sexton's contention is sound?—It amounts to 9,000*l*.

5703. You have added to the paper which you put in, appendices, with all of which we have dealt, I think?—Yes, I think so.

5704. Does anything arise upon them which you wish to mention particularly?—No, there is nothing further.

Valuation of mansions in England and Ireland.

5705. One thing that has caught my eye as requiring perhaps some explanation is the valuation of the mansions in England and Ireland respectively. Appendix VII. Some of them seem to be valued at a very curious rate; they are generally valued very low.

5706. Would you say, speaking generally of places you know, that those mansions are valued on anything approaching the same principle in Ireland and England?—I am afraid I could not make a comparison; I have tried to get the cost of some of those mansions, but I have not been able to do so. Some of them are very old historic mansions, and it is impossible to get at what they originally cost.

5707. These are the actual valuations are they not, on which taxes are paid?—Yes.

5708. (The O'Conor Don.) Do you think they would let at a higher rate than the valuations put down here?—I do not know that they would. I doubt it very much.

5709. (Chairman.) Either in England or Ireland?—Either in England or Ireland.

5710. (Sir David Barbour.) That is due to there being a limited demand for them, I suppose?—Yes, I suppose it is.

Effect of proposed ... of income ...

5711. (Lord Farrer.) These figures that you have given us at the foot of page 24, Ireland 4·6 and Great Britain 95·4, are the proportions as they would exist if your corrections were made, are they not?—That is so.

5712. Have you made out what difference it makes; it is something very small, is it not? You have given us here the proportion which Ireland would pay if she were assessed and taxed in the same way as Great Britain?—That is so.

5713. Can you give us the corresponding figures as to what she does pay; it is only a calculation?—It is one twenty-fifth, I think.

5714. It would be convenient to you in the comparison of what the alteration would be?—Yes, I will do so. I have it in Mr. Hamilton's paper.

5715. (The O'Conor Don.) I think you told us that you had been only two years at the Valuation Office, did you not?—Between two and three years.

5716. And, I suppose, previous to that you had no experience at all in connexion with valuation?—I had a good deal to do with valuing land for railways, and that kind of property.

Basis of valuation.

5717. But with regard to the manner in which the valuation was carried out, is not the evidence you give what you have learnt from others; it is not your own experience?—No; what I have learnt from others and reading the different reports of Sir Richard Griffith and my predecessors, and what I have found out from some men lately on the staff who were employed in the valuation, and what I have ascertained from the documents in my office and our old books.

5718. I think you told us that the first important valuation made by Sir Richard Griffith was based on a scale of prices arrived at by inquiry from the principal maritime markets of Ireland?—That is so.

5719. Can you tell us what those markets are?—I am sorry to say that I cannot.

5720. Is there no record?—There is no record I can find.

5721. You told us in connexion with the subsequent valuation that the schedule of prices was taken at 30 different towns, I think?—Yes.

5722. Is there any record of those towns, or of those prices?—I do not think there is, but if you wish I will try and ascertain.

5723. Under the townland valuation the whole of Ireland was valued excepting the county of Dublin, and all Munster excepting Clare, you say?—That is so under the townland valuation.

5724. The townland valuation did not set out the names of any of the occupiers, I believe?—No.

5725. It was simply the total aggregate value of the townland?—That is so.

5726. I think you have referred to the system under which the valuation was carried on by the valuers making what were called quality lots?—Yes.

5727. They divided the town land into lots according to the quality of the soil, did they not?—They did so.

5728. Was that system carried on in the counties which were not valued under the townland valuation?—Do you refer to the six counties now?

5729. Yes?—It was I believe.

5730. I was under the impression that your predecessor stated it was not, but you may be right?—I think so.

5731. Have you got records of those quality lots in your office?—Yes.

5732. You have got the maps showing them?—Yes.

G g 4

Mr. J. G. Barton.

21 Feb. 1895.

Books of valuations.

5733. And this valuation I think you take as was arrived at by very experienced men with great knowledge of the work?—So I understand.

5734. Did not Sir Richard Griffith take great pains to get the best men he could for carrying out the valuation?—Sir Richard Griffith describes in his evidence given in 1869, that when he commenced the valuation in the county Derry he got the very best men he could in the county who had been accustomed to valuing for sales, and he trained those men himself.

5735. Did he not form what was called a school of valuation?—He did, and trained these men at it.

5736. He got payment for this from the Treasury, did he not?—He did; he got 300*l.*, I think, for it from the Treasury.

5737. Then in order that the valuation might be uniform, he adopted the plan you have already mentioned, of testing the valuations of others who were not trained in this school by these skilled men, did he not?—Yes; practically that was his checking school; these men that he trained in the first instance.

5738. Have these maps and documents which you have showing the quality lots in each of the divisions into which the townlands were divided, ever been asked for by the Land Commission, or used by them in any way in their valuations?—I do not think so, but we use them ourselves every day.

5739. You have to use them of course when you are revising the tenement list?—Yes.

5740. And do you keep them up in perfect condition?—Yes.

5741. So that they would be capable of use at any time they might be required for any purposes?—Yes.

5742. After the townland valuation was stopped, and the Act of 1846 was passed, you told us that a certain number of counties were valued under it, but the valuation was never published?—Yes, the six counties.

5743. And that these counties were valued somewhat on the principle of the English system, as it is called of the beta annual value?—Yes.

5744. That I suppose was the rent, with deductions for taxes?—Yes.

5745. Have you got a record of that valuation in your office?—I think there are a few of the books left. There was a deduction made from that valuation and the valuation as it now stands in our books is not the exact valuation that was made then, but the valuation after the deduction was made to bring it in line with the valuation made after the Act of 1852.

5746. Can you tell us what was the system of bringing it into line?—I believe it was done in this way. There was a general reduction of either 10 or 15 per cent. taken off in each county.

5747. Was that the system?—That was the system I understand.

5748. They did not go into any particulars of particular holdings, but took off an average all round?—I believe so.

5749. Was that applied to each tenement?—That would apply to each tenement.

5750. *Pro rata* I suppose?—Yes.

5751. Have those counties that were so brought into line ever been altered since?—No.

5752. The valuation of those counties at the present time is the valuation under the Act of 1846 is it not, brought into line, as you say, by a sort of average deduction?—Exactly.

5753. (*Mr. Sexton.*) But there were two valuations under the Act of 1846, there was a valuation for the poor rate was there not?—Yes.

5754. Which I think was made the basis of bringing into line, was it not?—The valuation made for poor rate.

5755. The other was rejected was it?—Yes.

Adjourned for a short time.

5756. (*The O'Conor Don.*) You mentioned in your evidence in chief, and also in answer to a question from me, that the valuers divided the townlands into quality lots.

Mr. J. G. Barton.

21 Feb. 1895.

Books of valuations.

5757. And I think you stated that books were kept recording those qualities as well as maps?—They were.

5758. Did that extend to the whole of Ireland?—It extended to the whole of Ireland, I believe.

5759. Have you got the books and maps now of the whole of Ireland?—We have got the books of, I think, the whole of Ireland, except Ulster; the books of Ulster were, I believe, either burnt or destroyed, shortly after they were made. We have not got them at present in our office. It is generally supposed that when the books and documents were moved from Sir Richard Griffith's private house to the office in Ely Place, a certain proportion of these were destroyed, and those amongst others.

Valuation of Ulster.

5760. The valuation of Ulster you told us is higher than the rest of Ireland?—Yes.

5761. You gave some reasons for that and amongst others, you mentioned that the tenants' interest was taken into consideration?—I did not mention that in my evidence. It is in the *précis* of my evidence which you have before you, but I would rather strike that out. The fact that both Sir Richard Griffith and Sir John Ball Greene say in their evidence in 1869 that it was not taken into account is stronger evidence than I had that it was. I had certain evidence that it was, but that given by them is, I consider, the stronger.

5762. I took down that the occupier's interest was taken into consideration in making the valuation. I think you stated it to-day, but at all events you withdraw that, do you?—Yes, I withdraw that. I did not intend to state it.

5763. You say that prices that were the basis of the tenement valuation were taken from average prices in 40 market towns. Can you tell me how the details of these averages were obtained?—I am afraid I cannot.

Valuation of railways.

5764. With regard to the railways, how are they valued in Ireland?—The railways are valued for local taxation by our department, in this way. The gross profits are ascertained; from that, the expenditure is taken; from that, certain allowances are made for tenants' profits for interest on tenants' capital, and for depreciation of rolling stock. A percentage is allowed on the capital necessary to work the line, the tenants' capital, we call it, and certain other small deductions are made, and from the balance a valuation is arrived at.

5765. Are all these calculations made in your office?—Yes, by myself.

5766. Are the railway companies bound to furnish you the figures upon which you make these calculations?—That is so.

5767. I presume that that is a valuation which is constantly varying then?—That is a valuation which is constantly varying. Last year I valued two large railways, and the year before a smaller one.

5768. Do you know how the valuation of railways is made in England, is it on the same system?—I believe identically the same for local rating purposes.

5769. But this valuation in Ireland, is for Imperial purposes as well, is it not?—No, the assessment of railways for income tax is made under Schedule D on profits, and our valuation is not taken into account by the income tax authorities at all.

5770. Is it not?—No, the valuation of railways in Ireland, is, roughly speaking, 500,000*l.*; the assessment for Imperial taxation is, I think, something like 1,600,000*l.*

5771. Do not railway companies pay under Schedule A, at all?—I think not.

5772. The land which they hold then, is not taxed to income tax at all, is it?—No, it is entirely a question of profits. As I have already pointed out the reason that our valuation of land has in some years slightly decreased, is because this land has been struck out of the townland in which it was, owing to the railway companies being taxed on their profits.

5773. But with regard to the land on which the railways run, is not that land rated for local purposes or is it struck out for them also?—It is struck out for there also, except on certain railways, where there is only a local value, there being no profits.

5774. Where the railways make no profits?—Where the railways make no profits.

5775. (*Lord Farrer.*) Then they are rated on a proportion of their profits, are they?—They are rated on a proportion of their profits where these exceed the expenses.

5776. (*The O'Conor Don.*) Do you know what the proportion is?—I [illegible] reason, I think, is under half the net profits; that is to say, if a railway company's net profit for the year was [illegible] the valuation would be under [illegible], roughly speaking.

5777. The valuation under Schedule D?—No, our valuation. Of course I cannot answer as to the other; it does not come into my department at all.

5778. Do you not know how they are valued under Schedule D?—No.

5779. It is not you who makes the valuation then for the purposes of income tax at all?—No.

5780. What department makes that valuation?—I presume the income tax authorities.

5781. Do they come to you for any sources of information regarding them?—No, none.

5782. With regard to the revision of the valuation, under the revision of the valuation in Ireland you cannot make any alteration in the total value of the tenement?—No.

5783. And the revision simply consists in plotting the changes that have taken place within the year amongst the occupiers?—Yes, as regards land.

5784. How is it, if that be so, the valuation of land in Ireland appears, I think, by one of these returns at the end of your paper to be considerably different. I see here, taking Appendix 4, the valuation in 1864 was 12,[illegible] and the valuation in 1891 was 14,[illegible]. How do you account for that difference?—That is the valuation of all rateable property in Ireland; that includes houses.

5785. Would you say that the difference there is in the main due to houses?—Entirely due to houses, railways, and other rateable property liable to change.

5786. And there is practically no difference in the valuation of 1864 and the valuation of 1891 as regards land, is there?—There would be any, except in the way I explained to you just now where a railway has no profits.

5787. Now with regard to houses, will you explain to the Commission how the revision is made with regard to houses where alterations have been made?—The way in which the revision is made is as follows: If it is a very small change and the house is valued comparatively with others in the neighbourhood, and not too low, the cost of the new portion is calculated and added. If there is any considerable change, or if it is a new house, the rent is ascertained, the cost of the building is ascertained from local sources, and it is also ascertained from measurements. With these three factors before us we can calculate the valuation the house ought to bear, and we make a deduction to make it relative to other houses in the locality district.

5788. Do you make a deduction from what you consider ought to be the fair value, because the house before had been undervalued?—Because the whole district is undervalued.

5789. What is that deduction; what does it amount to. I think you have a table here, table 6?—Yes, that table 6 merely gives the few cases we have dealt with up to the present this year, I do not think there is any great value to be put on the totals; it merely shows we do make deductions, but generally speaking the deduction all over Ireland is from 15 up to 30 per cent.

5790. I see here in your table you put all over Ireland the per-centage deduction at 22 per cent.—if you look at your figures you will find, I think, that the per-centage is wrong?—As I said before, I do not think much weight should be attached to these totals, for this reason, that to arrive at a fair average it would be necessary to have the number of cases in each town proportionate to its size.

5791. (*Lord Farrer.*) Is that deduction made after a valuation founded upon the actual rent paid?—Yes, either the ascertained rent or the calculated rent.

5792. To what extent does cost of construction enter into your valuation, and to what extent does rent enter into it, because of course they are two different items?—In every case now I try to ascertain both cost of construction and rent. Of course in a very large proportion of cases there is no rent paid, and we have to depend altogether on the cost of construction; but I arrive at a rent by a percentage on the cost of construction and compare that with the actual rents paid in the immediate neighbourhood.

5793. (*The O'Conor Don.*) When a new house is built in the city of Dublin, is that the system you adopt?—That is the system we adopt.

5794. So that you try to bring down the new houses to the same standard as existing ones, do you?—As nearly as possible. Property is becoming more valuable in certain portions of Dublin and is falling.

5795. (*Lord Farrer.*) Can you say what relation your valuation bears to the rent of houses in Dublin?—It varies very much in the different localities, but I should say that in what is the west end of Dublin, the fashionable part of Dublin, the valuation would be rather under two-thirds of the rent.

5796. (*Mr. Sexton.*) Of the gross rent?—Yes, of the gross rent.

5797. (*Lord Farrer.*) Of the actual rent paid?—Yes, of the actual rent paid, the occupier paying taxes and the landlord doing repairs.

5798. (*Chairman.*) It is generally called two-thirds, is it not?—Yes, I think that may be generally assumed.

5799. (*Lord Farrer.*) Is that rent paid upon a house where the tenant repairs, or does the landlord repair?—That varies, but as a rule the landlord repairs.

5800. (*The O'Conor Don.*) It would appear generally from your evidence that up to a certain period when rents began to be reduced the landowners of Ireland had an advantage in the valuation and that subsequently they were at a disadvantage in consequence of the value of land having fallen?—I think at present the landowners of Ireland have little or no advantage over their English brethren. In the north of Ireland they stand very much in the same position.

5801. And in Ireland the landowners pay half the poor rate, do they not?—Yes.

5802. And the whole of the poor rate on holdings of 4*l.*?—Yes; that you will see in Table IX. is deducted. The landlord's taxes are deducted in column No. 7.

5803. What table are you referring to?—Table 9.

5804. (*Mr. Sexton.*) You deduct it from the judicial rent in order to compare it with the valuation, do you?—Yes.

5805. (*The O'Conor Don.*) I suppose you have gone through that with regard to the small holdings where the whole rate is paid by the landlord?—Yes.

5806. In England were not the whole of these rates paid by the occupier?—Yes, I believe so. That was the reason why they were deducted for purposes of comparison.

5807. Do you know on what proportion of the lands of Ireland is the income tax now paid, is it paid upon the rental instead of upon the valuation?—I am afraid I could not say that exactly. You will see that there are some 18 counties now where the valuation is under the rental, as the gross, but of course there are numbers of cases in those counties where it is not under the valuation the figures in the Table (IX.) are totals, and unless one went over every individual tenancy it would be impossible to express an opinion of any value on this point.

Mr. J. G. Barton.

21 Feb. 1895.

Judicial rents.

5808. Would it not be hard to make a comparison between the judicial rents and the valuation, which would be worth anything?—It would.

5809. The judicial commissioners do not seem to have followed your valuation at all?—I do not know what they followed.

5810. At all events the dissimilarities are so great, even in the same locality that you could not make any reliable comparison between the two, could you?—No.

5811. And the percentages that are spoken of with regard to these two different valuations are therefore comparatively worthless?—In my opinion they are.

Assessment under Schedule B.

5812. With regard to Schedule B. you state that the number of holdings that would be assessable to income tax in Ireland under Schedule B. is extremely small inasmuch as the valuation must be 300*l.* or over?—Yes.

5813. Is not this calculation made by you upon the number of holdings that are returned to the Valuation Office?—Which calculations?

5814. The 1,000 holdings valued at 300*l.* and over?—Yes, from the returns which we have made.

5815. But is it not almost a general rule with regard to these large holdings that the same individual will have three or four of them?—It is quite possible; and I go on to state a little later that that is most likely the case. You will see all that in the next paragraph. "It is, however, apparent from the amount "of the tax that there are a considerable number of "persons occupying holdings of less value than 160*l.*, "who, having other sources of income (that may be "other holdings) are rendered liable and pay income "tax under Schedule B."

5816. In this case it is not correct to say "other sources of income." You have taken the number of separate holdings that have been returned to you, and not the number of farmers who occupy holdings?—That is quite so.

5817. And it may be the case, and certainly is the case I believe, that the number of occupiers of one or more holdings of over 160*l.* are more numerous than you put down here?—It is quite possible, but I do not think there are many. I think there are very few who hold more farms than one. There are landlords of course who have considerably more, but of tenant farmers I should think there are comparatively few.

5818. Perhaps I come from a county where we have more of them than there are in other counties. In my county we have a good many who have a considerable number of holdings. Did you know the state of the country at the time this tenement valuation was begun?—No, I did not.

Changes in occupation of land since 1846.

5819. I think Sir Richard Griffith stated in his evidence before that Committee to which you referred that there were enormous changes in the occupation of land in Ireland after the famine?—Yes, that was so.

5820. And in fact the valuation which was made in the years 1846 and so on, ought to be almost gone over again in consequence of the changes. The whole state of the country, he stated, was changed even during the progress of the valuation in consequence of the great emigration, people leaving the country and farms being consolidated, and so on?—That is so.

5821. Do you believe that to be the case?—Yes, I do; I know it as a fact, as these changes are now coming before me as boundary surveyor. In the counties of *Kerry* and *Cork*, for instance, the number of changes in the boundaries is very large.

5822. Would you think it too much to say that half the area of Ireland underwent changes at that time?—I should not like to express any opinion as to any exact amount.

5823. (*Mr. Sexton.*) You are an officer of the Government, are you not?—Yes, I am.

Constitution of Valuation Office.

5824. And I understand that since its foundation the Valuation Department has been a department of the State?—Yes.

5825. When was the income tax first levied in Ireland?—In 1853 the Act was passed; I suppose 1854 was the first year it was levied.

5826. Your department is paid by a vote of the House of Commons, is it?—It is.

5827. And the counties pay a part of the expense, do they?—They pay 8,000*l.* a year by imperative procurement.

5828. They have no discretion, have they?—They have no discretion.

5829. (*The O'Conor Don.*) That is a new system, is it not, since the Committee of 1869?—Yes, since the passing of 37 & 38 Vict. c. 70.

5830. But before that the counties had to pay half of any bill that was sent out from the Valuation Office?—Yes, I think half.

5831. It was a varying sum, was it not, depending on the work the Valuation Office stated was done in each county?—That is so, and the Act of 1837-38 provides, in the schedule, the amount each county shall have to pay.

5832. There was great objection to that, was there not, from the counties?—Yes.

5833. Did they not consider the proceeding inordinately expensive?—Yes.

5834. And then there was a fixed sum fixed for each county, was there?—Yes.

5835. (*Mr. Sexton.*) The counties never had any control over the remuneration of your department, had they?—No.

5836. Then I may say that from the time at which the valuation under the Act of 1852 began, income tax was levied in Ireland?—Well, yes, the next year.

5837. They were simultaneous?—The Valuation Act was passed a year before, and the valuation actually began in 1848; it began two years before.

5838. So that from the beginning of the operation of this Imperial department the amount of income tax paid out of Ireland depended upon the valuation made by the department?—As regards land and houses under Schedules A. and B.

5839. The scale of prices in the Act of 1852 was founded, I think you told us, upon general averages?—Yes.

5840. For about three years, 1849, 1850, and 1851?—Yes.

5841. Can you say whether the general average of each year was obtained by making an equation between the highest and the lowest price of the year? I am afraid I cannot answer that question.

5842. Assume that to have been done (and we have evidence already about it), may I not infer that if you strike a mean between the highest price of the year, when few commodities are sold, and the lowest price, when most are sold, the result will be a price higher than the farmer usually obtained?—It may be so.

5843. I believe the course of prices was progressive from 1852 up to 1865?—Yes, I believe that is so; I think that is borne out by facts.

5844. Improving all the time?—Yes.

5845. I think we have had it also that the valuation progressed during the time?—I think so.

5846. I do not know whether you suggest that the valuation was actually conducted all through these 15 years upon a scale of absolute prices?—I think that the Act scale influenced the valuation more or less all through these years.

5847. You have given us some of the instructions to the valuers, but not all of the important ones. For instance, Sir Richard Griffith instructed his valuers to "Value the land on a liberal scale, that is "to say, in the same manner as if employed by one "of the principal landlords of the county, who was "about to let the lands to solvent tenants on leases, "say of 21 years." Griffiths' Instructions of 1853 also laid down that "the total valuation of land and "buildings should not exceed the fair letting value as "to a solvent tenant." This shows that the "letting value" to be kept in view by the valuers. The

Mr. J. G. Barton. 21 Feb. 1895. Basis of valuation.

Instructions (p. 80) also declare that the total valuation of each separate tenement should be "the rent "which a liberal landlord would obtain from a solvent "tenant for a term of years." Do not these Instructions directly by their language point to the rent which may be obtained by a landlord at the time of the valuation?—Yes, to a certain extent they do. I think, as I explained before, that rent certainly was an element in the valuation.

5848. Sir Richard himself told the Committee in 1869 that the county of Dublin for instance was valued at a moderate rent value?—Yes.

5849. And he also said "We come up to the letting "rents of the principal landlords." Therefore you would not contest the conclusion that the scale in the Act of 1852 which ceased to be operative immediately because of a progress in prices ceased to affect the valuation, and that the valuations really were made upon what a tenant would probably pay upon the prices at the time of the valuation?—More or less it would certainly influence the valuation.

5850. The prices in the greater part of the period of the valuation were higher than they had been in recent years or are now, in Ireland, were they not?—Taking the prices in 1865, which I presume is the period you refer to.

5851. Wheat 12s. 4d. then and 6s. 9d. now?—I do not think wheat influences the question very much; take oats.

5852. Oats 7s. 6d. then, now 6s. 11d.; potatoes about the same; butter 110s. to 95s.; beef 65s. to 44s.; mutton 73s. to 53s.; and pork 56s. to 46s.?—Yes, but that is the year when the last county in Ireland was valued. The whole of Leinster, Munster, and Connaught had been done some years previously; therefore those prices could not influence the valuers who valued those three provinces.

5853. Not the prices of 1865, but the prices were progressive from 1853 to 1865?—They were.

5854. And the suggestion I make is that throughout the greater part of that period the prices were better than they have been in recent years in Ireland?—Without having the prices before me I cannot say exactly whether they were or not. I should say that would likely be about the same.

5855. There are two elements that enter into the calculation of the valuation as to which I wish to ask you a question. First taking local rates, by how much do the local rates in Ireland at the present time exceed what they were, or the maximum of what they were at the period of the valuation?—I can get that evidence.

5856. I dare say you can say from memory that there is a considerable increase?—I have not the figures before me.

5857. Assuming that there is a considerable increase, would not the difference, the increase in the local rates, have to be deducted now from any valuation made. Would not a valuation made now under that head be below the valuation made then by the difference?—Assuming that the land was of the same value now as it was then, it would be.

5858. I mean without any regard to the value of the land. In arriving at the valuation you previously deduct the local rates, do you not?—Yes.

5859. If there is a larger sum to deduct under the head of the local rates, other things being equal, the valuation would be lower?—Other things being equal, the value of the land being the same, it would be lower.

5860. Have you inquired at all into the cost of prices of labour in Ireland since the valuation was made?—I know that the price of labour has increased.

5861. We have it in evidence that the cost of labour has doubled in the last 40 years?—Yes, it has.

5862. If we may assume that the price of labour has doubled since the valuation was made, would not the increased price of labour have to come off the valuation now?—I do not think the price of labour has doubled since the valuation was completed, I think it has doubled since it commenced; but from the evidence of Sir Richard Griffith in 1869, I gathered that the price of labour had increased between 1852 and 1865, and that it had got up to a pretty high price at the latter date. I do not think it has doubled since.

5863. We have been told that in 40 years it has doubled, and I put this to you; whatever may have been the difference in the price of labour at that time and now, with the new valuation, the increased price of labour would operate to lower the valuation?—It would have that effect.

5864. Under the head of local rates, and under the head of cost of labour, the tenant now, other things being equal, would be entitled to a proportionately lower valuation than was made between 1852 and 1865?—If the valuation then was the same as it is now, it certainly would; that is to say, if there was no increase in the value from other causes.

Comparison between assessment in England and Ireland.

5865. Precisely, and we have seen with regard to a great part of the period prices have materially gone down. Now you suggest in one part of your proof, that you were about to institute a comparison between the basis of the assessment for income tax in Ireland and in England?—Yes.

5866. But having read your proof carefully, and listened to your evidence, I do not see that you have instituted any such comparison. You have given particulars about Ireland, but I do not see that you have at all referred to the system in England; have you any particular knowledge of the system in England?—Only from information I have gained from parties here who have to do with the raising of the taxes.

5867. In Ireland the valuation which operates to determine the amount of the income tax is made by officers of the Treasury, a department of the State, is it not?—Yes.

5868. Who are bound by their duty to see that nothing was undervalued in the Imperial interest?—That is to say that one of the ways in which income tax can be paid is so arranged—there are two ways in which income tax can be paid; a man in Ireland can pay either on the valuation, or he can pay on the rent.

5869. But your department has no power to affect the rent?—None whatever.

5870. So far as you are concerned, you are confined to the valuation; and in making that valuation you do effect an Imperial interest, namely, the yield of income tax?—Yes.

5871. Now in England I suppose you are aware, it is the fact that first the poor rate is fixed by the local guardians, and the assessment to the income tax is fixed and under the control of local justices of the peace, by local officers, having regard to the poor rate assessment?—Yes, it is not the same, but it has regard to it.

5872. I think I gather from your evidence that in regard to local taxes the only important question as between one valuation and another is that they should be relative?—It is.

5873. So it does not matter how low they are so long as they are all relatively low?—Yes.

5874. And as regards income the relative amount to each individual is of importance?—Yes.

5875. Does it not appear that when the assessment to income tax in England is made not by the State but by local parties it would be to their interests to keep the valuation down, because it would not hurt them locally whilst it would lower the amount of income tax. Do you think such a system is likely to yield so high a valuation as in Ireland?—So far as I know the local bodies do not keep the assessments down in England, the inclination is always to keep them as high as possible, because each person knows that the higher they keep them on their neighbours the less they have to pay themselves.

5876. What reason is there that the local body should not keep all the assessments relatively low so that they would bear an equal share of the local burdens, and be all relieved in respect of the income tax. Would not that be the natural tendency?—I

Mr. J. G. Barton.

21 Feb. 1895.

Comparison between assessment in England and Ireland.

think the natural tendency would be to keep them as high as possible.

5877. Why?—Because as to each new valuation that is made the tendency would be to make it higher than that before.

5878. So that they might pay more income tax?—No, so that they might individually pay less local rates.

5879. No, because the local rates they would have to pay would be equal, provided it was fairly relative between one person and another, high or low?—Yes.

5880. That end can be attained by a low valuation, and if the valuation is made high there is an increased burden of income tax?—But everybody's object is to put a little more on their neighbours and a little less on themselves.

5881. Within any rating area the valuation could be as low as you please on each tenement so long as it is relatively equally low, therefore is there not a temptation on local assessment bodies to make the valuation low, not affecting them locally, whilst it would relieve all of them from the payment of income tax?—I see your point that the income tax being the tax they most dread, they should keep the assessments low, so as to save themselves income tax whilst it does not matter what local rates they pay, because they are distributed relatively.

5882. That is the point?—I do not think that would be the case, because I think the income tax authorities have power to call in commissioners, and they have power to raise the assessment if they think it too low, and they do raise it considerably.

5883. There are such cases, but it is not usual that the local assessment operates?—I believe in England the assessment for income tax is something like 6,000,000*l.* over the local assessments.

5884. Have you ever inquired what relation the income tax assessment in Great Britain bears to the actual rent?—No, I have not. I cannot give it to you exactly.

5885. Much of your argument depends on the assumption that the English landlord pays income tax on the rent, does it not?—Yes.

5886. Of course that argument would be affected greatly, would it not, if you were to discover from public records that the amount of the rent paid in England in many cases very much exceeded the amount of income tax assessment?—I do not know why it should, but there may be cases where for reasons I know nothing about, that is so, but I understand, as a rule, it is the rent that is the assessment.

5887. There is a well known valuer, Mr. Hadley, who says he could give scores of cases where actually *bonâ fide* yearly rents were paid and the property not rated at half the amount of the rents?—I am sure the income tax authorities would be very glad to hear of those cases.

5888. I do not wish to pay you any unnecessary compliment, but do not you think the system in Ireland of which you are the head is very much more efficient for making the value correspond than the system in England?—I think the system in Ireland is a very good system.

5889. For the State?—Chiefly for local rating. I do not think it is for the State.

5890. So long as the assessments are relatively high or low it mattered nothing as we have agreed?—Yes.

5891. But the interest of the State comes in and makes it higher, does it not?—Yes.

5892. Then would you differ when I say that the system of an Imperial department in Ireland for income tax is more likely to produce the full value than a local system where the temptation is to make the assessment low so as to avoid income tax?—It might be if the valuation could be revised every year, but I do not think a system under which the valuation has stood for 40 years without any revision would be likely to do so.

5893. That is another question. During the whole of the 40 years, so far as my present argument goes, the point I put applies with equal force, because the department was all that time Imperial?—The department has no power to alter the amount of the valuation of land.

Mr. J. G. Barton.

21 Feb. 1895.

Comparison between assessment in England and Ireland.

5894. But in fixing the original valuation it had before its mind the knowledge that the amount of the assessment governed the yield of income tax?—I do not think it had; certainly it was not contemplated in the Act.

5895. No, but the income tax was being levied from the time the valuation began?—No, not from the time it began.

5896. Practically it began in 1854, and the valuation went on for 11 years afterwards?—I think you will find in the instructions issued to the valuers nothing was said about income tax at all.

5897. I do not say there was, but the point I put to you is, all the time the valuation was being made by Treasury officers they knew that the yield of income tax in Ireland would be governed by their assessments; is not that so?—Certainly; part of the time they were aware of that.

Incidence of taxation as between landlord and tenant.

5898. When you argue about the advantage that the Irish landlord has you seem to proceed on the assumption that the standard of rent in England and Ireland is the same, and that the landlord takes the same proportion of the produce for rent?—No, I start on the assumption that the rent the Irish landlord pays is the rent on which income tax would be assessed if he was in England. I do not touch the question of fair rent at all.

5899. But when you come to deal with the yield of income tax as a measure of the relative taxable capacity of two peoples, does it not become a very material question whether the proportion of the produce taken by the landlord in each country is the same?—Yes.

5900. When you come to regard income as a test of the general capacity of the whole community is it not a vital matter to consider whether the proportion of produce taken for rent is the same in both countries?—It is.

5901. And if it were true, as we find here, it is said that in England a fifth of the produce is so taken, and in Ireland one-third, would not that circumstance be of vital importance in determining the relative capacity of the tenants, who in England have four-fifths of the profit and in Ireland only two-thirds?—If it was the case it would.

5902. Also as to tenants' improvements, all improvements in Ireland are made by the tenant, are they not?—Practically, a great proportion of them.

5903. This valuation included, in the valuation of the holding, the improvements made by the tenant, did it not?—No, I think not. It is stated in the *précis* of my evidence that it did, but just before you came into the room I asked to withdraw that. I intended to withdraw it in my direct examination. Of course my evidence on that point is merely from what I have heard and read, and both Sir Richard Griffith and Sir John Ball Greene stated in their evidence before the Committee in 1869 it was not taken into account. I had some evidence that it was, but I think their evidence the stronger, and therefore I ask to withdraw that paragraph in the *précis*. That is on page 9.

5904. I think I should like to read the clause. "It must also be remembered that in the south the "larger proportion of the occupiers were yearly tenants "with no marketable interest in their holdings, whilst "in Ulster the occupiers had a large interest derived "from their improvements over and above the rents "they paid, and the value of which they could nearly "always obtain from an incoming tenant. This "interest was no doubt considered by the valuers "when working in the northern province"?—Yes.

5905. The valuer valued the holding as it stood, I suppose?—Yes.

5906. How was he to determine what improvements had been made by the tenants?—He was instructed in his instructions to make all allowances for the

tenants' improvements. You will see in the table of instructions he is told he must make a deduction for all improvements done by the tenant.

5907. But of course you are aware that the law at that time made all the improvements of the tenants the property of the landlord?—Yes.

5908. The landlord was entitled to charge rent upon every penny of the value of the improvements. There we have it from Sir Richard Griffith and others that the valuation approximated to the rent?—Yes, not the actual rent, but what he considered a fair rent which a solvent tenant would pay from year to year.

5909. Will you give me any answer that will give this Commission a glimpse of the mode by which a valuer went to value a holding at that time, without taking evidence from the tenant or anybody else, as to the improvements, could possibly have separated improvements made by the tenants from the corpus of the holding?—Except from information he got from the tenants, and I presume they got a certain amount of information from the tenants at the time.

5910. But is it not obvious that a question of that kind would be contentious, and evidence would have to be taken from the landlords also. Is there any trace of any such process?—Except in so far as the instructions required them to make those deductions.

5911. I submit to you that all the improvements of the tenants to the last penny were at that time the legal property of the landlord, that there is no hint in the Act of Parliament and no trace in the proceedings of the valuers of any distinction in the tenants' improvements and the holding. Can you find any?—No.

5912. I infer that the income tax assessment in Ireland includes the whole value added to the soil by the labour of the tenants, and that as tenants make no improvements in England, and the improvements are all the property of the landlord, there is a disparity in the comparison between England, where you simply assess the property of the landlord, and Ireland, where the assessment includes a great share of the property of the accompanying class, the tenants?—I think the fact that the decisions as to judicial rents in Ireland, have brought down the rents 20 per cent., rather goes to show that those improvements were deducted.

5913. I submit to you that there is a very great fallacy in your table of judicial rents, because I observe you have taken all the reductions since the Act of 1881 was passed?—Yes.

5914. Of course you must be aware that the operation of the Act of 1881 stands upon two levels different from each other, the one up to the year 1886 and the other since?—Yes.

5915. You know that the reductions in Ireland since 1886 have been far greater than before, do you not?—Yes, I believe they have.

5916. Taking the whole reductions—small ones in the earlier years and the high ones in later years—we reach the conclusion that the judicial rent and the valuation are about the same?—Yes.

5917. But suppose you had taken what is more to our present purpose—the rents as they have been fixed since the prices now operating began to prevail (that is, within the last seven years)—how, then, would the case be?—I have not the figures before me, but I should say most likely it might make a difference of 1 to 2 per cent. From my memory of the cases that have come under my notice before and since that time, I think it might about make that difference.

5918. Would it surprise you very much if I were to suggest that the difference between the reductions from 1881 to 1886, taken together, and the reductions from 1887 to now taken together, would be something nearer to 15 or 20 per cent. than 1 or 2 per cent.?—I do not see how that can be if the whole deductions were only 20 per cent.

5919. I can suggest an explanation to you. The reductions in the first years were small, and they operated to bring down the higher reductions of later years to a common level?—But I do not think any of the totals of reductions, if my memory serves me rightly, were less than 15 or 16 per cent., and therefore, taking the same amount of cases, it would naturally follow that the reductions those last years cannot be more than 25 or 26 per cent.

5920. I submit to you, that as the larger number of cases were heard in the earlier years, and the larger quantity of rent dealt with, that a small reduction upon a large rental, brought into a common sum with a great reduction upon a small rental, does operate to bring down the reductions of the later years?—Quite so.

5921. And I would suggest that the reductions of later years must be far higher than the earlier years?—They are higher, but I do not think they are more than five or six per cent., so far as I recollect.

5922. Have you any doubt from your information that if you were to take now, simply the rents reduced from 1886, and apply that adjustment on the very ingenious principle of your Table 9 to the whole of the rent of Ireland, that it would be found that the valuation of Ireland taken as a whole on that basis would now be considerably higher than the rent. Have you any doubt upon that?—I have considerable doubt.

5923. Do you feel able to give any stronger answer to the question?—No, I have a doubt; considerable doubt.

5924. Can you undertake to supply the Commission with a table such as your Table 9, showing the reductions in rent since 1886?—Yes.

5925. And applying the calculations of Table 9 to the whole rental of Ireland, assuming that the rents before 1886, and the rents that have not come into court at all, bear the same proportion to the valuation and would be subject to the same reduction?—Yes, I think so.

5926. (*Chairman.*) You could prepare such a table, could you?—I think so.

5927. (*Mr. Sexton.*) If such a table showed that the rents of Ireland now, if valued by the courts upon the basis of the reductions since 1886 are considerably lower than the valuation, that would take away the last shred of argument that the Irish landlord has any advantage in being assessed upon the valuation, would it not?—At present, but not in the past. It would show he has no advantage at present, that is to say, if every rent in Ireland was below the valuation, he would have no advantage because he would pay entirely on the rental, but if there was one rent in Ireland above the valuation, he still would have an advantage.

5928. You are speaking generally, are you not?—Yes, but unless you took every individual case you would not be able to arrive at a conclusion.

5929. As bearing on the question of the efficiency of valuation as a standard of value, it would show, judging by current circumstances, the valuation is higher than the value?—The valuations in certain parts of Ireland are higher than the rent of the land.

5930. Suppose you have to show that the gross amount of the valuation of Ireland, was say, 1,000,000*l.* in excess of the gross rent as adjusted, that would indicate, would it not, that so far as the valuation is the basis of the Income Tax Assessment it was excessive?—If it were only the basis it would be excessive.

5931. (*Chairman.*) That you can put in, an amended table, as Mr. Sexton suggests, can you?—Yes.

5932. (*Mr. Sexton.*) I think you have said somewhere, that where land has been reclaimed in Ireland the valuation has not been increased?—No, there have been one or two cases, I believe, where there has been a small nominal value put on some land which has been reclaimed. I have tried to find them, but if there are any, it is a mere bagatelle. It has not been generally done.

5933. You would not say, would you, that reclamation by the tenant ought to be included in the valuation for the purposes of income tax?—No, not for the purposes of income tax.

Mr. J. G. Barton.

21 Feb. 1895.

Judicial rents.

Case of reclaimed land.

Mr. J. G. Barton. [illegible] Feb. 1895. [illegible]

5034. I wish to ask you a few questions as to the instructions given by Sir Richard Griffith. In valuing farms in Ireland, you valued the buildings separately from the land, did you not?—We did.

5035. I suppose you know that is not done in England?—I know it is not.

5036. But you placed that the land value, however, was not to exceed the fair letting value?—Just so.

5037. What was the fair letting value at that time other than a rack rent?—The fair letting value was the produce that the land would produce less the cost of producing it, less the rates and taxes, and less a certain sum which represented interest on the tenant's capital.

5038. You mean the tenant's subsistence, he had no capital?—Yes, practically that.

5039. Have your researches enabled you to discover what proportion of either the gross or nett value of the produce was given to the tenant for subsistence, as a rule?—The only information I have on the subject is in the first valuation. It was stated in some instructions Sir Richard Griffith gave, that on certain qualities of land, which I will read you, a certain proportion was to be considered the nett value out of land produce, according to the following scale: On arable land valued at 20s. to 30s., he was to take a quarter as the rent, one-third being considered the rack rent; 10s. to 20s. he was to take a sixth, the rack rent being a fourth. Under 10s. he was to take an eighth, the rack rent being one-sixth. Pasture, 20s. to 30s., he was to take a half, and inferior mountain pasture a third.

5040. What relation did that proportion so taken as rent, bear to the subsistence allowance to the tenant?—I have always considered that it was one-half, that if the landlord got one-quarter, the tenant would get one-half.

5041. The tenant got double the rent?—Yes.

5042. But the gross produce was first taken?—The gross produce was first taken.

5043. And a reduction taken off that?—And a reduction taken off that.

5044. Sir Richard Griffith and others all said that they did not consider the cost of labour; how could they have taken off that without considering the cost of labour?—I think it must have been taken into account.

5045. (*The O'Conor Don.*) Is it a fact, that it was so stated?—I have read the evidence, and they say "yes" and "no."

5046. (*Mr. Sexton.*) This is distinct enough before the Select Committee of 1869. Mr. McCarthy Downing asks Sir John Ball Greene, "Can you say whether you took the question of labour at all into account?" and the answer was, "I should say we did not." That is distinct enough, surely?—Yes. But in one or two other later questions Sir Richard Griffith inferred he did so; I therefore leave it an open question.

5047. At any rate we cannot hold you responsible for the opinions of your predecessors. Let us assume that they took into consideration the cost of production?—Yes.

5048. Then we have the nett produce?—Yes.

5049. Then was this proportion gross or nett?—I think it is intended to be a proportion of the gross produce, but it is rather indefinite. I struck it out of my evidence because I was not very clear about it.

5050. In your type written proof you say they took the gross produce into account?—Yes, and I struck it out because I was not clear about it.

5051. As to this system of separate valuing of land and buildings, of course you will agree that the great majority in Ireland of the poorer class of tenants' houses, mud cabins and so on, had no value, except as a place for the tenant to live in?—Yes, and they are put in our books at a nominal value.

5052. What value do you put on these?—5s. to 1*l.* generally. We hardly ever enter anything in the books at less than 5s.

5053. Do you really think that a separate system of valuation of land and buildings did not operate to raise the valuation of the holding?—I do not think so. You see the value of the whole farm buildings in Ireland is about 1,000,000*l.*, and that includes all the gentlemen's mansions. If you take from that 1,000,000*l.* the mansions which I roughly estimate at 500,000*l.* you will find that the whole of the farmhouses are valued at about 500,000*l.*, which is about 1*l.* a house all round. As there are about half a million tenants, this would be about 1*l.* a house all round.

5054. If these poor dwellings were valued as places for the tenants to live while they were working the farm, would it not rather appear that the real value of these buildings was already included in the value of the land?—I think not under the instructions. If the valuer carried out the instructions, I do not see how it could be so.

5055. Were the mud cabins valued on a structural basis?—To a certain extent, but we had a scale [illegible] for these different classes of houses. We have different classes of houses dealt with in our instructions, and scales of prices under which a house of a certain class had a certain valuation; those cabins were usually valued from 5s. to 1*l.* The structural basis in Sir Richard Griffith's tables gives a very low valuation; it works out in such cases to about 1 per cent. on the capital expenditure.

5056. But the ordinary house of a small farmer adds nothing whatever to the value of the land, and the value of the land is the value of the holding?—I think the value of the house has been deducted.

5057. When you say that local circumstances were taken into account, such as climate and so on, of course your meaning is that these circumstances added to the valuation?—Added to or deducted from.

5058. How do you mean?—That it might add to, or it might deduct from. If a house was very far away from a market it lowered the valuation; if at medium distance it had no effect; if it was very close it raised it.

5059. Would not the tendency of such an instruction rather be to raise the value in case of proximity than to reduce it in case of distance?—I do not quite see why.

5060. Land under plantation and wood is assessed according to agricultural value?—Yes.

5061. I suppose you are aware that plantations and woods are not valued at all in England?—I am told they are valued as plantations. Mr. [illegible] told me yesterday that they were valued as plantations.

5062. I suppose that they are either not valued at all, or not valued at all on the same scale as in Ireland. Then turf bogs, I think, are sometimes valued both as pasture and as turbary?—I have never come across such a case; they are valued as turbary when the turf is sold; when it ceases to be sold they cease to be valued as turbary.

5063. At any rate, the turf bogs are valued as turbary, are they not?—When the turf is sold.

5064. At the time of the valuation, the turf bog which might be sold was valued as turbary which might be sold?—No.

5065. How was it valued?—It was not valued at all. It is one of the exemptions, unless it was used as pasture. You will find that it is stated in the Act, all turf bogs are to be exempted. I will give you the clause, it is No. 12, 13 & 16 Vict. c. 63.

5066. Unless it was used for sale?—Unless it was used for sale.

5067. Then where a turf bog was used for sale it was valued?—Yes; once they began to sell the turf, then it was valued.

5068. (*The O'Conor Don.*) What do you mean by "once they began," because this valuation was done 40 years ago, and has never been altered since?—The valuation of turf bogs has been altered since; it is being raised and lowered frequently; it is not treated as land. We consider that a removable hereditament which can be changed.

5069. (*Mr. Sexton.*) How is turf bog brought before you?—I had one case brought before me last

Mr. J. B. Greene.

8 Feb. 18[illegible].

[illegible]

work; two ratepayers of a district in Kerry stated that certain turf bogs were not fully rated. I inquired into the case and raised the value about 20*l*.

5070. The valuation was too low, was it?—The valuation was too low.

5071. How does that bear upon your general testimony that the total land valuation of a townland must not be altered?—This is not land value. Once the turf is sold, the bog ceases to be treated as land, and becomes a rateable hereditament liable to change.

5072. Is it only where the valuation is held to be too low that you intervene?—No, we intervene in far more cases where it is too high than where it is too low. I should like to give you the number of cases we dealt with last year where it was too high. The number of cases reduced or struck out was 9,303.

5073. What does that refer to?—Houses or turf bogs, fisheries, railways, canals, and all property liable to revision of its value. In Dublin in the last 10 years there have been 6,425 houses reduced in value out of a total of 25,000.

5074. Out of a total of 25,000 which came before you?—No, 25,000 is roughly the total number of houses in Dublin.

5075. Were those 6,425 in Dublin?—Those 6,425 were in Dublin.

5076. Supposing a turf bog is all cut away, the valuation may be abolished, may it not?—Yes, it will be abolished, unless it is a soil or pasturage.

Assessment of railways.

5077. Now as to railways and canals, what do you say as to the contention that the system of valuing railways and canals in Ireland gives far higher results than the system applied in England?—Our valuation of railways does not affect the valuation for income tax. Railways are assessed under Schedule D. Therefore our valuation only affects local rates, but our valuation of railways for local rates is, I think, rather lower than it is in England. I got a number of the English railway companies to send me in, for the last year, their receipts, and the rates that they paid, and from that I made out that for the principal English railways the local rates were 7·7 per cent. of the nett receipts; while in Ireland, on the five principal railways, they were 5·7 of the nett receipts.

5078. For the local rates?—For the local rates.

5079. Can you give any evidence as to the relative incidence of assessment on railways in Ireland and England for the purposes of income tax?—I cannot; it does not come within the scope of my department at all.

Valuation of property in cities.

5080. Now as to houses not connected with land, are you of opinion that the real cost of the repairs and maintenance of houses in cities, such as Dublin, is fully taken into account?—Yes, I think so. I take from a fourth to a sixth of the rent, generally a sixth; but where houses are old I take a fourth.

5081. You have told us that out of a total of 25,000 houses in Dublin you have actually reduced the valuation of 6,000 of them in a year?—No, in 10 years.

5082. It would show, would it not, incontestably, if you have reduced the value of a fourth of the houses in the city in 10 years, there is a decrease in their value?—Yes; yet the increase in the total value of the city is remarkable; in those 10 years it is 17,786*l*.

5083. I do not follow you?—The increase in the value of Dublin city in that 10 years, in spite of that reduction, has been 17,786*l*.

5084. Would not that appear to show that where parts of the city are progressive you have kept the value well up?—It would show that parts of the city are increasing very much more in value than the parts that are going down are depreciating.

5085. The increase in value in Dublin and the adjoining townships consists mainly of houses built in comparatively recent times, and fully valued, does it not?—I do not think they are fully valued.

5086. Valued in comparatively recent times?—Valued in comparatively recent times, but a deduction has been made every time to keep them relative to the old valuations.

5087. In the townships no such reduction was necessary, was there?—Yes, a very heavy reduction has been made.

Valuation of houses in cities.

5088. Are you disposed to commit yourself to a declaration that if you make full allowance in the city of Dublin for the cost of repairs in the old and somewhat dilapidated houses, for insurance, and for the local rates (now about 10*s*. in the pound), and taking those out of the rents, which is the system in Dublin, that the balance left of the rents will show you materially to increase the valuation of that city as a whole?—Certainly.

5089. I see by your table that the number of houses you have had to raise in Dublin for the year was 134. Were those cases of structural alterations?—No, they were new houses. I did not take in the cases of structural alterations, because it might affect the comparison.

5090. In the case of Dublin I take it there may be some progress in very obscure parts of the city, the better business quarters, but that the city as a whole has retrograded; and that parts of the city where there were family mansions and houses inhabited by wealthy families are now let in tenements?—A great part of the north of Dublin is in that position exactly, and there we have made there large reductions. I should say out of those 6,000 houses I mentioned as being reduced, much the largest proportion are on the north side of the city, which has depreciated in value considerably; but on the other hand the centre of Dublin, the business part, is increasing in value largely, and the valuations there would be doubled. In some portions of Dublin, about College Green, taking that as a centre, the valuations would be doubled if there was a valuation made to-morrow.

5091. On the other hand, is not there a very great part of Dublin where the cost of repairs and the local rates go far towards swallowing up the rent?—I do not think the cost of repairs in Dublin exceeds that of any other old city. The local rates are certainly 9*s*. in the pound. We have always deducted the local rates, and we have to take a percentage of new valuations to make them relative to the old. I merely state the facts I have before me.

5092. You admit, do you not, that it is a question of considerable complexity, taking together the element of unquestioned decline in a great part of the city and progress in another part?—I am very clear on the subject that there should be an increase in the valuation. I have had all parts of Ireland before me; in the last three years I have dealt with two or three thousand cases in every part of the country, and I have known the rent, the amount of maintenance the houses required, etc., and I am perfectly sure there would be an increase of 15 to 20 per cent. if a new valuation were made.

5093. (*Chairman.*) Is the population of Dublin decreasing?—Slightly, I think.

5094. (*Mr. Sexton.*) You make this observation in your first proof, "Even in cases of reductions due to "fall in rent, a further reduction beyond that suggested by the reduced rent is allowed, in order to "make the new valuation relative to those placed on "the adjoining premises"?—Yes.

5095. Is it not the case, when the rent of a house falls, it is part of a concurrent fall of rent in the neighbourhood?—Yes, generally.

5096. Then, if the reduction of the houses you value necessitates a reduction in the valuation, does it not follow if you had the other houses in the neighbourhood to value there would be a corresponding reduction?—So there is. I dealt with Mountjoy Square last year; I revised the value of two-thirds of the square at the same time, and reduced all the valuations some 10 per cent. below what we call the statutory valuation.

5097. Then what is the point of your argument?—I thought it was a little confusing, and that is why I struck it out of the second proof; but the point is this, that when I reduce to the statutory valuation houses which have fallen in value, I have also to make a

Mr. J. G. Barton. 21 Feb. 1895.

Valuation of houses in Dublin.

further reduction to make the reduced valuation relative to all the other houses in the city.

5998. That does not at all argue that the valuation of the other houses is too low, because the fact that you have had to reduce the rent of one house rather tends to show that the valuation of the other houses would have to be reduced if you had them in your hands?—I am afraid I did not make myself quite clear. Assuming that Dublin is a rateable area, and I have arrived at the conclusion that the valuations in Dublin generally are 10 to 15 per cent. below what is the rateable valuation——

5999. That is, that the whole valuation as a unit is that much less than what the sum of a real valuation would be?—Exactly. I then, in dealing with the new valuations, deduct 15 per cent. to make them relative to those on the other houses; and when I am dealing with the old valuations, which I have to reduce, I also deduct that 15 per cent. in addition to reducing them owing to the fall in rent.

6000. You make a larger reduction than rent would justify?—Exactly.

6001. Then it is only by reference to other neighbourhoods of the city that you could maintain the argument that the general valuation is too low?—You must take the rateable area in arriving at whatever deduction you are going to make. There is no part of Dublin which should be taxed more heavily than another part, and we take the rateable area of the whole city and make an average deduction.

6002. On the general question, have you read Dr. Grimshaw's evidence?—Not all of it; I have read a part of it.

Decline in value of agricultural produce.

6003. I suppose you are generally aware that he told us that the annual value of the crops and stock taken together now or of recent years is many millions a year lower than in the period during which the valuation was made?—I did not know that; it is very possible.

6004. Of course, if the annual value of what the tenant now produces in Ireland, crops and stock together, is many millions a year less than it used to be within the period when the valuation was made, that would point to a heavier reduction in the valuation being necessary, would it not?—If the valuation was a full one it would look rather like it.

6005. You have referred to the non-payment of rent since 1881 as reducing the yield of the income tax?—Yes.

6006. I suppose the operation of the Arrears Act of 1882, by which a large quantity was wiped out, contributed to that result?—I dare say. The matter was incidentally brought before me, and looking through the income tax returns I found that the amount of the tax written off through the Schedule of Discharge increased very much just about 1881. On inquiring the cause, I found it was owing to the tax only being paid since that date on the actual received, instead of the gross rental as previously.

6007. (*The O'Conor Don.*) With regard to those arrears struck out, is it not the fact that the landlords have paid the income tax upon them in a great many cases?—If due before 1881 they would have done so.

6008. (*Mr. Sexton.*) I suppose you mean nothing more than to suggest that as in England where the rents have been reduced by nearly one-fifth in the last 20 years, that abatements and voluntary reductions of rent have operated in this way; where the rent actually received is lower, I suppose he is entitled to be assessed on the rent?—Yes.

6009. I suppose you are aware of the immense falling off in the value of land in England since 1880?—Yes.

6010. The valuation of land in England increased between the time the Irish valuation was completed and 1880 by about five-and-a-half millions or a fifth, but then it went back 11,000,000*l.*, that is to say, that the increase in the valuation in England between the time when the Irish valuation closed and the prosperous period of 1880 was only half as much as the falling off has been since?—Yes.

Mr. J. G. Barton. 21 Feb. 1895.

Decline in value of agricultural produce.

6011. But the valuation of Ireland remains the same or rather it is 1,000,000*l.* more nominally than it was in 1865, which you say is due to houses?—The valuation is the same, but the houses were transferred by the income tax authorities from one account to another; that is to say, they were formerly charged under Schedule A. as houses, and they are now charged as land.

6012. The valuation of the land now is the same as it was when the valuation was completed, is it not?—Yes.

6013. [illegible] the valuation of England has fallen off in the same period from 46,000,000*l.* to 41,000,000*l.*, has it not?—Yes.

6014. Does it not seem that a corresponding reduction would have to be made in the valuation of Ireland now?—I think it very much depends upon the produce; the farmer in England cannot produce the same thing that the farmer in Ireland makes his profit out of. I think it was the great fall in the value of wheat that affected the English farmer, and we had not any such fall in Ireland, that is to say, wheat in Ireland is not a staple crop.

6015. But there has been a disastrous fall, has there not in things upon which Ireland mainly depends?—Yes, but I do not think it has been as great as the fall in the value of wheat in England.

6016. Perhaps you would say it is a matter of speculation, but if the valuation of Sir Richard Griffith followed, as we have evidence from himself, the course of prices and the course of rents between 1852 and 1865, and if the valuation of England has fallen by 5,000,000*l.* since 1865, whilst the valuation of Ireland has been left at the old figure, there appears no way of avoiding the conclusion that an annual valuation would materially reduce the assessment?—If you assume the valuation of Ireland and the rental of England in 1852 were on the same basis, that is so, but the valuation of Ireland between 1852 and 1865 and the rental of England at the same period were on very different basis.

6017. Still more would any argument prevail if it was the fact that the rent in Ireland to which the valuation approximated was a much higher proportion of the produce than the rent in England, would it not?—No, I do not think so. If the valuation in Ireland was a very low valuation in 1865, and the decrease in the rent of England and in Ireland was the same, the valuation in Ireland, unless it was still kept very low as compared to the rent, would not decrease by the same amount, and would still be a fair valuation.

6018. If the rent of Ireland at the time of its valuation was proportionately a higher rent than in England, and if the valuation in Ireland exceeded that rent, as it did, is it not evident that a new valuation now in which regard would be had to the basis of the rent, would accomplish a heavier reduction in the valuation of Ireland?—I do not think the valuation of Ireland exceeded the rent.

6019. It approximated to the rent, [illegible]—No, I think not at all; it was [illegible] below the rent, except in the north.

6020. At any rate, so far as the valuation approximated to the rent, if the basis of rent was higher in Ireland than in England, a re-valuation now in which regard would be had to the basis of rent in England, if lower than in Ireland, would operate to lower the valuation, would it not?—I do not see it.

6021. Does it not seem to be evident?—No, I think you must assume that the rent in England and the rent in Ireland at that date were on the same basis.

Effect of Land Purchase Acts.

6022. I am assuming they were not the same. I am asking you to assume that the proportion of produce taken off Ireland was higher than in England for rent; and therefore, so far as the valuation had regard to the rent, it was a higher valuation than would be imposed on England, and that if a new valuation were now had with reference to the basis of rent in England, if lower, that would operate to lower the valuation in Ireland. Now, as to your Table X.,

Mr. J. G. Barton. 11 Feb. 1895. Effect of Land Purchase Acts.

you offer here a suggestion as to the basis of comparison of the relative taxable capacity of Great Britain and Ireland. I must say, although the amount is small, the principle is important, and I fail to see why you add to the amount actually charged to duty, the amount that would have been paid if the sales had not been made. Certain property no doubt is transferred?—Yes.

6023. But how are you entitled to add that to the amount of income tax actually paid?—Because I have tried to get a basis of a tax upon the land, not on the income of the persons. That is a tax that represents a tax on the whole land of Ireland.

6024. Taking it, say, for 49 years to come, the man who bought that land will have to pay to the Treasury an annual amount corresponding to what was to be the rent, will he not?—Yes.

6025. It is obvious therefore, is it not, that the element in the value of that land, which properly forms the assessment to income tax, is no part of the wealth of Ireland for the next 49 years?—That is another question I think.

6026. Would you agree with me that in comparing the relative taxable capacity of these two countries upon the basis of the income tax, that you should proceed on the assumption that the incomes upon which the taxes are paid are expended in the countries in which the tax is raised?—I did not take that into consideration at all; it is merely the income tax raised on land.

6027. But as you have gone so far as to head your table, "Comparison of the relative taxable capacity of "Great Britain and Ireland," I should like to ask you if it were found that, say, one-third or one-half of the rental of Ireland goes to England to absentee landlords, and payment of interest, that circumstance would, of course, affect the calculation of the taxable capacity?—It might affect the capacity, but it would not affect the question of arriving at what the income tax of the two countries was.

6028. But you would agree with me, would you not, that the mere circumstance that income tax is paid in the country is no test of the capacity of that country if the income itself is not expended there?—I have no information as to how much of the income is expended in Ireland.

Tenant right.

6029. (*Lord Farrer.*) I think you said that where there is tenant right the tenant right forms no part of the valuation upon which income tax is paid?—Yes.

6030. Does that pay no income tax at all; does the tenant pay upon it?—The tenant is assessed under Schedule B. if his holding is over 150*l*. for his farm profits, but he is not assessed in any way for his tenant right upon it.

6031. Is that treated as part of his income?—No, it does not come in as part of his income in any way.

6032. Then he does not pay income tax upon that?—No, he only pays income tax upon one-third of the valuation of the farm which he holds and if that is not over 150*l*. (or 160*l*. it now is) he does not pay any income tax.

6033. A farm is worth so much plus so much tenant right is it not?—Yes.

6034. And is that tenant right taken into consideration in considering whether he shall pay income tax or not?—No, it is not taken into consideration at all.

6035. So that that part of the interest in the whole property does not pay income tax at all, does it?—No, that is so.

6036. That is a very considerable part of the property, is it not?—It is increasing.

6037. (*Mr. Sexton.*) Is there anything in the case of a tenant of land in Ireland or anywhere else which can be the subject of assessment to income tax except what is left to him out of the produce of the farm after he pays the rent?—That is all.

6038. (*Lord Farrer.*) But that which, where there is no tenant right, would form part either of the income of the tenant or income of the landlord, by reason of his being tenant right, escapes payment of income tax, does it not?—That is so.

Mr. J. G. Barton. 11 Feb. 1895. Tenant right.

6039. (*Mr. Currie.*) With reference to the absentee landlord he pays the income tax, does he not?—Yes.

6040. Can it be said to impoverish Ireland if you diminish the absentee landlord's income?—I presume, Mr. Sexton refers to the income he spent over here; not to the income tax.

Valuation of houses in London and Dublin.

6041. (*Lord Farrer.*) Have you ever made any comparison of the valuation of a house in Dublin, with the valuation of a house in London?—Only just from knowing what my friends in London pay for their houses and what my friends in Dublin pay for theirs.

6042. As far as you can judge, how do you think that the valuation in Dublin stands as compared with London?—The houses in the best squares in Dublin are valued at about 100*l*. or 120*l*. a year, and I should say the same class of houses here would be valued at nearly double that.

6043. How far does that depend upon cost of construction, and how far upon rent?—In those houses I am judging altogether by the rent. It is very hard in a city like Dublin to bring the question of construction in at all, because as a property becomes more or less fashionable, the houses cease to have the same rent value though the cost of construction remains the same.

6044. So that actual cost of construction has to be thrown aside in those cases has it not?—Yes.

6045. It is a question of demand and supply is it not and not of cost of construction?—It is a great check on our work to have the question of cost of construction before us. In factories and that class of property it is absolutely necessary.

6046. In the factories you have not the same means of judging what rent can be got as from the houses have you?—No, by no means.

6047. The real test of value, I suppose, is what can be got for a house in the market?—That is so, but cost of construction is a check in arriving at the result.

6048. But the real test for any values is what can be got for the thing in the market, is it not?—Yes, that is so.

6049. And, that is the case in Dublin as well as in London, I suppose?—It is.

6050. What relation does your valuation bear to the rent in Dublin as compared with the assessment in London to the rent in London?—Our valuation in relation to the rent in Dublin as I said before is about two-thirds.

6051. Do you know what it is in London?—I should say it was about four-fifths, roughly speaking.

6052. (*Mr. Sexton.*) Is the rent in each case the same; is it the rent without deducting the charges?—The tenant paying the taxes.

6053. When you speak of rent in this equation is the rent in each case the same rent, is it the gross rent?—I assume it to be the same; that is to say that the landlord does the repairs and the tenant pays the taxes.

6054. Then you would have to take off the cost of the repairs, would you not?—Yes.

6055. That would bring it down to the two-thirds?—Yes.

6056. The difference of one-third has to be reduced by the cost of repairs?—Yes.

6057. (*Lord Farrer.*) You are aware that in London a great controversy has been going on about the assessment of houses, are you not?—Yes.

6058. You are aware, are you not, that in London the Government officer has the right to interfere, and does come in?—Yes, I know he does.

6059. So that it is not quite true that each locality is left entirely to itself; the Government officer can interpose?—I think the Government officer can interpose everywhere to a certain extent; the Commissioner can, I think, interpose.

6060. (*Chairman.*) Under the Metropolitan Act he interposes all the way through, I think?—He does.

Mr. J. E. Barton. 21 Feb. 1895. Valuation of houses in London and Dublin.

6061. (*Mr. Sexton.*) Apart from the increased price of houses, due to fashion, have you any doubt that a man can get as cheap a house suitable to his condition and income in London as in Dublin?—It is a very hard question to answer. It is a common saying that you can live cheaper in London than anywhere else.

The witness withdrew.

Adjourned to to-morrow at 12 o'clock.

FOURTEENTH DAY.

Friday, 22nd February 1895.

At Committee Room B, House of Lords.

PRESENT:

THE RIGHT HON. HUGH C. E. CHILDERS, *Chairman.*

Lord Welby, G.C.B.
Lord Farrer.
The Right Hon. The O'Conor Don.
Sir David Barbour, K.C.S.I.
Thomas Sexton, Esq., M.P.
Henry F. Slattery, Esq.

Mr. R. H. Holland, *Secretary.*

Mr. W. F. Bailey called and examined.

Mr. W. F. Bailey. 22 Feb. 1895.

6062. (*Chairman.*) You are legal assistant land commissioner are you not?—Yes.

6063. How long have you been in that position?—Since the year 1887.

6064. You have studied the valuation and assessment of England and Ireland especially, have you not?—Yes. Since my appointment on the Land Commission the matter of the Government valuation has been brought specially to my notice as it of course arises more or less in the fixing of fair rents, and in that way I was led to study the question with some closeness.

6065. And that led you to study the English system as well as the Irish, did it not?—Yes, of course I do not pretend to as accurate and close a knowledge of the English system as that of the Irish, but I have tried to get some information with regard to the English system so as to arrive at a proper understanding as to the Irish system.

Valuations in Ireland.

6066. How many Irish valuations have there been in this century?—There have been three general valuations, the first townland valuation under the Act of 1826, which, however, was not commenced till 1830, owing to the absence of maps which were necessary for the carrying out of it; there were amending Acts from that time on in 1831, 1832, 1834, and 1836. Those all were concerned with the valuation of Irish land as comprised in townlands. The valuation of tenements was not undertaken until after the introduction of the poor law system which rendered it necessary that a tenement valuation should be carried out. That was commenced under the Act of 1846.

6067. At present you may say that the valuation system is complete in itself?—Yes.

6068. And applies to all parts of Ireland?—Yes, quite so.

6069. You would also say that it differs from the English system in being an official and Government system, would you not?—Yes, I think that makes a very considerable difference. In Ireland the valuation office is an office organised under special statutes, and is under the control of the Treasury. It is entrusted with the valuation of the entire rateable property of the country, lands, and houses, both for the purpose of local taxation and very largely for Imperial taxation, and of course it is carried out in a consecutive and regular system which cannot be expected to obtain in England, where the assessment of each district is left more or less to the local authorities.

6070. Then you would distinguish between the two systems that whereas in England the assessment and valuation is only partially a Government system, in Ireland it is thoroughly so?—Quite so.

Mr. W. F. Bailey. 22 Feb. 1895. Assessments under Sch. A. [illegible]

6071. With respect to the land under Schedule A., what are the amounts of the most recent assessments in the three kingdoms?—Taking the figures given in this paper which was put in before the Commission by Mr. Milner, the figures for the year 1892 were for England valuation of land 41,384,902*l*. In Scotland in the year 1892, the same year, the valuation of land is given as 6,318,281*l*., while in Ireland for the same year the valuation of land is given as 10,042,811*l*. From that it will be seen that the assessment of land in Ireland is about a fourth of the assessment of land in England, and is a third more than the assessment of land in Scotland.

6072. Do you look upon the Irish assessment as fair or too high as compared with the others?—The conclusion I have come to, so far as I can form an opinion, is that as compared with England the assessment of land in Ireland is too high.

6073. Has the assessment of land in Ireland altered much of recent years?—No; in fact it has not changed at all since 1855. There has been no change in the value of the land itself, and I may perhaps here explain what I should have to explain further on with reference to some tables that I intended to put in, namely, that the figures given in this table put in by Mr. Milner are in this respect a little misleading. On page 2 of that paper, No. 2 dealing with Ireland under the head of land, including tithes, it would appear that a very considerable rise had taken place since 1865 in the valuation of Irish land. It will be seen that in the year 1876 the valuation of land in Ireland is given at 9,383,670*l*., while the following year the valuation of land, including tithes, is given at 10,081,744*l*., that is, an increase of over 600,000*l*. in the year. When we are aware of the fact that no increase in the valuation of land has taken place, or can take place, under the present system in Ireland, these figures are a little puzzling but, as I think was explained by Mr. Barton yesterday, the income tax officials seem to have made a change in their method of making the accounts, and transferred from one column, that is, the second column, houses of about 600,000*l*. worth of the valuation to the first column under the head of lands, and as there is no note of that change in this return which

Mr. W. P. Bailey. 2 Feb. 1894. Assessments under Schedule A compared.

has been put before the Commission the matter, unless explained, is apt to lead to confusion.

6074. We will assume that that will be explained during our inquiry, but irrespective of that has any great change taken place of late years in the valuation of land in England and Scotland?—Yes. The valuation of land in England and Scotland has fallen over 20 per cent. between the years 1880 and 1893. While during the same period the valuation of Irish land has not altered, although during the same period the rental of Ireland has fallen by something over 20 per cent.

6075. (*Mr. Sexton.*) That is, so much as has been dealt with in the courts?—Quite so.

6076. (*Chairman.*) Going back to the year 1865, when the Irish valuation was completed, what do you find as to the figures of increase and decrease?—Comparing the year 1865 with the year 1893, which is the last available year, the valuation of land in England has fallen by between 11 and 12 per cent., and the valuation of land in Scotland has fallen by fully 8 per cent., while the valuation of land in Ireland having regard to these figures which I have just mentioned has not changed; it would appear to have risen; but it has practically remained unchanged.

6077. (*Sir David Barbour.*) I see the figures are 9,333,000*l.* the valuation for 1865, and 9,973,000*l.* for 1893; the two sets of figures I understand you to say are not comparable?—That is so.

6078. (*Mr. Sexton.*) I think Mr. Barton explained yesterday that the apparent increase in the valuation of Ireland was due to the increase of urban houses, not connected with land?—It would seem to me that they could hardly have transferred any of the urban houses, as there is a column given for houses in the return of Mr. Milner. I take it that the change must have been caused by the transfer of some purely agricultural houses, probably cottages and houses attached to the agricultural tenements. However, of course Mr. Barton could explain that.

6079. He told us that under the law the agricultural valuation of Ireland is unaltered, and cannot be altered, except so far as turf bog is concerned?—Quite so; but it would appear they have transferred houses which have been put under one column to another column, that is to say, the valuation of cabins, I suppose, and houses belonging to agricultural holdings.

(*Chairman.*) Perhaps Mr. Barton would be good enough to give in short the explanation.

(*Mr. Barton.*) I understand what actually happened was this: that previous to that year in the income-tax assessment in Ireland the land and farmhouses were all in separate columns, the land in the first column and houses in the second column, but after that year all the houses on the farms were added to the first column and now what is put down as lands only, includes farmhouses. That is what I believe to be the case.

(*Chairman.*) Not a separate living house, but only the farmhouses?

(*Mr. Barton.*) The farmhouses and the mansions on the different estates.

(*Chairman.*) Do these, in your opinion, account for the difference of 600,000*l.* a year.

(*Mr. Barton.*) That is so.

(*Mr. Sexton.*) Does that refer to Ireland and England?

(*Mr. Barton.*) I can only speak for Ireland.

(*Lord Welby.*) Is it not the case that in England the farmhouse, the houses belonging to the land, were always classed with the land.

(*Mr. Barton.*) Yes.

(*Lord Welby.*) And therefore the change made in Ireland was simply an assimilation of the practice in Ireland to that of England, namely, the classing along with the land of the houses belonging to the land.

(*Mr. Barton.*) That is so.

6080. (*Chairman to the Witness.*) Taking the earlier of the periods which we have had under discussion between 1864 and 1892; in the years 1865 and 1880 the percentage of increase in England, Scotland, and Ireland was about the same, was it not?—The percentage of increase in England and Scotland between 1864 and 1880 was something about 12 or 13 per cent., while according to Mr. Barton's explanation the valuation of Ireland remained unaltered as regards land.

6081. Except in respect of the method of arranging it?—Quite so.

6082. And in respect of that method there was an increase of 19 per cent., was there not?—Yes, if you take that into account.

6083. The landlord in Ireland only pays income tax upon the amount of his rent, when the rent is less than the valuation, does he not?—Yes, that is so.

6084. But the tenant is held to be the owner of the difference where there is a difference?—Yes, under the Act of 16 & 17 Vict. c. 34 the law is that where the landlord receives less rent than the valuation he only pays on that less rent, but the tenant, in law, is liable for the difference between the rent and the valuation.

6085. And in respect to his payment he is looked upon, is he not, as the owner of the difference?—Quite so.

6086. (*Sir David Barbour.*) Does he in practice have to pay on that difference, or does he come generally under the limit of exemption?—As a rule under the limit of exemption.

Basis of valuation in Ireland.

6087. (*Chairman.*) Will you give us briefly the comparison between the methods of assessment and valuation in Ireland and England, taking the Irish method first?—The Government valuation of Ireland under the Act of 1852 was, according to the words of the Act, intended to be made in a different manner as regards lands and houses. As regards land under the third section of the Act, it was intended it should be made "upon an estimate of the net annual value thereof "with reference to the average prices of the several "articles of agricultural produce herein-after speci"fied, all peculiar local circumstances in each case "being taken into consideration, and all rates, taxes, "and public charges, if any, except tithe-rentcharge "being paid by the tenant." Then it gives the scale of prices under which that valuation was to be made. Then, as regards houses and buildings, "The valua"tion shall be made upon an estimate of the net "annual value thereof, that is to say, the rent for "which, one year with another, the same might in its "actual state be reasonably expected to let from year "to year, the probable average annual cost of repairs, "insurance, and other expenses, if any, necessary to "maintain the hereditament in its actual state, and all "rates, taxes, and public charges, if any, except tithe"rentcharge being paid by the tenant." In accordance with that provision in the statute, the volume of instructions drawn up by Sir Richard Griffith, which are based upon previous volumes of instructions issued under the earlier valuation Acts, were issued for the instruction of the valuers. But it would appear to me, from my knowledge of the valuation, and the method in which it was carried out, so far as I can judge, that in reality the method of valuing the land was really altered for the method of valuing it in accordance with the prevailing prices at the time the valuation was made, and very largely it would appear to me that it was based upon the actual rental.

6088. The actual letting value?—The actual letting value; while on the other hand the valuation of houses was made, not upon the actual letting value, as apparently was intended to be the system of valuation, but it was made upon a very complex and carefully drawn up scale of cost of construction and price of material, which are given in Griffith's Instructions.

6089. Can you give any illustration of that departure from the original intention?—From what we can gather from the evidence of the instructions themselves, and the evidence given by Sir Richard Griffith and others before Parliamentary Committees of Inquiry, it would appear evident that the scale of prices was not adhered

Mr. W. F. Bailey.

27 Feb. 1895.

Basis of valuation in Ireland.

to, except to a very limited extent, in carrying out that valuation. In the original instructions of Griffith, issued to the valuers of 1830, the valuers were directed to "value the land on a liberal scale, that is to say, "in the same manner as if employed by one of the "principal landlords of the country, who was about to "let the lands to solvent tenants on leases, say, of 21 "years."

6090. (*Mr. Sexton.*) "Who was about to let the "lands"?—Yes, "who was about to let the lands." The original valuation of 1830 was carried out under that general instruction. Then, in the instructions of 1853, it was laid down by Griffith, on page 12, that it is to be borne in mind that "the total valuation of land "and buildings, exclusive of taxes, should not exceed "the fair letting value to a solvent tenant," which would seem to show that the letting value was to be kept in view by the valuers in making their valuation.

6091. (*Sir David Barbour.*) But simply as a maximum limit, I understand?—Yes, that was all, according to the instructions.

6092. The valuation of the land was to be made according to the system laid down; but if the valuation was more than the letting value, it was to be reduced to the letting value?—Quite so; but on page 80 of the same instructions he has a final instruction, in which he says, "It should be borne in mind that for each "separate tenement a similar conclusion is ultimately "to be arrived at, namely, that the value of land, "buildings, &c., as the case may be, when set forth in "the column for totals is the rent which a liberal "landlord would obtain from a solvent tenant for a "term of years."

6093. Not the actual rent?—No, the rent he would obtain.

6094. According to that system of valuation?—Quite so.

6095. (*Chairman.*) Have you any further evidence from the proceedings of the Committee of 1869 which would justify that view?—Before the Committee of 1869, which took a great deal of evidence from Sir John Ball Greene and Sir Richard Griffith, and, so far as one can judge from their evidence, the valuation was largely based on the rents at the time. For example, at Question 1566, speaking of the county Dublin, Sir Richard Griffith said it was valued "on a moderate "rent value," and when he was asked to explain the value of Ulster, which was admittedly higher than that of the other provinces, he said: "The fact is, the "improvement in agriculture was so great that the "valuers took a very high view of it. It has been "shown by a member of the Committee that our valua-"tion was, perhaps, on a scale too high, for it is equal "to the rents. I know that on an estate of my own "in the county of Londonderry my valuation was "higher than the rents." Then further on he says: "We came up to the letting rents of the principal "landlords." Then, in answer to Question 1577, "You valued, in fact, higher than the scale?" he said: "We did not leave the scale, but we took a "higher view of it, considering the improved state of "the agriculture of the country." I do not know exactly what he means by taking a higher view of it.

6096. (*Sir David Barbour.*) He was referring to increased produce perhaps?—The scale did not apply to produce. That explanation of it, at any rate, did not occur to himself.

6097. (*The O'Conor Don.*) You have read Sir Richard Griffith's evidence carefully, I suppose?—I have.

6098. And you must be aware that it is most contradictory?—From the evidence given in this volume (a great deal of it was drawn out by yourself as a member of the Committee), it is rather difficult to arrive at any clear understanding as to how the valuation was carried out.

6099. Would it not be easy from the evidence to quote other extracts quite in the contrary sense from the extracts which you have quoted?—It probably would be possible, but I read it through with the idea that the valuation was largely based on the rents, that was my idea when I commenced reading it, and it seemed to me from my reading of the evidence that that opinion was borne out.

Mr. W. F. Bailey.

27 Feb. 1895.

Basis of valuation in Ireland.

6100. (*Chairman.*) Do you found that entirely on the fact that between the valuation of Leinster and Munster, and the valuation of Ulster some time had elapsed in which land had risen very much in value?—Quite so. The valuation of Munster was commenced under the Act of 1846, the first Act for the valuation of tenements in Ireland, and, as I think was explained yesterday, six counties had been left unvalued under the earlier Townland Valuation Act. The valuation of these six counties was directed to be made in accordance with the Tenement Valuation Act of 1846. The valuation was commenced in 1846, and that valuation was the one that apparently still exists, probably with some alteration for the difference in the scale of prices in the different Acts. But the valuation of Ulster was not commenced until a much later period; in fact, some of the counties of Ulster were not completed until the year 1865; for example, the county of Armagh.

6101. And that, in your view, accounts for a good deal of the difference, does it?—Yes, I think it accounts for it almost altogether. The valuation of Ulster was admittedly from 15 to 25 per cent. higher than the valuation of the other provinces, and the only possible explanation of that difference, that I can see, is the difference in time at which the valuations were made.

6102. (*Sir David Barbour.*) At Question 1577 Sir Richard Griffith said: "We did not leave the scale, "but we took a higher view of it, considering the "improved state of the agriculture of the country." That would mean higher produce, would it not; it would not mean higher prices, but a larger quantity of produce?—Yes, of course it would also mean that, but the improvement in the amount of produce, I would hardly say, would be greater in 1860 than it was in 1852 and 1853.

6103. I was simply referring to what he states, which would give one the idea that he took a larger amount of produce, rightly or wrongly?—That is possible.

6104. (*Mr. Sexton.*) Would not larger produce with disproportionately lower prices mean a bad state of agriculture?—Yes; that is, it would be less profitable; there would be less rent-paying capacity.

6105. (*Chairman.*) I pass for the moment from the internal differences in Ireland to the comparison between, in fact, the Irish valuation system and the English valuation system; you wish, I think, to express that the Irish system is more unfavourable to the occupier than the English, do you not?—In my opinion the Irish system being, as I have said, a system carried out by a large and well-organised Government department is necessarily more stringent in its method of valuation. It will leave less property unvalued, or under-valued. The English system, of course, as I have said, is made in each locality, largely controlled by the local authorities.

Comparison with English system.

6106. Can you give us some illustrations of that?—Taking the English system, which of course every year is getting more perfect. I take it, as years go on, less property is left unvalued, and there is a greater improvement in the method, but notwithstanding that it is quite evident that with that greater stringency of valuation the gross valuation of land in England is still falling. Although you may have greater stringency the value every year is getting less, whereas in Ireland it is stationary, and there is no alteration at all.

6107. Going back a few years before the greater stringency was applied, can you point out any salient differences to the disadvantage of the Irish occupier?—It has been already pointed out, after estimating the value of agricultural holdings in England, it is not the practice to put a separate valuation on the buildings, while as we know in Ireland in all cases every building, even the mud-wall cabins on the

poorer holdings, have something put on them by way of valuation; and it is of course evident that a great deal of the value of those buildings attached to the small agricultural holdings is altogether dependent on the occupation of the land. Compared with the method adopted in England, of course it must make some considerable difference.

6108. Are houses in Ireland valued to any extent with reference to their structural cost?—Yes, in the instructions drawn by Sir Richard Griffith there are very careful tables given for the valuation of the houses, and rules are laid down. In the first of those instructions he says: "The absolute value of a build-"ing is equivalent to a fair per-centage on the amount "of money expended in the construction, and it varies "directly in proportion to the solidity of structure, "combined with age, state of repair, and capacity, as "shown in the following classification." Then he gives some very minute and complete classifications of the houses, and goes on to say: "It has been ascer-"tained that houses of one storey in height are more "valuable, that is, they let at a higher rent in pro-"portion to their cubical contents than houses of two "stories, and that houses of more than two stories "diminish in value as measured by their cubical "contents in proportion to their height."

6109. These are all houses let with land—not houses let separately?—Those rules would also apply to houses let separately. In fact the same rule, it appears, was applied to all classes of houses, whether let with land or let separately.

6110. Do you mean that the structural cost was considered in connexion with houses which were let separately?—Quite so.

6111. (*Lord Farrer.*) Structural cost apart from land?—Structural cost apart from land is checked by rent as Mr. Barton put it, with regard to houses let separately.

6112. (*Chairman.*) Then as to bog lands, was the Irish occupier put to a disadvantage compared to the English, do you think?—According to the method laid down in Sir Richard Griffith's instructions the valuation of bog lands (that is where the turf was cut for sale) were valued on the gross produce of the bog, less the cost of manufacture. Mr. Barton, I think, explained yesterday, that the Valuation Commissioners have interpreted the Act as enabling them to change the valuation of the bog lands where the bog is cut out; and of course if that is done it would reduce that grievance.

6113. (*Mr Sexton.*) Or to strike out the valuation?—Or to strike out the valuation.

6114. (*Chairman.*) Bog land was not subject to be valued and assessed, within seven years, I think, of its beginning to be improved?—The rule with regard to bog land, laid down in the section of the Act is that no turf or bog land used for cutting up turf shall be rateable, unless rent or other valuable consideration shall be payable for the same. The seven years rule applied to improvements.

6115. Then as to plantations, is there any rise as between England and Ireland?—The rule in England was apparently that plantations as a rule were not rated; but of recent years I understand that a change in that method has been adopted, and that plantations now are rateable; but I cannot say whether they are rateable as agricultural land, that is, having regard to the quality of the land under plantation, or having regard to the value of the timber, but certainly up to recent years, in the great majority of cases plantations in England were not rated at all.

6116. But you know the present law, do you not?—In Ireland, of course plantations have always been rated.

6117. In England, do you know the present law and practice?—I am not certain on the subject; but I know that, until recently, plantations were not rated. I am given to understand that a change was made recently.

6118. Going now from the general questions as to what were rated and valued, and how they were valued; will you pass to the system of valuation in England for local taxation, have you any point in respect to it to mention which you think gives England an advantage compared to Ireland?—In England the method of valuation, as I have already said, is carried out under the Act of 1836 for the purposes of poor law assessment. That of course has always been carried out by the local authorities. In the first place, the valuation list usually is prepared by the overseers of the parish. This is afterwards corrected by the assessment committee of the guardians of the union, and there was an appeal from them to the justices in quarter sessions, and so to the superior courts, but those valuations which were all made by the local authorities for a very long time were said to appear to have been very uneven and very uncertain, a very great deal of property not being valued at all, or being undervalued, and those who have experience of the English system of assessment and valuation are aware that there is no question connected with local government in England that has given rise to greater controversy than the question of local assessment. Of course with reference to the income tax, the income-tax valuation in England is carried out by different persons. It is carried out by commissioners who were appointed by local justices of the peace. There were general commissioners appointed and the Treasury were entitled, under certain circumstances, to appoint special commissioners to aid or help them, or to supervise them; and in some cases, where the local authorities did not make the proper appointment, at the proper time, the Inland Revenue surveyors were appointed to act; but all those persons in making their assessments for income tax were first supplied with the valuation criteria for poor-rate purposes, and, to a very large extent, it would seem that those persons formed the basis of the income-tax assessment.

6119. Then your impression is that in consequence of this great difference of system between assessment in England and the assessment in Ireland, the Irish occupier has been put to disadvantage as compared with the English occupier?—Yes, I think, without saying which is the best system, the Irish system is undoubtedly the much more complete one, and one that is the less likely to allow any property to escape valuation.

6120. Can you illustrate your argument from the assessment of mansions, or collieries, or railways?—With reference to those assessments in England it has very frequently been alleged by persons well acquainted with English valuation, that collieries and mansion houses have been very largely undervalued in England, and if that is so as a very large part of the wealth of England is in property of that description, which is undervalued, it gives the rate assessed to an uneven basis, as you allow a large share of the property of England to be undervalued, or not valued at all. Of course that is a disadvantage to the country which does not possess a similar class of property in a proportionate extent.

6121. With respect to collieries the number in Ireland is small, and hardly gives a comparison with the enormous colliery property in England, I presume?—No, but the fact of the collieries in Ireland being small or practically non-existent, of course, would put Ireland under a disadvantage as compared with England, if English collieries are under-assessed.

6122. But the comparison is not so good as it is with respect to mansions or houses, is it?—We have hardly any material for comparison as regards collieries, for we practically have none.

6123. You class together in your paper, quoting from Mr. Harley, who is rather an old authority, "Railways, collieries, mansion houses, and so forth," but let us take mansion houses, as to which there is ample material for comparison, do you think mansion houses are assessed and rated on a higher or lower rate in Ireland than in England?—Mansion houses I think are valued, as a rule, in Ireland with more Valuation of mansion houses.

Mr. W. F. Bailey.

22 Feb. 1895.

Valuation of mansion houses.

stringency than in England. The mansion houses both in England and Ireland, I should say, are valued at a very low rate, but I think that they are valued at a lower rate in England than they are in Ireland; that is, having regard of course to the different circumstances of the two countries, and their actual values.

6124. It is very difficult to compare one mansion house with another, is it not?—Yes.

6125. But Mr. Barton has given us, in his table No. VII., the principle of the valuation of mansion houses in England and Ireland; have you seen that?—No, I have not.

6126. Will you kindly look at it?—Referring to this table, and taking Eaton Hall, Chatsworth House, or places of that description, we have nothing in Ireland at all to compare with them.

6127. You do not compare with the great ones, but taking the well-known good mansion houses in Ireland, would you not say that the rate at which they are assessed is very low?—As to the higher ones given in this table, such as Downhill, in Londonderry, which is valued at 201*l*., and Rossmore Park in Monaghan, which I see is valued at 251*l*., the valuation of these, having regard to the amount of money that has been expended upon them is very low, undoubtedly, as compared to the valuation of other houses not to be classed as mansion houses; but I would say, on the spur of the moment, that the valuation even of these places, is proportionately higher than the valuation of any of the places given in England. I would hardly like to express a positive opinion on these subjects. I have not any personal knowledge of most of these houses in England.

6128. (*Lord Farrer.*) You have no personal knowledge of any of them?—No. But as to these Irish places I have seen most of them.

6129. (*Mr. Sexton.*) Some of them are ordinary dwelling houses, are they not?—Yes.

6130. And the English places are the great palaces of the country?—Yes.

6131. (*Sir David Barbour.*) Those given in that list are among the best in Ireland, are they not?—I think it gives about two from each county.

6132. (*Mr. Sexton.*) I know some of them, and they are ordinary dwelling-houses, are they not?—Yes; some of them in England would never class as great mansion houses.

6133. (*Chairman.*) Then, on the whole, do you think even as to mansion houses, the valuation is certainly not too low in Ireland?—No; of course the question of valuation of mansion houses is rather a difficult one. You have to consider what circumstances you have to take into account. You cannot take the cost of construction; you can hardly take the letting value, for in a great number of cases they have no letting value which would enable you to make a valuation.

6134. Practically, mansion houses have no letting value have they?—That is practically the case.

6135. I mean a letting value from year to year, which is the test in the Act?—Quite so.

6136. And practically that test cannot be applied to them, can it?—That is so.

6137. There is one more question arising on your paper. You say that the Irish Land Commissioners have, of late years, omitted any reference to Griffith's valuation?—Yes.

Judicial rents.

6138. What is the point of that remark?—At first the Land Commission required the tenants applying to the courts to have rents fixed, to state in their originating notices the Government valuation of their holdings. This was long regarded by many people, as part of the evidence in the case as to what the rent should be; but as time went on it became more and more evident to the Land Commission that the Government valuation was of very little use to them, and in many cases it was rather misleading, the only real utility of it being to show the amount of taxation that was paid out of the holding by the tenant. So in their annual report for the year ending 31st of March 1893, the Land Commission have got a paragraph in which they say this: "In the report of the "Land Commission in relation to proceedings under "the Act of 1881, for the year ending 22nd of "August 1892, the following passage occurs: "'Griffith's valuation, intended for purely fiscal "'purposes, was carried on in the years ranging from "'1852 to 1865, and the original variations which it "'discloses arising from the different periods at which "'it was made in the respective districts, as well as "'the great changes which have occurred in the "'circumstances of Ireland since its promulgation, "'lead us to regard it at the present day as an "'altogether untrustworthy basis to proceed upon in "'estimating a fair rent in individual cases.' For "'these reasons it is quite possible that in future we "'may find it advisable to omit any reference to the "'valuation in the tables annexed to our annual "'report." And then, in the report for the year 1893, they say: "Concurring in the views thus "stated, and as it has been found that in purchase "transactions, as well as in proceedings to fix judicial "rents, that a tenement valuation cannot, for various reasons, be always ascertained or stated with "accuracy in the form used in such cases, and in "order that misleading comparisons and miscomputations may be avoided, we have arrived at the conclusion on this occasion, and in future, to omit the "tables purporting to give the total valuation of each "county from the appendices to our annual report."

6139. (*Lord Welby.*) You say on page 1 of your precis, that the valuation of Ireland is, naturally, more strictly assessed than that of England, as it is carried out by a Government Department under the Treasury. Does not that statement require some qualification, when you take into consideration the fact that all English assessments are periodically revised, whereas the bulk of Irish assessments have remained unchanged. They are not in pari materia, are they?—To a certain extent that is so; you change the English valuation every three years, or more frequently, and each change, I take it, makes it more stringent than the previous one; but I had reference, of course, to the fact that in Ireland you have the entire country valued under one system.

6140. Quite so; but I want to call your attention to the fact that the Irish valuation remains unaltered?—Quite so.

6141. And the English valuation, as you say, is revised periodically, and, as you said just now, probably with greater stringency, which tells. I want to point out to you against your statement that the valuation is more strictly made in Ireland than in England?—But of course that assumes that the valuation in England, although it is more stringently assessed each time, still is assessed up to the stringency of the Irish system, which I do not think.

6142. But inasmuch as one assessment is never revised, and the other is, they are hardly comparable are they?—That may be so.

6143. You point out that the assessment of agricultural land in Ireland is nearly one-fourth of that of England. May I ask, do you use this as an argument that the valuation, as a test of the income or yield of agricultural land, is unfair to Ireland as compared to England; that is to say, that 10,000,000*l*. in the proportion to 40,000,000*l*. is an unfair one?—No; when I stated that, I was not thinking of the actual taxable amount of agricultural land in the two countries. To compare them in the way you are suggest, you would have to go into a careful inquiry as to the greater value of agricultural lands in the different districts of England as compared with the value of agricultural lands in different districts of Ireland. I merely state that as a general comparison.

6144. It looks, in the way it is put, as if you were putting it forward as rather a thing which would naturally strike one, that 10,000,000*l*., the assessment of Irish land, is high as compared with England. If that is not the gist of the argument I do not see why it is there?—I put it there for the purpose of showing the proportion of the gross valuation of Ireland as

Mr. W. F. Bailey. 22 Feb., 1895. Agricultural values compared.

compared with the gross valuation of England. Whether it is too high or too low, of course, would depend on further inquiry.

6144. I am only trying to get at what your object is in putting that down. You are merely stating a fact, are you?—I am merely stating a fact.

6145. Therefore, I take it, you do not put it forward as an argument that the value of agricultural land in Ireland is less than a fourth of the same value in England?—No, I would not like to put that forward as an argument unless I gave some grounds by going into the circumstances of the two countries.

6147. And you have not gone into those circumstances, have you?—Not sufficiently to enable me definitely to state that that proportion is, or is not, fair.

6148. May I call attention to one or two points bearing upon that, because it is rather interesting; do you know that, according to the last agricultural statistics, there are 15,000,000 acres of cultivated land in Ireland, as against 27,000,000 acres in England?—Yes, I am aware of that.

6149. You see it is more than a half?—Yes.

6150. And yet the assessment for income tax is as 10 to 40; that is not very high, is it?—No, but it would not be well to draw too strong a conclusion from that, because of course the same acre of land in England may have a different value to the same acre of land in Ireland and 27,000,000 acres of arable land in England may have a different value from 15,000,000 acres of arable land in Ireland.

6151. But *primâ facie* here you have the fact that the cultivated land in Ireland is half that of England, yet the assessment is only as 10 to 40?—Yes.

6152. And I think you would admit, would you not, that it is necessary to bring some proof that these 15,000,000 acres in Ireland produce so much less than the corresponding acres in England as to make the value of the land very much less?—That is perhaps one reason why I said I did not put that forward as an argument but merely as a statement of fact.

6153. I quite understand, but I am only bringing to your notice one or two circumstances which tend to show that 10,000,000*l.* is not at all a high valuation; and I begin by pointing out the fact that the quantity of agricultural land in Ireland is half that of England. But going a little bit further, do you know that the land under corn crops in Ireland is only one-fourth of that in England, and that land under green crops is not much less than a half?—Yes.

6154. The corn crops are the crops that are now less valuable, are they not?—Quite so.

6155. Therefore, pursuing my argument, first of all we have half as much land in Ireland as there is in England, and of that land in Ireland very much less is under non-paying crops than in England. That will shake the argument, will it not, that land in Ireland is worth less than in England?—I had somewhat present to my mind that in England a great deal of the land that is valued as agricultural land is land which lies more or less in proximity to some of those great manufacturing and other centres, where the value of the land would be very much greater, even agriculturally, than would be represented by the mere amount of produce that would come from it; and I would hardly like to make a statement that would bind me to any opinion on the mere fact that a certain number of acres in one country produce a certain crop as compared with a certain number of acres in the other country producing the same crop. I think it is too intricate a subject to make a general statement upon.

6156. Quite so, and after what you have told us, namely, that you did not bring this statement forward as a proof or an argument that the valuation of Ireland is too high, and I have brought forward an argument from my side in support of the view that the valuation is not too high, and in proof of that I have pointed to the amount of cultivated land, the nature of the cultivation on the land, it will be a point for the Commission to bear in mind, will it not, that the crops in Ireland are to a far greater extent than in England paying crops, namely, green crops?—Quite so.

Mr. W. F. Bailey. 22 Feb., 1895. Agricultural values compared.

6157. As another proof of the producing power of Ireland, and what is raised upon the land, I would call your attention to the fact of the proportion of the stock that is raised in Ireland to England. Let me take, in 1893, the cattle. England raises or keeps 4,780,000, Ireland keeps 4,500,000; those figures are very close to each other, are they not?—Yes.

6158. The total amount of stock England keeps is between 24,000,000 and 25,000,000, and the total amount of stock Ireland keeps is 10,500,000, which shows that the Irish land, at all events, keeps a much larger paying stock upon it comparatively than the English land, does it not?—Yes.

6159. That is all in proof, is it not, of what I am bringing before you, namely, not only is the proportion of Irish cultivated land to English cultivated land very much higher than the proportion shown in the income-tax assessment, but also that there is every proof, and fair proof, that those 14,000,000 acres in Ireland produce better paying crops, and sustain a larger comparative amount of stock than the English acreage?—Yes. I would not like to be taken as accepting your deductions unless I was able to consider them with some care.

6160. My figures are taken from the Agricultural Returns?—I accept the figures.

6161. (*Mr. Sexton.*) But not the inference?—I should like to think it out, of course.

6162. (*Lord Welby.*) Are you aware that the fall in value of land is greater in corn-growing districts as compared with pastoral districts?—Yes.

Percentages of increased valuation compared.

6163. The argument on page 2 of your paper, that in England the per-centage of increase in Irish valuation has been in the same ratio as England, now falls. You admit that 12 per cent. does not apply to Ireland, do you not?—Yes, as I stated earlier in day, no change has taken place apparently in the value of agricultural land in Ireland since 1865. I was misled upon these figures by the tables given.

6164. Quite so, and, therefore, that table has so far to be altered?—Yes.

6165. We must, therefore, come to the conclusion, must we not, that if the valuation of Irish land has not fallen like that of English and Scotch land of recent years, neither has it risen as the English and Scotch land rose in the preceding period of prosperity. That is shown by this table you know?—The only observation I would make with regard to that is, that the fall in the valuation of English and Scotch land since 1880 is much greater than the increase in its value was from 1865 to 1880. That is, that a greater fall has taken place in England and Scotland than the previous rise, while in Ireland no changes at all have taken place.

6166. (*The O'Conor Don.*) Taking the date of 1865 as the starting point?—Quite so.

Judicial rents and valuation.

6167. (*Lord Welby.*) Except that at the same time is it not the case that even the fixing of the judicial rents has not brought the rents down, as a rule, to the level of the valuation?—That is rather a difficult question; if you take the judicial rents as a whole, that is so.

6168. But remember, all your figures deal with Ireland as a whole?—Quite so. You are taking the judicial rents from 1881 to the present time.

6169. Therefore, inasmuch as you have, what you have not anywhere else, a most close examination of the value of land, and inasmuch as this close examination, so far as judicial rents are concerned, has not brought the rents down to to the valuation, it can hardly be said, can it, that the valuation is excessive?—Except to this extent, that rent and valuation are not in any way really to be regarded as synonymous. You could hardly say that the rent and the valuation of the same land should be the same.

6170. It is a very fair test of valuation, is it not, to take the rent that an independent authority puts upon it as representing its value?—Yes, but of course

Mr. W. F. Bailey. — 27 Feb. 1896. — Judicial rents and valuation.

there are various considerations that may affect a rent that would not affect the valuation; and there is this to be said also with reference to that table of comparisons of rent and valuation, that really it is very difficult, if not impossible, to make any fair comparison between the judicial rents and valuations in Ireland, owing to the fact that the valuations given in the Land Commission returns are so very inaccurate in a great number of cases. In my own experience, in fixing rents in Ireland, in a very large proportion of the cases we find that the valuation of the holdings given is quite inaccurate, from various circumstances. Owing to the fact that many of the valuations were made on the different portions of a tenement that existed in different townlands, you will find that it is impossible to get at the real valuation of the particular holding that comes before the court; and the result is, if you take those columns of valuations given in the Land Commission Returns they are full of errors; and I would not at all care to base any comparison on them.

6171. But still, in your paper you have brought forward as an argument the valuation as the ground upon which you base your opinion, and, therefore, you and I are only taking the same basis for consideration, namely, the valuation, and I point out that, with a careful survey by experts of what the value of the land should be, yet the rent as fixed upon the Griffith's valuation has not come down to the valuation?—Yes, if you take the entire period.

6172. (*Mr. Sexton.*) You never said that; in fact, you were proceeding to explain, I think, were you not, that in recent years the rent has been brought below the valuation?—What I was proceeding to say was this that more than half of the judicial rents that have been already fixed in Ireland were fixed prior to the 21st August 1885. If you take those cases they were, on the whole, fixed a great deal above the valuation in Ireland, in fact, in all the provinces except the province of Ulster, they were fixed very considerably above the Government valuation; but the rents fixed since 1885 would, I think, show a very different result. For example, if you take the cases fixed in the first four years of the Land Commission from the passing of the Land Act of 1881 down to the 21st August 1885, you will find that the judicial rents in the province of Ulster were 3 per cent. under the Government valuation of the same holdings, while, if you take the table Mr. Barton put in, of all the judicial rents fixed from the passing of the Act of 1881 down to March 1895, you will find that the rent of Ulster was nearly 9 per cent. below the Government valuation. If you take the province of Munster for the first four years, the judicial rents were fixed at 24 per cent. above the Government valuation; while, if you take the entire period they were only fixed at 13 per cent. above the same. If you take the province of Connaught for the first four years the judicial rents were fixed at 12 per cent. above the Government valuation; while, if you take the entire periods they were fixed at only a little over 2 per cent. above. In the province of Leinster for the first four years the rents were fixed 13 per cent. over the valuation, while taking the entire period from 1881 to 1895 they were fixed only 4 per cent. over Griffith's valuation. From that you will see that you have to divide the judicial rents of Ireland into two periods, namely, the period down to the 21st August 1885, and the period from then to the present time, and very different results will be seen.

6173. (*Chairman.*) May I ask you, parenthetically, a question. You and Mr. Barton, I think, both experienced some difficulty in comparing the valuation rents with the subsequent judicial rents. In fixing and notifying in the document which notified the judicial rent, was not the valuation always stated?—Yes, it is one of the circumstances required to be stated.

6174. And it always was stated was it?—In a great number of cases it is put in as "valuation unascertained." In a large number of cases you will find that.

6175. And that to a certain extent prejudices a very accurate and systematic comparison, does it not?—It does.

6176. (*Mr. Sexton.*) If those blanks were filled up the valuation would be seen to be still more different than appears, would it not?—Yes.

6177. (*Lord Welby.*) Then the result would be this that though the average deductions of rent leaves them still above the valuation yet the earlier reductions were not sufficient as compared with the later ones, and therefore supposing they had all been made at the same time the judicial rents would be very much lower on the average, which would probably take them down below the valuation, do I understand you to mean that?—That would follow from those figures.

6178. Do you put that as an answer to what I point out, that on the average the judicial rents as fixed are still above the valuation upon which I base the argument that the valuation could not be very much too high?—Yes.

6179. And you qualify my argument in that respect by saying that the judicial rents are too high?—Merely on the figures I have given you. Of course it is to be remembered that in the same period in England the valuation has fallen 15 per cent.

6180. You say that, though a landlord is not only paying to the extent of his rent, when the rent is less than the valuation, the tenant is held to be the owner to the extent of the difference. I think it has been agreed between the Commission and yourself that that is not a very important point, because the larger part of the tenants, anyhow, will escape, owing to being under the amount of rent, and therefore exempt altogether, will they not?—Quite so.

6181. Are you aware that practically no charge of that kind has ever been made by the Inland Revenue?—No I could not say.

6182. I believe that is so, is it not?—I merely stated what the section of the Act says.

6183. What leads you to say that in England the landlord is not usually assessed on the full rental?—In England there are deductions from the full rental in the majority of cases. — *Assessment in England.*

6184. (*Lord Farrer.*) Are you speaking of the gross value or the net value?—The gross. You have to deduct for rates and taxes, and repairs, and a variety of things which are specified.

6185. (*Lord Welby.*) There is a change, as you are aware, in the Act of 1894. Are you referring to a period before that. Do you mean that the landlord was assessed to income tax on a lower sum than the gross rental?—Oh no; what I said was or what I intended to say, was, that the assessment in England was intended to be on the landlord.

6186. It is not the case, from what I can learn, that there were, before the Act of 1894, deductions from the full rent in the majority of cases in England. Let me give you these figures?—Will you refer me to the page?

6187. (*Mr. Sexton.*) You cite two authorities on page 5, for your statement; you do not rest it on your own testimony, merely?—I quote Messrs. Boyle and Davies in their book on "The Principles of Rating," showing that the rent paid is not a fair test of valuation.

6188. (*Lord Welby.*) That is the test of valuation, but just look at the facts. The gross estimated rental of property in England in 1892–3, was 162,000,000*l.*; the rateable value, which is that upon which local taxation is paid, with a sixth taken off for repairs and various things of that kind, is 135,000,000*l.* The actual sum on which the landlord was assessed, was 167,000,000*l.*, so that, not only were there no deductions made from the gross estimated rental, but actually the Inland Revenue put the very large amount of 5,000,000*l.* on the gross estimated rental?—If those figures, which I take from you are right, that is so.

6189. Those figures appear in the report, do they not?—Quite so.

Mr. W. F. Bailey.

[illegible]

Assessment under Schedule B.

6190. You speak of excessive valuation of Ireland under Schedule B. May I point out to you that last year the amount charged in England under Schedule B was [illegible], and was only 26,000*l.* in Ireland? —[illegible].

6191. Would you contend that farming profits in Ireland are ten times less than those in England after what you have heard as to the acreage and the crops which are raised there. The figure of 262,000*l.* is the amount of assessment under Schedule B on farming in England, and 26,000*l.* in Ireland?—If I came that would also show that taxation in England and Ireland are on such entirely different principles that it is impossible for me to compare them.

6192. That is not quite an answer to the question? —I can hardly answer it otherwise.

6193. You say that the Irish assessment under Schedule B. is excessive, did you not?—Yes.

6194. How can it be excessive, if it is only 26,000*l.* in Ireland, as compared to 262,000*l.* in England?— That would be assuming that the two figures are absolutely comparable.

6195. Of course the obvious reason for it is, is it not, that in Ireland there being so many small holdings the Irish farmer does not pay income tax, in which case he is not too highly assessed?—I only intended to refer to the cases of where the Irish occupier was assessed; but if you take the entire country, your statement would modify it. I was only taking the cases where the assessment did operate.

6196. (*Mr. Sexton.*) England is a country of large farms which pay, and Ireland is not; that is the explanation, is it not?—Quite so.

6197. (*Lord Welby.*) But, so far as you would apply the whole argument, it has only a limited application, inasmuch as very few farmers come under it? —Yes, that is with reference to Schedule B., which is only a small matter.

Separate valuation of land and buildings.

6198. You say, in several particulars, the method of valuation in Ireland presses more hardly on the taxpayer than the method adopted in England; and you give us an instance, that in estimating the value of an agricultural holding in England, it would appear, it is not the practice to place a separate valuation on the buildings?—Yes.

6199. But in England it is assessed on the rack rental of the whole holding, and that, of course, includes a valuation of the buildings; is not that so?— Of course the question arises in Ireland that if a landlord is paying a rent on a holding, his rental covers the buildings; but, then, when the valuation authorities come in they put a separate valuation on the house which the landlord never asked any particular rent for.

6200. But you do not mean to say that the house in Ireland is counted twice over, do you?—It is doubtful whether it is not, because you first value the land as an equipped holding, and then you put a separate valuation on the house.

6201. But the house in Ireland is put apart from the land, otherwise the house would be counted twice?—Of course it is doubtful whether the valuation which is put upon the land, sore per acre, is not a valuation which is fixed at that arguable amount on the consideration that the holding, of which it is a part, is equipped with the proper buildings.

(*Lord Welby.*) Mr. Barton, you have heard Mr. Bailey say, as I understand him, that it is a question whether the assessment of the land in Ireland itself does not include a valuation of the farm buildings upon it in addition to which a separate valuation is put on the farm building itself; in that case, as I understand him, there might be a double valuation of the buildings—is that the case?

(*Mr. Barton.*) No, there is not a double valuation of the buildings. The valuation of the farm includes the buildings, though the buildings are set out in a separate column in Sir Richard Griffith's instructions to valuers, he specially states that the valuation of the farm, including the buildings, is to be the value that would be considered a fair rent to let to a solvent tenant at. I think that instruction has been read by the Witness to-day.

6202. (*Sir David Barbour to the Witness.*) I understand that the land was valued with reference to the produce on a certain scale of prices?—Quite so.

6203. But that could not include the houses, could it?—In valuing it in reference to the scale of prices you value the land, having regard to its productive capacity, and the productive capacity would include the houses.

6204. No, it is so much produce valued at so much, but it certainly impression all along was that the valuation never was carried out on that basis.

6205. But is not there the further condition laid down by Sir Richard Griffith that the total valuation of land and buildings should not exceed the fair letting value to a solvent tenant?—Of course that raises the further consideration as to what fair letting value meant, when Sir Richard Griffith wrote it.

(*Mr. Sexton.*) I want to ask you, Mr. Barton, if you can give any kind of reason why valuation in England estimates the value of land and buildings in one sum, and separates the value of the land from the value of the buildings in Ireland.

(*Mr. Barton.*) Do you mean at a previous date?

(*Mr. Sexton.*) I mean now the system includes land and buildings together in England, and in Ireland you take the land apart from the buildings, and then the buildings apart from the land—why do you do that?

(*Mr. Barton.*) We divide the land from the buildings in Ireland because we wish to have a separate rating for the buildings as distinguished from houses in Ireland; that is for the local rating. The object of the income-tax authorities, I understand, in bringing the buildings into the same column as the land was to assimilate the two assessments in Ireland and England. That was a matter, I think, done by them in 1869.

(*Mr. Sexton.*) Having heard Mr. Bailey's suggestion that the arable value put upon a farm in valuing it assumes that the farm is equipped, can you say that in valuing land in Ireland, in the first instance, separate from the houses, you value the land as if the houses were not there; or do you value it assuming that they are there.

(*Mr. Barton.*) I think in every case the land is valued according to what it would produce.

(*Mr. Sexton.*) As if there were no houses?

(*Mr. Barton.*) As if there were no houses. Then, the value of the houses is taken and the whole added together forms what is supposed to be the letting value of the farm; then the houses would be deducted and a separate valuation put upon them.

(*Mr. Sexton.*) Do you think there is no danger when valuers accustomed to value agricultural land as equipped, proceed to value land first and houses afterwards, that they will in estimating the value of the land take in practically or substantially, if not the whole, a part of the value of the buildings into the value of the land.

(*Mr. Barton.*) The system as laid down by Sir Richard Griffith was carried out (and I have no reason to think it was not), and they certainly would not.

(*Chairman.*) Practically the equipment is not valued twice over, is it?

(*Mr. Barton.*) I think not—in fact, I am sure it is not.

(*Sir David Barbour.*) Is the valuation of houses separately from the land due to the fact that that valuation of Sir Richard Griffith was a valuation according to a scale of prices; could you value the two together if you value on a scale of prices?

(*Mr. Barton.*) I think there would be a different system.

(*Mr. Sexton.*) Is there any sufficient reason why the land and the buildings in the case of an Irish holding should not be valued at once as one operation as a going concern?

(*Mr. Barton.*) There were reasons; in farms there were several houses, and it was necessary for registration purposes that houses should be subdivided.

Mr. W. F. Bailey.

22 Nov. 1894.

Separate valuation of land and buildings.

(*Mr. Sexton.*) But take the ordinary case.

(*Mr. Barton.*) That was carried out everywhere, there was a separate valuation put on the buildings.

(*Mr. Sexton.*) But is there any reason why the land and buildings, inasmuch as equipment is essentially an element in the value of land in the Irish farm, should not be valued together in one operation as a going concern as in England.

(*Mr. Barton.*) I think there is a reason with regard to local rating; there is no reason for Imperial rating as far as I can see.

(*Mr. Sexton.*) You might subdivide the figure afterwards, but is there any reason why you should not begin by estimating the value of the land and buildings together as a *going concern*, making what subdivision you please afterwards.

(*Mr. Barton.*) I do not see any reason why you should not.

(*Sir David Barbour.*) Except that the Act prescribes it.

(*Mr. Barton.*) Quite so.

(*The O'Conor Don.*) But is there not a reason, that the rating of the buildings were liable to be revised every year and that of the land was not?

(*Mr. Barton.*) Of course.

(*The O'Conor Don.*) And it was absolutely necessary to have a separate valuation of each, was it not?

(*Mr. Barton.*) Yes, for our local rating purposes it was absolutely necessary.

(*The O'Conor Don.*) And for Imperial rating too, because the houses are liable to change every year, are they not?

(*Mr. Barton.*) They are.

(*The O'Conor Don.*) They may be either improved, destroyed, or removed and a new valuation would be necessary according to the change which took place, which valuation would affect Imperial as well as local rating, would it not?

(*Mr. Barton.*) Yes.

(*Mr. Sexton.*) That would not prevent the repetition of the original process whenever there was a change, would it?

(*Mr. Barton.*) It would not prevent the separation of the houses if you made the valuation together. That would be another system of valuation.

(*Lord Welby.*) Do you alter the valuation of farm buildings?

(*Mr. Barton.*) Yes.

(*Lord Welby.*) You can do that, can you?

(*Mr. Barton.*) Yes, we can do so.

Adjourned for a short time.

6206. (*Lord Welby to the Witness.*) From the conversation which has taken place with you and Mr. Barton, I gather that in Ireland the valuation is on the land based upon agricultural value?—Yes.

6207. And houses are valued separately, whereas in England the assessment is based on the rack-rental which of course includes the value of the houses?—Yes.

6208. So far the house is not omitted in England?—No, it is valued as an equipped holding.

6209. You mentioned the fact that the houses are valued at their structural cost. Have you borne in mind the fact, as I think it is, that Sir Richard Griffith while he took the structural cost as the basis of calculation put a very low rate of interest upon that structural cost?—Yes, I have heard that stated, that the scale given was a low scale.

6210. I think as a general rule it is 2 per cent., and in some cases as little as 1 per cent., is it not?—I could not say the amount, but it was low I believe.

6211. That would have a considerable bearing in the result, would it not, because supposing it was a 500*l.* house, if the rate was only 2 per cent., the annual value would only be 10*l.*?—Yes, of course I do not know myself what it works out at, but I accept your figures.

Mr. W. F. Bailey.

22 Nov. 1894.

Valuation of bog lands and plantations.

6212. You call attention to the fact that pasturable bog is often valued in Ireland as pasture against the tenant and as turbary for sale against the landlord. Do you remember that where the turf is cut away the valuation is reduced?—Yes

6213. Therefore, so far as that goes, when the bog loses its value the valuation is reduced?—Yes, so I have heard. Mr. Barton stated that they have reduced in that case and I think it was the only case he mentioned in which they did.

6214. You mentioned the fact of plantations in England not being rated, but you have rather modified your view, have you not?—I have been informed of late they are.

6215. Not quite of late, it is since 1874?—Of course it was always a question in England as to whether they were rateable or assessable.

6216. The rating Act of 1874 makes the occupier of a plantation or wood rateable, does it not?—Just so. Some plantations were rated even before that, but it was the exception.

6217. Do I understand you from that to hold that they are not assessed to income tax?—I did not mean that; they are assessed of course for income tax under the second method.

Alleged under-assessment in England.

6218. Do you think the local committees which value land in England for rating purposes have a tendency to undervalue inasmuch as they are themselves ratepayers; do you think they are likely to lean to an undervaluation of the property of their neighbours, which would result in throwing a greater burden upon themselves?—I found my opinion largely on the fact of hearing so many cases of land being under-rated in England where it is rated by the local committees.

6219. You are aware, are you not, from the figures I have mentioned that the Income Tax Commissioners if they think that the valuation taken by the local committees not sufficient, put an extra value upon them?—Yes, I am aware they have the power to do so.

6220. Therefore inasmuch as the income-tax authorities are keen upon obtaining a full valuation for income-tax purposes, that result which you say is obtained in Ireland by the use of a Government department to insure strict valuation, you really have in England, have you not?—Yes, but I take it in England they are more dependent on the returns made them by the owners.

6221. But they go by actual rent receipts, do they not?—Yes, but of course in many cases actual rental would not form a good basis. I mean in many cases the actual rent of a holding is not at all equal to its value. The actual annual value of a holding is not always the same as the rent. There may be cases where the rent may be much less than the annual value, owing to a variety of circumstances, and you might have cases even where it might be the reverse.

6222. But still you must take the rental as representing the fair value of the land, especially in England, where the landlord would no doubt get as much as he could?—Taking it as a whole, in England it would be very fair.

6223. You have beside the local assessment committee, officers of the Inland Revenue, I should say, keen to mark any cases of undervaluation, with power to assess, have you not?—Yes. In some cases I take it the income-tax authorities have, to a large extent, taken over the valuation of the local authorities.

6224. I am not sure that you are quite alive to the fact that it is only under the Act of 1894 that allowances for repairs are deducted from the gross income tax assessment, and the taxpayer charged upon the balance only?—Yes.

6225. Up to that time, no allowance was made, was there?—Quite so.

Assessment of railways.

6226. You mentioned, I think, by way of illustration that railways are under-assessed. You know for purposes of income tax railway companies are taxed upon their net receipts, do you not?—Yes.

6227. Therefore, whatever they may pay to the rating authorities would not have any bearing upon the contribution to Imperial taxation, would it?—Quite so; I am aware that railways are assessed on a different system.

6228. (*Mr. Sexton.*) I understand that you consider when a valuation made by local persons becomes the foundation of an assessment for Imperial purposes, the valuation is likely to be lower than when it is made by Imperial officers?—Yes, that was my contention.

6229. From the outset of the valuation of Sir Richard Griffith it was conducted by a department directly under the control of the Treasury, was it not?—Yes.

6230. And aware that the amount of their valuation, although primarily intended for local purposes would measure the amount of the yield of Ireland to the income tax?—Yes, the valuation was almost synonymous with the introduction of income tax into Ireland.

6231. They were aware from the first that they were in effect and in practice valuers for the Treasury in Ireland, for the purpose of determining the yield of income tax?—Quite so.

6232. (*Lord Welby.*) But is it not the case that the present system of valuation began in 1847?—Six of the counties commenced in 1848.

6233. I mean the present law dated from 1847, did it not?—1852 was the date of the Valuation Act.

6234. That was before the levying of the income tax, was it not?—That was in 1853, but the valuation was not begun.

6235. But the law had passed before the income tax was thought of, had it not?—Yes.

6236. Therefore it was not passed with the view to the income tax?—No.

6237. (*Mr. Sexton.*) Whatever the view was the effect was clear. I am very glad Lord Welby has interposed. Five or six counties were valued under the Act of 1846, but it is not a fact that the valuation of these counties, although commenced in 1848 was not completed till 1853?—That is so.

6238. And we have heard from Mr. Barton, and I believe you agree that the valuation of those counties was brought into line by some process with the valuation directly under the Act of 1852?—Yes, they were altered to suit the new scale of prices.

6239. So that the circumstance that the valuation of these five counties was initiated, though not completed under the Act of 1846 does not establish any substantial difference between these and the other counties from our present point of view?—That would appear to be so.

6240. The system in England differs from that in Ireland, does it not, in this respect: that in Ireland the value of each holding in the country is measured by Imperial officers, and by them only. The Imperial officer knows that his valuation governs the amount of income tax to be paid by Ireland?—Yes.

6241. In England the system is not one of sole Imperial control, but merely of occasional intervention of the Imperial officer, is it not?—So I understand.

6242. Lord Welby has, I think, suggested to you that if local persons desire an unduly low valuation they would in some way injure themselves to the benefit of their neighbours. Now, taking the local persons who fix the valuation of any rateable area in England—I do not care what it is—would it not be the fact that these people would be well aware that if they made an equally low, or relatively low, valuation of all the holdings in the area, that would not affect the burden of local taxes as between one person and another?—Yes, that would appear to be so.

6243. Suppose you have to raise a rate of 100,000*l.* upon a rateable area of 100,000*l.*, and supposing that the value of that rate was set down at 50,000*l.* only, would not the rate fall equally on everybody whether the worth was 50,000*l.* or 100,000*l.*, providing that the holdings bore a relative proportion to each other?—Quite so.

6244. And whilst the local ratepayer was not affected locally, every local ratepayer would benefit in regard to income tax, in so far as the relation to his holding was the true value?—Yes.

6245. Is there not, therefore, a perpetual inducement to local valuers to value all holdings within the local area so low as that it would not affect the incidence of the local burden, whilst it would relieve every local ratepayer in regard to the Imperial burden?—Yes, that would appear to follow.

6246. Does that continue to be your impression as to the relative effect with regard to an assessment for Imperial purposes, between the working of the Irish department, which is Imperial, and the working of the English system where the English Commissioners only occasionally intervene in the working of the system?—Yes.

6247. (*Lord Welby.*) Mr. Sexton speaks of occasional interference. I think I am right, am I not, in saying that the Inland Revenue officers are present and have knowledge of all that goes on, and of the results arrived at in every case, and therefore it is not quite correct, is it, to put it as occasional interference, when they have the power of interference in every case and with every object to interfere and correct the assessment if there is a reason for it wherever they think it is too low?—Of course that depends upon, in actual practice, how far they do interfere.

6248. (*Lord Farrer.*) But you do not know how far they interfere?—I do not know at all, I have no knowledge about it at all, except that I know this, that the total difference between the poor law valuation in England and the income tax valuation is each year getting nearer and nearer, so that they are not very far apart at present.

6249. (*Lord Welby.*) What do you mean by the poor-law valuation?—The rateable value for poor-law purposes.

6250. The rateable value for poor-law purposes is 20,000,000 below the income tax?—But I mean that the difference between them is getting less and less.

6251. There will be a certain difference under this new Act in which allowance is made for repairs, and so forth, but, apart from that, I do not know that we can say it is approximating, can we?—From the figures given by Messrs. Wright and Hobhouse, it would appear to be so.

6252. (*Lord Farrer.*) Is it not the fact that the gross value and the rateable value are two totally different things, and that for all local purposes you make a certain deduction from the gross value in order to get at the rateable value?—Yes, undoubtedly.

6253. And that deduction is still made and continues. I forget exactly what it is, but it is a deduction on the ground that from the gross value has to be deducted the repairs which the landlord has to make, and certain other expenses?—Quite so.

6254. And that remains, does it not?—Yes.

6255. And the difference between the gross value and the rateable value does not diminish, that always continues, does it not?—But the totals, I take it, show that the two valuations are not so far apart now as they were some years ago.

6256. (*Lord Welby.*) I think a sixth, roughly, is taken off the gross value, is it not?—I have not the figures before me.

6257. I think that is the result; I have applied it to those figures, and it is a sixth?—Just so.

6258. (*Mr. Sexton.*) Of course you cannot be expected to have a close, still less an official knowledge of the system in England, but I apprehend you know this much that in Ireland the initiative and the sole action rest with the Imperial officers?—Yes.

6259. And in England the initiative is local, and the Imperial officer intervenes occasionally as a reviewing party only?—Yes.

6260. And do you adhere to your view that the former system is manifestly the one that will yield the largest results?—That certainly has been my view always. Of course any statements I have made with reference to the English system naturally are made from

Mr. W. J. Barton.
22 Feb. 1895.
Systems of valuation in England and Ireland compared.

Mr. W. F. Bailey.

25 Feb. 1896.

Systems of assessment in England and Ireland contrasted.

what I have tried to learn from looking at the different works on the subject, as I have no personal knowledge of the English system, while of course the Irish system I do know something about.

6261. But it is evident and undeniable, I take it, that a local authority by decreeing a valuation, however low, equally over the area, can make the incidence of local taxation low, and at the same time enable everybody, lowly taxed, to escape a portion of the Imperial burden?—Quite so, that seems to me to be so.

6262. Certain figures were put to you by Lord Welby, who pointed out that, whereas the gross estimated rental of property under Schedule A. was 162,000,000*l.*, the gross annual value of the property rateable was five millions more, but your contention, I understand, is that the poor-rate valuation in Ireland, which in the ordinary case, except where the rent is lower than the assessment, is a more stringent and searching test of value than what is called the gross estimated rental in England?—Yes.

6263. The value of Lord Welby's suggested argument would depend, would it not, on the extent to which it was found that what is called the gross estimated rental in England corresponds with the estimated value afforded by the poor-rate valuation in Ireland?—Yes.

6264. And there should be an inquisition into that before any conclusion could be arrived at?—Quite so.

6265. Lord Welby suggested that the English and the Irish assessment are not in *pari materia*, because the English valuations are revised periodically, and the Irish valuation has not been revised substantially since 1865; but for how many years now has the course of agricultural value been declining?—Certainly since before 1880.

6266. There was a slight and partial recovery in one or two years, I think, and then there followed, since 1886, a very heavy and continuous decline till now?—Yes.

6267. Of course, if these are not in *pari materia*, which cannot be denied, the advantage is, is it not, on the side of England, because in the period of falling prices she has had a periodical revision, whilst the valuation in Ireland has remained at the value at which it stood at an earlier period?—Yes.

Lord Welby's "area" method suggested.

6268. Lord Welby has suggested—I am sure he did not intend it as any searching test, but as a general indication—a comparison by area between England and Ireland?—Yes.

6269. Of course a moment's reflection will show, will it not, that no such comparison can be taken of any value simply as a question of area?—That is so. You might have the same acreable quantity of lands of entirely different values. The fact of there being the same number of acres would be in no way a test of their relative value.

6270. You have first to look to relative utility, have you not?—Yes.

6271. Then you have to look to the proportion of the different class and values of soil, and the total acreage?—Quite so.

6272. And in the third place, you have to remember that in Ireland only one-fifth of the population is urban, supplying a local market to the agriculturalist, whilst in England, from two-thirds to three-fourths of the population is urban, and a great home market is supplied?—Quite so.

6273. And, of course, the fact that the greater part of the soil of England is covered with great urban communities requiring agricultural produce, does give a market at the door of the agriculturalist, does it not?—Yes, I would say that the land in England round those great centres of population ought to have a very great increased value, a factor which the Irish have not got.

6274. And, of course, it develops market-gardening, and other branches of agricultural industry which result in a great profit?—Quite so.

6275. And which would not only increase, but multiply the value of land?—Yes.

Mr. W. F. Bailey.

25 Feb. 1896.

[illegible]

6276. The suggestion that, under Schedule B., the occupiers in England pay 249,000*l.*, while in Ireland they only pay 26,000*l.*, shows nothing more, does it, than that England contains a number of farmers who are such large proprietors that they come under the income tax, while the Irishman being so small a man, does not come under that tax?—That seems to me to be so.

Judicial rents and valuation.

6277. Some effort has been made to suggest that the judicial rent in Ireland continues to be above the valuation. I think it important, as you are a person entitled to speak with some authority, to ask if you can make it clear to us what is the present position with respect to valuation. In the first place, we have carefully to distinguish between the rents fixed between 1881 and 1886, before the last great disastrous fall began, and the rents fixed since 1886, and during the progress of that fall which is still continuing. You gave us some figures to-day, generally speaking, showing that the reductions up to 1886 did leave the rent still higher than the valuation?—Yes.

6278. You have shown us that though up to 1886, the larger number of cases were dealt with, and the larger amount of rental, yet that the reductions since 1886 in the smaller number of cases upon the smaller rental were so heavy as largely to affect the average of the whole bulk?—Yes, that is so.

6279. Does your knowledge enable you to say whether the reductions since 1886 taken by themselves without reference to the reductions of earlier years would show that judicial rents in Ireland, as fixed upon current values, that is, values since 1886, are lower than the valuation?—Without having the table made up by returns calculated the clear impression on my mind is that that is so—that the rents since 1886 are below the valuations in the great majority of cases.

6280. (*Sir Edward Hamilton.*) In all the provinces?—The only province as to which that might not hold good, is, I think, Munster, but even of late in a great number of sessions in Munster where I have looked at the returns for a month or two months, I have frequently noticed taking a small number of cases, say 50 or 100, that the judicial rents are below the valuation. Of course, to answer the question conclusively, you would have to calculate all the figures from 1886 down to the present time.

6281. (*Mr. Sexton.*) You have been a Land Commissioner, have you not, since 1890?—Yes.

6282. In various parts of the country?—Yes.

6283. Does your own administration leave on your mind the impression that rents are now materially lower than the valuation through Ireland?—Yes, that is clearly my impression.

6284. Mr. Barton submitted an ingenious table, Table Q, in which first comparing the valuation since 1881 with the valuation of the holdings operated upon, he showed that taking the totals, the valuation and the rent were approximate?—Yes.

6285. And applying that to the whole rental of Ireland, upon the assumption that the rent of the holdings which he was dealing with, stood in the same relation to the valuation of those holdings as the rent and valuation of the holdings dealt with, he proceeded to a further inference, that the landlord in Ireland scores on the assessment, by being entitled to take the valuation instead of the rent, that is to say, that upon his assumption, the valuation of all Ireland, if reduced on the basis of the reduction since 1881, would seem to be still lower than the rent. Now I ask you this: Suppose you applied to the whole rental of Ireland the scale of reduction since 1886, do you believe that the rent would now be substantially lower than the valuation, or in other words, do you believe that the option of being assessed upon the valuation is any longer any advantage whatever to the Irish landlord?—No, I do not think it is much, if any advantage now, that is, under the circumstances as you state them; if you were to apply the scale of reduction since 1886 to all the rents in Ireland,

I think it would probably remove the valuation altogether.

6286. Yet in fixing these rents you do still fix a rent upon a part of the improvements made by the tenant?—That is alleged.

6287. Do you usually give them a percentage on the cost of the work, and give the remainder to the landlord?—Yes.

6288. Yes, although the rent includes that, it has become lower than the valuation?—Yes, quite.

6289. Mr. Barton, in his cross-examination, said that the value of the tenant-right was included in the valuation, but in his oral evidence he withdrew from that position, and said it was not included in the valuation. I put it to him whether there was anything more to which value could be attached than the holding itself, and whether the valuer did not value the holding as it stood. Do you imagine he could have done anything else?—No, I do not.

6290. Is any evidence taken either from the tenant or the landlord as to the improvements made?—Certainly not, there is no machinery given by which such evidence could be taken.

6291. (*The O'Conor Don.*) Are you quite sure of that?—I am sure of it, except on appeals. Where there are appeals allowed from the primary valuation, evidence undoubtedly could be given, but in the primary valuation, reading over the instruction framed by Sir Richard Griffith, there is no machinery set forth by which such matters could be inquired into.

6292. Was it not one of the provisions of the Valuation Act that improvements made in the preceding seven years were not to be taken into consideration?—That is one of the provisions in the section, but I can find no machinery given in the instructions for the valuers to hold any inquiry. Probably if you found a certain piece of land reclaimed from a river or the sea, and they satisfied themselves in any way that that land was reclaimed within the seven years, I take it, under the section in the Act, the valuers could omit it from valuation, but I can find nothing in the instructions specifying how, and in what way, or by what machinery they were to make inquiries.

6293. What machinery would they require. Is it not clear it would be to the tenant's interest even as regards local rates, not to have his valuation raised on his improvements?—Yes.

6294. And would not he, in consequence, when the valuator came on his land, naturally tell him, "I have "made these improvements, and you must exclude "them"?—If the valuer was ready to accept the statement of one side without any inquiry, of course then the thing could be done, but we hardly look upon that as a feasible or possible method; he could not merely take a statement or hearsay evidence as to when the improvement was, or was not done.

6295. Are you aware that Mr. Greene, before the before the Committee in 1869 I think it was, distinctly stated that the occupancy-right or tenant-right was never taken into consideration?—Yes, I think I remember that statement being made by him.

6296. (*Mr. Sexton.*) In fixing rents, you conduct a searching inquisition upon oath as between the landlord and the tenant as to who made the improvements, do you not?—Yes.

6297. And you find that, of course, necessary?—Quite so, in fact in cases where the holding is inspected before the hearing under certain circumstances, statements are made to the Land Commissioners who go out on the land with regard to amounts alleged to be spent on improvements, and we find when we come into Court that a searching and difficult inquiry remains as to how far those statements are verifiable.

6298. Sir Richard Griffith and his staff had no authority under the law, had they, to conduct any judicial proceedings?—No, I can find none.

6299. And of course these would have been necessary in order to find out the ownership of any improvements?—Certainly, that is to do it in any way effectively.

6300. Is there any trace anywhere of anything done by Sir Richard Griffith and his staff, except the application of the judgment of the valuer to the holding as it stood including the improvements?—No, that is so.

6301. (*Sir David Barbour.*) If Sir Richard Griffith's valuators rejected a tenant's claim, had the tenant any right of appeal afterwards?—Yes, I have stated that. On the appeal there probably would have been that power. I am not aware, though, to what extent the right of appeal was availed of.

6302. (*Mr. Sexton.*) There was a general power of appeal against the valuation, was there not?—Just so, to quarter sessions.

6303. But is there any trace of any appeal grounded on a question of improvements?—I do not know of any.

6304. (*The O'Conor Don.*) Do you know anything about those appeals at all?—All I know about them is the statements I find in the evidence of Sir Richard Griffith and others who were examined before these committees.

6305. And do you find any statement of Sir Richard Griffith on this point?—I do not remember any.

6306. (*Mr. Sexton.*) Have you any doubt that the holding was valued as it stood?—That is my belief.

6307. And, therefore, included all improvements, no matter who made them?—That is my impression.

6308. That being so, and as the tenant right, whether in Ulster or anywhere else, can be nothing except a part of the value of the whole, it follows, I contend, that the valuation of Griffith included the valuation of the tenant right?—I think so.

6309. In fixing the rent, now, how do you deal with the tenant right. You fix the rent, I understand, as if a stranger wanted a farm?—Quite so, we fix the rent on what we suppose a solvent man would be willing to give for a holding, of course taking into account the various circumstances of the particular case which might affect it in different ways.

6310. Therefore, subject only to such percentage as you allow for improvements actually made by the tenant, the incorporeal tenant right, the tenant right other than the value of improvements, is included in the rent, is it?—Yes.

6311. Have you any doubt that the Irish rent and the Irish valuation both, are now considerably higher than the rent in England relatively?—I would hardly like to make any statement upon that, as my knowledge with regard to the English rents, of course, is mere hearsay, I have no actual knowledge of English rents which would enable [illegible] to make any such statement.

6312. Are you aware of any general current impression that the proportion of produce taken for rent in Ireland is higher than in England?—I have constantly heard it stated that larger proportions are taken in Ireland, but, as I say, there are certain circumstances connected with English farming which would, of course, explain the smaller share of gross produce that goes to rent. I would hardly like to give an opinion upon that without studying the English method.

6313. On the question of principle, if it were found that the Irish landlord takes a larger proportion of the produce for rent than the English landlord, and that consequently the English tenant after paying the cost of production, has a larger balance of the produce than the Irish tenant for subsistence, that consideration would of course affect the value of the yield of income tax as a measure of the capacity of the whole population in each country to bear fiscal burdens, would it not?—Yes, it would seem so.

6314. What do you say upon the practice which has prevailed in Ireland, of valuing badly-farmed land as if it were well-farmed?—That hardly seems to me to be a fair method to either landlord or tenant, as, of course, if you were to value land for its possibilities, you might value it far higher than its real income-paying power. If you were to value land

Mr. W. F. Bailey.

22 Feb. 1895.

Incidence of taxation as between landlord and tenant.

on its improvability, to put it so, you might value it much higher than the rent being paid for it would allow you, and landlord and tenant would both lose.

6315. And under this practice, Irish land has been valued in many cases, not at what it was worth at the time of the valuing, but what it might be made worth if improvements were judiciously applied to it?—Yes, that rule has been largely carried out, and I believe it has been admitted that it is so.

6316. We are told that it has been. What do you say on the practice of founding scales of prices in valuation Acts, and otherwise upon what are called general averages—averages taken from the highest and the lowest price of each year?—I do not much believe myself in that method of collecting prices; of course the usual criticism, and the fairly sound criticism is, if you take the average between the highest prices and the lowest prices, the highest price is taken where there is the least produce, and the lowest price where there is most produce, and certainly the mean between them would not represent the actual average price at all.

6317. It would represent more [illegible] received?—Quite right.

6318. If he sold the bulk of his produce at the time of year when the lowest price generally prevails, when the harvest is thrown on the market?—Quite so.

6319. What do you say on the suggestion that land reclaimed or improved by the tenant in Ireland has not been added to the valuation. Do you see any point in the suggestion that reclamations made by a non-income-tax paying class have not been added to the income tax assessment?—That is on the assumption that the amount of money spent on reclamation has added to the inherent value of the land.

6320. Yes?—One would naturally say, if you spent a large amount of money in reclaiming, or draining, or making any other agricultural improvements that it ought to add to the value of the land; but then you have to consider whether there was no change in the value of the land irrespective of those conditions. Undoubtedly you would have to add to your valuation the cost of those improvements, and the cost of that expenditure of money, but in Ireland, it would seem that that expenditure has been counter-balanced by other circumstances that have, to a more than corresponding degree, reduced the total value of the land.

6321. Moreover, these reclamations in Ireland are usually the subject of an annual expenditure to keep the land in condition, are they not?—That is so in a great number of cases.

6322. And at any rate if they were added to the valuation, the effect would be that the landlord would pay income tax upon property created by the tenant?—Yes, where the improvement was done by the tenants.

6323. Property undoubtedly belonging to the tenant would become subject to income tax, as if it were the property of the landlord?—That would be so.

Separate valuation of land and buildings.

6324. Upon the question of the separation of land and buildings in the valuation, you are the president of a court fixing rents, and of course you have great experience, have you not?—Yes.

6325. What do you say upon the suggestion that it is possible, by an acreable rate, which itself depends upon the value of produce, to fix the value of agricultural land without regard to the necessary equipment of the land, can you do it?—Of course in valuing land acreably, according to the produce, you must take into account that to produce so much out of an acre of land you require certain implements and instruments, and among those implements and instruments you might include the necessary buildings, the same as any other implement that is required.

6326. Do I suggest too much to you when I say that when the value of a holding is fixed upon an acreable rate, that that acreable rate fixed itself upon the value of produce does necessarily include the equipment of the holding?—I really do not see how you can say that an acre of land has got any value at all unless you take into account the fact that there must be some machinery for working it.

Mr. W. F. Bailey.

22 Feb. 1895.

Separate valuation of land and buildings.

6327. And therefore, when the land is valued separately upon this acreable rate, and the buildings valued afterwards, is there not some ground for thinking that a portion, at least, of the value of the buildings is twice included, first as necessary equipment as part of the acreable rate, and secondly in the separate value?—I think there is that danger. Of course I think also that it might be possible, if you kept it clearly in view in making your valuation, that you were to omit a certain part of the implements necessary for the cultivation and working of it you could do so; but I think that there is a good deal of risk that those who are carrying out a valuation might overlook that fact.

6328. In fact there would be no security unless the acreable rate were deliberately so fixed as to exclude equipment?—Yes.

6329. Now do you see any reason why the system in Ireland should not be the same as in England, where there is a good deal of ability applied to the consideration of these questions?—I do not.

6330. And that there should be a single valuation of land and buildings as a going concern?—Quite so. I quite see the reason suggested by The O'Conor Don, with reference to the constant changes in the value of buildings; but of course there are changes also in the value of the land.

6331. But after all does my suggestion involve any difficulty; if you make the integral calculation first as the value of the whole, how does that prevent subdivisions afterwards if they are required?—There is no reason why it should not be so.

6332. If you have one value for land and buildings together and it becomes necessary to re-value any building or buildings that can be done; a new item will be established and it will affect the main valuation?—Yes.

6333. Do you happen to know that the Select Committee of the House of Commons which inquired into this matter last year after hearing exhaustive evidence recommended that there should be in future in Ireland as in England, not a separate valuation of land and buildings, but a joint valuation of the two as a going concern?—Yes, I am aware of that.

Basis of valuation.

6334. When we are told that Griffith's valuation was not to exceed the fair letting value, what test or standard of the fair letting value was there at that time?—I think the words Griffith uses are they were to value in the same manner as if employed by one of the principal landlords of the county, who was about to let the lands to solvent tenants on leases, say, of 21 years. That was, more or less, the competitive value—what a man would get, of course limited by the fact that the tenant was to be a solvent one.

6335. It was to be as much as the pressure for land in Ireland would induce a solvent man to give, was it?—Yes.

6336. And the so-called fair-letting values of that time are the fair-letting values which have been reduced in the land courts—and some of them increased even afterwards in the prosperous years?—Yes.

6337. Have you any doubt that the local circumstances, such as altitude, climate, proximity and so forth, would be taken into account usually not to reduce, but to increase the valuation?—The instructions are very minute with reference to that, and there are tables of deduction and addition, I think, given; for example, as to altitude, if the land was over a certain number of feet in height there was to be a reduction per 1*l*. If it was at an altitude of from 800 to 900 feet it was a deduction of 5*d*. in the 1*l*., and when you come to 400 to 500 feet there was a deduction of 1*s*., and so on. Very minute tables indeed were drawn up with respect to those matters.

6338. The general effect, I submit to you, of the rules as to local circumstances was that they were taken into account more in the way of augmentation

Mr. W. F. Bailey. [illegible]

of value than reduction?—From that point of view I hardly have looked at it, so I could hardly say.

6339. Would you say that proximity to a town was more likely to increase a valuation than distance from a town was to reduce it?—I think Griffith takes the general average of about 5 or 6 miles as being supposed to be the average distance, and then he gives a careful scale for additions according to the size of the town and according to the number of miles the property is from it.

[illegible]

6340. I want to ask you a question or two about the towns. It has been suggested by the Commissioner of Valuation that the town valuation of Ireland might be increased if there were new valuations—in Dublin, I think he said, from 15 to 20 per cent.—and in Ulster something less. Now, so far as there is any progressiveness in Irish towns, it has occurred, I believe, in the townships of Dublin, in Belfast, and a few other towns of the north only—is not that so?—I think that is so.

6341. Is it not the fact that these townships about Dublin, and Belfast itself, have progressed mainly since Griffith's valuation was made?—Yes, I think so. Certainly, I can say mainly since then.

6342. And, therefore, the rents upon which the values are approximated were fixed in these cases upon the prosperous conditions of years more recent than the valuation?—Yes.

6343. Take, for instance (you know what I mean), Pembroke and places about Dublin?—Quite so.

6344. Does not that rather go to establish the presumption that there is nothing more prosperous now than at that time which would entitle an increase in the valuation of these towns?—Yes, because I do not know how frequently the valuation of these houses has been altered by the valuation office, but it would appear, if you take it that they were altered on the change of value, it is evident that they were valued at the most prosperous period.

6345. They appear to be altered only casually in the case of individual houses, and what I suggest to you is that the original valuation of these prosperous townships about Dublin and Belfast occurred at a time when rents were probably as high as they are now, owing to prosperity?—Yes.

6346. Do you know Dublin well?—Yes.

6347. The custom in Dublin is, is it not, for the landlord to pay all charges out of the rent?—Yes.

6348. Knowing what you do of the rents of Dublin and considering the local rates are about 10s. in the 1*l.*, and the old character of the city in connexion with repairs, do you think that the balance of rent left after repairs, insurance, and legal charges have been paid, would allow of any increase whatever in the valuation of Dublin?—Taking houses that I happen to know myself the rent of and making those additions in the valuations, having regard to the very high rates and taxes payable in Dublin (which come to 9s. or 10s. in the 1*l.*), and something for repairs and maintenance and insurance, it would seem to me that the valuation is quite high enough.

6349. Except Belfast and about four other towns in the north could it be said that the towns of Ireland now as compared with the period of Griffith's valuation are progressive?—No, if you take the test of population, certainly not, and of course with regard to a town the test of population is a very important one with reference to the value of houses.

6350. Would you say with reference to any town you know in Ireland, except as to three or four, that the rebuilding bears any satisfactory proportion to the decline or decay of buildings?—I think in most country towns I know of, the number of houses is decreasing.

6351. And in Dublin, as in most of the southern towns, are there large districts where houses formerly occupied by persons of good incomes have become mere broken-down tenements?—It is quite evident that it is so in Dublin. Streets that two generations ago were occupied by people of a fairly wealthy type have fallen into tenement houses, and they have lost a great deal of their value.

6352. Your opinion confirms my own observation so far as I know the country, that an increase in the urban valuation of Ireland could not equitably be made?—I think not.

6353. On the whole I mean?—On the whole, I should say not.

[illegible]

6354. One question generally upon Griffith's valuation. I believe the local rates even in 1852 were much less than they are now in Ireland?—Yes.

6355. And in the years that succeeded, between 1852 and 1865, whilst the valuation was in progress, the more progressive years of good prices, the rates bore only a very small proportion to what they are at present, did they not?—I think the rates were lower in 1865 than they were in 1852, but of course now they are very much higher.

6356. And so you deduct the local rates you would now have to deduct in any new valuation a much larger sum than in any time between 1852 and 1865, would you not?—Yes.

6357. Moreover I understand wages of labour within forty years have about doubled?—Yes, they have very largely increased.

6358. And in valuing the holdings now you would have to deduct from the gross value of the produce a far greater sum under the head of cost of production in order to arrive at the net value, would you not?—Yes.

6359. These circumstances would operate, would they not, to make a valuation, now, much lower than it was at any time between 1852 and 1865, apart from the heavy fall of prices in recent years?—Yes, I think it would.

6360. And the fall of prices would operate, would it not, to the same effect?—I do not see anything that make the valuation higher now than it was in 1852 or in 1865 irrespective of prices altogether, and I do not see anything that would cause you to raise the valuation.

6361. On the contrary, if rates are heavier and labour dearer, it would operate to reduce it, would it not?—Yes.

[illegible]

6362. I want to ask you a question or two upon Mr. Barton's Table 10. He gives us there what he calls income tax as a basis of comparison of the relative taxable capacity of Great Britain and Ireland, and you observe he opens with the actual charge; then he adds to the actual charge, for the purpose of comparison, the fall in amount of Income Tax paid because of sales of farms in Ireland under the Ashbourne and other Acts to the occupiers. Considering that those purchasers for 49 years will have to pay over to the Imperial Treasury a sum corresponding to the rent they paid to the landlord, do you see any reason why that sum should be added there in the measurement of the capacity of Ireland to bear general burdens. Do you see, he treats the farms which have been purchased by the occupiers as if they were still in the hands of the landlord and still paying income tax although they have passed into the hands of a non-income-tax paying class?—Just so.

6363. Do you agree that it ought to go in there to increase the measure of Ireland's capacity?—No, I do not see why it should. However, I suppose Mr. Barton had his reasons for putting it in, which I should like to consider before I definitely answer that question.

6364. If a man in England had 500*l.*, and instead of using it in a shop, he bought a piece of land, would you consider that the possession by him of that piece of land would be a reason for adding it to the income-tax assessment though he himself was not a person paying income tax at all?—There does not seem to be any reason for it, certainly.

[illegible]

6365. Then he makes an addition of "Saving due "to tax being assessed as regards landed property on "valuation, where same is under rent." You have told us upon your authority as a land commissioner

that if the reductions for the last seven years were applied to the whole rental of Ireland there would be no such saving?—Yes, that is so. I take it Mr. Burton has taken the sub-judicial rents from 1881 to the present time when making that calculation, but if you apply the circumstances which you put to me of the scale of reductions from 1881 to the present time to all the rents of Ireland I take it it would get rid of that altogether.

6366. It is not a perfectly safe basis to suggest to us as a guide at the present moment the deductions made in former years when the prices were higher and is not the true test of the current reductions made in rents in Ireland. As to schedule D. you have said already that, in your opinion, a new valuation could not rapidly be taken of the urban valuation of Ireland, and therefore that item in your judgment would disappear?—Quite so.

6367. Then generally when you consider the yield of income tax of the two countries as a basis of their taxable capacity of course you cannot ignore the question of where the income is spent?—Quite so.

6368. And if it were found that a great part of the rental of Ireland is expended out of Ireland to absentee landlords who live in other countries or to pay interest on mortgages or annuities due to mortgagees, that sum, as an equitable comparison would have to be deducted from the gross assessment in order to establish a fair comparison of wealth, would it not?—If you have a large expenditure of the rents out of the country then, undoubtedly, I take it, would largely affect the rights of the country to be charged on that account.

6369. In other words the yield of the income tax from a country cannot be taken as a measure of its capacity to bear taxation, except upon the assumption that the income upon which the tax is paid is spent in the country?—Yes; of course the difficulty I can see there is as to ascertaining where or how the income is spent. If you had a Table of incomes to show you where the income is spent and what portion of it you could then definitely measure it.

6370. I admit in the ordinary case there might be some difficulty, but in the case of Ireland it is notorious, is it not, that the great part of the body of landowners do live habitually out of the country, and that the land is mortgaged to a great part of its value to companies not trading in Ireland?—Yes, that is so.

6371. (*Lord Farrer.*) With regard to the last question put to you, if the money that comes from Ireland is spent out of Ireland there is any failure, as Mr. Sexton says, that that may not be a test of Ireland's capacity to pay, but it also secures, does it not, that persons in Ireland does not now pay that tax. If the money is spent by an absentee in London it is paid by the absentee in London, and not by Ireland, is it not. It cuts both ways, does it not?—Probably.

6372. Then with regard to the valuation of the rent I understand that everybody now may, if he pleases, pay upon his rent, and not upon his valuation? —Yes.

6373. Therefore really if we have got the thing cut by rent the valuation is of small importance, is it not?—Yes, as soon as you once get all the rents under the valuation.

6374. And supposing it were admitted for the sake of argument that we are not to go to the valuation, but that we are to go to rent, and that we do not make any distinction between valuation and rent, then we need not consider the Griffith's valuation at all we may fall back upon rent, may we not?—I think so as soon as you once get to that point.

6375. And whatever anyone chooses he may pay upon rent, may he not?—Yes.

6376. And the income tax assessment is on the rent, not on the valuation?—With the exception of the possible case of the occupier being charged on the difference between the rent and the valuation.

6377. Now let us go to the question of the occupier. There are two or three cases mentioned here where the landlord escapes income tax which he would otherwise have paid by reason of sales to the occupier or by reason that part of the value of the property is to be found in tenant right. In those cases there is no income tax paid, is there?—I hardly understand about the question of tenant right.

6378. Is not that income income tax is paid upon tenant right. A landlord pays so much less income tax because there is so much tenant right—that is so, is it not?—Hardly, for the reason that, in fixing the rent you do not deduct a special amount for tenant right.

6379. If there were no tenant right the landlord would receive a larger rent, and would pay upon that. A certain proportion of the value of the property has been transferred to the tenant, is not that so?—The saleable value and available values are different questions.

6380. By that means a certain part of the property which would otherwise belong to the landlord belongs to the tenant?—But the doubt is as to whether that amount has been deducted from the rent, that is, whether the rent is so much less because of the tenant right than it otherwise would be.

6381. The rent would be so much more if there were no tenant right, would it not?—Oh no.

6382. I want to get at the amount of income tax which is paid out of an estate in which there is a tenant right. For that part of the value of an estate which consists of tenant right the landlord pays no income tax does he?—The landlord pays income tax, we will take it, on his rent.

6383. And the tenant right belongs to the tenant does it not, not to the landlord?—But the question is whether the tenant right reduces the rent.

6384. Has the landlord pays only upon his rent, does he not?—Quite so.

6385. He does not pay on the tenant right, does he?—Certainly not.

6386. Does the tenant pay on the tenant right. No, because the tenant right is not part of the rent, I mean there is no tenant right there. Supposing you take up a holding on the borders of Ulster and a holding on the borders Leinster, side by side, except that one is in Ulster and the other in Leinster; one has a tenant right, we will suppose, and the other has not; there will be no difference in rent paid that you pay on them although one has tenant right and the other has not.

6387. But if you take the whole value of the holding there is first the landlord's share, which is the rent, and there is the tenant's share, which is the profit he can make plus his tenant right, is it not?—Yes, for saleable purposes, that is for the purposes of sale.

6388. On the sale of the property. Then when I want to get at is this. The landlord does not pay upon that part of the value of the holding which is tenant right. Do you agree with me there. He does pay if he comes within the range of the income tax upon that part of his profit which he makes by farming the land?—Yes, under Schedule B.

6389. But he pays nothing on the tenant right, does he?—No. I do not see why he should pay on the tenant right.

6390. Nor do I. I am only asking you as a matter of fact?—That is quite so.

6391. (*Mr. Sexton.*) Is there anything to value in a holding except the rent the landlord gets and balance of profit left to the tenant?—No, none that I see.

6392. The landlord pays income tax on the rent, does he not?—Yes.

6393. The tenant does not pay on the balance because his income does not reach the limit, that is the whole question?—Quite so.

6394. (*The O'Conor Don.*) But he does when it is, does he not?—Quite so.

6395. (*Lord Farrer.*) Have you any practical knowledge whatever of the mode of assessing values in London, say?—Oh no.

6396. You have spoken *à priori* of the probability that where property is locally assessed it will be assessed lower than where it is done by a Government

department?—Yes, an opinion backed up in my own mind by various pamphlets, arguments, and letters I have read, discussing the subject, but of course my knowledge is purely second hand.

6397. It is only derived from books, is it?—Quite so.

6398. Then you yourself know nothing whatever about London assessment, do you?—Of course, I have never had any opportunity of studying it except from books.

6399. And you do not know that every man on an assessment committee is jealous of his neighbour, and anxious to assess him at the highest value?—I suppose that is a consideration of human nature from which we may draw a general conclusion.

6400. And you do not know, do you, that every parish in London is also jealous of every other parish and anxious to assess it at a higher value?—No.

6401. You do not know, do you, that the London County Council have been engaged for years in endeavouring to equalise this assessment, and to get all the parishes assessed at their full value?—I take it that is so. Year after year efforts are made to make the assessments more stringent.

6402. Then when we go to the agricultural part of the country, do you know that the rating and assessment are under rating and assessment?—Yes.

6403. Do you know there are a number of parishes in each union?—Yes.

6404. And do you know that each of these parishes is jealous of one another just as the London parishes are. If, therefore, we are to go by *à priori* arguments you might guess that would be the case, might you not?—Of course I might guess that, and on the other hand, I might make the guess Mr. Sexton suggested to me.

6405. Do you know that lately there have been very great complaints (you may have seen Mr. Lefevre's letters in the paper) on the part of the agriculturists that the unions keep up the rating of the agricultural parts although the value has largely fallen?—Yes, I saw that, but of course the conclusion I drew in my own mind was that notwithstanding all this greater stringency and all these complaints the value of English land at the same time is going down. There has been a fall of 15 per cent. since 1883 in the valuation of English agricultural land.

6406. And the tendency of Mr. Lefevre's letters was to show, was it not, that the valuation of that land is keeping unfairly?—Quite so, and that it should come down still more.

6407. Do you not think that all these circumstances throw a doubt upon your *à priori* assumption that the local assessments will be less stringent than Imperial assessments?—No, I would hardly say so, because I think, although you may in some particular parishes and districts have these jealousies you speak of, notwithstanding that the fact that each locality has got the power of more or less assessing itself will still leave large opportunities for under-assessing land which Government probably would never give.

6408. Do you think the notion that the income tax in London might be slightly lowered if the whole assessment of London were below the mark of the rest of England, would be enough to prevent the different parishes in London and the County Council from seeing that the assessment was kept up for their own purposes?—It would show that the members of the local bodies were more wide-awake than perhaps they usually are to the general interests of the community.

6409. Have you any knowledge at all of the assessment in Dublin as compared with the assessment in London. Have you ever compared the assessment of London and Dublin houses?—No, I have not.

6410. You do not know anything about that, do you?—No.

6411. (*The O'Conor Don.*) I want to ask you a few questions with regard to the return to which you have alluded, presented by Mr. Milner. If you look at that return I think you will see it is practically a return showing the reductions which have been made on the English rental?—Yes.

Mr. W. F. Bailey.

12 Feb. 1896.

Rents and valuation.

6412. It appears from this return, does it not, that the total reductions which have been made up to the year 1893 is only 22 per cent?—Yes, from 1880.

6413. There was a gradual rise in the rents up to 1880, and then a diminution from 1880 down to 1893?—Quite so.

6414. And the total reductions in the English rents have therefore been only 22 per cent., have it not?—That is so.

6415. Now Mr. Sexton has spoken of the disastrous fall between 1895 and 1896 as compared with the fall preceding 1895. Will you look at that return and tell me does it not show that the English rents fell more between 1880 and 1886 than between 1886 and 1893?—Yes, taking those figures. You see, from 1884 to 1885 there was a considerable fall.

6416. In the next place the reduction that has been made by your body in Ireland has been on the whole 20 per cent. also?—Quite so.

6417. In reply to Lord Welby you admitted that very much more of the rent-paying crops are grown in England than in Ireland, did you not?—Yes, I assented to the figures that Lord Welby put.

6418. But is it not the fact that the great reduction in prices has been upon wheat and upon grain crops generally?—Yes, that is so.

6419. Is it not also a fact that in Ireland there is a very much less proportion of the land used in growing these crops than in England?—Yes. The proportions of tillage land in Ireland have been every year getting much less.

6420. And, consequently, we ought to expect that if the rents were reduced from natural causes, the rents in England would fall much more heavily than in Ireland?—Yes; of course Lord Farrer stated that there has been a great deal of objection in England that the assessments have not been brought down to the rents.

6421. But if we take this return as showing the fall in the rents, it would appear, would it not, that the reduction in the rental of England, although it ought to have been, if guided by natural causes, much larger than that in Ireland, has not been so?—Yes.

6422. The landlord also makes most of the improvements in England, does he not?—Yes.

6423. He lets the land like a going concern in full working order?—Quite so.

6424. Would you not naturally expect that where agricultural prices fall, the rents in a country where that was the rule, would be more likely to fall than in a country where the tenant did a considerable portion of the improvements and other works?—That is, where the landlord makes the improvements the fall in the rent ought to be the greater?

6425. Yes, it ought to be, ought it not?—On what principle?

6426. If the landlord makes all the improvements, and lets the land as a commercial concern, just as it stands, owning every thing in it, is he not more likely in good times to let the land up to the highest figure that it will fetch, and consequently when bad times come, and when natural causes produce a fall, should we not expect to find that that fall would be greater there than in a country where the opposite is the state of things with regard to the farming of the land?—I am not quite sure about that.

6427. But if that fact had any tendency, would it not naturally be in that direction?—It may be. Of course a tenant who has to make the improvements may, in bad times, hesitate to pay as high a rent as a tenant who got the land with the improvements made. I am not sure that I could say that is a general rule which I could assent to.

6428. The rents in Ireland, I suppose, were lowered very much after the famine, were they not?—Yes.

6429. That was about the time the rents would be the lowest, would they not?—Yes.

K k 4

Mr. W. F. Bailey.

18 Feb. 1895.

Rents and valuation.

6430. And the scale of prices upon which the valuation was made was taken at the time when the rents were lowest?—That is so.

6431. I believe it is part of the duty of your Commissioners at present—I do not know whether it was from the beginning—to take note, and record all changes made in the rents of the holdings which come up before them?—Yes, in most cases that is one of the first questions we ask.

6432. Can you tell the Commission what has been the result of your experience in that respect. Did you find in a large proportion of cases the rents had been raised, say since 1850?—We have great difficulty about that, for this reason, that we of course cannot take hearsay evidence—we are bound by the rules of law with regard to evidence—and in very few cases can we get evidence that we can accept and record with regard to changes of rent that have taken place before the last 20 years. A man will come and tell us that his rent has been reduced or raised; we ask him how he knows, and he says: "I was told so by my father." That evidence of course is ruled out. So that with the exception of changes which have taken place during the last 20 years, we hardly get any evidence.

6433. Is not the landlord always in a position to show you the changes which have taken place?—Sometimes; but very frequently the landlords omit to give us any evidence on the subject.

6434. But have you no idea in your own mind, or are there no records which would show the proportion of cases in which the rents were raised, say since 1850?—In the monthly returns made by the Land Commission of rents, the returns given of every rent fixed, wherever the evidence is such that it can be recorded—that is where it is legal evidence—it is recorded. The last change in rent is recorded, but you will find on looking over those returns, that the evidence is given in a very few cases.—Of course with reference to those cases, it would be possible to add them up, and find out the number of cases in which the evidence has been given, but I do not think it would be very valuable.

6435. Do those records show any large proportion of cases in which the rents were raised?—It varies very much. The general tendency is that, since 1850, any changes in rent that take place have been, more or less, rises up to 1881—from 1850 to 1880 any evidence we have as a rule is in the direction of a rise.

6436. But do those changes in rent form any large proportion of the whole?—No, they are not a large proportion as far as our books are concerned.

6437. If you look at this return of England and Wales, you will find that in 1892 the rental was practically about the same as it was in 1845. There is very little difference?—Yes.

6438. Do you think that the Irish rental as revised by your court is anything like as high as it was in 1856?—I can only state it very generally. I have really no evidence of what the rent was in 1856; but I am inclined to say that the rents we have been fixing in recent years are less.

6439. Then your evidence goes to show that the rents have been more reduced in Ireland than in England, does it not?—That is of course all on the assumption that the amount put down here as the valuation represents the rent which, I take it, is not admitted.

6440. Even if it did not represent the rental, I suppose it would represent the same proportion now as it did in previous years: there is no greater change in the proportion between the actual rent and the assessment now than there was say in 1880, is there?—Except that the valuations on the whole are higher now proportionately to the rent than they were then owing to the greater stringency with which the valuation is made in England.

6441. Are you aware of that from your own knowledge?—Yes; I am aware there has been far greater stringency in the valuation in England than there was at that time.

Mr. W. F. Bailey.

18 Feb. 1895.

Deductions by tenants ... landlord and tenant.

6442. Mr. Sexton asked you whether a larger proportion of the produce of the land was not taken in England by the farmer than in Ireland, and I think you answered that you had no knowledge upon that particular point, did you not?—Quite so.

6443. But supposing it were true, is it not the fact that the cost of the production to the tenant on account of his very high farming in England is much greater, as a rule, than the cost of production in Ireland?—Of course the circumstances are quite different.

6444. Entirely different?—Entirely different with respect to that. Of course on a large farm, an equipped farm, the relative cost would be far different from what it is on the small farms, such as we have in Ireland.

6445. Then if it were true that a larger proportion of the produce were taken by the landlord in Ireland than in England, still that would not prove that the rent was really higher in Ireland than in England, would it?—That fact in itself would not.

6446. (*Mr. Sexton.*) Unless it was a proportion of the net profits?—Yes; of course you would have to find that out.

Basis of valuation.

6447. (*The O'Conor Don.*) Do you consider the present tenement valuation of Ireland reliable as a standard either for taxes or rent?—No, I do not; I think the one great change that has taken place in the relative values of pasture and of tillage in itself would destroy its relative value, because when that valuation was carried out, tillage was far more valuable than pasture relatively speaking.

6448. I ask you whether you consider it reliable as a test for taxation purposes, or for fixing rent?—No.

6449. You do not think it is reliable for either?—No. I do not.

6450. And your ground for stating this is the difference between the relative values now of cattle and stock and grain and grain produce at the present time as compared with the time when the valuation was made?—That is the great cause, I think, of the unreliability of the valuation now; you see that by comparing Ulster with, say Munster. Ulster is mainly a tillage district. Munster is very largely a cattle raising district. In 1852, and from 1852 to 1860, when tillage was more valuable than pasture, relatively speaking, Ulster was valued at a higher rate proportionately than Munster. Now the result is that the valuation of Ulster is unquestionably far too high.

6451. That is on the supposition that the valuators valued according to the scale of prices, is it not?—Yes, or in accordance even with the rents; because I take it that the rents would naturally follow the particular article of produce that the farm was suitable for.

6452. And your Commission now do not set any value upon this valuation, you say?—No, none.

6453. Do you think that at any time it was reliable?—When it was made originally it may have been reliable enough, but the changes which have taken place, I think, have rendered it quite unreliable.

6454. Even in the same district?—Even in the same district.

6455. I am not comparing, now, the north with the south, but taking any particular county in Ireland, you do not think it is reliable in that county itself?—I think not; because even in the county you may have a difference from one farm to another with regard to what that farm is capable of doing, and the particular use to which the farm was more properly applied may have changed since the valuation was made.

6456. (*Mr. Sexton.*) Economic changes may have affected the use of the land?—Quite so.

6457. (*The O'Conor Don.*) According to the information given both to this Commission and the Committee in 1869, did not Sir Richard Griffith take the greatest possible pains to get the very best men to make the valuation?—Yes.

6458. And were they not all experienced men, who were trained to valuation?—Quite so.

Mr. W. F. Bailey.

2 Feb. 1898.

Valuations by Land Commission.

6459. Is that the case with regard to your Commissioners?—Yes, our Commissioners now are all men of very large experience.

6460. But were they so when they were first appointed; were they men who had undergone any course of training before?—Of course the effort was to get men who the Government thought had a large practical knowledge of farming, and of the value of land. One is always liable to make mistakes, but on the whole the present staff of the Land Commission, I should say, is composed of very experienced men.

6461. Has there been any instruction given to them upon what system they are to value?—No.

6462. Each man values, does he not, just as he thinks proper himself?—Upon what he thinks to be the value of the land from his own experience.

6463. And therefore there probably is a very great variety in the decisions at which they arrive?—That is, of course, quite possible; one man will not always take the same view as another.

6464. Do you think the valuations made by your body would be reliable for taxation purposes?—I think, with certain changes and alterations, they could be made reliable.

6465. Certain changes and alterations of what character?—I think, in a valuation for taxation, you have to take things into account that you would not take into account for rent purposes; for example, if you want to get at the value of a holding for taxation purposes, you have often to include things which you will not include in the rent. You have to include, I take it, in a valuation for taxation, the annual value of the holding as you find it; but the rent will not always mean that.

6466. But apart from that, do you consider from what you have stated about these gentlemen acting upon their own ideas, the valuation would be fairly relative if fixed upon their decisions—that they really do come to about the same relative valuation all round?—Of course I can only speak from my knowledge of my own colleagues with whom I have worked, and I must say, from my knowledge of them, I would have confidence in the relative character of their valuations.

6467. Do you think it would be desirable to base a valuation for taxation purposes upon valuations made by a body which a Committee of the House of Commons reported upon last year to the following effect: "No mode of valuation has been prescribed, either by "Parliament or otherwise, and consequently and of "necessity each individual administrator acts absolutely according to his own ideas of what may have "been intended, and there is neither a common understanding of the law, nor anything approaching to "uniformity of administration." Do you agree in that opinion?—That is not my evidence, that is the Committee's conclusion.

6468. Do you agree in that opinion of the Committee. I have read the opinion of the Committee of last year upon your body, and I ask you do you agree with it?—I certainly will not say that I agree with it. I say this, which might alter the matter that with reference to a great number of questions of valuation where no principles have been set forth in their judgment, individual Commissioners, the same as individual judges, in any matter may take different views, and that it is always advisable that either in the form of judgments or otherwise, principles should be laid down which would secure uniformity in valuation as well as uniformity in law, and if that were done it probably it would take away some of the objections that have been made by the Committee of the House of Commons.

6469. You think it would be desirable, do you, to have certain principles laid down?—Undoubtedly.

6470. And to have very detailed information given in all these decisions as to the ground on which the decision was arrived at?—Undoubtedly. I think the more information you give and the more the principles are stated the better.

6471. Assuming the valuations were made upon such principles by the Commissioners and Sub-Commissioners, do you consider that one and the same valuation would be suitable for taxation and for rent?—I do.

6472. Do you think that then the Valuation Office as a department might be done away with altogether?—No. I think for valuation purposes you require that there must be some body whose special duty it will be to go over the different buildings and tenements for valuation purposes, but I think you could work it in this way, that you might send to the Valuation Department the rents which are fixed by the Land Commission, or a schedule of them, and let the Valuation Office then so deal with them as may be necessary for the special purposes of assessment. I think without making a new valuation of Ireland with a new set of men you could effect the purpose.

6473. How would you deal with the lands that have not gone into your court. I believe half of Ireland has not gone into your court yet?—No, it has not such a proportion as that.

6474. (*Mr. Sexton.*) Half the rental, is it not?—Yes, half the rental.

6475. (*The O'Conor Don.*) That is what I meant?—Of course in the case of that land you would have to provide for a special valuation for the purposes of taxation.

6476. And do you think that a uniform system of valuation could be arrived at by having one half of the rental decided by one body and the other half of the rental decided by another?—There is no reason why both should be decided by the same body. I cannot see any objection to the valuers employed by the Land Commission also valuing the other portion that has not come into court for the purposes of taxation. With one set of valuers I think you could do both.

6477. And you think the valuers of the Land Commission Courts would be the best persons to employ to value the lands that have not come into court?—I take it the Valuation Office now possesses no land valuers who would go out and value land—as I understand it since 1865 no land valuation has ever been made, so that they do not possess land valuers now.

6478. Does not a great difficulty exist with regard to that. Is not there, now, for local taxation purposes, a great dissimilarity between the rents of land which have been reduced by your court and the rents that have not been? For local purposes the landlord has to pay the old valuation, although you have reduced the rent?—Yes.

6479. And then in other cases where there has been no reduction, there has been no new valuation, has there?—Quite so.

6480. Is it not the fact that at present there is an inequality as regards local taxes between the people who have had their rents reduced and those who have not?—Quite so.

6481. How would you propose to get over that?—I do not see any way of getting over it except by a re-valuation in the way I suggest.

6482. Do you not think a re-valuation of Ireland is absolutely necessary in some shape or form?—I certainly think so, but, as I said, I think that could be best carried out by having one valuation for rent and taxation, that is to say, sending the results of the valuation made by the Land Commission valuers to the Valuation Office, and let the Valuation Office deal with those valuations in accordance with the requirements for assessment purposes.

6483. How would you deal with the question of tenant's improvements?—That would be very easily managed. You would make your original valuation on the land as it stands, you would record that, and then you would make the proper deductions for tenant's improvements for rent purposes or whatever other change may be necessary in the circumstances of the case.

6484. Who should pay the local rates upon these improvements?—I take it that the local rates should be paid on the value of the tenement as it stands.

6485. And that there should be no rating put upon that portion of the value of the land which consists of tenant's improvements?—I do not say that. I

Mr. W. F. Bailey. 29 Feb. 1896. Valuation by Local Commissioners.

think that, probably, for purposes of local taxation, the land in its improved state should be valued. I think it is only fair that it should be valued for local taxation purposes as it stands.

6496. And that the landlord, therefore, should pay the rate upon the improvement which he does not get a consideration for in the rent?—Oh, no. As I say, as far as landlords are concerned, that proposal would necessitate some change in the law. I think it would be very unfair to make a landlord pay for what he was not getting—that would be very unjust.

6497. But I want to see how you propose to meet it?—If that difficulty arose you would have to alter the proportions of the local taxation that the landlord paid. I see no difficulty in doing that.

6498. I think you stated that the tenant right is not taken into consideration in fixing the rent, and I suppose you agree that it should not, that it is a saleable property, and one that has an actual value?—Yes. When we are speaking of what is known as tenant right in Ireland that has a saleable value, but of course in fixing a rent you are not to be taken as meaning to say "we put a competitive rent on the land." We certainly do not put a rent on the land that might be put by competition; we put a rent on it which it would be taken by a solvent man. And if he has got any right from his occupation or otherwise, that of course is a matter to be considered.

The witness withdrew.

Adjourned to Thursday, 7th March, at 11 o'clock.

FIFTEENTH DAY.

Thursday, 7th March 1895.

At Committee Room B, House of Lords.

PRESENT:

THE RIGHT HON. HUGH C. E. CHILDERS, *Chairman*.

LORD FARRER.	J. E. REDMOND, Esq., M.P.
LORD WELBY.	THOMAS SEXTON, Esq., M.P.
SIR DAVID BARBOUR, K.C.S.I.	GUSTAV W. WOLFF, Esq., M.P.
BERTRAM W. CURRIE, Esq.	HENRY F. SLATTERY, Esq.
CHARLES E. MARTIN, Esq.	

Mr. B. H. HOLLAND, *Secretary*.

Mr. MURROUGH O'BRIEN recalled and further examined.

Mr. Murrough O'Brien. 7 Mar. 1895. Church Fund items.

6499. (*Chairman*.) When you gave evidence before the Commission, now some weeks ago, your attention was specially called to the general financial relations between Great Britain and Ireland, but you now have submitted a memorandum as to a particular branch of the question about which I propose to examine you, going through your memorandum, so that the salient points may appear on our notes. I believe you wish to call attention to the transactions in connection with the Church Temporalities Fund, as illustrating the financial action of the Treasury, and the financial relations between Great Britain and Ireland; and I think you say that the principal part of that property may be divided into two classes, these are the tithe rentcharge, and the perpetuity rents. The tithe rentcharge amounted to how much?—The tithe rentcharge amounted to about 410,000*l*. a year, and the perpetuity rents to 131,000*l*. a year. There were some other items which I have not referred to particularly, such as rents of yearly tenancies and leaseholds.

6500. You described the tithe rentcharge as difficult to identify, and costly to collect, what, in your opinion, is the value of the tithe rentcharge; how many years' purchase is it worth?—Before the Church Act, tithe rentcharges were not saleable in the market for more than 17 years' purchase. Since the time of the Church Act, there have been very few, if any, sales in the market.

6501. And the tithe rentcharges were taken under the Church Act, as worth how many years' purchase?—The price fixed by the Church Act was 22½ years' purchase on the tithe rentcharge, and 25 years' purchase on the perpetuity rents.

6502. What, in your opinion, was the excess value so attributed to it?—The excess value put on by the estate, on the market value of these securities, was about two millions and three quarters, or three millions, I think.

6503. Did that take into consideration the liability of the charge to fall off?—At the time the Church Act passed, the rentcharge was variable with the price of corn as it is, I believe, in England. The right of varying that charge, was taken away not by the Church Act, but by the Church Amendment Act in 1872.

6504. And the operation of the two Acts, together with the great fall since in the value of the articles on which the calculation was made, has, in your opinion, made the excess charge about how much?—Very nearly 3,000,000*l*.

6505. Then, you also call attention, do you not, to the charges which have been since put, or were at the time put, upon the Church Fund, which were more properly charges upon the Consolidated Fund, which are these?—The charges which are referred to particularly as having been on the Imperial Revenue before, are the Maynooth Grant, in compensation for which 372,331*l*. was paid out of the Church Fund; and the Regium Donum, which had been a charge on the Imperial Fund since the time of Charles the Second.

6506. These were past charges, were they?—They had been annual charges on the Imperial Revenue.

Mr. Murrough O'Brien.

7 Mar. 1896.

Church Fund loans.

6497. But, in addition to these, charges were put upon the Church Fund which, in your opinion, ought more properly to have been charged on the Imperial Revenue, were there not?—A great many of the subsequent charges put on the Fund were in most cases purely temporary, such as famine, congested districts, or political emergencies. I think these would have to have been met out of the Imperial Fund, because it would have been quite indefensible to allow people to starve in Ireland when a revenue of [illegible] a year was being raised in the country. The thing could not have been defended, and, therefore, these relief loans and relief expenditure, would certainly have been paid out of the Imperial Revenue.

6498. Also, do you consider that the charges for intermediate education, and other subjects of that kind, which have fallen upon the Church Fund, ought to have fallen upon the Imperial Revenue?—I think the charges for education were matters which, considering the revenue that Ireland contributes, should have been paid out of that revenue.

6499. Could you name the charges to which you refer?—The principal charges are: Intermediate education, for which [illegible] was charged on the Church Fund at 3½ per cent.; National School Teachers' fund, [illegible] at 3 per cent. With regard to the Royal University, there was no principal sum fixed; but a yearly revenue of [illegible] was assigned to it out of the Church Fund. In addition to that the last charge imposed on the Church Fund is for the congested districts board which receives interest at 3½ per cent. on [illegible].

6500. Is it your position that these amounts which are charged on a special Irish Fund, ought equitably to have been charged on the general revenue of the country?—I do not say that; I say that the educational system in Ireland was such that a large expenditure was necessary, which would have been paid, I assume, out of the ordinary revenue of the country; instead of that it was put upon the Church Fund. It saved trouble, the fund was there, and it was a very convenient method of disposing of the educational question, so far as it has been disposed of.

6501. You also call attention to the rate of interest charged on the balance of debt due to the National Debt Commissioners, what is your point upon that?—The rate of interest which is payable to the National Debt Commissioners is 3½ per cent.; in one instance 3¼ per cent. I think so far as loans were made at all they should have been made at the lowest possible rate, so that England, as a sister, or mother country, should not make a profit out of those loans. They were made on the very best security, and the rate of interest should have been adapted to the lowest current rate of interest at which it was possible to lend. At the commencement of these loans I admit the rate of interest in the market was higher than it has been since, but of late years it has been below 3¼; and these loans have been very profitable to the National Debt Commissioners.

6502. And you think the rate of interest ought to have been reduced with the reduction of the current rate in the market, do you?—Certainly.

6503. And if per contra the rate of interest in the market had increased, you would have seen no objection to a larger charge, would you?—That is a point I have not considered, because it did not arise.

6504. You call attention to the loss in connection with the Church Fund. Will you explain to the Commission your point upon that?—The question of the value of the Church surplus fund arises every year I may say, in Parliament, when there are questions as to making further loans, or imposing further charges on it. Many estimates have been made and furnished to Parliament, but these are merely paper estimates. The Church Revenue consists of annual payments from several different classes of property, all practically landed property; the collection is uncertain and difficult. One of the reasons it is difficult is that the property out of which the revenue is payable is unidentified; in many cases we do not know what it is. As long as it is paid, it is paid; but if a question arises as to the liability of a person, it is very difficult to prove, and the result is there is a good deal of cost, and there ought to be a good deal more to make the income secure. The result has been that a considerable amount of loans have to be written off every year as irrecoverable, and in many instances the annual sum written off represents a capital sum lost. I think that this is partly due to a sufficient expenditure not having been made from the very commencement, in the collection and management of the Church Fund. To make it perfectly secure, the whole property should have been identified at first. That has not been done, and, in my opinion, there has never been a sufficient staff to collect, identify, and sell the Church property to the best advantage.

6505. Has the staff been considerably in your opinion below the mark?—The staff has I think been considerably below the mark, and below the mark in efficiency, because it has been largely composed of temporary men. There are many men who have been employed temporarily, who are liable to dismissal at a week's or a month's notice, who had been on the staff 10 or 15 years. That is not a system which leads to efficiency.

6506. This led to considerable arrears, and part of the arrear is, I suppose, a mere matter of outlay, and will be recovered, but part is worse than that, you think, do you?—Yes. By a recent decision of the Courts, when the Statute of Limitations runs against a debt that has accrued, the capital charge goes too; and the result is that a considerable part of the capital charge has been lost. I give you the amount that has been written off in each year, you will see that it has been since 1889 a gradually growing amount, at the same time the arrears have been diminished because greater strictness in payment has been enforced by the Land Commission.

6507. Are these arrears increasing or decreasing now?—The arrears are rather decreasing at present.

6508. Is that allowing for the process which you have described of their being written off and ceasing to be arrears?—Independently of what is written off; nothing is written off except what is absolutely irrecoverable; and, in addition to that, I think, the arrears have been pulled up within the last four years.

6509. There are three special cases, into which you divide the losses from arrears, are there not?—Yes, I think that the ultimate value of the fund will be affected by three principal causes: one is the interest on the mortgages, for three-fourths of the purchase money which was credited to tenant purchasers in some cases, owing to the fall in the value of agricultural land. The land on which the mortgages were secured has become of less value than the interest annually paid. In those cases we must anticipate a loss, and some losses have occurred.

6510. Even including the instalments which have been paid between the original loan and the present day?—Yes, if the Land Commission have to go into possession of this land, as they have in a few cases, and will have to do so in more, it means they make a loss; when it is not worth while continuing the payment on the mortgage, if they have to foreclose the mortgage they lose.

6511. That is the first point, then the second is—what?—The perpetuity rents are variable; they have not been varied until of late years, because the payers were not aware of the provisions for variability with the price of corn. Some of them are becoming aware of it, and more will, no doubt, do so. Since 1884 37 rents, amounting to [illegible] have been reduced under the provisions for variation to [illegible], a diminution of the capital value at 25 years' purchase of [illegible]. That will be an increasing item of loss.

6512. Then there is a third point?—In cases of sales of perpetuity rents under the Church Act, the Land Commission, even if they are thoroughly well secured rents, can no longer require payment or

redemption at 25 years' purchase, because the parties have a right to have the price fixed by arbitration, and it is very unlikely that 25 years' purchase will be obtained for them.

6513. There will, therefore, be under four heads which you give, a probable or a certain diminution in the surplus, will there?—A certain diminution in the surplus as estimated on paper.

6514. By what process would that be met, and the solvency of the fund secured?—I think there should be an immediate reduction of the rate of interest payable to the National Debt Commissioners, which is now 3½ per cent. on most of the debt. I think that ought to be reduced to the lowest possible rate, I should say 2½, or below that, I think, justice would require a refund of past payments at excessive rates; and then I think also that the church property establishment should be put upon an effective strength. I should like to draw attention to the figures I have given at page 3, as to the cost of collection. The whole charge is about three per cent. on the revenue. The mere cost of collection and sales amounts to 1½ per cent. Now I do not think any revenue of this kind, comprising a number of items varying from 1d. to 700l., and paid by 35,000 payers, could be collected for that sum. As a matter of business that could not be done; no agent would undertake to collect on those terms. When I compare it with other public revenues, I find that the cost of collecting and accounting for a rental of 515,900l. under the Court of Chancery was in 1890, 50,780l., or nearly 10 per cent. The cost of the Woods and Forests Department for collecting a gross income of 531,839l., amounts to 62,000l., or 11¼ per cent. of the revenue. I take these figures from Whitaker's Almanack, because the accounts of the Woods and Forests are so complicated and of so various kinds that I could not show the figures, but on examining them I came to the same conclusion. I find that the Woods and Forests Report for 1894, shows the cost of their collection in Ireland alone, they collect a yearly rental of 39,225l.; they pay their local collectors two per cent. upon that which amounts 790l.; incidental expenses come to 33l., making a total of 832l. Then the proportion of the vote of 22,000l. assigned in the Treasury return as the expense in Dublin of the Woods and Forests Department, is 2,798l.; that makes the total cost of collection and management of the Irish Revenue of 40,000l., about nine per cent. When I connect these figures, and my own experience of the cost of collecting a revenue from land with what is spent upon the Church collection, I say it is quite insufficient to do it efficiently and well; and my experience, from having had a good deal to do with the Church Fund property, is that it is a continual scramble.

6515. Would you say that the per-centage for cost of collection in the case of the Woods and Forests for instance, was really of a like character, and gave a fair comparison with the cost to the Church Fund?—As to part of the revenue it is. For instance, the Irish revenue is derived altogether, I think, from quit rents which are better secured than our tithe rent-charges. The cost in Ireland is 9 per cent.; in England the revenue that is collected locally—I forget the exact figure—is some hundreds of thousands of pounds, and an amount of some 2½ per cent. is paid to the local collectors, independent of the expense of the office which is provided for by the vote of Parliament. Therefore I say the mere per-centage paid to the local collectors for collecting an easily collected revenue is more than is spent on the whole of the church establishment and collection too.

6516. Summing up the points in your paper, you say that the Church Fund has been a source of profit to Great Britain, and a loss to Ireland. How would you illustrate that?—I think Great Britain has benefited by the transfer to the Church Fund of charges which previously fell on the Imperial Revenue; by the imposition on the Fund of other charges which would have fallen on the Public Revenue, and by the profit made on loans to Ireland, at an excessive rate of interest. When I say "excessive," I do not mean excessive as compared with the rates at which money can be secured from private lenders, but in excess of the rates at which public money can be borrowed.

6517. And per contra?—Ireland has lost, and this loss has fallen particularly on landowners by the artificial enhancement of the Church Fund, which I mentioned at first.

6518. Then you give a special cause of loss to Ireland based on a consideration of the country where the revenue is spent; will you amplify that a little?—It is part of the drain from Ireland to England resulting from the very centralised system of Government. Before 1869 the whole revenue of the Church was spent in Ireland; since then practically the whole revenue has been remitted to England, and the capital has been largely spent for purposes from which there is no economic return.

6519. You do not therefore believe, do you, that the system has really been a boon to Ireland?—I do not think it has. I think the disestablishment of the Church may have been a desirable thing, but the economic effect of it has not been advantageous to Ireland.

6520. How would you define the difference between Great Britain's and Ireland's requirements in this respect?—It appears to me that the prosperity of Great Britain depends on the maintenance and extension of her industries and commerce; the prosperity of Ireland on the development of her internal resources and the better organisation of her social, political, and economic system. Ireland contributes, without getting any return, to the wars, the forward and foreign policy of Great Britain. Her struggle is against want, occasional famines, and chronic distress. For the expenditure made to avert these calamities, or repair the damages done by them, expenditure on relief works, land improvement, arterial drainage, and grants in aid of distress, &c., Ireland has to pay 3½ per cent., yet the removal of the causes of poverty in Ireland is as legitimate a purpose for Imperial expenditure without charge as the wars and foreign policy to which Ireland has had to contribute for the development of Great Britain's industries and extension of her commerce.

6521. Then I believe you wish to add some words as to what is the great Irish difficulty in regard to financial matters?—The great difficulty in Ireland has always been her excessive poverty. That poverty exhibits itself in discontent. A prosperous people is seldom discontented even under unjust laws. The system of Imperial loans for temporary emergencies and charity tends to increase the poverty of Ireland, whose future income is mortgaged to pay interest on expenditure from which there is no return. There is no surer road to ruin for an individual than borrowing money to live upon, and most of these Imperial loans are practically made from time to time to enable the Irish people to live or relieve acute distress and avert disorder. Loans are almost annually made to keep the people quiet or to keep them alive. Yet this expenditure does not prevent the recurrence of famine, distress, and discontent; it rather tends to cause their recurrence, for each unremuneratively spent loan adds to the burdens on the incomes of the country, and it is well known that a great deal of the money nominally meant to be spent on reproductive works has been misspent and wasted.

6522. You sum up what you have said before by saying that the loans by the National Debt Commissioners on the security of the Church Fund are thoroughly well secured, and have been a profitable investment?—Yes, I think they have been a profitable investment.

6523. You give a rather remarkable figure as to the other public loans, and say that they amount to nearly 8,000,000l., and to the extent of between 6,000,000l. and 7,000,000l. the money is provided by Ireland out of the savings bank deposits. Will you explain that exactly?—The other public loans to Ireland, made through the Board of Works and Public Works Loan

Commissioners, amounted on 31st March 1893 to 7,881,258*l*. according to the return asked for by Mr. Smith Barry. The greater part of this amount is provided by Ireland from the deposits in the Irish Post Office Savings Bank, and balances from the savings banks in the hands of The National Debt Commissioners, amounting to 6,027,000*l*. Therefore a large part of the money that is lent to Ireland is really provided by Ireland. There is no liberality in the loans. Irish depositors invest their money here at 2½ per cent., and the National Debt Commissioners then lend it back at 3¼ per cent.

6324. It is, in your opinion, virtually Irish money, is it?—Virtually, and it simply goes to England first as a matter of book transaction, in consequence of the centralised system of government.

6325. (*Mr. Currie.*) You say that the National Debt Commissioners make a profit out of Ireland. Is it within your knowledge that the operations of the National Debt Commissioners result in a profit, generally?—I may say that they get money at 2½ per cent., and lend it at 3¼; there is a margin.

6326. But you are aware there are considerable considerable risks, such as the necessity of having to pay the money on demand, are not you?—There has been no risk in the loans made on the Irish Church Fund, because they are amply secured.

6327. I mean risk which they run in taking money repayable on demand. Their money is found, is it not mainly by the savings bank deposits?—Yes. I think the course of business shows they may depend on an annual amount, and from Ireland there has been an increasing amount for the last 30 years.

6328. But, as a matter fact, in the public accounts, does it appear that the operations of the National Debt Commissioners result in a profit?—That I could not say, as I have not the accounts before me.

6329. (*Lord Farrer.*) You say in the first part of your paper, that the Church Fund was over-valued?—So it appears to me.

6330. And that the returns are, to some extent, precarious?—I say that the price fixed by the statute, of 22½ years' purchase of the tithe rentcharge, was in excess of the market rate.

6331. The National Debt Commissioners, I suppose, lent on the security of this fund?—They lent on the security of this fund.

6332. Then anything that was precarious in the fund would reduce the value of the security, would it not?—It would depend on the margin there was. There was ample margin for all these loans, as has been proved by the way the Church Fund has worked out so far.

6333. You think, do you, notwithstanding the precarious nature of the returns, there was ample security, so that the National Debt Commissioners ought not to have taken anything more than the mere ordinary rate of interest, and that the interest not have been increased in order to indemnify them on account of the imperfection of the security?—If the National Debt Commissioners had lent money to the full value of the funds, I think they would have lost, as the Fund has lost money, but the National Debt Commissioners did not lend anything like the full value. They were like a prudent mortgagee.

6334. What margin was there?—I could not say exactly what margin there was to commence with, because these loans have been made from time to time, and as some have been paid off others have been added; but as the matter has worked out, they have had an ample margin; they were just as safe as a mortgagee lending on first-class property two-thirds, or one-third the capital value.

6335. I rather gather from the whole of your paper, that you think this business would have been much more economical and better managed if Ireland or the Irish had managed it for themselves, and the English Government had not intervened?—I think there is a good deal of waste in having the thing managed partly in Dublin, and partly in London.

6336. But, on the whole, if the Irish had had to manage it entirely themselves, and had to get the money for themselves, do you think they would have done it better and more economically than has been done through the instrumentality of the English National Debt Commissioners?—I have no doubt we could manage our financial affairs much better at home, because we are much better acquainted with our wants, and would manage them more prudently.

Mr. Barry O'Brien.

7 Mar. 1895.

Public loans.

6337. And you would have had no difficulty in getting money, would you?—I do not think there is any difficulty in raising money in Ireland. Of late years when some of the large municipalities have had power given to them to raise loans they have had no difficulty in raising money at a low rate of interest.

6338. (*Sir David Barbour.*) At page four of your memorandum you give various figures as to rental, do you not?—Yes.

6339. Do those figures represent the yearly claims, or the actual collections?—From 1883 to 1893, under the column headed "rental," the amount includes the sales. I thought it better to take them from the accounts as they have been printed. A change has been made in the method of keeping the accounts. That yearly rental represents the yearly amount received both from rental and sales. In 1891, 170,780*l*. is rental only; that is owing to a change made in the method of keeping the accounts.

6340. Then those figures represent the collections, and not the yearly demand?—It is the rental received I think, but I have not got that before me.

6341. If the solvency of the Church Fund is doubtful, the security of the National Debt Commissioners is not so very good?—That is not so at all, because after the National Debt Commissioners come several millions of money which are allocated to purposes with which the National Debt Commissioners have nothing whatever to do. Intermediate education in Ireland 1,000,000*l*.; National School Teachers Fund 1,300,000*l*.; congested districts board 1,500,000*l*.; Royal University, say, 700,000*l*.

6342. The National Debt Commissioners have the first claim, have they?—Certainly.

6343. If there is not sufficient left to meet the other claims, I suppose the Imperial Revenue would have to bear the loss?—That I could not say. It would depend upon Parliament, I suppose.

6344. (*Mr. Sexton.*) You stated that the amount held by the savings bank is some 6,027,000*l*.?—The amount returned in the official returns for Ireland, showing the total of the balances at the Post Office and Trustee Saving Banks on the 31st of December 1893 was 6,973,000*l*.

Returns to depositors.

6345. On which the depositors received 2½ per cent.?—Yes.

6346. And they receive 2½ to a certain extent because it is payable on demand?—Certainly.

6347. Is there any other mode by which the Irish people can get equal facilities for investing moneys payable on demand, at even considerable less than 2½ per cent?—I imagine that if the financial affairs of England and Ireland had been separated, Ireland would have done as every other civilised nation has done, established a Post Office Savings Bank. Until very recently the French Savings Bank gave 3 per cent. I do not know what rate of interest we should have given, but no doubt we should have given as good a rate as we could have afforded, in order to attract the money.

6348. But it is within your knowledge that other institutions existing in Ireland could receive the money on deposit from the Irish people at 3½ per cent. and practically repay it on demand?—I think the rates of interest chargeable by other institutions for money on demand vary very much. The banks will give 1 per cent., but many solvent building societies give more than 3½ per cent. I do not think we have many in Ireland, but still it is a common practice for building and loan societies to take money on deposit at a higher rate of interest.

L l 3

[illegible]

Mr. Murrough O'Brien.

7 Mar. 1896.

Savings banks deposits.

6549. Banks only allow 1 per cent. on deposits, and they are practically payable on demand equally as the savings bank, are they not?—I do not think the two businesses are at all comparable, the business of a bank and the business of a Government institution like the Post Office Savings Banks, are not comparable.

6550. What is the security that is given by the Government for the repayment of the savings bank deposits?—I suppose the revenues of the country.

6551. Is not the money practically largely invested in Consols, nearly nine-tenths of it?—I would say that a great deal of it was invested, as regards Ireland, by the National Debt Commissioners at 3½ per cent. in Ireland.

6552. That is not the return, the return is in Consols, is it not?—My impression is that they pay 2½ per cent. to their depositors, and we know as a matter of fact that they have lent 6,000,000*l.* or 7,000,000*l.* back to Ireland, not payable on demand, but repayable by instalments at 3½ per cent.

6553. Do you remember when a short time ago it was stated that banks, in order to afford greater security to the public, ought to keep larger cash deposits, and the matter was brought before the Bankers Association, it was stated that the security which was given by the Government by investing in Consols, was exactly the security which was given by the banks, and if large institutions, holding some six times as much as the 8,000,000*l.* can also give the same security to depositors and repay practically on demand, do you not think 2½ per cent. is a very excessive rate of interest?—I think at present the Post Office Bank would probably attract deposits at a lower rate of interest owing to the present plethora of money, but as regards the reserve and the moneys they must keep in hand to meet a call on those deposits, they are like other bankers, they must keep a reserve to meet a possible demand, but not an impossible one, just as a bank must retain some gold. But if all its liability were to be called up at once they would be bankrupt, which is a thing not contemplated in banking.

6554. What I want to ascertain is whether you think it is to the interest of the country that people should deposit money with the Government which is liable to repayment on demand or whether it would be to their interest to deposit it with other institutions?—I think the security given by Government Post Office Banks in every country is an advantage, because the public are unable to discriminate between sound and unsound banking establishments, and, as we all know, there have been very heavy losses made by people who have deposited money in order to get a higher rate of interest with building societies.

6555. What percentage do you think the losses of all the banks in the United Kingdom amount to within the last 100 years?—I do not know at all.

6556. Then how can you give an opinion as to the risk of depositing in banks?—I think I can; for instance, take the Glasgow Bank.

6557. Would it surprise you to hear that with regard to all the banks in the United Kingdom, even including the Glasgow Bank, for the last 50 years their assets have always realised over 75 per cent. of their indebtedness, exclusive of the calls on the shares?—Banks are not the only institutions that attract deposits from poor people, and it is just like the Government issuing a sound currency. The mass of people who handle coin are unable to estimate its value. I think it is a proper and advantageous thing for the Government of every country to establish these Post Office Savings Banks where poor people can deposit their money at a low rate of interest which always has been lower than the current rate.

Adjourned for a short time.

[illegible]

6558. (*Lord Welby.*) In your answer to the Chairman at Question 5411 you give a summary of the Treasury view of the financial relations between Great Britain and Ireland resulting in this; that Ireland contributed to Imperial services 1·01 in 1889, 3·04 in 1890, and 3·01 in 1893, and in an answer shortly afterwards I think you criticise that contribution, and state that a great many items are charged as Imperial services, which, in your opinion, should be classed as British services?—Yes.

Mr. Murrough O'Brien.

7 Mar. 1896.

[illegible]

6559. There is of course room for great difference of opinion upon that point, and I am rather anxious to divide the discussion, so as to arrive at some point at which we may agree. I should like to point out to you that there are two questions involved; one is what are the Imperial services to which Ireland should contribute; and the other what is the total sum which she does actually contribute. I want to take the latter point first, because I think there we deal with a question of fact?—May I say I have not a print of my evidence before me, but I may perhaps understand your question from my recollection. These tables have been prepared by the Treasury, and I do not think it is easy for us to criticise them. I drew attention to one or two instances from which, it seemed to me, Ireland derived no advantage from the expenditure which is set down as Imperial, although she is expected to contribute to it. I think I took the wine and the compensations. With regard to the Duchy of Lancaster and the Duchy of Cornwall, the revenues do not come into the account. They are appropriated, I believe, to the personal wants of members of the royal family, but yet Ireland contributes to the wine and the compensations—I merely took these as an example.

Irish contribution to Imperial services.

6560. This leads up to a question which I had asked before, but which I will repeat. I said there is, of course, room for a difference of opinion upon that point, and a legitimate difference of opinion, but I am anxious to endeavour to arrive at matters of fact, so that, if possible, we may be agreed up to a certain point. The discussion, I think, may be divided into two points: one, what are the Imperial services to which Ireland should contribute, and the other what is the total sum which she does actually contribute, the latter being a question of fact. Taking the latter point first, we have it that the revenue of Ireland is 7,614,000*l.*, of which 5,511,000*l.* is locally expended, so that Ireland only contributes to what may be called Imperial services 2,103,000*l.* I am taking the figures from page 31 of Sir Edward Hamilton's memorandum?—With reference to that, my remark was that a great deal of the expenditure in Ireland is really for Imperial purposes and not for Irish local purposes—I took the police as an example.

6561. I am only dealing now with the question of fact. You will see that the 2,103,000*l.* is the actual sum which actually comes over for Imperial purposes, whatever they may be?—Yes, and the conclusion I draw from that is, that, from a Treasury point of view, Ireland is only worth a couple of millions to the Empire.

6562. Do you think that 2,103,000*l.* is an excessive sum for Ireland to contribute to the expenditure of the Empire?—Yes, I think it is excessive. If you deal with what might be classified as Imperial services, I should put down a sum for defence, a small amount for foreign relations (for we are not very much interested in such matters) and postal services, which I think are most conveniently administered as an Imperial service. I think if we paid a proportion of the cost of those services it would be a sufficient contribution for Ireland to make to the Imperial expenditure, and that the whole of the rest of her revenues ought to be spent for Irish purposes proper.

6563. Do you think that 27 per cent., which is what is represented by 2,103,000*l.*, is an excessive sum for Ireland to pay towards defence, and those services which no doubt we might agree are Imperial?—Yes.

6564. Have you ever turned your attention at all to what Ireland did under Grattan's Parliament in the way of outlay on what we may call Imperial services, that is to say, debt and military services?—

No, I am not posted up in the figures of that time, but I understand that Ireland contributed to the military expenses, and not to the naval expenses.

6565. I particularly put them together as military and debt was entailed at the time.

6566. The average expenditure in the four years before 1793 (those being the four years of peace before the French war broke out) was 1,[illegible]*l.*, the average expenditure on debt and military services was as nearly as possible [illegible]*l.*, therefore she contributed to military services and debt at that time, nearly [illegible] per cent. of her expenditure, did she not?—I am not up in the figures of that time.

6567. The figures are before the Commission at the present moment, are they not?—Yes, I believe they have been put in before the Commission.

6568. Will you accept from me that those are the figures before the Commission?—Certainly, but I have turned my attention more to what Ireland ought now to contribute, and what is her present ability, and what it would be fair for her to contribute than to past history.

6569. At the same time you will observe the object of my question is that during those years, when she was under Grattan's Parliament, which has been generally held to represent the time when she had the greatest control over her own affairs, that was the state of things?—I think the control over her own affairs, at that time, was largely influenced by Great Britain. She had control for a very short time, and whatever readjustment may have been made at that time could only have been made to a small extent if she wanted to adjust her finances.

6570. But at all events reference is made to that time as compared with subsequent years?—I could not hold up that time as a pattern.

6571. At all events when she had a voice in her own affairs, you would agree, if these figures are correct, would you not, that she was laying out [illegible] per cent. of her expenditure on these two services?—I have no doubt your figures are correct, but that was a time of very large military expenditure all over Europe.

6572. Certainly not; it was the cheapest time. I may remind you that Joseph Hume called the attention of the British Parliament to that time as the model economical years before the French war?—Well it was a time when there were very large armies on foot in Europe. I am not prepared to contradict your statement, but it was a time when it was the custom of nations to make a very large expenditure on military purposes.

6573. I think you will find, so far as England is concerned, that it is not so?—A very short time afterwards, before the Union, there were [illegible] British troops in Ireland alone, for part of which we paid.

6574. I am particularly excepting those times and taking the time of perfect peace. The local expenditure, when it is made, is made in Ireland, is it not?—I would not quite agree to that, because some of it is made in England; for instance, where you have duplicate arrangements. There is, for instance, a Chief Secretary's office in Dublin, and a Chief Secretary's office in London. They are very small matters, perhaps, but there are other establishments of the same kind. I suppose we pay part of the expenses of the Treasury.

6575. No, I think that is not the case in the amount charged for local expenditure?—We are charged with part of the expenses of Parliament. Of course Irish business is done in Parliament.

6576. I think you are alluding there, are you not, to the Treasury estimate on account of Imperial services. The figure of [illegible]*l.*, I think I am right in saying, is money actually expended in Ireland. It is possible that includes the Irish Office, which is merely brought over here for convenience during the Parliamentary Session, but I think I am right in saying that that figure is money actually locally expended in Ireland. At all events you will agree, will you not, if I am right in saying it is spent in Ireland, that it is locally expended?—I agree there is a very large expenditure of the revenue derived from Ireland in Ireland.

6577. Then again a large part of the army is stationed in Ireland, larger than, it is admitted, is required for the garrison of Ireland. It is difficult for laymen to know how far that is the case, but considerable reference has been made and articles have been written on the subject. Dr. Giffen reckons that the garrison should be in proportion to the population as 1 to [illegible], and estimated that 3,000,000*l.* of public money was laid out in Ireland on military expenditure?—Yes, but I do not think that a large military force in Ireland is necessarily of advantage from an economic point of view.

6578. So far as money is laid out in Ireland, it is an advantage, is it not?—Certainly. I think if money is well laid out, it is an advantage; if it is badly laid out, it is a disadvantage to a country.

6579. So far it affords a market, does it not. I will only call attention to the fact that a considerable force is kept in Ireland, the outlay upon which takes place in Ireland?—The economic advantage of a military force in Ireland is very small; it affects the market price of such articles as are consumed by the military to an infinitesimal extent. The real advantage is a material advantage, which arises from the proximity of a large camp, enabling the farmers to farm better.

6580. Then you do not think, taking Dr. Giffen's statement for what it is worth, that a sum like 3,000,000*l.* is laid out in Ireland?—I think it is very likely it is laid out, but I think with regard to the military force, it is not an advantage on the whole, otherwise the more military we have in Ireland the better.

6581. Still it is expenditure in Ireland, is it not?—Certainly.

6582. You have criticised the terms on which loans were made out of the Church fund?—Yes, I have commented on the rate of interest that is still charged on the large loans made upon the security of the Church fund.

6583. I should like to call your attention to one or two considerations connected with that point. I think your answer upon that is No. 5538. Are you aware that the money which the National Debt Commissioners advance on public loans is chiefly derived from the Savings Bank funds?—So I understand.

6584. Are you aware that that is a trust fund which the Government is bound to administer with the utmost care?—Yes.

6585. Are you aware that in former times, in consequence of not sufficient attention being paid to that matter, there was a large deficit on the fund, which is now being made good by the taxpayers?—I was not aware of that, but I take it from you.

6586. They are now paying 80,000*l.* a year in order to make good this deficit. In the last 20 years or so greater care has been taken in that respect, in order to ensure that the fund is properly administered, and that an undue charge is not put on the taxpayers. Now the standard by which the Government work is this: Naturally speaking they are guided by the price of consols. Consols is the permanent security in which these funds are invested. At the time the loans were made, chiefly in 1870 and 1871, the price of consols was between 92 and 93 on the average. If the money, therefore, had been invested in consols (which, as I say, is the normal investment for the fund), it would have brought us up to the year 1888 something over 3¼ per cent. From 1888 to the present time (that is to say from the date of the conversion) it would have brought us a shade under 3 per cent. In addition to that, if, during those two years, the fund had been invested in consols, at the present moment the value of that investment would have been close on a million above the cost price. That is the standard, and the proper standard, by

Mr. [illegible] O'Brien.

9 May 1895.

Government expenditure in Ireland.

Military expenditure.

Cost of [illegible] in Ireland.

Public loans.

Mr. Murrough O'Brien. 7 Mar. 1895. Public loans.

which the Government judge of these things. What has been the result really of that loan? The rate of interest on the loan was somewhat higher than that which the Government could have got by investing in consols; but that is always the case, and ought always to be the case when you lend upon a terminable annuity, because I am sure you will agree with me it is a disadvantage when one has to replace capital over a long series of years without knowing beforehand at what prices we shall be able to replace the stock. As it so happened a very short time after that, the price of consols began to rise, and during a great part of the time their price was close upon 100l. Without working out the matter in detail, I think it is quite possible I am under the mark when I say that the fact of our having to re-invest this principal as it is gradually repaid, as compared to what would have happened if we had invested this money in consols in 1871, has left us at least 500,000l. to the bad, and I do not think you will find that, so far as the Savings Bank fund is concerned, the advantages of a higher rate of interest would have made up that difference, or placed the fund in the position in which it would have been if it had been so invested at once?—The way I look at it is that the deposits in the Savings Bank in Ireland amount to 7,000,000l.—somewhat under, for which the depositors get 2½ per cent., and so far as these sums are re-lent in Ireland, the rate received is 3½ per cent. I am quite unable to criticise all the arrangements of the Treasury, and their different investments and re-investments; but I merely point to the fact that there is no very great liberality in receiving from a country 7,000,000l. at 2½ per cent. and re-lending it at 3½ per cent. I think, considering the way our finances are at present arranged, it was a proper thing to re-lend the money. I understand it is the business of the Treasury to economise as much as possible, and they have a very hard struggle to do so.

6087. I am not aware it has ever been represented as a great act of liberality. It is a business act on both sides. A large sum of money was required by Ireland for the purpose of paying off the Church, and that was provided out of the Savings Bank fund, that being the available fund; is not that so?—It has been represented in Sir Edward Hamilton's memorandum (and I think it is frequently represented in Parliament) that Ireland has been treated with undue liberality in regard to loans. A great many loans have been made to Ireland, and I think, on the whole, they have had a very demoralising effect. The rate of interest has been low with reference to the market rate of interest; but looking on it as a loan from a sister or mother country, and having regard to the fact that we contribute such a very large revenue to England, I do not think there was any liberality in the matter. I do not know whether the Treasury claim any or not.

6088. I do not think the question of liberality has ever been raised in any shape or way?—It was part of Mr. Gladstone's contention when the question of the over-taxation of Ireland was brought before Parliament on some previous occasion that that would be to some extent met by treating Ireland with extra liberality in the matter of loans.

[redacted]

6089. You mentioned just now, did you not, that several of the services in Ireland charged for as local are more or less of an Imperial kind, and I think you mentioned, as an example, the constabulary?—I mentioned the constabulary and the expenses of the Lord Lieutenancy.

6090. To go back upon what has been said as to the amount which Ireland contributes, I would point out to you that whereas Irish expenditure on military services during the Grattan Parliament was 40 per cent., that at present the contribution which she makes to military services and debt is 27 per cent. of the revenue only, and even supposing we were to count on the ground put forward, say a million of the constabulary expenditure as rendered necessary by the Imperial system, we should still only arrive at a contribution from Ireland, including that of 40 per cent., should we not. Therefore even in that case we should still be much below the amount contributed in the time of peace under Grattan's Parliament, should we not?—The way I look at the matter is rather from a more general point of view. Here you have a country containing four and a half millions of inhabitants, you raise a revenue from that country, according to my estimate, of 9,000,000l., and yet that is not sufficient to pay for every possible Imperial expense, avert famines, and to develop its industries and resources. That seems to me to be a perfectly indefensible proposition. As I say, 9,000,000l. is contributed. I admit the contributions of Ireland is adjusted because the ultimate incidence of the tax no doubt is upon the consumer so far as this revenue is derived from articles that are taxed under customs or excise duty, but if the two countries were separated financially the whole revenue of 9,000,000l. would be credited to Ireland. If by the enterprise of her merchants or the development of her ports Customs duties are raised in Ireland or Excise duties are imposed, I think she should be credited with contributing an income of 9,000,000l. and not seven and three-quarter millions, and I say 9,000,000l. is ample to run any country upon with such wants as Ireland has.

6091. Of course we come there to a distinct difference of opinion. What would happen if the two countries were separated would be that the duty would be imposed in England on the spirits coming from Ireland into England in such a case as you put, and probably spirits would not come then, but at all events the duty would be paid here. England would not let the spirits off duty; that would come into the English revenue. But putting aside that point upon which we differ, and must differ radically and absolutely, the only point I want to bring before you is that even if we make a large allowance for the constabulary, still the sum that would be contributable to Imperial purposes would be very much less than that which obtained in very economic years and at a time when Ireland had more control over her affairs than she has ever had since, would it not?—With reference to the management of Ireland at that time it would be equally fair to refer to Macaulay's description of the Irish Parliament as the most corrupt and tyrannical assembly that ever sat in Europe, and I would not refer to that either as a time to be looked to as a precedent, or a body which we should now like to have governing the country.

6092. On the other hand I point out to you that constant reference is made by people not unfriendly to Ireland to that time as a time suitable for comparison?—I really think the practical question is what Ireland ought to contribute now, what she is able to contribute, and I should be very much inclined for my part never to refer to past controversies at all.

6093. You spoke of Ireland as being over-assessed as compared with England, when you were giving evidence in Ireland, did you not?—Yes. I should be glad to explain the ground on which it seems to me that the assessment is so, and I do not know whether I may do so by making a general explanation. I think it will save time. The assessment of Ireland, as the Commission know, was made by an Imperial Department, the Valuation Department, under the control of the Treasury. At the time it was made it was the opinion of a good many Irishmen that it was a very high assessment and that it followed the rent. I quoted the opinion of Mr. Senior as he was an English official with experience of Ireland. He had then been poor-law inspector for many years, and had great opportunities of watching the thing. He said Ireland then was more highly assessed in proportion to the produce of the land than England. I also quoted Mr. Hedley, who was a valuer of great experience who had visited Ireland. With reference to different classes of under-ratings, the under-rating of mansions has been, so far as I can read, a scandal of very long standing in England. Of course my information about the assessment of

Mr. Murrough O'Brien.

4 Dec. 1895.

Valuation in Ireland and England compared.

England is derived from the opinions of authorities and from such observations as I have made on occasional visits to England, where I always make it my business to ascertain the particulars of ratings, rents, and valuations, wherever I can. The under-rating of mansions is a scandal of such long standing that McCulloch in his work on "Taxation and Funding" refers to it, saying: "It is said that "not a few middle-class inns and hotels pay a larger "amount of duty than is paid by the most splendid "baronial residences." That was in 1840. Stuart Mill in his "Political Economy" refers to it, too. He says: "The public were greatly scandalised at "hearing that residences like Chatsworth and Belvoir "were only rated on an imaginary rent of 200l. a year, "under the pretext that they could not be let for more." Of course the comparisons before this Commission have been made as to the rateable value of Ireland, not merely at the present date but for several years since the Union. Attempts were made over and over again to rate this class of property, but as it is not built for letting and could not be let, there has been great difficulty about it. It was proposed over and over again that a percentage on the cost, or the present selling value, should be taken as the rateable value. That continued down to the year 1871. There was then a Rating and House Tax Bill before the House of Commons. Mr. Goschen said with reference to that: "There are many buildings and large houses "in the country districts which cannot be valued on a "calculation of what they would be let at from year to "year, and which in consequence escape paying on a "fair rateable value. It causes a considerable amount "of not unnatural irritation among the farmers, to see "large neighbouring property escape at a low rating for "this reason, while their own smaller farms are, as "they complain, highly rated."

6304. We are now dealing with the comparison between England and Ireland?—Yes.

6305. I do not mean to put anything into your mouth which you would not wish to say, but I should have inferred from your evidence that there was a difference in the treatment of England and Ireland in that respect?—The systems of rating are different, and I think the result has been that that class of property, for instance, has been very much under-rated in England and is still under-rated. You have an example this morning in the "Times," which, I think, exactly illustrates the whole of what I say, and that is with regard to the rating of the Imperial Institute. The Imperial Institute, with one of the finest sites in London, and an expenditure made on it, I believe, of about 1,000,000l., claims that it should not be rated at all because it could not be let. The matter went before the Middlesex Sessions, I think, and they put on it a value very low in comparison to the cost of a modern building, of 11,000l. a year, but apparently it was not rated at all until now.

6306. Confining the question to mansion-houses, I have here before me a list of the ratings. It may be very wrong not to rate these mansion-houses higher, but as we are comparing England with Ireland it does not matter if the Irish houses also are low rated, does it?—No, except that I wanted to draw attention to the contention in England that these big buildings and palaces, which are not buildings to be let, should not be rated at all. That contention is set up to the present day.

6307. But the point is the comparison as between England and Ireland. I have a list which Mr. Barton put in, to which I would call your attention. I will take Lismore Castle, in Ireland, rated at 170l.?—Lismore Castle is a very small building. It is built in a castellated style, but it is not as big as many an English villa.

6308. Then there is Curraghmore?—I have not seen Curraghmore, and I do not know its rating.

6309. I have a list of about 40 houses here?—I have received a few of them from Mr. Barton, and I find the highest rated house in Ireland is Powerscourt, which is 450l.

6310. Then take Muckross, 111l. When I come to the English houses (quite admitting what you say about the difficulty of letting them) they are all very much above the rating of the Irish houses?—But you must remember there is no comparison to be made between many of these palaces, such as Chatsworth, Raby Castle, and Blenheim Palace, with our houses in Ireland. They are piles of buildings which, with all their appurtenances, have cost 10 or 15 times as much as the best houses in Ireland.

6311. But then they are rated very much higher, are they not?—I admit that in Ireland there are some under-ratings, and that the ratings of mansion-houses as compared with the farm-houses of a local character in their neighbourhood are very low, but I have been examining the Government valuation in Ireland for 50 years with a view to the sale and letting of property, and comparing it with it, and the conclusion I have come to on the whole is that while there are some under-ratings there are a great many more over-ratings in Ireland.

6312. Of mansions?—Of mansions; a great many of the great mansions in Ireland are simply falling into decay, and would not let at all. The contention might be better made in Ireland that they would not let at all, because there is no market for such houses; they are not maintained in a condition for letting.

6313. You are aware, are you not, that that is also stated here, as one of the reasons why these great houses are rated low?—The reason alleged in England for not rating them is that they are so grand and magnificent, whereas ours are so decayed and so unattractive that they will not let.

6314. However, this list, which is an official list, shows, does it not, that these large houses of which you have been speaking, and about which you make rather a point as a proof of under-assessment in England, are very much higher rated than very considerable houses in Ireland, and that whatever may be said to that extent in England applies to Ireland; it is not easy to make a distinction between the two countries in the matter of assessment, is it?—But I might also point out that the local rating is much lower than the income-tax assessment. In some cases I think you will find it is not one-half.

6315. But we must bear in mind that we are talking about Imperial contributions?—Yes, except that Sir Edward Hamilton's memoranda deals with the whole burden of taxation, both local and Imperial. I have referred to Mr. Hadley's books, and in his last pamphlet he gives a great number of under-ratings, so late as 1880. This pamphlet shows that the under-rating extended not only to railways, but to other works which are so common in England. For instance, he gives here "mines of not rated at all," "ironworks, works," "annual rateable value, 550l." Then No. 8, "rated at 15l., and then on a reconsideration "at 1,275l." Then he gives a case of a brickworks, rated at 300l., which on reconsideration after the Union Assessment Act passed, was raised to 1,355l. He gives a great number of other instances. I have watched the rating cases in the papers, and I find the same things go on to the present day—that a great deal of property is under-assessed, and that there is a perpetual struggle to try and raise it, not always successfully. For instance, at the end of last year the London and South-Western Railway in one parish, [illegible], had been assessed at 1,315l. That was raised by the Appeal Court to 3,000l. There is a great deal of Government property, too, in England (more than in Ireland, I fancy) that is not assessed, or upon which [illegible] rates are paid. I find in the parish of St. Margaret's and St. John's, Westminster, the assessments upon the Government buildings were raised from 55,000l. to 99,000l. in January of this year. As I derive a good deal of my information from the statements of experts in the matter, I find in the evidence of the Agricultural Commission, Mr. Giffen says: "Assessments "never equal maximum rents. Assessments A and B

Mr. Murrough O'Brien.

4 Dec. 1895.

Valuation in Ireland and England compared.

Mr. Murrough O'Brien. 7 May 1895. Valuation in Ireland and England compared.

"are largely based on parochial assessments," which, I say, are low assessments. Up to the Union Chargeability Act of 1865, he says it was the practice in each parish to keep the assessment as low as possible. "The tendency of the income-tax people has been to "draw the rein tighter of late, but there are frequent "valuations which are below the actual rent." There is Mr. Giffen's opinion of the latest condition of affairs. Then Mr. Albert Pell, who I think was a Member of Parliament, and is a great authority on these matters, speaks of the difficulty of assessing railways, and mentions how the London and North-Western Railway Company's assessment was increased by about 20,000*l.* In the Union of Ely he says the Great Eastern Railway assessment was increased by 22,000*l.* Then at Question 17,011 he says he is sure railways are not assessed at their full value, nor canals, waterworks, &c.

6606. We are dealing now with the question of Imperial taxation; with regard to railways, the rating of them has nothing whatever to do with the matter, has it? Railways pay upon their earnings, and therefore, although the assessment may be, for anything I know, right or wrong with regard to local taxation, that is not a matter we are dealing with. The railways pay absolutely upon their earnings, do they not?—I quite understand that they do, but I think this is a question of the comparison of the assessments. For instance, Mr. Pell says attempts to raise the assessments of railways are often defeated by showing that other property in the same parish is undervalued. He mentions a case where they attempted to raise the assessment of a railway, but land that was rented at 2*l.* an acre was shown to be assessed at 15*s.* an acre, and so the railway company gained their case. Then, at Question 17,014, he says: "A great "deal of estate property is not sufficiently assessed." The Inland Revenue Report gives a comparison between the local and the income-tax assessments, that confirms the opinion which I have formed from reading Mr. Giffen's and Mr. Pell's evidence. That table shows that the deductions, allowances, abatements, and exemptions from the gross estimated rental (which, it appears to me, in England is very much less than the real rental) are very much less in Ireland than in England. I have made out a table from their statements, which shows that the gross estimated rental of all property rated locally in England is 151,586,362*l.*

6607. (*Mr. Sexton.*) For what year?—That is the Inland Revenue Report for 1894, Appendix, page 32. The rateable value of the same is 152,764,811*l.*—that is to say, one-sixth, or 31,000,000*l.* comes off. Nothing comes off the Irish assessment.

6608. (*Lord Farrer.*) That is for the purpose of local rating, is it not—that is the difference between gross value and rateable value?—Certainly.

6609. The rateable value has nothing to do with income tax, has it?—I beg your pardon. Mr. Pell, whom I quoted, or Mr. Giffen, says that the income-tax assessment is largely based upon the local ratings.

6610. But upon the gross value, not upon the rateable value?—Very good.

6611. (*Lord Welby.*) I think you will see in that Report what the income tax is actually assessed upon?—Certainly, and I have given it in this table, which I should like to put in. The rental of property rated but not assessed to Schedule A., is 29,500,255*l.* in England, that is one-sixth of the gross, whereas in Ireland there is only 543,493*l.*, that is one twenty-fourth of the gross assessment, not rated. Then there is the gross annual value assessed to Schedule A., 169,107,193*l.* in England and 13,612,049*l.* in Ireland. Deductions, abatements, and exemptions from that in England are 18,896,159*l.*, or one-ninth, and in Ireland 905,160*l.*, or one-fifteenth, that leaves the net annual value charged to Schedule A. 150,210,934*l.* in England, and the net amount in Ireland 12,706,889*l.* I will put in that table.

The table was handed in, and is as follows:—

	England.	Ireland.
	£	£
1. Gross estimated rental of all property rated locally.	151,586,363 (13,841,774)	13,141,088
2. Rateable value of same	152,764,811 1/6th off gross	13,841,658 not 1/6 off gross.
3. Rental of property rated but not assessed to Schedule A.	29,500,255 More than 1/6th off gross.	543,493 1/24th off gross.
4. Gross annual value assessed to Schedule A.	169,107,193	13,612,049
5. Deductions, abatements, and exemptions.	18,896,159 1/9th.	905,160 1/15th.
6. Net annual value charged to Schedule A.	150,210,934	12,706,889

Mr. Murrough O'Brien. 7 May 1895. Valuation in Ireland and England compared.

Then my initial starting point is that, on the whole, allowing for some under-ratings which there are in Ireland, our assessment is a high assessment, and in many cases far over the real value. In England 32,000,000*l.* is taken off the gross estimated rental to arrive at the rateable value. In Ireland nothing comes off from our assessment.

6612. (*Mr. Sexton.*) It is taken off the gross estimated rental to arrive at the rateable value, is it?—Yes, in Ireland nothing comes off.

6613. (*Lord Farrer.*) Does nothing come off with a view to local rates, do you mean, or with a view to income tax?—Nothing comes off either with the view to local rates or income tax.

6614. Is there no deduction made?—We have merely one assessment.

6615. Are local rates paid upon that?—Local rates are paid upon that.

6616. (*Lord Welby.*) Is that upon the valuation?—Yes. One-sixth of the property rated in England is not assessed to Schedule A.; in Ireland only one twenty-fourth escapes. In England the deductions, abatements, and exemptions from the gross annual value assessed under schedule amount to one-ninth, in Ireland only to one-fifteenth. Putting all these opinions and facts and my own observations, so far as I have been able to make observations, together, the conclusion I have come to is that a great deal of property in England escapes rating at its full value, and a little in Ireland.

6617. (*Chairman.*) Escapes rating, which is a different thing from taxability?—In Ireland, you see, having only one assessment, the matter is simple.

6618. (*Lord Farrer.*) Is your valuation both for the purposes of local rates and of the income tax (which are two quite different things) high as compared with England?—Yes.

6619. Is that what you mean?—Yes, certainly, I think so. I gave some figures to the Commission as to the under-assessment in London, which seems very large. I quoted Mr. Harper, whose statement was that there was a million and a half of annual value in London not assessed at all, on the ground that it produced no income. Of course it produced income in one sense; if it was in hand and was put into the market it would produce something.

6620. Is building-land in Ireland, say, in the neighbourhood of Dublin, which produces no rent, valued and assessed for income tax?—Yes, it would be taxed; but you must remember in comparing the two countries, that in Ireland we have not those large building sites, nor have we growing towns. There are only 15 towns in Ireland that have over 10,000 inhabitants.

6621. Take the town of Belfast, which is a growing town, and supposing there was a piece of ground which the owner chose to keep vacant, for which he received no rent but which would have a large capital value—how would that be treated?—I have no doubt it would escape in the same way.

6622. I ask that question because I feel pretty sure that Mr. Harper's statement has reference to that class of cases in London, which would be more

Mr. Murrough O'Brien.

7 May, 1896.

Valuation in Ireland and England compared.

exemptions than in Ireland?—Certainly. All our towns, with the exception of half-a-dozen, are decaying it seems to me, comparing the values in Ireland and Great Britain. The same thing would, to some extent, arise in Scotland, but the Scottish system is different again, and technical; but there I see in the evidence given on the Rating of Machinery Bill, that where a lease is made 21 years' duration, even if a fine has been paid upon it, the rent is taken as the assessment.

6623. (*Lord Farrer.*) May not we put what you have said in this way. There has been as we know, great complaint in London that property of that sort escapes local taxation?—Yes, so I have heard.

6624. And in consequence of its escaping local taxation in that way, there is a larger immunity from taxation of property of that kind in this country than in Ireland?—Certainly; that is what I mean. In these growing and thriving towns in England you have an immunity which we have not.

6625. (*Lord Welby.*) I want to keep to the assessment to income tax, because that is the real question between us. In Ireland, under Schedule A., the landlord has the option of paying income tax, either on his net rent after making allowance for the rate, or on the valuation, whichever is the lowest, has he not?—Yes.

6626. Therefore, no landlord, under Schedule A., pays on anything higher than the valuation, does he?—No, he only pays practically on what he gets.

6627. If the valuation is below what he gets, he only pays upon that?—Certainly.

6628. Therefore we may take the valuation, may we not, as the maximum?—Yes, but my impression is that, on the whole, landlords do not get more than the valuation, even if the nominal rental has been higher—that rents are not always well paid.

6629. But still that brings it back to the point, does it not, that the valuation is the maximum?—The valuation is the maximum.

6630. Griffith's valuation was based, among other considerations, on a scale of prices, was it not?—That was the main factor in it according to law.

6631. Those prices were fixed in the Act, were they not?—Yes.

6632. They were, in every instance, but one, wheat, were they not, and are, lower than those which are now ruling?—I think that is very probable. I have not the figures before me, but we all know that in Ireland the system laid down by the Act was not followed out, moreover it could not have been followed out for this reason: the Act says that the valuation shall be made with reference to a scale of prices, that is to say, it gives you some of the figures of the sum you are to do. You are to estimate what the produce of a farm is, and from that deduce your rateable value, taking the prices to rule the value of the whole produce, but the Act did not give you the materials for the sum; it did not give the cost of labour, which was an important factor. It did not give the rate of interest to be allowed on the farmer's capital, which is necessary to the production of the produce; you had not the materials for doing the sum, and everyone who has inquired into the valuation history in Ireland knows what they did was this: it was part of their instructions to record the rents, and I look on the valuation known as "Griffith's valuation" as being a rough record of the rents then paid.

6633. Was it not a factor. I did not ask if it was the basis?—The law prescribes that it should be made on a scale of prices.

6634. Therefore, so far as prices came into consideration, those prices were lower than the prices now ruling, except in the case of wheat, which in Ireland may be put out of the question?—Yes, the prices given in the Act are lower, but of course the price of labour has vastly increased, and so has the rate of taxation.

6635. It may be a question whether the rate of taxation has been increased, but so far as the prices came into the question, they were lower than they are now, therefore the valuation did not proceed, so far as prices was concerned, on an unfair basis, considering that it is a permanent one, did it?—It is quite manifest the prices were not followed, because when they valued in the year 1852 or 1854, which was the conclusion of the valuation, one of the allegations made by the Valuation Office people was that the valuation made was higher, because prices were higher, and therefore they did not adhere to the scale of prices they were expected to adhere to. Therefore you have the valuation of some parts of Ireland reputed to be very much higher than others.

6636. (*Sir David Barbour.*) Can you quote any passage in which the valuation officer said they used a higher scale of prices?—I do not think I can. I think, in the evidence given on the Richmond Commission, a table was put in showing the proposed additions intended to be made to the valuation in different parts of Ireland, in order to equalise it. No addition was to be made to any county in Ulster, on the ground that it had been valued later and higher.

6637. Did the valuation officers ever say they had used a higher scale of prices in Ulster?—That was the statement made by the head of the Valuation Office. Of course the valuation was made by a number of subordinate people; Griffith was not a valuer, but a civil engineer, and a geologist. The then head of the Valuation Office, Sir John Ball Greene, said so, and I will try and find the passage.

6638. (*Mr. Martin.*) If this valuation extended over a long period of years, the scale of prices had materially altered from the first valuation to the subsequent one, had it not?—The actual price obtained for the produce altered, but the scale of prices did not.

6639. (*Mr. Sexton.*) But you say it was not followed?—It was not followed. As a practical valuer you could not do a sum bringing out the value of land unless you have all the materials. You cannot do it on a scale of prices unless you have the cost of labour, the rate of interest on the tenant's capital; that is necessary to do the sum which is proposed to be done by the Act. Another very important thing is, from that scale of prices is left out altogether one of the largest crops in Ireland—potatoes, the value of which topped all other crops produced from cultivated land together.

6640. (*Lord Welby.*) At all events the result of it was, was it not, that the valuation was in general below the rents before the judicial rents were fixed?—I am not aware that they were, if you mean by "rents" rents actually paid. You will remember that in 1882 Parliament had to pass an Arrears Act, because rents had not been paid, and could not have been paid.

6641. But, as a matter of fact, taking the case in which rents were fixed, the valuations were in the proportion of 4,502,000*l.* to 5,750,000*l.*?—I do not think those figures are correct, because in all the returns given by the Land Commission down to the present date, while every rent is set out, every valuation is not set out. There are a number of cases where the valuation is not ascertained; therefore all you can conclude from the totals given in the Land Commission reports is that the valuation totals given would have been much higher, if every item had been put in, than it is. If you take up one of the Blue Books which gives all the things in detail you see on page after page columns of hundreds of pounds, under "Valuation not ascertained," which makes the totals perfectly worthless. The Land Commission have ceased to give those totals, though they have materials to give them more correctly than they did; it is a great pity they gave them at all, I think.

6642. Was it, or was it not, your view at that time that the rents, before the tenants came into court, were higher or lower than the valuation?—I do not think any general statement would be true. I know of properties where rents were never above the

Mr. Murrough O'Brien.

7 Mar. 1895.

Valuations in Ireland and England compared.

valuation, and I know of farms where they were three times the valuation.

6643. These figures come from the Land Commission, did they not?—I do not think official statistics are always correct; at any rate all statistics require explanation.

6644. (*Sir David Barbour.*) Do you know if, in making up these totals, they struck out farms in regard to which only the rent was given and not the valuation?—No, they returned the rent, but they did not put in the valuation, and the result is that the totals give you the total of the valuations so far as they were ascertained, but the total of the rents is right enough.

6645. The total of the valuations is too low, is it?—Yes, how much too low I could not tell you.

6646. (*Lord Welby.*) Then you do not say the rents were too low?—No, the rents were correct.

6647. And so far as the valuation was put in, it was correct, was it not; there were only certain omissions?—The figure is correct for each particular rent where it is put in for that rent, but where you have numbers of valuations left out your total will be wrong; therefore the valuation total is always less than it ought to be.

6648. In confirmation of what you say, have you ever compared those where the totals of both are in, and found that the valuation differs widely from the 25 per cent. which is here given?—I do not suppose there is any year in which the total valuation is correct; therefore you cannot compare the whole series.

6649. But as I understand in cases where the valuation is put in, it is correct?—Certainly. When I say correct, it presumably is correct.

6650. And where the rent is put in, it is correct, is it not?—The rent is always correct.

6651. Therefore when the valuation and the rent are both put in, and a comparison made, a fair judgment can be arrived at as to whether the proportion between the original valuation corresponded at all to that which your Commission has put in as the reduction, can it not?—I do not think it could, because, remember there are 300,000 or 400,000 rents fixed, I think. You cannot take a few of those and draw a conclusion as to the whole. My own impression is, that the valuation being so very unequal, you cannot form a comparison. At present there are numbers of rents fixed at 20, 30, 40, and 50 per cent. below the valuation.

6652. (*Chairman.*) Is it that the actual valuation is added up every page, or how is it the mistake occurs?—The judicial rents are published as fixed in volumes giving the acreage, valuation, and rent. Then those are totalled. For instance, here is one page in which out of about thirty rents there are five omissions of the valuation. There are a great many more glaring cases than that.

6653. (*Lord Welby.*) And have you no idea, looking at those and making allowance for those omitted, how far it would affect their per-centage which your Commission has given?—I do not think you could make any estimate, because there are a vast number of those books and the labour of extracting cases where the valuation was given and verifying those as to whether they were correct or not, would be enormous.

6654. We know that the rents are 5,756,000*l.*, and you will not go so far as to say, will you, they were not considerably above the valuation?—I admit they were above the valuation, but I do not think you can take the nominal rent of Ireland as having been the rent really paid during a series of years.

6655. A man need only pay upon the valuation: he would pay upon that most favourable to himself, would he not?—I think in the old days the landlord paid on his rental, or the valuation, but not necessarily on the rental he got. He paid on his nominal rental, and if that nominal rental was below the valuation, he paid upon that. But the rent he actually got is a different thing, as is evidenced by the Arrears Acts.

6656. The point I am anxious to find out is this: the landlord can pay upon the valuation, can he not?—Certainly.

6657. And the valuation, in the main, before the deductions were made, was below the rental, was it not?—I think it was generally below the nominal rent.

6658. And, therefore, so far, the law in Ireland was favourable to the income-tax payer, was it not?—No; that is the point which I say I do not go with you upon, because the landlord very often did not get his nominal rental. His nominal rental was above, but if he got the valuation of the property out of it as rent in a series of years, I think he did very well.

6659. Do you give that as an opinion or as a fact?—I give that as an opinion, having been acquainted with Irish estates for many years.

6660. (*Lord Farrer.*) If he does not get his rent does he pay. Does he pay on the full amount where there are abatements, or does he pay on the actual amount received?—I think he pays upon his nominal rental.

6661. Then, if he makes an abatement of 20 per cent., does he pay upon that?—That I could not say, because the income-tax people have relaxed of late years and rather changed their rules about that. In old days a man paid upon his nominal rental or valuation, which ever was the lowest.

6662. (*Lord Welby.*) After the great agricultural depression which took place about 1878 or 1879, as you say a considerable relaxation took place, and practically from that time income tax was only charged on the rent actually received, is not that so?—I notice that in the evidence given before the Agricultural Commission, it is stated if a man gets a temporary abatement he does not get his assessment reduced, therefore he pays on the annual rental; but if a landlord says, "I will reduce your rent," then the tax is paid on the reduced rent.

6663. On the other hand, we have seen from these figures of the Inland Revenue, that whereas the rateable value in England is, in the case I have been quoting, 136,000,000*l.*, the income tax is paid under schedule A. on 156,000,000*l.*, showing that the income-tax payer in England is paying very considerably more than the rateable value, whereas in Ireland the income-tax payer need not pay above the sum which corresponds to the rateable value, namely the valuation?—I do not think that is the conclusion I draw from this table I have put in. If the gross estimated rental of all property rated locally in England is 191,000,000*l.*, the net annual value charged to Schedule A. is 150,000,000*l.* What I want to draw attention to is this, that the gross annual value assessed to Schedule A. in the Report of the Income Tax is 168,000,000*l.* the deductions, abatements, and exemptions from that, reducing it to 150,000,000*l.*, come to 18,000,000*l.*; that is, a ninth comes off the gross annual value assessed to Schedule A. to reduce it to the net annual value charged to Schedule A. In Ireland, from the gross annual value assessed to Schedule A., only one-fifteenth comes off, leaving it 12,708,555*l.* Therefore I say that deductions, abatements, and exemptions, are larger in proportion from the gross annual value assessed to Schedule A. in England than they are in Ireland.

Incidence of taxation between Great Britain and Ireland.

6664. Then the Irishman has only to pay upon the valuation which is low, has he not?—The Irish valuation has always been a great puzzle to Englishmen, and a great cause of misery, I think, to Ireland. Because it was a Government valuation it was supposed to be a measure for everything.

6665. (*Lord Farrer.*) You say you do not want to go back to old times. What you say is, is it not, that under the present system of taxation, Ireland is charged more than she ought to be in proportion to her means?—I think so.

6666. You find fault with the principle which has been adopted by all statesmen since Mr. Pitt's time, namely, that the thing to be arrived at is identical taxation in the two countries. You say that as between

Mr. Murrough O'Brien.
7 Mar. 1895.
Incidence of taxation between Great Britain and Ireland.

the two countries identical taxation is not fair to Ireland, do you?—It is not. I say our circumstances and needs are entirely different, being an agricultural and a poor country.

6667. Do not take me as expressing any opinion, I merely wish to get your answer to this question. Supposing it is said that there are plenty of poor people in England as well as in Ireland, that what you are saying shows that the taxation on the poor of England is unfair, just as much as it shows that the taxation on the poor of Ireland is unfair; thus taking, for instance, the case of Wiltshire or Dorsetshire compared with Yorkshire or Lancashire, or the east as compared with the west part of London, the poorer parts of England are overtaxed as compared with the richer parts; how does the case of the poor man in Ireland differ from the case of the poor man in England; I want your answer on that?—My answer to that is that I think it is a question between classes as well as between countries, and that if you can divide people in England into the rich and the poor, the poor might very fairly say, "We are overtaxed in "proportion to our income." But the question at present before this Commission, I understood, was simply between England and Ireland.

6668. But if it were said that taking the tax off the poor man in Ireland would be putting something more on to the poor man in England, as would be the case if it is to come out of a common purse, what is your answer to that?—I do not think it would be so necessarily, because I maintain there is a great waste of money in your administration of Ireland; 8,000,000*l.* or 9,000,000*l.* is raised from Ireland, and all we ask to do is to contribute a fair proportion towards those public services from which we derive a benefit. I think it would be to the advantage of Great Britain financially to discharge herself of Irish affairs and Irish expenditure, and apart from things which would be reckoned purely Imperial matters, to let Irish revenue be expended in Ireland by Irishmen.

6669. You think such a saving might be made upon what is now wasteful expenditure in Ireland, as really to relieve Ireland to a very considerable extent from the grievance of which you complain, do you?—Certainly; and relieve England too.

6670. In trying to relieve Ireland from the taxation which you think now presses unfairly upon her, would you propose to go back upon what has been done in the way of equalising and identifying customs and excise?—I think if any re-arrangement is made it would be very convenient to have the Imperial Revenue raised on the same lines. What I should like to see this Commission report, and see done, would be that Ireland should contribute a certain fixed proportion of the Imperial Revenue, or a fixed sum revisable at periods to be reconsidered at some future date.

6671. As I understand, you would not wish to have a separate customs and excise for the two countries?—I should be very sorry to see anything of the kind.

6672. Income tax is another matter. What do you say as to that; do you wish to see that the same in the two countries, or would you leave that to be settled by an Irish Government?—I cannot say that I have considered the income-tax matter specially. It seems to me that the income tax is the fairest of all taxes.

6673. But you have not considered the question, have you, whether it is not necessary it should be the same in both countries?—I have not considered the matter.

6674. (*Mr. Sexton.*) What has been the extent of your official experience in connection with the valuing of land in Ireland?—I have been employed in valuing land, I may say, in Ireland, for 20 years. Before that I had experience of the value of land and agriculture in other countries.

6675. Have your official functions ever led you, both before and since you became a Land Commissioner, to take note of the valuation in every case in connexion with the rent?—I have been practically comparing the Government valuation with the actual value of land all my official life.

6676. With regard to the question of Lord Farrer as to poor people in England, you apprehend, I gather from your answer, that this is an inquiry not into the relative conditions of classes in England and Ireland, but into the relative capacity of England and Ireland, each considered as a unit?—Certainly.

6677. And whatever justice may require in the rearrangement of taxation in either country, as between one class and another, does not touch the question before the Commission, does it?—I do not think so. I should hope that whatever is just between classes, if done in England would be done in Ireland also.

6678. I gather from you that you are of opinion that Irish expenditure might be so diminished as to make it possible to diminish the burden upon Ireland, and at the same time that the Empire might sustain no particular loss?—I think that the revenue raised in Ireland is ample for all purposes, Imperial and local and it seems to me it would be a saving to Great Britain if Irish local affairs were managed in Ireland.

6679. We have it in evidence that Ireland is not worth 2,000,000*l.* a year to the Empire at present?—I should think that Ireland was a dead loss to the Empire, taking everything into consideration.

6680. I mean on the Treasury basis simply; and then we have it asserted that more than 3,000,000*l.* is spent on military expenditure in Ireland?—Yes.

6681. Which we are told would be unnecessary otherwise; but on that basis Ireland is a loss at present to the Empire, is she not?—I should think so.

6682. Do you think it easy to imagine reforms, political and otherwise, whereby the burden of the revenue might be diminished and the Empire still be a gainer?—I think so, taking into account the fact that retrenchment of any kind is always very difficult.

6683. Therefore do you affirm the conclusion to which Lord Farrer's questions invited you—that Ireland may be relieved and the Empire not prejudiced?—Without financial injury to the Empire I think that Ireland might be relieved.

Contribution of Ireland's Imperial services.

6684. Lord Welby raised the question as to what are the Imperial services to which Ireland should contribute—I understand your position to be that in the Treasury adjustment of charges as between Ireland and the United Kingdom, a number of charges are classed as Imperial which should be classed as English or British. Is that your position?—Yes.

Classification in Treasury Returns.

6685. Without asking you to attempt the task which I think no amateur could discharge, that is to say, to define the items in detail, I would ask you generally whether you say that items of expenditure which do not confer upon Ireland as much advantage as upon Great Britain (or at least some substantial advantage) ought to be taken out of the category of Imperial charges, and put into the category of British charges?—Certainly. I think that the column under the head of Imperial Services is the one which works out most unfairly to Ireland in this classification; because to expect Ireland to contribute towards services required by a wealthy country like England is not fair.

6686. Ireland being a country whose interests lie in internal development?—Wholly.

6687. Would you think it unfair that she should be held to contribute in proportion to her capacity to the expenses of the navy?—No, that puts my view correctly.

6688. And do you say that the Treasury classification ought to be re-adjusted from that point of view, in order to ascertain what is the true total of Imperial expenditure which Ireland ought to contribute?—Yes.

6689. (*Lord Welby.*) I think that the list drawn up by the Treasury was a list drawn up for consideration, and really for criticism, I do not think it was meant from the beginning to be a laying down that those were the Imperial Services, and therefore I

Mr. [illegible] 1 Mar 1895. [illegible]

think, a little criticism upon them and fair reasons given for the exclusion or modification of them would be rather welcome?—I do not think that the Treasury could have done anything else, because there is a great difficulty in separating Imperial Services by any other method unless they had definite instructions as what principle they were to act. But of course they adjusted the customs revenue so as to show only the taxation raised which was actually paid on articles of consumption, but they never thought of adjusting the Income Tax Return, though a large part, as I have tried to point out, of the income derived from Ireland is really English income; it is derived from Ireland, but altogether spent in England.

6690. (*Lord Farrer.*) Then that is paid in England by Englishmen, is it not, and not by Irishmen?—It is paid in Ireland.

6691. But if the income comes to England, the taxation is paid by Englishmen, is it not?—Yes, but it is reckoned as an indication of the wealth of Ireland.

6692. (*Sir David Barbour.*) You say that Ireland ought not to be required to contribute towards the navy?—I do not think I said that, but I say not to such an extent she is now charged.

6693. She does not contribute very largely, does she, at present?—The defence services are put down here I think, at 30,000,000*l*. I say that Ireland's need of a navy is small, as she has no commerce, and her need of an army is small from her geographical position and circumstances.

6694. (*Mr Sexton.*) With regard to these financial papers, whatever may be their accuracy, they are the basis of our inquiry, are they not?—Certainly, and are most interesting. The inquiry could not have been conducted without such information.

6695. And we accept them as the basis of discussion. The effect of your evidence, if acted upon, would be to reduce the total of Imperial charges to which Ireland should contribute?—Certainly.

6696. And thereby to increase the relative amount of her contribution to Imperial charges, if it were left as at present. The total of Imperial charges being reduced and her contribution remaining the same, it would appear that her contribution would be a larger percentage, would it not?—Certainly.

6697. On the other hand, you say that in this classification, many charges are included as Irish charges which ought to be classed as Imperial?—That is what appears now to be the case. In the first paper, for instance, the British Museum is charged as an Imperial service, but it seems to me it is entirely a local one.

6698. I am speaking now of the Irish charges. Again, without asking you to go into detail, I would ask you whether it is a general principle that so much of the cost of the administration of Ireland as arises out of the Imperial connection ought to be deducted from what we call Irish charges and classed as Imperial?—Certainly.

6699. And the best illustration is the police. It costs a million and a half I believe; but proportionately to the population of Great Britain, it ought to be 600,000*l*., ought it not?—I think about that; but you must remember it costs rather more than is charged here, because there is a local contribution of a varying amount for extra police, so that this does not really show the whole cost of the police.

6700. Then crime in Ireland is less in proportion to the population than in Great Britain, is it not?—It is so.

6701. Therefore, if the Irish police were utilised for local uses, according to the relative amount of crime, it would require less than 600,000*l*., would it not?—I should think it would require less in proportion than a country with large towns like England and Scotland.

6702. Would you say, therefore, that 1,000,000*l*. a year is spent upon the police owing entirely to the Imperial connexion and the political exigencies arising out of the Imperial connexion, and in no sense from the needs of Ireland?—I think when this table is readjusted, 1,000,000*l*. a year ought to be put down as for an Imperial service, or a British service.

6703. As we know, at times the costs of criminal prosecutions in Ireland are not relatively but absolutely larger than in the whole of Great Britain?—It has been very large in some years.

6704. Arising out of the political conditions resulting from the connexion?—Arising out of the political conditions and a stricter criminal law.

6705. All these charges being deducted from the Irish charges and attributed to Imperial expenditure, it would follow that the proportion of Irish revenue spent upon Irish uses would be much less than is stated by the Treasury?—It is less if you analyse the expenditure in the way you suggest.

6706. And the percentage, therefore, given to Imperial purposes would really be much greater than it appears to be at present?—I think so.

6707. Lord Welby brought you back to the pre-Union period, and he directed your attention to the fact that in the years before the French war, the military contribution of Ireland to the United Kingdom was more than half the revenue. You are aware, I presume, that before the beginning of the French war, the revenue raised in Ireland by taxes was not more than 1,000,000*l*. a year?—I am not sure of the figure, but I have read some of these papers, which show that.

6708. The Irish Parliament being able to discharge their civil government for half a million a year, gave the rest to an Imperial contribution. Would you be disposed to think that the liberality of the Irish Parliament of that day, in giving the surplus of their million of revenue after paying for the civil, affords any reason why seven millions of revenue should be granted now?—I do not see that it follows in the least, nor do I think that those times should be taken as a precedent in any way.

6709. I should like to put a few questions to you to show the course of taxation. Just before the French war broke out, the revenue of Ireland being 1,000,000*l*., and the population between 4,000,000 and 5,000,000, the taxation of the Irish people was between 4*s*. and 5*s*. per head, was it not?—I have not the figures before me, but that would appear to be so.

6710. How much is it now per head?—I reckon it is about 2*l*. per head, if you take the revenue raised in Ireland.

6711. Taking the revenue as adjusted by the Treasury, what would it be?—It would be 34*s*.

6712. So that the ordinary revenue of Ireland in a time of peace was 5*s*. a head, and now it is 34*s*. a head?—Yes, that would be seven times more.

6713. Are you aware that the taxation per head in Great Britain at the time of the Union was 3*l*. per head?—I am not, but I know it was very heavy at that time.

6714. How much is it now?—According to Treasury tables, it is now 2*l*. 11*s*. 6*d*. in England.

6715. Do you consider that the sevenfold increased taxation per head in Ireland, taken side by side with the fact that taxation, per head, in England has diminished since the Union, is a legitimate or tolerable result of a union which was held out to the Irish people as promising financial relief?—I think the financial results of the Union have been most disastrous to Ireland, and that that is pointed out so fully in Sir Edward Hamilton's paper that I imagined it was admitted by all parties.

6716. (*Sir David Barbour.*) The taxation of 5*s*. a head and the expenditure of 1,000,000*l*. yearly was some years before the Union. The expenditure in the year immediately preceding the Union was very much larger, was it not?—It was very much larger, owing to the disturbances in Ireland.

6717. (*Lord Welby.*) Mr. Sexton has put the question of the revenue paid per head in Great Britain at the time of the Union in the very middle and heat of the great war. Is that quite a fair date to take it from; is not the proper date to take it from years before the war broke out, because that would be

6731. Their clothes are sent from England, are they not?—Yes, and sometimes the food.

6732. And a great deal of the food?—Sometimes, I think, some of the food—it depends entirely on the contractors.

6733. And all the equipment?—All the equipments.

6734. So that a very small part of this figure of 3,000,000*l.* would really be expended in the country, would it?—I should think the principal expenditure would be on hay and oats.

6735. Do you think that excessive taxation is in any measure justified or palliated by the plea that, at any rate, even though it be excessive, a part of it is spent where it is raised?—I do not think that is any justification whatever. I think it is a very dangerous thing for a people to give the government its excessive revenue. In this case we have to do so.

6736. When you raise taxation you take incomes, do you not?—Certainly, and deprive the payers of the advantages which they would have derived from that income by either spending or saving it.

6737. When you spend a part of that income so taken in the country where the taxation is raised, you simply allow the people, instead of their incomes, the margin of profit that may result upon the transactions, do you not?—Certainly.

6738. The two things are incommensurable, are they not. Is the second point any compensation for the first?—None whatever.

6739. You were already questioned on the Church fund. Upon the general principle of loans to Ireland, do you say that it is any substantial return for excessive taxation that loans are made to Ireland?—I do not think it is any compensation for excessive taxation that loans are made, but with regard to the loans made in Ireland it seems to me they simply add to her burdens, because a great part of them have been unremuneratively spent. Public loans.

6740. If Irish local government were developed, and Irish local bodies had the same powers as in England, do you think it would be difficult for them to raise the money they require at reasonable rates?—I do not think there would be any difficulty whatever; Dublin and Belfast have raised the loans they require at 3½ and 3¾ per cent., and that stock now stands at a premium. Many of the smaller bodies who have power to do so, have also raised money without any difficulty. In the township I live in, a small township with a revenue of 8000*l.* a year, they are now proposing to issue stock to consolidate its loans, and expect to do so at 3½ per cent.

6741. (*Lord Farrer.*) Where is that?—Killiney.

6742. (*Mr. Sexton.*) Is there any force in the argument that although an excessive revenue may be raised in Ireland, at any rate Ireland receives cheap loans on what are considered easy terms?—I do not say that it is any compensation whatever.

6743. Taking the case of the Church fund, here was an Irish ecclesiastical corporation disestablished—the first thing, as I understand, was that the Imperial Legislature constituted an artificial value to the surplus?—Yes, they artificially enhanced the value of the security. Church fund loans.

6744. Putting a capital burden of about 1,000,000*l.* on the persons liable to pay these rents?—That was the effect of the Church Act, I think.

6745. (*Lord Welby.*) Are you referring to the tithe rentcharge?—The tithe and perpetuity rents.

Mr. Murrough O'Brien. 7 Mar. 1895. Church Fund loans.

6746. The tithes payable by the landlords?—Yes.

6747. (*Mr. Sexton.*) Having put that burden upon that class in Ireland, the next step was to relieve the Imperial purse of annual charges amounting to a capital value of 1,000,000*l.*, was it not?—Yes, by transferring them to the fund.

6748. Then the main bulk of the fund has been used since then for the purpose of meeting demands of famine, distress, and political exigency, which, if this fund had not existed and this Church had not been disestablished, would have to be met out of the Imperial purse?—I think most of the burden with which this fund has been encumbered would have had to be met out of the public revenue.

6749. It seems as if the Imperial Legislature availed itself of the reform of an Irish institution for the purpose of using the property of that institution to relieve the Imperial Exchequer, does it not?—I think they did so in fact, but I imagine it was to some extent the fault of the Irish members who did not represent that view in the House of Commons of the day. It is 20 or 30 years since that was done.

6750. Of course, being absorbed in your official duties, you may not be able to give such close attention to parliamentary matters as to be aware that representations of Irish members are not paid much attention to, especially in financial matters?—I think that is very probable.

6751. Then having transferred these Imperial charges to the Irish fund, the Imperial Parliament proceeded to allocate the fund for these Irish purposes, which otherwise would have fallen on the Imperial purse, and the next step was that the National Debt Commissioners, who could have borrowed money at that time, I think, at about 3 per cent., made advances amounting to about 11,000,000*l.* or 12,000,000*l.* and are charging now on these advances $3\frac{1}{2}$ per cent. interest?—They did, in fact, borrow part of the money at $2\frac{1}{2}$ per cent. so far as it was borrowed from Irish depositors. Three and a half per cent. it is suggested is charged to cover the risk of money at call and the cost of management. The risk of money at call is, of course, infinitesimal.

6752. The substantial fact is that the British Government can borrow as much as it wants at $2\frac{1}{2}$ per cent., is it not?—Yes.

6753. What can they borrow at now?—I should have to look at the prices of consols for the day, and I have not had time to do so.

6754. You know that $2\frac{3}{4}$ consols are about 104 or 105, are they not?—Yes, I think so.

6755. The rich country has lent to the poor one, on the security of this Church fund, about 12,000,000*l.*, and is charging now, is it not, upon these loans a rate of interest about 1 per cent. in excess of the value of money?—I think they are charging a rate of interest that certainly leaves them a profit.

6756. And you have noted the fact that this money so used is not even Imperial money, but it comes from Ireland out of the Savings Bank?—I do not think any of it is Imperial money. The money that is lent on the security of the Church fund is merely in anticipation of the realisation of that fund, and therefore, really, it is all Irish money. The money supplied from the Savings Bank depositors amounts to very nearly 7,000,000*l.*

6757. At any rate a sum equivalent to the sums advanced by the National Debt Commissioners, the Church fund, is in their hands, and also the deposits from the Irish Savings Banks?—That is so.

6758. And they pay $3\frac{1}{2}$ per cent. for that?—They pay $2\frac{1}{2}$ to the depositors.

6759. And they charge $3\frac{1}{2}$ to Ireland?—Yes.

6760. They use a sum equivalent to the savings of the Irish poor deposited in their hands as loans to Ireland on which they charge 1 per cent. more; is not that so?—I think the rate of interest charged has been higher on some of the loans; for instance, on the Lands Improvement loans made some years ago, my recollection is that the rate of interest charged was 4 per cent.

Mr. Murrough O'Brien. 7 Mar. 1895. Public loans.

6761. Are you aware that we have evidence before us (passing from the Church fund to the whole question of Treasury loans to Ireland), that upon the balance of 8,000,000*l.* now due by Ireland to the Treasury, there is an average interest charged at the moment of 3*l.* 11*s.* per cent.?—I was not aware that that was the case.

6762. Taking that as the evidence of the Chairman of the Board of Works, what observation do you make?—My impression about all these loans is that many are of no permanent advantage, and that a great many of them, including the loans under the Board of Works, produce no return; they have been spent to tide over some trouble or distress, and the future revenue of the country, or of the people who have got a part of these loans, is mortgaged to repay them.

6763. It was suggested to you that the National Debt Commissioners do not work at a profit; it appears, however, that they do achieve a profit in these particular transactions in Ireland, does it not?—One per cent. ought to leave a profit over management.

6764. Do you consider it fair that a profit should be exacted upon transactions of this character, in order that losses of the National Debt Commissioners in other spheres of action should be made good?—No, I think the money should be lent under the circumstances, at the lowest possible rate of interest, if the loans are made at all.

6765. And that if there be a deficiency on any part of the operations of the National Debt Commissioners, it should be met by an Imperial contribution, and not by charging an excessive rate of interest to one of the members of the Kingdom?—Certainly.

6766. (*Lord Welby.*) The Treasury contention would be that the loan was made at a loss?—It is made at a gross profit of 1 per cent. There may be expenses of management out of that.

6767. (*Mr. Sexton.*) I think Lord Welby was hardly accurate in suggesting to you that the bulk of these loans were transacted in 1871, was he not?—Yes; the loans have been made at different dates, commencing from 1869, but I have not the date of the different Acts, for instance, the Relief of Distress Act, under which a million and a quarter was lent, began in 1880; 16,000*l.* was lent in 1884–85, 5,000*l.* in 1886–87; and I fancy there is more money being advanced this year.

6768. Very many of these loans were advanced in recent years, when money had much decreased in value, were they not?—Some of the loans certainly were.

6769. No matter how far back we go, I believe it may be said, that the National Debt Commissioners took very good care, no matter what was the interest on consols, or how the money market stood, that they suffered no loss by reason of these loans. Lord Welby referred to the Savings Banks. I do not know whether you can give any evidence as to where that loss arose, whether it was British or Irish?—I do not know where the loss occurred.

6770. At any rate, taking the price of consols since 1870, have you any doubt that the loans made by the National Debt Commissioners at all times left some margin of profit?—I do not understand Lord Welby's reference to the investment in consols. It appears to me that the transaction is perfectly plain that there is so much money deposited at $2\frac{1}{2}$ per cent., which is re-lent at $3\frac{1}{2}$ and sometimes 4 per cent. for Irish purposes.

6771. Is it not curious, that whilst the National Debt Commissioners charge $3\frac{1}{2}$ per cent. to this Irish fund for moneys advanced, when a charge of interest is made on the fund and any money paid over, the allowance is only $2\frac{1}{2}$ per cent., say, as in the case of the Congested District Board. Can you discern any principle in that. If the National Debt Commissioners get $3\frac{1}{2}$ per cent., why should not the Congested District Board get more?—On business principles

Mr. Murrough O'Brien.

9 Mar. 1895.

Church loans.

they should have got more. The low rate of interest should have been on the debts that had priority and the higher rates on the debts that had not priority; but I imagine it was because there was a doubt about the sufficiency of the fund, and there was a great desire to preserve the fund for future emergencies.

6772. It appears to me that the effect of the policy and the high interest charged is to place the solvency of the fund in peril; is not that so?—I believe the ultimate surplus to be realised from this fund is a matter of doubt, and it is affected by the rate of interest that has been charged.

6773. At what would you fix a fair amount of refund for the excess over the market value of the money during the currency of these loans?—I suggest that the Treasury or the National Debt Commissioners should at once reduce the rate of interest to the lowest possible point. I think that would be one way in which justice would be done. I have not made any exact calculation, but in the past, I reckon the Church fund might have paid 30,000*l.* or 40,000*l.* less a year than it has done. That of course would have very largely increased the ultimate surplus to be realised from this Church fund.

6774. And it would have left a larger calculable surplus now?—Certainly.

6775. Taking it that these Church loans are made at this high rate, and that all the Treasury loans to Ireland are on an average of 3*l.* 11*s.* per cent., do you think that the imposition of excessive taxation is in any way qualified by lending money to Ireland from the Imperial revenue at a further profit; does it not seem rather to increase the tribute laid on that country than otherwise?—I do not think it is any justification for excessive taxation.

6776. It is adding to excessive taxation, profit, is it not?—Yes, on the assumption that we had to take these loans; which, I believe, as most of them were made in cases of emergency, practically we had to do.

6777. We had to take them because we were denied the local government and local power, which would have enabled us to utilise our own funds?—Certainly, it was the only means of public bodies getting funds to meet local distress.

Ireland and Sweden compared.

6778. Political liberties and local governments were denied, with the result of inflicting financial as well as other disadvantages. I should like to pass to a very interesting comparison which you made from a fiscal point of view, between Sweden and Ireland. You pointed out, I think, that the population of Sweden is about equal to that of Ireland?—The population of Sweden, in 1891, appears to have been 4,784,675, rather in excess of the Irish population at present.

6779. What is the annual revenue?—The Budget estimate for 1892 is given as 4,869,444*l.*; that amounts to 1*l.* 0*s.* 7*d.* a head.

6780. As against 34*s.* a head in Ireland?—Yes; but that includes receipts from the public railways. Excluding those railway receipts, which amount to 261,000*l.*, the rate of taxation would be 18*s.* 7*d.* a head, in fact, about 1*s.* 9*d.* of the revenue comes from railway receipts.

6781. Out of that revenue Sweden provides, I understand, workmen's insurance, and also expenses in relation to railways, which are not provided in this country?—The expenditure includes 777,000*l.* spent upon public worship; the payment of members amounts to 34,000*l.*; there is a certain contribution towards a workman's insurance fund recently established, and there is a certain outlay on railways. All this comes out of the revenue of, practically, 1*l.* a head.

6782. Sweden, therefore, a country with the same population as Ireland, out of a revenue of 1*l.* a head, as against a revenue of 34*s.* a head in Ireland, pays all the public charges, together with the cost of public worship, insurance for workmen and other things, and maintains an army and a navy?—Yes.

6783. (*Lord Farrer.*) Does that include the whole cost of governing Sweden?—Not local taxation; there is a certain amount of local taxation too.

6784. (*Chairman.*) How much is the interest on the debt?—I have not got the exact interest on the debt, but the expenditure under the head of finance is 918,000*l.* The Swedish debt has been largely spent upon railways, and it has borne interest at 4 per cent.

Mr. Murrough O'Brien.

9 Mar. 1895.

Ireland and Sweden compared.

6785. Which is a remunerative investment?—Yes; they are just now converting it into a $3\frac{1}{2}$ per cent. loan, and are giving notice to call in all the outstanding bonds of the 1880 loan.

6786. (*Lord Farrer.*) Have you compared the expenses of what we may call the civil government of Ireland with the expenses of the civil government of Sweden?—I took it, that when the army and navy are provided for, all the rest of it was what we should call civil expenditure.

6787. And that comes to how much?—A million and a half. That would leave 4,000,000*l.* in round numbers for the civil government, which includes a large expenditure on railways.

6788. (*Lord Welby.*) That is Sweden without Norway, is it?—That is Sweden without Norway.

6789. (*Mr. Sexton.*) Next to Great Britain, I believe, probably Sweden with Norway, has the largest mercantile marine, or certainly one of the largest in Europe?—I have read that she has the largest amount of merchant shipping, except Great Britain. I think she has a larger amount than the United States, but if not second in the world, she comes third.

6790. Then here we have two countries very much in the same latitude, the same climate, the same population, one at a cost of 1*l.* a head, paying the ordinary cost of administration, outlay on railways, insurance for workmen, cost of public worship, maintenance of army, and maintenance of navy for the protection of the second largest mercantile marine in Europe, and it does this at a cost of little more than half of the capitation cost of the other; is not that the case?—That is so. The similarity between the two countries in other circumstances is also remarkable. The local taxation in Sweden is pretty nearly the same as in Ireland. It amounts to less than two millions and a half.

6791. (*Lord Farrer.*) Is the great marine you spoke of Norwegian or Swedish?—The two countries together; they have together a large amount of merchant shipping.

6792. (*Lord Welby.*) If you draw deductions from the Norwegian plus Swedish marine, we ought to reckon in the Norwegian Budget too, ought we not?—I gave the figures of the Norwegian Budget.

6793. (*Mr. Sexton.*) If you do add the two together, how do they stand in relation to Great Britain?—They are less than Great Britain, but still they are very large; they are next to Great Britain.

6794. Will you proceed now to add Norway to the fiscal relationship?—The figures that I have taken as to Sweden are from one of the Foreign Office Reports. The figures as to Norway are taken from the Statesman's Year Book. It is a very similar country in its circumstances, and with a population of just about half Ireland. The population is 2,000,000, and its revenue 2,900,000*l.*

6795. That is very slightly over one-third of Ireland; the population is one-half, and the revenue about one-third, is it not?—Yes. Her army cost 433,000*l.*, and her navy 148,000*l.*

6796. The revenues of the two countries added together is not as large as the revenue collected in Ireland, and is not much larger than the revenue contributed by Ireland, as adjusted by the Treasury, is it?—No.

6797. Is there any way of accounting for this extraordinary disparity, except that Ireland, by reason of her political condition, is in such a state of discontent that it is found necessary, from the Imperial point of view, to raise these excessive taxes in order to spend them again upon a system of administration dictated by Imperial objects only?—I think Ireland is at a very great disadvantage from her political and financial connexion with a wealthy country so very differently circumstanced as Great Britain is, and that a great

Mr. Murrough O'Brien.

7 Mar. 1895.

Ireland and Sweden compared.

part of the expenditure of Great Britain has been in foreign wars, and in what I may call generally a forward policy—that is, one with which in Ireland we have very little concern, and to which I do not think we ought to be called upon to contribute. I think Ireland should reasonably contribute to any expenses for defence, but her principal danger of being attacked is from her connexion with England. The only time when she was invaded, that I know of in history, was in consequence of her connexion with England. The invasion was to injure England, not because Ireland was an attractive place to invade.

6798. That is in modern times?—Yes.

6799. My point was that the Imperial Government, because of its system, finds it necessary to maintain an expensive system of administration. Owing to the political system maintained in Ireland, does the Imperial Government find itself driven to maintain a more costly system of administration than need be if the government of Ireland was what the people desired?—Certainly; the habits of a nation are like those of an individual, and a wealthy country has a higher scale of taxation and payment for everything. That does not suit a poor person or a poor country in partnership with the richer partner.

6800. You say that it is only the connexion of Ireland with Great Britain that might make her the possible object of attack from any foreign power?—I cannot imagine any other reason. I do not suppose she would be an attractive possession, or one likely to be assailed by any foreign country on account of the aggressive character of her policy.

6801. In fact I think you have suggested in one of your points that she would be in as little danger as Iceland, have you not?—I do not think she would be in much more danger of attack than Iceland would be, if it were not for her connexion with England.

6802. In such circumstances, not having a mercantile marine or a foreign trade like Sweden, Ireland would have no need of an army or navy, would it?—I think Ireland would have need of a very small expenditure for the purpose of defence for many years.

6803. Therefore it appears probable, does it not, if her administration were reformed and reduced to the limit of expense required by the real needs of Ireland, that out of a revenue of 4,000,000*l.* (such as Sweden has) she might discharge the cost of her government and do many other things, such as supporting workmen's insurance, and so forth, which have been done in Sweden?—She would have an ample revenue for what she needs, above all other things, and that is the development of her internal resources, as well as to provide for social requirements, like workmen's insurance, old-age pensions, and in fact everything that modern thought points to.

6804. And do you think the great excess of revenue now charged upon her is due to the political conditions arising out of the Legislative Union?—Yes.

Adjourned to to-morrow at 11 o'clock.

Mr. Murrough O'Brien's evidence is continued at Question 6805.

SIXTEENTH DAY.

Friday, 8th March 1895.

At B Committee Room, House of Lords.

PRESENT:

THE RIGHT HON. HUGH C. E. CHILDERS, CHAIRMAN.

LORD FARRER.	CHARLES E. MARTIN, Esq.
LORD WELBY.	J. E. REDMOND, Esq., M.P.
SIR DAVID BARBOUR, K.C.S.I.	THOMAS SEXTON, Esq., M.P.

Mr. B. H. HOLLAND, *Secretary.*

Mr. MURROUGH O'BRIEN recalled and further examined.

Mr. Murrough O'Brien.

8 Mar. 1895.

Effect of penal laws on economic condition of Ireland.

6805. (*Mr. Sexton.*) I wish first to ask you a few particular questions touching upon points in your previous evidence. You spoke of the long continuing effect of the penal laws upon the economic condition of Ireland. Could you add anything as to the depression of the Catholic community long after emancipation had been granted?—The effect of emancipation was very trifling; it admitted Catholics to Parliament; 20 years after emancipation, Cobden, in one of his speeches, said that was the only benefit that had hitherto been derived from emancipation. John Bright held the same view, about 20 years after he said very much the same thing, that Protestant supremacy still prevailed, with the result, I think, of excluding Catholics from public life. Entrance into public life is one means of advancement of the people, and as they were excluded, the natural result in Ireland has been that a great many have emigrated. Bright, in 1845, which was long after emancipation, said in one of his speeches describing the state of Ireland and the relations of Catholics and Protestants, that "They have had everything Protestant; a Protestant clique dominant in the country; a "Protestant Viceroy to distribute places and emoluments amongst that Protestant clique; Protestant "judges who have polluted the seats of justice; "Protestant magistrates before whom the Catholic "peasant could not hope for justice." That describes the impression left upon an Englishman by the condition of the Catholics long after they had been theoretically admitted to equal rights.

6806. Do you think the proscription so long enforced against the mass of the people in Ireland has had an effect, which has not yet disappeared, upon their condition?—I do not think it has yet disappeared.

Wages of agricultural labour.

6807. Now I pass to the relative wages of the agricultural labourer. Could you add anything more to what you have said as to the relative wages of the agricultural labourer at present in Great Britain and in Ireland?—The only comparison to be made between labour in the two countries is, I think, agricultural labour, because we have very little other labour, and the most recent information in the way of giving

general figures is, I think, that in Mr. Little's report to the Labour Commission. He gives the average wages of ordinary labour in England at 15s. 11d.; in Wales 14s. 10d., and in Ireland at 10s.; that would make the average rate of wages 59 per cent. over Ireland for England, and 48 per cent. over Ireland for Wales. He adds also in his report what has not been taken into account: "In some Irish districts "there is insufficient employment. The demand for "labourers has decreased, the most able and intelligent "have emigrated; the physique of those who remain "has deteriorated." With reference to the living of the people, referring to England, he says: "In Ireland "a still lower average of cottage accommodation is "said to prevail."

6808. (Chairman.) Are you comparing purely agricultural labourers?—Yes.

6809. (*Lord Welby.*) What report are you quoting from?—From Mr. Little's report to the Labour Commission, summarised in the "Chamber of Agriculture Journal."

6810. (*Mr. Sexton.*) The wages of those engaged in industries non-agricultural, which prevail in England and scarcely exist in Ireland, would be higher still, would they not?—Such industries hardly exist in Ireland, and they would be very much higher than these figures for the artisans in the manufacturing parts of England.

6811. When you come to make a general comparison of labour, the existence of those industries in England, and their non-existence in Ireland, makes the comparison still more wide, does it not?—There are a large body of artisans in England, of which we have no similar class in Ireland.

6812. As to the important element of the precarious character of labour in Ireland, which you have illustrated already by reference to emigration, and to the migratory labourers who come every year to Great Britain, is it not the fact that in the Agricultural Labourers' Act, intended to provide houses and plots of land for labourers in Ireland, the Legislature has been obliged to recognise a few weeks of agricultural labour in the spring and harvest as constituting an agricultural labourer for the purposes of the Act?—I am not aware of the definition in the Act, but the provision of decent houses to a very small extent has, of course, added largely to the local taxation. In England the labourers' houses have been built by the landowners; in Ireland they are now being built at the expense of the general taxpayer, and have largely increased the rates in some districts.

6813. It is not the fact that we must hesitate even in considering 10s. a week, and bear in mind that it is only for a comparatively few weeks in the year that the Irish agricultural labourer throughout large portions of Ireland can rely on having employment?—I think 10s. a week is far above the average rate all over Ireland, and that Mr. Little's figure refers only to those who are in constant employment.

6814. Will you add anything to what you have said as to an important element in the wealth of England especially, that is to say the rating of railways, bearing in mind that we are considering Imperial taxation?—I think the inquiry has extended to local taxation as well, and as there is such an admixture of local and Imperial finance owing to the grants from the public revenue in aid of local taxation, the burden of local taxation has to be considered as well. The railways constitute such a large portion of the wealth of England that that seems to me very important. And there are other authorities besides those I have quoted. I should like to add a quotation from "Penfold on Rating." In the sixth edition an article is published at the end, in which the author says: "I have no "hesitation in asserting that if the matter were "thoroughly sifted, it would be found that railway "companies in England and Wales are escaping the "payment of local rates justly due to the extent of "1½ million pounds annually. What is true of railway companies is equally true, I believe, of gas and "water companies, though perhaps it may not be "quite to the same extent." I have compared from the railway returns of 1893 the rates and taxes paid by the Dublin, Wicklow, and Wexford Railway, the London and North Western Railway, and the Great Southern and Western Railway. The rates and taxes given in those returns amount to 3·6 per cent. on the gross receipts, and 8·5 on the net receipts of the Dublin, Wicklow, and Wexford Railway, a railway the reverse of prosperous. On the London and North Western the rates and taxes came to 2·7 per cent. on the gross receipts, and to 6·6 per cent. on the net receipts; on the Great Southern and Western Railway of Ireland, one of our most prosperous railways, the rates and taxes come to 3·38 per cent. on the gross receipts, and 7·4 per cent. on the net receipts. The table is handed in, and is as follows:—

From Railway Returns for 1893 [*C.* 7460.]

Railway.	Receipts.		Rates and Taxes.	Percentage of Rates and Taxes on	
	Gross.	Net.		Gross.	Net.
Dublin, Wicklow and Wexford, [illegible] m.	[illegible]	[illegible]	[illegible]	[illegible]	[illegible]
London and N.W. Railway, [illegible] m.	[illegible]	[illegible]	[illegible]	[illegible]	
Great Southern and Western (Ireland), [illegible] m.	[illegible]	[illegible]	[illegible]	[illegible]	

6815. (Chairman.) In Great Britain or in England does that include the passenger tax?—There is no passenger tax in Ireland. It does not include the passenger tax in Great Britain, which is given in a separate column.

6816. (*Lord Welby.*) When you say "rates and taxes," what do you include in "taxes"?—I take the figures as given in the railway returns, and I presume they are made up in the same way for each, and represent the same payments for each company.

6817. You exclude from your comparison the railway duty, which is a charge there in England, and you quote returns which use the words "rates and taxes" which does not include income tax, as we know?—No.

6818. I think that must be confined to local taxation only, must it not?—Certainly, I think it only refers to that. It is given in these returns under the head of "rates and taxes," and of course it must be remembered that a great deal more is got for the local taxation paid in England than in Ireland. In Ireland our local taxes are practically the poor rate and the county rate; in England these railways run through very large towns, and derive a great many benefits, and the people employed by them also derive benefits from the expenditure of the municipalities.

6819. (*Mr. Sexton.*) Are the taxes paid by the English railways and the taxes paid by the Irish railways in that computation the same?—They are all rates and taxes, exclusive of the passenger duty and and income tax.

6820. (*Lord Welby.*) What other taxes are there, do you know, using the phrase "taxes," which usually means Imperial, as against rates?—I have simply taken the heading from the returns, but I presume it means only the local rates.

6821. (*Mr. Sexton.*) Therefore the question of what Imperial taxes may be paid by these railways in England and not in Ireland does not enter into the issue, does it?—It does not enter into that comparison.

6822. The comparison is just, therefore, is it?—The comparison is just, perfectly just, taking into account that for the local taxation in England larger benefits are derived by the ratepayers.

6823. You have said in your general evidence that in considering the local taxation you must have regard not only to the amount of the burden imposed, but to the amount and value of the service rendered, which is greater in England?—Certainly.

6824. By reason of the greater development and greater efficiency of local government in this country;

Mr. Murrough O'Brien.

4 May 1895.

is that the reason?—That is the reason; there are larger services rendered.

6825. Have you said what you wished to say about the railways?—Yes, that is all I have to say about the railways.

Rating of cabins. Valuation of houses.

6826. In the Irish assessment of real property to income tax, the value of those thatched buildings, with which all those who know Ireland are familiar, is included; what do you say on that subject?—A large part of the buildings in Ireland, in the country parts, and in most of the villages, are of a very frail description; according to the census of 1891 there are 453,206 thatched cabins, of which 20,617 are mud cabins, with one room. A great number of these 200,000 thatched cabins, if the Public Health Acts were enforced, would neither have existence nor value.

6827. There are about, I think, one-third of the houses in the country, are they not; the houses are about 1,000,000 in number?—I have not the figure.

6828. Assuming the family to be five, the houses are about 1,000,000, and I should say that would represent one-third of the houses?—I should think they probably would, but the figures I have taken from the census are 20,617 mud cabins with one room, and 312,589 third-class houses, which are described as somewhat better than the mud cabins.

6829. Have these houses any letting value?—I think that the maintenance of these houses is as much as they are worth, and I think they would be worth nothing at all if the Public Health Act were enforced.

6830. Do they form a substantial part of the assessment to the Irish income tax?—They are a substantial part.

Cost of living in London and Dublin.

6831. Could you add anything more to what you have said as to the comparative cost of living in Dublin and in London. It is suggested here that the cost of living in London is higher than in Dublin, and in England higher than in Ireland, as a sort of general assumption?—I think it is a mistaken assumption. There was an inquiry by the Treasury into this matter in 1872, and I would like to read one or two passages from the report then made by the Departmental Commission of the Treasury. The Commission consisted of Mr. Stevenson Blackwood, Lord Monck, and Myles O'Reilly. They say: "The cost of living in Dublin "was undoubtedly less than in London until within "the last few years. We have sufficient evidence to "show that this is not now the case, and that even in "the matter of house accommodation the rents paid "by persons in the same rank of life, and with incomes "presumably similar to those of Civil Service clerks, "are not appreciably higher in London than they are "in Dublin." They then go on to say: "We have "come to the conclusion that there exists no reason, "based on local considerations, for giving salaries to "civil servants stationed in Dublin less in amount "than those assigned to persons in London performing "analogous duties." That report was signed by Lord Monck and O'Reilly. Mr. Stevenson Blackwood, in a separate report, mentions one of the facts that influenced him in coming to the same conclusion: "Further, we have ascertained that local taxation in "Dublin has risen from an average rate of 5s. 5d. in "the pound in 1852 to one of 9s. in the pound in "1872." He then goes on to say: "Apart, however, "from the question of similarity of pay on the ground "of similarity of duty, we have to state that, from the "evidence we have received, the cost of living in "Dublin appears to be very nearly, if not quite, equal "to that in London, and that even in the matter of "house accommodation, the rents paid by persons in "the same rank of life, and with incomes similar to "those of Civil Service clerks, are not appreciably "higher in London than they are in Dublin." They refer then to a list of prices.

6832. I think your evidence on the general question of cost of living is that it is not less in Ireland than in England?—I have consulted a great many people who have kept houses in Dublin and in London, and compared the budgets of people in similar positions, and the conclusion I have come to—in fact I am so informed by those who have kept houses in both places—is that it is just as dear to live in Dublin as in London, and some of them say rather dearer, because, even if the cost of articles is, as it sometimes is, somewhat less in Dublin, the quality is worse. Everything is provided to hand in London; there are greater facilities for distribution, and that, I think, is the chief cause of the greater cheapness of retail articles in London.

Mr. Murrough O'Brien.

4 May 1895.

Cost of living in London and Dublin.

6833. Coal, and many other important commodities, and even clothes, are imported from England, and therefore are probably dearer in England than here, are they not?—The clothes of the poor are very much dearer. The clothes of a few rich people who go to the fashionable tailors are probably dearer than in London, and people dress better in London.

6834. The clothing of the poor is more relevant to the inquiry?—The clothing of the poor, I think, is very much dearer in Ireland than in England.

6835. (*Lord Welby.*) Have you any ground on which you base that opinion?—By comparing the prices of rough clothes bought by workmen, and comparing such purchases as boots—most of our boots are imported from Northampton—I find they are cheaper in English country towns than they are in most Irish country towns.

6836. (*Sir David Barbour.*) Do not the shopkeepers make larger profits in Ireland under those circumstances?—I could not say. Of course, the volume of business is so very much larger in England that there is a quicker turn-over.

6837. (*Mr. Sexton.*) Even as compared with the last generation, or any previous one, a far greater part of the food of the country is imported, now is it not, such as tea, coffee, and sugar?—A very large part of the articles of ordinary consumption is imported, and is imported from England.

6838. And therefore, is presumably somewhat dearer than on the English market?—I think, another thing that adds to it in the internal parts of Ireland is that the railway rates are higher. I am not able to give figures, but there is a general complaint that the railway rates in Ireland are much higher than in England.

6839. That is, I believe, unquestionable?—I dare say you have sat upon some of the railway committees, but I only know generally.

6840. Upon the whole, even supposing the Irish agricultural labourer had his 10s. every week, which we know he has not, do you see any ground whatever for Sir Edward Hamilton's assumption that he can spare more out of that 10s. on what Sir Edward Hamilton is pleased to call luxuries, than the English labourer can out of his 15s. 11½d.?—It is a matter of wonder to everyone who is acquainted with the labouring classes in Ireland, how they subsist at all, and as to having money for luxuries, I do not see how they could have any.

6841. The mention of luxuries in connexion with the subject sounds a little sarcastic, does it not?—I think very.

Valuation and rents.

6842. Passing to another point, as to the relation of judicial rents to the rateable valuation; there was a Commission appointed under the presidency of Lord Cowper a few years ago, was there not?—Yes.

6843. What did they find with regard to about 200,000 rents which had been fixed by the Commission up to that time? What year was it?—They reported in 1887 I think; they sat at the end of 1886. Their report was to the effect that the rents fixed up to that time in five years were too high, and could not be paid. They must necessarily, therefore, have been high in relation to the productive value, and the present letting value of the farms, and must therefore have included the whole benefit derivable from the farms. The report was that these rents could not be paid, and the Government of the day passed an Act of Parliament which had the effect of reducing those rents for the following three years. Since then prices have continued to fall, and farmers' profits, in my opinion, have continued to diminish.

Mr. Murrough O'Brien. 4 Mar. 1895. Taxation and rents.

6844. When we compare the rents in England with the rents in Ireland to find a basis of relative taxable capacity, it should be remembered, should it not, that the improvements, equipments, and buildings in England, which form an element of the rent, are made by the landlord?—I think if you could get two identical farms in quality, in lands and equipment, one in Ireland and one in England, that the fair comparison to take would be this—the best authorities in England, such as Mr. Caird, the late Mr. Walter, who was a practical agriculturalist and landowner, estimated that the cost of the equipment of a farm with buildings was one-third of its total value. The landowner in England makes and maintains the building and equipments. The Irish farmer is at a disadvantage from his remoteness from the markets where his articles ultimately are consumed. I therefore take it that if a pound was a fair rent in England, first a third should come off (33 per cent.) for the cost of the buildings and equipments, if they have been provided by the tenant. Then I would take off the average cost of maintenance and repairs, which I gather from the Agricultural Commission amount to about 15 per cent., I would then take off 10 per cent. for remoteness from markets, which makes a difference in the ultimate selling price, and the Irish farmer is at a somewhat greater cost in importing manures and all agricultural implements, which are not manufactured in Ireland. For that I would add 5 per cent. I think that a fair comparison between land rented at a pound in England, if that was fair under English circumstances, would be that the farmer in Ireland, providing the buildings and equipment, maintaining and repairing the premises, and being at a disadvantage in markets, should pay about 8s. 6d. as the equivalent of the pound in England.

6845. (*Sir David Barbour.*) That is on the assumption that he is to make the same profit as an English farmer?—That is assuming he is to make the same profit as an English farmer, and assuming, which I do not say is always the case, that he has provided the equipments, though he generally has.

6846. (*Mr. Sexton.*) You have said what he could or should pay, what do you think he does pay in comparison with the pound in England?—I would rather not go into the question of what he does pay, because the variations of rent are so very great in Ireland that I do not think I can give a general answer to that question. I would rather not.

6847. Could you go so far as to say what is the difference, in your judgment, between the proportion of the gross produce of two such farms in England and in Ireland?—First I should say that the gross produce in Ireland is generally less, partly because of the disadvantages under which Irish farmers labour, partly because our climate is not, on the whole, so advantageous for farming. Mr. Clare Sewell Read, the well-known agriculturalist, told the Agricultural Commission that is now sitting that a tillage farmer could not live in England unless he made six or seven rents, that is to say, for the tillage farm he should pay a sixth or a seventh. I think there has always been a greater demand for Irish land, which is the only industry we have, and that competition has always kept rents higher—that a larger proportion of the gross produce goes to the landlord in Ireland than in England. I may say I am a landowner to a small extent. I happen to have land, and am unfortunately a landlord in two counties. Comparing that land with such similar land as I know of in England, I think the rents are a larger proportion of the gross produce.

6848. Have you any general idea what proportion the landlord does get in Ireland of the gross produce?—It was stated to the Committee on the Land Acts that the usual practice was to give the landlord a third of the gross produce. I do not think that is the case, because it could not be paid; it would be perfectly impossible that a tillage farm could pay a third of the gross produce to the landlord, but I believe that has been reckoned by valuers in the past as the proper proportion to be assigned to the landlord. Mr. Sexton, who I referred to before, stated in 1844, with reference to this valuation, that he thought a larger proportion of the gross produce went to the landlord in Ireland than in England. Many other English observers have said the same thing.

6849. Have you any doubt that the proportion taken by the landlord in Ireland as rent approximates more nearly to the one-third fixed by Irish valuers than to the one-sixth or one seventh which Mr. Clare Sewell Read thought would be the just proportion?—I think, on the whole, it is a true statement to make that a larger proportion of the gross produce finds its way ultimately into the pocket of the Irish landlord than into the pocket of the English landlord.

6850. Then, if the comparison be 8s. 6d. in Ireland and a pound in England, it would appear as the rents, where it is a pound in England, it would be more than a pound in Ireland, certainly not less?—My comparison is of farms of equal quality and equally equipped with buildings.

6851. At any rate, the actual proportions between England and Ireland are very far indeed from those which you say would be just, are they not?—A common proportion given on dairy farms in the south of Ireland, which are worked at considerable expense and with a large investment of capital, and are somewhat comparable with tillage farms (because you must have buildings, dairy apparatus, and a good deal of labour), is that two-fifths of the gross produce should go to the landlord, and that is frequently assigned to him as the fair rent of the farm by valuers.

6852. These 200,000 Irish judicial rents fixed by the Land Commission, which the Cowper Commission found to be so high that they could not be paid, are still payable, are they not?—They are still payable at law, if the owner thinks it right to enforce them.

6853. Without any diminution?—There was a diminution for three years.

6854. But that time has gone by, has it not?—There was a diminution in proportion to the fall, so far as it could be ascertained, in the prices of produce.

6855. These 200,000 rents, and all other rents in Ireland, include the bulk of the letting value added to the holding by the improvements of the tenant?—I am not prepared to give a general opinion as to that.

6856. I believe the practice of the sub-commissioners is only to allow a percentage on the outlay incurred in making an improvement, is it not?—The practice of the sub-commissioners, I fancy, is variable, and it is not easy to ascertain it, because the only means I should have of knowing what the sub-commissioners have done is from their reports, and they are framed in a somewhat vague manner which does not always make clear the principle on which they have acted.

6857. (*Chairman*). Referring to the actual rents now paid in the case of these 200,000 farms, you carefully, I noticed, used the words "are enforced at law." Do you mean that that is the customary thing?—No, I mean to say this: We all know very large arrears accumulate in Ireland, presumably because the rents have been higher than could have been paid. For instance in 1882 Parliament passed an Arrears Act which gave the owners of land, I forget whether it was three-quarters of a million or a million of money, and in consideration of that payment by the State to them, or through the State, or the Church Fund, a larger arrear (I fancy double that) was wiped out. Since then we know from the proceedings that continually go on in the courts that large arrears have occurred again.

6858. And are not insisted upon?—They are sometimes insisted upon and sometimes not. Cases have been before the courts within the last two or three months where 20 years arrears were sued for. Of course it would not follow that rent had not been paid for 20 years, there may have been payments each year, but gradually an arrear to that amount grew up.

Agricultural produce value and quantity.

6859. (*Mr. Sexton.*) You said yesterday that statistics often need explanation. Would it be your

Mr. Murrough O'Brien.

8 Mar. 1895.

Agricultural produce, value and quantity.

opinion that what we called the "prosperity statistics" in Ireland require a careful scrutiny?—I think they require a very careful scrutiny. I was astonished when this inquiry began, and I looked up the agricultural statistics which are reduced to the same basis in the statistical abstract, at finding that, notwithstanding what is evident from observation in Ireland, the produce per acre of almost every crop that is returned is given as very much larger. For instance, taking the year 1893, I find that the return per acre for wheat was 20 per cent. more in Ireland than in England; for barley 25 per cent.; for oats 24 per cent. more per acre; for beans 80 per cent. more per acre.

6860. Nearly double?—The exact figures are: Beans in England, 19·39 bushels; in Ireland, 35·85. I would imagine it is a misprint, but it is here.

6861. No, is it not a misprint; I have the previous year's report before me?—Then in peas Ireland is returned as growing less. Then potatoes, as to which one might have expected we grow more, we were returned as growing 30 per cent. less per acre. Turnips, which are particularly well cultivated in England, we were returned as growing 20 per cent. more, and mangold and beet also 30 per cent. more.

6862. I would like to draw your attention to a more remarkable figure than any of them. In 1893 in England, an acre is returned as yielding 1·06 ton of hay, and in Ireland 2·6; that is double the yield?—Yes.

6863. (*Sir David Barbour.*) The figures you have given are from the 1893 return, are they not?—Yes.

6864. Was not 1893 a special year?—1893 was a special year.

6865. 1893 was a year of great drought in England but not to the same extent in Ireland?—Certainly, and that is indicated by the hay yield in England, which was only 1 ton per acre, while in Ireland it is put down at 2 tons; but I must remind you that the drought affected some parts of Ireland very much. South of my own district there was practically no hay.

6866. Is there the same difference in regard to other crops?—There is the same difference generally in other years. I will give you the figures, taking them at random. In 1891, in wheat the number of bushels per acre was 31·26 in England, 32·34 in Ireland; barley 34·14 per acre in England, 41·04 in Ireland; oats 38·77 in England, 44·50 bushels per acre in Ireland; beans 29·05 bushels per acre in England, 43·43 in Ireland. They are generally more.

6867. And you say you think these figures are not correct?—I may say I have no doubt about it.

6868. Are the English figures wrong?—I only know from the criticisms I see passed upon the English agricultural statistics, that they are very untrustworthy. They are collected in a different manner in the two countries, and from the way they are collected in Ireland they could not possibly be correct, or anything more than a guess; and that a bad guess.

6869. (*Mr. Sexton.*) Would it be too much to say that they wear an aspect of absurdity?—I think they are perfectly absurd, and anybody who is acquainted with the method by which they are collected would know that they could not be accurate, and that it is money wasted collecting them in that way.

Mode of collecting agricultural statistics.

6870. Will you kindly inform the Commission of the reasons for making that statement. Tell us what you know of the mode?—The agricultural statistics are collected yearly by the police. It is quite evident that people going round to get this information can only get it by asking the farmers. It is quite impossible for a constable visiting a district to see every farmer; he has to take a great deal of it on hearsay. I am quite aware that many farmers who have been farming on a largish scale in Ireland for 20 or 30 years have never been asked, therefore the information must have been derived from their neighbours. Farmers very often do not know how many acres they have of each crop. That is a remark I see made by the Superintendent of the Census in America even, where one would expect farmers would be likely to know. That is one difficulty they have in collecting agricultural statistics there. In Ireland many farmers do not know how many acres of each crop they have got.

Mr. Murrough O'Brien.

8 Mar. 1895.

Mode of collecting agricultural statistics.

6871. And if they do, in many cases they are not asked, are they?—Their neighbours may be asked; it is a mere matter of hearsay. A constable, even if he visited every field, could not tell by looking at a field how many acres there are in it. You cannot tell by looking at an undulating piece of ground, or even if it is plane, how many acres there are in it; it is a difficult thing to estimate.

6872. What do they do?—The constable visits the district, and he makes the best inquiry he can. He has got to fill up his sheet, and he does it, but that he returns with any accuracy these things I am perfectly certain he does not.

6873. How do they arrive at the number of stock?—In the same way. They could not see the stock, which are scattered all over the country, and they must do that by inquiry too. It would be much easier to perform the simplest of all statistical operations; that is, to take a census of the people by going round and inquiring from the neighbours how many people there were in a district, and how many children they had, but the result of an inquiry of that kind would be perfectly useless.

6874. The information would be more likely to be accurate about children than stock, would it not?—Just so; but I say if the same method were adopted it would lead to a perfectly valueless result, and it is still more so in these agricultural estimates. These estimates are given of the produce, but the most skilled farmers are very much astray as to their own forecast when they come to measure their harvest, and police constables going round and looking at the crops can form nothing but a general opinion that the country and the crops look well or ill.

6875. (*Chairman.*) For how many years have the police been in charge of the collection of these statistics?—For a number of years, but I could not say how long.

6876. (*Mr. Sexton.*) Is it anything unusual to settle the amounts of the crops and stock of the present year by a guess founded on the figures for the previous year?—I do not know how the figures can ever be got excepting by correcting the guess or the estimate of the previous year made on some general information.

6877. I think you have gone so far as to say that the money is thrown away?—I think the money spent in collecting these agricultural statistics is thrown away, and yet those statistics are made the foundation of reasoning by our legislators and statesmen.

6878. They have formed, I think, the foundation of the vice-regal speeches in Ireland for a number of years?—And the speeches of members of Parliament too.

6879. (*Sir David Barbour.*) How do you account for the fact that the returns, from your point of view, seem to always exaggerate the produce?—I do not know at all.

6880. (*Mr. Sexton.*) Figures collected in the manner you have described, if they can be called figures, form, do they not, the foundation not only of speeches of statesmen (which might be not so important) but of the evidence given at public inquiries by such officials as the Registrar General, and also the statements published in the Statistical Abstracts as to the produce of Ireland?—Certainly, the Registrar General has to collect this information with the machinery put at his disposal by the Government. The Registrar General is a very competent and able man at figures, and I am sure he does his best with the material given him to work with.

Registrar General's [illegible]

6881. We had him before us lately, and were impressed by his ability as an arithmetician, though

some of his conclusions seem to be open to question. For example, he handed in a paper showing an estimate of the income of the Irish agriculturists for the year 1885. In that estimate he made the gross produce of crops and stock amount to 64,000,000*l*. in that year, and he put down 14,000,000*l*. for milk and its products, nearly one-fourth of the whole income of Ireland derived from milk and its produce. He was questioned as to how he arrived at that enormous figure, and all he could tell us was that there were 1,400,000 milch cows in the country; he put down 10*l*. for each, and debited the Irish farmer in that way. What do you say to that?—The statement published in the paper, which is the same as what you have stated, astonished people in Ireland. I think there are some manifest corrections to be made in it. One is, that if there are 1,400,000 milch cows in Ireland, every milch cow does not produce milk that year; there is always a percentage of casualties, or misses, which I would put at 20 per cent. Then with reference to the milk of a cow being worth 10*l*. a year, it seems to me an enormous estimate. I have frequently collected information as to the price obtained for the milk of cows, and I have checked that with returns obtained from some of the butter factories in Ireland, and I think that 6*l*. per cow would be a much truer figure. The amount of milk given by a cow in the milking season would seldom exceed 500 gallons, and I do not see how 10*l*. a head could be got as an average for that. The only places we have estimates of a regular price for milk for, are the butter factories. These only deal with cows fed on good land, because it does not pay to keep a butter factory in bad land; you must have a considerable number of cows in the district around, and therefore the milk of the cows outside that district would not be so valuable.

6882. Instead, therefore of 14,000,000*l*. of income, you would put down about 8,000,000*l*., would you?—I could not give an opinion, because cows vary so enormously, some giving a very small quantity of milk, for which it is difficult to find a market, while others that are well fed, at considerable expense, yield a large return of milk. But I would say that that estimate of 14,000,000*l*. was more like double the proper figure.

6883. (*Chairman*.) Have you in this connexion had an opportunity of referring to the produce of Denmark and Holland, which are more analogous to Ireland?—Not as to the yield returned from each cow.

6884. But as to the value of the milk, butter, and cheese produced?—No, I have not.

6885. (*Mr. Sexton*.) What figure would you substitute for the 14,000,000*l*.?—I would not give any exact figure, but I say that 6*l*. a cow would appear to me to be a full estimate of the value of the milk.

6886. Then even if there were no casualties or misses, as you have expressed it, the total would be 8,000,000*l*., and not 14,000,000*l*., would it?—Yes.

6887. (*Lord Welby*.) Under milk you include all milk produce, I suppose; you take the value of the produce of the cow?—Certainly; that is to say, butter or milk, but I have taken the Registrar General's statement as referring only to milk.

6888. In reference to what the Chairman asked just now, do you know, speaking of what may be produced by a country like Denmark, that Denmark, which is a small country as compared with Ireland, actually sends to this country alone in butter 6,000,000*l*. sterling?—Really.

6889. Therefore, it shows, does it not, that the cow produce of a small country may be large, inasmuch as that does not include what she sends elsewhere and consumes at home?—I confined my inquiry to what might be produced from a single cow. I can imagine a person living in a town falling into a natural error, and thinking that the value of milk was a large sum when it is sold by retail at the door. No doubt the value of milk, including the carriage, and deducting the cost of the retail business, under these circumstances, would exceed 10*l*.

6890. (*Mr. Sexton*.) Denmark stands in a unique position with regard to butter, does it not?—It makes very good butter, I believe.

6891. And has applied itself in a special manner, really, to that industry. At any rate, your calculation is founded on the number of cows given by the Registrar General, and the amount per cow, is it not?—It is.

6892. So that there is no speculation in your calculation as to the number of cows?—No.

6893. Did you make any observation upon his estimate of the value of oats, which he gave as seven million and a quarter?—If you are referring to the estimate given of the value of oats in 1885, there seems to me to have been a mistake made there. The Registrar General said that he took the price of oats from Thom's Directory. The price of oats given for that year in Thom's Directory is oats per barrel of 14 stone from 1st November 1885 to 1st November 1886 (which would be the crop for 1885), 10*s*. 10*d*.; 10*s*. 10*d*. per barrel of 14 stone would be somewhat less than 5*s*. 2*d*. per cwt.; while the Registrar General's estimate for oats that year is taken at 6*s*. a cwt., although he refers to the figure in Thom's Directory. That would make a difference of about million and a half in that estimate as to oats.

6894. On the other side of the account he put down 11,000,000*l*. for rent, and he explained that by saying the rent and taxes (by which I assume he meant local rates), are estimated at 11,000,000*l*., by making a deduction from the total on Griffith's valuation in consideration of the valuation of towns, and adding roughly a certain amount for taxes. I ventured to suggest to him that the figure of 11,000,000*l*. was inflated. What do you say upon it?—I could not express any opinion, because I do not think there are materials for guiding us as to what the rent is of farming land alone in Ireland.

6895. Do you think that the total agricultural rents of the country as they stand, together with the local rates, are represented by any such figure as 11,000,000*l*.?—I do not think I could give an opinion within 2,000,000*l*. or 3,000,000*l*., but I should say that probably 10,000,000*l*. is a common estimate for the rent of farming land. But unless you define what are urban areas and what is meant by farming land, whether it includes parks and pleasure grounds, I think it would be impossible to give a figure. If this calculation is meant to show what expenses farmers are at, to be deducted from their gross produce, you would, of course, have to add the taxes.

6896. Would you have any objection to send the Commission a memorandum of observations upon the estimate made by Dr. Grimshaw as to the income of an agriculturist in 1885 if you have any further observations to make?—I do not think I could undertake to do that.

6897. You have adverted to the fact that in the Act of Union the produce of income tax was designated as the best test of relative taxable capacity—produce you will observe—not the assessment. I believe the test afforded by produce puts Ireland lower in the scale of comparison than the test afforded by assessment, does it not?—Somewhat lower. Taxable capacity.

6898. Taking the assessment, I believe it is right to say, is it not, that the capacity of Ireland to bear taxation, as indicated by the income tax assessment, is about 4 per cent. of the capacity of England?—About that. I have given the figures as indicated by the assessments in the returns laid before me.

6899. And the same capacity is indicated, I think by the other direct taxes, such as stamps, is it not?—Yes, I think about the same figure is indicated.

6900. Is it the case that all the taxes taken together except those upon articles of consumption, indicate the same capacity, about 4 per cent. taking the assessment as it stands?—I think about that.

6901. If the proportions fixed by the Union had continued to operate to the end of 20 years, and if an income tax had then been in existence, the amount

Mr. Murrough O'Brien.

8 May 1895.

Estimate of Irish agricultural income.

tax would have been the test applied to determine the future taxation under the Act of Union, would it not? —Certainly.

6902. But it happened that by the proceedings connected with the debt, the arrangement of the Union was brought to an end in 1817, when income tax had not been imposed, and, therefore, that test was never brought into operation?—That is so.

6903. But it now indicates that the capacity of Ireland to bear taxation is about one-half which she has to bear at the present moment, does it not?—That is the conclusion I would draw from the figures unadjusted.

6904. Now you have given us grave cause to consider that they require adjustment, have you not?—I think with regard to the absentee rental, that income is English income, not Irish income.

6905. First, let us take the foundation of the matter. The rent in England is compared mainly with the Griffith valuation in Ireland, is it not?—Certainly.

6906. And the first figure that we reach in the English estimate is what is called gross estimated rental. Is that gross estimated rental the actual rent, or is it, as Mr. Giffen says, less than the actual rent? —I think it is less than the actual rent, because in the figures I gave you yesterday, we have some of the best authorities on the subject saying the rating is below the rent, where they have to estimate it. There are many cases where there is no rental; the owner is in occupation, and it is a self-assessed valuation to a large extent.

6907. Then the Irish valuation includes, does it not, a great part of the capital of the tenant invested in improvements on the land, which in England are made by the landlord?—There is no doubt that the valuation made in 1852 included everything on the land as it then stood, both the buildings, either good or bad, and everything that had been put up. They did not go into the question whether it had been improved by one person or another. It was not their function to determine a fair rent, and Sir John Ball Greene, in his evidence before the Richmond Commission, I think it was, stated that to be the case. But it is manifest from the law and the circumstances under which the valuation was conducted that the valuers did not fix fair rents, but that they fixed the letting value.

6908. The valuers valued the rents, and the rents being in Ireland upon a higher scale than in England, would you say, whether a landlord in Ireland is valued upon his valuation or upon his rent (for he has the option of taking whichever is the lower figure), that in either case the assessment is on a higher scale than what is called gross estimated rental in England?—I think that the valuation in Ireland is higher, as far as my inquiries into the matter have gone, than the assessment in England.

6909. Do you know of any other country in the world in which a system like that of Griffith's was applied to the valuation of land?—None whatever; in every country as to which I have inquired into the assessment system, they ascertain either what is the selling value of the land or what is its net letting value, and that is taken. In fact they record facts instead of prescribing what ought to be or what the officials deem should be the value.

6910. There is no such system in England or in Scotland, or in any other civilised country that you know of, is there?—Or in America, France, Switzerland, or Belgium, I believe.

6911. Did the Act of 1852 lay down any intelligent or intelligible plan of valuation?—It laid down a principle which I think could not be acted upon without giving more material. A theoretical calculation could be made, of course, of the produce of any farm, but all valuers are agreed that such a theoretical calculation is not a true guide to the value of land, for this reason, that the produce of every farm depends on the amount of capital with which it is worked. A man who is farming highly close to a town, may want to draw 60*l*. out of an acre of land before he gets a penny for himself. Another man may have a profit when he has produced 6*l*. an acre; therefore the produce of every farm depends largely on the amount of capital employed in working it, as well as on the skill and intelligence with which that capital is applied.

6912. The Act denoted nothing but prices, did it?—The Act denoted nothing but prices; it gave neither labour nor tax, nor the rate of interest to be allowed on the farmer's capital, all which are necessary factors in the sum that would have to be done.

6913. That may be partly due to the fact that, like other statutes, it was an Act passed in London to deal with an Irish question; it gave Griffith's staff no intelligible directions to put into the Act a scale of prices, but said no matter how many years the valuation occupies, when you are valuing you are to base your prices not on the prices of the time, but on the prices of 1852; is not that so?—Certainly, I imagine the system was an invention of Sir Richard Griffith.

6914. (*Chairman.*) Was not the system itself devised and recommended by Sir Richard Griffith?—Yes, I think so.

6915. It was not a London plan, was it?—It might have been suggested by Sir Richard Griffith, but I cannot imagine it would have been passed in Ireland if it could have been considered there. I do not suppose Irishmen had any hand in it.

6916. (*Mr. Sexton.*) Who was Sir Richard Griffith?—Sir Richard Griffith was a well known civil engineer and geologist of considerable note in Ireland.

6917. A scientific person, but not a land valuer?—Mr. Senior at the time drew attention to the absurdity of bringing in geological questions. You will find equally valuable soil on granite, on old sandstone, and on different geological formations, and therefore geology has nothing to do with the value of the land. It has something to do with the crops that may be growing, but the value of land depends upon other circumstances than the geological formation.

6918. (*Sir David Barbour.*) A knowledge of geology would not do him any harm if he were competent in other respects, would it?—Not the least; it would do him good.

6919. (*Mr. Sexton.*) But he had more to do with the surface of the earth than the interior?—I believe he was a very good geologist.

6920. (*Lord Welby.*) He was an engineer too, was he not?—He was an engineer.

6921. (*Mr. Sexton.*) As the Act gives no directions upon which any scheme can be founded, he set about making a scheme of his own, did he?—I presume he suggested that plan, but I cannot say how such a system came to be established.

6922. (*Lord Welby.*) I think you said just now that the value was based entirely on prices, but do you know that in the instructions issued in the Act it was stated that it was to be borne in mind that the letting value was to be taken as if the land were let to a solvent tenant?—Yes, but I do not think the system of valuing land and buildings separately led at all to an equitable valuation.

6923. That is not quite my question. I wish to call your attention to the fact that under the instructions issued to the valuers, prices were not to be the sole guide in fixing the valuation?—Under the Act the valuation was to be made according to the scale of prices, but as I have said, I believe what was really done was simply to record roughly the rents paid, and that Griffith's valuation may be taken as a rough record of the rents paid at the time it was made.

6924. Therefore, we should not be quite correct, should we, in saying it was based entirely on that schedule of prices, but that it was only an element?—I merely refer to the fact that the Act prescribes it should be made in that way, and no other.

6925. (*Sir David Barbour.*) If it was a record of the rents paid at the time, would not that show that for that time it was a fair valuation?—Certainly.

Mr. Murrough O'Brien.

4 Nov. 1893.

Valuation of land and houses.

but what a state England would be in if you had to work on a valuation which was made 40 years ago.

6926. (*Mr. Sexton.*) He instructed his valuers to record the rents, did he?—I do not say he instructed them. As a matter of fact, we know they followed the rents, and part of the information to be obtained by them was the rents payable. In fact, they could not have gone about the business without that.

6927. What did a fair letting value mean at that time? Did not it mean whatever a landlord could get from a tenant?—Certainly.

6928. There was no check on his will?—None.

6929. The population of Ireland at the beginning of Griffith's valuation must have been approaching to 8,000,000 must it not, and even up to 1864, when the valuation closed, it must have been 6,000,000, and there must have been a very intense competition for land?—There was, but the diminution during the time that the valuation went on did not affect the North of Ireland so very much; and one reason why the North of Ireland valuation is admitted to be higher than that in the south (I do not think it always is so, but in some cases it is) was that the linen industry and hand-loom weaving had been prevalent in the greater part of the North of Ireland for more than 100 years, and in the more prosperous times of that industry, people lived not by what they made out of the land, but by what they made by their looms. A man could easily earn 1*l.* a week then by his loom, and work on the land as well, and that led to the rents always being very high in the North of Ireland.

6930. (*Sir David Barbour.*) That hand weaving has ceased now, has it not?—It has not ceased, but it has practically ceased—there is some going on now.

6931. It has practically ceased for a long time?—For a long time.

6932. (*Mr. Sexton.*) Apart from the special case of Ulster, the rents everywhere were higher, were they not, at the period of the valuation?—I think the rents were high, but in some cases they became low in comparison with the value of the land where there were any extensive reclamations, for instance, some of the mountain land which has been cultivated.

6933. Take the ordinary case?—In the ordinary case I think the rents were high.

6934. Therefore in following the rents and in making the valuation, a rough record of the rent, the valuers did not assign to the land anything so low as what would be called its fair letting value now, did they?—No such expression was known in Ireland at the time.

6935. And if it had been known it would have had no such meaning as we attach to it, would it?—I do not suppose anyone foresaw a fair rent in those days.

6936. (*Lord Welby.*) I have not the actual words here, but I think the instructions mentioned "a fair letting value," did they not?—I could not say what the exact words were.

6937. This happened a long time ago, and there are very few persons living now, I suppose, who know how Griffith made his valuation. In answer to Mr. Sexton's question about the fair letting value, you said the phrase was not known, but I have it here before me?—I meant in the present sense. I have met a great many people who saw the valuation being made, and questioned them closely, and there is no doubt it was a very rough-and-ready procedure. Many people say that the valuer would stand in the middle of a valley and value the land all round. That has led to great inequalities. The valuation was made in a great hurry, by men who were insufficiently paid, and the result is, you find, where land is variable and broken up, an equal acreable rent is put on good and bad land alike, because, as I gather, a general view was taken of a place, and so much an acre put all round in many instances.

6938. (*Mr. Sexton.*) They recorded the existing rents, did they?—To a large extent.

6939. And to a large extent followed them?—Yes.

6940. The existing rents were the rents which landlords could obtain in a country where the pressure of the population made competition keen?—Certainly; the rent was fixed in a different method to what it is now.

6941. Sir Richard Griffith was a Treasury officer making a valuation upon which the assessment for income tax was to be founded, was he not?—That is so.

6942. What was the natural effect of that position. Was it not to induce Sir Richard and his staff to take care that the valuation was not any lower than they felt they could make it?—I do not think I can go into the question of what Sir Richard Griffith's relations with the Treasury were, but I think that a valuation made under those circumstances would probably be different from one made by local authorities.

6943. (*Lord Welby.*) In analysing that valuation it should be borne in mind that primarily it was intended for the levying of local taxation. In 1852, when the Valuation Act was passed, there was no Imperial property tax in Ireland, therefore it was rather difficult for Sir Richard Griffith to make his valuation with a view to a tax which did not exist, was it not?—The valuation went on until 1864.

6944. (*Mr. Sexton.*) Therefore eleven-twelfths of the valuation was conducted after income tax had been legalised, imposed, and levied, was it not?—May I give you a quotation here, which I think you asked me for, of Sir John Ball Greene to the Richmond Royal Commission on Agriculture. At question 28,114 he was asked, "No question was entertained as to whether "the improvements, buildings, or other permanent "improvements had been erected by the landlords or "tenants"; and the answer is, "No, we took them as "we found them, without inquiry as to whose "expense they were constructed at." Then the next question is, "Therefore the tenant's outlay is included "in the tenant's valuation?—Yes."

6945. Who devised the system of valuing the land and buildings separately?—I think that that was probably found convenient for statistical purposes for recording the number of houses, but I do not know whether Griffith invented it or not.

6946. What possible reason is there for valuing an agricultural house (that is, a house upon a farm), except at its letting or selling value as an agricultural house, which is neither let nor sold, except with the farm?—Lord Farrer has pointed out in his book on Mr. Goschen's Finance the great difficulty there is in valuing land and houses separately, because he says the ultimate basis of a valuer's knowledge must always be actual sales and lettings, and where land and houses are inseparably connected, as they are in the case of a farm, I think it leads to a very untrue result to put a value upon each separately. In London the question has been very much discussed, as Lord Farrer pointed out. Some valuers say they can do it, and others say they cannot; it is much easier to do it in London because you can ascertain what a site is worth, and land is let separately, and therefore there is some basis to go upon, but with respect to farms I do not think there is, and it is an untrue system.

6947. If a house in a town, or a house unconnected with agricultural land is to be valued, you would probably have some means of ascertaining what that house or such a house would let or sell for, and you have a basis of valuing?—Certainly.

6948. But in the case of houses on farms in Ireland, is there any basis of valuing a house separate from the land?—None. In most cases the house could not be let without the land; in many cases the land might be let without the house, but often it could not.

6949. According to the system of the Land Commission, of which you are one of the heads, you divide a farm according to the different qualities of land, do you not, and then assign an acreable rate to each acre of the farm. That acreable rate is founded, of course, upon the assumed value of the produce, is it not?—In many cases it is.

Mr. Murrough O'Brien. 1 May 1895. Valuation of land and houses.

6950. If the saleable rate is founded upon the value of the produce, the value of the produce of course includes the value of the buildings as well as the value of the land?—Of course the produce in a tillage farm or a dairy farm could not be obtained without the use of the necessary farm buildings. In the case of land of some qualities, prime feeding land, which is only used in summer, there is no occasion for buildings, except so far as tenants may require them for residence. A farm of that kind is just as profitable without a house, because there is no expense in maintaining buildings upon it.

6951. Taking the ordinary case where equipments and buildings are necessary to the working of a holding, the saleable rate founded on the value of the produce must have as much relation to the value of the buildings as to the value of the land, the buildings being an essential part of the working of the farm?—Of course.

6952. (*Sir David Barbour.*) Do you value a farm at the same rate whether the farm buildings are good or bad?—Certainly not. I think that on a farm where buildings are required, it is very important that the buildings should be suitable; at the same time I do not think that the buildings necessarily add to the profit derived from the farm. For instance, a man may have a good farm and live in a bad dwelling-house. If he has a better dwelling-house that costs a good deal, but he would live more comfortably.

6953. It is important for a farm to have good out-houses, is it not?—Certainly.

6954. And it makes a difference in the value of the farm?—Certainly.

6955. (*Mr. Sexton.*) Does it not appear that, by a system founded upon a principle, the conception of the mind of Sir Richard Griffith, that there is a prospect that the land will be first valued in such a way as to include a portion of the value of the buildings, and whilst you affect to ignore the buildings if they belong to the tenant they are substantially included in the value, and when they belong to the landlord there is a prospect that they may be added twice in the rent?—I think where the valuation is stated to be founded upon the produce there is great danger of that, and therefore it is a system I object to, and I think it is a great fault in Griffith's valuation. I think the houses might have been separately classified for any statistical purposes, but to put a valuation on the buildings and on the land separately was a mistake.

6956. Do you think that the system of valuation in Ireland should conform to the system of England, of Scotland, and of every other country, that land and buildings should be valued together as a unit in the first instance, and any adjustments or deductions requisite be afterwards made?—Certainly; I think the proper system is to value the whole farm as it stands, and then, with respect to a fair rent or repairs, to make any necessary deductions. It would save an enormous sum to Ireland if the system was adopted of recording the full letting value of every farm and making that hereafter the basis of the valuation as a substitute for Griffith's. The inequality of taxation arising from Griffith's valuation is now very great, and is a very crying evil.

6957. Do you mean from the Imperial point of view, as between one county and another?—For all purposes, and I say that if advantage was taken of the proceedings before the Land Commission to value on that system, to set out the full letting value of the farm as a basis for the future taxable value, it would save the cost of a new valuation of Ireland, which would probably amount to half a million.

6958. Do you think a valuation could be made in the way you say; do you think it would be worth while doing it?—Yes, I think it would; for I think inequality in taxation is a very great grievance, and I think it may be done in the way I suggest at very small expense.

6959. I should like to ask you whether if the operation of the Land Commission Courts were applied to the whole rental of Ireland upon the basis of the present prices, as they have been to almost half the rental of Ireland already, and if the reductions given since the great fall in values were applied to the whole rental of Ireland now, you have any doubt that the fair rate fixed by you, which you suggest as a foundation for future assessment, would be materially lower than the Griffith's valuation all over Ireland?—I do not suggest the fair rent to be fixed by the Land Court as the value for assessment. I say that the Land Commission, in fixing fair rents, should set out, as you propose, the full letting value of the farm as it stands. That should be the basis for taxation, possibly with an allowance for maintenance, which would vary according to the quality of the buildings.

6960. Judging of the course of rent reductions in rent since 1881, if the scale of reductions since 1881 were now applied to the whole rental of Ireland, what effect, in your judgment, would it produce in relation to the existing valuation?—I think that the existing valuation would be lowered.

6961. How much lower would the rents so fixed be than the valuation of Ireland as it stands?—I could not say how much, but I have no doubt that if the land were now valued for the purpose of taxation at its full letting value, less an allowance for maintenance and repairs, that Griffith's valuation for assessment, so far as agricultural land goes, would be reduced.

6962. Substantially reduced?—I would expect it to be substantially reduced; in some districts very much.

6963. I think you have told us that the prices ruling in 1854, when this valuation was completed, were upon the whole from a third to a fourth higher than they are now?—They were considerably higher.

6964. And the cost of labour has greatly risen since, has it not?—The cost of labour has increased, and taxation has increased.

6965. For these three reasons, apart from what you have just said, a valuation conducted now would necessitate a heavy reduction upon that of 1851, would it not?—But you must remember that these were not the prices given in the scale in the Act. These prices, I think—in fact the current rents, which, no doubt, were affected by those prices—were really taken as the valuation, and, for that reason, I say, it has always been admitted by the Valuation Office Authorities that the valuation was higher at the end of their proceedings than at the beginning.

6966. There was a currency also current in all the values, was there not, from 1852 to 1854?—There was.

6967. The rents for the latter years of the period approximated far more, did they not, to those later prices than the prices in the Act?—There were a number of reasons (amongst others the existence of the tenant-right custom in the North of Ireland) which led to the rents of that part being very much higher than in some others.

6968. It is admitted that the English assessment has fallen by about 15,000,000*l.* since 1880?—I think it has fallen more than 15,000,000*l.* I think it is over 18,000,000*l.* according to the last report of the Inland Revenue.

6969. My return goes up to 1893, and the difference is from 52,000,000*l.* to 41,000,000*l.*—about 11,000,000*l.* It is argued here, however, that although the Irish valuation (which has not been revised since 1851) would, if revised now, have to be reduced proportionately to the English valuation at least, in consequence of the fall in values since 1880, that as it was not revised during the earlier and prosperous years from 1854 to 1880, when, if it had been revised, it would have undergone an increase, that the decrease due to the fall in price since 1880 would leave the valuation very much where it is at present; what do you say to that argument?—I do not think that is the case, because the prices of some produce were higher even in the earlier part of the period during which the valuation was conducted. For instance, during the Crimean War wheat was

Mr. Murrough O'Brien. 4 May 1895. Valuation of land and houses.

at a very high price, and at that time we grew a large quantity in Ireland. In the years 1844 and 1845, for instance, Ireland exported 2,000,000*l*. worth of wheat to England, and wheat continued to be grown wherever it was profitable. During the Crimean War it was very profitable, indeed; I think it ran up to 80*l*. a ton. That affected the rents in all wheat-growing land.

6970. (*Lord Welby*). But the prices on which the valuation proceeded were those that were adopted at the time of the Act, were they not?—Yes, I am speaking of the rents, which I say were really roughly valued by the valuation.

6971. Mr. Sexton's question rather referred to the prices and the fact that they had gone up since 1865? —But more prices were high at the time of the Crimean War.

6972. (*Mr. Sexton.*) Lord Welby suggested that we should start from 1852, because the prices of 1852 were named in the Act. I put it to you that the rents in Ireland continually increased from 1852 to 1864, that the valuers followed the current prices and not the prices in the Act, and that much of the valuation of Ireland was influenced by the prices of the later years, which were much higher than they are now?—What I have said is that I believe the valuation followed the rents, the rents no doubt followed the prices. I have not got the figures before me, but of course the prices varied from year to year; I know that in the years of the Crimean War prices were very high, especially those for wheat. When you came on to the sixties, you had very high prices because of the flax industry in the North of Ireland, which was prospering then.

6973. On the point of the increase of the English valuation from 1864 to 1880 from 45,000,000*l*. to 52,000,000*l*., do you attribute that increase greatly to the extensive outlay made by English landlords in those 16 prosperous years on the equipment of the land?—My knowledge of the expenditure by English landlords of course is confined, as far as my own observation goes, to a very few cases, but the evidence given before the Agricultural Commission and the reports of the Assistant Commissioners who reported to that Commission, as to the expenditure on estates are most interesting. I gather that there has been a very very large expenditure on most English estates in the way of improvements, better equipments, and generally in expenditure that added to the letting value. But on the other hand it is stated with reference to some of these large estates, that, notwithstanding the large expenditure, the addition to the rent was very trifling. Therefore I do not know that the rents of farms were very much raised. I think that the total English valuation kept rising because of the great increase in the value of urban property, the continual piling up of the rateable values (they having always been very low) and large railway concerns and other works of that kind to which I referred yesterday. I think that piled up the assessment, for the evidence is that notwithstanding the very large expenditure by the English landlords, they charged no interest on it.

6974. To some extent what you call an enormous expenditure by the landlords might have affected the assessment, but chiefly it would have been brought up by the great accretion of population in towns and cities adding to the value of the land, would it not?—And the increase of urban properties generally.

6975. And no similar cause has operated in Ireland has it?—The opposite causes were in operation in Ireland, because all our towns have been decaying.

6976. And all our landlords have made no improvements, or nearly all of them?—Quite so.

6977. You do not assent, then, do you, to the proposition that the valuation of Ireland, if revised between 1864 and 1880, would have followed in any such forward course as the English valuation?—I do not think so.

6978. And therefore you maintain the position, do you, that the valuation of the valuation of Ireland between 1864 and now is not affected by the increase in the English valuation between 1864 and 1880, and no argument is to be drawn from that increase in England that a similar increase could have taken place in Ireland?—I do not think so.

6979. It is important that we should get from you clearly the result of these observations of yours upon the relative assessment of income tax as laid down in Appendix 32 to the Report of the Inland Revenue for 1894; Lord Welby has already called your attention to these figures. Have you got the report before you?—I think I put in a table which showed everything I had to say on the subject.

6980. Will you look at the table for a moment. In the comparison of the assessment to income tax between Great Britain and Ireland, we have first given to us the annual value of property for local assessments?—Yes.

6981. This is not without its importance, because Sir Edward Hamilton adds the amount of local taxation to the amount of Imperial taxation in order to make a final comparison, does he not?—Certainly.

6982. Now in England we have the total gross estimated rental of all property rated together at 191,000,000*l*. in round numbers?—Yes.

6983. You say that that gross estimated rental is short of the actual rent, do you?—That is what I gather from the experts to whose statements and evidence I referred yesterday.

6984. It compares, however, with the poor rate valuation in Ireland, which, according to your testimony, is now substantially in excess of what any fair rent would be?—Yes.

6985. Then the next figure we come to is the total rateable value of all property rated, and that is only 159,000,000*l*. in England, showing a deduction of 32,000,000*l*., or one-sixth, from what is called the gross?—Certainly.

6986. And on the other hand there is no corresponding deduction in Ireland, but the full amount of Griffith's valuation is actually applied to the local rating, is it not?—That is so.

6987. Then we come to the next figure, the gross estimated rental of property rated, but not assessed under Schedule A., that is to say, actual rental in the country which is not made the subject of income tax, that is, 29,000,000*l*. out of 191,000,000*l*., or between one-sixth and one-seventh, while the corresponding Irish figure is only 582,000*l*., or say, about $\frac{1}{25}$th?—$\frac{1}{25}$th, I think.

6988. So that there we have rental in England kept out of Schedule A. to the extent of 29,000,000*l*., where the corresponding rental in Ireland kept out of Schedule A. and therefore relieved from income tax, is only 500,000*l*. Then we come to the gross estimated rental of property rated and assessed under Schedule A.; that is in England 162,000,000*l*., is it not?—162,000,000*l*.

6989. Yes, the gross annual value of property rated to Schedule A. is 162,000,000*l*. in England, and in Ireland 13,612,000*l*., so that in England 29,000,000*l*., or one-sixth, is taken off the gross estimated rental in order to come to the income tax assessment, whilst in Ireland only 500,000*l*., or about $\frac{1}{25}$th is taken off. It therefore would appear, would it not, that the English gross estimated rental, although it is less than the true rental, has a deduction taken from it proportionately three times greater than the deduction from the excessive poor rate valuation, but higher than the rent in Ireland, in order to arrive at the income tax assessment?—That is what I think that table shows. I put in the table as a confirmation of the opinions I quoted yesterday.

6990. Then the deductions are 18,000,000*l*. in England, and only 900,000*l*. in Ireland. The net result is, gross estimated rental in England 191,000,000; amount made available for income tax assessment 150,000,000*l*., being 40,000,000*l*. taken off, or more than one-fifth of the gross; in Ireland, on the poor rate valuation, the gross is 14,190,000*l*.; amount made available to income tax 13,000,000*l*.; odd deduction

O 0 3

Mr. Murrough O'Brien. — 8 Mar. 1895. — Valuation of land and houses.

1,000,000*l*., or one-tenth off—one-tenth off the gross in Ireland, one-fifth off the gross in England, although the gross in England is less than the real rent and the valuation in Ireland is greater than the true rent; is that a just summary of the figures?—Yes, that is what I meant to convey by the table.

6991. For the reasons you have given, do you hold it to be essential to adjust the assessment before it can be made a basis of comparison of relative taxable capacity?—Certainly, I think that an adjustment should be made.

6992. Do you say that these agricultural Schedules A. and B. should have the Irish assessments reduced by one-fourth, with reference, firstly, to the higher assessment in Ireland than in England, and, secondly, to the fall in economic values since the valuation was made?—That seems to me a proper correction to make in order to compare the two valuations.

6993. Therefore off 15,300,000*l*., the gross amount of Schedules A. and B. in Ireland, you would take one-quarter, or 3,700,000*l*., to bring it to a level with the English assessment at the present time on the present prices; is that so?—That would bring it to about 11,600,000*l*.

Absenteeism.

6994. 11,600,000*l*. Then you come to the principle that the yield or assessment to income tax cannot be a fair test of taxable capacity between two countries unless so far as the income from which the tax is derived is spent in the country to which the tax is credited?—The income of the property held by absentees, I think, should properly be counted English income; in no sense is it Irish income except so far as it is lost to Ireland.

6995. Can you add anything to what you have said already upon the absentee rental?—I think I have under-estimated the absentee rental in putting it at 4,000,000*l*., but I admit the figures obtainable are not perfectly reliable. Absenteeism has been recognised as a very great economic evil in Ireland by every inquirer and visitor who has investigated the economic circumstances of Ireland. It has affected the prosperity of other countries, and led to disturbances there. I think the Chairman took part in putting an end to absenteeism in Prince Edwards Island, where the discontent arising from it had become very serious. But absenteeism in Ireland has continued for ages. Estimates have been made of it at various times. In Dalton's History of the County of Dublin, the amount of the absentee rental at different periods, according to the most approved authorities, is given in 1691 at 136,000*l*., the rental of Ireland being very small then, of course. In 1729 it was 627,799*l*.; in 1769 1,223,222*l*.; in 1804 3,000,000*l*.; in 1830 it was estimated at 4,000,000*l*., "and it is now, in 1838," he says "estimated nearer 5,000,000*l*."

6996. (*Chairman.*) Are these the whole of the absentee rents?—Those are the whole of the absentee rents so far as they could be estimated.

6997. (*Mr. Sexton.*) Of course you can not include in them, can you, the head rents payable by immediate lessors to the superior landlords?—There are many other payments of the same kind which it is difficult to ascertain, such as annuities to people living in England. These figures were supposed to represent merely the rental. That would be about a third of the rental of Ireland. Then if you take examples, one finds that that proportion is confirmed very much. Swift, in his day, said one-third of the rents of Ireland are spent in England, and, with other remittances, he says a full half of the income of the kingdom goes to England. Then Mr. Finlay Dun, who was a correspondent of the "Times" in the eighties, says in a book which he published on "Tenants in Ireland," "of the holders of estates exceeding 60 acres, about "one-third are absentees, who every year abstract "from their impoverished country upwards of "2,000,000*l*. The western counties are the strong-"hold of absenteeism. In Mayo, for example, nine "owners hold upwards of 20,000 acres each, amongst "them draw annually 100,000*l*. from this poor "western county, and spend not one-tenth of their "income on their estates." That would be about one-third of the rental of Mayo, the whole valuation in 1881 being 311,000. A return was furnished in 1872 of the absentee owners of properties in Ireland, which was known at the time to be very imperfect.

Mr. Murrough O'Brien. 8 Mar. 1895. Absenteeism.

6998. Was that a Parliamentary Return?—It was presented to the House of Commons on the 22nd of April 1872. I have only got a summary of it. The summary was given for years in Thom's Directory. It gives the absentee proprietors and their properties at 2,470,816*l*. That did not include public companies, and the greater part of the county of Derry was owned since the time of Charles I., I think, by London companies, who for many years drew almost the whole rental away from their estates. Most of them have sold now, but there still remains a residue of about 30,000*l*. a year, I think, owned by the companies exclusive of that belonging to the Irish society, who are supposed to spend their income for the benefit of the town of Derry. This return of two and a half millions worth of absentee rentals was confined to rural properties, out of a total valuation of 10,000,000*l*. I think it is reasonable to assume that a similar proportion of town properties was held, and taking a smaller proportion of the remaining valuation of Ireland, the amount of the absentee rental would be 3,431,716*l*. That is no doubt an under estimate, because the people who are set down as owners are the immediate lessors of the tenants. In many cases these men are paying superior rents to the original grantees, who live in England; therefore, that can only be taken as a minimum.

6999. I think I understood from you that you put the figure at 4,000,000*l*.?—I think I would be under the mark in deducting 4,000,000*l*., but, to be on the safe side, I put it down as 4,000,000*l*.

7,000. (*Chairman.*) That is 4,000,000*l*. out of how much, including the town properties?—That is 4,000,000*l*. out of 14,000,000*l*., which I take to be the valuation of the assessment of Ireland.

7001. (*Mr. Sexton.*) Swift's estimate of the proportion appears to have remained good, then?—I think it is pretty much the same.

7002. You are obliged, for want of information, to ignore the interest on mortgages held out of Ireland, and payments to incumbrancers generally, but without them you make a deduction of 4,000,000*l*., and under the two heads of "adjustments" (the fourth already stated and the 4,000,000*l*. now) you bring, do you not, the amount of assessments of Ireland under Schedules A. and B., for the purposes of this comparison, to 7,000,000*l*. a year?—Yes.

7003. And taking no note of the circumstance that under Schedule D., owing to the mass and volume of property in England, a great quantity of property escapes, you bring the total income tax assessment of Great Britain and Ireland in relation to this comparison as 1 to 31?—Yes, but as I say, I do not think I have sufficiently allowed for the absentee landlords. There is some information about mortgages. As we know, Irish mortgages in years gone by were a favourite investment for English capital, because the rate of interest was somewhat higher, and Mr. Giffen's evidence was that 14,000,000*l*. had been lost by the Insurance Companies alone. The total mortgage debt in Ireland has been estimated at various times as from 80,000,000*l*. to 120,000,000*l*., and it would be probably the same as many other countries; about half the value of the country is subject to mortgage, therefore I conclude, in addition to the 14,000,000*l*. which Mr. Giffen says the English Insurance Companies have lost in Ireland, a very much larger amount of money must be lost.

7004. Your calculation would have to be further adjusted by what might be ascertained to be the drain for mortgage interest, and for annuitants and other incumbrances, would it?—I think you could not ascertain it, but you could get materials for a guess.

7005. Do you think there would be any difficulty in getting from the Government, or the Courts in Ireland, a return of counties giving the names of the

Mr. Murrough O'Brien. 1 Dec. 1894.

immediate lessors with the area and valuation of their estates, and showing which have been for the last five years non-resident, and another return showing those who have been non-resident for, say, six months?—I should think it could be got, and it would enable this Commission to form an opinion of the subject.

7006. The Court of Chancery I believe can give a return of the properties under their control, with the valuation, rental, arrears, and so forth?—They could easily do that.

7007. Now you have brought us to the point at which Mr. Pitt's test, as deemed in the Act of Union, would give a relation of 1 to 31, without further adjustment being made, what do you say as to the incomes below the level of the income tax in Ireland, what would you be inclined to fix as the relation between the two countries as to incomes below the income tax level?—I think there could be no exact figure given in such a matter, but having regard to the well-known poverty and want of employment in Ireland, the low rate of wages, the fact that we have no class corresponding with the well paid artizans and tradesmen in this country, I think that $\frac{1}{60}$th would probably be the figure.

7008. The two elements, therefore, are 1 to 31 with regard to income tax, and 1 to 60 with regard to the community below the income tax level?—Yes.

7009. (*Lord Welby.*) Upon what do you base 1 to 60; what ground have you got for fixing that figure?—I take the probable earnings of the wage-earning classes and Mr. Giffen's estimate of the income and capital per head in Ireland, which I quoted to you when I was examined in Dublin.

7010. (*Mr. Sexton.*) He gave the average Irish income at 14l. and the average English income at 30l., did he not?—I think so.

7011. You deduct from that a subsistence allowance of 10l. each, which gives the taxable income of the Irishman as 4l. and that of the Englishman as 20l., or a proportion of 1 to 7?—Yes.

7012. That one-seventh, multiplied by a population which is only one-seventh, brings it up to $\frac{1}{49}$th or so, does it not?—Yes.

7013. Mr. Giffen's result was that the taxable capacity of Ireland, taken altogether, was about 1 to 53?—I think that was his figure.

7014. Have you observed that the Registrar General, Dr. Grimshaw, notwithstanding the observations which are to be made about the way in which he has inflated the income and reduced the expenditure side of the account for the Irish farmer, only gives a total income of 35,000,000l. for the whole agricultural population of Ireland; that is about 10l. a head?—I have not gone into the Registrar General's figures except as regards the cows and sows, which appeared to me to be rather remarkable.

7015. But you do adopt the principle and the calculation of Mr. Giffen, do you not?—Yes; I think his estimate seems a reasonable one.

7016. And is higher than that made by the Registrar General?—Except that, with regard to Mr. Giffen's estimate, it must be remembered that since he made it in 1883 Ireland has been losing ground in comparison with England. That, I thought, Mr. Giffen pointed out, but the losing of ground, I think, has been continued.

7017. So that a further estimate made now upon the same basis as he used 10 years ago would probably put us in a lower relation, would it?—I should imagine, following out Mr. Giffen's lines, it would, because our chief industry, agriculture, has become less and less prosperous.

Economic drain.

7018. Such being the results of the comparison upon the basis of income tax assessment and of taxable income to the population generally, have you made any calculation of what may be called the economic drain out of Ireland in addition to the taxation; and, if so, will you state it briefly to the Commission?—There are several payments on other accounts, which, I think, should be taken into account (for some of which there is some small return to Ireland and for others none) in addition to the absentee rental drain.

7019. Which you put at how much?—3,431,716l. according to the minimum amount we know, but which I think should be put at 4,000,000l. or 5,000,000l. Then there is the interest, which I take at 4½ per cent., on the English insurance companies' mortgages, estimated at 14,000,000l. That would be 630,000l. There are then the items I referred to yesterday—the average amount of interest paid yearly on the Church Fund, 219,824l.; the average annual repayment on capital for the last 12 years, 379,766l.; there are then the annual payments in respect of the Board of Works and public works' loans, 265,137l., for interest, according to Mr. Smith Barry's return in 1890, and 430,000l. repayment of capital. Of course, any benefit derivable from the expenditure of these loans is represented in the valuation returns, most of them having been spent upon the improvement of real property.

7020. (*Lord Welby.*) But the valuation is not changed, and that would not come in?—Certainly, because a large part of this is spent upon new buildings.

7021. But I think we must take that very carefully. We should know exactly what proportion has gone on new buildings, should we not?—Certainly. However, a considerable amount of it is spent not only on buildings, but in so far as it is spent in public works, it affects the present rental value of the country.

7022. (*Mr. Sexton.*) It goes to increase the income tax assessment, does it not?—Yes. Then there are the quitrents, amounting to 40,000l., and then there are the land loan annuities, which I take at 4 per cent. on 12,000,000l. = 480,000l. The remittances to England in the way of deposits in the Post Office and trustees savings banks, increased in the last 21 half years by 2,887,000l.; that is, on an average 254,760l. goes to England yearly to be invested at 2¾ per cent.

7023. (*Sir David Barbour.*) Do I understand you to say that the greater the increase in the amount of money deposited in the Irish savings banks the greater the economic drain on Ireland?—I point this out as a payment that is made yearly from Ireland to England. I also point out that we get 2½ per cent. interest upon it, but, as I mentioned yesterday, the money is lent back again to us at 3¼ per cent.

7024. I merely ask you if you look upon the fact that there is so much money deposited by the Irish people in the Post Office Savings Banks every year as an economic drain?—What I suggested yesterday was that this money would be deposited in Ireland if we had not the highly centralised system under which we live. As it is, it is a remittance from Ireland to England. There is then the interest at 1 per cent. on the Post Office and trustee savings banks deposit, on which 2½ per cent. interest is paid to the depositor, while we pay 3¼ per cent. back to the National Debt Commissioners; 1 per cent. upon that would be 84,000l. Then there are other items which, if it were possible, should be exhibited as part of the drain upon Ireland. There is the extra cost of Irish private Bills in London. 30 years ago Jonathan Pim, the then member for Dublin, brought the expense of these proceedings before the House of Commons. His estimate then was that the cost of proceedings in Parliament were about five times as much as they need be if they were conducted in Ireland, as he suggested.

7025. You show a total economic drain of about 8,000,000l. a year?—About that.

7026. The Imperial taxation, even as adjusted by the Treasury, is about 7,000,000l.; that makes 15,000,000l.?—Yes.

7027. The local taxation is about 3,000,000l., is it not?—Yes.

7028. That is 18,000,000l. a year in a country where the taxable income (that is, the total income, after a minimum allowance for subsistence) is 15,000,000l. a year according to Mr. Giffen?—I Taxable capacity.

4 Mar. 1895.

Taxable capacity.

understood Mr. Giffen's statement was that the whole taxable income of Ireland was absorbed.

7029. His statement was that the taxable income was about 15,000,000*l*. You have now shown, if you add together the Imperial and local revenue of 10,000,000*l*. and the economic drain of 5,000,000*l*., that it exceeds the revenue, and you say forms ground for the presumption that these levies trench upon what ought to be the means of subsistence?—I am sure they do.

7030. That necessitates a condition of chronic poverty, does it not?—Yes, which every visitor to Ireland is aware of, and I should think the Government of the country, too, because they are annually called upon to make loans to avert distress and famine and misery of one kind or another.

7031. Whilst that fiscal, economic, and financial condition prevails, do you think we ever can in Ireland be rid of the grinding poverty or the bare discontent which, according to human nature, must accompany it?—I do not think so. I think Mr. Giffen's statement that under the existing condition of things there can be no accumulation of capital in Ireland, is correct.

7032. You know, do you not, as the Treasury computation, by which the revenue of Ireland, collected at 9,000,000*l*., is adjusted down to about 7,000,000*l*., but as Lord Welby pointed out, there is no doubt if there were separate fiscal systems England would levy her excise duties in her own ports?—But I propose there should not be any separate fiscal systems, and you must remember if there were it would be the same thing, for we should levy duty on goods imported from England; therefore I do not think the observation was exactly applicable to my remark. I say each country should be credited with the capital which its enterprise raises. If the countries were separate, and England levied duties on Irish whiskeys and tobaccos, Ireland might do the same on other articles in return, but I should be very sorry to see any such course adopted.

7033. (*Mr. Sexton.*) Of course you are aware, so far as the adjustment of revenue of 9,000,000*l*. down to 7,000,000*l*. is concerned, the Treasury do what they please, and we have no means whatever of ascertaining on what basis they proceed, or whether their conclusions are correct?—I do not impute any unfair motives to the Treasury; I merely do not know how these adjustments are made. I believe they are explained in a memorandum which I must say I do not quite understand, because it is partly guesses and partly returns from traders.

7034. In reference to your argument that the trade of a country being developed by the enterprise of its manufacturers and merchants, by the efficiency of its local authorities and their expenditure, it would not be too much to expect that this revenue might be attributed to Ireland. I suppose you are aware that Mr. Gladstone in his speech on the Home Rule Bill of 1886 directly stated that, having regard to all that had happened, the amount of revenue on goods duty paid in Ireland, but consumed in Great Britain, might be equitably allowed as part of the revenue of Ireland?—I was not aware of the statement.

7035. You apply two tests to this question of capacity to bear taxation. You say it ought to depend first of all upon how much each country is able to pay, and, secondly, upon what proportional benefit each country receives from the public expenditure. Could you undertake at your leisure to go through the Treasury classification of expenditure with regard to the Irish Imperial contribution, and give us the benefit of your observations?—I regret to say I have very little leisure, and I do not think I could undertake to do it.

7036. You are a very striking illustration of the fact that the busiest man can find leisure more than the idle man. You have devoted yourself very efficiently to this study with which we are concerned. I will take the question of relative capacity now, and I would ask you, as a concluding question, what you would think, as the result of your evidence, Ireland could fairly be called upon to pay towards Imperial expenditure, first, upon the basis of the present system of payment into a common purse, secondly, upon the Home Rule basis, what her payment ought to be to Imperial charges out of a separate exchequer, which would have to bear the cost of Irish administration?—I do not know that I can give you a direct answer to that, because it would depend upon whether credit is to be given to Ireland for what I believe to be her past over-payments. These seem to me to amount to an enormous sum, and as a mere matter of justice I do not think any contribution whatever is due from Ireland to England [illegible] account of the over-payments for many years.

7037. Will you remind us of them?—I say for the last 25 years you may take it at 4,000,000*l*. a year, and at the beginning of the century it evidently was more than her present proportion, because it reduced Ireland to bankruptcy. However, I do not look upon that as anything except a theoretical opinion that England is in Ireland's debt. With regard to the amount that should be paid, I think some weight should be given to that opinion, and the theory of union between the two countries is just as fully preserved by a small payment as by a large one. According to the Treasury figures, Ireland is worth very little more to the Treasury than 2,000,000*l*. a year, or not quite that just now. It seems to me that if we contribute—I can only give an approximate opinion—a million to a million and a half for such Imperial services as we require, that is to say, the little requirements we have for defence, the very little requirements we have in connexion with foreign missions and postal services, which I think is also an Imperial matter, that these would be amply covered for Ireland by the payment of a million and a half.

7038. That is to say, assuming the present system to continue?—Assuming the present system to continue, and that any extra expense arising from the Imperial control of local affairs should be borne by the Empire, and not by the Irish revenue.

7039. (*Chairman.*) In two words, that Ireland should pay, out of her own revenues, her own expenditure, and contribute a million or a million and a half to the common fund?—That is so.

7040. (*Mr. Sexton.*) In the event of the establishment of a separate Legislature and a separate exchequer, of course they would then have the fixing of the amount of the Irish revenue, and out of that, whatever it was, you would have them pay a million and a half as a contribution to Imperial affairs?—It would depend on what was settled as being common objects of expenditure, and what proportion of benefit we derived from those common objects. I do not think I should like to give an opinion on a state of affairs that has not arisen.

7041. Would you say a general proportion of 1 to 60, qualified by what might be found to be the benefit derived from the Imperial expenditure?—Certainly.

7042. (*Sir David Barbour.*) You said, in answer to Mr. Sexton, that the amount of taxation in Ireland before the Union was very light, and the amount of revenue was small?—I have not the exact figures, but I have read them, and I believe that to be the case generally.

7043. No doubt you are aware that immediately before the Union the Irish expenditure was much higher than the Irish revenue?—I think that was due to the civil disturbances in Ireland.

7044. And the French War?—Which we have to pay for.

7045. But it was considerably higher—I merely want the fact. I do not know whether your attention has been called to a return showing the rate of increase of the Irish Debt for some time immediately before the Union, and immediately after the Union?—No, I have not got those figures before me.

7046. Because I find that the increase of the Irish Debt in the four years immediately preceding the

Union was 22 millions sterling, and in the four years immediately succeeding, it was not quite 18 millions sterling?—The four years preceding the Union were the years of the Irish Rebellion—two of them at any rate—the Rebellion was in 1798, and there was a very large expenditure then. I imagine it was put down by British troops; I think there were 200,000 British troops in Ireland, and we had to pay the expense of it.

7047. I merely point out that the rate of increase for the four years preceding the Union was greater than for the four years succeeding the Union. It may no doubt be due to the cause you mention?—Yes.

7048. I think you gave rather a low estimate of the character of the Irish Parliament just before the Union, did you not?—I quoted Macaulay's description of it, according to my recollection.

7049. And you quoted it with approval, did you not?—I quoted it to show that I do not look on the management of the country at that time as a precedent to be followed now.

7050. And the state of Ireland before the Union, I suppose you will admit was very unsatisfactory?—Very unsatisfactory, I think.

7051. Ireland at that time suffered from certain commercial disadvantages, did she not?—I do not know the dates of either the passing or the repeal of the laws which interfered with Ireland's commerce.

7052. Some of the laws had been repealed before that, and some of them existed, did they not?—No doubt.

7053. So that at that time there were some grounds for a union. The state of affairs was not satisfactory at the time the union was carried was it? Perhaps there may have been a better way to remedy the evils, but there were evils to be remedied, were there not?—"Satisfactory" is ambiguous—satisfactory to whom?

7054. I suppose the state of things just before the Union would be hardly satisfactory to anybody to look back upon?—No doubt it was an unsatisfactory state of affairs, but whether Ireland let alone could not have worked out her own salvation or not, I am not prepared to give an opinion; probably she would as every modern nation has done.

7055. There was a state of affairs existing, was there not, calling for some remedy?—Certainly, but the state of affairs was very bad all over the world at that time.

7056. I do not know whether you are aware that the avowed object of the Union was to bring about ultimately indiscriminate taxation, and a common exchequer?—I do not know. Whose object?

7057. The object of the British Government of the day as expressed, first, by Mr. Pitt, and secondly by Lord Castlereagh?—Yes, but I think the Irish people had a right to be consulted in accepting Mr. Pitt's or Lord Castlereagh's object.

7058. That may be, but I merely wish to bring out the fact that that was the avowed object. If I were to read to you what Lord Castlereagh said would you accept it as showing what the object was?—I should accept it, and I think it was a very great advantage to England to obtain the revenue of Ireland as a contribution to Imperial expenses.

7059. I should like to read you what Lord Castlereagh said when the matter was first discussed in the Irish House of Commons: "Were our entire expenditure common (which would happen if neither kingdom had any separate debts, or if their debts were in proportion to the ability) by no system whatever could they be made to contribute so strictly according to their means, as by being subject to the same taxes equally bearing upon the great objects of taxation in both countries." There you see Lord Castlereagh says that the fairest system of getting a contribution in proportion to the means of each country would be to make each country subject to the same taxes equally bearing on the great objects of taxation in both countries?—Very different ideas prevailed at that time as to the principle on which taxation should be levied from those which are current now-a-days; and many hopes and inducements were held out by Lord Castlereagh and the people who promoted the Union, which were not fulfilled.

7060. It has been stated that Lord Castlereagh said the best test of the ability of the two countries would be the produce of an income tax?—I think he said that in another speech.

7061. No, in the same speech. What he quoted was this; he said, the best test would be the same tax equally applied in both countries; such a system not being possible at the time, he cast about for the best criterion of the ability of the two countries, and took first of all income tax?—Yes.

7062. And after that, not having an income tax at the time, he took what he called the combined result of commerce and consumption?—Quite so.

7063. I understand you hold that though the system of taxation is the same in both countries now, yet that system is unfair to Ireland owing to her being a much poorer country than England?—That is my opinion.

7064. I think you said yesterday you did not wish to see different rates of excise or customs duties?—I think customs barriers are a misfortune between any nations, and I should not like to see a custom-house between England and Ireland.

7065. You also said you looked on the income tax as a fair tax, did you not?—I think an income tax, properly levied, is one of the fairest, but I should like to see exemptions; to exempt a minimum required for subsistence, and I would like to see it graduated.

7066. The present minimum of 160l. is high enough, is it not?—I think it is.

7067. You did not express any opinion about the taxes on property such as death duties, but I presume you do not object to duties of that sort, which are paid in proportion to the amount of property?—Perhaps you would excuse me; I should not discuss questions of taxation, but I think if the revenue is to be levied, it is the only way they can get the money; otherwise, I think, taking money just at a time when a family loses its breadwinner is, to some extent, an objectionable thing.

7068. I think your opinion was this, practically, that you thought under a different system the Irish revenue might be economically spent and spent with greater advantage to Ireland?—There is no question it would be more economically spent.

7069. And with greater advantage to Ireland?—Yes.

7070. I think you expressed the opinion that Great Britain would not lose and Ireland would gain very greatly if there were some system by which the bulk of the Irish revenue was left in the hands of a body of Irish representatives?—I think people generally can manage their own concerns better than other people can manage them for them, and the disadvantage of Ireland is very great, because you have English statesmen and the higher English officials, with their minds taken up with the concerns of a vast empire extending all over the world, dealing with Irish affairs. Ireland is a mere trifle to it, and I say it with humility, that they err through ignorance not through intention.

7071. I suppose you will admit that the financial question is not the only one to be considered in connexion with any proposal for leaving the Irish revenue in the hands of Irish representatives?—It is one of the most important questions, because the business of Governments is raising money and spending it on objects of common want.

7072. One of the most important, but not the sole question, is it?—Not the sole question, but still a large one.

7073. At any rate, I imagine the question of leaving the Irish revenue in the hands of Irish representatives is not one before this Commission, is it?—Certainly; I should say—not from the Home Rule point of view—all matters that can be dealt with locally should

&c. Very great difficulties arise from mixing up local and Imperial taxation, and the system of giving subventions from the Imperial revenue in aid of local taxation is very embarrassing, and takes away responsibility and the motive for economy from local bodies.

7074. I cannot find in the terms of the reference anything about local management of Irish revenue. Do you think that the individual Irishman has anything to complain of in the matter of taxation as compared the individual Englishman having the same income?—Certainly; I stated that he does not get the same advantage from the expenditure.

7075. In what way?—I will take the one matter of legislation. Irish legislation, I would say, in many matters is 20 years behind English legislation. Our grand jury is different, our management system is different. What a state of confusion this country would be in if you were taxed on a valuation made 40 years ago. Then I considered the great expense attending private Bills, but that is not the only expense, because the Irish enterprises which are dealt with by private Bills are of a small character compared with the large English enterprises. The expense of a hearing in London is so heavy that it deters people from undertaking municipal improvements and enterprises such as are carried out in England every day with great advantage to the public. All these are matters in which I consider we are 20 years behind England in our legislation; therefore, I say that the control of every detail of local matters by the Imperial Parliament, which is occupied by the affairs of the Empire, is of enormous disadvantage to Ireland.

7076. Your argument is not that the Irishman is overtaxed, but that the arrangements for legislation and administration generally are defective, especially as regards Ireland, is it not?—I have not said that Irishmen are not overtaxed, and I think some classes are taxed heavier than other classes in proportion to their incomes.

7077. (*Lord Welby.*) There was some misunderstanding at the beginning of your evidence to-day on the subject of the houses in Ireland?—Yes.

7078. You alluded to some of those houses as farms and the nature of them, but a question arose as to the definition of the third class, which I presume is not a very good class. As the definition was not given, and so perhaps they might be mixed up with mud cabins, I want to define the third class of houses. They are houses with two to four rooms with windows, are they not, and so far they are not a class of houses to be confounded with the mud cabins?—I think the description given in the census is that it is a somewhat better class of house, with one to four rooms, with windows. There are very many miserable cabins in Ireland with, I admit, four rooms, and it says "from one to four." The words I have quoted are taken from the Census of 1891.

7079. Mr. Sexton spoke of Griffith as being a Treasury officer; as a matter of fact, when his valuation was made he was not a Treasury officer, but a purely Irish officer. The Treasury at that moment had nothing to do with the matter, and he was appointed purely by the Irish Government to carry out the work of local taxation, was he not?—We look upon almost every official in Ireland as being an officer of the Treasury, inasmuch as he is paid by the Treasury, and his salary and prospects, so far as he is an official, depend upon the Treasury.

7080. That is not so. Mr. Sexton's question pointed to the idea that he was sent there by the Treasury to make a valuation with a view to Imperial taxation?—I did not understand that, but I understand that the Valuation Office now is a department of the Treasury; the Treasury controls them in everything.

7081. Mention has been made of Lord Castlereagh taking the income tax as the best test of the taxable capacity of the two countries. I want to call your attention to the fact that that is rather an academic opinion on his part, because practically, to all intents and purposes, there was no income tax at the time he said that, was there?—Quite so.

7082. Practically, neither Mr. Pitt nor Lord Castlereagh had any experience of the working of an income tax, and therefore I say it was an academic opinion upon a point on which he had no knowledge?—I suppose he was in advance of his time in recognising that the income tax was a good tax.

7083. But one must not put too much weight on a speculative opinion of that kind, must one? I think we have been rather confusing the matter, in that we, having an income tax, and being able to form an opinion on its value now, have attributed to Lord Castlereagh the same knowledge of its advantage. Then Mr. Sexton called your attention to the fact that property statistics wanted very careful analysing. We shall both be agreed, shall we not, that other statistics in the opposite direction want careful analysis as well?—I think it is necessary to understand how all statistics are collected before you can rely upon them.

7084. (*Lord Farrer.*) Especially if collected with a view to a particular object?—I do not know; for we you must take statistics which have been already prepared. If they are collected specially for an object, that is a different matter.

7085. (*Mr. Sexton.*) Will you hand in the paper which you have written on the matter, so that it may be subjected to the severest scrutiny which any member of the Commission desires to give it?—Yes.

7086. (*Chairman.*) In the Act of Union the prospect of testing the relative taxation and expenditure of England and Ireland on the income tax, or anything of that sort, was qualified, was it not, and there might be one of three methods, or a combination of three methods employed, the income tax being one, the exports and imports being the second, and the special duties on beer, spirits, sugar, wine, tea, tobacco, and malt in the two countries the third. Those three methods of division were laid down in the Seventh Article of the Act of Union, or any combination of them, were they not?—Certainly.

7087. So that it was not solely the income tax, was it?—No, but the extent of imports and exports has not been ascertainable.

7088. Since the abolition of internal custom-houses, of course that was impossible?—Nobody nowadays would dream of measuring the ability for taxation by a tax solely on articles of general consumption.

7089. What I meant was that in the Act of Union it was specially provided, was it not?—Yes, certainly.

(Adjourned for a short time.)

Mr. G. F. [illegible] called and examined.

7090. (*Chairman.*) You were in the English Income Tax Office, I believe, for some years, were you not?—I was for about [illegible] years.

7091. Did you then go to Dublin?—Yes, in June 1893.

7092. And you have been there in the Income Tax Office there, have you not?—Yes.

7093. You have therefore had rather unusual facilities for comparing the income tax system, both of assessment and collection, in Great Britain and Ireland, have you not?—That is so.

7094. Will you describe the method of making assessments under Schedule A. in England?—The Schedule A. assessments in England are made by a body of Commissioners called the Commissioners for the General Purposes of the Income Tax Act. At their first meeting in the year they appoint local assessors to act as assessors of income tax for the year then commencing. In years when a new assessment has to be made under Schedule A. they have a copy of the poor rate given them, together with forms of return, which it is their duty to serve on all occupiers of property within

the area for which they act. When they get these returns in, their duty is to examine them, and if not satisfied with the statement, if the statement is incomplete or wants amendment, they would have to return them to the persons who made the returns; but if they are satisfied they proceed to enter them in the columns provided for the purpose in the books of assessment. They would then go on to compare the amount of the actual rent where property is really let at a rack-rent with the gross poor rate upon such properties. If they find the gross poor rate really represents the full letting value, then in the case of properties that are not let, they would assess on the gross value in the poor rate assessment—not the rateable value, the gross value.

7095. (*Lord Welby.*) Then is in the case of the person occupying his own house, is it not?—That is so, but if an examination of the returns made in cases that are actually let at rack-rent shows that the gross poor rate is less than the real letting value, then their duty would be to reject the gross value entered in the poor rate, and to make an assessment upon such sum as in their judgment would represent the real letting value of the property as it stands at the time—the rack-rent value of the property including all improvements, no matter by whom those improvements were made.

7096. Then it is impossible, is it not, practically under that system, that any person should escape except by accident?—Except by human infirmity, which would render anything liable to mistake or accident. The system is intended to ensure that all property, whether the owner occupies or lets it, should be assessed up to the full rack-rent value.

7097. Have you often known of cases of assessment under Schedule A. in excess of the rent?—I have made them by the hundred myself. When the assessors have finished their work they bring their books in to the commissioners, and after that the books and the returns are handed to the surveyors of taxes; the surveyors of taxes are not local officers, they are permanent officials appointed by the Treasury, and the duty of a surveyor is to take all these returns and assessments and to go through them carefully and check them. In every case where the surveyor is of opinion that the assessor has failed to charge property up to its full value, it then becomes the surveyor's duty to amend the assessor's charge and increase it. Notice of the charges made in that manner is sent to the persons assessed, and they have the right to appeal to the body I referred to before, the Commissioners for the general purposes of the Income Tax Acts.

7098. (*Chairman.*) But you have nothing to do with the Special Commissioners under Schedule A., have you?—There is a section in the Income Tax Act of 1842 which states that in the event of no local commissioners acting, and the whole machinery of that Act being brought to a deadlock, in that case the Special Commissioners may step in and take upon themselves the functions of the General Purposes Commissioners.

7099. That is a sort of accidental exception, and the rule is the other way?—Yes, I do not think there has ever been a case in which the Special Commissioners have had to interpose.

7100. Then no allowance is made for deterioration or for the cost of collecting?—None whatever.

7101. The only allowance is under the last Budget of 1894?—Yes.

7102. Under which an allowance may be made for repairs?—That is so.

7103. (*Lord Farrer.*) I think you said you would often increase the assessment over the actual rent; have you often increased the assessment over the gross assessment to the poor rate?—Frequently.

7104. And never reduced it?—I have found cases in England where the rack-rent has been reduced to a sum below the gross poor rate (they are very exceptional); but if I were satisfied that the real rack-rent value of a given property at the present time was less than the poor rate now stands at, I should put it at the rack-rent; but I should always warn the person who was making the appeal to me that unless before the next new assessment he got the poor rate reduced, and by that means showed the poor rate people were satisfied, he would then be assessed on the gross poor rate value, subject to appeal to the General Commissioners.

7105. (*Chairman.*) What is the system in Ireland?—The system in Ireland is simply to follow Griffith's valuation.

7106. The landlord has the option of paying on one of two sums, has he not?—Yes, whichever he pleases; he can either pay on Griffith's valuation, or he can pay on the rent.

7107. Has he that absolute choice under all circumstances?—Yes, under all circumstances.

7108. Although one may be very much below the other?—Yes. What really happens is this: When an agent in Ireland gets a demand note in from the collector, he would take it in conjunction with his rent roll account, and take it item by item. If item No. 1 were let at a rent above the poor rate, he would simply pass it. Then item No. 2, if the rent were less than the valuation, he would object to, and claim a reduction on it. If there were 300 holdings, he would go through them, and pick out every individual charge where the poor law valuation was in excess of the rent, and he would demand a reduction on those, and those only.

7109. Is the result of that, that in many cases the payment is upon a very much less amount than it would be in England?—Yes; it has a very great effect.

7110. What sort of properties?—To begin with, even upon an estate where the present rents, for the sake of argument, are in the aggregate exactly equal to the valuation; even there we do not get the tax on the full valuation, because it always happens that some of the rents run a little above it and some a little below, and as we never get tax on more than the valuation, while the owner picks out those particular holdings let at rents below it, and says, "On those I shall not pay the duty as assessed," the result is, the Crown does not get the tax either on the full rental or the full valuation. The vast bulk of the occupiers are not chargeable to income tax at all; in 1893–4 the total number of occupiers assessed in Ireland was 719,019, and of that number 647,366 were wholly exempt; so that it was a matter of indifference to them whether the assessment was above the rent or not, because they paid nothing on account of the difference. Included in the remaining small percentage of about 10 per cent. are the whole of the assessments throughout Ireland, on owners who are rated as occupiers of their own property. I cannot say exactly what they would amount to, but it is quite certain that the number of *bonâ fide* rent-paying tenants who are liable to income tax in Ireland is very small indeed, and even those, if they do not make the profit on which they are assessed, have only to make out accounts to get the charge reduced.

7111. Is there anything in Ireland corresponding to the poor law assessment in England?—Only Griffith's valuation.

7112. So that there is no local assessment by assessment committees?—Nothing of the kind.

7113. (*Lord Welby.*) And there is no change made in that valuation, except in the event of new buildings put up?—Either new buildings being erected or buildings decreasing in value. You can get them diminished. I understand Mr. Barton's evidence to show that although they diminish them, they cannot increase them. If a new house is erected, it would be assessed when built.

7114. (*Chairman.*) Can any return be made showing the comparative variations in Schedule A. assessments in Ireland and in England?—No return could be made which would be really an exact statement, because we have no means of telling exactly what the rent is in Ireland. Under the circumstances we Government officials never hear what the rent is when it is above the valuation, we only hear of it when it drops below the valuation, and no matter how

Mr. G. F. Moore. [illegible]

Revision of assessments under Schedule A. in England.

Absence of assessment in Ireland.

Revision of valuation.

Rents and valuation in Ireland.

Mr. G. F. Horne.

8 Mar. 1895.

Rents and valuation in Ireland.

much it might be above, we should not be told what the rent was.

7115. (*Mr. Sexton.*) In order to induce you to accept the valuation as a basis of assessment, would not you require to be told what the rent was?—No, we have no option, we are bound to accept the valuation; we are compelled to.

7116. It is only when the rent is lower you hear what it is, is it?—Yes; and of course then it is quite at the free volition of the landowner, who simply does it in self-interest.

7117. (*Chairman.*) Taking the whole of the cases in which judicial rents have been fixed, how much are the present rents below the valuation?—Taking the whole of the cases in which judicial rents have been fixed, and deducting from those judicial rents the local rates that would be payable by the landlord out of the rent, I find that the present judicial rents net, would be 3·2 per cent. below the valuation for Ireland as a whole; that is, taking the estimate made by Mr. Barton, the head of the Valuation Office, as being the best figures which we can obtain—they may be correct or not—I am not in a position to dispute them, but taking them as correct, the present net judicial rents would be 3·2 per cent. below the valuation for Ireland.

7118. How does the valuation in those cases compare with the old rents?—The old rents were 5,754,300*l.*, and the valuation was 4,682,000*l.*, which shows a difference of 23·1 per cent.

7119. At present have you any reason to suppose that farms are assessed in Ireland at other than their fair value?—At the present time my opinion is that agricultural land in Ireland is about the same value, if we could get at the letting value disclosed by the actual rents, as the amount of the valuation. I think it is assessed at about its proper value.

7120. But under that optional system in past years, assuming the rents are fair rents, a large number escaped full assessment?—Yes; taking Mr. Barton's figures for many years, the under assessment would have amounted to about 1,580,800*l.* as compared with the amount that the assessments would have been made upon had the English system been in force in Ireland.

7121. Does that express the whole difference?—No, it would not express the whole difference, for the same rule comes into play again. Even in the best of times there were no doubt a certain number of holdings where the rent would be below the valuation, and no matter how much the aggregate rent of an estate might exceed the aggregate valuation, the landlord would always exercise his right to pick out the isolated cases, where the rent was below the valuation, and restrict his payment to the rent.

7122. As to house property, are the assessments very much below the rack-rent valuations?—We have every reason to believe, from an examination of the valuation with the rent in those cases in which we know the rent, that there is a very large discrepancy indeed.

Rents and valuation of house property in Dublin.

7123. You put in some papers, do you not, showing the rents and valuation of house property in Dublin?—Yes.

7124. One refers to Dublin, North, and the other to Dublin, South. Taking Dublin, South, first, you deal, I think, with a number of houses, the annual rent of which is 8,862*l.*?—That is so.

7125. How much is the valuation?—The rent being 8,862*l.*, the valuation is 4,108*l.*

7126. Then from the rent you have to deduct the rates, have you not?—Yes; I am not in a position to say exactly what the rates are upon the whole of those houses, but I have put it at 6*s.* 8*d.* as the best estimate I could make. I may say I have the exact particulars with regard to three of the townships among which these other townships lie, and the full rate paid in 1894 for Dalkey township was 6*s.* 11*d.*, for Killiney township 5*s.* 7*d.*, and for Bray township it was 5*s.* 2*d.* I think there is no doubt that in putting it at 6*s.* 8*d.* I am erring on the side of allowing too much rather than too little. But assuming it to be at 6*s.* 8*d.* in the pound, which of course would be on the valuation, not on the rent, the rates would come to 1,369*l.*, which would leave assessable (if the assessments were made on the English system) 7,521*l.* against a valuation, as it exists in Ireland, of 4,108*l.*

Mr. G. F. Horne.

8 Mar. 1895.

Rents and valuation of house property in Dublin.

7127. That is in this part of South Dublin?—Yes.

7128. The actual assessment valuation for rating is 4,108*l.*, and in England, after making all deductions, it would be 7,521*l.*?—That is so.

7129. Do you put that in as a fair comparison in your view?—I do. I should like to tell you how I got at these figures, because they are not figures that are picked in any shape. The reason why I only gave such a small number as 21 houses in the first statement I furnished was that it was prepared in a hurry. I had very short notice that I was to come over here. I had no time to do more myself than take this list, which I got from house agents, and check it as to two townships on the outskirts of Dublin, with which I had some acquaintance. The house agent's statement does not give the names of the owners of the property, and the poor rate assessment in many cases does not give the names of the houses, so that unless a person were acquainted with the neighbourhood, it would be no use for him to look in the valuation lists in order to identify properties of which the owners' names were not given.

7130. In England those can be identified, can they not?—They could to a better extent than in Ireland, with some little pains. The only ones I could trace myself were those 21 cases which are given in the appendix to my notes of evidence; but subsequently particulars of every case in which there was a clear unmistakeable, annual rent quoted, were sent to Dublin and the two surveyors in charge of the Dublin districts were asked to give the valuation of each case. In order to enable them to do that, they got the local collectors to come in, and the local collectors had information which enabled them to identify the properties. These lists which I have put before you include every case without exception which we can trace in the books where a yearly rent is given in the list by the agents; none of them are picked cases.

7131. And the percentage of reductions as compared with England is the difference between 7,500*l.* and 4,100*l.*, is it?—The valuation would have to be increased in that case by 83·15 per cent.

7132. And in the other case of North Dublin, what does that show?—There are very few houses given there, because North Dublin is not such a favourite locality for residence; there are not so many people living there as in the south, and this list which I had from the agent did not give many houses to let in the north; but I took out what I could from it, and that shows the increase would be 84·72 per cent.

7133. Is the Sackville Street district north of Dublin?—That is in the centre of Dublin. None of these properties are in Dublin proper. The list did not contain any that were to let in the heart of the city; of course in the heart of the city the rates run much higher; for instance, last year, within the limits to which the Dublin Corporation extends, on the north side the rates came to 9*s.* 2*d.*, and on the south side to 8*s.* 6*d.*, but that would only apply to the City of Dublin proper.

7134. What is the effect of the Finance Act of last year on the assessment in Ireland?—As regards houses that are let at a rent the section will be practically inoperative, because it enacts that where the rent is more than one-sixth above the amount of assessment no allowance shall be made, but with regard to all houses occupied by the owners the result of the 35th section of the Finance Act of 1894 will be to give them an allowance of one-sixth for repairs. Now that deduction has admittedly been made already in arriving at the valuation, so that the deduction will be allowed twice over.

Finance Act, 1894; allowance for repairs.

7135. Was that known when the Bill was brought in?—I can hardly see how it could not have been known, I think it must have been known.

Mr. H. P. [illegible] 4 Dec. 1895. Fiscal [illegible] of Ireland.

7136. (*Lord Farrer.*) And that is not the case in England, is it?—No; because in England the owner would be assessed up to the full letting value, just as if he had let the house.

7137. (*Lord Welby.*) Are you quite clear on the point that the deduction has already made in the valuation?—I think there is no doubt about that from Mr. Barton's evidence. He distinctly stated the other day in his evidence that the valuation was put on the net value of the property, not on the gross.

7138. Might I refer you to one paragraph from Mr. Barton's memorandum. Are you clear from his evidence and memorandum that an allowance for repairs was made in fixing the valuation?—Yes, I am. This is what Mr. Barton says in the wind up of his evidence. Speaking about item D, which is one of his returns, he says: "Item D shows the advantage to owners of house property in Ireland in being able to pay on the valuation instead of the gross rental as in Great Britain. This benefit is even greater than that enjoyed by the landowners, the former not only gaining by the amount being, say, 15 per cent. below the statutory valuation, but reaping the further benefit of the deduction for repairs and maintenance provided for in the valuation, which usually amounts to one-sixth of the rent. No such abatement is allowed under the Income Tax Act of 1842 in Great Britain."

7139. (*Chairman.*) Then unless Mr. Barton is entirely mistaken, which is not likely, do you affirm what you said just now, that the deduction is made twice over?—I adhere to that.

Assessment under Schedule D.

7140. As to Schedule D., can any comparison be made between the stringency of the assessment in Great Britain and the assessment in Ireland?—It is not possible to produce any figures which would prove anything exact with regard to that, but from my experience as a surveyor in both countries I consider that the assessment under Schedule D. is carried out with greater stringency in England than it is in Ireland, and there are two or three reasons which would conduce to it. In the first instance, there are no assessors in Ireland. The assessors being local men, who have lived all their lives in a particular locality, they would know a great deal more about the business of the people living in the locality than it would be possible for a surveyor to do, who is a comparative stranger and constantly shifted. In the next place, there being no local commissioners in Ireland, another great source of information is completely wanting. In all the great towns in England the commissioners are generally chosen from the leading merchants, and you get representatives of the different classes of trade which is carried on in the town, and between them the body of commissioners would represent an immense amount of local knowledge. There is nothing of that sort in Ireland.

7141. The commissioners advise, do they not?—One of the bodies of commissioners in England actually make the assessments, not the body called Commissioners for General Purposes, but another body called Additional Commissioners.

7142. Is the assessment made under their hand, as it were?—Yes; in England under Schedule D., except in a few cases where the taxpayer elects voluntarily to be assessed by the Special Commissioners, all the great mass of the assessments are made by commissioners who are called Additional Commissioners for Income Tax, who are local men who have a knowledge of the affairs of the neighbourhood.

7143. And it is done under their hand, as it were?—Yes.

7144. They actually do assess, do they?—They actually do assess. The surveyor has the right of making any representations to those commissioners he thinks proper, but the surveyor cannot over-ride their judgment.

7145. He can appeal to Somerset House, I suppose?—No, he cannot. They have absolute power to make assessments, and can over-ride the surveyor altogether on questions of fact.

7146. Neither in respect of deductions nor in respect of augmentation can you go beyond them?—No, we can do nothing; their power is absolute in making the assessment. If the surveyor is of opinion that they have allowed deductions which are absolutely illegal, and which the law does not allow them to make, he has the right of objecting to the body of commissioners called the General Purposes Commissioners; and if they give an erroneous decision in a pure matter of law, the surveyor could take the point of law into the Supreme Court.

Mr. H. P. [illegible] 4 Dec. 1895. Assessments under Schedule D.

7147. But he cannot take a point of judgment as to the amount of assessment, can he?—Never.

7148. (*Lord Welby.*) The commissioners are finally?—Yes, they have absolute power in everything except in matters of law.

7149. (*Chairman.*) With reference to another question connected with inland revenue taxation, there is no licence duty in Ireland, is there?—No.

7150. And there is no land tax?—There is no land tax.

7151. And there is no railway duty, I think?—There is no railway passenger duty.

Assessments in England and Ireland compared.

7152. (*Lord Farrer.*) Has your experience extended to London as well as to the country in England?—To a smaller extent. I have not had very much to do with London, but I have officiated in London.

7153. With regard to towns in England as well as to the country?—Yes.

7154. I gather that the general result of your evidence is that so far as concerns country districts, Ireland is not more heavily assessed than England?—That is so.

7155. And that as regards town districts Ireland is considerably less assessed than England?—That is so.

7156. That is your opinion, is it?—That is decidedly my opinion.

7157. (*Mr. Sexton.*) You are an Imperial officer, are you not?—Yes.

7158. How long has the department been Imperial?—Ever since the Act of 1842. In fact, surveyors of taxes were in existence before that, because in the old days surveyors of taxes used to have jurisdiction over what we now call the assessed taxes; but for a good many years past now surveyors of taxes have had nothing to do with any tax in England except land tax, inhabited house duty, and chiefly income tax.

System of valuation in Ireland and England compared.

7159. From the beginning, then, it appears this department, of which you are an officer, has been Imperial, and conducted the valuation, knowing that their valuation would govern the yield of income tax?—We have always made our own special valuation in England for income tax.

7160. I am speaking of Ireland now?—In Ireland we have no voice in the valuation.

7161. Do not you alter the valuation whenever it requires to be altered?—No, we cannot touch it.

7162. How is it done?—It is done by the Valuation Department. We have no voice whatever in it.

7163. You belong to the Income Tax Department then, do you?—Yes.

7164. As to the Valuation Office, that is an Imperial Department, is it not?—I am told it is. I know nothing of it, personally.

7165. And the valuation made by the Valuation Office in Ireland has from the beginning, of course, been applied to the purposes of income tax as well as to other purposes?—That is so.

7166. Your official connexion with Ireland began only in the year 1894, I believe?—Yes, that is so.

7167. Had you any previous knowledge of Ireland?—None whatever; I had never been there.

7168. The system of valuation, as you describe it, in England appears to be in the main a local system. The foundation of the system is the assessment to the poor rate, is it not?—No, I cannot admit that, because we reject the poor rate if we are not satisfied with it. We are not bound by it in the least.

7169. I know, but I say the "foundation"; it is the figure from which your proceedings are taken?—

Mr. G. F. Howe.

2 May 1895.

System of valuation in Ireland and England compared.

No, I could not admit that; it is not our foundation. We take it simply for the purpose of seeing that no properties escape our assessments which are assessed for the poor rate; and in the case of properties that are not let we use it for the purpose of comparison.

7170. We need not differ about the word "foundation." The assessment of the poor rate is the beginning of the operations, is it not?—Yes, in that way it is. The only objection I have to the word "foundation" is that it would seem to imply that any superstructure must be affected by it; and the point I wish to make clear is that in England, for Imperial purposes, we are in no way bound by the poor rate. We take it or reject it according as we find it trustworthy or untrustworthy.

7171. But it is the foundation on which the superstructure of all subsequent assessment is made?—I do not wish to quarrel about terms. Those are the conditions on which we make the assessment; we accept the poor rate if we are satisfied that it represents the full rack rent, and if we are not so satisfied we reject it.

7172. A copy of the poor rate assessment locally made is supplied to local assessors?—Yes.

7173. Who appoints the local assessors?—The Commissioners for the General Purposes of the Income Tax for the district in which the property is. There is an area called a division or hundred, which would comprise a certain number of parishes, and a staff of general commissioners act for this number of parishes.

7174. And they appoint the assessors, do they?—They appoint the assessors.

7175. How are they themselves appointed?—The Land Tax Commissioners appoint the General Purposes Commissioners and the Land Tax Commissioners themselves are appointed by Act of Parliament. Each year there is what is called a Name Act, I think, introduced.

7176. By whom?—I suppose it would be Treasury officials, I do not know.

7177. I believe that the representatives in Parliament of the various districts make a list, and that that list is accepted by the Treasury?—Yes.

7178. And these gentlemen who are so appointed, appoint commissioners for the general purposes?—Yes. In most cases you will find that the Land Tax Commissioners themselves are General Purposes Commissioners. There are exceptions to that rule, but I should say in the vast majority of cases the same gentlemen who act as Land Tax Commissioners also act as General Purposes Commissioners.

7179. They appear to be the local appointees of local appointees?—Yes. Of course vacancies in their ranks are filled up in the same way that they themselves were originally appointed.

7180. They are local men locally appointed and not paid?—That is so. When you say locally appointed, you are speaking of the General Purposes Commissioners? They are appointed by the Land Tax Commissioners, who are local gentlemen themselves.

7181. In matters of local taxation, so long as the assessment is relatively equal, no damage would be suffered by any local interest, would it?—Certainly not. It would not matter whether it was twice the value or half the value, or the full value; it makes not the slightest difference.

7182. On the other hand, if there were a low assessment for local purposes, it would tend to make lighter the burden of the income tax, would it not?—Certainly, if the Local Assessment was also the Imperial Assessment. Of course, we cannot assume that a given parish would submit to having light assessments made on one part and heavy on the other.

7183. The principle of my inquiry was, whether in case rating was relatively low or relatively high over a rating area, it would make no difference then to any individual?—It would not; but of course in that case, when we came to get the returns of rent, we should see at once that the ratings were below the actual rents, and when we came to deal with properties that were not let, we should simply refuse to accept the poor law valuation as the basis of assessment.

7184. Who fixes the salaries of the assessors?—Up to, I think, three or four years ago, they were paid by commission; but considerable objection was made, on the ground that payment by commission led these local assessors to an excess of zeal, which resulted in harm to the taxpayer.

7185. In what kind of harm?—It was asserted that in order to get a lot of poundage, they charged people a great deal more than the property was worth, and charged them more income tax under Schedule D. than their profits were likely to come up to in framing the local assessment. It was contended it was not right to make a man's remuneration depend on the amount he could wring out of the taxpayer.

7186. Obviously the effect of that system would be to make it to the interest of the officer to have a high assessment, would it not?—Certainly, I am told that complaint was made in Parliament, and about three or four years ago an Act was passed which abolished poundage to the only classes of officers remaining who were paid by poundage. There were three classes, assessors, collectors, and clerks to the commissioners; they were all paid by poundage, but an Act was passed some three years ago which fixed the amount of remuneration for these gentlemen at the amount of poundage they received in the preceding year or an average of years.

7187. (*Chairman.*) After a very long struggle I believe, was it not?—I believe it was. I am told the view held was that, so far from the local assessors letting the taxpayers off, they were stringing them up a good deal too high, but I am not expressing my own views in saying this.

7188. (*Mr. Sexton.*) When the local assessors, acting on the basis of the poor rate assessment, have framed the income tax assessment, your class of officers come in?—Yes.

7189. The local assessors put into your hands their returns and books of assessment?—Their duty is to give them up to the commissioners by whom they are appointed, who hand them to us. The result is the same; they pass from the local assessors to the surveyors of taxes.

7190. What do you call the returns?—The word "returns" as used there means the statements made by the different occupiers of the amount of rent that they pay for the properties they occupy, and the terms and conditions annexed to the letting, that is to say, the number of years for which the tenancy is to exist, and whether any premium was paid in consideration of the letting; also who has to pay the land tax, and sundry particulars of that sort, for which columns are provided in the returns.

7191. If the premises are not let at the time of the return, what statement does the occupier make?—Of course if the premises are not occupied no statement can be obtained. There is no person to give one; the return is only from the occupier, and if there is no occupier there is no return.

7192. If the premises are let, the occupier states what rent is paid, does he not?—That is so.

7193. Is that verified in any way?—In the great mass of cases it would not be. The Acts provide a penalty of 20*l.* and treble duty upon any one who makes a false return.

7194. Then the duties of surveyors of taxes are to examine these returns and to revise the books, are they not?—That is so.

7195. What are we to understand by an examination of the returns?—The surveyor goes carefully through them and sees that the assessor has extracted the particulars stated on the returns correctly, and put them into the books of assessment, and he examines the other columns on the return as to what the terms of tenancy are; for instance, if a tenant makes a note that in addition to paying his rent he has to pay the land tax, the probability is, it might escape the assessor's attention, but it would not escape the surveyor's; he would take note of it and add

the assessor to the rate in arriving at the value of the premises.

7196. If the premises are not let, what would the surveyor do, would he fix the assessment?—Yes, at what he considered would be the letting value if they were let.

7197. And if they are let does he put down the full rent?—Yes, or more than the full rent.

7198. Not less?—Not less.

7199. Possibly more?—Frequently more, but never less.

7200. The appeal from your decision would be to the Commissioners for General Purposes, would it not?—Yes.

7201. They are a local body of unpaid men, are they not?—They are a local body of unpaid men.

7202. And their decision would be final as against you on any question of value?—As against me it would, but not as against the appellant. The appellant, if he likes, may demand a valuation to be made; but I may say that that is so extremely rare that in the whole course of my 15 years work in England I only knew it done once.

7203. But if the appellant is dissatisfied with the assessment, the local commissioners have power to determine finally, have they not?—Yes.

7204. Therefore the system in England at its initiation being a system of valuation by local assessors for local purposes, and at its crown or summit being a final exercise of power by a local tribunal, may be described as a local system?—To that extent of course it is. Local people have a voice in the matter.

7205. A decisive voice?—Only within legal limits, because the surveyor of taxes would at once take a case to the Supreme Court if they attempted to go outside section 60, 5 & 6 Vict. c. 35, which lands them down.

7206. I quite appreciate that you have an appeal under law?—Yes, the law lays down the principles under which they are to act, and if they do not act upon them he can go to the court.

7207. (*Lord Farrer.*) What is section 60?—The clause runs:—"The annual value of lands, tene-"ments, hereditaments, or heritages charged under "Schedule A., shall be understood to be the rent "by the year at which the same are let at rack-rent, "if the amount of such rent shall have been fixed by "agreement commencing within the period of seven "years preceding the time of making the assessment; "but if the same are not so let at rack-rent, then at "the rack-rent at which the same are worth to be let by the year."

7208. (*Mr. Sexton.*) Does not that leave the assessment of values still in the hands of the local commissioners?—If the local commissioners say, in the case of a let place, "This is the rent," or in the case of a vacant place, "This is the rack-rent," is not that judgment final?—Certainly they would have no discretion whatever as to putting the place at less than the rent; but in the case of property not let at all, or property in the hands of the owner, then of course on the mere question of fact as to what the value was, the local commissioners' judgment is absolute.

7209. (*Lord Farrer.*) Supposing there is a rent, they cannot alter that fact, can they?—No, nor may they make their assessments at less than the rent.

7210. (*Mr. Sexton.*) Do you consider the system which you have described to be as efficient for the purposes of income tax as the system where every valuation is made by an Imperial officer?—I consider it far more efficient, judging by results. Comparing the result in England with the results in Ireland by my own experience, I consider it is infinitely more efficient.

7211. To what results do you refer?—The results that in one case we actually get assessments that are made upon the full annual value, and in the other we get imaginary assessments which, tried by every test we can put to them, have been, up to the present time, far below the letting value.

7212. That answer of yours involves an assumption as to the relation of the assessment in England and the poor rate valuation in Ireland to the value of the land, does it not?—Yes.

7213. As to the assessment in England, in the Inland Revenue Return, page 32 of the Appendix, we have first given for local assessment the gross estimated rental of all property rated at 151,000,000*l*. Is that the sum of the figure ascertained by those who assessed for the local poor rate?—Yes.

7214. Is that the actual rent or the rack-rent in the case of empty premises?—It is the estimated rack-rent. That is what the poor rate people consider to be the full letting value of the property.

7215. The rent of rented property and the full letting value of vacant property?—Yes.

7216. Do you consider it is that?—Our own tests as applied to it show that it is about 97 per cent. of what we should consider the full value, with one important proviso which I must make before we go further, namely, that that 151,000,000*l*. includes a very large class of property as to which we do not apply the test of rent at all, but the test of actual profits, namely, all coal mines, railways, quarries, and every description of property of that kind, which we assess to Income Tax not at all by the test of rent, but by the test of what the actual profit is. Here, of course, for poor rate purposes it would be brought in simply upon an estimate of the letting value. So that before you can compare the figures given for the gross estimated rental of property with the Schedule A. assessment, you must cut out that class of property which is not assessed at all under Schedule A., but which is assessable under Schedule D. for profits.

7217. It would be assessed here on letting value would it?—It would.

7218. What relation would such an assessment on letting values of collieries and other such property bear to the profits?—That is a question I could not possibly answer. No comparison is ever made for that purpose. Of course it would be very much less than the profits.

7219. This 151,000,000*l*., which is called gross estimated value, includes, does it not, a large quantity of property which is assessed upon letting value in this schedule and upon profits in Schedule D.?—Yes. The exact extent to which that is the case is that 29,150,235*l*. out of the 151,388,353*l*., consists of property which, although rated on a letting basis for poor rate purposes, for Imperial taxation comes in under another schedule, and is assessed on the full profits, without any deduction for the rents which are paid. We get tax on the rents and a good deal more than the rents, but not under this schedule.

7220. That important class of property only pays income tax on the actual profits?—Including rent. For instance, if a colliery paid 10,000*l*. a year rent, and the result of working was a loss, then we should restrict our assessment to the 10,000*l*. a year rent they paid; but if, after paying the 10,000*l*. rent, there was a profit of another 10,000*l*., then we should make an assessment of 20,000*l*. on them, of which they would get back the tax on 10,000*l*. by deduction when they paid the rent.

7221. The assessment then would be on the profit simply?—No, we should include the rent. We never make any deduction for rent. We make the assessment in one sum. If there were no profits that sum would be the rent or way-leave, or whatever they paid; if there were any profit, it would be in one sum, which would include those things and the profit as well.

7222. Deducting from the gross estimated rental for local purposes of 151,000,000*l*., this sum of 29,000,000*l*. odd, you come to a gross estimated rental of 122,000,000*l*. rated and assessed under Schedule A.?—Yes.

7223. And that assessment, as you say, is founded, in the case of vacant property, upon what you think the real rent would be, and in the case of rented property at not less than the rent?—Yes. Before we go further with that, I should like to draw the attention

Mr. G. R. Hume.

5 Mar. 1895.

Valuation and letting values in Ireland.

Mr. G. F. Howe.

8 May 1895.

Valuation and letting values in Ireland.

of the Commission as the fact that the poor rate assessment on the property which is both rated to the poor and assessed under Schedule A. of the income tax is 162,034,116*l*. Now, if you look at the next line but one, you will find that the gross annual value in the income tax Schedule A. assessments upon that same property is 167,925,000*l*., which works out as an increase of 3·63 per cent., and the inference that I draw from that is that at the present time the poor rate assessment is within 3·63 per cent. of the actual letting value of the property.

7224. What do you call the actual letting value of the property?—The rack-rent of the property.

7225. Do you mean the gross estimated rental?—No, what I mean by rack-rent is the annual rent which a tenant might reasonably be expected to pay, taking one year with another, if the tenant undertook to pay all usual tenant's rates and taxes and the landlord undertook to pay the land tax and bear the cost of repairs and insurance and all other expenses, if any, necessary to maintain the property in a state to command that rent.

7226. You observe that the gross amount assessed in Schedule A. is 168,000,000*l*., and that the gross estimated rental of all property rated is 191,000,000*l*.?—Yes.

7227. What would be your short explanation of the difference?—The explanation is that 23,500,255*l*., part of the 191,380,955*l*., belongs to a class of property that is not assessed under Schedule A. of the Income Tax Acts, but under Schedule D.; it does not escape taxation, only for the purposes of the Income Tax Acts it is brought in under another schedule, and assessed under other rules.

7228. Taking the corresponding case, we see that in Ireland the gross poor rate valuation of 14,000,000*l*. is only diminished to the extent of half a million?—That is so, because, of course, there are very few coal mines and that class of property in Ireland.

7229. That is one of the elements of comparison. Do you consider that you are in a position to say that the gross estimated rental of 191,000,000*l*. in England is not lower in relation to value than the 14,000,000*l*. in Ireland?—I should say it is higher.

7230. Have you any personal knowledge of the circumstances under which the valuation of Ireland is effected?—Personal knowledge, no, because I was not in Ireland, in fact, I was not alive at the time; but I see by the tables supplied by Mr. Barton that it was considerably below the real rent.

Basis of valuation in Ireland.

7231. I would prefer to have your own evidence so far as you can give us it. Mr. Barton is a new comer in the department he is in, like yourself, is he not; I mean his official experience is not long. I suppose you know of the Valuation Act of 1852?—Of course I do not know it in the same sense I know the Income Tax Acts, but I have a general knowledge of it.

7232. Do you know that the valuers were instructed to value according to a scale of prices given in the Act?—Yes.

7233. Do you know that they were instructed to record the actual rents?—No.

7234. You do not know that?—No, I was not aware of that.

7235. Do you know that the valuation occupied 12 years?—Yes, it did. I only got that information from this report of Mr. Barton's; I was not aware of it. I see the bulk of it was done before the 12 years, but in the case of one or two counties it did take 12 years. I see County Down was completed in 1864 and County Armagh in 1865.

7236. Do you happen to know that there was a great disparity as between the valuation of the different counties during that period?—I have seen it stated that Ulster was assessed at a higher rate than the southern counties.

7237. Have you examined the records with sufficient closeness to enable you to say whether or not the valuation, as the years went on, and the prices went up, followed the actual rents, which of course were ruled by the current prices?—No, I could not give any opinion upon that from my own personal knowledge.

Mr. G. F. Howe.

8 May 1895.

Rise of prices in Ireland.

7238. Have you any knowledge of the circumstance that the prices in Ireland from the Crimean War up to 1864 went on increasing?—Only from what I have seen stated in the course of this inquiry. It is only what one would expect, because I see the prices in England went up very much in the same time. I see the land, which was only assessed at 41,000,000*l*. in 1852, was assessed at 46,000,000*l*. in 1865, or 12 per cent. more, so that there is no doubt the same process went on in the two countries.

7239. What years have you named?—Those you were taking; those between the time when the Valuation Act was passed and when it was completed, namely, 1852 and 1865.

7240. What do you say to the evidence we have that the increase in English valuation was due to two circumstances, first, that the landlords in England made an enormous expenditure in the improvement of their land, and second, that there was an immense accretion of urban population in England, which increased the value of agricultural produce and land?—It might be so; I should not be prepared to contradict it; but as regard to that I might say, so far as we are concerned, whether the landlord made the improvement or the tenant, it would not affect our question of valuation, because we should value the land as it stood at the time we made the valuation.

7241. From your official point of view?—Yes.

7242. But for the purposes of this Commission, and for the purposes of considering how far a yield or assessment to income tax is a true basis of comparison of the taxable capacity of the two countries, it would be a relevant and vital question whether or not the improvement on which the assessment is founded, is made by the owner or the tenant, would it not?—Yes; I should say it is a matter of common knowledge that in England the landlord makes them and in Ireland the tenant makes them, as a rule.

7243. And if the improvements in England were made as charges in the rent, it would not be fair to value the improvements in Ireland, which are made by the tenants, in the same way?—I cannot admit that; because whatever I have seen in Ireland has led me to consider that to a great extent the valuation did not include the tenant's improvements.

7244. You think not?—I think not.

7245. Have you any knowledge of the proceedings of the Cowper Commission?—No.

7246. I put it to you that in 1887 the Cowper Commission reported that about 300,000*l*. rent fixed up to that time could not be paid?—Yes.

7247. That they were more than the improved value of the land?—That was rents; of course the valuation was not equal to the rent. I was speaking of the valuation; we have nothing whatever to do with rents; we cannot charge tax on the rents.

7248. But you know the rents have been brought down to a figure approximating to the valuation, do you not?—Not in 1887, as far as I know. Valuation and rents.

7249. I am alluding to 1887?—They are shown to be down now, that is that the Land Commission have fixed them down to the valuation in 1895, but I was not aware they had come down to the valuation in 1887, and I have never seen any evidence to show that they had.

7250. Have you examined separately the reductions up to 1887 and the reductions since?—No, I have had no means of doing so.

7251. Are you aware of the evidence of the heads of the Land Commission, that if the reductions since 1887 were applied to the whole of Ireland, the whole rental of Ireland would be substantially below the valuation?—I heard the evidence of Mr. O'Brien to that effect.

7252. I submit to you that even up to 1887 the reductions made in the rent did cause the rent to approximate to the valuation?—I was under the impression that was not so, but I could not produce figures to show it.

7253. If it be true, as Mr. O'Brien says, that the reductions up to now would bring the rent substantially below the valuation, it leads to the inference, does it not, that the reductions up to 1887 cannot have left the rents much better?—That depends on what the extent of the reductions have been since 1887 in comparison with those which had taken place before 1887.

7254. You are aware the number of cases heard since 1887 is small compared to the number before, are you not?—I suppose the number before was much greater than since 1887.

7255. And therefore that the average of reductions on the larger number of cases before 1887 would prevail in the main?—Of course it would have a great effect upon it.

7256. Therefore even the report of the Cowper Commission, in 1887, that the rents fixed up to that time were excessive, and could not be paid, although those rents included the value of the tenants improvements, would appear to show that the valuation, if it approximated to the rents, included them also?—If it approximated to the rents, yes.

7257. Are you aware that the prices during the latter part of the period of the valuation far exceeded what they had been in recent years or are at present in Ireland?—I have no personal knowledge of that. I have seen it stated here, but I know nothing about it personally of my own knowledge.

7258. If it were the case as stated to us, that the valuers followed the rents, and that the prices prevailing at the latter part of that time especially were much higher than they are now, and that the cost of labour has greatly increased, and local rates have greatly increased since then, would not all these things be elements making it necessary to reduce the valuation now upon revision?—They would undoubtedly be elements to that extent so far as they go, first of all to eliminate the difference, if any existed, between the valuation and the rent, and then of course if they tended to bring the rents below the valuation I should say certainly that the valuation should be revised.

7259. Does it not occur to you that a great deal of the considerations that must prevail in this matter are beyond your official cognizance?—Undoubtedly. I can only take the figures as I find them, and as they come to my knowledge.

7260. Have you, for instance, any knowledge on the question whether the rent in England, which is the basis of everything, bears the same relation to the total produce as it does in Ireland?—No; but what strikes me on that is that the income tax assessments in England are based on a competition rent, whereas in Ireland the rents are not competition rents, because a case frequently happens where a tenant goes into the Land Court of Ireland, gets a fair rent fixed, and comes outside and sells his holding for twice as much as the landlord can sell his fee simple; that proves conclusively that that rent does not represent the value of the property.

7261. But have you heard the evidence that the land valuers, after fixing the rent, take no notice of what the tenant pays, but fix the value of the whole thing as it stands?—You cannot compare an assessment made in England upon a competition rent, inclusive of all interests, with an assessment made in Ireland exclusive of a great deal of the property.

7262. But it is fixed at the fair value, is it not?—Not at the present time, otherwise how can a tenant go outside the court and get 25 or 30 years purchase on his interest? What does he sell? If the rent he has to pay is the full rent the property is worth, what is there to sell?

7263. If the land valuers tell you that if there are two farms side by side, one of them vacant in the hands of the landlord, and the other in the hands of the tenant, and they fix the two rents at the same figure, what plea is there for saying the rent is fixed lower?—I go by the notorious fact that when a tenant has a rent fixed by the Land Commissioners he has such a valuable commodity that the selling price will exceed the price of the fee simple of the land.

7264. That arises from the compensation; a tenant in England may be turned out?—A tenant in England has to take his land and hold it at a competition rent.

7265. That depends on the degree of the competition?—I admit there is greater competition in the one case than another, but one is a competition rent and the other is not.

7266. But in England the competition is between the landlords to get a tenant, is it not?—Just now.

7267. Surely that distinguishes the matter very much?—It may, or may not. I do not admit that without qualification. In the very worst of times, I believe, the Duke of Bedford has always had a number of applications for every farm that has fallen vacant.

7268. You have lost sight of the state of affairs of England, perhaps, lately?—No, I think not.

7269. You are not aware, perhaps, landlords are very glad to get tenants for the payment of the poor rate?—I am aware that in some cases it may be so, and in some not, but it depends to a great extent on the character of the landlord.

7270. But you know very well, I should say, looking to the variety of occupations in England and the many ways in which capital may be put, that the difficulty of landlords in England is to get tenants to pay any rent now?—Now, it may be; of course I admit there is nothing like the competition in England that there is in Ireland.

7271. And you would accept, would you not, the testimony of those who fix the rents, that the rent is fixed just the same for a farm in the landlord's hands as for a farm in which the tenant has a legal interest, and that would be a conclusive reply, would it not, to any suggestion that the rent is lowered because of any interest existing in the tenant?—I do not know; I do not think it would.

7272. Why not. Would you not take the word of the man who fixes the rent?—There are two farms you say, side by side, one of which is in the occupation of a tenant.

7273. And one of which is vacant, the total interest of which is in the hands of the landlord?—Under those circumstances who would apply to the Land Court to fix a fair rent.

7274. No one; but the evidence is that if there were two such farms, and they were called upon to fix the rent they would fix them the same?—Then if the vacant farm were let and the man in it acquired a tenant right, there is no doubt he could do with that farm what the other could do, go and sell his tenant right for a considerable sum.

7275. But it has not affected the amount of his rent, has it?—I do not see that it follows then that the rent in either case would represent the full value.

7276. What it shows is that no importance is attached to the existence of the tenant right, does it not?—And yet the tenant right would sell for an enormous sum.

7277. The Commissioners say comparatively they fix the rent in every case, whether a tenant right exists or not at the full rent, which a person going into the farm without an interest would be able to pay from year to year?—That being so, I cannot understand how it is that another tenant could afford to pay a large sum, on which he would have to pay interest for it.

7278. Does it not occur to you as possible that an English tenant expects to make a better living than an Irish tenant?—I do not think so.

7279. You do not think their scale of living is somewhat better, do you?—Of course they are larger farms. You would expect a man who farms 500 acres to live in better style than a man who farms 15 acres.

7280. Large or small, do you not think they are better off?—I do not think so.

7281. Does it not occur to you that the willingness of Irishmen to pay a price for the right of admission to a farm, even though the rent may be already up to the fair value, is probably due to their willingness to

Mr. G. F. Moore.

8 Mar. 1895.

Basis of valuation in England.

Tenant right.

Mr. G. F. Howe.

8 May, 1895.

Tenant Right.

accept a smaller profit and live in a poorer way, than would be tolerable in England?—It may be. I do not think I have any right to speak with authority, either for or against that view. I should think it is very possible that competition led them to pay some far in excess of what they ought to pay for the tenant right.

7282. And, therefore, if the farm is let at a fair letting value, it follows, does it not, that the residue left for the tenant to live upon will be decreased by the amount he has paid for the tenant right?—It does so. I may say in the case of England, when there was tremendous competition for farms in the same way as there has been in Ireland, the effect was to run the rents up tremendously, and no matter what extent they went up to, they were assessed for income tax up to the full rent. There was a competition for farms in England, although no doubt that competition has fallen off so as to be practically non-existent just now.

Causes of increase of assessment in England.

7282a. Bearing in mind that the figure of English assessment in the years between 1864 and 1880, in fact in recent times, was greatly due to the expenditure by landlords upon their holdings, and also greatly due to that enormous development of town life, would you say that any similar cause arose in the same period to justify an increase in the Irish assessment?—No; my idea is that in both countries the assessment should have gone by actual facts, that if, as a matter of fact, the rents in England increased, the assessments should increase accordingly; if they drop they should drop accordingly, and I think that is the proper system which should be in existence in Ireland as well as in England. I think it is just as unsatisfactory to have a hard and fast valuation, which you cannot drop in times of depression, as it is to have a hard and fast valuation which you cannot put up in times of prosperity.

7283. But if the rentals of England improved, as they enormously did, owing to the enormous expenditure, that must have increased the assessment?—It did increase the assessment, of course.

7284. And if great towns have sprung up in England and extended during the last 30 years, supplying a ready and remunerative market to the farmer for developing such profitable branches of industry such as flowers and market crops generally, that, of course, must have greatly increased the value of land in England?—The part of England I know best is the eastern counties, and I am quite sure that the great bulk of the farmers there would not admit their profits have been affected by the sources to which you allude. The great part of the farmers there go in for the ordinary corn crops or pasture; you will find very little in the shape of market gardening, or growing flowers, or anything of that sort there. The British farmer is a very conservative being. There may be parts of the country where that would apply, but it would not apply to the part that I know most about.

7285. But do you not know that every town, great or small, agricultural land acquires a special value?—Certainly, both in England and Ireland.

7286. But in Ireland the towns are decaying, and in England they are developing?—That is so; the same thing would apply in different degrees. I admit, when a great town like Birmingham grows up, the land for a radius of miles round it increases in value.

7287. I submit to you that the two great causes which are absent from Ireland, namely, the expenditure on the land and the large growth of these urban communities, have contributed to increase the assessment in England?—I do not contend for a moment, as the assessment on land in England jumped up from 41,000,000*l.* in 1852 to 52,000,000 in 1882, there were not causes to account for it. Whatever the causes were, the rents went up, and directly the rents went up, up went the income tax assessment.

7288. And you would hardly contest my suggestion, would you, that amongst the causes those I have mentioned were two powerful ones?—I should think probably that is so.

7289. There were no corresponding causes existing in Ireland, were there?—I suppose not.

Mr. G. F. Howe.

8 May, 1895.

Causes of increase of assessment in England.

7290. I suppose you know Ireland well enough to know that south and west of Dublin there is hardly a town that cannot be said to be declining?—They are stationary, at any rate, I suppose.

7291. I would be disposed to ask you to infer, therefore, that during the period within which the British assessment grew, no similar growth could have occurred in Ireland if there had been a revision?—Not to the same extent.

7292. Then the British assessment has declined?—Will you name the years. Do you mean from 1880 up to the present time?

7293. Yes?—Undoubtedly.

7294. From 52,000,000*l.* to 41,000,000*l.*?—Undoubtedly.

Valuation and judicial rents.

7295. Are you aware of the evidence, that if the reductions in rent during the last eight years could be applied now to the whole rental of Ireland, that those who administer the Land Acts have no doubt that the rental of Ireland would fall, as a whole, substantially below the figure of the valuation?—Yes, I heard that evidence.

7296. Then, if during the period of increase in Great Britain any similar causes operated in Ireland (for the agricultural depression has affected Ireland heavily since 1880), does it not seem to be impossible to avoid the conclusion that the valuation would have to be substantially reduced?—I think it would be probably reduced in some cases, but I believe there are still a great many cases where the valuation is below the rent. From the evidence you have had put before you, and the statistical accounts of what the rents actually have been up to the present time, the judicial rents have not actually brought them below; I mean, I suppose there will still be a good many cases in which the Commissioners will put the judicial rent above the valuation, although on the average we have the evidence of Mr. O'Brien that, in his opinion, the effect will be to reduce it below.

7297. Do you happen to know that in the returns for the Land Commission, on which all these comparisons of rent and valuation are founded, the rent is always put in of course, and that in the valuation column there are numerous blanks, where it has been impossible to ascertain the valuation, and that these blanks were more numerous in previous years?—I have seen it stated; it is not a matter of which I have any knowledge.

7298. Assuming that to be the case, it would make the valuation much larger than it appears to be in the totals, and therefore tend to bring it still more over the level of the rent, would it not?—I did not understand that in making up these tables put before you nothing was put in for the valuation in those cases.

7299. That is so?—If that is so it would have the effect you state.

7300. The evidence of Mr. O'Brien is conclusive. We, in fact, had before us a page of the book showing a dash where the valuation ought to be?—Yes. Then of course it would have the effect of increasing the valuation when you compared it with the amount of the rent.

7301. You will admit, will you not, that if the prices now in Ireland on real agricultural valuations are substantially lower than the Imperial valuation, if rates have increased and the price of labour increases, the valuation would have to come down?—Supposing it was a correct valuation at the time it was made, if it was high enough then, it would have to come down now.

7302. If they follow the rents?—Yes, I admit that.

Valuation of houses in towns.

7303. All this would apply to your observation that income tax is levied on individuals and not on communities, because if it was found that the valuation was excessive, that would bear on the capacity of Ireland to bear taxation as compared with England, tried by the same test. As to houses, I think your evidence goes further than that of Mr. Barton, does it not?—Yes, it does. Mr. Barton's evidence simply

Mr. G. F. [illegible] 4 Mar. 1895. [illegible]

was to the effect that there had been a deduction made for repairs, and so on, and that in his opinion the valuation would now be 15 or 20 per cent. higher if a revision were made, but Mr. Barton does not tell you what the reduction was for the repairs and maintenance of houses, and he does not give you any definite idea as to the precise basis on which the supposititious revised valuation was to be made.

7304. But is not he the commissioner of valuation?—Yes. I see that he does give you, as you have alluded to his evidence, a statement of valuation of rents of property valued in and around Dublin during 1894–95, and comparing the actual rent as stated by Mr. Barton, and the actual valuations as given by him of the work done during 1894, the rent is 50·65 per cent. above the valuation 13,392*l.* to 20,216*l.*

7305. It is a limited basis to go upon. He told us that he would not say the valuation of houses would be increased more than between 15 and 20 per cent.?—No, but he was not then speaking with reference to the English Standard of Assessment. Presumably his revised valuation would, like the old one, allow for maintenance and repairs.

7306. You say 50 per cent., do you?—Yes, I say 50, and I think if it were possible to get at the figures it would be still more; I think I am moderate in saying 50.

7307. When the Commissioner of Valuation and the Surveyor of Taxes upon a matter so closely related to their duties differ so widely, we may be excused if we feel some doubt, may we not?—Certainly. I have given reasons for my opinion. I have given a list of 100 houses of which we know the actual rents and the actual valuations. I may say that in some respects a surveyor of taxes has sources of information which would hardly perhaps come under Mr. Barton's observation, and that is with regard to the actual rents paid as shown in trading accounts produced in appeals under Schedule D.; for instance, a tradesman in the heart of the City of Dublin, when appealing, would have to show what his receipts were, and he would be entitled to charge against his receipts all his trade expenses, including the rent paid, although, of course, he would only pay in tax upon the valuation, and by that means it would be possible to obtain a good many particulars with regard to the rents now actually paid in the City of Dublin if time were given to do it. For instance, I said that those instances which I have given were not special cases picked out. If they were I should have to give very different figures. I heard of a case the other day of premises where the valuation was 6*l.* The landlord had an offer to take them for 15*l.*, but he demurred to that, and thought in addition the tenant ought to put a new roof on. That I consider to be an extreme case. I remember a case which came under my notice a year or two ago, when I was in charge of one of the Dublin districts, of a tradesman appealing against his Schedule D. assessment, producing accounts showing what his rent was. Now, he was the nominal owner of the premises in which he carried on his business, and the valuation of his premises was 105*l.* The two charges of head-rent and mortgage interest alone came to 215*l.*, so that he held as owner subject to a charge of 215*l.*, and yet the valuation was only 105*l.*

7308. I should think that tradesman was in a very special position; he was not a typical tradesman, was he?—I have no reason to think he was not.

7309. Have you any evidence to show that he was?—No, I cannot say anything about that. One, of course, would have to get a large mass of those cases given before you could rely much upon them. It might be a special case, but with regard to these 100 cases I have given now, they are certainly not picked cases, because I have taken all I could get.

[illegible] Schedule D.

7310. As you have touched upon Schedule D., do you think the self-made assessments under Schedule D. in a country like England, where the volume and number of assessable estates is so great, can have been as searching an assessment as in Ireland?—My opinion is that it is more searching. Taking the area, speaking roughly, Ireland is half the area of England, there are 18 surveyors in Ireland and 200 in England, with the result that in England each man has a much smaller area to supervise, and the consideration I have mentioned, namely, the existence in England of a number of bodies of local men, each of whom have special knowledge (speaking from what has come under my own personal knowledge), leads me to the conclusion that the assessments in England are certainly made in a more stringent manner than in Ireland.

Mr. G. F. [illegible] 4 Mar. 1895. Assessments under Schedule D.

7311. It has passed into a truism in the United States that the more populous and wealthy any community is, the more difficult it is to make an exhaustive assessment for income tax than it would be if the circumstances were similar, but if, in the one case you have a large body of local men, all of whom will give information, and in the other case you have none, the circumstances are not similar.

7312. But a surveyor in Ireland would keep his eyes open, and would easily know of all the circumstances of every case, while in England the number of people is so great that I should doubt whether any experience of staff would enable a surveyor to do that?—I only give my opinion for what it is worth, and I know it is an opinion to which my brother officers share.

7313. It is very much a matter of opinion. With regard to these houses in Dublin, may I ask you this generally: Do you really think that any revision of the valuation of houses in the country south of Dublin would increase the valuation?—Yes. Valuation of houses in Dublin.

7314. In the cities and towns?—Yes.

7315. In the City of Limerick?—Yes.

7316. In the City of Waterford?—The City of Waterford I know very little about.

7317. In the City of Cork?—I think it would in Cork decidedly.

7318. Do you not think that those cities, compared with what they were 30 years ago, when the rural population was larger, purchases made in towns were greater, and they had a more secure and larger rural community to depend upon them, were in a more prosperous condition than now?—They may have been, but I am taking the thing as a whole, and from the best evidence I can obtain, I should say that in the prosperous times the rents in Ireland were far and away above the valuation; the valuation was never anywhere near the rent.

7319. When made?—Yes, when made. The only test in these cases, of course, that is worth anything, is to get the actual figure of what a place is let for, and assessed at, and tried by that test, it certainly does appear that there is a very great discrepancy.

7320. I notice that your printed list of houses in Dublin is taken from houses to let by one of the leading firms?—Yes.

7321. What firm is that?—North.

7322. The valuation of the houses you have ascertained, have you?—Yes.

7323. And you have no doubt of the accuracy of this list?—I can speak positively myself for the 21 cases I have given here, and the others were ascertained by the surveyors and collectors. I have no doubt they are accurate.

7324. Could you identify the houses. Can you hand in a list afterwards, at your convenience, identifying those 21 houses?—Yes.

7325. It would be satisfactory for further inquiry, perhaps. What you call the full rent here was not a rent being actually paid by the tenant, was it?—The rents given in the list would be the rents which would be asked for the houses, the rent quoted in the list issued by the agent. I simply took those as the only means by which I could get at any considerable number of rents.

7326. This appears to be a comparison between a valuation and the rent, not paid, but asked for by the landlord?—I only know of one case on the list where the house has been actually let since, and there the

Mr. G. F. Moore.

4 May 1895.

Valuation of houses in towns.

actual letting is for the sum stated in the list. Of course I cannot say that it might not turn out that some of those others were let at a less sum; there may have been a reduction. I thought it best to state the full facts at the head, so that you might draw your own conclusions. I say that the statement is a "statement "showing the rent and the valuation of 21 houses in "the southern suburbs of Dublin, of which 19 are "taken at random from a list of houses to let," not actually let.

7327. Do you know the valuation of the City of Dublin and the City of Belfast in the aggregate?—No.

7328. I think I may put it to you that the valuation of Belfast is about three-quarters of a million, and the valuation of Dublin is about 100,000*l.* less, that is the municipal borough?—Yes.

7329. If that is so, Belfast, being a progressive town, recently valued because it only recently arose, and if it be true as Mr. Barton says, that the valuation of Belfast would not be increased more than 10 per cent., does not it seem to you that Dublin, which is not progressive, comes rather close to the proper figure?—Personally, from all I have been able to see, and from all the cases in which I have been able to compare rents with the valuation, in Dublin, I do not think the valuation is anywhere near the rent, and I am still of that opinion, after having read Mr. Barton's evidence.

7330. Belfast being progressive, and recently valued, being only 100,000*l.* more than Dublin, would you say Dublin is progressive?—I should say Dublin is progressive at the present time as regards houses. There is not anything very much going on, but I should think it is progressive rather than retrograde.

7331. Belfast is a great industrial centre, is it not?—Belfast has increased much more rapidly than Dublin.

7332. And has more industry, two great industries has it not?—Yes.

7333. Dublin has only one limited industry. Would you be disposed to say that the valuation of Dublin could be put very much over what is the present valuation of Belfast?—I really have no means of knowing anything about Belfast.

7334. I notice that all your houses are taken from the southern suburbs?—Not quite all the cases, there are a few from the north.

7335. It is impossible for us to analyse the particulars you have handed in in manuscript. In the printed heads of your evidence you have dealt with houses in the south, have you not?—Yes, simply because I could not trace them on the north.

7336. I have no doubt as a surveyor you know the whole place pretty well?—No, I do not think I can say that I know the north well.

7337. Do you not go there?—No, my work at the arrears branch would extend over the whole of Ireland, more or less, I should have just as much to do with Galway as with Dublin.

7338. Are you chiefly concerned with arrears alone?—Yes.

7339. Then your official duties do not bring you in direct relation with this class of work?—They have now and then, but not the whole time. My duties are in connexion with this class of work, but it is spread all over Ireland.

7340. Are there no surveyors on the staff who would have to do, as a matter of their daily functions, with this particular branch of the subject with which we are concerned?—Yes, there would be, if you take the Dublin surveyors, for instance; but they have not officiated in England, and know nothing about England.

7341. You are occupied with arrears all over Ireland, and there are other surveyors who are occupied in Dublin solely, yet you have come here and not them?—At times I have had to do with the current valuation in Dublin, but in the main my work is in connexion with the arrears branch.

7342. I am rather surprised that some surveyors who have had to do with the current valuation in Dublin have not come here, because it is obvious that you have had nothing to do with the valuation?—Excuse me, I have. I have as much to do with it as any surveyor has.

Mr. G. F. Moore.

4 May 1895.

Valuation of houses in towns.

7343. But if you have all Ireland for your province you must be more occupied with rural affairs, must you not?—But that is dealt with on the same basis of valuation. The general principle governs the mode of making income tax assessments just the same whether it is in Dublin or any other part.

7344. I should suppose the arrears are chiefly due from landowners, are they not?—That is so; but the principle which governs the assessment is exactly the same.

7345. Your time is occupied chiefly in connexion with arrears from landowners, is it not?—That is so, undoubtedly.

7346. No doubt you discharge those duties very efficiently, but I should say there are other members of the staff who have more direct knowledge of the circumstances of urban valuation than you have?—Of course they have been there longer. There are men who have lived in Ireland all their lives, and to that extent they have had more to do with it than I have, but in making the assessment there is so little to do. You simply get a copy of the valuation lists and make the tax assessments from it. The surveyor is bound to take the valuation list as he finds it.

7347. But you are occupied otherwise than in revising the assessment of the City of Dublin, are you not?—Yes.

7348. You know enough about Dublin, I presume, to know that the southern suburbs are the suburbs in which the wealthier inhabitants live, and that the northern side has gone in a great measure, and over large areas, to decay?—I know that the southern is the more fashionable suburb, and that of course the south is growing while the north is not growing.

7349. But you know that whole districts in the north formerly inhabited by wealthy families are now given over to poor tenants, do you not?—Yes.

7350. Would not that greatly affect a revised valuation of Dublin?—Undoubtedly it would, because no doubt there the rents are much nearer to the valuation than they are in the more fashionable parts.

7351. I should say there is no doubt that the valuation of a house in the northern side of Dublin, which was a family residence or mansion, and is now occupied by the poorest class, would have gone down?—Of course the Valuation Office have power to reduce it, and I have no doubt they have reduced those valuations. It is not as it is in the case of land, that a valuation, once made, must stand for ever, because the Valuation Office issue lots of hundreds of reductions they make every year in house property.

7352. The number appears to be very small?—I really do not know whether it is so or not, but I certainly could not contradict you.

Systems of valuation in Ireland and England compared.

7353. (*Lord Welby.*) Some questions were addressed to you on the subject of the poor rate being the basis of the assessment for income tax, and I think you rather demurred to that, and you would not go further than saying that it was the starting point?—That is so.

7354. In those cases, the poor rate assessment being the starting point, do you actually get rent receipts by which to check the poor-rate assessment?—We do not get rent receipts; we get statements of rent signed by the occupier. The occupier has to make a declaration that the rent is such and such an amount. We have an actual document signed by the occupier.

7355. The figures to which your attention has been called have been a great deal before us. Are not these the figures upon which we ought to fix our attention in dealing with the matter. First of all, after you have eliminated those headings which you assessed under Schedule A., you have a gross estimated rental of 162,000,000*l.*, which, may I put it, the Income Tax Commissioners have raised to 168,000,000*l.*?—That is so.

7356. The difference between 162,000,000*l.* and 168,000,000*l.* really represents, does it not, the action

Mr. G. F. Pearn. 4 Mar. 1895. Systems of assessment in Ireland and England compared.

of the Income Tax Commissioners in correcting the poor rate assessment?—That is so.

7357. As against that, the rateable value is only 133,000,000*l.*?—Yes.

7358. And these three figures really sum up the history of property assessable under Schedule A.?—That is so. I should like to say, with regard to that, that Griffith's valuation in Ireland is not analogous to the gross estimated rental of property in England, but to the rateable value.

7359. From your experience in both countries, and especially since you have pointed to Mr. Barton's evidence, that an allowance is made in the valuation for repairs, would not that bring us to this point, that the rateable value in England really corresponds to the valuation in Ireland?—It certainly does. I have looked back to see what the relative proportion would be years ago between the gross poor rate on property rated to the poor and assessed under Schedule A. and the Schedule A. assessments actually made, my object was to ascertain what the proportion was years ago, which now stands as 100 to 108, and I see that the earliest year in which the department ever called for that information was the year 1874–5. Now, I see for that year the gross poor rate value on property that was rated to the poor and assessed under Schedule A. was 131,007,789*l.*, and the Schedule A. assessment on the same property in 1874 was 121,882,107*l.*; the difference is 9,024,321*l.*, which is an increase upon the gross poor rate of 8·90 per cent. That shows that 20 years ago the local assessments were not made with quite as much strict accuracy as they are at the present time, because there were a greater number of cases in which in making the Crown assessment we refused to accept the local valuations.

7360. There has been a good deal of conversation as to comparing the assessment to income tax in Ireland, which practically corresponds with the valuation and the assessment in England, more especially as to what has been the effect of the provision in the English law which allows revision of the assessment from time to time. Do you think it would be possible to make a return, starting, we will say, from 1853, showing the valuation upon one side in Ireland, which, of course, is very much the same now as it was then, and on the other side the assessment of land under Schedule A. in 1853, in England and Scotland, with what it is now and what it was 20 years ago. The Commission have been told that the comparison between the assessment in England and Ireland is unfair to Ireland, because during the last 20 years there has been a large decrease under Schedule A. in England on account of depression, and the answer to that is, "Yes"; but between 1853 and 1873, or whatever the date was, there had been a very considerable increase. Do you think land under Schedule A. now would be assessable at less than it was in 1853?—Do you mean in England?

7361. Yes?—I can answer that question at once. Lands in England were assessed in 1853 at 41,449,290*l.*, and in 1893 they were assessed at 41,028,703*l.*

7362. Therefore you say they are very nearly the same, do you?—Very nearly; it is a slight decrease.

7363. And that compares with the valuation of Ireland, which is a stationary one?—Yes. I should say with regard to the figures given in this return as to the rent in Ireland, quoted by Mr. Bailey, and made the subject of his first statistical account in the heads of his evidence, this little difference is to be accounted for in the first place by the fact that up to 1876 farm-houses and buildings, rated with the land, were not included in the annual value of lands, whilst since that date they have been, and that really wipes away the great bulk of the difference between the valuation in 1862 and the valuation in 1893. As a matter of fact, as the valuation of land in Ireland cannot be changed, it is quite clear it must remain about the same, no matter how many years you take it apart.

7364. We have also had our attention called to the fact that a large amount of land unoccupied in great towns in England does not pay any rental, and it has been stated that that is a benefit on the part of England which Ireland does not get. What would be your view of that?—If no income is got from a place, I suppose you could hardly get a tax from it, could you. I am speaking now of land ruined or unoccupied?—As a general rule that land is assessed at its present value in its present condition, that is to say, if it were part of what had originally been a grass field it would be assessed at its agricultural value as accommodation grass land, and the tax would be paid on it. Of course no assessment is made on any theoretical value based upon a percentage of capital value; we have no power to charge a man upon what he might make by his property if he chose to put it to some other purpose, either in England or Ireland.

Mr. G. F. Pearn. 4 Mar. 1895. Systems of valuation in Ireland and England compared.

7365. And the land, if only agricultural, would only have an agricultural value?—That would be so.

7366. Can you tell us from your own knowledge what proportion of income tax in Ireland is paid on the valuation and not on the rental?—No, I could not say that.

7367. Do you think that information could be ascertained?—I do not know that that could be given; it would involve an enormous amount of work, because every single voucher throughout the country, numbering hundreds of thousands, would have to be examined in order to answer it.

7368. From your experience do you think as a rule it is paid on the valuation, or what?—In a large number of cases it is still paid on the valuation.

7369. And within your notice since judicial rents have been fixed, has the tendency been not to pay on the valuation but on the new rent?—There are still a great many cases in which the landlord elects to pay on the valuation.

Valuation of houses in Dublin.

7370. (*Mr. Martin.*) In reference to your appendix giving the amount of valuation of certain houses, are you aware that the Dublin house agents usually put down in their lists a very appreciably higher price than they mean to take for their houses?—No, I do not know that.

7371. Would it surprise you to hear that the custom is to accept a diminution of 25 to 50 per cent. on the prices asked?—Yes, I should be surprised to hear that. The only house I know of that has been actually let comprised in this list has been let at the price asked for it, that is No. 20.

7372. I have some experience in taking houses in Dublin, and no one would dream of giving the price the agents put in their list. Are there any cases where a larger demand is made on owners having land in their own hands than the ordinary rate of income tax on the valuation of such lands?—No.

7373. Is there any case where a demand is made of 9*d.* in the pound in addition to 8*d.*?—Under Schedule B.

7374. How do you come to place the land under the two schedules?—All land is liable to be placed under two schedules; in the case of an owner occupying his own land, he would be liable to the Schedule A. rate as owner, and Schedule B. rate as occupier.

7375. Even although he pays on the amount of his receipts?—We should not tax him on the amount of his receipts.

7376. But he had the land in his own hands, and let the grazing we will suppose?—In that case we should do this. He could either pay us under Schedule A. at 8*d.*, and Schedule B. at 3*d.*, or if he chose he could send us an statement, saying "I let the land at so much, "the cost of doing it is so much, the rate is so much, "and the net balance I get is so much, on which I "will pay you at 8*d.*," and if the amount came to less than the combined charge under A. and B. we should accept taxes on the receipts at 8*d.* We are constantly these having claims.

Deductions for repairs.

7377. Have you experienced any falling off in the receipts for income tax owing to the action of the Finance Act of last year, that is allowing one-eighth or

Mr. S. F. [illegible].
8 Mar. 1895.
Deductions for repairs.

one-sixth off for repairs?—Yes, that will make a very large falling off.

7378. Has it occurred up to the present?—Yes, allowance has been made in thousands of cases. There is a note at the bottom of the collectors demand notes calling the attention of the taxpayer to the fact that he is entitled to make a claim, and instructions have also been issued to the surveyors, telling them to give the necessary directions to the local collectors to make this alteration contemplated by the Act; but, to be perfectly candid, I know, as a matter of fact, that there are a great many cases in Ireland which will have to be adjusted by repayments; several cases have come under my notice where owners, in ignorance of what their rights were, have paid on the full charge. In England, where the assessments, in all cases, were made on the full letting value, there was no difficulty in correcting the books before delivery to the collectors, but in Ireland, as the Act says that these allowances shall not apply in cases where the disparity between the rent and valuation exceeds a certain proportion, namely, one-eighth and one-sixth, and as we have no means of knowing where the disparity does exceed it and where not, it was impossible for us to alter the books.

7379. (*Chairman.*) Is there in Ireland, especially in Dublin, anything analogous to the annual return, which, in London, all householders have to make to the parish authorities, with the details of the value and rent of their houses?—Nothing at all.

7380. That does not exist, does it?—That does not exist.

7381. You know, do you not, that it does in England?—Yes.

7382. And that we, in England, are put to the proof of the rateable value of our houses every five years?—Yes.

7383. There is no such thing in Ireland, is there?—There is no such thing in Ireland.

7384. It would be a beneficial change, would it not?—Of course, if we had that information, we should know at once what the real assessment should be, and it would save all this guessing.

7385. It is a return which is much objected to in England, do you think?—I do not think so. Speaking generally, there is nothing like the friction and trouble in the working of the Schedule A. assessment as the Schedule D.

7386. If you had your choice between the English system and the Irish system which would you, from the Crown point of view, choose?—I should choose the English system, because it admits of much greater accuracy.

7387. And it admits of adjustment from time to time, according to real value?—Yes.

7388. (*Mr. Sexton.*) With regard to reductions, exemptions, and abatements on page 32, I took you as far as the gross annual value assessed, 169,300,000*l.*?—Yes.

7389. That is subject to a deduction of 18,000,000*l.*, for abatements and exemptions, is it not?—Yes.

7390. That is to say, about one-ninth of the gross?—Yes.

7391. The Irish assessment of 13,612,000*l.* is subject to a deduction of 900,000*l.*, that is one-fifteenth of the gross?—Yes.

7392. If the English proportion of exemptions and abatements were the same as the Irish, one-fifteenth, it would be 11,000,000*l.*, not 18,000,000*l.*?—Yes, but I can explain that in a moment. You see the great bulk of that 18,300,000*l.* comes under the head of exemptions under 160*l.*, there is no less than 13,784,676*l.* of the total under that one head, of exemptions that simply arises from the fact that in England there are an enormous number of real property owners with incomes below the limit of taxation, whereas in all Ireland there are comparatively few such cases. The great bulk of property in Ireland is held by people whose incomes are not within the limits of exemption.

7393. But of the total exemptions of Ireland, 747,000*l.* arises under that head?—Yes, it does.

7394. The main exemption in Ireland, as in England, is under that head, and almost in the same proportion, is it not?—Yes.

7395. And the fact remains that the whole exemptions in England are proportionately nearly double to what they are in Ireland, does it not?—Yes, the reason of that is that the other exemptions here are included in the assessment in England, but not in Ireland. Now in Ireland, at the present time, it is the practice to leave out hospitals and public schools altogether. They are not put in, whereas in England there is 1,900,000*l.* assessed under that head. Then there is 494,000*l.* for land tax deduction, while there is no land tax payable in Ireland. With regard to these other things, the parochial rates, &c. as the tithe rentcharges, for instance, in Ireland the rentcharge is not assessed separately, and in England it is assessed separately. We cannot give them a deduction in this way, but it is made by way of repayment.

Mr. S. F. [illegible].
8 Mar. 1895.
Reference to the ruling.
Deductions from gross annual value.

The witness withdrew.

Adjourned to the 28th March.

SEVENTEENTH DAY.

Thursday, 28th March 1895.

At B Committee Room, House of Lords.

PRESENT:

THE RIGHT HON. HUGH C. E. CHILDERS, *Chairman*.

LORD WELBY.	J. E. REDMOND, Esq., M.P.
SIR DAVID BARBOUR, K.C.S.I.	THOMAS SEXTON, Esq., M.P.
THE HON. EDWARD BLAKE, M.P.	GUSTAV W. WOLFF, Esq., M.P.
BERTRAM W. CURRIE, Esq.	HENRY F. SLATTERY, Esq.

Mr. H. J. Morgan. 29 Mar. 1906. Action of County Council.

7399. To what extent have you personal experience of assessments under the different schedules of the income tax?—The action of the London County Council, in promoting uniformity of assessment, has brought their Estates and Valuation Department, to which I belong, into close communication with the local assessing authorities; and since 1890 all valuation lists deposited in London have been carefully examined by that department. In the discharge of my official duties, I am frequently present at the meetings of the local assessment committees, and at the sittings of the London Quarter Sessions devoted to assessment business; and I am well acquainted with the principles and practice of assessing property to income tax, under Schedule A., throughout the metropolis, as defined by the Valuation (Metropolis) Act, 1869.

7400. Beyond that district you also have experience, I think?—Some slight experience derived from, first, the assessment of property in other counties belonging to the London County Council, nearly all of which has been re-valued during the last six years, and secondly, examinations, for various purposes, of the valuation lists of parishes adjacent to the county of London, parishes which take the benefit of our main drainage system.

Assessment of property let on long leases.

7401. In the case of property in London let on long leases, in what way is so much of the annual letting value, which is not covered by the rent paid by the occupier, assessed to income tax?—Any value beyond the rent paid by the occupier should be included in the "gross value" column of the valuation list (which is, by the Act of 1869, section 45, conclusive evidence of value for income tax purposes), and in most London parishes this is now done. Such value (that is the value beyond the rent paid) is often represented by a premium paid by the occupier on entering, or by his expenditure of a stipulated sum in the improvement of the premises. In these cases there is a rule (suggested by the Assessment Conference) now generally applied, and its effect is to produce substantial fairness in the assessment. I do not know whether you wish me to explain what I mean by that rule and that Conference.

Action of County Council.

7402. If you please, and also would you state what the Assessment Conference was?—The Assessment Conference was convened by the London County Council, and was a conference between their Local Government and Taxation Committee and representatives of all the various assessing bodies in the metropolis. This Conference passed a series of resolutions, which were printed and circulated to all the London rating authorities, in the form of rules for practical guidance in arriving at the annual value of various classes of property. The principal end in view was to induce all the local authorities to follow the same practice, and thus ensure substantial uniformity. I have copies of those rules here, and if they will be of any use I will hand them in.

7403. Was the Assessment Conference successful?—Yes, I think I may say that it was successful in the sense that it arrived at practical unanimity in connection with those resolutions.

7404. Has it required legislation to enforce it or not?—In so far as those resolutions are concerned, not. There was a proposal before that Conference to amend the law, and they arrived practically at an agreed Bill, but these resolutions which I have now handed in are under the present law and would not in any way be interfered with by the Bill which was considered by that Conference, and which has been introduced, I believe, into the House of Commons this session.

7405. But the resolutions of the Conference, so far as they did require legislation have not been considered by any decision of the County Council yet, have they?—No. The Council felt that it would be wise on their part not to interfere with these resolutions in any way. Of course they had to come before the Council in order that a formal vote might be passed for their printing and issuing to all the rating authorities, and members of the Council then desired to make amendments and alterations, but it was felt by the great majority that it was undesirable to interfere at all with the work which had been done by the Assessment Conference.

7406. Therefore it is still in the power of each authority to apply these rules or not, as they think fit?—Certainly.

7407. (*Mr. Hinds.*) You say they have been generally applied, do you?—In fact they have been generally applied, but of course there has been no general re-valuation since those resolutions were passed. That re-valuation is about to take place this year.

7408. (*Chairman.*) I interrupted you in the middle of a previous answer. Perhaps you will conclude it?—As to the particular properties where the annual letting value is not covered by the rent paid by the occupier, I had mentioned two ways in which that might be accounted for, the premium and the outlay made on the premises; but it may happen, however, that the holder of a long lease will remain in occupation for many years, during which time the property increases in value. The only means available to the assessors for including such increase of value in their assessments are, first, a comparison with adjacent similar properties, if any, held at rack-rents; or, secondly, an expert valuation. There is, among the resolutions passed by the Assessment Conference, a rule suggesting that in the case of all leases more than five years old, special attention should be paid to that particular consideration.

Assessment of property let on long leases.

7409. Does property of this kind, in your opinion, pay income tax on its full annual letting value?—In the majority of London parishes rough justice is done, and has been done in the past. In others, part, at any rate, of the full annual value of such properties has escaped assessment in the past, but much of this class of error has been, and is now being, rectified. In certain wealthy districts, however, even at the present time, any value beyond the rent paid escapes assessment to a considerable extent, the principal offenders being the City of London Union and the parishes of St. Marylebone, St. James, Westminster and St. George, Hanover Square. It is believed, however, that they will conform to the rules laid down by the Assessment Conference in the forthcoming quinquennial re-valuation.

7410. When the principles of the Assessment Conference will practically be in force?—I can hardly use the word "enforced," but I believe that the vast majority of the parishes in London will voluntarily adopt those rules and carry them out.

7411. I said "in force," not "enforced." Is much property in London held, in your opinion, at rents in excess of its actual letting value, if in possession?—There is not much in the sense of proportion to the whole; but there are, no doubt, fairly numerous cases of this kind. They arise mainly, first, in the case of leasehold property, where unforeseen depreciation takes place during the currency of the lease; and, secondly, in the case of business premises, where tenants pay unduly high rents in order to avoid the necessity of removing an established business to a new address.

Assessment of freehold property.

7412. Does freehold property in London, in the actual occupation of its owners, bear an appreciable proportion to all the property in London?—Numerically, I think not; but with regard to value, I think the proportion is appreciable. Some of the largest and most valuable properties in London come under this head, while, on the other hand, building societies have had a tendency to multiply small owners during the last 30 or 40 years. Of course, if I am to include in this category—as I should, technically, be justified in doing—properties owned and occupied for public purposes by the Imperial Government, the local authorities, and other public or semipublic bodies such as railway, gas, and water companies, I should not hesitate to say that the proportion is fairly substantial in both senses.

7413. But as to residential property—houses in occupation—you would say it was very small, would you?—Very small indeed.

7414. Does such property, in your opinion, pay income tax on its full annual letting value?—As to small properties, yes; for they are readily comparable with adjacent similar properties let at rack-rents. As to more valuable properties, I think a large proportion of them in private hands are under-assessed; those belonging to the London County Council and the School Board for London are, if anything, too highly valued; but many buildings belonging to the local authorities are not fully assessed. Railways, docks, tramways, canals, gas and waterworks are, as a rule, kept up to the mark, as experts are usually employed to value them.

7415. Do large freehold private mansions, hotels, clubs, restaurants, and public houses pay income tax, in your opinion, on their full annual letting value?—On the whole, I think not. Freehold mansions in London are often under-assessed; but this is in some measure due to the fact that they are, for the most part, situated in parishes where other classes of property are also under-assessed. Hotels, clubs, and restaurants, in the City and West End, are not always fully valued; but in other districts there is less cause for complaint. Some assessment committees put them at a high figure, and appeals to quarter sessions are the consequence. The surveyors have great difficulty in dealing with properties of the descriptions set out in the question; and the rules drawn up by the Assessment Conference as to licensed premises (Nos. 5a, 6a, and 6c), under which an arbitrary proportion of the premium is converted into annual value and added to the rent, are not sufficient to ensure accuracy, which, in complicated cases, cannot be attained by a hard and fast rule. In following the rules, errors result, no doubt, in both directions; but the balance, in my opinion, is on the low side.

7416. You mean on the side of under-assessment?—Yes. I think, generally speaking, licensed property in London is somewhat under-assessed.

7417. Can you give the case of any particular place?—In the Fulham Union it has been the practice to take into account only one third of the premium instead of one half; but this will be altered at the forthcoming quinquennial re-valuation.

7418. Can you make any estimate of the annual value, assuming it to be utilised for building, of vacant land in London?—No reliable data are available for framing such an estimate. I have formed an opinion as to the quantity, though on somewhat slender grounds, to the effect that, excluding public open spaces and accommodation land within the curtilage of existing buildings, there are about 14,000 acres of vacant land in the county of London. But the greater part of this land is not, under present conditions, ripe for building operations; and consequently, while it has an increasing capital value, its annual value would be little more than it would fetch for agricultural purposes.

7419. When you say "ripe for building operations," do you mean liable to building operations, but not ready to be built upon at present?—The word "ripe" is in use among surveyors, means land which could now, if placed in the market, be let on building lease and ground rents created.

7420. It is land liable to be built upon. There is nothing legally, in these, to prevent its being built upon?—Certainly; perfectly liable.

7421. (Mr. Blake.) You mean the time has arrived when you can put it on the market with advantage?—That is my meaning.

7422. (Chairman.) On what principle is such land now assessed?—Land about to be built on is seldom or never assessed, except to land tax. But vacant land fit for immediate occupation as agricultural or accommodation land is assessed at its full annual value in nearly all districts.

7423. Can you give any information as to the assessment of country houses?—Not from personal experience.

7424. If assessments were made entirely by a central Government department instead of, as at present, by local elected bodies, subject to supervision by central officers, do you think that there would be greater approximation than at present between assessments and actual annual values?—I think the question applies rather to England generally, and is not applicable in some particulars to the case of London. There the assessment committees are not directly elected bodies, but are chosen by the members of vestries and boards of guardians from among themselves. Nor are they subject to supervision by central officers, though the metropolitan surveyors of taxes attend their meetings and possess special privileges for making objections (see the Act of 1869, sections 8, 18, and 32). These officers, having usually no expert qualification in valuation, are not always able—despite their ability—to check efficiently the action of the assessment committees. I have not considered the idea of having assessments made entirely by a central Government department. The desired approximation between assessments and actual annual value would, in my opinion, be best secured by the appointment of expert officials who might either act as the advisers of the local assessment committees, or form part of a municipal assessor's department, such as exists in Glasgow. The Valuation (Assessment) Bill, promoted by the London County Council, with the concurrence of the Assessment Conference, would provide facilities for such appointments, and would also throw upon the Council the duties of sending a representative—who would undoubtedly be an expert in values—to sit with each local assessment committee, and of assessing all hereditaments (such as railways) which extend through two or more parishes. Both provisions are introduced with a view to promoting uniformity, but they cannot fail to promote accuracy at the same time. Personally, I have a preference for the Glasgow system, modified to meet the needs of London; but the scheme embodied in the Bill would, to a large extent, have a similar effect, and, as it is the outcome of long and careful deliberation by many persons well versed in the subject, I attach the less importance to my own opinion.

7425. The Commission desire to ascertain, as nearly as practicable, the annual value of real estate in England. Do you think that, on the whole, the assessments to Schedule A. of the Income Tax form a fair standard of measurement?—The assessment to income tax under Schedule A. includes the average annual cost of repairs and insurance, and therefore represents, in this sense, more than the net annual value of real estate. On the other hand, various classes of property, such as parks, churches, &c., are exempt from assessment under Schedule A. But, on the whole, taking one thing with another, I think the present assessments under Schedule A. form as good a basis for determining annual value—so far as London property is concerned—as any with which I am acquainted. Assuming all property included in assessment at its full value, a deduction of one-sixth part from the gross annual value—as prescribed by the Finance Act of 1894—would have the closest possible approximation to the net annual value.

7426. (Mr. Currie.) Do I understand you to say that the value of residential property in such parishes as St. James', Westminster, Marylebone, and St. George's, Hanover Square, is on the increase at present?—The value I did not say is on the increase, but the existing value is not fully represented by the figures in the valuation list.

7427. But is it within your knowledge that leasehold houses have recently been sold in those districts at less than half what they commanded some 20 years ago?—Yes. On the other hand, there are many properties which are worth double what they were worth several years ago.

7428. But I understood you to mention the rating of houses was always on the increase, my experience is the other way?—Certainly.

7429. Within the last few years the saleable value of such houses as you describe has been decreasing very much, has it not?—I have no wish to give the

Mr. E. J. Harper.

9 May 1899.

Assessment and actual value.

impression that there was a steady increase in the value of residential property; all I have said is that the existing value of residential property is not fully represented in the valuations at present made. I believe that during the revaluation which has just commenced, and which will be brought to an end during the current year, there will be a very great reform in that respect.

7430. I understand you to say that one of the main factors upon which the valuation was based in the case of long leasehold residences was the purchase price?—Yes, the premium.

7431. If that premium is less than half, as I know it is in many cases, would not that represent that the premium was ... ?—No, for the reason that in many, many cases, with which I am personally familiar in particular at the west end of London, the premium whatever has been taken in account in assessing them, they have taken the rent only, and the annual value beyond that, represented by the premium, has hitherto escaped assessment altogether. The authorities are fully alive to that now, and I believe during the revaluation this year all those cases will be corrected, and that the valuation now proceeding, if it could be completed in time for the purposes of this Commission, would give you the nearest possible approximation to the actual value of London property.

7432. (*Chairman.*) The actual letting value of London property?—The actual letting value of London property.

7433. The letting value in the words of the statute?—The letting value in the words of the statute.

7434. (*Mr. Blake.*) Then I understand you to say, notwithstanding there has been in some quarters a considerable under-value, the depreciated value has not run down to the assessment value yet, but that the assessment value remains below even the depreciated value of the property?—That is quite so, and beyond that, while there has been depreciation in certain quarters, there has been appreciation in others, and so far the balance has been a slight increase as to property as a whole—not as to residential property only.

7435. (*Sir David Barbour.*) After the valuation is made, is it frequently corrected or does it last for a number of years?—It lasts for five years, unless there are any special reasons, such as the addition of a new storey to a house or something of that kind, when it is in the power of the overseers, in fact it is their duty, to make what is called a provisional list in order that the rates on the property may be forthwith claimed. Then every year those provisional lists are brought together in what is called a supplemental list, and that is added to the total of the previous full valuation.

7436. (*Chairman.*) But the change must be a visible change, must it not?—That is a legal question upon which I am hardly competent to express a final opinion. In practice that is how we regard it; the words of the Act are "is from any cause increased or "decreased in value." Those words seem to be wider, but cases which have been tested and carried to the High Court seem to throw some doubt on the wider construction that one is at first inclined to put on those words.

7437. (*Mr. Wolff.*) In answer to question 11, you said that the assessment committees were not subject to supervision by central officers, but that the surveyors of taxes attended their meetings, although these officers, not being experts, were not able always to check efficiently the action of the assessment committees. Then you said that the desired approximation between assessment and actual annual value would be best secured by the appointment of expert officers either as the advisers of the local assessment committees or as forming part of a municipal assessors' department. Do you think that would have the result of raising the assessment?—During the forthcoming valuation, I think, on the whole, it would.

7438. Then do you think on the whole the assessment is below the actual valuation?—At the present time.

7439. (*Lord Kelly.*) When will the forthcoming quinquennial valuation take place?—It has already commenced, the overseers have sent out their forms of return to the occupiers and, on getting them in, they are commencing in some parishes already to make out their lists.

7440. Therefore it will be completed this year?—It will be completed and deposited on the 31st of May, but that is subject of course to objections which any ratepayer may make to the various assessment committees.

7441. When that is put into force, do I understand you think that, taking London, the income tax will be fully and fairly charged upon London property?—I have every confidence that it will.

7442. And that the cases which you have pointed where properties have hitherto escaped full valuation will be remedied?—Yes.

7443. And therefore in answer to the evidence which has been put before us that income tax is not levied fully on real property and, I think, especially in London, below its value, it is likely that that will no longer, whatever it may have been worth in the past, be the case?—I believe it will not.

7444. (*Chairman.*) Would you say so as to mediate now that that belief is well founded that income tax is levied upon considerably less than the value?—I certainly should not employ the word "considerably." The total assessment to income tax under Schedule A in London at the present time is something over 40,000,000*l.*, and I do not suppose that any re-valuation (disregarding new buildings, which of course form some element in it), would add another million.

7445. Disregarding new buildings?—Disregarding new buildings. Of course new buildings come in as a matter of course as they are put up, but the mere correction of all present under-assessment I do not think would add more than a million to the existing forty millions.

7446. That is 2½ per cent.?—That is 2½ per cent.

7447. May I ask you incidentally, are the questions which are addressed to householders this year with the view to the preparation of that information upon the former form or has any change been made?—They appear to be, so far as I have seen them, on the former form. The list prepared by the County Council with the concurrence of the Assessment Conference took power to modify that form from time to time in order to obtain certain items of information that are not provided for on the existing form.

7448. Has that been done?—That has not been done on the forms issued for the forthcoming revaluation because there has been no authority to depart from the old form which was prescribed by the Act.

7449. So that the information may be more correct as it will be given this year, but it is practically the same information as has been obtained quinquennially for some time past, is it?—Yes. Of course the value of the quinquennial re-valuation consists in the skill and accuracy with which these returns, made by the occupiers, are checked by the officers responsible for making the list.

7450. The questions are searching questions, are they not?—The questions are searching questions so far as regards rent and annual value, but the question of premium, which is a very important one in certain parishes, is only dealt with by a question worded, if I remember rightly, somewhat in this form. "Was any "consideration other than the rent made for the "granting of the lease?" There are many people who do not know what the word "consideration" in that connexion means; others, no doubt, omit to reply of set purpose in order to escape assessment to a certain extent.

7451. And you think it would have been better if the question could have been more searching and put so clearly?—It is rather too formal and legal in shape at present.

Qq 4

Mr. E. J. Harper.

20 Mar. 1895.

Assessments and actual values.

7452. (*Lord Welby.*) You said that in some parishes the full annual value of properties had escaped assessment, I suppose that is due in fact to this, that the rent was fixed some time ago, probably on lease, and that rent continues to be charged, though in many cases the value of the house has considerably increased, and if it were re-let now it would fetch a higher rent, is that the reason why property escapes full assessment?—That is exactly the reason. You have a body of overseers sitting round the table with the occupier's return before them, they see the rent is so and so, and they write down the assessment at so and so, it is quite impossible for them to judge, sitting round the table, whether a property has increased or decreased in value.

7453. It has been rather held upon that ground that property has escaped full assessment on account of appreciation, but, passing to the question Mr. Currie put to you just now, on the other hand have not people been paying more than they ought to pay, because property has decreased. I will give you an instance in my mind. A friend of mine told me some time ago, of a house he gave 9,000*l.* for, in South Kensington. A certain number of years had lapsed, but the lease had not over depreciated, and he had leased it had recently realised 4,500*l.* That house must have depreciated very much in value, must it not? Supposing it to have been the same lease, the occupier of that house had been paying very much more income tax than the value of his house warranted, had he not?—That would be so in that case, but that is corrected to a certain extent by the right of objection given to every ratepayer. You see when a property is assessed too high, the ratepayer has the right to object before the assessment committee, and if he shows good grounds, the assessment is reduced. On the other hand, if it is too low, it is to the interest of no individual to object, and, consequently, hitherto he has escaped. These representatives sent by the London County Council to the assessment committees would, among their other duties, have to look after those cases where the assessment is too low.

7454. In such a case as I have mentioned, would the fact of the decreased capital value, which the occupier paid for the remainder of the lease be taken into consideration by the assessment committee?—Yes, and certainly we, as representing the Council, should ask for a reduction in the assessment, whether the ratepayer did so or not. Our object is, of course, to secure uniformity, and not necessarily a high assessment.

7455. But you say nobody has an interest in the case where property is under-assessed. Has not the Surveyor of Inland Revenue an interest in it?—Yes, the surveyors of taxes look after that very sharply, but they have only the returns to guide them. They are not surveyors, they have no expert knowledge as to the value of property, and all they can do is to see that the assessment is not lower than the rent. Where there is a premium paid, and it is not disclosed by the occupier, the surveyor of taxes is powerless.

7456. But under your new method of assessment which will come into force, you think this will be remedied, do you?—I hope it will.

Method of assessment.

7457. (*Mr. Sexton.*) I am sorry not to have heard your direct evidence, but I should like to ask you a few questions. Your personal knowledge on the matter of your evidence is confined, I think, to London and some parts adjacent to London?—Yes, practically.

7458. You have no connexion yourself with the assessment to income tax, have you?—No.

7459. Your function is simply to supervise assessments for the purpose of local rating, is it not?—No, not exactly. Of course the London County Council are simply acting in this direction in the interests of uniformity, and their only power—their only right to do so lies in the fact that they are ratepayers in the great majority of the London parishes and they are exercising the rights of ratepayers. They have no supervising authority, but they make use of their right of lodging objections to get into communication with the authorities who do make the lists, and with the authorities who determine the objections to those lists and bring moral pressure to bear upon them in the direction of uniformity.

Mr. E. J. Harper.

20 Mar. 1895.

Method of assessment.

7460. As persons who have a right to object legally afterwards, they suggest by preference a conference before?—That is exactly so.

7461. This uniformity at which they aim, does not, as you have just said, I think, in reply to Lord Welby, necessarily mean a full or higher assessment?—It means a full assessment—not an unduly high one.

7462. It does not necessarily mean, I think, even a full assessment, does it, but it means the assessment should be on the same principle?—Yes; but there is no safe road to uniformity except by taking the full assessment.

7463. Possibly. When these assessments are made by local authorities and when the local assessment may serve as the basis for the income tax levy, does it not rather seem that the local interest is in the low assessment as far as the income tax is concerned?—You see what is in the eye of the assessing bodies is generally the local rate, which is much more considerable than the income tax. I do not think the income tax consideration has much weight with them.

7464. Of course, if they are assessed unfairly, even upon a low basis, there would be a certain advantage would there not, I mean that the local rate is distributed in like manner over the assessment as if it were higher?—Certainly, and there has been a tendency, of course, in the past, for parishes where the rate is high, to be highly valued in order to keep the rate as low as possible and *vice versâ* where the rate is low, to value low in order to keep the rate in the *£* up.

7465. To give it the appearance of being up?—Yes.

7466. And in the other case to give it the appearance of being down?—Yes.

Revaluation of property of the County Council.

7467. I notice in your proof that nearly all the property belonging to the London County Council has been revalued during the last six years?—That is the property outside London.

7468. What has been the effect of the re-valuation?—A very considerable increase. The property referred to consists mainly of large outfall sewage works and lunatic asylums.

7469. Situated in counties adjoining Middlesex or counties near it?—Yes.

7470. Can you say whether that property, before its revaluation, had been valued for the purpose of assessment upon a basis uniform with the other property in those counties or districts?—No, it had not.

7471. Will you kindly say what the system was?—In the case of lunatic asylums the practice was under statute to rate them at precisely the amount at which they stood in the rate books when they were purchased by the asylum authority for the purpose of lunatic asylums, so that while there was no loss of rate or income tax owing to the fact of the property being taken for an asylum, there would be no increase in the future. That law was repealed in 1890 or 1891 by an amendment of the Lunacy Act, and that led to a revaluation of all our asylums. They are now assessed on the same principle as all other properties.

7472. Had your outfall works been under-valued before?—They had not been under-valued on the basis of the then decisions. Of course, the districts in which they were situated had previously made attempts to rate them at figures somewhat similar to the figures at which they stand now, and those being the days of the Metropolitan Board, there was strong resistance on their part to those high ratings, and the deciding case, I believe, was carried to the Queen's Bench Division, only. There the parishes stopped, they did not go on to the House of Lords being beaten in the Queen's Bench Division, or it may have been to the Court of Appeal. But during the last two years the parish of Erith, I think it was, carried an appeal to the House of Lords, and there succeeded to the extent that our outfall works have now to be rated on a percentage

of their capital value, which never falls below 3 per cent., but is generally something above it.

7473. Has that involved an increase in the valuation?—A very large increase indeed.

7474. Can you say whether similar property or other property to that owned by the County Council in those districts has been rated on the like principle before the revaluation. I mean does it seem likely to you, from your knowledge, if other property in those districts were re-valued in the same way there would be an increase in the valuation?—Of course other varieties have been revalued in the same way, and there has been a similar increase. With regard to the ordinary property, residential and other, in those districts, there may be some little under-assessment for rating purposes, but outside London the valuation lists made by the parishes do not bind the income tax people, and surveyors of taxes take care to see that the valuation is up to the proper amount for their purposes.

7475. If the assessment for local purposes outside London were low, the question whether the assessment was made full for income tax would depend on the efficiency of the surveyors for income tax, would it not?—Yes.

7476. But in London, I understand, another system operates, and that is a certain column of the local valuation list has to be taken by law for the income tax assessment?—Yes, that is so.

7477. How does that work?—It works in this way, that a surveyor of taxes (although he cannot actually put up the figure, if he is not satisfied with it) has a column set apart for his use in the list, and in that column, wherever he differs from the figures put down by the overseers, he puts down his figure, and there is a special clause in the Act saying that unless his valuation is disproved it is to stand.

7478. But when he does not put any figure in the column then the rent stands, of course, for the income tax assessment?—Yes, he is taken to concur in the valuation made by the overseers.

7479. There is no onus upon him, as it were, to interfere in every case; it is left to his discretion altogether, is it not?—It is left to his discretion, certainly.

7480. What means has the person liable to pay income tax of questioning the action of the surveyor?—If there is an alteration made in his assessment he has notice of it served upon him in sufficient time to enable him to serve the proper notice of objection and have his case considered by the assessment committee.

7481. Does the local assessment committee consider whether or not the entry made by the surveyor of income tax in the gross value column is accurate?—Certainly.

7482. Can they determine the matter?—They can determine the matter subject to the provisions of the Act to which I have already referred. There must be absolute disproof of the opinion of the surveyor of taxes before it can be set aside. The surveyor of taxes sits with the assessment committee when they are considering these matters.

7483. In what capacity does he sit, in a deliberative capacity?—In a deliberative capacity; but he does not vote.

7484. And he has no control, has he?—He has no control.

7485. Do they finally determine the question?—They finally determine the question.

7486. And the question they have finally to determine is how far they should permit a departure from their own assessment for the purposes of the Imperial tax?—Not from their own assessment. The overseers who make the lists and the assessment committee who hear the objections are different bodies.

7487. How far is the assessment committee concerned with the local valuation which has been altered by the surveyor for the purposes of income tax?—They are concerned in, and they have the duty of settling the list, making it accurate in every respect.

They have, in the words of the Act, to revise the list from beginning to end, and to make the total.

Mr. E. J. Harper.

21 Mar. 1898.

Method of assessment.

7488. Do they approve of the valuation which has been entered in the list before the surveyor makes the entry in the gross value column?—No; before the lists go to the assessment committees the surveyor of taxes is supposed to have made all his entries.

7489. So that both the entries come before them at the same time?—Yes.

7490. I see from your footnote that you expect a good deal from the conference which has been voluntarily convened between the County Council and the local assessing bodies?—Yes, I do.

7491. The object of it is simply, as you say, a series of uniformity?—Certainly.

7492. And the efficiency of that conference will depend entirely on the free accord of the parties?—Yes, it will; but I think you should bear in mind that the action that has been taken by the Council, not only in convening that conference, but in examining all the valuation lists for the past four years, has had a very good effect. In fact, the parishes, say, five years ago, in which there was considerable under-valuation, are now the foremost in putting their houses in order.

7493. Only time will show whether you are too sanguine, but at any rate there is no compulsion, everything depends on the free will and co-operation of all the parishes?—Certainly.

7494. I gather that you are of opinion that where the letting value in the case of a progressive property held on lease exceeds the rent, the property is often not fully assessed to the income tax?—Yes, that may be so.

7495. It seems rather an haphazard thing that everything should depend in London upon the filling in of this column by the surveyor, does it not. There is no kind of check upon him as to whether he ought to have made an entry in the gross value column or not, is there?—No, there is no check upon him; if he does not make it there is an end of it.

7496. Quite so. If there is no entry in his gross value column the other column seems to be all sufficient?—Subject to all the objections of the occupier.

7497. In the case where the increased value has been due to a premium paid by the tenant on entry, how do you say substantial fairness is secured on the assessment?—A percentage on that premium is added to the rent.

7498. What percentage?—It is calculated on a 5 per cent. basis according to the number of years that the lease has to run.

7499. A 5 per cent. basis upon the actual premium?—Upon the actual premium.

7500. (*Lord Welby.*) How does that work. Do you say there is an addition made to the actual rents on the ground of any extra premium that may be paid?—Any premium that may be paid. There is under those rules. Of course the trouble has been that in certain parishes the premiums have been disregarded in the past. I am speaking of the new rules now.

7501. It is by that means that you think the accuracy of which you have spoken will be obtained?—Certainly.

7502. (*Mr. Blake.*) That process is adopted only provided the increased letting value due to such outlay cannot be otherwise ascertained, is it not. That is Rule II.?—I think you are taking the rule which relates to freehold properties.

7503. (*Mr. Seaton.*) These rules have no binding force have they?—Of course they have no binding force at present.

7504. I daresay they are admirable rules, but are they followed?—I think in the majority of parishes, during the last 12 months, they have been followed, and I have every reason to believe that they will continue to be followed in the re-valuation that has just commenced.

7505. You think that they are followed now in some parishes, and you hope the others may follow

Mr. E. J. Harper.

28 May 1895.

Method of assessment.

those hereafter?—I know they are followed in the majority of parishes, and I think they will all come into line.

7506. (*Chairman.*) I put a question to you on that point—that it is intended to give them the force of law. I do not know whether you answered it?—We can hardly give this the force of law, but we are seeking power in the Valuation Amendment Bill to frame byelaws, and these would practically be the byelaws, and they then would have the force of law.

7507. (*Mr. Sexton.*) In the event of the Bill passing into law?—Yes.

7508. Then the effect of the operation of these principles is all a question for the future, is it not?—Not all a question for the future, because we believe that voluntarily they will be applied to to a very large extent.

7509. Except in so far as certain parishes may have applied them up to this time?—Yes, speaking to-day.

7510. In a case where it is not a question of a premium paid on entry, nor a question of the expenditure of a man in improving the premises, but where the accretion in value is due to causes outside the action of either landlord or occupier, how do you there secure the full assessment, or how is it secured for income tax?—At the present time, I do not think it is secured in such cases.

7511. Do you think the assessment does not include that increment?—I do not think it does. There are no facilities for the persons whose duty it is to make the valuation list ascertaining what the increment is. That is why we suggest that experts representing the County Council should sit with these bodies when they are making their list in order to supply them with that information. At present the overseers sit round the table, and make the lists from the occupiers' returns. We suggest that a gentleman with practical knowledge of the value of property, having viewed and surveyed all the property in the district previously, should sit with them, and from his knowledge supply the deficiencies in the occupiers' returns.

7512. Of course, even from the local point of view, I suppose something is lost, when from a casual reason an individual tenement is under-assessed?—Yes, something is lost.

Action of the County Council.

7513. So you think the County Council would have an interest in keeping this class of property up to its full assessment?—Not a pecuniary interest. When you spoke of a local interest my mind went to the vestries and parishes. Of course, if a property is under-assessed there a penny rate in the pound yields them so much less, but with regard to the Council, we simply make our precept, send it round to all the parishes, and they have to collect it for us, and it is a matter for them, not for us, as to whether one parish has to raise more and another less. We get the whole sum we want whether it is raised on an equitable assessment or not.

7514. Whatever their valuation may be they have to pay your precept?—Yes.

7515. Should I be right in saying that even as regards the vestries, the question whether any particular property is under-assessed does not concern them pecuniarily, because, as you have to get your precept, they also have to get their rate, but that the injustice would arise as between the individual under-assessed and those who might be fully assessed?—Yes.

7516. Only that?—Only that.

Assessment of property on long leases.

7517. I gather from you especially in wealthy parishes, such as St. George's, Hanover Square, the wealthiest parish in the world, probably, and in the city, that this leasehold property, which has increased in value, does escape full assessment generally?—Yes, it does at present.

7518. And your only hope is that they may, perhaps, conform to your rules?—I practically have the assurance of the gentleman who is mainly responsible for the preparation of their list that they will be kept up to the mark in this re-valuation.

Mr. E. J. Harper.

28 May 1895.

Assessment of property on long leases.

7519. When we look at the great, steady, and vast increase in the value of London as a whole, one is disposed to infer that the mass of this leasehold property, which has increased in value, must represent the great bulk of value in London?—Yes, no doubt it represents a large sum. We have some idea of it from the calculations we went into five years ago, when we appealed against the totals of the parish of St. George's, and also of other parishes.

7520. Can you give any idea of what the extent of your objection was? Although you acted only in the interests of what might be called symmetry, you had no pecuniary interest?—No, no interest except that of seeing justice done between the parishes, and on that score we asked that 231,000*l.* should be added in the case of St. George's, Hanover Square.

7521. (*Chairman.*) How much per cent. is that, roughly?—About 10 per cent.

7522. (*Mr. Currie.*) But you did not succeed in establishing that, did you?—We had no opportunity; we were ruled out of court on a technical point.

7523. (*Mr. Sexton.*) Did you ask for any advance in the case of any other parishes?—We asked in the case of Marylebone for an advance of 120,000*l.*

7524. And in St. James', Westminster?—No. In that case our examination was not made in sufficient time to enable us to lodge an appeal.

7525. What as to the City of London Union?—Our appeal asked for an addition there of 417,000*l.*

7526. What is that union?—That is the union of the whole of the very numerous parishes in the City proper—the old city, as it is called in Mr. Courtney's report.

7527. You are dealing now with the wealthiest spot in the world certainly, the City of London, and there you say the assessment was 400,000*l.* a year too low?—That was our contention. I think I ought to say that we do not now say, after our experience of the four years which have elapsed since we lodged those appeals, that those figures represented actually what we should have succeeded in gaining, had those appeals been carried to an issue. They were what we contended, and they may be taken as outside figures.

7528. Qualified by the observation that you had no pecuniary interest?—Certainly we had no pecuniary interest.

7529. Your motive was wholly public, was it?—Wholly.

Assessment of freehold property.

7530. There is a vast mass of freehold property in London, is there not, the heads of which you have noted in your evidence?—Yes.

7531. In the case of freehold property in the occupation of the owners, I understand that the ordinary security of the Income Tax Department does not exist. Although the surveyors of income tax in London have no such powers as they have elsewhere, do they as a matter of fact receive a return from the occupier of the rent paid?—The return which is made to the overseers has by law to be sent to the surveyor of taxes for his information.

7532. In the case where property is owned in freehold and is occupied by the owner, there is no such return, is there?—There is a return. Of course the return cannot disclose a rent, because it does not exist.

7533. What is the nature of the return in that case?—The owner is asked to state what in his opinion is the annual value.

7534. (*Chairman.*) It is on the same form, I think, is it not?—It is on the same form.

7535. (*Mr. Sexton.*) Have you the opportunity of examining these returns yourself?—Only in parishes where the Council is a ratepayer.

7536. I suppose you are a ratepayer in most parishes?—Yes, in most parishes.

7537. Can you see all the returns in each parish?—Yes.

7538. And do you?—We generally do.

7539. Would you make any observation on the returns made by freehold occupiers as compared with those made by rent-paying occupiers, that is to say,

the return made by a man whose own income tax is affected, and the return of a man whose return affects the income tax to be paid by another person?—Of course, as regards the returns made by occupiers of such rates, there is no possibility of their going away from the rent they pay. The occupier of his own freehold property naturally [illegible], as he is asked to [illegible] himself, to do so at the lowest possible figure. But of course you have to take into account the desire of the [illegible] who make the list, on the other hand, to assess him at a fair figure. The desire, I am quite sure, is in that direction, the ability is what is wanted.

7540. On the part of the local overseers?—Yes. They merely send experts in valuation to assist them.

7541. In the case of a small ordinary dwelling-house or shop they have the assistance afforded by the knowledge of what similar premises fetch?—Yes.

7542. But where the property is in any sense exceptional, a large mansion, or a great hotel, or a restaurant, a difficulty arises?—Certainly.

7543. And do you think the effect of that difficulty is that the premises are not fully assessed?—No doubt in many cases that is so. There are parishes which have the courage of their convictions, and they will put properties up to what they consider their fullest possible value, and the result is that the ratepayer appeals to sessions, and that keeps the parish in costs whether they succeed or whether they do not to a certain extent, but the majority of parishes of course fight shy of incurring those costs, and therefore they put the property down at such a figure as they hope the ratepayer will accept.

7544. I think you have given an admirable explanation. In your first phrase, "the courage of their convictions," I was disposed to believe that it was lost, but you have explained that in order to avoid conflict with the ratepayers the tendency would be to fix it low?—Well, as high as they safely can without incurring the cost of an appeal.

7545. Would you think that your income tax, depending upon such a system, is likely to be as full as in Ireland, where every assessment is valued by an Imperial officer with a direct view to income tax?—Of course that is a very short summary of what goes on in Ireland. I am afraid it does not furnish me with materials to compare the two cases.

7546. The element of the courage of one's convictions is absent, the Imperial officer does not care at all. But it is a matter of argument, and I will not press it upon you because I think your explanation is admirably clear, so far as your personal knowledge goes. I should like to ask a question about this vacant land. I think you said some years ago in evidence before a committee of the County Council, in answer to Mr. Tory, that you put the annual value of vacant land in London somewhere at half a million sterling?—Yes, I did, but that was for a very different purpose from the purposes of this Commission. That was a committee of the Council sitting to consider whether land could be valued separately from the buildings upon it, in order that it might be assessed to a new tax, and that committee simply wished to have a rough idea of all the land, valued on their basis, which was a basis of percentage on capital value where the annual value was not an equivalent for the capital value; whether the value of the land on their basis would reduce so much or so much more, and one had no hesitation in giving a very rough-and-ready answer to a question of that kind, because there was no question of doing justice between two bodies or two [illegible]. Before this Commission I should think something very much more accurate than anything I then said would be required.

7547. For the purpose we have now in view?—For the purpose now in view. As I say, the greater portion of that land was taken at a percentage on its capital value.

7548. You were dealing with vacant land?—We were dealing with vacant land.

7549. Simply as vacant land, without regarding whether it was ripe for building or not?—Not entirely without regard; but I lumped the two categories together. Of course, the great bulk of vacant land in London—about 10,000 acres of it or so—is not ripe for building and has a small annual value, though it has an increasing capital value, because of the probability that it will become ripe for building in the future.

7550. Can you separate a probability of an increased capital value from a expectation as to an increased annual value?—Certainly, in that particular case.

7551. You can look on it separately.

7552. Would you say that a piece of land, which may be built upon in a little time, has by reason of that fact a capital value for sale now larger than it would have if that probability did not exist?—Yes.

7553. But nevertheless, that that probability will leave its annual value only the actual value of agricultural land?—Yes, that is so.

7554. Is that your position?—That is my position, because no one would take it for building purposes now, and it could only be let as agricultural or accommodation land.

7555. Of course, if the time had come when the owner would let it for building, whether he was holding out for far more remunerative terms, then the increased capital value would also entail an increased annual value?—Then it would.

7556. Would that be recognised in the valuation?—Yes. All such land, I should treat, certainly, all together, making a valuation on the basis of the annual ground rent which the owner could obtain if he chose to put it on the market.

7557. In your local system of valuation, what happens now with this vacant land? First of all, what is the County of London?—The County of London is as defined by the Local Government Act of 1888.

7558. Can you give us some idea. Is it the metropolis?—Yes; it is the metropolis, including the City.

7559. And there is within the metropolis, you say, leaving out the public spaces and also leaving out the [illegible] of houses, 14,000 acres of vacant land?—Yes; I think so.

7560. It would appear to an ordinary observer, like myself, that that land would be now [illegible] destined to building—I mean that the destiny of that land would appear to be building?—Yes; the destiny of it is, certainly.

7561. You say that such land, as the land about to be built upon, is seldom or never assessed at all except to land tax?—That such land, but the land the future destiny of which is building is assessed as agricultural land; it is the land that is ripe for building, such land as you see in the City and Fleet Street, where houses are pulled down—vacant building land—that is not assessed at all.

7562. What do you call land ripe for building?—I mean land for which the landlord could get a ground rent tomorrow if he chose.

7563. That is to say, where people want to build now?—Yes, where people would be willing to build now if it were in the market.

7564. (*Lord Welby.*) Can you say how far the County of London extends outside the actual limits. Does it include, for instance, Finchley?—No, it does not. I think Hornsey Lane is about the most northerly point, and the Crystal Palace the most southerly.

7565. Does it include any of the marsh land on the banks of the river, which, I believe, is not at present altogether built upon?—Yes, it includes marsh land, not only on the banks of the Thames, but on the banks of the Lea.

7566. (*Mr. Norton.*) In the ordinary case in the County of London the agricultural value of a piece of land, I should think, would be a small fraction of the annual value of land that was ripe or ripening for building. Agricultural value is not very elastic, is it?—No, it is not very elastic, but, of course, there

Mr. E. J. Harper. [illegible] May, 1900. Values of [illegible] building land.

Mr. E. J. Harper. 3 Mar. 1896. Value of vacant building land.

is a higher rental value on land actually in or close to towns.

7567. Yes, what you call accommodation agricultural value, perhaps?—Yes.

7568. Or approximated value?—Yes.

7569. Still, taking a piece of land in or about London and valuing it at the highest rate in connexion with agriculture, and taking the relation of that value to the value of the same piece of land for building, the first would be, I suppose, a small fraction of the second?—Certainly, quite a small fraction.

7570. Have you any idea of what proportion of these 14,000 acres is valued now as ripe for building, and what proportion is valued simply as agricultural land?—What is ripe for building, with very very few exceptions, I believe, is not valued at all. I have, since I sent in my proof, obtained particulars of the figure at which the other 10,000 acres are at present valued, that is the 10,000 acres of vacant land which is not yet ripe for building, though it is in course of becoming so.

7571. It is included in the 14,000 acres is it?—Yes, it is included in the 14,000 acres. That amounts to 60,000*l.* in round figures.

7572. That is the annual value of that 10,000 acres?—That is the annual value of that 10,000 acres. That is what it stands at in the valuation lists to-day.

Method of assessment.

7573. Generally, I think, one may infer from your evidence that the system of assessment in regard to local rates, certainly in regard to Imperial tax, might with advantage be reformed and made more efficient?—I think in certain directions it might—in the directions I have already stated.

7574. Do you know that in Ireland the system of valuation does not admit of periodical revision?—I believe that is so.

7575. It has been unaltered for 40 years, and it is conducted by the Treasury Department by Imperial officers whose power is absolute subject to an appeal to a court. Does it not seem to you that that is a system of the highest degree of efficiency so far as concerns the interests of the tax receivers?—The element of weakness in that system appears to me to be that there is no regular revaluation, and the result of course, is, that where there are increases of value the tax receivers do not get the benefit, and where there are decreases of value the tax payers are unfairly treated. There must in such a period as 40 years be very great changes, especially in towns.

7576. We in Ireland believe we suffer heavily because of the lasting character of the valuation, but apart from the question of fluctuation, and assuming a revision, taking two systems, one depending on local action, and the other conducted by Imperial officers, and assuming, if you like, any facility for revision, does it not appear to you that the system conducted by Imperial officers, who know that their valuation will dictate the amount of the income tax, or any other Imperial tax which may from time to time be levied, more likely to be efficient from the Imperial point of view than the other system?—In my opinion it all turns upon the character of the Imperial officers appointed. If they are experts in valuation, I think probably they would obtain the nearest possible approximation to accuracy, but if they are not experts in valuation, as I believe they are not, I think that there is a certain advantage in the system which we have in London which submits the valuation lists to the revision of a body of men—the assessment committees appointed by the vestries—who bring to bear what local knowledge they have upon the valuation lists. That seems to me to be a system which has worked very well, and, as I say, it has not gone wrong in London from want of will, but simply for lack of the proper expert knowledge.

7577. Do you apply your observation generally that the surveyors of income tax have no expert knowledge?—In London I have not met any surveyors of taxes who put forward any claim to be valuers.

Mr. E. J. Harper. 3 Mar. 1896. Method of assessment.

7578. How do they become surveyors of taxes; are they promoted from the public service, or are they appointed from outside?—That I do not know; I have no knowledge about the appointments.

7579. Or about the qualifications?—Or about the qualifications.

7580. But you do know that they are not valuers, and they know nothing about it?—So far as the gentlemen who act in that capacity in London are concerned, they are not valuers.

7581. Have you noticed that a consciousness of a lack of experience on the part of the surveyors prevents them putting a high value on premises?—I have noticed that they confine themselves to interfering in cases where the return shows a higher rent than the figure put down by the overseers in the valuation list.

7582. In regard to Ireland the Commissioner of Valuation told us that the valuation of certain cities might be increased 15 or 20 per cent. if there were a new valuation now, and a surveyor told us that it could be increased 50 per cent. That is to say, the gentleman who was not an expert gave three times as great an increase in his estimate as the expert did. Would you say that was probably due to the circumstance that he was not an expert himself?—Of course I have not the pleasure of the gentleman's acquaintance, and should not like to pass an opinion upon him.

7583. So far as your opinion goes, if he has any experience he is an exception to his class?—As a surveyor of taxes.

7584. (*Lord Welby.*) You would rather hesitate to answer such questions, would you not, without seeing what the question put to him was and what his answer was?—Certainly.

7585. (*Sir David Barbour.*) You have no knowledge of the qualifications of the valuers or surveyors of taxes in Ireland, have you?—No; I have no knowledge of the Irish system at all.

7586. (*Mr. Sexton.*) But you have knowledge of the surveyors in London, have you not?—That is so.

7587. And you do not know anyone of them who is an expert in valuation?—That is so.

7588. One would suppose if a department had excellent and well qualified men in it, you would find them in London?—Yes.

7589. (*Chairman.*) Would you give the Commission a definition of an expert in valuation. If you were asked to choose an expert in valuation, who would you choose?—I should certainly go to the membership of the Surveyor's Institution, but, of course, within that institution there are differences. There are surveyors who call themselves mainly building surveyors, and others who are mainly valuation surveyors; the line is a very indefinite one. In fact, all surveyors are held to be competent to value property, but of course some of them have a great deal more to do with it than others, and those are much more efficient, and to be relied upon.

7590. Holding the very clear views you do, you would not find it difficult to find for the purpose of appointment a surveyor as an expert in valuation, would you?—No, I do not think I should.

7591. (*Mr. Sexton.*) Whether we speak of England, Ireland, or London, would you consider it desirable that the assessment which is to govern local and Imperial objects, ought to be arrived at if possible in communication between local representative bodies and experts well qualified for appointment?—Yes, that is my opinion.

7592. When you say that the deduction of one-sixth from the rental of land and houses allowed by the Finance Act of last year would leave the closest possible approximation to the net annual value, that of course rests entirely on the assumption, qualified in many respects by your evidence, that the actual assessment is the gross annual value?—Yes, I so qualify it in my answer. I say, "Assuming all property in-"cluded in the assessment at its full value, a deduction "of one-sixth," would give you the right thing.

Mr. W. J. Carver. 28 Mar. 1899. Assessments of property on short lease.

7593. We have seen from your evidence that that assumption is rather a general formula to enable you to present a theoretical conclusion than a statement of fact?—It cannot be a statement of fact at present, but I think in eight or nine months' time it will be a statement of fact. That assumption will be transformed into a statement of fact.

7594. And when that happens, of course we shall see what the total effect of the assessment to income will be?—Yes.

7595. (*Mr. Cramer.*) I understand you to say that there were some parishes in London in which the assessment committee took no notice of such things as premiums, and simply charged on the rent?—Yes.

7596. You do not mean to convey by that, do you, your belief that on the great leasehold estates in London there is any house which is only assessed on the ground rent?—No, certainly not.

7597. Then you must correct that statement, must you not. If they do not take cognizance of the premium paid, or outlay on repairs, and simply assess on the rent as returned by the occupier, that would imply, if the occupier returns the ground-rent, they would assess on that, and that surely is not in accordance with the fact?—It would be so obviously absurd for them to assess on the ground rent.

7598. The ground rent is the only rent paid on the great leasehold estates in London. Let me take one estate, which is a modern estate, the Cadogan Estate. You do not mean to say any one on the Cadogan Estate is assessed only upon his ground rent, do you?—No, certainly not.

7599. Or upon five times the ground rent?—I should not like to go as far as that. I believe the ground rents are high there.

7600. I am a tenant of the Crown, and I am assessed at seven times my ground rent?—That may very well be; but, especially in valuable property of that class, there is a great deal of dealing going on after the first lease is granted, by way of sub-lease, and it is only the return of the occupier on his particular sub-lease that is got by the overseers, and consequently the cases in which they have to frame an assessment on the return of the ground rent only are very very few in number indeed.

7601. I agree with you, but I understood you to say that there were parishes in which the assessment committee took no notice of anything but rent. It is certainly the fact that on many leasehold properties in London the ground rent is the only rent paid?—I did not wish to express it in that way; I do not know that I did. What I wished to say was that they did not take notice of ordinary premiums. I should not call the purchase money paid upon buildings erected on a lease an ordinary premium.

7602. Supposing a man having purchased a house sells it again the next year, would you then call it a premium?—No; he might get a profit in the nature of premium, but the bulk of the purchase money would be for the bricks and mortar, the house actually built, and a premium in the sense of being an increment of value apart from building.

7603. Premium does not mean the difference between ground rent and the letting value, but it means, does it, the sum expended on the erection of the house?—No, I think it means distinctly not the sum expended on the erection of the house, but where a house has been let at a rack rent on an ordinary 21 years' lease, let us say, and the rent when fixed was fair, it may be that in ten years' time the value of that house goes up 25 per cent. The lessee, if he wishes to part with his lease, can either sub-lease for the remaining 11 years at the higher rent, or instead of doing that he can simply assign the existing lease and take the difference capitalised as a premium. That is a premium pure and simple.

7604. That does not apply to the great estates such as the Duke of Westminster's and Lord Portman's, or the Cadogan property, those houses surely are not let upon 21 years' leases, but upon 99 years' leases, which leases in the course of the tenancy change hands many times do they not?—Of course, I have not had many dealings on the Duke of Westminster's Estate or on the Cadogan Estate, but I am not at all surprised to hear that property of that class does change hands frequently.

7605. And I should have imagined that the assessment committee would always take into consideration the terms upon which that property had changed hands?—I know in the case of the Cadogan Estate they do very carefully indeed.

7606. Your answer rather led me to suppose that you thought there were assessment committees who took no notice of such facts, and that therefore the implication was that they were under-assessed?—My intention was to say that certain assessment committees took no notice of premiums, pure and simple, in accordance with the definition I just now gave—that is a consideration paid in a capital sum—beyond the rent which does not represent a payment for the erection of a building. That, I think, has been disregarded in some parishes in the past, but I think that is entirely a thing of the past, and will never happen again.

7607. Then you do not think it is the case that in any part of London houses are at present assessed above their value in the cases I speak of?—There may be cases, such as the cases of companies and so forth, who do not care to take the trouble when they are over-assessed to object to that over-assessment, but they must be very very few in number.

7608. Is not the process of appeal rather an objectionable one?—The process is simple; they have simply to hand in their notice and appear personally before the assessment committee, lay the facts before them; the assessment committee will decide, and there is an end of it. They have simply to attend an hour or two before the assessment committee.

The witness withdrew.

Adjourned to to-morrow at 11 o'clock.

INDEX TO EVIDENCE.

INDEX TO APPENDICES

APPENDICES.

APPENDICES.

APPENDIX I.

A.—Memorandum presented to the Commission by Sir Edward Hamilton, K.C.B., in connection with the Evidence given by him.

PREFACE.

The Royal Commissioners, to whom the question of Irish Finance has been referred, may, in prosecuting the inquiry entrusted to them, find it useful to have before them some historical review of the financial relations which have subsisted between Great Britain and Ireland, and likewise some record of the fiscal changes which have taken place, as well as of the policy pursued and action taken by Parliament, during the period which is proposed to be investigated by the Commissioners.

It is in the hope of serving such purpose that this Memorandum has been written.

I have divided it into three Parts.

The first Part relates to the period (1782–1800), during which Ireland enjoyed legislative independence.

The second Part relates to the period (1800–16), during which, notwithstanding the legislative Union of the two countries, they remained financially separate, on certain terms prescribed by the Treaty of Union.

The third Part relates to the subsequent period, during which Great Britain and Ireland have (with certain exceptions) been treated as one country financially as well as constitutionally.

The main considerations, which in writing these pages I have endeavoured to keep steadily in view, have been to bring the facts together impartially as well as accurately, and to refrain as far as possible from drawing conclusions.

I wish to mention that I have received valuable and interesting information bearing on Part I. from Mr. R. W. A. Holmes (Treasury Remembrancer in Ireland), and from Mr. James Mills (of the Irish Record Office), who have examined the original documents relating to pre-Union finance, and that I have been ably aided throughout the Memorandum by Mr. W. Blain (of the Treasury).

E. W. HAMILTON.

Her Majesty's Treasury,
15th September 1894.

CONTENTS.

MEMORANDUM ON THE FINANCIAL RELATIONS BETWEEN GREAT BRITAIN AND IRELAND.

PART I.—1782–1800.

At the time when legislative independence was accorded to Ireland in 1782, though there was, as there always had been, reserved to the Sovereign the constitutional right of disposing of the Irish surplus revenue, yet that right was not being directly exercised, except, possibly, to a limited extent, in the granting of pensions. Indirectly, however, Ireland was contributing to the support of the Empire. For, by the order of the King, issued from time to time, Ireland was bound to maintain, and place at his disposal for service in England or abroad, a certain number of soldiers. This military aid, which Ireland was being called upon to afford in 1782, had been placed on a more distinct basis by an Act of the Irish Parliament passed in 1769 (9 Geo. III. c. 3); the Irish military establishment having, under that Act, been fixed at about 15,000 men, of whom 12,000 were always to be retained in Ireland, except in case of invasion or rebellion in England, while the remaining troops were to be held available for Imperial service. [illegible]

The establishment of the independence of the Irish Parliament naturally afforded an opportunity for reviewing the financial relations between Great Britain and Ireland. It might well have been deemed to be anomalous that Ireland should bear no part of the cost of the British Navy, which protected Irish commerce equally with British commerce, and it appears that the Prime Minister of England (Lord Shelburne) and the Lord Lieutenant of Ireland (Duke of Portland) of that day, impressed by this consideration, were strongly in favour of accompanying the grant of legislative independence with an arrangement for securing some more direct contribution from Ireland to Imperial expenditure. Lecky's Hist., Vol. VI., p. [illegible]

The excited state of feeling in that country at the time prevented the British Government from giving effect to their intentions; but the propriety of some such arrangement was recognised by the Irish Parliament itself. For, on the 27th May 1782, Mr. Grattan, who was all powerful in the newly constituted legislative body, proposed a vote of 100,000*l*., to be obtained by loan, for the purpose of raising 20,000 additional sailors for the Royal Navy. The proposal was duly adopted by the Irish House of Commons, though it appears from the report of a Committee which, in the following year, inquired into the use made of the grant, that only about half the money was actually spent, and that only about 7,000 men were actually raised. Irish Commons Journals, Vol. X., p. [illegible] and Vol. XI., p. [illegible]; also Irish Parliamentary Register [illegible], p. [illegible]

Mr. Grattan's proposal was immediately followed by a further offer of aid to England in another and less direct form. The Irish Parliament passed an Act (21 & 22 Geo. III. c. 38) which permitted the temporary withdrawal to England of 5,000 out of the 12,000 men borne on the Irish establishment for constant residence in Ireland. But only limited advantage was apparently likewise taken of this offer; and it was not renewed. Lecky's History, Vol. IV., p. [illegible]

About a year and a half later, in November 1783, a determined effort was made by the minority in the Irish House of Commons to reduce the numbers of the Irish military establishment. This movement in the direction of economy was powerfully supported by Mr. Flood; and it was argued in debate that then was the time—a time of peace—to effect a reduction, unless it was intended that Ireland was to be merely "a barrack to Great Britain." Mr. Grattan, however, opposed any reduction of Irish troops. It would, he thought, have an appearance of bad grace about it. "The Navy of "England," he said, "protects our trade, and we, as "an equivalent, pay 70,000*l*. a year to maintain the "troops destined to serve in the plantations. This is "not a dear purchase for partaking that which has "cost England so many millions." He carried his point, and the proposal of the Opposition was accordingly negatived. Irish Parliamentary [illegible]

Not long after this, the question of revising the financial relations of Ireland to Great Britain again engaged the attention of the British Government, of which Mr. Pitt had now become the head. It was raised in connexion with his proposal to revise the commercial relations of the two countries. He saw that the existing position of affairs might expose this country to a twofold danger. Ireland might, at any time, have withheld her military assistance. There was nothing to prevent her from imposing such duties on English goods as would practically close a market which was most important to Great Britain.

In view of these risks Mr. Pitt elaborated certain proposals whereby, in return for "an almost unlimited "communication of commercial advantages," Ireland should contribute from time to time "to the common "exigencies of the Empire." His idea, as explained to the Duke of Rutland (Lord Lieutenant of Ireland) on the 6th January 1785, was that "the future surplus "of the hereditary revenue," consisting mainly of Customs and Excise duties, should constitute the contribution. But such a contribution was "not to be "made a pretext for withdrawing any part of the aid "now given by the Irish Parliament . . . . in the "maintenance of the regiments upon the Irish establishment serving out of the kingdom . . . . and it was to be considered only as a means" for defraying "the ordinary expenses of the Empire in time of "peace"; Ireland being "still, in case of war or any "extraordinary emergency, called upon and expected "voluntarily to contribute, as in justice and policy she "ought, to such further exertions as the situation of "affairs and the general interests of the Empire may "from time to time require." Correspondence between Mr. Pitt and the Duke of Rutland, p. [illegible] Do. p. [illegible] and Lecky's History, Vol. VI., p. [illegible]

A proposal requiring Ireland to make a fixed contribution to Great Britain, though it was to be fixed in proportion to the growing means of the smaller kingdom, was, no doubt, a very delicate one. But the difficulties amid which the Lord Lieutenant anticipated on the part of Ireland, proved to be exaggerated.

The plan, formulated in ten resolutions, was brought before the Irish Parliament on the 7th February 1785. All foreign and colonial goods were to pass between Great Britain and Ireland without any increase of duty; and English and Irish domestic goods were to pass from one country to the other at the same rates of duty; while, whenever the hereditary revenue, amounting then to about 652,000*l*., should exceed a given sum, the excess was to "be appropriated in support of the naval "forces of the Empire in such manner as the Parliament "of this kingdom shall direct." Lecky's History, Vol. VI., p. [illegible] Irish Parliamentary Debates, Vol. IV., [illegible]

In deference to Mr. Grattan, the resolutions were so altered as to make the compulsory contribution in each year of peace conditional on there being first established an equilibrium between revenue and expenditure; while the hereditary revenue was to produce 656,000*l*. before any part of it could be appropriated to navy expenses. With these modifications, the resolutions passed the Irish Parliament with tolerably general concurrence; and, as evidence of the desire of that Parliament to fulfil the obligation of a contribution, additional taxes were imposed, calculated to yield 140,000*l*. a year.

This plan, for securing commercial equality between the two countries simultaneously with a contribution to Imperial expenditure from Ireland, was brought before the British House of Commons on the 22nd February 1785. At Westminster it met with much more opposition than it had in Dublin. It was denounced as ruinous to British trade; and the commercial classes throughout England were up in arms against it. In the course of the next three months the resolutions, in deference to this strong feeling, underwent alterations in a manner seriously detrimental to Ireland. Lecky's History, Vol. VI., p. [illegible]

When the resolutions, modified in this way, were returned to Dublin, they met with a reception very different from that which had been originally accorded to them by the Irish Parliament. It was felt that the plan in its present shape was not only establishing the ascendancy of the British Parliament over Irish commerce, but was virtually asking Ireland to surrender in a great measure the exclusive right of her Parliament to legislate for her. So strong was this

feeling, that the Bill embodying the altered resolutions had to be abandoned as soon as it was introduced.

With the abandonment of this Bill, the plan of securing from the Irish Parliament, on a settled basis, a contribution to imperial expenses fell to the ground; and, though the question of commercial equality was subsequently revived on two occasions by Mr. Grattan, first in 1790 and again in 1793, the original plan was never proceeded with.

[illegible] Accordingly, the maintenance of the Irish military establishment, with a fifth part of it liable to serve abroad, as fixed by the Irish Act of 1769, continued to constitute Ireland's sole contribution to Imperial services during the next eight years of peace.

[illegible] When, however, the French war broke out in 1793, the military establishment of Ireland was raised from 15,000 to 20,000 men, and a Bill was passed directing the enrolment, for four years, of a militia force of 16,000 men. This augmentation was the practical response made by the Irish Parliament to the Lord Lieutenant's message at the opening of the session, when he said that the King relied "with confidence on the firm and effectual support of the Irish "House of Commons, and on the zealous exertions of a "brave and loyal people in prosecuting a just and "necessary war."

[illegible] Two years later, the new Lord Lieutenant—Lord Fitzwilliam—in opening the session stated in his speech that the King believed so strongly in the loyalty and zeal of the Irish Parliament for his service, that he thought it "unnecessary to press" them "in any particular "manner to make a provision adequate to the present "awful situation of affairs." It is evident that this appeal likewise met with an adequate response; for later on in the year, in embodying in an address their views on the sudden recall of Lord Fitzwilliam and the conduct of the Irish Ministry, the Opposition made some significant allusions to the sacrifice which Ireland had made for the common cause. "In consequence of the "war," they said, "we have greatly added to our annual "taxes and increased near threefold the debt of the "nation. We have also assisted the Army and Navy of "the Empire with vast numbers of our people. . . . "In this year we continued to increase the annual taxes, "voted a loan of nearly two millions, granted a greater "force than ever was paid by Ireland."

[illegible] About the same time, Wolfe Tone made out that, during the first two years of the French war, no less than 200,000 men were raised in Ireland, of whom 80,000 were for the Navy alone. This assertion was, no doubt, a great exaggeration; nor is such exaggeration surprising, as it was his object to demonstrate that Ireland was the recruiting ground of Great Britain, and that consequently, if that ground fell into foreign hands, the naval supremacy of England would be at an end. But, according to a Return which was prepared under the instructions of Mr. Secretary Pelham, the number of men furnished by Ireland for naval and military service from the commencement of the war to 1796 was very considerable; for, though his estimate fell far short of Wolfe Tone's figures, there appeared to have been no less than 38,000 men furnished in all by Ireland, in addition to the 30,000 men required for the protection of her own shores.

Early in 1797, being challenged as to the measures which the Government intended to take for the mutual defence of Great Britain and Ireland, Mr. Pelham urged that the two countries should assist each other as occasion required. If Ireland wanted troops in the event of an attack, Great Britain, he said, should send some of her soldiers; and if Great Britain, on the other hand, should need assistance against an invading enemy, Ireland should lend her similar assistance.

By this time, there was the rebellion in Ireland as well as the French war to be reckoned with; and the military demands on Ireland were further increased. Numbers of English troops were sent to Ireland, and the cost of these was borne by that country. The Irish Yeomanry was constituted, and this force also involved a considerable charge. When the money Bill was receiving the Royal Assent, the Speaker of the Irish House of Commons made a speech, in which he referred to the unprecedented magnitude of the supplies granted by Ireland. "They go," he said, "to the full extent of "every service proposed by Government, and are given "with an unanimity and zeal which mark the unalter-"able determination of this kingdom to stand or fall "with Great Britain. . . . With the same una-"nimity we have voted the maintenance of an army "far greater than was ever kept up by this kingdom "during any preceding war; and we have continued "to them the augmentation of pay which was granted "by the last Parliament."

We must now turn to actual figures, and proceed to examine the public accounts of Ireland during her autonomy.

The following Table gives the annual revenue and expenditure of Ireland, under principal heads, during this time. The figures are taken from the well-known Return of Public Income and Expenditure presented to Parliament in 1869; and it should be mentioned that that Return, so far as it relates to pre-Union Irish income, was based upon the annual accounts of the Irish Treasury, which only gave the net payments from the Revenue Commissioners to the Irish Exchequer. As a considerable number of salaries, drawbacks, and other charges were paid by the Commissioners and their collectors out of gross receipts, the amounts of both revenue and (civil) expenditure in the following Table appear to be less than they actually were.

TABLE I. showing the REVENUE and EXPENDITURE of IRELAND in each year from 1782–3 to 1800–1 inclusive.

Year ending 25th March	Revenue (Converted into British Currency.)*				Expenditure. (Converted into British Currency.)*				Surplus (+) or Deficit (−).
	Customs and Excise.	Other Taxes.	Miscellaneous.	Total.	Debt Charges.	Civil Government.	Naval and Military Expenditure.	Total.	
	£	£	£	£	£	£	£	£	£
1783	736,858	68,746	301,838	1,106,564	128,876	383,566	609,312	1,313,797	−207,233
1784	812,681	50,854	301,593	1,214,860	127,216	546,074	468,865	1,142,300	−128,490
1785	764,834	40,941	83,237	993,844	130,386	876,392	960,827	1,209,704	−197,780
1786	869,380	70,826	188,496	1,127,648	141,632	426,381	608,361	1,176,815	−30,007
1787	932,313	58,806	216,347	1,226,466	129,683	447,230	609,374	1,177,509	+88,975
1788	875,591	80,616	198,069	1,253,282	112,767	657,906	590,647	1,360,215	−63,134
1789	910,187	78,786	341,408	1,310,411	143,948	566,737	571,036	1,282,821	−5,410
1790	871,852	74,780	334,095	1,337,381	140,321	456,634	526,718	1,123,864	+86,217
1791	1,090,082	90,902	232,464	1,410,477	127,827	368,833	678,847	1,494,087	−70,145
1792	975,054	95,885	500,581	1,568,414	143,173	548,377	614,240	1,305,066	−36,286
1793	934,391	94,498	634,862	1,363,806	152,287	516,855	484,246	1,363,409	+431
1794	876,499	79,871	220,415	1,176,872	146,307	635,364	743,929	1,595,669	−401,997
1795	1,118,189	97,855	367,741	1,472,513	214,429	746,873	1,363,166	2,325,668	−1,053,656
1796	1,166,377	105,718	857,467	1,544,279	344,078	765,163	1,843,899	2,852,968	−1,301,121
1797	1,273,402	120,878	358,869	1,753,120	409,296	983,137	3,032,136	4,131,253	−3,298,444
1798	1,390,146	113,044	580,182	2,084,099	828,651	714,772	3,404,700	4,747,323	−2,556,109
1799	1,559,179	117,369	424,585	2,140,719	768,273	679,560	3,963,856	5,300,088	−3,262,970
1800	2,408,861	167,343	441,564	3,017,734	1,283,582	1,425,019	4,546,738	6,264,986	−3,257,046
Three quarters ending 5th January 1801	1,564,318	143,663	457,195	2,104,169	1,140,834	952,616	2,737,196	4,630,855	−3,526,182

* 1l. British sterling equalled 1l. 1s. 8d. in Irish currency. Accordingly in order to translate into British currency sums denoted in Irish currency it is necessary to deduct 1/13th, or 1s. 6d. per 1l., from such sums. The two currencies were not assimilated until 1826, when the Act 6 Geo. IV. c. 79. was passed, providing that thenceforward all receipts, payments, contracts, and dealings should be made in British currency only. The figures throughout this memorandum are (unless expressly directed to the contrary) in British currency.

An examination of this Table clearly establishes two facts. It shows that during the first 11 years of legislative independence the expenditure of Ireland kept fairly level, averaging about 1½ millions per annum; and that thenceforward, until the Union was carried, the expenditure increased year by year, mainly under the head of military services, at a formidable rate—indeed, so much so that the total expenditure in 1799-1800 was five times greater than it was in 1792-3.

It may be fairly assumed that this great increase in the years preceding the Union was due to two causes—the war, which had been declared between this country and France on the 1st February 1793, and the disturbances in Ireland which culminated in rebellion.

On this assumption, it is possible to make some calculation of the amounts of expenditure in Ireland which may be attributed to the two causes respectively, though the calculation can only be founded on hypothesis.

The war with France was being waged throughout the period in question. It is difficult to assign an exact date to the outbreak of the home disturbances. But as the bill of costs usually follows in the wake of such outbreaks, and as the cost of the Yeomanry force, which was specially constituted to meet the insurrectionary movement, makes its first appearance in the accounts of 1797-8, it seems fair to take that year as the year in which the internal state of Ireland entailed specific expenditure of an extraordinary character. On this supposition, the increase of military expenditure in the years 1793-4, 1794-5, 1795-6, and 1796-7 would be wholly due to the French war; and in the later years it would be due to the French war and Irish disturbances combined. It may be contended that the rebellion practically received its death-blow at Vinegar Hill in June 1798; but many of its horrors continued in isolated districts, and troops were not likely to be withdrawn from disturbed districts for some time afterwards for fear of fresh outbreaks.

The sum annually expended on military services between 1783-4 and 1792-3 inclusive, amounted on an average to [illegible]; and, accordingly, I take this sum to represent the annual military expenditure, for which the Irish Parliament deemed it necessary to provide, at the end of last century, to meet Ireland's own requirements in normal times of peace.

In the year before the disturbances at home involved serious cost (1796-7), the military expenditure amounted to 2,030,000; and if the normal expenditure of 583,000l. be deducted, the remainder (viz., 1,447,000l.) would represent the extra expense to which Ireland was that year exposed in consequence of the war with France. I take this sum of 1,447,000l. to represent likewise the annual expense on account of the French war from the 25th March 1797 to 5th January 1801, and the expenditure incurred over and above these two sums of 583,000l. and 1,447,000l., in 1797-8, 1798-9, 1799-1800, and 1800-1 (three quarters of a year), may then be held to represent the cost of the disturbed state of Ireland herself.

These hypothetical calculations will be best followed when they are given in a tabulated form.

Year ending 25th March.	Estimated Military Expenditure in Ireland in Times of Peace.	Estimated Addition to Military Expenditure on account of the War with France.	Estimated Addition to Military Expenditure on account of the disturbed State of Ireland.	Total.
	£	£	£	£
1793-4	[illegible]	181,000	—	764,000
1794-5	[illegible]	[illegible]	—	[illegible]
1795-6	[illegible]	[illegible]	—	[illegible]
1796-7	[illegible]	1,447,000	—	[illegible]
1797-8	[illegible]	1,447,000 *[illegible]	[illegible]	[illegible]
1798-9	[illegible]	1,447,000	[illegible]	[illegible]
1799-1800	[illegible]	1,447,000	[illegible]	[illegible]
25th March 1800 to 5th January 1801 (three quarters)	[illegible]	[illegible]	[illegible]	[illegible]
Totals	[illegible]	[illegible]	[illegible]	[illegible]

* This sum is specially mentioned as relating to advances "prior to 1796-8 for army extraordinaries"; so I exclude it from the expenditure incurred in 1797-8. (See Parliamentary Paper, No. [illegible] of [illegible], Part I., p. [illegible].)

It will be seen from this statement that had the military expenditure during these 7¾ years been at the normal rate, it would have amounted in the aggregate to [illegible]. As a matter of fact it amounted to no less than [illegible], thus exceeding the normal amount by [illegible], or (in round figures) by [illegible] millions. Of this huge excess, six millions may be said to have been due to the disturbed and rebellious state of Ireland, and 10 millions to the war in which this country was engaged with France. The Vice-Treasurer's abstracts of accounts printed in the Irish Commons Journals have been carefully examined, and the result of the examination is to show that the amounts directly incurred in maintaining Irish regiments abroad, or in manning the fleet, were very insignificant. It may, therefore, be assumed that practically the whole of the extraordinary expenditure on account of the war with France was incurred in defending Ireland herself, and thus in defending the most vulnerable part of the King's home dominions.

There is one other subject to which special reference should be made before we approach the time of the Union, and that is, the state of the Irish Debt between 1783 and 1800.

The following table shows the nominal amount of Funded Debt and Unfunded Debt at the close of each financial year from the 25th March 1783 to the 5th January 1801.

TABLE II. showing the Amount of Funded and Unfunded Debt of Ireland outstanding at the end of each financial year from 1783-4 to 1800-1 inclusive.

1. Funded Debt.

Year ending 25th March.	Nominal Capital Stock outstanding at the close of each Financial Year.			Net Increase (+) or Decrease (−) in the Year.
	Funded in Ireland.	Funded in Great Britain.	Total.	
	£	£	£	
1784	[illegible]	—	[illegible]	
1785	[illegible]	—	[illegible]	
1786	[illegible]	—	[illegible]	− [illegible]
1787	[illegible]	—	[illegible]	+ [illegible]
1788	[illegible]	—	[illegible]	+ [illegible]
1789	[illegible]	—	[illegible]	− [illegible]
1790	[illegible]	—	[illegible]	—
1791	[illegible]	—	[illegible]	—
1792	[illegible]	—	[illegible]	—
1793	[illegible]	—	[illegible]	—
1794	[illegible]	—	[illegible]	+ [illegible]
1795	[illegible]	—	[illegible]	+ [illegible]

* Parliamentary Paper, No. [illegible] of [illegible], Part II., p. [illegible].
† Parliamentary Paper, No. C—[illegible], pp. [illegible].

1. *Funded Debt—cont.*

Year ending 25th March.	Nominal Capital Stock outstanding at the close of each Financial Year.*			Net Increase (+) or Decrease (−) in the Year.
	Funded in Ireland.	Funded in Great Britain.	Total.	
	£	£	£	£
1795	[illegible]	—	[illegible]	+ [illegible]
1796	[illegible]	—	[illegible]	+ [illegible]
1797	[illegible]	—	[illegible]	+ [illegible]
1798	[illegible]	[illegible]	[illegible]	+ [illegible]
1799	[illegible]	[illegible]	[illegible]	+ [illegible]
1800	[illegible]	[illegible]	[illegible]	+ [illegible]
To 5th January 1801 (three quarters).	[illegible]	[illegible]	[illegible]	+ [illegible]
	Aggregate increase in the period			+ [illegible]

* Parliamentary Paper, No. C.—8008, pp. 8-9.

2. *Unfunded Debt.*

—	Amount of Unfunded Debt outstanding.	Increase (+) or Decrease (−) in the Year.
	£	£
On 25th March 1783	507,649	—
" " 1784	552,126	+ 44,477
" " 1785	730,745	+ 178,615
" " 1786	774,400	+ 43,615
" " 1787	617,355	− 157,051
" " 1788	617,348	—
" " 1789	617,348	—
" " 1790	617,368	—

2. *Unfunded Debt—cont.*

—	Amount of Unfunded Debt outstanding.	Increase (+) or Decrease (−) in the Year.
	£	
On 25th March 1791	629,368	
" " 1792	627,348	—
" " 1793	627,348	—
" " 1794	904,233	+ 276,882
" " 1795	1,061,509	+ 157,541
" " 1796	1,107,102	+ 45,154
" " 1797	1,150,478	+ 33,600
" " 1798	658,775	− 501,707
" " 1799	896,477	+ 37,602
" " 1800	1,341,430	+ 425,921
On 5th January 1801 (3 quarters of a year)	1,699,926	+ 358,538
Aggregate increase in period	—	1,192,344

It will be seen from this Table that in the period under review the increase of the public debt in Ireland was most formidable.

	£
On the 5th January 1801, the Funded Debt stood at	26,841,211
and the Unfunded Debt at	1,699,926
amounting in the aggregate to	28,541,137
On the 25th March 1783 the aggregate amount had been only	1,917,754
So in about 18 years the Irish debt had been augmented by	26,623,379

and almost the whole of this increase occurred in the last eight years. It is evident, moreover, that the amount borrowed in these years was raised on very onerous terms, for the aggregate deficit did not amount to much more than 10½ millions.

PART II.—[illegible]

Some test of the relative positions of Great Britain and Ireland at the time when the Union of the two kingdoms was in contemplation is afforded by a comparison of their respective—(1) Populations, (2) Revenues, (3) Expenditures, and (4) Debts, at that date.*

1. Population.†

—	Great Britain.	Ireland.	Total.
Population in 1800	No. [illegible]	No. [illegible]	No. [illegible]
Relative proportions	[illegible]	1	[illegible]
Per cent. of total	[illegible]	[illegible]	[illegible]

2. Revenues.

—	Great Britain (year ending 5th January 1801).	Ireland (year ending 25th March 1800) (British Currency).	Total.
Revenues	£ [illegible]	£ [illegible]	£ [illegible]
Relative proportions	[illegible]	1	[illegible]
Per cent. of total	[illegible]	[illegible]	[illegible]
Per head of population	£ s. d. [illegible]	s. d. [illegible]	£ s. d. [illegible]

3. Expenditures (including Sinking Fund charges).

[illegible]

—	Great Britain (year ending 5th January 1801).	Ireland (year ending 25th March 1800) (British Currency).	Total.
Expenditures	£ [illegible]	£ [illegible]	£ [illegible]
Relative proportions	[illegible]	1	[illegible]
Per cent. of total	[illegible]	[illegible]	[illegible]

4. Debts.

(1) Nominal Amounts.

[illegible]

—	Great Britain (1st February 1801).	Ireland (5th January 1801).	Total.
Funded debt	£ [illegible]	£ [illegible]	£ [illegible]
Unfunded debt	[illegible]	[illegible]	[illegible]
Total	[illegible]	[illegible]	[illegible]
Relative proportions	[illegible]	1	[illegible]
Per cent. of total	[illegible]	[illegible]	[illegible]
Unexpired annuities	£ [illegible]	£ [illegible]	£ [illegible]

Note.—[illegible]

Description of Annuities.	Great Britain.			Ireland.		
	Amount of Annuities.	Years valued.	Capital Value.	Amount of Annuities.	Years valued.	Capital Value.
Long Annuities	[illegible]	[illegible]	[illegible]	[illegible]	[illegible]	[illegible]
Short Annuities	[illegible]	[illegible]	[illegible]	[illegible]	—	[illegible]
Exchequer Annuities	[illegible]	—	[illegible]	[illegible]	—	[illegible]
Bank Annuity	—	—	—	[illegible]	—	[illegible]
Total	[illegible]	—	[illegible]	[illegible]	—	[illegible]
Short Annuity (Imperial)	[illegible]	[illegible]	[illegible]	—	—	—
Total	[illegible]	—	[illegible]	[illegible]	—	[illegible]

* [illegible]

† [illegible]

Parliamentary Paper, No. 366 of 1869, Part I., pp. 332 and 333.

(3) *Annual Charges for Interest, Sinking Fund, and Management of Funded and Unfunded Debt.*

—	Great Britain (year ending 5th January 1801).	Ireland (year ending 25th March 1800).	Total.
	£	£	£
Annual charges -	21,500,790	1,232,232	[illegible]
Relative proportions.	17¾	1	18¾
Per cent. of total	94·68	5·32	100·00

Such, then, was the financial position of Ireland, relatively to Great Britain, when the British Government had decided to unite the Parliaments of the two countries.

The project for a legislative Union of the two countries was authoritatively announced in the British House of Commons for the first time on the 22nd January 1799, in a message from the King; and on the 31st January the measure was taken into consideration.

In moving on that day the resolutions relative to an Union, the Prime Minister and Chancellor of the Exchequer, Mr. Pitt, strenuously denied that the scheme was intended to bring Ireland under the burden of the English National Debt, or make her the subject of increased taxation. The debts of Great Britain and Ireland were to be kept separate; and the ordinary expenses of the United Kingdom in peace and war were to be defrayed by the countries in fixed proportions.

"It is in our power," he said, "to fix for any "number of years which shall be thought fit the "proportion by which the contribution of Ireland to "the expenses of the union shall be regulated; that "those proportions shall not be such as would make a "contribution greater than the necessary amount of "its own present expenses as a separate kingdom; "and even after that limited period the proportion of "the whole contribution from time to time might be "made to depend on the comparative produce in each "kingdom of such general taxes as might be thought "to afford the best criterion of their respective wealth.

"Or what I should hope to be found practicable, the "system of internal taxation in each country might "gradually be so equalised and assimilated, on the leading "articles, as to make all rules of specific proportion "unnecessary, and to secure that Ireland shall never "be taxed but in proportion as we tax ourselves."

The terms of the financial resolution which Mr. Pitt moved, were as follows:—

"That it would be fit to propose that the charge arising from the payment of the interest or sinking fund for the reduction of the principal of the debt incurred in either kingdom before the Union shall be separately defrayed by Great Britain and Ireland respectively. That for a number of years to be limited the future ordinary expenses of the United Kingdom in peace or war shall be defrayed by Great Britain and Ireland jointly, according to such proportions as shall be established by the respective Parliaments previous to the Union; and that after the expiration of the time to be so limited, the proportion shall not be liable to be varied, except according to such rules and principles as shall be in like manner agreed upon previous to the Union."

After nearly three weeks' discussion, but no very serious opposition, the resolutions were agreed to by the British House of Commons. They were carried still more easily in the House of Lords; and a joint Address of both Houses in favour of the Union was thereupon presented to the King.

Meanwhile the question had likewise been engaging the attention of the Irish Parliament, though no definite proposal had been submitted to it. At its meeting on the 22nd January 1799 the speech of the Lord Lieutenant had not gone beyond the expression of anxiety "for some permanent adjustment which may extend "the advantages enjoyed by our sister kingdom to "every part of this island." But the subject of an Union was the sole topic of debate, and Lord Castlereagh, the Chief Secretary to the Lord Lieutenant, announced that it was the intention of the Government to bring forward a measure.

The debate turned almost entirely on the constitutional issue, and no references of any great importance were made to the financial aspect of the proposal.

An amendment, moved by Mr. George Ponsonby, was only lost by a majority of one (106 to 105), and two days later, when the report on the Address was brought up, Sir Lawrence Parsons succeeded in carrying his motion to omit the paragraph referring to the projected Union.

In consequence of these proceedings in the Irish House of Commons, no real further progress was made in 1799 in either Parliament with the scheme for incorporating Ireland with Great Britain. But the subject was from time to time revived during the session; and, when the Regency Bill was under discussion, Lord Castlereagh made a speech in favour of the Union, in which he asked, "How was it possible "to conceive that the Empire should continue as at "present, while all parts of it were to receive equal "protection, and only one part of it was to suffer the "burdens of that protection? Must we not of necessity "and in justice look to some settlement of "Imperial contribution?"

Mr. Foster, the Speaker, also availed himself of the Regency Debate to deliver a speech in which he stated with much elaboration the case against the Union. One of the subjects which he considered most closely was the probable effect of the Union on the material prosperity of Ireland. In his opinion, it would almost certainly lead to an era of increased taxation. While one of the capital advantages of Ireland during the eighteenth century was that it was one of the most lightly taxed countries in Europe, he believed that this would now be changed, and Ireland would be made to contribute in an increased proportion to the expenses of the Empire. Lord Castlereagh, he said, "wants an Union in order to tax you and take your money"; and the Speaker dwelt on the great and manifest progress in material prosperity which had accompanied the latter days of the Irish Parliament. It had been its work "to raise this kingdom into prosperity, and keep it in "a steady and rapid advance, even beyond the utmost "hopes of its warmest advocates. . . . . The "general export rose in 74 years to 1782 from one to "five, and in the years after 1782 from five to ten . . . . ." It was all very well, he argued, to say that "you would depend on the articles you may "frame, to secure your trade and your purse"; but the very doctrine of the omnipotence of Parliament which was now so constantly urged, and which was necessary to justify the Union, reduced its articles to mere waste paper; because the United Parliament would have the power to alter or abrogate any article of the Union which it pleased, to abolish bounties, to amalgamate debts, or to raise the level of taxation as it desired, and a minority of a hundred Irish members would have no power to stay its decision.

When the subject of the Union was brought forward in the following year (1800), the articles of the Union, including the one dealing with the proposed financial arrangements, had assumed more definite shape.

It was on the 5th February that Lord Castlereagh made his principal explanation in the Irish House of Commons, when the message from the Lord Lieutenant strongly recommending a legislative union was under consideration.

He maintained that the first principle upon which the two kingdoms were to be incorporated in point of contribution was "that there should be no retrospect "in regard to expenses. Ireland is to have no concern "whatever with the past debt of Great Britain. . . . "Such is the liberality of Great Britain; but as to "the future it is expected that the two countries "should move forward together and unite with regard "to their expenses in the measure of their relative "abilities."

"It were to be wished that there was not an insurmountable "bar to a common system and a common "treasury, and that we could become, like counties of "the same kingdom, subject to the same system of "finances. Were our entire expenditure common "(which would happen if neither kingdom had any "separate debts, or if their debts were in proportion "to their ability) by no system whatever could they "be made to contribute so strictly according to their "means, as by being subject to the same taxes equally "bearing upon the great objects of taxation in both "countries." Such, however, is the disproportion of

"debts of the two kingdoms to each other at the present, that a common system for the present is impossible, nor could any system of equivalents be applied for equalising their contribution. It is therefore necessary that the debts of the two countries should be kept distinct, and, of course, that their taxation should be separate and proportionate. The great point, therefore, to be ascertained is the best criterion which can be formed of the relative means of the two countries in order to fix the relative proportions of their contributions."

He went on to say that he conceived the best possible criterion would be the produce of an income tax, levied on the same description of incomes in each country and equally well levied in both. In the absence, however, of that tax in Ireland, resort had to be had to some other test. "I consider that the criterion next in order is the joint result of commerce and consumption; and that this may be satisfactorily ascertained by a review of their exports and imports, together with the quantities and value of the chief articles of their consumption. I propose, then, to consider the proportion which those articles bear to each other, separately and conjointly, in Great Britain and Ireland; and if they nearly coincide, I shall take it for granted that the best means of deciding the relative ability of the two countries have been fairly taken."

He found that the result of comparing (1) the average annual value of the imports and exports of the two countries during the three latest years for which statistics were available, and (2) the average annual amount consumed during the same period of the principal dutiable articles (viz., malt, beer, spirits, wine, tobacco, and sugar), was as follows, viz.:—

—	Great Britain.	Ireland.
Average annual value of imports and exports - - -	£ 73,961,077	£ 10,903,901
Proportion (about) -	7	1
Average annual value of dutiable articles consumed - -	£ 16,624,663	£ 2,514,350
Proportion (about) -	7¾	to 1
Average of two proportions -	15	2
Percentage - -	88·24	11·76

As the mean of these proportions was 7½ to 1, it was proposed that Great Britain should contribute 15-17ths, and Ireland 2-17ths, to the "general expenses of the empire."

Having stated the principle of the financial arrangement, Lord Castlereagh went on to explain more in detail its provisions. "The past debts of the two countries," he said, "shall be borne by them respectively; and if we couple this liberal provision with the section of the Article, which gives to Ireland a participation in whatever sums may be produced from the territorial revenues of the dependencies of Great Britain in India, we must acknowledge not only the justice but the generosity of the terms."

As to the proportionate contributions of 15 and 2 respectively, Parliament was to have the power to revise the proportions at the end of 20 years, in case the proposed system might, "under different circumstances, prove to be both partial and disadvantageous." "By there being a provision for a revision, Ireland has the utmost possible security that she cannot be taxed beyond the measure of her comparative ability, and that the ratio of her contribution must ever correspond with her relative wealth and prosperity."

As to the disposal of any surplus Irish revenue, Lord Castlereagh favoured the accumulation of it owing to the different system of Great Britain and Ireland with respect to raising supplies. "Great Britain," he said, "has at length established the great principle of raising a great part of her supplies within the year; this island is not at present in a situation to adopt a similar system, the consequence of which is that the debt of Great Britain will hereafter increase in a much less degree and be more rapidly liquidated, whilst the debt of Ireland will be increasing with greater rapidity, especially if she shall continue a separate country; but as an Union will greatly diminish her expenses in time of peace it is proposed that the arrangement with respect to any surplus of revenue should be adopted, to prevent her too rapid accumulation of debt in time of war."

The article provides, he continued, "that all future loans, for the interest and liquidation of which, the respective countries have made provisions in the proportion of their respective contributions, shall be considered as joint debt; and, on the other hand, that, where they do not make corresponding provisions, their respective quotas of the sum so raised should remain a separate charge, in like manner as debt contracted previous to the Union."

He then referred to the provision that, when the separate debts of the two kingdoms should be either extinguished—(a sanguine expectation)—or be in the proportion of their respective contributions, the general expenses of the empire should be thenceforward levied by common taxes, in lieu of proportionate contributions. He proceeded to endeavour to remove any impression that, when either of these contingencies arose, common taxes with Great Britain would impose upon Ireland heavier burdens than she would otherwise be called upon to support; but the figures which he cited in support of his argument are not easy to follow. "It may happen, however," he said, "that if war should continue, and Ireland fund her supplies, whilst England raises a great part of hers within the year, and mortgages her income tax to their rapid reduction in peace, that the proportion of the debt of Ireland may rise, and her scale of taxation increase accordingly. In this case also the system of common taxation perfectly secures the interests of Ireland, being produced by natural causes and in no degree forced. It cannot impose any burthen on this country (Ireland), to which she must not in the ordinary course of her expenditure be liable; whilst the provision, which goes to preclude any article from being subject to a higher rate of duty in Ireland than the same article pays in Great Britain, will secure her from having the scale of her taxation raised above that of England, even though the natural progress of her expense should lead to it. And whilst Ireland is thus secured against any injustice in substituting a system of common taxes in lieu of proportionate contribution, the United Parliament will be enabled to make abatements in Ireland, as the Parliament of Great Britain always has done in Scotland since the Union; when, from local circumstances, the high duty cannot be levied without either rendering the revenue unproductive or pressing too hard upon the poorer classes."

In concluding his explanation of the financial provisions of the Treaty of Union, Lord Castlereagh adduced figures to show that, in times of war equally as in times of peace, Ireland ought to gain by the arrangement.

In a year of war like 1799, the expenditures of the two countries (exclusive of their separate debt charges) had been as follows:—

	£
Great Britain - - -	[illegible]
Ireland - - -	[illegible]
	[illegible]

Had this sum been met by the two countries in the proportion of 15 to 2—

	£
Great Britain's share would have been - -	33,[illegible],000
and Ireland's share	4,[illegible],000
	[illegible]

So Ireland would have saved [illegible].

Under the existing arrangements, the establishments in a year of peace should, he said, be—

	£
In Great Britain - -	7,[illegible],000
In Ireland - -	1,[illegible],000
	[illegible]

If the charge were to be borne in the ratio of 15 to 2,

	£
Great Britain's share would be - -	7,941,000
and Ireland's share	1,059,000
	9,000,000

So Ireland would save 442,000*l*.

Lord Castlereagh's speech was followed by a long debate, which lasted continuously for about 20 hours. In the course of it Sir John Parnell observed, that, under the proposed arrangements, Ireland's expenditure would have from the first to keep pace with Great Britain's, and at the end of 20 years Ireland would be entirely at the mercy of the United Parliament with only 100 Irish members against 540.

Mr. J. C. Beresford accused Lord Castlereagh of disingenuousness in his comparison of the National Debts. By carefully restricting himself to their relative proportions, Lord Castlereagh had made it appear that the Irish debt had increased much more rapidly than the English; but, if he had quoted their absolute amounts, it would have appeared that the actual increase of the Irish debt was of trifling amount.

The (Irish) Chancellor of the Exchequer said that the objection to subjecting Ireland to the taxes and debts of Great Britain might, if necessary, be removed by inserting in the Treaty of Union a stipulation that Ireland should be liable only to such portion of the public burthens as were suitable to her means and finances. This stipulation had been made in the case of Scotland and had been carefully observed. But, in his opinion, it would not be necessary for Ireland, whose natural resources were as good as those of England and would under the Union be equally developed.

At the close of this debate the Government secured a majority of 43, having 158 votes against 115 for the Opposition.

On the 17th February 1800, the Union proposals were considered in committee, and the Speaker, Mr. Foster, availed himself of this opportunity of delivering a very comprehensive speech against the measure of the Government. In the course of it he grappled with the argument that nothing but a Legislative Union could save Ireland from bankruptcy; and that the result of the Union would be an annual saving of a million in time of war, and half a million in time of peace. He held that it was not true that Irish finances were desperate. In Great Britain the National Debt had grown much more rapidly than in Ireland. In the six years ending the 5th January 1799, the British debt had been increased by 186,000,000*l*., while during the same period Irish debt had been increased by 14,000,000*l*. The liabilities, therefore, of the two kingdoms had been augmented by 200,000,000*l*. Ireland's share of these joint liabilities under the Union proposals (viz., 2-17ths) would have been 23,530,000*l*. instead of 14,000,000*l*. Accordingly if the Union had been accomplished in 1793, Ireland would have incurred 9½ millions more of indebtedness than she actually had done. Instead of bringing reduced taxation, the Union, he maintained, would add not less than 1½ millions to the annual taxation of the country.

This speech, however, had no effect on the division list, and the measure now slowly but surely made its way through the Irish House of Commons.

The resolution raising the difficult and delicate question of the relative contributions of the two countries was debated and agreed to at a single sitting on the 24th February 1800. Lord Castlereagh took this occasion to reply to Mr. Foster's calculations of the financial effect of the ministerial proposals. He stated that, instead of there being any fear that under the Union scheme the debt must increase much more rapidly than with a separate Parliament, Ireland would "in the next five years taken in the proportion "of two of war and three of peace," save under the Union nearly ten millions.

Mr. Foster, Sir J. Parnell, and others, maintained that the proportion to be imposed on Ireland was beyond her capacities; and an amendment was moved by Mr. J. C. Beresford that the contribution should be 2-20ths instead of 2-17ths. But the amendment was speedily negatived.

Before the resolutions reached their final stage in the Irish House of Commons Mr. Grattan, who throughout this session had been one of the warmest and most impressive opponents of the Union proposals, challenged Lord Castlereagh's statements in defence of the financial provisions. The Irish orator maintained, on the 19th March, that the idea of an Union was, from a financial point of view, founded upon two false principles: first, that the revenues of Ireland would not increase; and, secondly, that the expenses of the country were bound to grow. If the revenues were to decline under the Union, what, he asked, was to become of the national prosperity which was promised to flow from the Union? If they were not to decline, what became of the argument of impending bankruptcy? Lord Castlereagh had stated the Irish revenue for the year to be 2,500,000*l*. The cost of the last peace establishment had been 1,000,000*l*., and the interest of the debt was 1,400,000*l*. There was thus a margin of revenue over normal peace expenditure. But this margin disappeared in Lord Castlereagh's statement, because he arbitrarily estimated the establishment at 1,500,000*l*. instead of 1,000,000*l*. No ground had been shown for anticipating such an increase, and none could be conceived, unless indeed the Government contemplated an increase of military force, which would ill accord with the tranquilizing effects promised as the result of the Union. As to the proposed contribution from Ireland, the proportion of 2-17ths had been calculated on worthless data; and it was safe to say that the minister had overrated Ireland in contribution as he had overcharged her in establishments.

Meanwhile, in the Irish House of Lords, the Union proposals had met with much less opposition. Probably the most noteworthy incident of the debates in that House was the memorable speech made by Lord Clare on the 10th February 1800, when he brought forward the first resolution approving the Union. Two years before, he had described Ireland as advancing in prosperity more rapidly than any other in Europe, but he now painted its situation as desperate. He related the rapid rise of the national debt, and attributed the rise far less to the French war than to internal rebellion. "We have not three years of redemption," he said, "from bankruptcy or intolerable taxation . . . . If "England were at peace at this hour with all the "Powers of Europe . . . . you would be compelled "to maintain a war establishment for defence against "your own people." He maintained that the scale of expense rendered necessary by the rebellion was ruinous, and that, if it continued for three years, 1,100,000*l*. would have to be raised for the interest of the debt alone.

One hundred and one Irish Peers voted in the division, which gave the Government a majority of 49; and the resolutions passed through their remaining stages in the House of Lords with little discussion.

At the last stage a protest was entered on the Journal of that House by 20 Peers, and as the protest was specially directed against the financial arrangements, it may be well to quote a part of it.

"Dissentient.

*

"Secondly: Because, however willing we now are and always have been to contribute in proportion to our means to the support and defence of the empire, we hold it our bounden duty, before that we shall irrevocably enter into any engagement to take upon ourselves any particular proportion of the expenses of the empire, to ascertain the probable amount of such proportion, to enquire into the ability of Ireland to discharge the same, and to examine whether such part be proportionate to the relative abilities of the two nations. Upon such enquiry we find that the expenses incurred by Great Britain in the year 1799 amounted to upwards of 32 millions; and that which was incurred by Ireland in the said year amounted to upwards of six millions, two-seventeenths of which sums (the proposed proportion) amount to upwards of 4,500,000*l*., which, added to the present interest of the debt incurred by Ireland and the discharge of her annuities, amounting to 1,400,000*l*., and the interest of the loan of this year, amounting to above 130,000*l*., will make the annual charge upon Ireland to amount to 6,030,000*l*.; it appears to us that the produce of our revenue, including the estimated amount of the taxes laid on this session does not exceed 2,800,000*l*., and, consequently, they will fall short by 3,230,000*l*. of the sum necessary to discharge such proportionate part of the expenses of the empire. In order to ascertain the relative abilities of the two nations, their respective balances of trade

with the whole world have been compared, and it appears from thence that such balance in favour of Great Britain amounts to the sum of 14,800,000*l.*, and that such balance in favour of Ireland, according to the returns laid before this House, amounts to the sum of 509,322*l.* Taking, therefore, the balance of trade as a criterion of ability, the proportion would be as 29 to 1. Enquiry likewise having been made into the current cash in circulation in both kingdoms, it appears that in the year 1777 the current cash in Great Britain was calculated at 42,000,000*l.*, and it is computed by persons the best informed upon that subject in this kingdom that the current cash in Ireland may now amount to between 3,000,000*l.* and 2,500,000*l.*; taking it, therefore, at the latter, the proportion should be as 17 to 1. Considering it in another very essential point of view, the influx and efflux of money into the respective kingdoms it appears that Great Britain receives, by remittances to persons having property in the East and West Indies who reside in Great Britain 4,000,000 sterling. We do not know of any influx of money into Ireland, save that of 509,322*l.*, the balance of her trade, and it appears to us that she annually remits to Great Britain on account of her debts the sum of 720,000*l.*, and on account of the pay of 2,538 men serving in Great Britain the sum of 161,570*l.* These annual drains, together with the remittances to absentees (probably little short of two millions), we consider to have occasioned the high rate of exchange with Great Britain during the last 12 months, from three to five per cent. above par, notwithstanding that during that period three millions have been borrowed in Great Britain and remitted to Ireland. We do not know of any fund to resort to for raising the said deficiency of 3,358,000*l.*, save by taxation, in addition to which cannot in any considerable degree be supported; and by resorting to her landed property, the gross contents of which being but 11,000,000 plantation acres, we cannot estimate at more than the annual rent of 5,000,000*l.* We observe the large sums of money borrowed by Ireland within these few years have been for the most part raised in Great Britain, owing to the total disability of raising them in Ireland; the facility of obtaining money in Great Britain and the difficulty found in raising any in Ireland clearly demonstrate the opulence of the one nation and the poverty of the other. Under such circumstances it appears to us that, if this kingdom should take upon herself irrevocably the payment of two-seventeenths of such expenses, she will not have means to perform her engagements unless by charging her landed property with 10*s.* or 12*s.* in the pound; it must end in the draining from her her last guinea, in totally annihilating her trade for want of capital, in rendering the lands unproductive, and consequently in finally putting her into a state of bankruptcy. We think ourselves called upon to protest against a measure so ruinous to this country, and to place the responsibility for its consequences upon such persons as have brought it forward and supported it."

On the 27th March 1800 an address was voted by the two Irish Houses, informing His Majesty of the result of their deliberations; and this address, together with the resolutions of the Lords and Commons of Ireland, containing the terms proposed by them for an entire union between the two kingdoms, was communicated by His Majesty to the British Parliament on the 2nd of April.

In the speech which Mr. Pitt delivered on the 21st April, when the propositions of the Irish Parliament were under consideration at Westminster, he expressed his regret that the financial systems of the two countries could not be identified, owing to the different proportions of debt which they had respectively incurred, the different stages of civilization and commerce, and the different wealth of the two kingdoms. "To avoid suspicion," he said, "of unduly loading our sister kingdom with "more than her share of the expenses of the State, to "obviate all imputation of partiality . . . . . . " the Parliaments of both countries have fixed pro"portions to be paid by each for a limited time, at the "expiration of which it is presumed the finances of "each may so far approximate that they may be "assimilated and identified"; the proportions meanwhile being founded on "a blended and mixed con"sideration of population and revenue."

"The object of the financial arrangements was to effect "the gradual abolition of all distinction in finance and "revenue between the two countries, and to accelerate "the time when both countries form but one fund and "pay one uniform proportion of taxes throughout each.

"It is obvious, while there remains a disproportion of "debt, they cannot form one fund; that event cannot "take place, till by the operation of sinking funds this "disproportion is destroyed. Yet, Sir, as I have already "observed, the real value of the respective debts may be "alike, before they are of the same magnitude, because, "if our sinking fund will discharge our larger debt, be"fore the debt of Ireland can be discharged, though not "of equal magnitude, the greater debt discharged in the "shorter time may not surpass the less debt remaining "a longer time unpaid; and, whenever the real value shall "be alike, the finances of both countries may be assimi"lated and identified, and it will remain in the discretion "of the United Parliaments, to abolish all distinctions of "quotas and contributions, and to fix one rule of taxation "throughout the United Kingdom, subject merely to "such local abatements as from circumstances may "become necessary."

The resolutions agreed to by the British Houses of Parliament, and their joint address to the King, arrived in Ireland on the 12th May 1800.

Thereupon the Irish Parliament applied itself to embodying the resolutions in a Bill. On the 21st May Lord Castlereagh obtained leave, by a majority of 60, to bring in the Bill. It was read a second time on the 26th, and, on the motion made that day, that it should be committed, Mr. Grattan delivered a speech, in which he referred specially to the incongruities and imperfections of the Bill. Turning to the financial terms, he said that the proposal to fix Ireland's contribution at 2 to 15 was made without any data whatever that could warrant such a proposition. The papers before the House were unintelligible and conflicting. In the instances of tea, tobacco, and other articles, the value of the goods consumed was returned by one-third, and in other cases by one-half, more than the value of the same kind of goods imported. The differences were not reconciled. There was no explanation. In one set of papers the articles were valued with the charge of freight and duties added; in another set they were valued with these additions omitted. The comparison formed on imports and exports was no better. The average imports and exports of Great Britain, as given by Lord Castlereagh, were understated by about 6,000,000*l.*; those of Ireland had been overstated by about 2,000,000*l.* The proportion, therefore, being about 8 to 71 the proposed contribution was evidently unjust and fallacious. The contribution was estimated at about 4,500,000*l.* in time of war . . . "a "charge equal to the support of 126,000 soldiers, which "is near eight times as much as you paid in former wars, "so that you are to multiply your charge for the loss of "your Parliament . . . . Though I do not "think the means of this country are unequal to every "necessary expense, yet I do think they are inadequate "to that contributory expense which the Union stipu"lates. . . . . . The attempt will exhaust the "country, at the same time that it enslaves her. "Colour it as you please, Ireland will pay more than "she is able. . . . . . . Considering then the "terms of the Union, so far as they relate to revenue, "they amount to a continuation of the double establish"ment, an increase of the separate establishment, and "a military government, with a prospect of soon "ascending to the full taxes of England."

On the night that Mr. Grattan delivered this speech, the Bill was committed by a majority of 65.

Feeling that the continuation of the fight in Parliament was hopeless, but desiring to place on the journals of the House a full record of their case, the leaders of the Opposition in the Irish House of Commons, headed by Lord Corry, moved a lengthy address to the King on the 6th June. This address summarises so forcibly and clearly the arguments used at the end of the struggle against the financial proposals, that it may be well to cite a portion of it:—

. . . . . "The imposition of your Majesty's Ministers is still more glaring, in their having presumed to fix a proportion of contribution towards the general future expenses to be observed by the two kingdoms, in the ratio of one part by Ireland for every seven parts and a half by Britain.

"If they had any plausible grounds whereon they calculated this proportion, they have not deigned to lay them before your Parliament; and the usual and established forms of committees to investigate into matters of such intricate and extended calculation have been superseded by them.

"Your Majesty's faithful Commons are satisfied that the calculation is extremely erroneous; and this in a

Lowe's Review, Vol. VIII, p. 467.

Grattan's Speeches, Vol. IV, pp. 1, &c.

Grattan's Life, Vol. IV, p. [illegible]

just and fair inquiry into the comparative means of each country this kingdom ought not, and is not able, to contribute in anything like that proportion.

"They feel it a duty, too, to protest most solemnly against any arrangement of taxation on which they have had no documents, or made any inquiry, to guide their judgment, and in which, they understand, no consideration whatever has been had to the different legal interest of money in this kingdom, which causes a disadvantage of 20l. per cent. in procuring capital; nor to the relative quantity of shipping possessed and used by each country; nor to the export trade in foreign articles; nor to the extent of manufacture for home consumption; nor to the balance of trade, which shows the annual increase of its clear profit, and, of course, the annual increase of the fund it creates to contribute from; in all of which the means of Britain very far exceed the foregoing proportion, and particularly in the balance of trade, which, in Ireland, amounts to little more than half a million with all the world; but is stated by authority to have amounted to 14,800,000l. in Britain, exclusive of an annual influx of money from the East and West Indies, to the amount of four millions, to the proprietors resident in Britain; and of two millions from Ireland, to the proprietors of Irish estates resident there; and of another million from Ireland for the charges of her debt due in Britain; whereas the only known visible influx of money into Ireland is the above balance of trade of half a million only; and those two sums of two millions and one million, while they add to the wealth and means of Britain, unfortunately take away in the same amount from the ability of Ireland.

"Thus, had a due investigation been made, and a fair inquiry gone into, with a view to obtain a true knowledge of facts whereon to ground a just calculation, it would have appeared that this proportion for Ireland is not only unjust but far beyond what it will be in her power to discharge; and the rashness of your Majesty's Ministers in hazarding such a measure is the more to be lamented or wondered at, because, should Ireland engage to pay more than she is able to answer, the necessary consequence must be a rapid decrease of her capital, the decline of her trade, a failure in the produce of her taxes, and, in the end, her total bankruptcy; but, under such circumstances, she cannot be alone a bankrupt, and, should she fatally become so, by an injudicious or avaricious apportionment of contribution, Great Britain must share in her ruin, and our great and glorious empire be brought to the brink of destruction by an unavailing attempt to take from Ireland its constitution, and substitute a theoretic, visionary, and untried system in its room.

"We should, therefore, earnestly supplicate your Majesty to oblige your Ministers to defer the measure until a full and satisfactory investigation should be made, if we did not feel that it ought to be entirely relinquished, and that the injuries and dangers attending on it could not be removed by any change of that proportion, or reconciled by any modification of detail whatsoever." . . . . .

[illegible] This address was negatived by a majority of 58; and on the following day (7th June) the Bill was read a third time, and sent up to the Irish House of Lords. It passed quickly through its stages in that House, though not without there being lodged another protest by some of the Irish peers.

The Bill was then sent to Westminster, where it passed through both Houses of the British Parliament, and it received the Royal Assent on the 1st August 1800, the Articles of the Treaty of Union, which was to take effect as from the 1st January 1801, being embodied in the Act 39 & 40 Geo. III. c. 67.

According to the declarations of the spokesmen of the British Government, it was their intention in the matter of finance to treat Ireland, when united with Great Britain, not only justly but generously; and, it is evident that nothing but the inequality of the debts of the two countries deterred them from proposing an union of Exchequers as well as an union of Parliaments in 1800. On the other hand, it was predicted by the opponents of the measure that the Irish contribution would prove to be beyond the capacities of the country, and that rapidly increasing debt, speedy bankruptcy, and full British taxation were in store for Ireland. We shall see how far these predictions were fulfilled.

The exact terms of the 7th Article of the Treaty of Union, which prescribed the financial arrangements, were as follows:

"1. That it be the Seventh Article of Union, that the charge arising from the payment of the interest, and the sinking fund for the reduction of the principal, of the debt incurred in either kingdom before the Union, shall continue to be separately defrayed by Great Britain and Ireland respectively, except as hereinafter provided:

"2. That for the space of 20 years after the Union shall take place, the contribution of Great Britain and Ireland respectively, towards the expenditure of the United Kingdom in each year, shall be defrayed in the proportion of 15 parts for Great Britain, and two parts for Ireland; and that at the expiration of the said 20 years, the future expenditure of the United Kingdom (other than the interest and charges of the debt to which either country shall be separately liable) shall be defrayed in such proportion as the Parliament of the United Kingdom shall deem just and reasonable upon a comparison of the real value of the exports and imports of the respective countries, upon an average of the three years next preceding the period of revision; or on a comparison of the value of the quantities of the following articles consumed within the respective countries, on a similar average; *viz.*, beer, spirits, sugar, wine, tea, tobacco, and malt; or according to the aggregate proportion resulting from both these considerations combined; or on a comparison of the amount of income in each country, estimated from the produce for the same period of a general tax, if such shall have been imposed on the same descriptions of income in both countries; and that the Parliament of the United Kingdom shall afterwards proceed in like manner to revise and fix the said proportions according to the same rules, or any of them, at periods not more distant than twenty years nor less than seven years from each other; unless, previous to any such period, the Parliament of the United Kingdom shall have declared, as hereinafter provided, that the expenditure of the United Kingdom shall be defrayed indiscriminately, by equal taxes imposed on the like articles in both countries:

"3. That, for the defraying the said expenditure according to the rules above laid down, the revenues of Ireland shall hereafter constitute a Consolidated Fund, which shall be charged, in the first instance, with the interest of the debt of Ireland, and with the sinking fund applicable to the reduction of the said debt, and the remainder shall be applied towards defraying the proportion of the expenditure of the United Kingdom, to which Ireland may be liable in each year:

"4. That the proportion of contribution to which Great Britain and Ireland will be liable, shall be raised by such taxes in each country respectively, as the Parliament of the United Kingdom shall from time to time deem fit; provided always, that in regulating the taxes in each country, by which their respective proportions shall be levied, no article in Ireland shall be made liable to any new or additional duty, by which the whole amount of duty, payable thereon, would exceed the amount which will be thereafter payable in England on the like article:

"5. That, if at the end of any year any surplus shall accrue from the revenues of Ireland, after defraying the interest, sinking fund, and proportional contribution and separate charges to which the said country shall then be liable, taxes shall be taken off to the amount of such surplus, or the surplus shall be applied by the Parliament of the United Kingdom to local purposes in Ireland, or to make good any deficiency which may arise in the revenues of Ireland in time of peace, or be invested, by the Commissioners of the National Debt of Ireland, in the Funds, to accumulate for the benefit of Ireland at compound interest, in case of the contribution of Ireland in time of war; provided that the surplus so to accumulate shall at no future period be suffered to exceed the sum of five millions:

"6. That all monies to be raised after the Union, by loan, in peace or war, for the service of the United Kingdom by the Parliament thereof, shall be considered to be a joint debt, and the charges thereof shall be borne by the respective countries in the proportion of their respective contributions; provided that, if at any time, in raising their respective contributions hereby fixed for each country, the Parliament of the United Kingdom shall judge it fit to raise a greater proportion of such respective contributions in one country within the year than in the other, or to set apart a greater proportion of sinking fund for the liquidation of the whole or any part of the loan raised on account of the one country than of that raised on

account of the other country, then such part of the said loan, for the liquidation of which different provisions shall have been made for the respective countries, shall be kept distinct, and shall be borne by each separately, and only that part of the said loan be deemed joint and common, for the reduction of which the respective countries shall have made provision in the proportion of their respective contributions:

"7. That if at any future day the separate debt of each country respectively shall have been liquidated, or, if the values of their respective debts (estimated according to the amount of the interest and annuities attending the same, and of the sinking fund applicable to the reduction thereof, and to the period within which the whole capital of such debt shall appear to be redeemable by such sinking fund) shall be to each other in the same proportion with the respective contributions of each country respectively; or if the amount by which the value of the larger of such debts shall vary from such proportion shall not exceed one hundredth part of the said value; and if it shall appear to the Parliament of the United Kingdom, that the respective circumstances of the two countries will thenceforth admit of their contributing indiscriminately, by equal taxes imposed on the same articles in each, to the future expenditure of the United Kingdom, it shall be competent to the Parliament of the United Kingdom to declare, that all future expense thenceforth to be incurred, together with the interest and charges of all joint debts contracted previous to such declaration, shall be so defrayed indiscriminately by equal taxes imposed on the same articles in each country, and thenceforth from time to time, as circumstances may require, to impose and apply such taxes accordingly, subject only to such particular exemptions or abatements in Ireland, and in that part of Great Britain called Scotland, as circumstances may appear from time to time to demand:

"8. That, from the period of such declaration, it shall no longer be necessary to regulate the contribution of the two countries towards the future expenditure of the United Kingdom, according to any specific proportion, or according to any of the rules hereinbefore prescribed; provided, nevertheless, that the interest or charges which may remain on account of any part of the separate debt with which either country shall be chargeable, and which shall not be liquidated or consolidated proportionably as above, shall, until extinguished, continue to be defrayed by separate taxes in each country:

"9. That a sum not less than the sum which has been granted by the Parliament of Ireland on the average of six years immediately preceding the first day of January in the year one thousand eight hundred, in premiums for the internal encouragement of agriculture or manufactures, or for the maintaining institutions for pious and charitable purposes, shall be applied, for the period of twenty years after the Union, to such local purposes in Ireland, in such manner as the Parliament of the United Kingdom shall direct:

"10. That, from and after the first day of January one thousand eight hundred and one, all public revenue arising to the United Kingdom from the territorial dependencies thereof, and applied to the general expenditure of the United Kingdom, shall be so applied in the proportions of the respective contributions of the two countries."

The article is not so clearly worded in some respects as it might be; but the gist of it appears to be this:

Ref. of Parliamentary Papers, No. 251 of 1894. 1. The interest and sinking fund of the debts which had been incurred by Great Britain and Ireland previously to the Union were to continue to be separately defrayed by each kingdom.

2.—(1) For the next 20 years Great Britain and Ireland were to contribute jointly towards the expenditure of the United Kingdom in the respective proportions of 15 to 2; that is, Great Britain was to defray 15/17ths, or 88·24 per cent., and Ireland 2/17ths, or 11·76 per cent., of such expenditure.

(2) At the end of that term, unless it had been provided that the joint expenditure of the United Kingdom was to be indiscriminately defrayed by equal taxes in both countries, the respective contributions of Great Britain and Ireland to such expenditure were to be defrayed in such proportions as might be deemed by Parliament to be just and reasonable, upon a comparison of the respective resources of the two countries.

(3) Alternative bases of arriving at such just and reasonable proportions were indicated, viz.:—

a. The respective values of British and Irish exports and imports on the average of the latest three years; or

b. The respective values of the quantities consumed of beer, spirits, sugar, wine, tea, tobacco, and malt; or

A combination of both these considerations (which had been the basis adopted by Mr. Pitt and Lord Castlereagh for the first 20 years of the Union); or

d. The respective incomes of each country as ascertained from the yield of a general tax on income, if such a tax existed.

(4) A revision was to be subsequently made on a similar basis at intervals of not more than 20, or less than 7, years; unless, previously to any such period, Parliament had declared that the expenditure of the United Kingdom should be indiscriminately defrayed.

3. Irish revenues were to constitute a consolidated fund, on which the payments in respect of Ireland's pre-Union debt were to be the first charge, the remainder of the revenue being applicable to defray Ireland's contribution to the joint expenditure.

4. The respective contributions of the two countries were to be raised by taxes in each country, as Parliament might deem fit to impose; but no article in Ireland was to be taxed at a higher rate than it was taxed in England.

5. If, after Ireland had defrayed her pre-Union debt charge and proportional contribution to the joint expenditure of the United Kingdom, as well as the separate charges to which she was liable, there were a surplus, it was to be applied in one of several ways, viz.:—

a. In remission of taxation; or

b. to local purposes; or

c. in making good a deficiency of Irish revenue in time of peace; or

d. in building up a reserve fund, not exceeding five millions, to relieve Ireland's contribution in time of war.

6. All debt incurred by Parliament subsequently to the Union for the service of the United Kingdom, in peace or war, was to be considered a joint debt, and the charge thereof was to be borne by the two countries in the proportions of their respective contributions. But, if Parliament should raise a greater proportion of the contributions in one country within the year than in the other country, or should set aside a larger sinking fund for paying off the loan raised on account of one country than for paying off the loan raised on account of the other country, then the debt was to be kept distinct and the charge thereof to be borne separately.

7. If, in the future, the separate debts of Great Britain and Ireland should be liquidated, or if the values of those debts should be proportionate to the respective contributions of the two countries, or the amount by which the larger of the debts (i.e., the British Debt), were to vary from such proportion should not be more than a hundredth part,* then Parliament might declare, if the circumstances seemed to justify it, that all future expenses incurred in the United Kingdom should be defrayed indiscriminately by equal taxes imposed on the same articles in each country, and might impose and apply such taxes to those expenses, subject only to such exemptions or abatements in Ireland and also in Scotland, as the case might seem to require.

8. In the event of such a declaration by Parliament, the contributions of the two countries to the joint expenditure of the United Kingdom were not to be regulated in specific proportions, except as regards so much of the separate pre-Union debts as might neither be paid off nor consolidated; and the charges in respect of these debts were to be defrayed by separate taxes in each country.

9. A sum not less than the amount which the Irish Parliament had, during the six years ending the 1st January 1800, granted in aid of the encouragement of

* These limits contemplated a latitude of variation in the proportions between [illegible].

agriculture or manufacture, or of the maintenance of certain charitable institutions, was to be applied, for 20 years after the Union, to such local purposes in Ireland as Parliament might direct.

10. All public revenue, accruing to the United Kingdom from the territorial dependencies, and applied to the general expenditure of the United Kingdom, were to be applied in the proportions of the respective contributions of the two countries.

Such were apparently the financial provisions of the Treaty of Union. The next matters for consideration are, what were the steps taken for giving effect to these provisions, and what led to their alteration by Parliament in 1816?

[illegible margin note] The most important point connected with the operation of the 7th Article was the mode of apportioning the joint expenditure of the United Kingdom between the two countries.

The amounts estimated to be payable by each country were, in the first instance, agreed upon by the Chancellors of the Exchequer for Great Britain and Ireland, and stated in their annual budgets. Thereupon the necessary ways and means were provided, partly from revenue and partly from money raised by creation of debt, to meet those amounts and likewise the separate charges of each country. The intention evidently was that, at the close of every year, and as soon as the actual expenditure was ascertained, the accounts should be settled up, and the balance due from one country paid over to the other.

Some delay was of course necessary before a settlement could be made, but the delay was enhanced by the absence of any recognised or authorised tribunal for examining the accounts and determining the final proportions.

Indeed, there is no record of any attempt to arrive at a settlement during the first four years of the Union arrangements; the Chancellors of the Exchequer being apparently content to take the provisional estimates only.

In 1805 a Committee of the House of Commons was appointed to inquire into and report the amount of the joint charge from 1801; but this committee made no report.

Parliamentary Paper, No. [illegible] of 1806. In the next session (1806), a Committee was appointed to proceed further with the matter. They were directed not only to examine the state of things up to date, but also to consider the best means of ascertaining in future the amount of the balance that might be due from one country to the other at the expiration of each year.

The Committee found themselves unable in 1806 to report the joint charge, or to ascertain the situation of the two countries as to their expenditure, in consequence of an error in the formation of the accounts transmitted on the part of Ireland, in which the sums expended for services prior to the Union were not distinguished with sufficient exactness. They consequently recommended that the accounts should be presented in the next session, expressing their belief that the matter had been put in such a train as would enable them then to make a definite report.

Parliamentary Paper, No. [illegible] of 1811. Owing presumably to the intricacy of the subject, the presentation of the accounts was delayed until 1811. They were then referred to a new Committee, who were directed to inquire and report (1) what had been the increase of the debt in Ireland since the Union; (2) what had been the state of Irish Revenue; (3) what the taxes of Ireland were likely to yield in future; (4) what had been the expenditure in that country on its separate account and on its joint account with the United Kingdom; and also (5) what was the trade and navigation of Ireland.

In making their report, this Committee for the first time settled, subject to the final judgment of Parliament, the principles by which the account of the joint expenditure should be regulated, and they struck the balance between the two countries.

The main point, however, on which the Committee dwelt in their report was the rapid increase of the debt of Ireland during the preceding 10 years. In the course of that period it had nearly been trebled in its nominal amount. This was an increase far more rapid than the increase of the debt of Great Britain.

Indeed, the Committee presented actuarial calculations to show that the values of the respective debts of Great Britain and Ireland had very nearly assumed the proportions of their prescribed contributions to joint expenditure, viz., as 15 to 2; and this was the fact to which they drew the special attention of the House, not only because it appeared that it was consequently open to Parliament, under the 7th Article of the Treaty of Union (par. 7), to consolidate the debts and expenditures of the two countries, but because the wording of the provision was capable of an interpretation by which, if Parliament did not effect a consolidation then, it might be precluded from doing so afterwards.

The Committee also pointed out that, while the debt charge of Ireland had been so materially augmented the revenue of the country had latterly been falling off.

It was the opinion of the best-informed politicians of those days that, if Mr. Spencer Perceval had lived, the two exchequers would have been consolidated the next year. But, as a matter of fact, the only parliamentary action taken on the report of the Committee of 1811 was to reappoint the Committee in 1812, with similar, though not identical terms of reference. Walpole's History of England, Vol. I, p. [illegible]

It was, again, mainly the question of the debt of Ireland, and of the meaning to be attached to the words of the Act of Union applicable to future borrowing (7th Article, par. 4), to which the Committee addressed themselves. Parliamentary Paper, No. [illegible] of 1812.

"It appears," they said, "to have been the intention of the Legislature in these provisions" (viz., in par. 6 of 7th Article), "that all loans, which might be incurred after the Union, should, as far as possible, be raised upon the joint credit of the countries comprising the United Kingdom, and the charges to be incurred in consequence of them borne in the proportion of their respective contributions. It did not, however, escape the attention of the Parliaments of Great Britain and Ireland that circumstances might arise in which it might be expedient to raise a greater proportion of the respective contribution of one country within the year, than of that of the other, or to appropriate a larger sum to the liquidation of debt; and these cases must have been brought into the view of the Legislature by an actual situation of affairs at the time of the passing of the Act of Union, as at the same time a large sum was annually raised in Great Britain, by extraordinary war taxes, while no similar provision had been made in Ireland.

"To this state of things, the latter part of the clause applies, and directs that so much only of the loan shall be deemed joint and common for the reduction of which the respective countries shall have made provision in the proportion of their respective contributions: had no such provision been made, the consequence would have been, either that the revenue of each country must, at whatever inconvenience, have been raised so as to bear to that of the other the exact proportion of its respective contribution, which might obviously have occasioned great hardship to the country which was least wealthy, or least accustomed to taxation, or that the country, which, by means of extraordinary taxes, had made a provision within the year beyond its respective proportion, would, instead of deriving any benefit from such an exertion in diminishing the charge of future loans, have been obliged to bear its proportion of all the loans rendered necessary on the other country, in consequence of the want of such extraordinary taxes.

"These inconveniences have been avoided by the provision above referred to, and upon that provision the legislature of the United Kingdom appears uniformly to have acted; the respective proportion of contribution raised within the year having since the Union been usually much larger in Great Britain than in Ireland, in consequence of the great amount of war taxes in Great Britain . . . . , and in one year (1807) a much larger sinking fund having been provided for the liquidation of the British loan than was established in Ireland.

"It does not, indeed, appear that any part of the loans raised since the Union have (*sic*) been considered as joint debt; nor would it have made any other than a nominal difference, if so much of the Irish loan of each year as bore to the British loan the proportion of the respective contribution of Ireland, viz., 2 to 15, had been so considered; because the charge to be borne by Ireland, in respect of the two portions of the loan, viz., the joint and the separate portion, would in that case have been exactly equal to that which has been incurred on account of the Irish debt undivided."

The Committee continued their inquiries in 1813; but practically made no progress with them beyond bringing the accounts of the two countries up to date. Parliamentary Paper, No. [illegible] of 1813.

The Committee resumed their sittings in 1815; and the principal part of their report that year was also Parliamentary Paper, No. [illegible] of 1815.

devoted to the state of the debt in Ireland, and its bearing on the consolidation of the exchequers as contemplated by the Treaty of Union. They presented further actuarial calculations about the respective values of the Irish and British debts. According to those calculations, the proportions were as (about) 2 to 13 or 13½. So the Irish debt was actually in excess of the Union proportion of 2 to 15. The committee pointed out that, according to a literal interpretation of the 7th Article, it might be inferred that the time for a consolidation of exchequers had passed, inasmuch as consolidation was only intended when the debts of the two countries were in the proportions of their respective contributions to joint expenditure. But, having regard to the spirit of the arrangement, which was one of affording protection to the weaker country, the Committee held that Parliament still had the right of consolidating the debts and the expenditures of the two countries, notwithstanding that the debt of Ireland had gone beyond the Union proportion.

The further question was, whether the existence of such right being assumed, it was expedient that Parliament should exercise it. It was true that all the direct taxes levied in Great Britain had not been extended to Ireland, and that in some other respects Ireland was less heavily taxed. But on the great heads of revenue the rates in both countries had been nearly assimilated, and for several years past Ireland had advanced in permanent taxation more rapidly than Great Britain, notwithstanding the immense exertions of the latter country, and including the extraordinary and war taxes.

Such being the case, it appeared to the Committee that no practical benefit could possibly be obtained, for any part of the United Kingdom, by endeavouring to maintain a fixed proportion of expenditure, when that proportion had rapidly carried the debt of Ireland from a state of relative inferiority into a growing excess; and with a view to relieving Ireland from a burden which had proved too great, and to rendering her resources more productive, the Committee concluded their Report by passing a resolution in favour of there being a financial, as well as parliamentary, union between the two countries.

The terms of the resolution were as follows: "That "it is now become expedient that Parliament should "take into consideration so much of the 7th Article of "the Act of Union as respects the competence of Par-"liament under certain circumstances therein stated, "to declare, that all future expenditure of the United "Kingdom, together with all interest and charges of the "joint debt incurred previous to such declaration, shall "be defrayed indiscriminately by equal taxation imposed "on the same articles in each; subject to such parti-"cular exemptions or abatements in Ireland, and in "that part of Great Britain called Scotland, as cir-"cumstances may appear from time to time to "demand."

So emphatically worded a resolution, made by a Parliamentary Committee, naturally impelled the Government of the day to take some decided action; and on 20th May 1816, Mr. Vesey Fitzgerald, Chancellor of the Exchequer for Ireland, moved that the House of Commons should resolve itself into Committee, in order to take into consideration the 7th Article of the Act of Union and the report of the Irish Finance Committee, together with the accounts which they had presented.

In moving the resolutions for the consolidation of the British and Irish Exchequers, he referred to the fact that, owing to the extraordinary rapidity with which the Irish Debt had grown, the debts of the two countries had as early as 1811 reached the proportions which admitted of consolidation. It was, he said, only accident which had prevented the measure being carried out before 1816.

In 1815 the debts were in the proportion of 2 to 13, and in February 1816 in the proportion of 2 to 13½.

He gave illustrations of the endeavours made by Ireland to meet the increased burden thrown upon her since the Union. The year 1815 was a bad year in Ireland owing to agricultural depression, but even so it showed enormous developments under the great heads of Revenue. The gross produce of the Irish Revenue in 1815–16 he stated to be about 7,000,000*l.*, and, as the expenses of management were part of the joint charge, the whole of this sum was available for Ireland's debt charge and her contribution to joint expenditure.

Mr. Fitzgerald turned then to the comparison of sinking funds with a view to show that the sinking fund of Ireland was richer than that of England, so that the latter country would be a gainer by the consolidation. The incomes of the sinking funds he compared as follows:—

	Ireland.			Great Britain.
—	Applicable to Debt funded in Ireland.	Applicable to Debt funded in England.	Total.	
Income of Sinking Fund.	[illegible]	£ [illegible]	£ [illegible]	[illegible]
Proportion to Debt.	1 to [illegible]	1 to [illegible]	1 to [illegible]	1 to [illegible]

He thought that those who hoped much from the extension to Ireland of British taxes from which she had hitherto been exempt would be disappointed. There would be a diminution upon some of existing taxes, e.g., 350,000*l.* on houses and hearth money, the latter of which must cease if the house duty were extended. So far would the yield be from defraying the Irish contribution as fixed by the Union, that it would not even make up the existing deficiency in Irish net revenue.

Summing up, he said that at the Union Ireland hoped that her expenditure would be lightened. As a fact in the 15 years preceding the Union it amounted to 41,000,000*l.*, and in the 15 years after the Union to 148,000,000*l.* Her revenue had so far increased that it would in the 15 years, without loans, have discharged more than the expenditure of the 15 years before the Union. She had paid in taxes 78,000,000*l.*, being 47,000,000*l.* more than in the 15 years on which her contribution was calculated.

Lord Castlereagh, who had had so much to do with the Union arrangements, naturally took part in the debate. He was of course anxious to defend those arrangements. He pointed out that, if since the Union instead of 15 years of war there had been 15 years of peace, Ireland's expenditure would not have been greater than before the Union; and that with the war, even without the Union, her debt must have increased not less rapidly than it had done. This increase was a necessity in view of the fact that her internal service cost 4,000,000*l.* a year; and in raising her loans she would not have had the support of the English connexion. The calculations at the time of the Union had been made on the basis of the then existing national expenditure of 25,000,000*l.* a year; no one could then foresee the rapid rise in 15 years to 80,000,000*l.* The reason why Ireland's debt had risen more rapidly than England's was that the local advantages of England enabled her, not only to raise a greater proportion of supplies within the year, but to raise loans with special facility. p. [illegible]

The terms of the resolutions, which were moved by Mr. Fitzgerald on behalf of Lord Liverpool's Government, were as follows:—

"1. That it is the opinion of this Committee that the values of the respective debts of Great Britain and Ireland, estimated according to the provisions of the Acts of Union, have been, at a period subsequent to those Acts, in the same proportion to each other (within one-hundredth part of the said value) with the respective contributions of each country respectively, towards the annual expenditure of the United Kingdom; and that the respective circumstances of the two countries will henceforth admit of their contributing indiscriminately, by equal taxes imposed upon the same articles upon each, to the future expenditure of the United Kingdom, subject only to such particular exemptions or abatements in Ireland and in Scotland, as circumstances may appear from time to time to demand; and that it is no longer necessary to regulate the contribution of the two countries according to any specific proportion or according to the rules prescribed by the Acts of Union, with respect to such proportions. Annual Register, 1816, p. [illegible]

"2. That it is the opinion of this Committee that it is expedient that all expenses henceforth to be incurred, together with the interest and charges of all debts hitherto contracted, shall be so defrayed indiscriminately by equal taxes to be imposed on the same articles in each country; and that from time to time, as circumstances may require, such taxes should be imposed and applied accordingly, subject only to such exemptions and abatements in Ireland and Scotland as circumstances may appear to demand.

"3. That it is the opinion of this Committee that such legislative measures should be adopted as may be necessary to carry into further effect the purposes of the said Acts of Union, by consolidating the public revenues of Great Britain and Ireland into one fund, and applying the same to the general services of the United Kingdom."

These resolutions were agreed to, and on the 19th June a Bill was brought into the House of Commons for consolidating the debts and public revenues of the two Kingdoms. By the 20th June the Bill had passed through all its stages in that House; the only point which gave rise to any serious discussion being the proposed appointment of two new Lords of the Treasury in Whitehall and of a resident Vice-Treasurer in Ireland.

The Bill received the Royal Assent on the 1st July 1816; and it became the Act 56 Geo. 3. c. 98. Pursuant to that Act, all revenues in Great Britain and Ireland were, from and after the 5th January 1817, to constitute one general fund, called the Consolidated Fund of the United Kingdom; and that fund was to be charged with, and indiscriminately applied to, (1) the services of the British and Irish debts; (2) the Civil List; (3) all other services previously charged on the separate Consolidated Funds of the two Kingdoms; and (4) supply services of the United Kingdom generally.

The results of the working of the financial arrangements during the 16 years, in which the two Exchequers had been separate under an united Parliament, may now be reviewed; and they will perhaps be exhibited most conveniently in the following tables:—

TABLE I.—Showing the EXPENDITURE and REVENUE of GREAT BRITAIN in each of the 16 years ending the 5th January 1817.

Parliamentary Papers, No. 128 of 1864, p. 225, and No. 429 of 1864.

Year ending 5th January.	Separate Expenditure.	Joint Expenditure.	Total Expenditure.	Revenue.*	Deficit.
	£	£	£	£	£
1802 - - -	37,033,219	27,244,342	64,277,562	35,265,560	29,004,880
1803 - - -	26,134,004	27,229,894	53,363,200	34,744,357	18,606,153
1804 - - -	29,717,602	32,094,104	61,819,773	38,152,719	13,679,406
1805 - - -	28,149,634	34,433,371	62,621,065	45,972,214	16,693,724
1806 - - -	28,685,131	42,596,389	71,324,371	56,328,284	22,606,125
1807 - - -	30,303,373	41,611,309	72,074,685	55,702,138	12,372,737
1808 - - -	30,326,509	49,111,265	75,703,781	56,272,487	15,748,274
1809 - - -	31,449,830	48,777,359	73,660,012	61,346,583	18,363,728
1810 - - -	32,030,776	49,261,478	80,032,826	63,460,738	19,150,801
1811 - - -	34,161,369	51,399,475	86,711,884	64,123,708	12,143,685
1812 - - -	34,245,443	57,146,366	91,706,778	64,379,859	22,702,638
1813 - - -	37,371,427	61,892,554	96,263,981	64,279,975	30,003,463
1814 - - -	36,035,806	78,124,750	114,156,714	71,014,451	42,156,219
1815 - - -	40,033,363	77,589,413	117,613,827	72,177,549	40,032,332
1816 - - -	40,064,552	68,175,950	108,430,819	76,643,279	32,287,367
1817 - - -	42,833,538	35,427,965	78,363,004	63,318,595	15,037,459
Total - £	548,064,464	753,543,758	1,301,499,005	930,363,190	373,961,171

TABLE II.—Showing the EXPENDITURE and REVENUE of IRELAND in each of the 16 years ending the 5th January 1817.

Parliamentary Papers, No. 128 of 1864, p. 275, and No. 429 of 1864.

Year ending 5th January.	Separate Expenditure.	Joint Expenditure.	Arrears of Proportion of Joint Expenditure separately charged.	Total Expenditure.	Revenue.†	Deficit.
	£	£	£	£	£	£
1802 - -	3,279,603	4,349,187	—	7,628,808	3,186,351	4,441,157
1803 - -	3,036,186	3,539,153	—	6,575,363	4,095,248	2,576,582
1804 - -	2,401,637	3,376,164	—	5,877,781	3,673,496	2,304,273
1805 - -	2,494,677	5,350,744	—	7,845,131	3,733,950	4,111,171
1806 - -	2,040,379	5,053,071	—	7,707,244	3,902,317	3,903,689
1807 - -	3,036,907	4,944,379	—	6,979,127	4,209,733	2,770,254
1808 - -	3,145,386	5,244,396	—	6,397,544	4,280,835	3,117,293
1809 - -	3,609,159	4,831,542	—	6,540,379	5,162,041	4,173,308
1810 - -	3,639,083	5,714,087	—	5,837,078	5,061,804	4,573,773
1811 - -	3,481,201	7,824,103	1,276,000	10,424,228	4,767,441	5,756,587
1812 - -	4,345,317	7,540,463	1,495,000	11,600,599	3,947,784	6,292,328
1813 - -	4,483,355	3,509,325	1,455,376	12,456,485	3,030,841	3,723,809
1814 - -	4,923,234	3,815,429	1,603,653	13,842,433	6,532,346	6,318,844
1815 - -	5,107,046	6,263,623	1,458,348	12,577,201	6,488,144	6,313,064
1816 - -	5,365,744	6,892,831	2,107,257	17,003,252	6,566,778	10,458,294
1817 - -	6,540,837	4,672,654	2,104,065	13,137,859	5,564,843	8,272,535
Total £	61,348,350	83,014,232	12,788,273	160,727,004	77,844,154	81,883,671

* This column gives the amounts received into the British Exchequer without any deduction on account of the expenses of collecting the revenue. These expenses, though met in the first instance out of revenue, as they were incurred in the two Kingdoms, were subsequently charged against Great Britain and Ireland, according to their respective quotas, as part of the joint expenditure of the United Kingdom, because the cost of collection was proportionately greater in Ireland than in Great Britain.

† This column gives the amounts received into the Irish Exchequer without any deduction on account of the expenses of collecting the revenue. These expenses, though met in the first instance out of revenue, as they were incurred in the two Kingdoms, were subsequently charged against Great Britain and Ireland, according to their respective quotas, as part of the joint expenditure of the United Kingdom, because the cost of collection was proportionately greater in Ireland than in Great Britain.

TABLE III.—Summarising Tables I. and II.

—	Separate Expenditure.	Joint Expenditure.	Arrears of Proportion of Joint Expenditure separately charged.	Total Expenditure.	Revenue.	Deficit.
	£	£	£	£	£	£
Great Britain	[illegible]	[illegible]	—	[illegible]	[illegible]	[illegible]
Ireland	[illegible]	[illegible]	[illegible]	[illegible]	[illegible]	[illegible]
Two Kingdoms	[illegible]	[illegible]	[illegible]	[illegible]	[illegible]	[illegible]

TABLE IV.—Showing how the Proportions of the JOINT EXPENDITURE, in which GREAT BRITAIN and IRELAND were respectively liable, were met in each of the 16 years ending the 5th January 1817.

Parliamentary Papers, No. [illegible] of [illegible], p. [illegible], and No. [illegible] of [illegible].

Year ending 5th Jan.	Total Joint Expenditure.	Proportion payable under Treaty of Union. Great Britain [illegible]	Proportion payable under Treaty of Union. Ireland [illegible]	Amounts paid. Great Britain.	Amounts paid. Ireland.	Amounts paid more (+) or less (−) than Proportions payable. Great Britain.	Ireland. In the Year.	Ireland. In respect of Balances due in former Years.
	£	£	£	£	£	£	£	£
1802	31,[illegible]	27,[illegible]	3,[illegible]	27,344,[illegible]	4,[illegible]	− 344,004	+ 344,004	—
1803	30,[illegible]	27,[illegible]	3,[illegible]	27,[illegible]	3,[illegible]	+ [illegible]	− [illegible]	—
1804	[illegible]	[illegible]	[illegible]	[illegible]	[illegible]	− [illegible]	+ [illegible]	—
1805	[illegible]	[illegible]	[illegible]	[illegible]	[illegible]	− [illegible]	+ [illegible]	—
1806	47,[illegible]	41,[illegible]	[illegible]	42,[illegible]	[illegible]	+ [illegible]	− [illegible]	—
1807	[illegible]	[illegible]	[illegible]	[illegible]	[illegible]	+ [illegible]	− [illegible]	—
1808	47,[illegible]	[illegible]	[illegible]	[illegible]	[illegible]	+ [illegible]	− [illegible]	—
1809	[illegible]	[illegible]	[illegible]	[illegible]	[illegible]	+ [illegible]	− [illegible]	—
1810	[illegible]	[illegible]	[illegible]	[illegible]	[illegible]	+ [illegible]	− [illegible]	—
1811	[illegible]	[illegible]	[illegible]	[illegible]	[illegible]	+ 1,[illegible]	− 1,[illegible]	+ 1,[illegible]
1812	[illegible]	[illegible]	[illegible]	[illegible]	[illegible]	+ 1,[illegible]	− 1,[illegible]	+ 1,[illegible]
1813	[illegible]	[illegible]	[illegible]	[illegible]	[illegible]	+ [illegible]	− [illegible]	+ [illegible]
1814	[illegible]	[illegible]	[illegible]	[illegible]	[illegible]	+ [illegible]	− [illegible]	+ [illegible]
1815	[illegible]	[illegible]	[illegible]	77,[illegible]	[illegible]	+ [illegible]	− [illegible]	+ [illegible]
1816	[illegible]	[illegible]	[illegible]	[illegible]	[illegible]	+ [illegible]	− [illegible]	+ [illegible]
1817	[illegible]	[illegible]	[illegible]	[illegible]	[illegible]	+ [illegible]	− [illegible]	+ [illegible]
Total	[illegible]	[illegible]	[illegible]	[illegible]	[illegible]	+ [illegible]	− [illegible]	+ [illegible]
						Net balance due from Ireland on 5 January 1817.	− [illegible]	

Credit was given to Ireland on account of—
(1) imprest moneys repaid to the British Exchequer in 1802–17, viz. - - - £ [illegible]
and (2) overpayments made by Ireland in respect of long annuities, viz. - - - [illegible]
A further payment was made by Ireland on the Joint account in 1817–18, viz. - - [illegible]
[illegible]

So the balance found to be finally due from Ireland was - - - - [illegible]
And this was cancelled by the Act 57 Geo. 3, c. 48, s. 4.

Parliamentary Paper, No. [illegible], p. [illegible].

TABLE V.—Showing the INCREASES made to the Nominal Amounts of FUNDED DEBT and to the Amounts of the UNFUNDED DEBT, charged against GREAT BRITAIN and IRELAND in the 16 years ending January 1817.

Parliamentary Paper, No. [illegible] of [illegible].

Year ending January	Great Britain.	Ireland.	Total.
	£	£	£
1801	445,[illegible]	[illegible]	475,[illegible]
Relative proportions	[illegible]	1	[illegible]
1817	737,[illegible]	112,[illegible]	[illegible]
Relative proportions	[illegible]	1	[illegible]
Aggregate increase in 16 years.	[illegible]	[illegible]	[illegible]
Increase per cent.	[illegible]	[illegible]	[illegible]

NOTE.—The Amount of the National Debt valued [illegible] of Great Britain on the 5th January 1817 [illegible] with [illegible] on the 1st January 1801, thus showing a [illegible] in their capital value, and the [illegible] of Ireland on the 5th January 1817 [illegible] as compared with [illegible] on the 1st January 1801, thus showing an increase of [illegible] in their capital value. (See Parliamentary Paper, No. [illegible] of [illegible], pp. [illegible] and [illegible].)

[illegible]

TABLE VI.—Showing the Increase made in the [illegible] Duty Charges of Great Britain and Ireland in the [illegible] years ending January 1817.

—	Great Britain.	Ireland.	Total.
	£	£	£
At time of Union (see above, p. [illegible])	[illegible]	[illegible]	[illegible]
On 5th January 1817	[illegible]	[illegible]	[illegible]
Increase	[illegible]	[illegible]	[illegible]

TABLE VII.—Showing the Changes made in the Rates of the Principal Duties levied by Great Britain and Ireland from 18[illegible] to 18[illegible].

Rates of (Excise) Duty on Home-made Spirits per Gallon.

—	England.	Scotland. Lowlands.	Scotland. Highlands.	Ireland.
	s. d.	s. d.	s. d.	s. d.
[illegible]	[illegible]	[illegible]	[illegible]	[illegible]

Rates of (Customs and Excise) Duty on Foreign Spirits per Gallon (furnished by Board of Customs).

Year.	Kind of Spirit.	Great Britain.	Ireland.
		£ s. d.	s. d.
[illegible]	Brandy and Geneva	0 11 1	[illegible]
	Rum	0 [illegible] [illegible]	[illegible]
[illegible]	Brandy and Geneva	0 11 [illegible]	[illegible]
	Rum	[illegible]	[illegible]
[illegible]	Brandy and Geneva	[illegible]	[illegible]
	Rum	[illegible]	[illegible]
[illegible]	Brandy and Geneva	[illegible]	[illegible]
	Rum	[illegible]	[illegible]
[illegible]	Brandy and Geneva	[illegible]	[illegible]
	Rum	[illegible]	[illegible]
[illegible]	Brandy and Geneva	[illegible]	[illegible]
	Rum	[illegible]	[illegible]
[illegible]	Brandy and Geneva	[illegible]	[illegible]
	Rum	[illegible]	[illegible]
[illegible]	Brandy and Geneva	[illegible]	[illegible]
	Rum	[illegible]	[illegible]
[illegible]	Brandy and Geneva	[illegible]	[illegible]
	Rum	[illegible]	[illegible]
[illegible]	Brandy and Geneva	1 4 [illegible]	[illegible]
	Rum	[illegible]	[illegible]
[illegible]	Brandy and Geneva	[illegible]	[illegible]
	Rum	[illegible]	[illegible]
1814	Brandy and Geneva	[illegible]	[illegible]
	Rum	[illegible]	[illegible]

NOTE.—In the earlier years of the 19th century the rate of duty on Geneva spirits was slightly lower than that on brandy, but the difference was so small that the rate of duty on brandy is taken for both these spirits.

Rates of (Customs and Excise) Duty on Tea per lb.

Year.	Great Britain.	Ireland.
[illegible]	Sold at or above 2s. 6d. per lb., [illegible] per cent.; and at or under 2s. 6d., [illegible] per cent.	Purchased at or above 1s. 6d. per lb., [illegible] per cent.; and at or under [illegible], [illegible] per cent. ad val.
[illegible]	Sold at or above 2s. 6d. per lb., [illegible] per cent.; and at or under 2s. 6d., [illegible] per cent.	—
[illegible]	—	Purchased at or above 2s. 6d. per lb., [illegible] per cent. ad val.; and at or under 2s. 6d., [illegible] per cent.
[illegible]	[illegible] 2s. 6d. per cent. substituted for [illegible]; and [illegible] 2s. 6d. for [illegible].	—
[illegible]	[illegible] per cent. on all teas.	—
[illegible]	—	[illegible] per cent. ad val. on all teas.

NOTE.—These rates have been obtained specially from the Board of Customs.

[illegible]

[illegible]

RATES of DUTY on *Malt* per Bushel.

	England.	Scotland.	Ireland.
	s. d.	s. d.	s. d.
[illegible]	[illegible]	[illegible]	[illegible]
[illegible]	[illegible]	[illegible]	[illegible]
[illegible]	[illegible]	[illegible]	[illegible]
[illegible]	[illegible]	[illegible]	[illegible]
[illegible]	[illegible]	[illegible]	[illegible]
[illegible]	[illegible]	[illegible]	[illegible]
[illegible]	[illegible]	[illegible]	[illegible]

[illegible]

RATES of (CUSTOMS and EXCISE) DUTY on TOBACCO per lb.

Year.	Great Britain.	Ireland.	Year.	Great Britain.	Ireland.
	s. d.	s. d.		s. d.	s. d.
[illegible]	[illegible]	[illegible]	[illegible]	[illegible]	—
[illegible]	[illegible]	[illegible]	[illegible]	[illegible]	[illegible]
[illegible]	[illegible]	—	[illegible]	[illegible]	[illegible]
[illegible]	—	[illegible]			

[illegible]

RATES of *Income Tax* in the £.

Year.	Great Britain.	Ireland.
1799	10 per cent. on incomes of 200*l*. p.a. and upwards, with reduced and sliding scale on incomes between 60*l*. and 200*l*. p.a.	Nil.
1803	1s. in the £ on incomes of 150*l*. and upwards with varying rates from 3*d*. to 11½*d*. in £, on incomes between 60*l*. and 150*l*. p.a.	Nil.
1805	Graduated additions to preceding rates	Nil.
1806	10 per cent. on incomes of 150*l*. and upwards with abatements.	Nil.
1816	Repealed	—

TABLE VIII.—Showing the official Value of Imports into, and Exports from, GREAT BRITAIN and IRELAND respectively in 1816 as compared with the average annual value thereof in 1802.

—	Great Britain.	Ireland.	Total.
	£	£	£
Official value in 1802*	[illegible]	[illegible]	[illegible]
Proportion (about)	[illegible]	[illegible]	[illegible]
Official value in 1816	[illegible]	[illegible]	[illegible]
Proportion (about)	[illegible]	[illegible]	[illegible]
Increase (+) or decrease (−).	[illegible]	[illegible]	[illegible]

* [illegible]

It will have been seen from Table II. that the aggregate revenues raised in Ireland, during the 16 years following the Union, were less than half the aggregate amount of expenditure which she was called upon to meet during that period, notwithstanding that the country had, according to the prevalent allegation, been taxed to the utmost of her capacity. The consequence was that her debt had been quadrupled. [illegible]

Such a state of things shows that, at the end of that period, Ireland was practically reduced to a condition of bankruptcy; and the question which naturally suggests itself is, whether it was the manner in which the financial arrangement made at the time of the Union was worked, or whether it was the arrangement itself, which was at fault.

The mode in which effect was given to the provisions of the 7th Article of the Treaty has been severely criticised; and the principal points against which criticism has been directed are two points about which

the intention of the Article was not quite clear. The two points are these:—

1. Whether "the expenditure of the United Kingdom," towards which Great Britain and Ireland were to contribute in fixed proportions, was correctly calculated; that is, calculated in accordance with the meaning of the Article?
2. Whether it was the intention of the provision relating to debt incurred subsequently to the Union, that such debt should be, and only could be, joint debt?

It is necessary to examine both these points.

1. *The Joint Expenditure of the United Kingdom.*

In paragraph 5 of the 7th Article there is a reference to other charges than the pre-Union debt charges, which Ireland was to be required to defray separately. It is provided "that if at the end of any year any surplus shall accrue from the revenues of Ireland, after defraying the interest, sinking fund, and proportional contributions and *separate charges* to which the said country shall then be liable, taxes shall be taken off to the amount of such surplus, &c., &c." But the only charges specifically prescribed by the Article (par. 3) to be separately defrayed by Great Britain and Ireland respectively are the charges in respect of the debts incurred by the two countries previously to the Union. Moreover, paragraph 3 provides that "the remainder" (of the revenues of Ireland, *i.e.*, after the charges in respect of the interest and sinking fund of pre-Union Irish Debt had been met) "shall be applied towards defraying the proportion of the *expenditure of the United Kingdom* to which Ireland may be liable in each year."

It might be inferred from these two last provisions that "the expenditure of the United Kingdom," to which the two countries were jointly to contribute, was intended to represent the entire expenditure incurred, not only on Imperial services, but also on all local services in England, Scotland, and Ireland, other than the charges connected with the debts which Great Britain and Ireland had incurred previously to the Union.

But, whatever may have been the intention of the authors of the Treaty, it appears that the two countries were, as a matter of fact, made to defray separately certain other charges besides those debt charges.

Indeed, during the first two years of the new arrangement, though those years may be regarded as a transitional period, the other separate charges amounted to a considerable sum.

Great Britain was required to defray separately in 1801–2, not only the charges connected with the pre-Union debt, amounting to		£ 23,008,731
But also the following charges in respect of—	£	
(1) Civil List, &c.	65,977	
(2) Navy	8,270,971	
(3) Ordnance	632,969	
(4) Army	3,922,974	
(5) Miscellaneous services	1,606,933	
	14,027,403	
Less a charge connected with Irish loans	5,426	
		14,021,977
The separate expenditure of Great Britain, therefore, amounted in the aggregate for 1801–2 to		[illegible]
Ireland was required to defray separately in 1801–2, not only the charges connected with the pre-Union debt, amounting to		1,974,160
But also the following charges in respect of—		
(1) Purposes stipulated prior to the Union (in Irish currency)	£ 725,989	
(2) Civil List (do.)	183,155	
(3) Army (do.)	206,308	
(4) Miscellaneous services (in Irish currency)	194,391	
Total in Irish currency	[illegible]	
Total in British currency		[illegible]
The separate expenditure of Ireland, therefore, amounted in the aggregate for 1801–2 to		[illegible]

It will, however, be seen from the following table that the separate charges annually debited against Great Britain and Ireland respectively in addition to their pre-Union debt charges, were soon reduced to comparatively inappreciable amounts.

—	Great Britain.	Ireland.
	£	£
1801–2	14,034,000	1,470,000
1802–3	2,574,000	1,194,000
1803–4	2,833,000	488,000
1804–5	752,000	24,000
1805–6	1,431,000	27,000
1806–7	1,439,000	406,000
1807–8	515,000	54,000
1808–9	480,000	71,000
1809–10	1,411,000	49,000
1810–11	1,725,000	58,000
1811–12	524,000	163,000
1812–13	1,188,000	132,000
1813–14	461,000	94,000
1814–15	543,000	137,000
1815–16	516,000	94,000
1816–17	278,000	69,000
	30,626,000	4,375,000
Aggregate of sums separately charged.	35,001,000	

Although these separate charges were not large, except in the first three years, yet the aggregate amount of them, during the 16 years that the British and Irish Exchequers remained separate under the Union, was considerable, viz. 30,626,000*l.* against Great Britain, and 4,375,000*l.* against Ireland; and, as it is open to doubt whether it was not contrary to the spirit of the agreement to debit Great Britain and Ireland with any separate charges, besides their respective pre-Union debt charges, it might be argued that Ireland was not quite fairly treated in this respect. For, had the total of these charges, viz., 35,001,000*l.*, been charged against the two countries in the proportions of 15/17ths to 2/17ths, the respective shares of the two countries would have been—

	£
Great Britain	30,884,000
Ireland	4,117,000
	35,001,000

whereas, by being separately debited with them, Great Britain paid less, and Ireland paid more, than their prescribed shares by 258,000*l.* The amount, however, in question is not great, when spread over 16 years; and it must be remembered that there was an allusion to "separate charges" in paragraph 5.

2. *Debt incurred by the two Countries in 1801–17.*

Whether the debt incurred by Great Britain and Ireland, during the time that their Exchequers were separated under the Parliamentary Union, was treated as it was intended to be treated under the 7th Article, is a more doubtful point, and is a point which has been still more directly questioned.

The wording of the paragraph in the Article about borrowing subsequently to the Union is perhaps somewhat involved and obscure; but it is submitted that it must be read in the light (1) of the interpretation placed upon it by its authors, and (2) of the only practical manner in which the financial arrangements could be worked.

Lord Castlereagh's explanation of the provision about future debt has already been quoted. It may be convenient to quote his words again: "All future loans," he said, "for the interest and liquidation of which the respective countries have made provisions in the proportion of their respective contributions shall be considered as a joint debt; and on the other hand where they do not make corresponding provisions, their respective quotas of the sum so raised would remain a separate charge, in like manner as debt contracted previous to the Union."

Accordingly, it may be inferred that, on the assumption that a loan of 17,000,000*l.* were thereafter to be raised "for the service of the United Kingdom," and Parliament were to determine that the interest (5 per

[illegible] rate] and sinking fund (1 per cent.) should be borne by the two countries in the respective proportions of 15 to 2, the debt was to be considered a joint debt, Great Britain then paying annually 750,000l., and Ireland 100,000l., in respect of such loan.

On the other hand, if Parliament were to determine that Great Britain was to pay annually 850,000l. and Ireland [illegible], or that Great Britain was to pay [illegible] and Ireland [illegible], then the debt was to be treated as a separate debt; the consequence being that the separate liabilities of Great Britain would be separately and permanently increased by 15,000,000l. or 14,000,000l. and those of Ireland by 2,000,000l. or 3,000,000l., as the case might be, and that the annual charges for which each country would be liable in respect of the loans would not constitute part of the joint expenditure.

So far, then, as Imperial loans, or loans "for the "service of the United Kingdom," were concerned, the provisions seem to be tolerably [illegible].

But what is less clear is how far it was intended that either country might raise debt on its own account, not for local purposes, but to enable it to meet its share of the joint expenditure of the United Kingdom.

It is remarkable that, though the 7th Article of the Treaty provides distinctly enough for the disposal of an Irish surplus there was no direct provision for meeting a deficit; and unfortunately Ireland was, under the financial arrangements subsequent to the Treaty of Union, in a perpetual state of deficit.

But it is obvious that, unless more could be raised by taxation, the only way of meeting such a state of things was for Ireland to borrow, and borrow on her own account. Otherwise the terms of the Treaty could not have been observed. There may have been no specific power to enable Ireland to contract a loan separately from Great Britain, and it is probably owing to the absence of such power that it has been alleged that Ireland was unfairly treated as regards the burden of debt incurred subsequently to the Union; but the fact remains that, if the Irish revenue fell short of the charges thereon, resort to separate borrowing was the only means of enabling Ireland to pay what she was required to contribute to the joint expenditure.

A hypothetical illustration will make this contention more clear.

Let it be assumed that the joint expenditure to which Great Britain and Ireland had to contribute in a particular year amounted to 34,000,000l. Accordingly, Great Britain's share would have been 30,000,000l., and Ireland's share 4,000,000l. Let it further be assumed that, after the payment of the separate charges of Ireland, the balance of her revenue did not exceed 2,000,000l. Consequently, the other two millions required to make up her contribution would have had to be borrowed. Now, if it be held that this loan could only be a joint debt, and if the charge on account of it was 5 per cent., Ireland's share of the charge would have been 2/17ths of 100,000l., or 11,765l.; and the rest of the charge would have fallen on Great Britain. Accordingly, Great Britain would have had to contribute in the year not 30,000,000l., but 30,088,235l.; and Ireland would only have contributed 2,011,765l. instead of 4,000,000l.; while the future liability of Great Britain would have been permanently increased and that of Ireland permanently diminished.

It is tolerably evident that Lord Castlereagh foresaw the necessity of Ireland's borrowing on her own account; for, in alluding to the contingency of a continuance of war, he said that "the proportion of the "debt of Ireland may rise." Moreover, the Treaty (par. 7 of Article VII.), by providing for the contingency that the value of the debts of the two countries might assume the proportions respectively of their prescribed contributions, may be held to have contemplated an increase of the separate debt of Ireland, as well as a decrease of the separate debt of Great Britain. At any rate Mr. Grattan placed this interpretation on the provision; for, in his speech on the 26th May 1800, he scornfully referred to it as one that meant "that whenever the Minister shall raise the debt of "Ireland to an amount which shall be in the proportion of two to fifteen in relation to the permanent "debt of England (in three years of war they tell you "they will do it), then you are to be taxed as much as "England."

The conclusion, therefore, to be drawn is that, in the matter of debt, Ireland was treated in the only way in which it was possible to carry out the Union arrangements; and this seems to have been the view of the Committees which inquired into the financial condition of Ireland during the period of separate Exchequers subsequently to the Union, as well as of the [illegible] of Inquiry.

But not only in the matter of debt but also in the matter of taxation, it may, at any rate, be maintained that Ireland, as compared with Great Britain, received no harsh treatment at the hands of the United Parliament between 1800 and 1816.

First and foremost comes the question of the Income Tax. It is evident that in 1799 Mr. Pitt fully intended, Union or no Union, to extend that tax to Ireland. Indeed, he went so far as to make an estimate of its yield, which he put at not less than a million and perhaps a million and a half. His intention, however, was not carried out; nor does the proposal appear to have been revived subsequently. As a matter of fact, Ireland was entirely exempted from this tax throughout the whole period from 1798 to 1816, during which Englishmen and Scotchmen were almost continuously, not only subjected to it, but subjected to it severely, for the rate in Great Britain was 10 per cent., or 2s. in the £ on all incomes over 150l. Cornwallis Memoirs, Vol. III., p. [illegible]

That exemption by itself was a considerable boon to the Irish taxpayer in the early part of this century, though [illegible] that it was not the only exemption accorded to them. Neither the land tax nor the inhabited house duty was levied in Ireland, and she was not required to pay Excise duties charged on several articles in Great Britain, such as bricks, tiles, candles, glass, hops, leather, salt, and soap; while on such articles as foreign salt, spirits, tea, tobacco, and wine, which were dutiable articles in both countries, the rates of duty were lower in Ireland than in Great Britain. Parliamentary Paper [illegible]

A calculation has been made as to what Ireland would have had to pay had the same duties been levied in both countries and levied at uniform rates. Calculations of this kind are difficult to form, and when formed are apt to mislead. Perhaps the simplest way of stating the measure of relief accorded to Ireland in 1801–16 is this: The aggregate revenue raised in Great Britain in the 16 years ending the 5th January 1817 was [illegible]. If the revenue raised in Ireland had been raised at a rate proportionate to her quota of expenditure, viz., as 2 to 15— Do. Table I. above.

	£
the amount which ought to have been raised would have been	[illegible]
Instead of this, the amount actually raised was	[illegible]
or less by	[illegible]

Table II. above.

One other point remains to be noticed in connexion with the treatment accorded to Ireland by the British Government between 1800 and 1816. Except in the earlier years, she was continuously in arrears with her contribution to the joint expenditure of the United Kingdom. She does not appear to have been pressed to make good the arrears; no interest was charged in respect of them; and in the final balance sheet between the two countries during the period of separate Exchequers a sum of two millions was written off Ireland's account. Table IV. above.

It may be inferred from these various considerations that during that period there was no apparent disposition, on the part either of the Imperial Parliament or of the British Government, to carry out the Union arrangements otherwise than in the manner that would be least oppressive to Ireland. Such at any rate appears to have been the conclusion at which an impartial authority arrived. I allude to Mr. Chisholm, who was formerly Chief Clerk of the Exchequer, and to whom we owe more than to anybody else for the unravelling of the intricacy of the Public Accounts of the early part of this century. The opinion which he formed, after a long study of the question, was that "the provisions . . . were construed by "the several Parliamentary committees, and the actual "settlement of accounts was effected, upon principles "the most favourable to Ireland." Parliamentary Paper, No. [illegible] of [illegible], p. [illegible]

But this opinion was not only held by an official of the Imperial Exchequer long after the event. A similar conclusion was also formed nearer the time by a distinguished Irishman, who had himself been one of the ablest and sturdiest opponents of the Union in the last Irish Parliament, and who was a quarter of a century later able to review calmly the treatment of Ireland by the Imperial Parliament. In a debate in the House of Commons on

the 22nd April 1822, upon Sir John Newport's motion relating to the condition of Ireland, Mr. (afterwards Lord) Plunket said: "I had been afraid that the "interests of Ireland, on the abolition of her separate "legislature, would come to be discussed in a hostile "Parliament. But I can now state, and I wish when "I speak I could be heard by the whole of Ireland, "that during the time that I have sat in the United "Parliament I have found every question that related "to the interests or security of that country, enter- "tained with indulgence, and treated with the most "deliberate regard."

Life of Lord Plunket, Vol. II., p. 103.

He gave utterance to similar sentiments a few years later. From his seat in the House of Lords, when the question of the Roman Catholic claims was under discussion, Lord Plunket stated on the 1st June 1828: "I thought in the year 1800 that the Union was a "measure of party; that it would not be acted upon "fairly, and that the inferior country would be obliged "to suffer without redress. I have been most happily "disappointed. I hear of no instance in which, when "the interests of Ireland have been brought under the "consideration of the Imperial Parliament, those "interests have not been attended to with justice, "with favour, and almost with partiality."

p. 108.

The condition, then, to which Ireland was reduced in 1816 was probably not due to the manner in which effect had been given to the wording or intentions of the provisions of the Treaty of Union. It was due to the arrangement itself. By having had imposed upon her a quota of two-seventeenths of the joint expenditure of the United Kingdom, Ireland had, under that arrangement, been called upon to pay, in times of unprecedented expenditure, an amount which may be held to have been beyond her capacities to meet. Speaking to a motion about the window tax on the 23rd April 1822, Mr. Plunket referred to Ireland's share of joint expenditure under the Union as "a burden utterly disproportioned to her strength," and in 1822 a future Chancellor of the Exchequer, Mr. Goulburn, stated in Parliament that the quota was "now allowed on all hands" to have been more than Ireland was able to pay. The only alternative to plunging Ireland ruinously into debt would have been the imposition of still more taxes; but it was doubtful whether the taxation of the country had not been carried to the point beyond which further impositions would have ceased to be productive.

Hansard, 2nd Series, Vol. VI., p. 1422.

McCulloch's "Principles of Taxation."

It must, however, be remembered, in justice to the authors of the Treaty of Union, that they could not, and assuredly did not, foresee that the war in which Great Britain was engaged would last almost continuously for another 15 years; and further that, at the time, they took the most obvious standards, and probably the only available standards, by which the relative abilities of the two countries to contribute to the expenses of the United Kingdom could be fairly measured.

It is true that Lord Castlereagh's estimate of relative ability has been assailed on the ground that the period, which he took for comparing the resources of Ireland with those of Great Britain (viz., the average of the three years preceding the Union), was unfairly selected. It has been held that the presence of a large military force in Ireland, necessitated by the rebellion, created an increased consumption of articles of luxury which was transient and exceptional. It has, moreover, been pointed out that in his comparison he omitted to take into account certain sources of revenue like the stamp duties, post office receipts, and the tax on salt, which would have shown a much smaller proportion. Further than that; even the accuracy of Lord Castlereagh's estimate of Irish imports and exports at the time of the Union has been challenged, because he took the annual average to be 10,525,000*l*., whereas according to official statistics presented to Parliament in 1834 the average was only 8,314,000*l*. It appears that Lord Castlereagh's estimate of imports and exports was specially computed for the occasion; and the difference in the calculations of the combined totals is probably due to there having been pursued different methods of ascertaining the real value of imports, about which there was no authentic information until 1824. But in any case it is only fair to assume, and the assumption is borne out by his own words, that he took the best information available at the time, and what he considered at any rate to be the fairest test.

Speech for Westmeath Committee of Dublin by Mr. John Dillon, M.P.

Parliamentary Paper, No. 188 of 1834, p. 5. Parliamentary Paper, No. 213 of 1833, p. 113, and Lord Castlereagh's Memoirs, &c., Vol. II.

Very different judgments have been formed of the effect of consolidating the two Exchequers. It has, on the one hand, been held that it was the greatest boon ever conferred on one country by another. On the other hand, it has been called "a shameful transaction." It is probable that both these views are exaggerated ones.

Walpole's History of England, Vol. I., p. 462.

"Dublin Review," August 1861.

There is no question that, as compared with the Union arrangements the immediate result of the consolidation was to place Ireland in a comparatively solvent condition. At that time Ireland had to

	£	
meet separate charges to the amount of	6,500,000	Table II. above.
and she was liable to contribute to joint expenditure	4,700,000	Table IV. above.
Her total liabilities, therefore, were	11,200,000	
and as her revenue was only	5,561,000	Table II. above.
she had a deficit on the year of	5,640,000	

Such a deficit could only be met by an addition to her capital liabilities. Under the new arrangement, though she had to make over the whole of her existing revenue to the united Exchequer, she was relieved of having to pile up additional liabilities necessitated by annually recurring deficits, which amounted to over 5½ millions in the last year of the Union arrangements.

The case may be put in another way. Thus:—

	£	£	
The total expenditure of the two Kingdoms (in 1816–17) was		89,217,000	
(1.) Under the Union arrangement, the liability of Great Britain was:			Tables II. and IV. above.
a. Separate expenditure	42,936,000		
b. Joint expenditure (15/17ths)	35,162,000		
		78,098,000	
And that of Ireland was:			
a. Separate expenditure	6,530,000		
b. Joint expenditure (2/17ths)	4,686,000		
		11,216,000	

So, the respective proportions were, in round figures, as 7 (Great Britain) to 1 (Ireland).

	£
(2.) Under the new arrangement, Ireland was called upon to continue to pay the same revenue, viz.	5,504,000
and Great Britain became liable for the remainder	83,733,000
Total	89,237,000

Accordingly, the respective proportions were, in round figures, as 15 (Great Britain) to 1 (Ireland).

One of the main arguments used to prove that Ireland was unfairly treated by the consolidation of the Exchequers was that, under such arrangement, she was made to contribute to the charge connected with the pre-Union Debt of Great Britain. That charge was, at the time of the Union, 21,369,790*l*.; whereas the charge in respect of the Irish pre-Union Debt, at that time, was only 1,232,232*l*. Ireland, no doubt, was in no way concerned with the liabilities which Great Britain had incurred previously to the Union; and, therefore, to have saddled Ireland with any part of those liabilities, which were, according to the Union proportions, greatly in excess of Irish liabilities, seems *primâ facie* to admit of no justification. But, even had the pre-Union Debt charges of Great Britain and Ireland continued to be respectively debited against each country, Ireland must still have paid the same yearly sum, namely, the whole of her Revenue; the only difference being that her contribution to Imperial expenditure would have been slightly larger than under the actual scheme of consolidation.

	£	£
Thus: If from the total expenditure of the two kingdoms in 1816–17, viz.:—		89,237,000
there had been deducted those separate debt charges, which at the time of the Union, amounted to		
(a.) Great Britain	21,370,000	
and (b.) Ireland	1,233,000	
to		22,603,000
the remaining expenditure for which the two kingdoms would have been jointly liable would have been		66,714,000
As the revenue of Ireland amounted to		5,560,000
the balance available for meeting that joint liability, after deducting her separate debt charge, viz.		1,233,000
would have been		4,327,000

Consequently, the respective contributions to the joint expenditure would have been: Great Britain,

[illegible]; and Ireland, £[illegible], or as 14½ to 1, as compared with the proportions of 15 to 1 under the scheme of complete amalgamation. But whether the proportions were as 14½ to 1, or as 15 to 1, was of no moment. The real consideration was that each proportion compared most favourably, so far as Ireland was concerned, with the Union proportions of 7½ to 1; and this notwithstanding that Irish exports and imports, which had formed the principal test of the relative abilities of the two countries in 1800, had not fallen off in 1816.

The real argument which may be adduced against the arrangement of 1817 is that under it Ireland derived no immediate relief from taxation. It is true, it may be said, that she was extricated from bankruptcy; but, in the process of extrication, she derived no benefit that would be felt by the taxpayers. In those days, when the local expenditure in Ireland was comparatively small, it mattered little to them whether the money taken out of their pockets was applied to meet increasing debt charges of their own, or whether it was appropriated to other purposes. It was admitted that the proportion which Ireland had been called upon to pay under the Treaty of Union was excessively large, and it was held that in consequence she had been forced to the [illegible]. Accordingly, nothing short of an appreciable remission of her existing burdens could be any reparation for the past. Amount of [illegible]

However that may be, the practical and principal consideration to be borne in mind in connection with the consolidation of the British and Irish Exchequers in 1817, is that from that time Great Britain has been content to take whatever revenue Ireland has yielded, and in return to become responsible for the capital liabilities as well as for the administrative expenses of her poorer partner, while Ireland's contribution to Imperial expenditure has never since been a fixed quantity, but has been represented by the amount by which her true revenue has exceeded her own local expenditure.

One of the consequences of the amalgamation of the British and Irish Exchequers was to affect materially the basis of ascertaining the true financial relations of the two countries subsequently, and therefore it needs to be made the subject of special notice. So long as separate accounts were kept by the two countries, and their revenues administered by separate Treasuries, it was indispensable to levy Customs and Excise duties in the country where the dutiable article was to be consumed. Indeed, it was specially provided, in the 8th section of the 6th Article of the Treaty of Union, that all duties charged on the import of foreign or colonial goods into either country should, on their export to the other, be either drawn back, or the amount, if any be retained, should be placed to the credit of the country to which they should be exported, so long as the expenditure of the United Kingdom was defrayed by proportional contributions. It may be stated, by the way, that it has been questioned whether this provision was strictly observed between 1801 and 1817. But the Commissioners of Inquiry in 1822 into the Revenue arising in Ireland, could not find that there had been any departure from the provision.

Parliamentary Papers, No. [illegible] of 1890, p. 140.

[illegible] of 1823.

When the revenues of Great Britain and Ireland became consolidated, there was no reason why the intercourse between the two countries should be subjected to such fiscal regulations, which caused annoyance to the merchant, disadvantage to the community in Ireland, and an increase to collection expenses. Accordingly, new regulations were in due course framed, whereby all payment and repayment of duties in the cross-channel trade were to cease, except in the case of articles which were subject to different rates of duties.

But, from a statistical and economic point of view, a considerable inconvenience resulted from this free interchange of dutiable goods between one country and the other. Accounts of the quantities of articles shipped from Great Britain to Ireland, and *vice versâ*, ceased to be kept in 1825–6; and since then, in the absence of the data which those accounts afforded, there have been no really trustworthy means (except in the case of spirits, where the permit system is enforced) of computing the true revenue of each country. It is evident that Customs and Excise duties may be collected in Great Britain in respect of articles which are consumed in Ireland and *vice versâ*; and that in that case the revenue derived from the duty is properly to be credited, not to the country in which the duty is collected, but to the country in which the duty-paid article is consumed.

Attempts have been made in the "Financial Relations" papers, recently prepared and presented to the House of Commons, to adjust the amounts of revenue collected respectively in England, Scotland, and Ireland, so as to show what each country really contributes* to revenue; or, in other words, to give the *true revenue* of each country; and the basis of the adjustments is fully explained in the Parliamentary Papers No. 329 of 1891, No. 93 of 1892, No. 248 of 1893, and No. 8.6 of 1893. But it must always be borne in mind that those adjustments are, except in the case of spirits, founded for the most part on estimates and hypothetical calculations, and that the absence of a Customs *cordon* during the last 70 years greatly enhances the difficulty of dealing with the reference made to the present Royal Commission.

The amalgamation of the two Exchequers was followed by another fiscal reform, which it may be well to notice. There had originally been imposed "union" or "protecting" duties with a view to protecting the manufacturers of one country from the effects of the industry or the natural advantages of the other. These duties, which had been fixed by the Treaty of Union at 10 per cent., and which had been applied to articles either not manufactured, or manufactured only to a trifling degree in Ireland, were to be in force (and they were in force) until 1820. In that year the Act 1 Geo. IV. c. 45, though it temporarily continued those duties, provided for their gradual cessation and final extinction in 1840. As a matter of fact, the "union" duties were abolished in 1824 by the Acts 4 Geo. IV. c. 26, and 5 Geo. IV. c. 22.

Parliamentary Papers, No. [illegible] of 1822, and No. [illegible] of 1864, p. 126.

Though the Act (56 Geo. III. c. 98) which effected the consolidation of the British and Irish Exchequers did not refer to the future taxation of the two countries, yet the 7th Article of the Treaty of Union, as well as the resolutions carried in the House of Commons, on which the Act was founded, specially provided (as we have seen) that thenceforward the expenses of the United Kingdom were to be defrayed indiscriminately "by equal taxes to be imposed on the same articles in "each country," subject only to such exemptions and abatements in Ireland (and Scotland) as circumstances might appear to demand.

As a matter of fact, at no period from the year 1817 to the present time has Parliament imposed "equal taxes" on the two countries; and so the proviso about exemptions and abatements has never been ignored.

Ireland has been, and still is, wholly exempt from the land tax, from the inhabited house duty, from assessed taxes (since 1824), and from the railway passenger duty since its first imposition in 1832. It is true that, with these exceptions, Ireland has gradually become subjected to the same taxation as Great Britain. But for some and varying periods subsequently to 1817 the duties on several articles of consumption, and likewise the stamp duties, were levied at lower rates in Ireland than in Great Britain; while the re-imposition of the Income tax in Great Britain preceded its imposition in Ireland by eleven years.

It is now necessary to see how, and when, the process of assimilation has been carried into effect throughout the United Kingdom.

The rates of duty on Tobacco were equalised in 1819; and the Tea duties have also been levied at uniform rates in both countries from the time of the consolidation of the Exchequers.*

Stamp duties, consisting principally of the probate and legacy duties, and of the duties on deeds and other instruments, differed in Great Britain and Ireland for some years after as well as before 1817. It may be stated generally that the rates of duty were more favourable in Ireland than in Great Britain, but the differences were so numerous that it is not possible to summarise them in a convenient form. The rates were assimilated in 1842; and the previous differences are given in the 1st and 13th Reports of the Commissioners of Inland Revenue.

The process of equalisation under other heads requires to be noticed in greater detail.

(1.) *Spirit Duties.*

The duties in which the differences have been most marked, which have undergone most changes, and which affect Ireland more materially than any other impost, are the excise duties on home-made *Spirits*.

It may be convenient and interesting to enumerate in tabular form the changes which have taken place in these duties, since the consolidation of the Exchequers in 1817 down to the present time. Accordingly, the following table, which shows the various rates imposed per gallon in the three kingdoms, is given.

* The use of the word "contributes," though it may be the most natural antithesis to the word "collected," is open to objection, owing to its constantly being also used in connexion with the estimated "contribution" of each country to Imperial expenditure, as represented by the estimated balances of English, Scottish, and Irish Revenue which is available for such expenditure after the estimated local expenditure of each of the three Kingdoms has been met.

* As a matter of fact no duty was levied on Tea in Ireland during a few years, for between 1824 and 1836 the duty was entirely under the management of the Excise, and the whole of it during that period was collected in Great Britain.

Year	England		Scotland		Ireland		Remarks
	s.	d.	s.	d.	s.	d.	
[illegible]	10	[illegible]	6	[illegible]	[illegible]	[illegible]	Parliamentary Papers No. [illegible] of 18[illegible], p. [illegible], and No. [illegible] of 18[illegible], [illegible]
[illegible]	11	[illegible]	6	[illegible]	[illegible]	[illegible]	
[illegible]	11	[illegible]	7	[illegible]	[illegible]	[illegible]	
[illegible]	7	[illegible]	[illegible]	10	[illegible]	[illegible]	
[illegible]	7	[illegible]	3	4	[illegible]	[illegible]	
[illegible]	7	[illegible]	[illegible]	[illegible]	[illegible]	[illegible]	
[illegible]	7	10	[illegible]	[illegible]	[illegible]	[illegible]	
[illegible]	7	10	[illegible]	[illegible]	[illegible]	[illegible]	
[illegible]	7	10	[illegible]	[illegible]	[illegible]	[illegible]	
[illegible]	7	[illegible]	4	8	[illegible]	[illegible]	
[illegible]	7	10	4	[illegible]	4	[illegible]	
[illegible]	[illegible]	[illegible]	[illegible]	[illegible]	[illegible]	[illegible]	
[illegible]	[illegible]	[illegible]	[illegible]	[illegible]	[illegible]	[illegible]	
[illegible]	10	[illegible]	10	[illegible]	10	[illegible]	
[illegible]	10	[illegible]	10	[illegible]	10	[illegible]	
[illegible]	11	[illegible]	11	[illegible]	11	[illegible]	

NOTE.—[illegible]

It will be seen that, when the consolidation of the British and Irish Exchequers was effected in 1816-17, the rate of duty in Ireland (5s. 7½d. per gallon) was not much more than half the rate of duty in England (10s. 3d. per gallon). In the course of the next few years the difference was enhanced. Indeed, in 1823, and the following year, the duty in Ireland was only 2s. 4½d. per gallon, as compared with 11s. 8¼d. in England. Owing to the reduction of the duty in England to 7s. in 1825, the differences during the next 20 years became less marked.

During that period it was evidently in the minds of Chancellors of the Exchequer to equalise, or at any rate to bring more closely together, the rates of duty. What deterred them from making more attempts in that direction than they did, was apparently the fear of aggravating the evils of smuggling and illicit distillation, rather than consideration for Ireland. In 1842, Sir Robert Peel did raise the Irish rate from [illegible] to [illegible]; but he had to abandon the proposal the very next year.

During the following 10 years (1843-53), the duty on spirits in Ireland (2s. 8d. per gallon) was levied at a rate hardly more than one-third of the same duty in England (7s. 10d. per gallon); and it was Mr. Gladstone who, while admitting the difficulty of levelling up the duties, made the first serious attempt to carry, and did carry, a proposal to lessen the differential treatment of the two countries in this respect. He raised the duty in Ireland from 2s. 8d. to 3s. 4d. per gallon—the rate at which it had temporarily been imposed in 1842-3; and in so doing he claimed that it was amongst "the mightiest of aims" that no Irishman should be allowed to intoxicate himself for 2s. 8d. a gallon, when the Englishman could not do it. Though the Budget proposals as a whole were assailed from an Irish point of view, no great opposition was at the time offered to this portion he proposed to increase the spirit duties in Ireland.

The addition of 8d. per gallon on Irish spirits proved to be successful beyond expectation. It yielded more revenue than it was expected to yield; and the fears about smuggling were not realised. On the strength of that success, Mr. Gladstone imposed, without opposition, in the next year (1854) a further increase of 8d., bringing the duty up to 4s. per gallon.

The consumption of Irish spirits having increased in spite of these additions to the duties thereon, Sir G. C. Lewis, in 1855, again raised it to 6s. 2d. per gallon, as compared with a duty of 8s. per gallon on Scottish as well as English spirits; and three years later (1858), Mr. Disraeli succeeded in effecting a complete equalisation of the spirit duties in the three kingdoms. The discussion on the proposal did not indicate that Irish opinion was greatly opposed to his carrying the policy of his predecessors to its logical conclusion; and since then, though recent additions to the spirit duties have been held to fall with undue severity on Scotland and Ireland as compared with England, the question of reverting to differential treatment has not been seriously raised.

2. *Income Tax.*

The income tax, which had, in different forms, been imposed on Great Britain from 1798, had already been repealed when the British and Irish Exchequers were consolidated as from the 5th January 1817. It was one of the taxes, to the repeal of which precedence was given in 1816 on the conclusion of the War with France; and it was not re-imposed till 1842.

In re-imposing it that year, for the purposes of repairing the deficiency of revenue and of effecting fiscal reforms, Sir Robert Peel proposed that it should only apply to England and Scotland. He exempted Ireland from the tax on the ground that the machinery for its collection was not ready to hand in that country as it was in Great Britain. Ireland had not been subject to the former income tax, and she had no assessed taxes at all. The collection of the proposed income tax would, therefore, have required the creating of new machinery. Such a step was a serious one to take in the peculiar state of society in that country, and was one which he did not feel called upon to attempt, more especially as the tax was to be levied only for a temporary purpose, and was to be limited in duration to three years. As, however, Ireland was, in his belief, to be fairly as much as any part of the Empire by the reductions of taxation which he proposed, he held that she should bear her fair proportion of the increased revenue which had to be raised. This end he proposed to realise, by adding 1s. a gallon to the duty on Irish spirits—thus bringing the increase to those duties which had to be abandoned within 12 months—and by equalising the stamp duties in Ireland to those in England.

By the time that Mr. Gladstone was first installed at the Exchequer as Chancellor in 1853, the spirit duties in Ireland had for ten years been restored to their old rate and the stamp duties had been reduced all round. In view of these considerations he held that the time had come for extending the income tax to that country; the strictest demands of justice, he considered, required the extension. "The fact of a country being poor," he said, "was no argument *prima facie* against the application of the tax where that tax did not attach to the class that were poor in that country, but only attached to a class which, being defined by a certain amount of income, were actually richer as regarded the enjoyment of the necessaries and comforts of life than the corresponding class who paid the tax in England." At the same time, mainly as a set-off against this imposition, he relieved Ireland of all separate liability in respect of certain loans, called the "Consolidated Annuities," which had been raised in connection with the introduction of the Poor Law system into Ireland and with the terrible famine with which that country had been visited. The relief was equivalent to about [illegible] a year, representing the annual charge in respect of the "Consolidated Annuities" which amounted to about [illegible].

Great exception was taken to these proposals. It was urged that the "consolidated annuities" represented expenditure for Imperial purposes; that the abandonment of them, which only affected parts of Ireland, was a matter of justice quite apart from Budget considerations, and was no real *quid pro quo* for the imposition of the income tax throughout the country; that the "springs of industry," which the income tax had been intended by Sir R. Peel to set free, and which had thereby been set free, were British "springs," not Irish "springs;" for Ireland had scarcely any manufactures, and consequently her share in the remission of other taxation had been proportionately insignificant. By submitting to an income tax which was yielding [illegible], Great Britain had been relieved of other taxes to the amount of 12,000,000*l*. Ireland's participation in the relief had, it was estimated, been only 400,000*l*., or a thirtieth part of Great Britain's relief. According to that proportion, the outside amount due to be contributed by Ireland in return for benefits secured by the income tax was [illegible], and this amount was more than covered by the addition to her spirit duties.

Notwithstanding these objections, Mr. Gladstone carried his point by subjecting Ireland to the income tax.

While the process of assimilating the rates of taxation in both countries was being gradually effected, the financial treatment of Ireland by the Imperial Parliament was not greatly discussed as a whole. Indeed, the general question was only seriously raised on a few occasions, before the Committee of Inquiry was appointed in 1864.

Sir J. Newport brought the question before the House of Commons on the 22nd April 1822 by moving an address on the state of Ireland. He maintained that, while before the Union the progress of taxation in that kingdom had been very moderate, it had since increased infinitely. The result had been that landlords

Hansard, Vol. [illegible], pp. [illegible], &c.

Hansard, Vol. [illegible], p. [illegible]

Hansard, Vol. [illegible], pp. [illegible], &c.

Hansard, Vol. [illegible], pp. [illegible], &c.

Hansard, Vol. [illegible], pp. [illegible], &c.

Hansard, Vol. [illegible], p. [illegible]

Hansard, Vol. [illegible], p. [illegible]

Hansard, Vol. [illegible], pp. [illegible], &c.

Hansard, 2nd Series, Vol. VI., p. [illegible], &c.

had been driven out of the country, thus aggravating the long standing evils of absenteeism; and that the proceeds of duties imposed on Ireland had manifestly diminished. He had, he said, long warned the House that what would be reaped from such a system of taxing Ireland would be a "harvest of discontent, not of revenue." His predictions had, he maintained, been verified. He had been asked in 1816 when Ireland was going to repay the debt which England had contracted on her account since the Union; and he had said "never." Though raised nominally by Ireland, the debt had, in his view, really been raised by England, because Ireland had been charged more than double the amount of her just proportion of joint expenditure.

Mr. Goulburn in reply contended that Sir J. Newport had answered himself. That gentleman had admitted that, although Ireland was bound to contribute 2/17ths of such expenditure (which was now admitted on all hands to be more than she was able to do), yet Great Britain had since taken on herself the debt of Ireland; and Mr. Goulburn held that by that means Ireland had virtually been called upon to pay not 2/17ths, but 1/17th. How, he asked, could the system of taxation in Ireland have driven landlords out of the country? Why, the taxation in Great Britain was incalculably greater than in Ireland; and was it probable that men would fly from one country, taxed with comparative lightness, to another country where taxes were positively burthensome?

Hansard, Vol. XXII., pp. 1108.

Twelve years later, the question of Irish Finance was again raised, in connection with Mr. O'Connell's motion for a committee of inquiry with regard to the Union. It is to be noted that, in the debate on the Address in 1833, when he enumerated the grievances of Ireland which required immediate redress—and he enumerated no less than seven grievances—he made no mention of finance. But in the speech which he delivered on the 22nd April 1834, he devoted much time to the financial side of the terms of the Union and of Ireland's subsequent treatment. He reminded the House that the Irish anti-Union Lords had contended for a proportion of 1 to 18; and yet Ireland had been saddled with a quota of 2 to 17. He maintained that, had there been no Union, England would, in the last 34 years, have had to pay about 16,000,000l. annually of separate taxation, amounting in the aggregate to 544,000,000l.; while, in a Return just issued, the separate taxation, to which it was calculated that Great Britain had been subjected, amounted only to 335,317,000l. So the Union had saved England 213,000,000l. He pointed out that the same Return had made it appear that 29,000,000l. had been given to Ireland during the same period. This sum was arrived at by comparing the amount of revenue actually collected in that country with the amount which would have accrued, had her taxes been levied at the British rates. But, he urged, additions to taxation did not necessarily mean an increase of revenue. An attempt once made to raise 1,000,000l. from Ireland by increased taxation had actually resulted in a diminution of receipts by 300,000l. Moreover, he calculated that, since the Union, while in England the increase of taxation had been 20 per cent., in Ireland it had been 80 per cent., and that upon the necessaries of life. According to him, too, Ireland had fared equally ill in the matter of remissions of taxation since the conclusion of the war; for, while upwards of 37,000,000l. of taxation had been repealed in Great Britain, only about a million and a half had been remitted in Ireland. Lastly, by taking the report of the Committee on Irish Poor in 1830, he showed that, according to some of the figures furnished by that Committee, the increase in the consumption of standard commodities in Ireland as compared with England had, since the Union, been very different to what it had been before the Union. Thus:—

Parliamentary Paper, No. 464 of 1834.

Parliamentary Paper, No. 17 of 1830, pp. 143.

Commodities.	Before the Union (from 1784).		Since the Union (to 1830).	
	England.	Ireland.	England.	Ireland.
	Per cent.	Per cent.	Per cent.	Per cent.
Tea - -	+ 45	+ 54	+ 25	+ 34
Tobacco -	+ 64	+ 100	+ 27	− 37
Wine - -	+ 27	+ 74	+ 24	− 46
Sugar - -	+ 53	+ 57	+ 36	+ 10
Coffee - -	+ 73	+ 400	+ 1,800	+ 400

Increase (+) or decrease (−) per cent. of consumption.

It fell to Mr. Spring Rice, Secretary to the Treasury, to reply to Mr. O'Connell. The principal counter-argument which Mr. S. Rice brought forward with much emphasis and in great detail was the enormous weight of "peculiar taxation," which Great Britain had borne since the Union. He produced accounts to show that Great Britain had between 1801 and 1833 paid in the aggregate no less a sum than 448,000,000l. in excess of what she would have paid had her taxes been levied at the Irish rates only; and that she had also paid during that time taxes not imposed on Ireland to an aggregate amount of 673,000,000l. He accordingly made out that, from having had to pay some taxes at higher rates and other taxes not extended to Ireland, Great Britain had, during those 34 years, paid nearly 1,100,000,000l. in taxation, from which Ireland had been exempted. He admitted that such calculations were to some extent open to argument and controversy. For instance, Ireland had, no doubt, consumed a part of the articles on which this taxation had been levied in Great Britain. But the statement of Mr. O'Connell respecting the comparative amount of taxes repealed in the two countries was equally open to argument and controversy. He (Mr. Spring Rice), therefore, considered himself entitled to set one statement against the other. In face of the figures which he had adduced, how was it possible, he asked, to say that in matters of taxation there had been, on the part of the Imperial Parliament, any disregard of the interests of Ireland? As to the contention that, by the consolidation of Exchequers, Ireland had been unfairly saddled with the burden of the National Debt, he maintained that the real state of things would best be shown by comparing the charge for debt, which had fallen on Irish revenues during the last three years of separate Exchequers, with the charge which had fallen on those revenues during the first three years of consolidated Exchequers.

Hansard, Vol. XXII., pp. 1242, &c.

(1.) The amount payable by Ireland for Debt services before the consolidation was in the three years ending—

	£
5th January 1815 - - -	3,460,445
5th January 1816 - -	3,716,673
5th January 1817 - - -	4,068,914
Total - - -	11,229,393

(2.) The amount payable by Ireland for debt services after the consolidation was in the three years ending the—

	£	
5th January 1818 -	1,012,882*	
5th January 1819 - -	[illegible]*	
5th January 1820 -	1,128,852*	
		3,078,812
Accordingly, in the latter three years, the difference in favour of Ireland, as compared with the earlier three years, was not less a sum than - - -		8,565,461

The fact was, he said, that if the Exchequers had remained separate until 1820, the effect would have been to create an additional charge of 13,000,000l. on Ireland in respect of debt during those further three years. That sum must have been borrowed; so she necessarily would have added in a proportionate degree to the amount of her burdens. From 1817 there was an end to the question of joint and separate expenditure; and an end to the question of the 2/17th quota. The consolidation of Exchequers in that year had swept aside all calculations about the most proportions. Granting that there had been inequality or injustice towards Ireland in the Union quotas, the transfer of the debt for which Great Britain made herself jointly responsible in 1817 was, he maintained, alone much more than a sufficient counterpoise to any want of equality in 1800. How, he asked, could the arguments about the Union proportion be in the slightest degree applicable after the consolidation of the Exchequers?

The next occasion on which the Irish financial question was raised in Parliament was in 1853. When the order for committing the Income Tax Bill was read on the 25th May, Colonel Dunne moved an amendment to the effect that, before additional taxation was extended to Ireland, the fiscal relations and relative taxation of Great Britain and Ireland

Hansard, Vol. 127, pp. 104, &c.

* These sums apparently represented the annual surpluses of Irish Revenue over Irish Expenditure, and therefore the amounts available for the service of the debt out of those revenues.

should be first considered by a Select Committee. English Members of Parliament, he said, were very little acquainted with the actual condition of Ireland, which had not prospered to the same extent as England since the Union. He did not say that Ireland ought not to bear her fair share of taxation; but what he did say was that, before Ireland, just emerging from a great crisis, had the income tax extended to her, there should be a preliminary inquiry into her resources. Indeed, to extend it without such inquiry would be a breach of the articles of the Union, the terms of which had themselves been extremely injurious to Ireland and to the advantage of Great Britain. The requirements of England and the wars in which she engaged after the Union had raised the taxation of Ireland, year after year, to an enormous amount; while the reduction of it had been held out as one of the inducements to legislative incorporation with Great Britain. Nor had the expectations been realised of an increased foreign and colonial trade for Ireland. His object was not so much to deprecate taxation, as to call on the Government to ascertain previously what was the fair amount for Ireland to pay by the means pointed out in the Treaty of Union, the conditions of which had been nullified by the consolidation of the two Exchequers, and which had given Ireland the right—a right never, however, accorded to her—to have her taxation revised at intervals of not more than twenty years, nor less than seven years.

Mr. Fitzstephen French, who followed Colonel Dunne, said that the Irish representatives only asked that the engagements into which the British Government had entered with Ireland at the time of the Union should be fairly carried out; and that a competent tribunal should, accordingly, be appointed to decide on the mode by which Ireland, considering her relative capability, should be called upon to contribute to the support of the State.

p. [illegible] The Chancellor of the Exchequer, Mr. Gladstone, opposed the appointment of the Committee. After taking exception to Colonel Dunne's motion as an extremely unfortunate one in respect to its form and to the time at which it was made, Mr. Gladstone twitted previous speakers with having alluded to the 7th Article of the Treaty of Union, as if it were a new discovery, and with having omitted all reference to the proceedings which had subsequently taken place. They had been told, he said, that it was a very hard case that Ireland should pay 4,000,000*l.* or 5,000,000*l.* a year towards the general revenue of the empire; and that she would have been much better off, if her financial concerns had been kept entirely separate from those of the United Kingdom. What was the real state of things? Why, in 1815, just before the consolidation of the Debts and the Exchequers took place, the annual debt charge of Ireland, irrespective of one farthing of charges for military or civil government, was 5,000,000*l.*; and now, when she was called upon to pay a great deal less than she had been bound to pay for debt alone, it was deemed to be a gross injustice. He referred to Parliamentary Returns presented a few years previously, from which he was able to show that, if Ireland had been debited with the charge on account of her own debt as well as with her other charges, the annual assistance which the British Exchequer had rendered to her between 1817 and 1848 was from five to six millions in the earlier years, and from two to three millions in the later years. This being the case, he could not see that any Committee was wanted to inquire whether Ireland was paying more than her fair proportion of taxation. The matter was as clear as daylight at that moment.

Parliamentary Papers, [illegible]

Colonel Dunne's motion was negatived by a large majority; but undeterred by the small support which it received in 1853, he renewed it 10 years later.

Hansard, [illegible] On the 12th June 1863 he moved for a Committee to inquire into the causes of the depressed condition of Ireland and the effects of the taxation which she now bore. He quoted statistics of population, agriculture, exports and imports, and manufactures, to shew the falling-off in all these respects during the last 20 years. Nothing in Ireland had, he declared, increased except taxation. The total taxation of Ireland according to the Revenue returns was 7,000,000*l.* But this was far short of the real amount. Ireland had but little direct foreign trade in tea, wine, and other consumable articles. The greater part of these articles came from England after paying duty there, and so England was credited with duties which Ireland paid. Ireland should also be given credit for her share of the miscellaneous revenues, of receipts from Crown lands, of payments by colonies and foreign governments, and of the proceeds of old stores. If proper credit were assigned to her on these accounts, her true revenue, he said, would be found to be, not 7,000,000*l.*, but as much as 11,000,000*l.* The consolidation of the Exchequers effected in 1817 had not dispensed with the requirement in the Treaty of Union that the respective burdens of the countries should be revised after every 20 years; and even now, at the third recurrence of the stipulated period, a readjustment of debt and taxation should be made.

It again fell to Mr. Gladstone, as Chancellor of the Exchequer, to deal with this motion for inquiry. He demurred to the claim to have public money expended on (what he might call) geographical principles; but he quoted figures to show that, even on such principles, Ireland received very liberal treatment as compared with Great Britain. For there was annually spent 1,460,000*l.* for the local advantage of Ireland; whereas on England, with her much greater population, there was expended about 2,500,000*l.* a year. He maintained that the Revenue Returns gave the true version of the relative contributions of the two countries. There were plenty of bonded warehouses in Ireland, and the Irish tradesmen knew their business too well to import large quantities of duty-paid goods when they could get them in bond near their own doors. If, as Colonel Dunne contended, the Irish Customs revenue was really twice what the published returns showed, then she must be the richer country of the two, and the case would fall to the ground. The returns showed the payments per head of population of the respective taxes as follows:— p. [illegible]

—	Revenue Payment per Head of Population.					
	Customs.	Excise.	Stamps.	Land and Assessed Taxes.	Income Tax.	Total.
	s. d.	s. d.	s. d.	s. d.	s. d.	s. d.
Great Britain -	20 7	13 4	7 7	9 11	8 7½	51 7½
Ireland - -	7 11	8 10	1 10½	3d.	2 4½	22 1

Mr. Gladstone admitted that these figures were not incompatible with the view that there might be real inequality of taxation in Ireland, owing to the extensive poverty of her poorer population. But what were the facts? Ireland paid no tax that England did not pay; but England and Scotland both paid a considerable number of taxes that Ireland did not pay. It was true that the taxes in which equality had been established were those which bore upon the poorer classes, who in Ireland were poorer than the corresponding classes in Great Britain; while the exemptions were wholly in favour of the propertied classes, who were as well able to pay in Ireland as in Great Britain. But he maintained that, in Ireland's own interest, fiscal equality was the end to be kept in view; and that it was vain without equality of taxation to claim the exercise of full political equality. If there was not to be a revival of the former and "almost antediluvian state of things" before the consolidation of Exchequers was carried out, it must be shown in what way the present laws bore upon the face of their enactments injustice to Ireland; and he believed that this would be found impracticable, because the equity, liberality, and fairness of those laws had been proved. In conclusion, he intimated that there was one concession which he would be disposed to make out of regard for the special circumstances of Ireland; and that was the exercise of special liberality in loans of public money, where the security was unexceptionable.

Continuing the debate, Mr. Longfield said that the decline of Ireland's prosperity dated from 1853, and that its cause was the excessive taxation imposed since that year. He gave the following particulars to show how the pressure of taxation had increased:—

Year.	Population of Ireland.	Taxation of Ireland.	
		Total.	Per Head of Population.
		£	s. d.
1853	6,136,000	4,000,000	12 4
1862	5,650,000	7,004,000	23 0

p. [illegible] As regards Ireland's exemptions from British taxes, Mr. Maguire held that the quit rents in Ireland were the equivalent of the land tax, and that the exemption from house duty and assessed taxes was of little moment, as they would not yield in Ireland more than 50,000*l.* each, or 100,000*l.* in all.

At the conclusion of the debate, Colonel Dunne, in view of the late period of the session, withdrew his motion. But he returned to the question in the following year.

Hansard, Vol. [illegible], pp. [illegible]. On the [illegible] February 1864 he again moved for the appointment of a Select Committee, but the terms of the motion were somewhat different. He proposed on this occasion that the Committee should consider not only the taxation of Ireland, but how far it was in accordance with the provisions of the Treaty of Union, or just in reference to the resources of the country. In urging his proposal, he maintained that, in spite of the Consolidation Act of 1816, the Treaty of Union was as binding as it ever was, and that, in face of that Treaty, it was inconceivable how advantage had never yet been taken of the provision for revising the financial terms at least every 20 years. He considered that, under the altered circumstances of the country, a standard of comparison measured by the consumption of single articles, as had been prescribed by the terms of the Treaty, would be unjust, and he suggested that the valuation of property would be a fairer method of judging the question. After a short debate, in which it was admitted that any attempt to strike a debtor and creditor account between Great Britain and Ireland would lead to confusion and embarrassment, Mr. Gladstone, still Chancellor of the Exchequer, announced that the appointment of the Committee would be conceded; though the Government would not have recommended it of their own accord, inasmuch as it might tend to raise expectations which it might be found impracticable to fulfil. As regards, however, the terms of the Treaty of Union, he would not suppress his own opinion that they had been kept, and more than kept. The stipulation of that Treaty was that Ireland should raise $\frac{2}{17}$ths of the entire revenue of the United Kingdom, but he believed that it had in reality been about $\frac{1}{16}$th, and never higher than $\frac{1}{11}$th.

The Committee nominated to undertake the inquiry consisted of Colonel Dunne, Sir E. Grogan, Sir F. Heygate, Mr. Longfield, Mr. Hennessy, Sir G. Colthurst, Mr. Henley, the O'Conor Don, Mr. Banks Stanhope, Sir S. Northcote, Mr. Bowes, Sir R. Peel, and Mr. Lowe.

Parliamentary Papers, Nos. [illegible] of 1864, and [illegible] of 1865. The Committee sat for two years. They took a great deal of evidence. They presented many papers. They furnished many accounts. They drew several reports. But in the report which they finally adopted, they arrived at conclusions which perhaps may be said—and said, it is hoped, without any disrespect to the distinguished members constituting the Committee—to be somewhat impotent.

They practically disposed of the principal allegations brought against the operation of the Treaty of Union. They pointed out that, had Ireland after the Union been unable to borrow, and had she not borrowed, separately, her liability would have been the same, unless in violation of the Treaty she would have thrown upon Great Britain the burden of [illegible]ths of her own separate deficits, as well as of the joint expenditure of the United Kingdom. The Committee admitted that there might have been departures from the terms of the Treaty strictly interpreted, but they were technical departures, and they were not then matters of pressing importance. Ireland had, between 1801–16, suffered by the arrangement from not having raised by taxation as large a proportion of her contribution as Great Britain had met in that way; because, in the absence of further taxation, resort to constant loans was necessary; and those loans involved a charge not only for simple but for compound interest. The Committee also admitted that, had the Exchequers not been amalgamated in 1816, and had the previous system of raising revenue in Ireland been continued, the Irish separate debt would have continued to increase, until the country might have been crushed by it. They recognised that attention had been paid to the provision in the Treaty for allowing to Ireland certain abatements and exemptions from indiscriminate taxation. Ireland had been, and still was, exempt from some of the taxes to which Great Britain was subject. At the same time, there was the fact that in recent years the taxation of Ireland had been placed much more on an equality with that of Great Britain; and it was not surprising that this gradual levelling up of taxation had given rise to complaint. But when it came to saying whether the existing taxation was "just in reference "to the resources of the country," the Committee found themselves confronted with great difficulties. In the absence of any accounts of the trade between Great Britain and Ireland, the real value of the exports and imports of the two countries, relating only, as they did, to foreign and colonial trade, was no real criterion of the comparative wealth or resources of the two countries. All, therefore, that could be done was to adduce other tests which would more or less indicate, though they would not show with any real accuracy, the respective resources of Great Britain and Ireland. The tests which the Committee adduced may be summarised in the following table:—

Giving Various Tests of the Comparative Resources of Great Britain and Ireland in [illegible].

Year.	Basis of Proportion.	Great Britain.	Ireland.	Total.
[illegible] (Average).	Tonnage of Foreign Trade	[illegible]	[illegible]	[illegible]
	Percentage	[illegible]	[illegible]	[illegible]
[illegible]	Tonnage of Coasting Trade	[illegible]	[illegible]	[illegible]
	Percentage	[illegible]	[illegible]	[illegible]
[illegible] (Average).	Total Tonnage entering and leaving both Countries	[illegible]	[illegible]	[illegible]
	Percentage	[illegible]	[illegible]	[illegible]
[illegible] (Average).	Tonnage of Vessels belonging to both Countries	[illegible]	[illegible]	[illegible]
	Percentage	[illegible]	[illegible]	[illegible]
[illegible]	Property assessed to Income Tax	£ [illegible]	£ [illegible]	£ [illegible]
	Percentage	[illegible]	[illegible]	[illegible]
[illegible]	Accumulated deposits in Savings Banks	£ [illegible]	£ [illegible]	£ [illegible]
	Percentage	[illegible]	[illegible]	[illegible]

Giving Various Tests of the Comparative Resources of Great Britain and Ireland in 18[illegible]—contd.

Year.	Basis of Proportion.	Great Britain.	Ireland.	Total.
1894–95	Post Office Money Orders issued	£ [illegible]	£ [illegible]	£ [illegible]
	Percentage	[illegible]	[illegible]	100·00
1893	Gross Railway Receipts	£ [illegible]	£ [illegible]	£ [illegible]
	Percentage	[illegible]	[illegible]	100·00
1891–5 (Average).	Payments on account of Death Duties	£ [illegible]	£ [illegible]	£ [illegible]
	Percentage	[illegible]	[illegible]	100·00
1893–4	Gross ordinary Revenue	£ [illegible]	£ [illegible]	£ [illegible]
	Percentage	[illegible]	9·51	100·00
At time of Union.	Mean of proportions of average Imports and Exports, and of average value of dutiable articles consumed.	88·16	11·84	100·00

The Committee did not deny that Ireland had recently been suffering; but, in their opinion, it had not been shown that the suffering had been owing to pressure of taxation. It was probably more due to the unfavourable character of the seasons. Nor could they say that there was any tax in Ireland at that time which was materially interfering with the development of her industries, unless it was the excise duty on spirits. Moreover, if the principle of graduating taxation were recognised so as to relieve Ireland of a part of her burdens, it would be in part at the expense of adding to the burdens of the poor districts in Great Britain; and, if that principle were admitted as regards different parts of the United Kingdom, it would have to be admitted as regards individual taxpayers. As to spending more in Ireland, the Committee believed that more harm than good would result from it, at any rate as regards unproductive expenditure; for such expenditure, like that on naval arsenals, ought to be regarded from a national point of view, and incurred at the most suitable spot. It was different with reproductive expenditure. Though much had already been done in that way, there was no objection to doing still more, by the advance of public money for improving land and furthering arterial drainage.

Such were the conclusions at which the Select Committee arrived in 1865. These conclusions neither invited action, nor was any practical action taken upon them, except that some further impetus was given to the system of public loans in Ireland. It was no wonder, then, that the question of Irish Finance was soon revived in the House of Commons by the representatives of Ireland.

Two years later, in July 1867, Mr. McKenna returned to the charge, with a resolution to the effect that the increase of taxation in Ireland since 1841 had been great and disproportionate as compared with that of Great Britain. He took returns of taxation and population for 1841, 1851, and 1861, and deduced conclusions from them to show that the fiscal changes during that period had been greatly to the disadvantage of Ireland as compared with Great Britain. In 1841 the pressure of Imperial taxes per head of population had been 2l. 11s. in Great Britain and 10s 1d. in Ireland. In 1851 it had fallen to 2l. 5s. 9d. in Great Britain, but in Ireland it had risen to 13s. 2d.; while in 1861 the respective amounts were 2l. 13s. and 1l. 3s. 5d. In 20 years, therefore, according to these figures, the demand upon the inhabitant of Great Britain had been increased only by 2s., but upon the inhabitant of Ireland the increase had been no less than 13s. 4d., or more than his full contribution at the beginning of the period. It was observed by Mr. McKenna that the increase in Ireland from 10s. 1d. to 13s. 2d. during the first 10 years had taken place without the imposition of any fresh taxes during that time, thereby justifying Sir Robert Peel in his refusal to extend the income tax to that country in 1842. The much greater increase during the later 10 years was the result of the Budget of 1853, by which Mr. Gladstone "gave a shilling of relief with one hand "for the pound of taxes he extracted with the other." Mr. McKenna's endeavour, however, to measure the effect of taxation by the amount of individual payment met with no support in the debate. Even the members who agreed with his conclusions admitted that the test was a fallacious one. General Dunne, who as Colonel Dunne had presided over the Committee of 1864–65, maintained that the true test was the amount by which taxation had diminished the capital of the country; and he referred to a Parliamentary Return, showing that every pound sterling of income in Ireland was taxed to the extent of 6s. 3½d., but in England only to 4s. 0½d. Parliamentary Paper No. [illegible] of 1865.

Mr. Hunt, who, as Secretary to the Treasury, represented the Government in the debate, maintained that the increase of taxation, of which complaint had been made, was really evidence of increase of material prosperity. As regards the increasing proportion of taxation to population, he pointed out that it was the natural consequence of a decrease of population caused by the emigration of the poorer people, who contributed little to the revenue.

The motion was by leave withdrawn.

In March 1873 Sir Joseph McKenna (as he had then become) brought forward another resolution in the same sense, calling upon the Government to take measures to secure that each country of the United Kingdom should contribute to the Imperial Revenue in proportion to its actual means. He attributed the prevailing scepticism as to the reality of Ireland's grievance to the illusory evidences of her progress and prosperity contained in what he called the "Dublin Castle Statistics," returns which were misleading by reason of their incompleteness. He maintained that a fair test of Ireland's relative capacity was afforded by the amount of income subject to income tax. According to the income tax figures for 1872, the aggregate of such incomes in Great Britain amounted to [illegible]l., and in Ireland to 27,000,000l. Thus the tax-paying abilities of Great Britain and Ireland were in the ratio of seventeen to one; but their actual contributions to Imperial Revenue were nearly in the proportion of eight to one. Hansard, Vol. 187, p. [illegible].

He again adverted to the great increase of taxation in Ireland, as compared with Great Britain, since 1841; and he objected specially to the gradual raising of the duty on Irish spirits from 2s. 8d. in 1841 to 10s., while the duties on the alcoholic liquors in use in England had been greatly reduced.

Sir Stafford Northcote, who had drawn the Report of the Committee of 1864–5, now replied as Chancellor of the Exchequer. Admitting that the proportion of

Ireland's taxation to that of Great Britain was [illegible], he pointed out that the alterations in total expenditure in the two countries were in the ratio of 10s. for Ireland and 8s. for Great Britain. The calculation as to the increase of the duty on Irish spirits left out of account the large quantities of those spirits which were consumed in England. The proposal to test the proportions of taxation due from either country by the ratio of their aggregate incomes would have been suitable in the state of things before the amalgamation of the two Exchequers, but would not apply to the existing system, the principle of which was to apply the same taxes uniformly throughout the Kingdom. Under such a system, if taxes were borne in a different ratio by different parts of the Kingdom, it was not through any arbitrary rule of the Government, but through the following rule of the circumstances of the different parts and their means of payment. Taxes were of two kinds. There were those on property or income, and those on consumption. One part of the country could not be said to be more heavily taxed than another under the first kind of tax, so long as the assessment was the same; while, whatever difference of incidence there was, it was all in favour of Ireland; and, as regards taxes on consumption, they were paid entirely in proportion to the means of the consumer. The increase of Irish taxation since 1841, relatively to that of Great Britain, was due to the fact that Ireland had previously been exempted to a larger extent from the taxes paid in Great Britain; but after she had for so long had the benefit of that exemption, the time had come for her to bear her full share of the burdens of the Empire. He believed that, if the system were adopted for equitable distribution of taxation; and that, if that system were carried out with due regard to the distinctions still existing, as well as to the local distribution of the Imperial Revenue, Ireland would be a loser and not a gainer thereby.

Commenting on the argument of the Chancellor of the Exchequer that the system of taxation was self-acting, and that particular portions of the Kingdom could not be separately considered, Mr. Sullivan said that this state of things was the fulfilment of the prophecies of Mr Grattan and the Plunkets, who had told the Irish Parliament that incorporation with England would attach the wealth of Ireland to the greater wealth of England, and that, whereas Ireland under her own Parliament had a comparatively light taxation, she would, when joined to England, "stagger "under a weight which was a feather on the shoulders "of the wealthier people."

Mr. Lowe, as late Chancellor of the Exchequer, and as a member of the Committee of 1864-5, contended that the arguments of the Irish members rested on an obvious fallacy. They spoke of the taxation paid by England, by Scotland, and by Ireland. Whereas, of course, taxation was not paid by geographical districts but by individuals. To establish a case it must be shown that the individual Irishman was more heavily taxed than the individual Englishman in similar circumstances, and this proof could not be adduced.

Sir Joseph McKenna's motion was negatived without a division, and therefore it met with no better fate than the motion which he had brought forward eight years previously.

In June 1877 Mr. Mitchell Henry moved three resolutions to the effect that the taxation of Ireland was excessive, that it violated the promises made at the Union, and that it caused a drain of money out of the country, which made improvement hopeless. The first part of his speech was devoted to an account of Irish finance before the Union, and a criticism of the Union provisions. His statement of the present-day grievance followed on the lines of those which had been made in the previous debates, and the same may be said of Sir S. Northcote's reply.

In his speech Mr. Mitchell Henry had referred to the argument used by Mr. Lowe in the debate of 1874, that taxation was paid not by the country but by the people. This argument, he said, placed Ireland in the position of an English county; but her whole case rested upon the fact that she was a nation, united to Great Britain by a treaty, which provided that she should be taxed in proportion to her financial ability. Thus, it was not a question of individual taxation, but of the taxation of a nation. On this occasion, the motion made on Ireland's behalf was carried to a division, but it was rejected by a majority of 138 in a House of 194 members.

The next occasion on which the Irish finance question was brought before Parliament was in April 1882, when Sir Joseph McKenna, undeterred by the ill success with which his previous efforts had been rewarded, moved for a Committee of Inquiry. His resolution asserted that the imperial taxation of Great Britain was equivalent to the produce of an income tax of 2s. 6d. in the £, and that of Ireland to a tax of 5s. in the £. This contention he based on the figures in the last-issued return of comparative population and taxation (viz., that for 1871-82), and he attributed the disparity to the unjust principles introduced by the Budget of 1853, and especially to the enhanced duty on spirits. Before, however, he had concluded his speech, the House was counted out. Hansard, [illegible] Parliamentary [illegible]

Four years later Sir Joseph McKenna made one more attempt to enlist the sympathy of the House of Commons with Ireland in the matter of her financial relations to Great Britain. He brought the question forward by moving, on the 22nd February 1886, for Returns of Taxation and Population of Great Britain and Ireland in the years 1851, 1861, 1871, and 1881, and it met with very different treatment from that which had been accorded to it on former occasions. Leading members of both sides of the House took part in the discussion, and concurred in the opinion that the subject required, and ought to receive, earnest consideration. It had, of course, assumed greatly increased importance in view of the proposals which Mr. Gladstone was about to make for granting to Ireland a measure of self-government, which included the separation again of the two Exchequers. Hansard, [illegible]

Sir Joseph McKenna stated the case as in former years. He mentioned that Mr. Gladstone's statement on the repeal of the Malt Tax had revealed the fact that the tax on the English national beverage was only 2s. on the equivalent of a gallon of proof spirit as against 10s. on Irish spirits. He quoted Mr McLaren's Return for the year ending the 31st March 1883, which showed that in that year Ireland paid in Imperial taxation one-tenth as much as Great Britain, while, measured by her Income Tax assessment, her proportion should have been only one twenty-second. A Treasury Return of 24th April 1882 showed that each penny of Income Tax in Ireland yielded 80,000l., and in Great Britain 1,840,000l., twenty times as much. Parliamentary [illegible] Parliamentary [illegible]

Mr. Goschen showed that the comparison of Income Tax assessments was not itself a sufficient criterion, although it would be one of the elements in a thorough consideration.

Mr Fowler, Secretary to the Treasury, analysed the Revenue figures for 1884-85, adjusted as far as possible to give the true contributions. His conclusion was that Ireland, with a population of one-seventh of the United Kingdom, contributed one-eleventh of the gross Revenue, and less than one-twentieth of the Imperial charges. He preferred the Legacy and Succession Duty payments, as a test of wealth, to the Income Tax assessment.

Mr. Gladstone stated his opinion that the Union proportion of two-seventeenths was too high. He agreed with Mr. Fowler that the Legacy and Succession Duties were perhaps the fairest test of taxable capacity, but their amount was so variable that the comparison must be extended over a number of years. He had only added the figures for the last three years, and these showed property chargeable in Ireland 38,000,000l., in Great Britain 361,000,000l., or in the proportion of 1 to 12. He asked Irish members not to lose sight of the considerable advantages which Ireland had received by the use of Imperial credit.

On the conclusion of the discussion, the Returns were ordered. Parliamentary [illegible]

The question of the relative incidence of taxation in Great Britain and Ireland, and of the respective contributions of the two countries to Imperial expenditure, naturally occupied a foremost place in the debates on the Home Rule Bill of 1886, and likewise on the Home Rule Bill of 1893. But it seems unnecessary for present purposes to refer to these debates. In the first place, they are tolerably fresh in people's minds. In the second place, they had reference to specific schemes of British and Irish finance, which are not now in question.

Allusion, however, must be made to one step which was taken by the Government of the day in the interval that intervened between the production of Mr. Gladstone's two schemes, and that was the appointment of a Committee to consider the financial relations of the three kingdoms. This step was taken by Mr. Goschen

as Chancellor of the Exchequer in 1890, when on the 12th August, on his motion a Select Committee was appointed to consider the present financial relations of England, Scotland, and Ireland. The terms of reference comprised several points:

(1.) The amount and proportion of Imperial Revenue;
(2.) The revenue paid to local authorities;
(3.) The expenditure upon local services and collection of revenue;
(4.) The amount of State loans and State liabilities for local purposes;
(5.) The equity of the financial relations in regard to resources and population of each of the three kingdoms.

The Committee, whose instructions excluded, contrary to the appeals of Mr. Sexton, any inquiry into the past financial treatment of Ireland, was appointed too late in the session to admit of its commencing its labours in 1890 before Parliament was prorogued; and in the next two sessions, when the re-appointment of the Committee was brought forward, the motion was persistently opposed by Welsh members, who desired to have Wales treated as a separate financial entity. In consequence of this opposition, the late Government were prevented from securing the re-appointment of the Committee. By way, however, of breaking ground and furthering the inquiry ultimately, Mr. Goschen directed a Return, based on the terms of the reference to the original Committee, to be prepared and laid before the House of Commons. This Return was the first attempt made to adjust in detail the amounts of revenue collected in each of the three kingdoms, so as to show the true incidence of taxation in England, Scotland, and Ireland respectively, and it constituted the basis of the several Returns subsequently issued, and likewise known as "Financial Relations" papers. Parliamentary Paper, No. [illegible]

It is now time to turn to the consideration of the more important of the questions to which the Royal Commission will presumably have to address itself; and that is, the relative taxable capacities of Great Britain and Ireland. The difficulty of ascertaining the true state of things is as great now as it was in 1864-5, when the last inquiry was instituted; and it would be presumptuous on my part, as well as going beyond my province, if I offered any opinion purporting to solve the problem which a competent Committee of the House of Commons failed to solve 30 years ago. But it may be permissible to submit various statistics, which may assist the present Royal Commission in the prosecution of their inquiries.

I propose, in the first instance, to give the amounts of revenue collected annually in each country from 1817 down to the present time.

TABLE I.—Showing the REVENUE collected in GREAT BRITAIN and IRELAND respectively in each year from 1817-18 to 1893-94 (i.e., the net receipts after repayments, drawbacks, and allowances have been deducted, but without any deduction on account of collection expenses and of certain other charges, which were formerly paid out of Revenue in its progress to the Exchequer, instead of being voted, as now, and charged on the general revenues of the United Kingdom).

[Down to 1869-70 the figures in this Table are taken from the Annual Finance Accounts, and for the period 1870-71 to 1880-81 from Parliamentary Paper, No. [illegible] of 1891; while from 1881-82 to 1893-94 they have been furnished by the Departments.]

Year ending	Great Britain.	Ireland.	Total.
	£	£	£
5 January 1818	[illegible]	[illegible]	[illegible]
Per-centage	[illegible]	[illegible]	100
" 1819	[illegible]	[illegible]	[illegible]
Per-centage	[illegible]	[illegible]	100
" 1820	[illegible]	[illegible]	[illegible]
Per-centage	[illegible]	[illegible]	100
" 1821	[illegible]	[illegible]	[illegible]
Per-centage	[illegible]	[illegible]	100
" 1822	[illegible]	[illegible]	[illegible]
Per-centage	[illegible]	[illegible]	100
" 1823	[illegible]	[illegible]	[illegible]
Per-centage	[illegible]	[illegible]	100
" 1824	[illegible]	[illegible]	[illegible]
Per-centage	[illegible]	[illegible]	100
" 1825	[illegible]	[illegible]	[illegible]
Per-centage	[illegible]	[illegible]	100
" 1826	[illegible]	[illegible]	[illegible]
Per-centage	[illegible]	[illegible]	100
" 1827	[illegible]	[illegible]	[illegible]
Per-centage	[illegible]	[illegible]	100
" 1828	[illegible]	[illegible]	[illegible]
Per-centage	[illegible]	[illegible]	100
" 1829	[illegible]	[illegible]	[illegible]
Per-centage	[illegible]	[illegible]	100
" 1830	[illegible]	[illegible]	[illegible]
Per-centage	[illegible]	[illegible]	100
" 1831	[illegible]	[illegible]	[illegible]
Per-centage	[illegible]	[illegible]	100
" 1832	[illegible]	[illegible]	[illegible]
Per-centage	[illegible]	[illegible]	100
" 1833	[illegible]	[illegible]	[illegible]
Per-centage	[illegible]	[illegible]	100
" 1834	[illegible]	[illegible]	[illegible]
Per-centage	[illegible]	[illegible]	100

Year ending	Great Britain.	Ireland.	Total.
	£	£	£
5 January 1835	[illegible]	[illegible]	[illegible]
Per-centage	[illegible]	[illegible]	100
" 1836	[illegible]	[illegible]	[illegible]
Per-centage	[illegible]	[illegible]	100
" 1837	[illegible]	[illegible]	[illegible]
Per-centage	[illegible]	[illegible]	100
" 1838	[illegible]	[illegible]	[illegible]
Per-centage	[illegible]	[illegible]	100
" 1839	[illegible]	[illegible]	[illegible]
Per-centage	[illegible]	[illegible]	100
" 1840	[illegible]	[illegible]	[illegible]
Per-centage	[illegible]	[illegible]	100
" 1841	[illegible]	[illegible]	[illegible]
Per-centage	[illegible]	[illegible]	100
" 1842	[illegible]	[illegible]	[illegible]
Per-centage	[illegible]	[illegible]	100
" 1843	[illegible]	[illegible]	[illegible]
Per-centage	[illegible]	[illegible]	100
" 1844	[illegible]	[illegible]	[illegible]
Per-centage	[illegible]	[illegible]	100
" 1845	[illegible]	[illegible]	[illegible]
Per-centage	[illegible]	[illegible]	100
" 1846	[illegible]	[illegible]	[illegible]
Per-centage	[illegible]	[illegible]	100
" 1847	[illegible]	[illegible]	[illegible]
Per-centage	[illegible]	[illegible]	100
" 1848	[illegible]	[illegible]	[illegible]
Per-centage	[illegible]	[illegible]	100
" 1849	[illegible]	[illegible]	[illegible]
Per-centage	[illegible]	[illegible]	100
" 1850	[illegible]	[illegible]	[illegible]
Per-centage	[illegible]	[illegible]	100
" 1851	[illegible]	[illegible]	[illegible]
Per-centage	[illegible]	[illegible]	100

Year ending.	Great Britain.	Ireland.	Total.	Year ending.	Great Britain.	Ireland.	Total.
	£	£	£		£	£	£
5 January 1852 -	55,490,000	4,202,000	59,692,000	31 March 1873 -	65,136,000	7,067,000	72,203,000
Per-centage	92·62	7·38	100	Per-centage	90·21	9·79	100
" 1853 -	57,219,000	4,425,000	61,644,000	" 1874 -	68,188,000	7,311,000	75,499,000
Per-centage	92·82	7·18	100	Per-centage	89·66	10·34	100
" 1854 -	54,328,000	4,513,000	58,841,000	" 1875 -	66,960,000	7,980,000	74,940,000
Per-centage	91·95	8·05	100	Per-centage	89·36	10·64	100
Quarter to 5 April 1854 -	10,522,000	1,314,000	11,836,000	" 1876 -	66,722,000	8,277,000	74,999,000
Per-centage	91·10	8·90	100	Per-centage	89·25	10·75	100
Year ending 31 March 1855 -	59,186,000	5,202,000	64,388,000	" 1877 -	70,116,000	8,044,000	78,160,000
Per-centage	90·84	9·16	100	Per-centage	89·57	10·43	100
" 1856 -	63,177,000	6,501,000	70,415,000	" 1878 -	71,275,000	8,081,000	79,356,000
Per-centage	90·51	9·49	100	Per-centage	89·83	10·17	100
" 1857 -	63,672,000	6,545,000	70,217,000	" 1879 -	74,610,000	8,376,000	82,986,000
Per-centage	90·64	9·36	100	Per-centage	89·91	10·09	100
" 1858 -	61,407,000	6,298,000	68,105,000	" 1880 -	76,336,000	7,811,000	84,147,000
Per-centage	90·16	9·84	100	Per-centage	90·51	9·49	100
" 1859 -	58,538,000	6,449,000	65,221,000	" 1881 -	78,344,000	7,514,000	85,858,000
Per-centage	90·46	9·54	100	Per-centage	90·51	9·49	100
" 1860 -	63,209,000	7,344,000	70,607,000	" 1882 -	77,028,000	8,205,000	85,233,000
Per-centage	90·07	9·93	100	Per-centage	90·32	9·68	100
" 1861 -	63,881,000	6,566,000	70,447,000	" 1883 -	80,506,000	8,752,000	89,258,000
Per-centage	90·62	9·38	100	Per-centage	90·22	9·78	100
" 1862 -	63,065,000	6,719,000	69,784,000	" 1884 -	74,217,000	8,754,000	82,971,000
Per-centage	90·28	9·72	100	Per-centage	89·83	10·17	100
" 1863 -	64,028,000	6,225,000	70,273,000	" 1885 -	78,040,000	8,598,000	86,638,000
Per-centage	90·75	9·25	100	Per-centage	89·14	10·86	100
" 1864 -	64,140,000	6,480,000	70,640,000	" 1886 -	81,232,000	8,348,000	89,580,000
Per-centage	90·87	9·13	100	Per-centage	90·21	9·79	100
" 1865 -	58,775,000	6,469,000	70,244,000	" 1887 -	83,318,000	8,842,000	92,374,000
Per-centage	90·71	9·29	100	Per-centage	90·38	9·62	100
" 1866 -	61,479,000	6,493,000	67,972,000	" 1888 -	81,308,000	8,481,000	89,789,000
Per-centage	90·44	9·56	100	Per-centage	90·27	9·73	100
" 1867 -	63,338,000	6,812,000	69,420,000	" 1889 -	80,915,000*	8,465,000*	89,380,000*
Per-centage	90·19	9·81	100	Per-centage	90·53	9·47	100
" 1868 -	63,808,000	6,687,000	70,495,000	" 1890 -	85,870,000*	8,830,000*	94,700,000*
Per-centage	90·43	9·57	100	Per-centage	90·57	9·43	100
" 1869 -	65,830,000	7,152,000	72,982,000	" 1891 -	87,058,000*	9,213,000*	96,271,000*
Per-centage	90·18	9·82	100	Per-centage	90·43	9·57	100
" 1870 -	64,390,000	7,202,000	71,592,000	" 1892 -	86,281,000*	9,140,000*	95,421,000*
Per-centage	90·26	9·74	100	Per-centage	90·36	9·64	100
" 1871 -	61,585,000	7,294,000	70,379,000	" 1893 -	87,687,000*	9,048,000*	96,735,000*
Per-centage	89·63	10·37	100	Per-centage	90·39	9·61	100
" 1872 -	67,470,000	7,688,000	75,158,000	" 1894 -	88,651,000*	8,434,000*	[illegible]
Per-centage	89·78	10·22	100	Per-centage	90·29	9·71	100

* The figures of these years include the amounts of revenue collected by Imperial officers, which is assigned to local authorities.

It will be observed that the proportions of revenue collected in Great Britain and Ireland respectively, during the long period to which this Table relates, varied much less than might have been expected, regard being had to the facts that, in the course of that period, numerous fiscal changes took place, that the course of trade necessarily shifted, and that the relative populations of the two countries underwent material alteration. In the opening year (1817-18) the revenue collected in Ireland amounted to 9·55 per cent. of the entire revenue collected in the United Kingdom. In the last year (1893-4) it amounted to 9·71 per cent. The lowest figure which the per-centage reached was 7·21; that figure being touched in 1853-4. The highest figure which the per-centage reached was 10·75, and that was in 1875-6.

But, though these figures of revenue collected respectively in the two countries are interesting, and though they are the only figures on which a comparison of receipts based on facts can be uniformly made since 1816-17, yet they do not, and cannot, show the relative incidence of taxation on the inhabitants of the two countries during the whole period. In the first place, the population of Great Britain 75 years ago was only about double the population of Ireland; whereas now the population of Great Britain is about seven times as great as that of Ireland. In the second place, it must be remembered that, ever since 1825, when the two countries came to be treated as one country for commercial and customs purposes, and when, consequently, accounts of dutiable Articles shipped from one country to the other ceased to be kept, there have been no authentic means of ascertaining accurately how much of the revenue collected in one country on account of dutiable articles represents the true revenue belonging to that country. In the third place, part of the

revenue collected in Great Britain represents Imperial receipts, which belong to both countries.

It is true that, as spirits can only be moved under "permit," that system, which was described by the Commissioners of Inland Revenue in a report presented to Parliament last year, has made it possible to trace the movement of these dutiable articles, which constitute the largest and consequently most important head of such articles, and thus to credit to each country the revenue derived therefrom.* But, as regards the duties on other articles subject to customs and excise duties, and as regards some of the direct taxes, it is only quite recently that attempt has been made to adjust in detail the amounts of revenue collected in each country, so as to show the true local incidence of taxation; and even the adjustments then effected are necessarily based, not on actual statistics, because none exist, but on the best information obtainable from shipping and railway companies. The results of such adjustments are given in the "Financial Relations" papers which have been presented to Parliament in the course of the last two or three years, and they may be considered, at any rate, to be an approximation to facts.

It will be seen, then, that we have a fairly trustworthy basis, on which to compare the relative incidence of taxation in Great Britain and Ireland at the commencement and at the close of the period from the union of the British and Irish Exchequers down to the present time. For, at the commencement, accounts were kept, as if there were a Customs barrier, and for the last few years we have the adjusted accounts available.

Accordingly, I take one of the earlier years (1819-20) and the latest year (1893-4) for which the accounts are complete, and in Table II. I compare the true revenue of Great Britain with the true revenue of Ireland in those two years; the revenue estimated to be derived from Imperial sources being thus excluded.

The figures relating to 1819-20 are taken from Mr. J. A. Pease's Return, to which reference will be immediately made, and those relating to 1893-4 from Sir J. Hibbert's (Financial Relations) Return.

* In [illegible] the last remaining [illegible] of the "permit" system was removed, and accordingly the documents, on which the calculations about the removal of duty-paid spirits from one country to the other were based, were discontinued, with the result that [illegible]

The accounts in the "Financial Relations" papers relating to [illegible] and [illegible] were corrected, but the figures relating to previous years [illegible]

The returns, therefore, of duty-paid spirits moved from one part of the United Kingdom to other parts, from [illegible] when the duty on spirits in Great Britain and Ireland was equalised and the returns [illegible]

TABLE II.—Showing the true Revenue of GREAT BRITAIN and IRELAND respectively in 1819-20 and 1893-4.

Heads of Revenue.	1819-20.			1893-4.		
	Great Britain.	Ireland.	Total.	Great Britain.	Ireland.	Total.
1. Customs:	£	£	£	£	£	£
a. Exchequer Revenue	[illegible]	[illegible]	[illegible]	[illegible]	[illegible]	[illegible]
b. Local Taxation Revenue	—	—	—	[illegible]	[illegible]	[illegible]
Total	[illegible]	[illegible]	[illegible]	[illegible]	[illegible]	[illegible]
2. Excise:						
a. Exchequer Revenue	[illegible]	[illegible]	[illegible]	[illegible]	[illegible]	[illegible]
b. Local Taxation Revenue	—	—	—	[illegible]	[illegible]	[illegible]
Total	[illegible]	[illegible]	[illegible]	[illegible]	[illegible]	[illegible]
3. Stamps:						
a. Exchequer Revenue	[illegible]	[illegible]	[illegible]	[illegible]	[illegible]	[illegible]
b. Local Taxation Revenue	—	—	—	[illegible]	[illegible]	[illegible]
Total	[illegible]	[illegible]	[illegible]	[illegible]	[illegible]	[illegible]
4. Taxes (land, house, and assessed)	[illegible]	[illegible]	[illegible]	[illegible]	—	[illegible]
5. Income Tax	[illegible]	—	[illegible]	[illegible]	[illegible]	[illegible]
TOTAL TAX REVENUE	[illegible]	[illegible]	[illegible]	[illegible]	[illegible]	[illegible]
6. Post Office Services	[illegible]	[illegible]	[illegible]	[illegible]	[illegible]	[illegible]
7. Crown Lands	—	[illegible]	[illegible]	[illegible]	[illegible]	[illegible]
8. Miscellaneous	[illegible]	[illegible]	[illegible]	[illegible]	[illegible]	[illegible]
TOTAL NON-TAX REVENUE	[illegible]	[illegible]	[illegible]	[illegible]	[illegible]	[illegible]
GRAND TOTAL	[illegible]	[illegible]	[illegible]	[illegible]	[illegible]	[illegible]

NOTE.—The totals in Tables II. and III. cannot correspond with the totals in Table I., because that Table includes the whole of the revenue collected in Great Britain and Ireland respectively; whereas, in apportioning the true revenue of each country [illegible], Tables II. and III. necessarily exclude those receipts [illegible] collected in Great Britain which may be considered to be derived from Imperial sources, and cannot [illegible] to either kingdom.

TABLE III., summarising TABLE II.

Heads of Revenue.	1819–20.			1893–4.		
	Great Britain.	Ireland.	Total.	Great Britain.	Ireland.	Total.
	£	£	£	£	£	£
1. *Indirect Taxes*	[illegible]	[illegible]	[illegible]	[illegible]	[illegible]	[illegible]
Proportion per cent.	[illegible]	[illegible]	100	[illegible]	[illegible]	100
Per head of population	[illegible]	[illegible]	[illegible]	[illegible]	[illegible]	[illegible]
2. *Direct Taxes*	[illegible]	[illegible]	[illegible]	[illegible]	[illegible]	[illegible]
Proportion per cent.	[illegible]	[illegible]	100	[illegible]	4·10	100
Per head of population	[illegible]	[illegible]	[illegible]	[illegible]	[illegible]	[illegible]
3. *Total Tax Revenue*	[illegible]	[illegible]	[illegible]	[illegible]	[illegible]	[illegible]
Proportion per cent.	[illegible]	[illegible]	100	[illegible]	[illegible]	100
Per head of population	[illegible]	[illegible]	[illegible]	[illegible]	[illegible]	[illegible]
4. *Non-Tax Revenue*	[illegible]	[illegible]	[illegible]	[illegible]	[illegible]	[illegible]
5. TOTAL REVENUE	[illegible]	[illegible]	[illegible]	[illegible]	[illegible]	[illegible]
Proportion per cent.	[illegible]	[illegible]	100	[illegible]	[illegible]	100
Per head of population	[illegible]	[illegible]	[illegible]	[illegible]	[illegible]	[illegible]
Population (1821 and 1893)	[illegible]	[illegible]	[illegible]	[illegible]	[illegible]	[illegible]
Proportion per cent.	[illegible]	[illegible]	100	[illegible]	[illegible]	100

NOTE.—[illegible]

Hitherto, no attempt has been made to adjust the accounts of the years which intervened between 1819–20, when the Customs barrier was removed, and 1889–90. But the adjustment has recently been attempted, in order to comply with an order given by the House of Commons on the motion of Mr. J. A. Pease, M.P. In pursuance of that order, a memorandum, on which much print have been borrowed, has been prepared in the Treasury. It is necessarily based on a good many assumptions, and in some cases arbitrary assumptions; but it is the best solution of the problem that the Treasury can offer. As it would be superfluous to go over again here the ground which is covered by that memorandum, I need only make one general remark on the conclusions which it draws, with a view, more than anything else, to enjoin caution in the use of Table I. above, and to show how that table ought probably to be modified, in order to arrive more nearly at the true revenue of each country.

The calculations made by the Treasury tend to show that, immediately after the Customs barrier was removed, the amount of revenue which was derived from dutiable articles consumed in Ireland, but which was collected in Great Britain (called the Irish "uncredited revenue"), exceeded by about a million the amount of revenue which was derived from dutiable articles consumed in Great Britain, but which was collected in Ireland; that this so-called "uncredited revenue" belonging to Ireland, gradually dwindled during the next 40 years; and that since then the position has been reversed, so that the amount of revenue which is derived from articles consumed in Great Britain, but which is collected in Ireland, has exceeded, in an increasing ratio, the amount of revenue which is derived from articles consumed in Ireland, but which is collected in Great Britain, until the excess, which represents British "uncredited revenue," has reached about 1,800,000*l.*

The following Table IV. shows the changes which, on the assumption that the adjustments made in the Treasury Memorandum and the recent Financial Relations Papers are a fair approximation to facts, should be made in the amounts of revenue collected in the two Kingdoms.

TABLE IV.—Showing the estimated amounts by which the REVENUE collected in IRELAND has been more or less than the true REVENUE of the Country.

Year ending	Amount of Revenue collected in Ireland, but really paid by Inhabitants of Great Britain.	Amount of Revenue collected in Great Britain, but really paid by Inhabitants of Ireland.	The net Amount by which the Revenue collected in Ireland has been more (+) or less (–) than the amount really paid by her Inhabitants, and accordingly to be deducted from, or added to, such Revenue.
	£	£	£
5 Jan. 1820	Nil.	3,000	– [illegible]
„ 1830	153,000	1,216,000	– [illegible]
„ 1840	140,000	[illegible]	– [illegible]
„ 1850	121,000	644,000	– [illegible]
31 Mar. 1860	[illegible]	[illegible]	– [illegible]
„ 1870	[illegible]	701,000	– [illegible]
1880	[illegible]	[illegible]	+ [illegible]
1890	[illegible]	484,000	+ [illegible]
31 Mar. 1892	[illegible]	570,000	+ [illegible]
1893	[illegible]	[illegible]	+ [illegible]
1894	[illegible]	[illegible]	+ [illegible]

The next table applies these adjustments to the percentages of revenue collected in Great Britain and Ireland, which are given in Table I. of Part III. above; and it also takes into account the further adjustments in respect of Revenue which is attributable to imperial sources, and which being collected in Great Britain

should be deducted from the amount collected therein. I give these Imperial receipts as estimated in Mr. Pease's Return (page 20), and the Financial Relations papers:—

			£
Year ending 5th Jan.	1820	-	1,250,000
"	1830	-	893,000
"	1840	-	163,000
"	1850	-	734,000
Year ending 31st Mar.	1860	-	1,900,000
"	1870	-	2,800,000
"	1880	-	3,134,000
"	1890	-	1,898,000
Year ending 31st Mar.	1891	-	1,322,000
"	1892		1,324,000
	1893		1,214,000

TABLE V.—Comparing the percentages of TOTAL REVENUE collected in GREAT BRITAIN and IRELAND with the percentages of British and Irish Revenue, after adjustments have been made between the two countries and Imperial Receipts excluded.

Year ending	Proportions according to	Great Britain.	Ireland.	Total.
5 Jan. 1820	Revenue as collected	[illegible]	[illegible]	100
	Revenue as adjusted	[illegible]	[illegible]	100
" 1830	Revenue as collected	[illegible]	[illegible]	100
	Revenue as adjusted	[illegible]	[illegible]	100
" 1840	Revenue as collected	[illegible]	[illegible]	100
	Revenue as adjusted	[illegible]	[illegible]	100
1850	Revenue as collected	[illegible]	[illegible]	100
	Revenue as adjusted	[illegible]	[illegible]	100
31 March 1860	Revenue as collected	[illegible]	[illegible]	100
	Revenue as adjusted	[illegible]	[illegible]	100
1870	Revenue as collected	[illegible]	[illegible]	100
	Revenue as adjusted	[illegible]	[illegible]	100
1880	Revenue as collected	[illegible]	[illegible]	100
	Revenue as adjusted	[illegible]	[illegible]	100
1890	Revenue as collected	[illegible]	[illegible]	100
	Revenue as adjusted	[illegible]	[illegible]	100
31 March 1891	Revenue as collected	[illegible]	[illegible]	100
	Revenue as adjusted	[illegible]	[illegible]	100
1892	Revenue as collected	[illegible]	[illegible]	100
	Revenue as adjusted	[illegible]	[illegible]	100
1893	Revenue as collected	[illegible]	[illegible]	100
	Revenue as adjusted	[illegible]	[illegible]	100

We must now turn to the other side of the account. I only propose here to compare the expenditure on British and Irish services in two years. I take, as I did in the case of British and Irish revenue, the years 1819–20, and 1892–3, leaving the comparison of expenditure in the intervening years to be drawn from such accounts as may be separately laid before the Royal Commission, and from the Treasury Memorandum which is presented to Parliament as Mr. Pease's Return.

TABLE Va.—Showing the EXPENDITURE incurred on LOCAL SERVICES in GREAT BRITAIN and IRELAND respectively, in 1819–20 and 1892–3.

Expenditure.	1819–20.	1892–3.	Increase (+) or Decrease (−) as compared with 1819–20.
	£	£	£
1. On services in Great Britain:— (1.) Met out of Exchequer Revenue.			
a. Civil Government charges	[illegible]	[illegible]	[illegible]
b. Collection of taxes	[illegible]	[illegible]	[illegible]
c. Post Office services	[illegible]	[illegible]	[illegible]
(2.) Met out of Local Taxation Revenue.	Nil.	[illegible]	[illegible]
Total British services	[illegible]	[illegible]	[illegible]

TABLE Va.—cont.

Expenditure.	1819–20.	1892–3.	Increase (+) or Decrease (−) as compared with 1819–20.
	£	£	£
2. On services in Ireland:— (1.) Met out of Exchequer Revenue.			
a. Civil Government charges	[illegible]	[illegible]	[illegible]
b. Collection of taxes	[illegible]	[illegible]	[illegible]
c. Post Office services	[illegible]	[illegible]	[illegible]
(2.) Met out of Local Taxation Revenue.	Nil.	[illegible]	[illegible]
Total Irish services	[illegible]	[illegible]	[illegible]

The most noteworthy feature of this table is the relatively great increase which has taken place during a period of three-quarters of a century in the expenditure on Irish services not only actually, but relatively, to the expenditure on British services. In 1819–20 the cost of Civil Government and collection of revenue in Great Britain, with a population of [illegible], was [illegible], or [illegible] per head of population, and in Ireland, with a population of [illegible], it was [illegible] or [illegible] per head of population. In 1892–3 the cost to the State of administering Great Britain with a population of [illegible] was [illegible], or [illegible] per head of population, whereas the corresponding cost of administering Ireland, with a population of [illegible], was [illegible], or [illegible] per head of population. If we confine the comparison to Civil Government services borne by the State in both countries, thus excluding the expenses of collecting taxes and managing the postal services, which may be held to be Imperial services, the increased charge of Civil Government in Ireland is still more marked. In 1819–20 the Civil Government charges in Great Britain, with a population of [illegible], was [illegible], or [illegible] per head of population, and in Ireland, with a population of [illegible], it was [illegible] or [illegible] per head of population. In 1892–3 these charges in Great Britain, with a population of [illegible], were [illegible], or [illegible] per head of population, whereas in Ireland, with a population of [illegible], they amounted to [illegible], or [illegible] per head of population.

Having compared the true revenue of Great Britain and Ireland and the expenditure on British and Irish services in 1819–20 and 1892–3, we are now in a position to ascertain a most important fact. I allude to the respective contributions of Great Britain and Ireland to Imperial expenditure in these two years. It is obvious that the contributions must be represented by the amounts by which the true revenues of the two countries exceed respectively the expenditure on British and Irish services. The following Table gives the results.

TABLE VI.—Showing the contributions of GREAT BRITAIN and IRELAND respectively to Imperial Expenditure in 1819–20 and 1892–3.

(1.) 1819–20.

—	Great Britain.	Ireland.	Total.
	£	£	£
True revenue (Table II.)	[illegible]	[illegible]	[illegible]
Local expenditure (Table V.)	[illegible]	[illegible]	[illegible]
Balance available for Imperial expenditure.	[illegible]	[illegible]	[illegible]
Proportion per cent.	[illegible]	[illegible]	100
Contributions per head of population.	[illegible]	[illegible]	[illegible]

TABLE VI.—(2) 1892-3.

—	Great Britain.	Ireland.	Total.
	£	£	£
Tax revenue (Table IV.).	[illegible]	[illegible]	[illegible]
Local expenditure (Table V.).	[illegible]	[illegible]	[illegible]
Balance available for Imperial expenditure	[illegible]	[illegible]	[illegible]
Proportion per cent.	91·33	8·67	100
Contribution per head of population	£1 14s. 11d.	9s. 0d.	£1 11s. 9d.

It will be observed that the proportion per cent. of Ireland's contribution to Imperial expenditure as compared with the proportion of Great Britain's contribution, is appreciably less now than it was about three-quarters of a century ago. The decrease is, of course, due to the great increase of local expenditure in Ireland during the intervening period. But the contribution per head of population in Ireland has only been reduced from 10s. 10d. to 9s., or by (about) 17 per cent.; whereas in Great Britain the contribution per head has been reduced from 3l. 6s. 4d to 1l. 14s. 11d. or by (about) 50 per cent.

Historical comparisons of this kind are interesting; but what is more important, and has a more direct bearing on the practical considerations with which the Royal Commission have to deal is the present financial relations of the two countries; and so it will be well to examine somewhat more in detail both sides of the current public accounts of the two countries.

I deal first with the accounts of the Revenue which may properly be credited to Great Britain and Ireland respectively, continuing to take the year 1892-3, and embodying the comparison in Table VII.

TABLE VII.—Showing true Revenue of GREAT BRITAIN and IRELAND respectively in 1892-3 under its principal Heads. (Parliamentary Paper, No. 334 of 1893.)

Heads of Revenue.	Net Revenue.		Percentage.		Per Head of Population (Middle of 1892).	
	Great Britain.	Ireland.	Great Britain.	Ireland.	Great Britain.	Ireland.
(a.) TAX REVENUE.	£	£			£ s. d.	£ s. d.
I. Customs.						
Cocoa, &c., chicory and coffee	314,000	28,000	92·12	7·88	0 0 2·1	0 0 1·4
Dried fruits	395,000	43,000	89·82	10·18	0 0 2·2	0 0 2·2
Foreign spirits:— Exchequer Revenue	3,787,000	335,000				
Local Taxation Revenue	151,000	14,000				
	3,938,000	349,000	91·82	8·18	0 2 4	0 1 8
Tea	3,020,000	479,000	86·00	14·00	0 1 7	0 2 1
Tobacco	8,727,000	1,027,000	89·30	10·20	0 4 5	0 5 0
Wine	1,197,000	101,000	92·00	8·00	0 0 8·6	0 0 5·9
Other articles	45,000	9,000	87·86	12·14	0 0 0·31	0 0 0·31
Total Customs	17,437,000	2,028,000	87·89	12·11	0 10 4	0 10 4
II. Excise.						
Spirits:— Exchequer Revenue	14,171,000	2,334,000				
Local Taxation Revenue	450,000	107,000				
	14,918,000	2,242,000	84·94	15·16	0 [illegible] [illegible]	0 [illegible] [illegible]
Beer:— Exchequer Revenue	8,843,000	593,000				
Local Taxation Revenue	369,000	23,000				
	9,212,000	616,000	93·46	6·34	0 5 0	0 3 0
Licences, railway duty, &c.:— Exchequer Revenue	323,000	194,000				
Local Taxation Revenue	3,434,000	—				
	3,757,000	194,000	95·10	4·90	0 2 0	0 0 10
Total Excise	26,552,000	3,052,000	89·76	10·24	0 17 0	0 13 5
III. Stamps.						
Probate Duty:— Exchequer Revenue	7,398,000	360,000				
Local Taxation Revenue	3,320,000	100,000				
	6,318,000	300,000	95·76	4·24	0 3 5	0 0 10
Estate, legacy, and succession duty	5,868,000	258,000	95·14	4·86	0 3 3	0 1 1
General stamps	3,332,000	161,000	95·72	4·28	0 1 9	0 0 11
Total stamps	15,371,000	719,000	95·55	4·45	0 9 2	0 3 0
IV. Land Tax and House Duty.	2,438,000	—	100·00	—	0 1 5	Nil.

TABLE VII.—*cont.*

Heads of Revenue.	Net Revenue.		Percentages.		Per Head of Population (Middle of 1893).	
	Great Britain.	Ireland.	Great Britain.	Ireland.	Great Britain.	Ireland.
	£	£			£ s. d.	£ s. d.
F. Income Tax.						
Schedules A and B	[illegible]	[illegible]	[illegible]	[illegible]	[illegible]	[illegible]
Do. C and D	[illegible]	[illegible]	[illegible]	[illegible]	[illegible]	[illegible]
Do. E	[illegible]	[illegible]	[illegible]	[illegible]	[illegible]	[illegible]
Total Income Tax	12,7[illegible]	567,000	[illegible]	[illegible]	[illegible]	0 2 5
Total Tax Revenue	74,7[illegible]	[illegible]	91·74	8·26	[illegible]	[illegible]
(b.) Non-Tax Revenue.						
Post Office	[illegible]	[illegible]	[illegible]	[illegible]	0 5 10	[illegible]
Telegraphs	[illegible]	[illegible]	[illegible]	[illegible]	[illegible]	[illegible]
Crown Lands	[illegible]	[illegible]	[illegible]	[illegible]	[illegible]	[illegible]
Miscellaneous	[illegible]	[illegible]	[illegible]	[illegible]	[illegible]	[illegible]
Total Non-Tax Revenue	[illegible]	[illegible]	[illegible]	[illegible]	[illegible]	0 2 11
Aggregate Total of Revenue	[illegible]	[illegible]	[illegible]	[illegible]	2 15 10	1 12 11
Total Exchequer Revenue	[illegible]	[illegible]				
Total Local Taxation Revenue	[illegible]	[illegible]				

A comparison of the true revenue collected by the State in one country with that of another appears to be by itself an incomplete test of the incidence of fiscal burdens on their respective inhabitants; because a rate levied by a local authority is as much a burden on the persons liable to pay it as a tax imposed by the Government. It seems, therefore, proper that account should be taken of the relative amounts raised by means of local rates in Great Britain and Ireland; more especially as the State bears the entire cost of the Irish Constabulary and Dublin Metropolitan Police, while the cost of the British Police mainly constitutes a charge on rates.* It is not possible to separate completely the proceeds of rates from the proceeds of charges for gas and water undertakings; but the sums derived from these charges may be held to be analogous to part of the revenue collected by Imperial officers, which is equally derived from charges for services rendered, and so they may analogously be included in the Local revenue.

—	Great Britain.	Ireland.	Total.
	£	£	£
Amount raised from (1) rates and (2) gas and water undertakings.	[illegible]	[illegible]	[illegible]
Proportion per cent.	[illegible]	[illegible]	100
Per head of population.	£1 [illegible]	15s. 1d.	£1 [illegible]

NOTE.—These figures are the latest available figures. Those for England and Ireland relate to the year 1893-4, but those for Scotland to the year 1892-93. The total, therefore, for Great Britain must be regarded as approximate only.

It will be seen that, if these sums are added to the total revenue collected by Imperial authorities given in Table VII., the percentages of burdens will be slightly altered in favour of Ireland. Thus:—

—	Great Britain.	Ireland.	Total.
	£	£	£
1. Exchequer Revenue	[illegible]	[illegible]	[illegible]
2. Local Taxation Revenue	[illegible]	[illegible]	[illegible]
	[illegible]	[illegible]	[illegible]
3. Proceeds of Rates, &c.	[illegible]	[illegible]	[illegible]
Grand Total	[illegible]	[illegible]	[illegible]
Proportion per cent.	[illegible]	[illegible]	100
Per head of population	[illegible]	[illegible]	[illegible]

I now compare the expenditure side of the British and Irish accounts, giving the comparison in Table VIII.

TABLE VIII.—*Showing the* EXPENDITURE, *under its principal heads, on* SCOTCH *and* IRISH SERVICES *respectively in* 1893-4, *met out of* EXCHEQUER REVENUE.

Parliamentary Paper, No. [illegible] of [illegible].

—	Great Britain.	Ireland.	Total.
I. Charged on Consolidated Fund.	£	£	£
1. Annuities and pensions	[illegible]	[illegible]	[illegible]
2. Salaries and allowances	[illegible]	[illegible]	[illegible]
3. Courts of Justice	[illegible]	[illegible]	[illegible]
4. Miscellaneous	—	[illegible]	[illegible]
Total	[illegible]	[illegible]	[illegible]

* This statement would be modified as regards the Dublin Metropolitan Police, for there is a local police rate which produces about [illegible] a year, the proceeds of which are supplemented in aid of the vote of Parliament for its services.

—	Great Britain.	Ireland.	Total.
II. Civil.	£	£	£
Class I.—Public works and buildings	[illegible]	[illegible]	[illegible]
Class II.—Salaries and expenses of public departments	[illegible]	[illegible]	[illegible]
Class III.—Law and justice	[illegible]	[illegible]	[illegible]
Class IV.—Education, science and art	[illegible]	[illegible]	[illegible]
Class VI.—Non-effective and charitable services	[illegible]	[illegible]	[illegible]
Class VII.—Miscellaneous services	[illegible]	[illegible]	[illegible]
Total Civil Government charges	[illegible]	[illegible]	[illegible]
Collection of taxes	[illegible]	[illegible]	[illegible]
[illegible]	[illegible]	[illegible]	[illegible]
Grand Total	[illegible]	[illegible]	[illegible]

In order to arrive at the total cost of Civil Government in Great Britain and Ireland, which is met by revenue raised by the State, we must add the expenditure met out of the revenue which, though collected by Imperial officers, is paid over to the local taxation accounts. This expenditure must be measured by the amounts which, in pursuance of the Acts 51 & 52 Vict. c. 41., and c. 60., 52 & 53 Vict. c. 50., 53 Vict. c. 8., and 53 & 54 Vict. c. 60. are thus placed at the disposal of local authorities. Similarly, if we like to add the expenditure for which the local authorities provide out of their own resources, we must add the amounts raised from rates and local undertakings.

The following Table IX. makes these additions, and also shows the relative percentages of the costs and the relative cost per head of administering the two countries, exclusive of the expenses connected with the collection of taxes and the management of the postal services.

TABLE IX.—Showing the present Cost of Administering Great Britain and Ireland respectively.

—	Great Britain.	Ireland.	
1. Expenditure on local services met out of Exchequer Revenue, as given in Table VIII.	£ [illegible]	£ [illegible]	£ [illegible]
Percentage	[illegible]	[illegible]	100
Cost per head of population	[illegible]	[illegible]	[illegible]
2. Expenditure on local services met out of Local Taxation Revenue. (Parliamentary Paper, No. [illegible] of 1894.)	[illegible]	[illegible]	[illegible]
Total expenditure under (1) and (2).	[illegible]	[illegible]	[illegible]
Percentage	[illegible]	[illegible]	100
Cost per head of population	[illegible]	[illegible]	[illegible]
3. Expenditure on local services met out of rates, &c. (See preceding page.)	[illegible]	[illegible]	[illegible]
Total expenditure under (1), (2), and (3).	[illegible]	[illegible]	[illegible]
Percentage	[illegible]	[illegible]	100
Cost per head of population	[illegible]	[illegible]	[illegible]

It may be well now to revert briefly to the present contributions, out of the revenue truly derived from Great Britain and Ireland respectively, to Imperial expenditure.

Parliamentary Paper, No. [illegible] of 1894, p. [illegible].

The expenditure incurred on Imperial services in 1892-3 amounted to 62,067,000*l*.; and the principal heads under which it was incurred were as follows:—

		£
1. *National Debt Services*		25,200,000
2. *Naval and Military Services*:		
(1.) Army	17,690,000	
(2.) Navy	15,730,000	
		33,420,000
Civil Government Services		2,877,000
Imperial portion of Postal Services		570,000
TOTAL IMPERIAL SERVICES		62,067,000

The following Table X. shows the respective contributions of the two countries towards these Imperial services.

TABLE X.—Showing the present CONTRIBUTIONS of GREAT BRITAIN and IRELAND respectively to IMPERIAL EXPENDITURE.

—	Great Britain.	Ireland.	Total.
1. True or adjusted Exchequer Revenue (Table VII.)	£ [illegible]	£ [illegible]	£ [illegible]
2. True or adjusted Local Taxation Revenue (Table VII.)	[illegible]	[illegible]	[illegible]
Total true or adjusted revenue collected by Imperial officers.	[illegible]	[illegible]	[illegible]
3. *Deduct Local Expenditure met out of*— (1.) Exchequer Revenue (Table VIII.)	[illegible]	[illegible]	[illegible]
(2.) *Local Taxation Revenue*	[illegible]	[illegible]	[illegible]
Total Local Expenditure	[illegible]	[illegible]	[illegible]
4. Balance available for Imperial Expenditure, representing the respective contributions thereto of the two countries.	[illegible]	[illegible]	[illegible]
5. Proportions per cent. of contributions (Table VI.)	[illegible]	[illegible]	100
6. Contributions per head of population.	[illegible]	[illegible]	[illegible]

		£
It will be noticed that while the total expenditure on Imperial services in 1892-3, as represented by the amounts issued out of the Exchequer for those purposes, was		62,067,000
The joint contributions of the two countries amounted to		60,577,000
There is, therefore, a difference of which has to be accounted for.	£	1,490,000
In the first place, there were receipts derived from Imperial services, such as the profits from the Mint, interest on Imperial loans, Patent Stamps, and taxes paid by or in respect of persons domiciled abroad, which receipts were estimated to amount to	1,216,000	
In the second place, the amounts paid into the Exchequer in the year exceeded the actual net receipts, on which the "Financial Relations" Returns for 1892-3 was based by	254,000	
		1,470,000
The remaining balance of receipts over expenditure, viz.		20,000

represents the surplus of the year.

I now propose to adduce various standards of comparison, which may, in a general way, indicate the relative resources and taxable capacity of Great Britain and Ireland, and which may thus assist the Royal Commission in the prosecution of the more difficult part of their inquiry. I accordingly give the following tables:—

TABLE XI.—Showing the AMOUNT of PROPERTY assessed to Probate and Succession Duties in GREAT BRITAIN and IRELAND respectively in the three years ending the 31st March 1891, 1892, and 1893.*

(1.) Net value of Property upon which *Probate Duty* was charged.

Year ending	Great Britain.	Ireland.	Total.
	£	£	£
31 March 1891	[illegible]	[illegible]	[illegible]
" 1892	[illegible]	[illegible]	[illegible]
" 1893	[illegible]	[illegible]	[illegible]
Average	[illegible]	[illegible]	[illegible]
Percentage of Total	[illegible]	[illegible]	100

* The figures in this Table (XI.) and the next Table (XII.) have been furnished by the Inland Revenue Department.

(2.) Net value of Property assessed to Succession Duty.

Year ending	Great Britain.	Ireland.	Total.
	£	£	£
31 March 1891 -	43,345,000	4,719,000	48,0[illegible],000
" 1892 -	36,390,000	3,014,000	39,[illegible],000
" 1893 -	42,929,000	4,543,000	47,472,000
Average -	40,888,000	4,759,000	4[illegible],000
Per-centage of Total	90·[illegible]	[illegible]	100

(3.) Average net value of Property assessed to Probate and Succession Duties.

Average of three Years.	Great Britain.	Ireland.	Total.
	£	£	£
Value of property upon which Probate Duty was charged.	165,578,000	7,346,000	172,926,000
Value of property assessed to Succession Duty.	45,955,000	4,758,000	50,713,000
Aggregate average	211,[illegible],000	12,[illegible],000	22[illegible],[illegible],000
Per-centage of Total	94·[illegible]	[illegible]	100

TABLE XII.—Showing the NET AMOUNT of PROPERTY and INCOME charged under each SCHEDULE of the INCOME TAX ACTS in GREAT BRITAIN and IRELAND respectively during the three years ending the 31st March 1891, 1892, and 1893.

(1.) Schedule A.

(*Letting value of Lands, Tenements, and Hereditaments.*)

Year ending	Great Britain.	Ireland.	Total.
	£	£	£
31 March 1891 -	1[illegible],[illegible],000	12,[illegible],000	177,[illegible],000
" 1892 -	1[illegible],[illegible],000	12,[illegible],000	179,[illegible],000
" 1893 -	1[illegible],[illegible],000	12,[illegible],000	180,[illegible],000
Average -	166,417,000	12,[illegible],000	179,[illegible],000
Per-centage of Total	92·[illegible]	7·09	100

(2.) Schedule B.

(*Profits made by Occupiers out of Husbandry.*)

Year ending	Great Britain.	Ireland.	Total.
	£	£	£
31 March 1891 -	22,[illegible],000	2,[illegible],000	24,[illegible],000
" 1892 -	21,[illegible],000	2,[illegible],000	24,[illegible],000
" 1893 -	21,[illegible],000	2,[illegible],000	23,[illegible],000
Average -	21,[illegible],000	2,[illegible],000	24,[illegible],000
Per-centage of Total	89·7[illegible]	10·[illegible]	100

(3.) Schedule C.

(*Income derived from Government Stocks, &c.*)

Year ending	Great Britain.	Ireland.	Total.
	£	£	£
31 March 1891 -	40,[illegible],000	777,000	41,[illegible],000
" 1892 -	39,[illegible],000	7[illegible],000	40,[illegible],000
" 1893 -	39,[illegible],000	7[illegible],000	39,[illegible],000
Average -	39,[illegible],000	74[illegible],000	40,[illegible],000
Per-centage of Total	98·17	1·83	100

(4.) Schedule D.

(*Profits derived from Trades and Professions.*)

Year ending	Great Britain.	Ireland.	Total.
	£	£	£
31 March 1891 -	[illegible]	[illegible]	[illegible]
" 1892 -	[illegible]	[illegible]	[illegible]
" 1893 -	[illegible]	[illegible]	[illegible]
Average -	[illegible]	[illegible]	[illegible]
Per-centage of Total	97·[illegible]	[illegible]	100

(5.) Schedule E.

(*Official and other Salaries or Pensions.*)

Year ending	Great Britain.	Ireland.	Total.
	£	£	£
31 March 1891 -	3[illegible],[illegible],000	1,7[illegible],000	[illegible]
" 1892 -	3[illegible],[illegible],000	1,744,000	[illegible]
" 1893 -	37,[illegible],000	1,[illegible],000	[illegible]
Average -	3[illegible],[illegible],000	1,7[illegible],000	[illegible]
Per-centage of Total	9[illegible]	[illegible]	100

(6.) Summary of Averages.

Average of three Years.	Great Britain.	Ireland.	Total.
	£	£	£
Schedule A. -	166,417,000	12,[illegible],000	179,[illegible],000
" B. -	21,[illegible],000	2,[illegible],000	24,[illegible],000
" C. -	39,[illegible],000	74[illegible],000	40,[illegible],000
" D. -	[illegible]	[illegible]	[illegible]
" E. -	[illegible]	1,[illegible],000	[illegible]
Aggregate average	[illegible]	[illegible]	[illegible]
Per-centage of Total	9[illegible]	[illegible]	100

TABLE XIII.—Showing the ESTIMATED AMOUNT of CAPITAL in GREAT BRITAIN and IRELAND respectively in 1888. Mr. Giffen's Growth of Capital, pp. 11, [illegible]

—	Great Britain.	Ireland.	Total.
	£	£	£
Estimated amount of capital in 1888.	[illegible]	[illegible]	[illegible]
Proportions per cent.	[illegible]	[illegible]	[illegible]
	No.	No.	No.
Populations in 1888	[illegible]	[illegible]	[illegible]
	£	£	£
Amount of capital per head of population.	[illegible]	[illegible]	[illegible]

NOTE.—Mr. Giffen fully explains the basis on which he framed his estimate of capital in the three Kingdoms. The amounts per head in this table do not exactly correspond with those given by Mr. Giffen, owing to his having taken the population of 18[illegible] instead of that of 1888.

TABLE XIV.—Showing the AVERAGE GROSS RECEIPTS derived from RAILWAYS in GREAT BRITAIN and IRELAND respectively, in the years 1891, 1892, and 1893. Statistical Abstract, [illegible]

—	Great Britain.	Ireland.	Total.
	£	£	£
1891 - -	78,[illegible],000	3,[illegible],000	81,[illegible],000
1892 - -	[illegible],000	3,[illegible],000	[illegible],000
1893 - -	77,[illegible],000	3,[illegible],000	[illegible],000
Average -	78,[illegible],000	3,[illegible],000	[illegible],000
Per-centage -	9[illegible]·06	[illegible]	100

TABLE XV.—Showing the AMOUNTS with which DEPOSITORS in SAVINGS BANKS were CREDITED in GREAT BRITAIN and IRELAND respectively on the 31st December 1893.

Deposits in	Great Britain.	Ireland.	Total.
	£	£	£
Post Office Savings Banks.	74,[illegible]	[illegible]	[illegible]
Trustee Savings Banks.	[illegible]	[illegible]	[illegible]
Total - -	[illegible]	[illegible]	[illegible]
Per centage -	[illegible]	[illegible]	100

TABLE XVI.—Showing the NUMBER and AGGREGATE AMOUNT of MONEY ORDERS issued in GREAT BRITAIN and IRELAND respectively in 1893.

—	Great Britain.	Ireland.	Total.
Number of orders issued.	[illegible]	[illegible]	[illegible]
Proportion per cent.	[illegible]	[illegible]	100·00
Amount for which orders were issued.	£ [illegible]	£ [illegible]	£ [illegible]
Proportion per cent.	[illegible]	[illegible]	100·00

TABLE XVII.—Showing the NUMBER and AGGREGATE AMOUNT of POSTAL ORDERS issued in GREAT BRITAIN and IRELAND respectively in 1893.

—	Great Britain.	Ireland.	Total.
Number of orders issued.	[illegible]	[illegible]	[illegible]
Proportion per cent.	[illegible]	[illegible]	100·00
Amount for which orders were issued.	£ [illegible]	£ [illegible]	£ [illegible]
Proportion per cent.	95·27	4·73	100·00

TABLE XVIII.—Showing the ESTIMATED NUMBER of LETTERS, NEWSPAPERS, BOOK PACKETS, CIRCULARS, SAMPLES, and POST CARDS delivered by the POST OFFICE in GREAT BRITAIN and IRELAND respectively in 1893-4.

—	Great Britain.	Ireland.	Total.
Number delivered	[illegible]	[illegible]	[illegible]
Proportion per cent.	[illegible]	[illegible]	100·00

TABLE XIX.—Showing the NUMBER of TELEGRAPH MESSAGES forwarded from TELEGRAPH OFFICES in GREAT BRITAIN and IRELAND respectively in 1893-4.

—	Great Britain.	Ireland.	Total.
Number forwarded.	[illegible]	[illegible]	[illegible]
Proportion per cent.	[illegible]	[illegible]	100·00

TABLE XX.—Showing the NUMBER of PAUPERS in RECEIPT of RELIEF in GREAT BRITAIN and IRELAND respectively, in January [illegible]

—	Great Britain.	Ireland.	Total.
Number of Paupers.	[illegible]	[illegible]	[illegible]
Proportion per cent.	[illegible]	[illegible]	100·00

I now come to the consideration of a test which might be considered the most crucial of all tests whereby to gauge the relative resources of two countries; and that is, their respective incomes. But, as the materials for ascertaining the wages of the labouring population, the profits of the middle classes, and the revenue of capitalists are very difficult to handle, I shall be content to summarise the latest conclusions at which two high authorities on statistics and economic subjects have arrived on this complex question.

I will first cite the calculations which were made by Mr. Leone Levi in 1885, and then those of Mr. Giffen, relating to about the same period.

TABLE XXI.—Giving Mr. LEONE LEVI'S ESTIMATE of the TOTAL INCOMES of GREAT BRITAIN and IRELAND in 1882-3.

—	Great Britain.	Ireland.	Total.
1. Income assessed to Income Tax under Schedules A, B, D, and E.	£ [illegible]	£ [illegible]	£ [illegible]
Proportion per cent.	[illegible]	[illegible]	100
2. Estimated income of lower middle class.	[illegible]	[illegible]	[illegible]
Proportion per cent.	[illegible]	[illegible]	100
3. Earnings of the working classes.	[illegible]	[illegible]	[illegible]
Proportion per cent.	[illegible]	[illegible]	100
Total income -	[illegible]	[illegible]	[illegible]
	[illegible]	[illegible]	[illegible]
Population of [illegible] -	[illegible]	[illegible]	[illegible]
Income per head of population.	[illegible]	[illegible]	[illegible]

TABLE XXII.—Giving Mr. GIFFEN'S ESTIMATE of the TOTAL INCOMES of GREAT BRITAIN and IRELAND in 1881.*

—	Great Britain.	Ireland.	Total.
1. Income Tax incomes -	£ [illegible]	£ [illegible]	£ [illegible]
Proportion per cent. -	[illegible]	[illegible]	100
2. Trades and Professions below Income Tax.	[illegible]	[illegible]	[illegible]
Proportion per cent. -	[illegible]	[illegible]	100
3. Manual labour classes -	[illegible]	[illegible]	[illegible]
Proportion per cent. -	[illegible]	[illegible]	100
Total aggregate income -	[illegible]	[illegible]	[illegible]
Proportion per cent. -	[illegible]	[illegible]	100·00
Population in 1881 - -	[illegible]	[illegible]	[illegible]
Income per head of population.	[illegible]	[illegible]	[illegible]

* I should state that Mr. Giffen, in an article which he wrote in the "Nineteenth Century" of March [illegible] (p. [illegible]), says, in reference to this subject: "I have a strong feeling that in these figures, which were based [illegible] very much on what Mr. Dudley Baxter and Mr. Leone Levi had done, I gave too little to Great Britain, if not too much to Ireland."

Such were the estimates at which these distinguished computists arrived. I do not pretend to endorse, and still less to dispute, the accuracy of their calculations. But, however accurate they may be, I venture to doubt whether any very certain conclusions can be drawn from them as to the relative capacity of the two countries to bear taxation. The estimates unquestionably bring out in a very striking manner the relatively small income which the average Irishman enjoys, as compared with the income enjoyed by the average inhabitant of Great Britain. But "the taxable income" (to quote Mr. Giffen) "is the income remaining after "allowance for the subsistence necessary to maintain a "population upon a given standard of living"; and that minimum may vary greatly. It is quite conceivable that an Irishman with a weekly wage of only 10s. or 12s. may have a larger margin to spend as he pleases than an Englishman or Scotchman with a weekly wage of 18s. The Irishman may be able to house himself more cheaply. He may have less to spend on his food. His food may be cheaper. His clothing may cost him less. Therefore the amount of a man's income is not necessarily a test of his capacity to bear taxation.

Perhaps a better test of the amount which the taxpayer can afford to pay for being governed, protected, and educated, is the residue of income remaining after bare necessities of life have been met; and probably the best and readiest means of gauging that residue is to be found in the amount which he spends on luxuries. Now it so happens that the only dutiable articles of consumption are luxuries of the masses, unless tea be excepted from that category; and, as the amount of duty paid on each article is approximately ascertainable, it is possible to make an estimate of the amount which the people of Great Britain and Ireland respectively consume, and the amount which they respectively spend in buying it. I submit the estimate with much diffidence, and before I do so, I must explain the basis on which I proceed.

I take Tea first. I translate the estimated true receipts derived in Great Britain and Ireland respectively, from the tax on that commodity, as ascertained in the "Financial Relations" papers, into the amount consumed; and I then calculate the cost to the consumer of that amount. According to a number of representative price lists, and regard being had to the retail prices at which the article is supplied to the poorer classes, whose consumption makes up the great bulk of the total quantity consumed, I am advised that 1s. 11d. per lb. is fairly representative of the average price to the consumer; and I take that price to be the average price paid by inhabitants of both countries. Table XXIII. gives the result of that calculation.

TABLE XXIII.—Showing the estimated ANNUAL EXPENDITURE incurred on TEA by the INHABITANTS of GREAT BRITAIN and IRELAND respectively, as deduced from the adjusted REVENUE RETURNS for the year ending the 31st March 1893.

Tea.	Great Britain.	Ireland.	Total.
	Lbs.	lbs.	Lbs.
Amount consumed	[illegible]	[illegible]	[illegible]
Estimated cost at 1s. 11d. per lb.	[illegible]	[illegible]	[illegible]
Percentage of total	[illegible]	[illegible]	100
Per head of population	[illegible]	[illegible]	[illegible]

Tobacco is a more difficult article to deal with, because not only do the rates of duty differ, but there are also different rates of moisture. Moreover, the returns on which the "Financial Relations" papers are based have been more questioned as regards tobacco than as regards the other articles, which are known to pay duty in one kingdom and to be consumed in another. But I have been favoured by Mr Pinter, of the Board of Customs, with an estimate, in which the problem is reduced to its simplest form, and taking that estimate (which, of course, must be taken with much reserve) I am able to compile the following table.

TABLE XXIV.—Showing the estimated ANNUAL EXPENDITURE incurred on TOBACCO by the INHABITANTS of GREAT BRITAIN and IRELAND respectively, as deduced from the adjusted REVENUE RETURNS for the year ending the 31st March 1893. Parliamentary Paper No. [illegible]

Tobacco.	Great Britain.	Ireland.	Total.
	Lbs.	Lbs.	Lbs.
Amount consumed	[illegible]	[illegible]	[illegible]
Estimated cost*	[illegible]	[illegible]	[illegible]
Percentage of Total	[illegible]	[illegible]	100
Per head of population	[illegible]	[illegible]	[illegible]

* Average retail price of the various kinds of tobacco estimated for the United Kingdom as follows:—
Cigars - - - [illegible] per lb.
Cut and roll tobacco - - - [illegible] per lb.
Cigarettes, snuff, and other tobacco - - [illegible] per lb.

I next come to Alcoholic Drinks, from which I exclude wine, because it is not an article of general consumption. It is not, of course, possible to obtain information which can be regarded as more than an estimate of the respective "Drink Bills" of the two countries; and such estimate can only be based on a series of assumptions.

It is assumed that throughout the United Kingdom one gallon of spirits is sold outside a public-house for every three gallons consumed inside.

It is further assumed that every gallon sold by a publican in England is diluted with water to the extent of 30 per cent., thus entailing a reduction of strength from (say) proof to 30 under proof, and that this diluted spirit is sold at 3d. a glass or 9d. a gill; while the spirit consumed outside the public-house is taken to be sold at 18s. a gallon at proof. On these assumptions, the average cost of spirits to the consumer in England would work out at 30s. per gallon.

In Scotland and Ireland the spirits consumed are believed to be stronger, the dilution being to the estimated extent of 25 per cent. only. The sale price is computed to be 8d. a gill, and on similar principles to those applied to the English figures, the average cost of spirits to the Scotchman and Irishman would be 28s. per gallon.

Analogous assumptions have to be made with respect to beer. It is assumed that for every gallon of beer consumed outside a public-house four gallons are consumed inside; that the average charge made in a public-house is 1d. per glass, containing one-third of a pint; and that the price per gallon paid for beer consumed outside a public-house is 1s. 4d. Regard being had to these considerations, the authorities at Somerset House think that the average cost of beer to the consumer may be taken at 1s. 9d. per gallon in England and at 1s. 8d. in Scotland and Ireland, inasmuch as in those countries beer is of a somewhat higher gravity.

Table XXV. gives the results of these calculations about expenditure on alcoholic drinks.

TABLE XXV.—Showing the Estimated Annual Expenditure incurred on Spirits and Beer in Great Britain and Ireland respectively, as deduced from the adjusted Revenue Returns for the year ending the 31st March 1893.

1. Spirits.

Spirits.	Great Britain.		Ireland.	Total.
	England.	Scotland.		
Foreign Spirits (duty 10s. 4d. per gallon).	£	£	£	£
Exchequer Revenue	[illegible]	[illegible]	[illegible]	[illegible]
Local Taxation Revenue	[illegible]	[illegible]	[illegible]	[illegible]
Total Revenue	[illegible]	[illegible]	[illegible]	[illegible]
Gallons consumed	No. [illegible]	No. [illegible]	No. [illegible]	No. [illegible]
British Spirits (duty 10s. 6d. per gallon).	£	£	£	£
Exchequer Revenue	[illegible]	[illegible]	[illegible]	[illegible]
Local Taxation Revenue	[illegible]	[illegible]	[illegible]	[illegible]
Total Revenue	[illegible]	[illegible]	[illegible]	[illegible]
Gallons consumed	No. [illegible]	No. [illegible]	No. [illegible]	No. [illegible]
Total consumption (in gallons)	No. [illegible]	No. [illegible]	No. [illegible]	No. [illegible]
	£[illegible]	£[illegible]		
Total cost of consumption (estimated)*	£[illegible]		£[illegible]	£[illegible]
Percentage of total	[illegible]		[illegible]	[illegible]
Per head of population	£1 [illegible]		£1 [illegible]	£1 [illegible]

* Average retail price of spirits consumed at— [illegible] per gallon in England. [illegible] per gallon in Scotland and Ireland.

2. Beer.

Beer (Excise Duty 6s. 3d. per Barrel.)	Great Britain.		Ireland.	Total.
	England.	Scotland.		
	£	£	£	£
Exchequer Revenue	[illegible]	[illegible]	[illegible]	[illegible]
Local Taxation Revenue	[illegible]	[illegible]	[illegible]	[illegible]
Total Revenue	[illegible]	[illegible]	[illegible]	[illegible]
Barrels consumed	No. [illegible]	No. [illegible]	No. [illegible]	No. [illegible]
	£[illegible]	£[illegible]		
Cost of consumption (estimated)*	£[illegible]		£[illegible]	£[illegible]
Percentage of total	[illegible]		[illegible]	100
Per head of population	£2 [illegible]		£1 [illegible]	£2 [illegible]

* Average retail price of beer consumed at— [illegible] per gallon in England. [illegible] per gallon in Scotland and Ireland.

3. Spirits and Beer combined.

Amount Spent on	Great Britain.	Ireland.	Total.
	£	£	£
Spirits	[illegible]	[illegible]	[illegible]
Beer	[illegible]	[illegible]	[illegible]
Total	[illegible]	[illegible]	[illegible]
Percentage of total	[illegible]	[illegible]	100
Per head of population	[illegible]	[illegible]	[illegible]

I now summarise the foregoing calculations of the amounts expended on dutiable articles consumed by the masses.

TABLE XXVI.—Summarising Tables XXIV. and XXV.

Estimated Expenditure on	Great Britain.	Ireland.	Total.
	£	£	£
Tea	[illegible]	[illegible]	[illegible]
Tobacco	[illegible]	[illegible]	[illegible]
Spirits	[illegible]	[illegible]	[illegible]
Beer	[illegible]	[illegible]	[illegible]
Total	[illegible]	[illegible]	[illegible]
Percentage of total	[illegible]	[illegible]	100
Per head of population	[illegible]	[illegible]	[illegible]

Any record of the financial treatment of Ireland by the Imperial Government would be imperfect if no account were taken of the amount of public money which has been placed at the disposal of that country as loans, and still more as the amount of loans the repayment of which has not been exacted.

Accordingly, I append a table giving the amounts which, on the one hand, have been advanced, and which, on the other hand, have been repaid, have been remitted or written off, and may be expected to be repaid, in Great Britain and Ireland respectively, since the establishment of the system of State loans down to the 31st March 1893, according to the latest published account.

TABLE XXVII.—RELATING TO PUBLIC LOANS IN GREAT BRITAIN AND IRELAND.

To 31st March 1893.	Great Britain.	Ireland.	Total of Local Loans.
	£	£	£
Amount advanced	[illegible]	[illegible]	[illegible]
Percentage	[illegible]	[illegible]	100
Amount repaid	[illegible]	[illegible]	[illegible]
Percentage	[illegible]	[illegible]	100
Amount remitted or written off.	[illegible]	[illegible]	[illegible]
Percentage	[illegible]	[illegible]	100
Balance outstanding on 31 March 1893.	[illegible]	[illegible]	[illegible]
Percentage	[illegible]	[illegible]	100

It will be seen from this table that out of a total sum of [illegible] the State has advanced to the poorer but smaller kingdom [illegible] for local purposes, or [illegible] per cent. of the whole; and that no less than [illegible], or more than one-fifth of the amount advanced in Ireland, has, by being remitted or written off, been treated as a free grant, while only [illegible], or one fifty-eighth part of the amount advanced in Great Britain, has been so treated.

As it would be going beyond my province to attempt to draw any conclusions from the statistics which I have adduced, the figures must speak for themselves; and I conclude this dissertation on the financial relations of Great Britain and Ireland by giving a Table, which summarises the various proportions per cent., in order that they may be readily compared one with another.

TABLE XXVIII.—Summarising various PROPORTIONS per cent. in GREAT BRITAIN and IRELAND respectively.

—	Great Britain.	Ireland.	Total.
1. Property assessed to Death Duties (average of [illegible])	[illegible]	[illegible]	100
2. Property assessed to Income Tax (average of [illegible])	[illegible]	[illegible]	100
3. [illegible]	[illegible]	[illegible]	100
4. [illegible]	[illegible]	[illegible]	100
5. [illegible]	[illegible]	[illegible]	100
6. [illegible]	[illegible]	[illegible]	100
7. Amount of Postal Orders issued ([illegible])	[illegible]	[illegible]	100
8. Number of letters, &c. delivered by Post Office ([illegible])	[illegible]	[illegible]	100
9. Number of Telegrams ([illegible])	[illegible]	[illegible]	100
10. Number of [illegible]	[illegible]	[illegible]	100
11. [illegible]:			
(1.) Mr. [illegible]	[illegible]	[illegible]	100
(2.) Mr. [illegible]	[illegible]	[illegible]	100
12. [illegible]:			
(a.) [illegible]	[illegible]	[illegible]	100
(b.) [illegible]	[illegible]	[illegible]	100
(c.) [illegible]	[illegible]	[illegible]	100
(d.) [illegible]	[illegible]	[illegible]	100
Total	[illegible]	[illegible]	100
Population [illegible]	[illegible]	[illegible]	100
[illegible]:			
[illegible]	[illegible]	[illegible]	100
[illegible]	[illegible]	[illegible]	100
Total Taxes	[illegible]	[illegible]	100
Contributions to Imperial expenditure (limited).	[illegible]	[illegible]	100

Postscript.—The inquiries instituted by the Royal Commissioners tend to the conclusion that too much revenue has been credited to Ireland under the head of [illegible] in the "Financial Relations" papers, which have been already laid before Parliament. Should that conclusion be established, the true revenue of Ireland and consequently the Irish contribution to Imperial expenditure, will to some extent, perhaps to the extent of about [illegible] in [illegible], be reduced; while of course the true revenue of Great Britain and consequently the British contribution to Imperial expenditure will [illegible] be augmented. But it is not possible, or at any rate it is premature, to attempt any further adjustment under this head in the accounts of prior years.

LIST OF PARLIAMENTARY PAPERS AND RETURNS REFERRED TO IN THE FOREGOING MEMORANDUM.

Year and Number.	Title.
1806, No. 298 -	Report of the Committee appointed to examine and report the amount of the joint charge on the United Kingdom of Great Britain and Ireland between the 1st January 1801 and 1st January 1806; what proportion thereof has been defrayed by Great Britain and Ireland respectively, and what balance remains due from either part of the United Kingdom to the other, according to the provisions of the Act of 39 & 40 of His present Majesty, for the Union of Great Britain and Ireland; and likewise to consider of and report the best means of ascertaining in future the amount of such balance as may be due from Great Britain and Ireland respectively, at the expiration of each year.
1811, No. 262 -	Report from the Committee on accounts and papers relating to the public income and expenditure of Ireland (to 5th January 1811).
1812, No. 376 -	Second report from the same.
1813, No. 200 -	Report from the Committee on accounts and papers relating to the public income and expenditure of Ireland (to 5th January 1813).
1815, No. 214 -	Report from the Select Committee on the public income and expenditure of Ireland (to 5th January 1815).
1819, No. 73 -	Accounts of the total amount of the funded and unfunded debt of the United Kingdom of Great Britain and Ireland, as it stood on the 1st of February or 5th January in each year, from the year 1786 to 1819, both inclusive; distinguishing the amount of funded debt redeemed, and also the amount of interest and charges upon the unredeemed debt from the amount paid to the Commissioners for the Reduction of the National Debt on account of sinking fund or interest on redeemed debt, and distinguishing Great Britain from Ireland.
1822, No. 606 -	Third Report of the Commissioners of Inquiry into the collection and management of the revenue arising in Ireland.
1823, No. 624 -	Fourth Report of the same.
1830, No. 667 -	Report of the Select Committee on the state of the poor in Ireland; being a summary of the first, second, and third reports of evidence taken before that Committee, together with an Appendix and accounts and papers.
1834, No. 194 -	Papers relating to the income, expenditure, commerce, and trade of Ireland.
1844, No. 565 -	Report from the Select Committee appointed to examine into the present state of the tobacco trade, and to inquire what effects have been produced by the changes of the laws relating to it, and whether any and what legislative measures, compatible with the general interests of the country, may be advisable in order to promote trade or to check smuggling in tobacco, and to whom several petitions relative to the tobacco trade were referred.
1847, No. 192	Return showing the income from the various sources of revenue in Ireland; the expenditure under different heads; charges, and the excess or deficiency after defraying those charges, 1817 to 1846; also capital charge of the funded debt of Ireland from 1786 to 1817.
1849, No. 423	Accounts of the debt, income, and expenditure of Ireland from the Union to 1848, inclusive.
1852, No. 432	Return, showing the population, the gross receipt of the revenue (after deducting repayments, allowances, discounts, drawbacks, and bounties of the nature of drawbacks, and excluding therefrom miscellaneous receipts), and the rate per head of the population of such revenue; also the amount of property and profits assessed for Income tax, the amount of income per head of population and the poundage of said taxation on such income, for Great Britain, in the year ending the 31st day of March 1852; and similar Return for Ireland for the same year.
1864, No. 474	Returns showing the gross and net revenue of Great Britain in each year from 1801 to 1817, inclusive; the amount of the charge for the interest of the funded and unfunded debt due by Great Britain, and of the sinking fund applicable to the reduction of such debt in each of the said years; of the balance of revenue, after deduction of such interest and provision for the sinking fund, applicable to the payment of the proportion of the general expenditure of the United Kingdom for which Great Britain was liable, &c.; and similar returns for Ireland.
1864, No. 513	Report from the Select Committee appointed to consider the taxation of Ireland, and how far it is in accordance with the provisions of the Treaty of Union, or just in reference to the resources of the country; together with the proceedings of the Committee, minutes of evidence, and appendix.
1865, No. 330	Report of the Select Committee on the same subject in the following session; and who were instructed to inquire into the system upon which advances are made and repayments required by the Imperial Government for drainage and other works of public utility in Ireland; with the proceedings, minutes of evidence, and appendix.

Year and Number.	Title.
1864, No. 85 -	Return of the gross revenue of Ireland, excluding casual and miscellaneous receipts, for the years 1841, 1851, and 1861, respectively; and of the population of Ireland in each of those years; and a computation of the amount of such revenue raised in each of those years respectively for each head of the population.
1864, No. 331 -	Same for Great Britain.
1869, No. 366 -	Accounts of the net public income and expenditure of Great Britain in each financial year from 1688 to 5th January 1801; and of the other receipts into and issues from the Exchequer, distinguishing the amounts raised by creation of debt, and the amounts applied to the reduction of debt; showing also the balances at the beginning and end of each year:—similar accounts for Ireland, 1688 to 1800.—Accounts of the gross public income and expenditure of Great Britain for each financial year from 5th January 1801 to 5th January 1817; similar accounts for Ireland 1801 to 1819:—similar accounts for the United Kingdom for each year from 5th January 1801.
1870, No. C. 82-I.	Report of the Commissioners of Inland Revenue on the duties under their management for the years 1856 to 1869 inclusive; with some retrospective history and complete tables of accounts of the duties from their first imposition. Vol. II.
1874, No. 407 -	Return of the gross revenue of Ireland derived from taxation, and excluding casual and miscellaneous receipts, post office and telegraph receipts, Crown lands, and fees of courts of justice taken in stamps, for the years 1841, 1851, 1861, and 1871; and of the population of Ireland in those years, and a computation of the amount of such revenue in respect of each head of the population; and like return in respect of the revenue and population of Great Britain for the same years.
1878, No. 193 -	Account of the public income of Great Britain and Ireland in each year from the year 1871, showing separately the revenue derived from Great Britain and Ireland.
1882, No. 154 -	Return, showing the figures upon which the Chancellor of the Exchequer based, in his Budget speech of Monday 4th April 1881, his comparison of the progress of population, revenue, and expenditure, since 1841.
1884, No. 36 -	Return, respecting the duties on spirits, malt, wine, &c., together with the duty on tobacco and the excise license duties, in order to show, as regularly as can be ascertained, the proportion of the several items of revenue derived from England, Scotland, and Ireland, respectively, for the year ended 31st March 1883, and the results for each of the three Kingdoms; return of the net produce of each of the other sources of revenue derived from taxation, and the population of England, Scotland, and Ireland, respectively, as estimated by the Registrar-General for the middle of 1883. (This is one of the series of Mr. [illegible] Returns. The others of the series are [illegible].)
1886, No. 176	Return of the gross Imperial revenue of Ireland derived from taxation, and of the population of Ireland, for the years 1851, 1861, 1871, and 1881; and a like return for England and Scotland for the same years; and also Return of the gross revenue of England and Wales, of Scotland and of Ireland, respectively, raised by taxation for the year 1884-5, and of population, and of the average incidence of taxation of the population.
1891, No. 329	Memoranda and tables prepared by the Treasury and the Customs and Inland Revenue Departments in view of the proposed inquiry into the financial relations between *England, Scotland, and Ireland*.
1891, No. C. 6539.	Report by the Secretary and Comptroller-General of the proceedings of the Commissioners for the Reduction of the National Debt from 1786 to 31st March 1890.
1893, No. 97 -	Return, showing for the years ended the 31st day of March 1890, 1891, and 1892 respectively, (1) the amount contributed by *England, Scotland, and Ireland* respectively to the revenue collected by Imperial officers; (2) the expenditure on *English, Scottish, and Irish* services out of such revenue.
1893, No. 348	Report of the Commissioners of Inland Revenue to the Treasury, explaining an error in the "Financial Relations" returns of 1891 and 1893.
1893, No. 283	Return, showing the amount of the Irish debt and the British debt respectively at the time of the Union in 1801, and at the time of the amalgamation of the British and Irish Exchequers in 1817.
1893, No. 305	Return, showing for the year ended the 31st day of March 1893, revised figures of (1) the amount contributed by *England, Scotland, and Ireland* respectively to the revenue collected by Imperial officers; (2) the expenditure on *English, Scottish, and Irish* services met out of such revenue; and (3) the balances of revenue contributed by *England, Scotland, and Ireland* respectively, which are available for Imperial expenditure.
1893, No. 384	Return, showing for the year ended the 31st day of March 1892: (1) the amount contributed by *England, Scotland, and Ireland* respectively to the revenue collected by Imperial officers; (2) the expenditure on *English, Scottish, and Irish* services

Year and Number.	Title.	Year and Number.	Title.
	ture out of such revenue; and (3) the balances of revenue contributed by *England*, *Scotland*, and *Ireland* respectively, which are available for Imperial expenditure.	1894, No. 313	Memorandum by the Treasury on the subject of (1) the amounts contributed, so far as can be ascertained, by the inhabitants of Great Britain and Ireland respectively to the revenue collected by Imperial officers at intervals since the Union of the British and Irish Exchequers; (2) the expenditure out of the amounts so contributed upon local services in Great Britain and Ireland respectively; (3) the expenditure out of the amounts so contributed on Imperial services.
1894, No. 59 -	Accounts of receipts and payments by the Commissioners for the Reduction of the National Debt, in respect of the capital and income of the Local Loans Fund, for the year ended 31st March 1893; together with the Report of the Comptroller and Auditor-General thereon.		

B.—Tables showing the Revenue and Expenditure of Great Britain and Ireland severally from 1782–83 to 1893–94 inclusive, with Explanatory Memorandum.

Explanation of Tables relating to the Public Revenue and Expenditure of Great Britain and Ireland from 1782–3 to 1893–4 inclusive.

The following Tables, which are accounts of the Public Revenue and Expenditure of Great Britain and Ireland respectively, cover the three periods under the review of the Royal Commission.

1. Numbers I., II., and III. relate to the period (1782–1800) during which Ireland enjoyed legislative independence;

2. Numbers IV. and V. to the period (1800–16) during which the Exchequers of the two countries remained separate, notwithstanding the legislative union; and

3. Numbers VI., VII., VIII., and IX. to the subsequent period (1817–94), during which there has been one Exchequer for the United Kingdom; and Great Britain and Ireland have (with certain exceptions) been treated as one country financially.

One of the main objects kept in view in the preparation of these Tables has been to frame them, as far as possible, on an uniform basis, in order that like may be compared with like. It has been very difficult to attain this object owing to the many changes which have taken place in our financial system during the last 100 years, to imperfect records, and to discrepancies in Accounts. On account of these and other difficulties, the construction of the Tables has involved an amount of research, adjustment, and consideration, of which no conception can be formed when the results are merely viewed in tabular form.

I proceed to endeavour to explain the basis on which the Tables have been framed for each of the three periods, taking the periods in the reverse of their chronological order.

The Third Period (1817–94).

The figures in the Tables relating to the last five financial years (1889–90, 1890–1, 1891–2, 1892–3, and 1893–4) are taken from the recent Parliamentary Returns, known as the "Financial Relations Papers"; and it is on the general basis of those Returns that the Accounts of every fifth preceding year have been worked out. The operation has been very complicated and laborious for the quinquennial periods; and to have taken each year might have indefinitely delayed the presentation of the Tables.

It should be first explained what the figures in the Tables represent.

It should be remembered that there are, and necessarily so, two sets of Accounts relating to the Public Revenue and Expenditure.

1. There are the Accounts of *Exchequer Receipts* and *Exchequer Issues*; that is, the Accounts of (1) the amounts paid into the Exchequer between the 1st April and the 31st March by the Revenue Departments out of the cash received by them from their collectors; and (2) the amounts issued out of the Exchequer in the same period and placed at the disposal of spending Departments to enable them to carry on the services of the State. These Exchequer Accounts are closed every year on the evening of the 31st March; they are final; they are the Accounts on which the Annual Budget proceeds; and they constitute the basis of the Annual Finance Accounts.

2. As, however, it is obviously impossible to ascertain on a particular day of the year the exact yield of each tax and each branch of Revenue during the preceding 12 months inclusive of that day, and still more impossible to know on the 31st March the amount actually expended or properly brought to charge in the entire year, regard being had to the innumerable transactions connected with Expenditure which is incurred all over the world, the Exchequer Accounts are naturally supplemented, when the details have been received, (1) by an account of the true income of revenue under the various heads; that is, of *Net Receipts*, and (2) by accounts of *Audited Expenditure*.

The two sets of Accounts do not, and cannot, correspond exactly each year, but over a series of years the aggregate differences are immaterial.

As the "Financial Relations" Returns enter into details which are not separable in the Exchequer Accounts, the figures which they contain relating to Revenue represent *Net Receipts*, and they represent *Net Receipts* of the entire Revenue collected by Imperial officers, because in order to establish the relations of Great Britain and Ireland respectively it is necessary to take into account not only the Revenue which is raised for the purposes of the Imperial Exchequer, but also the Revenue which is under recent arrangements raised for, and assigned to, local authorities. Accordingly, *Net Receipts* have been adopted in the following Tables relating to Revenue throughout the period since the consolidation of the British and Irish Exchequers in 1817. But the figures in the Tables prior to 1854–5 will not correspond with the "Net Receipts" in the Annual Finance Accounts. For, prior to that year, the cost of collection and various various other charges, which now fall upon the Consolidated Fund or constitute voted services, were met out of Revenue in its progress to the Exchequer. Consequently, in order to maintain the comparison, the items of Expenditure which were formerly met in that manner have been added to the Expenditure, and the Revenue has been correspondingly increased.

It will be seen that, in the tables relating to the third period, the net Revenue of Great Britain and Ireland is classified under the heads of "Taxes (or duties) on commodities" and "other taxes" (or duties). The Royal Commissioners suggested a distinction between *indirect* and *direct* taxation; but the classification which I have adopted, while it practically serves the same end, seems preferable, inasmuch as there are some taxes (as for instance income duties) which, though paid by the persons from whom they are levied and thus constituting direct taxes, may be, or are, wholly or in part, shifted on to the shoulders of other persons, and thus really constitute indirect taxes.

It must, of course, be borne in mind in connection with the use of these Tables that the figures represent the amount of Revenue collected in Great Britain and Ireland respectively, and that such Revenue cannot correspond with the true Revenue derived from the inhabitants of each country; for, not only may the incidence of taxes which are collected in one country fall on inhabitants of the other country, but the collected Revenue may and does include Revenue which are not specifically assignable to either England, or Scotland, or Ireland, and which thus constitute Imperial Receipts.

In the Financial Relations Returns, attempt has been made to adjust the collected Revenue so as to arrive at an approximation to the true Revenue of the three Kingdoms; and in deference to an Order of the House of Commons, made at the instance of Mr. Joseph A. Pease, a more difficult task has recently been attempted, which has been to carry back the adjustments for Great Britain and Ireland in every tenth year from 1889–90 to 1819. The results, however, of these attempts can only be hypothetical; and, this being the case, it is clearly undesirable to present the results as Accounts apart from the explanation of the basis on which they are founded. For, Accounts should properly deal with ascertained facts only, and not with hypotheses. Consequently, the present Tables deal with collected Revenue, for which only there are really trustworthy statistics. No. [illegible] of 1894.

The figures which the Tables contain relating to Expenditure represent Exchequer Issues. The adoption of the Accounts of *Audited Expenditure* would give the facts in detail more accurately, and, indeed, in two out of the five years (viz., 1889–90 and 1890–1) for which the "Financial Relations" Returns have been prepared, those Accounts have been used in the Return moved for by Mr. Clancy, M.P., in 1893. But the analysed figures supplied by Departments to the Comptroller and Auditor-General do not go back further than 1889, and, therefore, in order to maintain uniformity, Exchequer Issues have been used throughout the third period; the figures for 1889–90 and 1890–1 being taken from the first Financial Relations Return presented to Parliament in 1891. No. [illegible] of 1893. No. [illegible] of 1891.

The figures in the Tables relating to Expenditure prior to 1854–5, will not correspond with the Exchequer Issues as given in the Finance Accounts, because (as has been already mentioned) the charges which were formerly met out of Revenue in its progress to the Exchequer have been added to the Expenditure side of the Accounts.

In the last five years, in order to make the comparison complete, it has been necessary to follow the precedent of the "Financial Relations" Papers, and to add to the Expenditure met out of the Exchequer, the Expenditure which is met out of the Local Taxation Revenue by local authorities, and which is to be measured by the amount thus placed at their disposal.

THE SECOND PERIOD (1800-16).

This period has in some respects presented less and in other respects presented more, difficulties than the third period.

On the one hand, the ground has already been gone over by a highly competent authority, Mr. Chisholm, who undertook the difficult task of analysing the old accounts 30 years ago, and who presented the results of his labours to the Select Committee on Taxation of Ireland in 1864. The Exchequers were still distinct; and therefore, British and Irish Services have not had to be separated. Moreover, the series of printed "Finance Accounts" goes back to this period.

On the other hand, the Finance Accounts were apparently compiled on no consistent principle, and were unbalanced; indeed, they remained unbalanced accounts until 1822. Again, it has been found difficult to follow the adjustments which Mr. Chisholm made, and to reconcile his figures with those in the Finance Accounts, which, however inconsistent and imperfect they may have been, must have constituted the basis of the Accounts rendered to the Select Committee in 1864.

It is evident that adjustments were necessary, because, in the first place, certain payments made by Ireland, though constituting Receipts into the British Exchequer, were not Revenue proper; and in the second place, special account had to be taken of the collection expenses which were met out of Revenue in its progress to the British and Irish Exchequers, and to which, as such expenses formed part of the Joint Expenditure of the United Kingdom, the two countries had to contribute in their prescribed quotas. There were other, though less material, elements of complication with which Mr. Chisholm must have been confronted. The figures in Mr. Chisholm's adjusted accounts are the figures given in the Memorandum which I have already presented to the Royal Commissioners; and they are reproduced in Tables IV. and V. appended hereto, but in greater detail.

The adjustments which were made by him will best, and indeed can only, be followed by an illustration. I take as an example the year 1810-11, which presents fewer difficulties than some of the other years.

GREAT BRITAIN REVENUE.		
The *British Exchequer Receipts* in that year were		£ [illegible]
Mr. Chisholm made deductions from and additions to this figure.		
He deducted—		
(a) money repaid by Ireland in respect of interest on loans raised for the service of that country in Great Britain	£ 2,448,471	
(b) one-third of Lottery Profits in Great Britain remitted to Ireland	174,177	
		[illegible]
		[illegible]
He added—		
(a) charges of collection met out of Revenue in its progress to the Exchequer	[illegible]	
(b) other charges similarly met	[illegible]	
(c) receipts from Ireland on account of quotas of Joint Expenditure	1,273,333	
		[illegible]
Total *Revenue* as given in these Tables (No. IV.) and the Memorandum		[illegible]
GREAT BRITAIN EXPENDITURE.		
The *British Expenditure* in 1810-11, according to the Finance Accounts was		[illegible]
Mr. Chisholm added—		
(a) the charges for collecting Revenue *	[illegible]	
(b) a charge in respect of interest, &c. on the Portuguese Loan	[illegible]	
		[illegible]
		[illegible]
He deducted—		
(a) the amount repaid by Ireland in respect of interest on loans raised for the service of that country in Great Britain	2,448,471	
(b) a sum issued to pay off some 3 per cent. annuities	[illegible]	
		[illegible]
Total *Expenditure* as given in these Tables (No. IV.) and the Memorandum		[illegible]
IRELAND REVENUE.		
The *Irish Exchequer Receipts* in 1810-11 according to the *Finance Accounts* were, exclusive of Appropriated Duties (in Irish Currency)		[illegible]
To this Mr. Chisholm added—		
(a) charges of Collection met out of Revenue in its progress to the Exchequer		[illegible]
(b) other charges similarly met		[illegible]
Total *Revenue* (in Irish Currency)		[illegible]
which, when translated into British currency, corresponds with the total given in these Tables (No. V.) and the Memorandum		[illegible]

* [illegible] the collection expenses met out of Revenue in its progress to the Exchequer were included in the Expenditure side of the Finance Accounts, and therefore do not need to be added here in order to reconcile Mr. Chisholm's figures with the Finance Accounts.

IRISH EXPENDITURE.

				£
The Irish Expenditure in 1810-11, according to the Finance Accounts, was				10,[illegible],421
Mr. Chisholm added—			£	
(a) the charges for collecting Revenue			877,507	
(b) the other charges met out of Revenue in its progress to the Exchequer	£ 312,714			
Less amount given in the expenditure statements in the Finance Accounts	[illegible]			
			127,437	
				1,004,944
				11,[illegible],365
He deducted—				
(a) Issues from "Appropriated Duties"			21,814	
(b) principal of Exchequer Bills			341,[illegible]	
Total Expenditure (in Irish currency)				11,29[illegible],864
which, when translated into British currency, corresponds with the total given in these Tables (No. V.) and the Memorandum				10,425,0[illegible]

It is neither necessary, nor possible with any real advantage, to criticise, at this distance of time and without access to Mr. Chisholm's original papers, the adjustments which he made. But the broad result of them was to credit the British and Irish Exchequers with the total Revenue proper, and to debit them with the total Expenditure proper; and thus the Accounts for this period accord in principle with the Accounts relating to the third period.

As during the second period (1800-16) Great Britain and Ireland, though both subject to the laws of the United Kingdom, were for fiscal purposes separate countries, the Revenue credited to each Kingdom (so far as it resulted from the proceeds of taxes) represented the incidence of taxation on the inhabitants of the two countries.

THE FIRST PERIOD (1782-1800).

In dealing with this period we have to deal with a period in which the Public Accounts are scanty and defective. There were no Finance Accounts in those days such as might be expected to have been published and presented to the Parliaments of Great Britain and Ireland. The most authentic records in existence of the Public Revenue and Expenditure in Great Britain prior to this century are the original Yearly Revenue Books of the Treasury, now deposited in original at the Record Offices. From these books Mr. Chisholm was enabled to compile the well-known Return of Public Income and Expenditure, which was issued in 1869, and in it to produce properly balanced Accounts for each year from 1688. These Accounts, however, are Accounts of the Revenue which found its way into the British and Irish Exchequers, and of the Expenditure which was met out of money issued from those Exchequers. They are, in short, Exchequer Cash Accounts. Until, therefore, the present financial system, whereby all Revenue is paid into the Exchequer, and all charges met therefrom, was introduced in 1854, these Accounts exclude the Revenue which was applied to meet collection expenses and other charges before it reached the Exchequer, and they thus exclude the Expenditure which was provided for in that manner.

Though the books of the British Treasury relating to last century do to a certain extent give the cost of collection, yet Mr. Chisholm came to the conclusion, when he made his exhaustive research, that the entries were so imperfect that "any attempt to state the total "amount of gross (British) Revenue would only tend to "mislead." So far, therefore, as Great Britain is concerned, we have to be content, for the early period under view, with Table I., which reproduces the figures contained in the Return of 1869, and which, as those figures are confined to the net Revenue and Expenditure, is, in this respect, inconsistent with the tables relating to the subsequent periods. No. 366 of 1869. Part II. p. [illegible]

In Ireland, however, renewed research has been made; and in addition to Table II., which is likewise a reproduction of the Accounts contained in the Return of 1869, it has been found possible to extract from the printed accounts appended to the Irish Commons Journals and the original "Quarterly Books" an abstract of the total Revenue (that is, the total net Receipts, whether paid into the Exchequer or appropriated to meet Expenditure), and to give the charges of collection and other payments made out of the Revenue in its progress to the Exchequer.

The result of this additional information is set out in Table III., which is practically an account of the Irish Revenue and Expenditure for the 18 years preceding the Union, on the basis of the Accounts relating to the other two later periods.

R. W. [illegible]

H.M. Treasury,
[illegible] February [illegible].

[illegible]

[illegible]

[illegible]	[illegible]								[illegible]					[illegible]
	[illegible]	[illegible]	[illegible]	[illegible]	[illegible]	[illegible]	[illegible]	[illegible]	[illegible]	[illegible]	[illegible]	[illegible]	[illegible]	[illegible]
	£	£	£	£	£	£	£	£	£	£	£	£	£	£
[illegible]	[illegible]	[illegible]	[illegible]	[illegible]	—	[illegible]	[illegible]	[illegible]	[illegible]	[illegible]	[illegible]	[illegible]	[illegible]	[illegible]
[illegible]	[illegible]	[illegible]	[illegible]	[illegible]	—	[illegible]	[illegible]	[illegible]	[illegible]	[illegible]	[illegible]	[illegible]	[illegible]	[illegible]
[illegible]	[illegible]	[illegible]	[illegible]	[illegible]	—	[illegible]	[illegible]	[illegible]	[illegible]	[illegible]	[illegible]	[illegible]	[illegible]	[illegible]
[illegible]	[illegible]	[illegible]	[illegible]	[illegible]	—	[illegible]	[illegible]	[illegible]	[illegible]	[illegible]	[illegible]	[illegible]	[illegible]	[illegible]
[illegible]	[illegible]	[illegible]	[illegible]	[illegible]	—	[illegible]	[illegible]	[illegible]	[illegible]	[illegible]	[illegible]	[illegible]	[illegible]	[illegible]
[illegible]	[illegible]	[illegible]	[illegible]	[illegible]	—	[illegible]	[illegible]	[illegible]	[illegible]	[illegible]	[illegible]	[illegible]	[illegible]	[illegible]
[illegible]	[illegible]	[illegible]	[illegible]	[illegible]	—	[illegible]	[illegible]	[illegible]	[illegible]	[illegible]	[illegible]	[illegible]	[illegible]	[illegible]
[illegible]	[illegible]	[illegible]	[illegible]	[illegible]	—	[illegible]	[illegible]	[illegible]	[illegible]	[illegible]	[illegible]	[illegible]	[illegible]	[illegible]
[illegible]	[illegible]	[illegible]	[illegible]	[illegible]	—	[illegible]	[illegible]	[illegible]	[illegible]	[illegible]	[illegible]	[illegible]	[illegible]	[illegible]
[illegible]	[illegible]	[illegible]	[illegible]	[illegible]	—	[illegible]	[illegible]	[illegible]	[illegible]	[illegible]	[illegible]	[illegible]	[illegible]	[illegible]
[illegible]	[illegible]	[illegible]	[illegible]	[illegible]	—	[illegible]	[illegible]	[illegible]	[illegible]	[illegible]	[illegible]	[illegible]	[illegible]	[illegible]
[illegible]	[illegible]	[illegible]	[illegible]	[illegible]	—	[illegible]	[illegible]	[illegible]	[illegible]	[illegible]	[illegible]	[illegible]	[illegible]	[illegible]
[illegible]	[illegible]	[illegible]	[illegible]	[illegible]	—	[illegible]	[illegible]	[illegible]	[illegible]	[illegible]	[illegible]	[illegible]	[illegible]	[illegible]
[illegible]	[illegible]	[illegible]	[illegible]	[illegible]	—	[illegible]	[illegible]	[illegible]	[illegible]	[illegible]	[illegible]	[illegible]	[illegible]	[illegible]
[illegible]	[illegible]	[illegible]	[illegible]	[illegible]	—	[illegible]	[illegible]	[illegible]	[illegible]	[illegible]	[illegible]	[illegible]	[illegible]	[illegible]
[illegible]	[illegible]	[illegible]	[illegible]	[illegible]	—	[illegible]	[illegible]	[illegible]	[illegible]	[illegible]	[illegible]	[illegible]	[illegible]	[illegible]
[illegible]	[illegible]	[illegible]	[illegible]	[illegible]	[illegible]	[illegible]	[illegible]	[illegible]	[illegible]	[illegible]	[illegible]	[illegible]	[illegible]	[illegible]
[illegible]	[illegible]	[illegible]	[illegible]	[illegible]	[illegible]	[illegible]	[illegible]	[illegible]	[illegible]	[illegible]	[illegible]	[illegible]	[illegible]	[illegible]
[illegible]	[illegible]	[illegible]	[illegible]	[illegible]	[illegible]	[illegible]	[illegible]	[illegible]	[illegible]	[illegible]	[illegible]	[illegible]	[illegible]	[illegible]

TABLE III.—[illegible]

[illegible]

[illegible]

[illegible]

[illegible]

[illegible]

[illegible]

[illegible]					[illegible]									
					[illegible]			[illegible]						
[illegible]	[illegible]	[illegible]	[illegible]	[illegible]	[illegible]	[illegible]	[illegible]	[illegible]	[illegible]	[illegible]	[illegible]	[illegible]	[illegible]	[illegible]
[illegible]	[illegible]	[illegible]	[illegible]	[illegible]	[illegible]	[illegible]	[illegible]	[illegible]	[illegible]	[illegible]	[illegible]	[illegible]	[illegible]	[illegible]
[illegible]	[illegible]	[illegible]	[illegible]	[illegible]	[illegible]	[illegible]	[illegible]	[illegible]	[illegible]	[illegible]	[illegible]	[illegible]	[illegible]	[illegible]
[illegible]	[illegible]	[illegible]	[illegible]	[illegible]	[illegible]	[illegible]	[illegible]	[illegible]	[illegible]	[illegible]	[illegible]	[illegible]	[illegible]	[illegible]
[illegible]	[illegible]	[illegible]	[illegible]	[illegible]	[illegible]	[illegible]	[illegible]	[illegible]	[illegible]	[illegible]	[illegible]	[illegible]	[illegible]	[illegible]
[illegible]	[illegible]	[illegible]	[illegible]	[illegible]	[illegible]	[illegible]	[illegible]	[illegible]	[illegible]	[illegible]	[illegible]	[illegible]	[illegible]	[illegible]
[illegible]	[illegible]	[illegible]	[illegible]	[illegible]	[illegible]	[illegible]	[illegible]	[illegible]	[illegible]	[illegible]	[illegible]	[illegible]	[illegible]	[illegible]
[illegible]	[illegible]	[illegible]	[illegible]	[illegible]	[illegible]	[illegible]	[illegible]	[illegible]	[illegible]	[illegible]	[illegible]	[illegible]	[illegible]	[illegible]
[illegible]	[illegible]	[illegible]	[illegible]	[illegible]	[illegible]	[illegible]	[illegible]	[illegible]	[illegible]	[illegible]	[illegible]	[illegible]	[illegible]	[illegible]
[illegible]	[illegible]	[illegible]	[illegible]	[illegible]	[illegible]	[illegible]	[illegible]	[illegible]	[illegible]	[illegible]	[illegible]	[illegible]	[illegible]	[illegible]
[illegible]	[illegible]	[illegible]	[illegible]	[illegible]	[illegible]	[illegible]	[illegible]	[illegible]	[illegible]	[illegible]	[illegible]	[illegible]	[illegible]	[illegible]
[illegible]	[illegible]	[illegible]	[illegible]	[illegible]	[illegible]	[illegible]	[illegible]	[illegible]	[illegible]	[illegible]	[illegible]	[illegible]	[illegible]	[illegible]
[illegible]	[illegible]	[illegible]	[illegible]	[illegible]	[illegible]	[illegible]	[illegible]	[illegible]	[illegible]	[illegible]	[illegible]	[illegible]	[illegible]	[illegible]
[illegible]	[illegible]	[illegible]	[illegible]	[illegible]	[illegible]	[illegible]	[illegible]	[illegible]	[illegible]	[illegible]	[illegible]	[illegible]	[illegible]	[illegible]
[illegible]	[illegible]	[illegible]	[illegible]	[illegible]	[illegible]	[illegible]	[illegible]	[illegible]	[illegible]	[illegible]	[illegible]	[illegible]	[illegible]	[illegible]
[illegible]	[illegible]	[illegible]	[illegible]	[illegible]	[illegible]	[illegible]	[illegible]	[illegible]	[illegible]	[illegible]	[illegible]	[illegible]	[illegible]	[illegible]
[illegible]	[illegible]	[illegible]	[illegible]	[illegible]	[illegible]	[illegible]	[illegible]	[illegible]	[illegible]	[illegible]	[illegible]	[illegible]	[illegible]	[illegible]

THIRD PERIOD (1817–1893-4.)

TABLE VI.—Showing the Revenue (Net Receipts) collected by Imperial Officers in Great Britain, exclusive of Imperial Receipts, quinquennially from 1819 to 1889-90, and annually thereafter to 1893-4 inclusive.

Year.	Taxes on Commodities.			Other Taxes.					Total Tax Revenue.	Non-Tax Revenue.	Total Revenue as Collected.
	Customs. 1.	Excise. 2.	Total. 3.	[illegible] 4.	Stamps. 5.	Land and Assessed Taxes. 6.	Property and Income Tax. 7.	Total. 8.	9.	10.	11.
	£	£	£	£	£	£	£	£	£	£	£
[illegible]	[illegible]	[illegible]	[illegible]	[illegible]	[illegible]	[illegible]	—	[illegible]	[illegible]	[illegible]	[illegible]
[illegible]	[illegible]	[illegible]	[illegible]	[illegible]	[illegible]	[illegible]	—	[illegible]	[illegible]	[illegible]	[illegible]
[illegible]	[illegible]	[illegible]	[illegible]	[illegible]	[illegible]	[illegible]	—	[illegible]	[illegible]	[illegible]	[illegible]
[illegible]	[illegible]	[illegible]	[illegible]	[illegible]	[illegible]	[illegible]	—	[illegible]	[illegible]	[illegible]	[illegible]
[illegible]	[illegible]	[illegible]	[illegible]	[illegible]	[illegible]	[illegible]	—	[illegible]	[illegible]	[illegible]	[illegible]
[illegible]	[illegible]	[illegible]	[illegible]	[illegible]	[illegible]	[illegible]	[illegible]	[illegible]	[illegible]	[illegible]	[illegible]
[illegible]	[illegible]	[illegible]	[illegible]	[illegible]	[illegible]	[illegible]	[illegible]	[illegible]	[illegible]	[illegible]	[illegible]
[illegible]	[illegible]	[illegible]	[illegible]	[illegible]	[illegible]	[illegible]	[illegible]	[illegible]	[illegible]	[illegible]	[illegible]
[illegible]	[illegible]	[illegible]	[illegible]	[illegible]	[illegible]	[illegible]	[illegible]	[illegible]	[illegible]	[illegible]	[illegible]
[illegible]	[illegible]	[illegible]	[illegible]	[illegible]	[illegible]	[illegible]	[illegible]	[illegible]	[illegible]	[illegible]	[illegible]
[illegible]	[illegible]	[illegible]	[illegible]	[illegible]	[illegible]	[illegible]	[illegible]	[illegible]	[illegible]	[illegible]	[illegible]
[illegible]	[illegible]	[illegible]	[illegible]	[illegible]	[illegible]	[illegible]	[illegible]	[illegible]	[illegible]	[illegible]	[illegible]
[illegible]	[illegible]	[illegible]	[illegible]	[illegible]	[illegible]	[illegible]	[illegible]	[illegible]	[illegible]	[illegible]	[illegible]
[illegible]	[illegible]	[illegible]	[illegible]	[illegible]	[illegible]	[illegible]	[illegible]	[illegible]	[illegible]	[illegible]	[illegible]
[illegible]	[illegible]	[illegible]	[illegible]	[illegible]	[illegible]	[illegible]	[illegible]	[illegible]	[illegible]	[illegible]	[illegible]
[illegible]	[illegible]	[illegible]	[illegible]	[illegible]	[illegible]	[illegible]	[illegible]	[illegible]	[illegible]	[illegible]	[illegible]
[illegible]	[illegible]	[illegible]	[illegible]	[illegible]	[illegible]	[illegible]	[illegible]	[illegible]	[illegible]	[illegible]	[illegible]
[illegible]	[illegible]	[illegible]	[illegible]	[illegible]	[illegible]	[illegible]	[illegible]	[illegible]	[illegible]	[illegible]	[illegible]
[illegible]	[illegible]	[illegible]	[illegible]	[illegible]	[illegible]	[illegible]	[illegible]	[illegible]	[illegible]	[illegible]	[illegible]

TABLE VII.—Showing the Revenue (Net Receipts) as collected by Imperial Officers in Ireland, exclusive of Imperial Receipts, quinquennially from 1819 to 1889-90, and annually thereafter to 1893-94 inclusive.

Year.	Taxes on Commodities.			Other Taxes.					Total Tax Revenue.	Non-Tax Revenue.	Appropriated Duties.	Total Revenue as Collected.
	Customs. 1.	Excise. 2.	Total. 3.	[illegible] 4.	Stamps. 5.	Land and Assessed Taxes. 6.	Property and Income Tax. 7.	Total. 8.	9.	10.	11.	12.
	£	£	£	£	£	£	£	£	£	£	£	£
[illegible]	[illegible]	[illegible]	[illegible]	[illegible]	[illegible]	[illegible]	—	[illegible]	[illegible]	[illegible]	[illegible]	[illegible]
[illegible]	[illegible]	[illegible]	[illegible]	[illegible]	[illegible]	[illegible]	—	[illegible]	[illegible]	[illegible]	—	[illegible]
[illegible]	[illegible]	[illegible]	[illegible]	[illegible]	[illegible]	—	—	[illegible]	[illegible]	[illegible]	—	[illegible]
[illegible]	[illegible]	[illegible]	[illegible]	[illegible]	[illegible]	—	—	[illegible]	[illegible]	[illegible]	—	[illegible]
[illegible]	[illegible]	[illegible]	[illegible]	[illegible]	[illegible]	—	—	[illegible]	[illegible]	[illegible]	—	[illegible]
[illegible]	[illegible]	[illegible]	[illegible]	[illegible]	[illegible]	—	—	[illegible]	[illegible]	[illegible]	—	[illegible]
[illegible]	[illegible]	[illegible]	[illegible]	[illegible]	[illegible]	—	—	[illegible]	[illegible]	[illegible]	—	[illegible]
[illegible]	[illegible]	[illegible]	[illegible]	[illegible]	[illegible]	—	[illegible]	[illegible]	[illegible]	[illegible]	—	[illegible]
[illegible]	[illegible]	[illegible]	[illegible]	[illegible]	[illegible]	—	[illegible]	[illegible]	[illegible]	[illegible]	—	[illegible]
[illegible]	[illegible]	[illegible]	[illegible]	[illegible]	[illegible]	—	[illegible]	[illegible]	[illegible]	[illegible]	—	[illegible]
[illegible]	[illegible]	[illegible]	[illegible]	[illegible]	[illegible]	—	[illegible]	[illegible]	[illegible]	[illegible]	—	[illegible]
[illegible]	[illegible]	[illegible]	[illegible]	[illegible]	[illegible]	—	[illegible]	[illegible]	[illegible]	[illegible]	—	[illegible]
[illegible]	[illegible]	[illegible]	[illegible]	[illegible]	[illegible]	—	[illegible]	[illegible]	[illegible]	[illegible]	—	[illegible]
[illegible]	[illegible]	[illegible]	[illegible]	[illegible]	[illegible]	—	[illegible]	[illegible]	[illegible]	[illegible]	—	[illegible]
[illegible]	[illegible]	[illegible]	[illegible]	[illegible]	[illegible]	—	[illegible]	[illegible]	[illegible]	[illegible]	—	[illegible]
[illegible]	[illegible]	[illegible]	[illegible]	[illegible]	[illegible]	—	[illegible]	[illegible]	[illegible]	[illegible]	—	[illegible]
[illegible]	[illegible]	[illegible]	[illegible]	[illegible]	[illegible]	—	[illegible]	[illegible]	[illegible]	[illegible]	—	[illegible]
[illegible]	[illegible]	[illegible]	[illegible]	[illegible]	[illegible]	—	[illegible]	[illegible]	[illegible]	[illegible]	—	[illegible]
[illegible]	[illegible]	[illegible]	[illegible]	[illegible]	[illegible]	—	[illegible]	[illegible]	[illegible]	[illegible]	—	[illegible]

TABLE VIII.—Showing the TOTAL REVENUE as collected by IMPERIAL OFFICERS in the UNITED KINGDOM, inclusive of IMPERIAL REVENUE, quinquennially from 1819 to 1869–70, and annually thenceforward to 1893–94, inclusive.

Year.	Imperial Receipts. Collected in Great Britain. 1.	Imperial Receipts. Collected in Ireland. 2.	Imperial Receipts. Total. 3.	Revenue as given in Tables VI. and VII. Great Britain. 4.	Revenue as given in Tables VI. and VII. Ireland. 5.	Revenue as given in Tables VI. and VII. Total. 6.	Total Revenue as collected. Great Britain. 7.	Total Revenue as collected. Ireland. 8.	Total Revenue as collected. Total, United Kingdom. 9.
	£	£	£	£	£	£	£	£	£
1819 to 5th Jan. 1820	[illegible]	[illegible]	[illegible]	[illegible]	[illegible]	[illegible]	[illegible]	[illegible]	[illegible]
1824 " " 1825	[illegible]	[illegible]	[illegible]	[illegible]	[illegible]	[illegible]	[illegible]	[illegible]	[illegible]
1829 " " 1830	[illegible]	[illegible]	[illegible]	[illegible]	[illegible]	[illegible]	[illegible]	[illegible]	[illegible]
1834 " " 1835	[illegible]	—	[illegible]	[illegible]	[illegible]	[illegible]	[illegible]	[illegible]	[illegible]
1839 " " 1840	[illegible]	—	[illegible]	[illegible]	[illegible]	[illegible]	[illegible]	[illegible]	[illegible]
1844 " " 1845	[illegible]	—	[illegible]	[illegible]	[illegible]	[illegible]	[illegible]	[illegible]	[illegible]
1849 " " 1850	[illegible]	—	[illegible]	[illegible]	[illegible]	[illegible]	[illegible]	[illegible]	[illegible]
1854–55 to 31 Mar. 1855	[illegible]	—	[illegible]	[illegible]	[illegible]	[illegible]	[illegible]	[illegible]	[illegible]
1859–60 " " 1860	[illegible]	—	[illegible]	[illegible]	[illegible]	[illegible]	[illegible]	[illegible]	[illegible]
1864–65 " " 1865	[illegible]	—	[illegible]	[illegible]	[illegible]	[illegible]	[illegible]	[illegible]	[illegible]
1869–70 " " 1870	[illegible]	—	[illegible]	[illegible]	[illegible]	[illegible]	[illegible]	[illegible]	[illegible]
1874–75 " " 1875	[illegible]	—	[illegible]	[illegible]	[illegible]	[illegible]	[illegible]	[illegible]	[illegible]
1879–80 " " 1880	[illegible]	—	[illegible]	[illegible]	[illegible]	[illegible]	[illegible]	[illegible]	[illegible]
1884–85 " " 1885	[illegible]	—	[illegible]	[illegible]	[illegible]	[illegible]	[illegible]	[illegible]	[illegible]
1889–90 " " 1890	[illegible]	—	[illegible]	[illegible]	[illegible]	[illegible]	[illegible]	[illegible]	[illegible]
1890–91 " " 1891	[illegible]	—	[illegible]	[illegible]	[illegible]	[illegible]	[illegible]	[illegible]	[illegible]
1891–92 " " 1892	[illegible]	—	[illegible]	[illegible]	[illegible]	[illegible]	[illegible]	[illegible]	[illegible]
1892–93 " " 1893	[illegible]	—	[illegible]	[illegible]	[illegible]	[illegible]	[illegible]	[illegible]	[illegible]
1893–94 " " 1894	[illegible]	—	[illegible]	[illegible]	[illegible]	[illegible]	[illegible]	[illegible]	[illegible]

* Exclusive of [illegible] repayment of Loan to [illegible]. † Including [illegible].

NOTES.

1. The figures of the last five years include, as explained in the remarks prefixed to the Tables, the amounts of Revenue which is assigned to local authorities, but which continues to be collected by Imperial officers.

2. It may be observed that the figures in column 9 of Table VIII., giving the total Revenue as collected in the United Kingdom, do not all tally with the figures given in Table I. of Part III. of the Memorandum (pp. 29 and 30) already presented to the Royal Commissioners. The differences proceed from the fact that the figures in that Memorandum were simply taken from the annual Finance Accounts, &c., without alteration; whereas the figures in this Table have necessarily been subject to adjustments in order to secure uniformity of treatment.

In most of the years reviewed, the discrepancies are immaterial, and cannot affect any inferences that may be drawn from the Revenues respectively collected in the two countries. But there are three years, viz., 1874–5, 1879–80, and 1884–5, in which the discrepancies are considerable, as will be seen by the following comparison:—

Year.	Totals in Memorandum previously presented.	Totals in Table VIII. above.	Less than Figures in Memorandum.
	£	£	£
1874–5	[illegible]	[illegible]	[illegible]
1879–80	[illegible]	[illegible]	[illegible]
1884–5	[illegible]	[illegible]	[illegible]

These discrepancies are almost wholly due to one cause, and the explanation is this: Previously to 1874–5 all receipts in respect of local loans were credited indiscriminately to the exchequer balances. In 1874 the interest was separated from the principal repaid, and, being properly considered as income, was credited to Revenue. In 1887 the Local Loans Fund was established, and thenceforward all receipts in respect of loans were carried to the credit of that fund. Accordingly, in these Tables, which have been framed on an uniform basis as far as possible, it has been necessary to exclude the temporary appropriation of interest on loans as Revenue between 1874–5 and 1887–8.

TABLE 16.—Showing the Expenditure of the United Kingdom, [illegible]

[illegible]

[illegible]

TABLE [illegible].—Showing the Distribution of the [illegible], &c.—continued.

[illegible]

[illegible]

[illegible]

[illegible]	[illegible]				[illegible]				[illegible]			
	[illegible]	[illegible]	[illegible]	[illegible]	[illegible]	[illegible]	[illegible]	[illegible]	[illegible]	[illegible]	[illegible]	[illegible]
	[illegible]	[illegible]	[illegible]	[illegible]	[illegible]	[illegible]	[illegible]	[illegible]	[illegible]	[illegible]	[illegible]	[illegible]
[illegible]	[illegible]	—	—	[illegible]	[illegible]	[illegible]	—	[illegible]	[illegible]	[illegible]	—	[illegible]
[illegible]												
[illegible]	[illegible]	—	—	[illegible]	[illegible]	—	[illegible]	[illegible]	[illegible]	—	[illegible]	[illegible]
[illegible]	[illegible]	—	—	[illegible]	[illegible]	—	[illegible]	[illegible]	[illegible]	—	[illegible]	[illegible]
[illegible]												
[illegible]	[illegible]	[illegible]	[illegible]	[illegible]	[illegible]	[illegible]	[illegible]	[illegible]	[illegible]	[illegible]	[illegible]	[illegible]
[illegible]	[illegible]	[illegible]	[illegible]	[illegible]	[illegible]	[illegible]	[illegible]	[illegible]	[illegible]	[illegible]	[illegible]	[illegible]
[illegible]	—	[illegible]	[illegible]	[illegible]	[illegible]	[illegible]	[illegible]	[illegible]	—	[illegible]	[illegible]	[illegible]
[illegible]	[illegible]	[illegible]	[illegible]	[illegible]	[illegible]	[illegible]	[illegible]	[illegible]	[illegible]	[illegible]	[illegible]	[illegible]
[illegible]	—	[illegible]	[illegible]	[illegible]	[illegible]	[illegible]	[illegible]	[illegible]	—	[illegible]	[illegible]	[illegible]
[illegible]	[illegible]	[illegible]	[illegible]	[illegible]	[illegible]	[illegible]	[illegible]	[illegible]	[illegible]	[illegible]	[illegible]	[illegible]
[illegible]	[illegible]	—	—	[illegible]	[illegible]	—	—	—	[illegible]	—	[illegible]	[illegible]
[illegible]	[illegible]	[illegible]	[illegible]	[illegible]	[illegible]	[illegible]	[illegible]	[illegible]	[illegible]	[illegible]	[illegible]	[illegible]

[illegible]

C.—Tables relating to the Funded and Unfunded Debt of Great Britain and Ireland during the period 1782–83 to 1816–17.

The following Tables, Nos. I. and II., show the nominal amount of the Funded and Unfunded Debt of Great Britain and Ireland respectively at the end of each financial year from 1782–83 to 1816–17; and Table No. III. shows the nominal amount of the Funded and Unfunded Debt in the United Kingdom at the end of each financial year from 1816–17 to 1835–36, inclusive.

The amount of the Funded Debt has been taken from Parliamentary Paper No. 366 of 1869, Part II., pp. 304–306, and Parliamentary Paper No. C.–6539 of 1891, pp. 72–77 and pp. 140–153.

The amount of the Unfunded Debt has been obtained from the original English and Irish records.

It will be observed that in the Tables included in this Appendix no account is taken of the Terminable Annuities. This omission is unavoidable, inasmuch as the calculation of their capital value in the years covered by the Tables has never, as yet, been attempted.

The state of the entire Debt of the United Kingdom from the year 1835–36, inclusive, down to the present time is fully given in Parliamentary Paper No. 312 of 1894; and it is therefore unnecessary to reproduce the figures here.

H.M. Treasury,
2nd January 1896.

E. W. HAMILTON.

Table No. 1.

Unfunded Debt.—Great Britain.

Amount outstanding at the end of each Financial Year from 10th October 1782 to 5th January 1817.

Years ended	Exchequer Bills. For Supply.	Exchequer Bills. In anticipation of Taxes and Duties.	Exchequer Bills. For Miscellaneous purposes.	Exchequer Bills. Total.	Navy Bills.	Ordnance Debentures.	Total Unfunded Debt.	Increase (+) or Decrease (−) in the Year.
10th October and 31st December—	£	£	£	£	£	£	£	£
1782	[illegible]	[illegible]	[illegible]	[illegible]	[illegible]	—	[illegible]	—
1783	[illegible]	[illegible]	[illegible]	[illegible]	[illegible]	—	[illegible]	[illegible]
1784	[illegible]	[illegible]	[illegible]	[illegible]	[illegible]	—	[illegible]	[illegible]
1785	[illegible]	[illegible]	[illegible]	[illegible]	[illegible]	—	[illegible]	[illegible]
1786	[illegible]	[illegible]	[illegible]	[illegible]	[illegible]	—	[illegible]	[illegible]
1787	[illegible]	[illegible]	[illegible]	[illegible]	[illegible]	[illegible]	[illegible]	[illegible]
1788	[illegible]	[illegible]	[illegible]	[illegible]	[illegible]	—	[illegible]	[illegible]
1789	[illegible]	[illegible]	[illegible]	[illegible]	[illegible]	[illegible]	[illegible]	[illegible]
1790	[illegible]	[illegible]	[illegible]	[illegible]	[illegible]	[illegible]	[illegible]	[illegible]
1791	[illegible]	[illegible]	[illegible]	[illegible]	[illegible]	—	[illegible]	[illegible]
1792	[illegible]	[illegible]	—	[illegible]	[illegible]	[illegible]	[illegible]	[illegible]
1793	[illegible]	[illegible]	[illegible]	[illegible]	[illegible]	[illegible]	[illegible]	[illegible]
1794	[illegible]	[illegible]	—	[illegible]	[illegible]	[illegible]	[illegible]	[illegible]
1795	[illegible]	[illegible]	[illegible]	[illegible]	[illegible]	[illegible]	[illegible]	[illegible]
1796	[illegible]	[illegible]	[illegible]	[illegible]	†	†	[illegible]	[illegible]
1797	[illegible]	[illegible]	[illegible]	[illegible]	—	—	[illegible]	[illegible]
1798	[illegible]	[illegible]	[illegible]	[illegible]	—	—	[illegible]	[illegible]
1799	[illegible]	[illegible]	[illegible]	[illegible]	—	—	[illegible]	[illegible]
Quarter to 5th January—								
1800	[illegible]	[illegible]	[illegible]	[illegible]	—	—	[illegible]	[illegible]
Year to 5th January—								
1801	[illegible]	[illegible]	—	[illegible]	—	—	[illegible]	[illegible]
1802	[illegible]	[illegible]	—	[illegible]	—	—	[illegible]	[illegible]
1803	[illegible]	[illegible]	—	[illegible]	—	—	[illegible]	[illegible]
1804	[illegible]	[illegible]	—	[illegible]	—	—	[illegible]	[illegible]
1805	[illegible]	[illegible]	—	[illegible]	—	—	[illegible]	[illegible]
1806	[illegible]	[illegible]	—	[illegible]	—	—	[illegible]	[illegible]
1807	[illegible]	[illegible]	—	[illegible]	—	—	[illegible]	[illegible]
1808	[illegible]	[illegible]	—	[illegible]	—	—	[illegible]	[illegible]
1809	[illegible]	[illegible]	—	[illegible]	—	—	[illegible]	[illegible]
1810	[illegible]	[illegible]	—	[illegible]	—	—	[illegible]	[illegible]
1811	[illegible]	[illegible]	—	[illegible]	—	—	[illegible]	[illegible]
1812	[illegible]	[illegible]	[illegible]	[illegible]	—	—	[illegible]	[illegible]
1813	[illegible]	[illegible]	—	[illegible]	—	—	[illegible]	[illegible]
1814	[illegible]	[illegible]	*[illegible]	[illegible]	—	—	[illegible]	[illegible]
1815	[illegible]	[illegible]	*[illegible]	[illegible]	—	—	[illegible]	[illegible]
1816	[illegible]	[illegible]	*[illegible]	[illegible]	—	—	[illegible]	[illegible]
1817	[illegible]	[illegible]	—	[illegible]	—	—	[illegible]	[illegible]

* Exchequer debentures issued under Acts 55 Geo. III. cc. 61 and 62.

† On the 31st December 1796 nearly the whole of the outstanding Navy Bills had been funded, and, as under the Act 37 Geo. III. c. 26, passed on 26th December 1796, the character of the Navy Bills was changed by limiting their currency to three calendar months, they have not been treated as forming part of the unfunded debt from that date. Ordnance debentures, being somewhat of the same nature as Navy Bills, have been similarly dealt with.

Funded and Unfunded Debt of Great Britain and Ireland.

Amount outstanding at the end of each Financial Year from [illegible] to 1816–17 Inclusive.

Year.	Great Britain.				Ireland.				Grand Total.
	Funded Debt.	Unfunded Debt.*	Total.	Increase (+) or Decrease (−) in the Year.	Funded Debt.	Unfunded Debt.†	Total.	Increase (+) or Decrease (−) in the Year.	
	£	£	£	£	£	£	£	£	£
[illegible]	[illegible]	[illegible]	[illegible]	—	[illegible]	[illegible]	[illegible]	—	[illegible]
[illegible]	[illegible]	[illegible]	[illegible]	[illegible]	[illegible]	[illegible]	[illegible]	[illegible]	[illegible]
[illegible]	[illegible]	[illegible]	[illegible]	[illegible]	[illegible]	[illegible]	[illegible]	[illegible]	[illegible]
[illegible]	[illegible]	[illegible]	[illegible]	[illegible]	[illegible]	[illegible]	[illegible]	[illegible]	[illegible]
[illegible]	[illegible]	[illegible]	[illegible]	[illegible]	[illegible]	[illegible]	[illegible]	[illegible]	[illegible]
[illegible]	[illegible]	[illegible]	[illegible]	[illegible]	[illegible]	[illegible]	[illegible]	[illegible]	[illegible]
[illegible]	[illegible]	[illegible]	[illegible]	[illegible]	[illegible]	[illegible]	[illegible]	—	[illegible]
[illegible]	[illegible]	[illegible]	[illegible]	[illegible]	[illegible]	[illegible]	[illegible]	—	[illegible]
[illegible]	[illegible]	[illegible]	[illegible]	[illegible]	[illegible]	[illegible]	[illegible]	—	[illegible]
[illegible]	[illegible]	[illegible]	[illegible]	[illegible]	[illegible]	[illegible]	[illegible]	—	[illegible]
[illegible]	[illegible]	[illegible]	[illegible]	[illegible]	[illegible]	[illegible]	[illegible]	[illegible]	[illegible]
[illegible]	[illegible]	[illegible]	[illegible]	[illegible]	[illegible]	[illegible]	[illegible]	[illegible]	[illegible]
[illegible]	[illegible]	[illegible]	[illegible]	[illegible]	[illegible]	[illegible]	[illegible]	[illegible]	[illegible]
[illegible]	[illegible]	[illegible]	[illegible]	[illegible]	[illegible]	[illegible]	[illegible]	[illegible]	[illegible]
[illegible]	[illegible]	[illegible]	[illegible]	[illegible]	[illegible]	[illegible]	[illegible]	[illegible]	[illegible]
[illegible]	[illegible]	[illegible]	[illegible]	[illegible]	[illegible]	[illegible]	[illegible]	[illegible]	[illegible]
[illegible]	[illegible]	[illegible]	[illegible]	[illegible]	[illegible]	[illegible]	[illegible]	[illegible]	[illegible]
[illegible]	[illegible]	[illegible]	[illegible]	[illegible]	[illegible]	[illegible]	[illegible]	[illegible]	[illegible]
[illegible]	[illegible]	[illegible]	[illegible]	[illegible]	[illegible]	[illegible]	[illegible]	[illegible]	[illegible]
Aggregate Increase in the period from [illegible] to [illegible]	[illegible]	[illegible]	[illegible]	—	[illegible]	[illegible]	[illegible]	—	[illegible]
[illegible]	[illegible]	[illegible]	[illegible]	[illegible]	[illegible]	[illegible]	[illegible]	[illegible]	[illegible]
[illegible]	[illegible]	[illegible]	[illegible]	[illegible]	[illegible]	[illegible]	[illegible]	[illegible]	[illegible]
[illegible]	[illegible]	[illegible]	[illegible]	[illegible]	[illegible]	[illegible]	[illegible]	[illegible]	[illegible]
[illegible]	[illegible]	[illegible]	[illegible]	[illegible]	[illegible]	[illegible]	[illegible]	[illegible]	[illegible]
[illegible]	[illegible]	[illegible]	[illegible]	[illegible]	[illegible]	[illegible]	[illegible]	[illegible]	[illegible]
[illegible]	[illegible]	[illegible]	[illegible]	[illegible]	[illegible]	—	[illegible]	[illegible]	[illegible]
[illegible]	[illegible]	[illegible]	[illegible]	[illegible]	[illegible]	[illegible]	[illegible]	[illegible]	[illegible]
[illegible]	[illegible]	[illegible]	[illegible]	[illegible]	[illegible]	[illegible]	[illegible]	[illegible]	[illegible]
[illegible]	[illegible]	[illegible]	[illegible]	[illegible]	[illegible]	[illegible]	[illegible]	[illegible]	[illegible]
[illegible]	[illegible]	[illegible]	[illegible]	[illegible]	[illegible]	[illegible]	[illegible]	[illegible]	[illegible]
[illegible]	[illegible]	[illegible]	[illegible]	[illegible]	[illegible]	[illegible]	[illegible]	[illegible]	[illegible]
[illegible]	[illegible]	[illegible]	[illegible]	[illegible]	[illegible]	[illegible]	[illegible]	[illegible]	[illegible]
[illegible]	[illegible]	[illegible]	[illegible]	[illegible]	[illegible]	[illegible]	[illegible]	[illegible]	[illegible]
[illegible]	[illegible]	[illegible]	[illegible]	[illegible]	[illegible]	[illegible]	[illegible]	[illegible]	[illegible]
[illegible]	[illegible]	[illegible]	[illegible]	[illegible]	[illegible]	[illegible]	[illegible]	[illegible]	[illegible]
1816–7	[illegible]	[illegible]	[illegible]	[illegible]	[illegible]	[illegible]	[illegible]	[illegible]	[illegible]
Aggregate Increase in the period from [illegible] to [illegible]	[illegible]	[illegible]	[illegible]	—	[illegible]	[illegible]	[illegible]	—	[illegible]

* For details of the Unfunded Debt of Great Britain, see Table No. 1.
† Irish Treasury Bills.
‡ Includes a loan of [illegible], in Stock which, though charged on Great Britain, was raised for Ireland in 1813.

TABLE No. III.

Funded and Unfunded Debt of the United Kingdom.

AMOUNT OUTSTANDING at the end of each FINANCIAL YEAR from 1816–7 to 1835–6 INCLUSIVE.

YEAR.	Funded Debt.	Unfunded Debt.	Total.	Increase (+) or Decrease (−) in the Year.
	£	£	£	£
1816–7	800,280,327	40,827,915	850,107,242	—
1817–8	780,631,391	62,641,304	843,272,695	− 6,834,547
1818–9	796,604,651	45,161,350	844,766,001	+ 1,493,306
1819–20	798,833,221	45,194,800	846,770,021	+ 1,062,030
1820–1	804,913,982	33,364,350	838,278,332	− 8,450,689
1821–2	798,463,711	32,670,731	831,134,442	− 7,143,890
1822–3	797,376,319	36,248,000	833,625,319	+ 2,490,877
1823–4	792,651,071	34,710,400	827,361,471	− 6,063,746
1824–5	782,207,268	37,968,200	820,175,468	− 7,486,006
1825–6	779,795,110	31,960,950	811,256,060	− 8,918,603
1826–7	785,011,063	25,131,650	810,142,713	− 1,054,127
1827–8	778,743,097	28,121,200	806,864,297	− 3,277,966
1828–9	773,680,417	27,841,000	801,447,417	− 5,307,880
1829–30	772,607,235	25,515,850	798,123,176	− 3,344,241
1830–1	758,880,804	27,285,250	786,166,054	− 11,957,122
1831–2	756,984,117	27,141,050	784,125,167	− 2,030,887
1832–3	755,601,330	27,805,800	783,400,630	− 724,528
1833–4	753,235,754	28,038,746	781,273,500	− 2,131,139
1834–5	745,226,616	29,227,351	774,453,967	− 6,424,633
1835–6	760,294,551	30,082,585	790,377,139	+ 15,923,272
Net Decrease in the period from 1816–7 to 1835–6	39,944,775	19,785,330	59,730,105	—

APPENDIX II.

A.—MEMORANDUM presented to the COMMISSION by Mr. MURROUGH O'BRIEN, in connection with the EVIDENCE given by HIM before the COMMISSION.

Irishmen have never ceased to protest against the fiscal arrangements imposed upon their country at the time of the Union. The exceptions recorded in Ireland's complaints and protests illustrate Burke's remark, that "when any community is subordinately connected "with another, the great danger of the connection is the "extreme pride and self-complacency of the superior, "which in all matters of controversy will probably "decide in its own favour."

At the Union, Ireland's contribution to the Imperial revenue was fixed at 2/17ths of the whole, in spite of the remonstrances of a large proportion of the Irish Lords and Commons.

A number of Irish peers, Foster, Grattan, and other prominent opponents of the Union, demonstrated the inability of Ireland to bear such a charge, and that in an united Parliament 100 Irish members would be powerless to protect Irish interests.

This forecast was justified; Ireland was unable, as had been foreseen, to meet the charge imposed on her, and her deficit was made up by annual borrowings on her account, until, the Irish debt having quadrupled while that of Great Britain had only doubled, the Exchequers of the two countries were consolidated in 1817.

In 1800, Great Britain's debt per head was 42l., Ireland's 3l. 13s. Ireland's pre-Union debt was less than 1/16th part of the total debt of the two kingdoms; after 17 years of British management it had risen to between 1/8th and 1/7th. Several select committees failed to disentangle the public accounts of this period; but it is clear that they were neither honest nor kept in accordance with the Treaty of Union, and it is more than probable that, in addition to the fiscal burden in excess of her capacity laid upon her, Ireland was improperly charged with loans which should have been debited to the two countries jointly. At any rate, Ireland, as foreseen by those who had the best means of forming an opinion, became bankrupt in 17 years. Taxation raised to the highest possible rate did not meet the charges laid on her.

Since the amalgamation of the Exchequers in 1817, the taxation of the two countries has been gradually assimilated, and with a few trifling exceptions, identical taxation now prevails throughout the United Kingdom. But indiscriminate taxation does not, and identical taxes do not, necessarily mean equality of taxation between two countries differing in their economic circumstances and social condition.

Ireland's complaint is that she is unequally taxed, having regard to her comparative capacity to bear taxation, and to the services which she obtains in return for the taxes she pays. Her financial position is as if a person with 20l. a year had to keep up an establishment in forced partnership with, on the same scale, and in the same style as another person with 10,000l. a year, contributing a proportion of every outlay the richer partner chose to make. The scaled expenditure that would amply suffice for all the necessities of the first, if living independently, would be ruinously insufficient for the same person in such a partnership. Comparison of Great Britain's and Ireland's economic position.

A D 4

Ireland, the poorest and least progressive country in civilised Europe, the only one whose population has for 40 years been continually diminishing, is fiscally linked with the richest country in the world. She is taxed and her revenue is spent as if she were an integral part of Great Britain, although her circumstances, her economic and social condition, and her needs, are wholly different.

The 7th Article of the Treaty of Union provided that after 20 years the just proportion of contribution to the revenue by each country was to be ascertained (as an alternative to other methods which are not applicable) by a comparison of the income of each country from the produce of a general tax, if such had been imposed. No such tax existed until 1853, when the income tax was extended to Ireland; and if her contribution was fixed upon that basis, Ireland would now be paying four millions instead of eight millions—one twenty-fourth instead of one-twelfth of the Imperial revenue.

Parliamentary Paper 329/'91 presents the Treasury view of the financial relations of the three kingdoms, and the Treasury's conclusions as to the respective contributions of each country. The following table is taken from this paper, the first published of the series:— "Financial Relations" Papers.

Summary for Three Years—Amounts and Percentages.

	England.			Scotland.			Ireland.		
—	[illegible]	[illegible]	[illegible]	[illegible]	[illegible]	[illegible]	[illegible]	[illegible]	[illegible]
Amount	£ [illegible]	£ [illegible]	£ [illegible]	£ [illegible]	£ [illegible]	£ [illegible]	£ [illegible]	£ [illegible]	£ [illegible]
Total revenue contributed by the three kingdoms.	Per cent. [illegible]	Per cent. [illegible]	Per cent. [illegible]	Per cent. [illegible]	Per cent. [illegible]	Per cent. [illegible]	Per cent. [illegible]	Per cent. [illegible]	Per cent. [illegible]
Amount	£ [illegible]	£ [illegible]	£ [illegible]	£ [illegible]	£ [illegible]	£ [illegible]	£ [illegible]	£ [illegible]	£ [illegible]
Total expenditure on English, Scottish, and Irish services.	Per cent. [illegible]	Per cent. [illegible]	Per cent. [illegible]	Per cent. [illegible]	Per cent. [illegible]	Per cent. [illegible]	Per cent. [illegible]	Per cent. [illegible]	Per cent. [illegible]
Amount	£ [illegible]	£ [illegible]	£ [illegible]	£ [illegible]	£ [illegible]	£ [illegible]	£ [illegible]	£ [illegible]	£ [illegible]
Contribution to Imperial services	Per cent. [illegible]	Per cent. [illegible]	Per cent. [illegible]	Per cent. [illegible]	Per cent. 11·[illegible]	Per cent. [illegible]	Per cent. [illegible]	Per cent. [illegible]	Per cent. [illegible]

The Treasury's estimate of the taxation paid per head of population is as follows:—

Amounts per Head of Population.

(Census 1891.)

Year.	England.	Scotland.	Ireland.	United Kingdom.
	£ s. d.	£ s. d.	£ s. d.	£ s. d.
[illegible]				
Total revenue contributed by the three kingdoms.	2 10 3	4 0 1	1 12 5	[illegible]
Total expenditure on English, Scottish, and Irish services.	0 14 6	0 14 9	1 1 8	[illegible]
Contribution to Imperial services.	1 17 8	1 18 4	0 10 17	1 12 4
[illegible]				
Total revenue contributed by the three kingdoms.	2 18 4	2 12 4	1 19 4	[illegible]
Total expenditure on English, Scottish, and Irish services.	0 19 10	0 15 9	1 4 4	[illegible]
Contribution to Imperial services.	1 16 10	1 14 8	0 0 8	1 18 8
[illegible]				
Total revenue contributed by the three kingdoms.	2 13 3	2 11 4	1 12 6	2 10 10
Total expenditure on English, Scottish, and Irish services.	0 13 10	0 12 10	1 7 0	[illegible]
Contribution to Imperial services.	1 18 5	1 18 7	0 8 6	1 16 10

These figures show that from the Treasury point of view Ireland contributes less per head and absolutely, year by year, to the Imperial services, and that Great Britain would be no loser if Ireland's annual contributions to the Imperial revenue were fixed considerably under 2,000,000l., and the balance of her actual revenue handed over to an Irish local authority to be spent as it thought fit. Both countries would benefit by such a re-adjustment of the administrative system.

But the Treasury classification of expenditure in Parliamentary Paper 329/'91, and other subsequent papers, is not a fair statement of the facts, even if the 4,000,000l. alleged to be spent on Irish services were justly, economically, and usefully laid out.

Under the head of Imperial services, absorbing 62,000,000l. of the total revenue, and the greater part being spent in England, are a number of items from which Ireland derives no benefit whatever, and many disadvantages; these items ought more properly to be classed as English or British services. Under the head of Irish services are large sums which should be classed as British or Imperial, for though the expenditure is in Ireland, it is made for Imperial reasons, not for the benefit of Irish citizens.

Ireland, a very poor, purely agricultural and pastoral country, has no need of the costly army and navy which the commerce, foreign relations, and policy of Great Britain require, and which her wealth can afford to maintain. Ireland should not be expected to contribute to these costly defence services, either in proportion to her population or her wealth; she derives but little advantage from them, and would scarcely be more in danger of invasion or aggression from other powers than Iceland is, but for her connexion with Great Britain. Ireland derives no benefit from much of Imperial expenditure.

I do not suggest that Ireland should pay nothing for these services, but that she should pay less than the amount now contributed. It would be difficult for anyone except a Treasury expert to examine and criticise all the items of expenditure as given in detail in the Financial Relation Papers. The title of account does not always denote the real object or cause of the expenditure. For example, the Wine and Tin Compensations of the Duchies of Cornwall and Lancaster do not indicate a service from which Ireland derives any benefit, yet these items are charged as Imperial services.

Objections, however, may fairly be made to the classification as Imperial services of—

1. The Civil List, Royal Annuities and Expenses. Ireland pays the Lord Lieutenant, as a substitute for royalty, a salary which is double that paid to the President of the United States. That, and all the expenses of his residence and household, are debited by the Treasury to Ireland, and on the same principle the expense of royalty should be classed as a British Service.
2. Parliament, whose location at Westminster is a disadvantage to Ireland, for it makes all Irish legislation more costly, dilatory, and less efficient than if Irish affairs were locally dealt with.
3. Public buildings in London, including the British Museum; Irishmen derive no more advantage from that than they do from public buildings in New York, or than an Englishman derives from the Royal Irish Academy.
4. Diplomatic, consular, and packet services, and all charges arising from the maintenance of establishments for the same purpose in both Dublin and London.

[illegible]

Among the expenses classed as Irish services, the principal charge to which objection may be taken is that for the police, kept up admittedly for British reasons as a semi-military force, at a cost far in excess of the requirements of Ireland, where, under a much stricter criminal code, in proportion to the population, there is less crime than in the rest of the United Kingdom. In England the cost of police is [illegible]., in Ireland, [illegible] per head. In Ireland the number of committals for trial in [illegible] was 1 in [illegible], and of convictions 1 in [illegible]; while in the rest of the United Kingdom the corresponding figures were 1 in [illegible] and 1 in [illegible]. If the Irish police were kept up at the same rate per head as in England, the cost would be [illegible] instead of [illegible], and still less if the force were in proportion to the crimes committed; so that at least one million of the police cost should be transferred from the Irish to the Imperial or British services column. Law charges and criminal prosecutions cost more for Ireland's [illegible] of people than for England's [illegible]. Most of this outlay is for political and British purposes, and should be so charged in the accounts.

The Civil establishments in Ireland are kept up on an Imperial scale and for British purposes, yet are charged by the Treasury exclusively to Ireland. And Ireland is charged with her share of a number of large items classed as Imperial, such as Boards of Trade, Privy Council Office, Treasury, Office of Works, which should more fairly be charged to British or English.

[illegible]

A readjustment of the Treasury's classification, charging Ireland only with the cost of the services she required, and from which she derived an advantage, would entirely alter the results and percentages deduced in Parliamentary Paper [illegible]. Imperial expenditure in Ireland is large, no doubt, but this does not compensate for over-taxation, unless the expenditure is necessary and beneficial to Ireland. The comparison of the per head taxation, giving the average Irishman's taxation at [illegible], against an Englishman's [illegible], tells nothing as to the equality of taxation in each country, unless the average income of individuals in each country is also known, and the services rendered by the State to each country. Ireland pays less per head than England, because her population consists of a larger proportion of poorer persons in every class of occupation and property.

[illegible]

The following table shows what Ireland's proportion of wealth is to that of the United Kingdom on a comparison of the income-tax assessment and produce in [illegible], with the amount of the assessment or produce of the tax per head in England and Ireland:—

FROM INLAND REVENUE REPORT TO MARCH [illegible].

	United Kingdom.	Ireland.	Ireland's Proportion.	Assessment per Head.	
				England.	Ireland.
POPULATION.					
Preliminary Report, Census [illegible].	[illegible]	[illegible]	1 : [illegible]		
Net Income-tax Assessment:	£	£			
Schedule A.	[illegible]	[illegible]	1 : [illegible]	[illegible]	[illegible]
„ B.	[illegible]	[illegible]	1 : [illegible]	[illegible]	[illegible]
„ C.	[illegible]	[illegible]	1 : [illegible]	[illegible]	[illegible]
„ D.	[illegible]	[illegible]	1 : [illegible]	[illegible]	[illegible]
„ E.	[illegible]	[illegible]	1 : [illegible]	[illegible]	[illegible]
Total £	[illegible]	[illegible]	1 : [illegible]	[illegible]	[illegible]
	£	£			
Assessment of houses and messuages.	[illegible]	[illegible]	1 : [illegible]	[illegible]	[illegible]
Nett receipts Property and Income-tax.	[illegible]	[illegible]	1 : [illegible]	[illegible]	
Property assessed to Probate and Succession Duty.	[illegible]	[illegible]	1 : [illegible]	[illegible]	[illegible]

[illegible]

Ireland's largest item is Schedule A. (nearly half of her total assessment). Under Schedule A. she is much more highly valued than England. In Ireland the assessment of land has remained unchanged for [illegible] years; and the assessment cannot be changed, although the value of land has fallen. In Great Britain the rateable value of land diminished by over [illegible] between [illegible] and [illegible]. The under-assessment of country mansions and of valuable urban building sites, so common in England, has no corresponding place in the Irish assessment. For example, in evidence to the Valuation Committee of the London County Council, Mr. [illegible] said: "The annual value of all vacant "land (in London) which is not assessed I have put "down very moderately at [illegible] annually." The Committee's Report stated that in the parish of Kensington there was vacant land worth for sale [illegible] practically not rated at all (Report of Land Valuation Committee, [illegible]). Ireland's assessment of buildings comprises a large number of [illegible] houses which have no net letting value, for the cost of maintenance would exceed the rent.

Under-assessment in England.

This comparative under-assessment in Great Britain extends to railways and other such works as well as to farms, mansions, and vacant lands. Mr. T. P. Hedley, one of the largest valuers in the North of England, says: "Comparing the valuation and amount of rates "payable by the Dublin, Wicklow, and Wexford Rail"way with the amounts paid by the two largest English "railway companies, the London and North-western "and the Great Western, it will be seen that the rates "paid as payable by the former are enormously in "excess of the latter, and that the difference is solely "to be attributed to the 'parochial principle' of rating "in England." Comparing different parts of the L. N. W. R. system with Irish railways, he says the assessable value of the Dublin, Wicklow, and Wexford Railway, in proportion to the receipts, is [illegible] times greater than that of the Shrewsbury and Hereford! (Local Taxation, by T. P. Hedley, [illegible].) In another pamphlet on the same subject, in [illegible], he says: "Whilst "the strictest supervision is exercised over expendi"ture, the assessment of properties to the rates is "seriously neglected. Whilst the guardians may not "expend a few shillings contrary to the consolidated "orders or to the prejudice of the ratepayers, they "may, by neglecting the proper assessment of pro"perties, prejudice the ratepayers to the extent of many "thousands of pounds." He then states that in [illegible] unions of Durham collieries were under-rated to the extent of [illegible]; and to show that these irregularities existed in other properties, he gives the rents paid and the rateable values in [illegible] cases, [illegible] being valued by his firm. In some instances the valuation is one-eleventh of the rent; the rents of the whole lot are [illegible] per cent. higher than the rateable values—[illegible] rental against [illegible] rateable value.

"Griffith's valuation."

The valuation of Ireland, though supposed to be made on an estimate of what the land would produce, really followed the rents, which were excessively high, owing to the competition for land among a larger population than Ireland has at present. Mr. Senior's remarks on Griffith's system of valuation may be quoted: "Though "Mr. Griffith does not avow the element of rent, I "believe he is in fact really guided by it"; and as to rent, "I take it a smaller portion of the produce "remains with the tenant in Ireland than in Scotland "or England" (Proceedings of Committee on Townland Valuation, [illegible]).

Ireland's assessment comparatively high.

To the Committee on Taxation in [illegible] Mr. Senior said, in answer to Q. [illegible], that Ireland was much higher valued than England.

A great deal of inferior tillage land which was then valued as such has since relapsed into heathy, sedgy, or rushy pasture, of far less value than it was assessed at when under cultivation. The assessment of land in Ireland has always been high as compared with that in England, so far as each assessment follows the rents. It was stated to the Land Committee of [illegible] to be the custom for the Irish landlord to get about one-third of the gross produce, while in England the proportion was stated to be one-fifth.

Though I do not think these figures are correct, they are true as to the fact of the Irish landlord receiving as rent a larger proportion of the gross produce than the English landlord.

To compare the assessment of Ireland and Great Britain, [illegible] at least should be taken off Schedule A. in Ireland, to correspond with the reduction of [illegible] in Great Britain since [illegible]; for this diminution applies only to agricultural land, and the assessment of that is not given separate from urban land.

[illegible]

The comparison of the local rateable values with the income-tax assessment at p. 32, Appendix to Inland Revenue Report, 1894, confirms what I have stated above as to England's lower assessment under Schedule A.

The gross "estimated" rental of all property locally rated in England is 191,358,342*l*. For the reasons given this "estimated" rental is below the real rental value.

The net assessment under Schedule A, compared with this is 150,[illegible]*l*., *i.e.*, 41,[illegible]*l*. less, or 21·5 per cent. less than the "estimated" gross rental.

Absentee rents.

Schedule A., moreover, includes an absentee rental variously estimated at from 3,000,000*l*. to 5,000,000*l*. This should be deducted from the Irish assessment in comparing the respective wealth of the two countries on this basis; to include it would be as logical as to charge a farmer with income tax on the rent he pays to his landlord as well as on the profits of occupation under Schedule B.

In relation to the capital value of landed estates, which in Ireland are not worth more than 17 years' purchase of the rental, owners have been paying nearly double as much income tax and succession duty as owners in England, where estates are worth nearly 30 years' purchase.

In the Peers' Dissent and Protest against the Union Resolutions in 1800, the absentee rental was estimated at 2,000,000*l*., being 33 per cent. of the then total estimated rental. Absenteeism has increased since the Union. A return made in 1872 notoriously under-estimated the value of estates owned by absentees, and although no exact figures on the question are now obtainable, it is clear that from an economic point of view not only the rentals of absentee owners, but the interest on mortgages owned by residents in Great Britain, as well as all annual charges paid to persons residing out of Ireland, should be deducted from Ireland's income-tax assessment in estimating her capacity for taxation. These rentals and charges are paid by the exportation of Irish produce, and the only return received by Ireland consists of bundles of rent receipts.

Under Schedule D, practically self-assessed from returns by the payers, it has often been remarked that in the returns of trade and business many taxable incomes escape observation in England, while in Ireland fewer do so, owing to the greater difficulty of escaping notice. This coincides with experience of such self-made assessments in the United States, where "the "larger the city the smaller is the proportion of such "property reached."*

Even as the total uncorrected amount of income-tax assessment stands, the rate of Imperial taxation to Ireland in 1890-91 was 6s. in the £, while that for England and Wales was only 2s. 1d.; yet the average income indicated by the assessment is in Ireland less than one-fourth the average income in England.

It is quite clear that Ireland has been paying to the Imperial revenue for many years more than double what she would have been paying in accordance with the strictest and most adverse interpretation of the Treaty of Union. If the excess payment for the last 40 years is estimated at 4,000,000*l*. a year, the debt due to Ireland at 3 per cent. interest would amount to 300,000,000*l*. sterling.

Income-tax as a criterion of taxable capacity.

In 1800, Lord Castlereagh said that the best criterion of the relative means of the two countries would be the produce of an income tax on the same description of incomes in each country. We have this now, and it is the only criterion of the kind. It is the best available so far as it goes, provided that the difference in value of the assessments is taken into account, and an adjustment made for the tax on incomes derived from but not spent in Ireland.

The income of an Irish absentee owner is in no sense indicative of so much wealth in Ireland. It represents so much produce taken from the country without any return whatever. This is an active cause of impoverishment; for a district owned by an absentee is like a farm the produce of which is sold year after year and no corresponding return made to keep up the fertility.

Otherwise, the aggregate incomes shown by the produce of the tax in each country is a measure of the wealth of the propertied classes only. Taxable incomes, so far as they are spent in Ireland, are distributed among the wage earners, shopkeepers, and industries of the country, and the amount per head so distributed in Ireland is, as the income-tax returns show, very much less than in the rest of Great Britain.

[illegible]

If it be asked why a resident in Ireland with 1,000*l*. a year should pay less taxes than an Englishman with the same income, the answer is that he does not receive the same advantages in return; and if it be asked why an Irish manual labourer should pay less than an English labourer, the answer is the same, and in addition that he has a very much smaller margin of taxable income. Public revenue should be measured not by what people are able but what they ought to give, and each person's contribution should depend upon the benefit received in return. An Irishman receives less benefit from all the great items of public expenditure than an Englishman; from the army, navy, and civil services, including the vast expenditure on public buildings in London, the centre of Government.

[illegible]

In respect of incomes and properties below the limits of taxation, there are few statistics for comparison, but it is undeniable that the average of such incomes is very much smaller, and that small properties are more rare than in Great Britain. Wages are much lower in Ireland; there is no class there corresponding to the highly paid artisans and mechanics who are so numerous in England.

According to Mr. Little's Report to the Labour Commission the wages of agricultural labourers are 58 per cent. higher in England, and 46 per cent. higher in Wales than in Ireland (Board of Agriculture Journal, p. [illegible]). The house accommodation for this class is immensely inferior in Ireland.

The estimate of agricultural wages does not take into account the number of persons who, during part of the year, earn nothing in Ireland.

[illegible]

From want of employment at home, Irishmen go in numbers every year to England, and even to the United States, for temporary work, and about a 1,000,000*l*. of the savings of the Irish poor are spent annually on the outfit and passage of the 60 or 70 thousand emigrants who leave Ireland for ever, a drain on the resources of her country directly attributable to the political condition of Ireland. The commercial, industrial, and domestic classes are all less well paid in Ireland than in England, and less numerous in proportion to the population.

Mr. Giffen's estimate.

In 1886, Mr. R. Giffen ("Nineteenth Century," March, 1886) estimated the taxable income of Ireland at 15 millions, or one fifty-third of Great Britain's taxable income of 800,000,000*l*.; the conclusions he came to, writing "exclusively from a British point of view," were, "that Ireland as a poor country was dispro-"portionately taxed, and that although the taxes of "the United Kingdom are technically indiscriminate, "nearly the whole taxable income of the Irish people "was absorbed by the State, and that under such con-"ditions there could be little accumulation in Ireland." From his figures it appears that equality of taxation would exist if the average Irishman paid one-seventh the amount paid by the average inhabitant of Great Britain. Ireland's poverty consists in the fact that she has many more poor inhabitants than Great Britain, and in estimating their capacity for taxation a deduction should be made from the gross income of the minimum necessary for subsistence.

Mr. Giffen estimated the income per head in Ireland at 14*l*. 6*s*. 8*d*., against 33*l*. 7*s*. 5*d*. in Great Britain; and capital per head at 90*l*. in Ireland, and 262*l*. in Great Britain. This estimate appears more than borne out by the results of the tables which I give farther on.

[illegible]

In the matter of drink, from which so large a part of the public revenue is raised, there is as great an inequality of taxation, arising out of a disregard of the differing habits of the three countries, as if an indiscriminate tax on tea were imposed on France and England, and it was then maintained that the tea-drinking and coffee-drinking nations were equally taxed. It is not the business of Government to decide what articles of general consumption shall be used, and in what proportions, but to apportion taxation equally among all classes.

Taxes on alcoholic drinks produce about 30,000,000*l*. a year, and deducing the amounts consumed per head from the Treasury estimates of revenue contributed by

* "[illegible]" by [illegible].

each division of the kingdom. In Parliamentary Paper 333 we have the following table:—

DUTY ON, AND AMOUNT OF, SPIRITS, BEER, AND WINE CONSUMED IN ENGLAND, SCOTLAND, AND IRELAND.

Articles.	England.		Scotland.		Ireland.	
	Duty.	Gallons.	Duty.	Gallons.	Duty.	Gallons.
	s. d.		s. d.		s. d.	
Spirits, Cordials, and Liqueurs	8 4	·8	17 1	1·36	11 0	1·0
Beer	7 5	32·4	1 4	12·88	2 8	13·
Wine	1 11	—	0 4½	—	0 2½	—
	16 [illegible]		19 9½		14 [illegible]	

The standard of taxation for drink is the alcoholic strength; but an exception is made in favour of the Englishman's principal drink; the tax upon this, at the usual specific gravity of 1·055 degrees, would, in proportion to its alcohol, be 1s. per gallon instead of 3d. Taking the above amounts consumed per head, if taxation was levied on the alcohol in beer at the same rate as on spirits, an Englishman would pay 1l. 5s. 6d. instead of 16s.; a Scotchman 1l. 1s. 5d. instead of 19s. 1d.; an Irishman, 1l. 7s. 11d. instead of 14s., as taxation on spirits and beer.

The Treasury's bias against Ireland.

On every occasion when the financial condition of Ireland has been brought before Parliament, it has been the duty of the Treasury Department to furnish English Ministers with figures, facts, and arguments against the Irish view of the question. The forces of tradition and prejudice are, therefore, very strong at the Treasury. The officials of that department alone have the means of getting the figures embodied in the returns. They are experts in this, and no outsider has the means of checking, or questioning, their figures, though he may demur to the conclusions drawn from them.

Sir E. Hamilton's interesting historical account of the financial relations between Great Britain and Ireland, shows that the Irish objections to the financial arrangement in 1800, were well founded. The Union led to an era of excessive taxation, and the conclusion he comes to (p. 32), that Ireland's bankruptcy was due to the terms of the arrangement, not to the way it was carried out, concedes the fact that the terms of Union were unfair, oppressive, and ruinous to Ireland.

Excessive taxation was one cause of the poverty of Ireland, and prevented the natural accumulation of capital during the early part of this century, when the foundations of England's wealth were being laid.

National wealth is of slow growth, and the effects of bad laws continue long after the laws themselves have ceased to exist. The penal laws co-operated with excessive taxation in preventing the growth of wealth. Arthur Young thought that these laws, preventing three-fourths of the population of Ireland from owning property, from gaining or keeping wealth, from holding public offices, from being educated, laws discouraging thrift and industry, contributed more to prevent progress in Ireland than all other causes together. "Where," he says, "is there a people in the world to "be found industrious in such a circumstance? If a "Catholic should accidentally gain wealth, the whole "kingdom should not afford him an opportunity of "investing it. These laws were directed," he said, "not against the Catholic religion, but against the "industry and prosperity of whoever professes that "religion. How is agriculture to flourish, manufactures to be established, or commerce to extend, under "a system which drove out of the kingdom all the "personal wealth of the Catholics, and prohibited their "industry within it."

No history of the economic and financial condition of Ireland should omit to take into account the effects of these laws in the past, and the remains of those effects at present.

However, a just estimate of the present relative capacity of Ireland to bear taxation, and of the amount she ought to contribute to the Imperial revenue for the services she receives, is of more importance than past history.

Sir E. Hamilton's statement shows that the revenue from Ireland is continually decreasing, while the Imperial expenditure on administration is increasing.

Difference between British and Irish local taxation.

His comparison of the local taxation in each country (p. 20) is not a fair one, for Ireland does not obtain the same services in quantity, or quality, that Great Britain does from her local authorities. In Ireland we have not a reformed Local Government as Great Britain has, under the County and Parish Councils Act, nor so extensive a system of municipal government. In roads, streets, bridges, drainage, water supplies, parks, markets, public lighting, and libraries, artisans' dwellings, education, and municipal enterprise, Ireland, is far behind the rest of the Empire.

Taking the income-tax assessment (unadjusted for absentee rents and agricultural depression) as a measure, the total Imperial and local taxation, 127,570,000l., amounts to 1s. 3d. in the pound for Great Britain; similar Irish taxation, 10,434,000l., amounts to 3s. in the pound.

Excessive cost of Irish administration on Imperial service.

According to the Treasury classification of expenditure (to the incorrectness of which I have already adverted), Irish administration costs much more than British, in proportion to population and wealth. The reasons are clear; Ireland is more distant from the centre of government, and is practically charged with a double set of establishments, in Dublin and in London. But the principal reason is that Ireland is, and always has been, governed in opposition to the wishes of the Irish people, and much of the expenditure charged against Ireland is really for Imperial purposes.

Tests of taxable capacity.

The chief tests of Ireland's capacity for taxation given by Sir E. Hamilton are, (1) from official statistics, the death duties, and income tax; (2) from unofficial sources, Mr. Giffen's well-known estimates of national income and capital. As to the first, no adjustment has been made for absentee property or over-assessment under Schedules A. and B.; but according to the unadjusted figures, Ireland's contribution to the revenue should be from 4½ to 5½ per cent. It has been from 7½ to 10 per cent. according to Sir E. Hamilton's tables at page 33. Mr. Giffen's estimate of national capital and income in 1882 shows an absolute proportion of from 4½ to 5½ per cent. and the per head capital and income of Ireland at one-third that of Great Britain. All these estimates concur to show that Ireland has been contributing at least twice as much as she ought to the Imperial revenue.

Cost of living in England and in Ireland.

As a set off, Sir E. Hamilton suggests that if the Irish working classes have smaller incomes, their houses, fuel, clothes, and food cost less than an Englishman's, and that an Irishman, out of 10s. or 12s. a week, may have more to spend on "luxuries" than an Englishman earning 15s. a week. The idea of a labouring man having "a margin to spend on his "pleasure" out of 12s. a week, which is more than the average agricultural wage in Ireland, is ludicrous. As to fuel, English coals are burned over a large part of Ireland, and so far the Irishman's fire costs nearly 50 per cent. more than the Englishman's. Arthur Young said turf was the most expensive kind of fuel, and it costs more now to win turf equivalent to a ton of English coal than the coal would cost, except in particularly favourable conditions. An Irishman's house, clothes, and food cost less than an Englishman's merely because they are infinitely worse. With the exception of potatoes, oats, and milk, most articles of common use are imported from England and cost the Irish consumer more. Ireland is still poor in the sense Mr. Senior used the word to the Committee on Taxation in 1864, as "a "country in which the mass of the people are worse fed, "worse lodged, worse clothed, worse paid than in any "other country he had visited." Its cheapness, so far as it exists, is what Arthur Young described as "the "cheapness of barbarity, backwardness, and ignorance."

In 1872, the Commissioners appointed to inquire into the condition of the Civil Service in Ireland, reported that the cost of living was not less in Dublin than in London; "living," including house-rent as well as articles of consumption [C. 789] 1873.

Treasury basis of taxable capacity unjust and fallacious.

Sir E. Hamilton's further test of Ireland's capacity for taxation derived from the per head expenditure on tea, tobacco, spirits, and beer is quite inconsistent with the principles of just taxation. He omits wine from the drink bill, and wine is much more largely drunk in England than in Ireland. If luxuries are to be taxed let them be taxed all round. I have already shown that the Englishman's drink, beer, is unfairly (as between the two countries) exempted from taxation. It is absurd to call articles of every-day use such as tea, tobacco, and alcoholic drinks, luxuries, and to make taxation depend, not on the services rendered by Government, or on the means of the taxpayer, but on the

quantity of certain arbitrarily selected articles consumed.

Public loans to Ireland.

As to the loans of public money, in respect of which it is claimed that Ireland has been treated with special liberality, they were made as a partial concession to the claim that Ireland was overtaxed, and because Irish local governing bodies had not the same power as English bodies of raising funds on their own security. They were made for political reasons, and to a large extent they have been unremuneratively and uselessly spent. "Much of the money lent was merely so much charity." (The Budget by A. J. Wilson, p. 139.)

The interest still paid on these loans, so far as they have been unremuneratively spent, is a dead loss to Ireland, a payment for which she gets no return.

It is evident that no one exact measure can be found for the comparative wealths of the two countries. So far as what each can pay is ascertainable, what each ought to pay would be a different amount depending on the benefits received from the joint expenditure on Imperial services.

Decreased assessment of Ireland.

Great Britain is rapidly increasing in population and wealth, Ireland is decreasing certainly in population, probably in wealth. In 1864, when the Committee on Taxation sat, Ireland's income-tax assessment was 22,014,594*l.*; if allowance be made for the present over-assessment under Schedule A., Ireland's assessment has increased hardly or not at all. In the same period Great Britain's assessment has more than doubled, having risen from 292,264,590*l.* to 597,933,[illegible]*l.*

As regards Ireland's assessment under Schedules A. and B., 1864 was a year of low prices. Comparing the prices of that year with those of 1892 (and prices are still lower now) the undermentioned articles were lower in 1892 than in 1864 by the following percentages:—Store cattle, 32 per cent.; fat cattle 22·5 per cent.; sheep, 31·7 per cent.; mutton, 24·6 per cent.; beef, 33 per cent.; butter, 18 per cent.; pork, 20·5 per cent.; flax, 39 per cent.; wheat, 20 per cent.; barley, 22 per cent.; oats increased by 13 per cent. (Barrington's *Farm Prices*, 1893).

Such a fall in prices means a much greater fall in farm profits and rent values; and, therefore, an assessment which some of the witnesses, Mr. Senior particularly, thought high in 1864, should be very much lower now.

Mr. Giffen held the same opinion, and said there was reason to believe Ireland was more highly valued than England ("Nineteenth Century," March, 1886).

Income and property better tests of taxable capacity than consumption.

There can be no question that the per head amount of income, property, and business transacted are much better tests of the capacity of a nation for taxation than the amounts per head consumed of such common articles of use as tea, tobacco, spirits, and beer. In fact, property is a better test of wealth than a man's wants as evidenced by his consumption of articles of common use.

In the following tables, I give some statistics chiefly taken from the last number of the Statistical Abstract. The figures are unadjusted; for, except as regards the income-tax tables, I have no means of arriving at those adjustments which the Treasury officials can obtain from the departments.

Table I. shows the proportion of Irish income and property to be from $\frac{1}{27}$ to $\frac{1}{35}$ part of the United Kingdom's; that the average Irish income is about one-third of the average English income; and that the contributors of Ireland to the Imperial revenue in twice as heavy a poundage on the income-tax assessment as the English contributors.

Table II. shows Ireland's wealth and business to range from $\frac{1}{8}$ to $\frac{1}{100}$ of that of the United Kingdom; and the per head comparison between England and Ireland to vary (succession duty excepted) from $\frac{1}{2}$ to $\frac{1}{20}$.

Table III. gives somewhat the same figures as Table I., but taken from a different source as a check on Table I.

Table IV. shows the continuing diminution of the population in Ireland, and that there is no reason, from the circumstances of, and crime in Ireland, why the ordinary government should cost more than in the other divisions of the kingdom.

I.

Comparison of Net Income-tax Assessments and Receipts in the United Kingdom, England and Ireland; the Amount per Head of Population in England and Ireland (Inland Revenue Report to 31st March 1893); Increase or Decrease since 1879 of Gross Assessments (Statistical Abstract, 41st No.); Income Tax and Death Duty Receipts for five years (Parliamentary Paper, 1893).

—	United Kingdom.	England.	Ireland.	Proportion Ireland to United Kingdom.	Per Head		Increase or Decrease in Gross Assessments since 1879.	
					England.	Ireland.	England.	Ireland.
	£	£	£		£	£	Per cent.	Per cent.
Schedule A.	173,493,721	140,399,252	13,714,792	1 to 26	5·9	2·7	+14·2	+3·3
" B.	14,972,962	13,130,677	2,414,290	1 to 7·9	·30	·59	—19	Nil.
" C.	39,577,245	39,333,458	713,730	1 to 54	1·29	·15	Not given separately.	
" D.	314,710,962	277,592,391	9,394,249	1 to 34·3	9·2	2·0	+62	+12
" E.	37,972,371	30,791,334	1,742,408	1 to 21·9	1·02	·38	Not given separately.	
Total	592,433,305	518,393,706	24,031,285	1 to 25·2	17·	5·2	+34	+3·3
	£	£	£		£	£		
Assessment of houses and messuages.	143,269,377	123,043,640	3,371,027	1 to 39	4·7	·85	+25	+14
Net receipts, income and property tax, 1892-3.	13,470,979	12,071,878 Great Britain.	535,086	1 to 24·3	·54	·15	—	—
Ditto for five years, 1888-93. Parliamentary Paper 324/93.	82,096,000	78,332,000	3,764,000	1 to 25·7	—	—	—	—
Death duties for five years, 1888-93. Parliamentary Paper 313/93.	46,122,000	43,428,000	2,093,000	1 to 21·5	1·51	·46	—	—

Exchequer Revenue contributed by England and Ireland respectively, as given by Parliamentary Paper 334/93, for year to 31st March 1893, and the Estimated Revenue for year to 31st March 1895 (Parliamentary Paper 118/94), and the Percentage which the Revenue for 1892-3 amounts to on the Income-tax Assessment of each Country.

—	England.	Ireland.	United Kingdom.
Revenue contributed 1892-3. Parliamentary Paper 334, 1893	£ 71,690,858	£ 7,506,151	£ [illegible]
Percentage ratio on Income-tax assessment	3s. 5d.	5s. 9d.	[illegible]
Estimated revenue, 1894-5	£ 74,877,000	£ 7,726,000	£ [illegible]

II.

Comparison of the Wealth and Progress of England and Ireland from the principal Tables in which separate Amounts are given for these Countries in the Statistical Abstract (41st Number, 1894). The figures are taken from the last year given in the Abstract.

Table in Statistical Abstract.	Property assessed during Years 1879-93 to	United Kingdom.	England.	Ireland.	Ireland's Proportion to United Kingdom.	Per Head. England.	Per Head. Ireland.
		£	£	£		£	£
16	Value of property assessed during 14 years, 1879-93 to — 1. Probate duty 2. Succession duty	000 omitted 1,664,170 500,116	000 omitted 1,498,805 404,458	000 omitted 79,636 34,991	1 to 21 1 to 9·3	47· 14·	[illegible] [illegible]
		£	£	£		£	£
[illegible]	Post Office Savings Bank capital	80,180,848	74,777,858	4,840,358	1 to 16·6	2·47	·94
[illegible]	Trustee Savings Bank capital	42,143,607	29,872,812	1,898,722	1 to 22·3	·99	·41
[illegible]	Government stock held for depositors in trustee banks.	1,822,402	1,161,374	88,561	1 to 48	·035	·007
		No.	No.	No.			
[illegible]	No. of accounts, post office banks	5,149,659	4,898,176	255,944	1 to 25·2	one in 5·6 persons	one in 19· persons.
		No.	No.	No.			
[illegible]	Ditto, trustee banks	1,421,145	1,043,820	64,305	1 to 22·2	one in 24 persons.	one in 59 persons.
		£	£	£		£	£
[illegible]	Railways—capital	971,323,585	808,083,237	38,738,819	1 to 25	26·8	8·4
	„ net receipts	34,905,773	28,941,803	1,373,177	1 to 25·1	·96	·29
[illegible]	Registered companies — paid up capital.	1,013,819,889	895,005,807	22,486,876	1 to 45·2	30·7	4·8
[illegible]	Building societies' liabilities	44,135,091	43,132,005	849,434	1 to 54·9	1·5	[illegible]
[illegible]	Industrial and provident societies' capital.	17,474,097	16,805,144	21,800	1 to 796·	·57	[illegible]
		Millions	Millions.	Millions.		No.	[illegible]
[illegible]	Letters delivered	1,822	1,505½	100½	1 to 17	53	[illegible]
		Tons.	Tons. (Great Britain.)	Tons.		Tons. (Great Britain.)	[illegible]
[illegible]	Tonnage of shipping at ports classified as "Principal Ports."	35,874,748	34,982,677	842,054	1 to 55	1·13	[illegible]

III.

Amount of Revenue contributed by England and Ireland in 1892-3 in respect of Stamps and the several Income-tax Schedules; the Proportion of Ireland's Contribution to the total United Kingdom Revenue under these heads, and the Amount per Head of Population contributed by England and Ireland in thousandths of 1l. Parliamentary Paper 334/93.

No. of Head in Parliamentary Paper, 334.	Head.	Amount contributed by United Kingdom.	Amount contributed by England.	Amount contributed by Ireland.	Ireland's Proportion to United Kingdom.	Amount per Head in ·001l. England.	Amount per Head in ·001l. Ireland.
	Stamps.	£	£	£			
[illegible]	Probate duty	2,808,020	2,656,800	90,620	1 to 24	87	23
[illegible]	Estate duty	1,204,863	1,098,540	42,819	1 to 29	36	9
[illegible]	Succession duty	4,497,897	3,941,809	143,658	1 to 19	128	30
[illegible]	General stamps	5,437,794	4,772,546	210,837	1 to 24·6	156	45
[illegible]	Total stamps	13,798,390	12,080,545	608,734	1 to 22·6	394	130
	Income Tax.	£	£	£			
11	Schedules A. and B.	6,388,110	5,372,252	289,085	1 to 18·0	179	[illegible]
[illegible]	Schedules C., D., and Government stocks, public companies' dividends, &c.	4,329,316	4,027,518	145,313	1 to 29·4	130	[illegible]
[illegible]	Schedule D.—trades and professions	7,335,925	6,015,730	103,746	1 to 63·2	190	19
[illegible]	Schedule E.—public offices and salaries	912,950	735,126	42,876	1 to 21·5	24	9
[illegible]	Total Income tax	19,428,276	17,412,876	588,920	1 to 34	579	125

IV.

POPULATION of ENGLAND, SCOTLAND, IRELAND, and the UNITED KINGDOM in 1891, with PER-CENTAGE of TOTAL POPULATION, and INCREASE or DECREASE since 1871. (Statistical Abstract, 1894, 41st No.)

	England.	Scotland.	Ireland.	United Kingdom.
Population	[illegible]	[illegible]	[illegible]	[illegible]
Proportion of total of United Kingdom	Per cent. [illegible]	Per cent. [illegible]	Per cent. [illegible]	Per cent. [illegible]
Variation since 1871	[illegible]	[illegible]	[illegible]	[illegible]

PROPORTION to POPULATION in ENGLAND, SCOTLAND, and IRELAND of BIRTHS, DEATHS, MARRIAGES, EMIGRANTS, POLICE, CRIMINALS, and CONVICTIONS (Statistical Abstract, 1894, 41st No.) in 1893.

—	England.	Scotland.	Ireland.
Births	[illegible]	[illegible]	[illegible]
Deaths	[illegible]	[illegible]	[illegible]
Marriages	[illegible]	[illegible]	[illegible]
Emigrants	[illegible]	[illegible]	[illegible]
Police	[illegible]	[illegible]	[illegible]
Committals for trial	[illegible]	[illegible]	[illegible]
Convictions	[illegible]	[illegible]	[illegible]

The income-tax receipts or assessment are, if any one test is to be taken, the most obviously just, provided deductions drawn from them are confined to the classes who have taxable incomes.

To compare the Irish assessment truly with England's or that of Great Britain, I should omit all Schedules A. and B. for the over-assessment, in comparison with Great Britain's lower and reduced assessment. This would bring Schedules A. and B. to [illegible]. From this [illegible] should come off for the abnormal rental and drain, leaving the assessment for A. and B. [illegible], and making the adjusted total [illegible]. [illegible] Irish abnormal rental added to Great Britain's assessment brings it up to [illegible], of which the Irish assessment would be [illegible] part.

On the basis of the income tax, under the seventh article of the Union, Ireland should have contributed less than [illegible] to the revenue in 1893–4 instead of over [illegible].

In respect of incomes and property under the limit of direct taxation, there is no direct evidence nor figures available for statistical comparison; but Mr. Giffen's estimate of the average Irish and English incomes and capital is more than borne out by the rates of wages mentioned in the Labour Commission Report, and by the well-known facts of the want of employment and general low wages in Ireland. Mr. Giffen thought his estimate probably too high for Ireland, and since 1885 incomes of Irish landlords and farmers have very much diminished, and consequently the prosperity also of all the classes depending on them, labourers, shopkeepers, &c. Taking round numbers, for no exact comparison can be made, the following table shows how the adjusted income-tax assessment of Ireland truly compares with the rest of the United Kingdom, and what the burden of total taxation is as shown by the poundage rate:—

COMPARISON of the ADJUSTED INCOME-TAX ASSESSMENT of the UNITED KINGDOM, GREAT BRITAIN, and IRELAND, and the POUNDAGE RATE of TAXATION, Imperial and Local, upon the ASSESSMENTS.

	United Kingdom.	Great Britain.	Ireland.	Proportion of Ireland to United Kingdom.	Assessment per head. Great Britain.	Assessment per head. Ireland.
	£	£	£			
Total adjusted income-tax assessment, 1894	[illegible]	[illegible]	[illegible]			[illegible]
Taxation Imperial revenue	[illegible]	[illegible]	[illegible]			
Local taxation	[illegible]	[illegible]	[illegible]			
Total taxation	[illegible]	[illegible]	[illegible]			
[illegible]	[illegible]					

That Ireland has been since the Union, and is now, overtaxed in comparison with Great Britain is true and indisputable; the only question seems to be to what extent. The income-tax figures indicate a proportion of 1 to 21 as Ireland's share of taxation, and for incomes below the limit of taxation the proportion would probably be about 1 to [illegible]. But what Ireland should pay to the Imperial revenue on terms of equal capacity for taxation must be qualified by the consideration that she does not and cannot derive an equal advantage with Great Britain from much of the Imperial expenditure.

The excessive cost of Imperial administration in Ireland, as shown in the Treasury tables, is due partly to the unfair way in which the expenditure is classified, but chiefly to the fact that Great Britain claims to regulate every matter great or small in Ireland, instead of leaving to the Irish taxpayers and their representatives all those matters of which the Irish must be better judges than the people of another country.

Ireland has only the semblance of constitutional Government, for she is still, as Sir John Parnell pointed out in 1800, entirely at the mercy of the United Parliament with only 100 members against 562.

The excessive cost of the British administration of Ireland is an arithmetical demonstration of the incapacity of Great Britain to govern Ireland, for no one would maintain to-day that Ireland has been well governed since the Union, and the present expense speaks for itself.

No adjustment of the financial relations of the two kingdoms could fairly be made without taking into consideration the past over-payments by Ireland. The misery and moral evils caused by over-taxation, and the mis-spending of the Irish revenue cannot be measured in money or expressed in figures. She has paid since the Union from 7 [illegible] to [illegible] per cent. of the Imperial revenue; whether the over-payment be taken at [illegible] a year for [illegible] years, or [illegible] for 40 years, Great Britain's debt to Ireland is only to be reckoned in hundreds of millions.

Taxation is no evil if the public services rendered in return are worth the money; but what result is to be seen in Ireland for her contributions to the revenue of the richest country in the world? In no other civilised country is a rapid and continual diminution of the population taken to be a sign of prosperity, and as I have already shown, the income-tax assessment has practically not increased at all since 1864.

Any advantage Ireland derives from her connexion with Great Britain is not political or administrative, but geographical, from her proximity to the markets of Great Britain.

It is often said that Ireland is as much interested in the army and navy expenditure as England is, as she is now an importer of cereal food, and requires the ocean highways kept open for this purpose. This is pure nonsense; Ireland could maintain double the present population. She used to grow corn not only for home

consumption, but for exportation, and would do so again if prices warranted it. A war, which were partially checked the importation of food into Great Britain, would be an immediate advantage to the Irish farmer. The proximity of the English markets was at one time an advantage to Ireland, but those markets are now open to all the world, and the present conditions of ocean carriage and freights are such as to have deprived the Irish farmer of the superior advantages he formerly possessed.

Ireland's requirements for defence may be compared with those of Sweden and Norway. Sweden's population, 4,784,981, is nearer that of Ireland than any other European country; her agricultural products much the same; but she has considerable commerce and mineral wealth. Her revenue is under 5,000,000*l*., her army costs 1,140,000*l*., and her navy 340,000*l*., both together about as much as the Irish police cost. Norway, with a population somewhat less than half Ireland's, viz., 2,001,000, has a revenue of 2,800,000*l*. Her army costs 435,000*l*.; her navy, 149,000*l*.

These two countries have a larger amount of merchant shipping than any European country except Great Britain. Comparing Ireland's condition with these countries, it must be remembered that Ireland has neither shipping, commerce, or neighbours against whom it would be necessary to keep up armies and navies.

The economic causes of Ireland's poverty and non-progression in prosperity, as compared with the rest of the United Kingdom, are—

1. Over-taxation for over 50 years.
2. Drain of absentee rental.
3. Bad laws, chiefly those which have prevented agricultural improvement and enterprise, and now maintain a system of land tenure under which no prudent person, whether landlord or tenant, ought to lay out money in the permanent improvement of land.
4. The fall in agricultural prices and farm profits.

The manifest symptoms of this poverty are—

1. A continually diminishing population.
2. Decaying towns and villages.
3. Emigration.
4. Migration of labourers for temporary employment to Great Britain and the United States.
5. Annually recurring distress, and periodical famines.
6. Persistent and unabated social and political discontent.
7. The appearance of the mass of people—their houses, clothes, and food.

It is doubtful whether Ireland has increased at all in wealth during the last 30 years, although, owing to the diminishing population, it may be shown statistically that there are more acres of land, pounds of valuation, miles of railway, &c. per head of population; but this is not prosperity.

No poor agricultural country such as Ireland could stand the continued drain of excessive taxation she has been subjected to and of remittances to absentees, without the economic effects of such unremunerative payments becoming evident. These payments are equivalent to a perpetual bad harvest or annual cattle plague. If the entire potato crop or the whole saleable produce of Ireland's live stock were annually carried away without return, or if absentee payments were made in one sum as a tribute, the magnitude of the economic drain would be clearly recognised. The evil is no less because these payments without return are made to a number of individuals or go to support the dignity, maintain the strength, and reduce the debt of Great Britain.

As to Ireland's chief industry, farming, she suffers far more than England from the agricultural depression which is admitted to exist there. There is no reason why she should not. The climate of Ireland is very much the same as that of England; the principal crops grown are of the same kind, but the English climate and markets make better farming profitable, and the growth of fruit, flowers, vegetables, and hops possible and profitable. Owing to the large urban population, the English farmer has better markets within easy reach, and his produce is worth more than the Irish farmer's at the prices of their consumption, the large English towns; for the Irish farmer has to bear the cost and risk of carriage. The English farmer has a more abundant supply of manure from the large towns and villages, and can, therefore, farm more highly and grow heavier crops. He can get his feeding stuffs, artificial manures, agricultural implements, and appliances more cheaply than the Irish farmer, for many of these things are imported to Ireland from England. Above all, the English farmer rents his land fully equipped with buildings, roads, gates, fences, and thoroughly drained. The farm equipments are renewed and maintained by the landowner other out of other resources than the rental of the agricultural estate.

Mr. R. P. Squarey thus describes the position of the English farmer to the Royal Commission on Agriculture, at Question 7301, "I think, as a rule, English land is so perfectly equipped that it has all that is wanted for its proper management and cultivation, and the tenant is simply called upon to apply himself to the more practical aspect of the question of cultivation." Yet with all these advantages the condition of English farmers is deplorable; over large areas of good farming land no rent is earned; many farmers are paying rent out of capital.

The Irish farmer, on the contrary, has to supply these equipments and adjuncts to the farm without which in England no tenant would be found to rent it; he bears the whole cost of repairs and maintenance; he has, therefore, to bear alone the loss that is shared between landowner and farmer in England. Consequently he has less capital available for cultivation, and what he does in the way of equipment, and improvements, and renewals, is often done in a half-hearted way, and imperfectly, for he is sinking his capital in another person's property. His farming is carried on in the face of difficulties that are inconceivable to the English farmer with his "perfectly equipped" land.

Irish farm buildings are mostly bad and thatched, costly to maintain, uncomfortable and unhealthy for man and beast; farms are imperfectly fenced, insufficiently drained, without gates or proper farm roads. The cost of production is, therefore, much more to the Irish farmer, the prices he obtains are at least 15 per cent. less than those obtained by the English farmer.

It is no wonder then that Irish farms and farm-steads have deteriorated in condition and repair, for the farmer has had less to spend in maintaining them. It is an arithmetical impossibility that the volume of business in country towns should not have decreased, for both landowners and farmers have had very much smaller incomes to spend of late years, and the fall in price of articles of common consumption has not been so great as to counterbalance the fall in profits of the landed interest. Experience and inquiry show that what is a priori probable, is actually the case, and in a comparison of the wealth of Great Britain and Ireland, the difference in the conditions of farming and in farm profits must not be left out of consideration.

The physical ability of the population, as well as their occupation, counts for much in measuring their means of wealth and capacity for taxation. The population of Ireland is mainly rural, and should be more robust and long-lived than the mainly urban population of England. That the reverse is the case is due to the general poverty of the country, and the annual elimination by emigration of the most able and enterprising of the population in the flower of youth. This is shown by the larger proportion in Ireland of blind, deaf-mutes, and lunatic or idiotic persons, and by the proportion of persons living who are over 65 years of age; for, though the absolute proportions of the latter are almost the same in England and Ireland, a more proper comparison would be between Ireland and the rural districts of England.

The following figures, from the General Report of the Census, England, give a comparison of the civil condition, occupations, infirmities, and pauperism in the three divisions of the United Kingdom, and the figures from the Registrar-General's Report show the

average births, deaths, and marriages for 20 years to 1891:—

[illegible]		England. Males.	England. Females.	Scotland. Males.	Scotland. Females.	Ireland. Males.	Ireland. Females.
Proportion per 1,000 living—							
Single		[illegible]	[illegible]	[illegible]	[illegible]	[illegible]	[illegible]
Married		[illegible]	[illegible]	[illegible]	[illegible]	[illegible]	[illegible]
Widowed		36	73	[illegible]	[illegible]	[illegible]	[illegible]
Professional		[illegible]		[illegible]		[illegible]	
Domestic		[illegible]		[illegible]		[illegible]	
Commercial		[illegible]		[illegible]		[illegible]	
Agricultural and fisher		[illegible]		[illegible]		[illegible]	
Industrial		[illegible]		[illegible]		[illegible]	
Unoccupied		[illegible]		[illegible]		[illegible]	
Paupers 65 years old and upwards at Census, 1891, per 1,000 living	Urban districts	[illegible]		Not ascertained.		[illegible]	
	Rural districts	[illegible]					
Proportion per 1,000,000 living							
Blind		[illegible]		[illegible]		[illegible]	

[illegible]	England. Males.	England. Females.	Scotland. Males.	Scotland. Females.	Ireland. Males.	Ireland. Females.
Proportion of 1,000,000 living— Deaf and dumb	[illegible]		[illegible]		[illegible]	
Mentally deranged	[illegible]		[illegible]		[illegible]	
In receipt of indoor relief	[illegible]		[illegible]		[illegible]	
In prison	[illegible]		[illegible]		[illegible]	

AVERAGE NUMBER of PERSONS MARRIED, of BIRTHS and of DEATHS to 1,000 PERSONS LIVING, in 20 Years from 1871–92. Registrar-General's Report, 1894, Table 20.

Persons Married, Births, and Deaths.	England.	Scotland.	Ireland.
[illegible]	[illegible]	[illegible]	[illegible]
[illegible]	[illegible]	[illegible]	[illegible]
Number of deaths	[illegible]	[illegible]	[illegible]
[illegible] 20 years, 1871–91			
Urban districts	[illegible]		
Rural districts	[illegible]		

B. SUPPLEMENTARY MEMORANDUM as to the CHURCH PROPERTY FUND and PUBLIC LOANS by Mr. MURROUGH O'BRIEN, in connection with the EVIDENCE given by HIM before the COMMISSION.

MEMORANDUM as to the CHURCH PROPERTY FUND and PUBLIC LOANS, by MURROUGH O'BRIEN.

The history of the Church Temporalities Fund is an example of the financial dealings of Great Britain with Ireland.

Tithe rent-charge and perpetuity rents.

The principal part of the property consisted of tithe rentcharge amounting to 410,000*l*. a year, and perpetuity and other rents amounting to 121,000*l*.

Tithe rentcharges, though a first charge on the land, were difficult to identify, costly to collect, and not easily saleable in the open market. As a rule, they were not worth more than 17 years' purchase.

Perpetuity rents were not worth more than 21 years' purchase (see O'Conor Don's Report to Bessborough Commissioners, page 62), and as the Church rents were variable with corn prices they are not worth as much as ordinary fee farm rents.

Artificial value to capital of the Church Fund.

The Church Act, however, fixed the price of tithe rentcharge at 22½ and that of perpetuity rents at 25 years' purchase, thus adding (410,000*l*. × 5½ and 121,000*l*. × 4) 2,739,000*l*. to the then market value of these securities.

The value of the Church Fund was thus artificially swollen, to the detriment of the owners of property subject to these charges.

Variation of tithe abolished.

By the Church Amendment Act, 1872, s. 6 (3), the right of varying the rentcharge was taken away. But for this Act the rentcharge of 410,000*l*. would now only be worth 287,000*l*., and its capital value at 17 years' purchase would be 4,879,000*l*., instead of 9,225,000*l*.

Nearly 4,500,000*l*. added to landowners' liabilities.

In fact, by the Church Acts, a capital sum of 4,375,000*l*. was imposed on the payers of tithe rentcharge and perpetuity rents in excess of the present market value of these securities.

Imperial charges transferred to Church Fund.

On the fund thus swollen were placed charges that had hitherto been paid out of the Imperial revenue, and subsequently other charges which must have been paid, if at all, from the same source.

Maynooth grant.

Regium Donum.

372,331*l*. was paid out of the Church Fund in lieu of the Maynooth grant hitherto paid out of the Imperial revenue, and 771,757*l*. for the Regium Donum, which had been a charge on the Imperial revenue since the time of Charles the Second.

Other charges on Church Fund.

The whole Church Fund has since been practically allocated for purposes which would otherwise have had to be met by grants from the Imperial revenue to meet temporary emergencies, such as famine and exceptional distress, or political emergencies affecting the peace of the United Kingdom; or to provide for the educational wants of Ireland, a primary want which, having regard to the history of education in Ireland and to her large contribution to the Imperial revenue, should have been paid from that source.

The National Debt Commissioners advanced the principal sums required to satisfy most of the charges imposed on the Church Fund, requiring interest at 4¼ per cent. on the greater part of their loans, and in no instance less than 3½; repayments of principal being made from time to time as funds were available.

The following amounts were advanced on the Church Fund and have been partially repaid with interest during the last 20 years:—

1. 9,000,000*l*. at 3½ per cent., the Irish Church Act Loan, applied to compensation of life interests, Maynooth grant, Regium Donum, and partial re-endowment of the Episcopal Church.
2. 50,302*l*. at 3½ per cent., relief of distressed unions.
3. 250,000*l*. at 3½ per cent., Sea Fisheries Act loan.
4. 20,000*l*. at 3½ per cent., Poor Relief Act.
5. 900,000*l*. at 3½ per cent., Arrears of Rent Act.
6. 700,000*l*. in 1880; 500,000*l*. in 1881; 50,000*l*. in 1883–4; 15,000*l*. in 1884–5; 3,500*l*. in 1886–7 — Relief of Distress Act. Total—1,271,000*l*. at 3¼ per cent.

Out of 11,476,802*l*. total loans from National Debt Commissioners, 7,215,620*l*. were paid off to March 1894.

The average annual amount of interest paid for 23 years to the National Debt Commissioners has been 216,031*l*.

The average annual amount of capital repaid during 19 years has been 379,769*l*.

These loans are unremunerative to Ireland; they were made to avert famine, relieve distress, or to get over some difficulty which embarrassed the Imperial Parliament for the moment; but they were a good investment for the British Treasury which not only got its interest at 3½ per cent., but has received back a large amount of the principal.

The landlords who were the payers of tithe rentcharge and perpetuity rents were unfairly mulcted by the excessive prices imposed for the redemption of these charges; redemption being compulsory, for, practically, no estate can be sold except upon terms of these charges being redeemed, and the right of varying the tithe rentcharge was taken away.

Further sums were charged directly on the Church Fund without the intervention of the the National Debt Commissioners, and for purposes which, if not economically remunerative, were at any rate useful and beneficial to Ireland; but in these cases Parliament reduced the rate of interest payable on the principal sums allocated, although the Treasury still maintains the high rates of interest charged on its loans.

These further charges are for—

	£	Yearly. £
(1.) Intermediate education - - -	1,0[illegible] at 3[illegible] %.	[illegible]
(2.) National School Teachers' Fund -	1,[illegible] at [illegible] %.	[illegible]
(3.) Congested Districts board - -	1,[illegible] at [illegible] %.	[illegible]
(4.) Royal University (in principal sum fixed) say - -	700,000	[illegible]
Total -	[illegible]	[illegible]

The interest payable on the balance of debt still due to the National Debt Commissioners for the year ending 31st March 1894 was [illegible], whereas if the rate was [illegible] per cent., it would have been [illegible] less.

The amounts paid as interest in former years were considerably more, as a large part of the principal sum has been repaid in each year since 1871.

Any ultimate surplus there should have been in the Church Fund has been largely reduced by the excess of interest (about [illegible] a year on an average) paid to the Treasury on the loans from the commencement.

At present the estimates of the value of the Church Fund show a considerable surplus, on paper; the estimate being made upon the assumption that the whole revenue will be collected and redemptions carried out at statutory prices. This is highly improbable.

The present Church revenue, amounting to about [illegible], is collected from [illegible] payers, the items varying from [illegible] to [illegible] a year. Much of the property out of which the revenue arises was unidentified, and in case of non-payment there is still difficulty and expense both in the actual identification of the lands and in fixing the liability on the particular person whose estate in the lands makes him liable for the charge.

In the [illegible] years to March 1894, [illegible] of revenue was "remitted or written off" from the Fund, and in many instances the capital sum represented by the annual amount written off has been lost.

Part of the loss is due to an unwise economy which kept the staff below an efficient strength. A full establishment on a permanent basis was necessary to keep arrears from accruing.

The cost of the collection and administration of the Church Property Fund, of which the ordinary income is estimated in Sir John Hibbert's return, No. [illegible], 1894, as [illegible], is about [illegible] a year. [illegible] is spent on collection proper and sales business, and [illegible] on identification of the lands liable and investigation of the personal liabilities to the charge.

The entire charge is [illegible] per cent. on the revenue, and the collection and sales expenses amount to only [illegible] per cent.

It will be clear to anyone acquainted with collection business that a complicated revenue derived from landed property, and consisting of several different classes of annual payments, most of which have to be collected twice a year, could not be efficiently collected for [illegible] per cent., nor collected, managed, identified, and sold for [illegible] per cent.

Comparing it with other collections, it may be noted that the cost of collecting and accounting for the rental of [illegible], under the Court of Chancery was, in 1894, [illegible], or nearly [illegible] per cent. (Lord Ardilaun's Return [illegible].)

The cost of the Woods and Forests Department, collecting a gross income of [illegible], amounts to [illegible], or [illegible] per cent. on the revenue ("Whitaker's Almanac," [illegible]).

Of the [illegible] persons employed in the Church Property branch, [illegible] are temporary clerks (many of them writers and Lower Division clerks, assigned to this department while waiting for permanent posts). The frequent changes, departures, and introduction for a short time of new hands, is very detrimental to the efficiency of the staff; many clerks remain for a short time and leave the establishment as soon as they have become acquainted with the current office work and practice, and are replaced by clerks who have to learn the rudiments of the work again at the expense of the efficiency of the entire staff.

The want of a sufficient permanent staff has been one cause of the arrears on and losses to the Church Fund. Part of these would not have occurred if a sufficient permanent staff had been fixed by the Treasury from the first. During the last four years about [illegible] a year has been remitted or written off, and the amount tends to increase.

The following table shows the rental for each year ending on 31st March [illegible], the arrears at end of the year, and the amount written off or remitted since [illegible]:—

Year.	Rental, as per Accounts.	Arrears at end of Year.	Remitted or Written off during Year.
	£	£	£ s. d.
[illegible]	[illegible]	[illegible]	[illegible]
[illegible]	[illegible]	[illegible]	[illegible]
[illegible]	[illegible]	[illegible]	[illegible]
[illegible]	[illegible]	[illegible]	[illegible]
[illegible]	[illegible]	[illegible]	[illegible]
[illegible]	[illegible]	[illegible]	[illegible]
[illegible]	[illegible]	[illegible]	[illegible]
[illegible]	[illegible]	[illegible]	[illegible]
[illegible]	[illegible]	[illegible]	[illegible]
[illegible]	[illegible]	[illegible]	[illegible]

Part of the arrears is not a bad debt; it is merely late in payment. But there is a considerable proportion where the number of annual payments in arrear is very large; and the arrear is not only in danger of being lost, but also the capital charge which it represents, as the following table, giving the number of cases and the amounts, where from six to over [illegible] years' annual payments are in arrear, 31st March 1894, shows:—

—	No. of Cases.	Six Years and under Twelve Years.	No. of Cases.	Twelve Years and over.	Totals. No. of Cases.	Totals. Amount.
		£ s. d.		£ s. d.		£ s. d.
Tithe rent-charges and [illegible]	[illegible]	[illegible]	[illegible]	[illegible]	[illegible]	[illegible]
Rents and interest on mortgages	[illegible]	[illegible]	[illegible]	[illegible]	[illegible]	[illegible]
	[illegible]	[illegible]	[illegible]	[illegible]	[illegible]	[illegible]

Thus, though a large part of the Church revenue is well secured and punctually collected, there is a "bad end" on the property the collection of which is difficult and costly, on which there will be ultimately a loss. Other circumstances will also make the real ultimate surplus less than that estimated.

(1.) The interest on the mortgages for three-fourths of the purchase money advanced to tenant purchasers has, in some cases, become more than the value of the premises purchased. Where the occupiers are dispossessed the premises must either be held by the Land Commission at a loss or sold for less than the value of the mortgage.

(2.) Perpetuity rents, amounting to nearly [illegible] a year, are liable to variation with the price of corn. Since 1884 [illegible] rents, amounting to [illegible], have been reduced under the provisions for variation to [illegible], a diminution of the capital value at 25 years' purchase of [illegible]. Many more of these rents will be reduced, for grantees have only lately become aware of their right to have the rents varied.

(3.) In cases of sales under the Purchase Acts, vendors can compel the redemption of perpetuity rents, and, as the price can be fixed at vendor's option by arbitration, it is unlikely that 25 years' purchase will be obtained for them.

For the reasons above stated the solvency of the Church Fund, subject to the payment of the charges already placed upon it, cannot be assumed.

There will be a certain diminution of the estimated surplus from—

(1.) Annual and principal sums found irrecoverable.

(2.) Diminution of perpetuity rents as the periods for variation come round.

(3.) Redemption of perpetuity rents at less than 25 years' purchase.

(4.) Sales of land where Land Commission obtain possession through default of payers.

What is required on the re-adjustment of Church Fund.

The solvency of the fund would be secured by—

(1.) Immediate reduction of the excessive rates of interest payable to the National Debt Commissioners.

(2.) Refund of past payments of interest at excessive rates.

(3.) Establishment of the Church property staff on a permanent basis at such a strength as would enable it to deal efficiently with collection of arrears and current revenue, investigations of liabilities, identification of lands liable, and sales.

Profit to Great Britain from Church Fund.

The Church Fund has been a source of profit to Great Britain and of loss to Ireland. Great Britain has benefited by the transfer to the Church Fund of charges which previously fell on the Imperial revenue, by the imposition on the fund of other charges which would have fallen on the Public revenue, and by the profit made on loans to Ireland at an excessive rate of interest. Ireland lost not only to the extent by which Great Britain benefited, but by the artificial embarrassment of the Church Fund by legislation.

Loss to Ireland.

Before 1869 the whole revenue of the Church was spent in Ireland; since then practically the whole revenue has been remitted to England, and the capital has been largely spent for purposes from which there is no economic return. The Episcopal community now tax themselves to the extent of about 160,000*l.* a year for the support of their Church.

Fallacy of alleged liberality of the loan system.

The loans made out of Imperial funds on the security of the Church Fund, as well as those made through the Board of Works, amounting to about 5,000,000*l.*, are illustrations of the alleged "liberality" with which it is said Ireland has been treated.

Difference between Great Britain's and Ireland's requirements.

The prosperity of Great Britain depends on the maintenance and extension of her industries and commerce; the prosperity of Ireland on the development of her internal resources and the better organisation of her social, political, and economic system. Ireland contributes, without getting any return, to the wars, the forward and foreign policy of Great Britain. Her struggle is against want, occasional famines, and chronic distress. For the expenditure made to avert these calamities, or repair the damages done by them, expenditure on relief works, land improvement, arterial drainage, and grants in aid of distress, &c., Ireland has to pay 3½ per cent.; yet the removal of the causes of poverty in Ireland is as legitimate a purpose for Imperial expenditure without charge as the wars and foreign policy to which Ireland has had to contribute for the development of Great Britain's industries and extension of her commerce.

The Irish difficulty, the cause of her chronic discontent, has always been her poverty. A prosperous people is seldom discontented even under unjust laws. The system of Imperial loans for temporary emergencies and charity tends to increase the poverty of Ireland, whose future income is mortgaged to pay interest on expenditure from which there is no return. There is no surer road to ruin for an individual than borrowing money to live upon; and most of these Imperial loans are practically made from time to time to enable the Irish people to live, or to relieve acute distress and avert disorder. Loans are almost annually made to keep the people quiet, or to keep them alive. Yet, this expenditure has not prevented the recurrence of famine, distress, and discontent; it rather tends to cause their recurrence, for such expenses entirely spent leave nothing in the hands or the income of the country, and it is well known that a great deal of the money nominally meant to be spent on reproductive works has been misspent and wasted.

The 11¼ millions lent by the National Debt Commissioners on the Church Fund were thoroughly well secured loans, and at 3½ per cent. interest were a profitable investment for the Treasury.

The other public loans to Ireland, through the Board of Works and Public Works Loans Commissioners, amounted on 31st March 1893, to 7,604,258*l.* (*Mr. Smith Barry's return*, 376, 1893). The greater part of this amount is provided by Ireland, for the deposits in the Irish Post Office Savings Bank, and balances from the trustee banks in the hands of the National Debt Commissioners, amount to 6,827,000*l.*—(*Registrar General's Return*, June 1894.)

APPENDIX III.

A.—Parliamentary Return C. 313 of 1894, being the Copy of Memorandum by the Treasury on the subject of (1) the Amounts contributed, so far as can be ascertained, by the Inhabitants of Great Britain and Ireland respectively to the Revenue collected by Imperial Officers at intervals since the Union of the British and Irish Exchequers; (2) the Expenditure out of the Amounts so contributed upon Local Services in Great Britain and Ireland respectively; (3) the Expenditure out of the Amounts so contributed on Imperial Services.

IMPERIAL REVENUE (COLLECTION AND EXPENDITURE), GREAT BRITAIN AND IRELAND.

Copy of Memorandum by the Treasury on the subject of (1) the Amounts contributed, so far as can be ascertained, by the Inhabitants of Great Britain and Ireland respectively to the Revenue collected by Imperial Officers at intervals since the Union of the British and Irish Exchequers; (2) the Expenditure out of the Amounts so contributed upon Local Services in Great Britain and Ireland respectively; (3) the Expenditure out of the Amounts so contributed on Imperial Services.

General Introduction.

1. The Order of the House of Commons, in pursuance of which this Memorandum has been prepared, is drawn nearly in the same terms as those under which have been prepared the Returns headed "Financial Relations (England, Scotland, and Ireland)," several of which have been published during the last few years.* In the present Order, however, no separation is attempted between England and Scotland, while the field of inquiry, instead of being confined to particular years,† is extended over the period of nearly 80 years which has elapsed since the Union of the British and Irish Exchequers on the 5th January 1817.

2. The object of this memorandum, as ordered by the House, is to provide materials for discussing the relations of Great Britain and Ireland to each other in the matter of national finance since the date when their public revenues were constituted a single fund, out of which were met both the common expenditure of the two and the separate expenditure of each. From this point of view the two islands must be regarded as a co-partnership, possessing a single banking account, drafts on which are applicable to the individual expenditure of the two partners as well as to the requirements of the partnership. Under the Order no question arises as the character of the several taxes from which the revenue is derived, nor as to the incidence of the taxation upon individuals or classes within the two communities. Nor, on the other hand, do any considerations arise as to the purpose or utility of any part of the expenditure; the Treasury is only required to class that expenditure as joint or separate. It has seemed convenient, and consonant with the intentions of the Order, to approach the question primarily from the Irish side.

3. The "Financial Relations" Returns referred to above cover the period from 1889 to the present date. The tables prepared for the present memorandum have,

* House of Commons, No. [illegible], Session 1891; Nos. [illegible], and [illegible] of Session 1893. [illegible]

† [illegible] the years 1890–91 and 1891–92 will be found in No. [illegible] of 1893, those for 1892–93 in No. [illegible], for 1893–94 in No. [illegible] of 1893, and for [illegible] in No. [illegible] of 1894.

for the most part, been taken at 10 years intervals back from 1889-90, viz. :—

For the year ended	31st	March	1880.	
"	"	31st	"	1870.
"	"	31st	"	1860.
For the year ended	5th	January	1850.	
"	"	5th	"	1840.
"	"	5th	"	1830.
"	"	5th	"	1820.

The figures of 1889-90 have been taken from Paper No. 93 of 1891. Figures for quinquennial intervals might, perhaps, have given a more complete view of the subject; but the preparation of such additional figures would have involved a great deal of labour and consideration, and, consequently, would have occasioned more time than was consistent with early production of the results. In the cases, however, of tea and tobacco it has been possible to refer to quinquennial statistics.

5. The principles and methods upon which the results contained in the "Financial Relations" Returns were obtained are explained in Paper No. 329 of 1891, and in the Memorandum produced as Paper No. 93 of 1891. It is only necessary here to observe that what is called in those papers "Revenue as contributed," is referred to in the present paper as "true revenue." This term is used in order to avoid the ambiguous use of the word "contribution," which is here adopted solely to mean the surplus available for Imperial expenditure after local charges have been met. These principles and methods have been adhered to in the present Memorandum so far as possible; but, speaking generally, in the figures of past years the lapse of time and the imperfections of the record render it more difficult to arrive with confidence at even approximate results. The nature of such difficulties, and the extent to which they affect the probable accuracy of conclusions, will be shown in subsequent portions of this Memorandum. At present it need only be said that, at least under the head of expenditure, the field of error appears on investigation to be narrower than might have been anticipated. The labour of analysis, and the risk of error, would both have been greatly increased if it had been desired to treat England and Scotland separately, as was done in the returns for later years; in fact, owing to the absence of published figures for Scotland apart from England, the work would have been almost impossible.

6. The figures submitted in response to the third head of the Order of the House supply an estimate of the surplus available for Imperial services out of the revenue contributed by the inhabitants of Great Britain and Ireland respectively. In other words they may be taken as the amounts contributed by the two countries towards the joint expenses of the partnership, Great Britain and Ireland being regarded for this purpose as separate entities.

4. It will be observed that no reference is made in what follows to the subject of loans from public funds for local objects. The terms of the Order do not in their natural sense refer to loans; and apart from that, the subject could only be dealt with by a separate discussion involving not only the consideration of the amount of benefit derived by localities from public loans, but also a calculation of the financial results of an actual system of loans to the lending fund. Where, however, an advance was made originally as a loan, but was subsequently turned into a local grant, these considerations do not apply, and the advance may be treated statistically as local expenditure to be included in the budget of the year. In the year 1879-80, under a system which existed from 1875 to 1887, the Exchequer Accounts of Revenue and Expenditure contain on the one side interest received from public loans, and on the other hand charges in respect of money borrowed for such loans. These items have, on the principles laid down in this and the next paragraph, been altogether excluded from the figures in the present memorandum.

7. In concluding this branch of the subject it may be remarked that, in the tables which follow, uniformity has been regarded as an important object in dealing with the comparative figures of different years. The great changes in the methods of presenting the Public Accounts have rendered this object difficult of attainment, and, further, have involved, especially in the earlier years, considerable departures from the published figures. Such discrepancies, however, are inevitable, and admit of ready explanation; and in the result it has been found possible to produce a fairly coherent series of figures for the purpose of complying with the Order of the House.

MATERIALS.

8. The principal source of information for the purposes of the present inquiry is, of course, the series of "Finance Accounts of the United Kingdom," which cover the whole period. These accounts have undergone many changes of form in the course of their history, three of which may be specially referred to here, in retrograde chronological order.

(a) In 1869-70 for the last time the "Gross Public Revenue" of Great Britain and that of Ireland were separately shown. The figures so given were merely the revenue as collected in the two islands, which may differ materially from that contributed by their respective inhabitants, the "true revenue"; and it was because of this fact, which was considered to render the accounts as they stood misleading, that the Public Accounts Committee of 1871 recommended in their First Report* that, among other changes, the separate statements for the two islands should be discontinued. This recommendation was carried into effect in the accounts for 1870-71 and subsequent years, but the separate statements, with all their defects, have been of the greatest service in the present inquiry, which indeed would have been almost impracticable in the absence of them. No such series of separate accounts has been kept for Scotland.

(b) In 1854 the date of the close of the financial year was altered from 5th January to 31st March under the authority of the Act 17 & 18 Vict. c. 94. Hence it is that in the present Memorandum there is a corresponding change between 1849 and 1859.

(c) Down to 1825 inclusive, the Trade Statistics which then and for many years later formed part of the "Finance Accounts," gave in a distinguishable form the cross-channel trade between Great Britain and Ireland, with values for the principal articles. Thus, for the first year (1819) discussed in this Memorandum, independent evidence exists as to the course of trade in dutiable goods between the two islands.

9. Between 1869-70 and 1889-90, the year for which the "Financial Relations" Returns, already referred to, begin, several returns were made on the motion of the late Mr. MacLaren and others, showing the amounts of sundry branches of revenue collected in Great Britain and Ireland respectively.† In these returns the heads of receipt are arranged in what now appears a somewhat capricious manner, while some items are omitted altogether; and another feature in these recurring returns is that, while the bulk of the figures refer to collection, in the case of British spirits alone an attempt is made to show the true revenue by the use of the special but somewhat doubtful statistics described in paragraph 16, of the movements of duty-paid spirits between the three kingdoms. These Returns, however, afford some information for the interval between 1869-70 and 1889-90.

10. The reports of the Committee on the Taxation of Ireland,‡ 1864 and 1865, include in the attached evidence and Appendices some remarks and statistics bearing on the subject now under consideration. But the attention of that Committee was mainly occupied with the Treaty of Union and the financial arrangements of the years 1801-1816; and in their proceedings but little consideration was given to the relations between special British or Irish expenditure on the one hand, and British and Irish revenue on the other. Reference may, however, be made in the volume of 1864 to p. 61 of the evidence (Wilson), and to Appendix, pp. 325, 328, 329 (Fisher), pp. 332 and following (Dwyer), and pp. 413, 414 (Chisholm); in the volume of 1865 to pp. xi., xii., xiv. (Report), and pp. 168, 169, 194-199 (Chisholm).

11. The great Return of Revenue and Expenditure, 1688-1869, prepared by Mr. H. W. Chisholm, contains some figures bearing on the separate revenue of Ireland during the period, at pp. 153 foll. of Part II. (House of Commons, 366-I. of 1869).

12. The three historical reports of the Board of Inland Revenue, published in 1857,§ 1870‖ (Part II.), and 1885,¶ give a considerable amount of information as to the collection of Excise, Stamps, and Taxes, under their several heads in the three kingdoms separately. These statistics are specially valuable for present purposes in the case of Income Tax (since its extension to Ireland in 1853) and of British spirits. As regards the last-named article special accounts have

* House of Commons, No. 201 of 1871; pp. 3, 4, 5; Questions [illegible].

† That for 1879-80 is House of Commons, No. [illegible] of 1882.

‡ House of Commons Papers, No. 513 of 1864, and No. 330 of 1865.

§ C.—2199. ‖ C.—82-I. ¶ C.—4474.

been kept since 1826 of the movements of duty-paid spirits between England, Scotland, and Ireland, by a method described in the Board's published Report of 6th June 1893.* The results have been published in the Board's Annual Reports, and, four times a year, in the Trade and Navigation Returns. Tables for a series of years will be found at p. 8 of the Report of 1870, Part II., and at p. 142 of the Report of 1893. The Report of 6th June 1893 also refers to certain defects in these results.

13. Besides these general sources of information, special reference has been made to Reports and Returns of the Commissioners of Woods for the Crown Revenue in Ireland (not distinguished in the Finance Accounts), and much information and advice has been supplied by the two Revenue Boards bearing on different points in connection with the relation between revenue as collected on the one hand and true revenue on the other.

REVENUE.

14. The first step towards forming an estimate of the true amounts paid, by the inhabitants of Great Britain and Ireland respectively, towards the revenue collected by imperial officers, is to obtain the figures of revenue as collected in the two islands. This has been done with approximate accuracy, and the results for Ireland, with percentages of Irish collections to those of the United Kingdom, are given in Table A. of Part I. of the Appendix to this memorandum. Table B. gives the figures under the main heads of receipt, while Table C. supplies the principal details in consecutive form. The following general observations should be made in connection with these tables.

(a.) The figures under the different heads represent net receipts, *i.e.*, the gross revenue collected in the year, less drawbacks, discounts, and other repayments which are merely repayments of revenue. In 1849 and earlier years, the cost of collection, which since 1854 has been voted by Parliament like other branches of expenditure, was generally treated as a deduction from the receipt under the corresponding head of revenue, and various other charges, which now fall upon the Consolidated Fund or upon annual votes of Parliament, were paid out of one head or another of the gross revenue in its progress to the Exchequer. In the table, all such items have been excluded from the deductions from gross revenue; they will be found under appropriate heads in the table of expenditure. This arrangement facilitates comparison between the different years comprised in the tables; its effect is, of course, to increase both sides of the account.

(b.) For a similar reason the receipts from fee stamps have been transferred in 1879-80 and former years from the head of Stamp Revenue to that of Miscellaneous Revenue, under which they have been most properly classified in recent years.

(c.) As regards the figures of Miscellaneous Revenue it should be observed that in the earlier years a considerable sum yielded by such receipts was applied in reduction of voted expenditure; that, subsequently, up to 1879-80 inclusive (of the years now under consideration), the tendency was towards paying such receipts into the exchequer and providing the corresponding expenditure in gross, thereby swelling both the revenue and the expenditure; and that in 1889-90 and subsequent years the tendency has been in the opposite direction. It would have taken too much time and labour to adjust these figures throughout on a uniform principle, and the attempt has consequently not been made.

15. The figures in Tables A., B., C. are not without value and interest, taken even as they stand. But it is matter of common knowledge that they do not represent the true incidence of taxation on the inhabitants of the two islands. Two examples, taken from indirect and direct taxation respectively, will suffice to illustrate this point. When an Englishman buys Irish whiskey he pays, in the price of his purchase, spirit duty which probably has been already collected in Ireland. When an Irishman invests his savings in an English railway company's stock, the income tax on that portion of his property is collected in Great Britain. The relation between the true and the apparent share of each kingdom in the national revenue has been fully discussed in recent years in connection with the "Financial Relations" Returns, already referred to; and on the result of such discussions the figures on page 4 of Return No. 93 of 1891 may be accepted to represent the probable true produce of the revenue in England, Scotland, and Ireland in 1889-90, subject to one source of error which will be explained in the next paragraph, and to any better results which further inquiry may supply.

	£
It appears that while the apparent revenue derived from Ireland in 1889-90 was . . .	9,0[illegible]
The true amount, according to the assumptions in the Return, may be taken at . . .	7,8[illegible]
Showing the material reduction of	1,142,272

Turning to the beginning of the period, the figures of collection in Table A. for the year 1819 may be accepted as approximating to the true yield of revenue derived from Ireland in that year. At that time, Great Britain and Ireland were for commercial and customs purposes treated as separate countries. When duty-paid foreign or colonial goods were transferred from one country to the other, the duty had to be paid in the second country as upon a direct importation from abroad, the duty collected in the first being subsequently "drawn back," *i.e.*, repaid; it may therefore be assumed that all the dutiable goods upon which duty was collected in either island were consumed therein, and there can have been at that time no other source of error worthy of consideration, except, perhaps, the incalculable one of smuggling.* Thus materials exist for an approximate estimate of the true revenue yielded by Ireland in the first and the last years covered by this memorandum; and it remains to consider what estimate can be found in regard to the intermediate years.

16. There is one correction to the "collection" figures materials for which are available throughout the period, and that is the one arising from British spirits. As explained in paragraph 12 of this memorandum, special statistics have been kept of the movements of duty-paid spirits between the three kingdoms since 1826, and fragmentary statistics are also available for earlier periods, during which the duty on spirits was lower in Ireland than in England. The conclusions drawn from these statistics were, until 1893, regarded by the Revenue Authorities as very approximately correct; but in that year a source of error was detected (explained in Paper No. 246 of 1893, already referred to), which indicated that the true revenue of Ireland was overstated in former figures, by an amount considerable in recent years (it was about 700,000*l*. in 1891-92). Before the final assimilation of the duties in 1858 there was but little field for this source of error. In 1819, as explained in the foregoing paragraph, the correction was nil, and in subsequent years the amounts to be deducted from the revenue collected in Ireland under the head of British spirits, and to be added to that in Great Britain, appear from the records of the Inland Revenue Authorities to be as follows:—

	£
1820, to 5th January 1830	176,421
1830, to 5th " 1840	140,207
1840, to 5th " 1850 . .	120,988
1st April 1850 to 31st March 1860 .	392,789
" 1860 " 1870 .	503,999
1870 " 1880 .	815,614
1880 " 1890 .	1,364,750

The rapid increase shown by these figures in the export of duty-paid spirits from Ireland to Great Britain since the assimilation of the duties is very noticeable, but is consistent with the general experience of the officers of Excise. As already stated, this increase would have appeared even greater, had the figures been more nearly correct.

17. If the correction given in the preceding paragraph be applied to the figures in Table A., the result is as shown in Table D., which may be described as the second approximation towards the true revenue yielded by Ireland. Beyond this point no statistics are available which bear directly on the problem under consideration; and it is therefore necessary, if any further progress is to be made, to proceed by means of

* House of Commons No. 246 of 1893.

* As to special evasion of duty in Ireland, reference may be made to the Reports of the Commission of Inquiry into the Revenue arising in Ireland, Paper No. 405 of 1822, pp. 10-21; Paper No. 606 of 1823, pp. 1-8; Paper No. 405 of 1824, pp. 3, 4-6.

assumptions. Such assumptions must mainly refer (a) to the course of trade between the two countries in duty-paid dutiable articles; (b) to changes in the habits of the two populations as regards the consumption of such articles.

18. The conditions under which the trades in the various kinds of dutiable goods are carried on differ so obviously and so widely as to make it impossible to attempt any general conclusions as to the course of such trades taken collectively. The histories of the tea trade and of the beer trade, for instance, can have but little in common. In order, therefore, to form any idea of the further corrections to be applied to Table D, it is necessary to consider separately the cases of the principal dutiable articles, taking them in the order in which they appear in the published accounts.

19. *Customs.*

The Customs duties in Great Britain and Ireland were finally made identical in 1824 (4 Geo. IV., c. 72), but do not appear to have differed materially in 1819. As already explained (paras. 8 (c) and 12), the two islands formed separate statistical areas for Customs purposes down to 1826.

(1.) *Foreign Spirits.*—On the average of the three calendar years 1890 to 1893, for which exact statistics are available, it appears that the quantity of foreign spirits on which duty was collected in Ireland differed by little more than ½ per cent. from the amount consumed therein. Passing to the beginning of the period under discussion, it appears from the Trade Returns of 1820–25 that the trade in foreign spirits between the two islands was small, and on balance insignificant. It seems, therefore, safe to assume that, since at both the beginning and the end of the period the revenue as collected in Great Britain and Ireland respectively represented approximately the true revenue from foreign spirits, the same held good during the intermediate period. No corrections, therefore, under this head need be made to the figures in Table D, for 1829 to 1879.

(2.) *Tea.*—It is well known that the import trade in this article has always been concentrated to a remarkable degree in the Port of London. In 1840, 94 per cent. of the imports of tea into the United Kingdom were entered at London, and in no year since 1856 has the proportion been less than 89 per cent. In 1829 to 1832 the published trade statistics of Ireland contain no separate entry for tea imported elsewhere than from Great Britain, and it may be taken as certain that such direct imports were practically non-existent. This was to be expected from the peculiar position which the tea trade occupied in the hands of the East India Company. Thus it may be assumed that throughout the period under consideration Ireland obtained practically the whole of her tea supplies from Great Britain; and the only open question is whether those supplies came over under bond or after payment of duty in Great Britain. In the first year of those included in the table, 1819, no movement was allowed between the two islands, except on payment of duty in the place of destination, and the quantity paying duty in Ireland may, therefore, be taken as the same as that consumed therein. In that year the duty collected per head of population was 1s. 9·36d. in Ireland as compared with 4s. 7·44d. per head in Great Britain, that is to say, the percentage ratio per head was 28 per cent. in Ireland, compared with 100 in Great Britain. Since that date the duties have been the same in the two countries, though several times altered for the United Kingdom; so that the problem to be solved may be described as the determination of the ratio of consumption per head in Ireland to that in Great Britain, such ratio being most conveniently stated in the form of a percentage. The "Financial Relations" Returns for 1889–90 give the true revenue per head of population as 2s. 8·16d. in Ireland and 2s. 4·98d. per head in Great Britain, that is to say, the percentage ratio per head was 114 in Ireland, compared with 100 in Great Britain.* According to these figures the proportion of tea drunk by the average Irishman as compared with the average inhabitant of Great Britain quadrupled in the course of the period of 70 years now under consideration. The next question which arises is, by what steps has this great increase, if and so far as it may be correct, been attained; and to this no precise answer can be given. If, however, the increase be assumed to have accrued at a uniform rate throughout the period, and the total tea revenue of the United Kingdom be redistributed on this assumption between Great Britain and Ireland, the results will be as shown in Table E.

It might be suggested that the statistics of collection would indicate the general course of the increase in consumption, but this does not seem to be the case. The percentages of collection per head in Ireland compared with Great Britain at quinquennial periods are shown in Table F. The increased collection between 1829 and 1849 shown in that table may or may not be attributable to the removal after the Famine of a large number of the poorest inhabitants of Ireland; but the drop between 1875 and 1879 can hardly be explained, except by an increase in the duty-paid consignments of tea from Great Britain to Ireland. Table E therefore represents the best suggestion which can be offered under this head, subject to the remark that the figures for 1829 and 1839 are probably somewhat too high, and that for 1859–60 somewhat too low.

(3.) *Tobacco.*—In this case, as in that of tea, the amount collected in Ireland in 1819 may be taken as the true Irish Revenue from this source in that year. The duty collected per head of population in Ireland in that year was 1s. 9·4d., and that in Great Britain 3s. 2·32d., that is to say, the percentage ratio per head was about 57 per cent. in Ireland, compared with 100 in Great Britain. For 1889–90 the figures in the "Financial Relations" Returns estimate the true Tobacco Revenue per head in Ireland at 5s. 2·24d. and that for Great Britain at 4s. 8·76d., the percentage ratio per head being about 112 per cent. in Ireland, compared with 100 in Great Britain. According to these figures the proportion of tobacco consumed by the average Irishman, as compared with the average inhabitant of Great Britain, almost doubled in the 70 years. The percentages of collection figures at quinquennial periods are shown in Table G.

Table G exhibits a continuous growth from 1819 to 1879 in the collection per head in Ireland as compared with Great Britain, with only a small set-back in 1849, perhaps not unconnected with the then recent Famine. The yields per head became equal in 1869–70; this was followed by an appreciable drop in the Irish proportion of 1874, which was made good again by 1884–85, since which year the collection in Ireland per head has exceeded that in Great Britain. The apparent fluctuations since 1870 are explained from information supplied by the Inland Revenue as due to (1) a loss of both home and export trade by Irish manufacturers, which is known to have occurred about twenty years ago; (2) a growth during more recent years in the production of the finer kinds of tobacco in Ireland, without any reduction in the manufacture of "roll" and other coarser descriptions. The figures of 1829 in both islands are so like those of 1819 as to indicate that there was at that period little or no trade on balance between the two islands in duty-paid tobacco. There appears to be no basis on which any correction could be applied to the figures of the years 1839 to 1859–60; it is, however, considered probable by the Revenue authorities that in 1869–70 there was a net excess export of duty-paid tobacco from Ireland, and that this state of things has continued since then. The "Financial Relations" figure of true Irish Tobacco Revenue for 1889–90 appears, in the light of statistics recently procured for a more recent period, to be probably too high; but at the present stage of matters no other definite figure can be suggested. Accordingly the figures of 1869–70 have been hypothetically adjusted so as to make the relative growth of consumption in Ireland proceed at a uniform rate from 1859–60 to 1889–90; with the result that 170,233*l.*, falls to be deducted from the collection figure of 1869–70, and 124,309*l.* to be added to that of 1879–80.

(4.) *Wine.*—It is difficult to arrive at any conclusion as to the corrections to be applied to the "collection" figures in respect of this item. Table H. shows remarkable variations in the proportion borne at various times by the Irish collection to the total for the United Kingdom. The collection figures of 1819 may, as previously explained, be taken to represent the true revenue of that year. A comparison of these figures with the statistics of population (Appendix, Part IV.) shows that the consumption per head in Ireland in 1819 (measured by the Customs duty-paid) bore the percentage ratio of about 62½ to the consumption per head throughout the United Kingdom, taken at 100; and, curiously enough, the corrected figures of 1889–90 work out to almost exactly the same proportion for that year. These facts suggest the assumption that for the period intervening between 1819 and 1889 the true wine revenue of Ireland should be taken, in round figures, at about 62½ per cent. of the amount proportionate to the population of Ireland compared with

* For figures and notes as to population, see Appendix Part IV.

that of the United Kingdom. The figures in the last two columns of Table H. have been prepared on this hypothesis.

(3.) *Sugar.*—This item was so long an important one in the tariff that it seems to require separate treatment. In 1819 the Irish Revenue derived from it was about 12 per cent. of the whole; in 1829 the collection in Ireland was about 9 per cent., with an unaltered population-ratio. The imports of sugar into Ireland were practically stationary between 1827 and 1830; about half came through Great Britain and the rest direct. As the relative conditions of the two islands remained substantially the same during this period, there seems no reason to suppose that the Irish consumption of sugar decreased in the proportion of 12 to 9; and if the consumption remained the same it follows that in 1829 about a quarter of the sugar consumed in Ireland was imported duty-paid from Great Britain. In 1819 the consumption per head in Ireland was about one-third of what it was in Great Britain, and the assumption is that the same proportion applied in 1829. It may perhaps be assumed that this proportion was unaltered in 1839, but that it was materially affected by the great rise in the average standard of living which followed the Famine; this follows somewhat the line suggested by the figures of tobacco. If the proportion be taken as one-half in 1849, two-thirds in 1859-60, and three-quarters in 1869-70, the results will be as shown in Table J. Here, again, the assumptions are of necessity arbitrary, and are only offered for what they are worth, in order to arrive at some figures for discussion. In any case the collection-figures are remarkable as showing the growth of the trade practice of sending sugar duty-paid from Great Britain to Ireland instead of direct importations or transhipment under bond. The duty was finally repealed in 1874.

(4.) *Other Customs Duties.*—There seems no means of distributing these with any confidence in the period between 1819 and 1859, so as to arrive at an estimate of the true Irish Revenue. The figures of 1819 show that the population-ratio cannot safely be adopted throughout, as in that year the Irish population, numbering about 32 per cent. of that of the United Kingdom, paid only about 11 per cent. of such Customs duties as are not separately distinguished in this memorandum. In 1829, when the population percentage was much the same as in 1819, the revenue collected in Ireland was only 4 per cent. of the whole. If the habits of the population of both islands remained unaltered during the decade, a sum of about 464,000*l.* should be added to the collection-figure of 1829 to obtain the true Irish Revenue, being 7 per cent. of the total receipt of 7,055,252*l.* The amount transferred from Great Britain to Ireland in the "Financial Relations" Return for 1889-90 is 93,319*l.*, or 9½ per cent. upon the total of 941,565*l.*, which represents the unclassified items, the amount to be transferred may perhaps be taken at 7 per cent. in 1839, 7½ per cent. in 1849, 8 per cent. in 1859-60, 8½ per cent. in 1869-70, and 9 per cent. in 1879-80. Table K. gives the corrections to be made on this very arbitrary hypothesis.

The great changes in the composition of this item took place between 1829 and 1849, in which period the revenue from these sources was reduced by 3,309,786*l.*, and between 1859 and 1869, when the reduction was 2,097,916*l.* The two principal unclassified items, since repealed, yielded the following amounts in 1839 and in 1859-60 respectively.

—	Great Britain (as collected).		Ireland (as collected).		United Kingdom.	
	£	Per Cent.	£	Per Cent.	£	Per Cent.
1839.						
[illegible]	[illegible]	[illegible]	[illegible]	[illegible]	[illegible]	[illegible]
[illegible]	[illegible]	[illegible]	[illegible]	[illegible]	[illegible]	[illegible]
1859-60.						
Corn	[illegible]	[illegible]	[illegible]	[illegible]	[illegible]	[illegible]
Timber	[illegible]	[illegible]	[illegible]	[illegible]	[illegible]	[illegible]

(Finance Accounts, 1840, pp. [illegible]; ditto, 1860, pp. [illegible].)

The variations in the proportions of both these articles between Great Britain and Ireland in the two years are curious, and perhaps may represent, more or less truly, the relative changes in the actual requirements of the two countries.

10.—Excise.

(1.) *British Spirits.*—This branch of the revenue has already been dealt with in paragraph 16. It has been matter of consideration whether an arbitrary correction should be here applied to the results of that paragraph in respect of the error explained in Paper No. 248 of 1893; but upon the whole it has appeared advisable to make no such attempt at present.

(2.) *Beer (including the former equivalents of the present Beer Duty*).*—Owing to the form in which the duty is assessed and collected, beer cannot practically be exported under bond; and as no "permits" are required for its removal from place to place, as is the case with spirits, no official statistics exist bearing on the question of the true Irish Revenue from this source. It is, however, well known that at present the Irish exports of beer largely exceed the imports, and information has been supplied from various sources sufficient to enable the Excise authorities to form an estimate for recent years of the net amount of duty collected in Ireland, but really paid by consumers in Great Britain. This item amounted in 1889-90, in round figures, to 149,000*l.* on a total for the United Kingdom of 9,400,000*l.*, and, in 1892-93, to 187,000*l.* on 9,800,000*l.*

Such information as has been procurable indicates that while the exports of beer from Ireland to Great Britain have increased considerably in the last 12 years, the imports from Great Britain to Ireland have been stationary. Thus, it is probable that the correction to the figures of 1879-80 should be at a considerably lower proportion than that for 1889-90, and so would perhaps not exceed 50,000*l.* on a total of 7,300,000*l.* Turning to the beginning of the period under consideration, it appears that in 1829 the Irish collection formed rather a higher percentage (7·2) of that of the United Kingdom than that of 1819 (6·4), the population ratios being about the same, but the rates of duty, which in 1819 were considerably higher in Great Britain than in Ireland, were, in 1829, uniform throughout the United Kingdom.† It is, therefore, desirable to compare the percentages of quantities, and as these are nearly the same (6·4 and 6·8) at the two periods (Inland Revenue Report, 1870, Part II., pages 16 and 17), it may be inferred that there was, in 1829, no important trade in beer (on the balance) between Great Britain and Ireland. In the years between 1829 and 1859 the figures of collection fluctuate in a rather puzzling manner, and do not suggest any definite conclusions as to the course of trade. In 1859 the Irish beer revenue was appreciably higher per head than in 1829, as compared with the figures for the United Kingdom, which fact may be accounted for by the improvement in the general condition of the population, and by a change of popular taste in favour of beer-drinking, without reference to any net export to Great Britain. Since 1859 there has been a considerable actual and relative increase in the Irish beer collection, probably due to a growth in the national taste for beer as well as to an increase in the export of that article. In order that the latter factor may not be neglected, it is proposed to deduct 50,000*l.* from the collection figures of 1879-80, and 25,000*l.* from those of 1869-70; these figures, of course, being purely conjectural.

(4.) *Licences.*—In this case the area of incidence clearly corresponds with the country of collection, and no correction, therefore, need be made to the collection-figures.

(5.) *Other items of Excise.*—In recent years the Railway Duty is the only important item under this head, and that has never been applied to Ireland; therefore for 1869-70, and 1879-80, as well as for 1889-90, the true Irish Revenue may be taken to correspond with the figures of collection. But in earlier years the unclassified amounts are much larger, and therefore require special consideration. The years 1819 to 1859-60 contain, under the head of Great Britain, sundry Excise duties not applicable to Ireland. The principal of these are as follows:—

Salt, repealed	1825
Beer, repealed	1830
Candles, repealed	1832
Bricks, repealed	1850
Soap, repealed	1853
Hops, repealed	1862

The incidence of such duties may safely be assumed to have lain solely on the part of the United Kingdom

* Except that Brewers' Licences are classed among Licences.
† They were finally assimilated in 1827.

to which they were confined, and no correction, therefore, is necessary in respect of them. In support of this treatment it may be mentioned that in all these cases a drawback was allowed on articles sent from Great Britain to Ireland, except hops, the trade in which enjoyed the equivalent advantage of being exempted from duty when sent from Great Britain to Ireland.

21. *Stamps.*

(1.) *Probate, Legacies, and Successions (Death Duties).*—In the "Financial Relations" papers the "collection" figures under this head are taken to represent the true revenue; and there seems no reason for departing from this method of treatment for the earlier years.

(2.) *General Stamps.*—In the "Financial Relations" papers an adjustment was made in view of what is believed to be the fact that more transactions by Irishmen in realised personal property pay duty in Great Britain than vice versâ; see pages 11 to 13 of the Return of 1891, and page 2 of Return No. 93 of 1893. This net adjustment is valued in those Returns at ·3 per cent. of that part of "General Stamp" Receipts estimated to arise from transactions in realised personal property; and that part is taken as one-fourth of the whole yield. There seems no better course than to take the same proportions for the whole of the period now under consideration. Upon this assumption the following amounts fall to be added to the stamp duties collected in Ireland.

		£		£
1819	[illegible]	3,211,394	=	2,408
1829	„	3,226,757	=	2,420
1839	„	3,196,987	=	2,398
1849	„	4,106,461	=	3,080
1859–60	„	4,422,500	=	3,316
1869–70	„	4,041,027	=	3,030
1879–80	„	4,206,395	=	3,154
1889–90	„	5,198,217	=	3,898

It will be seen that the amount of this correction is not important.

22. *Taxes.*

Under this head the only item which requires consideration is the Income Tax; the Land Tax, House Duty, and Assessed Taxes have never been extended to Ireland (except a small amount of Assessed Taxes in 1819), and their incidence is therefore obviously confined to Great Britain. The small residue of Pitt's Income Tax collected in Great Britain in 1819 (161,272*l.*) need not be considered; and therefore there is no occasion for any correction until 1849, when Sir Robert Peel's Income Tax, then confined to Great Britain, yielded 5,564,553*l.* The method adopted in 1891 for dealing with the Income Tax figures is explained on pp. 12 and 13 of the "Financial Relations" Return of that year (No. 331), and a small correction of that method made in 1893 is described on p. 2 of Return No. 93 of that year. The corrected method consists in applying the assumption that a net ·2 per cent. of the yield of Schedules C and D (Interest and Dividends), and of that of one-fifth of Schedule D (Trades and Professions), should be subtracted from the amount collected in Great Britain and added to that collected in Ireland in respect of the excess of Income Tax collected in Great Britain on property owned by Irishmen over Income Tax collected in Ireland on property owned by inhabitants of Great Britain. This net ·2 per cent. was arrived at from figures indicating that about ·3 per cent. was the amount of tax on Irishmen's property assessed in Great Britain, and about ·1 per cent. the amount of tax on property assessed in Ireland but belonging to inhabitants of Great Britain. On this basis the additions to be made to the Income Tax as collected in Ireland, to obtain the true revenue raised from Irishmen, would be as follows:—*

		£
1849 to 5 January 1850	say	5,790
1859–60		3,792
1869–70		5,307
1879–80		7,446
1889–90		10,112

* In 1849 the correction has to be the gross ·3 per cent. of the part of the tax affected, as there was then no Income Tax in Ireland. In 1859–60 a part of what is now Schedule D was under Schedule A, for which [illegible] allowance has been made in the above figures.

23. *Non-Tax Revenue.*

Post Office.—The revenue collected in Ireland is taken, as in the "Financial Relations" Returns, as the true revenue derived from Ireland, the expenditure on the other side of the account being treated in a similar manner.

Crown Lands.—The Finance Accounts do not distinguish between Great Britain and Ireland under this head; but the reports of the Commissioners of Woods enable the net yield of the hereditary property in Ireland to be stated with approximate accuracy in 1829 and subsequent years. For 1819 and 1829 the figures of gross receipts exist, but not those of the outgoings. It seems, however, safe to assume that the net yield in each of those years was about 50,000*l.*† The general tendency has been to dispose of Crown property in Ireland and invest the proceeds elsewhere; this item, therefore, tends to diminish. But in the financial calculations made for the Government of Ireland Bill, 1893, an allowance of 25,000*l.* a year was made for assumed interest on such investments.‡

Miscellaneous.—The items under this head have been analysed as for the "Financial Relations" Returns; there is no important field for doubt as to Irish share.

24. It is now possible to give figures which, on the principles of estimating suggested in this memorandum, may be discussed as a hypothetical approximation to the true revenue derived from Ireland in the years under consideration. Table L collects the various corrections which, under present assumptions, should be made to the figures in Table B, which latter represent the farthest point to which statistics can carry the investigation: and the following figures compare the results so arrived at with the collection-figures:—

Ireland.	Revenue as Collected (Table A).	Estimated true Revenue (Table L).	True Revenue more (+) or less (−) than Revenue as Collected.
	£	£	£
1819 to 5 Jan. 1820	5,[illegible]	5,[illegible]	+ [illegible]
1829 to 5 „ 1830	4,[illegible]	5,[illegible]	+ 1,[illegible]
1839 to 5 „ 1840	4,[illegible]	5,[illegible]	+ [illegible]
1849 to 5 „ 1850	4,[illegible]	4,[illegible]	+ [illegible]
1859–60—to 31 Mar.	7,[illegible]	7,[illegible]	+ [illegible]
1869–70—to 31 „	7,[illegible]	7,[illegible]	+ [illegible]
1879–80—to 31 „	7,[illegible]	7,[illegible]	− [illegible]
1889–90—to 31 „	8,[illegible]	7,[illegible]	− 1,[illegible]

It is interesting to observe how the balance of accounts between the two islands changes during the period. After the earliest year, in which the revenue collected is, as nearly as possible, the same as the true revenue, it appears at first that a large net amount of revenue which really came from Ireland was actually collected in Great Britain (that is what was called the "uncredited revenue"), but that this net addition to the apparent Irish revenue diminished steadily down to 1869–70, and that between 1870 and 1879 the balance turned the other way, so that in 1879–80 and 1889–90 the revenue collected in Ireland exceeded the true revenue, and such excess was much greater in 1889–90 than in 1879–80. It may be added that the excess has continued to increase since 1890.

This great change in the balance of revenue accounts between the two islands may be explained by two independent causes:—

(1.) The abolition or reduction of customs duties on foreign and colonial goods, for which London is the great entrepôt.

(2.) The growth of the Irish export trade in spirits, beer, and, to a less degree, tobacco.

25. Assuming the hypothetical estimates of true Revenue of Ireland given in the preceding paragraph, it is easy to arrive at the corresponding figures for Great Britain. For this purpose the figures of collection in Great Britain (shown in summary and detail in Tables M and N) should be corrected in respect of (*a*) the net amounts transferable to or from the account of Ireland, as given above; (*b*) the estimated amounts included in the revenue collected in Great Britain, which should be classified, by way of correction as

† Cf. [illegible] House of Commons, No. [illegible] of 18[illegible], and No. [illegible] of 18[illegible], may be compared with House of Commons, No. [illegible] of 18[illegible].

‡ House of Commons, No. [illegible] of 1893.

revenue derived from Imperial sources, each amount being arrived at, under all reserve, in the manner described in the "Financial Relations" papers. Tables O. and P. give these items, leading up to the following results:—

Estimated true Revenue of Great Britain.

	£
1819 to 5 January 1820	51,455,784
1829 to 5 " 1830	49,037,[illegible]
1839 to 5 " 1840	46,[illegible],412
1849 to 5 " 1850	51,870,[illegible]
1859–60 to 31 March 1860	61,[illegible],845
1869–70 to 31 " 1870	65,600,[illegible]
1879–80 to 31 " 1880	69,760,[illegible]
1889–90 to 31 " 1890	84,[illegible],809

26. The figures of revenue taken by themselves, even apart from the methods in which the revenue may be expended, afford no indication of the burthens laid on the people for the service of the State. They must be considered in the first place in relation to the numbers of the population; and, in the second, in relation to the taxable capacity of that population. As regards the first point the figures are as follows:—

—	Estimated true Revenue per Head. Great Britain. (1.)	Estimated true Revenue per Head. Ireland. (2.)	Percentage of (2) to (1).
	£ s. d.	£ s. d.	Per Cent.
1819 to 5 January 1820	3 13 6	0 15 4	20·2
1829 to 5 " 1830	3 0 4	0 14 9	33·3
1839 to 5 " 1840	2 8 11	0 12 3½	25·3
1849 to 5 " 1850	2 8 11½	0 14 5	25·4
1859–60 to 31 March 1860	2 13 2	1 0 7	39·1
1869–70 to 31 " 1870	2 10 4	1 7 5	54·5
1879–80 to 31 " 1880	2 8 11½	1 6 2	53·0
1889–90 to 31 " 1890	2 11 4½	1 15 3	68·9

A comparison between the first and second columns of this Table presents some interesting results. While the true revenue per head in Ireland appears to have rather more than doubled during the period covered by the memorandum, that in Great Britain has diminished by more than a fourth. Yet the amount raised per head in Ireland is still only two-thirds of that per head in Great Britain. The third column of the Table shows the relation between the taxation per head in the two countries in the form of percentages.

The question whether or how far the increase per head in Ireland implies an addition to the burthens laid upon the taxpayer in relation to his means depends upon many considerations, most of which lie outside the scope of the present memorandum; but the figures are submitted with all reserve as a basis for discussions as to the relative contributions of an average Irishman and an average inhabitant of Great Britain, respectively, to the Imperial revenue. The conclusions to be drawn from them, apart from controversial matter, are broadly as follows:—

1. Between the union of the Exchequers and the great Famine, the average Irishman paid between one-fifth and one-fourth as much as the average inhabitant of Great Britain. In the earlier years of this period the burthens on the taxpayer in Great Britain were swollen by the remains of the special taxation imposed during the great wars, which was never extended to Ireland.

2. By 1860 this proportion had risen to one-half. This rise may be ascribed to two causes:—

(a.) The great decrease in the poorest classes in Ireland, resulting in a rise in the average taxable capacity of the individual Irishman.

(b.) The removal of the special exemptions from taxation which Ireland had previously enjoyed under the heads of Spirit Duty and Income Tax.

3. By 1890 the proportion according to the Table had risen to two-thirds, but this figure is probably somewhat too high, in view of what is said in paragraph 16 as to British spirits and paragraph 19 (3) as to tobacco. Apart from the question whether, during the intervening period, the changes in taxation, taken in the aggregate, were such as to account for a relative increase of burthen on the Irishman, or the contrary, this growth may be explained by an increase in the relative wealth of the average Irishman as compared with the average inhabitant of Great Britain, or at least by a relatively increased tendency on the part of the former to consume dutiable articles.

EXPENDITURE.

27. Table A. in Part II. of the Appendix gives the Expenditure out of Imperial Revenue on Local Irish Services, so far as can be ascertained, for each of the eight years dealt with in this memorandum; and Table B. gives corresponding figures for Great Britain. As already mentioned in paragraph 4 above, the field of error in the matter of expenditure is a comparatively restricted one, but it would be impossible within reasonable compass to describe the various points which had to be discussed and decided in the process of arriving at the figures now submitted. Speaking broadly, these figures represent Exchequer Issues, except for 1889–90, when audited expenditure is available; but the old system of accounts was such as to render it very difficult to arrive at the expenditure properly belonging to a year even on the basis of Exchequer Issues; this is particularly the case for the years 1829, 1839, and 1849. It will be understood that the services which in former times were met out of the gross revenue, and which, as already explained, have not been treated in this memorandum as deductions from the revenue figures, are duly included as expenditure in Tables A. and B. An investigation of Local Loans transactions might result in an addition to the charge in either island, apart from the "voted grants" referred to in paragraph 6, which happen not to be important in any of the years here dealt with. That paragraph explains the reason why no such investigation has been attempted in the present memorandum.

These Tables show the following rates of expenditure per head of population in Ireland and Great Britain respectively, with the percentage ratio of the Irish figure to that for Great Britain:—

—	Expenditure per Head on Local Services. Great Britain. (1.)	Expenditure per Head on Local Services. Ireland. (2.)	Percentage of (2) to (1).
	£ s. d.	£ s. d.	Per Cent.
1819 to 5 January 1820	0 5 4½	0 4 7	78
1829 to 5 " 1830	0 5 3¾	0 5 6	88
1839 to 5 " 1840	0 4 10	0 4 4½	90
1849 to 5 " 1850	0 5 7½	0 6 10	121
1859–60 to 31 March 1860	0 7 4½	0 7 11¼	109
1869–70 to 31 " 1870	0 7 10	0 10 10	138
1879–80 to 31 " 1880	0 11 7	0 15 4	133
1889–90 to 31 " 1890	0 14 10½	1 0 0	140

The first noticeable point in these figures is the fact that at the beginning of the period the administration of Ireland cost the central Government appreciably less per head of population than that of Great Britain, whereas by 1849 the positions of the two countries in this respect were reversed. Since that date the average expenditure of the central Government for local purposes in Ireland per head has far exceeded that in Great Britain, and such excess has decidedly increased in recent years. One reason for this change, of an uncontroversial character, is the decrease of population in Ireland accompanying an increase in Great Britain. Establishments based on the respective populations of the two islands fifty years ago have not been materially altered since, neither reduced in Ireland as the population fell, nor increased with its growth in Great Britain. A notable example of this will be found in the judicial establishments. Secondly, it is to be observed that it was not until Ireland had become relatively more costly to govern than Great Britain that her special exemptions from Spirit Duty and Income Tax were removed; it does not, however, appear that this effective argument was employed at the date of such removal.

The general increase, shown over the whole period, and especially between 1859–70 and 1879–80, is not surprising in view of the great expansion in recent years of the functions and expenditure of the State in

regard to internal affairs, of which Elementary Education is the most striking example.

CONTRIBUTIONS TO IMPERIAL SERVICES.

28. In the "Financial Relations" Returns the contribution to Imperial services derived from any one of the three kingdoms has been arrived at by deducting from the true revenue of that kingdom collected by Imperial officers the local expenditure met out of that revenue; and a similar method seems proper to be used in the present memorandum.

Table A. and B., in Appendix, Part III., give the total amounts contributed, as estimated on the basis of the foregoing paragraphs of this memorandum. The amounts derived from Great Britain and Ireland respectively per head of population, and the percentage ratio between the two, are estimated to be as follows:—

—	Contribution per Head. Great Britain. (1.)			Contribution per Head. Ireland. (2.)			Percentage of (2) to (1).
	£	s.	d.	£	s.	d.	Per Cent.
1819 to 5 January 1820 -	[illegible]	[illegible]	[illegible]	0	10	10	16·5
1829 to 5 „ 1830 -	2	15	[illegible]	0	10	8	18·2
1839 to 5 „ 1840 -	2	5	[illegible]	0	8	10	19·5
1849 to 5 „ 1850 -	2	4	4	0	7	11	17·6
1859–60—to 31 March 1860.	2	5	[illegible]	0	15	[illegible]	40·7
1869–70—to 31 „ 1870.	2	3	[illegible]	0	18	7	[illegible]
1879–80—to 31 „ 1880.	1	15	[illegible]	0	15	[illegible]	[illegible]
1889–90—to 31 „ 1890.	1	18	[illegible]	0	11	5	[illegible]

These figures obviously fall into two groups, referring to the years before and after the assimilation of the Spirit Duties and the Income Tax in the two islands. In the first period the year 1819 is abnormal, because of the remains of war taxation in Great Britain, while in 1849 Ireland was, perhaps, still under the shadow of the great Famine. The figures of 1829 and 1839 suggest that during that period the average Irishman contributed towards Imperial services about one-fifth of the amount contributed by the average inhabitant of Great Britain. This would have been precisely fair, had the taxable capacity of the Irishman been one-fifth of that of the Briton; if it was higher, the division was unfair to Great Britain; if lower to Ireland. At the beginning of the second period the average Irishman contributed about 40*l.* towards Imperial services, and at the end of the period about 30*l.*, compared with every 100*l.* contributed by the average inhabitant of Great Britain, or in the ratio of two-fifths, diminishing to less than one-third. Whether these proportions have been on the whole fair, or otherwise, as between the two partners, is a question which will, doubtless, be discussed elsewhere.

CONCLUSION.

29. The results of the hypotheses set forth in this memorandum may perhaps be summed up once more in a form somewhat different from that adopted in preceding paragraphs. The following Table shows, for the years under consideration, how each 1,000*l.*, raised on these hypotheses by Imperial imposts from the inhabitants of Great Britain and Ireland respectively, was expended as between Local Services on the one hand and Imperial Services on the other.

—	Great Britain. Local.	Great Britain. Imperial.	Great Britain. Total.	Ireland. Local.	Ireland. Imperial.	Ireland. Total.
	£	£	£	£	£	£
1819 to 5 January 1820 -	[illegible]	[illegible]	1,000	[illegible]	[illegible]	1,000
1829 to 5 „ 1830 -	[illegible]	[illegible]	1,000	[illegible]	[illegible]	1,000
1839 to 5 „ 1840 -	[illegible]	[illegible]	1,000	[illegible]	[illegible]	1,000
1849 to 5 „ 1850 -	[illegible]	[illegible]	1,000	[illegible]	[illegible]	1,000
1859–60—to 31 March 1860	[illegible]	[illegible]	1,000	[illegible]	[illegible]	1,000
1869–70—to 31 „ 1870	[illegible]	[illegible]	1,000	[illegible]	[illegible]	1,000
1879–80—to 31 „ 1880	[illegible]	[illegible]	1,000	[illegible]	[illegible]	1,000
1889–90—to 31 „ 1890	[illegible]	713	1,000	[illegible]	[illegible]	1,000

These figures show the relative increase of local as compared with Imperial expenditure during the period under consideration, such increase being due on the one hand to the much larger field of duties now undertaken by the State in regard to the internal affairs of the community, and on the other to the decrease in debt charges and the relatively slow growth, during the period, of expenditure on defence. The figures also show how much more rapid has been the increase of internal expenditure in Ireland than in Great Britain.

30. In conclusion, it may be well to repeat that this memorandum does not profess to put forward authoritative decisions on the questions raised by the Order of the House. The intention has rather been to assist the discussion of those questions, not only by the preparation in a convenient form of figures bearing upon them, but also by the suggestion of definite hypotheses for the solution of the problems involved, leading to figured results. Each such hypothesis, however, should stand or fall on its own merits, without reference to the source from which it emanates.

Treasury Chambers, Whitehall,
August 1894.

APPENDIX.

PART I.—REVENUE.

TABLE A.—IRELAND—COLLECTION.

Revenue collected in Ireland, with Percentages to Total Revenue of the United Kingdom, and Amounts per Head of the Population of Ireland.

—	—	Per Cent.	Per Head.		
	£		£	s.	d.
1819 to 5 January 1820 -	[illegible]	[illegible]	-	15	[illegible]
1829 to 5 „ 1830 -	4,4[illegible]	[illegible]	-	11	4
1839 to 5 „ 1840 -	4,[illegible]	[illegible]	-	11	[illegible]
1849 to 5 „ 1850 -	4,[illegible]	[illegible]	-	15	[illegible]
1859–60—to 31 March -	7,[illegible]	10·[illegible]	1	4	[illegible]
1869–70—to 31 „ -	7,[illegible]	10·[illegible]	1	7	1
1879–80—to 31 „ -	7,[illegible]	[illegible]	1	10	[illegible]
1889–90—to 31 „ -	[illegible]	[illegible]	1	[illegible]	[illegible]

TABLE B.

Revenue as collected in Ireland under Principal Heads.

	1819.	1829.	1839.	1849.	1859–60.	1869–70.	*1879–80.	1889–90.
	£	£	£	£	£	£	£	£
Customs -	[illegible]	[illegible]	[illegible]	[illegible]	[illegible]	[illegible]	[illegible]	[illegible]
Excise -	[illegible]	[illegible]	[illegible]	[illegible]	[illegible]	[illegible]	[illegible]	[illegible]
Stamps (including Fee Stamps)	[illegible]	[illegible]	[illegible]	[illegible]	[illegible]	[illegible]	[illegible]	[illegible]
Taxes (Land, Assessed, and Income).	[illegible]	—	—	—	—	—	—	—
Property and Income Tax -	—	—	—	—	[illegible]	[illegible]	[illegible]	[illegible]
Total Revenue from Taxes	[illegible]	[illegible]	[illegible]	[illegible]	[illegible]	[illegible]	[illegible]	[illegible]

* See paragraph 8 of memorandum ad fin. † Including Local Taxation Revenue.

—	1819.	1829.	1830.	1840.	1859-60.	1869-70.	1879-80.	1889-90.
Post Office	214,921	204,222	227,849	141,351	246,161	551,117	429,200	[illegible]
Telegraph Service	—	—	—	—	—	4,364	92,859	[illegible]
Crown Lands	50,000	50,000	44,031	45,150	45,298	45,009	35,300	[illegible]
Miscellaneous (including Fee Stamps).	22,419	150,373	97,347	71,459	99,057	180,190	285,329	[illegible]
Total Non-Tax Revenue	289,308	404,593	309,227	262,950	390,425	798,597	843,734	1,043,283
Appropriated Duties for Local Objects.	10,404	—	—	—	—	—	—	—
Total Irish Revenue - £	5,255,009	4,461,917	4,324,150	4,308,291	7,097,904	7,331,013	7,831,679	9,005,969

Table C.—Details of Revenue as collected in Ireland.

—	1819.	1829.	1830.	1840.	1859-60.	1869-70.	1879-80.	1889-90.
Customs.	£	£	£	£	£	£	£	£
Spirits	93,123	90,768	29,859	22,348	89,447	339,700	249,097	234,330
Tea	433,979	*	487,290	303,154	769,573	893,582	610,085	792,935
Tobacco	§614,999	718,241	792,100	743,900	932,844	1,299,729	1,132,430	1,640,694
Sugar	492,285	443,472	409,031	304,294	179,130	203,731	—	—
Wine	903,582	191,144	190,397	145,158	144,758	130,758	172,903	95,521
‡Other Articles	729,120	307,329	113,815	192,560	135,484	65,440	15,112	15,353
Total Customs	2,475,994	1,505,194	2,016,109	2,171,199	2,299,304	2,643,974	1,997,317	2,307,912
Excise.								
Spirits	1,080,061	1,400,488	1,602,040	1,050,749	3,069,269	3,016,408	3,430,200	3,748,959
Malt (and Brewing Sugar in 1869-70 and 1879-80).	†180,600	270,679	296,039	262,810	348,044	290,470	468,411	‖744,720
Licences	183,542	136,504	171,811	94,036	167,945	190,530	159,790	182,591
‡Other Receipts	108,850	153,966	51,351	53,444	71,364	4,431	—	868
Total Excise	1,546,399	2,055,649	2,424,085	1,460,880	3,804,242	3,593,201	4,067,208	4,590,135
Stamps.								
Probate Duty	33,169	45,565	58,812	67,648	79,996	69,844	140,300	[illegible]
Legacy and Succession Duty	23,204	22,293	27,214	29,506	148,350	178,712	191,920	[illegible]
‡Other Stamps (excluding Fee Stamps).	470,309	356,609	357,432	331,061	378,758	259,894	211,712	[illegible]
Total Stamps	525,930	424,449	443,580	428,155	603,004	508,349	543,932	567,107
Taxes.								
Assessed Taxes	350,746	—	—	—	—	—	—	—
Income Tax.								
Schedules A., B., and E.	—	—	—	—	515,251	495,729	559,000	[illegible]
Schedules C. and D. (Public Companies).	—	—	—	—	41,565	47,898	75,000	[illegible]
Schedule D. (Trades and Professions).	—	—	—	—	156,190	129,490	111,000	[illegible]
Total Income Tax	—	—	—	—	714,008	672,115	695,000	554,795
Total Revenue from Taxes - £	4,908,319	4,026,363	4,824,953	4,040,198	6,720,475	6,272,227	6,987,045	7,963,686
Post Office	216,921	205,889	237,849	141,351	248,303	548,117	429,598	553,729
Post Office Telegraphs	—	—	—	—	—	4,964	92,858	327,987
Crown Lands	50,000	50,000	46,891	45,110	45,296	45,000	35,300	37,300
Miscellaneous	22,419	150,373	97,347	71,459	60,053	180,120	285,909	564,035
Total Non-Tax Revenue - £	289,338	406,262	382,287	257,920	353,426	778,201	843,734	1,043,283

* In this year the Tea Revenue was under the control of the Excise, and was all collected in England.
† Partly Excise. ‡ Including Miscellaneous Departmental receipts in all years except 1879-80 and 1889-90. § Beer Duty.

[illegible]

TABLE D.—IRELAND—BRITISH SPIRITS CORRECTED.

Revenue of Ireland, corrected so as to include the estimated true yield of the British Spirit Duties (para. 16), but otherwise based on the Revenue as collected; with percentages to Total Revenue of the United Kingdom, and Amounts per Head of the Population of Ireland.

—	Revenue as collected, Table A.	Deduction for British Spirits.	Revenue as corrected.	Per Cent.	Per Head.
	£	£	£		£ s. d.
1819	5,255,304	—	5,254,304	5·15	0 13 1
1829	4,488,217	122,421	4,365,796	7·77	0 11 0
1839	4,374,730	140,307	4,037,962	8·37	0 10 10
1849	4,890,891	170,988	4,317,303	7·42	0 17 10
1859-60	7,097,954	301,709	6,794,888	9·61	1 3 4
1869-70	7,855,084	301,894	6,887,022	9·32	1 3 3
1879-80	7,382,532	415,814	6,925,369	8·94	1 4 6
1889-90	9,665,982	1,094,214	7,624,172	8·19	1 12 3

TABLE E.—IRELAND—TEA.

—	As collected in Ireland.	IRELAND. Population Per Cent. of United Kingdom.	Assumed Ratio of Consumption per Head in Ireland to Great Britain.	Assumed true Irish Revenue.	Correction to Figures in Table D.
	£		Per Cent.	£	£
1819	455,576	39½	46	455,576	Nil.
1829	Nil*	32	56	655,170	+ 655,170
1839	497,480	31	41	598,127	+ 101,647
1846	698,164	24	50	746,258	+ 47,876
1859-60	780,278	20	51	723,000	− 58,099
1869-70	378,512	17	75	444,977	+ 105,695
1879-80	519,693	15	66	621,099	+ 635,510
1889-90	290,305	13½	114	559,671	+ 364,736

* At this time the tea duty was under the management of the Excise, and the whole of it was collected in England.

TABLE F.

Tea Duty collected per Head in Ireland, expressed as a percentage of that collected per Head in Great Britain.

1819 to 5 January 1820	26 per cent.
1824 to 5 " 1825	27 "
1829 to 5 1830	(Not ascertainable.)
1834 to 5 1835	" "
1839 to 5 1840	31 per cent.
1844 to 5 1845	38
1849 to 5 1850	41
1854 to 5 1855	36
1859-60	54
1864-65	65
1869-70	66
1875-76	55
1879-80	52
1885-86	48
1889-90	63
1893-94	49

TABLE G.

Tobacco Duty collected per Head in Ireland, expressed as a percentage of that collected per Head in Great Britain.

1819 to 5 January 1820	77 per cent.
1824 to 5 " 1825	58 "
1829 to 5 " 1830	57 "
1834 to 5 " 1835	56 "
1839 to 5 " 1840	65 "
1844 to 5 " 1845	66 "
1849 to 5 " 1850	58 "
1854 to 5 " 1855	67 "
1859-60	79 "
1864-65	89 "
1869-70	100
1874-75	75
1879-80	89
1885-86	100
1889-90	119
1893-94	134

TABLE H.—IRELAND—WINE.

YEAR.	Receipt, United Kingdom.	Collection, Ireland.	Per Cent. of Total.	Estimated true Irish Revenue. (Page 10 of Mem.)	Correction to Figures in Table D.
	£	£		£	£
1819 to 5 January 1820	1,029,304	100,962	14·9	300,281	Nil.
1829 to 5 " 1830	1,470,608	183,144	12·8	293,000	+ 110,856
1839 to 5 " 1840	1,848,730	150,599	8·3	328,870	+ 177,908
1849 to 5 " 1850	1,567,328	145,109	8·1	263,000	+ 122,004
1859-60 to 31 March 1860	1,814,257	146,738	8·0	204,000	− 57,144
1869-70 to 31 " 1870	1,475,404	150,752	10·3	187,000	+ 7,566
1879-80 to 31 " 1880	1,547,311	131,691	8·5	193,000	− 3,165
1889-90 to 31 " 1890	1,300,181	94,032	7·4	104,172	+ 2,182

TABLE I.—IRELAND—SUGAR.

	Duty collected in Ireland.	Assumed true Irish Revenue. (Page 18 of Mem.)	Correction to Figures in Table D.
	£	£	£
[illegible]	[illegible]	[illegible]	[illegible]
[illegible]	[illegible]	[illegible]	[illegible]
[illegible]	[illegible]	[illegible]	[illegible]
[illegible]	[illegible]	[illegible]	[illegible]
[illegible]	[illegible]	[illegible]	[illegible]
[illegible]	[illegible]	[illegible]	[illegible]

(Sugar duties abolished in 1874.)

TABLE K.—IRELAND—MISCELLANEOUS CUSTOMS.

Amount and percentage of Total Revenue proposed to be taken as representing Duty on Goods sent from Great Britain to Ireland (net) after payment of Duty in Great Britain.

	Total Receipt, United Kingdom.	Proposed Percentage.	Correction to Figures in Table D.
	£		£
1816 to 5 January 1820	6,874,416	—	[illegible]
1829 to 5 " 1830	7,038,136	7	[illegible]
1839 to 5 " 1840	4,879,345	7	[illegible]
1849 to 5 " 1850	3,479,479	7½	[illegible]
1859–60 to 31 March 1860	3,223,411	8	[illegible]
1869–70 to 31 " 1870	1,133,865	8½	[illegible]
1879–80 to 31 " 1880	893,214	8	[illegible]
1889–90 to 31 " 1890	941,395	9½	[illegible]

TABLE L.—IRISH REVENUE: SUMMARY OF HYPOTHETICAL CORRECTIONS TO FIGURES OF COLLECTION.

	Table D.	Foreign Spirits.	Tea.	Tobacco.	Wine.	Sugar.	Other Customs.	Beer.	Stamps.	Income Tax.	Total Corrections besides that for Spirits.	Estimated true Revenue.	Per Cent. of United Kingdom Revenue.	Per Head.
	£	£	£	£	£	£	£	£	£	£	£	£		£ s. d.
[illegible]	[illegible]	—	—	—	—	—	—	—	[illegible]	—	[illegible]	[illegible]	[illegible]	[illegible]
[illegible]	[illegible]	—	[illegible]	—	[illegible]	[illegible]	[illegible]	—	[illegible]	—	[illegible]	[illegible]	[illegible]	[illegible]
[illegible]	[illegible]	—	[illegible]	—	[illegible]	[illegible]	[illegible]	—	[illegible]	—	[illegible]	[illegible]	[illegible]	[illegible]
[illegible]	[illegible]	—	[illegible]	—	[illegible]	[illegible]	[illegible]	—	[illegible]	[illegible]	[illegible]	[illegible]	[illegible]	[illegible]
[illegible]	[illegible]	—	[illegible]	—	[illegible]	[illegible]	[illegible]	—	[illegible]	[illegible]	[illegible]	[illegible]	[illegible]	[illegible]
[illegible]	[illegible]	—	[illegible]	[illegible]	[illegible]	[illegible]	[illegible]	[illegible]	[illegible]	[illegible]	[illegible]	[illegible]	[illegible]	[illegible]
[illegible]	[illegible]	—	[illegible]	[illegible]	[illegible]	—	[illegible]	[illegible]	[illegible]	[illegible]	[illegible]	[illegible]	[illegible]	[illegible]
[illegible]	[illegible]	[illegible]	[illegible]	[illegible]	[illegible]	—	[illegible]	[illegible]	[illegible]	[illegible]	[illegible]	[illegible]	[illegible]	[illegible]

TABLE M.—REVENUE AS COLLECTED IN GREAT BRITAIN UNDER PRINCIPAL HEADS.

	1819.	1829.	1835.	1845.	1859–60.	1869–70.	1879–80.*	1889–90.
	£	£	£	£	£	£	£	£
Customs	13,111,748	20,080,309	21,387,874	20,691,742	[illegible]	[illegible]	[illegible]	[illegible]
Excise	17,310,818	18,409,539	[illegible]	[illegible]	17,019,335	[illegible]	[illegible]	[illegible]
Stamps (excluding Fee Stamps).	[illegible]	[illegible]	[illegible]	[illegible]	7,316,120	[illegible]	[illegible]	14,898,878‡
Taxes (Land, House, and Assessed).	7,774,376	[illegible]	[illegible]	4,388,110	[illegible]	[illegible]	[illegible]	[illegible]
Property and Income Tax*.	148,857	—	—	[illegible]	[illegible]	[illegible]	[illegible]	12,129,106
Total Revenue from Taxes.	[illegible]	[illegible]	[illegible]	[illegible]	[illegible]	[illegible]	[illegible]	[illegible]
Post Office	[illegible]	[illegible]	[illegible]	[illegible]	[illegible]	[illegible]	[illegible]	[illegible]
Telegraph Service	—	—	—	—	—	[illegible]	[illegible]	[illegible]
Crown Lands	—	[illegible]	[illegible]	[illegible]	[illegible]	[illegible]	[illegible]	[illegible]
Miscellaneous (including Fee Stamps).	1,317,745	[illegible]	[illegible]	[illegible]	[illegible]	[illegible]	[illegible]†	[illegible]†
Total Non-Tax Revenue.	[illegible]	[illegible]	[illegible]	[illegible]	[illegible]	[illegible]	[illegible]	14,850,471
TOTAL REVENUE - £	[illegible]	[illegible]	[illegible]	[illegible]	[illegible]	[illegible]	[illegible]	[illegible]

* *See* paragraph 8 of memorandum of fin. † Including interest on *Imperial* loans.
‡ Including Local Taxation Revenue.

TABLE N.—DETAILS OF TAX REVENUE AS COLLECTED IN GREAT BRITAIN.

—	1819.	1829.	1839.	1849.	1859-60.	1869-70.	1879-80.	1889-90.
I. CUSTOMS.	£	£	£	£	£	£	£	£
Spirits	[illegible]	[illegible]	[illegible]	[illegible]	[illegible]	[illegible]	[illegible]	[illegible]
Tea	[illegible]	[illegible]	[illegible]	[illegible]	[illegible]	[illegible]	[illegible]	[illegible]
Tobacco	[illegible]	[illegible]	[illegible]	[illegible]	[illegible]	[illegible]	[illegible]	[illegible]
Sugar	[illegible]	[illegible]	[illegible]	[illegible]	[illegible]	[illegible]		
Wine	[illegible]	[illegible]	[illegible]	[illegible]	[illegible]	[illegible]	[illegible]	[illegible]
Other Articles	[illegible]	[illegible]	[illegible]	[illegible]	[illegible]	[illegible]	[illegible]	[illegible]
Total Customs	[illegible]	[illegible]	[illegible]	[illegible]	[illegible]	[illegible]	[illegible]	[illegible]
II. EXCISE.								
Spirits	[illegible]	[illegible]	[illegible]	[illegible]	[illegible]	[illegible]	[illegible]	[illegible]
Malt (including Beer Duty in 1829 and 1889-90).	[illegible]	[illegible]	[illegible]	[illegible]	[illegible]	[illegible]	[illegible]	[illegible]
Licences	[illegible]	[illegible]	[illegible]	[illegible]	[illegible]	[illegible]	[illegible]	[illegible]§
Other Receipts	[illegible]	[illegible]	[illegible]	[illegible]	[illegible]	[illegible]	[illegible]	[illegible]
Total Excise	[illegible]	[illegible]	[illegible]	[illegible]	[illegible]	[illegible]	[illegible]	[illegible]
III. STAMPS.								
Probates	[illegible]	[illegible]	[illegible]	[illegible]	[illegible]	[illegible]	[illegible]	[illegible]‡
Legacies and Succession Duty	[illegible]	[illegible]	[illegible]	[illegible]	[illegible]	[illegible]	[illegible]	[illegible]
Other Stamps	[illegible]	[illegible]	[illegible]	[illegible]	[illegible]	[illegible]	[illegible]	[illegible]
Total Stamps	[illegible]	[illegible]	[illegible]	[illegible]	[illegible]	[illegible]	[illegible]	[illegible]
IV. TAXES.								
Land Tax	[illegible]	[illegible]	[illegible]	[illegible]	[illegible]	[illegible]	[illegible]	[illegible]
Assessed Taxes:— (a) Inhabited House Duty.	—	—	—	—	[illegible]	1,874,082	[illegible]	[illegible]
(b) Other Assessed Taxes.	[illegible]	[illegible]	[illegible]	[illegible]	[illegible]	[illegible]	—	—
Total Taxes	7,774,276	[illegible]	[illegible]	4,509,910	[illegible]	[illegible]	[illegible]	[illegible]
V. INCOME TAX.								
Schedules A., B., and E.	[illegible]	—	—	[illegible]	[illegible]	[illegible]	[illegible]	[illegible]
Schedules C. and D. (Public Companies)					[illegible]	[illegible]	[illegible]	[illegible]
Schedule D. (Trades and Professions)					[illegible]	[illegible]	[illegible]	[illegible]
Total Income Tax	[illegible]	—	—	[illegible]	[illegible]	[illegible]	[illegible]	[illegible]
TOTAL REVENUE FROM TAXES £	[illegible]	[illegible]	[illegible]	[illegible]	[illegible]	[illegible]	[illegible]	[illegible]

* From Excise. † Partly Excise. ‡ Including Local Taxation Revenue.
§ Besides 993,252l. under "Other Receipts, Excise."

TABLE O.—ESTIMATE OF TRUE REVENUE, GREAT BRITAIN.

—	Revenue as collected. (1.)	Correction for Ireland (Tables D. and E.). (2.)	Correction for Revenue attributable to Imperial Sources (Table F.). (3.)	Estimated true Revenue.
	£	£	£	£
[illegible]	[illegible]	[illegible]	[illegible]	[illegible]
[illegible]	[illegible]	[illegible]	[illegible]	[illegible]
[illegible]	[illegible]	[illegible]	[illegible]	[illegible]
[illegible]	[illegible]	[illegible]	[illegible]	[illegible]
[illegible]	[illegible]	[illegible]	[illegible]	[illegible]
[illegible]	[illegible]	[illegible]	[illegible]	[illegible]
[illegible]	[illegible]	[illegible]	[illegible]	[illegible]
[illegible]	[illegible]	[illegible]	[illegible]	[illegible]

TABLE F.—[illegible]

	Sums included in Miscellaneous Revenue.	Sums included in Revenue from Taxes.			Total.
		Customs?	[illegible]	[illegible]	
	£	£	£	£	£
1819 to 5 January 1820	*1,759,000	[illegible]	14,000	—	[illegible]
1829 to 5 " 1830	*200,849	[illegible]	[illegible]	—	[illegible]
1839 to 5 " 1840	144,033	[illegible]	[illegible]	—	[illegible]
1849 to 5 " 1850	558,442	[illegible]	[illegible]	[illegible]	[illegible]
1859-60 to 31 March 1860	1,758,971	[illegible]	[illegible]	[illegible]	[illegible]
1869-70 to 31 " 1870	2,070,661	[illegible]	[illegible]	[illegible]	[illegible]
1879-80 to 31 " 1880	2,648,894	[illegible]	[illegible]	[illegible]	[illegible]
1889-90 to 31 " 1890	1,287,037	[illegible]	[illegible]	[illegible]	[illegible]

* [illegible] in Ireland in 1819, and [illegible] in 1829, which sums are [illegible] from the figures in [illegible] Appendix.

PART II.—EXPENDITURE.

TABLE A.—IRELAND.

	1819.	1829.	1836.	1849.	1859-60.	1869-70.	*1879-80.	1889-90.
CIVIL GOVERNMENT CHARGES.	£	£	£	£	£	£	£	£
(a.) On Consolidated Fund	[illegible]	[illegible]	[illegible]	[illegible]	[illegible]	[illegible]	[illegible]	[illegible]
(b.) Voted	[illegible]	[illegible]	[illegible]	[illegible]	[illegible]	[illegible]	[illegible]	[illegible]
(c.) Out of Gross Revenues	[illegible]	[illegible]	[illegible]	[illegible]	—	—	—	—
(d.) Out of Local Taxation Revenues	—	—	—	—	—	—	—	[illegible]
Total Civil Government Charges £	[illegible]	[illegible]	[illegible]	[illegible]	[illegible]	[illegible]	[illegible]	[illegible]
Collection of Taxes	[illegible]	[illegible]	[illegible]	[illegible]	[illegible]	[illegible]	[illegible]	[illegible]
Post Office Services	[illegible]	[illegible]	[illegible]	[illegible]	[illegible]	[illegible]	[illegible]	[illegible]
Appropriated Duties	[illegible]	—	—	—	—	—	—	—
TOTAL IRISH EXPENDITURE £	[illegible]	[illegible]	[illegible]	[illegible]	[illegible]	[illegible]	[illegible]	[illegible]

* See paragraph 8 of memorandum ad fin.

TABLE B.—GREAT BRITAIN.

	1819.	1829.	1836.	1849.	1859-60.	1869-70.	*1879-80.	1889-90.
CIVIL GOVERNMENT CHARGES.	£	£	£	£	£	£	£	£
(a.) On Consolidated Fund	178,050	193,610	409,979	481,308	909,727	500,481	549,061	481,440
(b.) Voted	456,000	404,188	778,070	1,565,066	3,631,502	5,244,249	10,011,487	6,648,185
(c.) Out of Gross Revenues	479,161	420,743	275,475	231,809	—	—	—	—
(d.) Out of Local Taxation Revenues	—	—	—	—	—	—	—	4,969,213
(e.) Out of Crown Lands Revenues	48,040	—	—	—	—	—	—	—
Total Civil Government Charges £	1,138,471	1,082,333	1,456,327	2,278,783	4,541,102	5,746,709	10,510,148	15,110,229
COLLECTION OF TAXES.								
(a.) Customs	1,254,825	1,358,198	1,065,759	1,213,271	668,700	903,068	600,144	941,460
(b.) Inland Revenue	1,588,887	1,496,780	1,230,503	2,198,277	1,306,458	1,297,235	1,432,223	1,377,590
Total Collection of Taxes £	2,843,712	2,854,988	2,296,262	3,411,548	2,974,248	2,200,303	2,032,367	2,419,051
POST OFFICE SERVICES.								
(a.) Post Office	328,150	379,176	731,903	1,157,080	1,714,447	2,676,955	3,818,430	4,329,088
(b.) Telegraph Service	—	—	—	—	—	64,720	918,280	2,633,941
(c.) Packet Service	—	—	—	8,300	20,347	84,045	40,707	73,050
Total Post Office Services £	328,150	379,176	731,903	1,165,380	1,734,794	2,825,720	4,071,427	7,035,079
GRAND TOTAL, GREAT BRITAIN £	4,410,333	4,316,487	4,474,085	6,855,869	9,249,904	10,272,668	17,116,982	24,566,059

* See paragraph 8 of memorandum ad fin.

PART III.—CONTRIBUTION TO IMPERIAL SERVICES.

TABLE A.—IRELAND.

	Estimated true Revenue (Part I. Table I.)	Local Expenditure (Part II. Table A.)	Contribution.
	£	£	£
1819 to 5 January 1820	[illegible]	[illegible]	[illegible]
1829 to 5 ,, 1830	[illegible]	[illegible]	[illegible]
1839 to 5 ,, 1840	[illegible]	[illegible]	[illegible]
1849 to 5 ,, 1850	[illegible]	[illegible]	[illegible]
1859–60 to 31 March 1860	[illegible]	[illegible]	[illegible]
1869–70 to 31 ,, 1870	[illegible]	[illegible]	[illegible]
1879–80 to 31 ,, 1880	[illegible]	[illegible]	[illegible]
1889–90 to 31 ,, 1890	[illegible]	[illegible]	[illegible]

TABLE B.—GREAT BRITAIN.

—	Estimated true Revenue (Part I. Table G.)	Local Expenditure (Part II. Table B.)	Contribution.
	£	£	£
1819 to 5 January 1820	[illegible]	[illegible]	[illegible]
1829 to 5 ,, 1830	[illegible]	[illegible]	[illegible]
1839 to 5 ,, 1840	[illegible]	[illegible]	[illegible]
1849 to 5 ,, 1850	[illegible]	[illegible]	[illegible]
1859–60 to 31 March 1860	[illegible]	[illegible]	[illegible]
1869–70 to 31 ,, 1870	[illegible]	[illegible]	[illegible]
1879–80 to 31 ,, 1880	[illegible]	[illegible]	[illegible]
1889–90 to 31 ,, 1890	[illegible]	[illegible]	[illegible]

PART IV.—POPULATION.

Census of 5th April.	Great Britain.	Ireland.	United Kingdom.	Ireland. Per Cent. of United Kingdom.
1821	14,091,757	6,801,827	20,893,584	32½
1831	16,261,183	7,767,401	24,028,584	32
1841	18,534,332	8,175,124	26,709,456	31
1851	20,816,351	6,574,278	27,390,629	24
1861	23,128,518	5,798,967	28,927,485	20
1871	26,072,284	5,412,377	31,484,661	17
1881	29,710,012	5,174,836	34,884,848	15
1891	33,028,172	4,704,750	37,732,922	12½

The foregoing figures have been applied to the corresponding years of account discussed in the memorandum, i.e., the figures of 5th April 1821 to the financial year ended 5th January 1822, and so forth. In strictness the date at which the population should have been taken for the year ended 5th January 1820 should have been 5th July 1819, and so forth, down to the year ended 5th January 1830; for the year ended 31st March 1840 the date should have been 30th September 1839, and similarly in later years. But for the earlier portion of the period no estimate is available of the population at dates other than those of the actual census; while even for the later portion such an estimate can only be conjectural. For these reasons it has seemed best to adopt in the present memorandum the actual census figures, though not corresponding strictly with the financial years dealt with. The error due to the adoption of this course cannot be material in any case.

B.—PARLIAMENTARY RETURN (C. 314 of 1894) showing, for the Year ended the 31st day of March 1894; (1) the AMOUNT CONTRIBUTED by ENGLAND, SCOTLAND, and IRELAND, respectively, to the REVENUE collected by IMPERIAL OFFICERS; (2) the EXPENDITURE on ENGLISH, SCOTTISH, and IRISH SERVICES met out of such REVENUE; and (3) the BALANCES of REVENUE CONTRIBUTED by ENGLAND, SCOTLAND, and IRELAND, respectively, which are available for IMPERIAL EXPENDITURE (in continuation of PARLIAMENTARY PAPER, No. 334, of Session 1893–94).

PART I.—REVENUE, 1893–94.

1. EXCHEQUER REVENUE (Net Receipts).

[illegible]	As collected.					As contributed.				
	From Imperial Sources.	In England.	In Scotland.	In Ireland.	Total.	From Imperial Sources.	By England.	By Scotland.	By Ireland.	Total.
	£	£	£	£	£	£	£	£	£	£
Customs	—	[illegible]	[illegible]	[illegible]	[illegible]	—	[illegible]	[illegible]	[illegible]	[illegible]
Excise	—	[illegible]	[illegible]	[illegible]	[illegible]	—	[illegible]	[illegible]	[illegible]	[illegible]
Stamps	—	[illegible]	[illegible]	[illegible]	[illegible]	[illegible]	[illegible]	[illegible]	[illegible]	[illegible]
Land Tax	—	[illegible]	[illegible]	—	[illegible]	—	[illegible]	[illegible]	—	[illegible]
House Duty	—	[illegible]	[illegible]	—	[illegible]					
Income Tax	—	[illegible]	[illegible]	[illegible]	[illegible]	[illegible]	[illegible]	[illegible]	[illegible]	[illegible]
Total Revenue from Taxes	—	[illegible]	[illegible]	[illegible]	[illegible]	[illegible]	[illegible]	[illegible]	[illegible]	[illegible]
Post Office	—	[illegible]	[illegible]	[illegible]	[illegible]	—	[illegible]	[illegible]	[illegible]	[illegible]
Telegraphs	—	[illegible]	[illegible]	[illegible]	[illegible]	—	[illegible]	[illegible]	[illegible]	[illegible]
Crown Lands	—	[illegible]	[illegible]	[illegible]	[illegible]	—	[illegible]	[illegible]	[illegible]	[illegible]
Interest, &c.	[illegible]	—	—	—	[illegible]	[illegible]	—	—	—	[illegible]
Miscellaneous	[illegible]	[illegible]	[illegible]	[illegible]	[illegible]	[illegible]	[illegible]	[illegible]	[illegible]	[illegible]
Total Non-Tax Revenue	[illegible]	[illegible]	[illegible]	[illegible]	[illegible]	[illegible]	[illegible]	[illegible]	[illegible]	[illegible]
Total Exchequer Revenue	[illegible]	[illegible]	[illegible]	[illegible]	[illegible]	[illegible]	[illegible]	[illegible]	[illegible]	[illegible]

2. LOCAL TAXATION REVENUE (Net Receipts).

Customs	—	[illegible]	[illegible]	[illegible]	[illegible]	—	[illegible]	[illegible]	[illegible]	[illegible]
Excise	—	[illegible]	[illegible]	[illegible]	[illegible]	—	[illegible]	[illegible]	[illegible]	[illegible]
Stamps	—	[illegible]	[illegible]	[illegible]	[illegible]	[illegible]	[illegible]	[illegible]	[illegible]	[illegible]
Total Local Taxation Revenue	—	[illegible]	[illegible]	[illegible]	[illegible]	[illegible]	[illegible]	[illegible]	[illegible]	[illegible]

3. SUMMARY of REVENUE collected by IMPERIAL OFFICERS.

Exchequer	[illegible]	[illegible]	[illegible]	[illegible]	[illegible]	[illegible]	[illegible]	[illegible]	[illegible]	[illegible]
Local Taxation	—	[illegible]	[illegible]	[illegible]	[illegible]	[illegible]	[illegible]	[illegible]	[illegible]	[illegible]
GRAND TOTAL	[illegible]	[illegible]	[illegible]	[illegible]	[illegible]	[illegible]	[illegible]	[illegible]	[illegible]	[illegible]
Per Cent.	[illegible]	[illegible]	[illegible]	[illegible]	[illegible]	[illegible]	[illegible]	[illegible]	[illegible]	[illegible]

APPENDIX.—[illegible]

AMOUNT and PROPORTION of REVENUE contributed to the EXCHEQUER, Year 1893-94.

	Revenue (Net Receipt) as collected.				Revenue (Net Receipt) as allocated to [illegible] Contribution.				
	Collected in England.	Collected in Scotland.	Collected in Ireland.	Total.	Contributed by England.	Contributed by Scotland.	Contributed by Ireland.	Total.	
	£	£	£	£	£	£	£	£	
[illegible]	[illegible]	[illegible]	[illegible]	[illegible]	[illegible]	[illegible]	[illegible]	[illegible]	[illegible]
[illegible]	[illegible]	[illegible]	[illegible]	[illegible]	[illegible]	[illegible]	[illegible]	[illegible]	[illegible]
[illegible]	[illegible]	[illegible]	[illegible]	[illegible]	[illegible]	[illegible]	[illegible]	[illegible]	By population proportions.
[illegible]	[illegible]	[illegible]	[illegible]	[illegible]	[illegible]	[illegible]	[illegible]	[illegible]	[illegible]
[illegible]	[illegible]	[illegible]	[illegible]	[illegible]	[illegible]	[illegible]	[illegible]	[illegible]	[illegible]
[illegible]	[illegible]	[illegible]	[illegible]	[illegible]	[illegible]	[illegible]	[illegible]	[illegible]	[illegible]
[illegible]	[illegible]	[illegible]	[illegible]	[illegible]	[illegible]	[illegible]	[illegible]	[illegible]	[illegible]
[illegible]	[illegible]	[illegible]	[illegible]	[illegible]	[illegible]	[illegible]	[illegible]	[illegible]	By population proportions.
[illegible]	[illegible]	[illegible]	[illegible]	[illegible]	[illegible]	[illegible]	[illegible]	[illegible]	
Per Cent.	[illegible]	[illegible]	[illegible]	[illegible]	[illegible]	[illegible]	[illegible]	[illegible]	

* [illegible]

How calculated.	England.	Scotland.	Ireland.	Total.
	£	£	£	£
On old basis	[illegible]	[illegible]	[illegible]	[illegible]
On new basis	[illegible]	[illegible]	[illegible]	[illegible]
More (+) or less (−) than on the old basis	+ [illegible]	− [illegible]	− [illegible]	

MISCELLANEOUS REVENUE, 1893-94.

—	Derived from Imperial Sources.	Derived from England.	Derived from Scotland.	Derived from Ireland.	Total.
	£	£	£	£	£
Small Branches of the Hereditary Revenue	2,297	22,342	20,489	—	[illegible]
Bank of England	1,737	188,010	—	—	189,757
Naval Prize Fund	300	—	—	—	[illegible]
Transvaal	15,464	—	—	—	[illegible]
Contribution from Indian Revenue	19,927	—	—	—	[illegible]
Bankruptcy Act, 1883	—	32,437	—	—	[illegible]
Companies (Winding-up) Act, 1890	—	5,416	—	—	[illegible]
City of London Parochial Charities Act, 1883	—	1,070	—	—	[illegible]
Expenses of Administration of Local Loans	1,275	107	225	32,750	[illegible]
Westminster Improvements	—	1,208	—	—	[illegible]
Receipts by Civil Departments:					
Board of Supervision	—	—	244	—	244
Board of Trade	1,380	—	—	—	[illegible]
Civil List (Almshouses)	—	218	—	—	[illegible]
Civil Service Commission	37	—	—	—	37
Colonial Office	3,747	—	—	—	3,747
County Court Officers, &c., Ireland	—	—	—	1,718	[illegible]
Crofters Commission	—	—	379	—	[illegible]
Dundrum Criminal Lunatic Asylum	—	—	—	6	6
Education, England and Wales	—	602	—	—	[illegible]
Education, Scotland	—	—	11	—	[illegible]
Fishery Board, Scotland	—	—	7,363	—	[illegible]
Friendly Societies Registry	—	720	100	45	[illegible]
Carried forward	48,091	301,237	29,342	34,524	[illegible]

	Derived from Imperial Sources.	Derived from England.	Derived from Scotland.	Derived from Ireland.	Total.
	£	£	£	£	£
Brought forward	40,934	851,323	29,143	14,134	[illegible]
Receipts, &c.—*cont.*					
Harbours of Refuge	4,103	—	400	—	4,513
House of Commons	25,412	—	—	—	[illegible]
House of Lords	20,500	—	—	—	[illegible]
Land Commissioners, Ireland	—	—	—	100	100
Local Government Board, England	—	2,331	—	—	2,341
Merchant Shipping Acts	—	—	—	1	1
Mint	208,997	—	—	—	208,997
National Gallery, Ireland	—	—	—	34	34
Prisons	—	23,448	8,571	4,296	[illegible]
Public Works Loan Commissioners	—	7,318	1,500	—	[illegible]
Receiver of the Hereditary Revenue	—	1,133	—	—	[illegible]
Relief of Distress, Ireland	—	—	—	148	[illegible]
Register House Department, Edinburgh	—	—	38	—	38
Secretary for Scotland	—	—	87	—	87
Surveys of the United Kingdom	—	500	700	5,136	[illegible]
Treasury, &c.	13,839	—	5	33	[illegible]
Office of Works, England	—	3,340	—	—	[illegible]
Post Office Savings Banks	22,917	—	—	—	[illegible]
Savings and other Issues	400	1,711	14	105	[illegible]
Isle of Man	10,000	—	—	—	10,000
Greek Loan	13,800	—	—	—	13,800
Treasury Chest	314,742	—	—	—	314,742
Conscience Money	612	—	—	—	612
Casual Receipts	—	—	—	250	250
	879,670	773,508	36,416	65,842	1,756,436
Add—*Fee and Patent Stamps, as detailed below	178,150	480,739	41,599	88,086	818,165
Total Miscellaneous Revenue £	1,053,820	1,261,247	98,105	154,428	2,565,101
Per Cent., Total	50·41	37·96	4·51	6·72	100·00
Per Cent., England, Scotland, and Ireland	—	76·54	7·90	15·56	100·00
Fee and Patent Stamps:					
Admiralty Court, Ireland	—	—	—	20	20
Bankruptcy Court, Ireland	—	—	—	3,558	3,558
Board of Agriculture	—	4,553	78	—	4,631
Chancery Fund, Ireland	—	—	—	302	[illegible]
Civil Service Commission	8,697	—	—	—	8,697
Colonial Stock Act	60	—	—	—	60
Companies' Registration	—	12,031	2,590	1,707	[illegible]
County Courts, Ireland	—	—	—	20,653	[illegible]
Crofters Commission	—	—	74	—	74
†Crown Office in Chancery	—	4	—	—	4
District Audit	—	41,069	—	—	[illegible]
Edinburgh Gazette	—	—	2,809	—	[illegible]
Judgments Registry Fund	—	—	—	2,977	[illegible]
Judicature	—	264,920	1	37,773	[illegible]
Land Commission, Ireland	—	—	—	1,308	[illegible]
Land Registry	—	14,380	—	—	[illegible]
Law Courts, Scotland	—	—	19,431	—	[illegible]
London Gazette	—	22,504	—	—	[illegible]
Newspaper Registration	343	—	—	—	343
Police Courts, Metropolis	—	16,743	—	—	[illegible]
Public Record	—	547	—	805	[illegible]
Railway Commission	133	—	—	—	133
Register House, Scotland	—	—	44,146	—	44,146
Registration of Deeds	—	—	—	11,977	11,977
,, Title	—	—	—	197	197
Patents, Designs, and Trade Marks	168,986	—	—	—	[illegible]
Total Fee and Patent Stamps £	178,150	480,137	61,695	92,836	818,153

* Actual receipts in the year. † Repayment in excess of receipts.

1893-94.

Heads.	Revenue (Net Receipts) as collected.				Revenue (Net Receipts) as adjusted to show true Contribution.					Remarks.
	Collected in England.	Collected in Scotland.	Collected in Ireland.	Total.	Contributed from Imperial Sources.	Contributed by England.	Contributed by Scotland.	Contributed by Ireland.	Total.	
	£	£	£	£	£	£	£	£	£	
Customs:										
Tea	[illegible]	[illegible]	[illegible]	[illegible]	—	[illegible]	[illegible]	[illegible]	[illegible]	Adjusted like Exchequer Revenue.
Spirits	[illegible]	[illegible]	[illegible]	[illegible]	—	[illegible]	[illegible]	[illegible]	[illegible]	
	[illegible]	[illegible]	[illegible]	[illegible]	—	[illegible]	[illegible]	[illegible]	[illegible]	
Excise:										
Spirits	[illegible]	[illegible]	[illegible]	[illegible]	—	[illegible]	[illegible]	[illegible]	[illegible]	Ditto.
Beer	[illegible]	[illegible]	[illegible]	[illegible]	—	[illegible]	[illegible]	[illegible]	[illegible]	Ditto.
Licences	[illegible]	[illegible]	—	[illegible]	—	[illegible]	[illegible]	—	[illegible]	Revenue as collected.
	[illegible]	[illegible]	[illegible]	[illegible]	—	[illegible]	[illegible]	[illegible]	[illegible]	
Stamps:										
Probate Duty	[illegible]	[illegible]	[illegible]	[illegible]	[illegible]	[illegible]	[illegible]	[illegible]	[illegible]	Revenue as collected, with allowance made for [illegible]
Total £	[illegible]	[illegible]	[illegible]	[illegible]	[illegible]	[illegible]	[illegible]	[illegible]	[illegible]	[illegible] the United Kingdom.

Part II.—Expenditure.

1893-94.

(Exchequer Issues.)

	On Imperial Services.	On English Services.	On Scottish Services.	On Irish Services.	Total.
1. Met out of Exchequer Revenue:—	£	£	£	£	£
National Debt Charges	[illegible]	—	—	—	[illegible]
Naval and Military Charges:—					
(a.) Army	[illegible]	—	—	—	[illegible]
(b.) Navy	[illegible]	—	—	—	[illegible]
Civil Government Charges:—					
(a.) On Consolidated Fund	[illegible]	[illegible]	[illegible]	[illegible]	[illegible]
(b.) Voted	[illegible]	[illegible]	[illegible]	[illegible]	[illegible]
Total Civil Government Charges £	[illegible]	[illegible]	[illegible]	[illegible]	[illegible]
Collection of Taxes	—	[illegible]	[illegible]	[illegible]	[illegible]
Post Office Services	[illegible]	[illegible]	[illegible]	[illegible]	[illegible]
Total met out of Exchequer Revenue £	[illegible]	[illegible]	[illegible]	[illegible]	[illegible]
			[illegible]		

DETAILS OF NAVAL AND MILITARY CHARGES, 1893-94.

	Imperial.	English.	Scottish.	Irish.	Total.
	£	£	£	£	£
Army Services	17,[illegible]	—	—	—	[illegible]
Ordnance Factories	[illegible]	—	—	—	
Indian Army Pension Annuity	[illegible]	—	—	—	
Navy Services	14,[illegible]	—	—	—	[illegible]
Naval Defence Fund	1,[illegible]	—	—	—	
Total Naval and Military Charges - £	[illegible]	—	—	—	[illegible]

DETAILS OF CIVIL GOVERNMENT CHARGES, 1893-94.

(a) On Consolidated Fund.

	Imperial.	English.	Scottish.	Irish.	Total.
	£	£	£	£	£
Civil List	407,391	—	—	—	407,391
Annuities and Pensions:					
Annuities to the Royal Family	157,706	—	—	—	157,706
Pensions for Naval and Military Services	27,739	—	—	—	27,739
Pensions for Political and Civil Services	14,249	—	—	—	14,249
Pensions for Judicial Services	5,217	44,406	9,763	13,405	72,[illegible]
Compensations, Courts of Justice	—	25,790	—	4,483	30,273
Pensions, Diplomatic Services	2,600	—	—	—	2,600
Miscellaneous Pensions	2,447	—	[illegible]	—	2,[illegible]
Totals, Annuities and Pensions - £	2[illegible]	70,1[illegible]	10,[illegible]	17,[illegible]	[illegible]
Salaries and Allowances:					
Speaker, House of Commons	5,000	—	—	—	[illegible]
Exchequer and Audit Department	5,[illegible]	—	—	—	[illegible]
Clergy and Schools	4,[illegible]	—	17,[illegible]	—	[illegible]
Inspectors of Anatomy	—	370	[illegible]	473	[illegible]
Copyright Compensations	—	564	—	453	[illegible]
Salaries formerly on the Hereditary Revenues of Scotland	—	—	6,[illegible]	—	[illegible]
Land Revenue Allowances	—	748	[illegible]	150	[illegible]
Lord Lieutenant, Ireland	—	—	—	20,000	[illegible]
Queen's Colleges, Ireland	—	—	—	21,[illegible]	[illegible]
Miscellaneous	—	—	—	7[illegible]	[illegible]
Totals, Salaries and Allowances - £	[illegible]	1,[illegible]	[illegible]	4[illegible]	[illegible]
Courts of Justice Salaries	[illegible]	2[illegible]	[illegible]	[illegible]	[illegible]
Miscellaneous Services:					
Russian Dutch Loan	42,[illegible]	—	—	—	[illegible]
Greenwich Hospital	4,[illegible]	—	—	—	[illegible]
Duchy of Lancaster (Wine Compensation)	[illegible]	—	—	—	[illegible]
Duchy of Cornwall, &c. (Tin Compensation)	[illegible]	—	—	—	[illegible]
Public Offices Site Annuity	1[illegible]	—	—	—	[illegible]
Commutation of Perpetual Charges	[illegible]	—	—	—	[illegible]
Exchequer Contribution to Ireland	—	—	—	40,000	40,000
Totals, Miscellaneous Services - £	1[illegible]	—	—	40,000	[illegible]
Totals, Civil Government Charges on Consolidated Fund - £	[illegible]	[illegible]	[illegible]	[illegible]	[illegible]

(b) Voted.

[illegible]	Imperial.	English.	Scottish.	Irish.	Total.
CLASS I.	£	£	£	£	£
Royal Palaces and Marlborough House	—	36,790	730	—	[illegible]
Royal Parks, &c.	—	93,508	8,210	—	[illegible]
Houses of Parliament (Buildings)	36,556	—	—	—	[illegible]
Public Buildings	47,002	94,000	10,871	674	[illegible]
Admiralty, Extension of Buildings	48,171	—	—	—	[illegible]
Miscellaneous Legal Buildings (Great Britain).	—	45,303	7,500	—	[illegible]
Art and Science Buildings (Great Britain)	—	70,395	1,950	—	[illegible]
Diplomatic and Consular Buildings	28,159	—	—	—	[illegible]
Revenue Department Buildings (Great Britain).	—	304,364	25,300	—	[illegible]
Surveys of United Kingdom	4,273	124,246	50,173	60,950	[illegible]
Harbours under Board of Trade and Lighthouses Abroad	—	15,479	5,600	—	[illegible]
Peterhead Harbour	—	—	11,929	—	11,929
Rates on Government Property (United Kingdom).	1,900	207,500	4,065	36,172	245,539
Public Works and Buildings in Ireland	21,040	—	—	193,154	214,194
Railways (Ireland)	—	—	—	10,047	10,047
Total of Class I. £	253,469	955,142	137,135	313,914	1,617,532
CLASS II.					
ENGLAND.					
House of Lords Offices	26,484	—	—	—	[illegible]
House of Commons Offices	53,170	—	—	—	[illegible]
Treasury, &c.	37,500	20,072	3,500	1,500	[illegible]
Home Office, &c.	—	65,150	5,267	2,417	[illegible]
Foreign Office	69,282	—	—	—	[illegible]
Colonial Office	47,650	—	—	—	[illegible]
Privy Council Office, &c.	3,000	8,507	—	—	[illegible]
Board of Trade	167,320	5,350	—	—	[illegible]
Bankruptcy Department of the Board of Trade	—	—	—	—	—
Board of Agriculture	315	50,248	6,870	—	[illegible]
Charity Commission, &c.	—	32,949	—	—	[illegible]
Civil Service Commission	34,053	—	—	—	[illegible]
Exchequer and Audit Department	56,115	—	—	—	[illegible]
Friendly Societies Registry (United Kingdom)	—	5,304	365	860	[illegible]
Local Government Board	—	166,150	—	—	[illegible]
Lunacy Commission	—	15,417	—	—	[illegible]
Mercantile Marine Fund, Grant in Aid	50,000	—	—	—	[illegible]
Mint	77	—	—	—	77
National Debt Office	14,860	—	—	—	[illegible]
Public Works Loan Commission	—	8,023	1,148	—	[illegible]
Record Office	—	15,959	—	—	[illegible]
Registrar-General's Office	—	37,365	—	—	[illegible]
Stationery, &c., United Kingdom	987,500	193,934	21,090	35,000	[illegible]
Woods, Forests, &c., Office of	—	17,037	450	2,520	[illegible]
Works and Public Buildings, Office of	11,000	55,343	4,000	—	[illegible]
Secret Service	26,300	—	—	—	[illegible]
SCOTLAND.					
Secretary for Scotland's Office	—	—	10,625	—	[illegible]
Fishery Board	—	—	30,456	—	[illegible]
Lunacy Commission	—	—	3,679	—	[illegible]
Registrar-General's Office	—	—	7,195	—	[illegible]
Board of Supervision, &c.	—	—	4,324	—	[illegible]
IRELAND.					
Lord Lieutenant's Household	—	—	—	4,505	4,505
Chief Secretary's Office, &c.	—	—	—	41,114	41,114
Charitable Donations and Bequests Office	—	—	—	1,514	1,514
Local Government Board	—	—	—	134,945	134,945
Public Works Office	—	—	—	33,575	33,575
Record Office	—	—	—	5,004	5,004
Registrar-General's Office	—	—	—	15,041	15,041
Valuation and Boundary Survey	—	—	—	31,505	31,505
Total of Class II.	270,800	708,430	99,999	290,103	1,373,437
CLASS III.					
Law Charges	—	64,771	—	—	[illegible]
Miscellaneous Legal Expenses	19,150	36,127	—	33	[illegible]
Supreme Court of Judicature	—	353,135	—	—	[illegible]
Land Registry	—	3,164	—	—	[illegible]
County Courts	—	85,000	—	—	[illegible]
Police Courts (London and Sheerness)	—	2,354	—	—	[illegible]
Police (England and Wales)	—	56,152	—	—	[illegible]
Prisons (England and the Colonies)	5,570	461,548	—	—	[illegible]
Reformatory and Industrial Schools (Great Britain).	—	185,475	—	—	[illegible]
Broadmoor Criminal Lunatic Asylum	—	34,106	—	—	[illegible]

—	Imperial.	English.	Scotch.	Irish.	Total.
CLASS III.—contd.					
SCOTLAND.					
	£	£	£	£	£
Law Charges and Courts of Law	—	—	[illegible]	—	[illegible]
Register House, Edinburgh	—	—	[illegible]	—	[illegible]
[illegible] Commission	—	—	[illegible]	—	[illegible]
Prisons	—	—	[illegible]	—	[illegible]
IRELAND.					
Law Charges and Criminal Prosecutions	—	—	—	[illegible]	[illegible]
Supreme Court of Judicature and other Legal Departments	—	—	—	[illegible]	[illegible]
Land Commission	—	—	—	[illegible]	[illegible]
County Court Officers, &c.	—	—	—	[illegible]	[illegible]
Dublin Metropolitan Police (including Police Courts)	—	—	—	[illegible]	[illegible]
Constabulary	—	—	—	[illegible]	[illegible]
Prisons	—	—	—	[illegible]	[illegible]
Reformatory and Industrial Schools	—	—	—	[illegible]	[illegible]
Dundrum Criminal Lunatic Asylum	—	—	—	[illegible]	[illegible]
Total of Class III. £	[illegible]	[illegible]	[illegible]	[illegible]	[illegible]
CLASS IV.					
ENGLAND.					
Public Education (England and Wales)	—	[illegible]	—	—	[illegible]
Science and Art Department (United Kingdom)	—	[illegible]	[illegible]	[illegible]	[illegible]
British Museum	—	[illegible]	—	—	[illegible]
National Gallery	—	[illegible]	—	—	[illegible]
National Portrait Gallery	—	[illegible]	—	—	[illegible]
Scientific Investigations, &c. (United Kingdom)	[illegible]	[illegible]	[illegible]	[illegible]	[illegible]
London University	—	—	—	—	—
Universities and Colleges (Great Britain)	—	[illegible]	[illegible]	—	[illegible]
SCOTLAND.					
Public Education	—	—	[illegible]	—	[illegible]
National Gallery	—	—	[illegible]	—	[illegible]
IRELAND.					
Public Education	—	—	—	[illegible]	[illegible]
Endowed Schools Commissioners	—	—	—	[illegible]	[illegible]
National Gallery	—	—	—	[illegible]	[illegible]
Queen's Colleges	—	—	—	[illegible]	[illegible]
Total of Class IV. £	[illegible]	[illegible]	[illegible]	[illegible]	[illegible]
CLASS V.					
Diplomatic and Consular Services	[illegible]	—	—	—	[illegible]
Slave Trade Services	[illegible]	—	—	—	[illegible]
Colonial Services (including South Africa)	[illegible]	—	—	—	[illegible]
Subsidies to Telegraph Companies	[illegible]	—	—	—	[illegible]
Total of Class V. £	[illegible]	—	—	—	[illegible]
CLASS VI.					
Superannuation and Retired Allowances	[illegible]	[illegible]	[illegible]	[illegible]	[illegible]
Merchant Seamen's Fund Pensions	[illegible]	—	—	—	[illegible]
Friendly Societies Deficiency	[illegible]	—	—	—	[illegible]
Miscellaneous Charitable and other Allowances (Great Britain)	[illegible]	[illegible]	[illegible]	—	[illegible]
Pauper Lunatics (Ireland)	—	—	—	[illegible]	[illegible]
Hospitals and Charities (Ireland)	—	—	—	[illegible]	[illegible]
Total of Class VI. £	[illegible]	[illegible]	[illegible]	[illegible]	[illegible]
CLASS VII.					
Temporary Commissions	[illegible]	[illegible]	[illegible]	[illegible]	[illegible]
Miscellaneous Expenses	—	—	—	—	—
[illegible]	—	[illegible]	[illegible]	[illegible]	[illegible]
Repayments to Civil Contingencies Fund	[illegible]	[illegible]	—	[illegible]	[illegible]
Local Loans Fund	—	—	—	[illegible]	[illegible]
Highlands and Islands (Scotland) (Public Works and Communications)	—	—	[illegible]	—	[illegible]
Chicago Exhibition	[illegible]	—	—	—	[illegible]
Total of Class VII. £	[illegible]	[illegible]	[illegible]	[illegible]	[illegible]

	Imperial.	English.	Scottish.	Irish.	Total.
	£	£	£	£	£
Class I.	[illegible]	[illegible]	147,558	378,916	[illegible]
" II.	377,868	799,400	95,329	299,393	[illegible]
" III.	18,730	1,423,388	118,058	2,032,418	[illegible]
" IV.	33,300	7,237,359	1,110,499	1,230,349	[illegible]
" V.	831,380	—	—	—	[illegible]
" VI.	155,148	331,152	13,400	310,911	[illegible]
" VII.	40,400	57,347	41,300	19,580	[illegible]
Total Civil Government Charges Voted - £	2,062,[illegible]	10,400,[illegible]	1,623,474	4,045,[illegible]	[illegible]
Customs	—	435,000	56,063	49,758	[illegible]
Inland Revenue	—	1,497,[illegible]	[illegible]	187,[illegible]	[illegible]
Total Collection of Taxes - £	—	[illegible]	344,[illegible]	[illegible]	[illegible]
Post Office	—	5,440,000	718,000	358,720	[illegible]
Telegraph Service	—	2,024,[illegible]	309,[illegible]	179,000	[illegible]
Packet Service	501,000	24,000	90,000	54,000	[illegible]
Total Post Office Services - £	501,000	[illegible]	1,004,[illegible]	707,[illegible]	[illegible]
Total Revenue Departments - £	505,000	[illegible]	1,348,[illegible]	[illegible]	[illegible]

PART III.—CONTRIBUTION TO IMPERIAL SERVICES.

This Table shows the Balances of Revenue contributed by England, Scotland, and Ireland, respectively, which are available for Imperial Expenditure after the Local Expenditure of those Divisions of the United Kingdom has been met, according to the figures shown in Parts I. and II. of this Return:—

Year 1893–94.	England.	Per Cent.	Scotland.	Per Cent.	Ireland.	Per Cent.	Total.	Per Cent.
	£		£		£		£	
Total Revenue as contributed	[illegible]	[illegible]	[illegible]	[illegible]	[illegible]	[illegible]	[illegible]	[illegible]
Local Expenditure	[illegible]	[illegible]	[illegible]	[illegible]	[illegible]	[illegible]	[illegible]	[illegible]
Balance available for Imperial Expenditure	[illegible]	[illegible]	[illegible]	[illegible]	[illegible]	[illegible]	[illegible]	[illegible]

APPENDIX IV.

A.—MEMORANDUM and TABLES by Mr. T. J. PITTAR of the BOARD OF CUSTOMS with regard to the true Contribution to TOBACCO REVENUE by ENGLAND, SCOTLAND, and IRELAND respectively.

Mr. Pittar's memorandum explains the basis on which the calculations in the accompanying tables, relating to the estimated true revenue derivable from the duty on tobacco in each of the three kingdoms for the five years ending 1893-94 are made. But it must be understood that the Treasury and Board of Customs only submit the tables to the Royal Commission in deference to the express wish of the Commissioners, and that they do not hold themselves committed to the assumptions implied in those calculations.

The figures relating to the consumption of tobacco, based on the results which have recently been obtained from the tobacco manufacturers, may, and probably do, approximate more closely to the facts of 1893-94 than the corresponding figures deducible from the results which were obtained in 1891, through the railway and shipping returns. But, if the results obtained from the tobacco manufacturers for 1893-94 be applied to the four previous years, the conclusions to which the calculations point, necessarily become more hypothetical, and may be really no nearer the mark than the figures already given for those years.

Accordingly, having regard to this consideration and the obvious objections to there being two sets of hypothetical calculations for the same year, the Treasury and the Board of Customs would deprecate altering the figures in the Financial Relations Returns relating to 1889-90, 1890-91, 1891-92, and 1892-93, in the absence of the production of evidence from the manufacturers, directly bearing on the tobacco trade in each of those years.

JOHN A. KEMPE,
Deputy Chairman, Board of Customs.
E. W. HAMILTON,
29th January 1895. H.M. Treasury.

MEMORANDUM.

Statistical Office, Custom House,
London, 20th December 1894.

The Royal Commission on the Financial Relations of Great Britain and Ireland were desirous of receiving a return showing for each of the years since 1889-90 the consumption of tobacco in Ireland, the total of exports and imports of that article, and the balance, the resulting true contribution, and the rate per head of consumption in England, Scotland, and Ireland (1) by the new calculation based upon official inquiries made of the manufacturers and dealers, and (2) by the proportions known as those of the Railway and Shipping Returns (see Questions 1270 and 1281 in Minutes of Evidence).

The new inquiry has covered a period of 12 months, viz., the financial year 1893-94, and therefore it is

possible to state the imports, exports, balance, and true contribution for that year. But the Railway and Shipping Returns only extended over four months of the year 1890–91; they did not assume a total import or export for the 12 months, but treated the four months as an integral whole, applying for each kingdom its per-centage proportion of the total consumption of the four months to the total consumption of the United Kingdom for the 12 months. Thus no such comparative account of imports and exports by the respective methods can be given, because no account at all of imports and exports was formed in respect of any one of those years prior to 1893–94, except in the case of the first calculation as dealt with at page 5 of Parliamentary Paper 329 of 1891; but it is understood that the Royal Commission do not desire a comparison with that calculation.

With a view, however, of affording the desired information as nearly as possible, the following tables are annexed.

Table A. gives, in a comparative form, a statement of the amount of tobacco duty paid per head of the population in the United Kingdom, and in England, Scotland, and Ireland separately, (1) by using the proportions of revenue as deduced from the Railway and Shipping returns, and (2) by the proportions ascertained from the returns of the manufacturers and dealers for the year 1893–94.

The plan pursued in applying to the back years 1889–90 to 1892–93 the proportions of the new calculation for 1893–94 has been to ascertain the amount of tobacco duty paid per head of the population in 1893–94 both in the United Kingdom as a whole, and then separately in England, Scotland, and Ireland. As to these elements of the calculation there is no doubt, nor is there any doubt as to the consumption per head for the United Kingdom in the preceding years. With these data to work upon it has been taken that the amount of duty paid per head of the population in the United Kingdom in each of the years 1889–90, 1890–91, 1891–92, and 1892–93 will bear the same proportion to the amount paid per head in each of the constituent kingdoms in those years, as the payment per head for the United Kingdom in 1893–94 is known to bear to the payment per head in each constituent kingdom in that year.

Table B. gives a like comparative account, as between the two methods, of the aggregate contribution for each kingdom. As regards the years prior to 1893–94 these amounts have been arrived at by multiplying the duty paid per head of the population (shown in Table A.) by the population for each year as given in the 41st number of the Statistical Abstract.

It should be understood that the principal differences between the former calculation and the new one arise mainly from the better information which has been obtained as to the exports of manufactured tobacco from Ireland. The railway and shipping returns gave an export of 842,[illegible] lbs. in the four months, being at the rate of 2,[illegible] lbs. in the year 1890–91. The new inquiry gives an export from Ireland for 1893–94 of 4,[illegible] lbs., being 2,[illegible] lbs. more than the former. It must, however, be borne in mind that, according to the best judges, the export tobacco trade of Ireland had increased to a considerable extent in the intervening years.

By the railway and shipping returns the export of manufactured tobacco in the other direction, i.e., from Great Britain to Ireland, was at about the rate of 1,[illegible] lbs. for the year 1890–91, while the new inquiry gives for 1893–94 1,[illegible] lbs.

These are the principal items which affect to a large degree the final outcome of the new calculation, and differences between its result and the result by the former inquiries.

In addition to the foregoing, there are added in Appendix C. two tables drawn up in the form adopted in the Financial Relations papers. In these tables the new totals for tobacco (as given in Table B.) are included in place of those formerly given, together with the resulting altered totals of the estimated true contribution of Imperial Common Revenue from all sources for each division of the kingdom. Table C.

It only remains to be remarked that the application to the tobacco revenue of the years 1889–90 to 1892–93, of proportions which relate strictly to the revenue and consumption of 1893–94, cannot be defended as a statistical method. It is obviously open to the same objections as were urged against the application to the totals of other years of the railway proportions for four months of 1890–91. The population of England is rising at a certain rate; that of Scotland is rising at a different rate, whilst that of Ireland is falling; and again, the progress of industry, manufactures, and trade varies in different years. The division, therefore, of the revenue of the three countries by fixed proportions throughout a number of years, under such shifting conditions, must be productive of inaccuracy. No other way can be satisfactory in relation to the object of this inquiry, except the making of a fresh calculation on renewed investigation into the figures of each year. Whether that would be practicable is open to grave doubt.

T. J. PITTAR.

TABLE A.

TOBACCO.

COMPARATIVE STATEMENT showing per HEAD of the POPULATION the estimated true CONTRIBUTION to the TOBACCO REVENUE of ENGLAND, SCOTLAND, and IRELAND respectively for the Five Years 1889–90 to 1893–94, (1.) by the RAILWAY and SHIPPING RETURNS for the Four Months December 1890—March 1891, and (2.) by RETURNS of MANUFACTURERS and DEALERS for 1893–94.

Years.	Per Head of the United Kingdom.	England. 1. By Proportions of Railway and Shipping Returns.	England. 2. By Proportions of Returns of Manufacturers and Dealers for 12 Months, 1893–94.	England. 3. More or less by Methods referred to in Column 2.	Scotland. 1. By Proportions of Railway and Shipping Returns.	Scotland. 2. By Proportions of Returns of Manufacturers and Dealers for 12 Months, 1893–94.	Scotland. 3. More or less by Methods referred to in Column 2.	Ireland. 1. By Proportions of Railway and Shipping Returns.	Ireland. 2. By Proportions of Returns of Manufacturers and Dealers for 12 Months, 1893–94.	Ireland. 3. More or less by Methods referred to in Column 2.
	£ s. d.	£ s. d.	£ s. d.	£ s. d.	£ s. d.	£ s. d.	£ s. d.	£ s. d.	£ s. d.	£ s. d.
1889–90	[illegible]	[illegible]	[illegible]	+ [illegible]	[illegible]	[illegible]	– [illegible]	[illegible]	[illegible]	– [illegible]
1890–91	[illegible]	[illegible]	[illegible]	+ [illegible]	[illegible]	[illegible]	– [illegible]	[illegible]	[illegible]	– [illegible]
1891–92	[illegible]	[illegible]	[illegible]	+ [illegible]	[illegible]	[illegible]	– [illegible]	[illegible]	[illegible]	– [illegible]
1892–93	[illegible]	[illegible]	[illegible]	+ [illegible]	[illegible]	[illegible]	– [illegible]	[illegible]	[illegible]	– [illegible]
1893–94	[illegible]	[illegible]	[illegible]	+ [illegible]	[illegible]	[illegible]	– [illegible]	[illegible]	[illegible]	– [illegible]

Custom House, London,
20th December 1894.

TABLE B.

TOBACCO.

COMPARATIVE STATEMENT showing the estimated true CONTRIBUTION to the TOBACCO REVENUE of ENGLAND, SCOTLAND, and IRELAND respectively for the Two Years 1889-90 to 1890-91, (i.) by the RAILWAY and SHIPPING RETURNS for the Four Months December 1890—March 1891, and (ii.) by RETURNS of MANUFACTURERS and DEALERS for 1893-94.

Years.	England.			Scotland.			Ireland.		
	1.	2.	3.	1.	2.	3.	1.	2.	3.
	By Proportions of Railway and Shipping Returns.	By Proportions of Returns of Manufacturers and Dealers for 12 Months, 1893-94.	More or less by Methods employed in Column 2.	By Proportions of Railway and Shipping Returns.	By Proportions of Returns of Manufacturers and Dealers for 12 Months, 1893-94.	More or less by Methods employed in Column 2.	By Proportions of Railway and Shipping Returns.	By Proportions of Returns of Manufacturers and Dealers for 12 Months, 1893-94.	More or less by Methods employed in Column 2.
	£	£	£	£	£	£	£	£	£
1889-90 -	[illegible]	[illegible]	+ [illegible] per cent. + [illegible]	[illegible]	[illegible]	− [illegible] per cent. − [illegible]	[illegible]	[illegible]	− [illegible] per cent. − [illegible]
1890-91 -	[illegible]	[illegible]	+ [illegible] per cent. + [illegible]	[illegible]	[illegible]	− [illegible] per cent. − [illegible]	[illegible]	[illegible]	− [illegible] per cent. − [illegible]
1891-92 -	[illegible]	[illegible]	+ [illegible] per cent. + [illegible]	[illegible]	[illegible]	− [illegible] per cent. − [illegible]	[illegible]	[illegible]	− [illegible] per cent. − [illegible]
1892-93 -	[illegible]	[illegible]	+ [illegible] per cent. + [illegible]	[illegible]	[illegible]	− [illegible] per cent. − [illegible]	[illegible]	[illegible]	− [illegible] per cent. − [illegible]
1893-94 -	[illegible]	[illegible]	+ [illegible] per cent. + [illegible]	[illegible]	[illegible]	− [illegible] per cent. − [illegible]	[illegible]	[illegible]	− [illegible] per cent. − [illegible]

Custom House, London,
20th December 1894.

TABLE C.

CUSTOMS.

Year 18[illegible].

RETURN showing the AMOUNT of IMPERIAL CUSTOMS REVENUE collected in ENGLAND, SCOTLAND, and IRELAND respectively, together with the AMOUNT of the true CONTRIBUTIONS ascertained or estimated according to the several Methods described in the last Column hereof.

—	Revenue (Net Receipts) as collected.				Revenue (Net Amount) as adjusted to give true Contributions.				Remarks.
	Collected in England.	Collected in Scotland.	Collected in Ireland.	Total.	Contributed by England.	Contributed by Scotland.	Contributed by Ireland.	Total.	
	£	£	£	£	£	£	£	£	
Cocoa - -	[illegible]	[illegible]	[illegible]	[illegible]	[illegible]	[illegible]	[illegible]	[illegible]	By population proportions.
Chicory and coffee	[illegible]	[illegible]	[illegible]	[illegible]	[illegible]	[illegible]	[illegible]	[illegible]	[illegible]
Dried fruits - -	[illegible]	[illegible]	[illegible]	[illegible]	[illegible]	[illegible]	[illegible]	[illegible]	[illegible]
Foreign spirits -	[illegible]	[illegible]	[illegible]	[illegible]	[illegible]	[illegible]	[illegible]	[illegible]	[illegible]
Tea - -	[illegible]	[illegible]	[illegible]	[illegible]	[illegible]	[illegible]	[illegible]	[illegible]	[illegible]
Tobacco - -	[illegible]	[illegible]	[illegible]	[illegible]	[illegible]	[illegible]	[illegible]	[illegible]	[illegible]
Wine - -	[illegible]	[illegible]	[illegible]	[illegible]	[illegible]	[illegible]	[illegible]	[illegible]	[illegible]
All other articles -	[illegible]	[illegible]	[illegible]	[illegible]	[illegible]	[illegible]	[illegible]	[illegible]	By remaining proportions.
Total and average	[illegible]	[illegible]	[illegible]	[illegible]	[illegible]	[illegible]	[illegible]	[illegible]	
Per cent. - -	[illegible]	[illegible]	[illegible]	[illegible]	[illegible]	[illegible]	[illegible]	[illegible]	

Year [illegible].

—	Revenue (Net Receipts) as collected.				Revenue (Net Receipts) as estimated to give true Contribution.				Remarks.
	Collected in England.	Collected in Scotland.	Collected in Ireland.	Total.	Contributed by England.	Contributed by Scotland.	Contributed by Ireland.	Total.	
	£	£	£	£	£	£	£	£	
Cocoa	[illegible]	[illegible]	[illegible]	[illegible]	[illegible]	[illegible]	[illegible]	[illegible]	By population proportions.
Chicory and coffee	[illegible]	[illegible]	[illegible]	[illegible]	[illegible]	[illegible]	[illegible]	[illegible]	By proportions ascertained for [illegible], from Railway, &c. Returns. See Parliamentary Paper [illegible], page [illegible].
Dried fruits	[illegible]	[illegible]	[illegible]	[illegible]	[illegible]	[illegible]	[illegible]	[illegible]	By population proportions.
Foreign spirits	[illegible]	[illegible]	[illegible]	[illegible]	[illegible]	[illegible]	[illegible]	[illegible]	By proportions ascertained for [illegible].
Tea	[illegible]	[illegible]	[illegible]	[illegible]	[illegible]	[illegible]	[illegible]	[illegible]	By proportions ascertained for [illegible], from Railway, &c. Returns. See Parliamentary Paper [illegible], page [illegible].
Tobacco	[illegible]	[illegible]	[illegible]	[illegible]	[illegible]	[illegible]	[illegible]	[illegible]	By proportions ascertained for [illegible] upon inquiry made of manufacturers and dealers.
Wine	[illegible]	[illegible]	[illegible]	[illegible]	[illegible]	[illegible]	[illegible]	[illegible]	By proportions ascertained for [illegible], from Railway, &c. Returns. See Parliamentary Paper [illegible], page [illegible].
All other articles	[illegible]	[illegible]	[illegible]	[illegible]	[illegible]	[illegible]	[illegible]	[illegible]	By population proportions.
Total net receipts	[illegible]	[illegible]	[illegible]	[illegible]	[illegible]	[illegible]	[illegible]	[illegible]	
Per cent.	[illegible]	[illegible]	[illegible]	[illegible]	[illegible]	[illegible]	[illegible]	[illegible]	

Year [illegible].

	£	£	£	£	£	£	£	£	
Cocoa	[illegible]	[illegible]	[illegible]	[illegible]	[illegible]	[illegible]	[illegible]	[illegible]	By population proportions.
Chicory and coffee	[illegible]	[illegible]	[illegible]	[illegible]	[illegible]	[illegible]	[illegible]	[illegible]	By proportions ascertained for [illegible], from Railway, &c. Returns. See Parliamentary Paper [illegible], page [illegible].
Dried fruits	[illegible]	[illegible]	[illegible]	[illegible]	[illegible]	[illegible]	[illegible]	[illegible]	By population proportions.
Foreign spirits	[illegible]	[illegible]	[illegible]	[illegible]	[illegible]	[illegible]	[illegible]	[illegible]	By proportions ascertained for [illegible].
Tea	[illegible]	[illegible]	[illegible]	[illegible]	[illegible]	[illegible]	[illegible]	[illegible]	By proportions ascertained for [illegible], from Railway, &c. Returns. See Parliamentary Paper [illegible], page [illegible].
Tobacco	[illegible]	[illegible]	[illegible]	[illegible]	[illegible]	[illegible]	[illegible]	[illegible]	By proportions ascertained for [illegible] upon inquiry made of manufacturers and dealers.
Wine	[illegible]	[illegible]	[illegible]	[illegible]	[illegible]	[illegible]	[illegible]	[illegible]	By proportions ascertained for [illegible], from Railway, &c. Returns. See Parliamentary Paper [illegible], page [illegible].
All other articles	[illegible]	[illegible]	[illegible]	[illegible]	[illegible]	[illegible]	[illegible]	[illegible]	By population proportions.
Total net receipts	[illegible]	[illegible]	[illegible]	[illegible]	[illegible]	[illegible]	[illegible]	[illegible]	
Per cent.	[illegible]	[illegible]	[illegible]	[illegible]	[illegible]	[illegible]	[illegible]	[illegible]	

Year [illegible].

	£	£	£	£	£	£	£	£	
Cocoa	[illegible]	[illegible]	[illegible]	[illegible]	[illegible]	[illegible]	[illegible]	[illegible]	By population proportions.
Chicory and coffee	[illegible]	[illegible]	[illegible]	[illegible]	[illegible]	[illegible]	[illegible]	[illegible]	By proportions ascertained for [illegible], from Railway, &c. Returns. See Parliamentary Paper [illegible], page [illegible].
Dried fruits	[illegible]	[illegible]	[illegible]	[illegible]	[illegible]	[illegible]	[illegible]	[illegible]	By population proportions.
Foreign spirits	[illegible]	[illegible]	[illegible]	[illegible]	[illegible]	[illegible]	[illegible]	[illegible]	By proportions ascertained for [illegible].
Tea	[illegible]	[illegible]	[illegible]	[illegible]	[illegible]	[illegible]	[illegible]	[illegible]	By proportions ascertained for [illegible], from Railway, &c. Returns. See Parliamentary Paper [illegible], page [illegible].
Tobacco	[illegible]	[illegible]	[illegible]	[illegible]	[illegible]	[illegible]	[illegible]	[illegible]	By proportions ascertained for [illegible] upon inquiry made of manufacturers and dealers.
Wine	[illegible]	[illegible]	[illegible]	[illegible]	[illegible]	[illegible]	[illegible]	[illegible]	By proportions ascertained for [illegible], from Railway, &c. Returns. See Parliamentary Paper [illegible], page [illegible].
All other articles	[illegible]	[illegible]	[illegible]	[illegible]	[illegible]	[illegible]	[illegible]	[illegible]	By population proportions.
Total net receipts	[illegible]	[illegible]	[illegible]	[illegible]	[illegible]	[illegible]	[illegible]	[illegible]	
Per cent.	[illegible]	[illegible]	[illegible]	[illegible]	[illegible]	[illegible]	[illegible]	[illegible]	

Year 1893-94.

—	Revenue (Net Receipts) as collected.				Revenue (Net Receipts) as adjusted to give true Contribution.				Remarks.
	Collected in England.	Collected in Scotland.	Collected in Ireland.	Total.	Contributed by England.	Contributed by Scotland.	Contributed by Ireland.	Total.	
	£	£	£	£	£	£	£	£	
Cocoa	[illegible]	[illegible]	[illegible]	[illegible]	[illegible]	[illegible]	[illegible]	[illegible]	By population proportions.
Chicory and coffee	[illegible]	[illegible]	[illegible]	[illegible]	[illegible]	[illegible]	[illegible]	[illegible]	By proportions ascertained for [illegible], from Railway, &c., Returns. See Parliamentary Paper [illegible], page [illegible].
Dried fruits	[illegible]	[illegible]	[illegible]	[illegible]	[illegible]	[illegible]	[illegible]	[illegible]	By population proportions.
Foreign spirits	[illegible]	[illegible]	[illegible]	[illegible]	[illegible]	[illegible]	[illegible]	[illegible]	By proportions ascertained for 1893-94.
Tea	[illegible]	[illegible]	[illegible]	[illegible]	[illegible]	[illegible]	[illegible]	[illegible]	By proportions ascertained for [illegible], from Railway, &c., Returns. See Parliamentary Paper [illegible], page [illegible].
Tobacco	[illegible]	[illegible]	[illegible]	[illegible]	[illegible]	[illegible]	[illegible]	[illegible]	By proportions ascertained for [illegible], upon inquiries made of manufacturers and dealers.
Wine	[illegible]	[illegible]	[illegible]	[illegible]	[illegible]	[illegible]	[illegible]	[illegible]	By proportions ascertained for [illegible], from Railway, &c., Returns. See Parliamentary Paper [illegible], page [illegible].
All other articles	[illegible]	[illegible]	[illegible]	[illegible]	[illegible]	[illegible]	[illegible]	[illegible]	By population proportions.
Total net receipts	[illegible]	[illegible]	[illegible]	[illegible]	[illegible]	[illegible]	[illegible]	[illegible]	
Per cent.	[illegible]	[illegible]	[illegible]	[illegible]	[illegible]	[illegible]	[illegible]	[illegible]	

T. J. Pittar,
Principal of Statistical Office.

Custom House, London,
[illegible] December 1894.

B.—Account of Duty-paid Spirits removed from or to Ireland, &c., 1859-60 to 1893-94.

Year.	—	From Ireland: To England.	From Ireland: To Scotland.	To Ireland: From England.	To Ireland: From Scotland.	Excess Quantity of [illegible]	Quantity [illegible] in Ireland.	Consumption per Head: Ireland.	Consumption per Head: England.	Consumption per Head: Scotland.
		Proof Gallons.	Proof Gallons.	Proof Gallons.	Proof Gallons.	Proof Gallons.	Proof Gallons.	Proof Gallons.	Proof Gallons.	Proof Gallons.
1859-60		[illegible]	[illegible]	[illegible]	[illegible]	[illegible]	[illegible]	—	—	—
[illegible]		[illegible]	[illegible]	[illegible]	[illegible]	[illegible]	[illegible]	—	—	—
[illegible]		[illegible]	[illegible]	[illegible]	[illegible]	[illegible]	[illegible]	—	—	—
[illegible]		[illegible]	[illegible]	[illegible]	[illegible]	[illegible]	[illegible]	—	—	—
[illegible]		[illegible]	[illegible]	[illegible]	[illegible]	[illegible]	[illegible]	—	—	—
[illegible]		[illegible]	[illegible]	[illegible]	[illegible]	[illegible]	[illegible]	—	—	—
[illegible]		[illegible]	[illegible]	[illegible]	[illegible]	[illegible]	[illegible]	—	—	—
[illegible]		[illegible]	[illegible]	[illegible]	[illegible]	[illegible]	[illegible]	—	—	—
[illegible]		[illegible]	[illegible]	[illegible]	[illegible]	[illegible]	[illegible]	—	—	—
[illegible]		[illegible]	[illegible]	[illegible]	[illegible]	[illegible]	[illegible]	—	—	—
[illegible]		[illegible]	[illegible]	[illegible]	[illegible]	[illegible]	[illegible]	—	—	—
[illegible]		[illegible]	[illegible]	[illegible]	[illegible]	[illegible]	[illegible]	—	—	—
[illegible]		[illegible]	[illegible]	[illegible]	[illegible]	[illegible]	[illegible]	[illegible]	[illegible]	[illegible]
[illegible]		[illegible]	[illegible]	[illegible]	[illegible]	[illegible]	[illegible]	[illegible]	[illegible]	[illegible]
[illegible]		[illegible]	[illegible]	[illegible]	[illegible]	[illegible]	[illegible]	[illegible]	[illegible]	[illegible]
[illegible]		[illegible]	[illegible]	[illegible]	[illegible]	[illegible]	[illegible]	[illegible]	[illegible]	[illegible]
[illegible]		[illegible]	[illegible]	[illegible]	[illegible]	[illegible]	[illegible]	[illegible]	[illegible]	[illegible]
[illegible]		[illegible]	[illegible]	[illegible]	[illegible]	[illegible]	[illegible]	[illegible]	[illegible]	[illegible]
[illegible]		[illegible]	[illegible]	[illegible]	[illegible]	[illegible]	[illegible]	[illegible]	[illegible]	[illegible]
[illegible]		[illegible]	[illegible]	[illegible]	[illegible]	[illegible]	[illegible]	[illegible]	[illegible]	[illegible]
[illegible]		[illegible]	[illegible]	[illegible]	[illegible]	[illegible]	[illegible]	[illegible]	[illegible]	[illegible]
[illegible]		[illegible]	[illegible]	[illegible]	[illegible]	[illegible]	[illegible]	[illegible]	[illegible]	[illegible]
[illegible]		[illegible]	[illegible]	[illegible]	[illegible]	[illegible]	[illegible]	[illegible]	[illegible]	[illegible]
[illegible]		[illegible]	[illegible]	[illegible]	[illegible]	[illegible]	[illegible]	[illegible]	[illegible]	[illegible]
[illegible]		[illegible]	[illegible]	[illegible]	[illegible]	[illegible]	[illegible]	[illegible]	[illegible]	[illegible]
[illegible]		[illegible]	[illegible]	[illegible]	[illegible]	[illegible]	[illegible]	[illegible]	[illegible]	[illegible]
[illegible]		[illegible]	[illegible]	[illegible]	[illegible]	[illegible]	[illegible]	[illegible]	[illegible]	[illegible]
[illegible]		[illegible]	[illegible]	[illegible]	[illegible]	[illegible]	[illegible]	[illegible]	[illegible]	[illegible]
[illegible]		[illegible]	[illegible]	[illegible]	[illegible]	[illegible]	[illegible]	[illegible]	[illegible]	[illegible]
1893-94	Duty-paid	[illegible]	[illegible]	[illegible]	[illegible]	[illegible]	[illegible]	[illegible]	[illegible]	[illegible]
	Customs Warehouses	[illegible]	[illegible]	—	[illegible]					
		[illegible]	[illegible]	[illegible]	[illegible]					

Year.	—	From Ireland: To England.	From Ireland: To Scotland.	To Ireland: From England.	To Ireland: From Scotland.	Excess Quantities of Spirits paid [illegible] from Ireland.	Quantity retained for consumption as a Beverage in Ireland.	Consumption per Head: Ireland.	Consumption per Head: England.	Consumption per Head: Scotland.
		Proof Gallons.	Proof Gallons.	Proof Gallons.	Proof Gallons.	Proof Gallons.	Proof Gallons.	Proof Gallons.	Proof Gallons.	Proof Gallons.
[illegible]	Spirits	[illegible]	[illegible]	[illegible]	[illegible]	[illegible]	[illegible]	[illegible]	[illegible]	[illegible]
	Compound Warehouses	[illegible]	[illegible]	[illegible]	[illegible]					
		[illegible]	[illegible]	[illegible]	[illegible]					
[illegible]		[illegible]	[illegible]	[illegible]	[illegible]	[illegible]	[illegible]	[illegible]	[illegible]	[illegible]
[illegible]		[illegible]	[illegible]	[illegible]	[illegible]	[illegible]	[illegible]	[illegible]	[illegible]	[illegible]
[illegible]		[illegible]	[illegible]	[illegible]	[illegible]	[illegible]	[illegible]	[illegible]	[illegible]	[illegible]
[illegible]		[illegible]	[illegible]	[illegible]	[illegible]	[illegible]	[illegible]	[illegible]	[illegible]	[illegible]

C.—STATEMENT showing the AMOUNT of DUTY CONTRIBUTED per HEAD of POPULATION on TEA in ENGLAND, SCOTLAND, and IRELAND in each of the Years 1889–90 to 1892–93 inclusive.

Year.	England.	Scotland.	Ireland.	United Kingdom.
	s. d.	s. d.	s. d.	s. d.
1889–90 as per first return*	[illegible]	[illegible]	[illegible]	[illegible]
1889–90†	[illegible]	[illegible]	[illegible]	[illegible]
1890–91‡	[illegible]	[illegible]	[illegible]	[illegible]
Duty reduced from 6d. to 4d. per pound from the 1st May 1890.				
1891–92‡	1 9¼	1 6½	2 0¾	1 9¼
1892–93‡	1 9¼	1 7¾	2 0¾	1 9¼

* Paper 329 of 1891, page 6. † Paper 93 of 1890. ‡ Paper 334 of 1893.

Statistical Office,
Custom House, London,
19th July 1894.

T. J. PITTAR.

The bases on which the contributions have been calculated are those adopted in Parliamentary Papers 329 of 1891, 93 of 1890, and 334 of 1893.

APPENDIX V.

A.—STATEMENT of INLAND REVENUE DUTIES, &c. paid in ENGLAND and SCOTLAND in 1893–4, which were not leviable in IRELAND.

—	—	Net Produce, Year 1893–4: England.	Net Produce, Year 1893–4: Scotland.	Total for England and Scotland.
Excise.		£	£	£
Railway duty	—	[illegible]	[illegible]	[illegible]
Establishment Licences.				
Male servants	—	[illegible]	[illegible]	[illegible]
Carriages	—	[illegible]	[illegible]	[illegible]
Armorial bearings	—	[illegible]	[illegible]	[illegible]
Guns	—	[illegible]	[illegible]	[illegible]
Licences for sale of intoxicating liquors, &c.	Rates of duty in England, Scotland, and Ireland differ in several cases.	—	—	—
Licences for sale of patent medicines	—	[illegible]	[illegible]	[illegible]
Stamps.				
Legacy duty	1½ per cent. on succession is not levied in Ireland.	*	*	—
Patent medicine duty	—	[illegible]	[illegible]	[illegible]
Deed and other stamps	10 per cent. on succession is not levied in Ireland.	—	—	—
Carried forward		[illegible]	[illegible]	[illegible]

* Cannot be given.

—	—	Net Produce, Year 1893-4.		Total for England and Scotland.
		England.	Scotland.	
		£	£	£
Brought forward		1,329,245	130,718	1,460,[illegible]
Taxes.				
Land tax - - - - - -	—	985,[illegible]	23,[illegible]	1,009,211
Inhabited house duty - - - - -	—	1,345,[illegible]	94,[illegible]	1,440,[illegible]
Income tax - - - - - -	—	—	—	—
Schedule (A.)				
In England and Scotland the annual value is based on the rack rental. In Ireland the annual value is based on the Poor Rate valuation if the judicial rent is not fixed below it.	—	—	—	—
Schedule (B.)				
With tax at 7d. in £, the rate in force in England was 3½d. in the £. In Scotland and Ireland† it was 2½d. in the £.	—	—	—	—
	Total £	3,[illegible]	25[illegible]	4,[illegible]

† Under the Budget Bill, 1894, the rate under Schedule B. in England, Scotland, and Ireland for 1894-5 has been made uniform.

Inland Revenue,
23rd July 1894.

B.—Tables relating to Assessments to Income Tax in Great Britain and Ireland.

GENERAL NOTE.

The following tables, I. to IV., have been prepared under the supervision of the Inland Revenue Department from those down to the year ending 5th April 1869, contained in Mr. Goschen's report to the Treasury, presented as a Parliamentary Return, 470 of 1870, and reprinted as 201 of 1890, and from figures in continuation of those tables from the year ending the 5th April 1869 to the year ending 5th April 1893, which were put in by Mr. Milner, the Chairman of the Board of Inland Revenue, in connexion with the evidence given by him to the Commission. The figures represent the income tax assessments on the various kinds of property originally included in Schedule A.

The first two columns of table I., II., III., contain the assessments on lands and houses, which are based on annual value and which still remain in Schedule A.

Subsequently to the year ending 5th April 1866 the assessment to income tax in the case of railways has been made under Schedule D., and so, also, has been made the greater part of the assessment in respect of the "Other Property" formerly belonging to Schedule A., a head which includes mines, ironworks, gasworks, waterworks, canals, and similar property.

A further column has been added to the tables for the years subsequent to 1866, to show the proportion of such "Other Property" assessed under Schedule D.

Table IV. gives the totals of the assessment under all the heads in question for (1) Great Britain; (2) Ireland, subsequently to the year 1854, when Ireland first became subject to income tax.

B. H. Holland,
Secretary.

No. I.—ENGLAND AND WALES.

Account of the Annual Value (1) of Lands; and (2) of Houses in England and Wales assessed to Income Tax under Schedule A.; (3) of Railways assessed under Schedule A. previously to 5th April 1866, and for subsequent Years under Schedule D.; and (4) of "Other Property" (including Quarries, Mines, Ironworks, Gasworks, Waterworks, Canals, &c.), also assessed under Schedule A. previously to 5th April 1866, but for subsequent Years chiefly assessed under Schedule D.

Year ending 5th April.	Lands, including Tithes.*	Houses.	Railways.	"Other Property" as defined above.	Total.	Amount of "Other Property" transferred to Schedule D.	Remarks.
	£	£	£	£	£	£	
1843	37,[illegible]	14,[illegible]	—	1,[illegible]	53,[illegible]	—	—
1843	42,[illegible]	35,[illegible]	2,617,[illegible]	5,[illegible]	85,[illegible]	—	New assessments.
1844	42,[illegible]	35,[illegible]	2,617,[illegible]	5,[illegible]	85,[illegible]	—	—
1845	42,[illegible]	35,[illegible]	2,617,[illegible]	5,[illegible]	85,[illegible]	—	—
1846	42,[illegible]	36,[illegible]	3,[illegible]	6,[illegible]	88,[illegible]	—	New assessments.
1847	42,[illegible]	37,[illegible]	4,[illegible]	6,[illegible]	89,[illegible]	—	—
1848	41,[illegible]	37,[illegible]	5,[illegible]	6,[illegible]	91,[illegible]	—	—
1849	42,[illegible]	38,[illegible]	5,[illegible]	7,[illegible]	94,[illegible]	—	New assessments.
1850	42,[illegible]	38,[illegible]	5,[illegible]	7,[illegible]	94,[illegible]	—	—
1851	42,[illegible]	39,[illegible]	5,[illegible]	8,[illegible]	94,[illegible]	—	—
1852	42,[illegible]†	40,[illegible]	6,[illegible]	8,[illegible]	94,[illegible]	—	New assessments.
1853	42,[illegible]	40,[illegible]	7,[illegible]	8,[illegible]	96,[illegible]	—	—
1854	42,[illegible]	42,[illegible]	7,[illegible]	8,[illegible]	99,[illegible]	—	New assessments.
1855	42,[illegible]	43,[illegible]	8,[illegible]	7,[illegible]	100,[illegible]	—	—

* The figures of "Lands including Tithes" contained in this column differ slightly from those of "Lands" as given in the "Statistical Abstract." The cause of this discrepancy is that the present table comprises certain payments in the nature of tithes, not being tithe rentcharges, which are not included under the head of "Lands" in the "Statistical Abstract." This discrepancy is confined to the English figures, and does not affect the Scotch and Irish.

† The decrease in the valuation this year did not arise from the actual depreciation in the values, but from a difference in the mode of stating the accounts, by reason of which properties which had been previously included under the head of "Lands" were classified under other heads.

No. I.—ENGLAND AND WALES—continued.

Year ending 5th April.	Lands, including Tithes.	Houses.	Railways.	"Other Property" as defined above.	Total.	Amount of "Other Property" transferred to Schedule D.	Remarks.
	£	£	£	£	£	£	
[illegible]	[illegible]	[illegible]	[illegible]	[illegible]	[illegible]	—	—
[illegible]	[illegible]	[illegible]	[illegible]	[illegible]	[illegible]	—	—
[illegible]	[illegible]	[illegible]	[illegible]	[illegible]	[illegible]	—	New assessments.
[illegible]	[illegible]	[illegible]	[illegible]	[illegible]	[illegible]	—	—
[illegible]	[illegible]	[illegible]	[illegible]	[illegible]	[illegible]	—	—
[illegible]	[illegible]	[illegible]	[illegible]	[illegible]	[illegible]	—	—
[illegible]	[illegible]	[illegible]	[illegible]	[illegible]	[illegible]	—	New assessments.
[illegible]	[illegible]	[illegible]	[illegible]	[illegible]	[illegible]	—	—
[illegible]	[illegible]	[illegible]	[illegible]	[illegible]	[illegible]	—	—
[illegible]	[illegible]	[illegible]	[illegible]	[illegible]	[illegible]	—	New assessments.
[illegible]	[illegible]	[illegible]	[illegible]	[illegible]	[illegible]	—	—
[illegible]	[illegible]	[illegible]	[illegible]	[illegible]	[illegible]	[illegible]	—
[illegible]	[illegible]	[illegible]	[illegible]	[illegible]	[illegible]	[illegible]	New assessments.
[illegible]	[illegible]	[illegible]	[illegible]	[illegible]	[illegible]	[illegible]	—
[illegible]	[illegible]	[illegible]	[illegible]	[illegible]	[illegible]	[illegible]	—
[illegible]	[illegible]	[illegible]	[illegible]	[illegible]	[illegible]	[illegible]	New assessments.
[illegible]	[illegible]	[illegible]	[illegible]	[illegible]	[illegible]	[illegible]	Assessments for Metropolis revised.
[illegible]	[illegible]	[illegible]	[illegible]	[illegible]	[illegible]	[illegible]	—
[illegible]	[illegible]	[illegible]	[illegible]	[illegible]	[illegible]	[illegible]	New assessments, except Metropolis.
[illegible]	[illegible]	[illegible]	[illegible]	[illegible]	[illegible]	[illegible]	—
[illegible]	[illegible]	[illegible]	[illegible]	[illegible]	[illegible]	[illegible]	—
[illegible]	[illegible]	[illegible]	[illegible]	[illegible]	[illegible]	[illegible]	New assessments.
[illegible]	[illegible]	[illegible]	[illegible]	[illegible]	[illegible]	[illegible]	—
[illegible]	[illegible]	[illegible]	[illegible]	[illegible]	[illegible]	[illegible]	—
[illegible]	[illegible]	[illegible]	[illegible]	[illegible]	[illegible]	[illegible]	New assessments, except Metropolis.
[illegible]	[illegible]	[illegible]	[illegible]	[illegible]	[illegible]	[illegible]	—
[illegible]	[illegible]	[illegible]	[illegible]	[illegible]	[illegible]	[illegible]	New assessments for Metropolis.
[illegible]	[illegible]	[illegible]	[illegible]	[illegible]	[illegible]	[illegible]	New assessments, except Metropolis.
[illegible]	[illegible]	[illegible]	[illegible]	[illegible]	[illegible]	[illegible]	—
[illegible]	[illegible]	[illegible]	[illegible]	[illegible]	[illegible]	[illegible]	—
[illegible]	[illegible]	[illegible]	[illegible]	[illegible]	[illegible]	[illegible]	New assessments, except Metropolis.
[illegible]	[illegible]	[illegible]	[illegible]	[illegible]	[illegible]	[illegible]	New assessments for Metropolis.
[illegible]	[illegible]	[illegible]	[illegible]	[illegible]	[illegible]	[illegible]	—
[illegible]	[illegible]	[illegible]	[illegible]	[illegible]	[illegible]	[illegible]	New assessments, except Metropolis.
[illegible]	[illegible]	[illegible]	[illegible]	[illegible]	[illegible]	[illegible]	—
[illegible]	[illegible]	[illegible]	[illegible]	[illegible]	[illegible]	[illegible]	—
[illegible]	[illegible]	[illegible]	[illegible]	[illegible]	[illegible]	[illegible]	New assessments for Metropolis.
[illegible]	[illegible]	[illegible]	[illegible]	[illegible]	[illegible]	[illegible]	—

No. II.—SCOTLAND.

ACCOUNT of the ANNUAL VALUE (1) of LANDS; and (2) of HOUSES in SCOTLAND assessed to Income Tax under Schedule A.; (3) of RAILWAYS assessed under Schedule A. previously to 5th April 1866, and for subsequent Years under Schedule D.; and (4) of "OTHER PROPERTY" (including Quarries, Mines, Ironworks, Gasworks, Waterworks, Canals, &c.) also assessed under Schedule A. previously to 5th April 1866, but for subsequent Years chiefly assessed under Schedule D.

Year ending 5th April.	Lands, including Tithes.	Houses.	Railways.	"Other Property" as defined above.	Total.	Amount of "Other Property" transferred to Schedule D.	Remarks.
	£	£	£	£	£	£	
[illegible]	[illegible]	[illegible]	—	[illegible]	[illegible]	—	
[illegible]	[illegible]	[illegible]	[illegible]	[illegible]	[illegible]	—	
[illegible]	—	—	—	—	[illegible]	—	
[illegible]	—	—	—	—	[illegible]	—	
[illegible]	[illegible]	[illegible]	[illegible]	[illegible]	[illegible]	—	
[illegible]	—	—	—	—	[illegible]	—	
[illegible]	[illegible]	[illegible]	[illegible]	[illegible]	[illegible]	—	
[illegible]	[illegible]	[illegible]	[illegible]	[illegible]	[illegible]	—	
[illegible]	[illegible]	[illegible]	[illegible]	[illegible]	[illegible]	—	
[illegible]	[illegible]	[illegible]	[illegible]	[illegible]	[illegible]	—	
[illegible]	[illegible]	[illegible]	[illegible]	[illegible]	[illegible]	—	
[illegible]	[illegible]	[illegible]	[illegible]	[illegible]	[illegible]	—	
[illegible]	[illegible]	[illegible]	[illegible]	[illegible]	[illegible]	—	
[illegible]	[illegible]	[illegible]	[illegible]	[illegible]	[illegible]	—	
[illegible]	[illegible]	[illegible]	[illegible]	[illegible]	[illegible]	—	
[illegible]	[illegible]	[illegible]	[illegible]	[illegible]	[illegible]	—	
[illegible]	[illegible]	[illegible]	[illegible]	[illegible]	[illegible]	—	
[illegible]	[illegible]	[illegible]	[illegible]	[illegible]	[illegible]	—	

No. II.—SCOTLAND—continued.

Year ending 5th April.	Lands, including Tithes.	Houses.	Railways.	"Other Property" as defined above.	Total.	Amount of "Other Property" transferred to Schedule D.	Remarks.
	£	£	£	£	£	£	
1860	6,281,880	4,982,840	1,298,734	1,405,596	13,874,286	—	
1861	6,638,800	5,202,118	1,312,830	1,505,960	14,591,621	—	
1862	6,672,944	5,355,675	1,606,393	1,434,986	15,129,200	—	
1863	6,715,243	5,447,198	1,602,627	1,480,092	15,355,546	—	
1864	6,717,627	5,573,090	1,684,295	1,545,601	15,470,913	—	
1865	6,920,630	5,891,561	1,775,523	1,608,217	16,194,930	—	
1866	6,849,706	5,981,360	1,851,065	1,545,757	16,593,804	—	
1867	6,964,704	6,192,178	1,730,380	1,086,925	16,358,192	1,904,168	
1868	7,186,225	6,845,093	2,031,298	1,907,695	17,571,924	1,742,209	
1869	7,218,068	5,726,830	2,059,974	1,719,121	17,265,163	1,628,621	
1870	7,194,579	6,930,379	2,153,541	1,876,169	18,136,974	1,716,061	
1871	7,201,182	7,309,248	2,305,275	2,050,295	19,005,060	1,849,620	
1872	7,256,395	7,480,229	2,373,321	2,064,516	19,294,166	1,876,071	
1873	7,363,230	7,678,495	2,689,962	2,772,666	20,626,361	1,984,692	
1874	7,456,908	8,223,066	2,731,835	4,211,860	22,047,634	4,102,075	
1875	7,499,420	8,669,368	2,687,368	4,651,877	23,469,667	4,765,065	
1876	7,500,178	9,330,788	2,679,871	3,599,914	23,180,473	3,383,008	
1877	7,553,737	10,373,172	3,361,267	3,361,654	24,704,130	3,118,228	
1878	7,666,090	10,628,218	3,228,332	3,137,059	24,969,409	3,060,451	
1879	7,847,239	11,290,900	3,383,385	2,639,356	25,179,000	2,761,408	
1880	7,769,060	11,762,337	3,223,793	2,509,724	25,567,297	3,524,119	
1881	7,711,955	11,820,360	3,306,364	2,765,611	25,273,989	2,659,681	
1882	7,648,063	11,293,184	3,276,336	2,851,304	25,997,339	2,969,403	
1883	7,575,231	12,046,584	3,266,142	2,879,173	25,866,092	2,801,686	
1884	7,556,331	12,130,140	3,712,720	2,877,815	26,329,914	2,927,528	
1885	7,461,897	12,279,808	3,791,313	2,964,326	26,518,034	2,856,601	
1886	7,290,598	12,507,133	3,793,456	2,985,925	26,578,112	2,809,212	
1887	7,099,360	12,614,842	3,711,614	2,881,799	26,320,397	2,729,745	
1888	6,924,150	12,753,904	3,760,926	2,717,903	26,016,183	2,657,749	
1889	6,579,762	12,800,606	3,809,131	2,891,654	26,290,150	2,702,374	
1890	6,416,507	13,020,795	4,174,567	2,926,869	26,536,066	2,958,347	
1891	6,374,903	13,213,729	4,215,074	3,234,267	27,034,307	3,423,431	
1892	6,210,581	13,373,804	4,239,183	3,157,567	27,035,955	3,406,974	
1893	6,201,149	13,442,509	4,301,766	3,618,097	27,563,454	3,369,717	

No. III.—IRELAND.

Account of the Annual Value (1) of Lands; and (2) of Houses in Ireland assessed to Income Tax under Schedule A.; (3) of Railways assessed under Schedule A. previously to 5th April 1866, and for subsequent Years under Schedule D.; and (4) of "Other Property" (including Quarries, Mines, Ironworks, Gasworks, Waterworks, Canals, &c.), also assessed under Schedule A. previously to 5th April 1866, but for subsequent Years chiefly assessed under Schedule D.

Year ending 5th April.	Lands, including Tithes.	Houses.	Railways.	"Other Property" as defined above.	Total.	Amount of "Other Property" transferred to Schedule D.	Remarks.
	£	£	£	£	£	£	
1854	—	—	—	—	11,752,820	—	
1855	—	—	—	—	11,802,130	—	
1856	—	—	—	—	11,876,143	—	
1857	—	—	—	—	11,853,385	—	
1858	—	—	—	—	11,826,799	—	
1859	—	—	—	—	11,816,701	—	
1860	—	—	—	—	11,861,829	—	
1861	—	—	—	—	12,002,594	—	
1862	8,907,650	3,233,719	797,820	278,635	13,216,889	—	
1863	8,747,734	3,565,809	880,480	275,124	13,404,051	—	
1864	8,728,794	3,458,247	945,646	300,927	13,479,700	—	
1865	8,820,862	3,570,136	896,651	512,697	13,801,316	—	
1866	*9,142,809	3,440,529	987,859	309,247	13,870,618	—	
1867	*9,240,270	3,334,998	868,861	304,623	13,890,542	159,880	
1868	9,231,619	3,304,937	819,164	331,048	13,858,189	577,158	
1869	9,251,785	3,319,404	842,048	354,613	13,957,849	332,155	
1870	9,135,619	3,629,005	879,184	379,675	14,004,109	249,561	
1871	9,148,734	3,690,180	851,690	397,013	14,100,747	367,611	
1872	9,140,866	3,715,081	864,486	376,736	14,192,259	523,549	
1873	9,148,338	3,748,274	1,050,312	304,305	14,448,078	473,595	
1874	9,177,214	3,769,500	1,090,670	400,550	14,417,134	448,194	
1875	*9,304,600	3,501,358	1,092,257	391,092	14,449,303	522,319	
1876	9,383,670	3,512,082	1,082,416	497,919	14,576,187	481,397	
1877	*10,001,544	3,003,053	1,174,979	560,059	14,739,951	505,640	
1878	10,030,648	3,044,169	1,229,680	565,777	14,860,330	524,901	
1879	10,034,180	3,060,190	1,270,567	408,306	14,793,603	401,444	
1880	10,070,819	3,281,269	1,500,312	417,720	14,922,715	408,511	
1881	10,071,837	3,310,504	1,412,317	415,975	14,809,420	406,084	
1882	10,071,215	3,367,400	1,387,478	402,619	14,951,590	402,050	
1883	10,074,089	3,304,925	1,356,874	433,620	14,971,938	429,478	
1884	10,053,601	3,325,059	1,372,961	405,690	15,145,229	400,971	
1885	10,075,792	3,307,270	1,388,616	425,852	15,178,205	422,650	
1886	10,047,507	3,410,342	1,253,059	384,155	15,281,781	520,648	

* The apparent increase in the value of "Lands" in Ireland in these years is due to a transfer of certain property from the category of "Houses" to that of "Lands," and not to any change in the valuation.

No. III.—IRELAND—*continued.*

Year ending 5th April.	Lands, including Tithes.	Houses.	Railways.	"Other Property" as defined above.	Total.	Amount of "Other Property" transferred to Schedule D.	Remarks.
	£	£	£	£	£	£	
[illegible]	[illegible]	[illegible]	[illegible]	[illegible]	[illegible]	[illegible]	
[illegible]	[illegible]	[illegible]	[illegible]	[illegible]	[illegible]	[illegible]	
[illegible]	[illegible]	[illegible]	[illegible]	[illegible]	[illegible]	[illegible]	
[illegible]	[illegible]	[illegible]	[illegible]	[illegible]	[illegible]	[illegible]	
[illegible]	[illegible]	[illegible]	[illegible]	[illegible]	[illegible]	[illegible]	
[illegible]	[illegible]	[illegible]	[illegible]	[illegible]	[illegible]	[illegible]	
[illegible]	[illegible]	[illegible]	[illegible]	[illegible]	[illegible]	[illegible]	

No. IV.

TABLE showing the TOTAL GROSS ASSESSMENT to INCOME TAX (1) in GREAT BRITAIN; (2) in IRELAND, in respect of LANDS (including Tithes), HOUSES, RAILWAYS, and "OTHER PROPERTY" (including Quarries, Mines, Ironworks, Fisheries, Canals, Gasworks, &c.) from the Year 1854, when INCOME TAX was first extended to IRELAND, to the Year 1893.

Year ending 5th April.	Great Britain.	Ireland.	Year ending 5th April.	Great Britain.	Ireland.
	£	£		£	£
[illegible]	[illegible]	[illegible]	1874	[illegible]	[illegible]
[illegible]	[illegible]	[illegible]	1875	[illegible]	[illegible]
[illegible]	[illegible]	[illegible]	1876	[illegible]	[illegible]
[illegible]	[illegible]	[illegible]	1877	[illegible]	[illegible]
[illegible]	[illegible]	[illegible]	1878	[illegible]	[illegible]
[illegible]	[illegible]	[illegible]	1879	[illegible]	[illegible]
[illegible]	[illegible]	[illegible]	1880	[illegible]	[illegible]
[illegible]	[illegible]	[illegible]	1881	[illegible]	[illegible]
[illegible]	[illegible]	[illegible]	1882	[illegible]	[illegible]
[illegible]	[illegible]	[illegible]	1883	[illegible]	[illegible]
[illegible]	[illegible]	[illegible]	1884	[illegible]	[illegible]
[illegible]	[illegible]	[illegible]	1885	[illegible]	[illegible]
[illegible]	[illegible]	[illegible]	1886	[illegible]	[illegible]
[illegible]	[illegible]	[illegible]	1887	[illegible]	[illegible]
[illegible]	[illegible]	[illegible]	1888	[illegible]	[illegible]
[illegible]	[illegible]	[illegible]	1889	[illegible]	[illegible]
[illegible]	[illegible]	[illegible]	1890	[illegible]	[illegible]
[illegible]	[illegible]	[illegible]	1891	[illegible]	[illegible]
[illegible]	[illegible]	[illegible]	1892	[illegible]	[illegible]
[illegible]	[illegible]	[illegible]	1893	[illegible]	[illegible]

No. V.—INCOME TAX, [illegible]

A STATEMENT, taken from the [illegible] REPORT ([illegible]) of the COMMISSIONERS of INLAND REVENUE, showing the GROSS AMOUNT of PROPERTY and PROFITS assessed, and the NET AMOUNT charged to INCOME TAX under each SCHEDULE for the Year ended 5th April [illegible].

—	England. Gross Assessment.	England. Net Amount charged to Duty.	Scotland. Gross Assessment.	Scotland. Net Amount charged to Duty.	Ireland. Gross Assessment.	Ireland. Net Amount charged to Duty.	United Kingdom. Gross Assessment.	United Kingdom. Net Amount charged to Duty.	Amount of Duty charged at [illegible] in the £.	—
SCHEDULE A.	£	£	£	£	£	£	£	£	£	
Lands, &c.	[illegible]		[illegible]		[illegible]		[illegible]			
Messuages	[illegible]		[illegible]		[illegible]		[illegible]			
Tithes, &c.	[illegible]		–		[illegible]		[illegible]			
Manors, &c.	[illegible]		[illegible]		–		[illegible]			
Fines	[illegible]		–		[illegible]		[illegible]			
Other Profits from Lands	[illegible]		[illegible]		[illegible]		[illegible]			
Total Gross Assessment	[illegible]		[illegible]		[illegible]		[illegible]			
" Deductions	[illegible]		[illegible]		[illegible]		[illegible]			
		[illegible]		[illegible]		[illegible]		[illegible]	[illegible]	Schedule A.
SCHEDULE B.										
Lands, &c. ([illegible])	[illegible]		[illegible]		[illegible]		[illegible]			
Farmers, &c.	[illegible]		[illegible]		[illegible]		[illegible]			
Total Gross Assessment	[illegible]		[illegible]		[illegible]		[illegible]			
" Deductions	[illegible]		[illegible]		[illegible]		[illegible]			
		[illegible]		[illegible]		[illegible]		[illegible]	[illegible]	Schedule B.

* This amount be stated in detail for Schedules A. and B.
† [illegible]
‡ [illegible]

—	England. Gross Assessment.	England. Net Amount charged to Duty.	Scotland. Gross Assessment.	Scotland. Net Amount charged to Duty.	Ireland. Gross Assessment.	Ireland. Net Amount charged to Duty.	United Kingdom. Gross Assessment.	United Kingdom. Net Amount charged to Duty.	Amount of Duty charged at 6d. in the £.	
SCHEDULE C. (Home).	£	£	£	£	£	£	£	£	£	
Funded Debt and Terminable Annuities (including Life Annuities).	[illegible]		—		[illegible]		[illegible]			
Unfunded Debt	[illegible]		—		—		[illegible]			
Metropolitan Consolidated Annuities.	[illegible]		—		—		[illegible]			
Municipal Corporation, &c. Stocks.	[illegible]		—		—		[illegible]			
India Government Stocks and Loans.	[illegible]		—		[illegible]		[illegible]			
Indian Guaranteed Railways, Canal, and Irrigation Works.	[illegible]		—		—		[illegible]			
Foreign and Colonial Funds, &c.	[illegible]		—		—		[illegible]			
		[illegible]		—		[illegible]		[illegible]	[illegible]	Schedule C.
SCHEDULE D. Trades and Professions. Total Gross Assessment	[illegible]		[illegible]		[illegible]		[illegible]			
" Deductions	[illegible]		[illegible]		[illegible]		[illegible]			
		[illegible]		[illegible]		[illegible]		[illegible]	[illegible]	Trades, &c.
Particular Properties, Public Companies, &c. (1.) Concerns described in Rule No. 3, Schedule A. of Act 5 & 6 Vict. c. 35, viz.:—										
Quarries	[illegible]	[illegible]	[illegible]	[illegible]	[illegible]	[illegible]	[illegible]	[illegible]		
Mines	[illegible]	[illegible]	[illegible]	[illegible]	[illegible]	[illegible]	[illegible]	[illegible]		
Iron Works	[illegible]	[illegible]	[illegible]	[illegible]	—	—	[illegible]	[illegible]		
Gas Works	[illegible]	[illegible]	[illegible]	[illegible]	[illegible]	[illegible]	[illegible]	[illegible]		
Salt Springs or Works, and Alum Works.	[illegible]	[illegible]	[illegible]	[illegible]	[illegible]	[illegible]	[illegible]	[illegible]		
Water Works	[illegible]	[illegible]	[illegible]	[illegible]	[illegible]	[illegible]	[illegible]	[illegible]		
Canals, &c.	[illegible]	[illegible]	[illegible]	[illegible]	[illegible]	[illegible]	[illegible]	[illegible]		
Fishings and Shootings	[illegible]	[illegible]	[illegible]	[illegible]	[illegible]	[illegible]	[illegible]	[illegible]		
Markets, Tolls, &c.	[illegible]	[illegible]	[illegible]	[illegible]	[illegible]	[illegible]	[illegible]	[illegible]		
Cemeteries	[illegible]	[illegible]	[illegible]	[illegible]	—	—	[illegible]	[illegible]		
Total	[illegible]	[illegible]	[illegible]	[illegible]	[illegible]	[illegible]	[illegible]	[illegible]		
(2.) Public Companies being Concerns not described in Rule No. 3, Schedule A.	[illegible]	[illegible]	[illegible]	[illegible]	[illegible]	[illegible]	[illegible]	[illegible]		
(3.) Foreign and Colonial Securities and Possessions, and other Profits.	[illegible]	[illegible]	[illegible]	[illegible]	[illegible]	[illegible]	[illegible]	[illegible]		
(4.) Railways in United Kingdom.	[illegible]	[illegible]	[illegible]	[illegible]	[illegible]	[illegible]	[illegible]	[illegible]		
(5.) Railways out of United Kingdom.	[illegible]	[illegible]	[illegible]	[illegible]	[illegible]	[illegible]	[illegible]	[illegible]		
(6.) Interest paid out of rates, and other Interest.	[illegible]	[illegible]	[illegible]	[illegible]	[illegible]	[illegible]	[illegible]	[illegible]		
(7.) Other Profits	[illegible]	[illegible]	[illegible]	[illegible]	[illegible]	[illegible]	[illegible]	[illegible]		
Coupons (Act [illegible] Vict. c. [illegible], s. [illegible]).	[illegible]	[illegible]	[illegible]	[illegible]	[illegible]	[illegible]	[illegible]	[illegible]		
(8.) Lands (Act [illegible] Vict. c. [illegible], s. [illegible]).	[illegible]	[illegible]	[illegible]	[illegible]	[illegible]	[illegible]	[illegible]	[illegible]		
Total Gross Assessment, Particular Properties, &c.	[illegible]		[illegible]		[illegible]		[illegible]			
Total Deductions, Particular Properties, &c.	[illegible]		[illegible]		[illegible]		[illegible]			
		[illegible]		[illegible]		[illegible]		[illegible]	[illegible]	Public Companies, &c.
Total Assessment, Schedule D.	[illegible]		[illegible]		[illegible]		[illegible]			
Total Deductions, Schedule D.	[illegible]		[illegible]		[illegible]		[illegible]			
		[illegible]		[illegible]		[illegible]		[illegible]	[illegible]	Schedule D.
SCHEDULE E. Salaries, &c. Public Offices	[illegible]		[illegible]		[illegible]		[illegible]			
Other than Public Offices	[illegible]		[illegible]		[illegible]		[illegible]			
Total Gross Assessment.	[illegible]		[illegible]		[illegible]		[illegible]			
Total Deductions	[illegible]		[illegible]		[illegible]		[illegible]			
		[illegible]		[illegible]		[illegible]		[illegible]	[illegible]	Schedule E.
Total Gross Assessment for all Schedules.	[illegible]		[illegible]		[illegible]		[illegible]			
Total Deductions for all Schedules.	[illegible]		[illegible]		[illegible]		[illegible]			
		[illegible]		[illegible]		[illegible]		[illegible]	[illegible]	Total.

* This cannot be stated in detail for Schedules A. and B.
† A portion of this amount was formerly classified under "Foreign securities, &c.," and a further portion under Schedule C.

No. VI.

Gross Assessments to Income Tax, Great Britain and Ireland, [illegible] and [illegible]

Percentage of Schedules to Total

Years.	Schedule A. Lands, including Tithes commuted.	Schedule A. Tithes not commuted, Manors, and other Profits.	Schedule A. Messuages.	Schedule A. Total.	Schedule B.	Schedule C.	Schedule D.	Schedule E.	Total.
Great Britain.	£	£	£	£	£	£	£	£	£
[illegible] England	[illegible]	[illegible]	[illegible]	[illegible]	[illegible]	[illegible]	[illegible]	[illegible]	[illegible]
Scotland	[illegible]	[illegible]	[illegible]	[illegible]	[illegible]	—	[illegible]	[illegible]	[illegible]
	[illegible]	[illegible]	[illegible]	[illegible]	[illegible]	[illegible]	[illegible]	[illegible]	[illegible]
General percentage	—	—	—	[illegible]	[illegible]	[illegible]	[illegible]	[illegible]	[illegible]
Percentage, Schedule A. only	[illegible]	[illegible]	[illegible]	[illegible]	—	—	—	—	
[illegible] England	[illegible]	[illegible]	[illegible]	[illegible]	[illegible]	[illegible]	[illegible]	[illegible]	[illegible]
Scotland	[illegible]	[illegible]	[illegible]	[illegible]	[illegible]	—	[illegible]	[illegible]	[illegible]
	[illegible]	[illegible]	[illegible]	[illegible]	[illegible]	[illegible]	[illegible]	[illegible]	[illegible]
General percentage	—	—	—	[illegible]	[illegible]	[illegible]	[illegible]	[illegible]	[illegible]
Percentage, Schedule A. only	[illegible]	[illegible]	[illegible]	[illegible]	—	—		—	
Ireland. [illegible]	[illegible]	[illegible]	[illegible]	[illegible]	[illegible]	[illegible]	[illegible]	[illegible]	[illegible]
							[illegible]		
							[illegible]	[illegible]	[illegible]
General percentage	—	—	—	[illegible]	[illegible]	[illegible]	—	—	—
Percentage, Schedule A. only	[illegible]	[illegible]	[illegible]	[illegible]	—	—			
[illegible]	[illegible]	[illegible]	[illegible]	[illegible]	[illegible]	[illegible]	[illegible]	[illegible]	[illegible]
General percentage	—	—	—	[illegible]	[illegible]	[illegible]	[illegible]	[illegible]	[illegible]
Percentage, Schedule A. only	[illegible]	[illegible]	[illegible]	[illegible]	—	—	—	—	—

* [illegible]

† [illegible]

No. VII.

Gross Assessments to Income Tax, Great Britain and Ireland, [illegible] and [illegible]

Percentage Increase or Decrease in each Schedule

	Schedule A. Lands, including Tithes commuted.	Schedule A. Tithes not commuted, Manors, and other Profits.	Schedule A. Messuages.	Schedule A. Total.	Schedule B.	Schedule C.	Schedule D.	Schedule E.	Total.
Great Britain.	£	£	£	£	£	£	£	£	£
[illegible]	[illegible]	[illegible]	[illegible]	[illegible]	[illegible]	[illegible]	[illegible]	[illegible]	[illegible]
[illegible]	[illegible]	[illegible]	[illegible]	[illegible]	[illegible]	[illegible]	[illegible]	[illegible]	[illegible]
Increase or decrease	[illegible]	[illegible]	[illegible]	[illegible]	[illegible]	[illegible]	[illegible]	[illegible]	[illegible]
Increase or decrease per cent.	[illegible]	[illegible]	[illegible]	[illegible]	[illegible]	[illegible]	[illegible]	[illegible]	[illegible]
Ireland.									
[illegible]	[illegible]	[illegible]	[illegible]	[illegible]	[illegible]	[illegible]	[illegible]	[illegible]	[illegible]
[illegible]	[illegible]	[illegible]	[illegible]	[illegible]	[illegible]	[illegible]	[illegible]	[illegible]	[illegible]
Increase or decrease	[illegible]	[illegible]	[illegible]	[illegible]	[illegible]	[illegible]	[illegible]	[illegible]	[illegible]
Increase or decrease per cent.	[illegible]	[illegible]	[illegible]	[illegible]	[illegible]	[illegible] see Note A.	[illegible]	[illegible]	[illegible]

A.—[illegible]

C.—Stamps:—Net Receipt of Duties, 1861-2, and 1892-3.

	Probate Duty.	Estate Duty.	Legacy Duty.	Succession Duty.	Total Death Duties.	General Stamps.	Total Stamps.
	£	£	£	£	£	£	£
Great Britain.							
1861-2	[illegible]	—	[illegible]	[illegible]	[illegible]	[illegible]	[illegible]
*1892-3	[illegible]	[illegible]	[illegible]	[illegible]	[illegible]	[illegible]	[illegible]
					Percentage of increase		[illegible]
Ireland.							
1861-2	[illegible]	—	[illegible]	[illegible]	[illegible]	[illegible]	[illegible]
*1892-3	[illegible]	[illegible]	[illegible]	[illegible]	[illegible]	[illegible]	[illegible]
					Percentage of increase		[illegible]

* Including Local Taxation portion.

APPENDIX VI.

DOCUMENTS put in by Mr. J. C. Barton, of the Irish Valuation Office, in connection with the Evidence given by him before the Commission.

TABLE I.

Showing YEAR in which the TENEMENT VALUATION of each County was Commenced and Issued.

No.	County.	Year Commenced.	Year Issued.
1	Antrim,	1850	1859
2	Carrickfergus, Town,	—	1853
3	Armagh,	1853	1863
4	Carlow,	1851	1853
5	Cavan,	1856	1857
6	Clare,	1854	1856
7	Cork,	1848	1853
8	Cork, City,	—	1853
9	Donegal,	1855	1858
10	Down,	1853	1864
11	Dublin,	1848	1853
12	Dublin, City,	—	1854
13	Fermanagh,	1861	1863
14	Galway,	1855	1857
15	Galway, Town,	—	1856
16	Kerry,	1848	1853
17	Kildare,	1852	1851
18	Kilkenny,	1851	1853
19	Kilkenny, City,	—	1853
20	King's,	1853	1854
21	Leitrim,	1856	1861
22	Limerick,	1848	1853
23	Limerick, City,	—	1853
24	Londonderry,	1857	1859
25	Longford,	1853	1856
26	Louth,	1853	1856
27	Drogheda, Town,	—	1856
28	Mayo,	1856	1857
29	Meath,	1853	1855
30	Monaghan,	1858	1861
31	Queen's,	1851	1853
32	Roscommon,	1855	1858
33	Sligo,	1856	1858
34	Tipperary,	1848	1853
35	Tyrone,	1858	1860
36	Waterford,	1848	1853
37	Waterford, City,	—	1853
38	Westmeath,	1853	1856
39	Wexford,	1853	1854
40	Wicklow,	1853	1854

TABLE [illegible].

[illegible]

	[illegible]			[illegible]		[illegible]			[illegible]			[illegible]			[illegible]		
	[illegible]		[illegible]	[illegible]		[illegible]		[illegible]	[illegible]		[illegible]	[illegible]		[illegible]	[illegible]		[illegible]
	s.	d.	Per Cent.	s.	d.	s.	d.	Per Cent.	s.	d.	Per Cent.	s.	d.	Per Cent.	s.	d.	Per Cent.
Wheat,	[illegible]	[illegible]	[illegible]	[illegible]	[illegible]	13	[illegible]	[illegible]	[illegible]	[illegible]	[illegible]	[illegible]	[illegible]	[illegible]	[illegible]	[illegible]	[illegible]
Oats,	[illegible]	[illegible]	[illegible]	[illegible]	[illegible]	[illegible]	[illegible]	[illegible]	[illegible]	[illegible]	[illegible]	[illegible]	[illegible]	[illegible]	[illegible]	11	[illegible]
Barley,	[illegible]	[illegible]	[illegible]	[illegible]	[illegible]	[illegible]	[illegible]	[illegible]	[illegible]	[illegible]	[illegible]	[illegible]	[illegible]	[illegible]	[illegible]	[illegible]	[illegible]
Potatoes,	[illegible]	[illegible]	—	—		[illegible]	[illegible]	—	[illegible]	[illegible]	...	[illegible]	[illegible]	—	[illegible]	[illegible]	—
Butter,	[illegible]	[illegible]	[illegible]	[illegible]	[illegible]	[illegible]	[illegible]	[illegible]	[illegible]	[illegible]	[illegible]	[illegible]	[illegible]	[illegible]	[illegible]	[illegible]	[illegible]
Beef,	[illegible]	[illegible]	[illegible]	[illegible]	[illegible]	[illegible]	[illegible]	[illegible]	[illegible]	[illegible]	[illegible]	[illegible]	[illegible]	[illegible]	[illegible]	[illegible]	[illegible]
Mutton,	[illegible]	[illegible]	[illegible]	[illegible]	[illegible]	[illegible]	[illegible]	[illegible]	[illegible]	[illegible]	[illegible]	[illegible]	[illegible]	[illegible]	[illegible]	[illegible]	[illegible]
Pork,	[illegible]	[illegible]	[illegible]	[illegible]	[illegible]	[illegible]	[illegible]	[illegible]	[illegible]	[illegible]	[illegible]	[illegible]	[illegible]	[illegible]	[illegible]	7	[illegible]
Flax,	—		—	[illegible]	[illegible]	[illegible]	[illegible]	[illegible]	[illegible]	[illegible]	[illegible]	[illegible]	[illegible]	[illegible]	[illegible]		—

* [illegible]

§ [illegible]

TABLE III.

SHOWING AVERAGE POUNDAGE RATES of Poor's Rates and County Cess for Each Province in Ireland for the Years 1852, 1864, and 1870.

POOR'S RATE.

Province.	Poundage Rate in [illegible]	Poundage Rate in [illegible]	Poundage Rate in [illegible]	Percentage of Decrease in Poundage Rate from [illegible] to [illegible]
		s. d.	s. d.	
Ulster,	No detailed information for this year.	0 9½	1 1½	50 per cent.
Leinster,		1 1½	1 8¾	61 "
Munster,		1 5	2 6½	73 "
Connaught,		1 3½	2 0	57 "
Average for Ireland,	-	1 1½	1 10½	63 "

Total Expenditure of Poor's Rate for 1853, £1,113,172.
Do. do. 1863, £733,655.
Decreased percentage from 1853 to 1863, 53 per cent.

COUNTY CESS.

Province.	Poundage Rate in [illegible]	Poundage Rate in [illegible]	Poundage Rate in [illegible]	Percentage of Increase in Poundage Rate from [illegible] to [illegible]
		s. d.	s. d.	
Ulster,	No detailed information for this year.	1 0½	8 1	18 per cent.
Leinster,		1 6½	1 8¾	13 "
Munster,		1 9½	8 8½	50 "
Connaught,		1 9½	3 1½	55 "
Average for Ireland,	-	1 7½	2 1	30 "

Total Expenditure of County Cess for 1858, £864,176.
Do. do. 1865, £1,071,162.
Increased percentage from 1858 to 1865, 21 per cent.

TABLE IV

[illegible]

[illegible]	[illegible]	[illegible]	[illegible]	[illegible]	[illegible]	[illegible]	[illegible]	[illegible]	[illegible]	[illegible]	[illegible]
[illegible]	[illegible]	[illegible]	[illegible]	[illegible]	[illegible]	[illegible]	[illegible]	[illegible]	[illegible]	[illegible]	[illegible]
[illegible]	[illegible]	[illegible]	[illegible]	[illegible]	[illegible]	[illegible]	[illegible]	[illegible]	[illegible]	[illegible]	[illegible]

[illegible]

TABLE VI.

IRELAND.

HOUSE PROPERTY VALUED IN 1894-5.

Table showing Rent, Statutory Valuation, Actual Valuation, and Per-Centage of Reduction to make relative to existing Valuations.

Cities or Townships.	Number of cases quoted.	Total Rent* ascertained or estimated—Landlord doing repairs.	Total of Statutory Valuations.	Total of actual Valuations.	Per-centage of Reduction from Statutory to make relative to existing Valuations.
		£	£	£	
City of Dublin	[illegible]	[illegible]	[illegible]	[illegible]	[illegible]
Clontarf Township	14	[illegible]	[illegible]	[illegible]	[illegible]
Drumcondra Township	25	[illegible]	[illegible]	[illegible]	[illegible]
Kilmainham Township	6	[illegible]	[illegible]	[illegible]	[illegible]
Pembroke Township	35	[illegible]	[illegible]	[illegible]	[illegible]
Rathmines Township	[illegible]	[illegible]	[illegible]	[illegible]	[illegible]
Blackrock Township	[illegible]	[illegible]	[illegible]	[illegible]	[illegible]
Kingstown Township	8	[illegible]	143	[illegible]	[illegible]
City of Belfast	[illegible]	[illegible]	[illegible]	[illegible]	[illegible]
City of Londonderry	[illegible]	[illegible]	[illegible]	[illegible]	[illegible]
† City of Cork	[illegible]	[illegible]	[illegible]	[illegible]	[illegible]
City of Limerick	[illegible]	[illegible]	[illegible]	[illegible]	[illegible]
City of Waterford	4	[illegible]	[illegible]	97	[illegible]
Total of above			[illegible]	[illegible]	[illegible]

* The "Rent" in this column is the yearly rent, clear of rates and taxes, payable to the Landlord of the premises, he being responsible for maintenance, insurance, &c.

† The cases cited for the City of Cork are Valuations fixed prior to 1894-5, the Revision of the Valuation of this City for the present year not being completed.

Note.—Except as regards the Cities of Belfast and Cork the above comprise practically all the Valuations of new houses made out this year, in the above Cities and Townships, excluding those let by the week.

TABLE VII.

TABLE showing Valuation of some of the principal Country Mansions in Ireland and England.

IRELAND.

County.	Name of Mansion.	Rateable Valuation.	County.	Name of Mansion.	Rateable Valuation.
		£			£
Antrim,	Shane's Castle,	[illegible]	Limerick,	Adare Castle,	[illegible]
"	Glenarm Castle,	[illegible]	"	[illegible] Park,	[illegible]
Armagh,	Tynan Abbey,	[illegible]	Londonderry,	[illegible]	[illegible]
"	Gosford Castle,	[illegible]	"	[illegible]	[illegible]
Carlow,	Borris,	[illegible]	Longford,	[illegible]	[illegible]
"	Oak Park,	[illegible]	"	[illegible]	[illegible]
Cavan,	Castlesaunderson,	[illegible]	Louth,	[illegible] Hall,	[illegible]
"	Farnham,	[illegible]	"	[illegible]	[illegible]
Clare,	Dromoland Castle,	[illegible]	Mayo,	[illegible] House,	[illegible]
"	[illegible] House,	[illegible]	"	[illegible]	[illegible]
Cork,	Mitchelstown Castle,	[illegible]	Meath,	[illegible] Castle,	[illegible]
"	Castle Bernard,	[illegible]	"	[illegible] Castle,	[illegible]
Donegal,	[illegible]	[illegible]	Monaghan,	[illegible]	[illegible]
"	[illegible]	[illegible]	"	[illegible] Park,	[illegible]
Down,	Tollymore Park,	[illegible]	Queen's,	[illegible]	[illegible]
"	Castlewellan,	[illegible]	"	[illegible] Park,	[illegible]
Dublin,	Howth Castle,	[illegible]	Roscommon,	[illegible]	[illegible]
"	St. Anne's, Clontarf,	[illegible]	"	[illegible] Castle,	[illegible]
Fermanagh,	Crom Castle,	[illegible]	Sligo,	[illegible]	[illegible]
"	Florence Court,	[illegible]	"	[illegible]	[illegible]
Galway,	[illegible] Castle,	[illegible]	Tipperary,	[illegible]	[illegible]
"	[illegible]	[illegible]	"	[illegible] Abbey,	[illegible]
Kerry,	[illegible]	[illegible]	Tyrone,	[illegible]	[illegible]
"	Killarney House,	[illegible]	"	[illegible]	[illegible]
Kildare,	[illegible] House,	[illegible]	Waterford,	Lismore Castle,	[illegible]
"	Carton,	[illegible]	"	[illegible]	[illegible]
Kilkenny,	Kilkenny Castle,	[illegible]	Westmeath,	[illegible] Hall,	[illegible]
"	[illegible] Castle,	[illegible]	"	[illegible]	[illegible]
King's,	Birr Castle,	[illegible]	Wexford,	[illegible] Castle,	[illegible]
"	Charleville,	[illegible]	"	[illegible]	[illegible]
Leitrim,	[illegible]	[illegible]	Wicklow,	Powerscourt,	[illegible]
"	[illegible] Castle,	[illegible]	"	[illegible]	[illegible]

ENGLAND.

		£			£
Cheshire,	Eaton Hall,	3,300	Nottingham,	Clumber,	630
Derby,	Chatsworth House,	1,800	Oxford,	Blenheim Palace,	1,224
Durham,	Raby Castle,	713	Stafford,	Alton Towers,	511
Kent,	[illegible]	[illegible]	Sussex,	Petworth,	[illegible]
"	[illegible] Court,	[illegible]	Wilts,	Bowood House,	[illegible]
Herts,	Hatfield House,	[illegible]	"	Longleat,	[illegible]
Northumberland,	Alnwick Castle,	1,374	York,	[illegible]	[illegible]
[illegible]	Belvoir Castle,	1,382			

The above Valuations include mansions, stables, lodges, out-houses, and pleasure grounds and [illegible].

TABLE VIII.

Showing the Number of Cases in which Judicial Rents have been Fixed, up to the 31st March, [illegible], Total Acreage, Total Valuation, Percentage of Reduction in Rent, Former Rents, Judicial Rents, and their Percentage above or below the Valuation.

VALUATION TAKEN AS UNIT.

Province and County.	Number of Cases in which Judicial Rents have been fixed.	Acreage, Statute.	Tenement Valuation.	Former Rent.	Percentage above or below Valuation.	Judicial Rent.	Percentage above or below Valuation.	Percentage of Reduction in Rent.
Ulster:		Acres.	£	£		£		
Antrim,	[illegible]	[illegible]	[illegible]	[illegible]	[illegible] above	[illegible]	[illegible] below	[illegible]
Armagh,	[illegible]	[illegible]	[illegible]	[illegible]	[illegible] above	[illegible]	[illegible] below	[illegible]
Cavan,	[illegible]	[illegible]	[illegible]	[illegible]	[illegible] above	[illegible]	[illegible] below	[illegible]
Donegal,	[illegible]	[illegible]	[illegible]	[illegible]	[illegible] above	[illegible]	[illegible] below	[illegible]
Down,	[illegible]	[illegible]	[illegible]	[illegible]	[illegible] above	[illegible]	[illegible] below	[illegible]
Fermanagh,	[illegible]	[illegible]	[illegible]	[illegible]	[illegible] above	[illegible]	[illegible] below	[illegible]
Londonderry,	[illegible]	[illegible]	[illegible]	[illegible]	[illegible] above	[illegible]	[illegible] below	[illegible]
Monaghan,	[illegible]	[illegible]	[illegible]	[illegible]	[illegible] above	[illegible]	[illegible] below	[illegible]
Tyrone,	[illegible]	[illegible]	[illegible]	[illegible]	[illegible] above	[illegible]	[illegible] below	[illegible]
Total,	[illegible]	[illegible]	[illegible]	[illegible]	[illegible] above	[illegible]	[illegible] below	[illegible]
Leinster:								
Carlow,	[illegible]	[illegible]	[illegible]	[illegible]	[illegible] above	[illegible]	[illegible] above	[illegible]
Dublin,	[illegible]	[illegible]	[illegible]	[illegible]	[illegible] above	[illegible]	[illegible] above	[illegible]
Kildare,	[illegible]	[illegible]	[illegible]	[illegible]	[illegible] above	[illegible]	[illegible] above	[illegible]
Kilkenny,	[illegible]	[illegible]	[illegible]	[illegible]	[illegible] above	[illegible]	[illegible] below	[illegible]
King's,	[illegible]	[illegible]	[illegible]	[illegible]	[illegible] above	[illegible]	[illegible] above	[illegible]
Longford,	[illegible]	[illegible]	[illegible]	[illegible]	[illegible] above	[illegible]	[illegible] below	[illegible]
Louth,	[illegible]	[illegible]	[illegible]	[illegible]	[illegible] above	[illegible]	[illegible] above	[illegible]
Meath,	[illegible]	[illegible]	[illegible]	[illegible]	[illegible] above	[illegible]	[illegible] above	[illegible]
Queen's,	[illegible]	[illegible]	[illegible]	[illegible]	[illegible] above	[illegible]	[illegible] above	[illegible]
Westmeath,	[illegible]	[illegible]	[illegible]	[illegible]	[illegible] above	[illegible]	[illegible] above	[illegible]
Wexford,	[illegible]	[illegible]	[illegible]	[illegible]	[illegible] above	[illegible]	[illegible] above	[illegible]
Wicklow,	[illegible]	[illegible]	[illegible]	[illegible]	[illegible] above	[illegible]	[illegible] above	[illegible]
Total,	[illegible]	[illegible]	[illegible]	[illegible]	[illegible] above	[illegible]	[illegible] above	[illegible]
Connaught:								
Galway,	[illegible]	[illegible]	[illegible]	[illegible]	[illegible] above	[illegible]	[illegible] above	[illegible]
Leitrim,	[illegible]	[illegible]	[illegible]	[illegible]	[illegible] above	[illegible]	[illegible] below	[illegible]
Mayo,	[illegible]	[illegible]	[illegible]	[illegible]	[illegible] above	[illegible]	[illegible] above	[illegible]
Roscommon,	[illegible]	[illegible]	[illegible]	[illegible]	[illegible] above	[illegible]	[illegible] below	[illegible]
Sligo,	[illegible]	[illegible]	[illegible]	[illegible]	[illegible] above	[illegible]	[illegible] below	[illegible]
Total,	[illegible]	[illegible]	[illegible]	[illegible]	[illegible] above	[illegible]	[illegible] above	[illegible]
Munster:								
Clare,	[illegible]	[illegible]	[illegible]	[illegible]	[illegible] above	[illegible]	[illegible] above	[illegible]
Cork,	[illegible]	[illegible]	[illegible]	[illegible]	[illegible] above	[illegible]	[illegible] above	[illegible]
Kerry,	[illegible]	[illegible]	[illegible]	[illegible]	[illegible] above	[illegible]	[illegible] above	[illegible]
Limerick,	[illegible]	[illegible]	[illegible]	[illegible]	[illegible] above	[illegible]	[illegible] above	[illegible]
Tipperary,	[illegible]	[illegible]	[illegible]	[illegible]	[illegible] above	[illegible]	[illegible] above	[illegible]
Waterford,	[illegible]	[illegible]	[illegible]	[illegible]	[illegible] above	[illegible]	[illegible] above	[illegible]
Total,	[illegible]	[illegible]	[illegible]	[illegible]	[illegible] above	[illegible]	[illegible] above	[illegible]
SUMMARY.								
Ulster,	[illegible]	[illegible]	[illegible]	[illegible]	[illegible] above	[illegible]	[illegible] below	[illegible]
Leinster,	[illegible]	[illegible]	[illegible]	[illegible]	[illegible] above	[illegible]	[illegible] above	[illegible]
Connaught,	[illegible]	[illegible]	[illegible]	[illegible]	[illegible] above	[illegible]	[illegible] above	[illegible]
Munster,	[illegible]	[illegible]	[illegible]	[illegible]	[illegible] above	[illegible]	[illegible] above	[illegible]
TOTAL,	[illegible]	[illegible]	[illegible]	[illegible]	[illegible] above	[illegible]	[illegible] above	[illegible]

TABLE IX.

TABLE showing approximately the saving in the ASSESSMENT on which INCOME TAX is paid on LANDED PROPERTY in IRELAND under SCHEDULE A, owing to same being based on the VALUATION where it is below the RENTAL—the basis of assessment in GREAT BRITAIN.

NAMES of COUNTIES, &c.	Total Annual Valuation.	Estimated Valuation of Agricultural portion.	Portion which has been dealt with by Land Commission. Valuation.	Old Rent.	Reduced Rent.	Landlord's Rates.	Balance after deducting Rates being Rental on which Income Tax under Schedule A would be payable in Great Britain. Prior to 1881.	At present.	Approximate saving in amount of Assessment through Income Tax being paid on the Valuation and Rent. Prior to 1881.	At present.	Approximate amount on which Tax is saved on whole agricultural part of each County. Prior to 1881.	At present.
1	2	3	4	5	6	7	8	9	10	11	12	13
ULSTER:—												
Antrim	[illegible]	[illegible]	[illegible]	[illegible]	[illegible]	[illegible]	[illegible]	[illegible]	[illegible]	[illegible]	[illegible]	[illegible]
Armagh	[illegible]	[illegible]	[illegible]	[illegible]	[illegible]	[illegible]	[illegible]	[illegible]	[illegible]	[illegible]	[illegible]	[illegible]
Cavan	[illegible]	[illegible]	[illegible]	[illegible]	[illegible]	[illegible]	[illegible]	[illegible]	[illegible]	[illegible]	[illegible]	[illegible]
Donegal	[illegible]	[illegible]	[illegible]	[illegible]	[illegible]	[illegible]	[illegible]	[illegible]	[illegible]	[illegible]	[illegible]	[illegible]
Down	[illegible]	[illegible]	[illegible]	[illegible]	[illegible]	[illegible]	[illegible]	[illegible]	[illegible]	[illegible]	[illegible]	[illegible]
Fermanagh	[illegible]	[illegible]	[illegible]	[illegible]	[illegible]	[illegible]	[illegible]	[illegible]	[illegible]	[illegible]	[illegible]	[illegible]
Londonderry	[illegible]	[illegible]	[illegible]	[illegible]	[illegible]	[illegible]	[illegible]	[illegible]	[illegible]	[illegible]	[illegible]	[illegible]
Monaghan	[illegible]	[illegible]	[illegible]	[illegible]	[illegible]	[illegible]	[illegible]	[illegible]	[illegible]	[illegible]	[illegible]	[illegible]
Tyrone	[illegible]	[illegible]	[illegible]	[illegible]	[illegible]	[illegible]	[illegible]	[illegible]	[illegible]	[illegible]	[illegible]	[illegible]
Total	[illegible]	[illegible]	[illegible]	[illegible]	[illegible]	[illegible]	[illegible]	[illegible]	[illegible]	[illegible]	[illegible]	[illegible]
LEINSTER:—												
Carlow	[illegible]	[illegible]	[illegible]	[illegible]	[illegible]	[illegible]	[illegible]	[illegible]	[illegible]	[illegible]	[illegible]	[illegible]
Dublin	[illegible]	[illegible]	[illegible]	[illegible]	[illegible]	[illegible]	[illegible]	[illegible]	[illegible]	[illegible]	[illegible]	[illegible]
Kildare	[illegible]	[illegible]	[illegible]	[illegible]	[illegible]	[illegible]	[illegible]	[illegible]	[illegible]	[illegible]	[illegible]	[illegible]
Kilkenny	[illegible]	[illegible]	[illegible]	[illegible]	[illegible]	[illegible]	[illegible]	[illegible]	[illegible]	[illegible]	[illegible]	[illegible]
King's	[illegible]	[illegible]	[illegible]	[illegible]	[illegible]	[illegible]	[illegible]	[illegible]	[illegible]	[illegible]	[illegible]	[illegible]
Longford	[illegible]	[illegible]	[illegible]	[illegible]	[illegible]	[illegible]	[illegible]	[illegible]	[illegible]	[illegible]	[illegible]	[illegible]
Louth	[illegible]	[illegible]	[illegible]	[illegible]	[illegible]	[illegible]	[illegible]	[illegible]	[illegible]	[illegible]	[illegible]	[illegible]
Meath	[illegible]	[illegible]	[illegible]	[illegible]	[illegible]	[illegible]	[illegible]	[illegible]	[illegible]	[illegible]	[illegible]	[illegible]
Queen's	[illegible]	[illegible]	[illegible]	[illegible]	[illegible]	[illegible]	[illegible]	[illegible]	[illegible]	[illegible]	[illegible]	[illegible]
Westmeath	[illegible]	[illegible]	[illegible]	[illegible]	[illegible]	[illegible]	[illegible]	[illegible]	[illegible]	[illegible]	[illegible]	[illegible]
Wexford	[illegible]	[illegible]	[illegible]	[illegible]	[illegible]	[illegible]	[illegible]	[illegible]	[illegible]	[illegible]	[illegible]	[illegible]
Wicklow	[illegible]	[illegible]	[illegible]	[illegible]	[illegible]	[illegible]	[illegible]	[illegible]	[illegible]	[illegible]	[illegible]	[illegible]
Total	[illegible]	[illegible]	[illegible]	[illegible]	[illegible]	[illegible]	[illegible]	[illegible]	[illegible]	[illegible]	[illegible]	[illegible]
CONNAUGHT:—												
Galway	[illegible]	[illegible]	[illegible]	[illegible]	[illegible]	[illegible]	[illegible]	[illegible]	[illegible]	[illegible]	[illegible]	[illegible]
Leitrim	[illegible]	[illegible]	[illegible]	[illegible]	[illegible]	[illegible]	[illegible]	[illegible]	[illegible]	[illegible]	[illegible]	[illegible]
Mayo	[illegible]	[illegible]	[illegible]	[illegible]	[illegible]	[illegible]	[illegible]	[illegible]	[illegible]	[illegible]	[illegible]	[illegible]
Roscommon	[illegible]	[illegible]	[illegible]	[illegible]	[illegible]	[illegible]	[illegible]	[illegible]	[illegible]	[illegible]	[illegible]	[illegible]
Sligo	[illegible]	[illegible]	[illegible]	[illegible]	[illegible]	[illegible]	[illegible]	[illegible]	[illegible]	[illegible]	[illegible]	[illegible]
Total	[illegible]	[illegible]	[illegible]	[illegible]	[illegible]	[illegible]	[illegible]	[illegible]	[illegible]	[illegible]	[illegible]	[illegible]
MUNSTER:—												
Clare	[illegible]	[illegible]	[illegible]	[illegible]	[illegible]	[illegible]	[illegible]	[illegible]	[illegible]	[illegible]	[illegible]	[illegible]
Cork	[illegible]	[illegible]	[illegible]	[illegible]	[illegible]	[illegible]	[illegible]	[illegible]	[illegible]	[illegible]	[illegible]	[illegible]
Kerry	[illegible]	[illegible]	[illegible]	[illegible]	[illegible]	[illegible]	[illegible]	[illegible]	[illegible]	[illegible]	[illegible]	[illegible]
Limerick	[illegible]	[illegible]	[illegible]	[illegible]	[illegible]	[illegible]	[illegible]	[illegible]	[illegible]	[illegible]	[illegible]	[illegible]
Tipperary	[illegible]	[illegible]	[illegible]	[illegible]	[illegible]	[illegible]	[illegible]	[illegible]	[illegible]	[illegible]	[illegible]	[illegible]
Waterford	[illegible]	[illegible]	[illegible]	[illegible]	[illegible]	[illegible]	[illegible]	[illegible]	[illegible]	[illegible]	[illegible]	[illegible]
Total	[illegible]	[illegible]	[illegible]	[illegible]	[illegible]	[illegible]	[illegible]	[illegible]	[illegible]	[illegible]	[illegible]	[illegible]
SUMMARY.												
Ulster	[illegible]	[illegible]	[illegible]	[illegible]	[illegible]	[illegible]	[illegible]	[illegible]	[illegible]	[illegible]	[illegible]	[illegible]
Leinster	[illegible]	[illegible]	[illegible]	[illegible]	[illegible]	[illegible]	[illegible]	[illegible]	[illegible]	[illegible]	[illegible]	[illegible]
Connaught	[illegible]	[illegible]	[illegible]	[illegible]	[illegible]	[illegible]	[illegible]	[illegible]	[illegible]	[illegible]	[illegible]	[illegible]
Munster	[illegible]	[illegible]	[illegible]	[illegible]	[illegible]	[illegible]	[illegible]	[illegible]	[illegible]	[illegible]	[illegible]	[illegible]
TOTAL	[illegible]	[illegible]	[illegible]	[illegible]	[illegible]	[illegible]	[illegible]	[illegible]	[illegible]	[illegible]	[illegible]	[illegible]

NOTE.—[illegible]

TABLE X.

INCOME TAX

As a basis of comparison of the relative taxable capacity of Great Britain and Ireland.

Year 1891-92, ... Tax at 6d. in the £.

ESTIMATE showing the amount that would be charged to Duty in Ireland if the assessments were made on the same basis as in Great Britain, and Sales to Occupiers under the Land Purchase Acts had not taken place.

(IRELAND.)

	£
Schedule A.—	
(a.) Amount actually charged to Duty, ...	318,000
(b.) Add Fall in Amount charged to Duty between 1880 and 1892, consequent on Sales to Occupiers, ...	9,000
(c.) Add saving due to Tax being assessed as regards Landed Property on Valuation, where same is under Rent (Appendix IX.), ...	6,000
(d.) Add saving due to Tax being assessed as regards House Property on Valuation, same being under Rent, ...	18,000
Total, ...	351,000
(e.) Schedules C, D, and E,—Amount actually charged to Duty, . .	301,000
(Assessments on same basis as Great Britain).	
Total (less Schedule B), . .	642,000

GREAT BRITAIN.

(a.) Total Amount charged to Duty (less Schedule B), .	13,710,000

IRELAND, 4·6. GREAT BRITAIN, 95·4. (Say Ireland 1/21st of Great Britain).

Deducting (b) the proportion would be :—

IRELAND, 4·54. GREAT BRITAIN, 95·46 (Say Ireland 1/21st of Great Britain).

Deducting (b) and (c) the proportion would be :—

IRELAND, 4·5. GREAT BRITAIN, 95·5 (Say Ireland 1/21st of Great Britain).

Deducting (b), (c), and (d) the proportion would be :—

IRELAND, 4·37. GREAT BRITAIN, 95·63 (Say Ireland 1/22nd of Great Britain).

Schedule B being more or less a repetition of Schedule A has been deducted. To add it would not materially alter the proportion between the countries.

APPENDIX VII.

DOCUMENTS put in by Dr. Grimshaw, the Registrar-General of Ireland, in connexion with the Evidence given by him before the Commission.

I.

Special Papers with reference to the History of Population in Ireland.

(1.)

Estimated Population of Ireland in each of the 42 years, 1780–1821, based on the assumption that the yearly rate of increase was equal to the average rate of increase (1·615 per cent. of the estimated population in each year) between the Population (4,206,612) as returned by the Hearthmoney Collectors in 1791, and the Population (6,801,827) as shown by the Census of 1821.

Year.	Population.	Year.	Population.
1780, . .	[illegible]	1801, . .	4,937,533
1781, . .	3,563,541	1802, . .	5,017,269
1782, . .	3,611,543	1803, . .	5,098,293
1783, . .	3,700,376	1804, . .	5,180,630
1784, . .	3,760,165	1805, . .	5,264,278
1785, . .	3,820,938	1806, . .	5,349,294
1786, . .	3,882,673	1807, . .	5,435,684
1787, . .	3,945,404	1808, . .	5,523,470
1788, . .	4,009,139	1809, . .	5,612,681
1789, . .	4,073,926	1810, . .	5,703,322
1790, . .	4,139,728	1811, . .	5,795,435
1791, . .	4,206,612	1812, . .	5,889,019
1792, . .	4,274,546	1813, . .	5,984,129
1793, . .	4,343,580	1814, . .	6,080,767
1794, . .	4,413,729	1815, . .	6,178,967
1795, . .	4,485,009	1816, . .	6,278,753
1796, . .	4,557,441	1817, . .	6,380,150
1797, . .	4,631,043	1818, . .	6,483,183
1798, . .	4,705,834	1819, . .	6,587,877
1799, . .	4,781,832	1820, . .	6,694,259
1800, . .	4,859,058	1821, . .	6,801,440

POPULATION of IRELAND (including Army, Navy, and Merchant Seamen on shore and in port) estimated to the middle of each of the Years 1801 to 1884, inclusive:—

[illegible]	[illegible]			[illegible]	[illegible]			[illegible]	[illegible]		
	[illegible]	[illegible]	[illegible]		[illegible]	[illegible]	[illegible]		[illegible]	[illegible]	[illegible]
[illegible]	[illegible]	[illegible]	[illegible]	[illegible]	[illegible]	[illegible]	[illegible]	[illegible]	[illegible]	[illegible]	[illegible]
[illegible]	[illegible]	[illegible]	[illegible]	[illegible]	[illegible]	[illegible]	[illegible]	[illegible]	[illegible]	[illegible]	[illegible]
[illegible]	[illegible]	[illegible]	[illegible]	[illegible]	[illegible]	[illegible]	[illegible]	[illegible]	[illegible]	[illegible]	[illegible]
[illegible]	[illegible]	[illegible]	[illegible]	[illegible]	[illegible]	[illegible]	[illegible]	[illegible]	[illegible]	[illegible]	[illegible]
[illegible]	[illegible]	[illegible]	[illegible]	[illegible]	[illegible]	[illegible]	[illegible]	[illegible]	[illegible]	[illegible]	[illegible]
[illegible]	[illegible]	[illegible]	[illegible]	[illegible]	[illegible]	[illegible]	[illegible]	[illegible]	[illegible]	[illegible]	[illegible]
[illegible]	[illegible]	[illegible]	[illegible]	[illegible]	[illegible]	[illegible]	[illegible]	[illegible]	[illegible]	[illegible]	[illegible]
[illegible]	[illegible]	[illegible]	[illegible]	[illegible]	[illegible]	[illegible]	[illegible]	[illegible]	[illegible]	[illegible]	[illegible]
[illegible]	[illegible]	[illegible]	[illegible]	[illegible]	[illegible]	[illegible]	[illegible]	[illegible]	[illegible]	[illegible]	[illegible]
[illegible]	[illegible]	[illegible]	[illegible]	[illegible]	[illegible]	[illegible]	[illegible]	[illegible]	[illegible]	[illegible]	[illegible]
[illegible]	[illegible]	[illegible]	[illegible]	[illegible]	[illegible]	[illegible]	[illegible]	[illegible]	[illegible]	[illegible]	[illegible]
[illegible]	[illegible]	[illegible]	[illegible]	[illegible]	[illegible]	[illegible]	[illegible]	[illegible]	[illegible]	[illegible]	[illegible]
[illegible]	[illegible]	[illegible]	[illegible]	[illegible]	[illegible]	[illegible]	[illegible]	[illegible]	[illegible]	[illegible]	[illegible]
[illegible]	[illegible]	[illegible]	[illegible]	[illegible]	[illegible]	[illegible]	[illegible]	[illegible]	[illegible]	[illegible]	[illegible]
[illegible]	[illegible]	[illegible]	[illegible]	[illegible]	[illegible]	[illegible]	[illegible]	[illegible]	[illegible]	[illegible]	[illegible]
[illegible]	[illegible]	[illegible]	[illegible]	[illegible]	[illegible]	[illegible]	[illegible]	[illegible]	[illegible]	[illegible]	[illegible]
[illegible]	[illegible]	[illegible]	[illegible]	[illegible]	[illegible]	[illegible]	[illegible]	[illegible]	[illegible]	[illegible]	[illegible]
[illegible]	[illegible]	[illegible]	[illegible]	[illegible]	[illegible]	[illegible]	[illegible]	[illegible]	[illegible]	[illegible]	[illegible]
[illegible]	[illegible]	[illegible]	[illegible]	[illegible]	[illegible]	[illegible]	[illegible]	[illegible]	[illegible]	[illegible]	[illegible]
[illegible]	[illegible]	[illegible]	[illegible]	[illegible]	[illegible]	[illegible]	[illegible]	[illegible]	[illegible]	[illegible]	[illegible]
[illegible]	[illegible]	[illegible]	[illegible]	[illegible]	[illegible]	[illegible]	[illegible]	[illegible]	[illegible]	[illegible]	[illegible]
[illegible]	[illegible]	[illegible]	[illegible]	[illegible]	[illegible]	[illegible]	[illegible]	[illegible]	[illegible]	[illegible]	[illegible]
[illegible]	[illegible]	[illegible]	[illegible]	[illegible]	[illegible]	[illegible]	[illegible]	[illegible]	[illegible]	[illegible]	[illegible]
[illegible]	[illegible]	[illegible]	[illegible]	[illegible]	[illegible]	[illegible]	[illegible]	[illegible]	[illegible]	[illegible]	[illegible]
[illegible]	[illegible]	[illegible]	[illegible]	[illegible]	[illegible]	[illegible]	[illegible]	[illegible]	[illegible]	[illegible]	[illegible]
[illegible]	[illegible]	[illegible]	[illegible]	[illegible]	[illegible]	[illegible]	[illegible]	[illegible]	[illegible]	[illegible]	[illegible]
[illegible]	[illegible]	[illegible]	[illegible]	[illegible]	[illegible]	[illegible]	[illegible]	[illegible]	[illegible]	[illegible]	[illegible]
[illegible]	[illegible]	[illegible]	[illegible]								

[illegible]

[illegible]

[illegible]

[illegible]

[illegible]

[illegible]

(3.)

Population of Ireland at each Census, 1841–91 (inclusive) with the Decrease in each intercensal period.

Census Year.	Population.	Decrease.	
		Number.	Rate per cent.
1841,	8,175,124	—	—
1851,	6,552,385	1,622,739	19·8
1861,	5,798,967	753,418	11·5
1871,	5,412,377	386,590	6·7
1881,	5,174,836	237,541	4·4
1891,	4,704,750	470,086	9·1
Loss between 1841 and 1891,		3,470,374	42·5

(4.)

Table showing the Population of Civic Districts (i.e. Towns with a population of 2,000 or upwards) in Ireland, in each of the Census Years 1821 to 1891, with Increases and Decreases.

Year.	Towns with 2,000 and under 10,000 Inhabitants.		Towns of 10,000 Inhabitants and upwards.		All Towns with Population of 2,000 or upwards.	
	Population.	Increase (+), Decrease (−).	Population.	Increase (+), Decrease (−).	Population.	Increase (+), Decrease (−).
1821,	399,076	—	513,767	—	912,843	—
1831,	473,274	+ 74,198	636,324	+ 122,557	1,109,598	+ 196,755
1841,	516,459	+ 43,185	601,053	− 35,271	1,123,465	+ 13,867
1851,	545,584	+ 29,125	671,092	+ 70,039	1,216,676	+ 93,211
1861,	470,016	− 75,568	670,339	− 4,410	1,141,368	− 75,308
1871,	438,765	− 31,251	762,579	+ 92,237	1,201,344	+ 59,976
1881,	430,877	− 8,168	815,626	+ 49,367	1,246,503	+ 45,159
1891,	399,864	− 31,013	844,249	+ 28,623	1,244,113	− 2,390

(5.)

Table showing the Total Population, the Rural Population, and the Civic Population of Ireland, in each of the Census Years from 1821 to 1891, with the Increase or Decrease in the Rural and Civic Populations, respectively.

Year.	Total Population.	Rural Districts.		Civic Districts (all Towns with a population of 2,000 or upwards).	
		Population.	Increase (+), Decrease (−).	Population.	Increase (+), Decrease (−).
1821,	6,801,827	5,888,984	—	912,843	—
1831,	7,767,401	6,657,803	+ 768,819	1,109,598	+ 196,755
1841,	8,175,124	7,051,659	+ 393,856	1,123,465	+ 13,867
1851,	6,552,385	5,335,709	− 1,715,950	1,216,676	+ 93,211
1861,	5,798,967	4,657,599	− 678,110	1,141,368	− 75,308
1871,	5,412,377	4,211,033	− 446,566	1,201,344	+ 59,976
1881,	5,174,836	3,928,333	− 282,700	1,246,503	+ 45,159
1891,	4,704,750	3,460,637	− 467,696	1,244,113	− 2,390

2.—General Tables of Statistics referred to in his evidence by Dr. Grimshaw together with two Special Papers put in by him with reference to the value of the out-put of Agriculture in Ireland.

TABLE I.—Table showing the Number of Emigrants from Ireland in each Month, from 1st January, 1870, to 31st December, 1894.

Years.	January.	February.	March.	April.	May.	June.	July.	August.	September.	October.	November.	December.	Total.
[illegible]	[illegible]	[illegible]	[illegible]	[illegible]	[illegible]	[illegible]	[illegible]	[illegible]	[illegible]	[illegible]	[illegible]	[illegible]	[illegible]
[illegible]	[illegible]	[illegible]	[illegible]	[illegible]	[illegible]	[illegible]	[illegible]	[illegible]	[illegible]	[illegible]	[illegible]	[illegible]	[illegible]
[illegible]	[illegible]	[illegible]	[illegible]	[illegible]	[illegible]	[illegible]	[illegible]	[illegible]	[illegible]	[illegible]	[illegible]	[illegible]	[illegible]
[illegible]	[illegible]	[illegible]	[illegible]	[illegible]	[illegible]	[illegible]	[illegible]	[illegible]	[illegible]	[illegible]	[illegible]	[illegible]	[illegible]
[illegible]	[illegible]	[illegible]	[illegible]	[illegible]	[illegible]	[illegible]	[illegible]	[illegible]	[illegible]	[illegible]	[illegible]	[illegible]	[illegible]
*[illegible]	[illegible]	[illegible]	[illegible]	[illegible]	[illegible]	[illegible]	[illegible]	[illegible]	[illegible]	[illegible]	[illegible]	[illegible]	[illegible]
[illegible]	[illegible]	[illegible]	[illegible]	[illegible]	[illegible]	[illegible]	[illegible]	[illegible]	[illegible]	[illegible]	[illegible]	[illegible]	[illegible]
[illegible]	[illegible]	[illegible]	[illegible]	[illegible]	[illegible]	[illegible]	[illegible]	[illegible]	[illegible]	[illegible]	[illegible]	[illegible]	[illegible]
[illegible]	[illegible]	[illegible]	[illegible]	[illegible]	[illegible]	[illegible]	[illegible]	[illegible]	[illegible]	[illegible]	[illegible]	[illegible]	[illegible]
[illegible]	[illegible]	[illegible]	[illegible]	[illegible]	[illegible]	[illegible]	[illegible]	[illegible]	[illegible]	[illegible]	[illegible]	[illegible]	[illegible]
[illegible]	[illegible]	[illegible]	[illegible]	[illegible]	[illegible]	[illegible]	[illegible]	[illegible]	[illegible]	[illegible]	[illegible]	[illegible]	[illegible]
*[illegible]	[illegible]	[illegible]	[illegible]	[illegible]	[illegible]	[illegible]	[illegible]	[illegible]	[illegible]	[illegible]	[illegible]	[illegible]	[illegible]
*[illegible]	[illegible]	[illegible]	[illegible]	[illegible]	[illegible]	[illegible]	[illegible]	[illegible]	[illegible]	[illegible]	[illegible]	[illegible]	[illegible]
[illegible]	[illegible]	[illegible]	[illegible]	[illegible]	[illegible]	[illegible]	[illegible]	[illegible]	[illegible]	[illegible]	[illegible]	[illegible]	[illegible]
[illegible]	[illegible]	[illegible]	[illegible]	[illegible]	[illegible]	[illegible]	[illegible]	[illegible]	[illegible]	[illegible]	[illegible]	[illegible]	[illegible]
[illegible]	[illegible]	[illegible]	[illegible]	[illegible]	[illegible]	[illegible]	[illegible]	[illegible]	[illegible]	[illegible]	[illegible]	[illegible]	[illegible]
[illegible]	[illegible]	[illegible]	[illegible]	[illegible]	[illegible]	[illegible]	[illegible]	[illegible]	[illegible]	[illegible]	[illegible]	[illegible]	[illegible]
[illegible]	[illegible]	[illegible]	[illegible]	[illegible]	[illegible]	[illegible]	[illegible]	[illegible]	[illegible]	[illegible]	[illegible]	[illegible]	[illegible]
*[illegible]	[illegible]	[illegible]	[illegible]	[illegible]	[illegible]	[illegible]	[illegible]	[illegible]	[illegible]	[illegible]	[illegible]	[illegible]	[illegible]
*[illegible]	[illegible]	[illegible]	[illegible]	[illegible]	[illegible]	[illegible]	[illegible]	[illegible]	[illegible]	[illegible]	[illegible]	[illegible]	[illegible]
[illegible]	[illegible]	[illegible]	[illegible]	[illegible]	[illegible]	[illegible]	[illegible]	[illegible]	[illegible]	[illegible]	[illegible]	[illegible]	[illegible]
[illegible]	[illegible]	[illegible]	[illegible]	[illegible]	[illegible]	[illegible]	[illegible]	[illegible]	[illegible]	[illegible]	[illegible]	[illegible]	[illegible]
[illegible]	[illegible]	[illegible]	[illegible]	[illegible]	[illegible]	[illegible]	[illegible]	[illegible]	[illegible]	[illegible]	[illegible]	[illegible]	[illegible]
[illegible]	[illegible]	[illegible]	[illegible]	[illegible]	[illegible]	[illegible]	[illegible]	[illegible]	[illegible]	[illegible]	[illegible]	[illegible]	[illegible]
[illegible]	[illegible]	[illegible]	[illegible]	[illegible]	[illegible]	[illegible]	[illegible]	[illegible]	[illegible]	[illegible]	[illegible]	[illegible]	[illegible]
*[illegible]	[illegible]	[illegible]	[illegible]	[illegible]	[illegible]	[illegible]	[illegible]	[illegible]	[illegible]	[illegible]	[illegible]	[illegible]	[illegible]
*[illegible]	[illegible]	[illegible]	[illegible]	[illegible]	[illegible]	[illegible]	[illegible]	[illegible]	[illegible]	[illegible]	[illegible]	[illegible]	[illegible]
[illegible]	[illegible]	[illegible]	[illegible]	[illegible]	[illegible]	[illegible]	[illegible]	[illegible]	[illegible]	[illegible]	[illegible]	[illegible]	[illegible]
[illegible]	[illegible]	[illegible]	[illegible]	[illegible]	[illegible]	[illegible]	[illegible]	[illegible]	[illegible]	[illegible]	[illegible]	[illegible]	[illegible]
[illegible]	[illegible]	[illegible]	[illegible]	[illegible]	[illegible]	[illegible]	[illegible]	[illegible]	[illegible]	[illegible]	[illegible]	[illegible]	[illegible]
[illegible]	[illegible]	[illegible]	[illegible]	[illegible]	[illegible]	[illegible]	[illegible]	[illegible]	[illegible]	[illegible]	[illegible]	[illegible]	[illegible]
[illegible]	[illegible]	[illegible]	[illegible]	[illegible]	[illegible]	[illegible]	[illegible]	[illegible]	[illegible]	[illegible]	[illegible]	[illegible]	[illegible]
*[illegible]	[illegible]	[illegible]	[illegible]	[illegible]	[illegible]	[illegible]	[illegible]	[illegible]	[illegible]	[illegible]	[illegible]	[illegible]	[illegible]

* Averages for [illegible] years.

TABLE II.—Population of Towns of 10,000 Inhabitants and upwards in Ireland at each of the Censuses 1841–1891, both inclusive.

Date of Census.	No. of Towns.	Total Inhabitants.	Date of Census.	No. of Towns.	Total Inhabitants.
1841, . .	17	631,003	1871, .	19	735,810
1851, . .	16	674,871	1881, . .	19	814,896
1861, . .	16	670,323	1891, . .	18	844,949

TABLE III.—Towns in Ireland having a Population of 10,000 or upwards in any of the Six Census Years from 1841 to 1891, with the Total Population in Towns of that Class in each Census Year.

Town.	1821.	1831.	1841.	1851.	1861.	1871.	1881.	1891.
*Dublin City,	185,881	203,752	232,726	258,369	254,808	246,326	249,602	245,001
Rathmines and Rathgar,	–	–	–	–	–	20,508	24,370	27,796
Pembroke,	–	–	–	–	–	19,982	23,222	24,269
Kingstown,	–	–	–	10,453	12,180	16,378	18,586	17,352
Belfast,	37,277	53,287	75,308	100,301	121,602	174,412	208,122	255,950
*Cork,	100,658	107,041	80,720	85,745	80,121	78,642	80,124	75,345
*Limerick,	59,045	66,554	48,391	53,448	44,476	39,353	38,562	37,155
Londonderry,	–	14,020	15,196	19,888	20,875	25,242	29,162	33,200
*Waterford,	28,679	28,821	23,216	25,297	23,293	23,349	22,457	20,852
*Galway,	27,775	33,120	17,275	23,787	16,967	15,597	15,471	13,800
Newry,	10,013	13,134	11,972	13,191	12,162	13,364	14,808	12,961
Dundalk,	–	10,078	10,782	–	10,428	11,327	11,913	12,449
Lisburn,	–	–	–	–	–	–	10,755	12,250
*Drogheda,	18,118	17,365	17,300	16,847	14,740	13,510	12,297	11,873
Wexford,	–	10,673	11,252	12,471	11,673	12,077	12,163	11,545
Lurgan,	–	–	–	–	–	10,632	10,135	11,429
*Kilkenny,	23,230	23,741	19,071	19,975	14,174	12,710	12,299	11,048
Sligo,	–	15,152	12,272	11,104	10,693	10,670	10,808	10,274
Armagh,	–	–	10,948	–	–		10,070	–
Clonmel,	15,013	17,838	13,505	12,518	11,524	10,112	–	–
Queenstown,	–	–	–	11,428	–	10,334	–	–
Carlow,	–	–	10,409	–	–	–	–	–
Tralee,	–	–	11,363	–	10,309	–	–	–
Athlone,	–	11,362	–	–	–	–	–	–
Bandon,	10,179	12,617	–	–	–	–	–	–
Total,	513,557	626,534	601,022	671,633	670,383	752,719	814,925	846,849

* [illegible]

TABLE IV.—Showing the number of Houses in Ireland in each Census Year from 1821 to 1891, distinguishing the Inhabited, the Uninhabited, and Houses in Course of Erection.

Census Periods.	Houses.			
	Inhabited.	Uninhabited.	Building.	Total.
1821, . .	1,142,602	35,991	1,350	1,179,907
1831, . .	1,249,816	60,854	15,326	1,325,776
1841, . .	1,328,839	52,208	3,313	1,384,360
1851, . .	1,046,223	65,159	2,068	1,113,450
1861, . .	995,156	60,807	2,970	1,058,933
1871, . .	961,380	30,530	3,170	995,080
1881, . .	914,108	58,257	1,710	974,075
1891, . .	870,578	69,290	2,632	942,500

TABLE V.—Table showing the Number of First, Second, Third, and Fourth Class Inhabited Houses in each Census Year from 1841 to 1891.

Census Periods.	First Class.	Second Class.	Third Class.	Fourth Class.	Total.
1841, .	40,080	264,184	533,297	491,278	1,328,839
1851, .	50,164	318,758	541,712	135,589	1,046,223
1861, .	55,416	360,698	489,668	89,374	995,156
1871, .	50,483	373,113	382,043*	155,741*	961,380
1881, .	66,771	432,541	354,478	60,565	914,108
1891, .	73,740	455,632	313,580	20,617	870,578

TABLE VI.—House Accommodation in each Census Year from 1841 to 1891.

Years.	Number of Families Occupying Accommodation of the				
	First Class.	Second Class.	Third Class.	Fourth Class.	Total.
1841, .	31,333	241,664	574,386	425,326	1,272,709
1851, .	53,279	391,250	633,110	254,278	1,304,319
1861, .	64,303	383,440	653,498	157,098	1,158,300
1871, .	49,633	357,752	432,776*	227,379*	1,067,368
1881, .	57,073	400,863	448,247	90,393	953,074
1891, .	53,613	434,870	330,308	53,363	872,118

* See Questions [illegible], et seq., regarding difference of classification of Houses in 1871 and that used the other years.

Dublin, .	1841,	10·1	21·0	79·1	39·6
	1891,	11·1	50·0	29·0	11·9
Kildare, .	1841,	3·0	13·6	47·2	34·0
	1891,	8·4	45·6	41·0	4·6
Kilkenny,	1841,	2·3	11·4	41·0	32·1
	1891,	6·6	45·9	31·5	3·5
King's, .	1841,	2·3	19·0	50·5	32·1
	1891,	6·9	40·6	30·0	4·3
Longford,	1841,	1·7	15·1	46·4	36·3
	1891,	1·8	63·0	37·5	1·7
Louth, .	1841,	2·7	14·9	53·0	29·4
	1891,	7·6	44·7	43·6	4·3
Meath, .	1841,	3·0	10·9	47·3	33·9
	1891,	7·5	43·0	44·2	5·3
Queen's, .	1841,	2·2	18·0	46·7	33·1
	1891,	7·5	49·5	40·2	3·0
Westmeath,	1841,	1·9	17·8	45·3	35·0
	1891,	6·5	52·0	37·2	4·0
Wexford,	1841,	3·8	23·4	45·4	25·6
	1891,	9·7	36·0	38·7	3·6
Wicklow,	1841,	2·5	21·4	37·6	32·1
	1891,	9·9	37·5	37·6	4·6
PROVINCE OF MUNSTER:					
Clare, . .	1841,	0·6	13·5	31·7	53·0
	1891,	3·4	63·1	40·0	1·9
Cork, .	1841,	2·5	14·9	31·1	51·3
	1891,	5·0	61·0	33·6	0·7
Kerry, .	1841,	1·0	7·8	27·0	64·7
	1891,	3·7	38·4	48·5	10·1
Limerick, .	1841,	3·1	11·8	33·0	53·0
	1891,	6·6	17·8	38·7	9·1

TABLE VI.A.—Showing for the years 1841 and 1891 the percentage of Families in each County having 1st, 2nd, 3rd, and 4th Class House Accommodation respectively—continued.

County and Year.		Percentage of Families with House Accommodation of the			
		1st Class.	2nd Class.	3rd Class.	4th Class.
PROVINCE OF MUNSTER—con.					
Tipperary,	1841,	3·0	15·3	39·8	42·2
	1891,	7·3	51·9	33·4	4·5
Waterford,	1841,	3·9	20·3	36·8	38·0
	1891,	7·9	56·6	29·6	6·0
PROVINCE OF ULSTER:					
Antrim,	1841,	2·9	25·9	41·4	29·8
	1891,	7·4	64·6	26·0	1·9
Armagh,	1841,	1·7	20·0	47·6	30·7
	1891,	8·6	35·9	52·1	3·3
Cavan,	1841,	0·8	15·9	45·7	37·6
	1891,	4·4	50·8	41·5	3·6
Donegal,	1841,	0·6	13·6	39·9	45·7
	1891,	4·1	33·6	59·2	3·1
Down,	1841,	1·9	30·8	43·3	23·9
	1891,	7·7	63·4	28·0	0·9
Fermanagh,	1841,	0·6	19·6	39·6	40·4
	1891,	4·7	44·4	47·5	3·4
Londonderry,	1841,	1·9	22·6	39·7	36·1
	1891,	7·6	46·8	43·2	2·3
Monaghan,	1841,	1·0	18·7	49·0	31·3
	1891,	6·0	51·0	41·6	2·1
Tyrone,	1841,	1·1	19·8	43·2	35·1
	1891,	6·6	47·6	44·7	1·6
PROVINCE OF CONNAUGHT:					
Galway,	1841,	0·9	9·6	35·6	53·7
	1891,	4·0	40·6	48·6	6·7
Leitrim,	1841,	0·6	11·1	41·6	46·8
	1891,	3·1	63·1	31·6	2·0
Mayo,	1841,	0·6	6·1	32·0	61·3
	1891,	3·4	33·6	59·2	1·6
Roscommon,	1841,	0·7	8·5	43·6	47·2
	1891,	3·4	48·3	46·3	3·4
Sligo,	1841,	0·6	10·5	39·7	49·6
	1891,	3·7	43·9	49·6	2·9

TABLE VII.—[illegible]

[illegible]	[illegible]	[illegible]	[illegible]	[illegible]	[illegible]	[illegible]	[illegible]	[illegible]	[illegible]
	[illegible]	[illegible]	[illegible]	[illegible]	[illegible]	[illegible]	[illegible]	[illegible]	[illegible]
[illegible]	[illegible]	[illegible]	[illegible]	[illegible]	[illegible]	[illegible]	[illegible]	[illegible]	[illegible]
[illegible]	[illegible]	[illegible]	[illegible]	[illegible]	[illegible]	[illegible]	[illegible]	[illegible]	[illegible]
[illegible]	[illegible]	[illegible]	[illegible]	[illegible]	[illegible]	[illegible]	[illegible]	[illegible]	[illegible]
[illegible]					[illegible]	[illegible]	[illegible]	[illegible]	[illegible]
[illegible]	[illegible]	[illegible]	[illegible]	[illegible]	[illegible]	[illegible]	[illegible]	[illegible]	[illegible]
[illegible]					[illegible]	[illegible]	[illegible]	[illegible]	[illegible]
Total	[illegible]						[illegible]		

[illegible]

[illegible]

TABLE VIII.—Showing for Ireland for each of Six Decennial Census Years the Population, the Extent of Arable and Pasture Land, and the Valuation of such Land per Person of Population, exclusive of the Population of Large Towns.

Years.	Total Population.	Population of towns of 2,000 inhabitants and upwards.	Population less that of towns of 2,000 and upwards—country population.	Average acres per person of whole population.	Acreage of arable and pasture land.	Average acres of arable and pasture land per person of country population.	Valuation of arable and pasture land per person of country population.
	000 omitted.	000 omitted.	000 omitted.		000 omitted.		£
1841,	8,175	821	7,354	2·6	13,464	1·8	*—
1851, .	6,552	875	5,677	3·2	14,906	2·6	1·9
1861, .	5,799	670	5,129	3·6	15,424	3·0	2·2
1871, .	5,412	755	4,657	3·8	15,593	3·4	2·5
1881, .	5,175	815	4,360	4·0	15,271	3·5	2·6
1891, . .	4,705	845	3,860	4·5	15,117	3·9	3·0

Total area of Ireland, including rivers, lakes, and tideways, 21,000,000 Statute Acres. Valuation of arable and pasture land, £11,108,000.

* [illegible]

TABLE IX.—Showing the Distribution of Land in Ireland from 1847 to 1890—with Averages of the Acreage in each Year by Quinquennial and Decennial Periods.

Periods.	Cereal Crops.	Green Crops.	Flax.	Meadow and Clover.	Grass.	Total Land in use for Agriculture.	Woods and Plantations.	Fallow.	Bog, Mountain, Waste, Land, &c.
	Acres 000 omitted.	Acres 000 omitted.	Acres 000 omitted.	Acres 000 omitted.	Acres 000 omitted.	Acres 000 omitted.	Acres 000 omitted.	Acres 000 omitted.	Acres 000 omitted.
*1847–50, .	3,218	1,073	70	1,140	—	—	—	—	—
1851–55, .	2,897	1,425	140	1,273	(a) 9,297	(a) 15,060	(a) 305	(a) 111	(a) 4,804
1856–60, .	2,733	1,505	113	1,455	9,484	15,303	315	43	4,567
1861–65, .	2,419	1,505	273	1,589	9,705	15,199	318	36	4,537
1866–70, .	2,173	1,458	230	1,679	10,074	15,341	320	25	4,419
1871–75, .	1,960	1,418	133	1,854	10,223	15,718	329	15	4,356
1876–80, .	1,816	1,378	131	1,918	10,342	15,431	337	16	4,537
1881–85, .	1,689	1,258	111	1,976	10,163	15,201	330	22	4,773
1886–90, .	1,555	1,201	117	2,147	10,084	15,109	330	14	4,874
1851–60, .	2,810	1,503	126	1,349	9,385	15,169	310	58	4,685
1861–70, .	2,296	1,486	253	1,634	9,858	15,198	321	29	4,478
1871–80, .	1,903	1,388	137	1,886	10,285	15,571	337	16	4,450
1881–90, .	1,616	1,231	111	2,063	10,180	15,154	330	18	4,825

* Exclusive of the year 1848. (a) Exclusive of the year 1851.

TABLE X.—Showing by Quinquennial and Decennial Periods the Average Acreage per Person under the Several Heads of the Distribution of Land in Ireland in the Years 1847–90.

Period.	Average Acreage per Person.								
	Cereal Crops.	Green Crops.	Flax.	Meadow and Clover.	Grass.	Total Land in use for Agriculture.	Woods and Plantations.	Fallow.	Bog, Marsh, Waste, Roads, Fences, &c.
*1847–50, .	0·45	0·14	0·01	0·16	—	—	—	—	—
1851–55, .	0·47	0·33	0·02	0·20	(a) 1·49	(a) 2·41	(a) 0·05	(a) 0·03	(a) 0·77
1856–60, .	0·46	0·27	0·03	0·24	1·60	2·59	0·05	0·01	0·73
1861–65, .	0·43	0·26	0·04	0·28	1·70	2·70	0·06	0·01	0·80
1866–70, .	0·40	0·27	0·04	0·31	1·83	2·85	0·06	0·02	0·81
1871–75, .	0·37	0·27	0·05	0·35	1·91	2·95	0·06	0·02	0·80
1876–80, .	0·33	0·26	0·03	0·36	1·98	2·97	0·06	0·02	0·87
1881–85, .	0·32	0·25	0·03	0·39	2·05	3·05	0·07	0·02	0·96
1886–90, .	0·29	0·25	0·03	0·45	2·09	3·14	0·07	0·02	1·03
1851–60, .	0·46	0·25	0·03	0·23	1·55	2·50	0·05	0·01	0·77
1861–70, .	0·41	0·27	0·04	0·29	1·76	2·77	0·06	0·02	0·80
1871–80, .	0·35	0·26	0·03	0·34	1·94	2·94	0·06	0·02	0·83
1881–90, .	0·33	0·25	0·03	0·43	2·08	3·05	0·07	0·02	0·98

* Exclusive of the year 1848. (a) Exclusive of the year 1851.

TABLE XI.—*Extent under Cereal Crops.*—*Showing the Average Acreage under Cereal Crops in Ireland for the Years* 1847, 1849, *and* 1850, *and for Quinquennial and Decennial Periods from* 1851 *to* 1890.

Period.	Wheat.	Oats.	Barley.	Bere.	Rye.	Beans and Pease.	Total Cereals.
	Acres, 000 omitted.	Acres, 000 omitted.	Acres, 000 omitted.	Acres, 000 omitted.	Acres, 000 omitted.	Acres, 000 omitted.	Acres, 000 omitted.
*1847–50, .	579	2,135	279	56	17	67	3,133
1851–55, .	409	2,139	255	30	14	35	2,897
1856–60, .	513	1,970	168	5	19	14	2,733
1861–65, .	313	1,838	163	3	7	18	2,419
1866–70, .	277	1,680	194	2	8	13	2,173
1871–75, .	187	1,581	233	1	9	13	1,983
1876–80, .	144	1,415	227	1	9	10	1,814
1881–85, .	105	1,370	183	–	8	10	1,683
1886–90, .	83	1,278	177	–	13	6	1,555
1851–60, .	461	2,073	231	17	15	25	2,810
1861–70, .	295	1,759	168	3	7	14	2,294
1871–80, .	170	1,494	228	1	9	11	1,903
1881–90, .	93	1,326	183	–	10	8	1,618

* Exclusive of the year 1848.

TABLE XII.—*Yield of Cereal Crops.*—Showing the average yield per statute acre of the principal Cereal Crops grown in Ireland in the Years 1847, 1849, and 1850, and in each Quinquennial and Decennial Period in the Years 1851-1890.

Period.	Wheat.	Oats.	Barley.	Bere.	Rye.
	Cwts.	Cwts.	Cwts.	Cwts.	Cwts.
*1847-50, . .	12·6	13·5	17·9	16·7	20·1
1851-55, . .	14·0	14·9	16·1	16·5	20·0
1856-60, . .	12·5	12·4	14·9	14·9	13·5
1861-65, . .	11·4	11·7	14·3	14·4	8·9
1866-70, . .	12·5	12·3	15·9	13·6	10·7
1871-75, . .	13·0	13·1	14·6	15·8	12·0
1876-80, . .	16·4	13·9	15·6	10·5	12·1
1881-85, . .	14·4	13·6	15·9	14·1	11·5
1886-90, . .	16·0	13·8	10·6	13·2	12·1
1851-60, . .	13·4	13·3	15·4	15·7	12·6
1861-70, . .	11·6	12·0	15·1	13·0	10·3
1871-80, . .	13·7	13·1	15·0	15·6	11·5
1881-90, . .	14·7	12·6	15·6	13·4	11·7

* Exclusive of the year 1848.

TABLE XIII.—Showing the Acreage under Green Crops, Flax, and Meadow and Clover in Ireland, in Quinquennial and Decennial Averages from 1847 to 1890 inclusive.

(000 omitted.)

Period.	Average Acreage under						
	Potatoes.	Turnips.	Mangold and Beet.	Other Green Crops.	Total Green Crops.	Flax.	Meadow and Clover.
*1847-50, .	538	329	14	69	1,071	73	1,180
1851-55, .	933	367	37	83	1,428	140	1,273
1856-60, .	1,137	377	36	88	1,626	113	1,434
1861-65, .	1,054	347	14	84	1,506	113	1,529
1866-70, .	1,035	337	21	83	1,448	130	1,579
1871-75, .	930	337	37	73	1,418	123	1,641
1876-80, .	853	335	47	81	1,316	131	1,915
1881-85, .	819	300	38	81	1,338	111	1,970
1886-90, .	791	297	43	80	1,211	117	2,148
1851-60, .	1,040	353	35	65	1,508	125	1,349
1861-70, .	1,045	337	20	81	1,483	122	1,634
1871-80, .	903	331	42	91	1,368	127	1,890
1881-90, .	807	299	40	80	1,221	114	2,063

* Exclusive of the year 1848.

TABLE XIV.—Showing the Average Yield per Acre of the Principal Green Crops, Flax, and Hay grown in Ireland in the Years 1847, 1849, and 1850, and in Quinquennial and Decennial Periods from 1851 to 1890.

Period.	Potatoes.	Turnips.	Mangold and Beet.	Cabbage.	Flax.	Meadow and Clover.
	Tons.	Tons.	Tons.	Tons.	Stones of 14 lbs.	Tons.
*1847–50,	3·6	11·6	15·1	14·1	43·5	2·0
1851–55,	5·3	16·1	17·8	15·4	39·3	2·0
1856–60,	4·4	11·6	17·9	10·6	27·8	1·7
1861–65,	3·0	10·5	11·0	8·7	23·6	1·5
1866–70,	3·4	11·7	12·7	9·6	23·5	1·8
1871–75,	3·1	13·8	14·0	10·4	21·6	1·9
1876–80,	2·9	11·8	12·9	9·2	25·8	2·1
1881–85,	3·7	13·4	13·1	9·4	29·6	2·0
1886–90,	3·4	12·3	13·1	9·8	27·3	2·1
1851–60,	4·8	13·8	15·0	13·1	33·4	1·9
1861–70,	3·2	11·1	11·8	8·7	23·1	1·6
1871–80,	3·0	12·8	13·4	9·9	23·5	2·0
1881–90,	3·5	12·8	13·1	9·6	28·7	2·0

* Exclusive of the year 1848.

TABLE XV.—Showing under each Head the Number of Live Stock in Ireland in the Year 1841, the Average for the Three Years 1847–49–50, and the Averages for each Quinquennial and Decennial Period in the Forty Years 1851–90.

(000 omitted.)

Period.	Horses.	Mules.	Asses.	Cattle.	Sheep.	Pigs.	Goats.	Poultry.
1841 (only)	576	(a)	93	1,863	2,106	1,413	—	8,459
*1847–50	571	16a	127	2,750	1,848	783	183	5,771
1851–55	535	21	147	3,401	3,043	1,155	261	8,257
1856–60	607	19	150	3,540	3,365	1,224	231	8,558
1861–65	563	20	170	3,526	3,475	1,157	173	10,838
1866–70	539	20	171	3,727	4,500	1,429	199	10,758
1871–75	532	21	180	4,084	4,333	1,381	248	11,906
1876–80	538	24	182	4,018	3,834	1,277	271	13,523
1881–85	560	28	191	4,017	3,254	1,280	263	13,380
1886–90	555	30	204	4,135	3,597	1,401	270	14,474
1851–60	573	20	155	3,420	3,198	1,194	224	8,458
1861–70	555	20	170	3,596	4,038	1,153	187	10,473
1871–80	544	22	183	4,051	4,134	1,349	254	12,713
1881–90	548	29	197	4,116	3,435	1,341	277	14,107

* Exclusive of the year 1848.

(a) In the years 1841 and 1847 the mules were returned with the horses.

TABLE XVI.—Number of Live Stock in Ireland per Head of Population.

Periods.	Horses.	Mules.	Asses.	Cattle.	Sheep.	Pigs.	Goats.	Poultry.
1841 (only)	·07	—	·01	·23	·26	·17	—	1·03
*1847–50,	·07	·00	·02	·37	·26	·10	·03	·85
1851–55,	·09	·00	·02	·53	·49	·19	·03	1·33
1856–60,	·10	·00	·03	·61	·60	·20	·04	1·04
1861–65,	·10	·00	·03	·65	·61	·20	·03	1·73
1866–70,	·10	·00	·03	·68	·81	·22	·04	1·07
1871–75,	·10	·00	·03	·77	·81	·24	·06	2·03
1876–80,	·11	·00	·04	·78	·75	·23	·05	2·58
1881–85,	·11	·01	·01	·81	·65	·26	·05	2·70
1886–90,	·12	·01	·04	·86	·77	·29	·05	3·01
1851–60,	·08	·00	·03	·61	·54	·20	·04	1·48
1861–70,	·10	·00	·03	·63	·73	·21	·03	1·64
1871–80,	·10	·00	·03	·75	·78	·24	·05	2·41
1881–90,	·11	·01	·04	·84	·71	·27	·06	2·65

* [illegible]

TABLE XVII.—Showing the Number of Cattle and the Number of Acres of Pasture per Head thereof in each of the specified Years.

—	[illegible]	[illegible]	[illegible]	[illegible]	[illegible]	[illegible]
	000 omitted.	000 omitted.	000 omitted.	000 omitted.	000 omitted.	000 omitted.
Cattle, ...	1,863	2,967	3,472	3,976	3,957	4,449
Three Sheep equal one Head of Cattle, .	707	707	1,155	1,411	1,085	1,441
Total, .	2,560	3,674	4,627	5,387	5,042	5,891
Acres of Pasture, .	7,919*	8,719	9,534	10,071	10,075	10,315
No. of Acres per Head of Cattle, .	3·1	2·4	2·0	1·9	2·0	1·8

* Estimated.

Statement by Dr. Grimshaw with regard to the Value of Output of Irish Agriculture for certain Periods.

With reference to the changes in the value of the output of Irish agriculture since the agricultural statistics of Ireland were first collected in the year 1847, I went into the subject as carefully as its complexity allowed in an address I delivered to the Statistical Society of Ireland in the year 1888.

There were several disturbing causes at work during the first few years of the collection of agricultural statistics, which rendered them not so reliable as could be desired; therefore in the paper I referred to I commenced my review with the year 1851, thus giving at the time of the paper 38 clear years of agricultural returns, which I believe to be as accurate as any such large series of figures can be in Ireland or any other country.

I am now able to add five years more to these statistics, thus throwing further light upon this rather complicated subject. The agricultural statistics for the whole period have been handed in in connexion with the evidence already given.

I propose to analyse these figures, and from the results thus arrived at, in combination with information regarding standard prices of agricultural produce, to lay before you materials by which an approximate opinion may be formed as to the relative value of Irish agriculture in past and present times—first, as regards the total value of Irish agricultural produce; secondly, as regards its relation to the population. In order to do this, and as far as possible to obviate the disturbing elements of good and bad seasons, I have divided the years under consideration into a series of five-year periods, thus obtaining, for the purposes of my paper, seven such periods out of the 38 years referred to, and I can now, by an extension of the principle adopted in the paper, introduce a comparison for the last quinquennial period. The mode of procedure adopted is the following:—Having ascertained the annual average amount of agricultural produce and of live stock in Ireland during each of these five-year periods, I take as standard prices those published in "Purdon's Almanack," and where these are not available, then trustworthy figures from some other source, and treating them in a similar manner, apply the average prices thus obtained to the average produce and to the stock, and obtain an average annual value for the agricultural produce of Ireland during each of the five-year periods.

In order to obtain a clear view of the question at the time of the reading of the paper I dealt with three only of the five-year periods, namely, the first, 1851-55; the last, 1884-88; and the medium, 1866-70. In the first period there is a distinct disturbing cause which influenced prices during the years 1854-55, namely, the high prices caused by the Crimean war. The other periods appear to be only under the influence of ordinary meteorological and commercial causes. On the whole, I think I may claim that these three quinquennials are fair periods for which to strike averages, from which reliable conclusions may be deduced.

I have already pointed out the great change which has come over Irish agriculture during the past 50 years, and how tillage has decreased and how the production of live stock is increasing.

I am fully aware of the difficulties and fallacies attending attempts to estimate the value of agricultural produce from the available data as to prices.

I take the prices which have been carefully collected by the "Farmer's Gazette" and published in "Purdon's Almanack" as the most extensive and reliable set of standard prices available.

Using these and prices from other reliable sources examined and tested by high authorities on such matters, I have prepared these two tables.

Table A.—Average Amount of Produce, Price, and Value of Crops grown in Ireland in the Quinquennials 1851–5, 1866–70, 1884–8, and [illegible].

([illegible])

Description of Crops	1851-55			1866-70			1884-88			[illegible]		
	Amount of Produce.	Price.	Value.	Amount of Produce.	Price.	Value.	Amount of Produce.	Price.	Value.	Amount of Produce.	Price.	Value.
	Cwts.	£ s. d.	£	Cwts.	£ s. d.	£	Cwts.	£ s. d.	£	Cwts.	£ s. d.	£
Wheat,	[illegible]	[illegible]	[illegible]	[illegible]	[illegible]	[illegible]	[illegible]	[illegible]	[illegible]	[illegible]	[illegible]	[illegible]
Oats,	[illegible]	[illegible]	[illegible]	[illegible]	[illegible]	[illegible]	[illegible]	[illegible]	[illegible]	[illegible]	[illegible]	[illegible]
Barley,	[illegible]	[illegible]	[illegible]	[illegible]	[illegible]	[illegible]	[illegible]	[illegible]	[illegible]	[illegible]	[illegible]	[illegible]
Bere and Rye,	[illegible]	[illegible]	[illegible]	[illegible]	[illegible]	[illegible]	[illegible]	[illegible]	[illegible]	[illegible]	[illegible]	[illegible]
Beans and Peas,	[illegible]	[illegible]	[illegible]	[illegible]	[illegible]	[illegible]	[illegible]	[illegible]	[illegible]	[illegible]	[illegible]	[illegible]
	Tons.			Tons.			Tons.			Tons.		
Potatoes,	[illegible]	[illegible]	[illegible]	[illegible]	[illegible]	[illegible]	[illegible]	[illegible]	[illegible]	[illegible]	[illegible]	[illegible]
Turnips,	[illegible]	[illegible]	[illegible]	[illegible]	[illegible]	[illegible]	[illegible]	[illegible]	[illegible]	[illegible]	[illegible]	[illegible]
Mangold,	[illegible]	[illegible]	[illegible]	[illegible]	[illegible]	[illegible]	[illegible]	[illegible]	[illegible]	[illegible]	[illegible]	[illegible]
Flax,	[illegible]	[illegible]	[illegible]	[illegible]	[illegible]	[illegible]	[illegible]	[illegible]	[illegible]	[illegible]	[illegible]	[illegible]
Hay,	[illegible]	[illegible]	[illegible]	[illegible]	[illegible]	[illegible]	[illegible]	[illegible]	[illegible]	[illegible]	[illegible]	[illegible]
Total,	—	—	[illegible]	—	—	[illegible]	—	—	[illegible]	—	—	[illegible]

TABLE II.—Average Number, Price, and Value of Live Stock in Ireland in the Quinquennials 1851–5, 1866–70, 1884–8, and 1889–93.

(000 omitted from Numbers and Values.)

Description of Live Stock.	1851–55. Number.	1851–55. Price.	1851–55. Value.	1866–70. Number.	1866–70. Price.	1866–70. Value.	1884–8. Number.	1884–8. Price.	1884–8. Value.	1889–93. Number.	1889–93. Price.	1889–93. Value.
		£ s. d.	£		£ s. d.	£		£ s. d.	£		£ s. d.	£
Horses and Mules,	[illegible]	[illegible]	[illegible]	[illegible]	[illegible]	[illegible]	[illegible]	[illegible]	[illegible]	[illegible]	[illegible]	[illegible]
Asses,	[illegible]	[illegible]	[illegible]	[illegible]	[illegible]	[illegible]	[illegible]	[illegible]	[illegible]	[illegible]	[illegible]	[illegible]
Cattle,	[illegible]	[illegible]	[illegible]	[illegible]	[illegible]	[illegible]	[illegible]	[illegible]	[illegible]	[illegible]	[illegible]	[illegible]
Sheep,	[illegible]	[illegible]	[illegible]	[illegible]	[illegible]	[illegible]	[illegible]	[illegible]	[illegible]	[illegible]	[illegible]	[illegible]
Pigs,	[illegible]	[illegible]	[illegible]	[illegible]	[illegible]	[illegible]	[illegible]	[illegible]	[illegible]	[illegible]	[illegible]	[illegible]
Goats,	[illegible]	[illegible]	[illegible]	[illegible]	[illegible]	[illegible]	[illegible]	[illegible]	[illegible]	[illegible]	[illegible]	[illegible]
Poultry,	[illegible]	[illegible]	[illegible]	[illegible]	[illegible]	[illegible]	[illegible]	[illegible]	[illegible]	[illegible]	[illegible]	[illegible]
Total,	—	—	[illegible]	—	—	[illegible]	—	—	[illegible]	—	—	[illegible]

These tables are those used in my address of 1889 with five years added to enable the Commissioners to judge of how matters stood at the latest period.

Taking these four quinquennials and adding together the value of the stock and crops, we have the result shown in Table III.

TABLE III.—Average Value of Crops and of Stock in each year of the Quinquennial Periods, 1851–5, 1866–70, 1884–8, and 1889–93.

—	1851–55.	1866–70.	1884–88.	1889–93.
	£	£	£	£
Crops,	56,537,000	75,366,000	38,731,000	31,613,000
Stock,	23,348,000	29,430,000	35,837,000	34,312,000
Total,	77,885,000	104,796,000	81,879,000	62,366,000

The increase in the average of the second quinquennium over the first amounted to 1,114,000*l.*, or 1·4 per cent. The third quinquennium shows a decrease compared with both the first and the second. The decrease in the third compared with the first amounts to 4,806,000*l.*, or 6·4 per cent. The decrease in the third quinquennium compared with the second, amounts to 11,116,000*l.*, or 13·6 per cent. And in the period 1889–93, there was a further decrease of 2,514,000*l.*, showing the still further downward tendency in the total value of the agricultural output of Ireland.

It is not, however, quite fair to deal with crops and stock collectively, in this manner, as, in the ordinary course of business of the farmer, the crops (except those portions reserved for seed) are for sale or consumption within the year, whereas the live stock are only for partial sale or consumption each year, although some of their produce such as milk, butter, eggs, and wool, are for sale or consumption every year.

If we take crops by themselves, we find that their average annual value decreased from the first to the second quinquennium to the amount of 18,171,000*l.*, or 32·0 per cent., between the second and third to the extent of 9,513,000*l.*, or 21·2 per cent.; and between the first and third, to the amount of 22,783,000*l.*, or 36·9 per cent.

In the last period a further decrease of 1,108,000*l.* has taken place.

The great feature in this comparison between the average annual value of the crops in Ireland during the five years 1851–55 and 1889–93, is that there was a decrease of 24,924,000*l.*, or 40·8 per cent.

As it was the production of these crops which afforded employment for the greater portion of the population of Ireland in former times, it is interesting to note that the population decreased about 13·7 per cent. during the period between the Census of 1851 and that of 1891. As the great decrease of the population commenced immediately on and after the great famine of 1846–47, while the change of tillage land into stock-producing land cannot be said to have been established until some years later, it is an interesting fact that the estimated population decreased from 8,295,000 in the year 1845 to 4,708,000 in 1891, or to the extent of 3,590,000, or 43·3 per cent., a ratio closely corresponding with that (40·8 per cent.) representing the decrease of the value of tillage produce.

Turning to the value of live stock, we find that the rise in the average annual value between the first and second quinquennia, amounted to 20,281,000*l.*, or 31·3 per cent.; but when we compare the second and third periods, we find there is, in the latter, a diminution in the value to the extent of 3,802,000*l.*, or 9·4 per cent. Comparing the first period with the third, we find the increase in the latter over the former amounts to 16,479,000*l.*, or 41·9 per cent.; and while the value of live stock in the period of 1854–58 was 1,515,000*l.* more than in 1889–93, still the value in the latter period was 11,934,000*l.* more than that for a similar period 40 years ago. Thus the gain in the

total value of live stock, during 40 years, amounting to 14,964,000*l.*, has been more than counterbalanced by the loss in the annual value of tillage products, amounting to 23,894,000*l.*, leaving a net loss of 8,930,000*l.*, or 9·1 per cent.

Comparing these average values with the mean population, we have the results shown in Table IV., which shows the average value of agricultural produce per head of the mean population.

TABLE D.—Average Value per Head of Mean Population of Crops and Stock in each year of Four Quinquennial Periods.

—	1851-55.	1866-70.	1884-88.	1889-93.
	£	£	£	£
Crops, . . .	9·443	8·299	7·313	7·400
Stock, . . .	6·347	10·909	11·419	11·600
Total, .	15·790	19·208	18·732	19·000

From this we may fairly draw the conclusion that, while the aggregate value of live stock and agricultural products has diminished, the agriculturists, as a class, were individually better off in the second than in the first quinquennium, to the extent of 3·418*l.* per head of the population, worse off in the third than in the second, to the extent of 0·476*l.* per head, and better off in the third as compared with the first, to the extent of 2·942*l.* per head, and in the period 1889-93, 0·268*l.* better off than in the period which immediately preceded it, but showing a slight diminution from the good period of 1866-70.

We know that the labour expended in stock-raising is much less than the labour expended on tillage, and that all other things being equal, the cost of working an acre for tillage purposes is much greater than that of working an acre for the growth of live stock. On the other hand we know that there has been a rise in wages during the period we are considering, and again, we know that a large amount of hand labour has been replaced by the use of agricultural machinery of many kinds. It is quite impossible to make reasonably accurate estimates of these changing elements, and I have not attempted to do so; but I am informed by persons whose opinions are of great value that the increase of wages in the aggregate may be taken to counterbalance, or nearly counterbalance, the savings by the use of machinery, and the lesser number of hands employed on the present as compared with the past system of farming in Ireland.

I have mentioned the fact that in dealing with the money value of live stock, and combining it for general estimates of value with the produce of the crops, only a portion of the value is in the nature of an annual crop, so far as the animals themselves are concerned. We know, however, that live stock yield annual crops in the form of wool, milk, and its products, and eggs, all of which are either sold or consumed during the year.

In the year 1886 I made estimates of the value of the output of Irish agriculture in 1885, with the view of providing the means of estimating the annual profits derived therefrom. These estimates were, of course, only approximate. They were founded partly on published figures, such as I have used in compiling this paper, and partly on statements and information supplied by experienced agriculturists, salesmasters, and others, whose opinions were considered to be of especial value. Assuming that a certain proportion of the live stock are sold off each year, at a certain value, and placing values on certain products of live stock, such as milk, etc., already mentioned, sold or consumed during the year, and deducting from these the value of the crops consumed by those animals in producing these saleable articles we reduce both the value of crops, as given in Table I., and the value of our live stock, as given in Table II. Having done this we arrive at the results shown in Tables V. and VI.

TABLE E.—Average Annual Value of Crops, Stock, &c., disposed of, exclusive of the portion of the Crops used by Stock.

—	Average Annual Value in the Years		
	1851-55.	1866-70.	1884-88.
	£	£	£
Crops,	43,633,000	27,935,000	**16,466,000**
Stock, &c., .	28,325,000	44,279,000	**37,548,000**
Total, .	71,958,000	72,214,000	54,014,000

This table is arrived at by estimating the elements already referred to, as dealt with by me in 1886, and applying estimates to the averages for each of the selected quinquennial periods. We see here that, after allowing for the portion of the crops consumed by the stock, the estimated average value of the crops and stock, and products of stock sold or otherwise disposed of, was, in the first period, 71,958,000*l.* per annum; in the second, 72,214,000*l.* per annum, showing an increase of 256,000*l.*, or 0·3 per cent.; and in the third, 54,014,000*l.* per annum, which amount is 18,200,000*l.*, or 25·2 per cent. under the average value for the second period, and 17,944,000*l.*, or 24·9 per cent. under that for the first.

Dealing with these estimates, as with the previous series of figures in Tables I., II., and III., and making estimates of the average annual value per head of the population, we have Table VI.

TABLE F.—Average Annual Value per Head of the Population.

—	Average Annual Value in the Years		
	1851-55.	1866-70.	1884-88.
	£	£	£
Crops,*	7·044	6·111	**3·383**
Stock, &c., .	4·569	8·101	**7·660**
Total, .	11·613	14·212	11·043

* Exclusive of the portion used by Stock.

From this table it will be observed that there was a substantial though not very great increase in the average value per head in the second of the selected periods as compared with the first, and that in the third quinquennium the average value was slightly under that for the first, and considerably below that for the second, or 1866–70 period.

I regret to state that I am unable to continue Tables V. and VI. so as to represent the state of things in the quinquennial period 1889-93, as in order to do so a new survey of all the elements would require to be made, which time at present would not permit.

I have, however, drawn up this table (Table VII.) so as to show the per-centage of value sold, as given in Table V., to the total values, as given in Table III.

TABLE G.—Per-centage of Annual Value of Crops and Stock and Produce of Stock Sold to Value Produced.

Years.	Crops.	Stock.	Crops and Stock.
	Per cent.	Per cent.	Per cent.
1851–55,	74·6	72·0	73·5
1866–70,	61·6	74·6	66·4
1884–88,	49·1	67·3	59·0

It will be observed that the per-centage value of crops sold fell from 74·6 in 1851–55 to 61·6 in 1866–70, and further to 49·1 in 1884–88, and I have no doubt, as there has been a further decrease in tillage, that there would be a still further drop in the per-centage for the period 1889–93 if the means for making the estimate were available.

The per-centage of decrease in the value of stock and produce of stock sold to the total value of stock is not so great as in the tillage products, the per-centages sold for these periods, 1851–55, 1866–70, and 1884–88, being respectively 72·0, 74·6, and 67·3.

When crops and stock are taken together, the per-centages of value sold for the above periods to the total value of stocks and crops were respectively 73·5, 66·6, and 59·0 per cent.*

I quite admit the crudeness of these estimates, and in making them wherever I have had a doubt I have cast that doubt against the value of agriculture. I admit that the estimates made on the principles adopted in the construction of Tables V. and VI. tend to exaggerate the depression of agriculture in the third of the selected quinquennia.

In the first place, the prices adopted in making the estimates were all taken in good markets; in the second place, the means of communication have so vastly improved during the period which has elapsed between the years 1851 and 1888 that the market prices have been more equalised and new markets opened up; therefore there is every probability that the average values in the earlier years have been over-rated. This is especially true in the case of potatoes, the value of which, in the first period at market price, constituted nearly one-half of the total value of the produce of all crops, calculated on the principles I have adopted. We know, however, that but a small portion of the potato crop ever reached the market, and that had the whole of that large crop been placed on the market, no such price as 4l. 13s. 4d. per ton could possibly have been realised. Bearing this in mind, a large portion of the decline in the value of the crops between the first and the third period is accounted for. This affords a marked illustration of the difficulty of dealing with the subject under consideration. Again, while it is only the value of live stock consumed or sold, and the products of live stock consumed or sold, during the year which are taken, not the total, it must be remembered that a considerable capital in live stock has accumulated which would have no existence if the land used for pasture had remained under tillage. It also happens that the prices in the first selected period were favourably affected by the Crimean war, and that the period 1866–70 was a most favourable time for agriculturists.

* A considerable amount of the agricultural produce sold was exported [illegible] to Great Britain. [illegible]

[illegible] the following were exported in the year [illegible]:—

Cattle,	[illegible]
Pigs,	[illegible]
Sheep,	[illegible]

According to the best authorities the respective value of these animals per head was [illegible]. At these prices the result would be:—

	£
Cattle,	[illegible]
Pigs,	[illegible]
Sheep,	[illegible]
Total,	[illegible]

This estimate is exclusive of calves and lambs, of which there were large numbers.

The reason I leave the calves and lambs out of the estimate is, that I may be able to compare the figures with returns given in [illegible] Appendix, p. [illegible], for the year [illegible].

The number and value of cattle, pigs, and sheep, which may or may not include calves and lambs, exported for the year ended 5th January, [illegible] (i.e., practically for the year [illegible], or [illegible] years ago), was:—

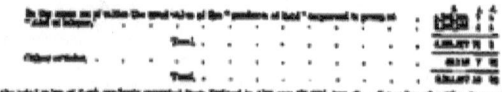

—	Number.	Value.
		£ s. d.
Bullocks and cows,	[illegible]	[illegible]
Pigs,	[illegible]	[illegible]
Sheep,	[illegible]	[illegible]
		[illegible]

In the same year the total value of the "produce of land" [illegible] "Land of Ireland,"	[illegible]
Total,	[illegible]
Other articles,	[illegible]
Total,	[illegible]

Thus the total value of Irish products exported from Ireland in [illegible] was [illegible], less than the value of cattle, sheep, and pigs since exported in [illegible].

A Paper put in by Dr. Grimshaw, Registrar-General for Ireland, with regard to the Income of Irish Agriculturists in the Year 1885.

The estimated gross value of the crops grown in Ireland in the year 1885 is 29,873,898l.; the value of milk and its products is taken as 14,174,810l.; that of the wool clip as 320,745l.; and of the eggs as 556,250l. The sum obtained for the live stock sold is estimated as 16,897,759l.; the total value of the crops and of the live stock disposed of during the year would, upon this calculation, amount to 61,823,462l.

The cost of production may be classed under three heads: (a) seed, artificial manure, food for live stock and wear and tear of vehicles and implements; (b) labour; (c) rent and taxes. The estimated expenses under these heads are: (a) 16,833,000l.; (b) 6,200,000l.; (c) 11,000,000l. Total, 34,033,000l.

Deducting this sum from the value of the crops and live stock as given above, the net income of the agriculturists of Ireland for the year would appear to have been 27,790,462l.

The following details afford information as to the process by which the above results have been arrived at:—

(1.) The produce of the crops has been ascertained from the Registrar-General's report on that subject, and the prices adopted, which are those used in Thom's Directory, are shown in the following table:—

Value of Agricultural Produce in 1885.

Crops	Total Produce.	Estimated Price.	Total Value.
	Cwts.	£ s. d.	£
Wheat, ...	1,097,179	0 9 0	493,730
Oats, ...	18,133,677	0 8 0	7,253,471
Barley, ...	2,883,937	0 7 6	1,081,476
Bere and Rye, . .	111,503	0 7 0	39,027
Beans and Peas, . .	134,630	0 11 6	77,412
Flax, ...	417,019	2 10 0	1,121,515
	Tons.		
Potatoes, . . .	3,170,758	2 10 0	7,926,895
Turnips, ...	3,561,783	0 12 0	2,137,070
Mangel Wurzel, . .	499,730	0 15 0	374,798
Hay, ...	4,156,075	2 5 0	9,351,169
Total, ...	—	—	29,873,898

(2.) The average yield of milk is estimated as 10l. worth per season from each milch cow; the number of cows in 1885 was 1,417,481, and the estimated value of the milk, therefore, 14,174,810l.

(3.) The wool clip is assumed to give an average of 4½ lbs. of wool per sheep; the number of sheep is taken as 2,138,298, and the total amount of wool consequently 9,622,341 lbs., which, at 8d. per lb., would be worth 320,745l.

(4.) It is assumed that one-fourth of the "ordinary fowl" were laying hens; the average number of eggs per hen per year is taken as 100, and the average price as 7s. 6d. per 100. On this estimate the sum received for eggs would amount to 556,250l.

(5.) As regards live stock. The total number of each kind in Ireland at a given period is known, and it is estimated that two-sevenths of the number of cattle and sheep, all of the pigs, and about two-thirds of the poultry are turned out and disposed of each year. The following table shows the total number of each kind of live stock (including horses), the estimated value thereof, the proportion disposed of during the year, and estimated amount received for same:—

Live Stock, 1895.

Description.	Number.	Price.	Total Value.	Proportion sold in Year.	Estimated Amount realised for Stock sold in Year.
		£ s. d.	£		£
Cattle, . .	4,358,751	10 0 0	43,587,510	Two-sevenths,	13,087,146
Sheep, . .	3,477,840	2 0 0	6,955,680	Two-sevenths,	1,987,337
Pigs, . .	1,369,123	1 0 0	1,369,123	All,	1,369,123
Horses, . .	547,132	15 0 0	8,206,980	—	[illegible]
Goats, . .	264,433	0 2 6	33,054	—	—
Poultry, . .	13,849,175	0 1 3	865,573	Two-thirds,	577,049
Asses, . .	197,121	2 0 0	394,242	—	—
Total, . .	—	—	60,613,161	—	16,797,739

The various items included under "cost of production" are set forth in the following statement:—

		£
(a.)	Seed, ...	2,000,000
	Oil Cake, Maize, &c., . .	1,108,000
	Artificial Manures, . .	400,000
	Agricultural Implements,	250,000
	Vehicles and Harness, . .	500,000
	Hay for use of Horses and Cattle,	6,000,000
	Turnips, ...	1,700,000
	Mangel, ...	375,000
	Oats for Horses, &c., .	3,000,000
		15,333,000
(b.)	Labour, ...	8,200,000
(c.)	Rent, ...	11,000,000
	Total, .	£34,533,000

(a.) The proportions of the various kinds of seed adopted for this estimate are those assumed in a letter from William J. Harris, Esq., which appeared in the "Economist" of 23rd January, 1896; the estimated outlay on oil cake, artificial manures, agricultural implements, vehicles, &c., is based on information kindly furnished by some of the principal agents and manufacturers in Dublin; the sum entered for hay is the value of two-thirds of the entire crop, this being the quantity estimated to have been used by cattle and sheep, and by horses engaged in agricultural work; and the sum set down for oats is the value of the quantities estimated to have been required for the horses last referred to, which numbered 363,000.;

(b.) The number of labourers is taken as 300,000 males and 30,000 females, the wages assumed for the former being 10s. per week, and for the latter 5s.

(c.) The rent and taxes are estimated at 11,000,000l. by making a deduction from the total of Griffith's valuation in consideration of the valuation of towns, and adding roughly a certain amount for taxes.

TABLE XVIII.—Showing by Quinquennial and Decennial Periods from 1841 to 1890, the Average Annual Quantity of Spirits Distilled and Beer Brewed in Ireland with their respective Proportions per head of the Population.

Period.	Whiskey. Average Annual No. of Gallons of Spirits Distilled.	Whiskey. Average Annual No. of Gallons per head of Population.	Beer. Average Annual No. of Barrels of Beer Brewed.	Beer. Average Annual No. of Barrels per head of Population.
	000 omitted.		000 omitted.	
1841–45, .	6,500	0·79	673 (a)	0·08
1846–50, .	7,834	1·03	810 (a)	0·11
1851–55, .	8,293	1·33	752 (a)	0·12
1856–60,	7,730	1·31	1,105	0·19
1861–65,	4,886	0·85	1,303	0·23
1866–70, .	6,565	1·20	1,520 (b)	0·28
1871–75, .	10,341	1·94	1,791	0·34
1876–80, .	11,138	2·12	2,069	0·39
1881–85,	9,717	1·93	2,116	0·42
1886–90, .	11,571	2·41	2,316	0·48
1841–50, .	7,167	0·90	741	0·09
1851–60,	8,011	1·33	929	0·15
1861–70, .	5,710	1·02	1,378 (c)	0·25
1871–80,	10,739	2·03	1,930	0·36
1881–90, .	10,644	2·16	2,215	0·45

(a) Estimated from Malt. (b) 3 years. (c) 8 years.

TABLE XIX.—Showing the Number of Woollen Factories, and of Persons employed therein in Ireland in the Years 1874, 1878, 1884, and 1889, with the Number of Spindles and Power Looms.

Year.	No. of Factories.	Spinning Spindles.	Doubling Spindles.	Power Looms.	Persons Employed.
1874, . . .	60	31,943	2,659	307	1,304
1878, . .	74	40,200	1,943	411	1,275
1884, . . .	141	50,922	6,543	763	3,138
1889, . .	67	61,099	11,129	028	3,443

TABLE XX.—Showing by Quinquennial and Decennial Periods the Average Number of Vessels and Boats, and of Men and Boys employed in the Deep Sea Fisheries of Ireland.

Periods.	Vessels and Boats.	Men and Boys.	Periods.	Vessels and Boats.	Men and Boys.
1861–65, . .	10,715	45,639	1856–60, . .	3,803	22,183
1866–70,* .	9,265	39,274			
1871–75, .	7,473	28,540	1861–70,† . .	10,049	42,921
1876–80, . .	5,880	23,126	1871–80, . .	6,678	25,833
1881–85, . .	4,964	22,384	1881–90, . .	6,863	23,123

* Four years' average only. † Nine years' average.

TABLE XXI.—Showing by Quinquennial and Decennial periods from 1841 to 1890 inclusive the Average Amount of Capital Invested in the Railways of Ireland, the Average Length of Lines open, the Number of Passengers carried, the aggregate Receipts, the Receipts per head of the Population, &c.

Periods.	Capital paid up.		Mileage.		Receipts.				
	Total.	Per head of Population.	Total Miles open.	Passengers per Mile.	Passengers and Mails.	Goods.	Total.	Per head of Population.	Per Mile.
	£ 000 omitted.	£	Miles.		£ 000 omitted.	£ 000 omitted.	£ 000 omitted.	£	£
1841–45,	–	–	(b) 35	135,625	–	–	(b) 77	0·01	3,800
1846–50,	–	–		28,452	(a) 215	(a) 131	303	0·04	1,131
1851–55,	(a) 14,780	2·44		799	455	303	780	0·13	1,013
1856–60,	18,061	3·07	1,159	4,954	719	608	1,271	0·21	1,037
1861–65,	23,913	4·19	1,679	3,797	950	563	1,543	0·27	918
1866–70,	(d) 27,030	4·94	(d) 1,947	3,609	(d) 1,123	(d) 799	(d) 1,924	0·35	995
1871–75,	28,996	5·44	2,021	3,661	1,365	1,096	2,461	0·46	1,177
1876–80,	33,156	6·11	2,325	3,524	1,431	1,271	2,703	0·51	1,189
1881–85,	35,608	6·99	2,501	3,014	1,491	1,256	2,747	0·55	1,098
1886–90,	34,101	7·60	2,628	1,851	1,547	1,326	2,873	0·60	1,085
1841–50,	–	–	(d) 184	48,365	(a) 215	(a) 161	(d) 305	0·03	1,638
1851–60,	(c) 17,137	2·89	984	4,160	600	605	1,006	0·17	1,031
1861–70,	(d) 25,314	4·53	(d) 1,798	3,107	(d) 1,033	(d) 678	(d) 1,731	0·31	983
1871–80,	30,373	5·77	2,173	3,476	1,398	1,183	2,581	0·49	1,183
1881–90,	35,854	7·26	2,564	1,920	1,619	1,291	2,810	0·57	1,096

(a) 7 years only. (b) 4 years only. (c) 7 years only. (d) 9 years only.

TABLE XXII.—Showing by Quinquennial and Decennial Periods from 1841 to 1890 the Average Tonnage of Vessels Entered and Cleared at the Ports of Ireland.

Periods.	Entered. Foreign Trade (with Cargoes and in Ballast).	Entered. Coasting Trade (with Cargoes only).	Cleared. Foreign Trade (with Cargoes and in Ballast).	Cleared. Coasting Trade (with Cargoes only).	Totals. Total Entered.	Totals. Total Cleared.	Totals. General Total.
	Tons 000 omitted.	Tons 000 omitted.	Tons 000 omitted.	Tons 000 omitted.	Tons 000 omitted.	Tons 000 omitted.	Tons 000 omitted.
1841–45, . .	330	1,840	160	1,400	2,180	1,560	3,720
1846–50, . .	440	2,340	230	1,830	2,780	2,000	4,780
1851–55, . .	410	2,720	190	1,950	3,160	2,240	5,400
1856–60, . .	480	3,160	180	2,330	3,620	2,500	6,120
1861–65, . .	580	3,700	200	2,610	4,280	2,840	7,120
1866–70, . .	620	4,120	200	3,000	4,760	3,200	7,960
1871–75, . .	810	4,530	380	3,380	5,340	3,740	9,080
1876–80, . .	1,220	5,140	480	4,340	6,360	5,020	11,380
1881–85, . .	920	5,220	340	4,020	6,140	4,300	10,600
1886–90, . .	848	5,137	334	3,851	5,985	4,187	10,172
1841–50, . .	330	2,140	270	1,510	2,470	1,780	4,250
1851–60, . .	460	2,930	230	2,110	3,390	2,370	5,760
1861–70, . .	620	3,910	200	2,810	4,530	3,020	7,550
1871–80, . .	850	4,870	520	3,860	5,920	4,380	10,300
1881–90, . .	884	5,202	338	3,935	6,065	4,273	10,385

TABLE XXIII.—Showing the Averages by Quinquennial and Decennial Periods from 1841 to 1890, the Amount of Cash Balances and Deposits in Joint Stock Banks, Post Office and Trustee Savings' Banks, and their proportion to the Population of Ireland.

Periods.	Banking Capital.	Deposits in Joint Stock Banks. Total.	Deposits in Joint Stock Banks. Per head of Population.	Deposits in Savings' Banks. Totals. Post Office.	Deposits in Savings' Banks. Totals. Trustee Banks.	Deposits in Savings' Banks. Totals. Post Office and Trustee Banks.	Deposits in Savings' Banks. Amount per head of Population.	Bank Note Circulation.
	£ 000 omitted.	£ 000 omitted.	£	£ 000 omitted.	£ 000 omitted.	£ 000 omitted.	£	£ 000 omitted.
1841–45, . .	—	7,008	0·85	—	2,545	2,545	0·31	—
1846–50, . .	4,774	7,649	0·99	—	2,019	2,019	0·31	—
1851–55, . .	4,923	10,781	1·73	—	1,515	1,515	0·24	—
1856–60, . .	4,949	14,730	2·90	—	1,690	1,890	0·28	(c) 7,226
1861–65, . .	(a) 5,348	16,331	2·79	(a) 152	2,036	2,148	0·35	8,191
1866–70, . .	6,356	22,391	4·09	378	2,503	2,170	0·40	6,943
1871–75, . .	6,637	30,109	5·84	867	2,076	2,943	0·45	7,660
1876–80, . .	6,620	31,529	6·05	1,335	2,147	3,473	0·68	7,117
1881–85, . .	7,038	30,849	6·15	2,073	2,033	4,174	0·83	7,255
1886–90, . .	7,021	31,443	6·84	3,315	2,019	5,231	1·09	6,644
1841–50, . .	(d) 4,354	7,276	0·97	—	2,181	2,181	0·27	—
1851–60, . .	4,943	12,756	2·10	—	1,703	1,703	0·28	(c) 7,224
1861–70, . .	(b) 5,908	18,856	3·26	(b) 276	1,914	2,162	0·39	6,548
1871–80, . .	8,747	30,968	5·84	1,101	2,100	3,210	0·61	7,363
1881–90, . .	7,021	31,146	6·53	2,642	2,035	4,677	0·95	6,949

(a) 3 years only. (b) 8 years only. (c) 3 years only. (d) 6 years only.

TABLE XXIV.—Showing by Quinquennial and Decennial Periods the Average Amount of Capital Invested in certain Stocks, and of Loans issued for Public Purposes in Ireland from 1841 to 1890, both years inclusive.

(000 omitted.)

Period.	Capital Paid up.		Government Stock held in Ireland.	Public Loans by			
	Banking.	Railway and Canals.		Commissioners of Public Works, Ireland.	Public Works Loan Commissioners.	Irish Land Commission.	Total.
	£	£	£	£	£	£	£
1841–45, .	–	–	33,320	366	123	–	489
1846–50, .	4,931	–	35,215	1,916	229	–	2,145
1851–55, .	4,832	‡14,750	36,141	436	102	–	[illegible]
1856–60, .	4,949	§18,061	40,763	247	153	–	[illegible]
1861–65, .	*5,316	22,818	37,633	224	120	–	344
1866–70, .	4,556	*27,030	36,908	296	104	–	400
1871–75, .	6,627	29,998	35,315	430	23		453
1876–80, .	6,834	32,164	32,483	919	8	–	927
1881–85, .	7,053	35,708	30,917	341	6	93	[illegible]
1886–90, .	7,034	36,103	28,616	619	13	1,213	[illegible]
1841–50, .	4,934	–	35,033	1,131	177	–	1,308
1851–60, .	6,945	‖17,177	39,463	341	¶136	–	[illegible]
1861–70, .	15,909	125,394	37,220	256	137	–	393
1871–80, .	6,741	30,575	34,033	674	¶16	–	687
1881–90, .	7,031	35,654	29,766	480	12	653	[illegible]

* 4 years only. † 6 years only. ‡ 3 years only. § 2 years only. ‖ 8 years only. ¶ 9 years only.

No.	[illegible]	Purpose for which advanced.	Total Amount advanced.	Total Principal repaid.	Total Interest paid.	Remitted.	Principal: In arrear: [illegible]	Principal: In arrear: Other arrears.	Principal: Not yet due.	Interest.	No.
		[illegible]	£ s. d.	£ s. d.	£ s. d.	£ s. d.	£ s. d.	£ s. d.	£ s. d.	£ s. d.	
[illegible]	[illegible]	[illegible]	[illegible]	[illegible]	[illegible]	[illegible]	[illegible]	[illegible]	[illegible]	[illegible]	[illegible]
[illegible]	[illegible]	[illegible]	[illegible]	[illegible]	[illegible]	[illegible]	[illegible]	[illegible]	[illegible]	[illegible]	[illegible]
[illegible]	[illegible]	[illegible]	[illegible]	[illegible]	[illegible]	[illegible]	[illegible]	[illegible]	[illegible]	[illegible]	[illegible]
[illegible]	[illegible]	[illegible]	[illegible]	[illegible]	[illegible]	[illegible]	[illegible]	[illegible]	[illegible]	[illegible]	[illegible]
[illegible]	[illegible]	[illegible]	[illegible]	[illegible]	[illegible]	[illegible]	[illegible]	[illegible]	[illegible]	[illegible]	[illegible]
[illegible]	[illegible]	[illegible]	[illegible]	[illegible]	[illegible]	[illegible]	[illegible]	[illegible]	[illegible]	[illegible]	[illegible]
[illegible]	[illegible]	[illegible]	[illegible]	[illegible]	[illegible]	[illegible]	[illegible]	[illegible]	[illegible]	[illegible]	[illegible]
		[illegible]	[illegible]	[illegible]	[illegible]	[illegible]	[illegible]	[illegible]	[illegible]	[illegible]	
		[illegible]									
[illegible]	[illegible]	[illegible]	[illegible]	[illegible]	[illegible]	[illegible]	[illegible]	[illegible]	[illegible]	[illegible]	[illegible]
[illegible]	[illegible]	[illegible]	[illegible]	[illegible]	[illegible]	[illegible]	[illegible]	[illegible]	[illegible]	[illegible]	[illegible]
[illegible]	[illegible]	[illegible]	[illegible]	[illegible]	[illegible]	[illegible]	[illegible]	[illegible]	[illegible]	[illegible]	[illegible]
[illegible]	[illegible]	[illegible]	[illegible]	[illegible]	[illegible]	[illegible]	[illegible]	[illegible]	[illegible]	[illegible]	[illegible]
[illegible]	[illegible]	[illegible]	[illegible]	[illegible]	[illegible]	[illegible]	[illegible]	[illegible]	[illegible]	[illegible]	[illegible]
[illegible]	[illegible]	[illegible]	[illegible]	[illegible]	[illegible]	[illegible]	[illegible]	[illegible]	[illegible]	[illegible]	[illegible]
		[illegible]	[illegible]	[illegible]	[illegible]	[illegible]	[illegible]	[illegible]	[illegible]	[illegible]	
		[illegible]	[illegible]	[illegible]	[illegible]	[illegible]					

No.	Acts under which Advances have been made.	Purpose for which advanced.	Total Amount advanced.	Total Principal repaid.	Total Interest paid.	Remitted.	Balance outstanding against Borrowers on March 31, [illegible].				
							Principal.				Interest.
							In Arrear.		Not yet due.		
							Written off (?) ... Local Loans Fund.	Other Loans.			
		II.—LOANS CHARGED (?) ...									
		Class II.—Loans (?) ...	£ s. d.	£ s. d.	£ s. d.	£ s. d.	£ s. d.	£ s. d.	£ s. d.		£ s. d.
[illegible]	[illegible]	Public health (?)	[illegible]	[illegible]	[illegible]	[illegible]	[illegible]	[illegible]	[illegible]		[illegible]
[illegible]	Do.	[illegible]	[illegible]	[illegible]	[illegible]	[illegible]	[illegible]	[illegible]	[illegible]		[illegible]
[illegible]	Do.	Relief of distress (?)	[illegible]	[illegible]	[illegible]	[illegible]	[illegible]	[illegible]	[illegible]		[illegible]
[illegible]	Do.	[illegible]	[illegible]	[illegible]	[illegible]	[illegible]	[illegible]	[illegible]	[illegible]		[illegible]
		Totals—Class II.	[illegible]	[illegible]	[illegible]	[illegible]	[illegible]	[illegible]	[illegible]		[illegible]
		Class III.—Loans (?) ...									
[illegible]	[illegible]	[illegible]	[illegible]	[illegible]	[illegible]	[illegible]	[illegible]	[illegible]	[illegible]		[illegible]
[illegible]	Do.	[illegible]	[illegible]	[illegible]	[illegible]	[illegible]	[illegible]	[illegible]	[illegible]		[illegible]
		Totals—Class III.	[illegible]	[illegible]	[illegible]	[illegible]	[illegible]	[illegible]	[illegible]		[illegible]
		Total (?) ...	[illegible]	[illegible]	[illegible]	[illegible]	[illegible]	[illegible]	[illegible]		[illegible]
		[illegible] Local Loans Fund / [illegible]	[illegible]	[illegible]	[illegible]	[illegible]		[illegible]			[illegible]

[illegible]
[illegible]

TABLE II.

STATEMENT showing the TOTAL AMOUNT ADVANCED by the COMMISSIONERS OF PUBLIC WORKS, IRELAND, VICE TREASURER, PAYMASTER OF CIVIL SERVICES, and PAYMASTER-GENERAL IN IRELAND on Closed Loan Services, the TOTAL REPAYMENTS, and the AMOUNT REMITTED.

Authorising Act.	Purpose of Loan.	Total Amount advanced.	Total Principal repaid.	Total Interest paid.	Total Amount remitted.	
	CLOSED LOAN SERVICES.	£ s. d.	£ s. d.	£ s. d.	£ s. d.	
[illegible]	Roads and bridges, repairs of	[illegible]	[illegible]	—	—	
[illegible]	Repairs of great roads	[illegible]	[illegible]	—	—	
[illegible]	[illegible], relief works	[illegible]	[illegible]	[illegible]	[illegible]	
[illegible]	Exchequer bills issued and cancelled	[illegible]	[illegible]	[illegible]	—	
[illegible]	Maynooth College	[illegible]	[illegible]	[illegible]	[illegible]	
[illegible]	Improvement of Shannon navigation	[illegible]	[illegible]	[illegible]	[illegible]	
[illegible]	Ecclesiastical Commissioners	[illegible]	[illegible]	[illegible]	—	
[illegible]	Employment of the labouring poor	[illegible]	[illegible]	[illegible]	[illegible]	
[illegible]	River drainage, preliminary expenses	[illegible]	[illegible]	—	[illegible]	
[illegible]	Commissioners of Wide Streets, Dublin	[illegible]	[illegible]	[illegible]	[illegible]	These advances were made by the Vice Treasurer, Paymaster of Civil Services, and Paymaster-General.
[illegible]	Relief of trade	[illegible]	[illegible]	—	[illegible]	
[illegible]	Boundary survey	[illegible]	[illegible]	[illegible]	[illegible]	
[illegible]	Suitors' Fund, Court of Exchequer (in aid of)	[illegible]	[illegible]	[illegible]	[illegible]	
[illegible]	Fishery piers, preliminary inquiries	[illegible]	[illegible]	—	—	
[illegible]	Trinity College, Dublin	[illegible]	[illegible]	—	—	
[illegible]	County Tyrone	[illegible]	[illegible]	—	—	
[illegible]	Londonderry, Mayor, &c. of	[illegible]	[illegible]	—	[illegible]	
[illegible]	[illegible], Dublin	[illegible]	[illegible]	[illegible]	[illegible]	
[illegible]	Tithe [illegible], expenses of	[illegible]	[illegible]	—	[illegible]	
[illegible]	Relief of clergy	[illegible]	[illegible]	—	[illegible]	
[illegible]	Fever hospitals	[illegible]	[illegible]	—	—	
[illegible]	Cholera expenses	[illegible]	[illegible]	—	[illegible]	
[illegible]	Board of First Fruits	[illegible]	[illegible]	[illegible]	[illegible]	
[illegible]	Insurrection Acts	[illegible]	[illegible]	—	[illegible]	
[illegible]	Peace Preservation Acts	[illegible]	[illegible]	—	[illegible]	
[illegible]	Constabulary	[illegible]	[illegible]	—	[illegible]	
[illegible]	Public Works	[illegible]	[illegible]	[illegible]	[illegible]	
[illegible]	Valuation of land and tenements	[illegible]	[illegible]	—	[illegible]	
[illegible]	Post roads	[illegible]	[illegible]	—	—	
[illegible]	Turnpike road debentures	[illegible]	[illegible]	[illegible]	[illegible]	
[illegible]	[illegible] turnpike road	[illegible]	—	—	[illegible]	
[illegible]	General rate in aid	[illegible]	[illegible]	—	—	
[illegible]	Gaols and bridewells	[illegible]	[illegible]	[illegible]	[illegible]	
[illegible]	Lunatic asylums support	[illegible]	[illegible]	[illegible]	—	
[illegible]	Temporary relief	[illegible]	[illegible]	—	[illegible]	
[illegible]	Consolidated annuities	[illegible]				
[illegible]	Distressed poor law unions	[illegible]				
[illegible]	Tithe composition	[illegible]	[illegible]	—	[illegible]	
[illegible]	Relief of distress	[illegible]	[illegible]	[illegible]	—	
	Total Closed Services	[illegible]	[illegible]	[illegible]	[illegible]	

TABLE III.

Summary of Loan Advances, Repayments, Remissions, &c. to 31st March 18[illegible].

—	Total Amount advanced.	Total Principal repaid.	Total Interest paid.	Remitted.	Balance outstanding ... 31st March [illegible]. Principal. In Arrear. Written off from the Balance of Loans of the Local Loans Fund.	Other Arrears.	Not yet due.	Interest.
Local Loans Fund.	£ s. d.	£ s. d.	£ s. d.	£ s. d.	£ s. d.	£ s. d.	£ s. d.	£ s. d.
Class I.:								
Loans secured on undertakings.	[illegible]	[illegible]	[illegible]	[illegible]	[illegible]	[illegible]	[illegible]	[illegible]
Class II.:								
Loans secured on rates.	[illegible]	[illegible]	[illegible]	[illegible]		[illegible]	[illegible]	[illegible]
Class III.:								
Loans secured on lands.	[illegible]	[illegible]	[illegible]	[illegible]	[illegible]	[illegible]	[illegible]	[illegible]
Class IV.:								
Miscellaneous loans	[illegible]	[illegible]	[illegible]	[illegible]	—	[illegible]	[illegible]	[illegible]
Total—Current and [illegible] services.	[illegible]	[illegible]	[illegible]	[illegible]	[illegible]	[illegible]	[illegible]	[illegible]
Total—Closed services.	[illegible]	[illegible]	[illegible]	[illegible]	—	—	—	—
Grand total—Local Loans Fund.	[illegible]	[illegible]	[illegible]	[illegible]	[illegible]	[illegible]	[illegible]	[illegible]
Church Fund Loans.								
Class II.:								
Loans secured on rates.	[illegible]	[illegible]	[illegible]	[illegible]	—	[illegible]	[illegible]	
Class III.:								
Loans secured on lands.	[illegible]	[illegible]	[illegible]	[illegible]		[illegible]	[illegible]	[illegible]
Total Church Fund Loans.	[illegible]	[illegible]	[illegible]	[illegible]	—	[illegible]	[illegible]	[illegible]
Grand total	[illegible]	[illegible]	[illegible]	[illegible]	[illegible]	[illegible]	[illegible]	[illegible]
					[illegible]			

TABLE IV.

STATEMENT showing the Rates of Interest chargeable on Loans advanced by the Commissioners of Public Works, Ireland, together with the Modes and Periods of Repayment.

No. of Account as per Table I.	Purpose of Loan.	Rate of Interest.	Observations.	Maximum Period of Repayment. Years.	Mode of Repayment.	Annual Payment per Cent. when Repayment is by Annuity. £ s. d.
	Local boards	4	- - -	[illegible]	*Instalments	—
	Inland navigation	4	- - -	[illegible]	Do.	—
	Railways	4	- - -	[illegible]	Do.	—
	Quarries, mines, and miscellaneous.	4	- - -	[illegible]	Do.	
	Harbours—					
	(a.) Commercial harbours	4	- - -	[illegible]	Do.	—
	(b.) Loans to pier authorities created by Harbour Act, 1883.	3½	- - -	50	Do.	—
	Reclamation of waste lands (See also Nos. 23 and 24.)	5	- - -	2 from completion of works.	Do.	—
7	Labourers' dwellings	—	Operations now carried on under Housing of Working Classes Act.	—	—	—
8	Housing of the working classes	[illegible]	- - -	[illegible]	Do.	—
		[illegible]	- - -	[illegible]	Do.	—
		[illegible]	- - -	40	Do.	—
		[illegible]	- - -	†50	Do.	—
	Grand juries of counties—					
	(a.) Roads and bridges	5	- - -	[illegible]	Annuity	[illegible]
	(b.) Court houses	4	- - -	1 from completion of works.	Do.	—
	(c.) Bridges between counties	5	- - -	[illegible]	Do.	[illegible]
10	Roads and bridges	5	- - -	[illegible]	*Instalments	—
11	Public buildings—					
	(a.) Reformatories	[illegible]	- - -	[illegible]	Do.	—
		[illegible]	- - -	[illegible]	Do.	—
		4	- - -	[illegible]	Do.	—
	(b.) Public libraries	5	- - -	[illegible]	Do.	—
	(c.) Industrial schools	3½	- - -	[illegible]	Do.	—
12	Fishery piers and harbours	5	- - -	[illegible]	Annuity	[illegible]
13	Public works loans (57 Geo. III. c. 34.)	—	No loans being made under this Act.	—	—	—
14	Repairs of post roads and bridges	4	- - -	2	Instalments	—
15	Repairs of fishery piers and harbours.	4	- - -	1 from completion of works.	Do.	—
16	Maintenance of navigation works	4	- - -	Do.	Do.	—
17	Lunatic asylum buildings—					
	(a.) Permanent works and purchase of land	[illegible]	- - -	[illegible]	Do.	—
		[illegible]	- - -	[illegible]	Do.	—
	(b.) Furniture, fittings, &c.	[illegible]	- - -	[illegible]	Do.	—
18	Artizans' dwellings	—	Operations now carried on under the Housing of the Working Classes Act.	—	—	—
19	Public Health—					
	(a.) Waterworks, sewerage, &c., &c.	[illegible]	- - -	[illegible]	*Instalments	
		[illegible]	- - -	[illegible]	Do.	—
		4	- - -	[illegible]	Do.	—
	(b.) Burial grounds	4	- - -	[illegible]	Do.	—
20	Emigration	[illegible]	- - -	[illegible]	Do.	—
		[illegible]	- - -	[illegible]	Do.	—
[illegible]	Labourers' Acts—					
	Erection of cottages by boards of guardians.	[illegible]	- - -	[illegible]	Annuity	[illegible]
		[illegible]	- - -	[illegible]	Do.	[illegible]
		[illegible]	- - -	[illegible]	Do.	[illegible]
[illegible]	Dispensary houses	[illegible]	- - -	[illegible]	Do.	[illegible]
[illegible]	River Drainage, 5 & 6 Vict. c. 89.	—	No loans are now made.	—	—	—
[illegible]	River Drainage, 26 & 27 Vict. c. 88.	4 during progress of works, subsequently 3½	- -	[illegible]	Annuity	[illegible]
				[illegible]	Do.	[illegible]

* i.e., equal instalments of principal with interest on balance outstanding.

† Only allowed to local authorities.

No. of Account as per Table I.	Purpose of Loan.	Rate of Interest.	Observations.	Maximum Period of Repayment. Years.	Mode of Repayment.	Annual Payment per Cent. when Repayment is by Annuity.
						£ s. d.
	River Drainage Maintenance—					
	(a.) Under 32 & 33 Vict. c. 42, for works carried out by Board of works	5	- - -	Not usually exceeding 22 years.	Annuity -	*11 [illegible]
	(b.) Loans to trustees -	4½	- - -	Not usually exceeding 18 years.	Do. -	*10 7 [illegible]
[illegible]	*Land Improvement*— Loans to landowners—					
	(a.) For sub-soiling, trenching, irrigation, embanking, fencing, and reclamation of waste lands.	3½ (about)	- - -	22	Do. -	[illegible]
	(b.) For farm buildings, houses and offices, scutch mills, labourers' dwellings, and planting	4¼ (about)	- - -	31	Do. -	[illegible]
		3½	- - -	35	Do. -	[illegible]
	(c.) For labourers' cottages erected by order of the Land Commission.	3½ (about)	- - -	34	Do. -	[illegible]
[illegible]	Land Improvement, preliminary expenses.	—	—	—	—	—
28	*Land Improvement*—					
	(a.) Loans to tenants for drainage.	3½ (about)	- - -	20	Annuity -	[illegible]
	(b.) Loans to companies for reclamation of waste lands.	3½	- - -	30	No loans yet made.	—
		3¾	- - -	35		
		4	- - -	40		
		4½	- - -	35		
29	Land Act, 1870 - - -	—	No loans now being made.	—	—	—
30	Glebe loans - - -	3½	- - -	35	Annuity -	[illegible]
31	Building schools - - -	—	No loans are now made.	—	—	—
32 & 33	Seed supply - - -	—	No loans are now made.	—	—	—
	National School Teachers' Residences.	3½	- - -	35	Do. -	[illegible]
35	Non-vested schools and training colleges.	3½	- - -	35	Do. -	[illegible]

* For 14 years.

TABLE V.

Board of Public Works, Ireland.

The following Statement shows the Rates of Interest chargeable on the several Advances making the aggregate outstanding Loan Balances on the 31st March 1894.—

	£
Free of interest - - - - - - -	13,473
3 per cent. - - - - - - -	5,000
[illegible] " - - - - - - -	1,4[illegible]
[illegible] " - - - - - - -	[illegible]
[illegible] " - - - - - - -	156,7[illegible]
[illegible] " - - - - - - -	2,348,[illegible]
[illegible] " - - - - - - -	763,[illegible]
4 " - - - - - - -	1,403,[illegible]
4½ " - - - - - - -	226,134
5 " - - - - - - -	49,682
Advances on which interest is deferred pending the completion of the works - - - - - -	98,306
Total Local Loans Fund - -	7,700,807
Church Fund Loans at 1 per cent. -	708,[illegible]
	[illegible]*

The average rate chargeable on the advances out of the Local Loans Fund was 3l. 11s. 2d. on the 31st March 1894. The interest realised in the year averaged 3l. 7s. 10d. per cent. on the principal sum outstanding on the 1st April 1893.

* Exclusive of [illegible] written off from the accounts of the assets of the Local Loans Fund.

TABLE VI.

Summary of the different Purposes for which Loans have been sanctioned by the Commissioners of Public Works in Ireland from [illegible] to [illegible].

Purposes of Loans.	[illegible]
CLASS I. [illegible]	[illegible]
CLASS II. [illegible]	[illegible]
CLASS III. [illegible]	[illegible]
CLASS IV. Miscellaneous Loans. [illegible]	[illegible]

TABLE VII.

Statement showing the Advances for the last five years on the six most important Loan Services administered by the Commissioners of Public Works, Ireland.

Year to 31st March.	Labourers' Dwellings in Towns Act and Housing of the Working Classes Act.	Labourers' Acts.	Public Health Acts.	Lunatic Asylums Buildings.	Land Improvement Loans to Landowners.	Land Improvement Loans to Tenants.
	1.	2.	3.	4.	5.	6.
	£	£	£	£	£	£
Total issued to 31st March 1889	587,081	[illegible]	1,581,811; Church Fund [illegible]	1,453,980	3,961,734; Church Fund [illegible]	[illegible]
In year to 31st March 1890	56,336	136,450	100,307	24,504	23,677	36,138
„ 1891	30,070	150,135	56,309	36,046	29,734	[illegible]
„ 1892	13,551	115,153	80,005	35,029	30,004	[illegible]
„ 1893	37,404	111,480	130,245	58,026	75,817	[illegible]
„ 1894	24,196	71,437	100,809	51,528	32,313	41,190
Total issued to 31st March 1894.	802,058	1,530,393	Church Fund 38,336; 2,079,046; 2,116,382	1,601,532	Church Fund 203,829; 4,196,153; 5,099,777	[illegible]

TABLE VIII.

(a.) Statement showing for the last 10 years the Amount voted by Parliament for the purpose of Loans to be advanced by the Commissioners of Public Works, Ireland, and the Sum actually issued on account of each Vote.

Currency of Vote.	Loan Vote. Authorising Act.	Amount.	Amount issued to meet actual Requirements.
		£	£
Part of years—			
1884 and 1885	47 & 48 Vict. c. 49.	1,200,000	740,000
1885 „ 1886	48 & 49 Vict. c. 65.	1,350,000	850,000
1886 „ 1887	49 & 50 Vict. c. 41.	1,200,000	690,000
1887 „ 1888	50 & 51 Vict. c. 57.	1,050,000	900,000
1888 „ 1889	51 & 52 Vict. c. 53.	1,000,000	850,000
1889 „ 1890	52 & 53 Vict. c. 71.	1,300,000	420,000
1890 „ 1891	53 & 54 Vict. c. 30.	1,000,000	655,000
1891 „ 1892	54 & 55 Vict. c. 58.	1,000,000	600,000
1892 „ 1893	55 & 56 Vict. c. 61.	950,000	860,000
1893 „ 1894	56 & 57 Vict. c. 24.	900,000	600,000

(b.) Statement showing for the last 10 years the total Repayments in respect of Loans advanced by the Commissioners of Public Works.

—	Total Repayments. Principal repaid.	Interest paid.	Total.
	£ s. d.	£ s. d.	£ s. d.
Year ended 31st March—			
1885	365,242 1 9	193,311 19 3	[illegible]
1886	375,060 7 9	[illegible]	587,335 15 5
1887	[illegible]	[illegible]	[illegible]
1888	[illegible]	[illegible]	[illegible]
1889	516,363 4 10	[illegible]	769,048 14 5
1890	478,119 6 1	[illegible]	745,961 15 5
1891	[illegible]	[illegible]	951,900 1 9
1892	590,745 7 6	[illegible]	853,837 17 3
1893	452,893 19 3	267,149 17 5	[illegible]
1894	453,479 4 4	244,765 14 11	697,344 15 3

TABLE XI.

STATEMENT of REMISSIONS up to the 31st March 1894 in respect of LOAN ADVANCES made through the BOARD of PUBLIC WORKS for IRELAND, or through the VICE-TREASURER, PAYMASTER of CIVIL SERVICES, and PAYMASTER GENERAL.

Purposes for which Advanced.	Amount Of Loan.	Amount Repaid.	Amount Remitted.	Authority for Remission or Write-off.
CLOSED SERVICES.	£ s. d.	£ s. d.	£ s. d.	
Grand Juries of Counties, Relief Works	226,105 15 11	65,871 16 1	160,679 1 10	Act 16 & 17 Vict. c. 75.
Maynooth College	18,643 10 9	2,735 6 10	15,857 9 9	Act 32 & 33 Vict. c. 42, s. 41 (Church Act).
Shannon Navigation	294,000 0 0	281,493 7 2	12,506 12 10	Act 42 & 43 Vict. c. 83.
Employment of the Labouring Poor	4,792,810 12 1	567,706 13 10	4,224,847 17 3	Acts 10 & 11 Vict. c. 87, and 16 & 17 Vict. c. 75.
River Drainage, Preliminary Expenses	25,000 0 0	6,728 6 10	18,271 13 2	Treasury Letter, 24th June 1853.
Commissioners of Wide Streets, Dublin	263,824 5 11	36,095 6 5	226,728 19 6	Act 40 & 41 Vict. c. 27.
Relief of Trade	279,075 7 7	245,770 17 6	33,304 9 10	Act 40 & 41 Vict. c. 27.
Dunleary Harbour	214,760 4 7	72,544 10 9	142,234 13 10	Act 40 & 41 Vict. c. 27.
Suitors' Fund, Court of Exchequer	190,431 10 6	550 6 2	189,880 4 11	Act 40 & 41 Vict. c. 27.
Londonderry, Mayor, &c. of	12,848 3 1	8,802 1 6	4,045 2 1	Private Act, 1843.
Corn Exchange, Dublin	7,848 3 1	218 4 6	7,629 18 7	Treasury Letters, 16th June 1838, and 11th May 1846.
Tithe Militia, Expenses of	5,188 15 0	5,098 14 6	10 0 4	Treasury Letter, 15th January 1846.
Relief of Clergy	48,500 0 0	15,404 0 11	33,095 19 1	Act 3 & 4 Will. 4. c. 100, and Treasury Letter, 15th January 1843.
Cholera Expenses	196,251 8 8	196,215 8 8	36 0 0	Treasury Letters, 20th January 1842, 24th October 1846, 20th December 1844, 27th February 1845.
Board of First Fruits	187,048 12 3	95,363 1 10	91,620 10 5	Act 4 Geo. 4 c. 98.
Incorporation Acts	23,582 0 0	22,911 18 10	673 1 2	Treasury Letter, 20th February 1852.
Fever Prevention Acts	650,287 11 8	636,530 15 6	14,300 16 6	Treasury Letters, 16th March and 14th September 1848.
[illegible]	3,723,609 15 6	2,500,146 12 10	723,947 3 6	Treasury Letter, 31st March 1851.
Public Works	380,615 3 10	355,892 13 1	24,792 10 9	Treasury Letter, 15th January 1848.
Valuation of Lands and Tenements	703,912 19 7	703,456 13 5	456 6 2	Treasury Minute, 6th September 1831, and Treasury Letter, 6th July 1875.
Turnpike Road Debentures	61,087 15 3	13,650 1 7	47,437 13 8	Treasury Letters, 22nd October 1857 and 7th March 1858.
South Turnpike Road	3,802 5 9	—	3,802 5 9	Treasury Letter, 4th May 1843.
Temporary Relief	940,333 18 3	528,181 7 11	787,870 11 1	Act 16 & 17 Vict. c. 75.
Consolidated Annuities	1,930 0 0			
Distressed Poor Law Unions	300,000 0 0			
Gaols and Bridewells	882,738 3 5	880,880 1 0	1,858 3 5	Treasury Letter, 22nd February 1842, and Act 6 & 7 Vict. c. 32.
Tithe Composition	379,451 9 7	51,794 4 6	327,726 14 1	Act 44 & 45 Vict. c. 35.
Total remissions on Closed Services	14,388,511 8 5	7,918,370 14 10	6,470,140 13 11	
OPEN SERVICES.				
(b.) Roads and Bridges (4,865l. 11s. 10d.):				
Dublin and Blessington Road	5,000 0 0	3,782 10 0	1,217 10 0	Act 15 & 16 Vict. c. 60.
Limerick Roads	2,000 0 0	150 18 1	1,849 1 11	Act 20 & 21 Vict. c. 15.
[illegible] Bridge	3,450 0 0	*1,850 14 7	1,599 0 0	Act 43 & 47 Vict. c. 42.
(b.) Inland Navigation:				
Ulster Canal	10,000 0 0	—	10,000 0 0	Act 54 & 55 Vict. c. 19.
(b.) Public Buildings (Roman Catholic Chapels).	85,000 0 0	83,045 2 1	1,954 17 11	Treasury Letters, 28th March 1854; 18th December, 12th March, and 20th April 1855; 7th December 1856; 5th August 1864; and 12th December 1868.
(b.) Harbours, Docks, &c. (74,886l. 2s. 4d.):				
Limerick Harbour	134,000 0 0	*27,853 7 0	56,865 4 2	Act 50 & 51 Vict. c. 54.
Galway Harbour	24,000 0 0	*7,917 5 1	8,822 14 10	Act 50 & 51 Vict. c. 55.
Ardglass Harbour	4,050 0 0	—	4,050 0 0	Act 40 & 41 Vict. c. 27.
(b.) Labourers' Dwellings (832l. 15s. 4d.):				
Timothy Moore	424 12 4	7 0 0	417 12 4	Act 44 & 45 Vict. c. 65.
Lough Allen Clay Works Company	423 6 0	6 4 3	417 15 6	Act 46 & 50 Vict. c. 45.
Carried forward	613,644 17 8	59,985 13 7	94,247 6 4	

Purposes for which Advanced.	Amount Of Loan.			Amount Repaid.			Amount Remitted.			Authority for Remission or [illegible]
	£	s.	d.	£	s.	d.	£	s.	d.	
Brought forward -	[illegible]	17	5	72,[illegible]	15	7	16,247	6	4	
(a.) River Drainage and Navigation, 5 & 6 Vict. c. 89.	2,[illegible]	7	5	*[illegible]	13	1	[illegible]	1	7	Acts 16 & 17 Vict. c. 130, 18 & 19 Vict. c. 110, 42 & 43 Vict. c. 35, 43 & 44 Vict. c. 4, and 46 & 47 Vict. c. 46.
(b.) River Drainage Maintenance -	49,[illegible]	5	4	*[illegible]	0	5	145	6	5	Act 44 & 45 Vict. c. 33, s. 3.
(c.) Public Works Loans, 57 Geo. 3. c. 34. (177,[illegible]l. [illegible]s. [illegible]d.)										
Repairs to Parish Churches -	1,[illegible]	7	9	[illegible]	[illegible]	9	140	13	0	Treasury Letter, 12th August 18[illegible].
Roads, Ballymoney Carberdine -	1,[illegible]	14	5	1,[illegible]	[illegible]	11	949	7	4	Treasury Letter, June 18[illegible].
Roads, Dublin to Navan -	5,[illegible]	13	10	4,[illegible]	11	4	1,143	2	6	Act 18 & 19 Vict. c. 98.
Grand Canal Company -	97,[illegible]	5	1	80,[illegible]	0	0	61,[illegible]	3	1	Act 7 & 8 Vict. c. 98.
Portumna Bridge -	3,[illegible]	4	6	2,[illegible]	4	1	1,[illegible]	0	7	Act 21 Vict. c. 34.
Limerick Bridge -	[illegible]	13	5	—			58,[illegible]	15	4	Act 20 & 21 Vict. c. 19.
Cork Street Improvements -	1[illegible]	13	8	6,[illegible]	13	6	10,[illegible]	0	0	Act 39 & 41 Vict. c. 27.
Fisney Canal -	1,[illegible]	10	6	[illegible]	13	6	[illegible]	18	10	
County Mayo, Court Houses -	5,[illegible]	0	0	2,[illegible]	17	4	[illegible]	2	6	
County Kilkenny, Roads -	3,[illegible]	9	3	2,[illegible]	0	3	[illegible]	9	4	
Toughal Bridge -	10,[illegible]	0	0	[illegible]	2	4	6,[illegible]	17	5	Act 42 & 43 Vict. c. 42.
Athlone Bridge -	4,[illegible]	0	0	—			4,[illegible]	0	0	Act 46 & 47 Vict. c. 42.
(f.) Land Improvement, Preliminary Expenses.	[illegible]	0	0	*[illegible]	2	7	[illegible]	3	5	Treasury Letters, 3rd May 18[illegible], and 10th September 1879.
(g.) Repairs of Fishery Piers:										
Kilkenny Pier -	344	14	2	—			344	14	2	Act 51 & 52 Vict. c. 38. Act 53 & 54 Vict. c. 10.
(h.) Lunatic Asylums Buildings -	1,[illegible]	4	0	*1,[illegible]	8	2	12,[illegible]	0	0	Treasury Letter, 14th December 185[illegible].
(i.) Building Schools ([illegible]l. [illegible]s. [illegible]d.):										
Dundalk Endowed School -	[illegible]	18	5	27	13	10	[illegible]	4	7	Act 40 & 41 Vict. c. 27.
New Ross Endowed School -	[illegible]	16	11	[illegible]	6	2	100	10	9	
Total remissions on Open Services -	4,214,[illegible]	13	1	2,[illegible]	12	7	1,[illegible]	17	11	
Total remissions on Closed Services -	—			—			6,[illegible]	13	11	
Irish Church Fund Loans -	—			—			25,[illegible]	11	6	
Total as shown in Table I. -	—			—			7,[illegible]	2	10	

* Repayments are still to be made on these particular loans.

The foregoing list does not include all the Loans made under the several services, only those Loans on which remissions have been made.

Closed Services are those on which advances cannot be made, and repayment have ceased.

Open Services include:—

(a.) Those on which no further advances can be made, though repayments have yet to come in.
(b.) Those on which advances can still be made.

TABLE X.

[illegible]

[illegible]

Lines	[illegible]	[illegible]	[illegible]	[illegible]	[illegible]	[illegible]	[illegible]	[illegible]	[illegible]	[illegible]	[illegible]	Remarks
1. Clogher Valley	[illegible]	[illegible]	[illegible]	[illegible]	[illegible]	[illegible]	[illegible]	[illegible]	[illegible]	[illegible]	[illegible]	[illegible]
				[illegible]	[illegible]	[illegible]	[illegible]	[illegible]	[illegible]	[illegible]	[illegible]	
2. [illegible]	[illegible]	[illegible]	[illegible]	[illegible]	[illegible]	[illegible]	[illegible]	[illegible]	[illegible]	[illegible]	[illegible]	[illegible]
				[illegible]	[illegible]	[illegible]	[illegible]	[illegible]	[illegible]	[illegible]	[illegible]	
3. West Clare	[illegible]	[illegible]	[illegible]	[illegible]	[illegible]	[illegible]	[illegible]	[illegible]	[illegible]	[illegible]	[illegible]	
5. [illegible]	[illegible]	[illegible]	[illegible]	[illegible]	—	[illegible]					[illegible]	
6. [illegible]	[illegible]	[illegible]	[illegible]	[illegible]	[illegible]	[illegible]	[illegible]	[illegible]	[illegible]	[illegible]	[illegible]	

[illegible]

[illegible]	[illegible]											[illegible]
	[illegible]	[illegible]	[illegible]	[illegible]	[illegible]	[illegible]	[illegible]	[illegible]	[illegible]	[illegible]	[illegible]	
[illegible]	[illegible]	[illegible]	[illegible]	[illegible]	[illegible]	[illegible]	[illegible]	[illegible]	[illegible]	[illegible]	—	
[illegible]	[illegible]	[illegible]	[illegible]	[illegible]	[illegible]	[illegible]	[illegible]	[illegible]	[illegible]	[illegible]	[illegible]	[illegible]
[illegible]	[illegible]	[illegible]	[illegible]	[illegible]	[illegible]	[illegible]	[illegible]	[illegible]	[illegible]	[illegible]	—	[illegible]
[illegible]	[illegible]	[illegible]	[illegible]	[illegible]	[illegible]	[illegible]	[illegible]	[illegible]	[illegible]	[illegible]	—	[illegible]
[illegible]	[illegible]	[illegible]	[illegible]	[illegible]	[illegible]	[illegible]	[illegible]	[illegible]	[illegible]	[illegible]	—	[illegible]
[illegible]	[illegible]	[illegible]	[illegible]	[illegible]	[illegible]	[illegible]	[illegible]	[illegible]	[illegible]	[illegible]	—	[illegible]

[illegible]

TABLE XI.

LIGHT RAILWAYS (IRELAND) ACT, 1889.

Name of Line.	Gauge.	Mileage.	By Government Grant.	By Local Guarantee.	By Working Company.
	ft. in.		£	£	
Galway and Clifden	5 3	48½	264,000	—	Balance of cost.
Killorglin and Valentia	5 3	26½	85,000	70,000	"
Headford and Kenmare	5 3	19¾	56,000	40,000	"
Bantry Bay Extension	5 3	1½	15,000	—	
Baltimore Extension	5 3	7¾	56,700	—	Nil.
Downpatrick and Ardglass	5 3	8	33,000	*17,000	"
Stranorlar and Glenties	3 0	24¼	116,000	1,000	"
Donegal and Killybegs	3 0	18¼	128,000	1,000	"
Collooney and Claremorris	5 3	47	198,000	120,000	Balance of cost.
Ballina and Killala	5 3	8	44,000	—	"
Westport and Mallaranny	5 3	18	131,000	—	"
Achill Extension	5 3	8¼	75,000	—	—
Preliminary expenses and contingencies	—	—	Estimate 25,000	—	—
Totals	—	236¾	1,232,600	249,000	—

* The Treasury contributes under the Act of 1883 two per cent. as a maximum in aid of Guaranteed Dividend, excepting in the case of the Downpatrick and Ardglass Line, in which the guarantee is 2 per cent. by the Grand Jury only.

APPENDIX X.

[illegible]

[illegible]

[illegible]	[illegible]	[illegible]	[illegible]	[illegible]	[illegible]	[illegible]	[illegible]
[illegible]	[illegible]	[illegible]	[illegible]	[illegible]	[illegible]	[illegible]	[illegible]
[illegible]	[illegible]						
[illegible]	[illegible]						
	[illegible]	[illegible]	[illegible]	[illegible]	[illegible]	[illegible]	[illegible]
[illegible]	[illegible]	[illegible]	[illegible]	[illegible]	[illegible]	[illegible]	[illegible]
[illegible]	[illegible]	[illegible]	[illegible]	[illegible]	[illegible]	[illegible]	[illegible]
[illegible]	[illegible]	[illegible]	[illegible]	[illegible]	[illegible]	[illegible]	[illegible]
[illegible]	[illegible]	[illegible]	[illegible]	[illegible]	[illegible]	[illegible]	[illegible]
[illegible]	[illegible]	[illegible]	[illegible]	[illegible]	[illegible]	[illegible]	[illegible]

Total amount written off or remitted . . . . Nil.

Present annual amount of payments in respect of outstanding balance, including replacement of capital and interest :—

Year ending 31st December.	Capital.	Interest.	Total.
	£ s. d.	£	£ s. d.
1895 - -	[illegible]	[illegible]	[illegible]
1896 - -	[illegible]	[illegible]	[illegible]
1897 - -	[illegible]	[illegible]	[illegible]
1898 - -	[illegible]	[illegible]	[illegible]
1899 - -	[illegible]	[illegible]	[illegible]
1900 - -	[illegible]	[illegible]	[illegible]
1901 - -	[illegible]	[illegible]	[illegible]
1902 - -	—	[illegible]	[illegible]
1903 - -	—	[illegible]	[illegible]
1904 - -	—	[illegible]	[illegible]
1905 - -	[illegible]	[illegible]	[illegible]
1906 - -	[illegible]	[illegible]	[illegible]
1907 - -	[illegible]	[illegible]	[illegible]
	[illegible]	[illegible]	[illegible]

	£
Balance due to depositors in Post Office Savings Banks in Ireland at 31st December, 1893 -	[illegible]
Estimated balance at 31st December, 1894	[illegible]
Balance due to depositors in Trustee Savings Banks in Ireland at 20th November, 1894 -	[illegible]

1st March 1895.

B.—LOCAL LOANS FUND, IRELAND.

Authority through whom Advance was made by National Debt Commissioners.	Total Amount advanced to 31st March 1894.	Total Amount of the Payments made from Ireland up to the 31st March 1894 in respect of such Advances, including Repayments of Capital and Interest.			Remitted up to 31st March 1894.	Balance outstanding on 31st March 1894.
		Capital.	Interest.	Total.		
	£	£	£	£	£	£
Commissioners of Public Works, Ireland.	[illegible]	[illegible]	[illegible]	[illegible]	[illegible]	[illegible]
Irish Land Commissioners under Land Purchase Acts.	[illegible]	[illegible]	[illegible]	[illegible]	Nil.	[illegible]
Total -	[illegible]	[illegible]	[illegible]	[illegible]	[illegible]	[illegible]
Public Works Loan Commissioners.	[illegible]	[illegible]	[illegible]	[illegible]	[illegible]	[illegible]
H.M.'s Treasury -	900,000	—	—	—	900,000	—
Grand Total - -	[illegible]	[illegible]	[illegible]	[illegible]	[illegible]	[illegible]

NOTE.—This table has been prepared from the summary of public loans on pages [illegible] of the Local Loans Fund accounts of the National Debt Commissioners for the year ended 31st March 1894 [illegible].

APPENDIX XI.

RELATIVE POPULATION of ENGLAND and WALES, SCOTLAND, IRELAND, and GREAT BRITAIN, respectively, for every fifth year between 1801 and 1891, inclusive, as obtained from the GENERAL REGISTER OFFICE, SOMERSET HOUSE.

Year.	England and Wales.	Scotland.	Great Britain (Total).	Ireland.	—	Year.	England and Wales.	Scotland.	Great Britain (Total).	Ireland.	—
[illegible]	[illegible]	[illegible]	[illegible]	[illegible]	Census.	[illegible]	[illegible]	[illegible]	[illegible]	[illegible]	Census.
[illegible]	[illegible]	[illegible]	[illegible]	[illegible]	Estimated.	[illegible]	[illegible]	[illegible]	[illegible]	[illegible]	Estimated.
[illegible]	[illegible]	[illegible]	[illegible]	[illegible]	Census.	[illegible]	[illegible]	[illegible]	[illegible]	[illegible]	Census.
[illegible]	[illegible]	[illegible]	[illegible]	[illegible]	Estimated.	[illegible]	[illegible]	[illegible]	[illegible]	[illegible]	Estimated.
[illegible]	[illegible]	[illegible]	[illegible]	[illegible]	Census.	[illegible]	[illegible]	[illegible]	[illegible]	[illegible]	Census.
[illegible]	[illegible]	[illegible]	[illegible]	[illegible]	Estimated.	[illegible]	[illegible]	[illegible]	[illegible]	[illegible]	Estimated.
[illegible]	[illegible]	[illegible]	[illegible]	[illegible]	Census.	[illegible]	[illegible]	[illegible]	[illegible]	[illegible]	Census.
[illegible]	[illegible]	[illegible]	[illegible]	[illegible]	Estimated.	[illegible]	[illegible]	—	—	—	Estimated.

CORRESPONDENCE WITH THE WAR OFFICE AS TO RELATIVE COST OF MILITARY ESTABLISHMENTS IN GREAT BRITAIN AND IRELAND.

21, Great George Street, S.W.,
February 1, 1896.

SIR,

I AM directed by this Commission to request that they may be furnished by the War Office with an estimate of the normal strength of the army in Ireland, and of the average annual cost of its pay and subsistence, and a similar estimate with regard to the militia.

Generally speaking the Commission desire to ascertain, as far as may be practicable, what is the total amount of the normal annual expenditure in Ireland in respect of all military objects, as compared with the expenditure in the rest of the United Kingdom, and they would be glad of any information which the War Office are able to supply with regard to this matter.

I am, &c.
(Signed) B. H. HOLLAND,
Secretary.

The Accountant General,
War Office, S.W.

114/Ireland/212.

War Office, Pall Mall, S.W.,
February 19, 1896.

SIR,

In reply to your letter of the 1st instant I am directed by the Secretary of State for War to enclose a statement showing the normal establishment of the of the Regular Army in Great Britain and Ireland respectively, and also of the militia in the two countries.

The statement further shows the amount of the normal annual expenditure on all military objects in Great Britain and in Ireland, exclusive of the expenditure under the Military Forces Localization Act, 1872, the Imperial Defence Act, 1888, and the Barracks Act, 1890, which must be regarded as abnormal.

I am to add that the sums 8,919,600l. and 1,049,100l. shown as pay, &c. of regular forces in Great Britain and Ireland respectively do not include military expenditure borne by the Indian Government to the estimated amount of 661,400l. in the former and 94,000l. in the latter, and that the sums 2,575,400l. and 302,600l. for non-effective pay, &c. are likewise exclusive of the Indian contribution towards effective charges. This contribution may be taken to cover further expenditure to the amount of 728,000l. in Great Britain and 91,400l. in Ireland.

I am, &c.
R. H. KNOX.

The Secretary of the Royal
Commission on the Financial
Relations between Great
Britain and Ireland,
21 Great George Street, S.W.

ESTABLISHMENT of REGULAR FORCES and MILITIA, in GREAT BRITAIN and IRELAND.

—	Great Britain.			Ireland.		
	Officers.	Men.	Total.	Officers.	Men.	Total.
Regular Army	[illegible]	[illegible]	[illegible]	[illegible]	[illegible]	[illegible]
Militia Perm. Staff	[illegible]	[illegible]	[illegible]	74	[illegible]	[illegible]
Militia	[illegible]	[illegible]	[illegible]	[illegible]	[illegible]	[illegible]
Total	[illegible]	[illegible]	[illegible]	[illegible]	[illegible]	[illegible]

NORMAL ANNUAL EXPENDITURE on all MILITARY OBJECTS in GREAT BRITAIN and IRELAND.

—	Great Britain.	Ireland.
	£	£
Pay, &c. of Regular Forces (including Permanent Staff of Militia)	8,919,600	1,049,100
Pay, &c. of Militia	[illegible]	[illegible]
Yeomanry and Volunteers	[illegible]	—
Supplies, stores, transport, &c.	[illegible]	[illegible]
Non-effective charges	[illegible]	[illegible]
Total	[illegible]	[illegible]

APPENDIX XIII.

EXTRACTS from SPEECHES made in the PARLIAMENTS of GREAT BRITAIN and IRELAND previously to the ACT of UNION in so far as they relate to the FINANCIAL RELATIONS of the two COUNTRIES.

In accordance with directions from the Commission I have endeavoured to collect from the debates in the British and Irish Parliaments which immediately preceded the Act of Union extracts of any importance from speeches with regard to the 7th or Financial Article of the Treaty of Union.

It seemed at the same time to be desirable to include some extracts from the speeches made with regard to the unsuccessful "Commercial propositions" of 1785, of which Sir Edward Hamilton has given an account on page 1 of his memorandum.

As he has pointed out, the idea of these propositions was to admit Ireland to some commercial advantages from which she was then still excluded, and to obtain in return a regular contribution from Ireland towards the support of the British Navy.

With regard to the debates in the Irish Parliament which immediately preceded the Union, it must be observed that the "Irish Parliamentary History," which contains a regular and consecutive report of the debates from the year 1781, came to an end on July 15th, 1797. Subsequent speeches down to the last meeting of the Irish Parliament have to be collected from separate publications of the pamphlet kind in the British Museum or elsewhere. Mr. Grattan's speeches are printed in the collection of 1822. The chief member of the Irish House of Commons who devoted himself in detail to the financial branch of the subject on the opposition side was Mr. Foster, then Speaker of the House, but who had at a previous time been Chancellor of the Irish Exchequer. The reports of his speeches are very full and apparently carefully revised by him for publication.

The extracts are arranged in three parts, viz.:—

Part I.—Debates on the Commercial Propositions of 1785, p. 1.

Part II.—Debates in the British Parliament in 1799 and 1800, relative to the Treaty of Union, p. 5.

Part III.—Debates in the Irish Parliament on the same subject, p. 8.

B. H. HOLLAND,
Secretary.

PART I.

DEBATES on the COMMERCIAL PROPOSITIONS in 1785.

MR. PITT, in his speech of 22nd February 1785, in bringing in the 11 resolutions as to commercial intercourse which had received the assent of the Irish Parliament, said (inter alia)—

"They would recollect that from the revolution to a "period within the memory of every man who heard "him, indeed, until these very few years, the system had "been that of debarring Ireland from the enjoyment and "use of her own resources; to make the kingdom completely subservient to the interest and opulence of "this country, without suffering her to share in the "bounties of nature, in the industry of her citizens, "or making them contribute to the general interests "and strength of the Empire. The system of cruel "and abominable restraint had, however, been exploded. "It was at once harsh and unjust, and it was as impolitic as it was oppressive; for however necessary "it might be to the partial benefit of districts in Britain, "it promoted not the real prosperity and strength of

"the Empire. That which had been the system counteracted the kindness of Providence, and suspended the industry and enterprise of man. Ireland was put under such restraint that she was shut out from every species of commerce; she was restrained from sending the produce of her own soil to foreign markets, and all correspondence with the colonies of Britain was prohibited to her, so that she could not derive their commodities but through the medium of Britain. This was the system which had prevailed, and this was the state of thraldom in which that country had been kept ever since the revolution. Some relaxation of the system, indeed, took place at an early period of the present century. Somewhat more of the restrictions were abated in the reign of George II.; but it was not until a later season to our own day, and indeed within the last seven years, that the system had been completely reversed."

Mr. *Pitt* then pointed out that the right of import from and export to foreign countries and British colonies had been conceded to Ireland, except that Ireland could not re-export British Colonial produce to Britain or receive it from Britain. This exception it was proposed to abolish so far as regarded America and Africa, but not with regard to the Asiatic trade, which was the monopoly of the East India Company. It was also proposed that English and Irish goods should pass freely from one country to the other, either freely or at duties which were the same in both countries.

In return for these advantages Ireland was to contribute any surplus over 656,000*l.* per annum of the "hereditary revenue" of Ireland towards the support of the navy. The Crown or "hereditary" parts of Irish revenue (which produced in 1783, 652,000*l.* per annum) was derived from customs, hearth tax, and inland excise, three branches of revenue which would, as Mr. Pitt calculated, increase with the increasing trade and prosperity of Ireland. (Parliamentary History, vol. 25, p. 327.)

Mr. *Pitt* said in the course of this speech (p. 316):

"There were but two possible systems for countries situated in relation to each other like Britain and Ireland. The one, of having the smaller completely subservient and subordinate to the greater—to make the one, as it were, an instrument of advantage, and to make all her efforts operate in favour of, and conduce merely to, the interest of the other. This system we had tried in respect to Ireland. The other was a participation and community of benefits and a system of equality and fairness, which, without tending to aggrandise the one or to depress the other, should seek the aggregate interests of the Empire. Such a situation of commercial equality in which there was to be a community of benefits demanded also a community of burthens, and it was this situation in which he desired to place the two countries. It was on that general basis that he was solicitous of moving the propositions which he held in his hand, to complete a system which had been left unfinished and defective."

Lord North and Mr. Fox.

Lord *North* and Mr. *Fox*, in the same debate, objected to the propositions, as not containing a sufficiently definite pledge on the part of Ireland to contribute to the support of the navy, and, in the same sense, was, among many other hostile petitions, a petition from Liverpool, setting forth (*inter alia*):

"That an equal participation in all the privileges and advantages of a community should, by every rule of right, reason, and justice include in it a mutual obligation to encourage, maintain, and defend those rights, and to contribute equally to their support; that the island of Great Britain, when first united in legislation, manufactures, navigation, and commerce became united also in taxation towards the general support of the common good; that admission of any neighbouring kingdom to a full share in all these rights without subjecting her to sustain a due proportion of the general burthen too, would be a great deviation from those principles upon which the union of this island was wisely founded, &c."

Mr. Pitt.

On May 12th, 1785, Mr. *Pitt* again brought forward the propositions, increased in number from 11 to 20, altered in many respects, and containing, *inter alia*, provisions that Ireland should enact all laws which had been or might be made by the British Parliament respecting navigation and Colonial trade. (Parliamentary History, vol. 25, p. 576). The leading principle, he said, was, "That a treaty should be concluded with Ireland by which that country should be put on a fair, equal, and impartial footing with Great Britain in point of commerce with respect to foreign countries and to our colonies; and as to the mutual intercourse between each other, that this equality should extend to manufactures, importation, and to exportation, and that Ireland in return for this concession should contribute her share towards the protection and security of the general commerce of the Empire."

In the course of this speech, in combating the argument that free trade between the countries would enable Ireland to compete successfully against English manufactures because less heavily taxed, Mr. *Pitt* made these observations (p. 586).

"He most earnestly entreated the House not to suffer themselves to be carried away with the idea that a poor country, merely because she enjoyed some comparative exemption from taxes, was therefore able to cope with a rich and powerful country; the fact, he was ready to contend, was by no means so; on the contrary, the smallest burthen on a poor country was to be considered, when compared with those of a rich one, by no means in a proportion with their several abilities; for, if one country exceeded another in wealth, population, and established commerce in a proportion of two to one, he was nearly convinced that that country would be able to bear near ten times the burthens that the other would be equal to."

Mr. Fox.

Mr. *Fox* opposed the plan mainly on the general grounds, (1) that it would be the loss of Irish legislative independence, as Ireland would have to follow our trade regulations; (2) that it would ruin many of the English manufactures.

The second of the 20 propositions, as they left the British Parliament, was thus:—

"That a full participation of commercial advantages should be permanently secured to Ireland whenever a provision, equally permanent and secure, shall be made by the Parliament of that Kingdom towards defraying, in proportion to its growing prosperity, the necessary expenses in time of peace, of protecting the trade and general interests of the Empire."

The 20th of these propositions was to the following effect:—

"That the appropriation of whatever sum the gross hereditary revenue of the kingdom of Ireland (the due collection thereof being secured by permanent provisions) shall produce . . . over and above the sum of 656,000*l.* in each year, towards the support of the naval force of the Empire, to be applied in such manner as the Parliament of Ireland shall direct, by an Act to be passed for that purpose, will be a satisfactory provision proportioned to the growing prosperity of that kingdom, towards defraying, in time of peace, the necessary expenses of protecting the trade and general interests of the Empire."

The resolutions were agreed to in committee, and on May 31st, 1785 were reported to the House.

Mr. Sheridan.

Mr. *Sheridan*, in the debate which followed, made the objection that Ireland would be tied down "to a specific provision for the support of the navy, which in all probability would in the end prove much less beneficial to this country than if Parliament had trusted to the generosity and liberality of Ireland." He also said that the grant of a perpetual specific sum would be a violation of the Irish constitution.

Lord North.

Lord *North* objected that England would be making commercial concessions in exchange for nothing, as the hereditary revenue would not produce any surplus.

Sir J. Erskine.

Sir *James Erskine* feared "That Irish freedom was the purchase to which the interests of England were to be sacrificed. He liked neither the purchase nor the terms; he neither wished us to resign our dear-bought commercial advantages, nor to infringe upon the liberties of others."

Mr. Sheridan.

Mr. *Sheridan* also said (p. 743) that if it was thought that the power of legislating as to particular objects should be lodged in one kingdom only, this should have been distinctly stated as the foundation of the treaty. "Instead of this all had been delusion, trick, and fallacy; a new scheme of commercial arrangement is proposed to the Irish as a boon, and the surrender of their constitution is tacked on to it as a mercantile regulation. Ireland newly escaped from harsh trepanals and severe discipline, is treated like a high-mettled horse, hard to catch; and the Irish Secretary is to return to the field, soothing and coaxing him, with a sieve of provender in one hand, but with a bridle in the other, ready to slip over his head while he is snapping at the food."

Mr. Fox.

Mr. *Fox*, in the same debate, summed up his views in this concluding sentence. "I will not barter English "commerce for Irish liberty; that is not the price I "would pay, nor is this the thing I would purchase" (p. 778, vol. 25).

The resolutions having been agreed to by the House of Commons, were communicated to the House of Lords, and a discussion with regard to them took place there on 7th June 1785 (vol. 25, p. 820).

Lord Abingdon.

Lord *Abingdon* (p. 825) violently attacked Mr. Fox for being the author of the policy by which the power of the British Parliament to legislate for Ireland in commercial matters was given up (20 Geo. III. c. 10) and the West India commerce had been opened to Ireland.

Lord Stormont.

Lord *Stormont* said that one objection to the plan was that it might be an obstacle in the way of eventual legislative union, "because every possible advantage "being held out by England to the Irish by the present "propositions, she could have nothing reserved by "which she might afterwards induce them to consent "to a union, after this she could have burthens only to "offer to Ireland a very bad inducement to a union of "legislatures. What was the true way of accomplishing "this object, which the learned Lord said was so much "coveted?—Was it not evidently by a reservation of "the good things which we possessed until the time "that Ireland shall be disposed to share our circum- "stances? That a full legislative union would be "ultimately as beneficial to Ireland as to this country "was what he sincerely believed; and he objected to "this scheme of intercourse because it would retard, "and in all probability render impracticable, that "more happy conjunction."

He also said, "A mutual monopoly had been formerly "the basis of our Colonial system; from this, in the "year 1780, we had thought proper, in some degree to "depart by permitting Ireland to maintain a direct "intercourse with our colonies . . . . More was "not thought of until the voluntary offer of the "present Ministry permitting them (the Irish) to "supply our markets with the produce of those colonies, "in the acquisition of which we had expended so much "blood and treasure."

He thought that "the immediate result of the new "system would be the emigration of our manufac- "turers to Ireland."

Lord Fitzwilliam.

Lord *Fitzwilliam* (p. 872) complained "as an English- "man, of the resolutions, as sharing with another "country that which every nation had a right and "ought, in common sense and common policy, to "retain to herself, not only the trade with our "colonies, but even our home market; nay, as mak- "ing that country an emporium for our own trade "with those very colonies, by allowing a circuitous "intercourse between them and us through Ireland."

Lord Sackville.

Lord *Sackville*, in the course of his speech, said, "It "had been said that these resolutions would restore "both countries to the same amity which prevailed "between England and Scotland. That, in his opinion, "was impossible. In the instance mentioned, the "legislation of the inferior was melted down into that "of the superior kingdom. But where two nations "were one, only on commercial principles, we knew "not by what means they could agree or harmonise in "any other. But where all their dependence was "placed in one and the same legislature, every source "of jealousy, suspicion, or distrust was for ever at an "end. He looked forward to this great interesting "and desirable event with anxiety, and should be "happy to see commissioners appointed by His Majesty "to negotiate and adjust this important object, to the "satisfaction, and for the infinite good of all parties "concerned."

Parliamentary Debates, Ireland, Vol. V., p. 354.

In August 1785 the 20 resolutions were brought before the Irish House of Commons in the shape of a Bill for establishing a treaty of commerce between Ireland and Great Britain, with the general object of making the trade between the two countries as free as possible, except as to export of corn, flour, &c., and of wool from England to Ireland, and of placing the same duties in each country on the export of foreign goods. Mr. *Orde*, in introducing these proposals said, that "he could have wished them still more "liberal. I could have wished that every sort of "distinction between the two countries was wiped "away, and a full and free community of rights and "profits established between them, but as circumstances "render that impracticable, it is necessary to look out "for something near it, and this system is the best "that has yet been devised."

Mr. Orde.

Mr. *Grattan* strongly opposed the treaty, which he considered would deprive Ireland of her free will in commercial policy, and said with reference to the above observations of Mr. Orde (p. 358): "It is here said "that the laws respecting commerce and navigation "should be similar, and inferred that Ireland should "subscribe the same laws as England on those subjects, "that is, the same law, the same legislature; but this "argument goes a great deal too far, it goes to the "army, for the Money Bill should be the same; it was "endeavoured to be extended to the collection of your "revenue, and is in time to be extended to your taxes; "it goes to the extinction of the most valuable part of "your parliamentary capacity, it is an union, a "creeping and incipient union; a virtual union "establishing one will in the general concerns of "commerce and navigation, and reposing that will in "the Parliament of Great Britain, an union where a "Parliament preserves its existence after it has lost "its authority, and our people are to pay for a parlia- "mentary establishment without any proportion of "parliamentary representation. In opposing the "right honourable gentleman's Bill I consider myself "to be opposing an union *in limine*."

The Bill was withdrawn in consequence of a vote of the Irish House of Commons.

Part II.

Debates in the British Parliament on the Union, 1799, 1800.

(1.) *January 1799.*

Mr. *Pitt's* speech in the debate on the proposed legislative union in January 1799 (Parliamentary History, vol. 34, p. 267), contained the following passage:—

"There is another consideration well worth attention. Consider what are the peculiar causes by which we have been enabled to resist the unequalled and eccentric efforts of France, without any diminution, nay, with an increase of our general prosperity—what but the great commercial resources which we possess? A measure then, which must communicate to such a mighty limb of the Empire as Ireland, all the commercial advantages which Great Britain possesses, which will open the markets of the one country to the other, which will give them both the common use of their capital, must, by infusing a large portion of wealth into Ireland consider- ably increase the resources and consequently the strength of the whole Empire."

In the same speech (p. 271) Mr. *Pitt* said:—

"Among the great and known defects of Ireland one of the most prominent features is its want of industry and capital; how are these wants to be supplied but by blending more closely with Ireland the industry and the capital of this country?"

In the same speech Mr. Pitt said (p. 268):—

"Sir, the only other general topic of objection is that upon which great pains have been taken to raise an alarm in Ireland. The idea that the main principle of the measure was to subject Ireland to a load of debt and an increase of taxes, and to expose her to the consequences of all our alleged difficulties and supposed necessities.

"Sir, I hope the zeal, the spirit, and the liberal and enlarged policy of this country has given ample proof that it is not from a pecuniary motive that we seek an union. If it is not desirable on the grounds there stated it cannot be recommended for the mere purpose of taxation; but, to quiet any jealousy on this subject, here again let us look to Scotland. Is there any instance where, with 45 members on her part and 513 on ours, that part of the United Kingdom has paid more than its proportion to the general burdens? Is it then, Sir, any ground of apprehension that we are likely to tax Ireland more heavily when she becomes associated with ourselves? To tax in its due propor- tion the whole of the Empire, to the utter exclusion of the idea of the predominance of one part of society over another, is the great characteristic of British finance, as equality of laws is of the British constitution.

"But, Sir, in addition to this, if we come to the details of this proposition, it is in our power to fix, for any number of years which shall be thought fit, the proportion by which the contribution of Ireland to the expenses of the State shall be regulated; that these proportions shall not be such as would make a contribution greater than the necessary amount of its own present necessary expenses as a separate kingdom; and, even after that limited period, the proportion of the whole contribution from time to time might be made to depend on the comparative produce, in each kingdom, of such general taxes as might be thought to afford the best criterion of their respective wealth. Or, what I should hope would be found practicable, the system of internal taxation in each country might gradually be so equalised and assimilated, on the leading articles, as to make all rules of specific proportions unnecessary, and to secure that Ireland shall never be taxed but in proportion as we tax ourselves."

Mr. *Pitt*, at the end of this speech, proposed nine resolutions, which were the foundations of the subsequent Articles of Union. The sixth of these resolutions related to duties on goods passing between the countries. The seventh was thus worded:

"That for the like purpose" (the union) "it would be fit to propose that the charge arising from the payment of the interest or sinking fund for the reduction of the principal of the debt incurred in either kingdom before the union, shall continue to be separately defrayed by Great Britain and Ireland respectively. That for a number of years to be limited, the future ordinary expenses of the United Kingdom in peace or war, shall be defrayed by Great Britain and Ireland jointly, according to such proportions as shall be established by the respective Parliaments previous to the union; and that after the expiration of the time to be so limited, the proportions shall not be liable to be varied, except according to such rates and principles as shall be in like manner agreed upon previous to the union."

When this resolution was proposed, Mr. *Corry* "objected to it as not precisely expressing that an "identity of taxation should take place between the "two countries."

"Mr. *Pitt* said that however proper it might be to fix at some distant period after the union such an identity of taxation, yet for the present it would be wise and politic not so far to offend existing local prejudices as to require immediately an equal portion of burthens to be sustained by Ireland, but to exact for the present only that proportion which Ireland hitherto paid in time of peace and war."—Parliamentary History, vol. 34, p. 267.

As Resolution 7 was settled in the House of Commons and communicated to the House of Lords its form was somewhat altered. The word "ordinary" was omitted before "expenses," and the last lines from after the words "so limited" were made to read thus (vol. 34, p. 516):—

"The mode of jointly defraying such expenses shall be regulated according to such rules and principles as shall be in like manner agreed upon previous to the union, for the purpose of establishing gradually a uniform system of taxation through every part of the United Kingdom."

Lord Grenville.

In the debate in the House of Lords on receiving these resolutions, Lord *Grenville* said (p. 661):—

"The next branch of the Royal authority regarded its fiscal power, that is, what related to the expenditure and administration of the public money. By the arrangement of 1782 in this particular, the unity of that part of the regal power of both kingdoms was completely annulled. This was an evil, however, that would be completely extinguished by an incorporated union; and in this part of the present system Ireland was peculiarly liable to feel an inconvenience—I mean with respect to loans. It was to this country that Ireland, in cases of necessity, must look for a supply, and the difficulty of negotiating them here must be increased, by the idea that the Irish Parliament was completely independent of this country. But in the event of a union, a system of mutual aid and accommodation in the line of finance would speedily be established."

(2.) *April* 1800.

Mr. Pitt.

In the debate in the House of Commons, April 1800, on the Articles of Union as passed through the Irish Parliament, Mr. *Pitt* said (Parliamentary History, vol. 35, p. 53), with regard to the 7th Article:—

"It were a circumstance much to be wished that the finances of both countries were so nearly alike that the system of both could be identified; but as from the different proportions of debt, and the different stages of civilisation and commerce, and the different wealth of the countries, that desirable object is rendered impracticable, at least for some time to come, it becomes an important question, would you defer the advantage of the union because you cannot at once carry it to the extent you would wish? Or will you defer it until by the increase of the debt of Ireland, and the decrease of the debt of England through the means of the sinking fund, the two countries had so far approximated to each other that an identity of finance might be established in the first instance? But, it had been said, what security can you give to Ireland for the performance of the conditions? If I were asked what security were necessary, without hesitation I would answer, none. The liberality, the justice, the honour of the people of Great Britain have never yet been found deficient. I would refer them to former precedents. I would desire them to look at our conduct towards those nations who have already incorporated with us, to Wales and to Scotland; that will convince them that there is the most perfect safety, even if there were no stipulation. But to avoid loading our sister kingdom with more than her due share of the expenses of the State, to obviate all imputation of partiality, particularly as on that ground the opposers of the union grounded one of their most important objections, the Parliaments of both countries have fixed the proportions to be paid by each for a limited time, at the expiration of which it is presumed the finances of each may so far approximate that they may be assimilated and identified; with a provision, nevertheless, that, if that desirable event can be effected sooner, the Imperial Parliament shall have power to make any future revision or alteration. It most certainly will be desirable to ascertain, in as exact a proportion as possible, the quantity to be paid by each country. The plan I have already proposed is, as I think, the best that can be devised, not taking it from any one criterion, but from a blended and mixed consideration of the population and the revenue. Upon this the proportions are founded, and the ratio fixed for 20 years, unless the Imperial Parliament shall make future regulations. And here it may be necessary to observe that the finances of both countries may be identified, although the debt of England should exceed by a large proportion the debt of Ireland, because by the rapid increase of the sinking fund it may be as soon discharged as the debt of Ireland, and a large debt sooner discharged will be equivalent to a smaller one requiring a longer term for payment. I have already stated that the proportion of contribution of Ireland is to England is as about 7½ to one; and this is calculated upon the consumption of the several articles, considered both as to their value, and their value as compared with their bulk, and upon those articles of general use which seem to afford the materials for the surest ground of calculation, such as malt, tea, sugar, and others of that description. It has appeared from this calculation that the proportion proposed in this resolution has been the proportion, as nearly as can be ascertained, in which Ireland has contributed during the present war. It must be most satisfactory, Sir, to consider that, in adopting this arrangement, the present existing system is not at all disturbed. It will continue in its accustomed proportion; and at the same time, for the security of Ireland, it is provided that any article shall not pay a greater tax than the same article pays at the same time in England. If there shall remain any surplus revenue after the current expenses are paid, it is to be appropriated either to the liquidation of the debt or for the purposes of national improvement for that country. There then remain some other regulations, which have for their object the gradual abolition of all distinction in finance and revenue between the two countries, and to accelerate the time when both countries form but one fund, and pay one uniform proportion of taxes throughout each. It is obvious while there remains a disproportion of debt, they cannot form one fund; that event cannot take place till by the operation of circumstances that disproportion is destroyed; yet, Sir, as I have already observed, the real value of the respective debts may be alike before they are of the same magnitude, because, if our sinking fund will discharge our larger debt, before the debt of Ireland can be discharged, though not of equal magnitude, the greater debt discharged in the shorter time may not surpass the lesser debt remaining a longer time unpaid; and whenever the real

value shall be alike, the finances of both countries may be assimilated and identified, and it will remain in the discretion of the united Parliament to abolish all distinctions of quotas and contributions, and fix one rate of taxation throughout the United Kingdom, subject merely to such local abatements as from circumstances may become necessary."

Dr. Laurence. On the separate consideration of Article 7 (p. 94) Dr. *Laurence* said that it was of the utmost consequence that the system which should be adopted should not operate unequally, and he had great fears that the one proposed would be very detrimental to Ireland. The standards which had been assumed were by no means just criterion of the respective wealth of the two countries. The amount of exports and imports only showed their mercantile wealth, and nothing could be inferred from their consumption of exciseable articles, as after paying all other taxes, Great Britain paid a tenth upon income, and was thus much abler to contribute than from the amount of her consumption one would be led to believe.

Mr. Pitt. Mr. *Pitt* admitted the impossibility of finding any one certain criterion of the wealth of the two countries. The utmost that could be done was to adopt the most reasonable one that could be found; and it was a great confirmation of his opinion that he had done so, since the learned gentleman, with all his ingenuity, had not been able to offer a better. The exports and imports proved the best criterion of mercantile wealth, and as an aid of that criterion, the home consumption was added. The demand must be a proportion to the population and wealth.

Dr. Laurence. Dr. *Laurence* said that it was the first time in the history of any legislative body, that it was proposed that taxes should be imposed by men who would not feel them; 100 members would tax Great Britain who were perfect strangers, and Ireland would be taxed by 558, with whom she was in no way connected. He then read a motion, which he might afterwards make, viz., that after the words "twenty years," there should be inserted "and the contributions to be paid by each "country shall be imposed by its own representatives."

Mr. Pitt. Mr. *Pitt* said he was surprised to hear such a dreadful remedy proposed for such a trifling inconvenience. What possibility was there of Ireland being oppressed since the amount of what she should pay was already fixed?

The resolution was subsequently agreed to without a division.

PART III.

DEBATES IN IRISH HOUSE OF COMMONS.

(1.) 22nd to 23rd *January* 1799.

The Lord Lieutenant's speech, after referring to the war, proceeded: "The more I have reflected on the situa-"tion and circumstances of this kingdom, considering on "the one hand the strength and stability of Great "Britain, and on the other those divisions which have "shaken Ireland to its foundation, the more anxious I "am for some permanent adjustment which may "extend the advantages enjoyed by a sister kingdom "to every part of this island.

"The unremitting industry with which our enemies "persevere in their avowed design of endeavouring to "effect a separation of this kingdom from Great Britain "must have engaged your particular attention, and "His Majesty commands me to express his earnest "hope that this consideration, joined to the sentiment "of mutual affection and common interest, may dispose "the Parliaments in both kingdoms to provide the "most effectual means of maintaining and improving a "connexion essential to their common security, and "of consolidating, as far as possible into one firm and "lasting fabric, the strength, the power, and the "resources of the British Empire."

Mr. Tighe. Mr. *Tighe*, in his speech on the address, said that the object of the British Minister was, "to sacrifice this "country to new schemes of desperate finance; he has "taxed Great Britain to the uttermost . . . he can go "no further; next year, therefore, he wishes to find his "resources in Ireland, and because he thinks the Irish "Parliament are too sparing of the money of the "people, he wishes to destroy the legislature, that this "country may be hereafter for ever taxed by a majority "of British representatives, who, in taxing us, will not "tax themselves, but will be ready to violate with "regard to us every constitutional principle, according "to the suggestions of a British Minister."

Mr. *Barrington* said that "The first measure of a "union must be taxation; the first act of Irish union a "tax of 10 per cent. on Irish property, not modified to "Irish circumstances by an Irish Parliament, but "calculated by a Scottish Minister and executed by a "British authority; the tax table of England will "become the excise book of Ireland, and the great "doubt will then be whether our wants or our burthens "are the greatest."

Mr. *Martin*, speaking in favour of the union, said that many persons had been led to disapprove of the measure by the idea that England would be enabled to tax Ireland at her pleasure, but he suggested that the terms of the union might secure to this country the "quantum of taxation which it shall be possible to the "united Parliaments in Britain to levy. The rate of "taxes here after the union may be infinitely less than "they are at present."

Mr. *Arthur Moore* compared the question of Irish with that of American legislative independence, and said, "The most striking similitude between the American "transactions and the concerns of our own country "appears to me to consist in the identity of object and "design against both. I think it is impossible not to "see that in this project the end and ultimate pursuit is "taxation, in which respect there is no demonstration "plainer than that Ireland would be at the mercy of "the British Parliament and Ministers to all intents "and purposes whatsoever, and after all, Sir, I do not "know that there is any appendage of legislation so "important and interesting to a nation as the imposi-"tion of taxes. But there are gentlemen who argue "that by our having a certain number of representa-"tives in the British Parliament we must be considered "as consenting to our own taxation. I am certain there "will be a number . . . who will consent to our "being taxed to any amount, but supposing the best "that can happen—supposing them all to dissent, can "the unanimous voice of the whole 100 secure this country "from any tax which the British representatives shall "think fit to impose upon it. . . . But then, "Sir, it is said, if our proportion of members in the "legislature will not secure us against British taxation, "the terms of the treaty may do so. I like not treaties "between the great and the humble, the strong and "the weak, the giant and the dwarf, the ties of plighted "faith are but a feeble barrier against the aggressions "of conscious power. . . . In England it was not "easy to find new resources, the luxury and industry "of the country are exhausted, capital and income have "been resorted to, what remains?—Ireland! yes!— "the generous hospitality, the social harmony of the "Irish nation must prepare for the tax-gatherer and "the tollcollector."

(2.) *April* 1799.

Mr. *Foster* (the Speaker of the Irish House of Commons) in a speech on 11th April 1799, said:—

"But the noble Lord has told us the real motives of the scheme of union, and I thank him for stating them so fairly. Ireland, he says, must contribute to every war, and the Minister won't trust to interest, affection, or connexion for guiding her conduct. He must have her purse within his own grasp. While 300 men hold it in Ireland he cannot put his hand into it, they are out of his reach, but let 100 of you carry it over and lay it at his feet, and then he will have the full and uncontrolled power. What, though you have given eight millions this year, a greater sum than any proportion of calculation calls for, yet it is no part of his finance system, and you may not do it hereafter when it might be a breach of trust in you to give it. Finance so occupies his mind that it is the ruling principle of all his measures, it attended the commercial system in the shape of a supply for Imperial concerns, and if you could contrive how to give him the purse of the nation, without extinguishing your Parliament, believe me you would hear no more of the union . . . . If a similarity of laws be an essential means of union it is already attained and zealously continued by the voluntary acts of both kingdoms. But the noble Lord wants more, he wants your purse and your trade, for the only question

of Imperial concern (the Regency excepted) which he has stated and the only one which Mr. Pitt in his speech has [illegible] even to suggest is that of war and treaty; and the only difficulty [illegible], as to war, is the want of power to tax you, and the only [illegible] and our treaties is to [illegible] or regulate trade, and then the whole [illegible] is discovered.

"He wants a union in order to tax you and take your money where he [illegible] your own representatives would deem it improper, and to force regulations on your trade which your own Parliament would consider injurious or partial; I never expected to have heard it so [illegible] acknowledged, and I trust that it will be thoroughly understood, that it is not your constitution he wants to take away for any supposed imperfection, but because it keeps the purse of the nation in the honest hands of an Irish Parliament. . . .

"Now laws, equal in appearance and phrase, may be very unequal in effect. I will instance [illegible] laws. Ireland is a young country, rising, and likely to rise, in wealth; it is her best plan to borrow money instead of raising an annual income to fund the war expenses, because the certain prospect of her increasing prosperity gives a moral certainty of her paying the debt gradually, and an increase of annual taxes in the necessary service might crush her enterprise. Britain is at maturity, the state of warfare has thrown the trade of the world into her hands, and there is no reason to expect it will increase upon a peace; perhaps the speculation of its decrease would not be chimerical; she therefore should take advantage of her temporary affluence, and by annual taxes, not by borrowing, make it support the yearly expenses of the war; a system, therefore, of taxation for the whole expenses of the year, though equal in appearance would be very unequal in effect." . . .

"If any man says that this union does not bring us back under the control of a British Parliament because we shall have the mockery of 100 representatives to sit among 558—I answer it is a mere imposition, a play on words. Is there a man can doubt that 100 must yield to 558, and that our sending such a shadow of representation will only give legal form to the power of the 558 to tax us? . . . Perhaps you would depend on the articles you may frame to secure your trade and your purse, but you must recollect that if the doctrine of the omnipotence of Parliament be just (and it has strong advocates) it will extend to the united Parliament, who will have the power therefore at its pleasure to alter any act of the union itself, and you must see that as no articles, so neither will the [illegible] of the union exist longer than while it is beneficial to Great Britain, but it will exist for ever, though Ireland find it injurious to her interest."

Lord Castlereagh, in the course of his reply to this speech said that Mr. Foster "states that Mr. Pitt's sole object was to lay his hands upon the purse of Ireland, whereas the resolutions produced by Mr. Pitt prove demonstrably the reverse. But does the right honourable gentleman contend that we are not to pursue a liberal system towards Great Britain? Does he mean to argue that the expense of Imperial protection is to fall on the shoulders of one member of the Empire alone, and that the other is to take no share of the burden? . . . I stated, Sir, that if the present principles of connection remain, they must be followed up by contribution. I showed the danger to the connection under that circumstance, and, in order to get rid of my argument, it must be contended that Ireland must ever remain separate, must ever be protected by England, and must never contribute to the Empire at all."

Mr. *Fitzgerald*[illegible] said, "It has also been argued that there cannot be proportional contribution for the general support of a war, while the two legislatures are distinct, and that Great Britain is obliged to bear nearly the whole weight. I do not think the Irish Parliament has shown any niggardliness in the expenditure of the public money or any want of liberality in contributing to the general defence of the Empire. This session of Parliament a sum of eight millions has been voted for the services of the State; the greatest sum ever voted by the British Parliament is fifty-two millions. Now, eight millions for Ireland is certainly as much as fifty millions for Great Britain in proportion to the wealth and resources of each kingdom, for no one will deny that the wealth and resources of Great Britain are seven times greater than those of Ireland. But there is a possibility that the Irish Parliament may hereafter not act so liberally, and for that possibility must the Irish Parliament be destroyed? But I will again repeat "the true and real cause why this union is so anxiously "desired, the British Minister wishes to become "despotic master of the Irish nation and the Irish "purse; that is the true cause why this measure is "pressed on the country, all the rest are mere "pretences."

(3.) *Debate in Irish House of Commons on the Address, 15th and 16th January 1800.*

Mr. [illegible], after remarking on the loss which the union would entail through increase of absenteeism, said, "Taxes will be increased. For whatever may be "agreed upon as the proportion of Ireland to contribute, we know that our taxes must advance as "[illegible] as they have done in Scotland; and "what the surplus of revenue may remain will be "remitted to the Treasury at Westminster. I cannot "[illegible] these consequences at less than [illegible] "Mr. Pitt has cast his eyes about on every side for "revenue. From the East India Company he has "obtained, I believe, an income of [illegible]. He has "got a large sum from the Bank of England for renewing its charter. Ever so long ago as the commercial propositions, he required [illegible] a year "from Ireland, and it cannot be supposed that he will "now be content with less than [illegible]."

Mr. *Grattan*, throughout his speech, which was the chief feature of this debate, assumed that the union would lead to a great increase of Irish taxation, but otherwise the matter was not directly discussed on that occasion.

(4.) *Debate of 5th and 6th February 1800.*

Lord Castlereagh introduced the articles of the treaty of union, the seventh of which related to the question of taxation. His speech, so far as relates to this question, was as follows:—

"I have thus shortly descanted upon that part of the plan which concerns the executive power, and the advantages which will be gained to Ireland in that essential part of the constitution, by adopting the measure of an union. If I were to follow the order of the resolutions, my next object would be to consider the formation of the Legislature; but, as the propositions I shall submit on this head, will be a great measure result from the consideration of the contributive powers of the island, I wish first to lay before the House those points which concern our finances and our commerce, and from these proceed to the legislative question.

"I shall now, therefore, state to the House the substance of the 7th Article which I mean to submit for their adoption, and which embraces the detail of the contribution which Ireland is to furnish to the general expenses of the Empire.

"The enemies of the measure of union, have founded much of their clamour upon the groundless supposition, that it is a mere financial project of the British Minister, to put his hands into the pockets of the Irish people. But, sir, I believe it will be found upon examination of the terms, that if any sacrifice be made, it will not be on the part of Ireland, but upon the part of Great Britain. The settlement which is offered, is that of advantage to Ireland; but it is offered not as a bribe, not upon the mercenary principle that Ireland would sacrifice what is essential to her happiness to any pecuniary consideration, but it is offered upon the fair and liberal ground of equal contribution.

"I shall then first consider upon what principles the two kingdoms are to be incorporated in point of contribution; secondly, the regulations which are to carry these principles into effect; and thirdly, I shall examine the operation of these regulations, as tending to increase or diminish the expenses of Ireland.

"The first principle which has been laid down by the liberality of the British Parliament is, that there should be no retrospect in regard to expenses. Ireland is to have no concern whatever with the past debt of Great Britain. All the wealth, all the territories, all the commercial power and advantages of Great Britain are to be fully laid open and communicated to Ireland, without demanding from her any contribution whatever to the support of that enormous debt, which she has contracted in acquiring and securing them. Such is the liberality of Great Britain; but as to the future it is expected that the two countries should move forward together and unite with regard to their expenses in the measure of their relative abilities.

"I should have considered it, sir, as a most valuable circumstance in this arrangement, if the two countries could at once have been so completely incorporated as not to be under the necessity of having distinct revenues. This principle made a part of the Scotch Union, and it was naturally felt to be of such importance that a great effort was made to equalise the circumstances of the two countries for that purpose. England had at that period a considerable debt; Scotland had none. An accurate calculation was therefore made of the sum which Scotland ought to receive as an indemnity for subjecting herself to the charges of the debt of England, and the sum being ascertained, was paid by England as an equivalent. The taxation of the two countries was accordingly subjected to the same scale, except in the article of land tax, which was fixed on a separate proportion. And this difference arose from the circumstance that the land tax in England was levied lightly and unequally, and the land tax in Scotland was levied strictly, so that, if the same rate of land tax had been imposed in Scotland as was imposed in England Scotland would have been taxed much more than her just proportion. I mention these circumstances in order to show the pains which were wisely taken to incorporate Scotland with England as far as possible in point of finance, and I lament that the circumstances of Great Britain and Ireland do not at present enable us to pursue the measure of identity with equal strictness.

"It were to be wished that there was not an insurmountable bar to a common system and a common treasury, and that we could become, like countries of the same kingdom, subject to the same system of finances. Were our entire expenditure common (which would happen if neither kingdom had any separate debts, or if their debts were in proportion to their ability) by no system whatever could they be made to contribute so strictly according to their means, as by being subject to the same taxes equally bearing upon the great objects of taxation in both countries. Such, however, is the disproportion of debts of the two kingdoms to each other at the present, that a common system for the present is impossible, nor could any system of equivalent be applied for equalising their contribution. It is, therefore, necessary that the debts of the two countries should be kept distinct, and, of course, that their taxation should be separate and proportionate. The great point, therefore, to be ascertained is the best criterion which can be formed of the relative means of the two countries in order to fix the relative proportions of their contributions.

"Sir, I conceive the best possible criterion of the relative means and ability of two countries to bear taxation would be the produce of an income tax levied on the same description of incomes in each, and equally well levied in both. This criterion, however, is not at present to be found in Ireland, nor is it likely that for some time our local circumstances will permit its operation. We must, therefore, resort to some other test.

"I consider that the criterion next in order is the joint result of commerce and consumption, and that this may be satisfactorily ascertained by a review of their exports and imports, together with the quantities and value of the chief articles of their consumption. I propose, then, to consider the proportion which those articles bear to each other, separately and conjointly, in Great Britain and Ireland; and if they nearly coincide, I shall take it for granted that the best means of deciding the relative ability of the two countries have been fairly taken.

"Upon a comparison of the average value of the imports and exports of Great Britain for three years, ending January 1799, compared with those of Ireland ending the 25th of March preceding, I find that the value of British commerce amounted to 73,961,889l.; of Irish commerce to 10,505,961l., and that they bear the proportion to each other of nearly 7 to 1.

"Upon a similar comparison of the values of the following articles, viz., malt, beer, spirits, wine, tea, tobacco, sugar, consumed in the respective countries, I find that the value of the British articles amounted to 46,891,528l.; of the Irish articles to 5,954,856l., which form a proportion of 7¾ to 1.

"The medium, therefore, or 7½ to 1, may be taken as the fair proportion; and I would maintain that upon this principle Great Britain ought to contribute 15 parts, and Ireland 2, to the general expenses of the Empire.

"Having stated the principle of the Article I shall now enumerate its provisions.

"The 1st section provides that the past debts of the two countries shall be borne by them respectively; and if we couple this liberal provision with the section of the Article, which gives to Ireland a participation in whatever sums may be produced from the territorial revenues of the dependencies of Great Britain in India, we must acknowledge not only the justice but the generosity of the terms.

"Great Britain holds out to Ireland a fair participation in all the advantages of the Empire without requiring the smallest participation in the burdens which she has incurred to procure them; and Ireland will acquire a revenue of 58,000l. a year, in ease of her own burdens, out of the revenue paid by the East India Company, from the territories subdued by British arms.

"The 2nd section will provide that the proportionate contribution of 15 to 2 shall continue for 20 years, in order that the system of the Union may acquire stability, before it be subjected to the slightest modification.

"When I stated the system of contributing on the principle of proportional ability, I was aware that a natural objection would arise, that however fair or liberal this system might appear at present, it might at a future period, and under different circumstances, prove to be both partial and disadvantageous. It is therefore intended, that the Imperial Parliament shall have a power to revise the proportion at the given period I have mentioned; but that the revision should be grounded upon the same principles upon which the original proportion is formed, and limited to the result of those principles. Our contributions, therefore, may hereafter vary according to our relative increased or diminished ability; but, until the period of a common taxation shall arise, the principles, and the basis of our contribution, are unalterably fixed. The only power reserved to the Imperial Parliament, is to examine and ascertain the criterion by which the abilities of the two countries are to be decided upon: the criterions themselves are to remain unaltered and unalterable, and, as they are of such a nature as that they cannot possibly fail of leading to a fair result, Ireland has by these means the utmost possible security, that she cannot be taxed beyond the measure of her comparative ability, and that the rate of her contribution must ever correspond with her relative wealth and prosperity.

"The 4th section will provide, that the revenues of Ireland should constitute a consolidated fund, which will be charged in the first place with the interest and sinking fund of the debt of Ireland, and be afterwards appropriated to its proportionate contribution. The 5th section gives power to the Imperial Parliament to impose such taxes in Ireland as may be necessary for her contingent; but that in no case it shall be enabled to impose higher taxes, after the Union, upon any article in Ireland, than the same article shall be liable to in Great Britain. The 6th section enumerates the manner in which any surplus of the revenues of Ireland may be applied. There are four considerations which occur with respect to any excess of revenue, which may take place. The first, and most obvious, is the diminution of taxes; the second, is the application of such excess to local purposes of ornament or improvement in Ireland; the third, is to provide against any possible failure of revenue, which may be expected in time of peace; the fourth, is to suffer such excess, or surplus, to accumulate at compound interest, in ease of our contribution in a future period of war. The reason which induces me to suggest the last method of disposing of any surplus of revenue, arises from the different systems of Great Britain and Ireland, with respect to raising their supplies.

"Great Britain has at length established the great principle of raising a great part of her supplies within the year; this island is not at present in a situation to adopt a similar system, the consequence of which is that the debt of Great Britain will hereafter increase in a much less degree and be more rapidly liquidated; whilst the debt of Ireland will be increasing with greater rapidity, especially if she shall continue a separate country; but as an Union will greatly diminish her expenses in time of peace, it is proposed that this arrangement with respect to any surplus of revenue, should be adopted, to prevent her too rapid accumulation of debt in time of war.

"The 7th section provides that all future loans, for the interest and liquidation of which the respective countries have made provisions in the proportion of their respective contributions, shall be considered as joint debt; and, on the other hand, that, where they

to pre make corresponding provisions, their respective quotas of the sum so raised should receive a separate charge, in like manner as debt contracted previous to the Union.

"The 8th section contains a provision that, when the separate debts of the two kingdoms shall be either extinguished, or in the proportion of their respective contributions, the general expenses of the Empire may be thenceforward borne by common taxes, in lieu of proportionate contribution. I have, Sir, already explained the importance of an assimilation of the taxes of the two kingdoms. The obstacle to the adoption of protocol has been stated to be the disparity of burdens, which arise from their respective debts, and which possibly may be removed by time. I shall, therefore, endeavour to obviate an impression which may be made, that common taxes with Great Britain will impose upon this kingdom heavier burdens than she would otherwise be called upon to support. Let the House then first consider that the charges of the debt of Great Britain amount to 20 millions a year, and the charges of the debt of Ireland to 1,300,000*l.*, British, a year, that common taxes are not to take place, till either the past and separate debts of both countries shall be liquidated, or till they shall become to each other in the proportion of their contributions, that is, in the ratio of 15 to 2. Before this can take place, the taxes of Great Britain must be reduced by the amount of 10 millions a year; in which case, the scale of her remaining taxation would be lowered to the scale of taxation in Ireland, and the adoption of British taxation would become a benefit; a similar result would take place, and to a greater degree, were the past debt of the two countries to be entirely liquidated; for, in this case, Ireland would be exonerated from taxes to the amount of 1,300,000*l.* a year, and Britain to the amount of 20 millions, and the system of common taxation would become still more beneficial to Ireland. It may happen, however, that if war should continue and Ireland fund her supplies, whilst England raises a great part of hers within the year, and mortgages her income tax to their rapid reduction in peace, that the proportion of the debt of Ireland may rise, and her scale of taxation increase accordingly. In that case, also, the system of common taxation perfectly secures the interests of Ireland, being produced by natural causes and in no degree forced. It cannot impose any burthens on this country (Ireland), to which she must not in the ordinary course of her expenditure be liable; whilst the provision, which goes to preclude any article from being subject to a higher rate of duty in Ireland than the same article pays in Great Britain, will exempt her from having the scale of her taxation raised above that of England, even though the natural progress of her expenses should lead to it. And whilst Ireland is thus secured against any injustice in establishing a system of common taxes in lieu of proportionate contribution, the United Parliament will be enabled to make abatements in Ireland, as the Parliament of Great Britain always has done to Scotland since the Union; when, from local circumstances, the high duty cannot be levied without either rendering the revenue unproductive or pressing too hard upon the poorer classes.

"It now, sir, remains for me to consider the operation and effect of this Article, and how far the proportion of $7\frac{1}{2}$ to 1 is favourable or otherwise to Ireland, considered with reference to the past expenses of the two countries, as also to their probable future expenditure.

"The peace establishment of Great Britain in the year preceding the war amounted to 3,805,744*l.*; that of Ireland amounted in the same year to 1,012,523*l.*

"The proportion of these sums is about $3\frac{3}{4}$ to 1. Upon an average of seven years, from the commencement of the war, Great Britain has expended each year 27,353,649*l.*; Ireland has expended 3,076,835*l.* The proportion of these sums is about 9 to 1. As, however, upon the experience of the past century, it is found that there are three years of peace to two of war; if we form our calculations upon this proportion, the past expenses of Great Britain and Ireland may be considered in the ratio of $7\frac{1}{2}$ to 1.

"Such is the result as to past expenditure. I shall now state what we may expect from the proportion of $7\frac{1}{2}$ to 1 in our future expenses. The expense of Great Britain for the year 1799 was 32,700,000*l.*; that of Ireland, 5,429,000*l.*

"If this expense had been borne in the proportion of $7\frac{1}{2}$ to 1, Great Britain would have expended 33,685,303*l.*; Ireland would have expended 4,491,363*l.*, and Ireland would have consequently saved 937,311*l.*, or 1,006,853*l.* in Irish currency.

"So long, sir, as the war shall last, and we shall continue separate from Great Britain, it is not possible to suppose that our expenses can be reduced; and, therefore, we shall in future expend more by one million a year than if we were united with Great Britain.

"I shall now advert to the probable future expenses of Ireland in time of peace; and, if we consider the advanced pay of the army, the increased charge of the militia, the necessity of keeping up some part of that formidable force, the yeomanry, we shall find it impossible to maintain a peace establishment of only 12,000 men at home, at a less charge than 1,300,000*l.* a year; and, if we were to increase our establishment to 20,000 men, the whole charge would amount to 1,500,000*l.* a year. Now, sir, from the best documents I have been able to procure, it appears that the peace establishment of Great Britain is likely to amount to about 7,800,000*l.*; and that of Ireland, 1,500,000*l.*; total, 9,302,000*l.*

"If this charge be borne in the ratio of $7\frac{1}{2}$ to 1, there would be a saving to Ireland of 414,000*l.* British, or nearly 500,000*l.* Irish currency.

"It may be asked, sir, how Great Britain can accede to an arrangement which seems calculated to charge her with nearly half a million in time of peace, and a million in time of war? The answer is, that Great Britain is willing to become one kingdom with Ireland, and contribute proportionably with this kingdom, according to their relative means. If the proportion of expense shall be rightly fixed and ascertained upon just principles, for every part of the Empire, it is immaterial to Great Britain where the expenditure takes place. If the internal circumstances of Ireland call for a large proportion of the army to be continued in this island, the expense will be greatest here. If the southern coast of England requires to be strengthened, the expenditure will be directed to that quarter; but can Scotland and other parts of the Empire, which equally contribute, but do not require any expensive protection, feel any challenge or jealousy that their state of security requires a less portion of troops, and a less proportion of expense than the more exposed or convulsed part of the two islands?

"Now, sir, let us for a moment turn to the situation of the public revenues. The produce of all the taxes in the last year amounted merely to 1,890,000*l.*, and the present charges of the debt alone are near 1,400,000*l.* Irish currency. I will, however, admit that the revenues of this kingdom have, during the present year, experienced an extraordinary increase; but it is not possible to suppose that the whole of this increase can be permanent, when it can be accounted for by the particular circumstances of the times. I will, however, suppose that the revenues may produce a permanent sum of 2,300,000*l.*—

	£
"The charge of our debt is - -	1,400,000
The peace establishment at the lowest computation will be -	1,500,000
Total expense	2,900,000

"So that, if we remain a separate state, we shall have an annual deficiency of 600,000*l.*, which we must endeavour to supply by new burdens upon the people: besides raising additional taxes of 250,000*l.* a year, so long as the war shall continue. If, on the contrary, we wisely unite with Great Britain, and agree in a system of contribution proportionate to our respective means, the future charge of our war expense will be diminished a million a year, and we shall be able to support our peace expenditure with a very slight addition to the present taxes. I now, then, confidently appeal to those gentlemen around me, who have a real stake in the interests and happiness of this country, and I trust they will seriously pause and deliberate before they suffer advantages like those which I have stated to be rejected without discussion, or to be decided by wild and senseless clamour."

Sir John Parnell said that "it had been contended "that Ireland must gain in a pecuniary point of view, "because her expenses would only be in the proportion "to those of England as 1 to $7\frac{1}{2}$; but this was a very "fallacious mode of reasoning; for as the expenses of "England increased those of Ireland must increase "also, and at the expiration of 20 years, Ireland would "be entirely at the mercy of the united Parliament, "to be taxed to whatever extent they thought fit; but "even if this project was calculated to procure "commercial advantages to Ireland, yet when it so "obviously attacked their independence he was sure "they would not agree to it."

Mr. J. G. Beresford said that, according to Lord Castlereagh, the proportion of taxation was to be as 15 to 2, and that consequently the taxes in Ireland would be less than they were at present, and adding "not being able from a loose statement of this kind to calculate whether the fact be so or not, I shall not attempt to examine or state anything on it; but I fear the country will find that, let the gross sum of taxation be what it may, the taxes will bear heavier on individuals than they at present do; indeed, the noble Lord himself reckons on not so reckon on the present increase of the revenue. I do not know on what his Lordship grounds his opinion that the present amount of the revenue is precarious, but I ground it in conclusion that the most of the landed property of the country will be drawn out of it by the adoption of such a measure, and when they are gone from it the revenue must fall, the import duties must diminish with the diminution of the consumption of imported articles, the other revenues will, of course, fail for the same reasons, and new taxes must be sought for, when from the absence of our men of property we are least able to bear them."

Mr. Edgeworth said that "to strengthen the two countries by a union their interests must be completely identified, their debts, taxes, commercial advantages and restraints, their current coin, everything which can be the object of legislative exertion, must be upon a perfect footing of equality. I know, Sir, that a Minister would not at all venture to propose such a bold and sweeping measure; but, Sir, he talks to you of our being equal in such a situation in 15 or 20 years. The debt of England the noble Lord has stated as bearing at the commencement of the war a proportion to the debt of Ireland, as 120 to 1, at present as 15 to 1. He therefore justly concludes that in a short time the debt of the two kingdoms must be exactly proportioned to their relative strength, riches, population. He might put this in a much stronger light, in 10 years before 1776, a period partly of peace and partly of war, the debt of Ireland has increased in a different proportion, in 10 years more, were our debt to follow the same proportion, it would amount to two hundred millions, and in 20 to two thousand millions. There must, therefore, Sir, be some fallacy in the common modes of calculations upon these subjects. Those who are in the least conversant with subjects of this nature must perceive that, if the debt of England were suddenly extinguished, it would create universal bankruptcy and confusion."

Mr. Edgeworth then went on to say that paradoxical as it might seem, Ireland did actually then "pay a very large share of the National Debt of Great Britain," and that the debt of England "gradually ceases to be a burthen, and, after certain periods of time, every addition to it becomes merely numerical, and encumbers neither the exertions of the State nor the industry of individuals."

(b.) *February* 1800.

Mr. Foster (the Speaker), in a speech on 17th February 1800 made in committee, after dwelling on the present independence of Ireland, said "If we adopt the proposed union and give up our Parliament we shall reverse our situation and have a theoretic independence with a practical and sure dependence, we shall be brought back to the miserable state in which we were when governed by the laws of another Parliament, sitting in another land, ruled by their will, not by our own; our purse, our trade, our properties, our very liberties at their disposal and under their control." . . . "It is curious to observe the noble Lord's arguments last year and now; our growing wealth was then held out by him as tending to render us too difficult to be governed by our present constitution; that, with its growth, our wealth, our consequence, our pride, and our power would increase, and there was the greater hurry for taking away our Parliament as that growth was advancing with rapid strides. Now, our poverty is made the pretence; we must take the union to save us from bankruptcy; we have not the means to go on for three years; we have overpaid our proportion of the war expense by a million a year, and of the peace expense by half a million. We have almost ruined the country by this profusion, and Britain, in proposing this measure, means to give us that million and half million, and hereafter to tax herself to pay it. Can any rational man believe such a story, or by which of these contradictory arguments will the noble Lord abide? . . . This argument of his seems to be a part of the general plan to vilify the Parliament in the eyes of the people, to tell the people that this House has granted their money too fast, that they must distrust us and lodge their purse in the hands of the British Parliament, who will be more paternal and faithful guardians of it. Is there any child so weak as to believe that he is in earnest, or that he means to load England to save Ireland?"

Mr. Foster then proceeded to argue that the union, instead of saving expense to Ireland, would increase it.

"The noble Lord states the relative ability of the two countries to bear taxation to be as 7½ to 1, and states the peace expenses to be as 5⅔ to 1, and the war expenses as 9 to 1, and taking the proportion of the years of war to the years of peace during the present century, he states the medium of 7½ to 1, which he establishes as the proportion of contribution, and Ireland is consequently to pay 2/17 and England 15/17 of the whole annual aggregate of expense of both kingdoms.

"He states the expenses of Britain to have been in the year (I suppose the last year) 32,706,000*l.*, and I take his statement as true, but I cannot find any paper which justifies his account of Ireland's expenses. I will therefore take them for the last year, which has been ascertained by the report of the committee of accounts, a year in which they were unusually great, owing to the extensive rebellion and the invasion which took place, and they appear by the return of the issues from the Treasury for all service, civil, military, and extraordinary, to have been 4,706,294*l.*, or in British money 4,347,000*l.*, making together 37,047,000*l.*; 2/17 whereof being 4,358,470*l.*, would have been our proportion had the union been in force, which exceeds by a trifle the sum we did actually pay.

"But he goes further, for in his calculation he states that our war proportion would be, British, 4,481,000*l.*, which exceeds the sum paid by us of 4,347,000*l.*, and consequently by his own statement of his beneficial arrangement which is to save us a million, we should pay more than he actually did pay to the amount of 145,000*l.*, or in Irish money 157,000*l.*

"But we have a better criterion than speculative calculation to show what would have been our actual situation on the 25th March last had this union proportion taken place at the beginning of the war.

	£
"Great Britain in six years to 5th January 1799 increased her debt in the sum of - - - - -	150,000,000
Ireland in six years to the 25th March 1799 increased her's 13,602,000*l.* or in British money, nearly - - -	[illegible]
Making together - - - -	[illegible]
2/17 whereof, or Ireland's proportion, would have been from 23,530,000*l.*, or in Irish money, nearly - - - -	25,100,000
But Ireland increased her debts only -	15,065,000
And the excess - - -	£10,408,000

would have been an additional debt, incurred by Ireland, had this blessed union taken place in 1793, an additional debt which, if averaged on the six years, makes an increased charge on each of 1,734,000*l.*, and this is one of the ways in which the noble Lord would give us a million a year.

"Again, Great Britain has imposed during these six years new permanent taxes to the nett amount of 7½ millions a year, 2/17 whereof must have been raised by Ireland amounting annually to 882,352*l.* British, or 955,801*l.* Irish, and this is another way the noble Lord in the generosity of his projected union would give us a million a year.

"Again, Great Britain has raised by temporary taxes, on imports and exports, and on income (or by mortgaging them) to the amount of 11½ millions a year, 2/17 whereof or 1,352,940*l.* British would have been Ireland's annual proportion.

	£
"Thus had we been fortunate enough to have been united, under the noble Lord's plan, in 1793, we should in the first place have been in debt in March last - -	10,408,000
more than we were, being an increase by the year of - - - - -	1,734,000
2ndly, we should have had permanent taxes imposed to the annual net produce of -	955,801
And 3rdly, we should have been forced last year to have imposed as further taxes -	1,465,685
Making together - - -	£14,157,324

"Whereas, if we take the calculations the noble Lord relies on for showing the revenues of the year, the

revenue of Ireland in 1799 exceeded that in 1793 by 700,000l., which being deducted from the [illegible], leaves 3,[illegible]l. annual increase. He would lessen our annual expense one million a year by increasing it near three millions and a half! . . . .

"Observe, too, that the noble Lord, to show [illegible] how near we are to bankruptcy tells us that we are running into debt faster than England. I have shown you the amount of each kingdom's increase of debt during the war, Ireland 14,000,000l. British; England 180,000,000l.; we ran only at the rate of one million for twelve and a half of hers, but he tells you we should have gone slower if we had quickened our pace, so as to go one for every seven and a half.

"And now I may dismiss his war calculations, and I trust I have made it clear as mathematical demonstration that, if this nation had been blessed with this union and its liberal accommodating proportion for Ireland, by his pretended free gift of one million a year, we should have been near 11,000,000l. more in debt than we are, and we should now be forced to raise about 2½ million more than we do at present, and we should have received no part of his boasted free gifts.

"Let us now go to his peace establishment, which he states at 1,500,000l. when the present war shall cease, but for which he produces no reasonable grounds; on the contrary, he allows the last peace establishment to have been only 1,012,000l. And there is no reason to suppose that all economy must cease, and that every war is to make the peace establishment half as large again as it was before.

"Let me remind you that in 1785, you determined by a resolution I had the honour to propose, as Chancellor of the Exchequer, that the revenue should be made equal to the expenses. You accordingly granted near 150,000l. a year new taxes, the debt then including 200,000l. voted, was 2,381,801l., and in 1793, at the end of the peace, it was only 2,344,[illegible]l. This shows you at once that the peace establishment was sufficient, and it is a conspicuous proof of the efficiency and wisdom of the Parliament, which you are called on to transport as a culprit, that it was capable of adhering during the whole peace to a steady system of economy, which advanced the trade and wealth of the kingdom. . . . .

"He takes the produce of all the taxes last year to 25th March 1799, at 1,800,000l., because such was the amount received at the Treasury, but by some fatality he forgets that the Treasury permitted the revenue collectors' balances to increase, so as to be 257,[illegible]l. more at the end of the year than at the beginning of it. This increase must have been part of the income of the year, and might have been received if called for; it should, therefore, be added to the Treasury receipts, and the whole year's net revenue would be 2,135,000l. He estimates the permanent increase of the revenue in 1800 at 450,000l., and he totally omits the lotteries, which may be reckoned at about 70,000l. profit, making altogether an increase of—

	£
	2,[illegible],000
The charges of the debt I state with him at - - - - - -	1,400,000
Which leaves - - -	1,[illegible],000

for peace establishment, and should this not prove sufficient, much more may be obtained by a better collection, and we should remember that this estimate of the revenues is taken from a year of rebellion and invasion.

"Where then is the mighty phantom of increased taxation, with which he would frighten us into his project, or where is the national bankruptcy with which he so kindly threatens us? One inference naturally occurs from this statement of the future peace expenses by the noble Lord, that the whole train of the kingdom's expenses is to remain, the Lord-Lieutenant, the State, the whole civil list, the officers, the Exchequer, in short everything but your Parliament, and I cannot too often or too strongly press upon you this truth, that the real question of the union is, Parliament or no Parliament! It is our Parliament they want to remove and nothing else.

"I have throughout followed his mode of calculation in order to render the comparison of my statement with his the more easy, and I have for this reason admitted his return of the debt as the total capital created, I mean at seventeen millions, which the Treasury states, instead of thirteen millions which the Accountant-General states . . . .

"I have also admitted his ratio of 1 to 7½ for the contribution, though he allows the real ratio is in war as 1 to 8. War expenses are much larger than those in peace, at his own calculations nearly as 4½ to 1; where then is the fairness of our paying two-fifteenths instead of two-seventeenths, when the expenses are 4,700,000l. a year, and making a saving in return when they are only 1,000,000l. and are to be at the utmost only 1,500,000l., particularly as there are but two years of saving or peace calculated for one of loss or war.

"Again, he says, he estimates the proportions on the joint grounds of commerce and consumption, but omits all internal commerce, which is much greater than the external, and even in the external he omits to calculate the tonnage of the shipping belonging to each kingdom, and rests solely on the value of the imports and exports, without regard to which country receives the profits of the carriage, though they constitute a material part of the value, and in consumption he omits the article of salt, which is one of very general use; the gross duties on it in the last year were [illegible]l. in Britain and [illegible],000l. in Ireland, or nearly 1 to [illegible]. The stamp duties arising from exchange of property, litigation, and insurance show in some sort the respective abilities, their gross amount in Great Britain last year was 2,000,000l. exclusive of post horses, hair powder, licences, &c., not adopted here or not affecting property in its transfer, and in Ireland only 137,[illegible]l., or as 1 to 15, yet these he has omitted. The post office also, was adopted by many of his friends in England as a criterion of the growing wealth of England, and I wonder at its escaping his attention. It produced last year in Britain [illegible],000l., in Ireland [illegible],000l., about 1 to 15.

"What effect any of these might have if added in order to form a mean proportion I won't say, but I am sure no means should be omitted which can be seized on to ascertain so material a point of negotiation as the contribution.

"I have now done with the dry subject of calculation, and I will ask were all the mighty benefits of revenue true, how are they to be conferred? The union won't change the total mass of expense of both nations in the war; no ship will be laid by, no regiment disbanded on account of it, all the force must remain while the war continues; if then Ireland is to pay less, Britain must pay more; if she is to save Ireland from threatened bankruptcy, she is thereby to draw herself nearer to it. Where then is our benefit? We must support her, for if she falls Ireland fall with her, consequently this supposed transfer will not serve us, if it weakens her. But it is all a delusion; can any man in his senses think that the Minister can call on Great Britain really to raise a million a year, to give it to Ireland who has not complained, and is willing herself to share her own load. . . . Besides, were it actually and bona fide to be given to Ireland, the proportion is to last only 20 years, or thereabouts, perhaps not nearly so long, and 20 years is a short period in the life of a nation. Well might a sagacious Minister, with a long lease, give a little boon during 20 years in order to get the entire command of the purse of a great nation for ever after. . . ."

(3.) March 1800.

Mr. *Foster* spoke again on the 19th March 1800, in committee, and said with regard to the 7th Article :— Mr. Foster

"To begin with the article of *contribution*, I will not enter into arguments that it is calculated on unfair or unjust ground, though I could, with ease, maintain that it is much more against us than it ought to be, even on the grounds on which it rests; and still more largely so if we compare the wealth of the two kingdoms, the comparative proportion of which can alone show the comparative ability to pay taxes. I say I will not enter into it, because the offer of it is such an imposition, such a palpable delusion, that I am astonished it could ever have been held out seriously as a favourable arrangement, for it is attended with provisions to destroy it before any benefit can arise from it; and be its advantages great or little, they must cease in three years or four at the most.

"The words in the 7th Article are that, if at any future time" the separate debts of each kingdom shall "have been liquidated, or the values of their respective "debts estimated according to the amount of their in- "terest and their annuities attending the same of the

'sinking fund applicable to the reduction thereof, and 'the period within which the whole capital of such 'debts shall appear to be redeemable by such sinking 'fund, shall be to each other in the same proportion 'with the respective contributions of each kingdom 'respectively, that is, of 7½ to 1, then it shall be competent for 'the said Parliament to declare that all future 'expenses thereafter to be incurred, together with the 'interest and charges of all joint debts contracted 'previous to such declaration shall be defrayed 'indiscriminately by equal taxes.'"

"The noble Lord who introduced it expressed his lamentations that the circumstances of Great Britain and Ireland did not enable us to pursue the measure of identity in the revenues with equal strictness as in the Scotch Union, and that the two countries could not at once be incorporated so as not to be under the necessity of having distinct revenues. It were to be wished, he said, that there was not an insurmountable bar to a common system and a common treasury; such, however, is the disproportion of the debts of the two kingdoms that a common system for the present is impossible.

"Hence then arose the necessity of a ratio of contribution; the unequal amount of the two debts occasioned distinct interests; and while those debts continue, their pressure being unequal, there can be no equal interest, and equal taxes would be unjust. But, contrary to this principle, the article says, we shall undergo equal taxation when these respective debts come to bear the proportion to each other, which is ascertained for our contribution, that is, of 1 to 7½.

"The British debt in January last was 351,389,604l. after deducting 42,904,316l. for the amount redeemed, and when the Irish debt arises to 46,162,612l. it will be in the proportion to it of 1 to 7½; but the Irish debt, as the noble Lord asserts, and as a pamphlet, said to be the speech of a great Law Lord, states in a minute calculation, will be 50,000,000l. in 1802, which is in a nearer proportion to 351,389,604l. than 1 to 7½; and therefore, in 1802, the delusion which is plausibly held out will vanish; we are to lose the advantage of paying one share only for 7½, and we are to commence a system of paying one for one, while the debts are to continue as 1 to 7½.

"Perhaps it may be said that the proportion of the principal due by each kingdom is not the only criterion, but that the value of the respective debts is to be estimated according to the amount of the interest and the annuities attending them. We will take it so and the result will be nearly the same.

"The annual charges of the British debt are stated in one of the returns on your table to have been on the 5th January 1800 above 20,000,000l. We are told by the noble Lord, and it appears by the same minute calculation I have mentioned that the annual charge of the Irish debt will be 2,775,755l. in 1804, which is within the proportion of 1 to 7½ of the British charge. So that even on this estimate we are to commence the burden of equal taxation with Great Britain in four years. But if we deduct the annual charges attendant on the debt redeemed by the sinking funds, the British charge is 17,000,000l., and the proportion will therefore be attained in less than three years. That is, the proportion will be attained whenever the charges of the Irish debt shall amount to 2,266,666l., but that speech tells us they will be 2,434,766l. in 1802; yet the noble Lord states in direct terms that, before common taxes can take place, the taxes of Great Britain must be reduced by ten millions a year. How is this to be reconciled, or am I wrong in calling it a delusion?

"Should the noble Lord urge that the value is to be estimated by another test—the period at which the respective capitals shall appear redeemable by the sinking fund, I will even meet him there. To go into the conjectures on the operation of the sinking fund is useless; it depends entirely on the value of stock at the moment of purchase, and there cannot be any reasonable ground for estimating future events and their influence on stock, but I may state that the sinking fund of Ireland ought to operate more rapidly than that of Britain; for, when the British sinking fund of one million was created in 1786, the debt was 238 millions, and, when the Irish fund of 100,000l. was appropriated in 1797, the Irish debt was 7,008,256l. The British fund therefore was $\frac{1}{238}$ part of the debt which it was to reduce, the Irish was $\frac{1}{70}$, and as to all debts incurred in each kingdom since the establishment of those funds, the provision in each is equal, being 1 per cent. on the capital created, and the operation therefore must be supposed equal. I don't mention the annual grant of 200,000l. to the British sinking fund; it is casual and would make very little difference to the argument. Take the matter therefore in any of the three views, of capital, annual charge, or sinking fund, you see the delusion clearly.

"The propositions offer us a proportion of contribution which, however more unfavourable to us than it ought to be, is certainly better than equal taxes; but it is so contrived that we are to lose it in three years. The cause which requires a contributive proportion is the different pressure of the debts; and yet when the debts are brought to press exactly in that contributive proportion it is to cease, as if no debt existed, and consequently there was no pressure. I was much at a loss to account for the anxiety manifested this session to state our debt at a higher nominal amount than heretofore, and to raise it from nineteen to twenty-five millions without increasing either the actual amount or the annual charge. We may now form a guess at the reason. It tended to accelerate the period of taking from us all benefit of proportional contribution and of making us subject to common taxation with Britain; and the mode of borrowing the whole of the supply this year (for the new taxes only pay the interest) tends materially to quicken our speed towards this period.

"In short the whole is a gross deception, unintentional, I will suppose, in the noble Lord (for I do not mean to charge him with deception), but the effect is equally prejudicial, and the reasoning is curious; the favourable proportion is given to us, as I have said, on account of the comparative greatness of the British debt—we owe only twenty-five millions, they owe 351—but when we shall owe 50, and they not above 340, we are to lose the benefit. We cannot bear equal taxation now, but when we double our debt in three years we shall be richer and more adequate to support it. Our increase of poverty, and their increase of wealth, are to bring on us an equality of condition, so as to bear an equality of taxes contrary to all reason; we are to increase our encumbrances in order to enjoy the full burden of equal taxation with Britain, and the period fixed on for our undertaking this burden is to be the moment of increased separate debt, and increased separate taxes in Ireland, when both our debts and taxes shall be doubled.

"To talk therefore of the justice or injustice of the contributive proportion would be an idle waste of time, and the Minister seems to think it would be as idle to attend to it, for unjustly as I believe it is calculated, unable as he has said, we are to go on without being bankrupt, which he tells us we must be, he has called on us this very session to borrow 4½ millions for the supplies of the year. When Britain borrows only 21½ millions, and we have voted taxes to nearly 300,000l., while she imposes only 550,000l., we borrow more than one-fifth of what she does, and we create a new revenue of almost six-sevenths of her whole additional taxes. If the kingdom is unequal to this exertion, if it so far exceeds the proportion which he admits we ought to contribute, why does he press us to it? Why does he allow our zeal to great so largely beyond our means, beyond our proportion of Imperial expense?"

After speaking at some length upon the 6th Article (commercial) of the treaty of union, Mr. Foster went on to say—

"In commerce then we clearly gain nothing and lose much, let us now examine revenue; the offer of one million a year in war and half a million in peace is too gross an imposition on our understanding to be believed; the attempt to delude us with the advantage of our contributing to general expenses in the proportion of only 1 to 7½, which I have exposed fully, was cloaked with some degree of plausibility, but this is brought forward without any covering to conceal its imposture; can any man, who appeals to his own reason think it possible that an union can give Great Britain the means of paying it, or that she would make such a sacrifice without a scheme of remuneration? Does the noble Lord's conduct justify his assertion? Look at the supplies of this year; England, as I have stated, raises twenty-one millions by loan and 550,000l. new taxes; Ireland 4½ millions by loan and 290,000l. new taxes. If the abilities of the two countries are in his favourite ratio of 1 to 7½, why does he call upon us to exceed the proportion of our abilities? Is it for England to save so much of her proportion? Or does he mean to show that England is not equally interested now, as she has ever been, in preserving us to the Empire, whether our Parliament be surrendered to her or not."

In answer to a reply by Lord Castlereagh, which does not seem to be reported, Mr. Foster spoke again on the same evening and said, *inter alia*—

"The noble Lord acknowledges that the contributive proportion between the kingdoms may cease in three years. He congratulates himself on my having proved it, and exults in the prospect that the separate interests of the nations are to be identified at once. He adds emphatically 'the sooner the taxes are equal the better,' and avows his hope that the burden is to fall on us in three years. I give him credit for this declaration, for I am sure he wishes so, but see the [illegible] of his argument. When the separate debts are extinguished the distinct interests which they create will certainly cease, and we are then to commence equal taxes; but the proposition says also that when the separate debts come to the proportion of contribution, $7\frac{1}{2}$ to 1, we are to commence equal taxes and, therefore, says the noble Lord, when we commence equal taxes the separate interests created by the debts will cease, applying the result of the one alternative to the other. No, Sir, as long as England owes $7\frac{1}{2}$ times as much as we do, so long do our separate interests in the debts continue, and so long should she pay $7\frac{1}{2}$ times as much as we do, and it would be the height of injustice that we should pay equal with her. Until then, the very proportion which she says identifies interest is founded on the distinctness of interest, else equality and not proportion would be the measure, and therefore, if the framers of these articles have artfully or inadvertently declared that on a certain proportion, which is a child of their own brain, taking place between the respective debts, our respective interests in those debts shall be deemed equal, though the very proportion declares them unequal, their saying it may show their folly, but can never make the debts nor the interests arising from them equal, nor destroy the distinctness they create.

"There is an absurdity in arguing on a debt as if it were wealth, and that when we attain the given proportion by becoming poorer, or doubling our debt from twenty-five to fifty millions, and England attains the same proportion by lessening hers, we grow wealthy thereby and are able to pay share for share, instead of paying only one share for every seven and a half."

In the same debate, the Articles of the Union having been agreed to, Mr. *Grattan* spoke against the motion that the chairman should leave the chair. After speaking on the general question, and arguing that the effect of Article 6, by abolishing or reducing the Irish protective duties, would be to injure the Irish manufactures, Mr. Grattan went on to say, "for the injuries "done to both" (your trade and your liberty), "the project of union proposes a compensation in revenue. England, it states, is to pay for your establishments in peace and war. A minister which has not [illegible] the British empire for near a century; England is to buy, and Ireland is to sell, the Irish constitution, and the empire of Great Britain and the freedom of Ireland are to be the victims; the empire is to lose what she wants, revenue; and you are to lose what you hold invaluable, constitution. When England communicates to Ireland the blessings of her trade, as in 1779, she lost nothing; she added to the stock of common industry; but when England parts with revenue, she loses what she gives, and you lose more than what you get; the idea, therefore, is inadmissible, the offer fraudulent. It is founded upon two principles, both of which are false; first, that the revenues of the country will not increase; second, that the expenses of the country must. As to the first, they say Ireland will be no longer able to support herself either in peace or war. In the last 20 years the revenues of Ireland have increased near fourfold, under the constitution of 1782. If they are to decline under the union in the next 20, what becomes of the national prosperity which is promised to flow from the union? Either their promise is true, and the union will increase the means of the country, and then what becomes of their argument? or their promise is false, and the union will diminish the means of the country, and then what should become of their union? So that they must either give up their argument or give up their measure.

"Let us see, however, what is this tremendous bankruptcy with which we are threatened. The revenues of this year they have stated to be 2,300,000*l.*, and the new taxes to be 300,000*l.* more, making together a net annual income of 2,600,000*l.* Now, the last peace establishment was not above 1,000,000*l.*, and the interest of the debt is not above 1,400,000*l.*; as they have under-rated the revenues of the country so they have over-rated her establishments; and they have estimated her future peace establishment at 1,[illegible]; they have increased, according to this estimate, the peace establishment one-third, for which they have given no adequate reason; they say the pay of the army has been augmented; that there will be a certain increase of expense in peace in consequence of the militia, and also in consequence of the [illegible] admitted; but these three items will not amount in peace to the difference of [illegible]. They have not attempted to produce any evidence to show that they will, nor can they; therefore, when they call upon you to acknowledge such a peace establishment, they call upon you for an opinion without any data or foundation whatsoever. The expenses of militia and [illegible] in peace, which they talk about but do not state, should produce a proportional reduction of the army, unless they propose, as I suspect they do, to make the establishment a military government, and to throw into this country a great proportion of the army of the empire, and they do hint, indeed, that your peace establishments must be 1,[illegible], and that you are not to have 12,000 regulars as formerly, but 20,000 effective regular troops.

"Thus they propose a war establishment in time of peace, as they have proposed a rebellion establishment in time of war, and form the estimate of their permanent establishments on the estimate of a permanent rebellion. They have already stated the productive effects, and now they state the tranquillizing consequences of a union—permanent disaffection, permanent military government. A minister states that he cannot administer the country according to the established constitution, or upon any revenue which the country can afford, and you are to make him a present of the Parliament, and to replace it by troops.

"Thus the union, when it defends itself, becomes a self-convicted measure. The projector tells you a military government and a military force, which the country will not be able to pay, and which Great Britain must, will be required in order to keep down those discontents which follow the union. I do acknowledge that some few years after the war it may be necessary to keep up a [illegible] force in Ireland. I do not know that it will; but if it should, I would consider such force the establishment of expediency, and not of permanency. It should be considered, like the martial law bill, or repeal of the habeas corpus bill, measures of the moment, and as these laws are not to be considered as your permanent constitution, so neither should that force be considered as your permanent establishment.

"With respect to the war establishment, the project holds out the saving of a million; on what grounds I cannot see; but let us proceed on the noble lord's calculations as if they were right. What will be the amount of that saving? His statement of the war establishment he cannot apply beyond the present war; you can collect something like a wish that the statement should be extended still farther, but nothing like an argument. Let us suppose, then, the present war to last for three years: for one you have provided already; in the remaining two you will, according to him, save 2,000,000*l.*; but you are to pay for the purchase of boroughs 1,500,000*l.*, so that your net saving for the surrender of your Parliament will be 500,000*l.* only. But this gain is founded upon a supposition that the noble lord's statements are right, and that the annual supply now voted is a million more than the annual contributionary supply projected; but his annual contributionary supply he states to be 4,[illegible] English, and the supply voted this year is 4,[illegible] Irish, so that his saving in time of war seems to be a perfect delusion. If you look back you will find that, upon his principle of contribution, we should in the present war, taking into consideration the taxes on exports and on income, and the permanent taxes raised this war in Great Britain, have raised, in addition to our former supplies, the annual income of above 3,000,000*l.* a year. Looking to the present moment, you see that you save nothing; and, looking prospectively, you see you pledge yourself to a principle of expense which is indefinite. You are to pay, I think he says, 4,400,000*l.* English in time of war, unless England should raise her expenses, and then you are to raise yours along with her. Let us, however, take the Irish contribution, and 4,400,000*l.* English; I should be glad to know whether this is to be expended on troops to be kept within the country or not? If on the former, it is a very bad disposition of the force of the empire, which cannot be justified but by rebellion and invasion, or the apprehension of both, and therefore never can be considered as the permanent application of His Majesty's forces. If the latter, that

[illegible]

is, if the money be to be expended on troops serving out of the country, how will you ever be able to bear so great a drain in addition to all your others; the drain of the absentees, the drain of the additional absentees, the drain of money paid for the interest of additional debt, and now the drain of the Irish contribution expended in other countries; so that, according to this plan, an invasion, or the apprehension of invasion or rebellion, are the only means to prevent bankruptcy. In every shape I view this question it is mischievous; and not less mischievous as the extinction of the Parliament of Ireland than as the corruption of the Parliament of Great Britain. You reduce your Commons by two-thirds, and you make the minister possess of the other; you calculate upon an immense Irish establishment in war, and an increased establishment in peace; thus you increase greatly the sources of influence, while you diminish the number of the persons on whom that influence is to operate; you keep up all the Irish establishments so augmented together, with all the establishments of Great Britain, and leave the double power to operate on one Parliament.

"The British House of Commons resolved some years ago, that the influence of the Crown had increased, and ought to be diminished. I understand it has considerably increased since. Some years ago, the number of placemen and pensioners in the Irish House of Commons were one hundred and ten; since that time the influence of the Crown has greatly increased in Ireland; and, according to the plan of union, the peace establishment is to increase one-third, and the military establishment infinitely beyond anything known in former wars. Thus, in addition to an influence which both countries felt to be truly alarming, and one country, in the resolutions of her representatives, declared to be so, do we see a vast accumulation formed, and forming to act on the reduced members of one legislature, thus rendered more compendious for the corruption of the minister, as the corruption of the minister is rendered more comprehensive and more decisive in the legislature; so that you lay a train for the downfall of the constitution of Great Britain, by the surrender of your own, whether you look to the military government, which is likely to take place in Ireland, to support this act of power, for such I must call the union, or to the tides of patronage, which are to accompany this act of power, and to add to tenfold the force of corruption, in conjunction, against the cause of liberty.

"I have mentioned the contributionary aid which is to follow this Union. I beg to consider, upon what proportion that contribution is founded. The noble lord who introduced the Union states it to be as two-fifteenths, or as a seventh and a half, but the grounds on which he formed his proportion, I own, do not satisfy me; his principal ground was a comparison of the respective exports and imports of the two countries, and he estimates the imports and exports of England, on an average of the three last years, at 75,000,000l., and those of Ireland at 10,000,000l., and something more. Mr. Pitt, in his calculation for his income tax, stated them at above 80,000,000l., and on that trade which was actually assessed, and we must suppose much that was not assessed. The noble lord has understated the export and import trade of England; he is also erroneous, inasmuch as he does not include tonnage, the proportion of which is beyond all comparison in favour of Great Britain. In the trade between Great Britain and this country, the tonnage and freight is almost entirely British; valuing, therefore, the imports from Great Britain to this country as a part of our trade, we ought to value the freight as her wealth, not ours, and it ought to be added to her export. He does not include in his estimate 1,000,000l. (it is a great deal more) imported into England to pay the absentees their rents from Ireland, and 4,000,000l. from the West Indies. He does not include in his plan of valuation of comparative wealth by trade the internal commerce of the two countries, which is to Great Britain a greater source of wealth than any other, and which, when we consider that Great Britain is in possession almost exclusively of her own markets, as far as relates to her manufactures, bears a prodigious proportion, we may assume, to the internal trade of Ireland. He says that it is difficult to obtain any knowledge on that subject; which would be a good reason for rejecting the Union, when so necessary a knowledge was impossible; but the fact is, Mr. Pitt, in his speech on the income tax, has obtained knowledge on that subject, at least knowledge enough for the purpose of taxation; and he states the value of the internal trade of his country to be 180,000,000l. There are other things of less consequence, but, however, of consequence notwithstanding, which he omits to state; for instance, he omits to state the profits of mines, minerals, timber, and shares in canals, which exist in Ireland in a very small degree of comparison, and which are rated to produce in England 2,000,000l. per annum. From all this what do I conclude? Not that the proportion of the wealth of Ireland is this quantity or that quantity, but that he has not given you any data whereon to conclude that the proportion of wealth in the two countries is the contribution recommended, namely, two-fifteenths or one-seventh and a half; on the contrary, I think you may safely say that he over-rates you in contribution, as he over-charges you in establishment."

On the 26th May Mr. *Grattan* spoke again on the Act of Union, and said with reference to the financial part of it:—

"If the principle of this Bill be innovation the terms of it are innovation likewise; the alteration in our system of commerce is innovation; the alteration in our system of revenue is innovation; the Bill teems with everything that is exceptionable; they talk to you, indeed, as if for liberty surrendered you were to break down under the weight of commercial acquisition; they talk to you, indeed, as if for liberty surrendered you were to carry off an immense portion of English revenue, and one million a year in war paid by England, in all deference, was to glad and to console you, and much silly and empty sound of that kind was rung in your ears; but what is the fact? that the terms of the union are aggravations of the union, the principal conditions are heavy contributions. Your financial conditions are dangerous experiments, and both such as you are perfectly competent to make, provided you are disposed to do so much mischief to your country; the revenue on the financial returns set out with the surrender of an availing revenue of 100,000l. a year, arising from the export of the raw material and the import of the manufacture, that is the best possible revenue that a nation can contrive; it adds the creation of a deficit of 80,000l. a year, the interest to pay a loan of one million and a half, to be paid for the purchase of boroughs, that is from one to two hundred thousand a year to be supplied by new taxes. The terms go on and propose a proportion of two to fifteen as the future contribution of Ireland; they do this without any data whatsoever which can warrant such a proposition. The data which are now before you, but which were not before you when you passed the resolution and when that proposition was laid, are unintelligible to the gentlemen to whom that data is furnished. Their papers, for instance, state the value of the consumption of the country in certain articles, by which they affect to ascertain its opulence to be so much; and other papers, which are also before the House, state the value to be so much less. In the instance of tea, of tobacco, and some other articles, the value of the goods consumed is returned by one-third, in some cases by one-half, more than the value of the same kind of goods imported. The difference may be reconcileable, but it is not reconciled, and the House votes for the proportion of the contribution which is founded on those very papers, without waiting for, without demanding, explanation. Suppose the cause, partly at least, of the incongruity is that in one set of papers they are valued subject to freight and tax, and in another set exempt from both. When the minister proceeds to value the ability of the country to pay taxes, he presents you with papers containing the value of the great articles, with the charge of freight and taxes embodied; but when he proceeds to state the balance of trade between England and Ireland he presents papers in which the freight and tax are omitted; thus coals (it is one amongst other instances) are valued at the pit mouths, and thus an apparent balance of trade is created in your favour, above 800,000l. more than the fact; so that by the double operation you are over-rated in commerce and over-rated in revenue. I say, therefore, that in fixing the proportion of relative contributions, so far as that proportion affected to found itself on the comparative consumption of the respective kingdoms, you had no data. When first you voted that proportion by way of resolution, you had not even papers; the majority of this House took the word of the minister without papers or documents, and on that word voted a 20 years' contribution. Since you proceeded by way of Bill, a member on this side of the House called for papers; the papers

are returned incongruous and unexplained, and now you vote the data which you don't understand, as before you voted without any data whatever. I speak of the comparisons on the articles of consumption; let us see whether you have better information on the comparison founded on the imports and exports. Here papers are submitted, but here the inland trade is omitted; it is calculated to amount in Britain to [illegible] a year; here also the re-export trade is omitted. It is valued at [illegible] per annum in Britain; in Ireland [illegible], in the year ending January 1799, it is valued at [illegible] in Britain. In the minister's calculation of national wealth to ground a tax on national income, it was included, I apprehend, as a distinct substantive source of wealth, and, if it were just to comprehend it with a view to impose tax, it is equally just to comprehend it with a view to ascertain a proportion; it is carried on by a distinct capital, it produces a distinct revenue; it is, by itself, a great trade; and it is almost the only one of some great commercial nations—Holland for instance. It is a greater evidence and greater source of wealth to make other nations pay for your industry, added to that of other countries, than out of the fruits of your industry to pay for the industry of those countries.

"But, without inquiring further into this head, without inquiring whether it be just to proceed on an average of three years, when it appears from a document, almost published under the name of Mr. Rose, that the imports and exports of Britain, in the year 1798, were not 73,000,000*l.*, but 80,000,000*l.*, and the re-exports not 11,[illegible], but [illegible]; while our trade is said to have declined, inasmuch as our revenue is said to have fallen [illegible]. Without inquiring into this, I say that the papers before you prove your contribution to be unjust; they set forth the imports and exports of Britain for the three years to have been 73,000,000*l.*, or that they form the proportion of two to fifteen. Now there should be added to that 73,000,000*l.* [illegible] per annum which Britain receives from the Indies and from Ireland; 4,000,000*l.* from the former and [illegible] in interest for public money lent, and over [illegible] in rent from the latter; this [illegible] is to be taken from the imports and exports of Ireland and to be added to those of Britain, which will make a proportion, not of 16 to 73, but of about 8 to 79; thus it follows that, whatever difficulty you may have in pronouncing the proportion of contribution, you can have no difficulty in pronouncing that the contribution you have ascertained is unjust and fallacious; and you can discover its injustice and fallacy by the very papers on which you have formed it; those papers ascertaining the proportion you have voted by the omission of [illegible] of British annual income. Thus has the House, under the direction of the minister, overcharged this country in contribution; having no sufficient evidence to estimate its contribution, but having complete evidence to impeach that contribution which it now imposes. And what is this contribution? It is valued at about [illegible] in war, in addition to the interest of your debt, which is [illegible] per annum; that is, equal to the charge of your establishment, four times greater than any past war establishment, a charge equal to the support of 128,000 soldiers, which is near eight times as much as you paid in former wars; so that you are to multiply your charge for the loss of your Parliament, or rather you are to pay the tribute of the slave; before this you raised the supply of freemen—a charge, I say, which if for troops to be kept in the country, establishes a military government as complete as in Russia; which will therefore render you a slave or a bankrupt, a military province of England, or a beggar, indeed both; for though I do not think the means of this country are unequal to every necessary expense, yet I do think they are inadequate to that contributory expense which the union stipulates. I do think they are unequal to a war contribution of [illegible] per annum; and I think the attempt will exhaust this country at the same time that it enslaves her. Colour it as you please, she will pay more than she is able; and she will pay for a force not to protect but to enslave.

"Do we know that the balance of our trade with all the world is but half a million in our favour, and that this half million is to supply the absentee drain of above two millions, which is to be greatly increased by the operation of the union, by which we are to pay not only absentee representation, but absentee establishment? Do we know that even now, when we borrow about [illegible] per annum from England, the exchange is greatly against us? Do we know that at this very moment the revenue has fallen [illegible], a fall which would be only occasional if your constitution were suffered to continue; but if the union and its new debts, contributions, absentees, military government, and military measures shall succeed, is ominous and alarming. Knowing all these, what have we done? We have overrated our country in wealth to over-rate her in contribution; to apply that contribution to the maintenance of a military to take away her liberty. I speak of the proposed war establishment. What is the proposed peace establishment? One-third greater than your peace establishments. Why one-third greater? The increased pay of 15,000 men, the peace establishment of a militia of 17,000 men, the skeleton of the yeomen corps, will not account for an increase of one-third, viz., of half a million. No ground whatever has been laid for it, except, indeed, a certain hint, which it may be expedient to mention. In peace, an army in Ireland of [illegible]—we understand that perfectly—an union army—a military establishment in peace, and a rebellion establishment in war; in fact, an army not for the people of Ireland, but put upon them; not to protect them, but to protect the progress of the minister against them; 'tis true it has been said that England will pay this additional expense, but what is that? The English minister will make his country assist in the subjugation of the Irish by force of arms; there is no great compliment in this; but rely on it that Ireland, like every enslaved country, will ultimately be compelled to pay for her own subjugation; robbery and [illegible] ever follow conquest; the country that loses her liberty loses her revenues. But if the terms of the financial part of the union were as beneficial as they are injurious, it would be of little moment, for there is an article that whenever the minister shall raise the debt of Ireland to an amount which shall be in the proportion of two to fifteen in relation to the permanent debt of England (in three years of war they tell you they will do it), then you are to be taxed as much as England. Considering then the terms of the union, so far as they relate to revenue, they amount to a continuation of the double establishment, an increase of the separate establishments, and a military government, with a prospect of soon succeeding to the full taxes of England."

Mr. Grattan then proceeded to refer to the loss which the Irish manufacturers would incur through the abolition of some protecting duties and the reduction of others under Article 6 of the Union, and to other matters, and then with reference to a speech by Mr. Pitt, went on to say:—

"The advantages predicted in revenue, like those in commerce, vanish also; the magnificent million of the speech of the Irish Secretary does not appear in the second oration of the British minister. He had indeed assumed a certain air of astonishment at the surprise that Britain sought to obtain revenue from other countries. He suffered his minister here to go a little further, and to teach us to think that England was impatient to get rid of revenue; that her turn now was to buy up constitutions; that she had become a chapman and dealer in liberty, and was willing to pay Ireland for her Parliament half a million in peace and one million per annum in war. I doubted the fact; I had not forgotten the American War; I had not forgotten the American Stamp Act; I had not forgotten Mr. G. Grenville's pamphlet, containing a proposal to tax Ireland as well as America; I had not forgotten the proposal of the present minister of England, contained in one of the propositions of 1785, namely, that the surplus of the hereditary revenue should go to England; when, therefore the same minister, in a state of twofold distress, disclaimed revenue, and when the minister here averred that England was to pay a compensation to Ireland, I did not believe either; but when the former disavows the latter, and, in his second speech, as printed, he is made to say that Ireland is to pay pretty much what she does now; that is to say, not as the minister here said, a million less, but above four times as much as she paid in any former war, and many times as much as she is able, and such an expense as the rebellion, not the war, produced—I say, when the minister sets forth such as our contribution hereafter, he does renounce all benefits predicted in finance with as much candour as he abandons all benefits predicted in commerce to result from his fatal measure of union."

www.ingramcontent.com/pod-product-compliance
Lightning Source LLC
Chambersburg PA
CBHW032008110726
47901CB00004B/1007
9783742831279